Oldest Living Confederate Widow Tells All

Oldest Living Confederate Widow Tells All

ALLAN GURGANUS

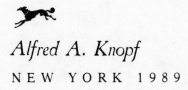

Alfred A. Knopf
NEW YORK 1989

Earlier versions of chapters from this work have been published by the following: "How to Leave" in Antaeus, "A Body Tends to Shine" in The Paris Review, "The Tailor and the Leg" in Southwest Review, "Fight Song" in The North American Review, "The Passable Kingdom" in MSS, "Love at 99" ("One Old Man in Here I Like") in The Leader, and two separate portions from "How to Return," one as "Under This Very Mall" in Harper's and the other as part of "Garden Sermon," an essay concerning the novel's historical sources, in The Iowa Review. "Good Help" was originally published as a chapbook by the North Carolina Wesleyan Press in a signed edition of 1,000, illustrated by the author; twenty-six alphabetized copies were accompanied by original drawings.
I appreciate the editors' early and abiding encouragement.

Library of Congress Cataloging-in-Publication Data
Gurganus, Allan.
   Oldest living Confederate widow tells all.
   1. United States—History—Civil War, 1861–1865—
Fiction. I. Title.
PS3557.U81404 1989 813'.54 88-45870
ISBN 0-394-54537-0
Manufactured in the United States of America
Published September 8, 1989
Reprinted Eight Times
Tenth Printing, November 1989

To my mother and father,
with gratitude for
standards and tenderness

And, with love, to Mona Simpson

Myth is gossip grown old.
—STANISLAW LEC

*What the American public always wants is a tragedy
with a happy ending.*
—W. DEAN HOWELLS to Edith Wharton
in conversation, *A Backward Glance*

CONTENTS

AUTHOR'S NOTE

It's a joy to thank my friends and most constant readers, people who greeted this work one chapter at a time: Eric Ashworth, Daisy Thorp, Jane Holding, Edmund Apffel, Andrea Simon, William Gurganus, Amanda Urban, Daniel Kaiser, William Carl Walker, Brian Zeger, Steven Cole, and especially Joanne Meschery. The work was midwifed by Elisabeth Sifton, its brilliant godmother.

Time is freedom. Freeing me during spans of this novel's writing were the Ingram Merrill Foundation and the National Endowment of the Arts. My colleagues at Sarah Lawrence College lovingly covered for me during a long absence. Many thanks, friends.

The Corporation of Yaddo gave me refuge years ago when I had only a Hermes portable, a clean face, and fairly good work habits. I began this book at Yaddo and am grateful for the place's kindness, its perfect sanctuary.

Books most often consulted: King James Bible, *A New and Complete Concordance of the Holy Scripture* by John Eadie (Glasgow, 1850), *All God's Dangers*, *Pissing in the Snow*, *The Children of Pride*. Shelby Foote's brilliant narrative history of the Civil War. *Battles and Leaders of the Civil War*, *Patriotic Gore*, *The Country Scrapbook*, *Children of Bladensfield*, *Aunt Arie*, *A Civil War Treasury*, The Federal Writers' Project Collected Slave Narratives, *Slave Life in Georgia*, newspapers and diaries of the period. Family letters. And, perhaps most useful for evoking the past, *The Montgomery Ward Catalogue of 1888* and *Images of War*, a complete photographic history of the struggle.

A word to the reader about historical accuracy. In testimony collected from former slaves during the 1930s' Federal Writers' Project, many recalled seeing Lincoln in the South during the Civil War. Fanny Burdock, ninety-one, of Valdosta, Georgia, remembered, "We been picking in the field when my brother he point to the road and then we seen Marse Abe coming all dusty and on foot. We run right to the fence and had the oak bucket and the dipper. When he draw up to us, he so tall, black eyes so sad. Didn't say not one word, just looked hard at all us, every one us crying. We give him nice cool water from the dipper. Then he nodded and set off and we just stood there till he get to being dust then nothing. After, didn't our owner or nobody credit it, but me and all my kin, we knowed. I still got the dipper to prove it."

In reality, Lincoln's foot tour of Georgia could not have happened. In this book, it can. Such scenes were told by hundreds of slaves. Such visitations remain, for me, truer than fact.

History is my starting point.

BOOK ONE

Nobody's

Perfect

Fight
Song

DIED ON ME finally. He had to.

Died doing his bad bugle imitation, calling for the maps, died bellowing orders at everybody, horses included, "Not over there, dunderdick, rations go here." Stayed bossy to the last. He would look down in bed, he'd command the sheets to roll back. They didn't.

—My poor husband, Captain Marsden, he perished one Election Day. Children were setting off firecrackers on our vacant lot. Cap believed it was Antietam flaring up on him again like a game knee. So he went happy, yelling March! to his men (all dead) and to me (not dead yet, thank you very much). It's about what I expected I reckon.

He'd been famous for years around here. The longer he lived the more he got on the local news, then the national noticed, black and white and in color. They brought cameras South and all these lights walked right into our home and his bedroom. Folks put TV makeup on him. He thought it was poison-ivy medicine. He hit the girl doing it.

I had to prime the Captain, make him tell his usuals. By then it was like getting your parrot going for company, you would say a key word and he'd chew it over, then you'd see it snag way in, and out whole favorites would crank—battle by battle—like rolls on some old player piano.

Strangers kept filing through our house, kept not wiping their feet, come to see the final vet of the War Betwixt States propped up. All them boys in blue were cold in Yankee earth. Captain had tricked the winning side by holding on the last, too proud to quit, maybe too cranky. Oh he was a sight—gray uniform bunched over his pajamas, beard wild as a hedge and white to match his cataracts grown big as ice cubes. Above the bed he'd hung a tintype of his missing buddy, he kept a rusty musket within easy reach. From a nail, one child-sized bugle dangled on its blood-red cord. Plus he had a dried twig off this tree where something bad happened.

A neighbor child brought Captain a fistful of dogtooth violets. I thanked her, set them in a bedside water glass. All day my old man kept squinting violets' way, smiling, swallowing—acting strange. Finally he waves me over, makes a scared face, nods towards blue flowers, whispers, "Lucy, baby spies!"

. . .

ESPECIALLY after that big Civil War moving picture come out in '39, folks couldn't get enough. I had strangers pumping me for aspirins and change of a dollar, and I offered everything. No spring chicken myself. A bookseller brought in every history of the war for Cap to sign, like he'd written it: The War. And you never knew which name my man would autograph next. One minute he was General P. G. T. Beauregard, next minute he'd be Captain Butler. And the bookdealer sold every last signature as real. —Honey, I had Yankees asking me for coffee, tea, and where was the bathroom. Got so I tacked up paper arrows in our hallway. Wrote out "Oldest surviving," etc., like pointing tourists to Mount Rushmore. Wrote "Toilets—men's and women's—please use same one—so you'd best lock the door, and gents, please do keep seat *up* when not needed, thank you. Only fair. Signed, Mrs. Marsden—wife of oldest surviving," etc.

One day I hear muttering on our third floor. I find a Northern newsgirl setting right on the bed alongside our blind son. "Wrong room." I hold open the bedroom door, "Our boy's a bit shy of strangers." She could probably tell. He had his head poked clear under the blankets. Says she in a voice like Brasso, "But we investigative types like to cover all the bases, madam." Her skirt was shorter than most decent panties used to be. I just bet you do, thought I, but, leading her back downstairs, I didn't like to say nothing at the time.

Captain Marsden was thirteen when the Confederacy called. You think he knew enough to stay home safe in civvies? No way. The only male mammals still at large in Falls, North Carolina, were either livestock or babies or our geezers left over from the 18 and 12 one, men still mighty big on John Paul Jones. My husband and his pal felt right overlooked. "We're ready," says the boys. Thirteen, and didn't even have to lie about their age. They had trigger fingers and some eyesight, didn't they? Was enough.

So Marsden trooped off with his best friend, a boy way prettier. The pal was Willie's age but older-seeming. Name of Ned Smythe. You could look him up. Both of them hailed from here, from Falls. Pressed into service in '62 when General Lee was already running out of living bodies to put the gray on and get shot at. —Those boys left town holding hands like girls that age would.

Their mothers had chose going-away gifts. My man's momma knitted him a Union Suit you couldn't call that in the South then, but it was. She brung along five wagonsful of slaves for saying goodbye to young Master Marsden. Knitting long johns she'd used patriotic colors, but instead of gray and red the woman picked red, white, and blue. Poor Lady Marsden didn't even understand secession and here she'd sent off her favorite to fight for it.

Ned's mother carried her best canary to the parade ground. She owned thirty-some, bred them. Wanted Ned to take a caged bird along for company. The head officer, polite as you please, wondered if battle conditions would be (folks later claimed he asked) "canary suitable." They were gentlemen then. Most of our Southern gentlemen got killed. For a while it stayed the polite thing to do and they couldn't not be polite. Being a gent in them times was like being a Catholic priest—more about what you couldn't do than what you could.

Mrs. Marsden asked the officer if these boys would have to fight in rainy weather. You know what he told her? "It depends." Now won't that tact? Honey, them days are gone.

Little Marsden dropped his home-knit long johns by the side the road not ten miles from home. Somebody brought them back. Was like that then. A stranger miles off would know who'd knit what for who and in which colors by mistake. Mrs. Marsden took it as a sign her boy'd been hurt and stripped already. She'd grown up overly rich. Still owned cooperative slaves. Lady Marsden had been encouraged to act batty-brained. She played piano like a pro, lived in a church-sized cupola-bedroom lined with white silk damask. Poor woman thought the North was nothing but icebergs. She pressed the brung-back long johns up against her throat, she told her favorite body servant, "My child'll freeze."

In a way she was right.

THE MORE the Captain got onto TVs, the more Mrs. Lucy here worked. Footprints all over my new beige carpet. Newsladies kept asking: What did *I* remember of the war, that war? I admitted as how I'd missed it by twenty-some years. I was born in 1885, and he was 1849. Well, when they heard this, they'd get kind of sour-faced and say, "oh," like it was my failing, like I was pretty lucky to have latched on to the last vet gets to live or breathe on either side.

His final thirty years I served as tour guide, and what I gave tours of was Captain Marsden. Kept hiding the bedpan, kept carding knots out of that beard, forever wrestling him into uniform and with Cap siccing the sentinels on me yet again.

Hoarse, he'd asked reporters, "Say . . . what o'clock is it?" They'd check their watches. I stopped them. "He means the year, folks, what year." "Oh," they looked from me to him to me. They seemed embarrassed, like it *shouldn't* be so late in the century. —Newsfolks acted like the recent lack of world progress was *their* fault. I know the feeling. Finally somebody did tell the year, and loud. Cap cupped a meaty palm behind one ear, sat straighter, "Say *what*?" When he heard it hollered again, my man heaved back into pillows and crossed his broad arms. Then Cap grinned out from under overhang eyebrows, he said, "Go *on*!"

I BEGGED reporters to please not use flashbulbs on him. Bright pops put him in a artillery frame of mind, shocked him into yelling for the horse brigade. But no sooner my back was turned, I'd see white light ricochet down the hallway, I'd hear folks scatter.

Off he'd go again. Northern camera crews had flashed him back to combat moods and then they left. I had to slip in and calm him as best I could. I sat, stroking his white hair, smoothing his white beard. I sat cooing the only word that ever helped: "Appomattox, Appomattox, Appomattox, baby." —It's a Indian word, you know. That's why it's so pretty.

2

NOWADAYS there's more commotion, folks coming to visit me. Just for me, too. Here you are with this recording machine set right on my bed. You way off on that plastic chair. Draw up nearer, sugar. —That's better. Good face. Oh, I know how mine looks now. All bunchy. But so is what's behind it. Don't they say the smarter you are, the more shriveled-up-like your brain gets? Well, child, if what's inside looks like what's hanging here on front, I figure I'm nearbout to genius level by now.

When my vet finally died (a violent death—another story), peace was such a novelty it scared me like a war would. Didn't know what to *do* with it. Walked around our house cleaning up after myself, but I'd always been the neat one. Every hallway knickknack looked shell-shocked with the silence weighing down our home. No mud on the beige rug now, I half missed it. Not a soul visited. Bad stroke, two broken hips—most of my friends got carried off in three bumpy months. And you know that one old lady living on alone in peace, why she ain't news anymore. First I hated being still. Now I'm getting more accustomed. Fact is, I like it. I love it quiet.

Turns out, that's what I was looking for all along. Funny, ain't it? Some of the old ones in here, they talk like a quiet house on a side street is the hardest thing in the world. To me, that lived in Poppa's home till Poppa passed me on to Cap Marsden's (which we soon filled up with babies and their noise), why a quiet house, it grew on me. Stopped sounding like what was missing, started being what I had. Soon the long hush got feeling better than church. You didn't even have to dress up and go out. It was all right there, all yours, sweet as a reward. Honey, I know I'm sounding like the selfish old woman I've become. But, believe me, it took work to get this way.

—So, you come to pump me for my news before I got too little wind to spill news with? Well, as for secrets, I admit I am rich, child. That's all the riches I've got—but on that score anyways, I am Mrs. Gotrocks. Still, a body can't give her secrets away twice, can she? They're either secrets or somebody else's. Others in here pride theirselves on knowing every grandchild's birth date. Some of our men can tell you how much tax they paid every unfair April for sixty-odd years. Me, I've mostly got his war stories and my peace ones. They're yet on tap. Knock wood (or in *this* room, rap yonder walnut-grained Formica).

But I can't see the percentages in spilling this amount of beans. What if I did tell: Maybe my old man's bad news, what war does, how it feels to be the last of something. What would I get for it? I know that smacks of greed, but I don't mind. I like being greedy. Turns out I was talented in that direction all along and never even knew.

See the sun in this nice room? Others want the corner rooms but I been given one. Polite young men wash my sheets twice a week, need it or no. This one, Jerome, quick, good-looking fellow the color of cinnamon toast, he comes in on Thursdays. He shows me the weekend disco routines he's planning. They're long! Last time, he takes off his orderly's jacket, underneath he's wearing a black-and-white T-shirt that spells:

> D I S C O
> A I N ' T
> D E A D
> Y E T !

I had to laugh. "Sounds like me," says I. He's going to get me one. Jerome hand-stitches quilts to order. Oh, he's versatile, Jerome is. Nights, he studies acting. I know you ain't supposed to say it but that child can flat dance. Jerome can jump from here to there just like that, like a deer, perfect. He says he feels like I'm his own grandma. Time's turnt me nearbout brown enough to be. Look at these speckledy marble-cake hands. I could be a mixed marriage all in myself. Yes, Jerome's a comfort. And the ladies with hairnets make my meals. Certain high school candy-stripers spill their love secrets Lucy's way. The things I've heard. Plus our director, he let me choose my own paint color for this room. I've had hints it looks, well, cheap. Is it too bright of a yellow for you? I don't think so either. I don't know what's wrong with these people.

Yeah, now all I got to do is sit here like a queen, watch young fellows dance, make statements to the Press or history majors, and eat what I didn't cook. Oh, I'll tell you straight, sugar, I'm getting used to it.

But, the story? It ain't just one. It's more to it than you think. Well, maybe a taste. Say once, as it so happens, Captain Marsden went to war with his best chum, say neither of them had even shaved yet, both so scared they walked hand in hand clear to Virginia, then Maryland. I probably told you before. They hiked into the valley of the shadow of death. Say all that, since all of it is so. Popular boys, not equally pretty nor equally rich (my homely little Marsden stood to inherit a passel of slaves and acreage, though you wouldn't of known it to look at him). Those boys were hair-triggered as five-dollar pistols. Tots, really.

In his younger life (till age forty-five, in there) my man stayed mighty tight-lipped about his war doings. Older, he'd speak of hardly nothing else. For breakfast toast, Willie wanted his bread burned jet-dark so he could call it "hardtack." Words like "forest" or "hood" stopped meaning anything but our Southern generals named that. By the end, my husband had gone back to battle, child. Lived there. He finally repeated his war tales so often, seemed like they happened to me (and to our nine civilian children), only neatened up considerable.

Just months from home kitchens, my boy was already a sharpshooter and Ned, the company mascot. These youngsters were well liked owing to nightly skits they did for others. Now, Ned had a way with a tune. Fellow soldiers loved him for being so liberal with the gift. His picture got lost when my old man's did. Odd what you lose. Ned was ringlets from the ears up, gold, and with this grin that *was* going to win him friends fast, girls specially. In the picture, he kept one hand on his hip, bugle propped there, head tipped kind of cocky, like in love with the photographer. Ned daily bugled the division awake. Then he upped and put men back to sleep again, some baby Gabriel. He had clear eyes as I remember and, you got to admit it, don't you, Mrs. Lucy Marsden's memory ain't half bad for somebody with ninety-odd years' mileage on it. —Yeah, every war has got them faces. Grins lit up from inside. Some eyes are so blue they don't even register on that poor-grade early film. Such stares show up nearbout clear and look slam through you. Faces oval as angels'. Too perfect to be local!

And every time you see a face like that? one that sets itself aside as overly excellent? one so full of rare high spirits? why—that's a face that ain't going to last. War looks over all the soldiers' pictures in advance. It takes the very best. Oh, quite a eye for beauty it's got. Picky picky picky.

Listen, it let *my* old man live, didn't it?

3

OKAY, look under my bed here. Get off that chair. I guess you're spryer than me by a century or so. Go on, door's closed, just us chickens. Yeah, now that there's his scabbard—the thing Cap kept his sword in till we hocked the sword part back in 19 and 31, had to. Starving.

Ain't fair that a person should live through the Civil War of one hunk of years and the Great Depression of the next batch, but Cap did. Had to. "The Great Depression." I'd like to know what was so great about it.

We ate dandelion greens for six years. He lost his livestock yard, sold his momma's last farm. Still I made the Captain, for that's what I had to call him (in bed and out), made him save back this here scabbard part for later, don't you know. He's long planted but now you turn up, "Later" come to chat.

Time was, I owned a tintype showed him wearing this, him hooked on to it, buck-toothed, grinning like a hero in advance of ever stepping off his folks' two thousand acres. Voice hadn't even changed yet. Imagine, still a soprano and already a soldier. Now you know that ain't right. Sword came clear up to his shoulder. Looked raw but mighty sweet, the cowlicks up and out like the crown on the Statue of Liberty later. What's happened to cowlicks? You don't see those anymore. Yes, blow-dryers, I guess. Now they'll blow-dry any baby's cowlicks to death. Never stand a chance. Three things missing off of children now: cowlicks, freckles, and stuttering. Used to every third child couldn't talk straight and was speckled as—well, as my old hand here. Now, not. Things change, weather's not what it was. Woman down the hall blames the astronauts going to-and-from through it. Did you see that rocket blow up with the people in it? Won't that sad? Their families were right there.

But wait, I'm wandering, the war, his war.

I MENTIONED NED. His beauty was kind of honorary. Men liked having him in sight, seemed *he* was what they fought for. Men claimed to be doing battle for the sakes of mothers, daughters, wives. (A likely story and a old one.) Ned was the nearest pretty thing. They watched him. The child'd idle around picking wildflowers, finding baby rabbits in the weeds. Even with artillery thunder rolling, he'd traipse off gathering a hatful of farmer's raspberries to give away later, mouth all red from sampling. Ned played the bugle perfect, his hair metal-yellow as the horn was. He did reveille not as punishment, more for the tune. Made a fellow's wartime waking easier.

Now, not six months into their enlistment, between rounds, boys found this swimming hole near a gristmill. Ned asked the commander for one morning off so everybody could horse around and bathe, horses included. Shock of shocks, the commander said Yes. Ned was one of the people people ofttimes say Yes to. (Myself, I've had a lifetime of "We'll see.") Ned got credit for the swim. Men all waded in, so glad after these many weeks of mud. This was up near Petersburg, Virginia, that they later called "Fort Hell" because it all got fought in holes and burrows underground. "Fort Hell" because it was one.

Ned drove twenty horses in shank-deep. My husband never told me that the whole division went swimming naked but I bet they did. You think the Confederate Army issued regulation-gray bathing suits back then? No way.

My man and this Ned were whooping, splashing, carrying on. If they'd been bosom friends when they left Falls, why they were beyond blood brothers now. Slept side by side, and when cannon fire got nearer and so loud, they'd scoot over and hold on to one another, all mashed cheek to jowl like puppies in a box—missing their old momma's teat and can't get close enough to suit them. My man claimed he'd start the sentence, Ned'd polish it off. Got to where their dreams rhymed. Was no surprise they dreamed of one hometown, of being safe in many different parts of it. They wore the selfsame boot size (4—I told you they were babies), and if their heels got blistered, they'd swap boots, giving one batch of calluses a rest, chafing up the other for a change.

Ned owned the singing voice, my poor husband croaked with one note only. Had the bellows but no control of it. His high and low notes come out only as louds and softs, poor thing. Back home in Baptist Youth Choir, these child-soldiers had stood side by side in civilian robes patterned on what we think the angels wear. Are angels civilian or military? Well, in *my* heaven, the robe is civvies. That much I know.

During his robe days, Ned had done most of the soprano solos. Girls grumbled but the choir leader mentioned how girls'd always be sopranos whereas Ned's sweet upward tones just wouldn't keep. "Gather your high notes whilst you may," the director told Ned. This choir honcho was New York–trained, somewhat of a sissy but musical as possible. He made my husband be "a mouth singer." Meaning my Willie could not get *near* a hymn. Will just had to stand there, cowlicks out, total quiet but with his lips moving. A lot.

Well, encamped with the division, the Falls boys worked out a routine based on all their Youth Choir practice. My husband did the gestures. Ned sang the song while standing before a open tent flap. Will would hide inside out of sight. Ned clasped hands behind his back. Marsden, after rolling up gray sleeves, would slide his bare arms under his pal's armpits. (You getting this?) From out front, you saw Ned's face and front, saw Willie's freckled arms. At the first perfect note, Marsden (glad to be hid, suddenly bold for one so bashful) made a first sweeping gesture. If, say, Ned's song run, oh maybe (I'm just making this part up) "My Heart Aches For You," then the right hand might point to Ned's left chest, flap there like a bird hurting, and then finally aim a "you" out at the tough-boy audience. Like that.

During civilian concerts in them days, people expected to weep. And in a city of tents, by campfire glow, on the night before a battle, to hear a boy whose voice might never get to change—well, what you asked and expected of a song went double.

DECADES later, survivors from my husband's division remembered Captain, not Ned, to be the singer. Our children, having heard their poppa's beagle baying in the bathtub, looked shocked. "Do one for us," visiting vets would beg my old man. "Sweetest Irish tenor south of Dublin. Willie's 'Last Rose of Summer' got us through many a rough night." Memory seems to work like that—meaning: wrong, for some of the right reasons. Of course, Captain Marsden refused to sing—but just from seeming modesty. He never corrected pals about his not being able to carry a tune in a bucket. And me, I didn't blame him.

Pecks of decades later, Captain was one of the last forty vets left alive. In homes across our land, others surrendered the battle of breathing. Before long, thanks to my good company, to time's wear and tear, plus his own meat-and-potato stubbornness, the list'd whittled down to ten, then six, with him still hanging on. Every day Cap scanned the Obits. Even prior to checking the Funnies and his "Andy Gump." And you know how he was about his "Andy Gump." Well, he was. For him, Obits soon became the Funnies, long as *he* won't listed. Whenever Cap found another Northerner had bit the dust, why he'd just chuckle. I'd hear him in there humming "The Old Reb" or "Who's Sorry Now?" Made his day. He'd asked me for a widgeon of celebration whiskey. Could he play with his scabbard today, please, please? My man held the *Falls Herald Traveler* so close to his beard you heard beard crackling against newsprint. He would eyeball the poor dead Yankee's photo. And my man's dark and final voice would tell that picture, "Weakling."

First my husband was the only non-vegetable Confederate left, then he was the final one alive on either side in any condition. More and more guests stopped by with ready-made questions. Around here, on the subject of the Civil War, every filling-station man's a expert.

They quizzed Captain: could General Braxton Bragg be clumsy as history shows? was hardtack all that rough on the teeth? what year did your average Reb foot soldier *know* the gray'd done dropped the ball? But grill me? Me, they'd corner to find out how you get back to Durham on the Interstate. Where could they buy decent bar-b-que to go?

Still, turns out I am something he never was. You know what? Well, see, there's the war and it gets holt of him, it shakes him something awful, and then he gets to grab *me* by the scruff of my neck. (He didn't *get* to, but I noticed he sure done it often enough anyway.) So, say, he's the last vet of that war, but me? Why, honey, I'm a veteran of the veteran.

I'm the last living veteran of the last living veteran of that war.

Probably a cheap kind of famous but, look, it's better than nothing.

Now he's gone. Around six o clock, at he-gets-home-for-supper time, I notice this the most. Even now, even after everything that had to happen, I halfway miss him. Don't it make you sick? But William More Marsden could be the most charming man in the world and I don't ever want to seem to talk just bad about him. That reflects terrible on the spouse, *I* think. I consider myself a loyal person. And there's nothing Lucy here is loyaler to than the idea that she *is* . . . loyal. If you catch my drift.

So, yeah, "charming." The fellow was not overpolite or knee-jerk kind, like me back then. But when he *did* do something tender, you sure noticed. It could break you sideways. Last reporters to interview Marsden told me he was the most charming *senile* man they'd ever met. In 19 and 21, I saw him drive our Model T over a rabbit and then get out and cry like a baby at what he'd done. Our children never forgot it. They stood sobbing by the roadside. Him kneeling on hot tarmac, him wearing his best summer poplin suit, and trying to breathe air into the creature (a trick learned at cockfights). Captain whispered to the victim, "I honked our horn. What were these long ears for?" Cap's beard was sticky and beautiful with rubies of rabbit blood.

Plus, he acted so good to his momma after what Sherman went and did to her. Captain also knew his way around a story, could be one of the funniest men alive. With me, child, that's a big part of "attractive." Question number one: Can he make you laugh on a regular basis? In my book, money and looks come way down the list after a decent daily giggle to keep the doctor away.

Sure, he did some things he regretted later. Haven't I and haven't you, child? True, murder might not top our particular list. But, taken all together, Marsden was a man. He had days and days like all of us.

Then Cap went and died. And myself? Well, less. "Close" only counts in horseshoes and hand grenades—but at this branch of the State Home, half dead still means half a loaf. Maybe I do look like I'm wearing canning alum for face powder (I won't *have* a mirror in this room). But Lucy here is still something that many folks from History would dearly love to be. I am alive, honey.

And unlike many a younger person, Mrs. Lucy knows it. Oh, child, I could blow the whistle on the world if I ever took a mind to. Forgive my speaking so strutting and bold, but remember, talk's about the single pleasure left me. My mouth is still a cakewalk, my mouth's both a deep gutter and a full-out waltz. And see, I liked saying even *that*.

—EVEN SO, honey? don't get your hopes up. Spare your batteries. You mustn't mind my being way too frank—but you ain't ready for this. I can nearbout look at you and tell. Open face, fresh skin, maybe the offspring of lawyers, even doctors. Such hopeful eyes—a tad tired but *more* hopeful for that. You think the world is a straight-A student. I see you're eager to do stuff right and behave professional. You're willing to sign a petition if you're really mad about something. A person that notices, you've got a sweet tooth for local color. Chestnuts opened on a roasting fire, Jack Frost taking off your toes. (Nobody believes in the Future no more, so they come in here trying to beat the bushes for some hokum called The Past. Bunk. *That* ain't a fair trade.)

Folks expect me to act all cute and all. Makes me sick. You don't see no African violets in *my* room, do you? Folks want I should tell them how to churn butter, what it was to weave cloth. How I saw some Indians onct. You think I'm going to play like that Miss Priss Betsy Ross? Momma always held her up as Miss Johnny-on-the-Spot, what women can do. Some glory. She just got to sew some more. They didn't let her featherstitch her name in that Constitution's lower left, I notice. She just made another quilt, warm stripes, a appliqué of stars, a quilt men chose to run up their erect old flagpole and fight for. One-track minds, men's ups and downs.

Honey, you don't want the truth. You're just hunting some sharp old gingham gal that'll fit onto a Sunday Supplement Ladies' Page. She'd tell you how to make gentle soap and slow candles. You think the past was just one long class in handicrafts? Oh, I've had others in here glad-handing me for household tips. Listen, as a child, I hated being near the candlemakers. Rendered fat stinks! Show me a butter churn or some margarine, I'll grab that margarine stick any day of the week. You ain't looking to hear my particular rough news. I ain't a antique, was never such a fine lady. I don't have no blue-book value whatever. All I am is stringy and cross—with a good memory for grudges. I'm no more than what you see: just old, old, old.

So, child, get this gear packed up, cut off your machine, leave. And no hard feelings. It's just—I'm too tired to lie, too vain to need to. Staying mad—that's a lot of what's kept me opening these eyes. See, I'm still waiting for a small last way of getting even.

I got news, honey, the world is a C – student. Everybody *but* it deserves the A's. So, get on out now. Bye.

4

NO? Oooo, I like seeing your jaw set. Good sign. Feeling underestimated? Welcome to the club—I am a charter member. Listen, the day I went ninety and somebody first called me a nonagenarian? I thought it meant I'd run out of claiming numbers, thought I'd hit some non-age—off time's mailing list. But *you* don't plan to be sold short, do you? Well, good. So you hate being pushed around, even from a bed by some creaky leather hinge weighing under eighty-nine, hunh?

Well, maybe we can work something out here. For today only, understand. My secretary tells me I ain't exactly got no national news conference scheduled between now and lunch. Look at you. Think you got some stuffing, do you? We all need to stay a little mad. Helps you know you ain't hand-picked—just lucky.

So, bracing for the whole truth and nothing but? Well, I didn't mean to tick you off none. It's just, you wouldn't believe the folks rush in here with their questions answered before they even ask. I get to talking about my babies dying, they'll shoo me over to household niceties.

LISTEN. I been steadily waiting for a certain person to turn up, the one who'll ask it right, who'll just say maybe, "yes?"

I can't be sure. But if you plan to hear a few more salty facts, Big Eyes, you'd best pull up a little closer. I ain't going to bite. Couldn't even gum you hard enough to make a mark. Just had to do a little test. Only got so many retellings in me. Can't be casting my old gems in just anybody's trough. At ninety-nine, you got to hold something back. What? I'm that old, hunh? Imagine, *me*? Well, you're the one with the facts and equipment. You have history on your side, all I got's my life.

Can you feature me this far up in years and still able to *notice* company? Machine's listening, ain't it? I can tell. Loose lips sink ships. Is this a Japanese one? I declare, nothing's what it was.

Come maybe two, three inches closer. Fine. No nearer, please. At my age, child, the suspense is everything.

ON THAT particular day I started, soldiers kept swimming in their millpond. A stone wheel ground corn toward being daily Confederate johnnycakes. Men stayed sloshing around the way men will when they been busy being scared and then, of a sudden, get a good chance not to be. Fellows freed up, hollering, were ducking one another. Men!—one minute killing each other, next minute all innocence, how do you figure it?

The sentinel on duty got to feeling so silly he fired a round of shots to celebrate. Everybody laughed. Pretty Ned shucked a rein from off one wading dray horse, he tied the four-foot leather thong to a sturdy sapling down near water. Made ready to swing off of it. He wanted to "cannonball," as my children call it. Called it.

Ned secured it good and tight, yelled that he got to dive first since swimming had been his idea. Nobody argued. Soldiers, older and younger with farmer's tans, hair full of soapsuds, stood chest-deep, hip-deep. They turned to see how big of a splash he'd make. They grinned. Ned got a goodly hold, he looped one arm in leather, wrist to elbow. Wore his bugle on its red sling full-time so he could signal during emergencies. Brass won't rust that much. He took a push off the mud shore. A slender naked boy, shiny-wet, hands and face catching bugle light. He heaved to get up a decent speed, ready to hurl hisself aloose for the largest plop possible.

Well, what noise others'd made, those shots fired, sounds of men acting so spunky for once, it had drawn three Yankees. They'd done set up sniper's shop in a old willow tree on the shore opposite. Dear me yes.

Course, you know.

NED SWINGS back a last time. For fun, the sentinel pulls off a blast straight up. Others start to whistling, slapping water, making Rebel yells. Ned, in this noise, gives a little shout that others think is for the fun of it, Ned keeps swinging, never letting loose, goes weaving way on out, then slinging in again and twisting funnier, more sideways every time. No man watching could tell Ned's high spirits from his flinching with them bullets finding every good soft part of him. Hogtied up in air, poor child was catching everything. The sentinel stopped his celebration firing. Swimmers ceased clapping. All went still. Finally plain weight pulled Ned down. Men groaned when he fell, disappointed at so poor a dive after all the practice. Still nobody knew. Only with Ned face-first and in too long did some man's foot nudge him, man saw stripes of dark all through the shallows, man yelled, "Child's been hit. They're here."

Then everybody plunged under. All but the caisson mules and horses—too stupid to—all but my man, my boy back then. He moved to carry out his pal. He lifted Ned from lake, lugged Ned right up onto slippery moss. Ned's bugle was draining brown water and all the color Ned had lost. The bugle belched out gore like it'd been wounded *for* Ned. The living boy didn't worry that things were splintering and popping open all around him, target number two. Didn't notice, bent across his friend.

The sentinel saw which tree smoke kept rolling from across the lake. He fired at drooping willow fronds till one lump of Yankee fell down splash into the water. Onshore Rebels grabbed knives from off their clothes. They swam over fast, they cut that Yankee in his manly parts like he had raped their boy, not shot him. They already missed their Ned. Seemed like he'd been nice-looking and in good voice for them. Their first lieutenant had to pull men off that sniper, then men tried to peel my naked little husband off the dead friend he kept propping up and holding on to. Willie kept pressing wet curls back from his buddy's forehead. Kept telling Ned which girls in Falls just couldn't live through news of this, which choir director couldn't. Didn't help.

"Ain't fair," he called down at the perfect face, two clear open eyes. So then—though nobody'd ever known young Marsden to do so before, the child swallowed hard, whispered at the rosy ear nearest, "Hey, help me out here, bud," bent closer, started singing, trying to. It sounded bad as expected—half-caw, much ache in it. Willie sounded plain pitiful and knew it but just hoped he might be interrupted. Didn't happen. Nothing left the dead boy's mouth but lake and a touch of pink, like when you brush your teeth too hard.

Others stood around dazed, still nude—so upset they all believed everyone but them was naked. Men cupped rough hands over their privates, like shielding these from so sorry a spectacle. Then young Marsden started slapping his friend's face side to side, and hard. Was striking like he'd just got peeved, swatting in the testing way a young cat worries what it's hurt and cornered. And only then did some of the platoon bend down, hands resting on the child's shoulder. "Quit," men said, sounding like the mommas of these boys. "Ain't fitting. Stop it now." Marsden kept striking that excellent face. Naked fellows finally had to wrestle a live child off the slack one. It took force to. Took seven strong men—weakened some by crying theirselves—but better nurses for that.

They had to fib about the burial spot so my boy wouldn't haul off and dig Ned up. That same night, Will did, did uncover the corpse. Private Marsden dragged it off into a clearing. Sunrise, the others found Willie, sitting there with it, Will talking quiet, his right hand pressed alongside its poor gray face. Odd how fast a best-loved "he" goes "it." And my man's later tragedy was trying too long to push that "it" back to being a real "he." Like long division, honey, you can't force a larger sum into a smaller one. Can't nobody *push* a chain along the ground.

Poor Willie Marsden, cowlicks a mess, seed packet of freckles, red-rimmed eyes, and a nose running unchecked (heir to sixty-one slaves!), he walked around numb for weeks. Boy was living through the battle of Antietam. Was not much more to him than three flies in the room with you, a little bother off at the edge. He saved back Ned's boots, tied them to his belt, wore them saddlebag fashion. Nights, he took to sleeping with his hands poked deep into them like high warming gloves.

Dawns he started sneaking far into the woods (and at real risk to hisself) just to practice bugle. This woke troops on both sides. Rebs compared Will's squawking to Ned's rise-and-shine played like some Foster ditty.

Fellows studied each other, pained at hearing how bad Will was. He'd begun from scratch (with no ear at all), kept trying over and over for reveille. Seemed to believe that when he finally got it right, he could maybe raise up every soul that war'd claimed so far. And this was only in '62. Three more greedy years of it waited ahead. By the end, it'd inhaled a respectable percentage of all males on our continent. Consider the 600,000 killed outright. One Rebel in three died. Artillery'd grown real advanced, honey. Medicine lagged back in the Middle Ages. The combination hurt or carted off nearbout twenty-three thousand in one day at Antietam. Twen-ty-three thousand. Imagine it, child. One time I tried counting on my fingers, just that single day's worth, hoping to get a feel for a number of that size? Honey, I quit way before lunch.

What a story, all them stories. But listen, before I settle into anything without my noticing—before I even consider getting rolling—if I was to, to tell you the first part, child, you, of all them ones that's asked—I'd be doing it not just for the fun of talking while a body still can. It wouldn't be just for Mrs. Lucy Marsden. No, it's more for them, my missing ones. If I should spill, it's like . . . to represent them. They'd want it known, I reckon. Even Captain would. Seems my family left me here to kind of keep their place. I'm one old parchmenty bookmark stuck right in the middle of a chapter where our particular group nodded off.

I made those many meals. Then you know what happened? Sounds crude. Is, honey. All my eaters died on me. I cleaned up behind folks all those years—and me, the right-neat one—then, of a sudden, there won't one set of bad habits left to mop up after. I always said I wanted a clean place. Well, now I'd got it. Of my nine children lived past babyhood, every last one has perished. And you know what of, child? Mostly natural causes. What nailed them was nothing fancier than—Time. My last three were in *their* old-age home right close by. My oldest girl stayed here with me—was the belle of this place till she went on, it'll be eight months next Thursday. Louisa.

Odd, that I'm left. I am, though. Still in the center, yet busy explaining—whether people want me to or not. Of course, now there ain't much left to be in the middle *of*.

You know what a mother's day is like, even with her brood gone? Well, I look at your sweater's nice color and I think, He will like this shade. I eat French toast for breakfast and think, She is crazy for her sweets. Many a pleasure harks on back to them. Might sound strange but fact is, I'm yet looking after their interests. It's almost like they voted for me. Too weak to stay on theirselves, they picked their scrappiest one to tarry here, to keep a eye out for their rights. A dead person still has rights, you know.

—That's part of why I hang on, stay honest, seek pleasure—it's for what of them is left in me. And, too, for what of me slid off when my kin did. Living or no, we got to represent each other. It's only right. The world is

. . . like the House of Representatives. I keep getting elected to it. I don't even know who's left alive to vote me in.

Is it you?

—Okay, well, Mrs. Lucy here is readier.

BUT, CHILD, remember, even sitting here in bed and bent this double, I still stand for them.

After Appomattox

*He drew me out of many waters. He delivered me from my strong
enemy, and from them which hated me: for they were too strong for
me.*

—PSALM 18:16—17

WHEN Willie Marsden did come around, his pal gone, the war still
healthy, that boy turned mean—both in battle and out. It's wrong
to say he'd changed into a grownup overnight—getting some age on you
should make you kinder and not worse, shouldn't it? But him, he came to
bitter.

Marsden asked that others please call him "Ned." When they wouldn't,
why he'd curse them something awful. Later, he told all this on hisself.
That's one thing I have to say about the Captain, he did admit stuff. He'd
call to me through our back screen door, "Lucy, guess what your loved one's
gone and done now." "No telling," was my usual answer, "go ahead and hurt
me with it." All his life, most of Cap's finer stories had *him* making the tale's
main mistake. Mine too. Him—mine.

Men finally buried Ned in a new spot (without even benefit of crossed
sticks, hoping to hide him from a friend's digging. This meant Ned's exact
burial spot was lost forever). Will dug up half the woods, looking. After this,
it got where men had to watch Willie to prevent his stealing out alone at
night. He went—silent as a genius Tuscarora—on one-boy raids against the
enemy. Hadn't gone fourteen. No need to even shave yet but here he was
crawling off into the dark to cut the throats of men his daddy's age, his
granddads'. Some nights Corporal Sal Smith, father of six, asked others'
help—they tied a flailing Willie onto his cot. They hoped to halt his slipping
off and getting killed. Seemed he wanted to copycat his one friend. Willie
planned going wherever his chum was—up to and including noplace
whatsoever.

The next few weeks, most everything that can happen to a soldier
jumped this particular one. He got taken prisoner with his buddy, Smith.
The day those two got loose, Will was shot in the left leg. He later fired on

a Yankee boy. Then—confused—Will pulled the bleeding victim right into his own hole and hiding place. Those kids were so scared they had to either get acquainted fast or strangle one another. They soon talked. Before the child died—he asked Willie to make sure that his heirloom pocket watch got returned to a waiting Northern family. Will held the watch and jotted the address when his target went and died on him. —All this would prove confusing to a fellow fifty-some. For a body thirteen . . . well, I started to say, Is this *fair*? That is one of my long-standing failings, honey. I can sit here in a bed at this charity rest home, me half blind and owning nothing much past old letters, Captain's scabbard, Momma's best brooch plus a sterling thimble or two. And I'll think back to what some loved one had to live through and—getting real riled—Lucy will holler, "Wait one . . . that ain't fair."

"Grow up," snaps a retired professor in here. "Don't you even know yet, Lucille? You, a resident of this hellhole. 'Fair'? At your age?"

My favorite candy-striper, newly fifteen, she calls me "super-innocent." Look, I don't have to put up with that! Ain't fair.

But the odd part, I never want to quit at least *expec*ting fairness. Even after all that's snagged me and mine, I want the lack of "fair" to always shock me. The best storytellers on earth, child, they've all stayed semi-furious defending something, expecting something—expecting something better.

ANYHOW, Marsden's losing Ned, his seeing what followed, it changed so much in him. Even war's ending didn't switch that around. When your appendix is gone, you've still got the scar proving right where knives went in to find it. Something was taken clear out of the child. And Reconstruction, honey, why it never reconstructed that. I spent my whole life trying and put it back and make it up to him. (I'm still trying. Hear me?) Well, news flash: You can't. Make it up to a person.

Hard to know what things were like back then. From here, child, it looks like how they fixed up Williamsburg all neater than a shopping mall. (Williamsburg! You can learn more about the past by studying a tenant farmer's unpainted house weathered silver, than by talking with some chipper summer-job college kid wearing a white wig.) You been to Gettysburg? one perfect dull old park now. But you think it looked like that or smelled that way? what with horses being horses and the people dying of them fevers nobody even had no titles for? In the fighting, if a boy got shot in his knee, say, and if lead was hard to get at? why, no time for fancy surgery, off that whole leg came. In every army doctor's bag, find a good-sized saw. Later, Captain remembered (both in bad dreams and stark awake) the piles and piles of hairy legs, whole separate arms—some more tanned than others—wedding rings still shining on the third fingers of some. Sights a child don't soon forget. Listen, honey, things was raw then. It was something.

• • •

SO AFTER the Civil War, so called—and I'll quit gabbing if you'll tell me what was so doggone civil about it—Mr. Marsden hiked clear home. Walked.

Onct back, Will got hisself bathed, pruned of wild-man hair that'd make Absalom look like some witch-hazeled drugstore smoothie. Home in Falls, the child hoped to try and set things right, blend in, play like nothing much had happened. During the stroll from Virginia, Will planned the rest of his days the way you'll do after getting one of life's big reprieves. Decision: Marsden's remaining years would be orderly and quiet as his last three had not. But even while mapping a clean future and trudging plantation-wards, Will picked up some southbound body lice.

A colored livery-stable worker helped the child to kill such mites, using diluted sheep dip. (It's a miracle anybody lived for even six weeks back then.) Our town barber, Stark of Stark's Scissor Tonsorium, sheared Will's dreadlocks. The ex-private felt ashamed to be seen publicly whilst looking so ragged. In a hotel room, with the help of the colored worker's carrying hot water upstairs, Willie bathed and rebathed. Nine rinses went from charcoal black to murksome gray, then semi-dinge till turning clear as teardrops. The boy watched layers float from him till it seemed war was just some mold or stain. Being so young, at first he thought he'd washed it off that easy.

Marsden wrote a letter, had it hand-delivered to Mr. Lucas of Lucas' All-Round Store. "Dear Mr. Luke, Yes I am back. You have surely heard as you always did hear most every little thing. So since I am . . . back, please bring me over a suit of clothes such as a fellow like myself would be wearing nowdays. I never was that fancy of a dresser. I am I fear perhaps a good deal out of touch lately. Socks too. I am truly back and truly yours Willie Marsden. O Yes Best to Doris. I am also good for this credit-wise and know I need not mention it but just do not care to take anything for granted in trying to start over right."

The black suit, the huge hat, the button-up boots looked like what a wax dummy in some store window would pick for itself. Dressed, shorn, talc-powdered by barber Stark pleased with one whole quarter's tip, Willie soon looked ready to attend a funeral, maybe his own. This getup became the Captain's civvie uniform for life. Honey, so few men have eyeballs for anything except the profit margin and is the lawn mowed. That was my Captain. A stranger, looking for a child of ours, once asked Marsden to please describe our little girl. Cap went, "Well," and held up fingers of one hand like for counting off the features of his well-loved flesh and blood. "Well, she's kind of . . . she's about the size you would expect of a person her particular age and weight. Now her hair is in between brown and not, only lighter, and the eyes . . . what *are* her eyes, honey? —But why am *I* trying this. Her own mother's standing right here. Men shouldn't have to *describe*." It's a point of view, honey.

And yet he slowly became one of the better storytellers in eastern North Carolina, which is—truth be told—saying something.

Just back from war, Marsden installed his momma in rented rooms.
He didn't talk to her about his own sad deeds in the historic mud of Virginia
and Maryland. She couldn't yet speak, which spared her mentioning bad
local luck—her getting in the path of Sherman's firebugs. The Marsden farm
had been leveled. Though she still lived and breathed, this lady's personal
best—her character, the priss and fun and fuss of her—was mostly leveled
too. Her ruined face and arms and chest spoke three words: Scorched Earth
Policy. In twelve minutes, she'd gone from Beauty to Monster. A story there.

So, two well-brought-up souls just sat together. He would clutch his
large hat on one knee. She would hold a teacup, sometimes a full one, more
often empty, always white and always Spode. She slept with this safe in her
palm like some child clutching its toy. And she never rolled upon or broke
the thing, and rumor has it she was buried holding her favorite bone china,
comforting in the casket with her.

Lady Marsden's two boardinghouse rooms were stocked with most of
her plantation's famous furniture. It'd been spared from Sherman's flames
by Mrs. Marsden's slave girl, one Castalia. The fine Empire fixtures had—
unlike poor Mrs. Marsden—escaped all fire damage except the stink of
smoke. (One time as a child of eleven, I was let in there. The rooms were
dark, thin paths ran betwixt best furnishings from a home of seventy-odd
rooms. The smell of the mansion's burning had lasted thirty years, was
sucked deep into brocades, it coated apple wood and glazed the gilt. These
rooms full of charcoal stink and marble masterpieces were occupied by a
woman whose face looked like a rawhide fleece-lined moccasin left six
months in the rain. Just the violence of her place's smell scared me witless.
This smell seemed so "old" to me at eleven. Seemed the war I sniffed harked
back to Sparta/Carthage, not just Charleston and Atlanta.) But I get ahead
of myself by getting behind. It's a pattern with me, sugar. Look, ain't nobody
perfect. Here at first I'm trying hard to keep this all set in line. It's tough,
being a good housekeeper for pretty much total chaos.

Alone together sat the Lady victim and her son. They rested, wordless,
three, four hours at a stretch. Aristocrats, they were on terms with silence.
They'd both grown up on the plantation, so far from anything but its own
self, silent, respected, feared. They now felt comforted by the passing clomp
of buggy traffic (Saturday was market day for the county's colored and its
white). The Marsdens liked sparrows' squabbling with happy domestic
meanness under boardinghouse eaves. Will sat fooling with his hatband.
Lady More Marsden dangled one empty teacup out in air like expecting
some slave (freed these several years now) to please come pour, please.

Fresh home, Marsden worked regular hours. Had to. Was the one way
he stayed half held together. Thank God for work! Willie yet owned the
timepiece of that Yankee boy he'd plugged. He kept the thing wound and
displayed on the mantel of his own rented rooms downtown. Years after
Appomattox, Will yet had the gold watch. He claimed that the moment for
returning it won't quite right, North-South mails still unsafe. Fact is, he

hated giving it up. Only souvenirs he owned were that and his sword and scabbard, his dead buddy's bugle, and a twig cut from one pondside tree where the bad thing happened.

Marsden was both a civilian child and a military grownup. He'd been hardened on each count by what he'd lost. He had only outlived his much-loved Ned by three war years. During that time, Willie'd seen so much, he'd had to hurt so many, the poor fellow got to thinking Ned had been his son!

That's how far in advance of your legal age a war can toss you.

And, oh dear, young William More Marsden remembered everything. Later I understood: a good memory is about one-third cure and two-thirds curse. My own memory, this very one I'm using, is my best handy example. You drop a child into the middle of a battle, he can't guess at the bigger reasons leading here—like maybe Northern factories vs. Southern farms.

A child just sees the results. I mean *sees* them.

Every passing minié, it'd stuck. That boy's brain was a savings account with waste in it: times of day, smoke, the whole map, horses lost, names of all his dead. True facts had snagged and abscessed, their sharp ends in. His poor young head was a pincushion calendar.

If they made my husband walk through one of these new aeroport X-ray machines checking for weaponry? why, just his memory would set it off.

Weird
for 1860

*Open thou mine eyes, that I may behold wondrous things out of thy
law. I am a stranger in the earth . . .*
— PSALM 119:18—19

HOME in Falls—three weeks after the waterhole shooting—Ned's
mother was still mailing her boy long letters. Mostly gossip
about nesting habits of her thirty-odd Harz Mountain canaries.

Telegraph lines were being cut then mended around Richmond. Headquarters favored military dispatches over condolence notes to thousands of
civilian mommas. If your boy is dead, finding out a month late is really a
type of favor, right? Such runs gents' logic anyway. I'll say more later about
gents' logic, where it parts ways with mine. Shortages in Falls meant folks
had already tried baking bread with acorn flour. "How's it taste?" somebody
asked concerning the first loaf. "Sort of like," a taster smacked, staring into
space, ". . . oak."

Local children claimed that Ned Smythe's mother used her back-yard
bird feeder to trap sparrows and thrushes. Children swore the widow then
chopped up birds' bodies, fed these to her canaries so they'd sing more larky
and free. When I was coming up, kids yet said this about her. Of course, I
knew it just won't true. Still, I pictured it so clear.

Now I don't want to say that Winona Smythe, the songbird breeder,
was a odd-type person but—fact is—even before her Ned perished in so sad
a manner and prior to grief's taking over, the lady had a knack for seeming
the wee-est bit weird. People wondered how Ned—so platinum and mild—
had sprung from this stubby grunch of a lady. Bound for school, Ned left
a yard where wisteria did what it jolly well pleased, where saplings claimed
the lawn. Ned whistled toward Lower Normal, orderly and starched, offering
greetings to Falls' citizens, milkmen included.

When people inquired about his widowed mom, Ned'd say, "Momma's
never been better, thank you. I'll mention your asking. Bound to please her."
Folks nodded, guessing just what Winona Smythe might sputter about the
idiots and hypocrites in this backward town. She fancied herself a thinker.

She'd grown up in Richmond and had never got over it. Some locals claimed she'd been a beauty when arriving here, a bride. Winona had been admired (if at all) for the tininess of her feet and the high number of books she put away. Her boy never seemed to notice the shouting matches his momma sparked in Lucas' All-Round Store. Winona Smythe, hands on hips, would corner perfect strangers: "And what are *you* web-footed inbreds gaping at?"

Ned even shrugged off the neighbors' petitions every spring. Summit Avenue's other fancy yards (two colored gardeners apiece) approached azalea season's ruddy peak. County wagons rattled to and fro before Falls' great homes—farm folks seemed amazed at everything that money can buy. Winona's place stunned beauty lovers. Weeds were chest-high. Come 1859, neighbors' letters again begged Mrs. Smythe to kindly have her lawn mowed "and timbered" (it'd got that bad).

The woman hadn't left her tangled yard since Ned marched off to war. All her groceries were delivered. She threw trash into her prissiest neighbors' yards. Popularity Plus, Winona won't. Fact is, even before she met her strange illegal destiny, she was considered semi-weird on the local level.

For then, I mean. Of course, what passes for strange nowadays is twelve octaves more so. Example being: one of my favorite volunteer candy-stripers here at the Home. "My fave," as she'd likely put it. Sweetest features you ever seen, but you know she went out and got herself a Mohawk hairdo? Fifteen years old. Then she just *had* to stick a pin clear through her right nostril, I'm not even talking about a brooch, child, I'm talking safety pin. And her daddy's a doctor!

The child still causes quite a stir when she sulks in here. Full of sighs and potential, this one. Jerome says she has a "advanced fashion sense." If that means turning your ears and nose into a hardware store, I guess she does. She's stayed right loyal to us, God love her. Me, I admire loyalty and remember it. I'm pleased the child wants to come in and help us—however she looks. Few along our hall still let her even read to them. I figure you can always close your eyes, during. Still, you know me, honey, I got to stare right at her. See, I'm trying and learn. I don't plan to be like some of these fuddy-duds in here. Some whine they just don't *get* the latest craze. Then they cross their arms, roll their eyes, and pray that death'll take them beyond fads.

She set here droning Dickens at me not two days back, hair up like a skunk taxidermied in butch wax. I said to her, "Zondro" (her real name is Sandra but she changed it just to have her way and feel in charge—something *I* understand). I go, "Zondro, is this new hairstyle a way of showing you feel . . . sad about the Indians?"

That got a major sigh.

"Why should *I* feel sad about some moldy old Indians? Hunh? Uh-oh, are *you* one? You could be. Indians have zillions of wrinkles too, maybe from living outdoors. But I don't even *know* any Indians, do you, Luce?" (I let these young ones call me what they will. I'm glad they speak to me at all.)

"None that're full-blooded." But I asked *why* that pelt set aslant young Zondro's noggin? I told her I won't judging, just keeping up. "Is your new 'do' maybe a sign of modern . . . sadness?"

"Hey, does it all always have to *mean* stuff? People your age never catch on. You think all of it always adds up to something. Read Zondro's lips. Start with zero, then go down from there. Everybody in here is old but you've really racked up the oldie-moldie points, hunh? You could've probably been next-door neighbors to the Flintstones."

"To the who?"

"Fred and Wilma Flintstone."

"I knew a Fred and Wilma. Lived out by the ice plant?"

"It's more like a joke. Only not." She was back to the hair—these young ones'll skip around on you. They get it from off the TV, channel hopping. "See, there's a guy at school that's completely drop-dead-looking, hunk city. So, see, he did it and then he caught so much flak, his four best friends got theirs shaved to keep him company and then—when I heard how people yelled things out of cars at them and threw beer bottles and stared and gave them such intensive heavy-duty static, well, one night I got super-bummed over it and I felt so, like, totally fritzed, I grabbed the pinking shears and then my mom's Lady Norelco and, well, the rest is history. We hang out at the Mall. People are so rude. We're just showing them that we're, you know, resisting it all. They feel that, and boy they just hate you for it. My friend, Jason? he keeps his unbelievably neat, his stretches from here to here. My boyfriend's is star-shaped."

"Your boyfriend's what, sugar?"

"His hair, dummy. Sorry. But you have a dirty mind. You do, Luce. Down and dirty. How can you be so old and still think about it just nonstop? I hope I don't, not then. Some days I'm sick of it already. You're always asking me this bizarre-o stuff. I've already told you way too much about him and me. Way way too. I don't know. I guess I hope you won't remember. Between visits. Others in here lose it week to week.

"I mostly just tell you stuff because you're here and can't move and I need to . . . to tell. But you? you always remember. It's not fair almost. I don't think you'd *use* it against me, but who can anybody trust? Remember about in the car, at night, that time in the car with the three of them? I'm sorry, Luce, but you keep hoping for more pay dirt. You keep expecting I'll be . . . *per*sonal. Jason wants to make his into a swastika but he's redheaded and did you ever try and make *your* red hair be a swastika?"

I admitted as how I hadn't, yet.

"Well, swastikas are super-hard to see unless you're standing right over the person or if they lean way down to *show* you, and that's not cool, especially not at the Mall. We're just there, minding our own business and these, like, hicks—do the rest. They start stuff. Sorry about unloading on 'hicks' too. Look, maybe we better just get back into this oldtimey story junk you keep asking for."

"Fine, sugar, didn't mean to pry none, just struggling to stay 'up to the minute.' It's a job, ain't it?"

Dickens is about to have Bill Sikes throttle little Oliver to death and Zondro reads this like tonight's TV listing, no, without that much juice. Her tone sounds a regular robot's—but at least her hair plans to be a prank. I *think* she means it partway as a joke. See, I'm trying and catch on. Darling? you got to really work at that to stay alive, don't you?

But, yeah, getting back—for around here, in 18 and 60–65, never leaving your small house, intermarrying canaries among theirselves to be your only conversation partners, letting your yard go to weeds then woods, plus later living on the wrong side of the law . . . well, for then and there, it did seem pretty do-funny. Not, I admit, a safety pin through the nose—but every age has got its own pet form of weirdness, honey.

There's styles in madness too.

2

HOW DID locals know that Mrs. Smythe's pretty son had been shot dead? They heard the lady's sounds, they saw her rolling around in the front yard's high weeds. The poor postman stood outside Winona's garden gate. He was just watching. Since telegraph lines were down, it'd fallen to this fellow—delivering the city limits' worst possible news. Such letters from General Headquarters/Richmond came in black-edged envelopes. You were at least spared the suspense of wondering what was *in* yours.

First the postman rung a corroded bell on the widow's rusted gate. Honeysuckle had already heaved her cast-iron fence ten inches off the ground. For the longest time, no answer—only canaries' scared cheeping from the glassed porch. Finally she did stomp out, but like interrupted from doing something pretty doggone big-time. The postman was holding out a fat letter, afraid to step onto the wooded lot. "I am," he said, "so sorry to be the one. It's this. One of these."

Living isolated like she did, the widow wouldn't of known what a black-rimmed envelope meant. Mrs. Smythe was a squat mug-shaped woman with a man's face but a baby's shoe size (4). She already wore black for the sake of a husband, dead these six years. She snatched the thing. Our mailman—armed with smelling salts and extra hankies—stayed to be of use. He watched the lady turn away from him and start reading. Even after a hiccup at seeing the first line, she kept on, bringing the pages closer and closer to her face till, by the end some minutes later, she fell directly off the brick path and—making such sounds—went climbing through her jungly yard. They say it was most terrible to see.

She didn't crawl toward her house but went lunging among underbrush, holding the letter stretched between either tiny hand, using elbows and knees to inchworm her weight along. Beloved birds indoors, hearing such cries, went nearabout crazy. Canaries had remained Winona's best and only friends. Her body stayed low to the ground—like some soldier's when air's plaited through with lead.

Neighbors heard, walked, come rushing. Among them my own mother—who was not that yet—a thin strict half-spoiled heiress whose mission in life was to later whip me into ladyship and grammar and who failed at both, poor thing. Folks found courage, finally pushed open a creaking gate, they lifted Mrs. Smythe from out the chest-high weeds of her un-lawn. They helped the lady up porch steps into her house. Nobody had ever been invited in. The grocery delivery boy claimed it was the worst-kept white household in town, no cleaning done, ever. Widow Smythe's staples were mostly oatmeal and pralines, plus birdseed purchased by the tow sack.

Entering, folks hushed from the shock ("Not our polite little Ned"). Folks silently remembered small neighborhood decencies of his. Bound for school, how clean Ned looked. True, he placed live pigeons in the schoolhouse desk drawer of "Witch" Beale. But when they flew at her, she laughed!

Visitors soon grew quieter from the pure strangeness of being in here. Overdue library books were stacked in columns clear to the ceiling. You wandered across scattered birdseed husks, in some spots inches deep. "Like sand on the beach," said Momma every time she retold this later, "thick as sand on the beach." The front parlor was paved with old newspapers, spongy layers that your shoes sunk into. This whole home seemed the whispery bottom of a single birdcage.

Some neighbor girls strolled right into Ned's room. They'd always wanted to. Nobody thought of keeping them out. Girls knew just where he'd slept. Hadn't they seen his lamp in here while he did homework for "Witch" Beale? Girls found the little cell real tidy, a few wooden toys, some pictures (a grizzly bear, a deer) cut from magazines and tacked up just so. One child touched the small oak bed's white blanket, found a single golden hair, she held it to daylight. Other girls gathered to touch it. "That's the sweetest thing I've ever seen," one said, and, sniffling, girls retreated with their prize.

Adults had propped up Mrs. Smythe—glassy-eyed—on a black horse-hair chaise that proved she must let her thirty German-but-filthy birds fly free right often. Neighbors—waving the postman's smelling salts under Winona's big chin—were promising casseroles. During hurricanes and house fires, minutes after hatchet murders, the ladies of Falls had and have one ready answer for survivors: a nice hot casserole. It still works, darling, and I'm glad for it, having eaten many a one since I got too old for anybody's letting me near a gas stove. (They tried calling me a public menace for cooking my own breakfast—alone at home, imagine!)

Neighbors were already forming shifts to come check on Mrs. Smythe. Somebody noticed her breath steady a bit, her nostrils spread. She suddenly bellowed, "You *made* him leave. My one child. I should've kept him back. You know what he looked like? How he sounded? You led the brass band to my front gate. You'll lose your war anyway. Watch. I just understood— I'll never see him again, will I? Tell me otherwise. I'll never get to wash his hair again. —Who asked you in here? Vultures, with their young. You swoop in the one time I'm too pained to stop you. Buzzards! Leeches and their leech babies!"

The group back-stepped quick over years of *Falls Herald Travelers*. Winona lurched, folks spilled down her brick steps. The committee of girls ran fast but guarded that one hair like it was some single lighted birthday candle. Everybody poured through the garden gate, feeling safer on the street. But Winona didn't leave her home. You could see her in there releasing all birds from their cages. She slammed her front door. Through porch-glass panes, neighbors saw a black dress now flocked across with beating yellow wings— the fragilest cloak and helmet of real lives. "Make my skin crawl," somebody said. Somebody else said, "She'd be a novel, but nobody'd believe it."

Won't two full days after the widow drove sympathizers from her yard, she posted a sign announcing that her songbirds were now for sale. (She'd been broke but hadn't admitted it till knowing her poor Ned was dead.) And it was that very evening, her watchful neighbors—ever vigilant for casserole reasons or new chapters in the not yet written Book of Here—noticed the addition.

Come morning there it sat in Winona Smythe's brambled side yard: a gray army tent propped—occupied.

3

I STILL own the letter. Winona willed it to my Captain. I got it next. Chain of command. Its writer was the gent who wondered aloud, would a war be "canary suitable," who stopped Rebs' carving up the Yankee sniper. See my bedside table's top drawer? Sometimes I call it The Archives. Sometimes I call it the top drawer. Fish out that whole musty bundle. You wouldn't believe what-all's in there. I'm sure I'd be surprised by half this mess. Look, time's turned my papers and me as brown as any good Cuba cigar. Here . . .

August 19, '62

Dear Mrs. Theodore Smythe,

We sorely regret to inform you that during the early PM of August 12, 18 and 62, your son, Private Ned Smythe, much beloved by his fellows-in-arms, was, in the line of duty, while being elevated to the rank of National Hero, deprived of his young life. The fatal skirmish took place roughly nine miles southeast of Cheatham, Virginia. The commandant (who was some distance from the locale of said incident) has asked me to explain that, at the time of your boy's death, young Ned had scaled a tree, apparently scouting enemy fortification on the far shore. It was then that Yankee miniés found and ended his valiant young life. He was killed at once, and, insofar as it is possible to tell such things, without apparent pain.

Though custom dictates that such letters as this inform the bereaved family of how respected and beloved their deceased soldier was, in Ned's case, the task proves especially easy (and therefore, Mrs. Smythe, most difficult). His beauty of character, of carriage, and of person were remarked upon by all. His trusting genial air and constitutional fineness provided each of us, during fatiguing manoeuvres, with an odd margin of quietude and consolation. His singing voice alone was a gift enjoyed by some of the Confederacy's highest-ranking officers. The night before he was taken from us, he sang for the men and with a perfect trusting composure that bespoke an admirable and genteel education.

He leaves behind a friend from your hometown, a boy as yet (these seven days after the shooting) only fitfully able to continue. If you will permit me a personal note in what should perhaps remain a more official communication.

Not long after one of our early victories, we had reason to encamp at a former mining camp along the Shenandoah Ridge. It had once been devoted to the excavation of either mica or gold. Its building showed the effects of years-previous abandonment. Pleased by this bivouac, both your son and his friend adopted, as boys will, a particular deserted cabin. They made it theirs during the four days we used the site.

The hut had been formerly employed, to judge from scales and a remaining chalkboard on its wall, as an ore-weighing station. Late one evening, as I was unable to sleep, I found myself pacing and smoking, feeling singularly homesick. I chose to wander our camp. I carried a lamp and, as I passed this roofless cabin, my light chanced to fall upon some bright surfaces within. I stepped through an open doorway. One full burlap sack, patterned with a felicitous checkerboard design, rested upon the table between your son and his friend. Both boys had fallen asleep while playing marathon checkers. The "pieces" were shards of crystal which the boys had collected at our various camps, much to the consternation of our fond commanding officer who warned as how the weight of such souvenirs might well slow the lads when they most needed speed.

On the aforementioned chalkboard, boys had marked up their scores. One youth's side was called, according to the legend, "The Official Falls, NC, Checker Team," and below it, a second such association had been titled, "The Other Official Falls, NC, Checker Team." I am myself the father of two daughters not far from the ages of the children I encountered that night. I stood in the hut looking down upon these boys intent on passing time while seeking to somehow encourage themselves. The sack holding their game had become a mutual pillow. Only boys' crooked arms prevented their young faces from pressing onto the quartz bits arranged between them. The children's muskets were propped, at the ready, in a far corner. Boys' fitful sleep would, I feared, stand them in poor stead for tomorrow's long march. And yet, stepping forward, about to wake them, I hesitated. Something in their slumber, their very trustfulness bespoke a similar moment I had experienced in my daughters' treehouse, one built with my own hands. I did not wake your son and his friend. I could not bear, Madam, to remind them of their current whereabouts and circumstance.

As with all of us here, the boys lately witnessed instances of carnage which—had we been forewarned in the quiet days before Sumter—would have seemed literally unendurable. And yet, one survives! I found the small moment I've described to be so peaceful and consoling. I felt nearly guilty at the peace I let it give me. But I have forgotten myself and my official function here. It is very late. Other chores are before me. I was writing of your son, a young gamesman making the best of an inhuman situation. Of course, it forever stays human because, human, we are here, having to endure it. I must end.

The camp is now so quiet, the countryside so peaceful. Even the twelve cannons I see across the way are all beaded with dew. It is inconceivable what noise and bloodshed might break upon us with first light. In addressing this to you, Madam, I seem to communicate with my own family and with all those persons I have written during these past two years. I have set down, usually at less length, roughly nine hundred such letters. I feel myself becoming half-accomplished at it. There are many things we should all remain quite bad at.

It is grievous to consider that my years of education, my early attempts at diary-keeping and at clarity of expression—enterprises so blithely and romantically undertaken in my privileged youth— should be thus enlisted. I recall my boyish Odes to various seasons, to various young ladies of my acquaintance. Odes! Were I now to try one, its subject might be the miracle that any person should have found the time and hope to ever attempt such a thing as an Ode!

Before first light, I must write three more families of three more men and boys I knew. If time proved less limited, I might send a second note of condolence to the mother of Private Marsden, so much a pair were those fine examples of Southern Boyhood. Please convey my sentiments. Her father, the late Judge More, was, I believe, in my father's class at Harvard College. They often traveled to school and home on the same holiday trains.

Closing, I can only leave you with reminders of the undoubted Rightness of our Cause. Be comforted, Madam, in understanding that your Child, while admittedly losing his life and being "untimely ripped"—has also Risen to the Threshold of that August Assemblage—The Martyrs to the Great Cause of Secession.

I remain most respectfully yours, a brother in grief, a fellow parent, an aspirant to glorious Honor and/or the Aforementioned Martyrdom Itself.

Officially and personally, Madam, I sign myself, with utmost sympathy,

First Lt. Vreeland Hester, CSA.
3:40 AM. In the White Oak Swamp,
somewhere Southeast of Gaines' Mill, Virginia

4

I MISS boiling my own water.

I been in here fourteen years and, previous to that, a stove was mostly where you'd find me, something to complain about slaving over a hot one of all day.

My husband liked his beef done nearbout raw—the children hated that. Seeing Captain's so pink, they always chanted, "Nosebleed, nosebleed." Where do kids come up with these things? *You* ever try doing a twelve-pound beef roast in your wood stove so meat's one end'll turn out red and the other a nice dark brown? Well, try. Mostly it's in how you stack your firewood.

But the water, the comfort of each morning's water boiling. —Back then, I'd be the first one awake naturally. The kids were babies, and me I won't much older. Dawn seemed my sloppy younger sister. Many's the day I beat her downstairs. Right off, I'd stoke kindling in my Wedgwood stove. From the pump, I'd fill one favorite white enamel saucepan rimmed with red. I always placed it on a back burner. (Otherwise little paws grab handles and scald little heads.) To be up and puttering in a big still-sleeping house, to hear the paper boy lob today's *Falls Herald Traveler* more or less onto our front porch, to hear his bike click off, followed by the toenails of his dog on Summit Avenue's bricks. To find that nighttime dark had gone a wet-wool gray as soon as you quit expecting light. From the window over my sink, our back yard looked to be a dresser drawer full of mist.

I was never one to use a kettle. (Teapot whistles make me nervous.) No, I liked to *see* my water boil. Pearl bubbles gather around its edges (a family reunion, resemblances galore). Then they send family representatives up top to check. Finally you have the whole thing twirling into necessary violence. I like to *smell* my water, feel its steam uncurl. At this early hour, water offered Lucy her best company. Times, water felt too perfect to be local—it seemed international or better. A spirit friend. I'd be making production-line school sandwiches. Lay down your two dozen bread slices in a row, get you a goodly glob of butter—then run along the table—coating every last one, target practice. I could do it while half asleep right now and from my wheelchair here.

My morning mood I gauged by water's speed in boiling. If it happened quick, I felt more "up." If it took forever, was going to be one of *them* days.

Odd, the kitchen sometimes felt more crowded *before* my cast of characters woke and scuffed downstairs. Somebody would soon admit to unfinished math homework, another might show first polka dots of chicken pox ("Momma, I don't *feel* so good"). But not yet, thank God. A crew of quieter, healthier ghosts rose with me, my list and honor roll trailing after, faint but real as steam. The water'd long ago been ready for coffee. I let it babble anyhow—just the way I let children natter about anything they pleased, me half listening to their staticky half-music. A jay bossed sparrows at our feeder. Later, Moxie, the Seeing Eye Labrador, would be underfoot—another mouth to stuff.

I was often tired. That I know. Looking back, you don't want to misremember and soften one little thing. That'd be wrong—I'd rather sound too harsh. And yet, I admit, at times and from this distance, misrecalling sure is tempting, child. Especially about our house before my others rose. The wall under the clock was penciled with their heights (changing each six months) but their initials constant. From this narrow bed-wide cell here, these partitions of yellow plywood, I recall my own home kitchen as being so huge—half a train depot and full of eastern light and, with water boiling, chummy-sounding as a fishbowl-sized reunion.

Once the twenty-odd pieces of breakfast toast were under way, once all lunch boxes and thermoses were lined up and latched shut, once each was tagged (Baby's full of complexion food, Louisa's with that extra sandwich she begged for despite her little weight problem), once the sun—following Lucy's good example—got the idea and trudged toward its monitor's position overhead, *then* I would allow myself a first cup of coffee. Dear God but it was excellent! Having done a bit of work already always made my java taste the better, child. At fifteen, I learned to take it black. That way you're freer. Freer of expecting extras. I had just one cup for starters but savored so before rushing upstairs on my unpopular mission of waking.

Throughout, I left the saucepan boiling away downstairs, on guard, chitter-chatter, giving itself away to kitchen air. Sometimes I'd refill the pan. I told myself such steam would be good for all our lungs . . . But too, I just liked the sound it made bubbling, a heart-to-heart with morning light, itself, me.

At this Home, staff people heat things up. We got no microwave at

Lanes' End Rest owing to six patients' pacemakers. So even now, even in this world of rockets and all, water takes just as long to boil. Some things never change, which is good. Personally, I want to be cremated. Studying water's boiling taught me how clean it'd all be. Fire will just have a conversation about you and with you, a real *thorough* conversation, I admit. You'll meet fire. Fire will take a shine to you. You're its subject. What will it say about you before it loses interest? I know how, in a quiet morning house, water makes party sounds, the angels of the elements all up and gossiping at dawn. Another-day-in-the-world's shoptalk.

If authorities let us have hot plates here in our cubicles, I swear I'd do me some water every morning of my life—just to smell and hear and feel it play across my face.

Child, I sure miss boiling my daily own. You know what water is?

Water's family.

5

MAYBE I told you how our charity Home got its peculiar name. All this property was once owned by a merchant family, name of Lane. Our leafy dead end of the road kept being called the Lanes' End of it. And when this cinder-block, glass-brick, and asphalt-roofed thingum got built on the cheap in 19 and 49, the name stuck. Lanes' End. —Nobody can tell me it's a friendly title for a body's final dwelling place. I don't like to talk against the officials but I think it's sloppy of them not to be a bit more sensitive and to change it. Might as well call it: Funeral Home Annex. Senility Central. Or something.

Reading the wooden sign's WELCOME TO LANES' END when your ambulance pulls up, well, it's harder on the new people. By now us veterans make jokes about it. You learn to. Maybe that's *why* we been around so long. That, and the love of our daytime TV show, *My Children, Right or Wrong*, plus little hallway scandals, and a basic knack for laughing things off. The old ones that can't, ofttimes they go first.

He who laughs—lasts.

RECENT-ARRIVED women tend to mix in quickest. Though sore from travel, they wonder, What *does* one wear to dinner? A sign of health. Newhere men take so much to heart. They care too much for their old idea of dignity—the dignity of a thirty-five-year-old boy, not somebody eighty-odd or over.

Darling, you got to keep revising downwards how much to expect. Or—no—just shifting what you'll settle for. I don't want to scare you about getting up to this particular thin-aired timberline of time. But let's put it this way: You got to be willing to change. Once *you* harden, the arteries do.

6

SEEN in downtown Falls, young Private Marsden was public now—pared of his mane, freed from passenger vermin (he almost missed them like they'd been his last war victims—and ones he might've saved, pets kept pearly in a jar). The boy dressed in civvies that at first felt uneasy as a robber's disguise. But Willie soon looked regular in street clothes as you or me. He buggied across three counties reclaiming family holdings. He knew—if you plan to make decent money—you got to at least *look* in charge.

Bound for his livestock yard, the boy passed other vets gathered in a pie-shaped park before our pretty Courthouse. Some got helped downtown by wives—these ladies were overjoyed to have their whole mornings quiet at home.

Two bachelors lived life in matching wicker hampers. Friends lugged these legless one-armed fellows towards the sunny public spot, left them out—to air all day like laundry. —Passing, the stringy young Marsden forever touched his big hat's brim and politely sidestepped this motley crew. Sure, he heard them jawing over old campaigns. He chose not to stop—seemed he had nothing much to add. Before the war, Will had considered these men cranks and yahoos. They seemed even more so afterwards. Only now— they felt the world owed them a living because they'd lost major battles in three states!

They did get strange respect downtown. Small girls sat there, listening big-eyed, keeping clear of awful brown tobacco juice that vets spit with infantryman's prideful aim. "Didn't get any *on* you, did I, peaches and cream? Will you look at this curly head, fellows? I tell you *that's* what we fought it for." Ladies placed dinner leavings and mended shirts on park benches nearby—like small offerings set near some religious type of shrine. Child, now War was done, these roustabouts finally had all the leverage some people ever ask of the world: at long last, subject matter.

So did Marsden but he kept his trap shut.

The two in laundry hampers rested beside each other sunny side up all day at Falls' dead center, soaking in whatever tales got told, both fleshy within oval baskets—like two huge willing nasty ears. Most of the vets had known young Ned. They'd heard about his mother's convulsions on hearing the news. They knew how Winona Smythe had—for the first time in years— ventured off her own property. She'd stormed downtown and right into the First Baptist's sanctuary during choir practice. She grabbed her donated art-glass pitcher and candlesticks from off the altar, all while screaming toward the steep-pitched roof, "I want him back, now. Or *else!*" This was the way our delicate choirmaster first learnt of young Ned's death. Winona won't exactly Mrs. Tact on tiptoes. The entire alto section had to help the poor director home. (In emergencies, you just couldn't count on the temperamental sopranos. Altos'll usually come through for you. I speak as one myself before time made my tunes go so colandered and crackledy.) Altos carried him up the steps to his one room as he taunted them, "That Smythe boy had more talent in his little finger than all you thirty years of dullard monotones combined. The voice at large in him. To lose his perfect pitch *and* the war! I loved him. Are you ladies shocked? Do be, please. Because, where does any of it *get* you, the keeping quiet? Where does it? Thirty years' painstaking musicianship. For what, for whom? Who notices, what use?" The altos considered crying but didn't, instead they cleared their throats, in perfect B natural, a tribute to him.

Altos found his room lined with three decades' pictures of the choir— Ned's curly head was real recent and proved much circled here and there in red. Two at a time, for days, altos sat beside the bachelor's bed, they feared he'd take his life. Near the bed, sudden casseroles cooled and hardened. Altos sat with him in pairs because he was, after all, a man alone and wearing pajamas (marked with cleft signs). These were churchgoing women, after all—even if they knew this bald lost gent was not exactly a major menace to unchaperoned womankind. Women were his best friends. That was it. Women stayed the ones he blamed and yet the ones he cried to.

Under their breaths, while the choirmaster slept, altos muttered: poor Winona was now cooking on a campfire in her yard, was sleeping—during summer storms and all—in a pup tent in her side yard. Somebody saw her patrolling her yard's edges at night, lifting before her a canary cage she seemed to mistake for a lantern, seeking the one just man.

COURTHOUSE SQUARE'S gimpy vets had spied Will Marsden walking blocks out of his way to avoid Winona Smythe's house. He'd been back nearly a month but still dreaded that first visit. And who could blame him? Willie spent his Saturdays visiting spots where Ned and him had played. Far out past the ice plant, clear beyond Silver Lake, young Marsden was seen to wander. His new black boots were muddy from patrolling ditches where two boys'd onct trapped crawfish. Some of the old "camps" had been reclaimed by fresh batches of kids—the way birds'll take over abandoned nests. Marsden seemingly approved. On the ground beside a tall sycamore, he left six dimes for the six black kids presently playing there. It was Nash County's steepest sycamore and famous for that (in Nash County). From its topmost seasick limbs, you could spy clear to the poorhouse, high over and beyond the river Tar, almost to the forty steepled churches of Rocky Mount. Ned had got fired on while swinging from a sycamore. All this mattered to the mumbling young Marsden now squatting in a ditch nearby. His gold watch, still on loan from the Northern dead, rested open before him. His big dark hat rested on a forked stick jammed into the mud. Willie stared as black kids tilted the whole treetop side to side—he wore a strange stricken look. Seemed he expected the sycamore and all its children to explode in about thirty seconds. He checked his watch. Something strange was going on with Willie Marsden, a bottling-up that'd pop out soon or later. Count on it—law of physics. And with Falls being the size it was, if somebody noticed him yonder alone in a ditch, this meant—in under two hours—most every single local soul had heard.

People worried about him, true. (There are certain men that get noticed because they expect too little from the world. You want to tell the fellow, "Hey, you're entitled. You especially." This lack of hoping attracts others. Seems Mr. Gloom is full of liquid secrets, banked inside him. Oh, to wheedle a few loose, it'd be like siphoning pure gold honey from a ugly dusty hive. Nurses, ministers, romantics, children—and fools—*will* move toward these ones. Watch.)

BASED on what I've seen here in Lanes' End Rest, I could write me a whole new Surgeon General's Warning for Your Health, like maybe: When you lose your looks, don't repeat *don't* expect to get treated as a beauty no more. Makes sense but you'd be surprised how strong a habit Habit is. (The physical beauty part is one thing the Lord never handed me and therefore never got to giggle whilst snatching back.) I try and warn former beauties, Find something else to get you through. Get *good* at something. Even if that means crafts—wood-burning yet another Sitting Bull's head onto yet another pine plaque that'd rather stay plain pine.

We have a rougher time trying to make our new-here men feel properly noticed. Notice is a kind of oxygen. The professor across the hall told me about a experiment done at some Mexican orphanage: won't no nurse allowed to touch the babies except whilst changing diapers or jamming bottles into their mouths—and you know, from want of notice, some of them children just died? Fact. Happens at this end of the production line too. It's hardest on your shyest widowers and bachelors.

Arriving alone, they keep to their rooms. Men have got this gift for prideful glumness, for rehashing long-done-with grudges. Dignity—the wrong kind—undoes many a gent, seems like. They arrive here and find four woman to each male—you think *that'*d give them the will to live! But no—regular happiness seems cheap to them. They don't trust it yet (and with some fellows creeping beyond ninety). Once and for all, darling, getting old ain't getting wise. I could give you a wheelchair tour from room to room and prove my point. No names, please.

First thing men notice is how our Home's roof leaks so bad. Come April showers, there's tin and plastic trash cans lined up for catching hallway water. Your chair wheels get soaked. Your hands go black with rubbery grit. Then men discover that the food here can, some Thursdays especially, nearbout gag a maggot. To gents, it starts seeming a plot against them personally.

Being fellows that had jobs and pension plans they've outlived, men hate knowing that they're on the dole. All their lives they've said how Folks that don't Work should Starve. Now they can't work but they ain't ready for what they been wishing on the shiftless of all races. It's especially hard on your registered Republicans. They think us others in here, poor as them, hold it *against* them, or else that we ain't fit company ourselves, also being this broke while this "mature."

After the new men have been socked in here two weeks, we know if they are going to get the joke or not. —The un-laughers? the what-did-I-do-to-deserve-this types? well, they just die out quicker. It's simple. But if you see a fellow take a little interest in *My Children, Right or Wrong*, if you catch him asking what happened to each character before he come in on the middle, and if he speaks to you at dinner in Multi-Purpose and makes it to breakfast a few days a week, if you learn what he done for a living and which part of it he was best at and what he misses most, well—maybe he's going to be with us for a while. He's in on the prank, see? and knows it ain't just a stunt at his expense. It's here for *him* to chuckle over too.

Trouble is: what a body has got to laugh off—grows bigger and bigger, don't it, child? Soon you have to be a regular glutton for cruelty jokes. You got to laugh at them wicked Helen Keller ones and *be* li'l Helen reading them by hand off of a waffle iron. Near the end, bad jokes practically come sit on you, hollering down, "*This* strike you as funny? that grab you? this break your funnybone or this? *this*?"

But "Lanes' End Rest"? I think the name is tacky and that the government should be ashamed and change it.

7

ONCE Marsden made sure his own mother was alive enough to carry on, hid safe in a boardinghouse with Mr. William Morris' wallpaper and a servant girl around the clock, he steeled hisself for visiting Ned's. Couldn't be a chore that even your smoothest boy looked forward to: There's all kinds of bravery and—for some boys—social calls require a gumption in the league with Battle Nerve. How do you tell a widow that her single child is dead? Is it better to blurt out one loaded sentence or to first roll a long talked mattress under her—*then* hit her with it, making her fall more safe?

Of course, Will had heard how she received the letter. He didn't yet know which of his division officers'd wrote the thing. Local talkers described in great detail how—on hearing—Winona flopped into front-yard weeds. And yet, Will felt the death had not yet been announced. Wouldn't seem true for the Widow Smythe till Marsden hisself strode over, knocked, told. He put the visit off for a while.

One evening, safe in darkness, he waited outside her gate and studied the side-yard campfire, saw a figure cooking one spitted duck or turkey, turning it slow with a soldier's own patience.

FIRST seeing Willie back on the streets of metropolitan Falls, most citizens didn't know him. Boy'd grown that much. He'd come home six foot one and turned grave as a young deacon. One local—seated on the often reenameled bench outside Lucas' All-Round Store—finally said, "Now I got it. I'm ready for a wager. Looks to me to be a Marsden—a Marsden out of a More. His late poppa's hatchet face under that pale skin his messed-up mother used to be so famous for. Any takers?"

Nowdays, it's hard to imagine a time or town where your own genes announced you at forty feet. Some ways, of course, it's awful, having seeming strangers know—on sight—which two clans combined to form the stew of you.

But—in the end, you knew you were home because home knew who you were.

AND WHERE am *I*? A glitter in my poppa's sea-green eyes—him still a towheaded farm boy far out into the poorest part of the swampiest county in either Carolina. I am the luster on the pearly nose of my rich infant momma (her rolled by in a white wicker baby carriage with its own attached white silk umbrella). Captain Marsden strides so far ahead of me in time, my own folks came of age noticing him around town, grown and sad, black-suited as a cast-iron weather vane—one character that children steered clear of.

FINALLY, fresh home and brilliantined, the young man set out, bracing hisself to do his duty. Will first stopped at Lucas', bought the widow some horehound candy. Then—looking like a longtime suitor trapped in clothes too-new—he strolled over, swallowing hard, unannounced.

Everybody knew exactly where he was bound, of course. They'd been waiting. A few people trailed him.

Marsden shoved into the yard, he overstepped bones of a dead campfire, he knocked on the tent's center pole, waited, cleared his throat, finally bent at his knees. Only a clot of blankets in there. At the house's front door, Willie tapped. Polite, neighbors hid behind the japonica bushes next door till something either did or did not happen next.

Winona at last opened. She looked like insomnia packed into one out-grown black dress. She wore cologne. She smelled terrible but tempting. Winona smelled that day like a jelly doughnut.

Will, standing on the lady's stoop, felt dizzy. He had to stare clear down at her. I *have* grown, he decided. He'd once arrived here and asked, "Ma'am, can Ned please come out and play?" Then he always gaped far up at Winona's great breakfront bosom, her solid chins. Today he felt perched on two high tin kitchen stools, his new God-given legs.

"I'm back," said he. "But, our Ned he's not. I've come to tell you. That. See. Something happened." Will began to explain, slow, about the millpond, the high spirits, mules being in already, that tree yonder, a loved one's swinging out over water. —Winona, not having asked Will into her home yet, screamed. Neighbors (who'd gathered owing to some sixth sense that gossip fodder sends, electric, in the air) left japonica's cover. Get those casseroles ready.

Canaries, hearing Winona, screaked. The widow ran deeper into her place. She tripped. Will followed. She barged away from him. She fell. He lifted her. She escaped. Winona struggled. She hit him on the shoulders. She screamed at him, "Deserter." She pushed Will hard. Then, turning, toppled. Will propped her up. She cursed him, "We sent you off together. *He* would be home today too. You were a unit. I distinctly told you, 'Guard him with your life.' Well, here's *yours*, all grown up and clumsy, nothing much to look at, but where's our Ned's, William? He started out so splendidly, he'll most certainly stay fine when you stop this prank. Show me. Where've you *hid* him?" And she pressed closer, poking through Will's jacket, her fingers digging far into the pockets of his new trousers. She held the gawky kid against hall wallpaper. He now clutched a candy sack up against his Adam's apple. Winona, finding no sign of her son anywhere on Will, soon struck his shoulders, his chest. He stood making low sounds, face so long, eyes half closed, head turned aside—expecting nothing, accepting everything. Only when Winona moved to knee him in his sudden grownup's groin did Will draw up one leg, block her jab.

She quit then. Seeing his blank features, Winona fell directly against him, sobbing in a way that scared canaries flying all over her house (only now did Marsden notice them, loose—circling her, trying to be her favorites, a black planet's beauty pageant of yellow moons). Seemed that birds would go crazy from her noise. Flying, they each gave off these flaky little mica chips of sound.

Out front, more neighbors glommed along the fence. Two men were eating sandwiches. It was getting to be a club. They worried now, less for the widow than her young visitor. "Poor thing," they said. "A whole war. And Winona to boot."

The front door stood open. Folks could hear her strange unnatural sounds—unnatural because they were (your hair standing on end, your arms' skin curdling) so natural, so often felt—and yet real seldom heard. Especially rare here on expensive Summit Avenue, where every bush was called topiary, where many people's first names were last names, where— unlike the county—no black dog was called Blackie and no white one Snowball. On this refined tree-lined street lived a person named Winona who would do absolutely anything she felt like, and anytime she chose. She should not be allowed to try such things and still have this remarkable address. Being weird, weird even for '65, made her a dangerous person, it meant she'd maybe probably come to a real bad end. Everybody knew this. Even Winona. Winona especially. But, honey, that made her just act the wilder.

Meanwhile, indoors, unknown to spectators but explained to me years later: Once Widow Winona had sobbed a sufficiency, once she'd begun acting semi-recovered, she grabbed the young man by what was left of his new-clipped hair. Right in the hall, whilst jerking his knobby head with each word spoke between her clamped teeth, she made Willie M. kneel, "Where/ were/you/when/they/got/him? Where, *were*, you?"

Soon listeners out front heard another sound, bass-baritone, buckling up under hers. "Now him too," folks told each other. Of a sudden her craziness—just railed against—got more dignified. (Emotions sure are mercury quicksilver.) Will's joining her in grief made neighbors see that—if *they* had lost a pretty only child like hers—maybe they'd feel nearbout as wronged.

But just then, plates started busting.

Neighbor dogs came running, barking. Breaking crockery hurt dogs' ears. Folks considered it selfish of her, pitching such a tantrum after she'd had so much time to prepare. Couldn't she just comfort a returned soldier? "*He* didn't kill her damn son," one fellow said.

"If you put her in a book," somebody shook a head sideways. A wit answered, "And I would, too, put her in one, if it'd get her out of *here*." Members of the Books and Issues Luncheon Club nodded.

U H - O H , here comes shy William More Marsden backing through Winona's front door, his hat is in hand, palms are lifted, trying and soothe her, all while ducking to keep tossed crockery from his general eyeball area. Then out the open door Will's just exited, one canary flutters. It lights in branches of a scrub tree growing on Winona's lawn. The watching crowd makes a sound blending "Ahhh" and "Uh-oh." Then neighbors hear Winona give a shrill two-fingered whistle. She hollers, "Von Himmel the Fourth, kindly get your butt back *in* here, I mean immediately if not sooner." And like magic, the bird flies direct through the door, precise as a thread entering its needle. For Pete's sake.

One green saucer (looking to be Limoges—which makes Summit matrons grunt all the more) rolls through air, spins just above a young man's scalp, finds solid brick footpath feet beyond him, and busts with dainty yet maximum noise. Marsden backs through the front gate and through well-wishers who've parted. "Sorry," he says. He holds his new black hat in both hands, keeps turning it round and round like some pot that he's trying and make perfect on a wheel. His strange sinking smile aims at all these people, seems to ask forgiveness on behalf of a bereaved hotheaded mother and for the whole conniption-causing war itself.

Bidding everybody a good day, Marsden resettles his Pilgrimish headgear and stalks back to work. A green platter big enough to hold a turkey dinner for fourteen divides on bricks into many more than fourteen portions. Neighbors—not wanting to again be called Buzzards and Their Leech Infants—leave quick.

Walking downtown, Will finds a sack of candy yet palsied in his grip. He must use his left hand to pry open the clawed right fist. Moving to his place of business, wearing outsized clothes, he looks like a kid disguised to seem somebody full-grown. Which is exactly what he was, darling—he'll turn sixteen next November.

HE'S THE MAN I married and, in telling this part, I see why. Later, it got harder, child. But, here, okay, true, I am yet his wife. And I still consider "Willie" to be a good name for a person's husband. Not like these ones now, where everybody sounds like trying for some slinky moving-picture star. Your off brands—"Nigel" or "DeWitt."

My home kitchen counter had tin cylinders lined on it. Spelled in a honest delft-blue script that hoped to look like cross-stitching: "Salt" "Sugar" "Corn Starch." I can still picture each tin and—between giant "Flour" and the smallest "Baking Soda," I can easily imagine it spelled out—a word: "Willie"—another daily staple.

8

SURVIVING friends of Will's dead poppa took aside the tight-lipped heir. They gave him one business tip, important when the currency is topsy-turvy as the South's was '65 to '71: Do Not Barter.

To the family stockyard poor farmers were bringing wads of useless Confederate money. (It's now available every Saturday nowadays at the Big Elk Browse 'n' Buy Mall Flea Market at higher than face value. Moral: don't *ever* throw nothing out, honey. You hear me?) Yankee money hadn't even healed itself yet. Farmers brought the best things they yet owned. Marsden decided to barter. Word spread. Word will. Soon his front office was heaped with silver tea sets massed under green canvas tarps. A stray red hen built her nest inside a crystal punch bowl. Hired hands made bets: when would the chicks hatch—you could see the eggs right in there under her. Around this nest, columns of Wedgwood dinner plates piled like huge coins, service for forty-eight cashed in to help buy one necessary ginger mule. Marsden's stable loft soon looked like Ali Baba's cave or a certain barn glittering with the Wise Men's safe-deposit loot. In straw: six busts of Dante wearing what looked like the same shower cap, Shakespeare bearded but bald (must be a comfort to bald men). The four marble Walter Scotts and six plaster Jeff Davises were going cheap.

Older merchants still held out for cash on the barrelhead. Marsden only trusted what was real. The war had taught him that, made him literal. Thanks to such trading, this boy who'd walked home from northern Virginia's Children's Crusade, he soon started growing richer. "No small talk," county folks said. "No *talk*. But a right straight shooter. He'll nod if you got something he wants. He'll hold up a certain number of fingers. That's the price. You take it or leave it, no hard feelings. Reckon the Feds cut his tongue out? I seen his mother at church one time, about the prettiest silliest woman in the history of the world, plus all of Nash County. Now a solid mass of scarring, so they say." Safe inside others' guessing about him, enjoying a type of skittish dignity, Will entered his twenties like a lamb, bounded out of his thirties like some lion. Once he crossed the threshold of forty, he finally commenced to publicly talk. He'd been rehearsing on Winona every single Thursday all those years, and at gunpoint, practically. Like late bloomers in everything, once the fellow let loose—he sure made up for lost time.

To his silent mother (and later to yours truly) Will spoke of a repeater nightmare that stuttered throughout time. He was attending some perfect local party, waltz orchestra playing loud, the room pretty and full of kind familiar women—when he saw three gray uniforms stuff the door. He saw his hostess drift towards soldiers of the non-victory army and then she read a little slip of paper and then pointed over heads to right here, at him. Will woke, sitting up grunting, "Won't. Go. Shoot *self* first. Shoot."

A FEW of the Courthouse vets had died. One of the basket cases had perished (the literal basket cases). Friends set his wicker in a coffin and the coffin in the ground. You suspected that the many grizzled talkers yet at it hadn't seen quite all the action that they bragged on. Their tales smacked less of a foot soldier's weedy ditchside view, more of on-high command gossip from, say, a *Harper's Illustrated Weekly*, only rewrote from the Southern slant. Skirmish by skirmish, vets' memories tend to spit and polish. You could hear the same stories come around again and again, heroism swelling by the minute.

History was daily being reshaped downtown, even by the quiet ones. That's one thing about tale-telling and history both: It takes two. Listening is belief. A body cannot go on record alone. You cannot tickle your own self. Try it. (I'm glad *you're* here. Lunch is soon. You booked, after?) Seemed every soldier telling in the town square believed the war'd been a wide bell— and he hisself the sounding clapper that'd given it all sound and meaning. Men had long since titled that long squabble "The War for Southern Independence." Even after we lost it, Falls' natives called it that—especially after we lost it.

Odd, Marsden's very silence first brought him a warrior's reputation. Pays to keep quiet. A hard lesson for some of us to learn. Folks watched Willie. Mothers told their daughters to pay him special attention. His fortune grew in plain sight. Plus, having got better-looking with age, he was now within calling distance of Not That Bad-Looking.

He did continuously right by his burnt momma. Lady More Marsden now went to bed at sunset, avoiding lamps and candles and the matches they required. Even ate her soups cold. Lady hung her fire-scorched coat of arms on a real plaster wall covered with paper featuring vines and sets of manifold blue birds, facing each other. Her and the wallpaper acted like nothing ugly had ever gone on hereabouts. (Wisdom and forgetfulness, they sometimes move hand in hand. My own smartness, such as it is, rests with remembering. But here in this Home, worked up with insomnia at 4 a.m., I too have prayed for the total eclipse of this memory. Of course, I never mean it long.)

Some Sundays, mother and son would be seen to buggy out towards their blackened homeplace. She had once been quite the talker—even considered "a conversationalist." Lady would sometimes sigh words, but only social ones: "Sends regrets." Some days she seemed not to know quite who she was. Other times she understood all too well. Willie spread a quilt on a low hill overlooking four smoke-black three-story chimneys. She held the empty white Spode teacup like it was some angel's egg that God had given her to guard. The two people ate long speechless lunches packed by Will's new maid and boyhood love, his mother's adored (overworked) former body servant, Castalia. Once the sun started to take its business elsewheres, here came two Marsdens back past the city-limits sign and toward streets' safety. Silent with each other, they were mighty glad to be so still, him in black and her—face hid beneath heavy veils—wearing a white silk wrapper she'd taken as her own kind of simplifying uniform when still a young girl of renowned good taste. Those were the times when a boy could love his mother right out in the open and say nice things into her ear and offer his arm and buy her pretty extras and even be admired for that. Why is it, child, that our present century has been so doggone hard on motherhood? I been a momma nine times over and I now want what they nowdays call "my perks."

Son Marsden had inherited three farms. Two of them, Sherman's forces had turned to little more than bumper crops of carbon. But even blacked, the acreage underneath still held, one river and six clear creeks yet flowed through them. Marsden owned the livestock yard that rented livery to folks unable to afford a personal horse yet. Plus, he had some beachfront sand on the Atlantic. Of course, he'd lost all his daddy's slaves (plus the children and grandbabies of his granddad's early investment—like split dividends). One-fortieth of all black folks in Falls were still called Marsden (the phone book even now is full of Cap's side-pocket kin).

Downtown, ex-slaves still answered to the name, but not so often, and never when called. Wandering Main Street, some older black people would touch their straw hats when their former boy-owner passed. Old people winced like still expecting a direct order from him. But Saturdays (market day, the day folks drank), younger colored people might wink Willie's way, giving him slow cagey grins. They could now say, "Afternoon, *Marse* Marsden. How it go? Seem like the top rail on the bottom. You working hard or hardly working?"

Once, two young fellows, sons of former Marsden house slaves, spit on the wooden sidewalk right before his shoes. "Back wages," one smiled. Courthouse vets seen it happen. They got excited, eager for a scrap. The one Reb left in a basket begged to have his hamper's head end lifted. But Marsden, chin up, took a giant step over the wet spots, just moseyed on his silent way.

9

HONEY, I got to say here: I believe things might've gone easier on us later if Wee Willie Marsden—fresh back from war—just hauled off his first day home and pitched what today's science calls a Major Nervous Breakdown.

Back then folks called it The Blues or else A Spell, or maybe Necessary Bed Rest. (Sometimes this rest could run on for decades. Many a local person took to the bed—pinned there by experience—and never quite got around to ever standing up again. Becoming a invalid was considered a right valid way of dealing with not being able to deal with not wanting to try and move one step from your bedroom ever again.)

If, when he first got home, Will had climbed to his upstairs four-poster out at The Lilacs, and if he'd had the meals brought in, if he'd spooned down soups and puddings—baby foods—if his single job had been no harder than watching sunlight move all day across a blank clean upstairs room— maybe recovery would've found him. If only he had called in a best friend and told all the gory banked-up tales. (A cow not milked for two days straight can start to die of souring unasked-for excess.) If Will had admitted to being so young, and gone ahead and cried a lot and let hisself be held by women like his momma (or better, by me—not within a stone's throw of yet being conceived—but willing, even so), then—however slow it took—young Will might've first stepped, leaning on the wallpaper for help, to his second-story window, then peeked at the post road's commerce till, finally feeling strong enough to creak down the spiral stairs onto the huge porch, he might first nod then wave then call at others still active with their roadbed lives. If only, by degree, Willie, hurting, could've been sucked back—gradual—into the healthy stupid lovely world!

But him? He just earned money. He made his downtown posture be the ramrod sort that mothers bullied their bunchy kids with. Him? The very Thursday after Winona chucked place settings his way and for years of Thursdays afterwards till the woman disappeared—here the vet hiked to- wards Winona's jungled yard. Weaned on duty, skilled at marching, this fellow was so knee-jerk male he never considered saying, "To heck with this. I need rest. Been clubbed back of my head and just want some quiet to mull it over in. Got severally jumped, feel weak, can't manage such mess yet! Count me down for a few months. Call me 'girlish,' go ahead."

Turned out: His best friend was no longer somebody you could cry to, having become instead somebody to cry over. Will's upstairs bedroom was now just so much open air for pigeons to enjoy and barn swallows to mea- sure off in swooping spins come evening. His momma'd never been able to cook him chicken soup even in her prime, though she might've liked the chore of decorating a sickbed tray with a sprig of lilac, say. Now she barely knew who she was (meaning—in the South after the war—who-all she'd been). So, Will, having grown many inches taller on the long walk home—the only child of his own mother and a single living memory of another lady's missing son—what could a fellow do?

He thought of *them*—is what. He walked to a weedy gate, he toted further candy and bad news. He forgot to know or help or nurse hisself.

I'm not blaming him. —No, what am I saying? Of *course* I blame him. But I guess I blame both him *and* circumstance, a ply that's famous for being hard to tug apart, sugar. I blame . . . the war, I reckon. *Some*thing should fess up. I blame, I blame . . . and yet that don't stop my feeling for the brave dumb boy. I want to call, "Sit down. You've earned it."

Instead, another Thursday afternoon devoted to selfish weird Winona Smythe.

NEWSPAPER serials of the day were full of bereaved mothers comforted by their dead sons' returned war pals. Ofttimes a killed boy's sister married her shot brother's handsome friend. The pal said, "Bill died in these arms, Irene, and you, his sister, will now live in them forever." The End.

But no citizen of Falls considered Will's weekly Thursday trips the least little bit romantic. He never missed. Neighbors would look for him just at one o'clock exactly. Years later, even during hailstorms, he'd appear, holding foodstuffs and—some said—a envelope of cash from his own bank account, crouching under some umbrella cut by falling pellets. Here he came on Christmas, if it fell on Thursday. Turned up during a hurricane named Pearla and, the week after, when Summit Avenue stood three feet deep in water—why, will you look here? a gent paddling a rowboat he then moored at her rusted garden gate and waded indoors wearing his duck hunter's hip boots, toting a sack of horehound like blood plasma you'd bring some shut-in.

Indoors, onct she'd seated the young boy, once she accepted his chicken, and the horehound had been offered, plus a beautiful piece of quartz crystal found near the spot where they'd both lost their only Ned, the sullen widow canted back against less than spic-and-span horsehair, said, "So. Now. Tell."

"Ma'am? Tell? Tell what, ma'am?"

"Tell all." Her tone meant it. "Every week I give the selfsame order."

Winona explained that a good possible starting place might be the day those two babies left here, marching, holding hands the way boys that age still will. The day a courtly officer refused to let canaries go along. She announced, right off, that if Ned *had* taken along Von Himmel I, her very best Harz Mountain warbler, if the boy'd agreed to use the rubberized cage cover she'd had made special to keep out Yankee dampness, she felt sure their Ned would be here yet, charming, alive, and far superior to this leaden "friend" who could only say, when asked a simple question, "Tell *what*?"

Will sat poker-stiff, right thoroughly tongue-tied. His mother'd onct been praised for the speed and nobility of her parlor talk. His poppa, with a scholar's streak, had been known to corner farm-equipment salesmen with ironic tales of the wandering Phoenicians' alphabet. And before trooping away from here, Will had hung out with a sociable buddy, plus a handsome talkative slave girl. But Will Marsden was always one to keep his mouth shut. Till now, he'd mostly profited from that.

"It's details I'll want from you," Winona said. "Start by reading the letter telling me my Ned got killed while he was scouting up a tree and you off somewhere swimming, I believe. I want to see you read this man's letter."

Her stubby hands popped open the top button of her ample black bodice. Will looked away quick. But he'd already glimpsed, blue with shadow, the double chin of his pal's momma's left breast. Her cologne was like several bakeshops and one of her breasts would have a larger waistline than young Willie's. She forced into his fist a black-edged envelope long since folded brown from handling.

Will saw the return address. "Not Lieutenant Hester." He shook his head.

"I suppose they shot him too." Winona was a blunt-type person, honey.

Marsden nodded. "You met him, ma'am. He's the one wondered would battle be 'canary suitable.' He got asked if we'd fight in rain, he said, 'Depends.' The very day before Lee signed it, Hester was eating in the officers' mess, ma'am. One thing about Hester—he knew when everybody's birthday was. He must have looked up our official dates, I guess, in records. But there on the field it surprises a fellow that anybody'd know, much less celebrate. Hester would do a little something. A candle on a johnnycake and everybody singing. It made you feel better, just did. He'd done that for our colonel. They were singing 'Happy Birthday' in there. Tent flaps were down. We weren't officers. We were outside but we could hear the song. The marksman couldn't have seen Hester. Was just luck. Bad luck for us."

So Will told Ned's mother that this here document would sure be a really hard thing for a person who just got home to read now, thanks anyway.

Was then that Winona Smythe rose, stepped nearer, got Will by the hair of his head. Tightening her grip, she moved him off the bird-messed couch and down onto a newspapered-and-feathered floor. He was soon kneeling square in front of her. She settled opposite him, like she was a queen of hearts in black on a black chaise. To be fair, she didn't know quite what she was doing, probably. No. They were both yet reeling from who they'd lost and how they lost him. Fully forty years down the line, they would still be reeling. Will didn't understand why such pain should be required—but he refused to break her hold or strike back or to leave. Must be part of a gent's duty. Being on all fours, panting, the letter wadded in his paw.

"Don't wrinkle it, you. Read me it. You can read, can't you?"

"Yes'm." Felt like a whole plug of his coarse brown cowlick might pop out, but this burning did give Will something to concentrate on. He was almost grateful to notice only one particular point of ache. She was right: Ned had been finer made.

With her fingers still locked around Will's bristly forelock, with his brow pressed most against her knee now, with Will's large hands tucked under the hollow a bent spine made as he stooped here on crusted *Herald Travelers*, he did open the envelope in a fumbling hasty way, half hoping she'd release him. And then, not knowing why, not planning to, Will Marsden kissed the black cloth stretched over her knee, she let loose of him. Breathing hard, his face a smeary mess, one sickening apologetic smile in force, he backed along the floor, patted behind him for the rocking chair's edge, got up onto the bobbling thing, pretending nothing'd happened. Willie told me decades later—when drunk, of course—that, as he clambered up, he found he'd experienced a certain manly stiffening below the waist. Part of it was grat-itude for so small a pain as yanked hair roots. Part of it was how much Winona looked just then like her dead boy. Only somebody who'd known both forever could really see it. Her voice's roll, ears' fleshy downy lobes. Then, shaking his head sideways, Willie opened the folded pages—reverently setting the envelope aside. Will read it for the first time. "Dear Mrs. Theodore Smythe, We sorely regret to inform you that during the early PM of August 12, 18 and 62, your son . . ." He halted. She barked, "You'll thank me later." Winona became like Miss Beale, the Athena of Falls Lower Normal, a teacher so hard and strict that everybody despised her while they "worked under her" but onct they'd lived through it—onct they found how much of the Rev. John Donne they'd memorized—locals claimed she was the best thing that'd ever got its claws into them. Who knows, child? maybe we love the hardest things we get to live through because we someway got to live through them?

I imagine the voice of the man I lived with all those years, honey. It drones like a ghost reading some account of its own onetime local life. By the time I knew him, the tone of voice was darker, harsher, rustier. But it'd stayed this same basic sound—low, slow, rich, a brownish river. Speech itself might later have gone fancier, in keeping with his fine family's claims. Three years talking in tents and ditches had erased fineness from a boy that young. But, especially at night, even in old age, his tone could sound—at its center—just as stunned and simple as the kid Winona cornered when he was civilian and fifteen. I imagine the untidy Smythe house going dim with afternoon, rubberneckers still pretending to promenade to and fro on the sidewalk out front, birds cheeping, Willie's labored breathing trying to get up the gumption needed, breath's cashing in its chips for simple animal sounds that could then be sent toward civilized human speech . . . "Well, ma'am, to start out with, you know, Sumter, well." He told War her way, tried. Inches at a go.

Across the dark room from him, Winona (a woman of steely wasted spirit, a person secretly starved for company, the secret kept even from herself), Winona listens, canted forward on the lime-crusted black couch, her face so still, her face a needy bottom-heavy blank.

so, when she'd broke him in some, broke him some, once she'd moved beyond his boy's brittle pride, she started pulling more of it out—in pieces,

the way a dentist goes in after a broken tooth that's got got got to come
out, and quick. Slow learner, Willie—the okay businessman, the starting-
to-be-adult, a son who acted kind to his own hurt mother—he'd begun,
Thursday to Thursday, learning to tell things. Describing first days of re-
cruitment, he'd find one detail in the mentioned mud and he'd set it aside
for refinding his next time through. He gathered these choice facts the way
he'd hoarded rock crystal off roadsides he marched along with Ned.

I sometimes wonder what might've come of him if Winona hadn't made
him. If allowed to keep stone-silent about his war.

Not sure.

One thing's certain, *I* never would've noticed him. He might've become
one of those returned Rebels—like the ones from this more recent war they
lost in Asia (it mostly happens to survivors of the *losing* side)—ones who
come unsnapped so suddenly, with a violent caving-in. A loud sound sets
them off. Two days back, while waiting for this Home's favorite soap show,
we heard the TV news about this boy over in Greensboro, handsome fellow
(they showed a yearbook picture) from a nice family, but who never held
a job after the Army, never quite "over" being in it years back. He never
quite got home from Asia—lost hisself somewhere in transit between Hawaii
and the California coast, in salt air over nobody's water. Regrets for what
they made him do. Do your duty and he did, poor thing. Boy walked into
his poppa's insurance office and opened fire with two hunting guns, got the
secretary and a meter man and his own poppa before he shot hisself. "Nice
boy but a loner," neighbors said after. "Eagle Scout but kind of kept to
hisself," they said. "Tried to fit in but couldn't really. Well known around
here but, now you think of it, had no real friends. Odd but neat." Hundred
years earlier, could've been William More Marsden, could've been if Winona
hadn't given him this way out, a steam-pressure release valve that let the
sense and poison free.

Later, this hard-won gift for telling gave the man a way to come near
other people. Nobody could believe a gift of gab suddenly spouting out of
old rock face. But first tales only started giving Willie joy after he'd been
through the whole war onct, and when he started going back, bumping into
things he'd skipped during the first muddy trudge, finding mineral clues
he'd left here and there—like Hansel and Gretel's dropped bread. He told
. . . was just one of the things we later had in common. Back in our happier
days, neighbors would pop in, hoping to find my husband and me jawing,
swapping tales, his trading tall ones and mine, medium high.

Nice to be considered entertaining. Nice to be funny when you know
that the world's so rough.

Some tell me I am a funny woman. Ha ha funny. Ha ha peculiar.

Ha ha.

THAT FIRST year of talk, if, in telling the widow his early battle tales, boy
Willie should lose his way, Winona might rise off the couch, come over,

matter-of-fact, crack him onct across the face. If that didn't start the story up again, leading with her knuckle and the wedding ring, several times, she lightly lovingly blacked one of his gray eyes. Winona didn't show no pleasure doing this—went at it like you lash your mule who's stopped midroad. But, look, she got him through the war. She even pulled Antietam out of him, whole and steaming, glad for air.

By his third time through, Will started seeing how the entire thing might be someday rendered into hoistable blocks, the way you break a permanent-seeming camp for fast traveling. One turned out as "The Man Who Loved His Wife Too Much." Another: "Simon's Immortal Pocket Watch." "Children During War." "Death of A Harpsichord." "The Tailor and the Leg." Bilge and mud started showing shiny forms hid down underneath . . . Looked to be nothing more than a bubble on some pool of mud but when you reached down for it, the shape lifted, came up whole and solid and right delicate—blown Venice glass had been hid there, waiting among blood flecks, swampy puddles, broken reeds, and heat-warped cannonballs.

Only later would Winona ask him to come sleep alongside her in the small tent.

10

HERE at Lanes' End, Jerome, our favorite orderly ever, black *or* white, picks up spare change doing commissioned Ex-Lax cab trips to the Rexall at Browse 'n' Buy Mall. He buys so much laxative on consignment, the clerks make rude jokes. Even the local-born black clerks do: "This man don't need another gross of Ex-Lax, he need a easy-to-take tablet form of atomic melt-down." One thing about jokes, child: There's only about seven of them, but they always seem to apply to most situations because—fact is—there's only really about seven of *them*.

Now I ain't criticizing Jerome, who's practically like my own grandson, understand—but he *is* a paid Home employee. You ofttimes find him missing from duty, shut in some room setting a wealthier lady's hair. (Plus dyeing several of the men's, truth be told. They pay him as much to keep quiet as they do for the rinse job—and Jerome, trustworthy, lets it get no further. Than me. Don't beg me for their names, please, sugar. My lips are sealed. Just use your eyeballs. One fellow, three doors down—on the left—he's as orange as I-Love-Lucy's.)

Jerome is saving up for his theater-seeing trip to London, England, next year or the one after. Him and Leonardo, his roommate, are going. Jerome's been salting cash away for it since he turned sixteen, quit high school, and found this jack-of-all-trades job. Born dirt-poor, the gentleman is touched by the wand of ambition and talent. It ain't no respecter of neighborhoods, child. Genius is a Democrat. —Our Jerome has Ideas. These are the people I like being near: the ones most *wanting* something.

Jerome is proudest of two virtues: his speaking voice, which is like black satin sheets that you worry will feel icky but onct you're under couldn't a crowbar get you out again. And his hands. "Zee golden digits," he says, imitating a German accent copied off some war-movie late show as he kisses his own knuckles. Have you ever seen so many gold signet rings on such dark perfect hands?

For a fee (75¢–$4.50 depending on how deep into it you really want him to go) Jerome will offer his so-called Swede massage. Some folks in here just about live for Jerome's weekly rub. Personally, makes me nervous to guess what a body (behind closed doors) gets for the full $4.50 (prior to tips). All I know is what I see and some of that, I tell. I *will* mention the scent of liniment and wintergreen alcohol trailing certain people's wheelchairs for days—plus crooked smiles that can last up to a week. Women *and* men! I won't say no more.

He did do my neck onct—a free sample. Had me yelling most unladylike. I give off more snap, crackle, and pops than the Kellogg's Tap Dance Academy. By the end I couldn't budge, just lay here groaning. Afterwards, I didn't know should I feel proud or guilty. Minnie Lytton admits that Jerome gets right up onto the bed with her "for better leverage."

" 'Onto' or 'into'?" asks our former physics professor, ever precise.

"You're the scientist." Min winks. "What have I got to do for you, a diagram?"

Jerome titles them Swede massages, I reckon he read that in some paperback. If our orderly, born in Falls' own Baby Africa, is a Swede—then I am Haile Selassie, Lion of Ethiopia, but let that go.

And finally, always looking out for geriatric cash, Jerome gives speech therapy for your stroke victims, those who can still explain about their having a little pin money to spare. The famous Talking Lessons were invented by Jerome after his auditing every drama course at Nash Tech. I hear he is their all-time Night School Star. If he signs up for a course, others flock to be in it. Jerome can do whole Shakespeare speeches like a perfect Englishman. (He memorizes off of gramophone records from the Public Library. Has hopes of getting known for it in New York.) Some folks along this hall doubt just how famous he's ever going to be beyond this hall. But his diction is a dream and his hands remain, for some, the one reason to go on.

Finally, about his speech lessons, I'll just say: Didn't Jerome get the Williston twins back to where they're able to do the Pledge of Allegiance straight through without stopping? The Williston girls were a year behind me at Falls Lower Normal. Here recent, both had strokes in the same week, both lost partial speech, seemed the same partial parts faltered in each. Nobody could believe things worked out so tidy—but, look, them girls've been dressing alike since 18 and something, eating the same foods, and sleeping in one bed (they still do, though the nurses don't like it one little bit, I hear). I reckon it follows that Williston illnesses would come on in a matched set too.

Well, them sisters now do that Pledge like nobody's business. Sad part, that's mostly *all* they do. They just shush other people ("outsiders" they call everybody but their own two selves) and they practice their Pledge. I mean they do it constant. A retired missionary in here, she scolded Jerome for not making it the Lord's Prayer. She said, "The twins might as well be building up some credits if they're going to parrot one thing all day. I'm patriotic as the next person but, Jerome (here, take this free tract, illustrated), there's higher things."

"Lord's Prayer's too long. I done clocked it," goes he in his toniest English accent, hand on a hip. "We speech pathologists choose shorter items so's our stroke victims can get they chops around stuff sooner. They loves the joy of quick accomplish-ment, for you information, Miss Know-It-All!"

Jerome criticized is a Jerome real high and mighty for about ten minutes. When you're self-made, you take blame harder. I know. Luckily, like me, he forgets insults fast enough. (We all need a short memory for some stuff, honey.)

Afterwards, Mrs. Missionary and myself counted on our fingers. He was right. Lord's Prayer's got fifteen lines not including Amen. We understood that, for the twins, fifteen—even Amen-less—would be overreaching. Anyhow them Willistons were clam-happy come July Fourth and Flag Day. See, our Home director let them lead.

OH, we've had some good times here. Strange, you can be right in the middle of one of history's golden ages and never even know. I mean, consider, darling: This we're *in* might be one. Well, it could.

11

DEACON-SOBER, home for some time now, the boy still hadn't told anybody but Winona a single fact about his doings '62–'65. If a good-natured stockyard employee pumped Marsden for news of his battle record, Cap might snatch his hat off the bentwood hat tree, he'd barge from the office, take long walks. Even during business hours, he headed towards woods where Ned and him had made the clever camps. Went on foot, Marsden, that owned so many horses.

Forced to mutter business lingo, you heard how his boy's voice had fallen two full octaves. His baritone didn't sound God-given but earned the way some smoker's voice gets baked far huskier. Only, Marsden's smoke was not your usual Turkish blend but such fumes as a horse artillery must breathe.

· · ·

(AND ME? I'm off doing my duty—getting myself born to odd yet decent people. It is up near 18 and 85. I can't wait till I am officially *in* this. Odd— even having gone this old—I can't imagine ever being *out* of it. Anyhow, owing to my birth, here comes a clear little sideways brook, feeding—cold and fresh—into the warm muddied river of Captain's widening life.)

AND IT was one noon—whilst he headed from a profitable shoat auction towards the People's and Farmers' National Bank—Cap stopped to tie his shoe. The man of few words paused in earshot of battle chatter. Sole propped against a pyramid of welded cannonballs, he must have heard the tail end to one warrior's flashy tale. Cap—twenty some years older than the war now, solid in the flesh and more mentally ripe—he maybe found them few words stronger than expected. You see, he stayed a while. He tied the other shoe's laces, untied it, double-knotted it anew.

Next day, the One Who Never Told was back for lunch hour, dawdling like somebody taking a survey of park benches. He settled nearby, listening in that solemn way he did everything, eating a brown-bag lunch Castalia had packed—but chewing slow—like he hoped to surprise the sandwich. He sat still, then remembered to take a few goodly chaws.

Men's stories commenced to working in him—you could tell. Some nail file that jiggles in a piggy bank's thin slot till—whammo—out showers this long-postponed silver jackpot. Every talker in that Courthouse Square exaggerated certain facts. That was how you put your mark on a tale—what you chose to taffy-pull, fluff up, squash down. Still, each vet understood how holy a true story is. Even the men that played most fast and loose, they respected a real one. Especially them. A liar's goal is to make up one that's half as good as Real Life's usual unusual. Ain't a secret, child: storytelling is one kind of revenge. Maybe losers get better at it than the winning side. Honey, us losers have to be.

WEEKLY practice with Winona (all those Thursdays among canary cages), it paid off during a late-night dinner at the Mayor's mansion (anniversary of Antietam). Marsden had drunk a extra glass of claret. He sat listening to the gent on his left, a man who'd never fought for anything more pressing than attention at such refined civilian parties. The mustached man made a quip about why we'd lost. Said our Southern aristocrats had been way too genteeeel to butcher like your cruder Yankee bulldogs would.

Marsden's fist went up. All talk hushed. He brought that hand down, grabbed a butter knife, chimed his emptied claret glass, said real loud, "I object, sir. Case in point, sir . . ."

Willie told a short if right heroic story. Next he recalled a second, longer one—and a third. Seemed a backlog waited, each tale with its hand up, calling, "Me. Me next, sir." (The tales he told were by now worked smooth as glass, perfected in a lady's parlor then a lady's tent.)

The Mayor's other guests slowly turned chairs to face a local fellow who, during the fish course and for his total lifetime previous, had been known as the silent type—then, since the war, as the strong and silent type. Even the offending dandy tipped back in his chair, crossed his arms, and listened, his head tilted like a dare. This was the beginning of it. Seemed public storytelling was a contagion young Marsden had picked up from gimpy Courthouse regulars, from the hurt and hurtful mother of a missing loved one.

The man talked real halting at first. Maybe the years' silence gave his speech—when it finally reached others' air—such feist and wallop. Willie's style was more straightforward than my own. I love the flourish of beginnings. He was mad for middles. Went straight there. Telling gets to be a habit. Soon it seemed natural to him and others, Private Willie Marsden's talking at last.

HAD TO BE night before he'd tell.

At the banquet, at your table, he'd place a fork opposite a soup bowl and make it be a tree beside a lake. Pepper from the shaker he'd sprinkle out to draw with, one antlike line crossing tablecloth connected snipers' willow roost to where snipers' shells would have to hit. Afterwards, a hostess cleaning up might sit at Cap Marsden's empty place, might study a pepper line, would touch it with her fingertip, maybe sneeze. Women longed to nurse him back to health, like peace was some simple rhubarb tonic, a recipe known from the inside out to females only. Men respected Cap, meaning they were just a little scared of him. They never onct corrected his war dates or place names, though all men felt they were true scholars of the fight. They never interrupted. Marsden had grown a lot. And when the gent got to rolling with his newfound battle tales, he looked even bulkier. Poor man left no fact out, couldn't. He'd hang forward, sometimes doing cannon sounds (you never laughed). Told how loud cannon concussions made horses' toilet habits change and nobody judged it unrefined, Cap's mentioning this even at Preacher's house. Cap would get to breathing from lower in, like a singer will, eyes half wet, him soon rocking back and forwards, with your finest crockery rearranged before him. Soup tureen: Sherman, who had burned Marsden's mother's china-doll face. The vinegar cruet was rebel General Johnston, who'd failed to prevent a pale beauty's being cooked. With tableware mustered into being serious battle-map toys, us guests leaned toward candlelight and him. —Oh, honey, everybody, ears to kneecaps, was soon cobbled with goose bumps. You admired the man about as much as you pitied him.

I COME IN around here. Housebroken, the one with pigtails, third from the end, all eyes.

HE DIDN'T clean war up a bit, nor did he add a drop of extra crimson. Just told it. Like the fellow says, facts are plain unbeatable. How some women fought in the war dressed as men. Nobody found out their real sex and they were right heroic and—after Appomattox—at least one brave lady-man-soldier of a Yank was offered a pension and died with the name of a regiment carved on her marker. Fact. Look it up. How—at Shiloh, after two short hours of battle, so much lead had flown through air at one single level—a whole woods, every single old-old tree and slender sapling, was sheared off even, perfect like the Lord's professional hedge clippers had swooped out of Heaven and passed over, strict.

Fact.

HIS THIRD tale of that first talkative evening opened something like this:

"They'd get too close. You'd yell for them to stay back. They wouldn't. You saw they had their muskets ready. Officers forced you to. Or maybe knowing that your friend nearby was watching. It could have been the scariness of someone's rushing over the hill at you. You could plainly see their faces. It might well be a nice face. It was. Sometimes a perfectly splendid face. Two of my three were a good deal better-looking than myself, which I handily admit is not that difficult. One wounded Yankee boy (shot by myself) later offered me his pocket watch. He was nearly as pretty as a girl, with silver-blond hair, not just the yellow kind which is certainly quite fine enough. After my dealings with this Northern boy—who actually gave me his watch—after that, why, every single time, I bent close, I checked. I felt it was my duty to remember the exact features of each fellow I shot.

"At that age, what did I know? They trained us to. The Lieutenant said, 'Don't pull on your trigger so hard, son, don't jerk it, Willie, that'll knock your sights all off. Just squeeze it, squeeze it like you'd squeeze your gal back home.'

"I told him that I'd joined our honorable Confederacy at thirteen, sir. I'd come in with my friend, sir, the little one over there. And, sir? I didn't exactly have 'a gal.' At least, not yet, sir. No time to.

" 'Well,' he said. 'Squeeze it like you love it. Nice and easy. Squeeze that trigger like it's everything you love. You do, as a gentleman, believe in love? You do love something, right, son?'

" 'Yes sir!' barks I.

"And two months after this particular shooting lesson, it happened. The Yankee I mentioned, one rendered an easier target by virtue of his bright watch chain and silver-blond curls, he walked directly my way. 'Go back,' I cried. 'Go back or I'll definitely have to, probably.' Well, he did not. I studied him along my sight—my hands they shook so. I was all but spastic, I was. The noise out there alone. I was in a hole and I let my musket's stock rest on the lip of the hole. Dirt at least was stationary except during jolts from the artillery breaking all around us. 'I am going to count to ten, or else.' I yelled it and he heard me too. I saw him hear me. Why didn't he stop then? I would've preferred that, I would have infinitely preferred not to hurt anybody. I hadn't previously. A flea I really wouldn't't've. Ask anyone local from before. I maintain that few people really want to, few of those who kill actually plan it. I begged that he not force me. He had a chance to go in any direction but my direction. But here he came. My finger, though in place, knew it absolutely couldn't. Even as it closed on metal, no, it simply could not. Unworthy of me, of my people. How harmless to contract the central joint of your right index finger. Here, you all try that, up and down this splendid table, let me see. Fine. I like to view others doing that in our present peaceful time. Ladies especially. You, madam, on the end, might I see your pretty forefinger do one minor little crooking? And the freckled little girl down there. Thank you. Yes, that helps. More claret for anybody else? It's really nothing, is it?—curl one digit inward. —There's a moment when you simply can't. It is followed by the moment when you know, to live you must.

"Oh my. I do seem to be holding forth here, do I not? Forgive me, mustn't really. Unlike myself. I know better. I was thirteen years old. It was difficult but also simpler maybe. Hard to explain. You should have been there. But, *No*. What am I saying? You *shouldn't've* been there. *I* should not have been. —Here endeth the lesson as they say on Church Street. I'll stop. Sorry. Growing garish in my waning years here."

Other diners did want to hear the rest.

This was at the Mayor's and it was late. The company was reasonably civilized and so the company begged for it. After sips of claret and several reassurances, he continued his murdering, his telling us it.

This beginning, spoken after dinner, during coffee and cigars, soon brought three black servants to a standstill at the table's edges, made certain ladies sit more forward—not caring how candlelight might show off the defects of a person's doubling chins and the crepe under your eyes. His telling the rest, it made men toy with watch fobs or cuff links, needing to be occupied, manually. The gathering had *asked* Marsden to continue, right? Probably it'd be better for *him* too. Men who hadn't gone to war felt shy about that now. Ones who had, they sat here beginning to remember things they'd chose not to, not inside Falls' city limits, which meant safety and a lawn-green truce. Nobody rose during the rest of Captain's sad little tale, nobody mentioned babysitters or went home early. Instead they kept very still and still more still. They took it like a medicine, a purge. This man was a big man, but the intimacy of what he admitted for all of us to hear, it was too huge even for so quilted a gent. But it sounded girlish, murder. Sounded *per*sonal. His tales were about how killing somebody kills the killed one— that's plain enough—but more about how the one that kills is killed then inch by inch, whittled down—even during a season when such killing is commendable. So, this handsome fellow was a killer, yet his table manners stayed right good throughout. In ending, Marsden turned to the sissified civilian and said, "So, sir, a body's being genteeel, sir, doesn't really figure in, sir, as I have suggested. Everybody here? forgive my going on. It is the anniversary of Antietam. That's what did it to me, I fear."

WILL had departed Falls the hushed and uglier pal of a perfect sleek little soprano. Now, grown, minus the friend, once he quit being a ventriloquist's dummy and finally found his voice, it worked.

Came the day he hit thirty-six, November 1885 (he was a Scorpio all over, sugar—whether you credit that mess or no), ex-Private Willie Marsden had been advanced by his excellent memory and a better imagination up to officer already. (Me? I was off somewheres getting myself diaper-trained.) By the time the century changed (oh, honey, we had such hopes for this one!), one rickety little private had been turned into a brassbound captain. His having money helped. Willie's daytime hush made his evening speaking voice seem more a event. The years had promoted Private Marsden, those and his way with his war's rude lore.

All his: "The Shoe Fits," "When the Colors Changed," "The Tailor and the Leg," "Sherman's Barbequeing Mother," a couple dozen others—I yet have them all by heart. Thinking back on his roster of favorites, it feels to Lucy here like Captain Marsden's bruise-gray Hit Parade. I can yet sing each tune—his way and mine.

One such—more or less in his own pitch and manner—still runs:

The Tailor
and the Leg

I MAGINE escaping from prison by walking through its open doors and you ain't even running. Guards let you loose for playing like it's regular: getting everything on earth you want. My husband, thirteen, plus a sidekick got chucked into a Yankee fortress. Escape, Willie told me later, seemed a form of flying at ground level. The hum of the world—river's running, bugs at click—seemed alarms that were *about* to screech news of your getaway but somehow didn't and became chums, pulling for you.

You've heard it said of some friend, "He'd give you a arm and a leg"? My husband claimed: The worse times are, the better friends you make. Lately when I read the newspapers, I figure we must be living through the golden age of buddyhood. Moral is: Hold on to your friends. You sure need them now.

AT WAR, Willie was a kid who said very little and feared very much. The more spooked he got, the fewer words he risked. He soon seemed mute. Big-eyed, he took in all the sights. Bodies stacked like cordwood, human hair snagged on barbed-wire fences: Those would scare anybody witless. His best hometown friend had just been shot. Wee Willie yet wandered in the haze from losing Ned. Our living boy had new beaverish adult teeth, a tendency to trip, and this squinty grin that tried to ward off harm. However charming, a smile cannot make friends with minié balls.

After his pal's death, Will found a new favorite in one Corporal S. Smith. This tailor-farmer hailed from North Carolina too. At forty, Salvador Smith was redheaded, moved all gangly, and had fathered six girls he talked about a lot. If you didn't watch him, he'd show you his daughters' daguerreotypes right during battle. Seemed like being a father—far from home—Sal had all this leftover guarding energy. Most of it he offered to my shivery cheerful Willie. Each night, before Corporal Smith could get to sleep, he made a walking tour of camp. He did it the way he'd checked on outbuildings and the barn of his sweet-potato farm near New Bern, North Carolina. Sal Smith would stop by Willie's tent, would ease two feet from the boy's cot and stand there listening hard for sleep's steady breathing. Sal liked to consider he'd someway "adopted" a young fellow soldier. Just made things more interesting, gave you this extra stake. (The world is full of our unofficial "chosen" children, child.) Sal Smith kept such attentions secret—but Willie was awake while Sal stood guard. The boy would fake mildish snores. And as can happen, in acting asleep to soothe your nearest well-wisher, a body sometimes drifts right off.

WILL forever loved Sal Smith for how—captured together—they got loose so perfect.

Simple: the two were on a stranger's farm chasing chickens to fill the company pot. Nothing more glamorous than that, nothing less necessary. Suddenly, where two cornered brown hens should be, twelve boots—connected to six Yanks and, higher, six muskets aimed. "Nobody home but us chickens. Come with us, gray boys."

The Yanks' prisoner-of-war camp was due south of Charlottesville. A girls' academy had been turned into this fort of bars and baffles. Led in, hands raised, the Rebs were brought before one Major Digby. He was all oratory and side whiskers. (Not to be confused with the General Burnside that barbers later named the sideburn for.) As Digby grilled the two about encampments, fortifications, their names and civilian jobs—how they might be most useful as prisoners—fellows studied the Major's nasty uniform. A rip run crosswise, opening his tunic. Though Digby wore dyed-to-match blue long johns underneath, he did look real shabby. Plus, his bare left knee played peekaboo through holes.

Smith said, "Home, I was the best non-Chinese tailor in New Bern, sir. I could salvage anything. I do mean anything," and he stared so hard at the scapegrace outfit, Digby finally went, "Oh, yes. Well. I once was a very particular dresser. Owned twenty stickpins, none less semi-precious than a tiger's eye. Now, down to this. It's the times, boys, it's these times . . ."

Smith winked. "While I'm in here (though I don't plan to stay long), let me set this rag aright for you, sir. Only thing I hate worse than spiffing up one of our finer-looking enemy officers is idleness. Ask Willie here. Why, I'm not just un-lazy, sir, I'm counter-lazy. Ask Will. Will?"

But Digby had opened a Bible. He explained the oath of Federal allegiance he was now bound to administer. Smith fidgeted and glared and said things loud. Willie studied his jumpy friend. Back in camp, Smith kept pretty quiet. To fellow enlistees, Smith always acted kind and mild, sewing on their buttons no matter how ornery each hellion was. But one thing Salvador Smith could not abide: a officer, any officer. If Sal hated Reb officers, he was all but boiling whilst this Digby yammered about reforming unregenerate Southerly hooliganism.

The room was filled with guards and muskets. Sal Smith tried getting around the desk to offer Digby a jolly back pat. When pistols discouraged this, the Corporal went, "Sir, was it Dickby, Digby? Us Southerners sure did give you ragged-looking Yankees a perfect conniption fit at Manassas, didn't we, though?" The Major called this insolent, especially from a man about to swear the Union his undying loyalty.

Digby's lecture rolled on when Smith butted in again: Us Rebs sure wiped you-all's noses in it at Manassas, huh?

Guards grabbed Smith, they held his hand onto the Bible. Oath finally done, Smith sweated and shook like a man forced to take poison. "Sir?" he asked, shivering, right hand still in the air. "Am I a good Yankee now?"

"I dearly hope so. They claim the Bible has unlimited power."

"Well, Major, Yankee to Yankee, didn't them Rebs just whup the living hell out of us at Manassas?"

Two days later on a inspection tour, Digby bobbed into Smith and Marsden's straw-lined cell. It'd been a classroom. A map of the world was painted on one wall. You could see that rich girls had daubed up each and every ocean. Just the word "Persia" in red cursive was a poem that filled a fellow with careful feelings. It made Sal Smith speak at length about six daughters' quirks and merits. The Major wore a even worse-looking uniform, carried the other tossed over his arm. "I wonder . . . in view of your professed sartorial ability and since nobody else here can . . ." Digby passed Smith the tatters, plus one needle and a spool of thread. "Scissors, you will understand—gent to gent—are simply not possible, under the circumstances."

"Say no more. Now my fun starts." Smith grinned. "Anything beats idleness, even helping out one of my fellow blue-bellied yellow-backed Yanks. Sir, you won't recognize this rag when Salvador Smith gets through with it."

"I suppose I should thank you."

Next morning, just past dawn, one dapper red-haired major of the Northern medical corps strolled away from camp. He led a young prisoner-assistant. This wandering officer acknowledged the gateway sentinel's salute, but he paused. "I seem to detect, Private, a touch of the pinkeye. Not good. Report to my tent during sick call at nine sharp. That clear, son?"

The guard saluted, then rubbed his eyes. "You know, I *thought* they were burning."

Next, the doctor and his aide wandered unarmed nearer Southern lines. Smith soon stripped so the uniform wouldn't get him kilt—he felt relieved to appear nearly naked and less a officer for that. Then the blue monogrammed jacket was carried to camp and hung outside the headquarters tent—a trophy. That whole day, Sal and Will—centers of attention—were considered clever as possible. "Tell us it again," troops asked.

The Private and the Corporal felt huge, reborn. My husband explained to me how: While you escape from what seemed your surefire doom, adrenaline makes the world almost too beautiful to bear. Overample brightness burns so far into your eyes it scratches your skull's inside rear curve. Light hangs over every tree and hillside like some stray fuel that you might gather in your arms and maybe eat. A thirteen-year-old boy, walking beside his trusty friend, felt like he was, oh, maybe a brand-new velvet pincushion, nearbout *wanting* shafts of steel in him. Nothing seemed too hard for you to stand. Pain would maybe register as pleasure, the way—leaving both school and jail—your first sight of a wet pretty woods at dawn came in, so new-looking it almost carved you up with tenderness.

Return was all grace and celebration.

Was the very morning my poor Will got shot.

THE skinny pip wandered out of camp, still feeling half drunk on the joy of slipping free. He found some berry bushes. Since his hometown buddy'd died, Will had started acting pushy, vague, and sometimes wild. Will remembered Sal and others tying him to the cot, preventing his night-time one-boy raids on Yankees. He drifted between acting passive as a small-town debutante ("stand over there, *smile*") and going haywire as any Mormon double-crossed. Some mornings, Willie woke up feeling all kitten-weak—others, he came to like a fist in boiling oil.

Only now that something decent had happened did Will start remembering how it felt: being just regular and human again. So, just before Antietam grabbed him, Will settled near blackberry bushes, was just commencing to gobble his fill. Came a sound—hoarse, buzzing past like a squirrel running on one tree limb overhead. Was then Private Willie Marsden noticed his left leg, from the knee down, had gone the red-purple of blackberries. For one second, feeling nothing bad yet, the boy told hisself, "It's just sweet berry juice. I spilled. I spilled a lot."

In the medic's tent, Will was visited by the orangey-pink corporal who'd stitched him clear of prison. Crusted sleep matted the corners of Sal's eyes. A good-sized twig stuck unnoticed in his hair. But Sal was one of those people whose grossness is part of their comedy and so is okay and—to Will now—almost dear. Yeah, "dear." Who *else* was there?

Smith touched the boy's forehead. "Free of frying pan, grabbed by fire, hunh, buddy? Sure wish I could sew it back right for you. I reckon it hurts plenty." Sal studied the matted pant leg ripped wide open.

First, Willie, not yet thirteen—still too ready to believe in textbook braveness—shook his head No.

"Not hurt? To be shot right in your leg and it don't smart?"

"Well, I was shot, Sal . . . but more *across* the leg."

"Hey, this is Sal, bud. Went slam *in*. Bound to be paining you something fierce, why just look at the swelling. Near big as your waist."

Willie finally nodded. He lay staring at the tent's top. All afternoon he'd tried counting its threads. His pal's fringe of red hair now tickled the edges of his view.

"Does," Will admitted. "Sure hurts plenty, Sal. Burns then freezes. And you know what? It's weak of me, I know," here he signaled Smith closer. "There's a black girl on our farm, name of Castalia—and I been thinking it'd sure be nice to see her face. She's not what anybody'd call beautiful but she is. Too, I can't help it, Sal—Momma's real bad in emergencies but . . . I do . . . just wish . . . she was here . . ."

"Nothing more natural in the world, buddy."

(I got to put in, child, how this tailor-farmer's full name run: Salvador Cortez Drake Magellan Smith. *His* mother read novels. She had dreamed of a gallant son. She'd got one. She had dreamed of a handsome son. That, she hadn't got. Willie loved looking up at Sal, whose Adam's apple was the size of a coffee mug. Sal's cowlicks shot out even wilder, his freckles more flapjack-scattered than Will's own.)

"SAL?" Will now spoke real soft to his visitor, like enemies were listening. "They'll try and take it. Off. I know they'll want to lop it from the knee down. Sal, I really wish they wouldn't. Sal, it just looks bad. But, hey, I'm *in* here. The person understands these things. If they'd just leave it on to heal, it will. Heal. But, cut clean off? nothing ever does. I'm not going to have a chance in heck, Sal, if they cut my whole blamed leg off."

This particular day, Salvador Smith looked worn, blue-green rings hammocked under either eye. A letter'd awaited his return from prison.

Good news and bad news—though, as ofttimes happens, child, in *my* life anyways, the show-off bad outdanced the wallflower good. Still, the good sure *was*: After six daughters, Sal's wife had hauled off and had twin boys. She joked she was going to "Junior" them both, naming one: Salvador Magellan Smith, the other: Cortez Drake Smith. Then the Corporal read how his farm had been foreclosed, how the one Chinese tailor left in charge of his New Bern shop had fallen in love with the alderman's stout wife and run off with her, nobody knew where to. Missing: the shop's cashbox and its best worsted.

The letter sketched barest facts, and Sal—tired from escaping, his mind dancing like a janglebones skeleton—made up the rest: A heavyset woman came in to have her overlong skirt altered, a lonely wife, her husband another volunteer in the 70th Carolina Regiment galloped off somewheres to the North. The happy little tailor, going down onto his hands and knees, was soon moving all around Mrs. Buxom like a toy train, his mouth—the cowcatcher—full of pins. This tidy Chinaman asked—in signs—if the woman needed her hem much shorter. She kept going, "Unh-hunh." She begun to feel his little child-dry hands work around across betwixt her ankles. Her big eyes closed. It was, Sal imagined, toasty in that cramped work space, just the clock ticking, a slow afternoon. Pinning made gentle bites and tugs around her calves. "Shorter still?" "Unh-hunh. Hem more." From the customer's toplofty view, the tailor soon seemed her own favorite infant, a pet, but old enough to vote. The more he worked around her shins, the more he seemed the best thing that'd ever happen to her next. Why not? She ordered: "Hem . . . hem." The tailor looked up from below. In this warm back room, the lady's big legs come to seem columns, something to get to the tops of the bottoms of. She was the slow boat from Shanghai, masted. She was a mighty excellent kind of transportation. The snug warm berth he'd stowaway and live in forever. Up skirt went, inch by inch, slowly back the hem did turn, everywhere his hot dry fingers, soon upon her thigh, thighs. Alterations. A mouth full of warm pins got nearer actual legs. To feel a boy's tape-measure breath on your bare innerest shanks. Pins burred like a mustache *between* his lips, pins thrummed words, "Shorter yet?" "Unh-hunh, baste it—baste it. Hem it, now." In a hot rear room full of buttonholes and dummies, one thing leads to another, natural as gravity. Everything that goes down must come up. A hand here, and then to lift him, kiss a mouth with possible straight pins still living in it. Same night, well dressed, they eloped, breezing towards Florida in a rental buggy piled with a Quaker cloakroom's worth of itchy winter cloth.

"Whoa." Smith shook his addled head. It all seemed too real to him. He felt hisself in jeopardy of fever, ruin, or a fit. He confessed to Will—once he managed imagining all this, he'd had to step into the woods to relieve certain husbandly feelings. Odd, that being robbed should register this way. During war nothing comes at you on the level. At a maggoty time like this, to think about the Love act! Here a man's sweet-potato farm was lost, his shop stripped, his wife—still laying in—reduced to a steady diet of yams mostly, the six girls passing croup amongst theirselves. Understandable, the bags under Smith's eyes as he now told all near Will's cot.

Trying for small talk, Sal mentioned the shame he'd felt last night: Newly returned to camp, he'd been corrected by a scholarly young society doctor. His nickname was "See and Saw," owing to a willingness to amputate. Men said he no sooner seen a wound than out his saw flashed. —"Herr Salvatore," he'd said, "you claim to find our ranks 'decimated.' A fine word, Corporal, and an ancient one, but incorrectly applied. 'Dec-imated'—means a rank's losing one man in ten. As in, oh, dec-imal points? Here, with us, however, it's more, what? three in ten? four in ten? But feel free to go on using it in whatever rough way suits you. Only seemed right to clarify."

This same well-groomed young Lieutenant now walked into the medical tent, nodded towards Smith, stooped nearer Willie's leg, shifting it side to side without once checking on the big-toothed face hooked to this same unit. Sal looked at nothing else.

"The lead, I fear, is all but bowed around the bone. It's going to be a difficult one, very difficult. We'll know more tomorrow. But whatever happens, young man, we shall count upon your continuing bravery."

The surgeon nodded, left. It was not like Will to cry in front of a fellow soldier. A boy thirteen wanted—more than any grownup might—not to act thirteen. Will cried. He took up Smith's yam-colored hand. He kissed its toughened knuckles. He breathed on the calluses like trying to make a whole new genie life spring from one thick, working paw. "Don't let them take it off me. If it stays on, it'll mend. I just know, Sal. Don't let him saw me up."

NEXT evening in the surgery tent.

A lantern at the patient's head. One by his feet. One near the spoiled left knee. The precise Lieutenant and a thick-wristed infantry aide enter.

Willie, made drunk to help him abide the pain, is face-up toward tent roof, is listening so. A doubled cloth is stuffed into his mouth to block all crying out. Willie's now too weak—with fever and the blood loss—to complain or defend life and limb, too weak for doing more than hearing everything go morbidly loud. He feels his eyes' water slide—back, across wispy sideburns, into ears, now filling.

"Overnight it's grown considerably worse. Here, some possible early signs of the gangrenous, son. Scalpel. Yes, lead is all but fused with shattered bone. The lead is killing you. It cannot be helped, son. I'm so sorry. Nurse, saw."

This here implement—pressed in hand—looked pretty much like any nickel-plated one you'd use for household carpentry.

Blade is placed two inches above Will's freckled knee. The Lieutenant plants his boots more solid on the ground to gain proper leverage for that first deep pull. Nurse clamps one hand on a boy's white foot, the other steadying his upper thigh. The Lieutenant draws back for the first stroke's squeal.

Tent bows inwardly. Tent flaps over Salvador Cortez Drake Magellan Smith. Who holds two pistols like a highwayman in a melodrama. Up alongside his either ear, barrels press beyond his face like snouts. Appreciating this spectacle, Willie, on the table—drunk, so scared—almost considers laughing once.

"Yes, Corporal?" asks the young doctor in white gloves. "Have we been apprehended by our Northern brethren? The reason I mention it, you seem to be holding two dueling pistols aimed very much my way."

"*You*'ve flat been 'apprehended,' sir. You're as tired as me. It's not you personally. It's just I've lost my farm. My dapper little tailor-helper has run off with our biggest customer plus them tweeds. I've lost so many friends already. I got six ailing daughters—one this boy's same age. They have nothing much past sweet potatoes to get them by. Meantime, I'm *here* and can't seem to help a soul. I'm duty-bound to shoot the ones in blue, sir. (I'd rather not. Is that wrong?) I can't find a single good and rightful step to take. Seems I've been born into the wrong time for doing any one thing decent. So this, sir, is what I plan to try. I know you're as worn out as me— which is going some. It's a sloppy time, sir, and we're all taking shortcuts. But not on Willie Marsden here. No shortcuts on that leg. He says it'll do better if you give it half a chance. He knows more than you. He's *in* there, it's his, sir. So, get the lead out, literal. Leave his leg be. Take as much care over this as you would during peacetime and if this was the President's boy and your whole standing, your life depended on it—because, sir? It does."

The Lieutenant tugged off both white gloves. In a low voice he hinted what a outrage this was. He mentioned professional dignity, codes of conduct, his father's being a surgeon too, so forth. "Here." He pointed toward a festering wound in lamplight, he tried passing Smith the gloves, tried handing Sal the shiny saw that had been through so much. "Be my guest."

A boy, mouth bunched with rag, looked at each speaker in turn, head shifting, fighting to follow the game fought over him, adding nothing to save hisself. But interested.

Smith's left-hand pistol nudged the surgeon back into place, his right pistol came to rest upon the Lieutenant's closest temple. "Sir? You hear the one about the dentist and the woman spooked of being hurt? No? Yeah, seems there's this dentist, see? It's the end of a long day. In comes the woman mentioned earlier. To him, this lady's just another mouth. He's all but yanked her jaw out of kilter and is picking around into them molars any old way. It's at that second he feels her pretty little hand slip into his white trousers and snag him by the goodly clump of his manly parts. He gets real careful about pulling the pick back out of her mouth so she can say, smiling, 'Now, we're not going to hurt each other, *are* we?'

"You do your best, sir. Just clean and dress it. You have others waiting in other tents. I hear some doctor sawing right nearby. Go whittle on anybody else tonight and till the cows come home. You got a reputation as being saw-happy, did you even know? Just spare our Willie here. We'll give him a month to heal. Me, I'm taking full responsibility."

"You? *You'll* take?"

But the doctor slid his gloves back on. Muttering about courts-martial, about these farmers, ingrates, he prodded—slowed, alert. He pulled out lead and bone in pieces. The lamps hissed, moths pelted glass, moth wings tickled a drenched patient, wings left brown and gold powder on damp pale skin. The boy stiffened, grunted but never bellowed onct. Compared to the saw, all this felt so easy, child.

The pistols were lifted clear up alongside Smith's ears, thumbs steadied barrels against each cheekbone. Sal looked ill from watching, sick from tiredness, agitated from going into and out of Yank prison camp so quick, worried over his shrunken business and swollen family—the more Will's leg bled, the louder that raw shot sounded thwunking in a tin dish, the better but more woozy did poor Sal feel. Finally a blob of metal the size of a dollar piece clanked real hard. When the doctor's red gloves came off at last, Smith blenched white, mildly handed pistols butt-first to the nurse, smiled, acting ashamed. Then, stretching out on the tent's sod floor, the Corporal passed over into a kind of fit. It lasted nine long minutes. St. Vitus, all akimbo. Chewed words, molars being castanets, a drowner's crackling. He kicked the operating table's 2 by 4 pine legs. The nurse held Smith's head, the young Lieutenant got hold of Smith's tongue. From off the table's edge—Willie stared down—soaked clear through, mouth yet jammed with whiskeyed cloth. Will was looking at his friend with such concern that, for a second, he left and almost lost his own pain. Then, of course, as happens, child, refound it.

(This near the front, such spasms as Sal's happened nastily often. Was probably the fear—the dailiness of fearing. Made some boys get real loud. You saw others just fall over with the shakes like this. Still others couldn't wake without being dunked into cold water—they *wanted* to stay out, they couldn't bear to remember all this mess waiting with first light. Everybody said that waking was the worst. Eyes opening, you thought you were back home, then you knew.)

When Smith, shy on memories of the night before, came to at 5 p.m. next day, he felt so much fresher. The Lieutenant Surgeon had not yet pressed charges. Will explained what had happened and Corporal Salvador Cortez Drake Magellan Smith went, "*I* did that? Must of borrowed Worley's dueling pistols. Well, good for me. Did you hear I have twin boys? It just sunk in. There's been so much of this *other* . . . imagine. Twins, little ugly redheaded mites maybe even worse-looking than me, poor things. Six girls, two boys, now that's a family, ain't it?" Grinning, Sal felt like something had been gained overnight—maybe his farm held on to, the Chinaman returned with new wool and a wagonful of coconuts and trained pet monkeys plus many tan-faced Florida lady customers, Vicksburg saved, something very good and mighty necessary won back. Sal's seizure had returned him to full spirits. —The world can be a friend that'll give you the shirt right off its back, honey, give you a arm or a leg.

Took weeks for the thing to start to sealing proper. You know how fast children heal. But even so, Willie gimped, then stepped and only finally (just in time for Antietam) tried and managed—walked on it. First destination: Salvador Smith. Who cheered.

MORAL: In hard times, friend, keep being friends to your friends. We sure do need us now.

> Hop hop hop
> jump jump jump
> Though scarred, the leg
> stayed on.
> The leg stayed on.
> The leg stayed on!

Nice
Local Boy

Y OU STILL like my room's color? Larry let me pick.
Mr. Laurence "Larry" Winch was our Home director. He supervised the first fourteen years of my eating this place's Thursday tripe
and rice. I've had complaints this tint is notches too "raw." Vote again. Not
too yaller a yellow? Well, ain't you kind. *I* like it. But considering how my
eyes have toned down lately, what's good taste for me might look heated
up to hootchy-kootchy for somebody your age. Along our cinder-block hallway, Larry allowed every soul to choose. One lady went for lilac with silver
trim, but did Larry even bat a eye? "Done," says he, like some wild gentle
king.

While Lar reigned, nobody exactly called Lanes' End a daily funfest—
but post-Larry we understood we'd onct had it pretty good. Except for
Thursday's tripe and Jell-O. (You know the new disease where young girls
won't eat, or else they do and upchuck right after? I never understood that
disease, except Thursdays.)

Of course, Larry made bad mistakes. True, the state got after him for
money matters. But, one nice thing, Larry Winch grew up local. Which
helps. Lar knew the family tree of every bad old apple on this hall.

With Carolinians, child, gene-knowledge means character-knowledge
means history-knowledge means destiny-knowledge. And you can quote me.
(Plus, feel free to tell my mother's toney maiden name, McCloud.)

If in 1929, say, a certain person's grandpa constantly stole stuff out of
Woolworth's (and this in a family that just had money to burn!) and if he
got caught more than onct and was ofttimes listed for it right in the local
paper's court docket, well, that certainly does not mean that all his kids and
grandkids must eventually be born sticky-fingered. No, nothing's that simple
in this double-whammy world.

However, when a local person's recent Tupperware party turned up short
by six cake stands, two colanders, and an as yet undisclosed number of
twirl-wind lettuce driers, local minds naturally turned to some likely candidates. Our Sheriff Cooper—whose poppa was Sheriff Cooper first—found
the total loot in the trunk of a certain Cadillac belonging to that dimestore
klepto's own great-granddaughter. No names, please. In this town, child, a

body don't need them. Gossip comes what they now call genetically encoded. Oh, I read. I keep up.

I'D SEEN Larry Winch's mother blossom, a pretty nervous only child from Summit Avenue, the best end. She married early, picked a bear of a metalworker who called her "Dollie," who soon sold most of her timber land, took to drink, and made fun of their one dimpled son in public. Mrs. Winch dressed her Laurence in velvet knickerbockers and silly tams. Folks never blamed *him*. Meantime Baby Larry doted on his wasting child of a momma. When she died young—her people *did*—Larry was onto thirty and back from college and had never really held a job. He meant to, of course. For a while, he lived off timber dividends. His mother's doctors' bills were harder to concentrate on paying—with the patient gone. Larry's poppa soon run off to Florida with a secretary (from First Methodist!). They took along the final lumber cash.

So Larry found hisself in possession of that big showplace home on Summit (fuel bills alone would eat you alive), he was a aging boy too unsteady for being even a waiter, he was eating only when invited out. —Well, everybody local pulled strings to get him the job here at Lanes' End. Falls felt that a boy who'd acted so kind to his momma deserved some kindness back. Outsiders might call this "undue local influence." Us locals call it justice.

Larry loved us calcified natives for witnessing his mom's fine upbringing, her quick decline. Laurence didn't need to study no file cabinet of residents' records. The day he walked in here, "Hi, Lar," said we. Our ruling wit went, "Well, will you look what the cat drug in." "Hello right back at you, folks. You all don't appear *much* worse than you always did," Lar winked.

If we mentioned his dead momma, Larry Winch acted proud as any boy. Afterwards, he'd beg to hear that same old tale. When young, she had enjoyed a certain fame—for hereabouts. She skipped everywhere, even into and out of church, while a tame squirrel rode her shoulder. The creature wore its own knitted cap. It loved that cap!

Listening, Larry sighed, feeling he'd been let onto a hallway lined with safe-deposit vaults, each yet holding a few stray factual jewels of her. We understood which tales Larry'd like to hear. Which—on pain of death—you'd never mention. He knew ours.

Outsiders might consider us to be too local of yokels. But knowing and being *known* (for generations' warp and woof), that can be a bind and yet one great abiding joy, sug. What with these malls, stuffed by total strangers, it's one joy that's withering fast.

SO ANYHOW, come parade time in 1899, twelve lady admirers paid a local tailor (Chinese, Falls' version of Sal's slippery employee) to make a uniform for Marsden. By then a prosperous Captain tipped the scales at a hundred and eighty-some pounds, stood six foot one, and you couldn't have fit one hairy solid leg of him into the child's suit I've got squirreled under this bed somewheres. You might say the Captain's reputation just expanded like his uniform had to. That officer's outfit was a show in itself. Nobody missed the young Willie, a stick-figure bugle boy whose mouth was too sour-sad to ever get reveille right.

First time I seriously noticed him in daylight Cap was wearing that particular suit. It had more brass buttons than a countinghouse, enough gold braid to bric-a-brac a altar with. Had those things like eaves on the shoulders, like graduation caps but for shoulders, you know those things. He owned a hat with this curly dove-gray feather growing right in it—wore his whole sword then, had on gloves as white as any white-bread new-rich debutante's. It was July, there was a full sun—he could hurt your eyes, the sun buttering him up so. Brown beard glossy as furniture. Boots so mirror-shiny seemed like they both had memories. All that fastened to a good-sized fleshy gent, oh, he was a one-man band for any woman's eyesight, honey.

Them days we liked a man with a little more meat on him, honey. Not like these boys you see now on the soap shows, so skinny it looks like they'd get tired from toting around all the hair mossing their chests. Our men then weren't just these pretty bony newts—a man then was *noticeable*.

You'd spy Cap in parades, on platforms with the Mayor, once when President McKinley came through by decorated train. And Marsden always wore Ned's bugle on a red cord crossing one shoulder—still loyal to the point of plain unhealthiness. Cap had swelled so far past boyhood, that horn now looked too tiny, like a your top-of-the-line play one from the Kress store. By now everybody local knew the story of it. During ceremonies and ribbon cuttings, Cap never give one speech, didn't have to, just sat. His mute looks were the whole story. He never told his now famous tales during daylight. I studied him. Dangling at his side, that bugle: Brassoed to a spectacle. Why, to me, Captain looked like a painting out of history. Re-touched—like history always is.

AND WHO was I? Good question. A wellborn if rough-talking child on the front row, gaping up. I'd get to noticing so hard I chewed the brush end of my braids till Momma slapped my hands back down to ladylike. Cap knew my daddy. Cap slowly understood that I was looking. I remember the first day Captain stared back. Gray eyes! Amber bits shot all across them. When he turned them on me, even though I was seated on the front row, I seemed to fall some inches into earth. I heard a new roaring around my head, a garland of fiddling crickets fastened over me like earmuffs. I couldn't hold his gaze for long, but sat—legs swinging—staring at the brickwork her-ringbone of our Courthouse Square. When I checked back, I saw: He liked that. My acting modest. His mouth had set. Man never blinked. His eyeball "had" me before I knew what "had" could fully mean. It still upsets me, excites me to remember. —I believed myself to be right bold and semi-clever. But, darling? from the start, Captain Marsden was strategy fine-toothed as Lee's. Me, I was Miss Chicken with Her Head Cut Off.

HE MIGHT be nearing fifty but—for all his war glory—the fellow still acted extra shy. Folks said as how three women, two of them rich, had come right out and proposed marriage to him. Cap Marsden didn't like that type of boldness one little bit. He lived alone, had a colored woman cook and clean for him. (She was named Marsden, too, but of course not because he'd upped and married her. Till right recent, he'd owned Castalia. They were the same age and once had been somewhat in love—but that's a later story, God willing. Was her admirers who'd spit at Cap's feet downtown, men miffed that Freedom had come and gone and their high-spirited Cassie was still bellied up to another bucketful of Marsden dirty dishes.)

Thing about Captain was, nobody knew him. Yes, by day he talked shop. Sure, he attended First Baptist onct a month, need it or no. Yeah, come weekend nights, he told the tales: How General Forrest got twenty-nine horses shot out from under him, but by Appomattox bragged he'd killed one Yankee more than he'd lost mounts—he'd stayed one human soul ahead. People respected Marsden way too much to take one jolly personal fact for granted. Nobody slapped *him* on the back, nobody called him anything but Captain. If you knew his first name was William (after his Latin scholar of a poppa), was hard to recollect ever hearing anybody downtown bray that name aloud. His staying so quiet left him wide open for whatever you most wanted him to be. Me? I had my own ideas.

Silent people can always lord it over gabbers like yours truly. You believe they *know* something. The more you natter around them, the sillier you feel, the more of a Buddha they commence to seem. —I'm thinking of you, for instance, darling. You and this machine that don't say nothing but must know something and just keep rolling along. I know it's hard to fit a word in edgeways with me on this here gabfest tear. You'll get your turn, after. I'm expecting to hear about your life, loves, the lessons and upsets. I want you to tell—all. Soon as the paint of this is dry. Or even tacky. —The quiet ones, they *do* know something. Know to keep their traps shut. They understand (he sure did) that speech'll never make a body seem as glamorous as a long smart hush. Still, only one thing's going to teach Lucy here to finally pipe down and join the strong-and-silents. And I'll breathe my last trying to talk Death out of *that*!

My chatterbox mind made the most of Captain's being still. Me, on his front row, maybe I *was* extra-young, all eyes—but seemed like I already knew his secret. I didn't even consider telling anybody, that's how powerful it was. And Captain's eyes soon let on: He knew I knew.

Bands played Sousa off-key, flags were snapping, President McKinley—a short portly man with a Presbyterian preacher's samish speaking voice—

he used a wealth of hand gestures. Everybody's eyes were fixed on our nation's Commander-and-Chief. Instead I studied a Captain perched up yonder, gleaming like for sale.

Nobody else knew, but hidden way under that solid mid-years rosy fellow yonder with the rusty beard I noticed, plain as anything, one skinny saddened child. The boy's wide-open eyes locked right on me. This pip had been there, locked like in a closet, hiding through the war. War'd been over for thirty-some years but the child still stood there listening, bug-eyed, waiting for the all-clear bugle. He still expected outside air to be clotted with miniés. The sensible baby soldier waited, scared so long, at constant attention. I blinked, seeing what I saw. Only place this living boy showed through was: in the Captain's adult eyes. Only person that saw him there was me. I checked around. Others yet studied poor Mr. McKinley, two years from assassination. Captain's face itself was only extras—just a beefy margin, tax-paying, full-grown. McKinley now said, ". . . honor to share the platform with your distinguished veterans," and flung one hand the Captain's way. Everybody joined me, looking at the soldier, but when others veered back to the President's podium, I stayed on—was then he really ladled sight my way.

Dear God, I feel it yet.

And when his eyeballs latched right square on mine, I flinched so. I'd seen in. I keeled back and then drew close again. Both his eyes said, "You finally? Help me, sister."

Hundreds of countryfolks milled about holding candied apples and souvenir fans courtesy of Black's Funeral Emporium—"Burying the community for fifty years from one convenient location." Momma, prim, overdressed, sat on my right, one hand idly centering her cameo. Poppa made joker's eyes at his best drinking buddy up there on the reviewing stand, Pop kept trying and get the man to giggle—the fellow stared clear into the sky, like praying to be spared the sight of Poppa sticking out his tongue while a U.S. President spoke. Instead Poppa made two fingers become devil's horns behind the Mayor's sister's hat before him, till Momma slapped Pop's hand down, sighed her usual "Rea-lly, Samuel." And not one soul was noticing how—when Captain looked my way—oh boy, bye-bye to brass bands, town square, right down and back and into him young Lucy here did go, a swimmer. Nobody knew! The adult man let me see—before a crowd of nine hundred—a child's message spelled there plain. Boy's eyes said, "Sister, please come in and help me out of this. I'm begging here." I heard that clearer than any old-man President. I'd been asked to do a favor for a boy my very age. And my two eyes said back, "Well, okay. I'll give my best try, buddy-ro."

That was pretty much it.

Momma spoke of Cap as a "mature" man. At fifty? No lie. Poppa, a well-known local card and storyteller hisself, had always envied Captain's war crimes (some material!). Pop said you sure had to admire a solid fellow done up in more gold braid than gift-wraps New York City come Christ-mastime. But, honey, all I saw was somebody else fifteen. A big-toothed boy whose hair no oil could tame, whose singing voice was nothing much to speak of. Willie stood there—one hushed semi-homely child—everything had froze for him back then. His face smarted, it'd just found out: War means nothing fancier than losing your best friend.

—SUG, you know what I wanted? Wanted in. What I someway planned: to tie a rope around my waist, to hook its other end around this bright sure year of 1899, to scramble back on down, right square into the dark and smoke, the tar smell, back to where, by feel only, I'd surely find that child (part brother, partly baby son, plus mostly my love of loves, my true med-icine) and, oh, I'd lug him out with me, him tucked under one arm, I'd hold that boy, all powder-burned and stunned past talking. I would bring him home safe, to live in peace. With me. In a nice white house.

Poppa really set the marriage up. Saw me looking, says, "You got your heart fixed on that one, don't you, my Runt Funny and Minute Hand?" I just studied my knuckles, ones scratched scabby from recent tree-house building. Lowered eyes were considered a Yes answer for girl of my age and class and time—I knew it, too. Child, if you are young and powerless enough, just saying nothing means: *Do what you plan with me.*

(I kept picturing how I would one day wash Cap's bitter gray eyes with water, two little porcelain eyecups Momma had at home. Those eyes of his would be red from flying metal slivers, red from seeing too many others' eyes lose quickness. How good the cool water would feel.)

I weighed eighty-six, ninety, in there—low nineties—pounds I mean, not years, not yet. I owned fourteen or twenty-some dresses. I was Poppa's hands-down favorite, was considered (by me, leastways) headstrong and somewhat funny when the need arose. Around our house, it arose right often. That was part of my power and still is. Pop called it "getting a rise out of people." Made me think of Lazarus. Had Jesus maybe stood at the mouth of the grave and cracked "a good one" and first heard a sound like pottery breaking and then a sucking in of wind till one bone knee got slapped and death-defying giggles echoed from the tomb? One honest and earned laugh to make a shroud go glad rags! "Getting a rise out of folks" meant making them laugh against their will. Especially then. It sometimes seemed my only power. I sure have clung to it.

After supper, Pop and me adjourned to porch or parlor. There, with Momma as our martyr audience, he'd smile, "*Do* somebody, Runt Funny."

I did. "Saw a teacher today and she runs something like . . . this." I demonstrated how the forceful Witch Beale rushed wrenlike all over town in thirty-foot lunges, stopping like wondering if she'd locked her boarding-house door, then dashing off again, refueled. Or how Luke Lucas straight-ened his apron straps with the finicky pride of a girl arranging her first formal's spaghetti straps. All these I stowed, then I mockingbirded back. To look at me downtown, you'd take me for any noisome freckle farm—background, no better. But I was sopping up pretensions, postures, voices. Pop guessed Witch in two seconds then minced through each of Pastor Saiterwaite's arty daughters, but not in order of age—so he'd make guessing harder. "Now *you* try each," he said. We took turns. By age fourteen, I felt I'd pretty much nailed every notable local silly citizen.

At fifteen I would discover the sixty percent of Falls I'd missed. The black majority. Had I skipped them out of mercy or through ignorance or both? A crash course waited dead ahead. I only wanted to "do" others for fun. But I soon found how others get "impersoned" (like "imprisoned") in the doer's body and for good. Many of these folks from then are dead—only not yet, not totally. My fingertips and neck muscles still imperson them a bit. Later, for their sakes, yours and mine especially, I'll do some. "Doing" people! Has a smutty kind of ring to it. Maybe that's why Pop liked it, why I love it so?

> *Here's the church, here's the steeple.*
> *Lingo and fidget, I'll do all the people.*

(The one time Poppa, newly wed, attended Momma's childhood Episcopal church, he—being so countrified—felt increasingly uneasy. Maybe, hoping to break him into Summit society, she overcoached him? This forced him to do something that nobody understood the purpose of, Poppa least of all: He started making farting noises with his mouth. Hushed, then lifelike and loud. Everybody knew who was "doing" these. Nobody knew why, either. "Our Father [plltt] who art in [seep-poi-ert] heaven," et cetera. During the Doxology, he ran out of church. Everybody felt relieved, even Momma. Being civilized humans, nobody ever mentioned it to my folks. Locals claimed my poppa would do nearbout *anything*. At the time, this struck me as right high praise. Momma soon lapsed into being Baptist. What choice? He sat quieter amongst the Dunkers. Shame and the Episcopals don't mix.)

Momma would look at me and Poppa "cutting up" on the porch. In her rocker, she sat studying her newest sheet music. She belonged to "Prelude of the Month" Club. Poppa made fun of this—claimed he planned signing up for "Chewing Tobacco of the Day" Club, or Spittoon of the Week. Poppa knew no limits. You think *I'm* bad! For this reason, Momma rarely showed signs of being non-deaf. "Today" (eyes still latched on her sheet music), "thanks to the beauty of this Prelude" (study, study), "your base stunts are lost on me, Samuel. I am impervious, cloaked in Spirit." He leaned nearer her chair, blowing breath at her face. "So, baby doll, what'd the chicken say to the egg? Heard this down at Lucas' from one of the slower Wilcox boys. Third from dimmest. Still, it's got more philosophy in it than John Harvard's college plus that new tune you're pretending to read." She tried concentrating harder, it always made her prettier, her finger traced the five-lined staff. "*Ask* me for this joke, Bianca. I know you'll lap this up. Beg Sammy."

She finally rolled her eyes, she closed her Preludio. "As if there were a choice. Just one." Momma kept her mouth all slotted, joyless. "All right, what was it? What did the chicken say to the egg?"

He bent nearer her smooth neck. "Said, 'You come first this time, I'll come first next time.' "

"Samuel! And in front of our Lucille. Really," and rocking her chair, she opened her score from Boston, finger falling back a bar or two then gliding on. "Why me?" she asked the mail-order music. "Of all the art-loving thinkers on earth, why should this particular ragweed love have been visited upon me?"

"Just lucky, I guess," he winked. She shuddered—40 percent of it pleasure. Correction, 48 percent.

She only really tantrumed for real when I said "ain't" again. Born monied, poor Momma hoped to make me a shiny debutante like she'd been in Raleigh, like Captain Marsden's mother had got to be in Charleston proper back in 1840. (Charleston rests higher than Raleigh on the local deb dream scale. Not that it matters any.) But I ask you, child, can imagine your Lucy here leading some prissy cotillion of whiny powder-shouldered society girls? I *tried* telling Momma that Coming Out would always be beyond me. I won't ever what you'd call a beauty. I was built short if sturdy, overaverage, not unclean. I was, turns out, just the kind of girl a longtime bachelor with many years' experience in judging character and livestock recognizes.

Anyhow, he acted mighty dashing and nice to me and I liked him for it. On night walks, he told me stories, ones he'd kept aside even from other grownups. Me and girls my age had always snickered when we saw Captain around town. He forever scared us with his old-fashioned auctioneer's tendency to appraise us. A soberness like the smell of smoke, it hinted that military good looks and big money still hadn't made his life no picnic. But the man sure kept a eye out for the most fetching of my classmates. When one of my girlfriends got old enough for him to tip his hat to—she felt his gray eyes on her like a mustard plaster mashed hot across her lower back, then lower, a sealed bid. Out of Captain's sight, we teased each other. "He looked at you the most, Shirley." "No, *you*, he stared right at your . . . middy knot." Then we collapsed into great sherbet scoops of giggles.

The older women who'd asked for Captain's hand in marriage? seeing me with him, they did just snub me dead on Falls' wooden sidewalks. Being fifteen, I liked that part a lot. Poppa soon called me Lady Engaged. He imitated me coming down the aisle and tripping on the carpet while gnawing on my braids' tips—he mimed a Lucy not able to say "I do" for all the hair stuffing her mouth. " 'Tain't funny," goes I. Momma cringed behind her April Preludio. She said there'd be no wedding if my grammar didn't take a hundred-and-eighty-degree turn toward something I'd not yet noticed, something known—in towns far more advanced than muddy Falls—as civilization. Ever hear of it?

Soon as company come visiting, Poppa started in on engagement jokes—

he took both parts. Odd thing was (and this should of tipped me off, but young as I was I missed it) my own father, flesh and blood, was way better at copying Captain Marsden than he was at doing me. He got Cap by going all stiff-backed, dropping chin against chest, holding elbows far away from ribs, and lowering his voice to sound formal, charbroiled. Me, Poppa would ape by skipping up and down our best parlor, by tripping over nothing, by twirling either braid. So far so good—but, still, Pop missed something basic. Hard to explain. All mimes know that the *real* imitation is what you do with your whole trunk—ain't just the fussy flibbertigibbet fingertip stuff.

Whilst engaged, I felt disappointed by the Me that he showed company— all the yeast and heat of True Lucille was missing. Underneath my freckles, I felt wild and turquoise as a rebel Indian princess, gorgeous, inky. In front of guests, disappointed, I'd rush over and punch Poppa really hard in his upper arm. Soon we got to tussling on the porch floor like two scrappy boys. Mother would then rise, set down her music, she'd lean back against a wall, one hand held to her throat and hiding her profile cameo like the brooch alone had disappointed her. "No, please, not again, you two, oh no. To our distinguished visitors, I can only say once more, I don't know them, either of them. Really. What did a woman do to earn this? It's far beyond seeming droll anymore. What possesses you two to . . . ? Lucille will be a Mrs. in two weeks' time, and with a good-sized scab on one knee. Look at her. A tragedy. I can't live like this. Sometimes your pranks suffocate me. Look. I'm suffocating, I tell you."

Family life!

Poppa paid a secret visit on the County Registrar of Deeds (the listing of who owned what). Red-haired Poppa bobbed home with his best cat-on-the-canary-farm grin. "Exceptional man, this finance of your, gal. Sterling character."

A typical joke of Poppa's—saying "finance" for "fiancé."

And I thought *I*'d chosen Captain William More Marsden!

I STILL believed I could rescue the boy in him. Bring him out, literal. Little Miss Search Party. I figured I was mightier than any old war. After all, war was over. And me? Why, I'd just begun. Fifteen, that's the age when the only world event that counts is whatever mood you're in that day. I was in love. I was confused. I thought *he* was fifteen and I was fifty. Oh Lord. We married.

—WHICH came first, child, the rooster or the egg?

YOU KNOW what comes on at one? Why, *My Children, Right or Wrong*. It's one full hour of sin and eating out in restaurants. I hear it's about the most famous of all soap shows. In here it sure is.

When I got sentenced to this Home, it'll be fourteen years ago, I wouldn't go near Multi-Purpose, not while no soap program was busying the TV set.

Owing to excess pride, I kept to my bed during every installment. Others could be heard in there, laughing and oohing and aahing. Just burned me up: "Fools, nobody on it is *real!*" I remember back in the twenties and thirties, neighbor women forever listened at *Mary Worth* on the wireless. While I hung up children's clothes in our back yard, neighbors tried to trap me into gossiping about some people made up to sell Oxydol! I just smirked. I explained that I had nine children and one man in that real house yonder, they kept *me* guessing. "Just you wait," my lonely next-door neighbor smiled, poor Ruth, brimming with some secret knowledge.

Pride can keep a person off to herself. Folks in here couldn't eat breakfast without referring to Lance this and Alexandra that. First I thought these two must be a orderly and nurse that livened up all rooms but mine. Just actors on a screen. Well, I grew more determined not to be no softhead, never to break down and join the wheelchair traffic jam at 12:45 p.m. Sheep.

And due to such false pride, I missed the show where Debbie got born! There's no going back. We pay for our mistakes. Soon enough, one orderly friend, no, one friend who is a orderly, he offered me a dare. Jerome claimed I was afraid of popular entertainment—like my momma with her airs and sheet music, trying and be grand and all. "Ha!" goes I. Somebody else offered me ten cents if I'd come see their show just onct. Woman claimed she wanted to discuss a particular character with me afterwards, needed my expert opinion on that scamp Dr. Marcus. See, *his* fault is—if it's got a skirt on it, he has to at least *try*. Some women in here say he's downright attractive (they think any doctor is). These old women claim that, slick and heartless as Marcus is, they'd *know* not to expect any permanent relationship off him. They say that, if he asked, well, *they* wouldn't mind. Just once. For experience's sake. Talk's cheap.

Anyhow, I made fun of folks that forgot their own living children and could speak of nothing else but Pleasantville this and that. So not two days after I accepted Jerome's dare and then the dime, just two days into the show (20¢) I'm gumming through my midweek chicken à la king when I hear myself go, "All Lance needs is the love of a good woman, and you know I hate to say it but I worry over that day-care center owner and the way he keeps young Debbie mashed so much *on* his lap. True, he teaches her the alphabet real patient but his mustache is sneaky and it's just something fishy about that one." You could hear others' gloating laugh as they chanted, "We got Lucy, we got Lucy." Like kids! Well, I hung my head. Seemed I was already a *My Children, Right or Wrong* goner. For me, child, since then, there's been no looking back. If you got a habit you can manage for free and from your wheelchair, why not?

EVERY rest home in this area enjoys its own pet show. Others hooked on *Children, Right* send notes here, seeking pen pals. Everybody has a favorite adult character they want to discuss in detail but Debbie stays the child that holds all Pleasantville together. The main show here at Lanes' End Rest used to be *The Edge of Night*. Then *My Children* came on. First day, our Magnavox in its overhead rack lit up with Lance minus his shirt and Dr. Marcus minus his (during some young bride's ob/gyn examination yet!). Well, that turned the tide. Later, our men—to show they had noticed but with reasons cleaner than us ladies'—they said, "Young Lance there must swim." Minnie fires back, "For exercise? with Stacey, Alexandria, Sara, and Chichi the Spanish-speaking maid around? For exercise, Lance doesn't *have* to swim."

That got a laugh in Multi-Purpose till others shushed Minnie. She always breaks in with the loudest comments. I blame her 70 percent deafness. One woman couldn't help correcting Min anyway: "It's not Alexandria. It's Alexandra. Everybody knows that. We've told and told you. Four actresses have played in her for the past six years but her *name* has stayed Alexandra. Alexandria is a city in Virginia."

"Egypt," Professor Taw puts in.

Everybody's got to be right! Especially at this age.

The Edge of Night was our hallway's bread and butter for nineteen years till the vote went against it. Majority rules. With ours being a poorhouse home, we only have the one set. Well, *Night* diehards sure took it personal. You know what one woman did? You won't believe me but would I invent it? would I bother to? She couldn't afford her own TV set and she loved the people on *Edge* better than any living soul. So the first day *Children* came on to a full house waiting for more Lance "skin," this stubborn woman wheeled herself to the nurse's rolling medication cart (abandoned because staff was watching *My Children* too). She snatched many pills, swallowed everything, including one paper nut cup.

They had to pump her stomach. Unconscious, she begged for *Edge of Night* —I believe I'm mostly telling this to give me time to collect my present self for what comes next in the life of a young girl.

Bull Run
Honeymoon

*I sleep, but my heart waketh: it is the voice of my beloved
that knocketh, saying, Open to me, my sister, my
love, my dove, my undefiled: for my head is filled
with dew, and my locks with the drops of the night.*
—SONG OF SOLOMON 5:2

QUITE the ceremony, quite a write-up. Pictures, everything. Even
Raleigh sent reporters. Nobody knew how my mother'd swung
that. Must of partly been the Captain's community standing. Part was probably a little trick of Momma's called cash bribery. (I suspect she sent the
Raleigh society reporter a voucher for her prepaid carriage round trip, plus
some tidbit of inherited personal jewelry.)

Leaving church, I found a short hallway made of ex-Confederate swords
crossed over our heads. I couldn't really see the fun in that. My three unwed
aunts (the local pinnacle of pianistic education) had made my traveling
outfit by hand. It was silk-lined, a plaid organdy, the envy of all. I didn't
feel worthy of it, really. Adulthood felt like Halloween. My three kind homely
aunts praised me as smart. What did *they* know? Everybody made me think
I'd picked him. I guess I someway did. I was near the age he'd been when
war ended. I soon caught on fast enough—like young Marsden had to. I
came to after our first battle. That's what I called the honeymoon. That was
the storming of Fort Sumter all right and guess who played the fort?

Wedding trip clear to Georgia. By train then buggy. Talk about dust.
And me in the excellent new dress (it wearing me), dove-gray piping, ankle-
length hem, the short bolero-ish jacket, cute. Cap acted real polite. Every
ten miles he asked did I want watering, like I was some thirsty filly or had
a bladder condition. He kept touching the brim of his big black hat each
time he looked my way. I mostly wanted to get alone with his eyes, wanted
to leave the rude suet remainder of him (them pink extra hundred and
ninety-odd pounds) in the hotel hallway on some gilt chair where nobody
ever sat. I would only save the parts of him I trusted. Oh, I thought I was
getting a pup for Christmas: I didn't know what a war *was*.

Holding reins, Captain told me secret plans for turning his livestock slaughter pen into the Chicago of the South. Sounded good to me. I listened and was pleased with him. We looked nice together. Folks noticed. Then night came on. How old are you?

—Will you check out this spotted hand beginning to wobble? Things I'm telling happened miles of decades back. A world ago. Feels about as recent as a sneeze. Oh dear, what time does your watch say? We only got a short while till the lunch chime sounds. My, how time flies when I'm doing all the talking. You booked for afterwards? Because, see, I believe I'm only getting started here.

This recording machine looks too small to be American. So it *is* Japanese. See, living on a little island means they make the tiny things better, saves precious space. Oh, I read. They're steadier workers than Americans are now. The winning-side Yankees are finally learning what it's like to be beat by choicer equipment and finer factories. Be good for Northerners' character, a bit of competition. Now it's *their* turn for a little Appomattox ash-eating. Things shift. Woman down the hall blames these recent weather changes on the astronauts going back and forth in it. I said that, I remember. Slipping. You get tired. Lunch soon. Lunch helps.

Still, I always figured I would tell my story to equipment homemade as me. How much film, tape, or whatever you got stowed in this contraption? Enough to string a whole long gabby life along? Because—listen, I'm deciding here—if you got the stuff to maybe try and glue them to, I sure got some things that want saving. Maybe I do only have the four good teeth left but, darling, I own around one million examples.

There's a old woman down the hall—not the astronaut one, another— I mean a real old woman (you think *I'm* bad) and she's sealed in what we used to call a iron lung. Now it's named "a life-support system." That's what stories are for me now—a goodly air bubble safe-deposited inside most every one. I now have stories like I onct had me children—a crowded table waiting, each with allergies and appetites. Oh, I could flat burn this little Japanese's ears.

But, first, draw a little closer. You think I've forgot the honeymoon part, don't you? No, just stalling. I ain't all that feebleminded quite yet. Just cowardly at times. You know how honeymoons are, honeymoons then, anyways. Nowadays there's no shocks left. That, I figure, is better than the surprise element. Jerome will soon come fetch me for lunch and then *My Children, Right or Wrong*. You ever watch? Be honest.

So. Honeymoon, him and me, a one-girl battle of Bull Run and you can guess who the bull was and what he aimed to run at. Now, in Northern histories of the war, they say, "Yanks at Fort Sumter were fired upon without no cause nor provocation." Darling, that was me all over. And on my back to boot. Concerning bees and facts and birds and life, nobody told us girls zip. Zero. We had to find out at the time.

Nice hotel outside Atlanta. Soon as we arrived, Captain found him another Antietam-surviving vet. They seemed to sniff each other out like brother dogs. Well, the two men started comparing notes, hill by dull and bloody hill. Captain left me in a tearoom off the lobby—all potted palms, polished brass, tassels on the tassels. I sat arranging my pearl-gray hem over my buttoned boots so everything'd look its best. My braids were hogtied in a honeymoon bun, Momma's strong hands had secured them there to keep me from gnawing on them whilst nervous. (Momma said, "I don't want to *hear* you had hair in your mouth, understand me?" Poppa demonstrated a person fishing a single curly one off the tongue. Momma blanched like this was smutty—a prediction for me. Myself, I only caught on a good bit later and I didn't think it was either funny or too kind.)

Setting there waiting for Captain to quit talking tactics, I bet I was prettier than I thought I was. Everybody fifteen is basically pretty, ain't they? Just nod. Captain finally got our luggage upstairs with a handsome bellhop's help. But when Cap came back down (hurrying so he could continue battle chat), he'd left the wallet in his dusty greatcoat. He called me over while jawing with the Georgian. (Odd that every lobby and bar had another Antietam survivor when you remember how the twenty-three thousand got killed in that one day.) Cap asked me would I please run up and fetch his money. He handed me the room key. I felt flattered, like I was his favorite trusted daughter, not his wife.

Upstairs, I fumbled in his pocket. First I found a sealed envelope with our Falls druggist's script across the back: "Have Leander hand-deliver to stockyard . . . French Letters for Capt. Marsden's Honeymoon." I shook the thing. I didn't know that my husband could read French—I imagined him quoting foreign mail at me like poems. Another skill to be impressed by.

Next I pulled out a hinged leather thing all worn from handling. I took it to a window, hit the little latch. It opened on a shiny tintype—a beautiful person stood pleased-looking under a mat of ringlets like a halo, only loopy with too much body. The choir robe's starched collar rested open, the face wore only half a smirk. The face looked like it'd just started to consider becoming conceited but had decided against it and yet wanted to be given the wee-est bit of credit—even for *that*.

Downstairs again, I handed Captain his billfold to pay for the several whiskeys he had ordered hisself and the new friend. Then I mentioned as how I'd found this too—I pulled out the picture case. He snatched it so fast his huge hand made a testy blur. He checked to see if I'd hurt that daguerreotype, he spun to see if the other vet—off at a pastry cart—might've noticed my mistake in bringing the picture.

I had to ask, "Who is she?"

"She!" says he, half roaring with a laugh. "I like that, she! This isn't just some she, Mrs. This is my dearest friend on earth, ever. Was male as I am now. My late friend, Ned. I've told you."

"You said he was pretty. But I thought you meant only to you." I grew quieter. Slow, my hand lifted to my own cheek, fingertips comparing this decent living face with the one saved under glass. Fingers knowing which would always be the plainer. If I'd had a braid loose, I would have gnawed the thing damp or brushed my thin lips with it, for comfort. "It's just," I told my husband. "I never before saw his likeness. It's fact . . . a real beauty."

"He was." The Captain opened the picture, pulled it nearer to gray eyes. "*Is*. —Waiter, some tea and cookies for the little lady here. Thank you. That all right, tea and cookies?"

Then there was further war talk. "Did you by chance know Gunnery Sergeant John B. Morris, exceptional fellow, spine aplenty, severally wounded, and assuredly blessed with grit to spare, was he. Notably clever with his hands, too. Why, I believe it was on the eve of our first day's battle, a lateral jamming had occurred in a firing pin on one particularly testy . . ." They really talked like that. History'd turned their daily talk to tin. How little bearing it had on anything that mattered, child. I tried to appear listening. Mostly I wanted to dunk my cookie in my tea. Didn't dare. "You're married," I told myself, and it was like I'd said "you're royal" or "you're dead."

Then it got darker. Then we were headed (Cap and me) toward being locked in the same room as man and wife. I saw two sleek bellhops my own age watching us and laughing, knowing more than I did. "In for it now," the prettiest one said and made his eyebrows go. —Could you slide a wee bit nearer, honey? Fine. I need to look at somebody during.

CAP and me were no sooner alone together. He locked the door. His husbandly happiness seemed exaggerated by recent whiskeys, he leaned back against the door he'd locked. He whipped off his necktie then its stickpin and flicked those down. He grinned whilst the long unfastening commenced. Pants unbuttoned in them days. There were many buttons on those pants but—even so, child—not near enough.

You could've knocked me over with a feather when I saw what-all had to fit where. He stepped nearer. A tumor, tree-root deformity. He had definite plans for what to do with which parts. I figured *he'd* thought up the deed. I didn't have no idea on earth it was what you'd call a . . . classic activity.

He was pushing fifty-one, and I mean pushing. Game as any dozen itchy roosters. And me? Skin-and-bones pitiful—no bigger than a dime. What-all he wanted to get me doing, honey, it was just this side of surgery. (You know when I said how, in battle, if lead was hard to get at, docs just took the whole leg off? Well, was something like that, only in reverse, like going in and using the whole blunt leg instead of tweezers.) Somebody had saved *his* leg, so why could this fellow not, in turn, save me?

His hairy shoulders, crops of bristles sprouting on his back—my thin white ankles bent way up against them massy shoulders. Oh dear me. Oh dear dear *dear* me oh my. Cannot imagine, you cannot. Of course you can, but even so. Man had to mash a feather pillow in my mouth, see, I was screaming, not as a polite sign he should ease off, no, screaming to bring outside help in through yonder bolted door. Men's pictures are up post offices for slimmer offenses than he tried on me that night. The hotel manager would not have cared to hear what noise I had banked up in me by morning. You think that when Cap got done with it onct, he stopped? No way. Seemed he hoped to prove what a live wire he still was, whatever his age. He offered steady proof of what I might expect for good, for life. At fifty, he could've given goat-glands lessons. Was his first honeymoon, and it was mine. Only, he'd been practicing up since 1860. Me, I was innocent as mutton.

How old are you again, how much time we got left? I know I asked before—but, on both counts, it's forever changing.

RIGHT after, he dropped off to sleep and still on top of me. Talk about a heavy sleeper. I thought he'd died on me. I felt myself to be a small brown hearthside throw rug caught under the hugest possible loudest-patterned hotel-lobby carpet—Rhode Island trapped underneath and way out in the middle of all gaudy Texas.

I lay looking up past one shoulder's fuzz. Hotel ceiling had plaster baby angels mashed across it. Like a pie meringue of wings, curls, chubby elbows. I pitied those angels—bare to strangers' eyes night after night. I felt for everybody. I thought, Well, this is married life so called. I remembered my mother, awake in our house and missing me, having to make do with Poppa's stunts and fond teasing. I really could've wept for her. Chances were, she'd been through this mess too. —Jokers, mates were *all* jokers underneath, just waiting to try stuff, sick!

I heard horses knocking in their stable out back. On the hotel's first-floor veranda, tipsy salesmen bragged about their wares. A man and a woman one room away kept speaking in low tones—real angry but locked forever at this extra-reasonable level, sounding the fiercer for that. Maybe a brother and sister? No, married probably. I heard him snarl, "I'll never get over it this time . . . never." You could tell that they just loved to fight, how it was mostly what they had. I listened only because: no choice. My right arm had gone pins and needles from the pure weight of Captain. My chest was getting rheumy. But from the waist down, I burned so. Thigh muscles popped and spasmed like frog legs come alive in their final frying-pan jig.

Then my right side, ear to hip, just went. Bye, it snuffed past stinging. Below between, a hurt kept really hurting. My throbbing seemed sharp as other people's sounds. I wondered that them nearby folks couldn't hear it. Seemed odd that the manager didn't come running to help me, didn't summon the Atlanta police then telegraph my momma. Not a soul arrived. Momma? I was under a man who felt like a convention of boulders. It was legal, this. I was under a man my folks had passed me on to, for him to use this way for life.

I dared not reach down betwixt sheet and, with my good left hand, touch my opened self. I should've got right up and done some serious rinsing. But I didn't know how to wash proper. They never told you nothing then. Did they think that, by sparing you certain news, those facts'd bypass you? I'm not sure which world my well-intended folks kept schooling me for, but—so far, honey—I ain't yet hit its outmost border. Still, flat on my back, I knew my plan. Manners aside, simple self-defense come clear enough.

My awake half would pull its sister 50 percent free of Captain. Next (I coached myself) place both your bare feet onto floorboards, girl. The cold'll give you spunk. Why, if you see a fallen dray horse trapped under a cart on the street, you try and help it get aloose. Anybody decent will. So now save yourself—you're at least that good. You're a animal, minimum, which means you deserve *some*thing.

Your carpetbag is packed except for the silver hairbrush and your new *Child's Garden of Verses* from the aunts. Plus, you might just rescue some of them nice baby hotel soaps as souvenirs. Dress fast and quiet, slip on out. By train or on foot, get home, girl, as best you can—go right to the unmarried aunts' big house. (I would forever refuse to knock at my own folks' front door. Poppa was in there. Why did I blame Poppa most for this? He should've hinted. Momma probably couldn't. Everybody at the wedding knew. All smiling, winking so. Everybody but me. Me and my innocent untouched aunts.) Except for them, I figured nobody else'd want me now. Used goods, marked way down. First, when the three unwed sisters saw me alone on their porch, they'd scold. And I wouldn't blame them. "You left Captain Marsden, catch of the year, before one single night was over—why, Lucille?"

But when they stepped outside, and once I told them exactly what-all he tried to pull on me (I wouldn't have to spell out how that particular stunt had hurt a girl), aunts'd either swoon or else throw up on the lilac bushes. *Then* they would take me in. For keeps. To live in a clean white house forever. They'd hide a person safe from men for good. —I pictured all of this till I felt ready for escape. By then I knew I was strong and mad enough to live alone for life.

I felt I knew how slaves had breathed real shallow whilst sneaking North and free of a owning master. Anatomy-wise, seemed like what'd just been opened in me *was* the Underground Railway. My left hand's fingers now hooked under hotel bedsprings, got a goodly grip, pried the rest of me two inches freer. My jostling underneath him made the Captain stir, made him say something. Asleep, he muttered right down towards my neck.

His breath was like the air from a big commercial greenhouse— sweetish, possible, trapped-smelling. He mumbled words I couldn't under- stand. The next-door couple kept on bickering, voices getting lower as they meant it more. Stabled horses cleared their foot-long sinuses. Drunk hawk- ers stumbled on the street, letting out a few sample yahoos. —And Captain told me where I should put up our tent.

He said it real plain. I straightened beneath him. Was like hearing a strange man with a extra-deep voice speak out of the darkness in the same rented room with you, same bed. It *was* that. —Under here, numb, I was both his legal bride and what they nowadays call "a abused child." And it was then I understood—my aunts hadn't given me the Stevenson poems as a wedding present to replace my old worn-out copy. No, the morocco-bound book won't even meant for me. Was for other children, younger than me, ones I was going to have to have. But, see, *I* wanted it. I loved those poems, knew most by heart. And till that very second, I thought the Child whose garden of verses it'd always be was me alone.

The man above me spoke. I listened for one reason only. Pinned, I had to. I knew it was the war that he was in—he spoke of how a brook ran near the camp, he named which horses had lost shoes. Then his tone changed, something bumped inside the dream. His body quaked, the huge calf muscles locked in tics. Captain's voice grew much more lively by degree, moving up like notes from lower to mid-high to pure-tee screech. He yelled for chums to please take cover, fast. He sounded like somebody new, somebody more my age. Soon he was just hollering full out and I mean *loud*.

The couple one room away hushed their fighting. They mumbled in a more united way, guessing that some nightmared child had screamed one chamber off. Then they dropped back to accusing one another with yet more clever venom spirit.

What went on inside Cap's dream came out to me in bits and inches. Even when he paused, when deeper sleep let him lose interest a while, it all hooked up. When speaking started again, I understood just which direction the enemy was advancing from—a hotel room's northeast corner. He muttered how some rabbits and four deer had scampered through camp from that way—a sure sign of right massive enemy onslaught. "Smith, Ned. Get ready, boys. Here goes again. Do wish it wouldn't. Uh-oh, it sure is, though." Some enemies arrived on horseback. Many more on foot. Pinned, I listened all the full night long.

After a while, I didn't have to. Maybe from fright, my whole right side came back alive again, hello. I could have slid free, might have dressed quick, grabbed my nicest things, just run. Poppa'd given me a gold piece I'd hid in my bag's lining. Considering my getaway, I still paid attention. My thin shanks were cold, twitching now with questions only a doctor could answer. And yet I listened. I did, child. My young eyes stayed so wide open for so long, their outer edges dried. I forgot to blink. Couldn't hardly swallow—soon felt like *I* was talking.

Captain's night voice had this mildness floating over it. "Bring water, could be trapped . . . right good while. Stay down, you fools. *Told* you, keep flat. *I* don't plan to clean up your dying mess. No joke, over there."

Compared to Cap's daylight tone, this was like holding a jar of October cider up beside one of aged molasses.

Seemed familiar. Then I knew, of course—it was the *sound* of those boy eyes I'd seen.

Braced awake, I knew when Northern forces drew closer. I guessed which of Captain's friends were hiding where, when they'd been shot at, then when one got blasted for sure. How real it felt—his voice vibrating into my ribs. I kept my bearings all night long and by 4 a.m. could've sketched his whole battle onto the ceiling overtop them baby angels. His pain was like a map. It lifted and kind of led me a few inches free of my own hurt— pinned beneath it. At least for a while it did.

Odd, I hadn't known he had any. Pain, I mean. Everybody told me how his family'd had the great plantation before Sherman's burning desire to tour local mansions. Everybody promised me that Captain was respected, handsome, rich, a civic somebody. So where did the pain part come in? Sure, I'd heard his war stories often enough. But good as he'd got at telling them, each by now seemed smoothed almost official. Even the raggedness of his ripe voice could feel expert as a singer's tricks.

It's one thing getting a body's battle facts, another hearing the very voice of Then in motion. The squeal of being trapped in a hole, of being that young, that spooked, and not expecting to get even twenty minutes more of life, but greedy, oh, mighty greedy for more. For the right to make further mistakes.

His weight still crushed me. But now I started working to support it. Womanhood! My head and chest moved free. I wedged the left hand loose. But instead of reaching under sheets to touch my own casualty self, I craned up and over, found his forehead. Found it bunched in ridges like a fist. At my touch, I felt it smooth some. Just like that. What a strange new power this seemed to offer young me. A joy to hear his squeaks and warnings ease, the snores take over.

I knew that my pain tonight was—for my age group—equal to his. I knew that war seemed his excuse. But even then, I figured: no excuse ever excuses your hurting other people. Still, he'd once been young and in deep trouble. Here, now, so was I. From the waist down, I felt novocained with the damage this old man had shot my way. But, considering the boy my age, a boy like myself—in a definite bind—that night, forgiveness interested me.

Forgiveness! Honey, I thought I had invented it.

Sleeping, he no longer believed that my touch meant I wanted a rematch at wrestling. With Mr. Marsden awake, I couldn't act this kind towards him without courting the old goat's pouncing. One last time, Cap piped, "Duck. Or you'll be hurt. Don't. Oh don't get hurt."

I touched his big closed eyes. I told them, "Won't. We won't. I promise."

If I hadn't jostled him whilst trying and save myself, he might never have spoke out in his sleep. I might never have known. —In some ways, sure, he was just another slave-driving pile-driving villain. But, too, he'd stayed a child damaged early on. That night, he seemed all heavy and all light at once. Which of the two would I pick to see and stay with? Maybe both, a boy and man dancing forever on each other's toes.

Finally, the sun—without even meaning to—helped me. Sun turned those young angels overhead as pink as raw roast beef, made them seem beef-real. I knew my pain was a match for the sleeper's piled atop me. Equal pain for equal work! But I calmed myself by whispering verse till the hotel roused in knocks and sweepings. Tears creeped from eyes' far corners and tickled both my ears full. And yet I kept on quoting, quoting one of those I knew:

> My bed is like a little boat.
> Nurse helps me in when I embark.
> She girds me in my sailor's coat
> And starts me in the dark.
>
> At night I go on board and say
> Good night to all my friends on shore.
> I shut my eyes and sail away
> And see and hear no more . . .

When he woke, heaved sideways, scratched hisself while looking around, saying, "Where the . . . ? Oh," when he sat up—his broad bare back to me, it felt almost matter-of-fact—with me still here, a stiff beside him. Felt semi-natural, seemed like what it was already . . . a kind of marriage.

We ate breakfast with the other vet. I had just got my Purple Heart in secret, purple something all right. I sat sipping tea, nibbling on a scone. Above the marble tabletop, I was Miss Teacake Priss. Underneath it: the Circus Lady That Gets Nightly Sawed in Half, only for real. Seemed the Captain hoped to hold off discussing what'd happened upstairs, wanted to postpone asking how I was, had I endured it. All my busy forgiveness in the dark meant I'd got not one wink of sleep. He'd snored right through. He said he sure felt fit this morning. "Nothing like a good night's log-sawing," Captain stretched. The other veteran, a gentleman, at least had the decency to lower his eyes and look away from me.

Was three miles clear of town before I spoke. We were riding north along Sherman's southbound route. So near to Atlanta, everything'd been burned twice. Soil still looked pitchy. No tree in sight stood over twenty feet tall. You'd see fine old trunks but they were only charcoal. I sat waiting for some news from my bridegroom. I sat thinking this must be a omen— tooling through a war zone on our first married morning outdoors.

Three miles and many trees of the sapling class later, he says, "Things," then quits. "Things do get easier, child, with practice they do. We'll have you relaxed in no time, we'll get you kind of . . . a little . . ."

I finished for him, "Broke in? Kind of broke in?"

Cap said he'd planned to state it a good deal nicer than that but, yeah, relaxed, whatever. He sat so straight-backed then, he got to fiddling with the reins. The horses' ears stayed up like horses were listening in. Let them.

"You'll see," he tells me. "Time helps, child. Things improve. You'll get used to everything. Maybe even me included. It's a sort of bill of goods, the whole married setup. You take the easy with the less so. I might not be smooth, but I'm not a bad man, either. Of course, I guess I'd be the last to know, if I were . . . but still . . ."

His crabbed tenderish voice showed me he was trying for my sake. But why hadn't this not-bad man helped me out last night? I kept still, ashamed of sounding like a bad sport. Nobody hates being a bad sport like a fifteen-year-old tomboy whose momma is a fainter. I looked over at him.

Now, for me today, child, a fellow of fifty would appear practically an infant. But to a girl so young, one who's known no sleep the night before, a girl just split netherwise with no more ceremony than a melon rolled off the roof, Mr. Marsden looked as old as I do right now. Maybe even longer in the tooth.

A bright morning, and he sat there, mahogany brown, steel gray, meat red—green country pulling past him. Lines fanned out this side's bright eye, lines printed there from his squinting at the world three times longer than I'd been alive. Oh, I knew the fellow half liked me. But, too, I figured he liked Momma's money—and me, her only child. (I understood that Momma's bratty childhood fame and snooty ways made folks forever believe her to be piles richer than she was.)

And I wanted to like this man back. I did. Right off, I knew it'd go way easier on a person if she could. So I smoothed my skirt over either knee and tried again to feel how good we looked together. Nobody, studying us today, could probably tell. Unless them handsome bellhops peeked, then snitched. So I told myself, "Enjoy the view, darling." (I believe it was the first time I ever spoke that overused word of mine "darling" to any living soul, and I said it whilst trying a mothering rescue of my own self.)

Was then I saw the stain. It'd spread from underneath me all up around and halfway across my lap—gray piping was now sogged purple with it. I couldn't look down no longer. "Enjoy the view, view, the view." I only stared at farmland, a third-degree war burn we buggied through. I saw a woman behind a cabin, she boiled clothes in a black pot. Her broomstick poked one family's thankless filthy shirts. Agewise, she fell betwixt Momma and me. Something about this white lady standing on history's scorched dirt, something in how—this early in the day—she stooped (so willing!) toward the steam of others' dinge. It made me want to scream for her, for the Captain back then (a child I saw would not rush out at my first invitation), and to scream for me, oh yeah, me too. Then I couldn't help but to notice— I was. Screaming. The washing woman jumped. When she turned my way, part of me went, "Oops," another figured, "Good. Stare! I'm being kidnapped. And everybody agrees it ought to happen. Come help a girl. I'm bleeding here. I need another lady's aid, please, ma'am."

Beside me, as I hollered wave on wave of it, spit fleeing in strings and spots of light, whilst I sat pointing at the colorful ruined lap of me and then to the man and back to damage done by him, Cap appeared right palsied. He lost all color, he give our mare and gelding one steadying cluck, "There, boys." He gawked like I was some lunatic lady that needed chaining to a attic wall for her own sake and others'. Oh and it was my good dress too. The traveling outfit my unwed aunts had spent two months of nights on their side porch making be so perfect. Soaked clear through. Me, bumping on that buckboard seat after all I'd been through down there last night, dress wet heavy in broad daylight and I ain't talking with perspiration either, honey. —The night before, he'd called out, "Don't. Oh don't get hurt." Right good advice. One wise child warning another. A voice I recognized like I had known his boy's eyesight. And I figured I should now definitely duck or dodge or hide myself, but where? Where was safety? Honey, from then on, there won't no cover anyplace for me. Darling, I was on my own for good. All of this was legal. It'd grabbed me oh so soon, so soon.

THESE Japanese machines understand plain English? Should I talk less bold about activities in B-E-D? Okay, I'll say all of it straight out. You can trim the troubling parts after. I ain't foulmouthed by nature, but it's time for total facts. Seems like I'm finally getting limbered up some. Okay, okay here, child.

I do have a load of stuff to spill before my breath takes its long-overdue vacation. Unless I'm wrong, and if you're willing—it might partly get told your way, child. Seems a miracle, but here I am—still trusting strangers at my age. Well, a body's got to. No matter what. That's the bargain. Good honest face you have here. Keep it that way.

FEELS easier with you settled closer. Look, you don't think I'm just some mean old gossip, do you? Because I'm not, not really. Gossip's what woes and vices happen to strangers. Stories come from nearer. They're from in here, up here, and yeah, Lordy, down there too. Maybe especially from down there.

My stories are mostly housebroken, they know the key's hid right under our Welcome mat because who'd think to look in a place so bold and innocent? Plus, all *my* stories are true. That's what bowls you over, ain't it? Keep your tales around long enough, they won't go bad on you like leftover food. Oh no, they'll improve, honey, they'll upgrade nearbout to legend— Mr. Bread Mold shifted clear uptown to Mrs. Pencillin.

And young as you are compared to me, you better get *your* stories in order, child. Because a person's life, it's just about a week. You're getting dressed for school on Monday morning, Momma's two rooms off calling, "You'll be late again, sister, and no written excuse from home this go-round, Miss Molasses in January," and by the time you try and put your foot through your pantaloon's other leg hole, you find it hard to straighten up because you're a woman of eighty-odd and your spine, why it's rusting already. Here you are, Momma long gone, no hope of another note of excuse ever again, and you're still stepping into schoolgirl britches so out-of-date they look plain silly, even to you. You perk and find yourself alone because, hey, it's late on Thursday and I mean your only Thursday, ever, child.

Now, for me it's about Sunday evening—late. Always did despise Monday mornings. So, just cover your wristwatch till you hear Mrs. Lucy croak, "The End."

Unnecessary Roughness

My kinfolk have failed, and my familiar friends have
forgotten me. They that dwell in mine house, and my
maids, count me for a stranger: I am an alien in their
sight. I called my servant, and he gave me no answer . . .

—JOB 19:14–16

OUR back-from-the-honeymoon buggy pulls up before Captain's
two-storied home. This place must be semi-mine now. Our evening of return, Falls mostly sleeps. Wake up, everybody, your Lucy's back!
I hadn't expected brass bands. Still, one familiar face—somebody waving
might be nice. My only fun: a little celebration waiting yonder on the lighted
Marsden porch.

Christmas come early, candles burn at every window. Flanking the front
door, five-foot magnolia branches stand in buckets. White waxy flowers
bloom big as Captain's head, beard included. I limp up front steps. I'd rinsed
my new dress as good as I could manage. I remembered Momma's saying,
"Only ice water might stun blood sufficient so your stain won't be permanent." Oh, but I feel eager to get alone in a house at least partway my own.

First, Cap throws open a wide front door. "Upsy-daisy," the man scoops
me off my feet. I pretend not to like this (that's just my way) but I do (my
way too). I'm grinning when he strides me to the center of a dim entryway,
when he sets me down before this huge black woman, candlelit. Who?

Arms crossed, the gloomy one snorts, sounds bored at the first sight of
me. She wears two necklaces, sizable glass earrings, and a red head kerchief.
The chrome-yellow blouse binds every which way. One purple gypsy sash
girds her center. A polka-dot green skirt has cloth enough for covering any
couch. Honey, to ever get color-coordinated, these clothes wouldn't just
need some tactful saleslady, they'd require a treaty.

She's onto two hundred pounds. It mounts up. Cap sets me before her
like this here's a relay and she gets me next. Then off he strides to read his
mail. Seems she's considering eating me for a snack but worries I've been

left out in the air too long. Shy, I smile, legs yet weak from certain marital activities.

My husband, flipping through letters, remarks over his shoulder, "You two know each other."

"No," I speak soft. "I don't believe we've had the . . ." Big woman roughly shucks me of my wrap.

"What, haven't met?" Cap acts surprised.

"No way." Billy goat gruff, her voice goes deep as his. Loamy with that long a history.

"Well, *now* you have. Castalia, may I present my young wife, Mrs. Marsden? Lucy, Castalia. Cassie here's been with me since . . . well, since forever, right, Cas? Yes, sir, if the years could speak . . ."

She growls, "Years can, you don't play you cards right." Then these two stand facing one another and are laughing—the concord of a lifetime stretches betwixt them. They chuckle at a single pitch: like some accordion shaken with violence to sound its jolliest.

And me? I'm in everybody's way. I feel that to my very molars. I touch my neck's bun. I figure: Lucy, about one-eighth of a polite little simper will do nicely just now. So I risk it. But Large Person notices, she blisters me with such a look, like I been caught eavesdropping. "Pleasure," grins I. Meaning "Pleasure to meet you." Nobody much hears.

My husband stands by a candlelit hall table, his massive back is toward me, the ivory blade goes ripping into four pounds of business mail. Castalia has stacked it just so beneath a ivory letter opener. "Seem to have received eight or nine paternity suits in ten days. Roughly the usual number." Appears he's made a joke for his celery-stalk wife and pumpkin-coach maid. Don't neither one exactly fall out laughing.

The front hall is underfurnished—a bachelor just sleeps here. That ex-bachelor is yonder muttering about bills and more bills—about others' mistakes. "I *told* that dunderdick 'in escrow,' now look what's he gone and done. I swear, you leave them for a minute—"

I'm scared to turn towards Castalia. Somewhere deeper in this house, apples must be boiling on a stove. Smells nice. Rooms away, is that possible gardenias? But as my face begins to open with smells' pleasure, the woman steps before me, gives a shake to earbobs large as cut-glass doorknobs. Eyes hold steady over the big jaw. Castalia's pillowy mouth might hint at Song of Songs but, child, these eyes form chutes that send you straight to a reckoning called: Revelations.

Candlelight shows her off in ledges. She allows Lucy sufficient time to understand how much of her is here, how serious it mostly is. I do.

Now her boss's back is turned, she tilts nearer me. Up close, her head—red cloth flagging its dome—looks the size and shape of a small fire hydrant. This face arching on front seems a mask made from bent dark woods, a disturbed violin maker's work. Some breasts!

Her scalloped edges bring to mind Momma's favorite portrait of Henry

VIII, hands lording it over hips, baggy clothes clinging to the globe of him like being all crepey Nations of the World. Castalia's breath smells of marigold (she *eats* marigolds?). Hoarse breath explains, "See me in this house? I been here. I permanent. —Who *you* kidding?"

Captain, hearing silence, wheels around, "Now now, girls." He grins like he's expected strife, considers it right cute. "Listen, and listen reasonably hard here. You two *will* get along, do you understand me? I mean—you're so abidingly alike or I never would've chanced bringing you two under a single roof. I'll lay odds you all will soon be just like . . . this." He raises two fingers. They spastic across each other. Two form one pinkish stump. I quake.

"Oh, I'm sure," I try sounding like Goodwill itself. "I mean, I've heard so much *about* . . ." I pivot.

She ain't there.

ON THE second floor, my hot bath waited. Somebody'd carried each heated bucketful upstairs. I felt nervous about that. Being waited on never seemed worth the awkwardness of having help nearby constantly *watching* you. My own mother lived in fear of black people. Wouldn't have one in the house. Anyway, how did this woman know exactly when Cap and me would drag in, dusty from Georgia? Is it hard to keep this many gallons warm so long?

The corrugated tub smelled of lemon juice. A single gardenia floated on top. Set inside its petals, one white birthday candle burned. I stood staring as if down some well. I longed to crawl between the satin sheets of that white flower. Like a girl in some illustration by Mr. Walter Crane, I'd sail away for good. After my honeymoon of service, such kindnesses made a body feel weepy. Castalia wedged in through the doorway behind me, arms crossed like some harem's strongman guard. I praised her thoughtfulness. She shrugged, "Just be my duty to. His momma never got near no bath without they be gardenias in it. Winters, had to have us a greenhouseful. She was worth it. Believe me, gal, ain't got nothing to do with *you*."

Castalia offered to help me undress. My hand flew up, shielded a top collar button. I said, oh, I could probably manage undoing my own self, but thank you *so* much. (I thought, I'd rather strip naked on the Falls Courthouse steps in January and before a lynching party than have this particular person see my over-many ribs and calcium-deposit knees.)

A secret pasteboard sign had been tied behind the honeymoon getaway buggy. One of Cap's hired men put it there. Everywhere we went, folks smiled and pointed. This pleased me. I didn't know as how this hidden placard read, "May tonight's Bedtime be like a Kitchen Table—all Legs and no Drawers!" —Hours later, during a rest stop, finding the thing, I tore it into bits. I stood gasping, grinning myself sick from shame. Hundreds had seen it!

Now another stranger waited to undo my travel clothes. I turned. Castalia's size made her forever seem standing one yard closer to you. Wet eyes burned, bloodshot in the unglossy face. Eyesight seemed some privilege granted late in life. You know them haunted-house portraits where certain ancestors' canvas eyes get snipped from behind—then some stranger's peepers fester back there, watching you? Castalia's amber eyes didn't so much live inside her head as stare *through* it.

I decided: Bad stuff has happened to this woman. Considering her eyeballs' haywire heat, you didn't need no genius to help guess that.

Finally, mumbling, shaking the jeweled head sideways, she left. I locked that door so fast. I listened. Glacier bulk creaked slow downstairs. Safe, I stripped pronto, climbed into the tub. I spoke kind to a gardenia candle boat, "Well, hi, you. Ain't you nice for staying up so late to be in here with Lucy." When my overutilized lower sector hit uppermost hot water, ooh but I did hiss, squint, thrash. I drowned the candle's flame, said, "Sorry." Both eyes closed, I tucked a wet flower back of one semi-prominent ear. Gardenia smelled peppery yet sweet. "There, there, Lucille," said Lucille here. I tried remembering what words my mother used when I was sick. I needed me a nice soothing nickname to goo-goo at myself. Who *else* would?

When you been bouncing in a train or buggy, you know how onct you stop, the world still seems to rattle forwards awhile, surfaces gliding towards congealing nowhere fast? This tub now felt set on a dozen axles spinning down Atlantic Coastline Railroad tracks. Maybe rude signs, hooked to the caboose, caused dirty-minded trackside watchers to hee-haw my way. Our buggy's other plaque had announced, "Grand opening tonight!" Tell me, child, was I a prude to mind? Any girl fifteen that survived so recent a breaking and entering, she's earned a bout of sopping self-pity. Prior to marriage, I had lived with my folks two blocks away. Those years now seemed like happy solitude. Here recent, all my beds and baths were supervised by different grownups, training me in your quicker ways of getting naked. That much I could do myself.

Seated in wet, I told myself, "This is Falls, North Carolina, you're home safe, right?" All the way back, I believed that finally getting inside the city limits might save me! So, in hot water, I tried staying attractive and deserving, I still felt mighty willing to be spared. "Welcome back, Lucy Married, darling," Lucy Married said, her tone lacking total sincerity maybe.

How to Return

And what man is he that hath planted a vineyard, and hath
not yet eaten of it? let him also go and return unto his house . . .
— DEUTERONOMY 20:6

D URING the long trip back from Georgia, Captain had paid courtesy calls on fourteen small-time Livestock Barons. Every three
counties boasted one. Captain knew the pedigree and pig-broking repute of
each. New at wifeness, I tried acting deeply interested. I have always wanted
to do right. A failing, it turns out.

From my present ripe-to-ptomained age, I recall these Barons as being
rolled into a single well-fed gent. He wore a checkedy suit loud as the tin
sign for some new chewing tobacco. He spoke from under orange-bristled
mustaches that corkscrewed on either end like pigs' tails. The dandy didn't
know his face hair copied backsides of the pork that'd so fattened his fortune.
(I reckon all of us are daily paying homage to things we ain't yet recognized,
child. Vanity is sensible. It hides so much from us.) Pig Baron squired my
hubby and me around a hog-parlor breeding station he claimed to've invented. But we viewed the same model sty from county to county. "Finer
than many *homes* in our area," the similar Pork Lord joked over and over.
The more times I got introduced to him, the more I longed for a town that
knew its scab-kneed Lucy by name, and on sight, and from one hundred
yards up any tree she climbed.

Finally our buggy creaked within four miles of home. I'd been steadily
asking, "Are we near it yet, halfway, more?" Cap rolled his eyes but told.
My heartbeats clocked the whittling distance. I sat up stiffer, cleared my
throat like some speech was soon expected. I pinned such rebel-tendril hair
as had escaped the mother bun. Preparing for what?

I onct heard life described as "a horizontal fall." Our toppling towards
home that afternoon seemed as destined as gravity.

So far, no vista looked familiar. Just typical crops, rural mailboxes
boasting Scotch-Irish names, zinnias collaring your finer farm homes. Ambitious ladies out this way copied yard fads from off my home street, Summit

Avenue, Falls real estate's top de la tip. Today I saw watery holes sunk in some farmyards, holes edged with metal wagonwheel rims and surrounded by marigold borders. From one such puddle, a sunfish broke water. I understood—Falls' trend towards goldfish ponds was being honored way out here. Why did this make me feel proud yet melancholy?

I scouted for landmarks I might know. Just more red dirt, a countrified sky being light and massive over acreage stretched taut in all directions. At 4 p.m., June heat had finally lost its ambition. And I sat waiting for some noisy welcome party's approach. I kept clearing my throat. My old man asked me was it the dust?

"Nervous is all. You *sure* we're nearbout there, sir?"

"The signs for Hedgepath's will appear in a minute and a half. Then perhaps you'll believe me and stop asking. *How* old are you?" But primping his beard, getting ready to greet any acquaintances, Marsden seemed pleased by my innocent excitement. His pleasure made me want to keep such pleasure to myself. In short, we'd really started being married, child.

A one-lane dirt road—a fringe of battered grass along its center. Coming at us, three pretty sisters on one threadbare asthma-gasping mule. Passing them, a old man whose jowls bounced atop his frisky palomino—horse tail all silver-white, streaming perfect in its breeze. Beyond roadside ditches, low scrub woods: loblolly pine, beech, sassafras, sumac, unappreciated Queen Anne's lace. The forest smelled musty, secret, welcoming. Woods smelled of living mushrooms and of Tuscarora ghosts. In 1900, so much of Carolina was still as outwardsly wild as I felt inwardsly. I was a secretly disguised Indian princess. I was a dark beauty, safe under straw-toned hair and a spy's zillion false freckles. Nobody would ever know me. I would see to that.

Jostled by a washboard roadbed, I sat hoping that our hill town up ahead might make certain things up to me. Maybe Falls would prove a tourniquet, it'd put the brakes on certain bedtime poisons just released in me. To be made a un-virgin before you ever understood you *were* one, no fair. I didn't really crave seeing my parents (they'd given Cap my hand in marriage, my hand and every other part). But Home, yeah. That. A new start in a safe place. I clutched my carpet sack. Hid under my Stevenson poems, hotel soap, and, wound in tissue paper, fourteen prisms rescued from the windows of my childhood bedroom.

Meantime, farmland's blankness did soothe a person some. Two counties—flat as kitchen tables. Roadside ditches bristled with blackberry vines and—if you looked close—lightning bugs showed among the shadows. Waking bugs blinked, practicing their on/off switches. Soon, darkness would lift these creatures out of homely shade. Lack of light would turn the world into their free-range home.

It's 5:40 p.m., June 15, 1900. It's 89 degrees. My bloomers are stuffed with strips of the *Atlanta Constitution* to absorb stray embarrassing losses. And here I start the happy recognizing.

We round a bend. Sure enough, my Captain's right. We pass four sooted chimneys of a famous plantation home, Captain's, once called The Lilacs. Sherman burned every surface not brick. Virginia creeper vines and mud dauber wasps' nests now bind and clot each exposed hearth. Vandals long ago stripped white onyx off the hearth facings. Rumor claims all our county bats sleep in these three-story hollows. Their bricks have been continuously falling all my life and everybody else's but won't end their brave topple for some years. (A inspiration to us all, Rome itself took nearly eight hundred years to fall. Gives me faith that I might hang on by the skin of my former teeth for maybe nine more months!)

Under a bridge, the gargling Indian Creek. It always lowers this road's summer temperature by eight to ten degrees. Some black kids fish down there, solemn planning the size of today's catch. The creek offers you a smell of bilge and honeysuckle, equal parts. (Here, two little Mayos drowned whilst hoping to get saved by two young Wilguses who plunged right in but went down too. Not one of them kids could swim but in the frenzy of ending, all forgot it.) Such facts—who died where—do tend to ground a returning person. Lore hereabouts often means gore hereabouts.

(Odd, I'm remembering the goose-down pillow from my room at home. If I asked my folks' permission to take it forever into Captain's house and bed, would everybody think this real, real weak of me?)

Ahead, a final feature before the River Road turns and shows us Home: signs for Hedgepath's Veg-table Stand, hooray! I shift with pleasure—Georgia newspaper crackles considerable. Hedgepath announcements will claim these next three miles before the promised stand itself turns up.

Signs sure overprepare a person. Hundreds of them stutter about Hedgepath's definitely coming up, yeah, folks, get ready, hungry yet? this'll mean your last country chance for produce, ever. "Thousands of satickfied costumers over Time."

Hedgepath's spelling is so awful it makes us town kids feel superior. (We love to see adults' mistakes made on so grand a scale. We always beg our folks to stop and buy something from any poor hicks *this* dumb.) "Ocri!" "Punkms!" "Peenup Buttur!" I swear to God, that bad.

It's really just another part of Hedgepath's strategy! Old man H. figures: You might believe he's as poor at math as at spelling, therefore you'll stop and try to gyp him.

The old geezer is justly famous for his homegrown watermelons. (Locals claim that bourbon's someway shot into the pink of each. Even teetotalers get hooked, especially them.) I greet my favorite of Hedgepath's signboards. A huge melon is shown over two powder-blue snow-flecked words: "ICe CoLT!"

To paint your own personal slice of Hedgepath melon, first slap on a yard-long grin of pink—use high-gloss enamel to make it look more cold and slippery. The slice's crescent moon of outer skin is no more than a thin green curving line. Let your sign's white background paint rush in to be the rind of whitewall sickled betwixt green and pink. Then overtop the now dried pink, you'll have the final fun—doing hundreds of speckledy black seeds (a joy for farm kids—daubing during one whole choreless rainy afternoon indoors). If you climb down off your buggy and stoop close enough, you'll see: No brush is used for the black paint. Seeds are no more than many children's fertile fingertips.

Most everybody stops at Hedgepath's. You nearbout have to. The stand features twelve-holer privies for white folks—ventilated, wasp-free. (Six-holers for our colored customers.) Road narrows where Hedgepath placed his colorful vegetable ambush. He'll *see* you slipping by—he ain't above hollering at you, either, "Tight wad. Go on, then. But I'm sure *telling* everbody."

So, you rein your horses partway owing to gratitude for any prank strung out so far. Signs' mottoes, boasts, and corny come-ons have made dull fields into a stupid (funny) human progress three miles long. That's surely worth *some*thing, darling.

Turns out: Hedgepath's lean-to has less timber in it than do most of his nine hundred promissory billboards. You get down anyhow—doubtful, pleased, half bullied into doing this, not minding but pretending to. "Free Wader for you Hosres! Road diwrecksions free of chage."

Right off, you find you're remembered from your last visit. "Well, well, if it ain't . . ." And you're called, if possible, by name, called that loud and many times. Captain eases our team toward ditch bank where lightning bugs show bolder now that day's losing face. He gets down to stretch. Of course he's recognized right off. Seems like mute farmland itself has spoke his name and—by extension—mine.

Mr. Hedgepath weighs ninety-some pounds, he seems as springy, tragic, appealing, and overpopulated as the awful coiled flypaper dangling everywhere. Mrs. Hedgepath weighs more than the umpteen bushels of gaudy produce she sits amongst like one more mound of. These oldsters boss around their dozen towheaded children who sack goodies, weigh these, sweetly overcharge you. To perfect strangers milling here, black or white, the senior Hedgepaths say, "Seems like we should *know* you." And the very second any stranger admits a name, older Hedgepaths snap fingers, look at each other, nod. "Knew it. *Strong* family resemblance. The very ones."

Which makes visitors feel good. It's a trick. Guests recognize this but are semi-flattered anyhow. They're pleased enough to buy a little something. Which is all them Hedgepaths ever intend. About to leave, even Cap shells out a few pennies for sun-warm tomatoes—ones so unlike these Styrofoam things you get in markets nowdays. (That's the modern world all over, child, growing food for how it *looks*. Once you've bought a California tomato, and tasted its blank chalk, you been exceptionally well suckered—can't take it back.)

Ones stuffed into our bag this evening are spotty, marred by picking—

but so full of a ornery over-alive red-dirt flavor. They're definitely "from around here." Maybe a pound of such tomatoes don't in 19 and 00 seem worth a whole nickel—still you hand five cents to the nearest Hedgepath. And you pay because of a kind of happy pity. It tells you you are home. Again you have found this bargain of a joke.

—Uh-oh, we're almost in sight of town, it's just beyond that turn! Falls lies directly ahead unless the place burnt or is some dream I've had for fifteen years running. Leaning forward across my honeymoon valise, careful not to squinch new produce—I squint around a bushy curve. "Oh, look," I say, more to myself than him. He does, though, look. —First I love his joy at being back. Then I think I love *him*. —It's easier if you love people. Remember that.

Falls—a cusp or bump—becomes one definite green swelling. It's inlaid right on the horizon going sunset pink, Falls shines with gas streetlamps being turned on one by one. Our road straightens—like owing to respect. All roads (in Nash County) lead to Falls—or out of it. Our buggy veers rightward. My left shoulder touches my husband's solid right one. I allow that to continue. I'm pleased recalling: Since Captain Marsden is from Falls too, however much we might could differ through our life ahead, we'll at least have this. A language spoke by just eleven hundred other souls on earth. (Plus you, child. See, I am slowly teaching you that ramshackle romance language. Ready or not, by the end of this and me, you'll be right hideously fluent. You will then have to take Forgetting Lessons. I am ninety-nine, and mine are scheduled straight ahead.)

Evening—perfect hour for return. Daylight has held on long enough to see us to our door and then retire upstairs like some good servant.

"Looks splendid waiting, does it not, Lucille? I assume you're reasonably happy to be back."

"Yes, sir," I nod. "It's nice knowing . . . everything. I mean, where stuff will be and all."

He adds: "Ten days away were just too long. I miscalculated. Could well have made it seven. Five perhaps—and with less business, more pleasure. In future I'll remember my mistake."

"For your *next* honeymoon?" In sight of home, I grow more sassy. My panties rustle like some Woolworth Easter Basket's clean excelsior.

"For my next with you, Lucille. In, say, ten years, we'll do it all again." When he sees I don't exactly hop for joy, Cap adds: "Only better . . . A person learns . . ."

Learns what? I want to ask but I am semi-scared to know. Besides, I'm too busy straightening the skirt's waistband, getting my attention pinned. Eyes are latched on the strange hill town ahead gleaming conch pink, valuable, porcupinish with competing church steeples.

Dead ahead, disguised as some hicks' make-do watering hole, I recognize it, child: the celestial city.

2

REMEMBERING the homecoming, still waiting for its comforts, I'd dozed in the bath, knees tucked under my chin. I heard two folks still downstairs, talking, catching up like brother and sister or worse, gently teasing each other.

Once I dried, once I saved a face-down gardenia from drowning, once I put on night things and unlocked, allowing a door-rapping homeowner into his own bedroom, I noticed some provisions set yonder on the hallway floor.

Castalia'd left a marbleized tin basin full of hot water—two thick towels stretched overtop to keep it steamy. Nearby, on a pretty saucer painted with cardinals and berries, one yellow bar of strong lye soap. I undid a crystal cruet, I sniffed the splash of vinegar set here like for to dress some salad. Old-style birth control, it was.

By now, of course, my maidenhead was just a singed and burning memory. And yet I understood nothing about the fertile seepage once a person's seal gets broke. Concerning nature, I knew the names of every woodland bird and flower from Manteo to Murfreesboro. But I recognized not one plumbing fact about that nearest feisty animal, my waist-down self. Those days, child, if you'd asked me what "douche" meant, I might've guessed: "The French word for a product of Holland?"

So after Cap climbed into the four-poster big as a yacht boat, after he said kindly, "Welcome home forever, my chosen bride," after he then grabbed me yet again for a little housewarming romp—I someway managed to crawl back out the bed. I took up that basin's hot water, went in and washed my hair with it! Castalia's hints at wifely hygiene were lost on me. Later, when motherhood struck, you could've knocked me over with somebody else's feather. Did I think that having my hair squeaky-clean might keep me a simple and skinny girl forever? I didn't think. Just trusted. The Think part often comes *after* the Trust part, don't you find? Think can take a larger and larger cut of a person's energy while the percentage of Trust sometimes wanes and thins and whittles.

I opened eyes the next day early, found my old new husband dressed for commerce. He rubbed his hands together, ready to traipse downstairs toward Castalia's java and ample breakfast (I could smell corn fritters and bacon coaxing him through floorboards). Soon the front door would slam— Cap bound for work—he'd leave me alone all day . . . with her.

A handsome witch-hazeled man now settled on my side of the bed, brown beard showing comb's teeth marks. "*You* mustn't get up, Lucille. I intend to make sure you're spoiled and most shamelessly. Especially here at first. Enjoy it, my Lucille. Come eleven o'clock, I plan to study the clock in my office. I'll picture you as being still quite warm here under my coverlet.

Ours. I'd prefer it, I think, if you were to move over and sleep on my side. Maybe even slip into one of my Egyptian-cotton nightshirts. Charming, yes. Third drawer from the top. Quite a picture you'll make for an old working-man. I daresay I shall be smiling from seven till six. But will I explain my doing so to any living soul downtown? Never, my Lucille."

"Yeah, but won't they know anyways, mister?" I whispered, though we were two married people alone on the bed. "I mean, your first day back off a wedding trip and all? With you fifty whatever you are (no offense) and me just gone fifteen? . . . Even if you was to smile just a tad, they'll guess, sir. So *please* don't even smirk none. Grinning means telling." I clutched his beefy paw. Bristles growing thick on its back were surprisingly soft. I kissed the baldest knuckles, I told the hand, heavy as a Sunday beef roast, "Something happened to me in Atlanta, sir. I don't yet half know what it was. But I beg you—don't let *on* to anybody. Even if some nasty men ask. Please, sir, don't snitch on me." He lifted my braid's brush end—he dabbed it over the tip of my nose. Tears stood in his gray eyes. This amazed me.

He said that I moved him so, did I even know? And, he added, very little had stirred him thusly since the sixties. Cap said my modesty—probably a source of genuine pain to me just now—simply made me mean more to him. Made *it* mean more. He said we were our own secret, forever. Marriage was private-like. We could do whatever we liked for and to each other, see? Nobody would know. "Not even the maid?" I asked, quiet. He smiled, considering this a joke. Cap said my first day's job would be just staying snug-as-bug-in-rug right here abed, all right? Castalia herself would bring up a tray for me. I just had to say how I liked my eggs—he'd pass along my order. I swallowed, hard.

I was to wear whichever of his nightshirts I liked best, ones she'd ironed so perfect (no starch for sleepwear, ever). "And do definitely leave your pigtails trailing down like this, Lucille. You appear no more than nine years old, especially mornings when your face is a bit puffed as it now is. So many freckles. How can I explain your appeal to you? Probably imprudent to even try. Lovely effect altogether, though. Your charm's probably the last thing you recognize. I'm sure I remain quite blind to my own, such as it is, or was. And I do thank you in advance—I'll be picturing you in bed here every hour on the hour and half hour. Agreed? You wake for that alone. Then roll directly over and, in your most spirited manner, drop straight back to sleep.

"And should you, while I'm gone . . . take the notion (don't mind Captain's mentioning such things) to . . . touch yourself or whatever . . . feel free. Do. Only natural in a person of your age. I shan't be home for hours, can't be helped. 'Absence makes the heart' . . . and so forth. Now, is our day's schedule quite coordinated? You're to trust the chiming of the old Seth Thomas downstairs. Leaving, I shall set my pocket watch by him. We'll be . . . connected seven to six. This little gambit pleases you, does it? Now, give us a long parting kiss. Excellent. Oh, my dear girl. So, is Lucille amused by our first day's battle plan?"

I nodded.

Look. What the heck *else* was I going to do?

3

WELL, a routine commenced. He lumbered down them steps, ate hearty amid the clank of silver on crockery. Lively talk, half-bawdy laughs from my two elders. Then off he waltzed to the World of Earn. He left Lucy here in the House of Pay. Left me unprotected from two hundred pounds of dusky grudge presently a-storming round the kitchen below. I'd never wanted a servant to boss.

Once Cap closed his home's front door, once he strolled, whistling, toward a garden gate, when he stepped onto sidewalk where I heard him greet three other walking-to-work gents by first names, once he moved past earshot, that same second such a racket of plate clattering and chair shifting banged from one floor under.

Last night I'd asked Cap if this Castalia person lived in. "Not now," Cap said. My thoughts wrapped clear around these words. At least she'd been banished—maybe for *that* I should feel grateful? Years earlier, his family had owned her, a slave child purchased at age three—imported like some handy portable Afro agricultural product. This much I'd already got out of Cap whilst under covers: From age ten onward, she served Captain's spoilt beautiful momma as her main "body servant," whatever that meant. Years after Emancipation, Cap hisself bought Castalia a cottage seven blocks and a continent away downhill in Baby Africa. She now worked here six and a half days a week, leaving our ready-made dinner—on day seven—warming in the oven. What *else* could I learn about the venom factory presently bowling butter churns around the kitchen?

I'd just been given direct orders to keep in bed—prisoner of sheets till shops' closing time. Well, that type slackness just won't within my personal makeup, honey, not even on day number one. Sure, I was tired. Sure, seeing my own bloomers across the way—lined with black and white and red all over—made me feel unwell. Yeah, I was scared to face Big Woman downstairs, fixing me either breakfast or arsenic or the two in one. But if not now, when?

Even so—keeping to my own truce side of the huge four-poster, I did dawdle a while. My palms pressed flat over mattress edges, legs kept swinging like a kid's would. I was. A kid. I wondered how I might could ever make a older sadder person such as her admire and maybe even enjoy a person such as snub-nosed little me.

Meantime, down the oak stairwell, a certain helper now chose to drop a twenty-pound frying pan. Seemed to take metal two full minutes to cease making every single sound that crashing metal can.

There are many kinds of wake-up calls. This, child, had been one of them.

4

ALMOST home, my husband he'd touched far corners of his brown beard like some Catholic might tap forehead and shoulder blades. The man had half grinned behind whiskers—maybe as excited as me about being back? I pictured him, a beardless boy of fifteen, hiking home from a war in Virginia and on foot, so eager to see Falls. Maybe even more thrilled than I was tonight, safe back from my bloody Bull Run Honeymoon?

Captain checked his pocket watch. "You'll soon be properly greeted, my Lucille. I tarried back at old Hedgepath's in hopes of making precisely this happen." And—grand as some junior-trainee God—the gent smiled, pointed one forefinger at the hill—*now*.

Sure enough, bells of our churches commenced a Babel of clanging. My breath all but locked. Gongs from far ends of Falls unfolded, overlapping in air like petals of some metal artichoke. Bells chimed slow or fast according to denomination. (Years later, I understood how much my own notion of each religion had got shaped by whatever order its bell announced the hour, and in what tone. Nobody can now tell me that this won't decided partly by theology, not just via each church's sexton's zeal or sloth.) Though all these outfits were Christian, none could agree. Not even on the time of day— much less the angel dance-attendance records atop a much-contested straight-pin head.

First Baptist always sounded off the earliest, maybe as one way of continuously staying *First*. (Those days, most good American bells were cast around Philadelphia and cost you a good bit. Some of Falls' earliest examples had got melted down for cannonballs during the war. There *was* a cut-rate bell broker in Birmingham—but, like my granddad Angus McCloud believed, you always get what you pay for.) Baptist bells won't meant to lull you into no false cheer. Their bronze seemed mixed with pig iron and brass. Tart notes scolded you: Years are dicey, Hell is real, Time will go on gonging just this quick, so Get Right with God, Quick, Brimstone Bait. (No Baptist steeple ever bothered to announce the quarter hour at fifteen and forty-five after. Fundamentalists only registered their clocks' basic bottom and top— hell or high water.)

The choicest bell in town was the rich Episcopalians'. A masterpiece, it was big as two wheelbarrows joined like famous hands, in prayer. Bronze pure as a museum statue's, its tone come mellow and boozy, old as Europe. It had a most forgiving aftermath—like a retiring senator taking it all back. Sometimes (Mondays especially) it failed to even ring. The sexton, like All Saints Episcopal's parishioners, drank and admitted so. All Saints' building was Tudor, its steeple antique brick, Falls' tallest. Nearby towers—Lutheran's starch and Methodist's high-collar—were white frame. (Locally brick was considered far classier than wood.) These two white churches forever seemed swan-necked on tiptoe, both turned toward All Saints. White steeples near the brick one seemed ladies in cloth coats claiming not to *want* the floor-length fur that they keep ogling.

Falls' Catholics (all nine families) met, secret as Masons, in a different home each week. (We heard as how they moved their 24-carat life-sized Mary statue under cover of darkness each Saturday night. Nobody'd ever seen it.) The local Jews—prosperous, learned, standoffish except whilst in their stores—buggied to Raleigh fifteen times a year for their non-Sunday Sabbath. This was mostly so their children could meet children of like faith. (A trusted Gentile head clerk was left to manage big Saturday sales in the clothing emporium and to lock up.) Our twenty Jews had a odd place of local worship. Wearing clothes too fine to ever be sold by a store as local as theirs, they gathered in one stone gazebo behind the Eksteins' giant home. This gazebo had a latticework extra-pointed star above its roof. The star was covered in climbing yellow roses that seemed to try disguising this symbol as any old genteel trellis. No bell drew attention to their rose-draped gazebo synagogue. We heard they discussed novels and poems in their services. Strange.

Finally, our Presbyterians didn't plan to let no bell get *near* their church. They considered such bauble trappings frivolous. And this too, child, seemed pretty much in keeping and predestined.

(No black church owned any bells larger than the hand-held school-house kind. Black churches *sang* their steeples.)

So: Our first evening back, and from a mile off, how clear we heard each set of chiming move across wide fields, plowing air. How plain we knew each steeple's voice and what each meant beyond the time it told.

Pink sunset sky made the green hill waiting up ahead look blue. Blunt hillside cast a shadow half a mile wide. And into this stripe of membership shade we kept straight to a straight road, our buggy aimed us right on home.

It wouldn't last. None of it. But did we know that on this balmy, palmy evening June of 1900? Those two open zeroes were wide eyes greedy to be filled by anything grand. Our town itself would not. Last. The hill itself wouldn't. And us, least of all. So far, true, I have. But will not. For all that long. Take my word for it. The person herself knows.

I'm using all my last-stand salt-lick energy on this and you.

Even the churches I've mentioned as being on Church Street—they too have gone the way of all flesh. No fair.

By late Truman/early Eisenhower, in there, suburban churches' unlimited parking had begun to suck the faithful out their way—great space-age-looking buildings. Even the Baptists built one shaped like some science-fiction nun's wide-flaring headdress. Don't ask me why. First Baptist downtown lost its life to make way for the Church Street Sears store and its huge parking lot that only ever fills clear up at Christmas anyway.

Them forlorn old Houses of Worship left standing downtown have been turned into (a) Belfry Decorators, AID—"with window treatment and interior advice for institutions and the discerning individual," and (b) Stained Glass Disco Supper Club. (My favorite dancing orderly in here, Jerome, he calls it the *very* Stained Glass Disco.)

Christ once drove certain money changers from the temples. Seems our temples drove out to be near our money-changing malls. Modren times!

Of our great downtown Houses of the Lord, only All Saints stays in use (traditionalists still rule there and have long held potent seats on our City Council). Only their Tudor tower, where Daddy made the farting noises, stood long enough to qualify for a national landmark, it being brick and all. The bell is now rung just on Sundays, only for late service (nearby heathen sleepers complained about the 8 a.m. racket and put a end to that around the time poor John Kennedy got shot). Not even the Episcopals can afford to keep a bell ringer on duty round the clock every fifteen minutes—are you kidding? with these unions and all? Nothing's what it was. Used to, a blind man could get the Falls time told him free all day!

But not yet, not gone yet, thank you . . . it's still the evening of our return. 1900. Here is the church, here is the steeple—I open my mouth and still hear its people.

5

TO FACE Castalia Marsden. I got out of the bed. At some point, you have to. Floor was cold under bare feet. I needed that. I stood at the mirror and, even to myself, looked like a sleepy kid—mostly bone. I just wanted Castalia (pushing three kitchen chairs back and forth across kitchen floor) to like me. Is this so much to ask? That, I'm afraid, child, has always been my particular cross to bear. Some folks don't even notice who's fond of them, who-all is staring daggers their way. But me? if a imported Yankee clerk at the Mall acts grumpy, I worry over it for weeks.

I guessed Castalia's life hadn't exactly been no picnic of extras. The night before troubled me, finding her, arms locked across her davenport chest, ready to be sourly useful in the dim foyer. Castalia'd growled like some spoiled old house pet the day a new pup bounds indoors fluffy-frisky then stops dead.

I now slipped into my simplest blue dress ("understate by two" was Momma's final words of fashion and moral advice for her only child, bound into marriage—not a breath about biology). I used my new silver hairbrush—"M" engraved loopy as a bow across its back. In my washing-up room, for courage I sniffed violet-scented baby soaps saved from Atlanta's Honeymoon Hotel of Horrors. I hung six prisms from the window sash. I breathed deep, made my mirror face: Try and look like Mrs. Married and Christian. Ready, you? Pinning up braids, I forced myself downstairs, I made as much noise as possible, not wanting to startle Castalia none, hoping to clear the coast. I even hummed, then worried this might just aggravate the woman.

"Morning?" calls I down several hallways, not sure which leads to the kitchen. Spying a lino rug's checkered corner, I tiptoed that way.

Her body seemed arranged to offer me a hemorrhaging double-dare on first sight. She leaned far back against the front of a ten-burner stove, arms yet resting on the mighty bosom, lips pursed like the purest form of hard rubber. One gold dance slipper beat time, a steady clockly tap, irked silly. I smiled so hard I practically got a sore throat. "Hi" was about the best I could manage.

Though bright, Miss Castalia's clothes looked plainer than last night's Indian blanket of a Joseph's cloak. I now understood, she'd been dressed up special for Captain's return. This worried me. For her sake, his, and yeah, mine. Saddening to think of Castalia's liking Cap so much she'd bother helping him celebrate the arrival of unpopular *me*. Her face now looked the way burning wires smell.

"Hi," a child bride repeated. "Captain's gone, I reckon?" (I *knew* this. Why'd I ask? Don't you hate yourself sometimes? Why can't we just keep quiet? Why can't *I*?)

No answer.

Behind her, along the stove's top and covering the wall beyond, dozens of ceramic and paper redbirds—figurines, picture cutouts from calendars and such.

Castalia finally spoke. Her voice parted like dark fur. "You usually sleeps so late?"

My smile got marked down to a grin. I pointed at the big Seth Thomas yonder. "But, Miss Castalia, ma'am, it's six forty-six a.m."

A pause.

"You usually sleeps so late?"

She judged how I'd taken this. Then Castalia spun around with the unlikely buoy grace of a real sensitive fat person. She flopped a brick-sized hunk of butter onto hot griddle. "Over easy? Fried? What? Quick. Some us ain't got the full day long to lounge in. Some us works."

Still on my feet, I pulled nearer. I found myself speaking to her back. Its shape buckled, frilly-edged as veal too long in a hot pan. I later credited the first day's boldness to my yet being sore and half asleep. "Ma'am? Ma'am, we don't even know each other. Please, I want us to be friends . . . or at least not to start out so doggone harsh. Really. Don't mind my speaking too frank but I bet we'll soon get used to things, our both staying here in his house. But doing like *this*, why, we'll just wear each other down. It'd be such a waste. Let's commence peaceable, umkay? You could teach me a whole lot. I've never onct harmed you, nor you me. So, 'Peace.' All right?" (Maybe what I said was shorter. But close to this.)

Seen from behind, her apron straps made two X's like the answer No doubled. "Do *that* be what she want! And on her first morning? Well, dreaming's free, girl. But I been wanting all kind of things. Hoping to be, oh, say a angel made of light, with snow for she wings, and maybe hummingbird feathers for the nappy hair under the arms of her, why not? But I keeps wishing into one hand, spitting in the other, and Cassie can't help but notice which one keep filling up the quickest. So what else you craves, skin and bones? How you wants these eggs? Get snapping here. Some us earns a living."

My mother often judged other people's servants as being "insolent." I always felt like if I ever personally saw this particular trend, I'd probably recognize it too. Well, honey, I felt like I'd just recognized it.

Settling quieter at the table, I went, "Maybe sunny side up? *That's* surely a fitting way to start so bright a June morning, ain't it?" I sounded exactly like Momma on her rare disgusting "good days," but I didn't mind this once. False cheer is still about the best I can muster for company prior to 7 a.m.

Butter, frying on the far side of this person, sounded like a snarl crackling in her very eyes and sinuses. "Sunny side? Do that be a remark from our Stick Bride or how she like her eggs, which? Fast."

"Whatever's easiest for you, ma'am."

Not turning, Cas told me she could make most anything I pleased. She'd whip me up a ten-ingredient omelette—fresh dill torn from out back—didn't bother *her* one little bit. "Look," she explained to the stove's redbird gallery. "Look"—she stuffed a good-sized log into the firebox with no more strain than if handling kindling. "Look, you, *one* us might's well be getting what she want. Seem like it ain't ever gone be me. Your trouble is you ain't learnt to *boss* folks yet. You best start. That you territory. Bossing stay one thing Castalia can't train you in. Had no practice. Either white folks got it in that depart-ment or they don't. You? don't."

Grinding pepper in a mill, she sneezed with whiplash suddenness five times. Needing a hanky, she scuffed to her corner closet. Seemed the place she hung her coat and kept secret stuff. All this I guessed from how she worried I might look inside. She used her wide back as a natural barricade. I didn't even try peeking whilst she stood there honking into several cleaning rags. I kept very still.

Sitting in a clean and sunny kitchen of a strange man's home—about to be fed by a woman even stranger—I felt one white-hot pinprick wiggle through the lining of my stomach's lower left. —This, I figured, is how a young person's crop of ulcers begins. Hi, history.

6

NIGGERTOWN. What was I to make of Niggertown? By now, the night of our luxurious honeymoon return, Falls' streetlamps were all lit. (They'd been lit by our hard-drinking lamplighter—whose name and sad tale as a sixty-year-old momma's boy it pleased but weighed on me to know.) Our hill town's smoky bottom sat ringed by squat unpainted boxes. Oh yeah, I told myself as we pulled nearer, I'd clean forgot it in my ten days elsewhere: Niggertown.

Shacks seemed dropped here by some landslide. Maybe mansions on high had leaned off Summit's ritzy cliff and relieved theirselves. Such lathing mounds as rolled downhill and landed at bottom: these were where the colored people got to live.

Odd, you had to pass through this poorest zone to get uphill towards Courthouse Square and our fashionable shopping district. At night, a visitor didn't need to notice Baby Africa owing to its well-planned lack of street-lamps (City Council's cleverness).

To hide the eyesore during daylight, a windbreak of high trees got planted annually. Our Ladies' Garden Club hoped to screen the colored district from Falls' visitors but come February, when things grew coldest around here, the latest expensive trees always got chopped down for Baby Africa's kindling. (Along with coal in bathtubs—this became a favorite local example of black folks' shortsighted sloth.) But even *I*, even as a kid, figured this much out: residents of Baby Africa just liked to see *out* of Baby Africa. Quick-growing poplars prevented that.

OUR RIG now passed a city-limits sign (Pop. 1103, Bird Sanct, 4 Mles Blw Sea Lvl, Wlcme). I twisted my carat-and-a-half diamond around so it'd show. Nervous habit, my palming it. The prize had been his mother's. It had outlived the plantation fire. I imagined somebody seeing me and remarking, "Lucy has been off experiencing concerts in advanced Atlanta. She sure does look it too. But not acting the least little bit stuck-up, not our Lucille." Instead, the dark, stillness, the odor of well water, two mosquitoes harmonizing near my ear.

Cap clucked tired horses on through the colored district—eager to get beyond it. But all of Falls now seemed more mortally my Home. Every last inch of it would matter now. When a person returns, only this greedy first glance teaches her to *see* it all again.

Ahead, ten black children ducked behind roadside weeds. Hearing our carriage, they giggled. I teetered forward, bottom crackling newsprint. A wallet had been tied to a long string, and as our buggy clopped nearer, one boy tossed the billfold in our path. Just as we drew even—he yanked his line. Billfold flopped across horses' path. Horse hooves totally trounced the thing. I turned back just as kids rushed out, surprised, to study damage done their wallet. I wanted to explain: no, your passing sucker has to be on foot, sillies.

(White boys ofttimes played this stunt on solitary black people hiking downhill after a day's work as Falls' maids or gardeners. White boys hoped some adult would spy the wallet, hang around whistling, finally bend toward it as the thing leapt like a frog in heat. Boys hoped the victims would bolt—

superstitious, arms up—screaming straight downhill. But for what reason? why? By now, the trick had ceased to work. News got out. Black folks just stepped over the dozen or so dime-store diamond bracelets, ladies' handbags left mid-sidewalk leashed and twitching in advance.)

Kids grouped back yonder rubbing their trampled wallet, they sure worried me. They still had lots to learn. Embarrassed for and by them, I chose to repalm my show-off diamond.

June being mosquito season, Baby Africa residents were burning rags to keep bugs out of homes lacking window screens. Smoke sealed off three hundred rusting tin-roofed shanties. On one porch, a granny woman lit her pipe, flame briefly showed a great nobbly crowd of dark heads, shoulders. Folks spoke from porch to porch like sampan owners docked close by.

Conversation had this expecting kind of tone. Rising voices seemed to guess that something fine or terrible would happen soon. (A honeymoon return didn't exactly turn no heads. And I admit that—vain, fifteen—I felt a wee bit disappointed.)

Did folks expect some unpredicted hurricane, or white-hot heaven settling early? *Some*thing sure felt due, overdue. I heard it in folks' rising tones tonight. Us Uphill whites spoke mostly in consonants, fencing t's, hedging h's. From porches yonder, black people's mutterings ran more towards the honey marrow of old a, e, i, o, u. From darkness, the open hope of vowels made quite a music.

We passed through this zone too quick. I held the rose-stitched satchel against me like I had some lapdog or baby or baby lapdog. I accidentally squeezed tomatoes too hard, then scanned a brown bag for signs of bleeding. I watched unlighted shacks drift past. In my chest and throat, I felt some edgy new attention gathering. Honeymoon travails had made me see these make-do huts afresh. They meant something new to me. I couldn't yet say what.

7

PARSLEY jaunty off to one side, Castalia's dill omelette turned out perfect. But, though the item had genius in its making, every mouthful beyond the first tasted exactly like ash and cat hair. Castalia watched me eat. She tilted back against her cast-iron locomotive of a stove, redbirds spiking its upper edge. She rested there, armed Xed, her whole shape bolted across stove's front like she herself was some mammoth cowcatcher about to plow across the checkerboard floor and flatten me.

I chewed. Rechewed. She'd made a four-egg omelette. Out of spite. I dared not leave one morsel. Waiting to wash my dish, she glared this way, then cleaned her fingernails with a huge handy butcher knife. When I finished, thirty minutes later, Castalia didn't ask but told me, "Perfeck eggs, right? *Say* it."

I nodded, had to. "Perfeck." My compliment pleased her in a grim way. Then the worst happened. She smiled, it proved the scariest part so far.

Outside I heard our milkman jingle by. I wished I was a milkman or his horse or even white milk safe behind clear glass.

What made her smile so poisonous was this: Beauty! Four square unexpected inches of it lingered. Two inches bracketed, witty and mild, the corners of her generous mouth. Two underlit her arched and hoppy eyes. True, only this much surface space had managed to stay beautiful. But that fraction sure upset a girl. Her ugliness, a person could get used to. I'd already started trying, child. But the shift toward something else destroyed my early progress. I slowly understood: Castalia's Ugliness has been built brick by brick. She's *chose* to look like this! But hints at what she'd been before still managed peeking over the self-made Ugly Wall. Could somebody this size, this bitter, have ever enjoyed beauty's head start? If so, where'd it all gone? To be whose fuel? What was eating her? Did *that* make her eat so? Across the hundreds of monument pounds—four square original inches rode intact.

But . . . those spoke volumes, even to a child my age.

Darling, how can I put this? I want to get it right. Imagine that all of ancient Greece got lost in a bad earthquake—every temple, column, scroll. All lost except one statue's white marble kneecap. It is now placed, cool, into your open hand. That's it—no more. And yet, holding this one clue, I believe you could someway *feel* all ancient Greece—its proportions, ideals, and rightness coming through your palm's willing skin.

Looking at her four sleek unlost inches, I knew: Lucy, you've come in at the end of something. It was once real complicated, it was a pageant big as the Grand Opera that your unwed aunts live and breathe, it was something readily silly as Opera because it was that game for being swamped by typhoon feelings. Overrun by Castalia-sized emotions, Castalia-sized reasons, Castalia-sized crimes. And you, Lucy, have slipped in for Standing Room near the finale of Act Five.

But, child? oh, I wanted to know *all* of it. I did. I wanted in: for each clue of how Miss Cassie Marsden here had rode the boat from Adult Africa to her doing whatever a baby body servant/slave once did, to her settling downhill in Baby Africa, to her just making those perfect eggs for somebody as new to this and undeserving and scared as me.

Behind her willed and bloated false front, glaring at my chewing over here, waited what? waited who? I felt like I would someday maybe drag that other out, unwilling, into local light—that first beauty, kicking, naked, African, intact. To live near me, safe and fun, in a white house.

I might now be eating ash and cat hair. I might seem powerless so early in the morning but, my molars at grind: I knew, someday, I'd know.

That's all. That's how it started.

8

LOOK, home from honeymoon bliss, *are* you ready to enter the commercial district proper? You feeling sufficiently ripe to greet Falls' equivalent of Parthenons and "Ladies' Mile" in New York City? Can you *take* the excitement? I can't, hardly. We must pass the Courthouse Square's unsavory side: Robinson's Billiards for Gentlemen. Somebody at the piano playing one of the new rags. (My piano-teaching aunts have got hold of rag sheet music. Advanced, tolerant, unmarried, they have chose to praise said "rag's antic architecture." A smallish local scandal done resulted amongst the culturally clued in.)

We see the giant gilded horseshoe over Marsden's Livery Estab. and Livestock. Here's the town square (thirty streetlamps lit to serve those shoppers of all races with hard dollars to spend). At the latest attraction, a single water fountain, the line of county thrill-seekers is short. You'll note the central statue "To Our War Dead." (A economy move, four words meant to make one marble upright cover all past and any future wars we might survive.) Now look down the incline off on your left, Falls' single pink stucco structure not in Baby Africa: Lolly's Palais de Beauté Féminine de Falls. (Lolly was in love with the Prince of Wales and had corresponded with him. I got to tell you more about that precious homely Lolly later.) There goes Harbison's Baked Goods—fresh (plus day- or week-old discount doughnuts).

Next door down, in the window with one draped dummy:

CHINESE TAILOR FOR MEN AND THEIR NICE LADIES (all welcome)
Wong "Red" "Jake Wade" "Shortstop" or "Riceyman" *Chow*
—prop.

A coal oil lamp burns in back. Hear the busy foot-treadle Singer? It could have hiked him clear home to China by now. He wishes! Bent there, a elf-sized man wearing very round eyeglasses, black hair seamed with a white center part, a fellow mild to the point of appearing terrified full-time.

"Red" can stitch any garment to fit anybody, perfect. He made Cap's adult war uniform. Ball gowns he sewed the titanic Mercer twins made them look no worse than statuesque. A miracle, art! But Wong Chow works just as hard at altering hisself to suit our edgy local will. Fifteen years ago, he got off the train nine stops early. Wong had already rented his storefront yonder when he discovered Falls won't Raleigh. (To him, they sounded alike.) Local wits claimed he'd got the Wong station. They flattered him with local-yokel nicknames meant to help the shy outsider seem more "human." Afraid to offend, Wong accepted all pet names. Called "Shortstop," did Wong really know what one was? Local rubes yelled insults, he smiled anyhow. Having shelled out his only cash for rent-deposit (not refundable), he stayed put for forty years. Many people do, for reasons much less good. The Chinese invented firecrackers, and bad boys gave Wong many reasons to feel homesick. Frequent cherry bombs exploded down the chimney of his shop/home. Lots of laughs. "You *scare* poor Riceyman," Riceyman smiled, shaking. Boys said, "Yeah, that was the general idea."

Jake Wade's prices are so reasonable, somebody really should *tell* him, but nobody quite has yet. He's a local success story. Whenever folks mention how ours is sure a land of opportunity okay, they call over Riceyman as their best handy example. He slinks nearer, low to the earth like a whippet ofttimes whipped. He comes over, wary, grinning very wide. Keeps pointing to his eyeglasses like these'll stop harm. Tough to understand him through teeth, smile, accent. Shortstop says, "How you doing, Jake Wade's good buddy? I your buddy still, hunh? hunh?" Stranger in a even stranger land, Red showed up once at First Baptist and tried singing hymns and couldn't really, and made members feel real weird. So did his eating off the café's plates and briefly seeking a non-Chinese girlfriend (horsey Lolly, of the Palais de Beauté). Silent glares sure cut down on Shortstop's social life.

Once when I was a real little girl, I came upon Red at sunset in the alley behind his small store. Mr. Chow sat on his back step eating noodles from a bowl, sat stitching these into his mouth via two sticks. Food moved, a steady white lanyard, threading one tailor's mouthy buttonhole. He sat unseen, nicknameless, non-smiling, glasses off, blinkish, curled there, staring out at a daisied cowfield, Meadows' Pasture, which is now the interchange of US 64 and Interstate 95. He was so alone and just blank. Imagine living thirty-odd years away from family and, maybe worse, hidden from your own language. I felt his daydreams to be far-reaching as a Chinese scroll stitched every inch by hand, gift-wrapping the world from here to his birthplace. He never saw me. I ran home as fearful as if I'd come upon somebody naked, somebody naked and hurt. That's our tailor.

We now clatter past "Works of Bert—Blacksmith of Choice. Bert . . . Prop." Rental horses pull us under the arching brag of Bert's wrought-iron masterpiece. It's a mammoth sign made after being described by our twelve-member City Council. It spans two lanes of traffic—its motto greets shoppers and likely water fountain users. This major example of the smithy's riveting art will later grace Falls' only postcard. The thing is black iron filigree and its legend cannot be easily read against a nighttime sky. Notice Bert's fine work, the Eiffel Tower's crosshatched conviction, Old English lettering cut from heavy-gauge sheet iron. Several letters are now half blocked by sparrows' beardy nests that, tonight, give our arch a certain Wild Man of Borneo carnival look.

Thing says:

YOU HAVE JUST ENTERED THE GATEWAY TO THE BREADBASKET

OF THE PEANUT BELT!

Falls is Educational, Falls is Fun.

Fourteen Christian-Owned Stores Offer Finest Wares.
It is Us for Commerce, Us For Culture.
Get the Smartest of World Merchandise, Leave Your Cares in Falls.
A Double-Warm Falls Welcome!

Bad children steadily dare each other to spoil the sign but cleverly. Considering a half ton of bolts, nuts, and sprockets, you never hope to remove even one comma that'll surely outlast even Judgment Day's full stop. Instead us kids cover certain letters with cardboard. You force exposed words to spell what *you* want.

The best such stunt I recall eclipsed much of the line "Get the Smartest of World Merchandise, Leave Your Cares in Falls." It soon read: "Get . . . Smart . . . Leave . . . Falls." I doubt that Mr. Da Vinci, after putting final touches on his Mona Lisa, received more backslapping credit in li'l downtown Vinci (Italy) than did our young rapscallions the morning after.

"How'd it even *come* to you, Junior?"

"Oh, simple, nothing much. I saw it in a golden dream from God, is all. Why?"

The culprits were mildly scolded but not before our Mayor admitted, yeah, it'd been a "pretty good one." He honored the sheriff's request to let this one instance of hooliganism stay up through the weekend. White farmers and black sharecroppers were soon streaming into town and doing the turn-of-the-century equivalent of taking Polaroid pictures: *looking hard*, then shaking their heads and *looking hard* again.

Boys were famous clear to Monday morning. Weekend business jumped by fifteen percent.

When electricity came in later, a natural first downtown project: let's go light Bert's sign with 450 tungsten bulbs! The forward-looking shop-teacher who'd rigged the thing climbed overhead for the grand illumination. A good-sized evening crowd gathered. The line around the water-bubbler shrank briefly. Adults stood open-mouthed, practically panting for a suitable Edison-Ford-type display of Future Progress. Oh how we believed in today's silvery Now whilst sunk back there in that mud Then!

Our metal monument was jungly with primitive wiring, all voices hushed. The trim young manual-arts teacher perched proud there, winked down at his delighted bride who'd hired a photographer out of her own pocket. The teacher signaled, the cameraman aimed, and somebody hit the power switch. Our future-looking citizen (ignorant of how short a fuse said future really has) learned something sudden about the glamorous jeopardy of a coming age. We all discovered that this particular iron made a pure conductor. The teacher was killed—instantly, so I'm told. The photograph, of a molten lightning bolt boiling mushroom-shaped above midtown, proved overexposed. WW I lay dead ahead. If we had kept that photo of pure light, pure release and rage, we might've learned something urgent: a brochure for the coming Spectacle. But who ever learns at the time, child?

The sign survived its un-illumination. In metal's twistiness and stubborn lace, in the way Bert made its edging of six hundred used horseshoes' doily toothsome rows, you could see the man's lifetime of shoeing beasts, his years spent fixing hay balers and, during hard times, making simple doorstep bootwipes. You saw all the rivets Bert ever put into any busted item that'd looked too weak to accept even *one* mending tack. That doggone Bert! Gigantic yet tender. (Hardly able to speak three-word sentences, he had once, at age ten, made some baffled girl a Valentine card out of shredded lard cans, *metal*.) Bert was blessed with the hidden heart of a artist clanging in him like All Saints Episcopal's pure bronze bell. Why Bertram, a bachelor living with Mom till age forty-two, later went and did what he did to the youngest Harbison boy—no, the second from the youngest—that's anybody's guess.

But Bert's metal message outlived even his own endless prison term. He eventually slipped free of four federal prisons. Iron bars were his pals, his joy, and hobby. They yielded as the younger Harbison (a beauty, everyone admitted) had not. Bert could've given Houdini lessons. Once loose, he got recaptured listlessly. It was the challenge, really. He *had* to be working with metal. Escape was just his latest excuse. Finally the Feds wised up as a homespun ballad, "The Legend of the Slippery Smithie," gained favor in state pens clear to Canada, a song that brought on a faddish spate of files in pies. Feds stuck Bert in solitary in a new cell, entirely cement. He stayed right beside its only metal, one iron doorlatch he kept stroking. But that was only three inches square, just a pig-iron alloy, impure and not enough to sustain an artist. Cut off from the Gilded Age, Bert let cement's damp hit him like rusting guilt itself. Nostalgia for the grandly metallic took poor Bert off quick.

"Get . . . Smart . . . Leave . . . Falls." This I recalled my first night home, minus a hymen. Was poor Bert telling me something?

9

I'LL STATE what's overevident: Hell hath no fury like a servant wronged.

I'd charged onto the scene just in time to catch grief for Miss Castalia's years of Marsden slavery. But me? *I'd* never owned her. Never rented her. Never really wanted her in this house. "Hi," I had grinned. Well, honey, that didn't exactly bowl her over with my charm. So I decided, I'd learn hard facts, but quiet and eventual. The one wise thing to try at the start: Keep well out of this storm cloud's way. I called myself "darling" a lot then. "Darling Lucy? now you just let this Castalia person get used to having you around, okay, darl? Only fair. She's got definite seniority. Then, gradual-like, maybe the two of you will make peace. A little Appomattox coffee sipping at that kitchen table. Right, darling? Right."

I was fifteen. Fifteen means: in a hurry. Fifteen and lonely in a big house, that makes you in a extra hurry.

I thought the founding of our major friendship might take us, oh, three weeks to a month, tops.

Live and hope.

THE WEDDING presents were yet lined on borrowed banquet tables in my parents' parlor. People still arrived to look at them. In Captain's place, two blocks away, I felt myself to be a convict remembering some former freestyle life.

I was shut up alone all day, feeling bartered and nicked. I was visited by my legal parents on Friday-night state occasions, and then only with my husband's advance permission. Captain chaperoned my time with them. I'd been a wife fully two weeks. My folks were eating here at the Captain's house and I was expected to ring a little bell that meant Castalia should come in and clear away our soup bowls. I jiggled the bell once, wincing at how bossy four inches of silver can sound. In she barged through the swinging door, her wide back hitting it with such a slap, my folks both jumped. I grinned, worried. I tried and help Castalia lift my soup plate and, in doing so, knocked over the bell and dropped my napkin. "Oops," said I. Captain and Poppa were talking about a sewage bond issue or something fascinating like that. Mother stared at Castalia, not trusting her a inch. Momma—victim of a childhood accident involving blacks—swore Good Help was impossible to get now, postbellum. And Castalia, stooping beside me to retrieve the napkin, was whispering hot against my ear, "Touch that ding-dong one more time tonight, gal, you done for, hear me?"

"Ah-ha," I said, and I giggled.

Next course change, I rose, pushed toward the kitchen. Cap asked why I didn't just ring (he'd trained me before my folks showed up). "This seems less formal-like," I smiled. Momma groaned.

I swung open the portholed door. "Castalia, if it's convenient, I believe we're about r . . ." At the stove, back half towards me, she was wolfing down what looked to be three doughnuts at onct. She meanwhile held two ceramic redbirds near her face. Mouth white with powdered sugar, she'd been whispering to them birds. "Oops," went I. "Fish course's done." She turned full on me, her eyes each offered me a separate hex. My destiny itself went cross-eyed.

She had to swallow major portion of doughnuts but, gulping done, she spoke in bass tones. Her mouth let powdered sugar fly before it like them big-faced snow-blowing Winters you see—full-cheeked in the upper left corners of old maps. Mouth said, "Ever hear of knocking, brought up . . . barn?" Then the mouth chewed more, more.

10

I DIDN'T like to whine to my husband concerning a certain person's domestic sniping. I was afraid my Captain would stop liking me—I was afraid he'd keep *on* liking me.

From my upstairs windows, I'd see other girls my age go idling towards the schoolyard's swing set. They looked up at this house. I hid behind new eyelet curtain, ashamed to be envied and lonely, both.

Eager to get myself a schedule (besides recalling a bearded gent every time Seth Thomas chimed), I soon noticed what other married ladies did at this tony end of Summit. For now I copied them. Desperate, a body tends to fall back into lockstep, hoping to blend in whilst trying and gather strength for later's wild lunge elsewhere. (Running-away-from-home already interested me.) Wives of young Summit lawyers and businessmen tended to read novels from two to four each afternoon. (Reading a novel *before* breakfast was considered a wickedness done only at the bawdy-house four miles from Falls, a establishment known as Miss Pettibone's Young Christian Ladies' Academy pour les Arts Equestriennes. More about which later.) So early in my job as Mrs., who was *I* to argue with daily novel reading? Seemed a form of playing that wouldn't let all Falls see you shinny up some sap-covered tree in your best dress.

After lunch, once Cap had hiked back downtown to work (oh, how happy I grew—seeing him charge in around one, full of news of dollars, generous with low stableboy jokes), off I'd run to hide in a dark front parlor.

I lifted the book before my freckled face. Street sounds held me for a while: the Thorps's yardmen (identical twins) raking in rhythm. Some child rolling her metal hoop along our sidewalk. But soon these ribbon sounds fell away like lines allowing one soft dark hot-air balloon to rise, drifting free. Words on the page had just quit being words, were panting past language into that breathing life of their own when—uh-oh—I spied the many crystal baguettes in our chandelier get to shifting, tremblish overhead. Soon they chattered like molars left at large in Antarctica. By now, all I held was a husk of paper, coded squiggles stamped across it. Could've been Egyptian Braille. I'd only lost: meaning, fun, my place forever.

Into the murky parlor, one huge shape comes thundering, its back toward me. This wide person starts sweeping—up dust flies all over my reading room. Said person gets within six feet of my chaise (where I hadn't been hurting a fly, only trying to please). Hearing me shift while fighting back a sneeze from the sudden dust—she jumps about three feet straight up, one hand clamped against her independent bosom.

"Oohf," she snaps, "you sure give *me* a turn. . . . If it's one thing Cassie hate, it be a sneak, sneak."

Accused, of course, I closed my novel, one finger marking my place.

Again I apologized. I asked for lessons. Maybe I could learn . . . to cook?—
or even do dishes, anything. My mother (a glutton for housework herself)
hadn't prepared me so hot. Couldn't I help Miss Castalia around the house,
please?

"You?" She grins, looking me over. "Help?"

Then Castalia rumbles out, muttering about underhandedness, pure-
tee laziness. "Lucy, darling, give her time," I told myself. The crosser Cassie
treated me, the more honorary "darlings" I issued my own self. In silence,
deeply personally alone, I soon grew right obnoxious with those.

Since Castalia jumped at the sight of me every afternoon for weeks, got
hard to believe I'd surprised her all that much. I begun worrying: Maybe
Peace won't going to come so easy as I'd thought.

Along with English novels full of mist and manners, I snuggled up and
read my husband's boyhood letters from the front. They made me feel
different about the charming fifty-one-year-old who had lunch with me, who
lifted my nightgown's hem from behind without exactly asking. The ink was
brownish red like pokeberries or blood. Words' plainness was the plainness
I still saw sometimes in good gray eyes across the oilclothed table from me.

Nov. 24, '63
near by Barryville, Va.

Dear Momma,

I am not so great a letter writer but wanted to. Since it winter
we are in winter camp which means log houses instead of tents.
This is better with the ground frozen hard instead of being mud
you wade through. It is strange that both sides agree not to fight
so much in the cold weather. You wonder why they couldn't just
stretch it out to be in the Spring too. We had four inches of snow
and a snowball fight that knocked out one tooth of Sal Smith. He
is my best friend since they got Ned. We all spent four hours doing
snowballs like it was a real battle. Some fellows put rocks and
pinecombs in theirs which why it hurt. Some think it is only fun if
you can get hurt doing it. They often gamble their pay away. Luck
is everything here. A man with the camera came through in a wagon
draped in black cloth like a hearse and set up for getting your
pictures made right in it. My friends posed but they posed like they
were fighting one another with bayonets at the throat of the best
pal. They had a good time but I cannot see the fun of doing it when
in winter you get not to. But I didn't like to say anything Momma
and maybe it is just me. The food is better now we are at one place
longer. Dinner is usually just sowbelly and hardtack. The hardtack
comes in barrels stamped B.C. That stand for Brigade Commissary.
But Sal and others swear that the B.C. shows when these crackers
got made that many years back. It sure taste it believe me. You have
to either soak hardtack in water first or brake it up with your butt

I mean your rifle butt Momma. Or else using a rock. To fry bits in
bacon grease is nice if you have the bacon to get grease out of. For
coffee we must now use parched corn or burned rye. Molasses is
all there is to be the sugar in it. We are out of most things now. I
am better stomach wise than that last letter. What we called The
Trots at home here they call The Tennessee Quickstep. We have a
pet dog we found named Spy because when we were camp near
Yankees up in Cheatham he came back with a Yankee bone in his
mouth. They had given it to him! Sal says Spy sure does work both
sides of the fence which is smart.

A good pet would mean even more out here than my pony at
home did. If I had one I would take better care of it than I did
Dobbin. I would name a good new dog Old Jeff or else after you or
Castalia. Say hi to her. You are both so in my thoughts. Here it is
like I am just going through the motions but am really safe with
you back there. Even if something happen to me which it won't I
feel that the best part of me never even left the homeplace or Falls.
That part will be staying safe with you. I can only think of home
food compared to here though it is probably not even so good at
table on The Lilacs anymore. It sure seem a long time since I saw
the house and walk down to our part of the river. I am fourteen
soon! but it someway seems longer than thirteen whole years since
I could do all that. I am yours and still here. I got the socks. What
yellow ones! Now I am ending this and sleeping some. Your boy
Willie.

We had passed under the rainbow arch of jailer's cast iron. Now here
came Lucas' dear old All-Round Store, forever Falls' best-known central
establishment. "Meet you at the store" means Luke's. Tonight I started understanding something: Might Lucas' seems so locally well stocked because
Falls' other shops offer next to nothing?

During the Atlanta honeymoon, I'd spied a good-sized store that sold
only *straw* hats (and then just ones for men!). Now, for the first time in my
short life, the skimpiness of Lucas' All-Round stock, the potent joke of Bert's
overgrand sign back yonder, the lack of window screens in Niggertown—
all this hit me like a small pie chucked right at my freckled local forehead.

I was busy wondering: Had the Captain here beside me always understood the joke of this place? Had he—for years—chose not to honor it with
snickers? Is that the bargain living here required? Keep a straight face
forever? Pretend that Lucas' *is* World's Finest. Should a body pretend that
a hill town's social highs and lows ain't laid out simple as a fatal chart? To
be a *sober* citizen of Falls didn't seem too fair a trade. At the very least, local
tackiness should entertain a local person offered little else!

I was real young, right freshly married. Others here probably considered
me Mrs. Lucy Lucky. I *was* semi-rich and back home partway safe. My

spouse was held to be a pillar of this vertical town. So, child, why should I suddenly feel so let down and tense? I slowly saw what we had going here: Why, Falls was just a town, won't it!

Like all them other ones glimpsed from out our steamy train window. Here were just more streets edged with yet other immortal civic elms. Porch lamps now burned all along fair Summit—less to welcome company, more to keep it at a distance. Light said, "We gave, we gave."

Falls was probably well intended as any soul at large in it, but just about that messed up too. A Athens city-state, I understood, we won't. Not yet.

Our team clattered, glad, along Summit brick and cobblestones: Here I'd started, here I would now probably live as Mrs. Married forever. Here I'd maybe end my days—and I was supposed to want to! Why should this bill of goods now so fill me with dread?

The more things Lucy recognized, the less sure she felt. If you can't make yourself feel at home when you're first and most freshly home, then when can you? We passed my aunts' boxy run-down house—the so-called Angus McCloud Mansion. Ha, place hadn't had a lick of paint since '81. Humongous homes said: White and Us, White and more Us.

Honeymoon's hostage. Having skimmed through a unbreezy Baby Africa, why should my own birthright, blocks ahead, make me feel so jittery?

Falls' white district won't really titled that—was just called mostly, well, Falls. It featured 1900's surest sign of civic progress: four gas streetlamps per block. (Unlit, Black Town *was* at night. The finer black homes seemed ones near enough the border to benefit from borrowed light.)

"Home," Captain said, and shifted reins into his left hand, the right mitt reached over and touched my neck's bun. I appreciated it.

Our rig was suddenly flanked by rows of enameled garden gates, by gardenias in hedges, by metal hitching posts that showed a single black stableboy painted in different overly bright clothes. We passed the goldfish ponds country ladies muddily copied. Gaslit sidewalks looked prim and creased as pathways made of damask tablecloths laid end to end for blocks.

We drew near Doc Collier's home, usual music greeted us. How glad I felt. Doc's homely daughters, twins of forty-five, played flute duets late into each summer night. Tonight was no exception. All a small town's joy and grief, child, lives in them four words: "Tonight was no exception." Plump sisters dueted by heart, not even candlelight required.

"The 'girls' are at it. In fine form too," Captain said what was right evident but I forgave him.

Their music went—soft as a moth's path, over wet flowers and across dim adjoining yards. Their sound was so perfect with longing, you sometimes saw young men hanging around, jumping to peek over Doc Collier's intentionally tall hedge. Forgetting Collier twins' daytime looks, boys were drawn here for the simple joy of healthy sighing.

Come daylight, spying Doc's stern devoted girls downtown (ladies who dressed as identical as two dolls on one store shelf, who favored overmuch suedey face powder and endured undergarments so argumentative with whalebone stays these corsets seemed nearbout . . . legislative), you felt like last night's music must've been a mistake, somebody else's. Until the next evening, no exception, when in passing onct more you heard all that skilled and wasted sweetness uncurl above wet grass. You sighed again because you believed again.

I now fought a urge to shout encouragement over the hedge and towards their breathy porch. I didn't—it might've stopped them.

Our buggy cut past a big elm's tree house that me and my best girlfriend had built not many years before. Strange to note how this tree's trunk and branches won't much different from ten thousand others I'd seen branching out twixt here and Georgia.

Homes—with porch lights lit—appeared to swing past our buggy seat. We seemed still, the houses moved on by us like huge white lanterns on parade. Real estate told us all its twisty histories. For Cap and me, each tale was sweet as Colliers' curling music, was plain as any Hedgepath plaque promising "from around here" fruit.

Third mansion on the left? The home of Falls' fourth-richest man, a guy who should know better but ofttimes *does* go steal useless carded buttons and boot hooks from Woolworth's and is then caught by the saleswomen that just love turning in a leading citizen.

Now, next *door* at 526 . . . Stop me, please, darling. I could go right on, and probably already have. A map of habits, faults. I'll just say this tour means more (to me) because I'm showing you certain sights no late-in-the-century bus can ever drive you past again. Gone.

Tell you what. This'll be a forward flash in Time's strange unguided missile of a tour. Them Collier twins just fluting away back there? They will, five years hence, run off at age fifty with a single skinny paper boy sixteen years old and wholly unmusical. Fact. A boy whose aim whilst chucking *Herald Traveler*s over their steeplechase-high hedge impressed them first. This trio elopement eventually killed Doc Collier, did so as literal as a lead slug to the brain. Finished Doc, a man many, many others of us relied on. Everybody blamed the paper boy, who took "the girls" to Florida, where them three adopted a pretty Cuban baby and lived (if I am to believe what I been told, and if *I* don't, my trusting child, who the heck *will*?) not unhappily ever after.

Forward by nine years or eleven, I forget exactly which: Somebody hungry stopped at Hedgepath's out near Indian Creek and somebody later found both senior Hedgepaths shot dead among the bright bushel baskets. They'd been robbed, stripped of their change aprons. A untold number of vegetables probably got pinched too, but who could say how many? I guess that Mr. Hedgepath had just spoke his usual to some fugitive, said, "Seems like we should *know* you," which brought out some outlaw's forty-five. After the funeral, as laden with flowers as the stand'd bear, Hedgepath's dozen children took over the vegetable shack but it won't ever the same and—you will not be surprised to hear—the institution has since closed. That's part of what'll have to happen onct its dark date comes due ahead.

So.

Home. I mean by that: stories that you know, the stories that *know* you know them. So you both can hush—can pass on by each other with gentle understanding. Meaning: you can gloat but very quiet, and in perfect taste.

I MEMORIZED my husband's war mail home. Nights, I asked him for tales of life on the slave-days plantation. I was hoping to get news of my helper's early years. She soon interested more than he did. Cap now took me for granted. I'd gone Fact. Castalia honored me with cunning daily hate I half appreciated.

My fourth married week, she offered to clean my new silver hairbrush, said only a blind person wouldn't notice how filthy the thing was. Well, I figured this little chore might help to bring us closer together. In a new red-rimmed white enameled pot atop her wood-burning stove, she boiled my wedding gift for going on fifty minutes. Half hour into this brush's Saint Joan purging, the kitchen begun smelling of my hair, my skin flakes, my hygiene, then my whole short lifetime. Castalia's comment was: to throw open seven windows and then stand flapping the back door, to and fro, fanning hard. And all while holding her nose. Doing this, she laughed. Whilst successfully torturing me, Castalia's pleasure sometimes led her to lighten up some. But if I—spying this—grinned any, she clamped down that much harder. I wanted to make her laugh full out and legal and just onct. It soon become my life's new goal.

(Child, did you ever get a full taste or whiff of your own basic dander? Too much of it can startle you into thinking, Me, direct from the tube? Am I fully *that* much me? I wanted to splash vanilla extract all over the steamy cabinets. I grew so embarrassed, it seemed nearbout funny, even to *me*.)

Then I couldn't help notice—my English brush's badger bristles floated, doing a circle dance amongst the churning foam. "Uh-oh," I pointed, smiled, tried not to sound real accusing, "unless I'm very much mistaken . . ." and I jumped up and down once, pointing at damage. Using pickle tongs, Castalia fished forth one sterling handle, bald now. "Dingy thing. Look like its time had done come."

That night I sneaked behind their (my) (our) house, spared a monogrammed silver stem from out the trash. Still have it around here somewhere. Odd, what you save.

DAYS, I had her "helping" me. Nights, I had him helping hisself to me. Ain't we got fun.

Soon the single hiding place left young Lucille—awake or asleep—was far into them blessed novels. I never wanted to leave their inner hearths. "Little did young Gwendolyn know that stormy first night in the Baron's castle, how, waiting just beyond the thick stone wall, a . . ." Some books seemed squat cozy galleons, sails sewn of woolly broadcloth. Others were Arab tents made from windblown sand-battered bellying chiffon. In my ideal sheltering book, I would want one wing done in every style—stone, glass, sod, igloo ice. There should be lots of different fresh foods stocked along feast tables in each annex. I love it when the prisoners of a story have to, like me, eat.

Though my young eyes were good, I'd pull double pages close before my face—wanting to live back of mule's blinders. After lunch, I all but galloped to my dim front parlor. I kicked shoes off, settled on a chaise, drew my knees clear up to my chin and book. I finally learned to lock the door to prevent a certain cleaner's zeal. And I would soon be oh so suddenly lost to the worries of the local. The novel dwellers' Gothic woes made my own ones seem no worse than introductory bunions.

A helpful somebody must of noticed my single source of joy. —The day before, in this here book, a governess was about to be trampled whilst wandering some foggy pasturelands of England. Today that very volume so full of danger, tea, and first wives was gone. On my hands and knees, I checked everywheres. Finally I worked up nerve sufficient to go quiz Big Woman, gentle-like. Barefoot, I padded towards the kitchen door.

Then, seeing what I saw, I wanted to evaporate like the water boiling on yonder stove. I'd found Miss Castalia talking to twenty some redbirds lined like targets atop her stove. I went dead-still. Ignorant of being watched, the woman bent largely forward, her curtsy making manifold accordion pleats of most substantial flesh. Then she crossed herself and stood quietly a-muttering, "Redbirdness, Give her Strength what sufficient unto this here sad redbird day, O redbirds of the Reba Woman, see me through it and . . ." I eased inches over against hall wallpaper, my mouth open, palms flattened against walls. Seemed I was witnessing something nobody ought to see.

I planned sneaking off when Cassie rose fast, grabbed a sugar canister off the counter, gobbled two big handfuls straight. Made me feel ill to imagine how that tasted going down. Burned probably. Then she clawed around inside whilst talking to herself about somebody by the name of Miss Reba Holy Red of Bird of Red. I prayed for amnesia. Then I prayed to know who Reba was. If Castalia was to whip around and catch me here, she'd kill me. Yeah, she'd scald me with the water chortling yonder. From white sugar, the woman pulled one spiny dark item. It had several points to it, thing appeared barnacled. Little threads of sugar kept spilling from all holes of it. She kissed the item. Then, doing a strange agile spin, Castalia turned most massively in place three times. Sugar flung loops of white into daylight, sugar sissing across linoleum. This gave me a chance to try and slip off towards my safe distant parlor.

Failing to either breathe or notice not doing so, I was tiptoeing backwards, barefoot, frowning at each chance of floorboard's creaking. I figured: Castalia must glue hairs over every cupboard door before daily leaving work.

How had she turned our kitchen, our personal food into redbird burnt offerings and some strange altar? Someday soon, I'd have to check all that. Really I would. I'd scout the closet where she hung her coat and stacked her gear. I just needed planning time was all, I just needed some voodoo information and somebody else's courage, nothing more.

"Who that?"

I flinched. "Just me. *Me* coming to see *you*, matter fact. Funny you should mention it." My fake and shiniest girl voice.

I thumped her way real loud, no choice. I only longed to retreat inside the tree house of my missing novel, to read my hubby's boyhood war letters, to pull the rope ladder up behind. Noisy as my advance was, I decided to maybe hum some for good measure. (Hum a hymn.) I found her there, face set, arms crossed, leaning against the stove, real ready for me. "Singing in the house again?"

"*The Church's One Foundation!*" I justified myself, tried.

"Singing in the house *again*? I believe Castalia done tolt you how nervous that makes the folks what's forced to be around you all the day. What you want *now*?"

I explained about a good book's being gone.

Sighing, mumbling, flats of wrists riding hips, Castalia charged across the lino's gritty worship-service sugar. She headed for the front parlor, lunged in, turned, stood facing me while thumping one fingernail against a glass-front bookcase. Shelves showed many volumes the selfsame color as the novel I'd described.

"You got you a whole roomful. Why you so set on *that* one?"

HONEY? Honey, something had to give.

I decided: I'd either get under the brown skin of her secrets or maybe kill her, one. But, considering her girth and energy, I'd surely need help to kill the help.

11

NEXT novel, I hid under Captain's bed pillow upstairs. Got so I really wanted to tattle. On her. To him: "You wouldn't *believe* the hoops that chunky witch puts me through most mornings." But, see, that felt cowardly. I had just been a schoolgirl and schoolkids have a code about snitching. Seemed wrong—my going against her, easing over to the Other Side. (And which side might that be? I wondered. The white side? The man side? Boss side? Sunny-side-of-the-street side? And won't I at least white and the rightful mistress of this gloomy manor? Didn't *I* have rights? Why should my acting out my rightful part trouble me so bad?) Call it a overdeveloped sense of justice. My momma's people were big-time owners. Poppa's—natives of Bear Grass, North Carolina—they mostly rented (when they could afford to). Odd it should be the renters of this world that seemed my nearest kin. I dearly hated going over anybody's head, even over the noggin of a woman daily mangling me with such sleek and growing skill I half admired it.

"There's reasons," I muttered aloud some mornings. "There's reasons," I still tell myself today. Such a idea ain't to everybody's taste. It just means that history interests a person—history being "a few reasons why." Also means you got a inborn sense of pattern. (Pattern is really just "repetition"— one line is just a line, but forty lines at cross-purposes mean "plaid." One crank with a fixed idea is a crank, four hundred "a movement.")

Look, what I'm saying: Seemed I needed me a project. It'd keep a young newlywed organized, might let me finally learn to breathe deep inside my own house or his, or ours, all three of ours. One midnight, I re-decided: My first mission would be tracing one enemy's twisty route through life. I planned to either figure her or else know why I couldn't. Lucy'd find Miss Castalia Marsden's good side or learn why it'd been amputated early and by who.

I sat bolt upright in the bed beside my snorfling rosy pudding of a spreading man. I whispered, "I'll inves tigate." I was picturing myself tip-toeing around Falls by night, a spyglass mashed against my fifteen-year-old's oily nose. On the trail of—what? maybe that Moriarty Mastermind called Grief, Fate, or Luck or the slippery Past—*you* fill in the blank. What *does* make everybody be so much what they are? Rebs liked to ruin Yankee train tracks, crowbarring metal into silly airborne loops that soon got known as Sherman's hairpins. What force is always making split ends of our earnest single necessary paths? That's the very force I planned to trail.

How could I of known that—right then—it was already trailing me?

NEXT morning, chewing hard, I studied the woman. She sensed the change: "What *you* after, doughface?" I'd become Marse Audubon and her a wild turkey in a low tree.

I understood at least one fact about Castalia of the clashy clothes worn like posters of petition gripes. She was the single person in all of Falls (Cap included) who'd forever let me know *exactly* where I stood with her. All over town, others talked dishonest about money or religion. They denied that their families were farmers new to Falls. Everybody—white or black—lived on the slant about something.

But not her. Only that person yonder, bulldog mean, guarded as a walking fort, ruder than seemed possible in either Carolina—only she might be a fitting model for me—and why? Because she'd already showed herself to be—a genius of a enemy, child. Beloved enemy.

The Civil War and the First World One, those were the last wars where the general of one side kept his opposite general's portrait in his tent. When he mapped strategy—or even when just at supper by his lonesome, he turned up his oil lamp—he studied the sly and worthy features of his counterpart.

When your enemy—like ours nowdays—ceases having a nose, two eyes, one mouth, then you got troubles. You're up against a dervish and a ghost, a evil empire. Me, in my time, us in our time—we were lucky. We knew the shoe size of the opposition.

Castalia tortured me in ways direct and sidelong. (She starched my pillowcase but not his.) And yet I told myself, Castalia never lied. Seemed she couldn't. Even to save herself. I'd already sneaked a few truths out of Captain: how during plantation days a black girl's backtalk ofttimes got her whipped, how his own mother loved Castalia best of all because of such steady sass and helpless dignity. And how this made things go way harder on the saucy girl child.

I learned how Castalia ran away from home and managed to get clear to Pennsylvania and how she got brought home in irons and how she rode back to the farm between Yankee bounty hunters, how she rode up the lane past the Big House and how all the other slaves disobeyed stiff overseer Winch and ran to the field's edge to wave and watch her and how she held her head high like queen Marie Antoinette (if poor Marie had been both noble *and* right). My husband—who I loved more the more he told me about his main slave girl—said how his mother had sent money downstairs—via Uncle Primus, the black butler, on a silver tray—for the bounty hunters but would not "receive" them. How she then called for Castalia at once and how Lady More Marsden ordered her own porcelain bathtub to be filled with hot water and fine oils and with all the gardenia blooms floating virgin-white on top and how she helped the silent sullen springy young black girl to undress and how Lady Marsden cried when the hot water—striking the pink flesh wounds around the young woman's wrists and ankles—made the strict black girl to suck in air. They both cried—for different reasons, naturally. And finally how Lady Marsden, not caring that the sloshing grimy water had spoiled her own white satin wrapper, finally leaned toward a twisted little tar-black ear protected by its picket of braids, and how she whispered, "I'll make you anything you like on this plantation. Anything you want to be, now you're home with me, I'll make you that, agreed? You desire to replace Primus as head of house slaves? Done. You want to be something other than my body servant? Done too. You care to be in sole charge of the herb garden or my cutting garden? What? Name it, Castalia mine, anything. I fear I perpetually fail to understand you. Don't leave again. What is it you want me to let you *be*, girl?"

Castalia's wide mouth was suddenly where her homely little ear had hung and—neck-deep in suds and flowers and balms—her broad dark mouth breathed into the mistress's pink slot mouth. "Free."

"That's not in my power." The lady of the manor rose from beside the steaming tub. "Anything else. But that, my dear one, is quite, you see, beyond my will. I cannot make you an exception. I can go right up to the very edge of that. But 'free,' you'll understand . . . if I caved in on that, you see, my much-missed one, much-*loved* one . . . then where would it end? That's Solomon blind in the temple. When that the keystone goes, it all falls. Bluntly put, it's you or me, and much as I've pined for your company and much as I admire how far you got from me, I still choose in favor of *moi-même*, I fear. If and when that changes, you shall, I promise, be the very first to know, Cassie mine. Now—welcome home—such as it is, and do enjoy the remainder of your bath."

"Castalia," Castalia said to the retreating white-satin back. "Castalia she appreciate you being blunt. That good. 'You or me.' That show you learned *some*thing from Castalia's taking off and all."

A maid to *us* now, Castalia still expected all of this, and daily. Her redbird worship hinted at some long wait still honored. Sometimes, child, I'd catch her—arms crossed, head tilted, face glazed—but perked like listening to a sound starting from far off and maybe getting nearer. She'd be studying the big round kitchen clock. Something on her massy features told me she won't listening to the past then—but was scouting for the future. Any future.

So few folks I knew then (and even fewer now) believed in a future. *I* never did. My Sherman's hairpin mind figured out that all the good clues really rested back yonder. I imagined over my shoulder back to Carolina 1840–80 as the source of anything we might expect ahead. But her? she yet believed that something good was due her, just around time's bend. Next month, next decade.

Here she was, waxing and sweeping for others. She was already in her early fifties maybe—though she looked decades younger than my man. But instead of feeling shortchanged, Castalia's long, long wait seemed to half prop up her hopes. Sure, her doubts were plainly huge as these here hopes, both had long since widened like her body. Her hope upset me, like her four square inches of beauty did. I wanted to shake her, ask, "What are you waiting for? Don't you see it's over? Where'd you learn to believe like this? Notice what's happened to you. Wise up." Something about her holding out for the impossible reward—it made me mad for her, then *at* her. *I* seemed lucky but felt so little joy in it. She had so doggone little, and yet there was some quality like royalty waiting to return in glory to some deserved throne. I can't explain it, not exactly. But I did notice, child.

Not since I composed school papers for the late great Witch Beale at Lower Normal, not since those history assignments drove nosy kids like me into asking frenzies, not since then had Lucy so wanted to know a set of facts. And this much come clear as I sat up in bed that midnight staring straight at (and into) darkness: If I could figure out Castalia, I'd maybe know more about my husband here beside me. If I could ever get half under the rock of him, my own foreground would sure be a clearer row to hoe for life.

So, beneath all of it, I had personal Lucy easement at heart. I don't admit this, child, for apology—I mention it to brag. History is self-interest.

Even then I saw that my own stake was with the others. Harry Houdini—lowered in some bank safe into a river—didn't wait till *then* to figure out the lock. He'd worked on that while still safe on dry land. He did his homework before being lowered to likely death. I would now do mine. I had a hunch that us three—him, Castalia, me—Wynken, Blynken, Nod on this unlikely life raft, we all someway/somewhere overlapped. We would go down together.

I felt it even then—a Mississippi of ice water waiting far, far ahead.

I had my work before me. I had my wits about me. Now . . .

12

NEXT morning, my head full of her that day's color scheme: salmon pink, cobalt blue, turquoise, and silver jewelry, the pale purple of a foxglove's throat, I set about my crude detective work outside the home.

And Nancy Drew Her Own Conclusions, sugar.

Castalia always did marketing on Mondays. I announced I would be downtown and shopping too. "Do tell," she muttered. She was putting on her tiniest hat, red. (The dressier the occasion, I noticed, the more Carter's Little Liver Pill-sized did Castalia's hats shrink.) I followed her outdoors, she hadn't said I could but didn't quite forbid it. Once, midstride halfway to the Courthouse Square, she spun around and stared my way. Basket looped over one wrist, she set heavy hands on stouter hips and rolled her overexpressive eyes, showed total disgust with tagalong me.

"Free country," I announced from thirty feet.

"That what *she* think!" come the tired answer.

Her wicker shopping basket looked suitable for carting home a living goose or John the Baptist's head, unshampooed. When Castalia Marsden stormed into a shop, causing the door's bell to ring with extra alarm, one moment's silence fell among the salesgents in their boaters and aprons. Smiles faded, jokes hung open like drawbridges halfway there.

She shut the door behind her like preventing any other customer from ever getting in here. Closing time, and she'd best be treated right. Castalia seemed to possess blackmail material on every white (and black) salesclerk in this town. (As a possible former beauty, as the total recall of all other maids' gossip for three counties and fifty-some years, plus a darned good guesser, Castalia controlled whatever dirt could be dug up on most all males in buggying distance. Her first glance at salesmen said, "Who you kidding?" Her glance said, "All males are guilty until proven guilty." Weird enough, I noticed, menkind sure seemed to agree. They gave back sheepish looks or tense ones. But innocence? they knew not of, to go biblical for a sec. And if the man *hadn't* erred quite yet, Castalia could determine exactly what he'd do *if* allowed. This was power, darling. She carried a headful of which girls' or even boys' hindquarters this one strapping church-deacon dude at the counter *had* been known to check out whenever he believed—mistakenly in fishbowl Falls, North Carolina—the coast was clear. Castalia's knowing this part gave her lots more clout. Was another way of believing in the future—

her prediction of each upcoming crime and carnal fall. Her counting on his *knowing* that she knew!)

This meant, among other stuff, that Castalia got—in stores, from such men—real deals.

I learned this on my Monday number one.

The white butcher served her *before* helping a waiting Caucasian lady— and all while he gave Mrs. Whitey a silent look that hinted, "I'll explain later. You'll thank me for getting her out of here first."

Clerks usually granted Castalia the prices that she named. Manliness meant a little wrangle—especially if white customers were present. But, by now, this late in her life (and fifty-odd seemed ancient to me at fifteen) Castalia pretty much got what she wanted. At least on the price of turnips. As I followed, respectful, store to store, it seemed turnips stood for other things she might get cheap from the world, eventually.

She paid me no mind at all, she looked right through me. Which was fine with me. What I couldn't get together: her power on one hand and, on the other, her being just a maid.

She stormed into the sawdust of Harbison's Day-Old Doughnuts and tried to bargain on account of her buying a gross of those. A gross of three-day-old cherry-jelly doughnuts! I should say so. "Gross" is one of Zondro's favorite words. I told you about Zondro, with the Mohawk? She admits that none of her pals who hang around the Mall or at Falls Country Day High even use "gross" anymore. But she says *she* still relies on it and cannot quit, just feels loyal to it.

I wondered: Was Castalia trying and save pennies for Captain or for her sake? If such cash was hers, what would it buy? A getaway to Liberia? Or New York City? Some new house built higher on this hill? Retirement? Her send-off funeral? Her surly sons' weekend pleasures? What?

This investigation I'd undertook owing to boredom soon claimed me like a fever. Falls Lower Normal had never considered me its prize pupil, but—restless, left with so many hours on my hands—I soon begun to find the England in my novels anemic compared to Castalia Marsden's un-manners and her Afro color schemes. I soon followed this woman at distances both reckless and safe. I'd turned into Madame Curie and Jane Addams of Hull-House, mixed, all while staying as determined (and flat-chested) as either Hardy Boy. (Now, looking back, I see I won't just being gumshoe to her history. What I was really looking into was, child, my own coming slavey wifely shopping cooking washing-up kid-bearing future. Now I see that. But who, even among great detectives stuck like ambered flies inside their own lives, can ever really know that at the time?)

ONE night, Cap said without prompting, "So, how are you and Castalia getting on? Like a veritable house afire, I'd wager. I predicted great things, you'll recall. But I'm deducing by your present facial expression, all the counties have not yet been heard from. Nobody ever called Castalia 'sweetness and light.' But I suppose she's training you at certain chores around the house . . . little kitchen skills, what have you?"

I give him a hard look. "I reckon she's trying to teach me *something*. Ain't clear just what. Maybe that it's her turf here, and you are too some days. —No, it's okay, basically. She cooks perfect. Even Momma claims to've never seen a house this size so clean and with a staff of one and you know how Momma is about black folks. Castalia and myself we're here together all day long. Still, I don't figure we're quite ready to be stranded together on no life raft."

"She'd assuredly sink it," he chuckled. I give him one stern-wifey clamp-mouthed look. (How quick I'd learned that, honey, a natural.) But, secretly, I admit it pleased me: hearing my old man speak somewhat ill of this woman he'd known for life. I hated feeling relieved by his joke at her expense. It won't worthy of her, it won't worthy of me. But I dreaded hearing him praise her at my expense. She could cook, I couldn't. She knew the world, I was new even to *not* knowing it. And yet, scared as I felt around her, hard as I found facing Big Person (mornings especially), a new kind of pride kept me from whining to Cap about certain of her cruelties. He had owned her. I— on the slant—had just rehired her. Someway, my own code (one I was forever making up right in the minute) kept a black person's present-day employer from complaining to her onetime owner. I had scruples from the start, my darling listener. Only a few reasons I'm worth listening to: scruples (and the woes they bring), plus what Jerome calls my "strong visual memory," and one very dirty mind.

Now, with my pillow beside Cap's, I fought so hard to seem casual: I sounded almost exhausted.

"There's something *about* her, ain't there?" said I, and waited, hoping I looked semi-cute. He didn't help a bit. "You know?" I touched his quilt. He turned half away from me, one fist curled under his head and beard. But finally he nodded, almost shy. He told the ivy wallpaper, "Always has been . . . That's the thing. It's still hidden under all that weight someplace. It's a secret the wench has always kept. Unfair. Used to drive my mother absolutely mad. I once heard Momma tell Castalia, both of them laughing over it too, Momma said, 'No, darling, you've got things con*fused*, I believe. You see, *I* am the aristocrat and you are actually here to *help* me.' And Cassie said, 'You the boss and I the slave? That it?' They giggled, actually.

"In some way no Yankee could ever catch, we all understood each other perfectly then—but that, I suppose, constituted the mystery of everything that Sherman burned. The invaders ended it. I can't believe how much has changed in my short life."

"Short?!" I joked, fifteen.

"Oh yes, that." I made a mental note: no further age jokes, Luce.

So I turned our topic elsewhere, asking after his business, some ship-ment of quarter horses he'd been waiting for (all to get his confidence, don't you see?). Then, sly, I put in, "Now where exactly'd you say Castalia lived downhill?" I was in search of what I had to know. I had become the very sneak she'd called me, and all in service of her interesting me.

Cap right off described her house, then, dozing, did half a double take. "Why?"

"Case of emergency or something. Curious, mostly. I wish I knew a little more . . . I don't feel like I'm really . . . *ben*efiting from being around her. You know me, sir. I got to have all the facts on everybody."

He shifted my way then. "You've probably gathered quite a little file on your old man already, I daresay. God knows what you tell your intimates about me."

"What inmates?" I bent over, kissed his forehead, smirked. I did this to relax him mainly. I did it not out of any true love—but the odd thing, soon as I did so, I felt that. That other. I loved him because I'd learned how to loosen him up some. I could. I guessed that he would tell a few stray facts about a person whose mystery presently held me in some way my husband as yet did not.

"Well," he started, slow, ripe voice dark as dark Karo syrup, never more beautiful to me than it sounded just then. Under our shared covers, I took his closest hand, my intimate, my inmate. "One thing, she's ever done precisely what she wanted. Cas caught absolute and total hell for it often enough, I can tell you. Which never seemed to stop her. That was part of her power, or a sign of it perhaps. Her family believed itself to have been the leading lights back in some African hellhole. Cas's sense of herself must have come in part from that. We called her mother Queen Esther because the woman behaved like one. Doing scullery work with her nose higher in the air than Mother's was—which was a stretch, my dear. Unlike Cassie, she was gorgeous, the mother. I mean, Castalia had something and got much masculine attention and enjoyed what my mother called 'presence.' But Queen Esther—you could dress her in a gunnysack and take her downtown and make her walk beside my own Lady Mother done up in her full satin and her white ostrich feathers. Every man, woman, and child would've stared at Queen Esther. Needless to say, she was not Mother's favorite shopping companion. Esther never left the farm till she escaped. Our overseer blamed Cassie, Winch was forever gunning for Castalia. Queen Esther was caught. Then Castalia ran away, got clear to Pennsylvania. You had to hand it to her. Mother was so proud of how many state lines Cassie had crossed. Mother got out my father's atlas and marked Castalia's route in secret, proud. She forgave Cassie, reinstated her as body servant, though I'm not sure how *Castalia* felt about that particular honor. Cassie refused to be forgiven. She said Mother could either set her free or pay for it in Cassie moods. Mother needed her. Northerners would call it twisted and it was, I suppose. Love is always a kind of bondage anyway, is it not? Maybe that's facile. Still, it was she who saved my mother. When the end came, I mean, at The Lilacs. But you know all this probably, know from that school paper you tried doing."

"Castalia wouldn't talk to me then. Others told me she never spoke about Back Then. Won't hardly mention it now. And you, sir, for my History Theme, you wouldn't cooperate much either, remember?"

"I didn't know you then. I was less of a teller. When Castalia was out there on the farm, we were all something like in love with her. I certainly was. It must surprise you, hearing so—you, having only seen the woman in her present shape. I hope you won't feel jealous. I only tell you this because, child, you must see by now just how central you are to me. You have my heart forever and that's fixed. All this other is just ancient history. Put on the pounds over time, Cas has, and me too, Lord knows. As a boy who weighed a hundred and ten maximum when Lee signed—I should understand how size sneaks onto a person. The days are pounds. Still, with her it yet shocks me sometimes. I walk into our kitchen, yours and mine, I look at her—especially from the back—I marvel she can be the same person. I know I've changed and . . . thickened, Lucille, inside and out. But she was so quick and springy and such a fox. Resourceful, I mean. To look back on yourselves as kids, you cannot quite believe you're the same ones. Difficult to properly express. To someone your age. But I almost grieve less for myself than I do for the person she was and what she's settled into. You'll say I had a hand in that, no doubt. And maybe that's true. I do believe in free will. She chooses to work for me. You know I pay her very well, by the by? Yes, I must do so secretly or we'd throw off the entire pay scale on Summit. My friends would never let me live it down. I had the little cottage built for her not long after I got back from the war. They were living, our black people from The Lilacs, in absolute squalor down by the river. You should've seen the village they built out of scrap lumber and shipping crates, what have you. . . . Oh, I'm not so bad to her as you sometimes seem to think."

"What'd I *say*?"

"You need not speak one word with those little ice-pick eyes of yours. Someday I'm afraid that the two of you, you and Castalia . . . someday I wouldn't be in the least surprised if you were to . . . almost as a revenge on me . . . might try . . ."

"What? Gang up on you?"

"Something. Something worse. She's capable, don't underestimate her perversity. She's extremely negative. I should know. —We'll continue this line of thought later. You asked about her *then*, remember? Mother couldn't bear to be alone. When Cas ran off, Mother hired two white men to go find her—less as punishment, more to try enticing her back. Everybody out on River Road considered that my parents were far too kind to slaves, especially their house ones. Mother and Cassie squabbled constantly. But like family, it's hard to make clear to anybody these days. The two were with each other all day long, at each other's throats. Mother was a trial to us all with her headaches and her airs. Castalia was tough as nails through most of it, grumpy, though in a lighter way than the fat old thing is now. Not 'old,' she's just my age. But she and Mother had an understanding of some sort. We loved each other then. You can't tell that now to people who weren't out there. 'Slavery,' 'ownership,' the moderns can't get past terms that do, admittedly, look at best so-so on paper. That far into countryside, *We* were what we had. Given that, you find a way to mostly get along. To be amused by each other. And if one of you is the least remarkable, it's noticed, she's soon idolized almost. She became a cult with us, your present housemaid.

"But to answer you, yes, I did love her then. Winch tried to, shall we say, 'fix me up with her' before I went off to war. Is this shocking? I don't know anymore. But you asked. Winch planned ordering Castalia to come upstairs to my bedroom, at night . . . Does this upset you? Maybe this is tactically mistaken, laying all this out. *She'd* tell you, if she ever comes to respect you enough. Not that she won't, mind you. Takes time: You have the goods but it takes absolute ages with her. No, Winch had worked for my poppa long enough to feel that he, the overseer, could not lay his hands on the younger black girls till my Owner Father had been given first dibs. Father availed himself fairly frequently. It might sound dreadful from here, to you. But we lived there on those two thousand acres side by side. You get to know people, often better than you'd planned.

"She *was* sent to me. I was just a boy. It was two days before Ned and myself left Falls together. There'd been a birthday party for Mother. Winch told me, when the party ended, to expect Castalia would arrive upstairs in my bed. 'What for?' I asked in dead earnest, Lucille. He laughed his wild Irish laugh. He'd started as an indentured servant over from County Cork but it hadn't given him much sympathy for our black folks. He had his pick of the girls. I got very scared. I wanted her to *want* to come and see me, not simply follow orders. She was as old as me but, unlike our other girls, physically she'd always kept to herself. On the farm, she fought off all interested gents, black and white, my father included. And my poppa owned her. But when you own a person, it's not the best circumstance for being convinced of their free will in *picking* you, if you get my drift. Not like you choosing me of your own volition, you see. I said good night to our last guests. Mother had retired hours earlier though it was her party—one of her tricks, disappearing. She always got a migraine on her birthday. A tradition. I was so nervous I could hardly walk to my own room. I used the banister like some old man. I knew I'd soon be hiking clear to Virginia. I wanted something to remember, something extra. She and I had been pals all over the place. We played rafts down on the river. Mother saw that Cassie was released from work whenever we played—but it was typical of Cas that she never assumed in advance that we'd be playing on a given day. She was always in the kitchen, doing some chore. She never came to me. I always had to go to her. She was twelve and in lots of ways the most powerful person on the whole two thousand acres. How does one explain powerful people? You don't know how they get this way, you just know they're powerful because . . . they have the power! She did. Wonderful-looking then.

Tall and springy and with her arms always crossed and her head back, judging, sort of judging. —Are you sure you want to hear this, child? You won't mind? It happened so far back. I have nothing to hide from you. I want you in on everything. You're sure?"

"Sure," I said but worried underneath. He was settling in now, looking not at me but towards the foot of our four-poster like she stood there, young and beautiful and sent up to his mansion chamber.

Uh-oh.

"Before I touched the doorknob I felt her in there, in my bed waiting. One just knew. I was exactly as innocent as she. That was part of it, I wanted this to be the first occurrence for both of us. It was my choice. But was it hers? if you catch my drift? I wasn't quite old enough to truly *do* anything but wanted to start with her. We'd been picked for each other before birth, it seemed. Everything threw us together around the acreage. She was so obviously superior and bright and, as I've said, not beautiful exactly but, yes, beautiful, taken altogether, potent, somehow in charge of everybody though technically, of course, still a slave. *Our* slave.

"Now I see she, in doing what she did, Castalia simply wanted to feel she had some control in this. A little control—especially for a girl convinced that she'd descended from royalty—even if that royalty was from some doodledy-squat Africa backwater. I think it's true, her royal claim. At least she believes it to this day, which accounts for her carrying on like Catherine the Great all over this town—a town, to this day, absolutely terrified of her. Do you *doubt* I overpay her, my Lucille? Poppa always said that she and Momma got on like a house afire because they both believed in divine right and considered themselves its finest local proofs.

"But I could feel her through the door, I could, waiting for me. She knew I'd leave for war on Friday, that I'd be back, if at all, quite changed. She knew this from experience. Hadn't she got clear to Pennsylvania? I'd only make it to Maryland! I knew next to nothing except that she was in there for me, and that I wanted her a good deal. I think Castalia also wanted it to happen. I know she did.

"But she was so proud even then. She longed to have a choice in the whole matter. Winch had probably presented this tryst as partly my suggestion though it came only from him. Of course, he saw that she drove me up the very wall. So it was partly me. But what she did was ill-advised. Still, it meant she'd made up something for herself, she'd provided her own part in our meeting. At my present age, I understand that better and I like her for it. But at the time . . . no. I opened the door and whispered towards my oak four-poster I would inherit—actually, come to think of it, this four-poster we are in, Lucille. I was whispering to a girl I would have inherited—had not events intervened. (About those events I have mixed emotions. Owning most of the others was one thing I could probably stomach even now. But owning her? Even then she made us know she was un-owned.) Anyhow, I'm dawdling the way you do when *you* tell things, Lucy. I tiptoed over. Winch had provided her a nice white muslin nightgown and the older black women in the quarter—who loved the romance of this meeting of the twain, who considered it our actual honeymoon—had ironed the nightgown and teased her mercilessly all day long (she told me later). Instead, Cas had left the dress downstairs outdoors. She was hiding under the quilt—had covers pulled clear up over her head. You see, she was probably already embarrassed, she'd got herself up as the African princess she steadily considered she was. Castalia knew about as much about Africa and its rituals and how one conducted oneself over there as you and I do, Lucille. She'd made up her whole history from what she knew around The Lilacs. Which was all she knew, altogether. So, she'd daubed her face with stripes of red clay. She'd stuffed two cardinals' worth of red feathers in her nappy hair, and in her pubic terrain (is this too much for a girl your age?) she'd put white chicken feathers so her . . . mound, what have you, was turned absolutely white. Like some Plains Indian, or some Falls child at Halloween. And I pictured her in this muslin dress I must've heard about in advance, with her long hair flowing down her back, except she didn't have long hair and it was not about to flow anywhere but was pure wire . . . Anyway, I had one picture of the honeymoon bride, she had quite another.

"I lit a candle by the bed. I held it up. She was under this tent of sheets. I said, idiotic but nervous, 'Is that you, Castalia?'

" 'Nope,' came her answer. 'It Princess Castalia in she native garb.'

" 'Sounds good to me,' I said, or something like that. I thought she meant 'naked,' 'birthday suit.' When I pulled the quilts aside and saw this Hottentot clogged with mud and chicken plucking, I screamed. *She* screamed, I dropped the candle. She jumped out of bed and dodged past me, out the door. She passed Mother in the hall, who *really* screamed and swore till her last days she'd seen the ghost of a Tuscarora goddess in our dark hall. That was our connubial bliss. That's about the size of it. It's almost as if we got the whole romance over with by hollering instead of doing any full deed. It took us twenty years to even mention this and then we practically expired laughing. But the moment was gone, our moment. Anyhow, you asked, Lucille.

"What got me onto all this? I nearly forgot. Your asking? Why am I even telling you this—so few weeks into our marriage, if at all? Because I trust you and want you to know everything about me.

"I don't know about having you two together all day. Some nights, you're glazed. I see you're thinking of her. I was your age once and I recognize the signs. She respects you. She's said the most ghastly things about you—a recognition. But, enjoy her food and cleaning, and learn from her, because, past a certain point, she's absolutely out of here. I want you to think of me, Lucille. One of the pleasures of *not* owning them, Lucille, is—you can fire them."

How still I kept, listening for more. And when I heard him clearing his throat, already half regretting what he'd spilled, I at once faked sleeping—

long steady breaths. I finally heard him snort, pleased to look down, find me shut-eyed, to believe he'd maybe bored me into darkness. This way, I'd get more from him, about her. Later. But all in time. I must never seem to press.

He had told me where she lived. I now knew where to find her downhill. But, first, he woke me, a hand on my left leg under our sheets. I then understood, it was another form of the barter that Cap practiced at his stockyard. A tale of her for the tail of little me.

Well, a deal's a deal. I'd started the night with a maid at the stove and wound up with a real princess in my history.

Seemed a bargain for just letting him again.

13

TRIALS and errors, some mornings after I ate her eggs like medicine administered, I rose up and said, "I believe I'm going out. If anybody asks for me please explain I'll be back by one for Captain's lunchtime." Funny, ain't it—though I'd grown up in a house without no servant, I still knew how to announce such things. The knowledge must be waiting—like a tasseled service bell pull—in the genes.

I heard Castalia snorf, huff, doubting my mission. But it seemed I *did* have some appointment urgent as Cap's daily dealings at his bustling livestock yard.

Around the street corner, I stood buttoning on white gloves, nodding at ladies who'd been wandering downtown to look at the same clothes in the same fifteen stores for years of such mornings. I tried and appear busy but slowly knew what'd pulled me onto the street, what'd made me feel so excited since I woke beside the Cap at five.

I wanted to play. I really wanted to just go somewhere and haul off and play. But how exactly? Seemed like in six weeks I'd clean forgot the method.

Fifteen, I was. But kids stayed younger longer then. The week of my wedding I'd climbed every tree I could, guessing in advance that Mrs. Married in a Dress couldn't exactly go with a monkey's ease up any scary limb she picked.

Now, stranded between running wild and sitting still in a guarded parlor, I moped around the corner from a house whose address seemed assigned to me for life. I counted lacy peaks in the Thorps' cast-iron fence here. My white glove's first two fingers pretended to be a human runner's legs hopping from one point to the other. Aloud, I said, "Being grown's no fun."

NEXT morning, Mrs. Married sat reading in the parlor when a flat-featured plump young white man walked right into the room. I jumped up, stood facing him. He held his hat and wore clean coveralls. I could see that he was shaking like a person joking about shaking. He had to lean against the doorjamb and was grinning to apologize. He mumbled the word "wife" and, ashamed at being barefoot, I admitted as how I was that . . . here . . . the wife.

"Mid . . . wife?"

"No, his first. Just plain wife."

"Because I was told she worked here and was a colored lady. The mid-one. Doc Collier is away from town and his girls they sent me here for a midwife and gosh but I'm in one terrible rush. This Captain Marsden's place, right?" Then Castalia was behind him, blocking doorway, wiping broad dark hands on the tiniest of white tea towels.

"How far along she?" Castalia asked.

He just nodded Yes, almost a spasm—his head wagged up and down so much. "Thank you, oh, very far along, thank you, yes, please do help us." He nodded so hard he nearbout knocked his own weight forward.

"Where she at?"

"My wagon's out front." Castalia hurried to the kitchen, preparing.

He turned around and grinned wild-eyed at me. "Thank you for letting me have her." Have? At first I thought he meant "have," like "have a girl baby," or even "have" like his wife. Then I decided he must mean my letting him have my maid, taking her off duty. I considered thanking him for that.

She bobbed in under a red hat so small it seemed like something else. Castalia toted what looked to be a lunch pail. "Ready. Where we bound for?"

"I got my wagon out front."

"So you say, but where that be heading us *to*, you?"

"She's in it. She's way past walking. Please, please hurry, it's started. I can't seem to make anybody under*stand* me here today, please."

"LONNIE!" A scream cut our neighborhood to green ribbons. "One's most out, LONNIE!"

"Twins, Doc *said* it'd be." But he spoke to where Castalia had just stood.

He raced after her. Now, rushing, confused, barefoot, I followed them down Cap's front-porch steps. I still held my novel, tight.

Castalia moved like hot oil on glass. Never saw anything like it. Her jolt of speed—her running on tiptoe in gold dance slippers—it scared and stirred me. I speeded along our brick walkway after her. Maybe I could *do* something for a change! She straddled the wagon bed already, calm, looking down at something while she prodded through her lunch pail.

But when Castalia noticed me, her entire upper body shifted this way. She fixed me with a look. It was different from her usual punishing stare. It said, "Oh, the little one." It *saw* me. In this emergency, I'd been spared whatever I usually stood for. I was just a girl fifteen hurrying to be of use, knowing next to nothing. But *meaning* well.

"You," she called. "Go back in the house, child. Do this. Now. Boil water, yeah, go boil water. That you job."

I minded her. Right off. I closed the front doors and leaned back against them, one hand over my chest. I would help! I'd be good help. Won't any question of my not doing what she'd just ordered. Even while the girl out there screamed, "Lonnie, oh Jesus, why two?" I was lost inside Castalia's new tone of voice. I found the red-rimmed saucepan where she'd martyred my brush. I filled it at the kitchen pump, I set it on a hot stove. But mostly I thought of how she'd spoke to me. Once the water boiled, I risked stealing back out, a towel wrapped around the pan's handle. Into the farm wife's screaming, I hollered, "Water, boiling water—like you said." I set the saucepan on the sidewalk near their wagon, hurried back up on the porch where Castalia seemed to want me stationed.

From here I could freely study the mule-drawn cart stopped at a angle before our garden gate. Something important was happening under cover of the wagon's rough side planks. I heard a girl scream straight up, then heard her say she sure regretted doing that on a street like this, then do it again way worse. Her husband stooped beside her in the wagon. His head kept checking from the wife's face down to her jolted body where Castalia worked, then back mostly at the girl's face. He gazed down hard, like his wife's face itself was changing from a big egg into some hatching yellow chick. All I could really see was her blanched fist, vined around his red one. And he was crying, "I *knew* we should of started out earlier. You just had to scrub that one last floor, you." He laughed while crying, saying it.

Lower in the cart, I watched Castalia's broad back struggling between uplifted dead-white knees. In the window of a house directly across Summit, one old couple held aside lace curtains and peeked but didn't exactly rush out as volunteers. All at once, Castalia rocked back like some fisherman when he heaves his catch from one element into another. She reeled backwards most powerfully, buttocks flattening against her upper calves. She moved with such force that the wagon's springs squeaked, its platform tilting so I worried all of them might topple out its back. Her red hat popped clean off and rolled—a pill—along brick street.

Castalia pitched hard forward, then suddenly held up a slick red sea creature spiraled to a trailing coral-colored line. She held this prize high in everybody's noon air—like some fisherman showing off a catch in his own element. As her right hand bound the thing's fin end, her left paddled the back till its wide mouth (seeming the whole front third) gave one unsealing hiccup. Then came a sound that seemed far bigger than its little fishy source. The sound was too human for me to quite abide or admit or stand—a wail so real and familiar it caused the old couple watching yonder to look at each other, nod, then smile and let their drapery drop.

Castalia turned the little noisemaker rightside up. She propped it in her lap. Using her apron, she seriously smeared at its eyes and nose. Then, after straightening a tangle in its line, she bowed more forward, seemed to place it on the mother's chest. Castalia next straightened, hands joined before her. She tipped her head, seeming to enjoy a bloody sight hidden from me. I wanted to see.

I hardly heard the poor farm girl's sounds begin again. I just stood here on a unfurnished porch, jiggling two cool white porcelain doorknobs. I was remembering the tone of Castalia's voice. (The miles and woes, the many uses of the laughs packed in it!) If the four surface inches of her beauty could be stuffed into a humid sound—it might be as slippery and deep but bell-clear as her direct order to me. That now seemed a song compared to usual growls she aimed my way. "You, child. Go back into the house. Do this. Now. That you job." I'd hardly met her, but standing here, I already *missed* her so. Hers was suddenly the voice of the one person on earth I most wanted to know.

14

NEXT afternoon was Castalia's half-day off. She was bound home to do laundry for the two grown cranky sons she called "my big boys." "Have a nice . . . one," I added as she trailed home lugging about ten pounds of leftovers. (She'd stashed our dinner for tonight in the warming oven.)

"Have a nice *what*? I hates folks what says mess they don't even *mean*. You go try to have a nice whatever you wanted *me* to have one of, you." And snorted, slamming the door. But, child, to my ears—since delivery of Billy and Barney, yesterday's twins—Castalia sounded kinder than she ever had before.

I waited till the garden gate creaked, till—trudging downhill—she joined another off-duty maid ripe with gossip for their joint hike downhill. I waited till Castalia couldn't possibly come back for nothing she'd forgot. Then I waited six minutes *past* that, and six more slow ones.

Finally I set down the novel I'd pretended to read. I glided barefoot to the kitchen and toward her personal closet, four feet to the stove's left. That cast-iron thing—her dark friend and spy in here—seemed to be watching, like it might could snitch. First I checked around the closet's seams for possible hairs glued on. Anything might give away my snooping. Not the least my being the World's All-Time Worst Liar.

Finding no likely booby traps, slow, I chanced opening the closet door. I expected almost anything—a sound, a humongous out-flopping bile-green snake, you name it. I found three loaded shelves and, below, a tangle of mops and brooms, one splintered gold-topped walking stick. Down among buckets, three ruined pairs of ladies' shoes very seriously run down at the heels.

On the top shelf here: a half-gallon jar of clear liquid. Across its label, a skull and crossbones hand-drawn in smudgy lead pencil. I slid this aside, took down the tin lunch bucket she'd used to help release them twins (now the talk of Summit Avenue). Inside: twine, three pair of scissors each in its own cotton-lined case, some needles big as a upholsterer's, lots of black catgutty thread that looked like sixty-pound fishing line, a pair of what appeared to be tongs, much gauze and adhesive tape, eye drops, smelling salts, a single baby pacifier—in them days called a sugar tit. Seemed too simple a catalogue of tools for a job so important—no better than other cleaning gear packed here. Behind clear poison, I set her lunch pail back most careful right where it'd been.

I kept checking over my shoulder and into the bright kitchen. Black-and-white lino. The big Seth Thomas clicked like egging me on. Horse hooves punished Summit's cobblestones. Coast seemed mostly clear.

Hooked to the closet's door, cleaning rags brightly colored as her clothes—the beautiful hues of Israel's twelve tribes intermarried. Tacked nearby, one pastel picture of a mild Jesus knee-deep in sheep. Beside Him, a pretty black model clipped from some magazine pomade ad, her face's silhouette jutting out so bold. The hand-sketched map of Africa I first took to show a crudely done water pistol pointing downwards. This map had one star penciled (red) at its western edge—a star much wider than the tiny river it seemed meant to mark.

On Castalia's top shelf, brilliant hatpins were stuck in a man's sock stuffed with fir needles that I sniffed. A heavy-bound maroon volume was called *You and Your Live Minks: For Profit and As Exceptional Pets*. Charts showed a person how to build proper ventilated running cages. One sketch demonstrated the male mounting position over a glazed-faced female coiled almost C-shaped underneath—and willingly, it seemed. (Animals, darling— what are you going to *do* with them? Us?) One picture gave you a cutaway of mink innards, blind babies were pictured as packed in yonder, chummy, blind, piglet-like. Was a chapter on your delivering the babies if Mother Mink herself couldn't get it right. But most diagrams concerned how to skin your exceptional pets without messing up their pelts. Pages were nubbled with flecks of food—like this had been a favorite cookbook used too near ingredients. Heavy black graphite stars studded the margins. Hand-jotted notes ran: *It say this but I lost me four doing it. Double they feed. Anybody know that!*

I stood here smiling. Was like flipping through my own school history textbook with its inked funny faces and frequent: "I doubt that very much. Them and who else's Army. Yeah? well so prove it."

I placed every single object exactly where I'd found it. Maybe owing to nervousness, each item I touched seemed to mean more than it should. Each thing's texture and color caused it to appear one of a kind, even her brooms, even her sour mops. Here you had your usual scouring supplies. (Except for saved cardinal and blue jay feathers—jammed into a wad of clay like a badminton birdie. Back of it—easy to miss in one corner—I touched a old-timey store-bought paper doll—a blond girl in a camisole, smiling in a open pointless way. Her figure was rigid, about a foot tall. My fingers noticed a new texture—staples pressed into her cardboard, no, pins had been pushed in till they burred and braided a surface. Metal had partway rusted under the thing's arms and down between her stiff and perfect straight legs. Extra gingerly, I put that right back.)

Kids shouted in the alley behind our house and I leapt a right good distance, then—hand over my mouth—laughed at myself. Still, I hurried through the rest. I just had to see whatever else she'd pack-ratted away. Had to view it whilst my nerves held, child. Witnessing what I did of yesterday's births had someway given me courage. Seemed I'd never find the gumption for such a inventory again. Quick: two hairnets flecked with gold, some rainbow-tinted emory boards that appeared to have been chewed for snacks. I found a four-leaf clover preserved in waxed paper. I found ruby-red nail polish and two photogravure pictures showing cardinal birds in flight. I found one smooth jawbone off what might've been a deer or goat. I found a New Testament torn, by force, out of a Bible and held together with pink rubber bands.

That was it.

Well, I centered the bottle of clear poison (cleaning fluid?), shut the closet door—feeling relieved, even considering the paper doll. I'd chose not to be bothered by that. For one thing, it looked a good deal older than I was, pins in it had rusted years before I ever stumbled onto the scene. Weirdly winded but feeling cheerful, I leaned back against the counter. Then I begun noticing delft-blue canisters of cooking staples lined—small to large—within easy reach. Out of SUGAR, I'd seen her fish a certain spiny something. But no way could I go direct to it. If this had all been occurring at night, especially during a thunder-and-lightning storm, it *wouldn't* of been. No way did I possess that caliber of brass. Daylight proved plenty rough enough. I kept listening to the ticking of the Seth Thomas in its nice round fruitwood case. Now it seemed to parse out question marks, tinny fishhooked shapes. A nice cup of tea? I felt spooked of going near SUGAR without some darn good reason. "I *live* here," I said aloud, mad-sounding. (But then, I've always been superstitious, am, still am, way too much so not to go ahead and admit it. Seems like the more modern this here century has got, darling, the more Dark to Middle Ages it's become. And me? Interested in magic and in self-defense. I've kept abreast.)

Into the stove I stuffed kindling, twists of old *Herald Travelers*. Lighting these, I filled a new saucepan that now seemed semi-holy from its uses in yesterday's births. Having heated water for Billy and Barney's arrival, I felt easier around a stove that'd always seemed so much Castalia's home base. I mention this because today was the first time I ever lit this famous wood stove that I myself would slave over so many years to come. (Before I got the Amana gas one almost too late to enjoy.)

Only after my tea was steeping did I dare barefoot it to the counter. Slow-moving, like trying and not alarm the blue-and-white china-looking tin cylinder marked SUGAR—I prized off its lid, I eased my whole hand in. Fingers struck a buried metal ladle that made me jump. Then, irked by my own sissiness, I jammed the scoop aside and touched a spinier-type item.

My fist, sifting white from out its every fold, slowly pulled something heavy toward daylight. Here we had a shell-crusted crucifix four inches long, made of splintery matchwood. A decal at its top said "Souvenir of Nags Head NC." Glued across it, dozens of tiny openmouthed shells. (The cross seemed filmed or coated like it'd been baked in something brown, cured for days at a low heat—like my poor hairbrush.) Dry sugar threaded from every pearly mouth of every shell. Mounted to the cross's back—one cutout cardboard picture. It showed the head of a redbird in profile against some dogwood blossoms. This'd been snipped from a magazine, glued to cardboard, varnished so many times it'd got stiff then glassy. It had then been wired behind the little Christ.

He was made of greening brass. Details of His thorn crown and loincloth seemed rubbed away by handling. Strips of fur—fur as good as possible— mink—were glued over the beard of Him. Strung to His body by kite string— six baby teeth. Teeth'd been drilled straight through so that these lines would fit and hold teeth close against His ribs. Baby molars wedged, large-looking, bunched under His either spindly outstretched arm. Jesus' open palms, both his X-ed feet, His spiny crown had all been daubed any old way with ruby-red fingernail polish. His crotch just shone gory with it. Across the redbird under-plaque, red nail lacquer spelled the words: "Reba Know Better. Reba Be The Real Inproved One HIM." The brown fur of His pelt beard shifted under Lucy's up-close breath. His mouth was open like from screaming and His upturned eyes were such awful bloody holes and I threw that thing straight into white powder and clamped its lid on so doggone quick. Couldn't believe I'd held it in my actual hand so long!

I mashed down the tin top hard, held it there for one full minute. You can never be too safe. I listened—pretending to worry that Cap might come in at the front door—but knowing in my heart I really now expected to hear muffled coin-sized cries from a screamer in and under glittery white mounds. Heebie-jeebie-ville, child.

Daintily then, so daintily, I carried my clinking cup and saucer from out that kitchen. Off quick to anyplace else, somewhere privater and darker. After sliding shut both rolling parlor doors, making sure the velvet drapes stayed drawn, I drank cold tea with greedy slurps. I meant to prove I was still here, yet basically fine. Lucy Mean-as-ever. For forty minutes, it was just me there in the dim room, deciding something hard—but not sure what. Not yet.

My husband found me, tense across my neck and shoulders, staring noplace. He turned on the gas lamp without asking after my mood. "Who died?" he asked. Cap then told me a new joke from downtown about two gentlemen sheep ranchers. The standing prank ran as how a man's loving relations with a ewe felt lots like real human coupling. So two ranchers are on horseback and they come across a ewe lamb caught in barbed wire, her hindquarter up and jammed right swayingly their way.

One rancher nods down in her direction. "Bill? I sure do wish that it was night and she was Lillian Russell."

"Heck," says Bill. "I just wish it was night."

I laughed so hard my husband stared at me. I slacked off quick then, wiping my damp eyes. "Good one," says I, confused. "Wish it was *night*! Good one. You're lucky you get to hear jokes."

He looked at me hard. "What have *you* been into? And what, young lady, has she told you? —If she ever turned you against me, she'd be out of here so fast. —But, enough of that.—How was *your* day? What did she leave the two of us for supper?"

"I ain't peeked!" I spoke too loud. "Corn beef and cabbage."

15

RETURNING from the honeymoon, I needed to believe in *some*thing. What besides *Here* could somebody like young Lucille claim? Surely not yet *Us*, not when that two-letter word included the mammoth mystery man seated here in the buggy, to my left. As for the comfort and safety of just *Me*? well, sure, later that became the underpinning of whatever story I am trying and tell you here. Otherwise, what would any of this mean? But at fifteen, I was yet too much in my own foreground for seeming of much value to myself. Hadn't yet noticed how I was, first of all, a Citizen of Myself. Later I'd discover that and with a vengeance, child. Takes time, though, but in story time, I'll try.

Back from Atlanta, noplace felt rightly mine. Maybe only downhill Baby Africa with its black-and-blue porch dreams, its unlit paths, the generations piled up like rich leaf-mold layers waiting to be turned onto some diamond lamp oil for the future.

Summit Avenue's deserted sidewalks seemed gaslit less to show you where to stroll after sunset. I wondered: What had made me consider Falls so doggone rare? Maybe I just loved the town for being the one that'd let *me* start in it.

"Things look exceptionally lovely tonight, do they not, Lucille?" His deep voice scared me. Cap didn't turn my way, just accepted my two bobbing nods.

To sit here, my engagement ring lighting up one streetlamp at a time— dying between—to feel that Falls won't that great, it made my own body feel less healthy.

(I pictured farm families coming miles to town in strawy open wagon beds. After a full day's work, they arrived Friday and Saturday evenings just in time to see Summit's huge white homes and tidy yards at sunset. Then they took usual evening spins towards the Square's one hardworking free water fountain and then looked over towards Lucas'. Then they faced the drive six miles back out into mule-drawn darkness. Their children stretched out in the wagon's back, hands laced behind heads, kids laid flat in dungy straw whilst looking up at stars that are both local and yet not. I imagine them: feeling pretty satisfied with what they'd seen in Falls! The responsibility I felt, picturing all this, knowing better now.)

I pulled my satchel closer and knew: Lucy, this town couldn't save you if it tried. And it won't try. It'd sooner send you down the drain, and it'll call that Entertainment. Good clean fun.

I told myself, Falls has spent its best efforts getting you hitched. If you now try retreating into some little private home, if you ever try and go and live alone or even move in with your aunts, this whole village will fight to keep you from staying separate. With any town this small, you got to either live smack-dab in the thick of others, or else you'd best go pack.

Maybe the Atlanta trip had cost me more than one little coin of membrane from a certain central location? Maybe I'd also been robbed of what we all need, child. A urgent feeling: "Me? why, I'm right unique—certainly in my pleasures but even in my pain, maybe especially in my pain." That, honey, a body's got to hold on to at *any* cost. "I deserve saving": That should be forever tattooed across your heart in prize-taking Palmer script.

"Gateway To The Breadbasket Of The Peanut Belt!" I'd onct held that boosters' sign to be so proudly serious I'd of pledged allegiance to it. Now, less . . . But what *new* reverence might replace it? I needed a fast Belief substitute. China painting? Love? What?

I NOTICED Cap had turned his rig a block out of our way, bound over to check on Winona Smythe. Being as I was *in* his buggy, I tended to go right along. No lights, her yard won't just a tangle now, more a private pie of woods. Evening felt cooler, I bundled arms around myself. Now coming up, four homes beyond Winona's, the big white frame place where I'd been raised. A house like other houses, really.

Except that my folks' two downstairs lamps still glowed at 9:15 p.m. One'd be set on Momma's polished grand piano, making ebony gleam like some fine boat made totally of ambitious crude oil congealed on tiptoe. Another lamp glorified Poppa's tobacco-brown easy chair, the lead-front bookcase housing his *Compleat Wild West Adventures*. On its bottom shelf, I lovingly recall each of Momma's outsized art books: *Pompeii, Architectural Treasures of France, Every American Child's Sistine, Guido Reni Saints, Holbein's Portraits of English Royals and Notables*. ("Lucille, don't you even *consider* touching these folios with those filthy farm paws. Go wash.")

I now expected that my recent husband, heavy-bodied and silent beside me, would rein horses to a halt. He'd toss a rose-patterned carpetsack onto sidewalk before my homeplace. Maybe he would let me take along tomatoes as my consolation prize.

His tired rich voice would announce, "No hard feelings, Lucille. Sometimes these things work out, occasionally not. In your case, young lady, I fear—not. We will surely be seeing each other around town. We will most certainly say only the most discreet and positive things about each other, will we not? And there's nothing personal in any of it. It's actually been quite real in certain ways. Nobody's fault. Many thanks for your efforts and so forth . . ."

Then I would climb down—feeling as glad as troubled—I would be slow-moving owing to strained muscles at the inner bases of my upper legs. I would gently hoist my satchel full of souvenir soaps and kiddie poems—I'd be careful with the gift tomatoes. I'd walk on mossy bricks betwixt our boxwoods forever trimmed sleek as store-bought cheeses. Up wood steps I'd go into my folks' bright home—without even using the knocker, without even needing to wave back at a man whose buggy'd already creaked off into the dark toward a home legally his. For life I'd live deeply alone as "Jake" "Riceyman" Chow.

But no, Cap kept clucking hired animals directly past. Wait. So. Well. Okay. But, oh dear. Still . . . What'd you expect? But, well—bye-bye, everything usual and smooth!

Child, I fought down wildest feelings. Entire fits got swallowed. A beaver's twiggy dam was spinning in me. Only by force of great will did your Lucy stifle another mudball urge to scream, wake everybody, throw stuff, tantrum-hard. Somewhere beneath my upper ribs, one small green bud of Rage come peeping out, said, "Jump down now. Run, fool. If he tries and stop you, hurt the villain. He's already really wounded you. It'd be self-defense, ain't nobody's fault."

Instead, dignity. Instead, we are definitely moving towards his place. I beg myself to be Reasonable, I nag me in the voice of my own mother. I cannot let no grown man (with actual claims on me) see my head fling back to study the parents' glowing lamps. No way will I jerk around for a last view of our yard, our wide porch, its twelve mismatched rockers. I don't want to seem to notice a upstairs window now dark, a lacy private only child's bedroom that will now stay forever unlit. Vacancy.

Instead to just gaze forward—chin held high, reminding myself what Adult Strength might be going to eventually cost a girl for good.

We approach ex-bachelor Marsden's place. I know it by sight . . . yard joylessly maintained by one helper (alternate Tuesdays). No flowers or shrubs. Front porch without one stick of easy furniture on it. But as we draw near porch light, a odd thing happens. When his house appears ahead and to our left, soon as I understand how somebody's taken care and time (a woman's touch?) to set one candle in each window (tying back drapes so as not to start no fire), once I see magnolia boughs all banked just so around his broad front door, I change.

You do.

Sometimes.

That quick.

Tonight as always, it registers in the body—that's how a person knows it's happening right deep. Some large inward locket swings wide open behind my sternum. "Come in." Air feels cooler in my nostrils. How much older I have grown during ten hard days! Odd that it should make me feel so much more tender towards all the saddening local stuff I see. I do, though. (Child, I now believe that this here tenderness should have been instantly awarded to my own self. But—typical of me, of us gals back then—I instantly turned such benefits right back over to the male-owned world. Like a dowry passing out of my open palm. "Here," I said that night.)

HORSES do a U-turn before Cap's lighted house. I climb on down, slow-moving as somebody lots older than fifteen, but somebody determined. In Atlanta, I'd failed to keep my self from harm. Now I just wanted to guard somebody or something else.

Falls seemed a candidate.

I now saw clear through its sham, its pitiful and stupid sweetness. The narrow comfy too opinionated streets. Even its cruelties, snobbery—the works. And right away, I chose to offer it the pity *I* needed. (Giving myself full credit and sympathy would've shamed me or, worse, it might have driven me mad. It's always been a risk with me. I've fought it steady. When Zondro come in here lately with the poems of a girl, a mother, who stuck her head in the oven and done away with herself before she reached age thirty-two, I shut the book, I told my candy-striper, "This girl's got nothing to teach me. I despise a quitter, especially one with kids sleeping a few rooms off, why, she might've gassed *them*.") No, that first night back, allowed to feel the least bit sorry for myself, I might've flown apart like most anybody weak. I'd soon have been just so much goose down blowing off in ragtag hunks downhill, rolling past Baby Africa's porches, drifting into peanut and to-bacco fields, snagging across dead stubble.

I figured: I will stay on here in town a while. I'll try and shield *it*. And without its even knowing or noticing. I'd do this just to save something. Fresh back, I required a mission. My husband would now manage livestock and his holdings. I'd assign myself this task. I now hobble towards a porch, my satchel and tomatoes pulled against me like parts of a baby sleeping, pitied in my arms. "There, there," I half whispered to bruised tomatoes.

Falls still believes itself to be remarkable, a tad more perfect than any other town this size on earth! (Till right up recent, I'd considered my own self just that secretly remarkable. Silly maybe, but right understandable.) And yet this first night back, I love Falls the way you love a child who's flawed with flaws you know were your flaws first. You figure, *some*thing must be spared. If nothing more than the good story of how it all got lost.

Falls holds itself to be, minimum, a masterpiece of world painting.

(—Darling? you know what? At the very best, it's just one right nice place mat.)

But *I* would never snitch.

And so, if, in telling you the rest of my life spent mostly here, if I sometimes seem to overenjoy our particular little town's littleness—it ain't that I don't *know* no better. Hey, I mean, *I* could've traveled more farther distances than I did. I could've gone more to the north than Norfolk, more southerly than Laurinburg, North Carolina (besides Atlanta *twice*, so far, and in a real aeroplane last time). Why, even later when I ran away from Captain—I dearly hated leaving *it*. If I could've taken this whole place along inside my carpetbag, I would've.

Honeymoon ending, I decide: I will do my level best on the local level— I'll aid the Gateway To The Breadbasket Of et cetera. I will try hiding a rude newfound fact. Finding: You know Falls proper? my home turf and best sidekick? Lucy's lifelong contract and her single decent subject?—why, sugar, *Falls won't even worth writing home about.*

LOOK, don't tell.

16

MY HUBBY hadn't named her street number—Black Town was innocent of curb and guttering and you described paths' twist mostly in relation to wells or trees or river's route. Homes here sprung up like mushrooms in chummy brown clumps, house backs often turned to the path. Unlike Summit with its white manses set even and frontal as perfect teeth.

Black people's dogs came down off porches and barked at me and nipped my hem just the way white folks' animals nattered maids and gardeners wandering uphill to clean white-owned rooms and lawns. "Hi, boy," Lucy said to a particularly nasty half pit bull.

Porches seemed held up with things meant for other uses. I saw a group of broomsticks joined by wire and used to support one eave. Porches were littered with hand-crank wringers for washing clothes. White-owned clothes were stretched on lines everywhere, in rows like soldiers.

Then I saw the place Cap had described as having the two gloomy sons forever on its porch. I saw animal cages stretched around her home's foundation. The shanty was built on six uneasy-looking mounds of bricks (some salvaged from the fiery sight of The Lilacs). The place tilted. Mink cages seemed built of newer wood, tin roofing less rusted than the home's. These cages were covered with window screening the house lacked and I could see long scurrying forms do a quick rush down a twelve-foot straightaway. Pens were built off the ground on sawhorses—barbed wire around each support, keeping neighbor dogs away. Dogs were now only interested at me—smiling—wincing at the center of them, eager to learn more about my help.

In the whole neighborhood I'd seen no female older than twelve or younger than eighty—only men of all ages. All the able-bodied women were uphill fixing lunch for me and mine. Castalia's eldest sons sat on the porch looking out at me. I considered waving but thought better of it. One boy had a face scar—pink and C-shaped—visible from forty feet.

The shanty sat back in a willow grove. Its rear yard sloped towards the river Tar bright to blinding at 11:30 a.m. The front porch held a jungle's worth of houseplants grown into leggy trees and bushes. From one rusted Maxwell House can, I saw geraniums blooming on six-foot stems. Seated amongst this flowery tangle—sons sat very still, hands open on their knees. I just stood here, not waving, not turning back, ignoring the dogs still yapping nearby. Men looked past me. The house stood so far off dirt I could see the river shiny beyond and under it. The whole place soon looked resting on the water like some battered square old boat being tested. The only motors might be them two solemn not-bad-looking fellows who started rocking in their chairs as I watched—pistons charging up for Saturday night. More than onct Cap had rose at 3 a.m. to post bail for one of them.

Behind pots of flowering plants, I saw stacks of signs. Stolen road directions, advertisements. One looked like a ad for Hedgepath's squashes. Signs were used to plug in rotted wood along the house.

As I watched—stooping to pitch a pebble toward a bulldog getting entirely too near my ankles—one son rose, flipped through stacked signs, held up one: "Caution: Men at Work."

He showed it to his brother, whose face told nothing. Then he found another, lifted that my way. "Those Peddling and Soliciting Will Be Prosecuted to the Maximum Extent of the Law."

I waved, smirking—as glad for a joke as the next person. I turned to leave, waving back just to show I'd come by choice and would now go only owing to my own free will. Dogs had let me get in this far but now seemed to block my path and I heard Cas's sons laugh. I swung my handbag at arm's length, hoping this'd seem a show of force, if pitiful. I found a stick and carried that.

When I stepped off the eroded dirt and onto wood sidewalks and found the red-brick herringboned streets that led me back to town, I felt sad at just how pleased I was to be home, white.

I dreaded going back to Cap's huge house right yet. I'd told Castalia I'd be out all day, it'd only make her smug to see me turn up early. The novels—ones my mother had force-fed me as a child—ones I'd come to read out of boredom since married life grabbed me—now seemed dull and easy, too cheap a escape. The wit of Castalia's big boys holding up rude signs—even the sound of dogs still yapping back downhill—those made the smoothness of this painted green world seem too simple.

Today downtown, when gents touched their hat brims, I accepted, said, "Fine morning to you, sir." I took their homage as my mother did, my due. The Chinese tailor was out on the sidewalk showing a bolt of fabric to a customer in honest daylight and they greeted me and I loved being greeted and known and I felt safe. Only my gratefulness let me understand how scared I'd been and still was. I yet felt I had a mission.

I might have resented my husband telling me about his frustrated "honeymoon" at age thirteen with a girl then about my own honeymooning age. But I didn't. I liked him better for admitting it. Made me feel more grown. Made him seem a sight more worthy.

I think that sleeping with my husband had unlocked some tenderness I was not yet ready to award to him alone. So here I was running around looking for someplace to give it, like you give old clothes to the Salvation Army while bragging there's nothing Wrong with them except you're being bored of them.

Wasted, I was, wasted.

I STOPPED by Lucas' and stole something. Had no idea why. The first small thing I could slip into my handbag, it slipped into my handbag. In the alley beside the store, hid behind packing crates and the chopped purple paper fruit came in by train—I checked to see what I'd grabbed. Sardines in oil. I used the can's key, uncoiled the thing and, with my bare hands, fed myself one whole fish at a time—how delicious they were, greasy with amber oil, salty. I craved salt then. I'd been feeling queasy around ten each morning. I stood here slurping down the ill-gotten food. My face must be a slippery mess. I bent forward so as not to get none on my dress front. I wiped hands on boards of Lucas' store siding. I kicked the can under shipping litter and stalked home the back way, sure I must look varnished from that delicious tacky lunch, sure I must look guilty for theft and my confused mission to Baby Africa.

I had told her I'd stay out, gone some place to play. Home early, I'd now wash up a bit, stay busy, silent.

She won't in the kitchen. Bread baked and the whole house smelled yeasty, possible. How bright the day had grown and how relieved I was to find her out somewhere, probably bullying shopkeepers who always treated her like explosives experts brought a sparking black round bomb seen in the funnies constantly.

Going upstairs, feeling shaky, I unpinned my braids, dropped my handbag on the bed and opened the washing-up room door.

Castalia wheeled on me, whole and entire—stripped to the waist, her blouse tucked into skirt's elastic. She was covered with water and soap and high gloss and it was hard to "read" where her arms stopped and neck ended and her breasts began. Prisms confused things further by throwing great tints and rainbow wens across the springy bulk of her. On the counter, violet and lilac soaps I'd saved from the hotel, these laid out like sample candies, most scrubbed down to nothing. How do I describe the great mahogany body, its curves and weights and browning counterweights—all this in a white-tile room to set it off more. For a second I couldn't tell what was what, which a breast, where. Everything seemed locked in spongy rings like soft targets or a Saturn ringed with human breasty flesh. Nipples gave me bearings—they were violent pink and big as drawer pulls or shot glasses, over-turned. Ribs beneath looked muscled as a man's from years of work.

All this I've taken time to describe was mine in a flash and we could both hear the downstairs Seth Thomas go one o'clock. Then I closed the door on her, her mouth left open, I closed the door, taking care I shouldn't slam it, not wanting her to feel she'd been nabbed or judged. The bathroom had been sloppy with tossed water, prism reflections doubled in standing wet. I leaned back against the very door of a room with her in it. I had no breath. There'd been so much of her, seemed my wind all flew out through my eyes trying to embrace or describe. Honey, I might of been some shocked boy. You'd think I'd never laid eyes on a lady's form before, much less *been* one. But in some ways I hadn't. Seen it. Not like that, the real thing.

Our house was so quiet. I could hear her in yonder—recovered—back to ladling the soap off her. I leaned here listening to so light a sound as water dripping off those great smooth shapes.

If, before I headed down to Baby Africa this morning, somebody had said, "Excuse me, Mrs. Lucy, but we're doing a personal survey. See, we have it from a real good source that in something like three hours you'll walk into a room and see your archenemy Castalia without no shirt on and what do you think you're going to *do*, seeing that?" Well, I'd of answered, oh, maybe, "Faint," or "Scream," or "Upchuck!"

I'd of been wrong. I now breathed funny, felt winded like the morning was a preparation. The beautiful four inches that showed in her face was just Coming Attractions for this bulk hid lavish under colorful wraps.

I told myself it was only the surprise element that'd got me.

I now dashed downstairs, pinning hair back up, trying to give her room for drying off, regaining dignity.

I settled at the kitchen table, feeling lonely and shy, face still greasy as a cat caught eating fish. Agitated. Hearing her slow creak down the steps, how old her footfalls sounded, and yet how full of promise her mammoth younger body seemed. I placed my hands on the table. I dreaded ever seeing her again, especially with clothes all on. I dreaded speech. I wanted to tell her every little thing that'd befell me since I left the house.

My each breath skimmed just a dime's worth from every dollar's lungful. I pressed knees together. She hurried to her stove like that was her home plate and safe, the redbirds clean and cheap and perfect and secret with a meaning that was hers only.

Then, leaning back against black cast iron—hands braced on its cool top—she turned on me. The front of her orange blouse was wet and this made me sick—no, not sick, but something. I *wanted* to breathe. I just couldn't remember—between breaths—how.

Seemed I had to talk. I would tell her how I'd gone downhill and seen her handsome oldest sons, I'd praise their looks, yeah, what momma could resist that?

"I . . . went and saw your big boys."

"*That* what you calls them?" she said, and laughed.

Oh Lord. It was something, the size of her laugh, big as a working two-man saw. It came out of her whole—everything she'd been saving back. As mean as she had acted, that'd been just the back side of this part ringing towards me now, like all Falls' church bells. When I saw the fun of this, how she didn't even mind my blundering in on her, that she won't the least bit ashamed of using keepsake soap or bathing during workhours, I said, "Your big boys, yeah, a good one." I laughed. I felt weak then weaker, hands over my face, sucking air, but grateful.

After seeing her, after eating them sardines, after cackling so, I slipped upstairs, faint but grateful. How strange I'd felt of late, a kind of secret fizzing in my lower body. I now slept, but woke at dusk to see a man's shape looming over me. I snatched up the covers, half-hid. "Sources tell me you were strolling all over Niggertown in a great mess of barking dogs, presumably down there looking for her home, am I correct in this?"

I told him I'd been curious. "Curiosity," he bent and whispered at my neck in a way I didn't like, "curiosity killed the cat and also the pussy. What have you two been doing behind my back here all day? You think I can't smell something when I come home from work?" I told him I had no idea what he meant. I told him walking Falls' streets was my right. I told him I had nothing else to do. He said I would, very soon. He planned to purge the house of her. He said I *represented* him. No wife of his was going to be nipped at by hounds down there. I would be occupied with cleaning now, with cooking now. I explained that, true, she interested me, but nothing else. I dreaded saying that I'd caught her lathered, that the spread of her had stirred and scared me—and sickened me a little—but had scared and stirred me too. Darling? I didn't yet know him good enough to level with him yet. I hadn't told him about missing two periods. I'd asked nobody what that meant. I wondered would I die and where the leaving blood stayed put, and I suspected, don't laugh at me, child, cancer. Being fifteen, my first thought, as he strode downstairs and fired my valuable ally in this big barn (that's what she now seemed), my thought ran: I will die of cancer and, boy, *he'll* be sorry.

I stole halfway down the broad staircase and listened as he told this woman he'd known since birth, he'd owned since birth and then lost then hired, "I'll write you an excellent letter of reference." "How long a one?" she asked, and made me wonder. He didn't answer and I guessed she was having him on someway. "You sacking me for what I didn't do," she said. "Three-quarters pay till I find something better or even not. Them's my terms, slughead. Don't and you looking at Miss Mouth."

He said that sounded fair. What did she have over him? He asked if she needed help moving her stuff, and Castalia told him to send for her boys and to lend them one of Cap's rental wagons and a mule. "When you wanting me out you house, sir?" "Now would be nice. You and her, it's a very bad mix. No hard feelings. Nobody's fault." "No?" she said, and the great clatter of cookware started and our back door slammed and the fruitwood Seth Thomas chimed 7 p.m. and I moved down the steps and towards her.

I was a brave little girl. She had supper simmering deep in the closed slots of the black stove and I come and stood there in the open doorway.

"I heard," I said. Castalia was alone in the kitchen.

I was very tired but I braced anyway, expecting physical assault. I stood here, almost wanting it. She started to unload her private closet. I knew every item in there and I guessed how, tomorrow morning, the sight of that space empty would make me feel way lonelier than now even. It seemed like she hadn't heard me but—light-headed—I grabbed a kitchen chair and pulled it away from the table. I didn't want to look like some employer waiting to be fed. The lamp needed lighting. I dared not move. I heard neighbors talking over the back-yard fences two yards down and laughing. It was the cicadas' one-in-seven-year appearance and they were making their insane, building noises all over town. There was enough ruddy light left to show me a packing maid, and when she glanced over here, all her fury at me was missing. I'd ceased mattering. Punishing and testing me now seemed part of her former job description maybe. For one second I wondered if the Captain put her up to it, some torture meant to form me faster as a tough little adult. She wrapped her mink-raising handbook in a clean striped rag and tucked it in a cardboard box and I saw she'd packed most everything except the clear bottle with the liquid and the skull-and-bone warning.

"What'll you *do*?" I asked. She shook her head, made a sound like some steam iron snorting to life. "Sit." "Sounds nice." "You oughts to know." But all the edge was missing from that tone I'd got to know so good.

I considered saying, "Will you show me how to make a omelette?" but thought better of it. Instead I heard a girl ask one departing older woman, seasoned enough to be the girl's great-grandma, "What does it mean when the person misses two sets of monthlies and the sight of food makes her want to turn kind of inside out? And, Cassie, it's like this big horse pill is dissolving down in here, like kind of burning or bubbling. What *does* that mean?"

I saw her turn. I saw her arms cross and then unfold so either wrist now rested, fond, on either hip. She shook her head sideways once, so hard she swayed whilst saying, "White people!"

And before she grabbed (I knew she would) the bottle full of toxic gin-clear liquid, before she guzzled that, a huge woman—just a bulgesome silhouette in this room full of early evening—she stepped before my chair and told me (without once lifting hands off hips to demonstrate the ins and outs) all about what went where and what swam towards a what and how long it took to ripen into humanhood and what a fetus two months old would have and not have on it and roughly when I could expect it, and what humans felt like, coming out of humans.

How still things got then, even the cicadas tapered down a bit. First words I said after learning all that in a few solemn phrases and knowing my delivery date, said, "And you won't be here." Then I hid my face behind my hands. I couldn't help it. She had more on her mind than silly me, but oh this house would seem a jail without her in it with me.

When palms parted, I saw her back at the closet, heard clicks and grunts and saw her upper body heave back and a glint and she was drinking that whole bottle down and I was now a leopard in the air. I was not on feet but leaping from the sitting position to the falling and I'd got her massy ankles and I pulled her down as the bottle shattered against a far enameled wall. The sound of her full weight coming down against and beside me (but not *on* me, proper, Lord be praised) was weirdly gentle—plop drub thump thump—like rain, or water boiling.

"Whoof, girl," she said. "You done spoilt my brew."

"No, *poi*son, spit it out. We're not worth that."

She told me it was moonshine brewed out on The Lilacs from stolen corn, by slaves around 1860. She'd been saving it, disguised, the way maids will, as cleaning fluid. Now I'd spilled it. Had I gone through her things? Must've, if I'd seen the markings. "Yes, ma'am," I said. I finally told her not to forget her crucifixion amongst the staples high on yonder counter.

I kept waiting for the old anger. I expected to be blamed for the firing and the spillage and for knowing way too little. Instead, her voice was lighter and less crabbed, far younger than I'd ever heard it. I asked her, bold— having gotten big answers already tonight—what the redbird meant and who this Reba was and would I ever meet her and might she, Castalia, ever come for supper once I learned to cook some? "Fat chance," she laughed, cynical but merry.

Maybe fumes from spilt corn liquor made us drunk a bit, the room reeked as she answered me, told me odds and ends, my first corners of the story of how a girl from Africa with great expectations *feels* waking up as body servant to the likes of my hubby and his persnickety intelligent momma. My bone side was slatted against her dough-sponge side. I some way smelled of mineral oil and day-old underclothes and a touch of vanilla extract. She smelled of moonshine and of asters.

There's a seam where the bitter and the lovely join, and her voice, her scent, her size all seemed tonight right there. And she was just beginning to explain—off duty—I should've *seen* the expression on my own face when my hairbrush lost its bristles, she was just conceding that—as a torturee and house slave—I hadn't been com*plete*ly without some kind of aptitude, when we heard this stirring in the hall, a muttering that locked us both and caused us to half-cling to one another among broken glass and puddled corn brew, when here came a lit lantern, held by the house owner, him followed by two gloomy young black men.

When Captain entered his own kitchen, stepped on glass, smelled booze in pools and saw it fringing drips down the walls, when he found two females clutching on the floor beside the stove, he took one step backward and said,

"Mother of God." Someway it struck us as funny, his shock. Made us giggle some, two girls.

And as we saw the color leave a face beside the lamp's smudged flue, Cas thought to call, "Get them cigars ready, Poppa-daddy." First he didn't understand. Then I was pointed to. "She gravid."

"That helps. A little," he said. The men were offering hands so we might stand again and she was soon gone. I heard him walk her to the wagon waiting on Summit. Sons carried out her personal effects. I was left here with the lamp in a kitchen full of broken glass and, seeing the broom yonder, being—preg, fifteen—a regular little Cinderella, child, I started cleaning up my kitchen for my life.

A WHILE BACK, when you first started coming and see me, you said I ought to spill my tidbits for "history's sake." Oh, I don't need that big a excuse. I like talking. Only got one subject: what happened next. Besides, "History," who's she? I been breathing a while, never met her once. I just saw people waking up for work and hoping to doze those twenty minutes extra. Later, *you* traipse in by the back door—loaded with names and dates and reasons. Then all that's up in front of you appears to be history.

But at the time, child, history's just keeping your rooms neat and hoping company'll give you a little notice so you can tuck your extras under the bed. What you call history is really just the luxury of afterwards. History is how food the soldiers gobbled at 11 a.m. sets with them at two when the battle starts, how one snack's heartburn changes everybody's aim. Honey, history ain't so historical. It's just us breaking even, just us trying.

Darling, you know what history is?

History is lunch.

BOOK TWO

Time

Does

That

Simon's Splendid
Pocket Watch,
Its Fate

*Now faith is the substance of things hoped
for, the evidence of things not seen.*

—HEBREWS 11:1

C AP HE TOLD ME over time in many ways and tries, this. Man
said:

THEY'D GET too close, Lucille. You'd yell for them to stay back. They
wouldn't. You saw they had their muskets ready. Officers forced you to or
perhaps knowing that all your friends nearby were watching. Maybe just
the scariness of another body rushing over the hill at you. You could see
their faces. It might well be a nice face. Frequently it was. Two of my three
were a good deal better-looking than myself, which I admit is not that
difficult. One had a pipe clenched in his teeth. I took it out and slipped it
in his tunic. Seemed only decent. The boy that gave me his pocket watch,
his features were regular and plain. He had silver-blond hair and not just
the yellow-blond sort which is certainly nice enough. Afterwards, every time,
I bent down and checked. I felt it was my manly duty, recollecting the
features of each fellow I shot.

At that age, what did I know? I mean they trained us to. The Lieutenant
said, "Don't pull on your trigger so hard, son, not to jerk it, Willie, that'll
knock your sights all off. Just squeeze it, squeeze it like you love it, like
you'd squeeze your gal back home. You do believe in love, boy? As a gent,
you do *love* something, right, son?"

"Yes, sir!" I barked.

In those times, a boy thirteen was bashful as a child now might be, oh,
say around seven. Imagine—seven and out shooting strangers. Before the
war, my father wouldn't let me fire at quail. I couldn't even target-practice

the bottles (nice green ones) lined along a wall behind our lilac hedge. Poppa said no boy should hunt before he'd shaved. A razor hadn't touched my chin yet, and I had already killed three. I sense that you think less of me for that, but I'll explain, girl, I'll venture to.

You can be innocent of knowing about the birds and bees and so forth, and still manage shooting others effectively. Wartime was not a bit like what your schoolbooks doubtless try and tell you, Lucy. One thing, it was far and away muddier. To recall, it seems Virginia and Maryland were mud puddles with state capitals. We had far less food than anybody admits. Half of our division—the ones left standing—suffered scurvy by the end. You hear how an army moves on its stomach? Well, in that case, for the last two years we had, as you might put it, not a leg to stand on. We got corn pulled out of any field we passed (farmers and their children stood right in the road too, begging us not to steal it). We ate dandelion greens. Bad food, plus being fairly often scared my three years in, it meant at night I'd sit up in my blanket. A chopping noise had waked me. I'd come to smiling, Lucille, I believed the sound was my own bossy mother having servants cut up apples to be pies in our home kitchen. But it was simply my new adult teeth chattering. I would stretch back out, eyes open, arms locked against my sides. I'd get quite spastic, shivering so, and in July.

Antietam Creek, they named the battles after nearby bodies of water, villages, and churches. By then I was an old hand. My first few months in I had missed my folks' farm but—after even half a year—it got so I'd lay awake missing the time when I *missed* everything the most. I was so young, the last thing that happened seemed the largest thing of all.

Had a plunge-loading flintlock, adult-sized, unlike me. You come to and it's already in progress. You'd find yourself resting belly-down in a fairly comfortable ditch. I became a connoisseur of gullies, holes, burrows like rodents might enjoy. "A good hole." Rebs fought each other for first dibs on the perfect gully. A decent makeshift grave, hand-dug, might, if picked correctly, keep you out of yours a little longer. And it is in just such a rut, with other soldiers bent double or hunched flat, dodging mostly left to right before your view, it's there, in sight of the Dunkers' church, that you spy one stiff-legged fine-looking Yankee boy. Notable because he's coming right along the farm fence and towards your chosen hole here. "Hey," you call clear across the meadow at the soldier fated for you. "Hey, this spot is mine. I dug it and am in it, go away, or else."

But the fine boy in blue acts deaf. He moves nearer. In a type of trance. So, go ahead—chuck a handy rock at him, Lucille. Better that than a more permanent volley. You do, the stone strikes him quite effectively on his upper leg. Not noticing, he comes right on.

He's one of dozens, hundreds out there—but he has your name on him. You see it. Your battle happens on this afternoon in a meadow full of flowers—seems odd. How the bees and monarch butterflies don't notice one thing strange. They fly, busy, in circles from flower to weed among the blurred lines of bullets. One big yellow farm dog, dragging its broken rope, pads everywhere, nose down, tail going. Yesterday this was a pasture, mostly his. The field's being beautiful makes combat here (using that beauty to be cover) seem a good deal less necessary, my girl. The stillness of the hot day makes this scrambling feel uglier and crabbier, smaller. There's such a thing as knowing when to quit but, uh-oh, that blond boy has been lockstepping, he has marched twenty-two feet closer since we checked last.

"Turn back," you cup hand to mouth. "Look, do, because, or else, see?"

To be thirteen, underfed, so subject to long fits of nervous shakes. And now his rifle has shifted, its butt moves against his shoulder as he strides. There is the minute when you doubt you can think straight, followed by a sharp second when—to live, you know you must. You have been trained to squeeze that trigger like it's everything you love. You'd best fire now. In deciding not to shoot, you're opting not to live a minute longer. Is that what you want, is it, Lucy?

Okay then, give a warning shot. You'd better. You tell yourself, while mashing a beloved musket into place, barrel steady on your ditch's bank, "This is just a way of wishing that one sleepwalking soldier elsewhere, not dead, more just *gone*."

His gun is fixed right on your head. Two ticklish inches between your eyes know this. You wince a bit and fire above him. Doesn't even slow the fucker down. Excuse me. His face stays very dull and you holler at it, "I told you, go back, last chance, don't make me."

You shut both eyes after using them to the very best of your ability, to aim, I mean. It's really just one closing of one forefinger. Don't jerk, mustn't jerk. Squeeze. How smartly guns are made—so little does so much. Off it bucks against you. Musket's kick forever makes you, the shooter, feel, for one bruised second, shot.

Peeking, you feel surprised then proud, then scared, and finally shamed to see your chosen boy heave sharply left and sharp backwards. His small cap and long musket go in opposite directions, landing among clumps of black-eyed Susans.

One blue uniform now rests face-up, heaving, blinking in a meadow that's all blooming yellow-gold and green. Around him, others run, aim, scream, grab themselves, rush off. The farm hound trots over, sniffs the fallen boy and—tail wagging—lumbers away, paws huge, tongue out, happy. Your hurt soldier's face looks fine, his chest not. Face dry, chest wetly opened in its upper right. You see this as he tries to prop himself on either elbow, and looks down at his chest as if staring a great distance. Then he gets interested, squinting toward this ditch of yours, a location where a crucial shot has flown from. Uh-oh. With his hat lost, blond hair standing in a funny crest, he tries standing, finds that too hard then starts to crawl this way. Really uh-oh. Bad tactics. He appears rational but puzzled by the logic of events that dropped him on his back and opened his young chest. Now, to yourself, safe behind your fringe of ditch-bank weeds and Johnny-jump-ups, you say simply, "Don't." You see he's not yet felt the full pain of being hit. He will, you know. You know this without pleasure, full of bitterness for him, though you yourself just shot him. Lucille? *you* figure all this out. I will simply tell it plainly and fast.

Earlier, while walking, a target, his face looked very vacant. Downed, it is all lit up with this strange intelligence, a care. Features are smarting but the pain seems almost some social embarrassment. Officers surely taught him *never* to move upright during firing, *always* dodge while advancing, do obliques, think obliques. Now he's shaking his head sideways, perhaps remembering the rules as he drags over here. Either elbow pulls the upper body. He's talking to himself and there's an expression like a smile, but not a smile. You hoot instructions, try and guide him back toward his own lines. Under his pulled weight, a trail of wildflowers flatten. It's terrible to see his pale grin as he gets nearer—like he's recognized you. You picture yourself out there. Just now, a running Yankee tramples one whole leg of him. Volleys keep detonating left and right. He's about to crawl directly into cross fire, he's about to get his goddam head blown off. Excuse me.

And here we go, Lucille, here's part I never manage to understand. It's from your being thirteen perhaps. It's pure insanity as you find somebody like yourself—but far, far stupider—leaping from your ditch's safety, running through the noisy open, hollering at this boy (far bigger up close), "Here, let me." He sees gray above him, scrambles backward, squeals, pats all around him, finds his musket's too far off, grabs a rock instead, holds this up—his eyes too huge to bear—tries tossing it. The thing falls inches short, of course. He keeps crying up at you, "No more. No more now, sir."

"Let me. Really. Here," which means setting down your musket as you get a grip, as, without permission, you pull this boy to safety. Seeing how his chest is opened, you have grabbed him boot-first. You pull him face-up by either long leg—he is bouncing, groaning from the pain of being dragged. Till the both of you fall backwards, you in first, gasping, grateful, it's your ditch again. Just then cannons really start and a great din of battle roars over where he was. And you look out to where your musket is. Oh dear.

What the fuck have you done? Pardon me, miss. Separated from your rifle, you've just pulled a Yankee stranger in this hole with you, is what. A mouse drags a cat through the small slit into its very home and has to know then it is certainly a stupid mouse and probably quite soon a dead one too!

You both hear you're both panting. Even above the pumping of lead over the ditch you occupy—the sound of troubled breath, your own, means most. You are very scared to look directly at each other. Terrified, no doubt, for different sets of reasons but both sets quite likely very good. It hurts to turn your neck but finally you do, so slow in hopes that—hand to hand— he won't now try to kill you back. Disarmed, in a hole, two boys, one hurt, one less so, stare at each other. Your mouths are both open like screaming, but they're embarrassed to make sounds while doing so. You see how, up close, the other kid has blond-silver hair, thick dark eyebrows, spiky lashes.

This is plain since these eyes are definitely on you. His damaged right arm and shoulder shake, St. Vitus, uncontrolled. You recognize your own nighttime teeth chomping.

Then you do something pitiful. You smile at him. It is a disgusting display but all you can think of. He says, "Some mess, hunh?"

He chances grinning in hopes you won't do him worse harm. The Yankee's sweating a lot, clear drops are set side to side across his forehead. He seems to know where he is and how he erred by becoming so willing a target. He seems to feel that he will now—for his mistakes—be killed. Soon. Maybe bayoneted. With one red palm, he covers his weird smile. But he doesn't apologize or plead. He hasn't yet noticed how, in saving him (from your own shooting him), you dropped your musket way, way out there in the harmful open.

As a sign, you hold up both your hands toward him—palms foremost, wrists exposed to prove you mean no harm, not *now*. Not now you've probably killed him once. Enough. Some mess all right. Does he even know that it was you who plugged him? You hope he'll blame most anybody else.

Missing your cartridge belt, powder, rifle, you turn and see those out there sunning among daisies, you just say, "Boy."

Then he notices that you're disarmed as he is. You want to ask advice. "Would it be all that dumb to dive back out in open fire and try for it?" Space above this ditch now coughs and whistles, it's fairly stuttering with flying damage far too quick to see but oh you hear it. Smoke leaves traces till it's like looking up out of a basket made of smoke. Some mess you're in.

Jangled, and despite yourself, you feel a need to explain or ask. You tell your predicament to somebody you just blasted into a state a good deal worse than yours. He tells you it'd be risky to go back for the gun but adds as how, considering, he *would* say that, and grins a form of laugh.

You look at him and snort appreciation for a little wit out here in this shithole situation. Excuse me. Some shithole. "Yeah, you *would* tell me not to." And you feel freer to confess what an idiot you've been. "Why'd I do that? Hester *told* us." And your guest nods, eyes half shut, "Me too. Till five minutes back, I thought I was fairly smart. Thing is, you freeze, you know?"

In order to hear him better, you'd best slide inches nearer but, check first, is there a knife on him? The kid keeps clawing at his tunic's dampening front, maybe trying to stanch the wound. You say, "Look, uh, you won't hurt me if I help you out here, right?"

"No," he, fifteen or so, says back. "Can't now . . ." So you bend across, undo his each brass button, holding your own breath all during, closing your eyes, like the hole you opened in his chest might send out one gruesome smell.

He fumbles for some item in his uniform's sogged right and then out into summer daylight pulls a very large gold pocket watch. The chain follows, crackling beady sounds. How it shines in the sunshine in this muddy hole.

Just from how he holds it you can see it really is a good one. First he wipes a bit of his own grape-tinted gore off its yellow casing and onto his driest sleeve. Then, greedy, the kid presses a timepiece against one whole ear. Finally he nods, eyes closing from pleasure. "Johnny Reb didn't even scratch it," he says, hurting your feelings some. He tells you how his father left it to him. His voice is just becoming manly, starting to break and deepen.

Six great explosions rock your hiding place. The boy barely notices.

"Look." Instead he presses some latch and the watch's gold lid springs open—yellow light, a coin's worth, swings across his face. Chimes play three bars of a hymn. Harmony and all. The owner smiles. Above cannons' rumbling and the shouts of others, over that farm dog's barking, you get this sweet tense little chiming. It makes you flinch. Pleasure seems completely out of place. You feel your own face strain and break, unused to really smiling. You've all but forgotten melody since your friend got killed.

"Plus, look." He wants to show you something. Just then a cannonade, the worst yet, pelts everything nearby and overturns a length of fencing. Dirt clods pepper you. When smoke clears, the Yankee (you're starting to think of him as *your* Yankee) is still staring at the watch. You see how his eyes wear tossed grit, it's all across their fronts. He looks from you to the watch, unaware of dirt in eyes. Tell him to blink. Ask his name. "Simon," he says and does blink, good-natured. "Nice picture on the lid." He shows you a hunting scene, enameled (one stag chased by six eager hounds). Above the swerving second hand, a small compass proves due north—a Yankee watch okay. And under that the phases of the moon are gauged in a slot. Spiky letters say the thing was made in Germany. It looks it.

He thanks you for pulling it and him to safety and you don't correct him. He holds the watch against his ear and nods, pleased with its ticking, as if eavesdropping on his own continuing heart. He talks some and you see that his spittle has blood in it. You are close enough to offer your canteen. This means pouring water into his cracked mouth. Afterwards, not recalling how you managed (apart from rank adrenaline), you two kids just talk. Seems natural. He mentions sledding, how he loves it and is considered pretty good at home. You try a joke on him.

Q: Why does the ocean stay real mad?

A: Because it has been crossed so many times.

Simon starts to laugh (he's Private Simon Utt from Malden, Massachusetts), but then the laugh falls back in on itself, it hurts him to, so he nods. You wonder how it happened: You two's winding up in this same rut in Virginia. You all should be in school, not here, and he agrees. Your complaints are similar: rotten recent food, one earlier flesh wound quickly healed (you mention your leg because it'll maybe make Simon feel better about *his* now being hurt). He speaks of a mother and three sisters. Then he seems to sleep but wakes describing the house, the sisters' bell-ringing choir. His late poppa was a preacher, bought the watch in Germany, went to seminary there. Simon praises one big icy slope near his home. Winters, a boy can sled down it and be carried—lickedy-split—half a mile, easy.

This ditch was your home six hours before you dragged him into it. Strange, but it feels such a relief to talk, even to this unexpected type of company. Odd, your hole (nobody would understand it) almost seems safer now for Simon's being in it. One boy from each side. Maybe he's talking too much, using up his life to speak of fishing through holes cut in the ice of winter ponds. Surely is hot out here. Then, after seeming to sleep, Simon asks if he might ask you one big favor, huh? Will you make sure—if anything should happen to him, not that it will—promise to get his timepiece here sent home safe? Simon says his best friends would do this but some got transferred, hurt or worse. Anyway, he might not be found here in a Southern ditch and all. So *would* you, huh? And he tells you which trouser pocket holds a home address. He admits—head trying not to quake so much—he's getting real scared now.

You agree to mail the watch but say he'll come out of this just fine. You add you're never wrong about these things. "Say you will?" he begs.

"I will. Honest."

"Say that you'll get out their address and see it's buttoned in your pocket? Buttoned."

"Sure. You bet, Simon. Word on it."

"Uh-oh, hold my hand, please," and you do. By now you're so much *for* Simon, you know? "Hold it, please. Play like we're at home. Say you'll get it there. Having it will help them. Having something. Say we're home, Will."

"You're safe at home. You've got somebody here. I'll guard this damn watch with my life, Simon. You see if I don't. You sure found the right person."

Simon nods then and his spine arches till it's straight. He rears up into sun. He mumbles about sleds, a hill, is it hot out here or is it just him? "Here we go," he says, then his nose is pink and it's a terrible nosebleed.

Worse than that.

To see us from above the ditch, Lucy, it'd look like two wrestling—a Reb and a Yank, young, thrashing one another good. But it's just me holding him for dear life. Putting hands where he's least hurt and hugging there. You hear it run out, like a fuel going. Then you can release him. You can admire the thick dark lashes and the brows and keep the flies off for a while and see the fronts of eyes where life shows wittiest, the fronts that soon cloud over to be just surfaces, like the ground nearby, the roots of weeds along the ditch. No better, no worse.

The dog bounds past and then runs off, its tie rope sogged in gore the rope's dragged through. A voice nearby says, "Sara? This is it, Sara. Sara?" And then there is a great yelling and it is too loud and unembarrassed for a man's and you guess as how the farm dog has got his. Shells toss great buckling geysers of black earth. In the silence after, in the char of cannon

stink, you smell a clover sweetness, you hear bee wings going in the ditch-
bank flowers, bees still out here, workaday busy instead of staying in their
hives during this field's one day of war. There's a Dunkers' church set down
there on the creek at meadow's bottom and a marksman chooses to fire at
its bell. Then others do until you're hearing Hester holler at your pals, fools,
don't waste rounds on bronze, for God's sake. He says get ready to advance.
Soon you are going to have to leave this ditch and Simon.

You can now have this beautiful watch and you feel guilty for it but
glad. The address is still there in his pocket. Simon's mouth hangs open.
His right cheek rests flush to brown ditch bank and is muddied. The pink
face has lost no rosiness, not yet. Near his left hand, high up by the collar
you unbuttoned, he still grips his preacher father's timepiece. He's kept it
clear of his own darkening lower clothes. You unsnag the long gold chain
from around pale fingers already locking. For the address, you must reach
directly into poor Simon's britches. He has fouled himself. It is embarrassing
and exceedingly unpleasant to reach into the pocket of another boy. Especially another one who's dead and you helped kill. No, not "helped"—
"killed" outright. Remember that. A woman's name and street facts are
written on a scrap of blue envelope, simple block letters, his—preparing for
emergency. Into your breast pocket you commend this scrap, buttoning as
he said do. For good measure—best to tip over, listen closer for his heart.
A person never knows. This is what the doctors do in books. Then, yes, your
eyes closed to concentrate, you do hear the faintest almost singing knock.
He's back! Company. Until you understand, no, it's the lovely heavy German
watch you're clutching in one hand, that sweats. Pocket the timepiece. Its
weight is that of two good-sized hen's eggs, it has that same sturdy-fragile
cool feel.

Voices you know now discuss moving. From one ditch quite nearby,
it's good old Sal Smith hollering your name. Fun to call, "Alive, Sal! Here!"

"Well, knock me over with a feather," Sal barks back. "You got through
it!"

"Yeah. Through it," you cry back. "Some mess, huh?"

"Say that again."

"Some mess."

"Card!"

NOT KNOWING what else to do, you prop Simon Utt (nobody you know
knows him at all or understands what-all has happened here, and that is
fine, that will help save your soldier's reputation, consorting with the enemy
and all), get him vertical against the ditch's edge. That way he'll look natural
and dignified while waiting for Northern gatherers to find him. Cross his
arms over the chest (because adults do that with bodies, though you're not
sure why, but you do it anyway). Make sure the boy's head shows up above
this hollow's flowered lip. He's got to be discovered if he's to get Christian

burial. Something should be said now but it's hard recalling even one stray tag of liturgy.

Others bellow for you. "Moving out," they call. Lieutenant Hester, usually so calm, sounds hoarse from yelling.

First, though you're no Catholic, make the sign of the cross—over your own front and then his. Touch Simon's forehead, his regulation belt buckle, then press opposite shoulders, including his wettest one. Close his mouth. Ease his head back against flowers that flatten from this much dead weight. Using your right thumb, press down each eyelid. Since there is a batter of dirt mixed across the white and blue of either eye, first use one of your sleeves to wipe grit out. "There."

At home before the war, you buried dead pets in Poppa's cigar boxes under Mother's lilacs, each creature important beneath its two crossed sticks. You have no other burying experience. Your division is leaving you, there's a roll call hole to hole. You killed this boy. Why lie? And there's a human need to speak something out loud. And, though alone now, you feel stage fright as if listened to by him and his whole family. You try, "Private Simon P. Utt. It could've been me. We didn't either of us mean it, did we? They just put us out here, so we did. I *will* get your watch home. Cross my heart and . . . cross my heart. I'm sorry now for what I did here. Boy, I never should've joined up. *This* happens. Now I see clearer, but I'll do right by you, Simon. Bye and . . . amen? Sure, amen."

Are the watch and address fastened in your breast pocket? With one hand cupped over those for good measure, scramble up across your ditch's edge and out into lethal air. You hustle, doubled small, then opening with rangy speed into this space. It seems like you were born and have always lived till now inside that flower-bordered hole. Running, you're feeling like some released animal, almost a dancer and perfect. Rush toward the musket and the belt you grab while running. Moving well you are, these things are warmed from sunlight. Startling to find them hot as a person is alive. Due east, a woods is burning black and gold. You stumble into a clearing behind other men who, looking over shoulders, half smile, cough your name as welcome. They *know* you! It's still you, to look at anyway.

What you've done to him, it doesn't show yet.

FROM your new hollow ninety feet nearer a smoking woods, you can easily look back across the meadow. You can easily see just where you were with him and where he—facing straight toward you—still sits.

You avoid noticing a poor yellow dog's legs-up remains.

Instead concentrate on the old hole. It calms you to stare—above the fringe of golden grasses, flowers, and butterflies—monarchs and cabbage ones—to see Simon's bright hair, his funny crest moved by breeze so it seems almost alive, and, hey, it could be, couldn't it?

Take out his watch, your watch, a luxury in hand. You wait for orders.

How smooth this metal feels. You can see how the soft gold has been nicked by years of use. Open it to hear the chimes, a pretty human sound like some toy shop has just opened on a battlefield.

Your new hole rests four hundred miles due northeast of your folks' farm. You are still thirteen, you take a risk, you hold the watch up so Simon'll see that it's still fine. Working. Miniés are yet firing here and there. A coarse "whoosh" you've almost learned to love since Sal said: Every one you hear: it hasn't killed you! (though you do recall the sound of that one going in your leg).

Now you risk your arm to prove to him his watch is safe. You hold it into air that's worrisome and cross. Chain dangling, you squeeze the watch like it's most everything you love. "See?" you call. No answer. Then you do something you know is pretty dumb. You yourself stand up. Whole. You pop up vertical long enough to get hit if you're going to. And just so you can wave towards him better, show his watch to him, your watch. His hair's so real-looking. It *is* real, stupid, human hair, just not alive. You get the shakes then. You want to tell somebody about what happened, it's nobody's fault. Sit down. You've done your duty. The watch is a good watch and it lives with you now.

"I will be worthy of Simon's watch, Simon." In the middle of Antietam you speak this to the watch. And toward the corpse you made a corpse, you wave, you holler, "Over here, Simon. Look. It's me. It's me."

2

NOW, my dimplenook, daffodil, and listener, to tell the rest myself. Slipping into something more comfortable. Doing *his* wears me down. The responsibility! Soon as I say a line that has the old man's exact and factual ring, soon as I do one sentence with his own low-gravity weights and balances, I decide, "Well, at least *that's* just like him." Then the next three get thrown all off. Ask me to imitate most any soul on earth but his and him. Our kids used to try and bribe me to do Jolson, going down on one knee—a mammy praising Mammy. I'm a sight better at the voice of FDR—complete with blue wireless's static and that warm brown bourbon/maple running safe underneath, "My fellow Americans . . ." Better at Mr. Roosevelt than at doing my own man I lived and battled with so long. Still, truth is, I'm closer to sounding like Captain Marsden than anybody else is—not that there's a heap of competition.

Same evening of the afternoon when Will exposed hisself to major miniés to prove to Simon that the mainspring had stayed sprung, he settled near his company's bonfire. It'd got built one mile from the meadow where the young body was yet stiffening in one hole of it. Will commenced writing a long letter to a Mrs. Utt. Will redone the thing fully four times till it come near to sounding right concerned and a bit official.

Dear Mrs. Utt,

Something bad happened on the afternoon of September Seventeenth, 18 and 62. It was in a field close by near here. He was square in the line of duty when your son Simon (Utt) lost his brave young life. He sure was defending his own country when that happened and I am going to try and tell you more how it came to pass, see . . .

Didn't it seem strange to Will—taking so Federal a tone with this far-off widow? During the whole war, Marsden had only wrote his own momma around ten times and each try took him many days. But this felt weirdly natural, spending so much time over one piece of mail. Seemed a fellow's duty to, even if these particular grieving strangers happened to be the worst kind, Yankee ones.

Will hunkered nearer his fireside friends. To them, he read the thing aloud. He skipped the victim's name. He asked did the letter sound like somebody older than thirteen had wrote it? Sure, they said.

Young Marsden, concentrating, tongue pressed between beaver teeth, used a borrowed pen and ink bottle, he'd tried describing young Simon's last earthly moments. Will told Mrs. Utt how her boy's final thoughts had been of his family, which was true enough. The note never did get around to mentioning who'd shot young Simon. How could a single letter tell: how a good Yank and one okay Reb wound up in the selfsame ditch, see? and how they never really tried no strangling of each other but instead had a good long talk? Will hisself hardly understood this, so he surely couldn't try and spell it out for some grown lady he'd never met.

Staring into flames, Will wondered what he'd answer if some court-martial pressed him: "Why didn't I try and *keep* hurting him?" Private Marsden explained it this way in his head: The shooting happened *before* them two spirited youngsters got introduced and all, see? Before they knew each other and joked around, talked stuff over. Otherwise it wouldn't have.

So, true, Marsden did announce the death but failed to mention the killer's exact name. It was wartime. Nobody expected to know just who shot who. Someday he would have to fess up to this act maybe. But, Will told hisself, the whole story could only be spoke aloud to the Rev. Utt's widow and daughters face to face. The brunt of total news seemed too much for one lightweight page to bear up North now.

I picture my Willie, hunched over a writing board at the fire's far edge. Paper was in short supply and so (true to the custom of the time) he cross-wrote the letter, lines working like a plaid of woven words. The lost picture of him from then showed a kid looking plenty unloved. Thirteen, he appeared younger, boy was freckles' very convention center.

Seeming made mostly of cartilage, he was one of them boys with sleep crusted in the corners of their eyes and it stayed there till some adult said wipe it. Few fellow soldiers cared enough to notice. None past Sal, and sometimes dashing Hester. Mirrors scare boys this age. With good reason. Many things scare them. War and puberty befell poor Willie almost at once. Put it this way: You have seen my husband. Around every swimming pool or pond in present-day America, just at five o'clock closing time, down near water's edge, you've spied a kid skin and bones, eleven years old (actually a young thirteen). His arms are coiled around his chest, his teeth just knocking in his head, them lips are hinting toward the bluish, his dough-white skin's drawn up knotty as a plucked duck's skin after a day of Frigidaire. Child's been in water since opening time this a.m. and now—freezing most to death—fleshless, knowing he should go dry off and head home—he still so hates to leave. He stands, pitiful without knowing it, at the edge of others' splashing. Here's a boy hating to miss even a minute of strangers' grab-ass fun. Boy seems to know everybody present, though nobody present quite knows or notices him. You wonder—just by looking at his overmany ribs, by seeing how unsupervised he looks—"Where's this child's *mother*?" So you—adult—slip up to him and bend alongside, say, voice kindly, what them lifeguards should've spoken hours back, "Don't you think it's time you dried off, son? Probably cold, right?" He jumps like fearing nasty strangers that his dirty-minded folks have warned him of. And then, finally hearing you, he nods, shows that, yeah, he should go in, he knows he's hurting. But when you turn and resettle on your chaise, he's still right down there by the water, stick arms crossed, dancing from foot to foot, back clinching from the chills—and smiling out at all them other fun lovers. And not one of them is missing him. If a single swimmer called, "Hey, pal, over here! Come back in!" he'd hurl hisself and, with six more minutes' exposure, would get fished out by the lifeguards, stiffened, his nipples and nails the gray-blue of used carbon paper and him smiling, embarrassed at beginning here, in public, to be dead. —*That* boy.

so, anyhoo: Letter done, Willie made the envelope hisself. Child used brown wrapping stock borrowed from the company's jolly cook, a man not long for this world. Will mixed glue from snitched flour and free ditch water. Will found some nice heartwood planks. Found them in a barn where he got caught in cross fire, spent two thirsty nights. On the floor, out of Yank sight lines, he used pegs and brads from a barn workbench. Will fashioned a solid little pine box, one just the right size to mail home a heavy watch. He'd never had much training at The Lilacs, where a boy complained that slaves got to shoe the horses and do all the fun stuff. Will used his rifle's butt to be a hammer. (He'd run out of ammo anyways.)

Later, during idle minutes around camp, he would poke the tips of tenpenny nails into a handy fire. He'd get them red-hot and—holding these with wooden tongs he made—Will commenced burning little pictures all over the outside of Simon's official ship-his-watch-home crate.

This container was six inches by four deep. Every inch, slow, got covered with pictures that—to others' eyes—looked blurred as any old-timer's tattoo smudged by decades of outrushing body heat. To Will, of course, these seemed little master drawings. Into soft pine he scored cabins, barns, animals both wild and tame, a large home ridged with columns, blooming bushes, sunflowers that shot high as houses. No people were shown. Will told hisself he couldn't draw a person good enough, not yet. That'd be the test of entering the big league, artist-wise, to risk committing some*body*. The child felt handicapped: his one art supply was—Sherman's own—plain fire.

Before our private wrapped this careful box in oiled paper using double-knotted twine and wiring, he decided Simon's watch should be well wound first. Thing had a eight-day movement. If the postman hurried, this timepiece might fall into Utt family hands whilst yet ticking.

The Friday after the Wednesday shooting, Will noticed that the masterpiece was losing time. This spooked him. If it wound clear down, that maybe meant some second death—his own. Seemed a relay. He had to get the watch home *right*.

He found the key hooked to its fat-linked gold chain. (A iron key that looked cheap and ugly, worker bee, compared to all that gold. But what good was gold without its good iron help?) Will worried he might break the trusted item by overwinding. So he prowled, checking for soldiers' watch fobs. Simon's watch had changed how Will saw others. While asking several gents the time, Will checked the quality of their timepieces. Most disappointed and he refused to accept their advice about the hour. He quizzed one grizzled vet for the o'clock. This fellow turned, leering, "Why? You in a rush for another set-to? Want to do in another little Yank like that last you bagged then pulled into your hole to finish off. Oh, we saw, Attila Junior. I like that, he's bloodthirsty ripe for another run at Yanks. We got a fierce 'un here, boys."

Men laughed half-nasty laughs. Made hand-to-hand sound smutty. Marsden hurried off, all he could do was his usual: pretending not to hear.

Officers had set up a table in a root cellar's far corner. (They always seemed to need a *table* to hold official papers or they couldn't think clear.) Will usually stayed away from higher-ups. Oh sure, he listened when they told him to line up, the boy did whatever dangerous they said do. But spying a fine platinum chain leading to the vest pocket of First Lieutenant Hester, Will slinked over whippet-shy and asked.

"Time? Surely, son." Hester's eyes were kind as he pulled forth this beautiful saucer-sized timepiece—but thin as a mint, it was. Willie yanked forth Simon's watch, he used the stem, he set its hand then let hisself be observed to fiddle with its key. "You've forgotten how, Willie, between windings? Here." Hester took Will's watch, set the key into its opened crystal's face. Hester twisted Simon's timepiece counterclockwise with a ratcheting that sounded like many toe bones popping. Will tried not wincing, he had to trust the First Lieutenant. Handing back the treasure, Hester said, "Fine instrument, Marsden."

"Yes, sir. Thank you, sir. It was his father's, sir."

"Oh, family thing, is it? Your granddad's. Yes, it looks to be. A hunting family. Keeps good time, does it? Imported, I see."

"Yes, sir. It's German and was made in Germany. And I'm trying and take care of it right."

"You do just that, Private. A superb watch is a comfort during times as bad as ours."

"Yes sir, sir."

WILL waited in line to mail it. He knew the Utt survivors would sure relish this keepsake. But, oh, but he hated giving it up. It *did* seem like some family thing, passed on. His own. He'd got into a habit: Whilst pinned behind woodpiles or in other gullies, Will would take the thing out, he'd mash its fine ringing clicks against one ear. Will would sometimes set to oiling its nice crate, admiring his own burned scenes around the edges. He made the watch his homework. Why did it soothe him so? It should make him feel bad but didn't, lonely like he was. It meted out the moon's phases, it showed a moon man's face grinning. He liked its hymn, "Work For the Night Is Coming." Good advice. German chimes sent out fanning gauzy rings, bongzz, bongzz. Such sounds made the watch seem larger than its own good given size. How fertile and continuingly egglike its nice weight felt in a person's hand or pocket.

Now, patient, Will stood moping in the long line for mailing stuff. He held his bundle chest-high in a treasuring Wise Man pose. He'd copied out the exact address from Simon's blue slip. Will had used his own best Lower Normal script. He laid his folded explaining letter up top so Simon's family would find that, even prior to touching coiled chain and a watch, still ticking, he hoped, ticking clear to Malden. Will had sealed his box's paper wrapping, caulking it in candle wax. Now, in December, men's breath made gray clouds, scalloped. Did Northern fellows out in this same weather see their own breaths as official blue?

Odd, it was only whilst approaching the postal tent, only when he stood feeling proud in this line one-eighth of a mile long, only then did Willie— slow—begin to understand a few right crucial facts. These come to him in small tick-tock degrees, then gonged. To his parcel, lifted near a private's freckled face, one mouth announced, "Uh-oh. *More* mess."

See, he'd just figured out—a Southern soldier couldn't post no package to no town in no Massachusetts, fool! Not even a small nice-looking box like this would inspire Yank mailmen to cooperate with Reb ones. Rebs would call the Southerner sending it North a Yank spy, maybe. Only when Marsden tallied how many days and months it'd taken him to catch on to this (September 17 to December 20, '62), only then did Wee Willie Marsden, Private, CSA, feel his first caving-in and weak-kneed shame. Regret, postponed, caught him across the back of his head. Who killed one Private Simon Utt?

Not I, said Cock Robin. Cross my heart and hope . . . cross my heart, not I.

All around Will, other fellows talked of far-off wives, of love-letter sweethearts (first cousins, but who cared!), of their old pappies left in charge of stores and probably losing everybody's shirt. Holding their own homebound letters, how stirred and loud and full of fire men acted! One boy had drawn some Christmas holly on his envelope and this got passed along. "That's *good*. Looks like it'd prick you almost." Soldiers behaved like this was some lottery queue. They each expected to win big. After all, one letter sent home from the front usually got you three civvie notes in return—from others' itchy wives, from the town mayor, good odds for a gambling man: three to one. Nobody noticed the new stillness of a kid with cowlicks, holding a bundle like he had his entire family in there, shrunk, politely eating supper, maybe even soup. Will's busyness in getting this item wrapped for Simon's kin, it'd tricked Will good. Softened the rude fact of what he'd done. The single good deed of a watch's return had started seeming to nearbout balance out the crime, cancel it. The shooting had been, of course, a legal crime—committed during a declared war, but even so . . . Will left line. He felt uneasy on his legs. He moved off and sat, back mashed against a wagon wheel's spokes, Will sat staring ahead whilst squeezing this nice homemade crate against his front. Wadded in one hand, Confederate money he'd planned to use for postage, a bill now damp. Other soldiers shuffled forward joshing, shoving one another, each holding something meant for others.

Imagine, Marsden told me years later, imagine thinking that you've justified shooting a live person by working hard to be your victim's belated shipping clerk! But that's just how far off course a decent fellow's decency can drift during indecent times.

(And, child, I figure: If that applied in 18 and 62, if fellow feeling had slipped that far back, then what-all must we worry over today? How far off the compass's pure course has recent Kindness drifted?)

3

WILL lived out the war, he wanted to and did. He had one extra reason to try hanging on. He must last till North-South mail routes healed. Appomattox would mean: One stamp fits all. For the rest of the war, he shot not nobody else. Boy vowed: If it came down to them or him onct more, then this go-round *they* were in luck. Instead, he mostly hid in holes—not bothering to fire back except when his officers stood close. Then he shot into the air and over all heads blond and otherwise. Usually he curled deep into ruts and—unobserved—just waited till smoke cleared. Hid, he polished the watch and listened to it like for company and wisdom. He sternly compared the real moon to the watch's painted moon and marveled that a old-time German should know about these recent modern months.

War ended and stillness suddenly got scarier than noise. It made the watch mean even more when you understood how hard it'd been to *hear* this thing during shelling and how valiant it'd been over all that mess. You felt the silence couldn't last. Will, as you well know, walked home from Virginia proper, walked clear to Falls, and in something under seven weeks, given all the wrong turns he made. He stood, hungry, in Nutbush, Virginia, on a sidewalk between a bakeshop and a pawnbroker. Will was holding his wood burner's case and its eighteen-carat prize nestled clicksome among straw inside. Will stared from racks of other people's gems and timepieces displayed in one window to three dozen hot caramel rolls steaming next door. (He could get all those for this one watch, he bet. A Yankee's watch, true, but who'd know?) Will scanned window to window till he felt dizzy, then got hiccups, which made him laugh and let him concentrate on hiccups and not cashing in young Master Utt's one heirloom message to his waiting folks. "Honest," Will had promised Simon, and meant it.

The very day that mutual mail routes recommenced in '65, Will, home again, posted his homemade envelope. It looked stained like it'd been to war and back, which it flat had. He sealed it safe inside a finer parchment one, knowing that Simon's sisters and mother would appreciate the smudged history of one letter carried all those miles. Off it went with too much superstitious postage paid, off went the letter he had wrote just days after shooting their young Simon dead. He had not seen fit to add a postwar postscript saying, "Oh yeah and you should know I killed him." Timing still seemed wrong.

Instead Will mentioned: once sending valuable stuff seemed safer, he *would* mail Simon's watch. Their getting this letter would be a test-like. "Meantime," he wrote strangers, "believe it or not, it has only lost three seconds since Sept. 17, '62! Simon would feel mighty proud, I bet."

You won't be shocked to know that postal delivery proved pretty spotty during Reconstruction. Certain Yank mailmen felt like any bulky item shipped from the Deep South was one form of personal war compensation. (Meaning they stole stuff.) Southern postal workers didn't act a mite more honest. (I put this in so you'll see I got me a pretty balanced mind, child. I *want* to be fair.) Nothing a body sent was guaranteed safe. Even so, Mrs. Utt's letter by return mail reached Will, prompt for then.

Hers was a real graceful and accomplished bulletin—long, too. It sounded like what she was, wife of a small-town preacher, a man dead but still beloved and daily mentioned. The note had a round Bible tone and was a regular fruitcake stuffed with quotes and scripture, citrusy bits of preserved poems. The letter talked about Utt family gratitude, it offered funny endearing facts about the departed boy. Willie, reading it again and again, would stand before the mantel of his rented civilian rooms. Was a mantel where the perfect gold watch now sat honored in its charred picture-book case (varnished by the lanolin of a young soldier's frequent handling). Mirror backed the timepiece and Will found he could, whilst reading aloud, study his own face in the glass. "Is this a guilty face?" he asked the face. Mrs. Utt's words seemed honorary, a dead boy's mother writes back and in a most beautiful hand. Felt almost like getting a note from Lincoln or somebody. Will showed the letter to his own mother.

About his killing Simon, Will had yet told no living soul, at least not in so many words. Oh sure, for Winona's sake he went, "We all did things we might wonder about now." But this was as far as he vented it. Sure, he *wanted* to tell, but kept deciding, "The time's not right"—and wondered what he meant.

Meanwhile he had the fine watch cleaned. He so worried the local jeweler to be careful, the man drove Will from a shop whose window still held slave-hocked trinkets stolen from The Lilacs.

Will rarely wore the watch, a token of respect. Whenever visitors admired it above his fireplace, the growing boy nodded, "Yeah, a good one okay, was a kind of gift." Each time Will heard tell of another local parcel being snapped up by them greedy Federal mails, he postponed mailing Simon's treasure North. Another week, a further six months, you know how postponing postpones itself. Soon, was going on 18 and 66. Time! Simon would've been nearbout eighteen by now. Will hisself stood six feet and some tall, gone huger across the back and chest, had a baritone voice as charcoal-dark as Sherman's leavings, dark as the marks that molten ten-penny nails make in heart pine. Will told hisself, "Simon Utt will never stop being fifteen."

Letters from the ladies Utt drew still more mail from him, a regular exchange. He rose to the occasion. He rewrote mail and worried over his bad spelling. Some mornings, while hiking to the livery stable, Will found he half envied Simon his license to rest. —To go right from childhood to war to earning a living, it meant you'd missed so many things.

That spring, a good white rental horse escaped from Marsden's stable. Will and two hirelings went seeking the mare. Will, in black civvies now, wandered to a meadow just behind Falls' shopping district. Wildflowers came clear up to stores' backsides where crates were stacked and rats seemed happy. Willie stepped on something hidden in high weeds, a FOR SALE sign. He looked up from it to this "desirable property." Nothing had ever been "done" with this border. It slid downhill from the business zone to the river Tar. Today a group of older black women, wearing huge straw hats, fished from a flat rock stuck out into willows' shade. (Here a local nursemaid once drowned herself.) White kids, dashing from ditch to holes, yelled orders at each other, playing "fort." Nearby, wild roses, black-eyed Susans, and Johnny-jump-ups bloomed. Those and the nameless grasses that seemed nothing much till passing wind made stroking pets of them. Shopping parents often said to kids, "Go play." That meant here. Back when the Fourth of July meant something other than the fall of Vicksburg, celebrations happened here. Started at 11 a.m. with family picnics and ended with midnight fireworks launched from rowboats, one of which traditionally caught fire and burned to prove what a rowdy time had been had by all. "See that boat burn last night?" Marsden kept one shoe sole flat on FOR SALE, his head swerving, scouting. Around his knees, daisies worked by noisy bumblebees and silent cabbage butterflies. He wanted this territory, and as a tribute: to do *nothing* with. The tract was known as Meadows' Pasture after the Mr. Meadows whose farm all this'd been. Someway, land's being called Meadows' Pasture seemed to double the plot's weedy sweetness.

Such acreage resting cheek by jowl with Falls' commercial district (all twelve stores) forever made the town seem prettier and safer, bigger. Child, you know how vacant lots are . . . you never appreciate them till they leave off being vacant. Then you see how the whole balance of a neighborhood once pivoted on that lost innocent space. You ofttimes notice when it's just too late. (Like civilian life regretted once your military one's begun.)

Willie heard kids playing "fort" behind the high weeds, he saw one old woman catch a little silver bream too small to keep then slip it right into her bucket. Willie decided. This place would serve as secret monument to Ned and Simon. A Southern boy might build a courthouse pillar marking some Rebel pal lost in the fight. But he was not allowed to raise no park statue saluting a young Yank he had bagged (and then been decorated for). That'd be double-dipping. So Meadows' Pasture would—quiet-like—become the Simon P. Utt Memorial Park. All this could stay a secret from the very folks that used it. It'd never come to locals that this greenery and river bend had been spared for them.

And yet, foot mashed on the sign—"This Attractive Location Can Be Commercially Developed to Suit *Your* Company's Needs"—much as Will wanted to act here, as willing as he felt to cash in some rental homes he'd inherited, big a bargain as this plot probably still was in long-range terms, something held him back. The offer wouldn't last, he'd need a while to swing this size down payment—best hurry—and yet he felt a powerful limit. He stood here, sun full in his face and warming his dark business suit's shoulders. (His employees led the recovered white horse—long since forgotten—along the River Road.) Willie Marsden hoped to own this plot but, local operator and sentimental person, felt he had no right to it. Not yet. Seemed one last important chore needed tending to before he might view hisself as the type civilian who *can* haul off and concoct grand secret plans. "Soon." He left Meadows' Pasture, hangdog, "I'll be getting it for Simon soon."

That's when he knew. He guessed he had to take the watch back. Personally take it, and confess.

Three unwed older Utt sisters had worked a sampler mailed South. They wrote on the parcel's paper just what was inside and the unvaluable item slipped right through, unstole. Framed in black lacquer, it showed a girl, hands balled to eyes, bent under a weeping willow. It was stitched with Simon's full name, rank, division number, and dates (opening and shutting years were set so close together, it seemed like Simon's start and end were cross-eyed, all but exchangeable).

Will wondered what to *do* with this here needlecraft. He passed it on to his scarred quiet mother for safekeeping. Boys did that then.

Will's rooms had nothing very fine in them except the watch. Across its lid a stag was almost but forever *not* caught by hounds. "Uh-oh," he told the timepiece, knowing what he had to do and dreading that so much. He'd take it up there and if he got the chance, in decency, he'd tell them what he'd done to Simon P. Utt, Private, USA. Then he'd come home and save that perfect field for Simon's sake.

4

WILL waited for some invitation to go North. The ladies Utt asked often. That was not enough. His last summons had come in the form of a draft to go up there and win the war of Yankee aggression. He was still so scared of the old enemy. He hadn't left his own three-county area since dragging home from Appomattox and the gloomy sight of a Lee gone weepy.

The more Utt gifts and news come South, the more Willie longed to tell some local soul the whole truth, nothing but. He'd been paying visits to Winona but held off spelling out events that happened after her Ned died. It someway undercut his promise of mourning his favorite Reb. Will had been decorated for ending the life of Simon Utt. Embarrassed him. The day after the shooting, soldier buddies'd gathered, and pumped Private Marsden for details. They'd seen Will—from *their* holes—wing the Northerner. They'd seen Will drag the pretty skinny fellow who'd tried and brain Will with a rock, drag the Yank down into a handy ditch. Risked his life, Will did—to polish off the boy newly plugged. Later, running, men spied the same Yankee child sitting in the ditch, propped up stiff, eyes shut, a perfect goner. Everybody praised unlikely Willie for his brutal work. Unshaved, guys had hung around grinning, asking did Will choke the boy, or what? "Naw, nothing like that," Will said. "Not much to tell. Natural causes."

"Yeah, natural for *you* to cause them. Tell us how you done it."

Hester commenced petitioning for a medal then—conspicuous valor, imperiling his person in pursuit of the enemy—a medal Willie kept here on the mantel. It never seemed to Will he'd got the medals *because* he had the watch. He'd have the medal long after he'd returned the watch—this helped.

By now the ladies Utt were writing Mrs. Lady Marsden herself, praising a son who'd bother corresponding with the family of a boy who'd died in Willie's very arms. "Be proud of him," Widow Utt instructed Widow Marsden.

The invitation to go North came. It was 1868 already and Will Marsden still had his eye on Meadows' Pasture (there'd been serious nibble and the Merchants' Association considered buying it "for further merchandising expansion purposes," but it'd remained as yet unsold).

Willie and his mother were asked to attend a family reunion to be held up near Alexandria, Virginia. The old lady claimed this was too far in Will-knew-which-direction for her blood. Her burned face had healed a bit but Lady stayed hidden from all. She was far too vain to permit Virginia relations, much less Charleston ones—those who recalled her for that perfect white skin—to see brown blots and red stains ruining her hands, giving neck and forehead the sheen of parchment.

Will reread the invitation whilst looking in his mantel mirror. He propped the engraved card beside a boy-made case. Leaning here, he did some makeshift push-ups, his own face coming nearer glass (pores) and leaving it (head and shoulders grown grosser than he could quite believe).

When he stood before his momma's rocker, Will told of heading North for visiting with her own kin. Then he explained, beyond that, he intended meeting with the ladies Utt. Lady More commenced whimpering. She hugged her son by the knees. Innocent of many spoken words, she still begged Willie not to venture North. He'd gone once before and only got as far as Maryland—and look what badness grabbed him there. She mimed out *mailing* the watch North, or maybe he should hire some young enterprising black worker to take it up that far. As he stood here, Will heard her strange hollow noises, he felt her working on his pant cuffs. When he checked, Lady More Marsden, still in this world but not always quite of it, had slipped the white silk belt off her silk wrapper. Lady had tied one end to the rocking chair's runner. The other she'd tethered to her young survivor's leg. To keep him. He made a funny game of hopping off from her and stopping dead but, even while he did this to cheer her, he felt her scaredness pass into him. She sat, face hid back of hands. Did Will really want to go up there? Would they let him freely leave? If he confessed, would he become the North's last prisoner of war?

5

BEING a man of his word, Will Marsden stepped onto the Atlantic Coastline's spiffiest club car, every brass spittoon polished to the point of being way overqualified for this line of work. He wore a new suit bought from Lucas' off a wax dummy. Will picked a jacket with pockets cut roomy enough to hold a little handmade cask that had come to seem almost as valuable as the German clockwork wonder it'd protected so well.

Now, glad for a window seat, Will has stopped by his reunion (they're all alike and need not be spelled out here) and is headed up more North by train, this time to Malden, Massachusetts, itself. The Utts are waiting. He's told his kinfolk in Alexandria he'll be back in time to buggy South with them.

ASIDE from earlier sightseeing on foot near Antietam Creek, Maryland—Willie'd never set foot north of the Virginia line. Falls'd always felt quite north enough, thank you. What he saw from this slow train to Boston started scaring him. The shock part was, child: plain streets, simple trees and houses, regular horses, rivers running blue and brown, even barbershops striped the same two-tone as Stark's Scissor Tonsorium. He'd expected—what? bands and drill-unit soldiers busying every town square. Will expected more Yankee homes to be painted holy Federal blue. Will felt like Northern shadows should be someway denser, maybe proving bluer than your sunnier Southern gray ones. Slow, along the train ride to Malden, young Marsden understood how much the color of a Yankee uniform had, like four years' cataracts, tinted and blurred his whole picture of Unionists' pastures, Federal cities. In Delaware, he saw a splendid magnolia tree all starred with full white blooms. He felt tricked. If the whole North looks just like the South, what had all that whole mess been about? Though his moneyed family once knew the North real well, though his granddad, Judge More, attended Harvard College, Will had grown up when the South kept to itself, all haughty, separate. The boy should've known better but didn't.

He stood windblown between train cars, lashed by cinders, keeping clear of Yankees. The more northerly this train got—the more Willie feared that his drawl might bring him bodily harm. He refused to eat in the dining car. Waiters wanted you to order out loud, and with three strangers right at your table, the three then tried and "draw you out." No thanks. Besides, who knew what they might slip into the food of a reverse scallywag, a carpetbagger with a boxed watch rattling on his person? Willie kept one palm cupped over the plugged pocket of his new brown suit. If people looked at him, he stared away. In his trouser pocket, he had many bills of Confederate money, like some ID badge to give him anchoring strength. Sitting near the Pullman window, staring out like somebody on their first weekend jaunt to Mars, Willie felt like a unemployed spy still sneaking peeks but doing it freelance now, on no side at all, and noticing what for who?

The trek from Alexandria took him nearly three days, seemed weeks. One reason time did so funny, the boy refused to eat. Anything Yankee. He would drink train water in small paper cups but only after he saw children do it, and when they seemed to live afterwards, rushing back for more. Willie understood right off, he'd not brought sufficient money. Overnight on reaching Boston, he couldn't afford a hotel and so slept sitting upright at the South Station (not the North one). He had his return ticket, he figured maybe he'd come so poorly prepared as a kind of accidental penance. He'd brought plenty of folding money but it was mostly the losing kind, Jeff Davis on it, already the stuff of bad and bitter jokes.

Will traveled by buggy then another short-line train then wagon again and finally, on foot, he entered a little town outside of Boston. There was still country all around the burg called Malden. He had wired ahead from Washington.

Once past Malden's city-limits sign, Will heard the watch grow louder. Or maybe it was just Will's being off trains and wagons, plus maybe hunger.

Still, the instrument sounded as if it knew what home was. Will kept his right hand, like for comforting the thing, on its decorated pine crypt. Five and a half years'd done slipped by since Marsden nailed this crate together while waiting rescue inside a surrounded barn. By now, Simon Utt would be twenty. (But, of course, Simon wouldn't ever be—he'd never have to.)

Will showed a stranger the Utts' address (he still dared not speak). The Yankee quacked instructions. Will nodded and, lips moving, went over his prepared speech again. Today, at last, he'd tell. He had found, in three years of Winona practice every Thursday, telling was good for what ailed you, the soul and so forth. Under his big black hat, he felt like some foreigner, a hawker of bad goods, an undertaker and a bounty hunter—mixed.

6

DEAD Simon's mother, still dressed in mourning, proved stout and pointy, sleek as a seal. She paced her cottage porch, waiting. Though Simon's dad had been deceased these many years, his family yet lived in a brick home beside a matching church. The Utt homeplace looked small but extra tidy. Like a cottage on a candy tin. It sported yellow flowers spilling from window boxes. Great honor-guard stands of rouge-tinted hollyhocks surrounded the place.

Slowed, tugging at his stiff white collar, Will now slid through the Utt garden gate. Their home looked like Simon had described it. Will took off his hat, held it to his chest, grinned a tinny awful grin (he felt this falseness and it pained him into grinning wider, faker). His features felt haywire and might do anything, already busy showing guilt first thing. He felt that awful swimming sense you get sometimes in church or at a overfancy concert where you *know* you are about to jump up screaming something nasty.

Three dark older sisters, each in black wool, all wearing hair lifted into buns, stood, grave and smiling behind Simon's exact eyebrows. Their faces looked like early tries at getting his one right. They lined up on the porch, eager to shake Will's hand. Ladies smiled varieties of one fixed searching smile. Sisters had, they admitted right off, memorized all Will's finer letters. Plainly they'd spent time imagining the last person to have seen their young brother alive. The Utts had allowed theirselves certain romantic thoughts concerning this striking Southern person. Ladies must've seen how bad Will's spelling was (they were all teachers!) but they knew his words come right from the heart—which helps you overlook a lot. There's many kinds of grammar, child.

"Here he is at last," Mrs. Utt sighed. "An answered prayer. We dearly hope that this might prove but the first of many visits, 'son.' But we consider today your true homecoming, William—if I might call you William?" William, he nodded. Child—what choice?

Entering the house, smells of baking, of standards, righteous cleanliness. Lining this hallway, seminary diplomas written in foreign languages. Even the cottage's plaster walls looked fresh-scrubbed. Will was glad he'd bought him a brown suit for this. Apart from business black, he only had a dressy gray one and he saw right off how that'd be rude, gray here. The brown did feel a little tight now. He toyed with his new black hat, its brim (a planter's sunproof one) was wider than most worn this far north. Mrs. Utt's fine voice explained that owing to William's kindnesses since Appomattox, he'd given this grieving household the greatest comfort, did he know? He'd made their several crosses easier to endure. "Would it embarrass you, William, to understand how knowing you has smoothed most every acrimony one might tend to continue feeling toward the other side?"

"The other *cause*, Mother," an older sister corrected.

"Yes, 'cause,' certainly . . . they coached me to say that," she laughed. "But with you I need not stand on ceremony, sir. I feel that to my very heart and am so grateful for your coming all this distance." The ladies in black each pulled forth fresh-ironed hankies folded into triangles, getting ready. It seemed to Will a cue.

The widow led him to one corner of a dim family parlor. Here stood a little shrine to the dead boy soldier: cuff links, a small oak bear riding a sled (a toy Simon'd carved—with a good deal more skill, Willie feared, than his own watch crate showed), some blue baby booties, childhood daguerreotypes, two school essay prizes and, beneath them, the papers themselves, showing a fat steady script. The same design of sampler the sisters'd sent Willie hung framed above this altar. Flanking relics, two candles burned. Swallowing, wiping his wet palms along his pant legs, Will said, bold, "There's something I better tell you right off. Something I reckon you all should've known all along." "Splendid," said Mrs. Utt, "just as you wish," but seemed to wait on something else. Then Will remembered. The gawky civilian reached into his pocket then, he heard the lining start to rip, he fished forth the homemade box, turned to Simon's sleek mother and handed it over. He said, "Here. I told him I would. And now I have."

Thanking him, she quickly set aside the wood-burned cask Will had made and decorated with such care. Right disappointing, her ignoring all the work he'd put into it. Mrs. Utt cradled a clicking watch in the palm of her right hand. Relieved as Will felt, he was also pained some to see another person touch it. He almost felt that she was getting to touch his personal privates. Odd. The chain trailed down her dark sleeve. She looked over at her three quiet daughters. One nodded. Permission. Mrs. Utt hit the latch. Time showed itself. Gold popped open in a rush of holy music almost perfumy, squirts of something pure unleashed in the close air of a Yankee parlor. Two sisters reached out and quick took hold of each other's arms. One sucked air as if she'd heard her brother speak (and maybe, within that, her father's voice cased within Simon's own). Against long dark dresses, white handkerchiefs shivered and knotted.

Moving slow and certain as some preacher at communion, Mrs. Utt faced the shrine and placed Simon's watch atop its own coiled chain and at the very center. She spoke a simple prayer aloud and, after her Amen, wept in a orderly, almost planned-seeming way. Odd squeaks bellowed out of her, half-barks like a schooled seal might sound. Everybody waited. When she'd finished, everybody sat and acted right cheered.

Draperies got pulled wide open. Will decided he'd now tell. Had to. The whole story. Sure did seem high time. Trying to live a life in Falls with Simon's watch still ticking on Will's mantel—it'd seemed, well, like a form of bigamy. In some way, Will's own freedom—to buy land, to haul off and conduct a life both legal and civilian, personal—all that depended on his fearless honesty right this second.

"I've got to say something out, ladies," Willie Marsden, hat in hand, announced just as the food arrived. You could see it'd taken ladies whole days to make these pastries. Tea biscuits, heart-shaped, gleamed with gems of careful red jam on top. Beside these, round discs, frosted to look like watch faces. One had a little toothpicked drawing of a deer. Ladies had remembered the deer but forgot the chasing hounds.

"Yes, do tell us all. Lovely. We must get to know each other ever so much better. Yes, but first, you have to be famished, considering the miles you've come just to be here with us."

The Widow Utt held a silver tray spread with buttery crumpets, browned just so, and still more watch shapes with little baked-on winding stems. Will understood: He hadn't really had a meal or anything in three and a half days. Now, at the sight of all this thoughtful food, he felt half faint. Still, eating seemed out of the question. But as trays of other sweets appeared—he started understanding just how truly hard his telling this would be here. He refused cookies. He saw it hurt their feelings, so he added, "Later, maybe . . . looks beautiful, you-all sure eat beautiful up here . . ." He was playing the hick, child. They laughed but seemed confused. "Well," he cleared his throat and picked up one of each treat. Ladies breathed again. "Well," he smiled, "there's much to say, seems like."

To sit here, your hat on one knee, big left hand full of sweets crumbling, with Simon's one sister on your left and another to your right, with others facing you head-on, and you a person still not old but aging fast under these gray-blue Bible-believing eyes all trying and make you out to be a hero . . .

"So," the widow spoke.

Earlier, on the porch, lined up, these sisters had seemed much alike. Now differences came clear. They soon grew lively—for flinty New England matrons (a style right mineral and fixed compared to the animal-and-flora of Southern womanhood's humid waltzier type of heat). The oldest sister announced: Will might find amusing certain stories concerning her boarding-school pupils during wartime. It seems that one little girl misheard the word "Rebel" as "Rubble." She imagined the advancing Rubble forces to be squadrons of gray stone men, formed of roots and mud, marching against far softer animal Northerners! Everybody laughed. Will laughed—

late—but somewhat harder than the rest. He sat shaking his head No to prove this was just *like* children, was it not? Then he nodded Yes. Rubble.

Sisters had been saving some one tale apiece. Each told each with an easy lightness. Their grace felt painful. He waited for his opening. He leaned forward like a runner at the starting line. Cookies crumbled in his left fist. The sisters' smoothness made him feel more heavy, murderous and coarse. He'd once been two years younger than their Simon. Simon had been ten to twelve years younger than these sisters here. Now Will was already three and a half years older than Simon had been when he got shot dead by a certain nearby person. Will, sitting here, did figures in his head till he felt sick from tallying ("I *should* eat"). The age of fifteen seemed something to forever subtract from any future age of Will Marsden's. Oh, but Will wanted out of here. Just run! Some mess. He felt embarrassed by his own superstitions. Would these teachers believe he'd expected many Northern houses to be painted blue? That he'd expected Yanks to still be swaggering around in war regalia? (Back home, gray uniforms were now illegal, only that prevented their being worn daily by many die-hard vets.)

Ladies mentioned the room upstairs where Will would sleep tonight. It overlooked the churchyard and cemetery where Simon's new marker stood. Will wondered if Simon's body had been shipped back up here, but there was no gentle way to ask. Ladies' interest in the watch hinted that Simon's body like so many others had been buried in a hurry at the time. Willie grinned at further mention of that Rubble story. Wasn't *he* that? A gray boy born out of a rocky hole. Compared to these fine ladies with their polished chintz and lace doilies, Will felt made of pond scum, scabby tree bark, stones—a Rubble soldier sure enough.

"There really is something, like I said before, I've got to say out to you, ladies. It's something hard." He spoke too loud but at least he'd started. This room sure did seem—maybe owing to Will's not eating for some days—to be drawing very far away and yet closing slow around his ankles like a set of shackles would. He recalled his mother trying to tie him safe in Falls.

"Fine, please tell," the Widow Utt smiled. "The second everybody gets here," and she twisted toward a knock at the door, she touched her neck's bun. "Fine—it's *op*-en."

Neighbors started arriving. Soon in came two dozen more parishioners, the present minister, a whole children's bell-ringing group from the sisters' Academy, plus many brass bells in pine crates. Fully forty-five people filed in. More and more kept pushing toward young Marsden, eager to get introduced. Since he'd wadded pastry in his right hand, he used his left and saw people wonder if this might be due to war wounds. Folks stared at Willie—like looking for traces of Simon on him—seeking some family resemblance.

Babies were held up for Will to kiss and they looked like normal babies, like present-day Rubble ones but fatter here. They'd won. Their folks had. Shy at being fussed over, Will kissed each child quick. His manners—while right good for a boy from a large farm outside Falls, North Carolina, pop. 1,100—had undergone some rough sea change during war. Now his own manners didn't seem (to him, anyhow) quite wide or fine or deep enough for this event. For this, you'd need to be a statesman or, at least, a leading candidate for mayor.

Will answered direct questions simply, trying to make his accent lessen as much as he could without feeling like a fake. Grinning till his jaws ached, Will begun finding first reasons not to tell.

Soon every hallway, the whole cottage staircase, jostled with talking Yankee people, their tones all right angles and hurtful sharp turns. A little choir of girls stepped forward, showing more white gloves than there seemed sets of legal hands among them. Gloves shook brass bells, doing two popular songs of the South. It upset the North Carolina murderer among them. The sound of ringing metal recalled a watch's fine hymn, it was like parade-ground marches or country church bells struck by miniés. Children played music that, four years back, would've got a Yank arrested. All this helped Will see how rough a public confession would now be.

Oh, but even with this houseful, he longed to fess up to murdering the neighborhood favorite. These folks were eager for the war to feel ended. They liked welcoming a onetime Rubble come North on this awkward mission. Willie knew: In downtown Falls just now, a confessed Yankee soldier would be snubbed at best, stoned at worst. These folks seemed to consider his visit civilizing, a rite they'd waited on.

The preacher who'd replaced Rev. Utt now rose and in a voice less rich than it seemed to plan to be, announced he'd quote a recent poem from *The Atlantic Monthly*. Rev. said it expressed the feelings of all persons present and, he was glad to say, it'd been penned by his second cousin, a Mr. Finch. The pastor cleared his throat to urge baby bell ringers to keep gloves off those clanky bells for now.

> No more shall the war cry sever,
> Or the winding rivers be red.
> They banish our anger forever
> When they laurel the graves of our dead!
> Under the sod and the dew,
> Waiting the judgment day,
> Love and tears for the Blue,
> Tears and love for the Gray!

Will noticed that many around the room were upset. Even men, backed against the walls, looked near tears and Willie understood, jolted: they'd been soldiers too. They stood watching him. They could've killed him then and they tried but couldn't. They might squash this Rubble yet. He'd come this deep into enemy territory, unarmed. Marsden fought back such fears in a roomful of girl bell ringers. Elbows pressed hard to ribs (he needed to half hurt hisself to keep concentrating proper). He waited only for the chance to leave. By now, a body's spilling facts seemed nigh on to impossible.

Others spoke of Simon. They smiled as Will sat picturing his dead friend. By now, however undeserved, he considered Simon a friend, a friend in passing. He listened to tales of Simon's rowdy kindness, he imagined Simon's chapped mouth moving, sounding something out for Will alone. Lips went, "These people here have suffered enough. Let them *like* you, buddy. Is that really so hard? They need to like somebody living and not just miss me dead." Seemed to make sense.

"I guess you all heard the one about why the ocean stays so cross and all?" There was a hush. Will understood he'd broke into the Widow Utt telling Simon stories. "Sorry." Will turned, but she smiled.

"No, please, tell, why? —Why does the ocean stay . . . angry, was it? Why?" Smiling, she glanced around, proving to others how pleased she was that their guest of honor—clumsy though he be with his fistful of dough— was trying to "enter in."

"Why? 'cause the ocean's been . . ." Then, ashamed, Will mumbled.

Others wanted to laugh but had to ask, "Because what?"

"It's mad because it's been crossed so many times. —See, 'crossed.' "

Then chuckles. Eyes cut toward each other, proving they liked Will's trying, even if he did mess up right bad.

"Good one," the preacher said. "We'll have to see that one enjoys an afterlife in some future sermon."

His wife remarked, "He always says that." Everybody laughed. You could tell the pastor didn't like to be corrected, which made it funnier. Will started feeling like these really were real people here.

Mrs. Utt continued her tale. "Out from dawn to dusk and year round too. We had one dreadful hurricane that got this far, remember, was it '59? Yes, '59, and our boy tied himself to the top of the oak tree, the huge one, past the church's east gate, so he might see it all better. Julia somehow knew he was up there, didn't you, dear? I got a ladder. Already boughs were snapping. Once we got him in this house and once I'd whipped him savagely, I'm not ashamed to admit, I asked our Simon how he'd even expected to live through a storm that size. You know what he said, remember?"

Sisters on either side of Will—his honor guard—nodded, knowing Simon stories like catechism.

"He said, 'Oh, Momma, I could have gotten used to it!' —Can you fancy? Oh, we've had many a smile over that. *'Used* to it!' "

Willie, who'd shot him, sat here, swallowing. "Hardly a saint, our Simon," one sister smiled. But her saying this made Willie feel his friend, a preacher's son, was *more* a saint. Mrs. Utt confessed that Simon had got most, if not all the family beauty for maybe three generations. Sisters nodded, smiling, plain faces pleased to remember their brother's slightly finer looks. "Our only silverhead," one said. A man mentioned Simon's gift for whittling and handstands. Neighbors mentioned his volunteering to babysit and such.

Marsden felt these comments to be aimed at him. He nodded in a few places. Big raw faces all around praised Simon. A baby crawling near Will's shoes untied one lace. When the mother corrected her child, Will grinned. He'd started shaking from nerves and hunger but still felt unworthy of fine food. His wool suit grew soaked clear through (was it hot in here or was it just him?). Slow droplets trickled down his spine, over ribs and out starched cuff, sliding toward a fist of dough gone solid now. If only they would let me speak, Will decided as a buxom lovely lady schoolteacher rose to describe "the firecracker incident." Others laughed. Grinning, Willie practically panted. More neighbors came packing in, standing on tiptoe to see the Living Reb. The teacher was saying Simon loved sledding "to a fault. It seems our Simon skipped class one day after a lovely snow, that eager to slide down our steepest hill, a sheet of veritable ice it was by then. It also happened, as things would have it, that Boston's truant officer, the *head* one, had stopped for a hot toddy at Gerson's Inn. His sleigh was out front waiting, tied at the slope's very bottom, you see, when young Simon, the rogue, comes lickedy-split down the ice, never guessing that the sleigh square in his way belonged to . . ."

"I killed him."

A creak and stiffening. Faces, still smiling, guessing the likely outcome of this story, turn, slow, towards the honored guest, turn your way. They keep grinning, not believing this they've heard. Silence starts off half cordial. Yanks believe you—socially ill at ease in this fine setting—have maybe leapt onto another subject. Yeah, you were speaking of another whole person. A war so often confused its survivors, right?

Mrs. Utt, yet smiling, clears her throat, a sign that you should either relax or hush or explain further, please. The teacher, yet standing, blinks, waits to finish her dull tale. The Widow Utt—a good hostess—slides forward on her chintz side chair, hands clasped in lap, mouth pursed—not unkind— and she just nods. Like going, "You now have the floor." The front of your white shirt (folks are definitely noticing) has got so soaked that people can see the pink of your chest, air bubbles, a nipple maybe. Pull your jacket shut. After swallowing a few times, sit here studying your hands, preparing what to say. But the hands (that did it) look so huge, haired, veiny things new-grown and stuck out in the air for strangers to see. Hide the hands. For two whole minutes there comes just the sounds of a hallway clock, of the shrine's candles guttering, four babies chattering over nothing much, a daintier clicking from the unsheathed German watch across the room. "Let them *like* you," the watch still says to you alone. It's not too late to call this all a blunder, to change subjects and save everything.

Children playing on the floor slowly notice stillness and their own sounds stop. The baby at your shoes, watchful, keeps hold of your laces.

"I tried and be kind to him. But first I shot him. I could say, We had to then. I might say that both our sides made us. But, fact is, *I* did it. —See, then we ended up in this one ditch together, soon we talked and all. I don't guess Simon even knew it was me got him. And I never told. He had enough weighing on him right then. He gave me his watch to send up here to you-all. Then the war ended not a minute too soon. And once I could afford to and it seemed safe, I hand-brought it to you. Now you've got it over there. I did what I said. I never stop thinking of what happened. Feels now like it didn't really have to. But at the time, it's different. It wouldn't happen now. But, look, it did. I wasn't expecting to travel here and tell all this and then have you people forgive me right away. That'd be asking too much and I know it. See, I only made the trip so I could say it to you ladies face to face. I didn't know others would be here, and I appreciate that, but it sure makes things harder. Simon's watch is delivered. He did love that watch. So, yes, ma'ams, I helped Simon but only afterwards. You should know. You do now. Still, I figure if Simon hadn't been such a nice fellow, I probably wouldn't have walked and ridden up all this far. I've never been this far up before—North, I mean. That's because of Simon, who he was, not just because of what I did to him. So. That's about it. And, look, ladies— the other people here—I don't mind saying—telling you all this, it's maybe even harder than doing that other at the time, almost. Now you'll hate me. I would too. Saying I'm sorry—that's not the half of it. Well . . ."

Speak no other sound. Folks in this here parlor seem locked stiff. They stare only directly ahead. You can hear one person's molars grinding. Babies who acted pleased when your talking broke the hush just now, wait for reasonable gabble to recommence. When doesn't nothing happen, some children start sniffling, looking around for parents. The baby near your shoe gets scooped up, toted out right quick, the mother glad for some excuse to leave here, leave you.

Neighbor ladies, helping in the kitchen, are the lasts to hear. You know the very moment when whispered news reaches them. The whole house is now so pained and silent that the street's horse traffic, a few jays squabbling in a back garden, sound extra colorful and noisy, right attractive. To be outdoors, to fly off!

Standing neighbors back nearer the walls, just like you expected. This sudden moat has opened all around the couch where you wait. Simon's sisters are on your left and right. The left-hand girl now rises, excuses herself, hurries to the back yard. She's out there making piping shrieks into her handkerchief. She does it alone, not wanting to embarrass you or anybody.

Two children in gloves knock two bells over and then right them. A great deal of time seems to pass, only real, real slow. Dear Lord, let us die or get on with things, one. Mrs. Utt, saying nothing, finally struggles to her feet. She looks unsteady and two neighbor ladies reach to help but she signals, No, she's fine. The widow, appearing both royal and tipsy, wobbles to her own front door.

"I'm sorry," she says, loud, to the air of her hallway.

That preacher rises. " 'Love and tears for the Blue, tears and love for the Gray,' Widow Utt?"

"Shut up," says Mrs. Utt, sounding patient and very tired. "This is my house. I do things here. Mr. Marsden, for delivering our watch, we thank you. Goodbye, Mr. Marsden."

The two seated daughters stand and form a row beside the open door. Mrs. Utt's emotion registers by making her face look neutral, almost bored with you. She holds the door open to its widest. Light seems brassbound, gaudy, full of welcome. Rude as you. You try and rise now. Can you? You really should've eaten. It's a long way home, you. First lean across the tray that still holds cookies. Empty a crumbly wad of stuff from your right hand, brush it with the left. Next, stand—straight-backed, try—dazed, now move past parishioners. They turn their heads aside without meaning to or noticing. It's like they need to keep from breathing any air your nose and mouth have tainted. They loved Simon. You killed Simon. Makes sense.

Hardest yet: Approach three waiting women. Nod once. Not to touch them or they'll scream. Best use the porch rail, slow, ease down stairs, then drag along the brick path, unfastening the garden gate. Finally, how grateful for the street. To pull on your big black hat, leveling its brim. You can only move with a great solemn slowness now. Admitting the truth—instead of lightening a person like you'd hoped—has flat quadrupled the pull of Northern gravity, enemy. Every step requires a decision, means a chore, a treaty. How many shoe movements are now between you and the desired sane southerly direction?

Oh, just to reach that far street corner. Once there, turn back, since you need to know. The crowd stands mashed on the front porch, all watching hard, most mouths open. The one sister who stepped out back now studies you from behind a side-yard fence. To see the Southern soldier leave, she's parted hollyhocks. Everybody bunched on the porch holds on to one another. All but the children. For one second, you feel almost wicked—yeah, pretty mean. You know that if you reached quick into your jacket pocket, like going for a pistol, they'd all dive clear off that porch and into flowering shrubs. Be kind of fun to see. For one second, feeling giddy (it's full sun and lack of food and your hurt feelings), you consider doing this. But cruelty passes (takes too much energy). It passes as it mostly does with you. Sometimes it seems things might go simpler for you if it *stayed*, the meanness. If so, you never would've come up here for this.

Maybe you had to. Maybe you'll be glad. Maybe it was all to help you forget Simon. You pat for his watch in your ripped pocket. Seems somebody stole it from you. You lift one arm, but slow so as not to spook one soul. You choose to wave. You need to see what folks'll do back. Three adults, not family but neighbors, react with half-mast hoisting of their wrists. But those hands fall quick and in shooing gestures: Go 'way. Only children hand-flap back at once, not knowing better yet. Nobody stops them. Then the lone sister in the side yard—invisible to those on the porch facing you—she nods, she releases blooming stalks. Those close quick before her face. —Not planning it or understanding why—somebody like you is taking off a new brown jacket. As others watch, the like-you person out here in the sun lays that on the dusty Yankee road. Next shed the fine black hat, place it atop the coat. Only now can you turn. You can finally leave here. It's done. In this world, anyway, you know you'll never see or hear from any of these folks again.

Mostly you will miss your mascot watch, which *is* Simon, or was.

IT's a neighborhood. To walk, hatless, in shirt sleeves, feeling harmless and addled but real old, to aim straight ahead, wherever that way winds up going. To feel, at noon, so like a ghost. And not even your own ghost. It's the sun, you tell yourself. It's not eating, it's being in the wrong place at the worst possible time. Later you'll learn you've had a fever these four days but, for now, as usual you blame yourself.

You soon find the street gives way to a river's edge. Docks far off and here are two huge factories. Smoked red brick and massive chimneys that push out smoke as black as the war's worst. There are many windows so workers inside can see to work. In most windows, corners of silver machines keep turning.

You are down near water, then you see how in every window, beside the silver loom that she must operate, one small girl stands looking out— one head per window looking at you hard like in some uh-oh dream. One child, seeing you notice her, waves. Notice how her right hand wears a metal bracelet. She's a child and has no discipline (like you at twelve). For her own good, it looks like the Yankee factory has hooked her to her machine until some whistle sounds. Big gold letters set in brick over the windows full of children spell: "McClellan's Indigo Works, Unltd."

Water lapping over a nearby dam and hissing through far waterwheels that drive the factory—it's blue, but blue as anything store-bought. Factories like this one won the Feds' war for them. Maybe this plant helped dye the uniforms that made one side's soldiers not in gray. With nothing to lose now, you ease down a mudbank and stand, shoes sunk into the blue marshy shore. River's bottom mud is so blue it's gone purplish, seems furry from leaked tannic chemicals. Then, slow, you see how certain logs angling your way fourteen feet offshore are really fishes, pretty good-sized ones.

Maybe it's your hunger, or the being numbed from wanting to be liked back there (or, if not liked, forgiven), maybe it's the sun or your being too far from home farms and cozy Falls, maybe it's being in this risky zone of industries that mean your country's future. Whatever makes it so, there are many good-sized carp just under this tinged water and they are looking right at you. Chemicals have turned each fish a bitter poison-blue. To see them clearer, you must wade out three feet more. Soon as your shoes and stockings are soaked blue-black, you know you should've taken them off first. No matter. This far north, who'll see?

Fish don't shy or backswim but hover out there, studying you like during some appointment you have kept. They hover in this strange formal horse-shoe shape, gathered like some tribunal. There's something odd about them and—dim at first—you notice they don't have usual pointy thick-lipped fish heads. No, their front ends seem shovel-shaped as human faces. You see how their eyes ride high in front, how their noses are long. Their eyes, unblinking, seem intelligent, fixed right on you here.

Mouths are going like chewing the fouled water they'd rather not, they're belching taint, trying to find a last safe pure part. Then, left to right, you start to recognize the faces. Features of men you knew during the war, the guys that didn't make it. Is this a fever? Third from the left is one you shot who had the pipe in his mouth, and on one end, you read Ned's pale dimpled gaze. He's being punished. Seems your war dead have been sent here, swim-ming in the country's future, living in the upstream leavings of a dye works. Three down, Simon's face, the dark brows all but joining at the center. How he gapes at you, fins fastened just beneath his jaw. Then all the fishes, dorsal fins going, churn up bottom storms of gravel. Swimming in place, they reverse to look up at the mill's four smokestacks, dark towers billowing darkness, shooting flames, spreading a yellow soot that takes itself to be some golden future.

People downstream drink this blue. People nearby breathe this stink. Your side, the farm side, lost to this. This is what it is now, and will be.

Maybe this is everybody's punishment for a civil war. Factories that helped make arms now turn to this and get better at it. You turn your back on all the children in the windows chained to moneymaking gear. You wade out of the leakage future. Think of home. Remember Meadows' Pasture waiting, pure.

You've seen what you've seen here. On dry land—your shoes are squish-ing with Yankee progress, some mess. You—innocent of food, stripped of your timepiece—find the return ticket in one pants pocket, find it's soaked half blue. You wander through six ordinary neighborhoods till one woman comes right up to you. Her hat is covered with a Eden of false fruit, smaller than life-sized (manufactured), and she tips her head and the harvest clacks and she asks if you are lost or have you been in some accident "or what?" She gives you the chance to answer. "Oh," she nods into your silence, "an-other veteran? You were *in* it, right? Yes, we see this all too often. What you boys gave!" You nod at "veteran." You try asking about the train depot but instead sign something with your hand. She calls her young son and he leads you there. The child takes your hand as if he knows he leads a blinded person, which you have sort of become, given all you have been through here lately. Much of it will never be explainable, even by yourself and *to* yourself, much less to some talky magpie little lady you will marry and who'll ask to hear it, to hear all.

The boy pulls you towards a station's gilded cage with a glass front. One black man is swabbing off the depot's white marble floor, the child leads you across its wet. A silence seems to follow. You stare back and see a Yank crowd looking your way. Blue-saturated footprints trail right here to you, no mistaking blame. A captive ticket taker in his gilded cage is thick-lipped under a green visor—fish-faced in a strange glass tank. You pull out your return ticket stub, half dyed blue. "Is it still good?"

Your relatives, leaving the reunion, are supposed to give you a buggy ride home. Somehow you manage to turn up just as they stand fussing in the lobby counting baggage. You wear no hat, you're in shirt sleeves with suspenders out for all to see, your brown trousers are stained most black to the knees, your dark shoes look blue. "What'd, you breaststroke South?" your so-called witty cousin says (because he wants to be called witty, not through any wit or merit of his own). Then you're in the back of wagon, jostling home. They seem to know they mustn't ask you how it went.

7

ONLY when kinfolks cross the unmarked Carolina border, oh Lord, just the smell of that, the sweetness of home turf and actual honest green after all the nasty acid-blue—it does sure press in towards you like a starter cure.

Only now do you revive some. You feel less watched. You say to kin, "I will never go North again. I make a solemn oath before you-all." Nodding. You see they're scared of you. They maybe smell it on you, how you killed three people.

They also smell you—plain you. You lift one arm and ooh-ee, too much. You sniff the fear—it's partly chicken soup, part it's pig iron, mixed. Fear stinks. "Fine," the witty cousin says. "As you wish, you never have to leave home ever again. Suit yourself."

"Thank you. I will never depart our holy state. Here, the monsters can't find *me*."

Nobody talks until reaching the town of Norlina, where you water horses. You haven't eaten anything for five days. Afterwhile, a person stops missing it.

Back home, Cuthrell's Jewelry Pawn Store won't be open until nine. It's 6 a.m. Your relations drop you off, glad to. Few Fallsites up yet. Or is it Fallsians? Your mother once said, "Well, I know these small-timers and *I* call them The Fallen."

You can hardly wait to buy the town's best watch, the platinum one, Swiss made. Here, you don't need cash. Your face means credit.

This early, Meadows' Pasture is all dew. Later today you'll do the banking paperwork required to buy this acreage, a tribute.

To wander out into this field that you know will, by sunset, be yours—meaning everybody's. Simon's, Ned's, the war dead and the civvie living. Through sedge and past wild roses' thorns, downhill to water. Pant legs wet, two rabbits brazen, sunning in a clearing. One old apple tree grows tilted near the river Tar's shore. Already green pips hang here. Though they're sour and you must chew about ten of these to get one apple's worth of nourishment, your stomach growls, grateful. Your tree, your apples, in your own civilian stomach. This river is called the Tar for the black deposits found downstream—tar British soldiers cursed, tar that slowed Brits, made them name the whole state Tarheel. But though the name is dark, its water runs as clear as anything, a lens enlarging the clean bottom, silver minnows there, harmless, just fish.

Near one rock, a glove is tacked. It has fish scales on it—somebody wore the thing while scaling their catch. A little note says, "This anybody's?" You tell yourself they wouldn't *do* that, not up there.

Find a place in high weeds. Still in shirt-sleeves, it's comforting to hug your knees and blue-stained pant cuffs. Lean back against the tree. There are meadowlarks. Church bells signal 8 a.m. in different denominations' register.

—NO ARMY will ever take you again. If a fresh war breaks out (and you, alas, suspect one will) you would sooner put your sons (as yet unborn, admittedly) on ships to foreign countries, Africa, anyplace. Anything is better than losing a boy to death—or even *not* losing him, even just letting him go through it, letting him come home with a headful of this you have. The town comes alive with sticky tender commercial life behind you—brooms on entryways, awning squeaking up, somewhere a cash register tries its tinny heartless music.

When you wake, the sun says early afternoon. You've slept so long. Maybe there's still a breakfast to be had, three eggs, wheat toast, grits, raspberry jam, lots of serious coffee. Now to go and buy the Swiss watch you've long studied at Cuthrell's, a instrument that doesn't show the moon, but chimes. Merciful, it doesn't warn you with "Work For the Night Is Coming" (as if you didn't know that). Swiss, it's jeweled to be quiet. This is good as the other one, more modern maybe but just as fine in its own way, right? Then you'll go to the bank to buy Meadows' Pasture for everybody and yourself.

YOU'RE wolfing breakfast served by a waitress, her little daughter, Lolly, crimping her doll's hair in one corner. The widowed waitress knows your entire story or thinks she does (that in itself a comfort). "I love to see a man *eat*," she says, and you chew, looking her over, like considering doling that fine favor her way. "Eat *food*," she says, and you both laugh, you with your mouthful. You must go see Mother, to prove you lived, you're back. This waitress's every Southern "sugar" helps you feel resettled and more real. You wipe your mouth on the cloth napkin and lean back. Out the window you know every soul you see and many wave. "Back?" some mouth through glass.

"Back," you nod.

You open the velvet cask, you set the hands of your new watch by the big round café clock. To hold the timepiece to your ear and close your eyes, learning its voice, not borrowed, bought.

"New?" the waitress asks.

"Sure is. Swiss. They never go to war, you know, the Swiss."

"How they do that, you reckon?"

"Just smart, I guess. Not sure—I'll have to look into it. —But, yeah, I think this one's going to keep real good time."

Later, during a very needed bath, you find that your own legs are—up to the hairy kneecap, one showing that awful scar—tinted blue. Like a centaur, you're half animal till—six latherings and a scrub brush later—blueness floats off. It's gone, with that fearful tannic foreign smell.

—So, child, this's been the story of Simon's splendid pocket watch. Its fate, its travels.

The end.

One Old Man
in Here
I Like

We took sweet counsel together, and walked
unto the house of God in company.
— PSALM 55:14

MALES are frailer and shorter-lived, overly talented at the pride
that depresses. So there ain't many non-bedridden men here at
Lanes'. Them that's here get noticed. Some things never change. Where's
the justice?

We have twenty-nine women and twelve men left, last count. Counting
is something you got to do most every breakfast. "Well, friends, what's the
latest bloodshed box score? Did poor Nineteen make it through the night?"
We use this shorthand—useful, considering the room turnover owing to
excess death. Every person first gets known by the number over their door.
If they last three months, you go ahead and memorize their name.

"You mean the *new* Nineteen? That last one—gloomy Gus—he hardly
got unpacked."

"But I thought our only recent new one was Thirty-nine."

"Thirty-nine? Fool, you're slipping. *I* am Thirty-nine. Six straight years
I've been Thirty-nine."

"You and Jack Benny. Jell-O Again."

My own favorite male stays Twenty-one, Professor Taw. It ain't escaped
me: Other ladies in here like him too. Thirteen and Thirty especially. That
Thirteen is shameless and throws herself at people and I pity her for it. One
thing about Twenty-one, he has the kind of cynical sense of humor that lets
a body squeak through tiny spaces, expecting nothing, settling for what little
comes. "You *see*?" he says when the worst turns up. It often does. That way,
he makes nothing seem a predicted something—perpetual-motion machine.

The fellow is also the very encyclopedia come alive. A lot of folks read
books, but how many remember all the good lines? Taw once confessed to

taking three pills of chelated zinc every day of his life. He's popped them ever since—at the age of thirty-eight—he first forgot something. He offered me free zinc. "Not that *you* need it," Taw told me, a first compliment. I may be vainest about my memory—which is most of what little I've got left to brag on, child. He was shrewd, knowing what I'd tolerate anybody's praising. And he knew it just days after coming in here on a stretcher.

Now I *do* take zinc, when I remember to. And I ain't much worse off than I was back when Taw got dragged in here looking like a condemned man. Even now, Taw drools some. How else can I say it? Look, nobody's ideal. The poor man's skin is yellow as Lifebuoy soap. He was one of the Why Me? types I mentioned. The kind that seems to think he's got a life sentence to serve out—which is true enough. These ones want to get loose early, they think dying's like parole. So they die.

Well, Professor Taw didn't. Or least, he ain't yet. Us two tease each other something merciless. Others can't stand to be around us long. Fine with me. I could wish that the man was in better health. Just my luck, finally hearing the long-awaited song, then catching its very last stanza.

Fact is, the makers of Camel cigarettes—his brand from the twenties on—should pay to keep this gent off our nation's streets where others might hear his unfiltered cough. He's lost a lung and a half. He's still got a three-pack-a-day habit. I don't want to talk about it. If you're a person's friend, you don't harp on things you know are past their ever changing. Sure, it hurts you, but you keep still.

Professor Wendell Taw is the one person at Lanes' that has a fame bigger than local. Very first day he arrived, while he was still in Admissions yelling at the staff, our head nurse stopped in here with my pills. She told me about his prizes in physics. She explained he was part Cherokee and had never married. He'd lost his pension by investing in some microscope that'd split atoms, or could *see* atoms get split or something. I noticed him missing the next day's breakfast then the next. Bad sign. I smelled tobacco fumes coming out under his door. I figured Twenty-one's number was all but up. I'd caught a glimpse of him—a hard man and a proud one. Maybe you'll be disappointed in me, sugar, but I've always felt drawn to a certain kind of Ornery. Man. Being right tough myself, I forever believe that I can get under the rock of them. Takes one to know one, all that. A kind gentle easygoing helpful type man—now I *appreciate* one. I know the world needs more. I love them for friends—like Jerome, everybody's favorite orderly, black or white. Like Larry. But such generous boys don't quite get my motor purring, get that flint to sparking heat. It still happens even at my age. You'd be surprised. Maybe you'd feel disgusted, honey. But Time'll change that. You'll be happy when it's you.

Taw's third day here, with me being naturally nosy and too old to feel ashamed of it, your Lucy decides to talk with him just onct before he passes. The Professor wouldn't even leave his room to see our soap show. When two ladies walkered in and begged him to come watch it, when they told him about Carlo's roadster going over the cliff maybe for real this go-round and about the Uptons' marriage problems because of what happened *one time only* between Raphaela Upton and the randy car mechanic during a thunderstorm upstate—which was, the ladies tried telling Taw, to prove how liberal they were, nobody's fault—he just laughed at them. He called them Porridge Brains, he threw the book at them. Literal. Propped wheezing in bed, it was all the man could reach. "And then he threatened to—something—on us," one later explained. "Tell, Maude."

"To spit right on us," Maude admitted, looking at her hands.

"Thank you, Maude," her friend said, and Maude added as how she felt better for saying it.

Well, I had me a crude thought. From our Bookmobile Lady (Tuesdays and Thursdays) I checked out *Beginning Physics*. It was a pretty powder-blue color, the jacket. I tried reading the first six chapters—to help me show off. I soon give up. At Normal School, I never even got far past fractions. Well, physics with its drag times and force fields made me feel satisfied but overfull like I'd ate twelve pounds of chicken and pastry and the pastry lumps was opening a chicken-and-pastry franchise at the bottom of my stomach. So, what I did, I memorized (and this was even *before* zinc's help) some test questions stuck between chapters. "What *is* energy?" run one. I admit: lately I'd been wondering that myself. Maybe you noticed that—unlike many a other old person—I never talk about my physical complaints. That, I believe, is why I snag a bit more company than most along this hall. I'm lucky. But I will say this—six months ago, I was not in no pink of health, bodily or otherwise. You get bored. Your body does. You ask it to do something usual—like digest this, please. It goes, "Why *should* I? *Again?*" So, the big Yawn was really setting in for good when I noticed Taw. —The hardest part is a old animal's keeping properly interested. You can decide to.

Book in my lap in my chair, I knock at his door. No answer. Unlimited time passed. I finally called, "Get decent. It's just somebody." Without waiting to be asked, I wheeled right in. He'd brought nothing with him but half dozen old-time sandbag-bottomed ashtrays (already full), a good set of German binoculars (in a case like a rifle's), plus around four hundred books and many a notepad. Not one family photo. He might have been a silverfish that gets its nourishment direct from nibbling paper. Or from Camels. My chair met smoke thick as a mad scientist's experiment in a movie show. And back of haze, like the bush that burned but won't ever all the way consumed, him—half Cherokee, all bone, part genius. I was sure of it. I *needed* him to be one.

From out the foggy gray, one long yellow-orange hand pointed back towards that door I'd just used. "You plan to interest me in something. You intend to 'draw him out.' Spare me. Do. 'A sense of duty is useful in work but offensive in personal relations.'—Bertrand Russell. Close the door behind you. Madam? I spit on you and your Welcome Wagon." In bed, he turned away.

Sure, it was a poor greeting. But his voice gave off the color of a plum fifteen minutes before it's going to be overripe—if you can catch the thing the very second it's most perfectly ready, you know it'll give you everything and just for finding it in time. Still, true, sure, the stranger had been extra surly.

I threw my wheels into reverse. I had mostly backed into hall again when I stopped. He must of seen me hesitate. Then, I promise you, I heard him clear his throat and chest—a sound I will not wish on any future human ears (a warehouseful of cellophane is wadded at onct). And he did. Spit. A big parchment-colored corner piece of something landed on lino not three inches from my left wheel. I looked down at the thing. "You *are* rude," I said. "Ain't you a nasty old thing to do that, hocking oysters at *me!*"

Well, then, I took as big a breath as my small but clearer lungs would accept and, with my best slippers and the chair's chrome footrest still in his room, I chanced it, navigated right towards his bed. "Prepare to duck," I told myself. I was considering giving the man a second chance, I figured what *else* is there to do till *My Children* come on at one?

Finally went, "Hi! I'm taking me a physics course by correspondence? and I'm doing so bad that even the mailman laughs. I need to lift a few answers off of you, like it or no, and if you spit again and especially if you get any *on* me, I'll . . . do something. I ain't saying what but you don't want to test me, hear? —Okay, now for starters: Why is gravity so great and what *is* energy?"

Safe behind smoke, he looked my way—it was the most bored expression I have ever seen on any human face, alive or dead.

Silent, he downed about half a cigarette with one slimy inhale, the whole front end flared to prove it was dying right into the dead part where all its million kin had been perishing since 19 and 21. Lanes' End for Camels. Odd, watching, I felt sorrier for that weed than for him.

Professor Taw and me both waited a right long time to know what might happen next. Finally he goes, "You don't require a physics lesson. You need a hearing aid and some fierce training at manners. Secondly, you could use acting lessons. That is the feeblest ploy imaginable. A course by mail. Who put that idea into your head? The director, who called me 'new boy on campus'? Or the swishy black orderly, who thinks this mausoleum is a popularity contest—with his menu of 'optional' services? Massages indeed. Who sent you?"

I held my own. I stared Taw down, tried. With the smoke between us, I couldn't really tell who was winning—a mercy. "Yeah?" says I, trying to sound tough, knowing I won't making too good sense. "Well, Buster Brown, look, between us—off the record—I'll leave if you slip me just the one. Okay. I believe I'll go with: What *is* energy?"

"If I knew that, would I be sealed into this crypt? Would I look like this? Would I put up with every senile hag's rolling in here feigning an interest in my subject? There've been others, you know. Don't fancy yourself as

being in the least unique. Does your book even concern physics? I seriously
doubt it."

"Is the Pope Cath'lic, you raunchy old . . . cigarette butt."

"Hold up the text, then, which is it? And don't you dare touch me, you.
Just place it on the southeast corner of the bed." I flung it down—like
granting him something major and not liking that one little bit.

He grabbed *Beginning Physics*, twisted away from me, moaned, "Oh
God, not the Tripler edition. No. No!" And he gawked at me like this might
be some great first joke we shared.

"Yeah, the Triplet," smirks I. "What *of* it?"

"For openers, it's roughly twenty-eight or -nine years out of date."

"Well, who ain't, mister? —You're *not*, I guess?"

"Certain old women might shrug off thirty years of hard-fought break-
throughs. I can't afford to. Three decades back, you were probably already
well past noticing. Look at your face. You have so many ruptured capillaries,
you appear suntanned. You seem to be roughly what? a hundred and eighteen or nineteen, very roughly. —You, only thirty years out of date! don't
flatter yourself, Nefertiti. And she uses the *Tripler*! Well, I spit on your
edition."

"Don't you dare. It's the Public Library's. I'll get fined."

"Why torture me, why now? Bernie Tripler is retired to West Palm Beach
in a hacienda on the proceeds of interest earned by this first edition alone.
He and his wife, Olga—ghastly enterprising woman—threw this thing together during one of their college summer vacations. Years ago we were all
in school together. Their timing was incredible. The ninth edition Wilkinson
was thoroughly fatigued (we all made jokes about it) but every college
somehow used it anyway. While *I* was fighting to get my name into such
texts, the Triplers, totally superficial climbing types, stole off, did a com-
pilation of lowest-common-denominator survey facts, and proceeded to retire in style. —The Tripler edition, and you dare bring me this!"

Knowing I was in semi-over my head, I decided to keep still—maybe
racking up a bit more accidental credit. For good measure, I crossed my
arms, like Castalia taught me. —Ruptured capiltaries? Is *that* what's turnt
me brown as a yam?

He paused. "Out," he said.

"No," I went. "I need tutoring and I ain't leaving till I get me at least
jigger of it."

"You're tremendously hostile. Your face and age have made you as bitter
as gall, haven't they?"

"Maybe they have, maybe they ain't. But I'm here to stay." Then I remembered a song off of Easy Listening radio. " 'Did you say I had a lot to
learn? Well, don't think I'm a-trying not to learn . . . Teach me tonight.' "
(I'm not sure why I told him this. But when a person spits at you, it makes
you do strange.)

"She's totally senile. She's speaking doggerel. She . . ." Then I saw him decide something, that maybe I was harmless. (It's a mistake others have made and later paid for dearly.) Old Professor Taw—squinting in the blue globe of his personal smoke—using a bone finger stained saffron from sixty years' nicotine, flipped to the back of my book, quick as any cardsharp. Throwing my textbook open on the bed's nearest edge, his witty hand then pointed, whisked away. For a man his age, Taw had very few liver spots. I give his Indian blood full credit.

I read aloud. "The Taw Effect (in combustion)."

Bent over his bed, with my eyes so far gone, I was ashamed of needing to stoop three inches from the words. I next felt pleased but scared. —To have your name in somebody else's library book and them wheeling it around in their chair's side pocket, not even knowing. It was something.

I never before imagined I might meet anybody with their name someplace safe, permanent, on record for as long as the world rolls forwards. The Triplers—Bernie and Olga (see how quick a study I can be when I get all hopped up around celebrities?)—they'd showed Taw's formula and under it had printed a paragraph—a short one, true, but a paragraph—and in a book for beginners. Someway, that seemed to me better than getting your work wrote up in a rule book for more higher-ups. It meant that this ruined-looking wheezy man had—while teaching college in a small Tennessee hill town—managed to get in on the ground floor of . . . well, the Physical World, or something.

"How . . ." I hesitated to make a fool of myself, but then, like always, threw caution aside, just jumped even into physics, feet-first. (Honey, if I kept my dignity safe on every single subject I'm ignorant of, why, I'd never say *any*thing.) "How, sir . . . did you think it up? Or whatever."

"One doesn't 'think it up,' Rebecca of Sunnybrook. One *notices*."

(I felt a chill, being, my own self, a fan of noticing.)

"It had been present all along. It only required someone's saying, 'There. That,' and then describing it for the record. It's not like a work of art. 'Art is *I*—science is *us*.' I simply added one more inch onto the temple. This," he pointed to the tiny equation, four two-storied numbers and a bridging equal mark, "describes the single new thing I observed. But, enough self-promotion. Before you leave, I have two questions for you—Miss, Mrs.?"

"Mrs. but the Mister he done died."

"More the fool he. First, your name, and secondly, why, oh why are you still in here plaguing me? Did I not tell you to leave? Do you *like* being spat on? Some do, I'm told. Leave, now. Why are you here? Who sent you?"

"Number one . . ." (*I* could enter into the scientific spirit, child.) "Name's Lucy Marsden. To you, Lucille. No, Mrs. Marsden. The Widow Mrs. Marsden. Number two: It ain't ruptured capillaries, it's rouge, intentional rouge. Plus, I'm here because (A) I'm just nosy, which is lucky, because (B) it keeps the air going into and *out* of your nose, and . . . well, because, well . . . (D)"

"(C)."

"No, sir, (D). I *meant* (D)."

"You slipped and you're covering. I can't abide that. Did you or did you not just now make a slack and probably senile mistake?"

"Yeah, well, it won't happen again, all right, ashtray mouth?" And I grabbed my book, my Tripler, and reverse-wheelied right out of there.

One thing I remember from my days of flirting and the receded high tide of the lovey-dovey: You got to always leave them feeling your womanly mystery. *Burn* them with it. I figured maybe the first glimpse of me had rekindled a will to live in Taw's ruined chest. Darling, I wouldn't of gone back in there, even if I heard the man begging.

Of course, I didn't. Hear him. All I heard: coughing. As coughs go—if most along this hall sound the size of potholes in the road—Taw's was the Carlsbad Caverns. You couldn't believe a man so thin could go down so deep. But, being me and needing this, I even let his cough seem less a tax paid for my visit than some small tribute to it. I'd upset him? Okay. He had noticed he was living, hadn't he? That'd do for now.

How to explain all this to a person young as you? I figured it'd been a start. Every great journey begins with that first humble bunion. Twenty-one. Well, well.

I REMEMBER rolling then to our Visitors' Lounge, nobody around—my powder-blue Tripler pressed against me. I sat staring at the aquarium's two surviving angelfish. Used to be a crowd in there. The two drifted around and around noplace particular, half studying one another, circling only their earlier circles but at least in there together. A bubbler coughed in gasps considered healthy for sea life. And setting here before green water, hugging my physics like some new Bible, I started to know: I *hoped* for something, and after so long without a plan.

I pictured more purposeful breakfasts, lunches, dinners in Multi-Purpose. For onct, physics seemed on my side, something held me straighter in my chair.

And odd: I knew that I would have to live a while longer. Just to see how it all turned out. "What is energy?" . . . Well, partly it's the central heating system hid inside the question "What'll happen next?" The most optimistic question in the world!

Something had just changed me. I bent forwards from my chair. I did a silly thing. I pressed my creasy lips against cold glass. First the fish darted off, then calmed each other. Finally they drifted nearer, checking what my mouth was. Food? Maybe something good.

But, darling, why *him*? A yellow crank, a chain smoker who spit on folks? A man who'd lost all but half a lung? Somebody penniless and vain and mean? Still, I'd got interested against my will. I needed to know more. A person she still feels things. I'd seen something I wanted.

DON'T laugh at me.

The
Passable
Kingdom

The wolf also shall dwell with the lamb, and
the leopard shall lie down with the kid, and
the calf and the young lion and the fatling
together, and a little child shall lead them.
                                  —ISAIAH 11:6

D OC COLLIER attended me during that first pregnancy and he
did fine till my eager-beaver daughter arrived early. Doc was off
someplace in the country, hard to trace. And here *I* was, waddling around
the house in socks wet from the water fallen with a great playful weight
(like the sound Castalia made that time I tackled her). So I asked a neighbor
to fetch Cassie, but quick. I saw her basin first, then the two dark hands
gripping it, and all the rest of her came sudden in the door, wider than
when last we met, and she clanged the basin down onto the floor beside
my bed and pointed at the basin. "Goes in there," she said then laughed.

Cap had been in the room, I sent him somewhere. Also banished my
own mother, who, no good in emergencies, was literally tearing her best
hankie to shreds. Both these folks appeared right grateful for Castalia's
presence. I looked up at her holding the brass alarm clock, timing my
contractions—totally involved with my lower body, my crowning child, my
legs' position. Cas kept checking from lower Lucy regions to the clock's face
like seeking some family resemblance—but she was not studying *me*. I can't
tell you how relieving I found this, darling, having somebody treat me just
. . . factual. It let me know: Every drunk downtown on Saturday had costs
some poor woman nine months, then this. Put it all in perspective. I now
wanted to do good for my child and Castalia, in that order. The big woman
was in control down there and her sympathy was impersonal. That someway
made it feel just enormous, bigger even than skinny me felt: subleased to

a girl child weighing (you ready?) nine pounds and two ounces, and a first child too.

Smarts.

Beneath me, as Cassie got me stooping over the enamel basin white as me and round as Mother Earth, as she got me to squat like black women delivered then—I studied the ivory-colored palms of her black-backed hands. An amazing sight (when, once, I briefly took leave of the pain whilst on the verge of passing out). Beneath me I saw colors—the beet-blue baby's advancing pliant head, the cord so red it seemed orange, and glossed with my own entrail leavings plus the baby's packing slop and luster, plus those coal-toned male-sized hands easing a child out of my unlikely! Then pain reclaimed me as raw matter. My entire nervous system went on red alert, and the niceties of coloring lost all charm. Loan-shark oxygen threatened to call back its controlling interest in my lungs' continuing.

I saw Castalia's satchel full of items familiar from the closet in my kitchen, the needle and thread now meant something new. She doused a terry rag with wintergreen, she pressed into its fold real mint leaves from her yard and, with my child squalling in my arms, the feel of Cassie's hands mashing compress across my forehead meant a benediction that could only be delivered by a child-bearing woman to another who's just managed that. "Thank you," I said to the ceiling, meaning her. "Welcome," came her umber voice without a trace of usual irony. But then I knew she hadn't said "You're welcome" to my gratitude, she was greeting the little goon in my arms. "Louisa," I said, "for the lady what wrote *Little Women*." "Good enough," Castalia told me. I asked her to say the name out loud to make it real. She did, first to me and then to her, right close near Louisa, who quieted. "She know," Cas remarked.

"*Who* know?," I needed it again. "Louisa do." I laid here under mint and wintergreen and how glad I was that Doc had been far out, important and untraceable, in Edgecombe County. Captain and my mother were soon close up, and it hurt me to notice how, between their sides, under their arms, a shape retreated, gathering equipment and stealing towards our parlor. (I'd never wanted a servant around, and I certainly did not want *her* being just a servant.) "Not yet." I reached toward Castalia's great cascading mass of back. So these other white adults called her in again, they acted understanding but disturbed. "I still here, not to fret none, Baby Momma."

"Good. Stay."

I needed her here to tell me that this strange wizened mewing toadish . . . *shape* was complete, regular. Human. Just having Cassie's bulk near the bed let me relax finally, sobbing but not crying, pure release, and a single thought rose up out of my head, child: *This is my house*. I won't no longer a bartered kid adults could trick or bully. I was the mother to Louisa first and foremost, though I'd never even got to tell the girl one story yet. My child. And lying there, so calmly, I knew: I would kill to keep her being safe with me in a nice white house forever. *Mine*.

Then I saw I had been yelling that. I looked around my bed and my mother wept to see me made a mother with a child helpless as she had been a child. My husband shook his head with pride or shock and his huge Reb-gray eyes were wet too. Only Castalia's burned dry, amused. She was getting a kick out of me yelping *Mine*. I made a face at her. We laughed. It caught the others out.

THIS I must say:

Having babies is one thing in life I *know* I didn't make up.

I do have this tendency to embroider on the decent muslin truth. You noticed? My momma was born right well-off, so to me, she's a heiress. Poppa loved his low pranks—he come to seem nearbout the Mark Twain of the Piedmont. But, if anything, I draw back from overstating the pain and wonder (they can amount to the same thing) of toting then spilling nine six-to-ten-pound young ones. And me myself just ninety-six pounds dripping wet when the waters broke!

How children get here—in my wildest fever dreams, I couldn't have invented. (If you put it in a made-up book . . . who'd believe?)

Folks oohed and aahed that somebody skinny as me could have so many children so fast. I figure it's like a jar of olives, once you get the first worked loose, others topple free more easy. —Folks don't call it labor for nothing. Only my favorite midwife give me comfort. Any hour of the day or night, Castalia'd come running with her basin, all two-eighty-odd pounds of her on the move PDQ, her yelling, "Hold off, Cassie's come, goes in here." That helped. You know how some doctors say a person can't remember pain from one hurt to the next? Ha. For pain, I got a photogenic memory.

SOON as each of my children could talk, I started coaching them in their sums and figures. A Normal School teacher once told me I had a real knack for things mathematical. One day and one day only, she swore I was real college material. I run home and told Poppa. He must have thought my teacher said College of Material—wanted to send me off to sewing school in Rocky Mount. Even with that much training, I'd of been extra thrilled.

I always did have a good attitude. That's been my problem, see. My regrets come not from what I did wrong, but every silly thing I did right. Odd, how all along I figured I was a one-girl rebellion, little Miss Red Mischief. It's insulting to look back and see: They considered me Miss Easy to Boss. My golden award—if I ever get one—turns out to be: Best Actress in a Supporting Role. And all along they told me it was the starring part!

> We built a ship upon the stairs
> All made of the back-bedroom chairs,
> And filled it full of sofa pillows
> To go a-sailing on the billows.

> We took a saw and several nails,
> And water in the nursery pails,
> And Tom said, "Let us also take
> An apple and a slice of cake—"
> Which was enough for Tom and me
> To go a-sailing on, till tea.
>
> We sailed for days and days
> And had the very best of plays.
> But Tom fell out and hurt his knee,
> So there was no one left but me.

Meaning, I was a married lady, alone in a house, making the best of it.

SEEMS the more you learn, the less you know, and five years into marriage I was *still* in bed with Captain Marsden. Still serving under him. During daylight, he could be okay company. His stories got better with practice, a good thing—since he repeated them right often. Times, I liked having him underfoot. Right after breakfast, he'd stand, pull at the double V's his vest bottom made—then, serious, the man would draw out his platinum pocket watch, set it by our kitchen's Seth Thomas. There was something in his steady look then, preparing to leave the house for work, not really wanting to—like taking our strength into the world with him. The man could charm a person—little jokes he'd heard. He'd come home from a buying trip and tell the children that he'd seen one farmer who had hogs so skinny the man had to knot their tails to keep them from sliding out the cracks in the fence. "Lucy," he tipped back in his kitchen chair. "Yesterday I was privileged to meet the world's foremost sheep counter. Fastest in our nation. I asked his secret and, you know, he actually told it to me."

Our children, eating pancakes, listened. "And what *was* his secret, Captain?" (We had it down.)

"Man said, 'It's easy. I just count their hooves and divide by four.' "

I laughed. The older kids frowned, the younger ones still waiting.

Sometimes Cap would hoist our two oldests—each a armful—and then turn in one place till he got so dizzy he had to tilt against the mantelpiece, laughing—taking great bites of household air. Kids wailing, "More, harder, Poppa," the youngests begging to go next. —But this was during daylight. Later, when you get your children in bed and off to sleep, later, when the decks were cleared, child, watch out.

He might have worked long hours, maybe he rode across three filthy counties buying decent shoats, mules. But you could not tucker out that old soldier. All was never quiet on *his* western front! Well up into his fifties, a fellow still randy as three billies at rut. Some nights I'd beat retreat to my sewing room off the kitchen, my only refuge. I had the key. I'd spread a pallet on the floor. Soon, he knocked on the door. He'd ask, of his own knocking, "Who *is* it?" A tender charming joke, he thought. The man wouldn't stay out of there even if I locked, even if I propped a chair under the doorknob. I blocked the entry with my foot-treadle Singer. Fellow could not take a hint.

Cap had a history of battle tactics on his side, had a bull's own strength. I was the china shop this particular bull had got used to. I thought about them signs in porcelain gift stores: "Sorry, folks, but: You break it, you bought it." Well, he had bought it before he broke it. Bought it so he could break it in good. Captain would just jimmy up the window. "Hi," he'd say, stepping in, standing there, grinning like I couldn't guess what-all he planned for us, me. "Just happened to be passing by. Couldn't help notice your light on, Missy. I've certainly been missing you," grins he.

"You ain't been missing *me*," I says. "You might be missing something but it ain't me. Least, ain't *much* of me."

"But . . ." He toyed with his watch chain, studied the floor, rocking his upper body to and fro like a schoolboy doing Diction. "But it's one of my favorite parts."

"So I noticed."

He steps nearer, squats down by my pallet, says, hoarser, "Can't I just *look* at it?"

What's a woman to do? You can't live with them. You can't live without. But you can't live. —To put it mildly, sugar, the honeymoon was over.

THESE DAYS they call it lovemaking, don't they? Used to, that meant just the kissing part, the warm-up. Titles change, styles in it shift, but that particular shenanigan has sure stayed popular right along. Well, after a while, you quit the struggling, you see it's maybe bigger than the both of you. Even bigger than him—which is going some. For one thing, it's free. They *really* love it in poor countries. It don't demand no expensive regulation gear but what you got on you. —Finally a woman has to learn to just lean back into it—either that or leave home. Relaxed, it sure hurts less. And there were times, I got to admit, I found out how to catch him, how to dash on by and wait ahead, toe-tapping, miles in front and ready for my Captain to rush up red-faced, wheezing like the horse cavalry, and finish the famous race my old man did so dearly love to run. He seemed to need it—proof sure he was still alive. It was a kind of punch clock for a man of fifty-some. I was a kind of punch clock.

Honey, when he traveled on the road for three nights straight, I'd finish the dishes, get the last of our kids' pajamaed, I'd stay longer than usual tucking them in. I would come downstairs, and every pine knot's popping of house timbers, every dog barking a block off would be filling in this odd new time—a welcome silence but, too, strange, don't you know? Them old songs might call it "Lack of a man." To me it was more "Lack of somebody." He happened to be it—that give him standing—faults and all. And when I moved from lamp to lamp, dousing household lights, the place seemed darker than usual with just me downstairs. I didn't miss it (didn't exactly want him to jump out of a hall closet, grinning, "I been homesick for something, guess what?"). I just missed his extra stir and weight—call it ballast.

He knew too much about card games and horse races. One night in bed he'd told me how folks invented the saying "To get somebody's goat." Seems that racehorses are keyed-up, high-strung creatures—jumpy about being shipped from track to track. So trainers give the thoroughbreds their own pet—another small life to fit into their stall each night: a goat. It soothes, this mascot, comes to be familiar and a constant. Well, bad men, the night before some race, they know how they can sure upset a competition horse. They steal into the stall, they kidnap the champion's beloved goat. The racehorse won't catch one wink one of sleep. "To get your goat." Nights that Captain was on the road, seemed my own was gone. The old goat. I slept shallower. Missed him and—only the slant-like, I reckon I got to miss that other part, too.

Yet, once he come home and however I cooperated, it never seemed enough. Captain believed Bed to be a type of siege. During, he'd mutter down at me, sometimes in a not-nice voice. Some evenings, he growled like I was a Yankee boy he'd trapped behind Rubble lines, a boy foe he planned to finish off from the back in a whole new way.

Later when one of our sons went out for high school football, I learned the name of a penalty: "unnecessary roughness." On me, Cap was still making Northerners pay. I was the middleman trapped between wartime and tonight. Sometimes he'd get my wrists wrestled flat to mattress, veins up. I'd call, "Look, ease off, I promise I ain't going anyplace, okay?"

Honey, for him it was all a flanking action.

Afterwards, Cap would roll my way, might lift one braid end from my unraveled bun, would try brushing my closed eyes with it, ask me how I was. But he didn't really want my facts. Poor thing longed for compliments, like craving good grades from his Normal School teacher. —You know how women get blamed for being too monthly-moody, for staying too near mirrors? Look, I described the Captain's dress uniform, didn't I? Well, they don't call it a *dress* uniform for nothing. Men have always held the patent for sullenness. Why, war itself is a form of pouting.

As for mirrors, men invented those. There's that myth boy that looked into a pond's top and fell flat in love with his reflected self. He figured the only thing on earth better than hisself was hisself twice. Thought he was so pretty he took the name of a flower. He did. In sulking and raw vanity, men could give us women lessons for life. Oh, don't get me on the subject of it, please.

I'm sure that Captain tried. But in bed he was like a stamp collector born with mittens on. A steam locomotive trying to hop up onto your knees and pass as a lapdog. Just wouldn't fit. Too much of everything. We never truly dovetailed at the mouths or lower. Teeth always knocking, bones in the wrong spots. He was twice my weight, going on three times my age. I don't want to dwell on this.

He kept a few old muskets right under our bed. Sometimes, during, I'd think of them—deadly—just inches below, antique and maybe loaded, cocked, and each one listening.

Times, in bed, my man wanted to try something "new." Like somebody in a restaurant holding the menu, accustomed to ordering roast chicken only—now snapping at the waitress, "What's *new* here?"

"New" meant tighter fits when use had broke in this or that.

"New" meant having your head shoved down onto such bulks as seemed a fire hydrant's own. This too raw for you?—go read Hallmark—this is my life. "New" could—a few times at his drunkest—mean a message itch of beard cleansing me like some angel of steel wool. Now, I think back on how strict we looked by day and at church and it strikes me how basically wild we were come night. Times, it shamed me. Times, it hurt me. Times, it felt like canopy of daylight and pure oxygen overtop our carved and squeaking bedstead. What I liked best: It was just us. Nobody would need to know. It was—at its best—like some legal playpen for adults.

Of course, I was a very young girl starting out. He was busy seriously corrupting the morals of a minor. Many a night—to be honest—it was with the minor's full consent. We had married. Richer or poorer, in sickie or in health.

Last week I looked at the Mall's supermarket's magazine racks: It's just naked people squirming on everything. Folks forget to notice. It's like them dreams where you go to church nude and nobody cares. Disappointing, really. The soap shows on the TV set, dear as I love my best one, it's basically about their all hopping into each other's beds. I don't like to say it but "soap" is what they mostly need. Bedroom's secrets are hanging out most everywhere. But, darling, to the menu question: "What's *new* here?" My answer is: Nothing. We tried it all in 18 and 97.

When it meant more.

January sometime 63, Virginia

Dear Momma,

Christmas was the same as other days. I never knew it could be but don't know what I expected. My socks are warm but sure very yellow and Sal and others say my legs look like a chickens. You say you want to know more than my being fine and asking How are you. Well maybe the strangest part here is games we played with Yankees. Before they moved, just a river kept their winter camp from ours. Since we had tobacco but no real coffee somebody got the idea of trading. Sal Smith my friend is good with his hands and made a little boat one foot square sealed with candle wax. He used his last good handkerchief to be its sail set up in sticks. He was once a tailor and sewed the sails in two minutes flat and the boat floated level. He put in a sacthel sathchel sachtel sachtel sack of tobacco he could spare and wrote a note that said *Yankees I am trusting you to do right and send me this same sack but full of real coffee.*

He went down by the reads reeds and used a stick to launch it so he could not be shot so easy. Sal sent it on across. It took over thirty minutes for it to drift about sixty some feet but we waited in the bullrushes. What else did we have to do? You know it came back! With coffee too. You never tasted anything better after our stuff made from parched rye. Its being brown and in tin mugs is about the one thing that lets ours try and even pass for coffee. Well we groaned with how good real coffee is. No wonder Yanks so often win lately. You feel stronger after it. Momma breakfasts before leaving I could never even have one sip. You said Too Young. Ha ha now. Well pretty soon we had a whole nice little navy going back and forth. Swaps and no hard feelings. First the fellows on our side of the river were scared to stand in the open for fear of getting shot but then we understood that anybody silly enough to sail these things would probably not mess up a good time by blowing your blamed head off. Soon we were waving at each other and trying to holler. Men put notes in stick rafts and the commerce was brisk, as Lt. Hester puts it. He knows how to put it evertime. The Yank notes were funny at first but one of our boys from the moutains which tends to be a hard type of fellow but good fighters he got somebody to write something for him. He never went to school. The thing he sail over said *Say Yanks have you got yourselves any nigger wives yet? We think maybe they would improve the Yankee breed a bit.*

Then a message came back that said *Say Reb why don't you people wear uniforms instead of those gray rags?*

Reb answer drifted over, *Who do you think we are anyways, a set of damn fools to put on our good clothes to go out and kill damn dogs in?* Then the shooting commenced. Our fleet of pretty boats got pretty much blown out of the water. It nice while it lasted. Like their not fighting during winter it made you wonder why it couldn't just go on like that. Well it is soon time for dirll drill which I hate but happens every Sunday like it or not. I would rather be there with you having rare roast beef and pudding and red wine from Poppa's cellar and with the good silver and flowers in the middle of the table so high we can hardly see each other over them. Sunday afternoon and your piano playing. Even jokes you memorized from mailorder books. I think I like those jokes now. Momma I sure know why they put the sick in homesick. It is like a disease for me sometimes around sunset especially. You keep right on being my mother don't you? Even after all the bad things I have had to do. They told us we should for the Confederaecy. You said to do what they tell me and I have. Everything that was just regular at home seems like remembering heaven. Winters go easier on a fellow. Which is why I wanted to write before the thaw changes one thing. I bet you never believed I could do so many pages at once did you Momma? It took me days to. You can do a lot of things you never knew you could till it's time. Yesterday I found the best rock kristl crsytl quarts I ever have. Well so long.

I wanted to send this one on off. Do not for one minute doubt that I am stay your loving son and Willie.

Seventeen years after Appomattox, my husband still meant to. Meant to go see old Sal Smith of New Bern, that leg-saving friend. But you know how it is with time and chores and excellent intentions. Those days, New Bern won't a two-hour car ride. It hid back of virgin woods, washed-out bridges, hairpin curves threading around the property lines of the powerful. Finally Will wound up there for the usual reason: moneymaking. He'd come to peddle overpriced peafowl to the takeover-type Yanks who'd bought the few river-front plantations Sherm's boys had spared.

Imagine it, you're on a leg that Sal saved. You're seventeen years and several pounds beyond the War. You turn a corner and here comes a banker-type, surrounded by yes-men holding clipboards, asking him questions. This gent wore a ground-dragging leather-looking coat. His face was framed in a starchy white collar and underwritten by a vulgar nugget stickpin. His hair looked dyed a hard brown, laid flat by grease. Fellow's right leg was wooden, but rosewood, mind you, and polished like some revered parlor furniture. The face, hopeless, had stayed yam-raw and comedy ugly.

Marsden, unrecognizably civilian, grown awful far past his own bony boyhood shakes, rushed this citizen and, practically breathless, called, "Why *has* the ocean stayed so doggone mad?"

The prosperous gentleman stopped dead. One portion of his tinted hair slowly unpasted and, like some bug's antenna, lifted as Will watched. The telltale cowlick! The gent touched my Willie's shoulders and checked behind this young out-of-towner. Maybe seeking a boy back there like Will had hid—all except his arms—in arrears of Private Ned Smythe, that kid almost irksomely perfect.

"Because it's been crossed so many times. —You?" Sal asked. "Grown? Better looking'n me, nice *hair*. You okay basically, pal?"

They fell against each other and wept there while the yes-men acted shy and a bit bored. Marsden found his tears falling on a leather coat that smelled of rubber. Tears became instant beads. Some tricky coat. Will asked Salvador Cortez Drake Magellan Smith, "Where'd your leg go, and what'd the money come from?" Old friends get to ask straight questions very soon.

During the ride to Sal's country house, another story unfolded. You tired of them yet? Sal got home from Surrender on a overcrowded troop train, Rebs a wasp-like swarm on every metal inch of it. The train crossed a war-hurt bridge. Here a locomotive gave up its ghost, went loco right into the creek taking all down with it. It chose Sal's favorite leg to fall upon. Which proved almost lucky. Because it also picked sixteen torsos to crush, plus four soldiers' favorite heads. What's a leg, really? Sal came home dead broke and partly missing. He gimped into a tailor shop ransacked of tweeds by one sly loverboy assistant. The shop contained a calendar (last year's), cups of China tea grown blue with mold, back bills for buttons, and— jammed on a rear wall's nail, this: a four-inch square of black rubber tarp, which tended, unbacked, to split and droop. It had been fused, by steam iron maybe, to a four-inch square of good hundred-percent cotton duck. With it on the nail, our Florida-hidden Chinaman had left this note: "Maybe do a gobbet for the day rain come down sky? Make hole soot. Sorry rob you. You nice me." Mr. Smith took this paper home and read it to his loving hungry family. "Gobbet" they guessed meant garment. "Make whole suit"?

Thusly, dimplenook, great ideas get translated into reality (then bank accounts). Stripped of tweeds, Sal gained one watertight notion, a idea vivid to a man who'd just lived four wet years out of doors in sooty holes. His daughters helped him try and join floppy rubber onto good white gauze. Many vile-smelling fusions later, Sal borrowed money, secretly. He traveled with his smartest Spanish-speaking daughter by schooner to what's consid- ered Ecuador today. Latex contacts were made before the Smiths, taking on twin boys and the wife at Norfolk, sailed up north to mills in Massa- chusetts. Visiting D.C., Sal did a little patenting. The man who'd stopped one operation with borrowed dueling pistols started many other operations in civvie life. Magellan Drake, et cetera, proved worthy of his name.

At his large new house, he treated Will to Madeira and the company of daughters whose pictures he'd showed often from First Manassas to Ap- pomattox. Girls took after their pretty mother, as did the twin sons, now onto twenty. The new house was a monument of cold good taste. But joined to it by a lattice veranda was Sal's family starter cabin. Adjourning to this humbler tacky spot, the large handsome family grew louder. This place was solid family pictures, keepsakes. Its mantel was a mess of doilies and gim- cracks, seven obscene sets of ladies' thighs carved from forked sticks (their history comes later).

"Life's been strange yet kind," Sal touched his rosewood pegleg. "The thing that's bothered me most about our years together, Willie, son: my hair! Why did no one tell me? When I turned up here, my Emily was critical. She found sticks in it, big sticks. The color too was terrible. I'm now 'ash- brown,' much more like it. But, children, shall we explain to Willie what's the only stuff that helps me keep it mostly flat?" A nod all-round. Sal led them with his index finger, "*Ax*le-grease!"

Sal Smith and his sons showed Will some fine new rifles. They'd just been goose hunting and what Will later recalled the best was: one humble cabin's kitchen table heaped with sixteen dead Canada geese and teals. Daughters plucked and plucked. Someday, imagine having sons, someday to hunt ducks with your fine sons!

Will arrived back in Falls a downtown novelty. Him, all over in black rubber which, inside, meant tender white cloth. Behind each great man, a back-up lady keeping him all flexible. Will prayed for rain and—while folks hid under storefront porticos, applauding—he sloshed back and forth, crossing and recrossing puddled North Church Street, shouting, "Nothing to it!"

Given life's surprises, why *had* the ocean stayed so mad?

2

SOMETIMES on our Home outings to the Old Mall, I'll see a group of Viet vets near the fountain and its palms. The water splashing seems to soothe them. Though other folks'd like to settle there, nobody argues with these skinny men in fatigues and civvy mufti, mixed. Fatigues, the right word.

They look a lot like the vets I done described lolling in our Courthouse Square after that earlier war. A lot. One thing about a life stretched long as mine, you see things come around many, many times: here's those selfsame starved-out missing-something warrior faces. —The Rebs and the South Asian vets, they both lost. Makes your being home-and-hurting mean something different. You win, you're forgiven more. Lose, means you've lost, both in your own head and in others'.

These moping boys were not necessarily no geniuses before getting shipped to Asia (or Maryland). Maybe that's why they were the ones that *went*. They grew up in churches, grew up being told: Freedom is worth saving, ladies and children first, standards, decency, rules, gentlemanly honor. Their home-boy waffle-iron brain motors purred along patriotic. All was well. Then, shipped to the front, they were told: to preserve home standards and women and kids, they should bypass all they'd been taught. In a civilian civil-type war, this might mean hurting non-home women and kids and gents, this could mean lining up suspected enemies against thatch walls and taking no chances, no prisoners. The boys' brain motors still worked, chugging hard to try and fit all this new stuff together, find a way of blending what seemed opposites. But, once home, the brain rebelled. It still *looked* like a waffle iron. But it was a implement that'd briefly had a city's worth of voltage pulse through it, knocking it right widely haywire. Motor still goes but all circuits are blackened, fused. So as a vet, you sit in the middle of the Courthouse Square, where ladies leave you mended shirts and leftovers, or near the Mall fountain that sounds like Asia's jungle rain. You people-watch the shoppers, Americans you gave your all to save. You see them call their children away from your spot. You see they're scared of what your saving them has done to you, guy.

I want to park my wheelchair among them and offer, "I know. I lived with one, my last husband, he suffered it too." I'm scared to bother them. They're in groups at the Old Mall, whispering, laughing, talking in infantry lingo decades after that stopped meaning anything to anybody but them. They lost. It shows, you smell this shame and rage they trail. What they're missing is what Rebs also lacked at the end of theirs, the real belief, reward. They now slouch out there in the temple of sales and busyness and maybe feel like they're yet guarding it and us. They were kids, and men told them to do a thing. Good literal boys, far from home, they did.

Now, out of work, living with Mom, forty-five years old, hooked on cough medicine or whatever at the Mall can be pilfered quick, they're glad for the fountain and the Oriental palms. They're most glad for each other. They lost a struggle. Everybody lost, lost them. They're out yonder every day. Waiting for the circuits of the head to heal. Waiting to be salaried as our guards. Waiting for a better war to come and make them right again.

Meanwhile I learned about survival training my husband had offered weird Winona Smythe in her back yard. Folks said her boast of the "town brain" only meant "a morbid streak." Being the single intellectual in a village of eleven hundred souls ain't much fun, especially when one thousand and ninety-nine of those don't think you're all that smart. —One year after Will's return, Winona got lessons in how soldiers ate and slept and took care of personal toilet needs. She used her army surplus "trenching tool," made small latrines under the wisteria. "Don't you want to know how it went, the *al fresco* . . . release, William?" Grieved, he made a sound. She answered, "Like clockwork. I faced the neighbors' house and thought pure thoughts and, well, clockwork."

"Yes, ma'am," was his only comeback.

She wanted to live entirely off mushrooms and berries found in her tangled yard. She ordered hardtack, and when the Lucas delivery boy come back empty-handed, she asked for Luke's explanation. He claimed such soldiers as has lived through war vowed they'd rather die than touch a piece of hardtack ever again. Winona's note said: "Order it and I'll swap you my second-best singer."

Two days later, Luke, in his apron, turned up early morning hours when he someway knew her caged birds warbled best. He used Winona's mingy parlor, took the bird he wanted in there so's he could hear its song unwoven from all others'. Sly one, Luke. He carried away the cage while passing Winona a tow sack that clattered as if full of roofing slates. She rushed past her three ignored neighbor ladies' greetings as they supervised maids hanging wet laundry. Tent flaps lowered, Winona took a hunk and bit, rebit, then sat there chewing and chewing. You had to. It was the flavor of mourning itself—soapy, harsh, and blank in the mouth. Metal and brewer's yeast, surf foam plus a trace of tar. Had the taste of history. Outside, the cicadas were already at it, throwing up these sheets and jagged stacks of sound. Made a tent over this two-man job where a big-jawed lady, all in dusty widow's weeds, sat cross-legged chewing chewing chewing on it. It lathered and stuck and became different slow-dawning colors in her mouth. Strange to be out here eating Then, eating Him.

And it was the following Saturday that everyone in two miles heard the gun go off in Widow Smythe's back yard at 3 a.m. Mindful of how grieved she'd been, aware of certain recent unsavory trends around her lawn (the neighbors' children had peeped from their highest pecan trees and reported seeing her do every manner of personal no-no under the wisteria—and all whilst carrying a old double-ought shotgun). The children were scolded for lying. (If you wrote a book . . .)

A quick committee formed—in nightshirts and robes. The group ventured forth to check on the source of so dreadful and window-rattling a blast. It was considered a godless hour in the best neighborhood of a small town this size one century back, and it would be today, child. No nice person phones another nice person after 10 p.m. unless there's been a death. Folks—appearing Tuscarora-tribal in their curling papers and eye cream—rung Winona's front-gate bell. Not waiting long, they stormed around to the side yard. Canaries—all thirty-six were out here with her, tonight massed in a pyramid of cages beneath a tarp like their own tent. Stunned by the blast, they still chittered, scared. Here beside a lantern, one smiling widow set cross-legged as any Indian. She looked exceedingly alive. Her tent straddled a hole with a big feather-bed bolster spilling out at one end. She'd dragged a low bookcase into the yard, the thing filled with favorite volumes of verse, mostly overdue from the library, and, on top of the case, all the art glass snatched from First Baptist's high altar. In lamp's glow she sat massaging her right shoulder—maybe where the rifle'd kicked considerable. She was smiling, constant.

"Thank God you're all right," said the Mayor's brother-in-law, a man who often introduced himself: "I am the Mayor of Falls' only brother-in-law, and who are you?" "We dreaded the worst. What's gone on, a thief, an altercation, some nigger intruder, what? Because: Not to fear, Widow Smythe, the neighborhood menfolk have gathered."

"That's what I keep a gun here for. Actually, a woodchuck. A monster woodchuck," she grinned even harder, the first time in recent memory. Her pleasure spooked folks worse than any usual sourpuss gloom. "And happily I nabbed one fat enough to feed me for many days to come." Then with a strange low chuckle, Winona Smythe reached into the grave of bedding. By its tail, she snatched forth a furred and dripping creature. The thing was bigger than some hunting dogs and it sent half the crowd scampering backwards, hiding behind each other, tightening belts of terry robes and letting loose a few squeals and several deeply felt "icch" sounds. For years neighbors had sworn that something near the size of hog was burrowing here in the Smythes' yard. Folks claimed this beast staged savage night raids on hybrid dahlias all along the street. "I can't *keep* dahlias," ladies complained.

One Christian woman, now clutching her nightdress shut at the neck, fought back her own disgust. "My dear Mrs. Smythe, if it's come to this kind of hunger, we have, you'll recall, regularly offered you casseroles, and for some years now. My squash one with the bread-crumb topping is, if I do say so my . . ."

"I like the taste of game," Winona gloated. "Especially homegrown game I nailed myself. Game's better when it's fresh, don't you find?" Then Winona couldn't but tell the truth: "This is the first time I've ever shot a firearm. And, beginner's luck, here I've realized a week of dinners, plus the pelt." Cheered, she moved to clean her double-barrel.

The Widow Smythe emptied her yard almost at once.

3

HONEY, I believe some men put on wars just to have a topic afterwards. My husband went and lived long enough to finally hear the Great War called that.

"Great?" Captain Marsden would snap. "They name this French thing Great and our only one on native soil gets downgraded to plain Civil? Why, that's not even patriotic."

My man's peacetime memory lost many a house key but it recollected the whereabouts of every roadhouse in either Carolina. A tale-telling vet could get free bourbon after dark. Captain Marsden's peacetime memory forgot to pay our grocery bills on time, but, child, his wartime one was a Dewey decimal system of musket balls. Every minute from '61 to '65 had schooled Cap in how to tell it true.

I heard his tales so often they've stayed more real than, say, the dirty looks our grocer gave me. From back of piled-up goods bought for seven children, then nine, I grinned at Luke Lucas of Lucas' All-Round Store. "Mr. Luke," says I, "this'll just be another charge."

The grocer—speaking of my husband's wartime fame and civilian slack—goes, "Lucy, the Light Brigade said that too, said, 'This'll just be another charge,' and look where it got them."

I decided to forget this part. You can see, I haven't.

A body learns to stress what you'd call the Upbeat. Maybe thanks to that, I still love my husband. Left on its own, Memory tends to make—not war—but many little treaties.

Captain Marsden had quite the mouth on him you get a few under his belt. Nobody had to force them down with no funnel, either. After our fifth child came, Cap swilled even more. Not sad, mind you, no, he just loved having five. He'd tell strangers about it, show the pictures. Be out celebrating three nights to the week. You'd think he'd won the lottery. First he would offer drinking pals free servings of his Antietam gore, then he'd swoop on home, corner our children. Finally I run clear out of patience.

Still, his tales could make a knot-tying merit badge out of anybody's heart. Since '65 and boyhood, he'd just expanded into all the space that respectful civilian ears awarded him. Others' listening held my husband up like ropes do the big top. After Lee signed it, Marsden stood taller, spread, gone huge with stories. By Appomattox, he'd only just begun to shave. Home, the beard sprouted like his lore did. Cap acted proud of his civvy whiskers, first brown then white. Heaped at the doorstep of his face, beard looked rolling and massy as a small woodpile. Each story would make him finger yet another corner of that great tangle. You definitely noticed my man's size. Had pores the size as dimes, fingernails tough and flat as baby garden trowels. Folks sometimes complained to me about his tall tales. Well, I say, a person this size can't help it.

Cap forever chose the wrong time for lovemaking and tale-telling. But on both counts, I'd usually hang around anyway. Don't ask me why. It's the foreground questions that're hardest to answer. Love—blame love. Times, I hated myself, but soon as he offered our kids "Once . . ." I usually gave in anywhere from twenty to thirty percent. You would've too.

—Know something, sugar? Stories only happen to the people who can tell them.

NOW, here I am, socked into this Home so called.

But I'm still semi-perked up, I would yet feel ripe for hearing his old rust-and-velvet voice. Even now, I know his war wounds by heart like the forty-eight states' capitals. Other stuff, I've dropped. Can't even remember all my Normal School teachers, which embarrasses a onetime not-that-bad student. Whole summers I have lost like items left off your grocery list. But what stays put are my hardships with the man, plus his tales. Like pets, each one got named. And, child, most every one still comes when called.

I'd best hurry. Soon they'll be bringing the wheelchair to rush me off for lunch. Today Tuesday? Oh Lord, that means chili con carne just as sure as the Pope's Cath'lic and a wild bird goes to the bathroom in the woods.

Anyhow, he'd reel home from a smoky roadhouse or some duck hunt. Out the bed he'd fish our brood, him calling, "Poppa's story time, bedtime story time."

"*War*time story," I'd add. "And if you give these young ones dreams again, *you're* getting up, not nobody else."

Later, our kids considered this their happiest memory of Poppa. Typical. They took it as a great compliment, his springing them from the sack after I'd teased and threatened them into it. They didn't know that their grizzled hero was somewhat lubricated. But in them days, drink mostly made him livelier and sometimes tender. Later, not—but that's another story.

With young ones nested all around him in their pink-and-blue pj's, some sitting on his huge shoes, others folding and unfolding his pant cuffs full of dirt, horse oats, and cattail fluff from duck blinds, with him breathing out great warrior whiffs of sentiment, 150 proof, he'd grin at us. "Now . . . ," he'd rub his huge hands together.

I was hovering nearby like some WCTU worker hanging around outside a barroom where I myself would never dare set foot. Then his fingers commenced to testing different corners of the beard, a phone operator plugging about for the right trunk line. He finally cleared his throat, man started.

The story was always one we'd heard—seemed we'd been born knowing them like catechism. I guess that, chapter and verse, Captain's were no gorier than the Brothers Grimm's or Mr. Andersen's. My own favorite peaceful poems are still Mr. R. L. Stevenson's *Child's Garden of Verses*. I said that. But even in nice Mr. Stevenson's stories, each boy's life only catches your deepest interest when a pirate is about to slit that sweet child's throat. —What makes a story good ain't what makes a person good. Why is that?

With crickets clicking their own low-lying sagas outdoors, with the noisy world of Falls, North Carolina, commerce asleep except for our town's ten misers clinking through their coins (lamps off to save more money yet), my late husband—one huge arm wrapping two daughters, the other bundling thin sons—remembered aloud how "Once . . ."

THE HOUSING from a shell ricocheted against this stone embankment in Virginia, struck one enlistee square in the right side of his young head. The boy heard church bells, a parlor full of whistling canaries, a choir singing, "Cleft for me, cleft for me, cleft for me." He pitched forward into a low gully. Others, rushing past, saw the homely kid topple but they couldn't stop. Cap explained that—whilst falling—he seemed to recognize the boots of all the men and boys he knew. It surprised little Marsden: how much of each fellow showed in his boots—polished or not, original issue or traded for, pointed with citified smartness or blunt from miles of country trying. And just before he passed out, the child decided: Every boot . . . is the portrait of the person wearing it.

When the child come to, he noticed black ants working on a red arm. Only the tickling told him finally: They're eating *your* arm, fool. His shoulder spasmed, he smeared ants off. "Not yet, you," he yelled at bugs. "Not Willie Marsden's time just yet." (The War Betwixt States was, for American ants, the golden age.)

From this boy's low place, he looked out on a clearing thick with evening mist. Then he peeked up at sky. After such a nasty battle, the sky burned black as earth. Dirt itself was misted and, this late in the day, looked a milky sky blue. Marsden's arms, which should've been white-boy-colored, appeared scaly as tree bark, dingy from explosion's soot. Meantime—in a grove across the way—trees, split by shelling, had peeled open to show the pinky-yellow tint of your standard white folks' flesh. Confusing. Just before the boy passed out, he closed both eyes, tried making everything go back to being its own rightful color.

"Oh," Captain, grown now, overgrown, adds to his captive listeners. "I forgot how—it being evening and all—my gray uniform in such light looked pure blue. Now, children, how would *you* all feel if the sky appeared like black dirt while the dirt kept trying to be sky? And if you, that'd spent your whole recent life trying and honor the Southern side, found all along it seemed you had been wearing Yankee blue? How would *that* make a person feel, do you suppose?"

"Funny," says our oldest boy.

"Correct," the Boss answers. Younger kids snap their fingers, sorry *they* didn't chance what their brother did and maybe get some extra credit. I stand here, worrying.

So anyhow the boy in blue passed out. Which is blackness. He comes around again in a camp hospital. Which first registers as its tinny sounds, then turns the opposite of blackness, which breaks into separate tints, becoming a place, yourself alive in that place, one row of cots. Crippled people rest on the cots. Some watch you wake. Over on the ground near a surgeon's tent, you see another pile of amputated legs and arms. Some of the hands are open, some are closed. They look like they don't know they're dead yet. Maybe you don't, either.

Boy Marsden spies—propped in a basin—one shaving mirror. He hollers for the orderly to bring it fast, please. In its round frame, a pink face— some freckles—regular. "Thank you, General Jesus H. Christ. I'm white!" he screams. "Sky's blue. Dirt's dark and back where dirt belongs. I was black but now I'm white, was black but now I'm me!"

Everybody laughed. Even fellows hurting the most considered this to be "a good one." Bandaged like the mummies of Egypt, some man (it was hard to tell which) said, "Well, little colored fellow, I'm glad at least *you* got something out'n this damn war!"

See, others didn't know the story behind his saying it: the story of how if a shell casing hits you hard enough and in one certain rear part of your young head, every color in the world can mutiny, change places on you.

"Well," goes the teller to his blinking ragamuffins (two dozed off, during). "That'll start us. Being one from then. Not the best by far and I'm the first to admit it. Something's missing, never have been quite sure what. You all bored? You even *hear* it?"

"Sure, and, Poppa? Poppa, I bet you sure felt . . . 'funny,' " Baby puts in.

"You can bank on that, sweetheart." Our vet is definitely not feeling no present pain. "All right, would you all like another or not? Either way's fine, just be honest."

Loud cheering. Anything to stay up. I say, "One more and one more only. Understand?" I cross my arms. But I've said all this *after* his friction-resisting "Once . . ." Nobody's listening.

OKAY, this one will be about how a man loved his wife too much.

Okay, once there was just such a person, once there lived the very fellow who loved his wife so much, he cried each night. He did. He'd get to sniffling then whimpering for her, called her name out loud, he sure did tire most everybody in his tent. Boy didn't have a picture of her but described the wife constantly. Men began to call this boy by his wife's name, "Dora." *His* name was Donald, so they didn't have to change much. He spoke of his young bride's fine cooking (baking was a specialty), he mentioned her posture, her blue-ribbon needlework. Donald said every person in their hometown knew: *He* didn't deserve such a spouse. Don claimed it only showed another proof of Dora's decency.

Some mail waited in Norfolk. Don got a package from home. Dora—for reasons known best to her (maybe Donald had asked for it?)—sent one of her better dresses. It was a pretty blue, some lace like iceberg lettuce at its sleeves and throat. For memory's sake, and maybe owing to happiness, Donald—standing among men reading their letters—stripped naked, then put on Dora's dress. Men stared but said nothing as Don now strolled from group to group describing how well his wife moved, trying to *show* his buddies, all while admitting that he, of course, could never look so good in her finery as the stately Dora did herself.

He told tentmates (who didn't want to know) how the skirt especially smelled just *like* Dora. Now he had her garment in hand, Don cried less. He cheered right up. Don finally became a pretty good soldier. He could concentrate at last, and he gave Dora full credit. General Forrest swept through, inspecting the division. He stopped before Donald. Bedford Forrest—a crusty old killer with bad grammar and a grudge that, during wartime, served him well—reached out. He poked and fidgeted with lumps across young Donald's lower tunic. Forrest seemed peeved by so chubby a infantryman during so rough a campaign. Out from under gray worsted, a entire skirt fell—blue, its hem unfurled, dainty, draping clear to the ground. Don's dress hid Don's soldier boots, Don's dress covered Don's soldier sword.

"What *is* it?" The General backed away. "*Whose* is it?"

Angry-sounding, his chin lifted, Don spoke. "This," he said, harsh, "is Dora's. We are all good soldiers here, sir, but we're backed up by many *other* people you can't always see. This . . . is Dora's. And I, for one, am not ashamed of her!"

There was a second when it could have gone either way. Maybe Forrest was about to slap Donald for being far stranger than any decent Rebel should. But the steadiness of Don's stare while posing, pouty in blue (the enemy color!), why, it sobered the great man. Of Don's explanation, the General said, "Oh." Then, turning toward a nearby colonel, Forrest went, "We've got us some billets opening in Richmond. This fellow seems a prime candidate for such spy work."

Donald (and his dress) were carted out of camp that very night. Nobody ever saw him again.

At the war's butt end, Jefferson Davis tried giving his Yankee posse the slip. He threw on his wife's raincloak, tossed a shawl over his bare head (it was raining, and he suffered bad neuralgia). Well, Northern papers claimed that old Jeff had been caught escaping in women's clothes. That can hurt any man's reputation. After the war, P. T. Barnum (lacking shame) added a side act to his midway: it showed a large homely fellow whose nose was as beaked as Jefferson D.'s. Onstage, this actor stole, tiptoeing from Yankee guards, while wearing a huge hoopskirt, bows and lace, much rouge, and the world's orangest wig. One soldier notices the humongous shoe size of this belle, the other guard says, "There goes the ugliest white woman I've ever seen," then they grab Jeff. Hearing about this later, the division—spread by civilian life—would think of Donald.

Odd, only *after* young Donald had left camp did his clothing habits come to seem a wee bit funny. While he'd modeled his loved one's outfit, while he'd used her hem beneath his face as nightly pillow—there was something saddening but half familiar about poor Don. You sort of understood a man so homesick for women that he'd wear what they did. While he sashayed through camp, hadn't nobody laughed. Fellows remembered, it'd been right nice having such a pretty outfit so close by. Miles from any woman, in this countryside of muddiness, mules, and blood—a lady's dress became a holy thing.

And afterward, men found they understood exactly how Dora herself must look. They knew her political opinions, favorite jokes, how her face was poreless except just under the eyes, what color her hair turned at each summer's golden end. Donald taught his buddies how to really love a person such as Dora. And men came to feel that she, too, had been a hearty member of their own division—one of its finest.

"BEDTIME for all civilian children," I cry, loud. "No ifs, ands, or buts."

"*One* more?" Louisa begs, holding her hands prayer-wise. "I want the 'Death of the Harpsichord' one. I'm sorry but I do. I just really . . . crave it."

"Too long," her poppa's reasonable for once. I been standing off to one side, like if I'm on my feet maybe I can draw some of the next tale's harm to me, clear of my children. "No," Captain's saying. "I believe I'll end with . . ." and waits, eyes locked on the upturned faces still awake.

" 'The Right-Sized Shoe'?" Our pretty oldest boy raises a hand.

"Well, *I* prefer to title it 'The Shoe That Fits,' but right, pal," Captain grins, half shy with pleasure. "You guessed it."

I stomp once. "They never sleep after some of these. Especially 'The Shoe Fits.' They'll have the dreams. You *know* that. Please, honey—this time, don't."

I'm already transporting certain wee ones toward the stairs when he begins it. Twins wiggle awake, not planning to miss a thing. Baby proves too fast for me. Back down steps they're stumbling. "Once . . ." He wins again:

ONCE, a red-haired Northerner, about forty, sat slumped against this road-side tree stump. He was still alive but clutched his whole opened chest, he rocked side to side with pain. The fellow's rifle had fallen out of reach. He begged a passing file of Southerners to please step over, hand him the gun, or else help finish him, fast. He kept crying aloud, about the pain, "You cannot imagine, boys. No way you can imagine it."

One ragged Rebel heard the Yank's pleading, called, "What'll you *give* me to?" Then he noticed the wounded Yankee's boots. Probably pulled off a dead Southern cavalry officer, they looked nearly new. Fine buttery English leather.

"Hey." The young Reb stalked nearer, stared down. "What size of a foot you got, partner?" Screaming it, the hurt man told.

"You're in luck, pal. Afterwards, can I have these?" And standing before the sitting man, Johnny Reb lightly kicked at unworn upturned soles.

"Please. Yes, please. Yours. Free. Please."

And so this bargain was struck. Begging the boy to hurry, the Northerner reached up and out, grabbed the Rebel's rifle muzzle, pressed its metal to his own temple, crying, "Yes, now, yes," and hung there, eager, gasping, acting glad all during. One shot did it. With blue smoke still hanging in the roadside air, the Rebel plunked down beside the dead man.

He tugged off his own worn boots, he chucked them into a ditch, he removed the better ones and, with such plain childlike happiness, pulled them on. "There"—he stood, kept striding back and forth, kept studying his own tired feet. These boots' luxury, the comfort they'd already given him, it moved the fellow till he laughed then coughed then cried. He kept wiping his eyes with the back of either dirty fist, he kept stepping to and fro across the road, kept testing out this ease he'd all but forgot.

"Perfect," he kept sobbing. "Perfect, perfect."

I'M SCREAMING, "You promised to leave off your bloodiest ones. Just look how big-eyed the twins've got. Up them stairs with the bunch of you. Sir? I'm sick to death of your moth-eaten War. And on a school night!"

Then I help one huge ex-soldier lug living children towards blankets, pillows, dicey dreams.

I mutter at the back before me: Since a War's spoilt *his* childhood, seems strange, Cap's wanting to muddy his own kids' with it. Hearing this charge, not turning, Captain explains straight ahead, "Look, it was my chance in history. What do you want from me, woman? Just because you never got *your* big moment, don't try to rob me of mine."

I wonder, Is it bad for our kids to know the truth so soon? Thanks to their pop's grim stories, will the world go easier or tougher on them? In my either arm, I tote bug-eyed twins. One whispers, "The Yankee *asked* for it, right? So that makes it better. Hunh, Momma, hunh?" I say we'll go over this at breakfast. For now, let's think of finer *sleepy*-time topics, okay?

Other kids follow, a pajama caravan. Baby pouts, "Baby want more war one."

What can a momma hope to offer instead? Right off, I'm quoting a

Stevenson poem, my best late-night balm. My poem hopes to be meat tenderizer, dream sweetener. I study young ones' footed pj's dangling from their daddy's massy grip. I want these children spared. I chant my ditty toward my husband's muscled back—like that's the world—like I'm now asking it to let these babies all go safe. My poem's "The Pleasant Land of Counterpane" by Mr. Robert Louis Stevenson.

> When I was sick and lay a-bed,
> I had two pillows at my head,
> And all my toys beside me lay
> To keep me happy all the day.
>
> And sometimes for an hour or so
> I watched my leaden soldiers go
> With different uniforms and drills
> Among the bedclothes, through the hills,
>
> And sometimes sent my ships in fleets
> All up and down among the sheets,
> Or brought my trees and houses out,
> And planted cities all about.
>
> I was the giant great and still
> That sits upon the pillow-hill,
> And sees before him, dale and plain,
> The pleasant land of counterpane.

Whilst we put kids to bed, I remember: When I first memorized this, I was five, couldn't read yet. I believed that "Counterpane" was spelled like "Pain"—with the I left in. I heard: The pleasant land of counter-pain, of not ever hurting. Only as a grownup, only when reading it aloud to little ones while trying and brighten Captain's rougher bedtime tales—only then did I see the word in print. I went, "Oh dear." Turns out, a counterpane is just a fancy quilt. Won't such a noun as my pet, made-up "counter-pain." —And don't I know there's no such place on earth as one where nothing ever hurts?

Still, I chose to hold in mind my peaceable kingdom—even if it *had* been founded on a mistake about the dictionary and human nature. I went on telling our children about this pleasant land of anti-hurt. That was where I wanted us to stay. Right off, it was so real to me. Still is. Some days, honey, it sure seems truer than this newspaper-headline world, this assigned one.

Kids helped me to invent: *Our* national flag would be a homemade quilt, or maybe a fine blue dress flying from a pole. Our national seal is a warm pie. Our official flower? Either the hollyhock or the sweet pea (we can't decide betwixt them, and don't want to hurt either's feelings). Ours would be the Lion lying down with the Lamb land. Every night before getting my brood to sleep, we'd all add another orchid pavilion, tree house, or band shell. It's a very clean place.

You might say: It'll be a lot like here, honey. Home, only kind of defanged.

SO ONCE Captain scuffs downstairs to bed after planting kids beneath sheets, I linger a minute, I ask for further aid in thinking up our nation, still invisible, but with liberty and justice for all. Kids help me zone it. Seems to relax them like it does me. I hope to bypass any coming nightmares about folks' basic meanness. It's what I've always had to offer: the idea of a true safe home, of acting decent, a treaty spread—quilt-wise—border to border. My talent is this garden spot I am still making up.

Finally, I quote the poem a last time, slower. Where's the war in *me*? —The time our garden shed caught fire, I tried and put it out. When my children beat up a new neighbor kid, I staged a little Appomattox on our vacant lot. First two years of marriage, I wouldn't let my man keep even a squirrel gun in the house. Sure, I act as cross and short-fused as the next person but, hey, I don't *want* to. I clean up after myself.

Captain claimed he'd had his moment, he'd fought for a whole nationality. He said: History allows some folks their one great chance. He got his. So what should I say mine has been?

HERE before the rolling chair swings low to sweep these eighty-odd pounds to lunch, I want to finally name my moment. *It* seems right important in history, too. —Yeah, I believe I know the title. Mine ain't just penned up inside the dates of '61–'65. It's longer and I hope'll go on clear forever. —Child, I think I'll name my own . . . "The Civil Peace."

> I'm yet the giant great and still
> That sits upon the pillow-hill,
> And sees before her, dale and plain,
> The pleasant land of counter-pain.

Black,
White,
and Lilac

*Woe unto him that buildeth his house by
unrighteousness, and his chamber by wrong,
that useth his neighbor's service without
wages, and giveth him not for his work.*
—JEREMIAH 22:13

WHAT'S black, white, and lilac? Honey, you think I'm feeding you
a riddle—like how newspapers are black and white and read all
over? No, this has a story for its answer. And a story, if truly and funnily
so—why that'll never gyp you.

Starts in 18 and 96. I'm yet a scabby freckled menace of a schoolgirl.
Don't push me. Our teacher goes, "Thirty-five years ago, what occurred in
literal hearing distance of us at Falls Lower Normal? I might offer one hint—
it is like Lazarus in appearing, sounding, and smelling dead but in not being
moribund quite yet."

Up shoots many a peacetime hand. "The war! Our Struggle for Southern
Independence, which fizzled but probably just for now."

"Absolutely. And as there are many persons in our vicinity who fought
or lived through said struggle—an assignment follows: For Tuesday, and I
do not mean Wednesday, my farm-town slugabeds—go and find yourselves
one. Ask calibrated questions, take shrewd notes. 'History is the science of
what only happens once.' I shall need dates, reasons, food, and clothing of
the period. I want a fifteen-pager, minimum—and punctuated to within an
inch of its life. Please include a liberal sprinkling of the semicolons you all
find so mystifyingly difficult. You are setting down a national document.
—Boys are to pick male survivors—girls not . . . I mean, girls, females. The
finished product *will* be here at the southeast corner of my desk, bright and
early on which day, class?" We answered.

Bobo Kingston sighed, "Ma'am? Ma'am. That's hard."

We liked calling Miss Beale's ambitions for us "strict." In 1840, during her local girlhood, whilst wearing a arty black cape meant to hide her crippled back, Beale got nicknamed "Witch." It stuck. Nicknames do here.

Anyhow, right off, I knew my war subject. I'd choose me Lady Marsden. She'd onct ranked among North and South Carolina's richest people, male or no.

The victim now lived at Falls' best rooming house, rent paid by her war-vet son (yet unrecognized to be my future husband). The Mangum Arms offered genteel quiet, seconds at dinners, towels aplenty. Even so: Lady Marsden had sure declined. During her famous Charleston debut in '40, the woman had "come out." During a famous local fire in '65, she had "come down." I found this to be of real human interest: Losing everything's romantic. (Or so I thought till it later jumped me.)

Borrowing Poppa's finest whittling knife, I sharpened three new yellow pencils. I even rebraided the left pigtail that forever curled sideways. Then young Lucille (not pretty but leastways clean) set out with a starter list: forty-five hard strict questions.

This happened in late fall (the season) in early Falls (the town). Time was, people burned leaves. You could. Time was, our village's thousand elms hadn't yet been carried off like by delayed plague from Egypt. Stately trees yet met and mingled over all streets leading to my topic. Time was, time was . . . Time. A humidity you moved through. Darling? when you're young, the world seems planned.

In gutter pyramids of dried leaves, my every step crunched the Present, plundering layers of a smoke-and-leather-smelling past.

Like all good cub reporters, I'd wrote ahead for a appointment.

LUCY tiptoed into the boardinghouse—steep, coolish, manifoldly doilied. On one door, a engraved card: "Lady E. M. Marsden"—crucified betwixt rusted straight pins. Before knocking, I wised up, snuck back out, settled on a porch rocker. Mangum Arms residents sometimes dignified these chairs after supper—but, you know, not one soul ever rocked. That's classy, honey. A way your Lucy here will never be.

I actively did not bob to and fro. Why hadn't every girl in my class picked Lady Marsden? Owing to burn scars, my subject was sometimes called the Mummy. She never left that room in yonder. Folks claimed the poor thing's mind was yet fogged owing to Sherman's one smoky afternoon of local excess.

Our double-daring teacher lived somewheres in this very Mangum Arms. What if Witch nabbed me slumped out here? Imagine the shame: caught slacking off on your national document.

Remembering the black cape helped steel me. Every town the size of Falls (1,100 souls) yet has a her, Athena Genius. Adults bring in astronomy questions and, proud, their five-legged calves. Our settler of bets had a dowager's hump. Witch suffered teeth so bucked she never grinned without

one palm's quick geisha dart, screening mouth's pleasure. For me, her doubled back seemed a brain's card-catalogue annex. I loved her—but feared *I*
might turn out this bright, this dromedary homely. Child? sometimes—in
a town so small—getting known as smart means being very brave.

Thanks to Beale's example, a surge of boldness sent me plunging indoors, made me pound three times upon a living mummy's door. Uh-oh.

After what felt as long as it'd took the Ancient World to mellow then
rot into this present second, after I considered yelling "Trick or Treat" and
running (it *was* October), the door opened one inch. The center of a black
maid's pretty face. Face goes, "Is you . . . the question girl?"

I smiled, "I sure is . . . am." (Got goose bumps just from being called
that. I thought, Ooh but this'd please Miss Beale.)

When in doubt concerning a password, child? try "Yes." Door swung
open on a rental room heaped with a mansion's furniture. The serving girl,
about my age, called at somebody hid under piled ormolu, bronze, brocade,
"Mrs. Lady? We must be living right. —Comp'ny!"

Then I got handed a paint chart, samples of whites and off-whites. The
maid passed me this like some everyday ticket of admission. I noticed: it
was grimed from others' nervous handling.

"Thank you."

The room had no room in it. Sixty gilt ballroom side chairs were stacked
to the ceiling, like a family of skinny Chinese acrobats. Before me, Biedermeier apple-wood lowboys, busts of emperors looking white and in need
of seasoning as hard-boiled eggs. One huge dead palm plant failed to notice
it'd browned in 18 and 65. On the far mantel, a glass gondola big enough
to sail Baby Moses through bulrushes, clear enough to show him bottom
mud. Nearer by, in two rows like army surplus, six marquetry armoires
(each offering a different frolic activity of three shepherdesses in one glade—
with not no sheep in sight). A narrow path wedged, broken-backed, betwixt.
Seemed if Lucy didn't know the next password, she'd be mashed by wardrobes. Inside such closets, great chandeliers dangled, lead crystal idly
clinked. Against yonder hearth, a dozen family portraits tipped any old way,
puritans scowling at the undignity of doing ramshackle headstands.

"You visiting the hallway, comp'ny?"

I tried a star reporter's winning smile. Stepping in, I found a floor paved
with Turkey rugs twelve inches deep, some muddy. Felt like the unasked-
for luxury of walking on a stranger's bed.

This wallpapered warehouse stunk of lemon oil, of cloves nailing oranges, some elegant underlying ash. Each knickknack smelled smoke-cured
as any Smithfield ham. The maid in a lace cap, stepping on her own long
apron, slammed the door, locked it, led me along armoires' narrow avenue.
I already missed the hallway. We seemed bound towards the farthest end
of this collection, a corner where the burned collector was herself collected—
so much cornered dust.

. . .

HALFWAY to my topic, the guide disappeared. I might of known. She'd dodged rightwards, either between armoires or into one. Across my path, the mirrored door of one chifforobe swung open. This room was pretty dim. Mirror creaked closer, blocked my way like some great unlatching wing.

I remember stepping aside to let the approaching stranger pass, then seeing a bowlegged girl do the same. I studied a scuffed pigtailed child clutching her pad, a list of questions, pencils, the paint chart like her underworld passport. Eyes bulged, the jaw slacked open in a way her mother would call "defective-appearing, Lucille."

How crude the outer husk of your own intelligence shows up. From deep indoors, your mind can feel so glassy, quick, and rare. (Even with me up to this age, with my outside edges slacked and melting—still, in *here*, child, it's ofttimes yet all mercury, a dance!)

—I peeked past armoire hinges, I saw my black Virgil wink then crook her finger. The door clapped shut totally behind me. I regretted that.

In a smoke-and-cedar-smelling box, blind, I backstepped onto quilts and—of a sudden knew—"The maid sleeps here. They consider it to be her room." Which broke my heart. I figured: Miss Beale? God love you, with your bucked back and humped teeth, I believe your Lucy's *onto* something.

From outside, a shrillness first seemed wind-down-chimney, tooting, "Who, who?"

Honey, by now I had goose bumps big as pearl tapioca. The maid opened our door just long enough to answer: "Be somebody bout wallpapering you mansion's third-best parlor, silly, if you gots to know. A question girl come to axt you all bout colors."

Onct our armoire was locked shut, I heard whispering. Listening, I pretty much had to. A mouth this close left mist in my ear's conchy turnings. One free black hand fumbled cross my shoulder, stroked my left braid. In hisses, I learnt, "Sshe sstill look right bad. Sshe sstill think we out yonder at The Lilacss. Sstill think that Ssherman's menss was Englissh, wass Cornwalliss' oness. Sstill think the housse they burnt, the dresss they torched been her momma'ss, not herss. Sshe think thiss room so crowded cause the resst sshe house yet being redid by you decoratorss from Charlesston. Gotss to be mosst careful what you ssay. Wantss to know how sshe got hurt so bad? axt after sshe momma. —Lady Marsden don't alwayss know her's *her* yet, sssee?"

"OH," I said in a street voice, then, ashamed, shushed, "oh."

Honey, I had no more idea what she meant than the man in the moon. But I figured—it'd be like on-the-job training, you fake it till you know it so good that it's soon faking *you*.

She touched my hand: If I agreed to these here terms, I could put any question I liked to the hurt one yonder. If not, this'd be a fine time to pleasse leave. —Well, I agreed, sugar. Wouldn't you? Took gumption—being as I was just eleven in 18 and 96. But what choice? When a body's this nose-deep in the scent of Story, why get shy? To this day—dead-elm-leaf brown as years've turnt me—I still love the ring of that: *"Is you the question girl?"*

Oh yeah, child. Time has bent me double as hairpin. Time's twisted me out of a statement and into a request. But—Lord knows, I'm the question girl yet.

SO LOOK, this much said: What *is* black and white and lilac? See, because—that's what I got out of it. That's how I come to finally organize my "Modern History" report.

First, it seemed so neat:

White'd be Lady Marsden's plantation mansion, Greek Revival, six miles northeast of Falls, happy on its personal hill above our river. This home can still be seen in many paintings. Old Mall Antiques owns three, even as we speak (as I do). And, child, the prices dealers are asking scare me near-bout as bad as anything I'm going to tell you here.

The mistress of the manor, number two in her class at St. Cecilia's Christian Finishing in Richmond, encouraged artists to set up easels on her wide front lawn. Slaves brung picnic lunches to any painter smart enough to do the Marsden home. Marsden slaves did. White is the Anglo-Saxon-type lady that owned the two-thousand-acre spread and so loved the image of both it and her.

Freed slaves—thirty-odd years later, rocking on *their* porch, looking out at a piano crate/chicken coop in the front yard—they claimed she hadn't been all that bad. Hobbies kept her clear of the worst mischief. Her mansion's seventy-odd rooms each housed a novelty clock—marble, bronze, quartz. All showed subjects from mythology. Swans mounted Leda ladies every quarter hour. Hercules' flat tummy was a walleyed German pocket watch. Under Phaëthon's chariot, pendulums swung, cheery as the hearts of peasants, solemn as famous necessary manly parts.

Mrs. Marsden hand-cranked every cloisonné Apollo herself. *"Some*body has to do it." Thursday (the day that gear wound down) Lady would actually rise before noon, she'd string a opera jailer's worth of keys around her neck. She'd tug on a green visor purchased from Falls' one pawnbroker. "Something about it appealed to me." Mrs. Marsden laughed at her own paleness tinted fishy green. "Hideous, no?" And off she'd scuff to wind parlors' seven-day-movement masterpieces.

—Lady'd taken a two-year correspondence course in horology. Slaves made fun of the word, though they knew their mistress's chastity was total, dull. Strange that the woman, usually so professionally helpless, could fix most any timepiece. Neighbors brung Lady their stalled locket watches. She worked in her high bed, visor tugged low, black eyepiece screwed into her all but albino face. Favorite tools: sterling sugar tongs and her eyebrow tweezers. When, at the quarter hour, seventy-odd clocks chimed (scaring guests), Lady's eyes would close. She seemed to sleep-talk at a handy slave, "Castalia, do run fetch me the bronze Hungarian Proteus, southeast parlor. It's lately changeable as I. Six and a half seconds slow again. —Those Hungarians."

If slaves fell sick, was Lady Marsden nursed them. They got stretchered to a third-floor bedroom off her tower conservatory. Lady spoon-fed them broth, she'd read aloud from *The Arabian Nights*, she'd mop dark brows. And for a full week. —Local gentlewomen, learning about this, turned briefly coolish towards Mrs. Marsden. Lady just loved that. All the river crowd had heard how a Marsden slave girl onct admired Mistress's diamond brooch— the thing was whipped off, pressed into a work-toughened hand, "Yours now."

Along with horology, knitting, piano, and doing jigsaw puzzles of Europe vistas, Lady fainted. Slaves noticed: Mrs. Marsden never collapsed whilst alone. She might drop from the strain of a week spent healing others but she forever toppled *towards* them slaves still strong enough to catch her.

Anybody who's ever nursed a not too sick patient knows how the first six to seven days—if you got nothing else to do—can be almost semi-engaging. Fluff their pillows, arrange the flowers. It's that second Monday, child—grimness gets under the bed, sinks teeth into your ankles. But by then, see, Lady Marsden herself had fallen over, was reclining in her forty-windowed room in her canopied ivory four-poster, was recovering from the week spent helping others to recover.

Lady's Greek and Latin proved good enough to savor her husband's puns, live ones in dead languages. —True, she could sometimes sound vain about her "attainments," as she calt them. But Marsden freed folks later swore that when relaxed, Lady acted charming and unguarded as a child. She'd always felt easiest around her *baby* slaves. With grown ones, Lady considered herself friendly and confidential but she was ofttimes only flirting. They knew this. She didn't. When men marched off to war, Lady used her female slaves for whetstones to keep Flirting's blade edge keen. As flirting goes, hers was—everybody yet says—real good of its kind. Dry.

ON RAINY days, Lady called her twelve youngest black children into the Big House for a homemade treat: Catacombs. This game meant servants' lining up all tables from a single mansion floor—every lowboy, drop-leaf sideboard, candlestand. Sheets were then thrown overtop, both seams drooping clear to the Oriental rugs (Caucasians, mostly). Next, into this long hide-and-seek catacomb, one frail lady was seen to crawl on all fours. Lady always wore a white silk wrapper for both at-homes and state occasions. "At my present age, clothes decisions strike me as pure nuisance—uniformity so frees the mind for higher things." Only when she'd hid good could her wee ones enter on their hands and knees, gigglish, tense, seeking It. She was always It. When you own sixty-one people—to them, you stay forever It. Thunder broke above slate-mansard roofing. Rain drummed window glass. All went blue white blue with lightning. Who cared? Hooray for Catacombs!

A cloth cave stretched into and out of many a parlor, the cave dead-ended in closets then turned back, winding off along cool halls. Sheets glowed white as the life-sized statuary Caesars lined near it, gesturing. Hid in such shelter, serenaded by clocks' godly foggy chiming, Lady Marsden and her children played for hours. They made up rules as they went.

(The South before the war had mighty rigid codes: Slave owners, feeling none too firm on the Ethics end, got mighty interested in Manners. Manners made a kind of crucifying corset that promoted Lady's perfect posture, that held her, chafed but upright, in her lofty place. So, ooh, but it must of felt good, honey—flouting rules, acting wild again, inventing a new ungirdled world beneath the chair rail.)

Thunder brung baby shrieks. Catacomb players scared each other breathless. Inside the tributaries of sheets, players pretended that any outside noise was a Roman centurion come to torture them for worshipping correct. If you stomped your shoe near some busy percale crossroads, what grunts and scramblings you set off.

On their feet, shut out of the game, slave women cleaned like usual—venturing to sheets' very edges. From the white cave of monograms and table legs, women heard their owner: "I dare you to! You darling scamps, no shame, you *would* try to get me, would you not? Here they come. The tawny Lions of Rome. Oh no. I shall pounce upon you first. Beware, the Darkling Creature from the Roman Swamps Approacheth!" Babies yowled, scattering, palms and knees drubbed carpeted parquet.

Slave women—rolling eyes at one another—must of felt glad at least to have their young ones brung indoors and spared a wet day's duties. —Then ivory swans mounted sterling Ledas, then seventy-odd chimes hid within bronze wings, gold globes, and sterling clouds—all told four-thirty. (Was a unanimous vote, but hardly sung in unison.) Then tea and cake got slipped under one sheet's hem. Refreshments were left in a different spot each day—just part of Lady's Instructions: "Something about it appeals to me."

Good game of Catacombs could run you clear till dusk. You knew it was ended when dark children shot from under far-flung sheets. Kids acted giddied by their day of fun. It seemed a form of travel. Their mommas later recalled having a right hard time getting young ones to sleep them nights. Babies grew so sassy from the privilege of hours spent tickling and threatening It (all in fun, of course).

Onct children scattered, the adult staff knew to strip draperies off all tables. In this way, at a new location each rainy evening, as time itself slaved away inside the Big-House excuse of mantelpiece gods and animals, servants found her, collapsed, sometimes grinning, sometimes drowsing already, sometimes pinching her nose's bridge—hinting at future migraines. Black women then lugged Lady to a bath kept warm since noon. Though the game tired her, though she often needed the whole next day to recuperate, Lady Marsden forever explained: " 'My children' rely on me. With great gifts go great responsibilities. I would not disappoint my Little Xerxes, Diana, or Baby Venus for all the glories of the ancient world."

Her husband had received a classical education at John Harvard's college.

· · ·

FAMOUS for three-week headaches, three-day parties, and her perfect cream complexion (no peaches ever got mentioned as being allowed in or near that cream), Lady wore white silk year round. I said that, honey. It come from China. I probably said that too. Even the fine cotton raised on her two thousand acres, even if it barely touched her baby skin—gave Lady hives. True, she did knit wool—but only whilst wearing gloves and for others' wear. She patiently explained, to touch it made her go right lilac-y with brocades of rashes. (Maybe this, I just thought of it, is why no shepherdess got shown as having a single sheep on any of her art or furniture.)

While playing their game, slave children—in coarse homespuns—loved to tickle It. They loved to feel It's perfect whispery gown. It believed they touched her to touch her. Since her husband's death, since her boy went for a soldier—the Mistress of The Lilacs got touched right seldom. She was soothed only by the dark hands that—along with polishing imported furniture—maintained her beauty, famous in both Carolinas and three adjacent southeast counties of Virginia. Plus amongst sundry cousins. The South is mostly the South's cousins, honey.

Every fifth day, Lady Marsden's hair—three and a half feet long—got oiled, its fine ends snipped. Each noon, at her waking, these fair locks were plaited through with roped pearls, real ones inherited by her late daddy, Judge More. He was a direct descendant of Sir Thomas More, the martyr— I put this in my school paper—linking ancient and modern history in a way that really tickled the Witch. —About Lady's daddy, a local joke had run: "That man can judge more than any Judge More I know." Which is another story.

As for his only child, the heiress . . . born white as a new glove in a store box . . . Well, she planned to stay that way. White. Theme number one: *White*. As this here history paper of mine will try and show, she could not. Stay. White. But boy, she really, really wanted to.

2

THERE IS, you won't be shocked, a story back of this.

3

BLACK (now we're getting somewheres) means (as of April 7, 18 and 65) the tint of folks that Lady Marsden (so white) yet owned but won't legally allowed to. She tried keeping her helpers as wound up tight as collector's-item clocks, all tunnel-visioned in one unending game of Catacombs. Without black help, she would have been totally lonesome. She'd of starved. *She* didn't know how to work the well to draw the water then build a fire to heat the bath to bathe in daily. Only a few of her staff hadn't yet run off.

By dawn, April 7, '65, Sherman's men (wearing blue) had crossed the Carolina border on horsebacks of all colors. Soldiers were headed here to plunder final Piedmont plantation-strongholds, including a certain grand white three-story home set on a green hill, river view. Yank torches planned to free the last black folks working this showplace.

Till a month earlier, meaning March of '65 (to be historical about it), the Marsdens' two thousand acres had claimed sixty-one slaves. In midnight dribs and drabs, playing their own game of Underground Railway Catacombs, some crawled into the woods, they guided five stolen covered rowboats upriver, they traveled late-night post roads further north. Even Uncle Primus, the Marsdens' courtly favorite, too old to run off, too loyal to . . . he run. Seemed he'd been saving up for years. Others—disgusted by his lifetime's toadying—laughed to see him sprint.

Just four women and six children still wash and fluff their Lady and her high white meringue of house. You'll meet them presently. —Hey, Miss Beale, wherever you are, I'm really getting organized this go-round, I deserve a right good grade, hint hint. See: we're already at Theme number two: Black = slave folks' faces and bodies. Plus Black stands for the scorched-earth policy about to happen right here. But blackest of all (I learned from Castalia, Evidence Anne, and other ex-slaves I quizzed), blackest of everything might be the white heart dark enough to try and own lock, stock, and barrel another human. Some nerve.

I should mention that Evidence Anne's given name was Diana but her pale skin and gray Marsden eyes caused Cassie, her momma, to choose the self-explaining attention-getting *Evidence*.

Our strict teacher drilled Who?What?Why?Where? into her pupils' cloudy hookwormed heads. (She left out Which? maybe because she'd heard tell of her nickname.) At age eleven I filled twenty-six pages (way over the required fifteen) with every W but the crucial Why? That one, honey, this wrinkled question girl is gnawing over yet.

MOST everything I learned concerning Whiteness and Mrs. Marsden (Lady was her given name because the Judge claimed she'd looked so perfectly prissy in her first organdied crib) I squeezed out of black eyewitnesses. The lady herself had been a serious talker till the major mishap, which this is. I later went and pumped many others about a day when the mistress's boudoir's white-brocaded walls come tumbling down around her eggshell-pale and ofttimes Humpty-empty head. —No, enough of that type talk. See, I'm trying and put a gag on the Flowery. That was Witch Beale's biggest complaint concerning my "current events" report of 1896. I later got to know many of the people mentioned in my theme. That would change my history paper's history. —And seeing as you are probably my last chance to tell stuff right, I want to get it perfect this go-round. I'm yet benefiting from certain harsh, if constructive, teacher comments wrote by lamplight in Beale's garden efficiency at the Mangum Arms in late October of '96. Child, concerning the Farfetched or the Flowery, remind me to muzzle myself. Just clear your throat, I'll tamp it back. I'll try.

"TAKING the bare bones of historicity—not unlike those scholars who construct an entire dinosaur on the basis of some stray tibia—our young Lucille herein employs her own highly coloristic if rusticated narrative energy. Lucille indulges a willingness to chance others' motives, to inhabit their very flaws. She can be borne along, despite a severe case of grammatical rickets, by her propulsive inventiveness, her own hapless mythomania. That said, what else might a reader seek in Lucille's 'national document'? Alas, a great deal. We, of the Falls, NC, greater school system are not purists. In a town of Falls' size and prideful backwardness, we cannot afford to be. This is not Richmond. This is not even Raleigh. Realistically put, I have lost two students in the past four years to death by tapeworm. In such a milieu, how foolish This Reader would be to expect any pupil gifted with the natural tonal grandeur of a Gibbon, say, or the chaste lucent prose of a Carlyle. That stated, and a good bit conceded already, the question remains, Is Lucille's historic tale-told view even remotely authentic? Alas, if our little pupil does have a gift, it is, I fear, not a profound cerebral one, but perhaps a propensity 'comique.' If her grammar does not improve, she is, I fear, going to *need* this ready mirth, as the world in general and Falls in particular deals harshly enough with the articulate. Especially with the articulate. Folk wit, an asset, doubtless, is no substitute for assiduous intellection, my young Lucille. One thinks of Novalis' advice, highly applicable in light of our Confederate topic: 'After losing a war, one should only write comedies.' However ultimately bogus they might be as period re-creations, one *is* caught up in these tawdry puppet masques Lucille stages with such typical bumptious joy. Having conceded our young friend's knack at interviewing and her gift for remarking a oddity, we did find this paper a bit much. It has qualities in common with her September *Ancient* History thesis, 'Pompeii—The Last Resort, or They Never Knew What Hit Them.' This reader is still not clear how sardonically Lucille intended her flip subheading. If she did not view it as wildly irreverent, then she is in even worse intellectual jeopardy than I—grimly overqualified for this line of work, grotesquely underpaid by this anti-progressive school system—care to deal with here. The present essay, I am pleased to remark, lacks an habitual slangy lowness. It partakes of Lucille's narrative compulsion (remarked elsewhere, in her Citizenship report, as 'talking in class'). That admitted, I fear that even with the rest of our year's improvement, even with my own steadying and diligent help— help that has, at best, qualified certain local sows' ears, if not for consideration as silk purses, then at least as more nearly wallet-quality pigskin— even given my Pygmalion to her home-carved Galatea, our Lucille will never a scholar make. An issue must be faced. Certain moments herein remain, no other word will do, 'cheap.' Speak to This Reader after class for specifics as they occur to me. I appreciate, Lucille, that you are a child positively febrile with a story-telling mission. Isn't there the old Genoese proverb that runs: 'Light is half a companion'? Yes. There is. It literally refers, I believe, to the companionability of sunshine. But I apply it to my little locals who —from underneath the heavy bushel known as Falls—still somehow shine. It will, I fear, be all that This Reader ever really knows of luminous company. Your earnestness is dear and sometimes heart-wrenching. Why is it that the closer to historic truth your papers venture, the more they grieve me—the more I long to protect you from all you must discover? No one can say you haven't tried. Given that, I must ask Where, oh where, Lucille, is the requisite 'liberal sprinkling' of our friend the semicolon? After everything that This Reader has attempted for your betterment (the sleepless hours uncounted), be truthful, can you even use a semicolon? And, past that, might you ever come to love, yes *love* a semicolon—one set in precisely the right spot, one bridging parallel ideas? 'Love,' in This Reader's opinion, is not too strong a term. You already dote upon History. Now you must learn to embrace, yes, embrace Punctuation,/.;:!

"Punctuation is, my young Lucille, quite probably all the control, weaponry, and, yes, the summa of allure that we more sensitive women of Falls will ever exercise. My dear, do learn to enjoy it."

4

so: finally, what is Lilac?

Well, come late April/early May, lilacs are. It being spring in 18 and 65, these bushes begun popping open everywheres, unasked for yet exceptional as Nature's been being since Adam served as first plantation gardener (Jan. 10000 B.C.).

We're talking eight-foot hedges of Marsden lilacs rolling downhill— stretching from the post road clean around farm's lily ponds, skirting the mansion proper—edging its wide lawn and running flush to riverbank where some blooms—like privileged winners of a bushes' race—tipped in and took a drink. (I'm making this part of our story be picture-book pretty in a semi-Woolworth's way since the next stuff is right grim. Honey, that's both a threat and a promise.)

Yeah, lilacs, quite the spectacle for eye and nose, eleven hundred hybrid shrubs planted in 1821, fertilized with bonemeal, tended by slave labor, and doing just fine. Some jealous neighbor had teased Lady: She must be burying her dead slaves under them bushes, so burly did they grow.

This plantation was *called* The Lilacs. The Marsdens pretended there won't another such bush blooming for counties around. And true, none rose to being such Junior Trees. The six-hundred-yard-long hedge had been featured—with its own engraving—in *Jennings' Notable Curios and Vistas of the American South* (1856). Its author, a English lady, believed her hosts at finer homes across the territory. She wrote of hearing contented slaves—after a happy day's work—playing banjos in many a Quarter.

If Uncle Primus, head gardener, bought lilac bushes from Rocky Mount's best nursery, and if any one tried blooming white, well, into the fire went that pretender. White was Lady M.'s color. Black, her slaves'. Purple did her lilacs grow. Goal: keeping all three shades in place, no blending. Separate but separate. —You know the three-toned ice cream you see nowadays—lined like a contest, each tint trying to give them others the cold shoulder? Like that. But, hey, onct blurring starts, bye-bye to the total setup. Darling? Melting is real hard to reverse. Take the word of somebody my age.

Ingredient number three: Lilac. —Now we're cooking.

Baked Alaska.

DOES such plantation lore seem ancient history, lava cold as Pompeii's? Listen, honey, even now, with a housing project and one corner of a mall sealed overtop The Lilacs' former two thousand acres, some of its bushes yet survive.

At the Big Elk Browse 'n' Buy Mall's parking lot's east end, around a few of them stainless-steel lampposts stuck out lonely in the tar, come spring you'll spy green heart-shaped leaves pushing up for air. The strength of things!

Next year in early or mid April, please notice certain purple stunted blooms. A testament to . . . something. Maybe: How stubborn beauty is. Maybe: How this Yankee-operated Mall (my favorite orderly here, he just told me the whole shebang is owned outright by a syndicate from *Japan*) still can't squelch the tints and odors of a region. Maybe it shows: How, onct you write you a fifteen-pager that runs overlong, you notice this here local topic ever after. Or maybe something else. *You* decide. I got my hands full, telling.

"Cheap," which part did she mean? Surely History itself played fast and loose to plunk a mall over the manor in question. History did, though. Look it up. Under acres of car lot, and rushing through titanic pipes, a river got corseted by cunning Northern engineers (or Nipponese ones). This now allows shoppers (my wheelchair among them, I'll admit) to swarm through cheap boutiques set smack where shad onct swum, where lilacs by the dockside bloomed.

And on this very spot, my darling history buff—in the spring of 18 and 60—you might have seen, out near what's presently the off-ramp curving past Dunkin' Donuts (I swear I've never set foot in the place—mainly because I'm on wheels), you could have seen one lady wearing white, studied by a army of shirtless black runners. They awaited her signal. The lady was deciding on her lilacs' coming-out date. Escorted by white parasols edged with Brussels lace, wearing the first known pair of sunglasses at large in eastern North Carolina—called "smoked" (a prediction)—Lady M. strolled and finally nodded that, yes, her eleven hundred bushes *would* reach their cumulus peak on the Saturday forthcoming. Was then she give her royal hand-jiggle wave. Was then slave runners trotted off, bound up and down the river road towards your choicest farm-owning gentry twixt here and New Bern, practically.

Whenever she required her strong male slaves to do showy chores like today's Lilac-Time marathon run, Lady asked them to please go shirtless. Was due to one reason (her favorite). "Something about it appeals to me," she tapped a fingertip to chin. The Lilacs owned fourteen blooded saddle horses and uncounted mules—but the dark young men scattered on bare feet, their fine chests showing.

And on the proper Saturday morning, here come everybody by water. Guests had to. Lady More Marsden—owner of keys to clocks, to barns, to platinum lockets, to rental buildings—she always got her way. Well, almost always.

WHEN a beautiful house burns, remember its last great party.

BEFORE

THE WIDOW Marsden's Lilac-Time Gala was a beloved tradition hereabouts—but then too, so was slavery. White folks advanced in pale painted boats paddled by dozens of black men that they, whites, also owned. Swans from roadside lily ponds had been hog-tied (panicked wings could break a child's arm) then set loose on the river Tar to "decorate and enliven."

Lady kept striving for what used to be called a Effect. When you own two thousand riverfront acres and the sixty-odd people to spiff them up proper, a Effect is lots more possible. The lawn (pride and joy of Uncle Primus, known for his dignity and for speaking a good bit of Latin and Greek, taught him by his scholar owner) was almost too green. From the pergolaed pier, you saw many white-clothed tables scaling a hill toward the mansion. Some had masterpiece clocks set on them, just for show. Tables were laid with cold pheasant, watercressy finger foods, sweets sufficient to give the Greater Raleigh Area sugar shock. Blown-glass swans and Venetian gondolas served as punch bowls' centerpieces (some near big enough for a slave child to sail away in—and don't think they hadn't thought about it).

Thirty hired musicians—boated south from Richmond and paid a pretty penny—drifted on the far bank in five covered rowboats (ones later stole by runaways, remember?). The band played a long liquidly suitable selection by Mr. Handel that—non-musical as I am—even *I* can guess. (Classical music makes me nervous as a cat. Does it you? Keeps going up and down, up and down. I want to tell it, Find a location you feel for and just *stay*.)

Lady's son, Willie, and his friend, Ned, begged to help servants with boat hooks when the crowds arrived. For boys aged ten, a boat hook means a good time. Slaves wore white livery today plus powdered wigs—leftovers from last century. Young fellows in stiff toupees with tails like comets, boys with brown chests bared, rolled one white carpet uphill: it'd cushion the six-hundred-yard promenade that Lady herself would soon lead.

She now reached for a sip of water and, thanks to young Castalia's watchfulness, the leaded-crystal glass was pressed in Lady's hand. Our hostess, waiting for first boats, went to sit. A gilt Venetian chair poked under her just in time—Zelia's work, despite the old woman's sneezing: wig's cornstarch.

Guests saw their blanched hostess from afar, right out there on The Lilacs' dock. She practiced her non-tiring wave, one learned from a ladies' weekly article about crowned heads' hardship (all that dreary crowd-waving). Considering Lady's fragile health, guests murmured, "Bless her soul, she's in the *sun*, she's come right down near *water*."

Wearing white as usual, she was shaded by two white parasols held in strong black hands. Lady's welcoming voice sounded husky, darker than her paper-white skin. From behind migraine-preventing smoked lenses, she forced a set of pleasant dimples into view, she seemed tipsy with such light, "I don't care how many doctors warned against . . . I simply had to come out my-*self*."

Fine-boned as a child, wound in a colorless silk wrapper, she'd been—folks knew—something of the spitfire in her younger days. When Judge More refused her a dress she considered Life or Death, Lady took her riding crop to him—it was the start of her daddy's deepest esteem. He loved to show off one lasting stripe across his neck, "Know who gave me that?" The strict Judge left her everything.

Now at least *seeming* milder, Lady teased and scolded guests. Her favorite cousin, Mabry, suffered gout. He advanced by boat—one hugely bandaged foot propped before him in the prow like some great tribute ham he'd brung. Lady called everybody by name, by *all* their names. "Why, if it's not my cousin Mabry Walter Scott Dumas More himself, you quixotic rogue, you." (Hers was a family of readers, honey.) She accepted funeral-huge bouquets, she blew dry kisses at boats of late arrivers. She sent Little Xerxes paddling a raftful of juleps toward musicians yonder, men who—mouths full of reeds and hands full of bows—could only look longingly down at the sweating silver cups where mint wilted.

All guests knew who would be here, who would not, and why. Everybody remarked—like polite company did then—on their hostess's ageless beauty. In this case, pretty much true. Of course, Lady pooh-poohed each compliment, "Flattery will get you *hard*ly anywhere, you shameless scallywag." She was a gentleperson of her Class and Age, child. No worse than most.

Folks considered her a firebrand liberal: She hadn't hired a tutor for her son but let Will attend the Falls public schools. Willie, a awkward boy, refused to take advantage of his handsome parents' position. Said he'd rather see his buddy, Ned, each day than be admitted early to John Harvard's college. —Lady, bountiful, ordered whole crates of oranges sent to her slaves on Christmas Eve—oranges being a great rarity hereabouts in 1860. From her ivory four-poster she insisted on settling all plantation disputes herself. Odd, she was considered fairly fair-minded. The Judge's daughter used a solid-silver hairbrush for her gavel, a breakfast bed tray as her bench. Sometimes, recovering from migraine, she wore a blindfold to spare herself daylight's harm. She'd preside from her canopied bed, robed in white, listening—blind. Some wronged slave wife told all. Lady's upper face stayed placid behind silky bandaging. She nodded like clockwork, adding many a human "Hmm." "And *when* you found him behind the pig parlor kissing her yet again, *cara mia*, how must *that* have made poor you feel? Be specific."

Today, her braided locks—never seriously cut—ride high in the latticed chignon. All tresses pivot on crossed mother-of-pearl chopsticks (said to be "decidedly original"), those and two yard-long ropes of hog-tying heirloom pearls. Lady, just gone thirty-eight, can look nineteen in certain light. And safe under parasols, she totes that particular light all around the property with her. Leading first guests up a famous *allée* of shocking purple, her face seems innocent even of laugh lines. Though Mrs. Marsden is known as a Man's Lady, she can befriend certain attractive young women. Now—calling over two—she squires them toward the lilac spectacle while offering beauty tips. "Remember, girls, nothing better emphasizes a refined complexion than a set of bare and preferably lightly oiled adjacent Nubian torsos. Happily, my Neptune and Marcus Aurelius here just adore this aspect of their work, the vagabonds. It shows, I believe. These young men are vain as Cousin Mabry's peacocks, *d'accord*, you rascals? Oh, *I* see you smiling, Marc. See Marc smile, girls?"

CHILD, this here's brutal. But what's the point of telling your in-laws truth if you can't, like my favorite candy-striper says, "let a certain amount hang out"? This happened back when white was White and should've known better. Before Black thought to call itself beautiful (at least in public). When Lilac, three weeks per spring, meant eleven hundred uphill bushes busting a gusset on a fancy farm. When all three tones entwined their most wildly for this here party. —Same tints will figure in the April when everything burns. Each person I afterward quizzed about Lady's peacetime galas— concerts and whist games running three full days (you slept over in her seventy-nine-room home)—they all mentioned how everything seemed so . . . well, so black and white and lilac. Which is why I brung it up.

Now I've risked glutting you with three calendar-art tones. (Was it *this* part of my paper that Witch Beale held to be most cheap? Hope not, *I* like it.) Let's simplify a bit, child—the way, say, fire does.

2

IN THE April of 1865, no such party done occurred. No food to serve, few slaves to serve it. The entire skilled band from Richmond had scattered into ragtag Secesh marching corps, drafted to be the front-line buglers so often shot. Not one guest boated upriver. No gent promised Lady that he'd sniffed her lilac *allée*'s perfume from the usual two miles upriver.

This year only uninvited Yanks were expected. Due any hour, any minute. The post road out front was wired, so few folks dared travel it. People were scared of Sherman's fire brigade. His company's job, child, was to start the fires, not end them.

Richmond, meanwhile, burned. (Miss Beale, I'm trying to offer some hard glittery facts no history lover can deny. But *this*, to my mind, could prove the cheapest part so far. Anybody can look up a fact, not everybody can *make* one up correct.) Yes, all records show—retreating Rebs torched Richmond's last warehouses. Yanks, entering the handsome fallen town (so smashed by cannon lobs it appeared a dress rehearsal for Dresden eighty years later), fought flames—just to save the town they'd won. Fire is a franchise, honey. Like these new Yankee- and Japanese-owned Malls, fire wants to open branches everywhere.

APRIL FOOLS' DAY ('65) seemed a final prank on the Confederacy. (Sounds good, don't it? Who says I'll never be no scholar?) Virginia was a whoopee cushion and the boys in gray were way too tired to keep standing. (Oh well.) Lee—American history's finest single mind for strategy (the North admitted it, even then)—was pinned by Sheridan, but good. One whole flange of infantry had stoppered Robert E.'s single exit.

Lincoln, walking quiet within a big armed guard, was seen on the very streets of Richmond. Him here? Abe gangled upstairs and sat at Jeff Davis' abandoned desk. History don't tell us if one President, linking fingers behind his head, rocking back in the chair, groaned with pleasure, then clomped huge feet onto the other's desk. But if so, who can blame him?

Lincoln next headed to the home of General Pickett, CSA, a boy Abe hisself had squeezed into West Point years before the war. Knocking. Mrs. Pickett (who was kin to me on my mother's people's side—her name was LaSalle Corbett Pickett—you think Lady E. More Marsden is bad) was a harum-scarum mess that day. She'd been down to her last slave (breaks your heart, don't it?) and that loyal maid had just run off like the rest. So Mrs. Pickett herself, holding the baby, was forced to open her own front door. "Is this the home of General Pickett?" "I am his wife and this is his heir." Spoke like a heroine.

First she seen a man so tall his clothes quit fitting about six feet up. Then she knew him. Imagine being the wife of a Confederate big shot and finding Lincoln—his presence in Richmond itself a secret—on your very porch. Well, she eased back, took in air (or so her memoir claims), and gasped, "The President!"

"Not really," said he, grinning that grin of his.

Now, to my mind, darling, if the war had come down to choosing one leader's face, that of Lee (perfect classic aristocrat dignity) or Lincoln (happenstance, insomnia, weather, everything that's homemade in personal character), the North would still have won and won big. Lincoln owned two eyes, the usual number of noses and mouths, and yet—from his every picture: trial and error, History itself looks out at you.

My favorite quick Lincoln fact is how: onct war quit, he invited the North's leading hero-soldiers to the White House. Glory hounds—some on crutches, some on canes—arrived expecting medals, guns, or money. Or all three. After a few commending words, Lincoln led vets down the hall—into a room piled with toys, the finest and most costly baby amusements then made. "Each hero, please, take one home to a child." Brave hurt men, disturbed, left carrying exceptional dolls, sleds, hobbyhorses. This is fact. —My Lee one's even briefer: The handsomest of Virginians had retired to being a college president. In town, one young mother held up her infant, she asked Lee for a philosophy of life to later tell her son. Without pausing, the great man said, "Teach him to deny himself." —Different visions. You choose which suits you.

So: True, Robert E.'s features shone perfect as the rosy Jesus in Sunday-school lithos. But Lincoln's wins.

Mr. Lincoln's smile is like a muddy country crossroad that—when rain has stopped—dries to show you every single wagon, bird, and walker that has ever passed across it.

"No, ma'am, not the President," says a tall stranger of hisself. "Just one old friend of your husband's, come to inquire after your health, to see if there's anything you need."

Mrs. Pickett was naturally too proud for begging favors off this kingpin enemy. But her male-missing youngster reached right out—not knowing no better. The guest gladly took this ten-pound Confederate. Abe was, you saw, a father who could deny his own sons nothing. He asked Mrs. Pickett to please inform her husband that his old friend forgave Pickett's maybe picking maybe the wrong side. And why? "No better reason than the color of this baby's eyes." See, they were blue, not gray. Grinning his crossroads of a grin, the caller handed back her child, said, "Good day, ma'am," left.

MEANTIME, Lee's men scout amongst theirselves for something un-dingy enough—towel, shirt, hankie?—to be read by enemy as a *White* (in keeping with our theme, Miss Beale) flag of surrender. Sherman had just took Raleigh—eighty-nine miles southwest of The Lilacs and thirty-three from my bed right here. Honey, it should be pointed out that Sherman's local foot soldiers hadn't yet heard tell of Lee's getting cornered. Little did they know that the entire Struggle would end in two days flat. Otherwise, men might've spared the mansion in question. But "mights" don't belong in no national document testifying to what went on because it had to, honey, had to.

A good percentage of Sherman's fire-eaters were Westerners. They'd hiked East to fight—they'd *walked* East. Sherman's supply quartermasters were forced to order larger-sized shoes for such pioneer boys, their feet run that much bigger than Eastern gents'. Fact. Sherm had some discipline probs. Frontier types *would* talk back to any pipsqueak officer—"You call West Point *West*, Lieutenant Lily-livered Boot Suck?" That type lip. Rough customers, see. And just such ragged homesteaders will soon burn The Lilacs—"cheap" or not—while you—if you choose—get a ringside seat.

So, watch.

3

AROUND two o'clock, on April 7, '65, the day it all come undone, rain happened hereabouts. To be historical and exact: a April shower done occurred. It would—history tells us—bring later, among other things, May flowers. The lilac hedge hung coated in raindrop. You've seen lilacs wet by rain? Perfect—a mingling of diamond bracelets and Concord grapes.

My school paper puts the white lady upstairs at her usual morning spot. She's playing the German concert grand piano that come upriver from Wilmington on a barge nearbout overattended as Miss Cleopatra's own. Because something about it appealed to her, Lady had the Bechstein painted frost white.

Being right melodic with aid from a Foster favorite, Lady—outliving one headache before bogging down in the next—banters at two slave women (one young, one old), both cleaning this huge upstairs bedroom. Castalia, 110 percent alive, just gone fifteen, hums, moves springy as a switch, keeps dusting a white mantel mobbed with Stratfordshire shepherdesses. She cleans them in spunky slaps (she never ever breaks one, knowing exactly how much force each can take). The older slave—one Zelia—trims tips from blooming lilac branches, makes a great arrangement meant to dress up this pale tower room. The owner talks. As ever. At day's end, slave women—safe in the quarter—moan, "Ooh, she got some mouth on her, don't she? Chaw you ear off, you let her." Till today, they ain't had much choice.

Pitching into a piano reduction of a lush orchestra arrangement of the ever-popular "Last Rose of Summer," Lady chatters at them across her own spilled music. Speaks of a son sent off to war, mentions her dead sainted husband, says peace is overdue. The only good local parties are wartime bandage rollings and everybody *knows* she's allergic to cotton. Wartime food's a bore. Plus, you can't get sheet music by mail. Her black helpers nod for once, today acting almost interested. Neither woman listens. Both concentrate instead on a moving-day racket from downstairs.

—The smell of smoke enters.

One dark Z shape of fume poses midair, hard to miss in this upper room whose very walls are white silk brocade. With the boss lady safe in her floor-length silk, with music straining forth in perfumed clustered chords, considering the paleness of pearls wound artful in her hair and the chopsticks' sheeny X behind her head, the only spots of color come from rolled wool in a corner knitting basket (still showing red/white/blue used to stitch Willie's farewell long johns), the lilac branches bright with rain, plus two dark nervous women's brown clothes, red head rags. And now this smoke.

White ivory keys are literally darker than the player's fingers. Head down, acting ignorant of Yanks' upriver housewarmings, Lady appears about the whitest white woman on earth. I maybe said that. She will not allow her nose to twitch at sudden carbon. Mrs. L. E. M. Marsden plays on, pretending today ain't the day it all ends. Cross-handing her keyboard—she watches the black women. From their sharp motions and sudden readiness to fake listening—Lady understands: Soon. She's had a note from the plantation four miles upriver. "Lady, Prepare in whatever way you might, my dear. While Nero fiddles the pagans are probably already burning Rocky Mount. Knowing, my gout all but roars. May our cause and bloodline live. Your devoted servant, Cousin Mabry."

Changing pianistic selections for her maids' sakes (she worries over their attention span), Lady tells herself, "I have always treated these and my other people fairly. I've nursed them through kidney colic and the toothache. And who hardly ever forgets a slave birthday? Yes, they will doubtless remember such an owner's kindness." One such favor: Lady has never allowed the word "slave" to be uttered within any slave's hearing—not even by Winch, the former taskmaster charged with lashing them. Other owners along the river Tar call The Lilacs' blacks "Marsden's freedmen." Lady is pleased to recollect how her late husband spoiled his "people" so.

Clear back in '59, he gave the staff their Sunday mornings off! It was, other owners saw, the beginning of the end hereabouts. Local slave morale went pure to pieces—others felt jealous of the privileged few. Whatever faint banjo music yet lingered in county quarters soon withered from hearing.

"A vision befell me," explained the quiet book-loving Dr. Marsden. (This happened during the Morning Prayers he required for his slaves' religious instruction.) "Last night, your humble master was visited with a dream concerning many dark sheep and a single shining good shepherd. In this case: poorly portrayed by, well, me, Ours Truly. I don't often interpret my dreams as being *eo ipso* true . . . Uncle Primus, would you perhaps care to translate *eo ipso* for our friends?"

Primus, white-haired, courtly, rose up smiling, "Marse, why, *eo ipso* don't hardly be worth no lingering over, do it?—mean just," he shrugged, grinning, ". . . *eo ipso*, sir!" and sat back down. Other slaves stared at the old man.

"Excellent, Primus," Marse Marsden laughed cleaning his pince-nez. "Of course, that was beneath your skills . . . Forgive me. —So, in light of my dream, considering the bounty of last season's cotton yields, which did our general coffers so fill, and admitting the ancient truth '*Salve Lucrum*' . . . Care to bother with *that*, Primus?"

"Now, that," the gardener-butler saw fit to stand again, "that be the words what say . . . Oh, to make it go down easiest, might could run . . . 'Profit mean joy'? Somethin long them lines. From de Greek."

Marse Marsden didn't correct him.

Castalia, vigilant, groaned. Primus never taught the others. Just hoarded facts. Cassie now mumbled, "Primus say: It from the Greek. I say: If it from him, it from de Geek."

Some giggling done resulted. Uncle turnt, give Castalia a spiked look, in English, signifying "Later."

"Excellent," Dr. Marsden wore on. "At least to Yours Truly, the dream means this: Christus, in my revised opinion, would surely have given *His* 'people' a portion of *their* Sundays off. Ergo. To wit: Begone, Ours Truly. Fly forth, do as you wish till noon!"

No translating needed, quite a scattering done occurred. Dr. Marsden was left behind his makeshift altar, feebly straightening papers. His lady wife set alone at the downstairs spinet she played for her "people's" moral and artistic uplift. (These came to the same thing, Mrs. Lady liked to tell visitors.) Young Willie, bored out of his skull and dressed in a red acolyte gown that made him feel like a perfect circus monkey, stood holding the five-foot silver candlesnuffer before a great bank of religious flame.

Suddenly the Marsdens, alone together, heard—in the whole house— no sound but Marsden breath. Gone the happy hobnailed bustle, the nice sense of audience that a big staff gives. Even the kitchen building out back got real silent. Marsdens looked at each other. Did this mean Sunday dinner would be delayed?

"Alone at last?" Lady risked a little joke.

"*Now* can I take off this doggoned tent?" young Willie asked.

"In point of fact," Dr. Marsden give a weakened smile, "I meant *after* the service, but no matter."

Slaves tilling adjacent acreage looked at the Marsden fields, unworked during a Sabbath's whole first half. County production fizzled. Neighboring owners remarked it. Even Lady's port-loving Cousin Mabry tut-tutted. Locals never quite forgave Dr. Marsden, with his smudged pince-nez and his break-fast-nook busts of eggshell-white philosophers. (People claimed he talked to statues in statue-languages dead as the statues.)

At All Saints Episcopal, other bosses asked: Why'd Marsden go dragging Jesus off His Pedestal-and-Cross down into muddy local labor questions? Besides, what'd Christ ever known about how to work folks? Only had a skeleton crew of twelve and most day He had to feed them (loaves and fishes) out of pocket.

4

IN 1859, Dr. Marsden started naming his babies after old-timey gods and generals. Before, he'd titled slaves for such Carolina cities as had elected his several brothers to be their mayors. Charlotte, she didn't come out too bad. Castalia, the town, claimed fewer citizens than The Lilacs did before the first runaways run away. But the person everybody felt sorriest for was poor L.S. When she finally begged Dr. Marsden, he said, yes, she could just be called by the initials. Poor woman complained that—come suppertime— shouldn't nobody have to hear her loved ones holler into evening air, "Oh, Leaksville-Spray, Leaksville-Spray!"

Dr. Marsden died one Monday after lecturing slaves on the corruptions of the Greek style in Wedgwood decoration. His staff hadn't exactly found this talk no laughfest, honey. He led house slaves up the spiral stairs, he pointed out one figure on a huge jasper vase niched there. Dr. M. reported Wedgwood's saying, "Fig leaves are not enough." Thanks to priggishness, Josiah Wedgwood made Priapus hisself wear a toga and flowers, under-cutting all that god's erotic oomph. Since slaves didn't know who Priapus was, Dr. Marsden alone laughed at his own remark. No slave smiled till Little Xerxes—standing on stairs above the Dr.—exactly mimed the boss man's blinky chuckling. *Then* slaves giggled. Causing their owner to chortle so hard his pince-nez fell, caught by its black grosgrain cord. The following morning, whilst translating yet more unappreciated Horace upstairs, the man hunched forwards, spilling ink across a hundred white lost pages.

Lady called in all workers from far-flung cotton and indigo fields. "The tragedy, long-dreaded, has, my people, befallen us. His heart was ever a frail one. We must, now help, each other, to be brave." She then offered her staff a full free day to mourn their fallen Leader. Twenty-four hours off!

Slaves chose to grieve via picnics near the lily-pad ponds. Some ex-pressed their loss by taking up abandoned bones and banjos. Others could only be consoled by pantry raids, by climbing the huge magnolias out front, by sitting up there chewing turkey drumsticks. It was, even Lady admitted, not a pretty sight. Children had the run of the place. Venus, Xerxes, and Baby Juno were seen bouncing on a imitation Roman chaise in the second-from-best east parlor. Such noise!

Buggies full of other slave-owning whites soon clomped back and forth along The Lilacs' post-road fences. A early form of traffic jam done occurred. Gentry studied the gardenia funeral wreath, big as a wagon wheel, hung from one of the mansion's four solid-marble columns. This announcement seemed at odds with the perfect carnival tumbling everywheres.

To owners parked on the highroad, grumbling in their dogcarts and covered phaetons—how strange it must've been to view slave children bob-bling in the gallery's twenty-four rocking chairs (and waving like from some

resort hotel, the rascals!). Odd to see adult blacks sleeping on the ponds'
wet banks, collapsed upon Oriental rugs dragged from out the big house's
marble foyer. Some slaves sat fishing by the lily pools, hooking giant golden
carp brought in vats from Richmond via China. Dozens of huge goldfish
now thrashed on the red-lacquered Chinese footbridge. Off nearer woods,
two bad boys were seen to roast a formerly white swan, one set free downriver for reasons of its showy whiteness alone.

Even Widow Marsden—weeping at her upstairs window—found slaves'
single day off a curious and, to her mind, right increasingly pagan spectacle.
She wanted to ask somebody nearby, "Is *this* how they'd utilize their so-
called freedom?" But since she'd given even Castalia, her body servant, a
holiday, since her son was presently away on some choir trip with his pretty
friend Ned—there won't nobody to hear the young widow's questions.

Would her slaves consider returning to the fields at dawn? And how
might a person go about *making* them? Short of charging Overseer Winch
to please get out the whips, please. (Dashing young Winch was presently
on a buying trip to Fayetteville—slave buying—and Lady feared that, even
considering her husband's death, the taskmaster might act real cross about
such liberality as her grief had inspired.) It was, she saw now, hard to offer
them just the one day's charity—packing your "people" from total license
back to usual labor. Lady, weeping in her turret with its view of distant
profitable fields, idly wished her people would work for one reason alone:
their love of her. It would so simplify their lot. (And hers.) But even Lady
wondered how much longer a certain pitch of service might could last.

Widow Marsden compared the threat of emancipation with her own
doubts about death itself. Yes, you heard how eventually everybody dies—
but one somehow felt, privately of course, and even on the day of a young
spouse's passing—that perhaps with proper discipline and good rest, with
a determined playing of one's scales, with decent cheerful help from "one's
people" . . . that, well, maybe one wouldn't. Die. Why *should* one? Must it
end, this easy glide she'd known for life? Her duties weren't far from the
swan's, a bird presently being rotisseried on the green stick out front. Profession: to be white and graceful in shape, to reign over a peaceful mirrored
surface, to represent refined charm—and to glide, forever glide (weather
permitting).

Watching from her third-floor window, Lady felt disappointed that
these, her people, had not chose to rue their master's end a bit more actively.
Lady E. More Marsden mourned. (Nobody knew her middle name and,
despising it so, she'd burned her birth record and defaced a family Bible to
hide the ugly thing.) She decided that slaves' grief should be noisier, a tad
more primitive. Alas, Lady now saw, her dear, if childish friends still had
much to learn.

So, hoping to help release their pent-up regret (it must *really* be pent
up by now), remembering her own favorite phrase: "With great gifts go great
responsibilities," Lady ordered her grand piano shifted down three flights

and placed on the first floor's flagstone portico. Asked to supervise, Castalia took a quick, if grumblish break from spearfishing.

Lady hinted: perhaps the young movers *should* go shirtless. Even today, even this borne down with woe, child, something about that yet appealed to her. The Lilacs' rosewood spiral staircase had been carved by a family of imported Germans in just three weeks. (They even cleaned up after theirselves. "So German," Lady had told locals—though she'd never met a native German before. She just wanted to sound knowledgeable. Surely we can forgive her *that*.) The stairs were fully wide enough to let twelve men (ten stubbornly wearing shirts today) stomp along bearing a clanging, seemingly grief-stricken concert grand. Lady felt that on the whole plantation, only herself and this precious instrument truly mourned.

The piano was stationed at her porch's very center. As the sun set, whilst sitting framed here amid overgrown magnolia boughs, torchlit by her only two shirtless workers, Lady offered funeral airs wrote at the deaths of English rulers. She'd refused to wear black clothes. She owned none. Besides *he* would've wanted her the way he'd known her—a White Woman— bleached even further by widow's pallor. Playing for her gathered staff, head tossing so much (it was plain she'd never guessed at slave quarter's Imitate How She Toss Her Head Around contests), with pearls agleam in torchlight, Lady felt moved by music's gift for reaching all walks of life. All.

Doing a piece called "Consolation," the woman was stirred at a talent often praised by her subtlest houseguests. She felt every inch the artist, till noticing that out yonder on their rugs (fact is, *her* rugs), except for children scaling magnolias' limbs and rudely beginning to toss red seeds into a white piano's working parts, her slaves all slept. So much for a captive audience. She stared down from the stage-porch at her "people" who'd gorged all day on swan plus goldfish, deep-fat-fried. (Darling, like the time her two white Pomeranians disappeared one midnight, she hadn't liked to say anything too critical at the time.) Lady studied snoring folks drunk on leisure, worn out by testing the limits of their only full day off, ever.

Till now. Till right this second. April 7, 18 and 65.

5

AT A PIANO long since muscled back upstairs, Lady plays impromptus, "Royal Fireworks" reductions, whatevers, ballades. A smell of burning drifts (one octave stronger than before) through twenty windows on this round room's river side. Today the mistress does all the repeats, hoping to slow this thaw toward Freedom. Castalia, her large face eager to be satisfied, moves in that wiry inspired way she has. Snitching sugar-coated almonds from a silver dish, she still swats her duster across froufrou figurines. Cassie's shoulders are wide as a man's. Cheekbones bow out in a style right regal. Her eyes are so alive they first seem a warning till you notice the deep joke, the wild pleasure burning in them today.

Zelia—fleshless as a stick, older than some hills, spreads a lilac bouquet that has become, since we last checked, big as any mummer's headdress. Both black women straighten now and—eyes fastened—sniff. Lady, working not to notice, plays a good bit louder. —We all got our ways of dealing with disaster, child. Some folks pace, some crochet. What's yours?

Since knee-high to nothing, Mistress has suffered migraines. I said so. She sure feels one coming on. A regular masterpiece. Her bedchamber's forty windows hang muffled with negligee material. Filters let in only playful minor sunshine, and halt the rough stuff. Her bedside table is piled with silk blindfolds. Staring toward the pagan sun can give Lady Marsden a three-day blinder almost at onct.

Now smoke—its source being, sad to say, Cousin Mabry's mock-Gothic dockside "folly" at Shadowlawn—cuts bolder through gauze window shades.

Lady Marsden has a pet remark, one that Cassie picked up early on. Lady uses it to explain the hardship of widowhood, the sadness of having her only child—thirteen—sent off to soldiering, the pain of running so huge a plantation alone, trying to do right by her "people" whilst living through this tacky needless war and eating so poor—okra done in every sauce invented by God or Frenchmen. She says it again, massaging the bridge of her nose. The free hand plays on, right valiant: "With great gifts go great responsibilities. 'To whom much is given, much shall be required.'"

The Good Book mentions this, and so did the Widow Marsden right often.

Lady tells Castalia she's getting an especially dreadful one. She feels that famous burning sensation in her nostrils, the first sign and one that has, she believes, been described to Cas before.

"My dear, you cannot imagine these—you, who are health itself. I hear that Yankees are actually *in* our state, the verminous infestations (oh—don't you two gape so. Your little friend here picks things up from out of the very air). Sherman seems a poison in one's own bloodstream. I fear the onslaught of a grand mal that will outdo even my worst. Who can ever forget the one last June? —At the start of even a typical spell the world resembles perhaps a white dinner plate—clean, round, shiny with Spodey light playing all across its surface. But then, oh dear, from one edge—usually the lower left—single black mouthfuls gobble at brightness till all is bitten into, bitten away. Till I must rest here as my whole life is eaten in veritable plugs. Plugs, I tell you. —At the end, there remains but a single mouthful of perfect whiteness. Mightn't that be spared me? Well? Might it not? Don't just stand there mooning, you two. No! I am spared nothing. A black jaw swoops down upon even that and when this final wedge is ingested, well, *you've* attended me often enough, Castalia, you know all too well what happens next, my child. After so many years as my handpicked confidante, you *should* know."

"You faints," Cassie cuts her eyes at the older serving woman. Zelia smirks, hacking lilacs' stem ends with a new right surgical energy. "You faints into somebody's arms," Castalia adds. "And you gets so weak you can't even hardly . . . talk. Now that be *weak*."

Missing the little joke, Lady rolls on, "*Justement*. And yet, as I always say . . ."

"To who much got givened, much gone be required."

"You speak my mind. My very mind, child. Castalia, there are times when you open your mouth and I hear the music of the spheres. I hear exactly what *I* would say."

Today, Castalia laughs in swallowed rushes, moves with jumpy turns, the elbows angle out. Her head tilts on its smooth axis, eyes are quick to flutter closed. Cas wants to keep her senses steeplechasing over eleven hundred lilacs' perfume. That heavy smell now seems the enemy, a kind of cage slung up around this vast white house.

Fumes grow thicker. Cassie perks to usual sounds, acts eager to miss the new knocks and odd draggings from downstairs. Making music in this chamber's center, Lady Marsden don't quite see the great evacuation underway.

6

BY PEELING back one window's migraine strainer, Cas looks down onto quite a parade. Other slaves are emptying best things from The Lilacs' first floor. Last night, Castalia herself ordered the job done, "Gone be our nest egg in the next world." She promised—if others would help unload the mansion—her and Zelia'd try keeping Lady Busybody busy. Busy with Cassie's famous true and semi-true tales of the crossing from Africa—busy with spanky-new lies, with anything that worked.

Old Zelia had said, "Let fire gobble every nasty stick of it." Castalia snapped, "We ain't been cleaning this fine mess for all these years just to see it fry for being Hers. We Hers too. And *we* couldn't help it."

House slaves upriver have sent news: Silver is already being buried. At places like Mabry's Shadowlawn, this could mean digging a all-day trench. Last night, Marsden slaves voted: This house's silver will be left to Inferno's happy-go-lucky elbow grease. Women had spent so much of their lives keeping blackness off the julep cups, salvers, fish platters for two hundred. Well, not no more! Only shy Baby Venus asked that one thing not be polished off by fire—the silver service used on rainy days to send tea towards players of Catacombs.

Baby Venus got voted down.

CASSIE now studies workers filing across the lawn—greenery commencing to sprout first dandelions since Uncle Primus and his six garden helpers trotted North last month. Castalia—way up here, seeing what others choose to save—longs to shout orders. (Ain't often you get warned that your place will burn at 3 p.m., letting you pick from amongst what'll otherwise soon be soot.) Through the window, it's clear to Cas—the women left downstairs might've lemon-oiled these items for thirty years, but they sure don't understand what Best means. She wonders, Maybe I been made a monster snob like her, *by* her. Castalia has served as Lady Marsden's body servant for ten of her seventeen slave years. And during all the days of standing behind Mistress at the oval pier glass, long evenings of brushing the famous pale brown hair two hundred strokes a thick handful, Castalia has someway picked up (like a disease) more stray facts than she's ever needed knowing. Till today. By heart, she's got the words that Lady speaks with such reverent boldness. Things ours: Wedgwood. Sèvres. Majolica. Aubusson. Ormolu. Why should such syllables chime so in a young head kidnapped out of Africa at age three? Why do these words—ones Cassie can't rightly recollect ever *not* understanding—sound to her someway tribal? personal? African?

"*I* knows just what wants saving." Pretending to dust, Cas settles her forehead nearer gauze drawn drum-tight over the third floor's splendid view.

Meanwhile, Little Xerxes is lugging a busted cuckoo clock from out the back scullery. And here comes Baby Venus with one dented copper coal bucket worn over her head. She's most stomping on the heels of two older women who tote a dead-ordinary oak hall table. Why *that*? Cas goes to yell a whole litany of things worth salvaging, then recollects last night's other show of hands.

Question: Since Freedom would be theirs today, should folks run off early or serve out last hours by playacting through usual routines? Should they tell Mrs. Whitey or keep her in the dark a little longer? Well, everybody chose to carry on. Being slaves of a self-styled lady actress—having lived for years in this imagined pageant play, the drama part appealed to them. Anyhow, their mistress stayed at such a pitch of regular hysteria, especially since Marse Marsden died and Will marched off, if she knew the end was near, she'd only make the final minutes of unfreedom harder on everybody. Herself included.

Castalia had announced today's schedule: "Fire gone get here round three o'clock if we to believe what we been told from upriver. And I, for one, do. I ready to try and trust all kind of things. This house gone be cooked medium to well done by teatime. After that, please call me: Young Miss New York City–bound!"

Following last night's vote in the quarter, everybody talked loud, they waltzed around. Baby Venus rode grown women's shoulders. Using a broom handle and tin basin, Zelia done some right spunky percussion. Little Xerxes copied Uncle Primus' formal butler-bowing from the waist. But then, *anybody* could do Primus.

7

LADY counted Xerxes among the all-time favorite slaves she'd ever inherited or personally purchased. And that made quite a crowd. Of all her black children, only Little Xerxes got invited to high tea on odd days between white visitors. Local gentry called him the best copycat living, boy had more lives than nine. The lad could imitate other people imitating him imitating other people. (Odd, at a glance you'd know all parties and only later wonder *how*.)

Though eleven years old, Xerxes stood just one inch taller than a yard. Ain't too many gentle ways to say it, sugar: He was semi-funny-looking. Skin and bones, the quick-moving boy had sizable ears and a studious indoor glee that reminded Lady Marsden of her dead husband, Xerxes' likely poppa.

Everybody (including Lady's guests) asked the child to please mime so-and-so. A slave, he obliged. Black folks claimed: to see Xerxes "do" you meant courting your own death. In the quarter, the child was real good about warning friends so's they could shut their eyes, could sit real still, braced, suddenly surrounded by hacksaw laughing, shoved a bit yet never daring to peek. Was like your looking in the mirror with your eyes closed.

After midnight, in the safety of the quarter, performing by a single candle, Xerxes most often did Lady. With oh such fierce attention. If the jumpy boy was her novelty-clock possession, she was sure his masterpiece. (As a prod to action and a reason for rising, child, Revenge should not never be underrated.) Xerxes caught her rich surprisingly deep voice, her precise tiny hands, the way she tossed her head—now finicky, now with passion.

One morning Xerxes overheard her say, "Gentlemen always wear neckties." Next day and ever after, the child sported a ascot made from three of Master's cast-off hankies. Wearing this, he turned up at the Big House for his usual cleaning of Marsdens' shoes. Others teased Xerxes till Mistress called his little neck gear "valiant." Then others muttered instead.

The child had finally quit entering slaves' Toss You Head Like Her contests—giving the adults a chance. Unlike me, Xerxes rarely exaggerated. This dryness made his imitations start off scarier and soon get funnier. Castalia spent the most time alone with Mistress. Cas had all kinds of secret noticings and she tried passing these along to the boy wizard.

Begged to do Mistress, Xerxes would sometimes sulk, refusing. (All comics, child, want to be took *partway* serious—I should know.) Cassie bribed the child—offering her own meal rations. "*Please* first do Mistress play the piano slow, then Mistress reading verse while eye-deep in too bubbly of a bubble bath. You know the one. Then to wind up with Mistress Gets June's Big Old Headache. In that order, boy." And thin Cas, stomach growling—having sacrificed tonight's fried okra—would rock back like royalty, arms crossed, her face already practicing its ready grin, so eager to be satisfied.

When slaves pleaded for Xerxes' choicest, they didn't call, "Do her." They begged, "Do it. Do *it* now." Cassie felt sad that Lady'd never get to see Xerxes' version of Her Ownership. "The Mrs. might could learn so much from it."

Some nights, the boy's act was good enough so, next morning, slaves stared extra hard at their mistress. (Smiling, she checked her hairdo's linchpin chopsticks, she stood whispering, "What?")

Uncle Primus—usually right hard and strict—gave the little actor time off from slave garden duty. A artist, Xerxes never took no shortcuts, boy stayed busier than anybody. So much to know and notice!

In one outbuilding used for harness tack, a large mirror was kept locked. It won't chipped or broken. Seemed like some political prisoner: harmless except for its views.

Lady had banished the thing. "It fattens. Considerably. Here I had it shipped from France via Boston, I expected a soupçon's loyalty. But what does it see fit to do? Add seven pounds. Per arm. I simply won't have it." —Passing the hut, you'd hear Lady's nearly lifelike voice asking Lady's mirror, "What? *What?*" in forty different mothy ways. —Darling, if you watched Little Xerxes long enough he could almost teach you how to love her.

DURING private wee-hours sessions, long after Winch and his underlings were off drinking in far cabins, why did black folks keep going over Lady's fussbudget extremes? Would they ever reclaim a smidgen of their lifetimes' time spent humoring Judge More's only child?

Xerxes could copy whatever he saw or imagined (which means: Anything). But the child never considered any slave—hisself least of all—half so much fun to do as Lady. His hit parade included: *Lady gives away jewels and oranges*. In Xerxes' strange imitation, these gift items were always someway stitched to Lady's silk wrapper. In saying, "Here—just for you," she had to tear shreds off of her clothes. Soon she tried screening bad rips with one hand while passing on more treats. Dipping far into her capital, she was soon left jaybird naked.

Tonight—his last unfree one—Xerxes stayed mighty wound up. He fairly chugged. For once, our imp of talent overdid. Hey, nobody's perfect. Laughing just encouraged the famous migraine trick.

Standing, Xerxes mashed the bridge of his nose. Others spoke a chorus, "Uh-oh, look like she getting one her blinders, sure. Poor canary bird. Reckon it a bad one?" Xerxes, eyes closed, nodded Yes, give off a single peep of pain.

Folks drew into a circle, like preparing to catch this Lady bound to fall. But when Xerxes' staggering begun—nose and forehead bunched, free arm trailing in a comic goldfish-graceful way—wouldn't nobody save him. Xerxes give each person a chance. Each sidestepped helping. He just reeled on to the next, next. Finally, run out of help, he collapsed, but only by getting down real slow onto the stone floor, careful not to muss clothes or the imaginary eighteen-inch-high hairdo he kept touching, organized air.

Safely fallen, the big-eared Lady pitched a real conniption fit, coming around just long enough to fret with pearls and say, "What? I *is* shocked!" Finally it did die, but with many comic froggy kick-spasms. You had to of been there, probably. Everybody laughed. Slaves practically had to.

Honey, after such fun, couldn't nobody sleep. Felt like the night before Christmas/Sunday mornings off/plus Marse Marsden's deathday—all combined and spiced. Winded from celebrating in this windowless dormitory, lit by one candle, folks finally grew silent. They settled on corn-husk mattresses, turned away from each other, and commenced by degree to mumbling quiet prayers. Slaves' beliefs smoothed African memories with handpicked Christian leftovers. Mud-and-blood tones bled through pastel Episcopalian hymns. Slaves had made up the necessary religion. Who else would do it for them?

8

FOLKS chanted a favorite ditty only when alone together:

> I got one mind for Master to see.
> The other one I know is me.

Recipe: take one part strong tribe lore—shades of red and black. Stir in dainty candy colors from the Big House's paintings of the Jesus Man. Mix to taste.

The Lilacs' Slaves' Hero and Liberator would look a bit like that well-known stripped bachelor painted on a tree (one of the pictures Castalia, now fidgeting with her ostrich-feather duster, waited to see hauled from out the northwest parlor).

Slaves' expected Saint would also favor the missing Master Willie— innocent but guilty—a boy who'd trooped off towards Virginia, battling so inherited slaves might stay here and his years longer. Seemed odd that *his* freckled face had someway got into the home-brewed picture of today's Freeing Agent. But there it was. (Will's first toddler steps had been aimed toward the bathhouse on mornings when dark women all scrubbed. At age three, he loitered around outside—stripped bare, escaped from his white nurse, trying and act real casual while—behind cupped hands—his boy's part stood at honorary attention. Black men shook their heads, "Take after his poppa. Already know what *he* like." Mrs. Marsden later tantrumed to prevent her son's sleeping alongside young friends in the quarter on non-school nights. Oh, but he begged. —All this got remembered.)

Black folks at The Lilacs didn't think of Northern forces as separate soldiers. No, a single useful giant seemed likelier. In 18 and 60, the predicted Savior's swart limbs had lengthened. His beard blackened. The farm's workers had just seen their first engraving of Marse Lincoln.

They'd learned about Him from Mabry's valet. But everybody'd misheard the name as "Abraham, Linking." The Lilacs' ex-African blacksmith repeated his own version. Had to do with busting chains, with being soldered in the elsewhere place where you belonged. Slaves all knew how a oldendays Abraham had been the sourdough starter culture for a great line. Seemed this new Abe would found another tougher tribe. He'd link the from-around-here freed folks with some Balm of Gilead strengthening to the North. Your chains'd return to being African bauble jewelry. The Lost Tribe, found, would be spared, heated, coupled, annealed—Today.

Child, it all stayed vague as that, and—for these folks—as powerful.

CLEANING, using ostrich plumes abducted from Africa for decoration and duty, Castalia now awaits His striding in. He'll come cleansing a lighted path. He'll be bare, dusky, tall as any plains-dwelling African but bound in a semi-Tuscarora semi-Jesus loincloth. He'll smile safe and sweet behind a boy's untested face. He'll arrive on long stilt Abe legs, high-stepping over lily ponds eaten free of goldfishes and swans. He'll come to set this house in order—and how? with one accusing finger's Lordly touch, to set the house afire.

Off towards waiting carts down there ("Castalia, I believe I am speaking to you. I *have* been. You daily grow more absentminded, more like me, my dear. I do feel a bleariness setting in, I need distracting. Might I hear about *your* coming out—from Africa, *mia cara* Scheherazade?"), down there and out into daylight marches a George III library ladder, six pitted convex mirrors from Revolution days, a stained-glass fire screen that only slaves seem to find beautiful. There goes a hand-blown punch-bowl gondola.

Off to the safety of the woods marches a family oil portrait—Little Xerxes' barefoot strut beneath the white male ancestor. This puritan's stiff white collar is padlocked in a halo of gold frame. The face seems none too pleased about them stubby black legs saving it. Xerxes, spying Cassie in this high window, peeks around the painting's gilded edge. He makes his own features go fish-mouthed/sniffy as the picture. The child's free arm crooks, bracketing his real face—one now shaped like the fake face he makes seem more real than his born own. Next, shrugging, moving off, in one instant he's forgot it all.

"I hears you. I on my way. So you wants your Cassie's Africa, hunh? —Zelia, sug, them flowers looks fine enough for now. You may to be adjourn." And the fifteen-year-old winks at the eighty-year-old, who nods, purses her mouth, tiptoes out, apron corners lifted between fingertips, making a joke of her own exaggerated courtesy, maybe Zelia's last.

9

WHITE and black, with Lilac looking on, are now alone together.

Lady still plays something Spanishy, she slides over, bares a fresh section of warmed piano bench. The mistress is feeling feverish with the coming on of migraine, the coming in of Yankees, the coming out of her Servant Problem's true start. These two young women, one white, one black, know so much about each other. It's suddenly become a burden. Monthlies' peculiarities, the men that both consider flirting with on weekly shopping trips, the allergies and prides and clashing moody woes of each. By now, one's freedom from the other will mean dying or amnesia.

"Please," smiles Lady. "This time. Right here, close by me." Her left hand pats white brocade three times.

Cassie chooses to stand near the white instrument she keeps uselessly dusting. Her ostrich feathers cause thwunks among living wires. Cassie stares down at her owner's profile.

Lady, grinning, leaves off playing, tilts her noggin leftward (Xerxes has taught Cas to notice: for flirting it's always left—for direct orders steadily right). Many men have found this real attractive. For Castalia it's just *"that old trick."*

"What? You're looking at . . . what? my hair, friend? Do you prefer it up like this? I am told that lifting it does give me some added 'height,' or at least the illusion of that—which I can certainly live with. —Don't you find, or do you? Be candid."

"But you done always wore it like this. Why you axting Castalia today?"

"Because, my dear, if you believed it to be wrong for a my-shaped face, I might . . . change it. I very well could, and just on your say-so. People consider me so fixed in my habits. But I'm capable of altering, even of improving. If you convinced me, I mean. Castalia? Simply show me how."

Women look at each other for a long while. Seems Cassie might now speak, might offer to save this lady from coming flames. Seems that Lady, a educated human person after all, is about to, what, apologize, repent?

"No, ma'am—you done dressed your hair like this forever. Probably be too late. Folks wouldn't rightly reco'nize you—you chop it off or let it run free down you back. Cassie figures you too far gone for changing nothing now."

Then Castalia can't halt herself. "Know what you needs? —Spending about a half a hour watching Xerxes do you."

" 'Do' me? I haven't heard that since my poor husband died. Certainly Xerxes 'does' my shoes. But you probably mean 'imitate.' The scamp goes after everybody else, why shouldn't he ape his mistress? I'm flattered, actually. He knows I dote upon him. So acute, our Xerxes—he even gets the voices, does he not? —I suppose . . . in simulating me . . . he's frightfully accurate?"

Cassie, grinning, nods. " 'Frightfully' be bout right."

"Well, then," Lady strikes a chord for effect, "that *is* something to anticipate. He's certainly shameless when he does, oh, you, for instance. You've seen that, of course. No? Oh dear me, yes. First he wedges his elbows out, *comme ça*, then he frowns and smiles at once, like *so*."

> Oh wad some power the giftie gie us
> To see oursels as others see us!
> —Burns

Castalia has heard the Scottish poet quoted all her life. But today she chooses to say, "Burns? Burns?"

White stares at Black. Smoke is a hammock pulled from one corner of this room to the other. Black/White—who will blink the first? Merciful, Castalia changes subjects. "I reckon you bout ready for you story, bout me?"

"Oh, do, yes. Notice how my hands shake? Ivory from middle C on up is quite slick with dew."

A slave's feather duster strikes piano's rim. " 'Dew'! How come you always only 'dews' while Castalia here steadily sweats?"

"I'm sure I haven't the faintest notion what you mean. But, please, my story . . . concerning you, of course. Tell."

Cas is mindful how them others voted not to snitch. Still, she can't help it, she commences her Slave's Tale like so: "White folks' Bible say, 'In my father's house is many mansions.' But, Missy, for now, down here, this the only one you got. And, ma'am? It just about to burn. You ready?" Then comes a tale of pillage, strangers in a even stranger land.

Smoke from upriver curls indoors, sharper gusts. Strange dry metal smells still can't dent the sweetness of eleven hundred blooming lilac trees. Castalia will stay busy till the end of her story and of this plantation—they'll last about the selfsame time.

She calls her tale "The Tribe That Answers" and I will tell it to you later, God willing. Halfway through, Cas yells downstairs for scalding water, soap, a scrub brush. Dusting, she's decided, just ain't hard enough for your last minutes. On all fours, she serves the end of her life sentence. She refuses Lady's offers: the whole piano bench, a garnet brooch, some candied almonds . . . On hands and knees, Cas feels she has—since age three—been locked into this crawl space minus headroom, a game of Catacombs that hides rooms' beauty from the very person assigned for life to clean them.

Lady Marsden, not sure what else to do at the end, amid the epileptic clinking of seventy-odd clocks (they begin to make her nervous), replays most all music she knows and somewhat up-tempo. Castalia scrubs around white silk slippers—blurring—frantic on brass pedals.

THE CHAMBER door opens. Both women turn. Getting to her feet again after a good hour's tale-telling, Cas appears winded. So does Lady, reduced to timider tinnier scales. And now, coming past a white onyx hearth and silver andirons, across Aubusson carpets faded almost white—Miss Zelia edges unannounced, on all fours.

She checks over one shoulder like somebody being followed. Seems shots might soon pour through all forty filtered windows of this third-floor bedchamber. Leaning on the table where her mammoth bouquet now fans, the old woman gets to standing. Zelia, sometimes called just Z—which is how her name sounds spoken hereabouts—the onetime wet nurse and nanny to Lady, parts flowers. Her small face, a brown and beaten punching bag, is half hid behind purple blooms. Face announces, "They nearbout here. Best to hide youself, you."

Lady leaves off playing. Ain't Castalia's story just offered her a lesson in Marsden mistakes and the world's unfairness? She knows full well who "they" are—so couldn't Lady yield this once? But don't you find, darling—the more cornered folks feel, the more rigid and rule-making they'll grow? "You are speaking to me this way? You didn't so much as knock. You've certainly had better training at announcing guests in using their full names, ranks, titles. I hate mentioning these little lapses of yours, but this is just not *like* you, Zelia mine."

"Z don't know no names *to* nounce. Only come in here out the kindness Zelia heart. What I trying and say: *They Here, Bitch!*"

The old woman flops back onto all fours, goes scuddling towards doorway. Lady, vexed, leans past the piano's edge to watch. Crawling, Zelia growls, "Got a good mind to . . . I got me a good mind . . ." Then she scoots right back past the instrument, Z rises behind the seated player and, with one serious yank, Z tugs out the Xed chopsticks. Pearls spiral ackety-acking down, a whole hairdo flops around shoulders. Mrs. Marsden grabs at fallen braids, mashes pearls against her pale neck, yelling, "Tell me the meaning of this, you. What possible *mean*ing?"

Miss Z, shy again, staring all around, seems to hear something like cannons' advance—collapses onto hands and knees, is quick past the great iceberg piano, eases out the door, closes it behind her, quietly. Polite.

THIS ROOM smells of too much spring. You can hear the river running at the bottom of the lawn. Comes a scream from the foreyard. Cas pulls Lady's limp hand from the hairdo it's trying to resurrect. Clocks throb fire-drill bongs through all three stories. Cassie jerks her mistress onto slippered feet, gets the woman out into the corridor, scurries past a row of Caesars whose spears and rods of office signal toward the exit.

Running, it's Lady Marsden, "Meaning whom? Not Yankees on my land. *We're* here. This is the South. Go tell them."

Once down her famous spiral staircase, she notices: rooms have been stripped. Ignoring all she's just been told, Mrs. Marsden blames the enemy. *Let her*, Cassie decides.

"Northern scoundrel hellhound thieves!" Lady screeches before even seeing one.

10

I AM pleased to say, I got my theme in by Tuesday, early. The schoolyard milled with others holding their "national documents," some wrapped by mommas in waxed paper like fine foods. Even Bobo Kingston, sixteen years old, proudly showed his burlap binder, though his penmanship looked done in charcoal. "Lucy? My topic lost both legs and a pinkie fingertip at Vicksburg. Still got some mouth, though."

Myself, I did twenty accompanying watercolor sketches (India ink swirling wild to be tragedy's smoke). I painted my report's elm-wood binder the correct tricolors. Poppa helped me put the hardware-store brass hinges on. Then Pop claimed these looked too new to hold "history" (even the history of a war just thirty years past ending). So, Poppa, a Xerxes copycat artist in his way, took steel wool to them. "You'll spoilt their *fin*ish, Samuel," Mother complained. With a ball peen hammer, Pop was giving each hinge three to six goodly cracks.

"There," he backed off, squinting. "Damaged sufficient. Lucy, History always takes its cut. I did it *for* it this go-round. Now you can call yours History."

I WORKED in everything but a semicolon. Now explain to me again about semicolons.

AFTER

ON THE top step of the portico, both women go still. Out in the yard, six children and Zelia stand pointing, heads back, mouths open to the sky. Seems the North is coming down as hail, honey. By tiptoeing forward, by leaning past a solid-marble column, Lady notices the million flakes. Some are big as pillows, some are round as logs—all black. Down drift the ashes of plantations lost already.

Countryside seals itself so quiet—exactly like the few times when true snow has fallen here. Children jump, snatching at dark crusts. Z wobbles over, grabs her mistress's silk shoulders, shifts the other's body in a useful new direction. First, Lady studies the woods apparently on fire, her woods.

But past that, beyond four clotheslines' soot-specked sheets, Lady finally sees: great cyclone shapes.

Two miles up into the sky they go. Twisty, pitch-dark columns, contained, set miles from one another. Understanding the river's distances and twists—every child can point to a pike of black smoke, can name the mansion that this smoke just was. Xerxes quotes now, in a almost unfamiliar voice (his own). The boy's arm moves from one to one. "Be:

Bynum Hall,
Cool Spring,
Ten Oaks,
Ivanhoe Acres,
Wisteria,
Ashland,
Greenwood."

And nearest, he names Cousin Mabry's Shadowlawn, just four miles off but already up there in the sky for all to see.

Old Zelia says, "And here we done started bleaching the spring linens yesterday. Wouldn't you just know it?" Z lets go of Lady Marsden and, craning forward, pokes a drifting ball of ash. She grins, old blue-black gums exposed. "Why, Missy, looks to be you nice plump Cousin Mabry come a-calling," then Z clamps one hand over her mouth, unsure should she risk this cackle. It's all banked up—steam-pressurized—pending eighty years.

2

"WALKING PAPERS!" Three young black men wave from the post road. They're rushing so towards Falls.

"Ooh, now it done started, sure," Zelia chances a one-step hop. The squinting mistress (new to sun) still gapes towards the great upriver fires. "There's been a mistake," Lady says, but to herself. Z again takes hold of pale shoulders, turns this wild-haired woman toward a road where ten more black folks hurry. Lady cups one hand to screen her eyes. For some reason, she belches. "Excuse me," she says.

More freed slaves bound along carrying sacks, chairs, babies, chickens. A great holiday chatter. Some folks stop near Marsden lily ponds. Drinking, they wave uphill at The Lilacs' staff—shy and stunned here, unsure of Freedom's etiquette. One old man points towards Lady, cries, "You-all gots her where you wants her?"

"Sure do!" Zelia tightens the grip.

Freed folks call, "Come on—before they burns *you* out. You can now. They be by here directly."

Miss Zelia hollers, "Listen. What they like?"

One answer drifts up-lawn, "They gods."

• • •

SOON you see local white folks in closed buggies, faces hid, whipping horses bloody in their hurry to get by. Lady has no one best female friend. She's been admired and feared and "cultivated" but not too loved, child. Now, no white neighbor—in saving theirselves—even thinks to stop for this here self-sufficient beauty.

Carriages cut past black people wearing former owners' clothes. Dusky bare feet labor under white satin hoopskirts. Two fellows sport top hats, tipping brims at one another, linking arms then circling. A single file of children march with the graveness of Three Kings. They hold fistfuls of silver forks and knives clutched chest-high, strange nosegays. Bound for Falls, one girl tries guiding six white geese. But something's changed. Holding her switch overhead, the child's arms are raised, she backs before six red beaks taking lazy swipes at her dark legs.

Mrs. Marsden watches. Her two small hands keep trying to become a generous sun hat. She half whispers, "Tea. —And a bath after."

Darling? Nobody exactly jumps. Near the road, two young men are tearing fencing from The Lilacs' front gate. One tries to break a rail off Mrs. Marsden's adored Chinese footbridge. He can't do it, so instead he kicks a slat loose and, pretending not to have hurt his foot, hobbles back, laughing, to his friend.

It's now that Lady spies two older gents carrying the biggest grandfather clock anybody's ever seen hereabouts. The thing has a pitched roof like a johnny house—appears near the size of one, even to its hinged front door's swinging open. Just behind, a tiny girl wearing a mammoth feathered bonnet carries the clock's brass pendulum directly before her face, stepping so very proud.

Mrs. Marsden's silks suddenly rustle alive. "But that's Cousin Mabry's. From the foyer at Shadowlawn. I worked on it myself, remember? Here, Cassie, run tell those two to report to me immediately. That's our dear Mabry's prized property. It came from England. Remember how he waited? Yes, instruct them to bring that here to me this instant."

Mrs. Marsden's arm is out. Is pointing at the world of lawbreakers.

Her own slaves give each other slow-burn looks. They commence to back away from her. Castalia's face has never been more neutral. This scares Lady more than any bad-day rampage. Mistress, seeing her people change, falters back up her veranda's stairs. Height will surely prove a advantage— even "height" will, the illusion. From the third step, Lady uses her child voice, "I'd just kill for a bowl of consommé. Even bouillon. I . . ." And waits.

Nobody moves. Since the summer of '61, they've lacked the needed chicken stock. When no soul budges to help her, Lady mutters, talks, then screams. Her headache swells with her own volume, child. What she yowls is what it all comes down to finally, it's too blunt by half but we've each of us felt it at our laziest: She screeches, "You people *will* do as you're told and *now!*"

Her arm is yet extended. She points down, face to face. And yet her people, features impartial to the point of deadness, back off further. Some women call their children, babies Lady helped to name. Venus pulls aside. Evidence Anne—formerly Diana—runs to Castalia, hides her face in apron. Little Xerxes jogs away, stands panting, gaping back over his shoulder, shaking his head No so hard he nearly falls.

Her voice smoothed musical and mild again, Lady asks who has nursed these youngsters through the croup, who offered them not inexpensive Christmas oranges, and who, pray tell, invented Catacombs just for their amusement? "Birthdays, who hardly ever forgets? Come here to me, my favorites.—At once," and smiles, and tilts her whole head to the left, thinking this might help.

Honey, it don't seem to.

Take a second, child: Imagine her migraine.

FROM this perch above the yard, Mrs. Marsden focuses on Xerxes. "I've been informed. I am prepared. You shall find your old friend just a terribly good sport."

His back is to her, the child's face buckles. "Who tolt?" It's a artless bleat from a child so skillful. Turning, he scans dark faces.

Cassie confesses, "Go on, Xerxes baby. It gone do her good for you to do it of her. So . . . do," but Cassie sounds unsure.

"Yes, please. Now," Lady claps onct. She arranges her long hem just so, like posing for a portrait. "Mr. Blake claims, 'Imitation is criticism.' I can withstand it. Which is why I've been such a good owner to you all for all these years. There, I'm quite prepared. Just see if I don't do terribly well." Smiling, she becomes a model of posture, it seems that some thorned corset is holding her in place.

They all stare at the child. Others smile like they theirselves are now expected to perform. He's three feet one inch tall and, out in brightness, seems a toy of hisself, so shy now. Somebody nudges him. Xerxes grins a shamed sickening grin—first at others, then, slow, on up to her. "Hi," he says.

First he straightens his famous hankie ascot. Xerxes faces Lady, takes some time to shake hisself limber, knees give a bit—warming up. Smiling, it seems like he has finally turned pro. This could be the moment he's done waited on forever.

The post road streams with runners, hollering. And yet here, in a separate slower side zone, this odd command performance rolls on. And something about that sure appeals to her.

Midair, Xerxes settles, places fingertips, conjuring a keyboard. (Recognizing the activity, Lady nods, confident she always looks especially well at her instrument.) Xerxes gives his skull one spoilt sultry toss. Just one. And Lady, up yonder—still smiling at the phantom fingerings—cringes from this flung head, finds her mouth relaxed considerable. By accident, just for one second, and even before Xerxes can go on, Lady's face distorts the way a dog's will when you blow into its eyes.

Seeing this, picturing hisself midyard squatting at the foot pedals of nothing, pinned betwixt relations' head-wagging smirks and his owner's congealed smile, Xerxes suddenly doubles over. It's something like a cramp. He wheels away from Lady. Seems to be laughing, till you hear him heave. Is it weeping or a sickness?

Lady's face restores itself: Xerxes apparently regrets. That quick, all's well. Lady has never appeared more beautiful. Holding on to her silk hem, she shifts it with a huff. Chin up, the owner actually says, "*Et tu*, Xerxes?" —Look, nobody's perfect. Just now, Lady E. M. Marsden feels more fully herself than maybe ever before. Says she, "Now that, I think, will about do it."

BUT here comes Zelia, easing up them steps, spindle arms out—balancing like walking on a clothesline tightrope. Spry Z climbs very slow. She might be stealing up on some ninety-five-pound cottonmouth disguised in this white dress. "Mrs. Lady? Z got something *for* you." And spits.

Wetness pills along dry silk. Lady leans forward, wrists cross at her Empire waist, she stares down—amazed, child, as if a sapphire has been hocked on her.

Unchaperoned sun falls across the Widow Marsden's bowed unaccustomed head. "What?" She retreats, upward a step. "Why now? what's it *for*? Be direct. You shall find me not unreasonable."

Then the bolder children edge nearer, one stair step at a time. You can see their little jaws working, cheeks puckered. Xerxes, face still wet from crying, his back yet clenching, meekly tiptoes up, joins others. When Mistress grimaces his way, Xerxes offers, slack-mouthed, "Hi you do?"

She can tell what they want. What kind of hostess would she be otherwise? And maybe hoping to forestall big changes through little social sacrifices, Lady E. More Marsden's face opens. A determined brilliant smile displays itself, happier for a lifetime's successes. She must somehow get through this, must discover the graceful gesture hidden even in this most unsavory of situations. It will not do to shirk one's Christian duty now. Her face gives off a happiness seen mostly at piano or during Catacombs with these same youngsters. Lady spreads her own white hem, she makes things easier.

Three children, eyes on her, spit in turn, comparing damage. The target herself bends forward, seeming interested in levels and amounts. Children hear her smallest silky voice, "So we've come to this, my darlings. —Oh, for tea, a bath, please. I'm simply not myself today."

Then she tries something else. "Zelia, when Momma died bearing me— you allowed me your milk, Zelia. Your very milk."

"Milk be spent, but here, Z gone give you little something extra," and spits again, does a quickstep. Next the old black woman's voice falls deeper than a man's. "My boy he drownded running off. Winch caught Zelia with the chicken Zelia stole, he lashed Z till it took Zelia near a whole year to get back half right. You-all ain't let Zelia know nothing Zelia *need* to. You · done locked Z up. Seem like it been a most long time . . ."

"Yes, but not *me*, Zelia. Not I. This is how things work here where we've lived together. How could a baby in your arms have invented it? I was born to my part, just as you to yours, old friend. —I've loved you all. I love you all. Surely that counts?"

But people just gape at the lady on her steps. And Mrs. Marsden seems to suddenly recollect how bad she must look. Slow, like hoping others won't notice a person's trying to improve, she touches long pearly plaits. "What?" She gathers up the chignon's collapse. "What?" She checks her nightdress's seams for evenness. "Tell your Lady *what*." —Darling? she thinks the world's done come unloose because her hair has!

"Seem like . . . with great gifts . . ." Castalia says.

As the mistress of The Lilacs begins to sway. Down three steps she waltzes, silk tears lightly over stones' rough nap, her arms spread wide. Her people know the game. She'll need to be on their level for it to work proper. Sure enough, down into the yard their Lady totters. How she swerves from one to one, turning, reeling, woozy in her dancing slippers. How rehearsed it seems. Lady staggers like a drunkard teetering from one dark person to the next. Adults ease back a step, children must take two reverse steps to avoid her.

Not one soul is left in range of maybe even catching Lady M.

She now understands that if she drops, she falls. And: Lady is deciding to give way anyhow when, that same second, she hears laughing. Lady spins to see a thirty-seven-inch black shadow of herself flopping directly behind, gasping, spastic, a giddy headless hen. "Am I all *that* bad?" Should she dodge over, slap the child—should she faint, or both? And Lady's just about to take responsibility for her own falling . . . when hoofbeats punish the lily ponds' bridge.

"It them!"

3

FROM the post road, black people cheer, cackling at how Marsden freed folks bolt off, dragging children after. Cassie yells, *"We free! I free!"*

In one second, only two figures are someway left in sight before the sunlit columns. Castalia, smooth, solid, breathing like she's just sprinted a marathon—and beside her, this thin white woman in white, one hand still fidgeting to make sense of a hairdo. "Just *look* at me," the lady says. "A perfect mess, and today!"

That fast, all others are tucked back of a tall hedge. They squeal, "Cassie, over here. Save youself, gal!"

"Well, I fear that Yankees are simply not welcome in my home." Lady uses the back of one hand to test her brow for fever. Cassie snatches that wrist, tries running the Mistress one hundred yards toward lilacs.

"Castalia, you goose, I'd never get that far. In *my* condition?"

So, by simply stepping left, by dipping under one housefront magnolia, Cassie disappears. Through shiny green—one strong black hand reaches into sun, hooks a pale lady round her waist, jerks hard. Inside the tree's strange hollow, White prepares to scream, Black clamps a palm across White's mouth.

Yankees fire one warning shot. White mouth calms some.

Yanks will plainly shoot any owner trying to halt their torching duties. Castalia and Lady now wait inside a snug magnolia that grows against one marble pillar. Leaves are leathery, tenting clear to the ground. Like Catacombs, this hiding spot makes much of outside sounds. A second shot is heard. Cassie's already going up a branch, she's ten, then twelve, fifteen feet off the ground. One bough at a time she pulls the other person up. That one—totally supported by a single arm—yet uses the free hand to furiously work her hair.

"Hep youself or be dead, one," Cas settles the widow in a crotch of limbs. Lady shakes. Leaves take up her jitters.

Mistress whispers, "Not those Satans from the North, not here? Tell me it's not so, Castalia."

"It so."

"Well, go explain: we *live* here. You're so sensible, people listen to you. I don't even think you understand how persuasive and bright you really are. I've been meaning for the longest time to mention it. Tell them how happy we've been. Haven't we? This is our home. You mostly grew up here. I grew up here. Reason with them. Your moment is at hand."

Lady, reaching for the shoulders of the person beneath her, nearbout topples from her roost. Castalia curses, stops this spill. Castalia feels she has forever braced her mistress into some uneasy spot overhead. Castalia finds her own hands around a pale spongy throat. Can't quite stop strong thumbs. Thumbs press, slightly, testing. Cas sees the woman's cheeks color, nostril wings tint pink, a pretty mouth comes opens. There's no scream, not a bit of scratching. Instead, the mistress bends forward, polite, as if to beg.

All Lady's body weight now pivots through a fair neck—she presses her own lips down over Cassie's upturned fuller set. First it seems that Lady's pleading for air. Castalia's thumbs relax, not quite meaning to. Then, slow, Cas understands: the mouth—on and across hers—plans more than leaching. See, Lady's trying to kiss Castalia Marsden. Hard. It *is* a kiss, too. After Cassie's first disgust, she decides this one does pack a certain damp conviction. Hmmm.

Cas considers herself a right expert kisser. (Most everybody does but eighty-five percent are dead wrong, honey. We just hate to tell them others otherwise, don't we?) Castalia has practiced with black men her age and older, black girls her age and younger, and—unwillingly—with this here lady's husband. More happy-like she's tried it with this woman's son. And Cassie of a sudden understands that both males' mild smoochy talent might come—through learning or inheritance—from this very mouth Cas is now in.

Cassie, stunned by everything, waits on the branch below, ready for the smack to end. Around her upturned face, unlatched braids, chains of cool pearls lick and tickle—a strange shared curtain.

Lady finishes and, winded, primly backhands wetness off her pointed chin. "Castalia, I know" (breath) "you're trying to save me. I'm not certain" (breath) "why. But bless you. And you *will* be rewarded. With all I own. I tell you now: when this unpleasantness is over, we shall run off together. Just you and me. You're the only one I've ever known how to love."

"Well, gal, you gots to get better at it than *that*! Look, was you proposing just now? Something 'long them lines?"

"It *is* unconventional. But then, I've always been considered outré."

"Well, Castalia's answer's *No*. You clear on that?" And Cas is down the tree so quick. Horses gallop from around behind the house and right up portico's stone steps. Cas bolts into the open towards a frothy hedge that's absolutely hollering encouragement.

4

"WAS IT NOT Dionysius of Halicarnassus, Lucille, who described History as 'philosophy teaching by example'? Yes, it was. At times our Lucille's personal variant seems to hold History most notable for its myriad rags-to-riches stories. But no. Both here and in her lurid Pompeiian effort, Lucille clearly prefers riches-to-rags themes. I am pleased that she has expunged from this essay a favorite locution which so marred her earlier effort. That being: 'Little did they know.' The expression had been utilized no less than fourteen times when This Reader saw fit to cease counting. 'Little did they know that 79 A.D. suppertime when they set (sic) down to a hot meal how blamed (sic) hot it *would* be.' Really, Lucille. Even for you, this is stooping! In light of my own exceptional early training, in view of my current wages, I must refrain from offering further comment here. History's hindsight often tempts us, Lucille, to make such facile formulations. Others have found sufficient restraint to abstain from these belated gloatings. Yes, Pompeii, like its sister city Herculaneum (a town missing from your paper, and why? only because archaeologists have found it less perfectly preserved than your topic city), *was* a resort town notorious for its bawdy establishments, its profusion of sublime statuary. Yes, you are correct to view Pompeii as a resort, a city dedicated to pleasure. But does this justify your joy at seeing it smothered from consciousness? Ask yourself: Why, Lucille, the glee? As in her graphic (if savage) account of Vesuvian revenge, Lucille's fiery conclusion of 'Black, White, and Lilac,' as she calls it, also hints at moral retaliation. But, Lucille, put the question to yourself: *Are* the wicked punished? Does one woman's hereditary subscription to the peculiar institution called slavery make her so fitting a victim for avenging justice? If a mind lofty and democratic as Mr. Jefferson's was incapable of freeing Jefferson slaves except by posthumous decree, why should we expect a profoundly sheltered, profoundly small-town woman to prove more exemplary? Perhaps the virtuous *are* rewarded in Lucille's papers and her fantasy life. However, sharing, as I do, her literal hometown (if not her moral nature's black-and-whiteness), This Reader is hard pressed to find many visible examples. Lucille understands Emerson's edict that there is, per se, no history, only biography. She has found a fitting and all too mortal hometown subject. But do stay after school, my dear girl, and name for your Miss Beale here just one virtuous Falls citizen who has overtly benefited from said virtue.

"Lucille's paper can be, like Lucille personally, dogged, pugnacious, well-intentioned. But economic realities? Prevailing social attitudes? Ethical soundings?

"I would send you to Goethe's splendid epigram, related both to your title and to his color theory. As you doubtless recall from Thursday's class discussion (while other teachers on our hall were forcing their unfortunates to try nothing more instructive than another drear round of, "Row, Row, Row Your Boat"), Goethe's color theory, unlike his competitor's, Newton's, proved fallacious. But perhaps Mr. Goethe's is all the more poetically profound for that (meaning: there might yet be hope for you and your well-meaning *Black, White, Lilac*). Think about this, my dear Lucille.

"Goethe puts it thusly: 'Colors are the deeds and suffering of light.' "

5

CASTALIA, well hid back of lilacs, blots lips onto her homespun apron, muttering, "That Lady'll try anything, seem like." Cas expects the mistress to now pop out and challenge visitors, "Have we *met*, sirs?" Cassie strains for a better view of heroes. She's heard how handsome Yankees are. The closer Northerners have got, wilder rumors of their beauty. Crouching, Cas fully expects the giant Young Linking.

He'll come to set finally this place afire with one finger's pointing—the way a touchy God creates Adam in one oleograph upstairs.

What had sounded—on the Chinese bridge—like a regiment now whittled into four ragged fellows. Two are old, fattish. All need shaving. The youngest and best-looking, missing a leg, appears tied to his saddle. Blue uniform's left sleeve is also pinned up empty.

A petticoat flies from this raider's saddlebag. Maybe a souvenir of some upriver outrage? The man halts his horse near the library's French door. Slowed by missing one arm, he empties a canteen's coal oil onto this dainty apparel. When it's sogged good, he lights the thing and—horse shying— heaves it. A flaming crinoline seems to walk on air indoors. The horse Castalia recognizes. Ain't no Northern animal but a dancy white Arabian from Cousin Mabry's Shadowlawn, four miles north.

Smoke—a nice blue plume of it—comes rolling lazy out one library window—hangs in air like searching for a purpose—then, seeming reminded of something by the view, curls back indoors, gets busy. Regulation-gray fumes soon hide the magnolia Cassie's studying. Eyes shut, gagging behind her apron, she yet faces one clouded tree: Is Lady going to die? Should she?

Ex-slaves hold one another. Faces streaming in this haze, they choke, watching a house they know so good commence to end. All burning homes— when you understand they can't be saved, and were maybe even set for insurance's sake—are right interesting to watch, don't you find, child? *I* do. And how much more a fire must mean to slaves who've used up lifetimes maintaining the mansion's spit and polish.

From first-floor windows, blue light soon fountains. Light is easily taking out the bubbled windowpanes. First breakage chimes beautiful and spotty as them salvaged chandeliers hid in gunnysacks in woods. Fire now tests a solid-marble pillar. Fire'll soon try scorching a magnolia and its mothy rider. Indoors, seventy-odd clocks suddenly sound a ragged group-question, like maybe plea-bargaining. Riders in the house laugh at how such chiming scared them.

What must she be *doing* up there? If she outlives all this, will she finally learn some basic lessons? Cassie feels curious, without exactly wanting to. Honey, the healthiest people in the world are the ones most interested in others. It's helped me live this long.

How can so many noble-looking flames have sprung from four such scruffy men? Cassie hears soldiers barking jokes and stories at each other, Yankee accents mystify her. Maybe men's being near so many mammoth fires has charred and hardened their words. Cas recalls the medicinal-sound- ing Greek her master used to jabber round this place.

Two dozen rocking chairs become horses' obstacle course. Yanks sure are having fun. Animals cobble down stone steps—not twelve feet from Lady's tree. When torchbearers saunter off towards the barn (where Old Z wanted to hide furniture), Castalia bolts from kneeling, aims towards a middle-distance clothesline, pays no mind to friends' shouts, "Come back, Cassie. How bout saving you own self."

Ears roaring, brain a-fuel, feeling herself the sudden leading actor on these two thousand acres, Cas runs smack under one clothesline and past it, now wearing a soggy percale sheet. Arms out, wetness curved against her, Cassie again goes, gasping, under warming leaves and, hid now, pant- ing, stares up where she left a certain person.

Looking down from on high, cross-braced by dark boughs, the face

appears blank as yards and yards of white now drooping long as any chris-
tening gown. Lady, so pleased to see somebody she admires, grins, "You're
back. You'll stay, my dear. I do thank you."

Castalia, disgusted while half laughing, scrambles up lower limbs.
"Wrap youself in this."

Mistress reaches for the cloth. "But, my dear, it feels . . . quite wet."

"That's cause fire's hot and dry, you dizzy doo-doo! Cause you so *near*
a fire!"

"Clever you. Why didn't *I* think of that." And the Widow Marsden does
as told but expects praise for it. Chill brings just one squeal. When horses
pound back this way, Cassie clatters straight down—nearbout falling—she's
out in the open, she's chugging toward a hedge's encouraging cries. Onct
safe, gasping hard, onct screened by lilacs, familiar hands settle all over
her—pats, strokes.

WHY, it might could be asked, are ex-slaves hiding from the very forces
come to free them? Good question. It's partly owing to years of Lady's talk
about the Barbarous Tartars North of Maryland. Partway cause of these
black people's own history with invading forces: example being them whites
what slipped up a African river and tricked these souls onto a ship, and
over here (Cassie's tale). So, black people at The Lilacs, while right happy
about being freed, whilst plenty ready to believe in a future, still choose to
hide, thank you very much. Considering the favors History's paid them so
far, it makes a certain amount of sense.

"She living?" Zelia asks.

"Ain't dead." Others snort. Evidence Anne asks, "Did Lady want that
sheet so she could play Catacombs?"

"Something like that, baby. She in real deep hiding just now."

BEYOND soldiers' prancy foreground silhouettes, slaves see the barn become
a dawn.

Soldiers don't guess: somebody is listening from fifty foot up a eighty-
foot magnolia not twelve foot from where their horses presently paw. Raid-
ers are waiting till the mansion catches proper. Arsonists talk about recent
letters from home, about what they plan doing out West onct this running-
down war is won. (It's the usual: Men intend to own everything for as far
as the eye can see. America!)

They been being patriotic firebugs for so long, you'd think this chore
would tire them. But, honey, fire ain't ever routine. (Neither is land, water,
or air—ask farmers, fishers, weather gals.) Hoping to get better at such
house burning, being the type gents that *do* want to own clear to the horizon,
they're yet studying flames' progress. Improving on the next plantation's
torching, fellows talk about their kids and hearths.

How soon, sugar, the terrible becomes routine. We've all got this dangerous built-in talent: for turning horrors into errands. You hear folks won-

der how the Germans could've *done* it? I believe part of the answer is: They made extermination be a nine-to-five activity. You know, salaries? Lunch breaks? And the staff came and did their job and went home and ate supper and slept and woke and came back and did their job and went home and ate their supper and slept and woke and came back and did their job. —That's partly how you get anything done, especially a chore what's dreadful, dreadful. —Honey? we've all got to be real careful of what we can get used to.

ALONE, hid good, Mrs. M., my mother-in-law-to-be, saw nothing of her barn's burning, was probably shaking from both fear and the sheet's chill. I bet she tucked monogrammed percale around her. (Careless, Cas has brung her a guest-room cotton sheet, not the usual silk.) I imagine Lady tried and "toga" the cloth so that, if found here by Yanks or even by Fire, she'd look in charge, "at home." She had lived forever from the outside in. Ethics started in her morning mirror. "What to *do* about one's waning looks today?" Now, treed, she has time sufficient to fix the hairdo Z yanked loose. Who'll see Lady's toilette now? But Lady can't. Improve herself. She's never learned, she's never had to. She picked a hairstyle that nowdays might be called "labor-intensive." She can only fiddle with the braids that droop around her face. Now she uses one fine plait to bind the others. Odd to understand, her woven hairdo is semi-African.

Lady E. More Marsden hears the barn's first roar, thinks about her dead husband, her son away at soldiering. She's set up so high, the arms are crossed over her knees—she's like a person in the privy, not exactly thinking, not exactly not, just there.

"Dear," she says, quiet. "Oh dear my oh me."

6

IN ASSIGNING us the paper, Teacher Beale forced her pupils to imagine War's effect on everybody it grabbed. Bobo Kingston, class bad boy for so many held-back years that he'd become the class bad *man*, raised one knotty arm and spoke, a bass deep enough to rattle windowpanes. "Even . . . *Sherman?*"

We always tried to trip up Witch. It was a education how we never really could. Everything we considered a good trick question, she named a lapse of the moral imagination. Every trap we set for our beloved spinster, she gladly jumped right into—then she called up at us from the crude pit we'd dug. Witch kept hollering news of cave paintings down there, saying how all Pompeii's citizens had been made perfect statues by the killing ash and how she could see them extra good from down inside. Grumbling some, we were all soon lowering ourselfs right into the hollow, ready for a tour, even a tour of the grave we'd laid for her.

"*Especially* Sherman. *Tout comprendre, tout pardonner.* Are you aware, for instance, gallant Bobo, that Sherman endured such dreadful asthma he was medically required to burn 'niter papers' in his tent of an evening just to permit himself to breathe properly? How many of you children personally suffer or know someone who suffers asthma? Fine. Then you'll feel a bit more for a gentleman in a tent, deprived of oxygen, buffeted by workaday battle smoke. Doubtless you've heard, Bobo, how the surrender terms Sherman proffered General Joseph alias 'Joe' Johnston in Raleigh, not forty miles from where I now stand and you now slouch—sit up and learn, Monsieur Bobo—were so rife with toleration that Northern newspapers soon branded Sherman 'Handmaiden to the South.' Sherman was subsequently jeered during the victory review of Federals through Washington. Yes, history's never black and white, nor even gray and blue, my intuitive one. There's always more to know, especially about the villains. Perhaps you all have sensed this from your earliest fairy-tale reading. How bland those virtuous heroines, how riveting, heated, and familiar are the crones and gnomes and witches. No giggling, class. Is Sherman our enemy? You decide. Once we depreciate others as being wholly unlike ourselves, we've succumbed to the same flattening they've practiced on us. We cannot have enemies if we choose not to.

"I speak from experience as a person who grew up in a town superstitious as the Dark Ages and Old Salem conjoined. Your town. Quite early in my professional life here, a decision required making. Would I view Ignorance as the Enemy, or would I blame the practicing ignoramuses themselves? I hate no one. I hate only stupidity, imprecision. Had I blamed the stupid, the religious, the congenitally vague for their Disease, I daresay I should by now have worn myself into oblivion. The tendency to blame gnaws more readily into the Blamer than the Blamee.

"Concerning Sherman, Mr. Bobo, you, of all my favorite misunderstood people, should surely grasp that villains in the world's eyes can actually be Lambs, albeit huge Lambs."

Others chuckled. (Bobo Kingston had him a police record. Peeping Tomism, breaking/entering.)

"So, monsieur, if it is human—and it all is, up to and including a perfect saturated human evil—then it rests within our understanding. If it lies within the bounds of human understanding (and what that is human does not?), then it is, however painfully, forgivable. And should it prove even tangentially forgivable, then we must must must forgive it.'"

"Ma'am? I sure as heck wish *you'd* been my last judge down to the Courthouse, but . . . *Sherman?* Miss Beale? He burned *your* people's place. I fish out near the chimleys of it."

"Chim-neys. That's hardly unique to the family Beale. Children, how many of you lost family property to Sherman's following orders?"

From a class of thirty, eighteen fists lifted. Eleven-year-old hands, knuckled—these thirty years after. "And how many of you, had chores been reversed, had you been given similar orders, had you hoped to end the war more quickly and save precious lives by sacrificing mere property, had you been dispatched into Northern regions among its finest homes all conveniently arrayed in a single riverside row, how many of you would have done precisely what Sherman did?"

Bobo's huge hand shot up first. Then, for good measure, he whipped out the kitchen matches he used to light his home-rolt cigarettes, he struck one in plain sight. Any other Lower Normal School teacher would've got Bobo reexpelled just for "matches in class." Witch Beale only waited for the thing to burn down, to singe Bo's horny fingers, to make him cuss once then throw it toward our window ledge's sprouting sweet potato.

"Attention, my War Crimes Tribunal. A confession has been rendered, a life, albeit a Northern one, now rests in your hands. How many choose to exonerate our volatile Goth of a young officer here? Search your hearts, young judges. Here's one Bobo Kingston, Jr., admitted Yankee arsonist, throwing his life upon the mercy of this our Southern court. Our heritage is infinitely richer in culture and civilized graces than was the winning side's. Alas, however, our refinement sprang from a feudal system basing the well-being of a few upon the ownership of many. Yet even now we remain a more literate lively culture than the child-hiring factories that vanquished us. Having survived Tragedy's wheel of fire, we are now ready for new health. This single hope has kept your Old Lady Beale (oh, I know you've given me various epithets) coming here to you day after day for these fifty years. I feel it. The Periclean Age is just about to crest, my pillars of the new Doric order. That stated, here languishes the apparent assassin of our riverside hilltop temples," she gestured.

Bobo set scratching one ear, not able to follow how he'd just become the very guy he'd called the scummiest of lowlifes. Witch stepped over, placed a hand on Bo's massive shoulder. (She touched us all and often—unlike other teachers.) Now, stroking sad Bobo's gristle—with Bo half smiling, sleepy-acting—the Genius of Falls Lower Normal asked us, in a slow and glowing final curtain of a voice, "Can you forgive him?"

It carried.

7

IF SHE could teach me to cozy up to *Sherman*, seems I might feel more for poor Lady Marsden, treed. The house about to burn was one that I, by marriage, would have owned and occupied. Maybe just the way Bobo hated Sherman (jealous of the General's pyromaniac free license), I shy away from Lady Marsden. Probably there's more of Mrs. Priss in me than I feel easy with.

The Book says we're all dead level in the eyes of God. Our Forefathers claimed everybody's created equal (of course, by the time you get delivered nine months later, seems like social class, skin color, looks, and health have pretty much knocked the pins out from under Conception's fair shake). A decent tale maker should—like the Constitution, God Almighty, or Witch Beale's philosophy—offer what was once called Equal Opportunity Employment. Except for twists of fate, the villains could, along the way, have become the hero-saints, or vice versa. Versa vice. I want to know what, close to burning, Lady Marsden felt.

It's our duty, imagining each other.

So, I admit, yeah, I *partway* know what Lady E. More Marsden, out on a literal limb—April 7, 1865, 3:45 p.m.—sat hoping.

SHE intended to be rescued. (It's everybody plan.) Maybe she deserved it. (Probably we all do.)

THE HELPER Lady pictured wouldn't look like Castalia's darkling Linking Youth. Maybe Lady's hero was some knight from Walter Scott or Dumas, the Daddy. Lady lived so accustomed to Service. She sure needed it now. Her saint would share with Cassie's Christ's haberdashers' thorns and blood. But Lady's feudal warlord would also enjoy her dead husband's knowledge and surface wit. He'd have the strict Christian nobleness of Robert Edward Lee hisself. Lady's Man would boast the flashiness of J. E. B. Stuart, the fierceness of Nathan Bedford Forrest (a future founder of the Klan), hybridized with General Mosby's scholarship, bolstered by Beauregard's manners—and on and on. Okay . . . so: Where is he?

Clinging to this trunk, one ear turned toward her Chinese bridge, ready for the tattoo of chivalry's silver hooves, the mistress can't help picturing all her nearby rooms. She must know: even He can't save them now.

Lady Marsden imagines rooms so clear—they might be her own lungs' brocaded linings, satiny-corridored intestine walls. "My interiors!"

In downstairs chambers, she understands: ain't too much left but side tables, tacked carpet runners veering room to room and meant to guard her parquet between parties. But on The Lilacs' second floor and third—everything rests just where it's been since her dead mother's time.

Now, holding on to this tree like it might save her (it is *hers*, after all) —forehead pressed to bark the way a lady in her childhood picture book leaned against back armor plates of a saddled knight galloping her off from danger, with the face well masked by Castalia's wet sheet—Lady's eyes close, eyes are tearing with first saw-toothed whiffs. Her tree starts rolling, a strange storm of wind currents sucking—scrolling—through the opened lower house. And she hears everything she ever owned start ending.

(When this lady turns in bed at night, when one of her fine bones crackles, she surely knows if it was her elbow or the third vertebra down. Like that, nested this close to furnishings nearly as dear to her as her own skeleton—Lady Marsden reads each pop. Child, her last moments of being so alive become near-miracles of hearing.) You know how lobsters make no sound till plunged—brightening from black to red—into their final boiling pot? Lady's things become a martyrs' choir.

Over sounds of edgy Yankee talk, over the un-noise of the awaited prince's white blooded horse from Upperville or Lexington—Lady hears exactly how each lowboy takes to high flame, finds she'd really rather not know. What each hiss means. Lady finds she just can't quit this farewell map making. Goodbye, four jasper Wedgwood compotes set into stairwell's niches. See you, Priapus overdressed. Goodbye, Empire ormolu, ivory-colored Louis-the-umpty-umpth thus-and-so pulled from earlier fires at earlier castles and brung to safety here. So long, Della Robbia choirboys belting out Latin hymns from the study's frieze. Toodle-do, the Ter Borch oil picture of a lady wearing white come evening, cloth silk-pursing last light. So long beauty, order, swan life, god-and-goddessy clocks.

With this much carbon combing past her, Lady's eyes are shut, but oh her head is so alive. It almost hurts, this final surge. Feels like it's her blood's own museum inventory. Lady's ears already fill with blowing grit, her braids' brush ends begin to coil—they smell metallic from the heat. Seems the kiln this home's become is changing *her* into some semiprecious store-bought thing. She's finally and truly turning "It."

Lady hears Yankees gossip from close by—hears slaves mumble, awe-struck, yards away. Her winding sheet crackles, suddenly unwet due west, seems to be browning like meringue in a low oven. Before smoke overcomes her, it teases, sharpens all sensations. She finds a strange new calm—and Lady wonders: "Perhaps this is what it's like when one is close to dying. This is how one's body comes to its own rescue, chemical toddies that hostess you through your own exit. Could I be thinking of last moments because these ones happen to be mine? Wouldn't *that* be odd."

Meanwhile, she knows exactly what's become swan-song smoke in every room and with what sort of sigh, which tint of flame, and at what turncoat speed. Morocco-leather-bound books downstairs, her husband's greatest joy, a lending library for Combustion now. ("Illiterate scamps, they spared the ladder but not the Gutenberg Bible!" She refused teaching slaves to read, claiming it'd interfere with their natural dignity.) Lady hears books—burn-ing somewhat alphabetical from floor to ceiling—perish in a frying roar. Seems like world literature ain't dry at all, but victual as bacon.

She knows when doilies quarter like dinner guests' napkins folded after a final satisfying course. In ending, buckled veneer suddenly lies flat. And under carpet, a long-lost key finds itself at the very last second, glows molten orange, "So. *Here* I am! I never doubted it."

One second-floor Dutch painting, a lady in white satin, burns bright blue, but its gold-leafed frame—on the job till the very end—puts off a yellow light, continuously framing blue damage. The owner, eyes shut like some Lady Oracle, knows what's turned black, what's whitening, which item curls purplish at its edges. (Myself, I own some family snapshots, a shawl, the cameo Momma give me, my husband's scabbard and bugle, some sterling thimbles. Still, they're mine. They make me guess: Hell for a collector must be hearing fire collecting on and under every item you love.)

Poor thing (are those my two favorite words, darling?) keeps breathing, coughing through cotton gone warm, hot, now singeing. She shivers—heat registers as one terrible chill. Lady believes she must now become choice butter smeared onto magnolia log, or maybe a cinder flying on to warn other gentlefolk downriver. She has time to recall one neighbor's scolding, "You *must* use your conservatory's white brocade lining to help bandage our South's bleeding boys." Lips now sound out, "Should have, should have." Words you tend to utter whilst your house burns.

"At least my headache's cured. Small blessings," and it finally strikes her—if she *does* get through—she'll wake in a landscape minus house, minus Bechstein grand, without a living son maybe, surely sans husband, without no clothes, all slaves gone. Dying loses some of its former sting.

Idly, idly, like she has all the time on earth, Lady E. More Marsden tells herself concerning death, "Well, *some*thing about it appeals to me."

Tree's roasty creak lets Mistress know: her magnolia has now gone over to the other side. Lost in smoke, she curls around the trunk. Worse heat tans her fingers, sets the pearls to sizzling. Last of all—hot in silk, slick with dew, renowned for perfect pallid skin—Mrs. Marsden hears it leave her ownership and this world's: the concert grand, black painted white, probably charred darker than its starting ebony. She hears her signed masterpiece come plunging through three floors—riding a sound like Hell's idea of Music.

8

YANKEES whoop at this sign of progress. Horses back off. Oh, honey, the heat! Third-floor roof begins to slack. Then it bows. Caves in. Sparks braid up two hundred yards. Nearby lilacs are already cooked but good. Soldiers clap. All but the boy whose single arm must hold the reins. He pats his Arabian's flank. The horse bolts. Off go others. A yodeling gallop across the Chinese bridge. Troops turn right, towards Falls. Towards the next farm. Is The Lilacs' punishment now over? Has Freedom started yet?

On the hedge's cooler side, black people sure cling to each other. Through purple blooms, they see the familiar house offer a glut of smoke to the sky's map. By stealing into the open, by turning to stare downriver, freed folks view a hundred miles of rich folks' disasters.

Ownership of people as property has just ended. Long live un-owner-ship! Odd, but property itself has died somewhat like people do. In picture books, the souls of the departing go smearing up—birds—vertical into air. White houses have left the world in just this way, smudged black, straight up. A windless afternoon and these great stripes, each half a acre wide, rise far apart at the river's finest bends. Like proud figures in pain, they keep to theirselves, columns of a single mammoth temple. And only when each pillar floats far up (we're talking miles, child) does it begin to sidle over toward the others. That high, a mild gray roof forms—transparent, weightless—tipped on jet-black uprights. —This former home now sets its vertical in place.

Freed women and children cannot quit holding one another. Their hiding seems done forever. Getting near as heat allows, don't nobody cry. Ain't one soul laughing. Out the mansion's every white hole, a separate stem of darkness rises. This house is spoked like a black candelabrum. Children see the mansion playing Catacombs. It has started being un-adult, it is coming down onto its hands and knees. The Big House ain't now.

CASTALIA inches close enough to understand: the famous solid-marble pillars are only veneered. She stares right into a hollow post—four foot wide, its inner curve shows home-cast brick, round pine cross braces. Who ever considered there'd be shortcuts here? Who knew all this could end so easy, like any *house* would?

Zelia points. Upstairs, on the former third floor, you can see the music room's exposed white onyx hearth. Lady's mantel still holds its French clock. The pink porcelain shepherdesses so recently well dusted are now lined like some minstrel show, all black-faced. Between the silver andirons yonder, almost comical, part of a ceiling beam must've dropped—a small fire burns just exactly where a fire should. All this happens eighty feet above you, held stark against the sky.

For ex-slaves, seeing the great white place crack to pieces feels joyful, scary. It's like the moon has died. (What good is the moon? And yet . . . you're used to it.)

In smoke, Old Zelia creeps nearer a particular tree, apron swaddling her mouth. Folks move like they onct tiptoed past the mistress's bedchamber during migraine. Heat makes people get closer only in measured sidesteps. They hear a dying mansion suck and gobble on its self.

"No," says Little Xerxes, not yet able to believe.

"Oh yeah. Be so," one woman says.

Then to make it truer for hisself, the boy tries mouth sounds copying so huge a housefire, "Ssnaffle, hump sheeee-crimpicle—poik. —Um-kay. More *like* it."

Must be four-thirty, the hour for high tea. Certain clocks—on fire and otherwise—still chime their duty. Xerxes then "does" time, too.

Smoke this thick ain't a mist, it's a new place you might could stand on like a stage or staircase. Folks breathe through wet pillow slips grabbed off the line. Adults hold children's hands, fearful that such whey-thick fumes will claim the wee ones as revenge. People risk the heat's full brunt. They now stand grouped twenty feet from a tree all flames.

IN EXODUS, Moses finds the bush that burns but ain't ever quite destroyed. Ex-Marsden slaves study a magnolia busy consuming itself. But today, see, *that's* the speaking miracle: Hers burns just like the four huge ones flanking it. She ain't being spared a thing. Fire, turns out, won't just another family friend that owed Judge More a favor.

Her hiding place has lost its houseward side. Only a few silver-hot twigs stay put. Everybody scans these for the near-albino person Castalia hid. Nothing's left but a charred trunk crisscrossed with fire's favorite lizard-skin design. There's one small flaking bulge, sheet's top and bottom merged with smoking bark.

Castalia moves to climb but—first branch up—burns her palm so bad she hops back down and dances—cussing, shaking fingers in the air. She wrestles off her apron, rips it, binds her palms with rags, then, well wrapped fingers to wrists, scutters right back up. Old Z, eyes shaded from the heat, stands quiet, staring overhead. Her untoothed mouth keeps opening and closing like a doubting extra eye. Maybe Z will now be punished for certain sassinesses earlier. She don't yet understand: she's free. Z could be flying to town. Honey, how long will it take her, greeting her own freedom?

Children hold on to women's skirts, needing company. If Lady's body *has* gone to smoke—just another vapor in the black tower rising off this site—well, that's one thing, that's clean and fitting, if terrible. But to come across her bacon-strip remains—that, the children don't want to see. Maybe when kids are aged eighty or even fifteen, when they have been snapped at and misused long as Zelia or Cassie, well all right. But not yet. Lady Marsden should've gracefully become, well, a dew. Resolved into a dew. Castalia goes on up hand over hand.

At The Lilacs' Galas' end, Cas helped Lady plot ways of bidding guests adieu gracefully. Cassie'd seen it happen often: The hostess would go halfway up her famous spiral stairs, hurrying to fetch a poetry book for somebody in the foyer. Then a wave, a flash of white hem—the last this party'd glimpse of her. Woman hated goodbyes. Her specialty was pretty dockside greetings. She could not endure departures, even if she knew she'd see the folks to-morrow. Guests—staring up—were slow to understand they'd just witnessed another swift exit. "Well," somebody'd say. "My," they'd say. And Cassie would then order Uncle Primus to go fetch gentry's hats, to wave down-lawn at bored slave boatmen. Oars up, fellows—party's over.

FLAPPING at tree smoke, Cas nears her ex-boss's last known whereabouts. Blue billows still go hard on the eyes. Where Lady sat wound in soggy white, nothing's left but a flaking tumor. Its outer shell catches light from the first floor's continuous uproar. Heat keeps others backed fifteen feet into the yard, arms raised, palms flat to shield faces. Against the savage orange light (okay, Miss Beale, maybe "savage" *is* going too far) others see Castalia, in black silhouette, straddling a tree's black prong, dramatic against a . . . savage orange.

The lump Cas studies seems some tree-gall rising, three and a half feet long. Browned past crispness, it has turned the weathered steel blue you sometimes see on old hornets' nests. "Look like she cooked," Cassie calls down. Z hollers, "That be the *first* cooking she ever done." Two children laugh, then cover their mouths. Everybody waits for news, everybody holds hands.

Why are these people bothering to check? Couldn't they be dashing towards a new life in Falls? Yeah, sure could. From a third-floor showcase, Lady's art-glass collection—many rainbow-tinted Roman jars and medicine vials—busts, shooting-gallery sounds, ripe sweetish pops like notes strung on the hot air.

This close, Cassie can study a baked cocoon. She's catching sounds furniture flopping in three directions before diving through a burning floor's best hole. But she listens hardest for somebody on the ground—somebody who'll tell her what to try next. —Sharp and willful as this young woman is, she's forever been instructed what to do. Since age three, since the long boat trip over: steady instructions. Who will give her orders now? Little Xerxes down yonder? Old Miss Zelia?

So, instead—Cas takes in extra breath (her back's so heated, homespuns stick against the skin, her red head rag is wet to black). Staring first at loved ones foreshortened in the yard—Cas—slow—lifts her rag-bound hand nearer ash. Up close, Lady's sheet yet shows its every thread fused into a layered page of soot. Castalia touches. Ash topples a light gray crust across her thighs. Seeing what she sees, Cas draws back, all but loses her grip.

She is posed on something's face side. Ash, a fragile coffin lid, has dropped to show one dark mummy's face—aimed at Cassie's. The thing's eyes seem melted shut. Firelight shows too much. Its skin is really oh Lord God so charred. Cassie just goes, "Ooooh!"

"Wha . . . ?" Zelia, below, jumps a single time, proves she means it. "Tell."

Castalia bends closer, dares to blow on the shape. Ash's next layer clears, the exposed form seems made of pitch. Cassie's breath shoots confetti flakes to all sides. She turns away, half choking. White bits drift down on the upturned features of black children and women. Folks now chance the heat at this tree's very roots. Arms screening faces, folks are impatient at being so near a inferno. They're too eager to stay back. Still, no soul feels willing to climb up, to settle beside Cassie, to stare damage in its face.

One tarry arm winds around the trunk. It clings so. Heat has sheared away a silk gown's front. Castalia must look at the ivory of exposed rib bones. Great glittery welts show where a person's breasts once stood. Blisters rise big as brandy snifters, hang bottom-heavy with odd trapped liquors. Yellow firelight plays over the sheen of blisters.

Its hair is lost. A skull shape is all homely facets, crisped blacked ears poke out, unhid (the hairdo's unpretty secret). Cassie sees six yard-long braids, turned white by such temperatures, drooping across branches below. Pearls in plaits have fused to wizened baby teeth. The diamond ring—still in place—looks bigger for such charring shrinkage all around it.

The face of this oily carcass rests not ten inches from Castalia's own. Cassie's big features (so eager to be satisfied) wince but gape right back, unblinking at her mortal enemy and owner. Lady was always a hard woman to be owned by—but, child? maybe they all are.

What now makes Castalia cry aloud ain't fear. It ain't rank happiness. It's something she's not counted on. Gaping at this punished shape forces forces forces her to yell, "Poor thing." Cas screams this, trying to dodge a terrible and unexpected pity. Castalia yells to make herself feel safer from the sight. She's furious at seeing all of this the first of anybody. "I just *won't*," she cries too late. "Answer's *no*, you hear?" Mostly, she's disgusted at her dizzy-making sympathy for ninety pounds of human scar. All this was supposed to end. Where's the Freedom part? Who will Freedom be?

HEARING Castalia scream, others back off for a better view.

"Burnt alive, I reckon," Zelia states, not asking.

That magic word "alive" makes Cassie wonder.

She draws even nearer to this husk. Trying not to fall, eyes clamped steady on the friends below, Castalia presses her right ear to a chest's central blister. Her voice soon roars, competing with fire's strong voice.

"Be a miracle. But, you-all? she alive. And guess what else? Could be the most strange of everything. You know Lady Marsden? Well, she done been broilt as black as us!"

From below comes cheers and clapping—maybe on both counts.

SIX children trot over with the burled-oak George III library ladder. "Go easy up yonder," comes a croaky warning. "Cause this, Old Zelia gots to see." Takes many minutes—unlatching one bone arm from round its log. Working the toasted body down is like trying to unpin a brittle bird nest from a spot where it's been built over many a weaving season. People clump onto/around/underneath the ladder. Black hands lift, black faces raise, all try lowering a helpless something—frail, dark, flaking.

Z fetches damp sheets but Cassie warns that, raw as this crisp thing is, sheets'll maybe stick to it. Little Evidence Anne hurries towards the stream, fishes out cheesecloth sacks of new butter sunk underwater to cool. Round yellow ingots have been made in a press, each embossed with fleur-de-lis lilac boughs hog-tied at bottom with a rope of pearls—the plantation's crest.

KITCHEN help, body servants, furniture polishers are all now basting it.

"Go slow down there, you young ones. When a chicken cook too long, you know how the meat try and pull off them rubber bones?" Castalia watches children's stub fingers smear ankles' spurred points.

Lady's always been tiny. But without the broad and trailing extra yards of silk, without her fanning forth of culture and menace, minus flirting, missing zigzag moods, the constant orders, and especially without no hair, she looks—face up to sun, under so many dark ministering hands—like some charbroiled pullet, a nasty little antique idol, or (while I'm going in for the flowery—sorry, Miss Beale, can't help myself) maybe a meteor what's come light-years in one cannoned instant.

Her attendants' lives have been used up in brushing long hair before the pier glasses convenient on each floor (plus one hid within the dock's lattice pagoda). Women have patted, smoothed, and dried her after bathing—but never with the interest of today—not never has Lady been handled with such relish, care, and tenderness.

See, she is now black. It was ever their daydream. Xerxes' wish made so. That being granted makes folks think this Freedom stuff is going to work just fine, right quick.

How cheerful and bold they move—trying to revive her, doubting that they can.

BY NOW, heat from three stories' burning has fried front sides off the hedge's eight hundred feet. Only lilac bushes down near river or out by post road have escaped withering. Lord God, the smell! Child, it clamped onto/over you like a sugar-watered felt glove—custom-made for your whole body. *Smelled* overly purple as the purple prose this is about to become, if I don't tread more careful.

The smell grew to such a heated pitch of Southern jasmined sugariness, you got nearbout sick. With today's bonfire, flowers took on corpses' tinge, worse for the famous terrible sweetness underneath. Made you wonder why anybody'd plant eleven hundred lilacs, and why you yourself had—on other such April days—bent your face into a foamy bush, pulled plush blooms against your nose, moaned over How Good Life Is Sometimes. Then sneezed.

In twenty minutes' heat, this has happened: the balance it has tipped. Everything's changed. Bitter carbon now seems pure relief—some mascot. Of a sudden, smoke has turned into such a honest scent—proportions and a purpose to it. Lilacs planted in 18 and 21 for their scent now reek worse than any old run-over skunk. Compared with that, the purging swipe of ash has grown so elegant.

Till smoke smell took over complete, freed slaves, smudging butter on a crusted body, gulped air through their open mouths. They did it partway from disgust at seeing the singed pubis of a lady what'd owned them, part it was from fear that all this sweetness-unto-sickness (O lilac, thou smell right sick) rose from out of *her*.

Riding heat straight up, slave owning ends in a final honeyed glut. And ooh, child, it just stenched to highest heaven!

9

WHEN I first picked the title of this Modern History theme, I felt well pleased with its tidiness: three permanent colors. I figured they'd divvy facts up amongst theirselves, three corrals. Only halfway through did it strike me: tints'd have to change places. "Uh-oh," said my overly organized eleven-year-old mind. "You won't get no decent grade from Witch if you prop a whole paper around things that've got to trade off *being* one another. Ain't near neat enough."

Now I see I was wrong. Like often happens, what shoves you into a simple idea is not what—when it grows way messier and complicated—keeps you rolling on with it. Marriage, for instance.

To learn about White, go ask Black, vice versa. Each color is the brick beside/above/below/another, separate brick and yet all set in one wall.

So: What *is* black and white and lilac?

Well, the house and owner have lost any claim to Whiteness. Both've turnt glossy black as tar babies. Black folks still *are*, okay, but they're feeling heaps cheerier about it now that river's real estate and bosses are also signing on as black—a fad.

Lilacs ain't no more. That color. —And what smells good?

Soot and ash now outstrip perfume.

What is sweet and what is bitter?

What is just and what is just not fair?

Even the colors of the world can switch headquarters and meanings on you and in minutes. The right answer one second is such a wrong answer the very next.

History's one of them subjects requires regular questions to help a body stay abreast. Meaning: Let's keep on our toes and remain dancing. Let's not wait for others to grill us in advance for the right answers. We'll prepare, revise, stay game for a little Ethics exam every second of our lives. Whenever Witch Beale pitched into some chalk talk about the Enlightenment, say, she'd smile, shielding from sight her huge dictionary of a mouth, she'd go, "You *will* be tested on this."

Tiring, but true of every moment of your life, darling. *Experience is a pop quiz you ain't ever quite prepared for.* But you always pass by the skin of your teeth anyhow. Who ever gets held back? —Time itself is a social promotion.

Maybe a better center-question might run: What's ever *just* Black or White and Lilac for long?

Q: According to Mr. Goethe, according to the Witch, why does one see-through prism bruise forth so easy with two dozen perfect jewelry-store tints?

A: The deeds and sufferings of light make colors. By the time sunlight reaches us, it is beautiful old news. We get tanned, healed, fed by the sun's own long spent ricochet history.

10

ZELIA, house expert at furniture polishing, tries daubing the ebony victim (fetus-homely, fetus-slippery) with wet rags. Just like Cassie predicted—cloth gums onto/into it/her. Poor little critter seems fashioned of black shoe wax. Its legs, stretched out on a sheet, might be wavery twin licorices. Castalia smears grease along crackled limbs, across more blisters that've bloomed. Cas whips off her own red dew rag. With the headcloth, she hides a pate's singed roots.

"There go the last of our sweet butter," Old Z says. "Six pounds, for this."

Children find a rosewood door. It's been knocked flat by mounted Yanks. Folks plunk the mistress onto it. Off they cart her to a less smoky place, one that Sherman's men have purposely spared: the slaves' quarter.

This got left—and, like a joke, so did the smokehouse. One precious ham yet hangs there. Zelia, remembering certain of her earlier rudenesses to Lady, now acts semi-scared of the burned one. Fact is, Z hides. Then, like trying and make up, the old woman reappears with a sample from the icehouse (great white hunks of it someway survived the hut's very burning). Zelia presses coolness between the maimed one's split lips, she wets the teeth and gums, blacked by inhaled soot.

Quiet, children stay busy, studying. To see it naked, to see it bald-headed, to see it black—means seeing Lady truly helpless, not just playing-like. Odd, you can stare right *at* Mistress, without that helmet zone of sharp blue eyes looking ownership your way. Children linger close, their faces solemn. Winch the overseer used to scare them, using a marsh-dwelling mossy hag (excellent for keeping ghost-believing ex-Africans indoors at night). How strange—children's finding that, right along, this threatened Bogey Demon of the Swamp was real. Was no animal or spirit or clockly goddess. All along, the farm's monster won't nobody but Her Ownership.

CASTALIA, usually the ablest of talkers, suddenly says next to nothing. She is full of glares and misgivings. Others feel her watching everything, a grave new trying-it-out manner. Since Cassie turned ten, one of her bodyservant chores has been attending Lady's monthly needs. With Mistress so allergic to cotton, only silk would do for her home-rolt napkins. Before wartime, all the used monthly rags got burnt. But lately—what with silk become so scarce—Castalia's dutifully washed out and rerolled each one. You take a eighteen-inch pennant of white silk, you (yeah, I mean *you*), you trim it to five inches wide. You twirl this tight as possible, doubling many absorbing layers whilst you spin and spin the thing. Set aside a goodly supply by the twenty-sixth.

Question: Should one able-bodied person (you, for instance) *have* to take another's furled bloodied silk and unroll the monthly banners into a bucket of boiling water, lye, bleach, blueing? (Harder if this lady boss ain't even no blood kin to you.) Is Castalia remembering all this whilst setting staring at the newly blacked one yonder? Is Cassie deciding the date when her and the others should leave here, leave it?

Dr. Marsden onct mentioned how in olden Greek days certain unwanted girl babies got "exposed"—meaning left naked on mountainsides. If a girl child was someway rescued (by a shepherdess or such), well, more power to her. Most didn't. Civilization, child! —Exposed at last, either Lady E. More Marsden will live or no. Whatever happens, that's now *her* job.

Lady weighs so little, even the children can drag her on that door. Roped to the makeshift sled, pressed inside a buttered sheet, she is pulled all over—still unconscious. Describing the spoilt acreage, wee ones jatter back her way. They give Mistress a tour of her personal ruins: blacksmith forge, dovecote, pierside pergola. Just the way Lady onct fussed over new black babies, bouncing and spoiling them, loving to dance them around—young ones now use her. They set her down near this gateway, try itching her awake with clover stems. From the post road, it must look like young ones have gone and dug up some ancient black woman's corpse. Kids are being real artful with the body, arranging it curled here, propped humorous over yonder.

In the days of Catacombs, kids tickled Lady just to feel her yards of silk, a guardian cloud. Now, Xerxes dares the other children to press even one of their fingertips onto certain crusts congealing—like tree's sap—round her chest and head. From the dead magnolia, using a bamboo fishing pole, Xerxes pries loose a single whitened braid. The black pearls chittering brittle in it are cooked tear-shaped. Just a child after all, Little Xerxes chases other kids, them shrieking from the snaking bobbling thing—a life—at the stick's springy end.

11

THE FIRST night is real hard. Ex-slaves sleep just inside the edge of the fire's wide beacon. A corner of far woods glows orange-pink. From downhill lily pools, frogs go crazy piping piping. On the post road—all night long you hear strange buggies rattle closer, stop, somebody gaping uphill toward the great pile of molten third-floor newels, stairways hotfooting it nowhere—then such buggies clatter off. People sleep in shifts. Like the house needs company. Like they do.

Dawn cheers everybody considerable. Waking folks file over, one by one, to check on a nude woman glazed black. Even children stumble first to her—just the way gardeners in late April, say, will trot, still half asleep, out to their dewy patch. Anything come up yet? In one night, Everything

Can Change. This, honey, we all partly and continually believe. Otherwise, could we stand it?

That first morning, Lady is tugged into the sun she's always dreaded. Might help to dry the worst places on her arms and chest. Ex-ownees settle in a powwow horseshoe to examine her up close. Why? Because they can now. For the first time in her thirty-eight semi-invalid years, others listen at her heart's beating with cheerful peasant steadiness. Makes a body feel bitter, recalling her years of so-called frailness. She ain't opened either eye. "It sure do *look* dead," Evidence says.

For onct, mothers quit fussing at their noisy little ones. Seems that Behaving has sprung from Lady's white Spode and from the overseer's whip. With these gone, with Lady so past caring, laws feel like runaways gone North. But, honey, rules are really just circling back, tiptoeing. Comes around, goes around. Revolutions do like that, don't you know. And freed folks—beginning to suspect this—sure quiet down. You see women looking over shoulders. They seem fearful that one person's happiness might some-way leach all others'. They're used to Lady's airy comfort being fueled by their own cellar lack of it. Now every time somebody grins or seems to have a minute's fun, others turn her way, "What *she* planning?" Daylight here must mean it's night back home in Africa. "Where was Moses when the lights went out? Standing in the corner with his shirttail out."

12

EVERY black person in Marsden ownership long ago got sized up, if lazily. Castalia: quick, bossy, sharp, hard. Zelia: a cloud in a pocket—half again too vague. Xerxes . . . etc. Judged, each slave then turnt into a canny actor, determined to get along by playing out the owner's decision. Colors are the deeds and sufferings of light.

These parts got perfected above nearbout any other Lilacs skill. Lady was such a genius at her own tender temperamental role, she forever ex-pected a good show from others.

So, what happens when the landlord that called you "handsome" or "featherbrained" slides past noticing? With your audience and management gone—you can start over. But how, honey? Maybe this is why these folks keep so still and sulky two days past the fire. They act worried: what if friends make them *continue* whatever disposition they choose to try out first. Used to working for a single lady, seems like one of them must now rise up, try taking over Lady's role.

Old Miss Zelia appears to suddenly want the job. Z keeps stick-figuring to and from the woods, face caged in with plans, hands fisted, pouchy eyes alive. Castalia, a young woman who's been the group's main steady opinion, acts semi-disgusted, watching Z want it so bad. Others figure: the head-honcho-ette job should only go to somebody that wouldn't ever choose it.

Only then will you be safe from your own kind becoming a worse copy of Lady.

One thing's sure: The first Freedom is Insomnia. What's the second Freedom? When does the Flight part come? Where's the fun?

USED TO doing everything in groups, even having dormitory married relations in sight and earshot of each other, folks now start stealing off by theirselves. One by one, women and children trail toward the woods like seeking whatever answers are stowed out yonder with the furniture. In the Big House, these items just meant a set of chores. But finding them out here, it's magic, like stumbling onto Pompeii's stopped-clock luxury made into preserves for you.

Old Zelia, alone, in woods, turns back the tarp, chooses a fine salmon-pink wing chair. Once in it, she pulls tarp's canvas back over her gray head. It's like Catacombs—she's listening, cynical but interested. A wood thrush sings nearby. Z hopes the wild bird and this satin chair will whisper some secrets, offering strengths she now needs. Z is onto eighty-one. Seems her chance has finally found her. Nights, she can't hardly sleep for the ambitions working in her head—wishes whining, noisy as a market Saturday in Falls. Alone now, under the cover, touching her own beef-jerky face and bagpipe throat, Miss Zelia cries. From the excitement. It's a pink wing chair. She daydreams of flying.

"WHEN we leaving?" Xerxes asks that midnight.

Cassie answers, "When we knows how."

13

FIRST black stragglers are seen wandering the post road, headed *out* of Falls and pretty doggone quick. Castalia spies folks that traipsed to town three days before. Now here they come lugging a small fellow on a stretcher. Strangers hint, he has been shot for stealing bread. But when The Lilacs' group draws near, asking about Freedom, wanting some of liberation's How To's, the group is plainly laughed at. One man says, "Ladies, I invites you to hike in, try it for youselfs. You has to make it up while you goes. Seem like that what Freedom mean. I dearly hopes you-all is better at it than this winged baby brother mine done been."

Studying the downhill road, Baby Venus later asks, "Where do that Young Linking Man be?" Grownups stare her way. No adult has ever described the holy bearded giant they've been waiting on. Venus—honey-colored, with Evidence's own big gray Marsden eyes—has siphoned news from nowhere, the way kids do. All servants here have specialized in asking questions whose answers they well know. Each now suspects that this child is putting them on.

Cassie's neutral face sure worries her friends. One noon, she suddenly rises and goes kicking a dried pumpkin up and down the farm road till there's little left of pumpkin. She's grumbling to herself. Others see her squat then, making water in plain view the way children will, ignoring a nice privy still out back. She daubs her cheekbones with chalky mud from the riverbank, like Tuscarora war paint. "You sick?" Xerxes calls.

"I a pure-blood African princess. Who you, mongrel?" For some reason, he laughs at this. Then so does she. Which makes the others feel only a little easier.

I said how, before the fall of the House of Lilacs, Castalia got along by being semi-rude, flirting with danger, her back a cat-o'-nine-tails' copybook. How Old Zelia inched through by clowning, blinking then scratching her grizzled head, seeming charmingly forgetful all these years. In Z's early days, with Lady's sensible mother in charge, rumor claimed Zelia was somebody else—sharp, ordered, fine-looking—her role was then more like Cassie's under pre-burn Lady. Questions: Has the main thing a body's been known for at The Lilacs now been proved as wrong as slavery? How much gumption will it take for, say, Little Xerxes, just gone eleven, to decide he ain't naturally the crafty actor Lady noticed at age three (and, by noticing so grandly, part-invented)? And if the child picks to sober some, will he be doing that only out of spite? —Honey, which talent of yours, praised and shaped by your bosses, got sized up correct? Does the basic cruelty of a lady's owning you cancel everything she's ever guessed, predicted, or loved about you? Can you love a owned one? Can you own a loved one?

Now it's Cassie who seems ready to sit in one sunny spot and go blank. The young woman acts bone-tired. Odd, she ain't even noticed her exhaustedness till right now.

Zelia, suddenly faster-moving, begins directing others about. She sweeps the quarter (first person since the fire to touch a broom by choice). Nobody acts on Z's commands but everybody watches her. "Miss Zelia, who *you* now?" Xerxes asks, meaning it, ready to revise his imitation of the overly easy-to-copy old-time Z.

14

WOMEN watch their children pull back Lady's cloth. Women let them. It's day four after the mansion's fall. Kids scan a scarred shape—they act saddened by such damage. Children stare hard at each other, then back at her. Venus soon gets to giggling. Next, young ones are just rolling all around. One child quits laughing long enough to huff, "She . . . sure . . . got . . . one . . . nappy pussy."

This just doubles them up. But, hooting, they run off quick. Each feels scared the boss is only playing possum. Maybe the fire's been staged, a test of loyalty. If so, they've surely flunked. She'll wake, she'll have them lashed, she'll shut them in the root cellar, where slaves once got weeks of solitary punishment, where some died.

Three days after torches left their mark on her home and person, whilst ex-Marsden helpers set cooking greens here in the sun, Lady—with long frightening tearing sounds—opens one eye, then the other. Children, turning, scream. Whites of Lady's eyes have been so seared by heat they show the exact color of her blood. It's like looking through the side of a clear gondola punch bowl at whatever liquid it guards. Eyes' centers have stayed their own pale whitish blue. Her face is red, black, gray like the head of a ugly hybrid duck Mabry kept on his lily pool—one that folks felt sorriest for, one they threw extra bread and cake. She now studies a cooking pot, sees people scrambling away from her, then—straining so hard to focus or to understand—her whole head topples forward. She is snoring like a sailor. Even Zelia laughs, relieved. "Whoo," goes Z. "Look like she done drawed in bad fumes from all them jewels in the vault, see. Rubies flown, for punishment, to she very eyes." Zelia checks to see how many appreciate her explaining.

Squatting, Castalia snorts, shifts to one side, won't add nothing.

BY DAY, Xerxes scrubs his hankie ascot, preparing for town like it's some show he's willing to do but only if properly begged. Z, prodding through charcoal at the Big House's edge, finds a copper cask holding relics of the master: his pince-nez—glass intact, grosgrain ribbon burnt. Z now puts specs on the way a teacher might, pinching the end of her flat nose. Children sashay around her, asking (hoping—like all of us—to finally be discovered), "Can you see me clear? How I look?"

But farsighted Zelia only squints towards the Big House's hazy foundation. Z scratches her head, then points. "Hey, wait. What that stuff between the bricks?"

It's been Z's duty for the last thirty years, rising first on Thursday mornings, to light the breakfast fire. (The kitchen outbuilding has burned to the ground four times before. It sets a safe sixty feet behind the mansion to spare grease fire's spreading.) Since Sherman killed the clocks, don't nobody remember just what day of the week it is. (Sunday mornings off gave slaves their one weekly drop stitch.) But even so, early this Thursday morning (Z's duty day), when the light hangs sour and gray over pinewoods due east, one crabbed body does stagger from the quarter. Rubbing sleep from eyes, she sets the suddenly necessary spectacles in place.

Half asleep, she's edged toward the cook shack. Z is hoisting two big logs and some kindling off a unburned pile.

Then Old Z notices. Gone. It's all of it gone.

Die-hard frogs still croon from ponds. Rags of mist soften the woods' far edge. Every sooty blade of grass looks glassy with dew. And right then, from six spots all across Nash County, six surviving roosters offer peaked and rusty songs towards the sun. (They think, if birds *do* think, that they sound pretty good. Males, they hate each other's songs. Each believes he ain't just announcing the day but he's personally carving it, by voice, by will. Like me, someway hoping that everything I can rest here in my bed and try describing is therefore someway *so*. Poor birds, they're a lot everybody else, child. —We all think life is *for* us!)

Well, Zelia sure tosses down that heavy firewood, she twirls on one ankle broomstick-thin. She crooks a thumb under either arm like for to pull at new suspenders, and—head thrown back, arms flapping like stunted bantam wings—yodels her own creaking "EEE err eee err eeee. —Z Be Freee!"

Then, hand holding the pince-nez in place, head lowered like a person on some mighty major mission, Zelia nearbout runs, determined, back to bed.

15

YOU MIGHT could wonder, darling, why these folks ain't yet hightailed it. They could. But from their hillside, looking down onto the river road, they've already seen twenty-odd more black folks who dashed to Falls three days before come drooping, raging back.

Retreaters, noticing Marsden freed folks still huddled near a uphill fire, try and make their strides appear more sure. One spiffy young fellow stops for water. Using a stick, he skims the ashy lid off one lily pond's corner. He was owned by Mabry—a gent who chose to stay high in his burning mansion's cupola, a gent who shouted benedictions on his land while, somewhat late, giving his slaves their freedom, then (believing hisself to be captain of a great white-tiered sinking ship) rode to the ground in Shadowlawn's great house.

Mabry's ex-valet now claims: center-city Falls is one ripe mess. Black folks, expecting their due, keep meeting white folks busy being bad losers. Whites are now hiring armed guards (freed slaves seeking work). Guards patrol white porches. They sleep in white-owned garden houses, preventing such white/black blurring as fires out this way have unloosed. Falls' commercial street is prone to pushing and stealing, with outsized punishments for both. Two hangings took place in the Courthouse Square last Monday alone. Was the sheriff's day off.

"If you does move to town? and should you walk on the street? and do it be a Monday? don't you even take the time of day from nobody. Hear?"

"They owes us." Zelia's head swings southwest towards Falls. The young man laughs. "If *anybody* do, them what owned you owes you." He points uphill to snaggled steaming columns, planks yet smoldering these days later. Lady Marsden snoozes against a sunlit stuccoed wall nearby. Nobody mentions how "they" still live close by—in her, it. Nobody much remembers.

News of the hangings naturally scares folks here. Anyhow, they've always wondered what this farm would feel like without chores to make a body hop. They vote to stay on till Lady changes: either by getting well enough to understand or by dying. Whichever comes first.

Many post-road walkers are headed North, bound for what? the President's promised linking? But Castalia guesses most are wandering right back to woods around the plantations they know—spots where possums are slow enough to stone or club, where bright sunfish bite real quick. Freed folks require a good feeding before gallivanting toward New York City town.

Seeing the Falls exodus, free folks on this hill stare at one another and then over to their sleeping mistress—like blaming her. Maybe they're still seeking Lady's permission to clear out. Maybe they're waiting to take a rock and crush her skull but just ain't learned that yet.

THE SLAVE garden yet offers baby carrots, fresh greens, volunteer zinnias colorful here and there. After Marsden work dawn to dusk, black people tended this plot by lamplight. Seems a year ago, it's been under a week. Slaves could keep whatever sprung from their own acreage—Winch often remarked how large their yield stood compared with Master's. Now this food alone sustains them. The two-hundred-acre cornfield was set ablaze when woods did.

Baby Venus spies a single smart chicken. It's among the last uneaten ones at the end of the county. The hen is wandering among blacked stalks, seeking unsinged cobs. Hearing Venus, the bird hides itself, maybe hoping to be taken for a hefty sparrow. Then the chicken proves too quick for Venus' short legs. Hungering after something not collards, the others later quiz Venus. Seems she's sighted some white meat angel. "Were it fat?" "Fat as . . . a pig." "And I reckon it looked to be a good-eating chicken?" "Look like one tasty bird, eyes already the color of giblet gravy. Be some kind of good eating, could I of catched it. But that thing run fast as . . ."

"The wind?" Xerxes is excellent at physical likeness but language-wise he's got to get better than that, child.

For now, folks patrol the old acreage, quiet, hunting food, wondering who to try and be next. Some sleep long hours—never having got to nap before. It bores them pretty quick. Abraham Linking didn't bust your chains so you could cut freestyle ZZZ's all day. Seems you should at least be resting up *for* something. Even Xerxes ain't hisself—meaning: he is only that. He forgets to be funny. Friends fail to force him. He's just another big-eared watchful boy, eleven, no better. Evidence Anne finds a charbroiled piano keyboard, drags it back to the quarter, fakes playing. Huge chimneys still smokestack a factory's worth of fumes. Freedom seems: the right to be bored.

16

SIXTH DAY after the fire, while everybody hunkers in the quarter's foreyard making hike-to-Falls plans, while children weave clover garland around Lady's scaly head (she now blinks awake for ten minutes of every hour), a shrill cry lifts from out the woods. In one second, everyone but Lady is well hid. Such ghosty screeking, "Heeere y'all, heeere y'all!" Cassie soon says, "It peacocks. Be one of Cousin Mabry's, probly hiding out from all these fire." Hungry freed people look at one another, are soon running over furrows brittle with last year's cotton stalks, so useless to your empty stomach.

Evidence Anne is first to spy the bird. Up a sycamore, all tinsel-tailed and heavenish with blues, the creature's wingtips look right charred. Sounds like it's weeping, screaming bad news, hoping for human help. When children shinny up, the bird flies straight down, flopping something pitiful and is soon being turned on a spit.

The bird is studied by a underfed Lady. She's been making do with greens stuffed into her mouth, jaw then held until, eyes watering, she swallows. "Tough," Zelia admits, rechewing fowl. "Swanses, goldfishes, peabirds. Look like show stuff would be tender, don't it? But maybe that why it just *for* show. Least this ain't collards. When I gets my mansion in town, I never wants to taste another green or smell not one more lilac. Make Z sick. Now, don't you all be bringing me none from *you*-all's mansions, hear?"

After the meal, feeling more than usually satisfied, wearing blue-green feathers jabbed among basket-perfect corn rows, folks again name which in-town home will be theirs. They say what mansion they'll store firewood in, which they'll chop up *for* firewood. They argue over what day of the week to use as their "at-homes." "You all can't have Mondays. Zelia here done claimed it. Something tells Z: streets ain't none too safe that day. So, you all come see *me*. Six days left, fight among youselfs. Miss Zelia here's too old to lose her first argument since sliding free."

Women describe the great dances in their homes and then, idle, feeling large and sure and safe, turn to watch their former mistress. Evening is here—a great spun-gold sky backs four uphill chimneys. One shape hunkers five feet off. Red-eyed, the creature keeps blinking this way, probably seeing but little. "And you," Z calls. "Miss Cinder-ella gal, eavesdropping yonder, *you* ain't invited to any of Zelia's high teas, not never. For all you talk about manners, you been steadily so rude to your old Z here."

Children step over to check on Lady's healing skin. First they shoo away the day's last flies. Evidence Anne borrows Xerxes' neckcloth, tries and blindfold the messed-up one. Now that Lady looks so bad, you'd think blindfolding might soothe her. But since fire, she just hates that. Whenever white swims down before her face, she screams, rips cloth away, eager to see whatever she can.

Finally, tired of fanning bugs away, being just a kid after all, Evidence bends, pinches Lady. Tries it just to see what the mistress'll do. What Lady does is: look back. Not even like saying, "Why'd you try that?" Instead: "You did that to me, didn't you? All right. I noticed." One way she's still herself—old reflex—the head, coquettish, still tilts left like it did when she really wanted something out of you. A fraction of her is still in there trying to flirt all this out of being true.

Lady's eyeballs are splotched with brown papery scraps. Doesn't bother her a bit. Castalia will stoop before her, daub at these, using skirt's doubled edge. Lady's head seems as clogged with crisp ash as that wasp-nest winding cloth they found her in. Xerxes, hearing how labored her breath comes, sacrifices one-third of his last ascot, holds it to her nose, "Blow, you. Your own good." First, she fights him (weirdly strong, she is—a cornered swan can break your wrist with one wing's swipe). When Lady finally does honk, the cloth shows not just color but enough black woody bits to start another fire. Mostly she just sets here—brittle arms stuck out to either side like some baby bird might (must hurt when a arm touches her bared ribs). In Winch's burnt cabin one unbroken bottle of witch hazel is found. Women gather, try and clean Mistress's skin. How richly black is she going to be for good? Lady's face—onct described as "poreless"—now shows a million fine specks—each dent and eye fold plugged with fine blown soot. She battles, squeaking, head doubled against one shoulder. Layers of black then sepia then gray scrub off but women soon hit the dark unchanging underscars. They see that only on paper, only technically, child, will Lady E. More Marsden ever be a lily-white again.

"We getting bout ready to," Z tells young ones. She stands, stretching like somebody waking from a eighty-year snooze. Z means leave, leave here.

This group has stayed on in the slave quarters a full ten days after the blaze. Folks've been pulling Lady out into fullest sunlight—thinking maybe it'll heal her stickier burns. Though she has hid from sun for her whole lifetime, she seems to like it now. A little wizened bald-headed charcoal-colored crone, she looks ancient, shivery. She goes crawling on all fours towards a warm spot. She stays hid beneath her sheet like in a game of Catacombs played nude, played solitaire, and minus furniture. Around the yard, she knows where heat lives minute to minute. On hands and knees, she tags after it all day like some battered cat. Lady seems cured of the onetime nervous energy that made her such a fussbudget, gossip, and key-board twinklefingers. She can now rest for whole hours, eyes shut, mouth sealed, face tipped up to meet whatever warmth Old Sol allows her. She soaks it in, nearbout like information, child—like finally accepting dictation, some lesson from the light.

17

THE MORNING before leaving, little ones pull over pine sawhorses. Kids wrestle sooty sheets off the lines and make a short draped tunnel. Castalia, washing a broken gravy boat, wanders nearer, curious.

Do children think the burnt one might now crawl under their cloth, Catacombed into motion by memory? But she just slumps over there, studying whatever far-off blur the children make. Young ones soon grow tired of trying and improve It. They just climb into the tent. Onct clear from the victim's birdy stare, their mischief starts sounding regular.

Somebody (*has* to be Xerxes, feeling hisself again in trying out others) squeals, "Why, la-dee-dah, here come my dusky lions of de Roaming swamps. They after me, they dare not. Uh-oh. Dey do dare! Well hush my li'l mouth. Planning and eat *Me* for they canapés?! You know not. Consommé moi? I bound to be tough as shoe leather. Just *look* at me today, with this headache and my hair a perfeck mess. I gone give *some*body bad gas, sure."

Castalia, quiet, arms crossed, listens, notices the rules have shifted. Children, lost under sheets, have picked one "It." Freed young ones still can't imagine this game played among equals. Ain't no fun without some feared and central It to hide from, then pounce upon. When children do crawl out, they slowly see her yonder, alive and somewhat in person. Disappointing: Lady's homeliness, one raw breast exposed. Cover it, please. Did children think their game under percale might help and heal her? Almost unwilling, they mope towards her resting place, they group all round.

"Ain't she pitiful? She sure sadder than any *we* ever was." Evidence Anne, Baby Venus, Little Xerxes covey right before her. Clover crowns from earlier have all dried flat. She looks up at them, no judgment in her former-judging eyes. Her head moves from face to face, holding on each for maybe a full half minute. Seems she's hoping she can finally notice something. Seems that Lady guesses she *should* remember what these dark witty shapes might mean. —But she can't yet. And, understanding this much, Lady blinks, breathes one breath deeper than the rest, then tips on back. She'll wait. She accepts that. You can see her lose even the small earlier interest. You can read her like a child of one. She acts so willing to sit quiet till it all, at last, comes clear to her again.

Ruined—how patient she has grown!

Old Z cuts through clumped children. Her right foot prods the buttery percale. "We leaving, but what to do with *this* leftover?"

Castalia rises, paces to and fro. Others watch. "All right. We gone try four things." Using powerful fingers, Cassie counts. Behind her, pacing to and fro, Xerxes counts. "First show her how to get water up out the well. Then we points to where collards grows, teach her how and build a fire, how to cook her up a mess of greens. After that, we free and gone. All right by you?"

A show of hands: agreed.

So, pleased, folks drag the former mistress to her well. Xerxes and Venus act real proud in operating rope and pulley, going slow for her sake. Then Xerxes steps two feet aside, repeats it all—in air. Does Lady notice? Spirited, everybody rushes to the garden, where Cas pulls a few choice collard leaves. Being trained to build a fire (Fire!), Lady whimpers, she's blocked from trying to scuttle away. Z, squinting through the pince-nez she often cleans on her apron, ain't sure how she feels about these lessons. Arms crossed, she stands to one side, tapping a finger against her toothless mouth.

Now that the ex-mistress is in love with sun, freed folks (for reasons all their own) try and keep her out of it. The sun still seems a African national. (Didn't it follow their slave boat—serving as the guard, God, and sponsor?) They already loved Sun back when Lady, still sullen under parasols, yet snubbed it, fought to keep Sun in its place.

18

ELEVEN days after the fire comes the afternoon of leaving. Children make extra-secret jaunts to the woods. Like going to a zoo, or visiting some charming friend in jail. How strange the furnishings look resting out here, half under tarps. The brookside glade makes treasures seem more valuable and perfect. A test for beautiful furniture: Does it still look beautiful in a beautiful woods?

Children coax canvas aside. They bounce on upholstery. Inlaid drawers, they fill with pinecones. For kids, it all seems some ghosty tea party they've finally been invited to. A red velvet footstool rests beside a clump of even greener velvet moss. Evidence has hung sixty apple-green Spode teacups by their handles from one thorn tree's briars. Honey, a breeze convenes a banquet of clinking. Doubled Oriental rugs fly from boughs, patterned bold as flags of Africa.

The coveted ham, now soaked, cooked, prepared, has disappeared from out the smokehouse. "Bet It got it," Zelia nodded towards a silent one. "And don't play dumb with me, you. I onto you tricks."

The neighbor's chicken—glad Yanks are gone, maybe thinking a sacrificed peacock has sated folks' hunger for fowl—sneaked out of woods, come pecking around a former mistress's black little feet, her toe bones singed like a baked fish's dainty fins. Chicken never knew what hit it. A farewell lunch.

The hostess/mistress's scars now bubble, crusted. Though naked, her body wears a tweed of scabs. First hair is sprouting back—it grows white. "Be from the shock," Castalia tells children. They touch the fuzz, keep shooing away wasps and bluebottles that—working Lady's eyes—bother her so little but sure annoy her former children. Castalia reties the red bandanna under the old owner's chin. "O Lady," Castalia gives a great luxurious sigh, "be so much I could tell you now. You done lost all you pretties, the house, you Europe clocks, the clothes. But what's way the worst, you done forever lost you only Castalia. Cas been being so good to you, Cas never did get paid. *Why* so good, you reckon? I don't know that my own self." Cassie studies the thousand dark dots sunk into a tight forehead and neck, the strange comic raccoon mask framing onetime famous eyes. Eyes, half aware of being watched, shut hard, pleading maybe, Don't notice me now.

Watching, Zelia snaps her fingers. "I know what I plans giving her for *my* going-way present. Why Z didn't think of it sooner? Getting old, seem like. Be right back. This gone to be rich." And trudges off speaking fondly only to herself.

Widow Marsden's one-and-a-half-carat diamond ring has outlived heat's tribulation. Pearls might've melted into popcorn kernels but the diamond glimmers more perfect than before. Mistress onct bragged on its winking tints: "Notice the 'fire'?" Now youngsters—weaving her with farewell clover loops, decking the bandanna with crowns—shift Lady's scarred hand, admire how the gem catches sun just so—how it squirts local rainbow (the long-suffering light) all over a mud-daubed ocher wall.

Everybody hears a cotton cart come rattling from the woods, Zelia pulling like a coolie. She's brung a needlepointed coat of arms—Lady's maiden name, More. This item's three feet square, finely framed. The old one unloads it easy enough but needs help with the hundred-and-fifty-pound mirror.

Pre-fire, women rushed this out of Lady's first-floor dressing room. Was her favorite pier glass. Lady always admitted to her women, "Only the profoundly vain, my friends, understand: no two mirrors are alike. And only we, the truly unapologetic, can name our especial favorites from over the years. I remember one beveled one in Charleston, five feet square it was and positively wasted, exiled on my aunt's landing. A genius of a glass when it came to showing me the me I intend. You know I've rejected several. I will *not* be distorted by something I myself purchased. I just won't, I tell you—fair warning."

This—her champion flatterer—is full length, oval. It rides a mahogany base and frame. Borders are inlaid: three shepherdesses lounge in one glen, holding ribboned crooks, no sheep in sight.

Zelia oversees its being grappled to the ground then pulled nearer, rocked until it's plunked right square before her. Lady rests tipped against the quarter's outside wall. Glass swivels, locking down down. In its lower eight, there she sort of is—blacked like a stage comic's blacked front tooth. Can she find a way to *notice*? Old Z reaches over, whips a borrowed head rag off Lady's pate. Z grins, "Better. Much."

Castalia stoops beside her former mistress, nods at the reflection, half purrs to *it*, not the dark nub herself, "There you is. And here's us ones, standing all round, see?" Xerxes, unable to resist the pleasure of greeting his own raw-material self, grimaces through eight test faces, fast. But he spares Lady his imitation of her face *now*.

"We leaving," Cassie explains. "You gone stay right here. You yours now. Satisfied?"

"No kindness!" Zelia yells. "I ain't having no mushy tone of voice. Where kindness been hiding these eighty years? Why it should pop out today?" And, squatting, Z elbows Castalia aside. "Lookie," Old Z's gnawed fingernail thumps glass. "Know who *that* be? —Three guesses, first two don't count. Missy? Do something about this toasted little muffin appeal to you?"

Requires many minutes for two ruby eyes, their strange pale centers, to settle on the skin of silver glass. Z holds a pince-nez before these eyes. "Do that help?" Lady keeps checking others' faces, hoping for instructions, knowing *some*thing is expected—not yet rightly understanding what. Children tilt closer. Kids make sure their faces (inside a shepherdess frame) register well above their old-time owner's.

(Black women watch theirselves, each one maybe wondering how this, her own fine face, will now aid or hurt her in downtown Falls. A female slave's being beautiful only drew the Master then Winch and his crew—in that hand-me-down order. And yet, surely, for a *freed* lady, all this beauty's going to help, right?)

One mirror holds a row of interlacing faces, totem-poled.

Lady checks from those higher in the glass to a little crisped one down here at the bottom. "Oh yeah, you catching on *now*," Z nods hard. "Quit beating round the bush for that fussy other one. She gone. This all what left."

Lady blinks. Everybody strains more forward. Lady cocks her head like a challenged bird or animal. She swallows hard. Honey, it's grown so tense and still here in the yard. Evidence Anne slips off into the garden, gets well clear of mirror's sight and others' hearing. She stands crying, not rightly knowing why. Then—wiping her face on one homespun sleeve—she hurries back. The child understands: This here's her History happening. Mustn't miss a time you know your folks are going to talk about forever.

Evidence finds Lady bent more forward, Lady is about to touch the bluish glass. Something in her upper face has half unfastened. Others murmur, squatting now, heads a-bobbing. Through festered eyes, Lady studies them, she clearly wants to please. Finally she presses one blistered palm across this picture of somebody cooked. A diagonal of lost lanolin smears cold glass. She shifts her head one way then the other—like trying to catch the mirror at some mistake. Watchers recollect these same blue eyes fixing on any slave's serving accidents at dinner parties, hard and strict. "Later," blue eyes had said. This is later.

She now levels the famous stare at her own self. She is seeing *some*thing. Next she squirms so, tries getting away. "Ooh noo you don't. Yeah, folks. It happening," Zelia rubs hands together then holds Lady fast. Everybody packs in closer. Dust under Lady darkens. Nobody mentions it. Bare feet sidestep sudden tributaries.

Then, slow, like scared of being wrong—slouching lower—Lady gives off one questioning sound, checking others' faces. You know the optimistic way a question rises at its end?

"Yeah. It you. You *now*. Ain't she smart?" Z slaps a thigh. And Lady—maybe troubled by being laughed at, maybe (thanks to pain) starting to understand she's still alive—turns her head aside and does something strange.

For the first time since the fire, whilst gazing up and around at the faces grinning down on her, leaning back against the quarter's wall and twisting far aside in hopes of losing the mirror, she cries. But everybody later swore—what rolled out them tear holes was purest black—jet pearls tipping down either cheek. A matched set—one moving faster than its mate. Poisoned through and through with all that this plantation has become—blackness empties from her eyes, bitter half-pints just gushing.

NOW FOLKS can leave. It's the sign they've waited on.

Freed people wander, a last tour of woods and the root cellar where certain punished kinfolk died. One yellow-headed Yankee boy gallops up on a sorrel, seeking provisions. He rides right past the blackened lady cringing away from a mirror's plank of light. He sees a headcloth slipped back showing a pitiful stubbled dome. Boy calls from his horse, "How you faring, Mammy? Where's the grub at?" Blinking, she don't answer. "Now now, act nice to Robbie. After what my people did for your people, what'll you give us?" Shrugging—he's gone. Others, watching, can ease out of the woods again. They lift their bundles.

"Time come, Mrs. We the last," Castalia announces. "Off for to seek our fortune." Cassie's tone rolls out amber-sounding, round-edged. "Afterwhile, you ever come up to New York City town, New York the State? why, you and me can go riding on a red trolley car together, side by side, shopping, everything. By the time you get there, I gone know the whole map of streets. New York a island inside rivers. We go down look at the boats. Cas might save up for riding on one. Sail home to Africa, a garden that'd sure put *this* weed heap to shame. So, bye, place. We done lived here for White plenty long enough. —Lady, seems like I ought to tell you something. But now, Cas can't for the life of her remember what that be. Oh well. Just . . . Bye."

Around Lady, children now pile tiny unripe fruit from her orchard.

"Here," says Baby Venus, "these you apples. Growing yonder, them's collards. We trained you to cook greens, remember? —So long, good luck. Seem like you gone need it. Us too, probly."

The little ones have gathered pebbles. White rocks are held to be the rarest hereabouts. Pale pinks and yellows get lined up nearby—a circle, like for keeping back wild animals or spirits. Evidence Anne sets down one pet cricket in a jar. Propped nearby, the snaggletoothed keyboard. One framed family coat of arms is settled closer as a charm and badge. Two women, holding sacks, run over, aim the mirror more direct at Lady. A bright oval plays across her scrubby surface. With one hand, she shields her eyes. She moves to pad away from such glare. But the two women—easy as you'd block a toddling child—drag her directly back. They press their former owner face to face with glass.

Old Zelia stubs off first, not saying bye to nobody. Halfway cross the red Chinese bridge, she pivots, drags clean back uphill to Lady, bends nearer, takes up Lady's matted left hand. Seems Z is asking for some final handshake or a Lady benediction. "You all got my son drownded that time he try and run off. Your momma, her momma, and now you done kept Miss Zelia busy here for all these years. You all made me do what I wouldn't of, could I of picked. Starting, I was smart. How you gone pay Zelia back for Zelia's long life, Missy? You didn't know it but, ma'am? you never could afford me. Well, Z gone hep you try. Them others got they whole young lifes left them. Zelia's nearbout gone."

It's the ring she's after, twisting hard. She jerks this hand like it's a glove she might could peel off, tote to Falls, and hock. But fire's done got so close. Scar tissue is confused—gold band and diamond all scrambled with skin, scab, finger bone. Ring won't budge. So, snorting, Z finally lets the wrist drop. Swearing, she stomps away. Lady, distracted, lifts that hand, studies where she's just been touched.

Then Old Zelia's going for good. Judge More's early mistress is seen to hobble over the bridge spanning soot-clogged ponds. On the far side, she stoops at a gardenia bush, takes up a missing ham. Under one arm—Z lugs the single prize she's managed claiming (and only by cheating others). Lady Marsden ordered that this delicacy must be kept back till her soldier son marched home victorious. A hog would have to serve as Confederates' fatted calf.

Miss Zelia can barely hold on to the salted slippery thing. She hauls it tipped against her in one arm, crooked there like a infant. It's what she's got after eighty years—her severance-type pay. —Z onct diapered Lady. Zelia nursed the fretful pretty child (while Z's own son, Lady's half brother, cried in his hammock for what milk was left). Now, making a right turn, bound for Falls, Zelia only thinks to spit on the roadside. Hard. Twice.

Castalia tells the children, "Hold hands, get ready." Ex-slaves planned taking along the furniture but without no horse to pull a cart, with most of the saved things being such good size, you couldn't lug enough today to make it worth your trouble. Only six miles to freedom, but six walked miles are still six miles. (Along the route to Falls, they'll see Marse Mabry's grandfather clock, heaved into a ditch and jumped on, splintered to matchwood.)

Folks did save, from under tarps, one gold cigarette box shaped like a scallop shell, half heavy as a cannonball. They left the green enameled frog, them hand-blown swans and gondolas, the Turkey carpets yet flying in trees for any takers.

. . .

EACH PERSON'S brung along one green-banded demitasse and saucer of Spode: this stuff was always easier to clean than the silver. It is yet so pretty you can't quite blame *it* for everything. People carry all the gifts Lady gave— busted castoffs and a few good birthday ones. Tucked into a tow sack, the Wedgwood gravy boat Castalia broke when she was ten and got so lashed for. It's been mended with such care it looks less spoilt than Cassie's back where the lashes' curving marks still show. Rumors along the river claim: Lady onct handed a jewel to the slave girl that admired it. Cassie wears the item today—a small ivory brooch, a miniature: some English gent's favorite hunting dog, and behind the hound's bristled ears, a great house painted, half hid, in mist.

Who can say what waits in Falls? Nobody here's got a lick of money. Ain't one person leaving now that's ever held more than three coins at a time. In Falls, there'll be no ready place to live. These people's skills are whatever slavery's trained them for. If they do have a genius, it might be their gift for necessary acting.

Slaves leave because they can. Considering rumors of in-town hangings, of household guards and squatters' villages, they're scared to set off, sure. But, honey, they're ashamed of having stayed out here this long.

Castalia lifts Baby Venus to her shoulders. The group stares down on a certain little woman. Her upturned face is flaking like a pane of isinglass. "It gone sing come night," Evidence Anne points at the cricket jar. "That might could help you through."

Then everybody moves away. Lady E. More Marsden is yet propped— her itchy back rests against stucco. She is left near a cook pot, a tin ladle for water, the busted keyboard, a glassed needleworked coat of arms, one overly life-sized mirror. Close by, the pebbles, a jar, some baby apples. This will have to be her kit for the world. She leans against the quarter's chamber her husband used as his famous "nap" chamber. To this spot, he brought the young slave girls who helped him rest at midday.

Honey, Lady's "people" became, for a while, her people—the only ones. Now off they trudge. She squints, seems to try and concentrate. Her split lips work, trying parts of words. Some women on the Chinese bridge turn back, others won't, two swear long curses against the place, its owner. All children wave, not knowing no better. Xerxes, feeling fully hisself again— the sieve that others elegantly pour through—signals at Lady in her own old manner. It is that spare-your-energy hand jiggle Lady learnt from a Godey's magazine, proving: being royalty ain't easy. You can say that again.

Spying others' exit, Lady goes even stiller. Her eyes are working better, more able to find middle distances. Slow, she shifts one bone arm, she lets that wrist rise. First the hand appears to point, accusing. Her brow knots. She then tries copying Xerxes' copy of her. She's trying hard to keep her people in view. She seems to partway guess she's being left. She knows enough to want to stop it.

Castalia looks back just in time to see the former mistress manage. Lady has specialized in lush hellos, quick exits. Does she think she can woo folks back to help her? Does courtesy always hide a command? Cassie tells the children, "She alone now." Everybody understands, in Lady's forty-three years the woman has never spent one solitary night here on these grounds. She's now waving so careful. Arm held in place, only the wrist gives a sidelong clockwork jiggle. Zelia, a good ways off, shifts, spies this last try at grandness. Yelling nothing, but yelling it real loud, Z gallops back to the property line, nearly drops her ham, yanks up many blooming roadside tulips, bulbs and all. Others join her, carrying flowers off, tossing them down, jumping on them for good measure. Ain't no horse to steal and furniture's too heavy. A few road's edge lilacs have stayed unsinged. But won't nobody touch these. (Forty years from now, the scent of lilac sachet sold downtown at Lucas' All-Round Store will still turn these women's stomachs.)

Children wave as long as they can, long as mommas'll let them. Lady, noticing, tries to blow them the kisses she onct awarded guests arriving in white pleasure boats.

The huddled group strides away in sun. Their heads are lifted, their shoulders set. They are taking broad steps with such sudden strength. Buttoning their tattered clothes to the neck (one way of getting formal for town), they help each other along. Folks march off double-file. Today they're real particular about how they look. The post road twists then disappears into deep-shadowed evergreens. And on it, so do they.

Uphill, alone, and until dark, Lady keeps steadily waving. Her left hand must soon prop up the right elbow. She continues trying. It's a mechanical signal, only half understood even to itself. And yet she does it, does it.

Soon, dew. The night gets her. She's lost somewheres inside of that. And still she tries and wave. She nods off, exhausted, wakes, signals towards nothing for a while. As promised—that trapped cricket sings. But its icy noise gives little comfort. Locked up, the bug sings just one piping question, particular and familiar. It sings, "Why *me*? Why *me*? Why *me*?"

19

MAYBE it's "cheap" to bust in here and say so, honey, but you know Little Xerxes? Well, he would become famous. He appeared as a vaudeville sand dancer/mimic playing the Albee circuit thirty-odd years down the pike. Taking full credit for inventing hisself, he dropped "Marsden" but kept the made-up-sounding "Little Xerxes." (His moniker later trailed a REG. U.S. PAT. OFF. Famous for copying others, Xerxes didn't plan on nobody's doing that to him.)

In Raleigh, during a museum trip when I was ten, my folks took me to see him. Xerxes was headlining at the Gold Leaf Theatre (named for tobacco, the quietly cancer-causing cash crop then). Small-town life is such that my own parents bought tickets just because this starring black man hailed from Falls or near it—just because they knew Captain Will Marsden good enough to speak to him downtown.

Xerxes' name run second from the top. Fine print claimed he was fresh home from entertaining the Crowned Heads, whoever they are. Riding a long drumroll, he twirled out dancing to beat all. By now grown to five foot even, he was a black/white pinwheel whirring/grinning inches off the floor. Now forty, his hair'd turned white as if cornstarched. His pointy child's-sized white shoes were so shiny. White satin tails, white top hat, white bow tie, something to see. Only his hands and face showed very brown/blue/black. —Theater!

Xerxes strewed his own danced path with sand from out his pockets, white sand—fine and store-bought as any Mall pet-shop aquarium's. His whirligig entrance drew a great mild roar and sigh from black people in their separate balcony above us. They were invisible but tremendously heard, being our immediate roof.

Xerxes talked straight at us—confiding, leering—all while pinching yet more friction-cutting whiteness from deep pockets. He tossed it like Diamond Jim flinging fat-man tips—like we were the ducks and swans floating on our dark pond and he was feeding us from up yonder on that lighted shore. Soft white dance slippers did continuously whisper over powder—easy, sleepy, skillful, secret. My. He soon commenced to imitating all the big politicians and show folks of our day.

Unlike your usual show-business whitey (black-faced to mime blacks), Xerxes, doing whites, never stooped to paint *his* black face pale. Didn't need to. Where was the art, the sport in that? Ooh, *his* white folks made you want to cry, "Yes, but . . ." Made you feel worse than blacks must of done, seeing some half-drunk cracker in burnt cork play Uncle Happy-Go-Lucky.

Xerxes' whites were locked and vain and limited, not meaning to be, hardly noticing. He did "The Belle," floppy as a fileted perch, and yet . . . half dignified, dry. Commercial gents in our audience—the prewar gentry's loud moneyed replacements—howled, "Just *like* them." As if the old-time landowners had already become a strange and comic race all to theirselves.

Xerxes' paleface copies were dead accurate—a good surgeon that's already cut you and is washing up across the room when you ask, "Sir? uh, has it started yet?" Xerxes kept each portrait small and short, a wicked series he lined up, like a row of perfect clocks. He left grandness for his own hostly manner that framed each weak white subject. Little Xerxes never mimed one black person, funny or not. Some white folks claimed that, when it came to doing colored people, Xerxes couldn't. Black folks said he wouldn't.

Since I was only ten, Xerxes' impressions of famous whites stayed Greek to me. But I did notice that even my momma giggled (a accomplishment), though she did it into a hankie (like being sick). Poppa, a amateur-hour comic hisself, sat shaking his head, muttering, saddened, "It's beyond anything. He's way better'n me. A whole different class. How does he *do* it, you reckon? Mirrors? Don't you figure he must just live in front of mirrors?"

"Practice," Momma whispered from behind her white hankie nested in a whiter glove. "And remember, Samuel, he *needs* this. Both for a living and as possible revenge. I mean, he *has* to be better than a contented, privileged person such as yourself."

"Is *that* what I am? Well, hot dog. You know, I been wondering!"

A braid-chewing child remembers this best: At stage's right and left stood the American flag and a North Carolina state one. Dancing, mid-imitation, nearing his act's smooth end, Xerxes seemed to suddenly notice the Stars and Stripes. He sand-skated hippety over alongside the flag. Seemed he'd sneaked up on a live vain white person who'd most hate being copied.

One broad sandman grin widened Xerxes' face—you seen Idea flare off over his head. His act won't a bit like your usual banjo and bones high jinks from them days. His dignity was such—it seemed he'd paid admission to see and giggle at us white ticket holders. (Unlike Poppa and me, Xerxes always underplayed.) For him, in black and white, every motion seemed ink-brushed, shorthand, semi-Japanese.

He straightened beside red/white/blue. One cheap-gilt eagle set atop the varnished pine stave. You seen Xerxes check out a flag entire, then—tip to bottom—copy it one feature at a time. He froze, by half-inches. His head went Eagle—big old ears sticking forth like wings almost. Doing slanted stripes, one shoulder canted high, the other flagging, slackened. Tuxedo tails hung twin pennant-dividends behind. He went onto a single foot and stuck there, face being eagle, chest a proud tired angled cloth, leg the pole of all. What is a flag but a sheet, percale, appliquéd? Just a sheet, but it expects you'll go to war and die over its three simple colors. Well, honey, by the end, I was ready to Pledge *him* Allegiance.

Sure, there'd been other flags on other stages—but someway you felt this was the first night Xerxes had noticed. Seemed like the two of you had thought this up together. He'd become It. And his being It so perfect made you wonder all the more who He must be!

Closing—Xerxes tippy-tapped over, spilling diamondy glitter like the tracks his wit left. He did the state flag, fast—making it the shyer local wife of a bolder better-traveled national one. Then off the stage he pinwheeled, spotlit, spinning.

Someway you knew he'd learnt this the way the best things get learnt—by using all of it to stay alive as hard as a body can. Try learning to tap-dance on the edge of a windy cliff. Either you really will, child, or you really won't.

AFTERWARD, my folks and me hurried to the stage door. Though this happened in December, we willingly waited outside for what—to a child—seemed ages. Everybody's winter breath showed white—even black folks', kept off to one side. Momma uncapped her best pen so Mr. Xerxes Reg.

U.S. Pat. Off. might sign our 5¢ souvenir program. Eighty people milled around, one wit in each group feebly trying and imitate His recent imitations.

Underlings bustled out first, clearing the way. A silence done resulted. After a goodly sobering wait, the star attraction finally appeared. He looked the size of a serious child. He wore one ice-creamy Cheshire-cat white fur coat tossed casual around his shoulders. His neck trailed a white silk scarf, its fringe almost touching alley's cinders but not quite, not quite.

Following Xerxes was a tall beauty, a high-yellow boy carrying white calfskin valises, plus two tissue-paper megaphones binding dozens of white roses. Black admirers, rowdy earlier, hushed as if some spirit had drifted by. The sandman glided in a private party of local whites, rich-looking Raleighites joking overloud to entertain him. The star smiled a lidded little Buddha smile but sure seemed bushed from what he'd just offered us. By now, even Xerxes' ugliness seemed another angle in his smart exotic plan. He appeared a person made milder, kinder by a lifetime's steadying respect. You saw he expected years more of it.

He floated by, all foamy fur, the armada of whites setting off Xerxes' rare dark. He was being escorted to Black Bottom's Chitterling Palace, Raleigh's one colored gin joint where your wilder wealthy white folks sometimes slummed.

Poppa jammed our program forward but too late. "Maestro would prefer not." The flower-bearing boy sure sounded Yankeefied and pure. Others near us seemed disappointed too. One rawboned white man called, "Who *pays* for it?" then whispered a bad word. The fellow seemed to forget he'd just waited thirty-odd minutes to see this particular wizard of that particular race. "Now now," my mother let the rude man hear her scolding.

But to us she said, "Well, I like *that*."

"No, we mustn't mind," Poppa told her. "He's a real busy man, he's earned the right to be. —I think it's definitely mirrors. Yeah, instead of a mind he's got him a . . . magnifying mirror. Can't *start* stuff, just gives back. It's a service he pervides us. —Still, truth is, some mirrors are better'n others."

I probably picked the wrong place to break in and tell this, Miss Beale, but at my advanced age a body can get so artful in waiting for the perfect opening, she forgets to recall it ever again. So—slid in on friction-cutting sand, here, pinwheeling—it is, was, is. Taa-daa.

20

A MANSION takes weeks burning to the ground. Fire, that superior unworkman, leveled the Big House two years and one month faster than sixty skilled slaves had took to build it. In The Lilacs' quarter come night, Lady (if we can still call her that and we can, child, can't we?) would hear another wing of the house finally give way—one uprushing splinterish din. Red sparks spiraled far above the litter. Then, head moving so slow, long after all uplifted ash had settled, minutes past new kindling dumping onto red coals for yet more chatty burning—Lady would register the sound, her scarred face slowly turning that way four minutes late.

She stayed sane enough to find a walking stick, to search out staples, to gimp around the place on her burned soles. She'd crab her way from the quarter where she felt safest—out into a weedy slave garden. She'd been left to get along on greens her slaves had grown to feed theirselves. White cabbage butterflies (one black spot per wing) daily made lace of collards. Lady accepted them as fellow diners, her company, co-workers.

Most hours, she just sat, her eyes closed, trailing sun around the quarter's foreyard. In olden days, except for clock-winding Thursdays, she rarely woke before noon. Now, wrapped in grimy percales, Lady M. would climb the hill above the former barn to wait for dawn's first heat. When it found her, she made sated back-of-the-throat sounds—greeting. Times, she waved due east. Times, she seemed to think that Day itself, a gentleman caller, had come here just to see her.

She sometimes noticed the sheets' embroidered overlapped initials. She mistook these for a spider, she'd whimper, twist aside, use a handy stone to beat at her name's letters. Exploring, lost in the woods, she onct found a cave. In the poplar grove, Lady happened on a great green tarp. When she saw—poking out from under the cloth—a blond claw holding a brass ball—she went crying off splashing across the brook. Smoke from the mansion's foundation always helped lead a person home to her slave's quarter.

Lady's burned feet soon grew infected, she learnt to get around by walking on the sides of them, by depending more on her stick, partly crawling on all fours. Her hands and knees, tops of feet and fronts of ankles, soon grew nicked then callused. Afternoons, she'd settle in daylight (like a duty) picking at the scars. Her features seemed caulked almost neutral by such burns. The surface of her face was like ceramic, a clay mask some half-talented child might make—the usual two eyes, one nose, one mouth, but recognizable mostly as a pounded *try* at looking human.

Lady's drinking water has always been hauled from the artesian well yonder. Till children showed her, she didn't know how such a thing quite worked. She still doesn't rightly know. Just onct—while courting young Dr. Marsden—she'd paused here long enough to throw some coins down its cool stone mouth. Her black folks, piqued and moody, watched good money fall, hoping a penny or two might find the bucket.

Now, instead of fretting with well's rope and pulley, Lady just caned herself downhill, moving almost on ankles to spare her soles. Giving up on the stick, she then crawled the last sixty feet. It could take her twenty minutes getting to the nearest roadside lily pond. She would settle at one edge, she'd ease her lower face into dark water, sipping sipping, a mind not much bigger than its present thirst. Her mouth in, bloodshot eyes moved—constant—

side to side across the water's surface. Like expecting to be prevented even from this comfort. Drinking with great slurping sounds, not aware of offending anybody, she just bent here drinking—watchful, animal, innocent.

THIS SIDE of Falls, Castalia and them others found refuge by the river. They soon discovered: Whites who'd owned best houses still owned those, and pretty well planned to continue, thank you very much. When Zelia, ham under one arm, creaked up the front walk of the downtown mansion she'd chose as the site of her at-home Mondays—when she got rudely stopped by two young black fellows holding rifles—the old woman quick invented the name of some local white family she was seeking. Then, hoisting salted pork, old Z about-faced, fast.

She later admitted: The only name that'd come to her when challenged: Marsden. Telling this to Castalia and the rest, Zelia cried while laughing— swearing, cackling, angered, striking her own upper legs. Others sat watching, surprised.

Z had been forever famous for her absentminded mistakes. Early on, she figured: Lady would love owning somebody even more forgetful than herself. But nobody could rightly remember Zelia's ever *admitting* to a slip-up, much less crying over it. Now, some strange perfectionist was showing up in their slouchy toothless Z. This awed them others. They studied Zelia's torment over speaking "Marsden" when cornered. They watched bony fists beat fleshless thighs. Cassie reached out, stopped her, "It ain't just you, Z. Don't *blame* youself so bad, gal. You didn't cook all this up."

Getting to Falls, Z had refused speaking to The Lilacs' other black folks. Walking quick, she'd led them down the road, not onct glancing back—not helping to shepherd the children, tending only her own excellent mood and heavy ham. Onct arrived downtown, others had seen Z shuffling back and forth in front of high-priced shops, avoided by white and black passersby, talking vividly at herself, peering into the braggart windows of Lucas' All-Round Store, seeking what? Something new to buy? But after two days, the old woman finally did sidle over, join them. Z threw down scrappy leavings of the home-cured ham. Children sure pounced. Seemed Zelia'd already eaten about sixteen pounds' worth in forty-eight hours. Freedom's mighty hungry-making.

Was then, flopping down, Zelia told them how it burned her up: offering Lady's password name to them first guards. Others felt pleased to try and soothe her. She'd never permitted that before. Maybe she had acted different as a girl. Everybody'd heard tell how handsome Z'd onct been during Judge More's youth (meaning her own). But it sure seemed doubtful—with no tintype nor oil picture to prove her beauty. (Some poor folks' tragedies is having no more proof of early looks and health than what their present bodies show. Which, honey, speaking for my own photo album of ouches here, don't seem near evidence enough.)

Miss Z explained: she'd already found work, cleaning a funeral home.

Others give each other side glances. How quick their oldest one had got her city bearings! Seemed Z was finally coming to, growing up—at eighty-one. When praised, she only shrugged, made a mouth. "In Z's mind, Z been getting steadily ready right along. Sure done had sufficient *time* to. Anyhow, you can't grow your wings while you up in air using them, can you? No, a body wants to sprout her set some seasons before. Get them like you wants them. Grow you some that's stiff as buckram, smooth as ice, as looking glass. Then, airy time come on, you holler, 'Don't *push* me no more,' and off and up you goes. By then you got forty ostrich-feather dusters corn-rowed under you either arm, helping to row you properly up. —Oh yeah, I had to molt a many a mountain of feathers before I got to use this last fine set. You looking at one old bird what has *flown*," and she made elbows do like wings. Z rocked back laughing (ackle-ackle) as others stared hard at her—understanding, not understanding—but laughing along. Children jumped up, ran circles with their strong young arms out straight. "I right high up. How high up is you?" Venus asked Evidence.

OTHER freed slaves kept wandering in from sundry county plantations. Hundreds of ragged folks unseen till now, hundreds that you'd someway felt were out there, being owned on other farms. The sense of them yonder had given ballast to your every lunge and hunger, each irk and chore matched yours. They shared your secret craving for this finally flying free.

Most now camped in a single riverside marsh. Odd how geography can say the same thing to so many promised-land strangers at onct: "*Here*." Was a place somebody must own but didn't nobody claim. Nobody but mosquitoes. The joke here run: One ex-slave was woken by hazy whisperings in her shack's corner—she seen two bugs as big as German shepherds and smart enough to talk that over. The one bug buzzzzes, "Should we ought to eat her here or carry her back?" Other one goes, "Here. Cause you know what'll happen if we tote her home? Them big ones'll get her."

The very day black folks arrived in Falls, they scattered, seeking jobs downtown and along fancy Summit Avenue. They used many a polished brass door knocker: ones shaped like pinecones, ladies' hands with rings on, Greek goat gods' smirky horny heads. Some of these showplace homes hired up to three laundresses to primp a family of four. One heavy-bodied Christian black woman with a good singing voice and steady disposition, age fifty-one, mother of eight—her duty: ironing four daily changes of puff-sleeve crinolines for a white child, three.

Little Xerxes auditioned as third-to-the-top shoe-clean boy at Stark's Scissor Tonsorium. For starters, entering the place, he tugged out his hankie ascot so it'd serve as a funny little sudden barber bib. Right hungry, eager to be hired, he told a joke (about mosquitoes), then he done some sailor hornpipe steps (God know where he learnt *that* on The Lilacs—maybe from his folks who'd seen the boatmen what had brung his kin from Africa?).

His jig occurred among tile floor's dark and white and blondy curls. His jig swept white-man fleece into a tidy pile—artful, useful.

Little Xerxes then offered imitations of the two barbers presently clipping. Since one of these fellows was fat and loud, the other all boned and prissy, Xerxes' deeper skills won't really called into play (nor will Lucy's, sugar). The child ventured copying each barber in ways that brung cheap if ready laughs. And Xerxes done it all without offending them too mortally. (A art in itself, getting folks to recognize theirselves without your forcing them to go jump off some bridge.)

Xerxes wisely refrained from "doing" Old Man Stark. The boss, appreciating such tact, went, "I reckon this little blackamoor just copied *you*-all to a tee, hunh, Shep and Edgar? Be a fine one to have around if we can keep it from aping the customers. Little joke there. You're hired. Stay this cute and you'll earn your way, Shinola." If Little Xerxes ever planned to quit being funny, he figured he couldn't exactly afford to try that just yet, child, not quite yet.

Cassie, already fighting to save up her New York City fare, soon done extra ironing (piecework) for the Mayor's second cousin. By nights she helped scrub and sweep the understocked aisles of Lucas' All-Round Store. Castalia found a dwelling place for The Lilacs' skeleton crew. It was well made, pine. It'd housed First Baptist's new grand piano when that got shipped from Philadelphia before the war. Cas and Zelia and three other women and all their children carried, dragged, and rolled the crate end over end (with rest breaks) from back of Lucas' clear to the river encampment one mile downhill. They decorated it with the late Cousin Mabry's late peacock's tail feathers. Emerald-green Spode demitasses and a Wedgwood gravy boat hung from nails (bent just so) hammered with Z's shoe sole.

Was here, at the base of a hummock topped by famous Summit Avenue and its thousand elm saplings, ex-slaves gathered. Here they'd someday build their real-life houses. (Once such homes looked done, the owner of this tract—quiet for so long—would arrive to collect back rents.) And right here, ex-Marsden slaves would one day use the same piano crate to coop fat chickens while I, a child of eleven, rocking a porch rocker, asked some hard strict questions.

This riverside community got known, even in its camptown squatter days, as Baby Africa. Whites in passing wagons studied the heavy mist from evening rags burnt to keep your biggest mosquitoes away. Whites studied the settlement's thatch and boxes—huts set into three wide circles amongst high grass. They saw black women washing white folks' clothes on river rocks, they saw naked babies running unsupervised, spearfishing all day for dinner. Whites claimed it looked like their idea of something pretty doggone tribal, some kind of Africa, but a baby one. And freed slaves, set loose to reinvent who-all they'd be (at least whilst alone together), refound certain habits long considered clean forgot. One ancient blue-black man grabbed some reeds at random, said, "I'm gone weave us a fish trap," and he did and it worked perfect—letting fish in, but leaving no room for their turning around, slipping out. The old one then sat gaping, shocked at his yet having in him: the whole first person he'd been from the whole first nation he had known. History's a raffle. History's a Fire Sale.

Nights, folks gathered near huge burning logs—listening to seasoned ancient ones tell all. Each farm boasted its own genius talker. Some really were. (Ex-slaves from one plantation would promote their own tale-teller as Baby Africa's very best.) The Lilacs' freed folks chose Castalia.

Ex-slaves' stories remembered the Other World. They were right quick to forget a bondage just ended. Stories swarmed with upright animals— clever ones enjoying human traits, beasts forever getting out of terrible binds, like having not no food now, no steady place to live. Even the plaguing mosquitoes got turned real quick into jokes. To stand them: You give the bloodsuckers extra comic credit. You let them fly *and* talk—so when a non-speaker bites you, you can say, "Oh, only this."

Strange that a white man should get famous for first writing down these freed-slave animal tales. But no, not strange at all. Look at young Mr. Elvis, God rest his soul. At age nineteen, and after being born into the cracker race, that child got full credit for personally inventing a hundred and fifty years of black folks' blues. Smart boy.

21

THE WINDOW of Cuthrell's Jewelry/Pawnshop (the very store where Lady's bought spare cogs and her green visor for clock repair, the store where Cap would later find his platinum Swiss replacement watch) it was now a pyr-amid of treasures bought mighty cheap. Here rested a gold scallop-shaped cigarette box half heavy as a cannonball. Venus, Xerxes, and the others would stop here with new little friends, would point through dusty glass whilst saying, low, "That ours."

Seeking extra odd jobs, you soon learnt: In-town bosses had to know who'd owned you till last week. Your old owner's name served as a letter of reference. Didn't matter if your particular bigwig, like Lady out yonder doing God-knows-what, was beyond writing a note concerning your work ways. The black folks who'd hiked from farms too far off, they couldn't find no work till others coached them—offering names from plantations closer in.

Felt shaming for Castalia and Z to get their first paid jobs by mentioning the formerly flashy Lady E. M. Marsden. In town, the woman was disliked and admired because of how few city dwellers ever got invited to her lilac boating parties. Odd, the more snobby your old owner'd been considered, the quicker did in-town whites hire you. Of course, Falls' whites also craved good gossip, juicy news about what-all off-color had gone on in a Greek Revival castle of that size.

Lady's name always brung a nod. "Well, well . . . Judge More's little girl? Spitfire, good skin. Gave each slave a crate of oranges, so we hear. Handed a hen's-egg diamond to one of her girls. Still, a demanding person to work for, I bet. I remember one time she pitched a temper tantrum right in church. Her poppa must've finally whispered about it's being God's house, she yelled at the top of her lungs, 'I don't care *whose* shack it is. I'm p-ssed.' Look, you ain't expecting fruit and jewels on *this* job, are you? And, miss, do you just iron shirts, or do you just *love* ironing shirts? Your old boss make it through the sadness out there?"

"Well, sir, far we know, she ain't dead."

NIGHTS, Zelia straightened reception rooms at Falls' second-best white funeral home. Place smelled of tuberoses, floor wax, and mice. Maybe only a premises-owning mortician can love a darkened funeral parlor at 3 a.m. Zelia's African aunts had filled her head with lore about ancestor ghosts, the nasty dispositions of the dead. "They jealous." Z forever brung along Evidence Anne and Baby Venus to keep her noisy company. These children wouldn't stay out of them display-room coffins. (Girls called the boxes boats. Girls had ofttimes heard Cassie's tale of the big one what'd delivered their relations to this, the Un-world.) Z finally gave up trying to scare kids clear of coffins. She just made them take off their shoes before climbing into white-satin-lined barges. Girls had the natural good taste to prefer the highest-priced ones down at the end—lots more tassels, your extra quilting, and Belgian lacy foot pillows. Comforted by sounds of kids' playing, Z closed the door, scuffed off to dust and polish the heavy thankless receiving-room furniture.

Miss Zelia had refused to clean them tile-lined back chambers where the unhappy "work" got done. "Ain't enough money in all Falls," she crossed her arms. Hearing this, the white owner's spoilt son chose to play a trick on her. One night, he set up this freshly dead fat man on a parlor love seat, nude. About to clean in there, seeing the shape propped yonder, Zelia waited. From the hall, she finally screamed for him to wake right up, get some clothes on, go home. Or else. She finally used her broom with the longest handle. "You drunk? sick? what?" she prodded the sleeper. When he flopped forward onto the marble floor face-first with such a rancid smack, Zelia screamed, "Z knew it, Z been tricked again." She grabbed all personal cleaning gear and, cussing, ran clear to the river, pulling along two little girls who squealed, "What happened? Tell, Auntie Z." Next morning, the prank player was there rapping knuckles on a certain piano crate's top. His daddy'd forced him to come apologize to a cleaner as good as Miss Zelia. Boy's daddy had threatened to make him call on the distinguished dead man's wife, personally explaining how a body, considered extremely deceased since last Wednesday, had hauled off and broke its nose. Z crossed her arms, "Never.

Only if you was to ask me back extra *nice*." "Okay," the boy bent nearer, whispering. "Just don't tell, ma'am."

By day, The Lilacs' children helped do wash. (Shirts 2¢, skirts 4¢, dresses with two or more darts and/or lace sleeves and collars 7¢. Not no exceptions, neither.) Girls strung clotheslines near the riverbank. They stood guard whilst white gentlemen's ghosty business shirts took forever to wave dry. For now, ex-Marsden workers lived in the piano crate. They pulled a tarp over its leakiest end, they found painters' drop cloths to serve as blankets and felt grateful that Freedom had seen fit to find them in mild April. Looking toward coming cold months, they were happy at least for each other's warmth.

Every Saturday night, survivors of the Marsden fire pooled their coins, slowly counting change aloud, learning just what money meant. Most everything. They'd bicker over what to spend on what. Shouting matches broke out. Finally knowing how much the group had, each would slump out into the dark and bury her own wages, only each knew where. —You think these folks were going to stash their savings in a white man's bank?

22

THE VERY first day Cassie migrated to Falls six weeks before, she turned up at a livery stable. It was yet owned and leased by the family Marsden. The blond fellow in charge had a shovel-shaped face and a enamel stickpin. Looked exactly like a shiny-green beetle that just loved grazing on this particular blue necktie.

Castalia squared off with the manager. "Mister, I blonged to Lady Marsden. All The Lilacs' furniture's yet hid a quarter mile off the farm road back due northeast among a poplar grove. It still mostly resting safe under canvas." She ordered him to rush wagons out there before rain spoilt all that finery, hear?

Did Cassie mean to collect a ready cash reward? A starter nest egg for this, the un-world? Was she saving them nice things on behalf of Wee Willie Marsden, CSA, now walking home from a war that—church bells tolling mighty mournful—had just ended? If she hoped to peddle treasures, then why'd Cas come and reported these to family interests? Castalia won't accustomed to driving no bargains. She'd never handled money—none past the two-per-year Christmas coins, plus a half-dollar onct found when raising a bucket out the well. So, after Castalia said her say for this dandy middle-aged horse boarder, she paused, solid shoulders squared—hoping that such information might could be worth something.

The fellow looked over a dark rangy young woman. Well built, a strong grooved neck, features smoothed like something steadily handled and— almost by accident—burnished nice. She won't exactly beautiful but my she looked complete. Hers was a big face that yet expected to be satisfied and didn't yet know as how, in some circles, that never actually happens. She was young. Years of asking permission made her seem younger yet.

The fellow noticed her wild-fox country air, noticed them elbows jammed partway out—ready to help side-jump whatever trick tried hopping her. Her breasts would be pert sour-apple high-riders, thighs round as milled black-walnut logs. She had on men's work boots. At her homespuns' top button, Castalia wore a brooch: some dog's-head painting. The man saw furrowed rows of braids, this crop of loops—a tenant farm of a hairdo. Her bright black asking eyes met his and—after a tussle—his backed off the first. He'd seen others like her, too innocent to be ashamed yet. It made them pitifully attractive. You wanted to help out. That in itself brung them harm. A gent hoped to screen such a girl's decency from *other* gents' wanting some. He would protect his ward from men even worse than him. There always were some. "I'll keep her innocent while getting her a bit readier for the next ones, afterwards. —Broke in good." Oh, don't get me on this subject, honey, really. Neither logic nor kindness got invented by horny small-town bachelors mid-April. You can quote me.

Hands on hips, Castalia cleared her throat and stayed put, breathing, right aware of breathing. The spiffy little manager touched his tiepin, risked winking at her. Man said, "I got a little office in here, little cot back in here. Welcome to Falls, gal."

Castalia give no sign of having heard, none beyond a extra-bored look. Then—in a trick learnt off Z—Cas crossed her arms. The fellow found her all the finer-looking for this show of toughness. And even while trying to get whatever he might off this girl, the man did partly pity her. Complicated, ain't it? Even among con artists, you find all these seasick degrees of fellow feeling.

The manager figured: This slave girl might be basically sharp and stubborn, but she sure had lots to learn. If only she'd walked in here saying, "I know where Lady Marsden's treasure's hid, you maybe interested?" He would've stepped to the till (in a little office with its stained cot). He would have gone, "Let's talk turkey here, miss. I got something you need, you got something I want. *You* might be free now, but everything else cost money. How much it seem worth to you?"

But Castalia hadn't said that. Ain't transactions interesting? I sometimes think that Business is the business of the world. We're all of us negotiating toward *some*thing twenty-four hours a day. Poor Cas was still behaving like a good servant, still expecting rewards for doing things now considered honorable by owners only. She guessed this, but hadn't yet understood the newer rules. And, child, won't nobody exactly rushing out to teach her. So the fellow grinned, rewinked, thanked her. When she still didn't budge, her right foot tapping like a pendulum, the man asked her name, promising she'd someway be rewarded. "You *best* to remember Castalia here," it was all she could think of.

Finally, she did turn, she did leave. She knew she'd just given away her life's one advantage. First she stalked around Meadows' Pasture then she stepped into the alley behind Falls' row of stores. Castalia stared at a wooden wall. She had just handed over thousands of dollars' worth of goods, she'd failed the friends what'd picked her as their talker. "Seem like I just being born, I doing so silly," she struck dry boards. "Ain't rightly fair."

THE LIVERY manager believed her enough so he buggied out that same afternoon, checked. After a little stumbling about, feeling uneasy while touching his beetle stickpin, he found the first floor's loot stashed under poplars in a streamside huddle. He eased canvas off one blond Biedermeier desk, it had more boxes and columns and niches than does many a hillside city. Nearer the brook, one clear-glass life-sized swan curlicued like some ice carving just done. Under the tarp hunched a weirdly real-looking ceramic pug-dog doorstop, goggle-eyed and smug. But here, right within reach, our stable manager saw gleaming on a red red velvet footstool beside a hill of greenest moss: the all-time masterpiece.

One enameled emerald frog rested: its eyes were of beaten yellow-gold, each spot along its back had been lovingly tooled with glimmering copperish ridges—the thing was detailed down to its separate ball-tipped toes. For the visitor, a great admirer of the enameler's art, this frog seemed about the most stealable and splendid thing he'd ever viewed in either Carolina. Breath fusing, the man slowly crouched for it—it hopped straight up in air, plunked into the stream, paddled off. Darling, like to scared that man to death. He needed to sit down. Lucky for him, seventy-odd chairs waited right out here in the woods.

He never glimpsed the other human being yet hid in the uphill quarter— owner of his leased stable, a woman setting cross-legged chewing greens with a great reasoned slowness. Same day, the livery fellow summoned three rental wagons to collect the bounty and he already had it stored in his dry hayloft when a ruinous May downpour broke. The downpour proved to Cassie and the others where their crate home dripped its worst. Somebody joked, "Good day to hie indoors for a fine long game of Catacombs." Relations and friends sat bunched against each other at the carton's driest end. Under their awning, a sour little fire sputtered. Its fumes, timid about getting wet, curled back under, causing all eyes here to water without much noticing.

Since most of the women worked nights, they usually rose around four each afternoon. Their breakfast was discounted day-old Harbison rolls and donuts, plus the tea presently being brewed. Today it had been made from sassafras roots dug by Venus downriver.

High tea had ever been Lady E. More Marsden's favorite time of day. By 4:30 p.m. she was usually fully awake. "I believe warm baths and hot tea *so* help organize a person's thinking, don't you find?" Even when Lady played Catacombs, a teapot in its chintz cozy was slipped under the sheets' hems. If she had no white company on a given day, she invited selected slave women—and young Xerxes—upstairs for "conversation." Topics were assigned: Duty, Immortality, The Transforming Powers of Art, Duty. Rule number one: No giggling.

Lady, It, forever poured.

By now, for freed folks stooped around this fire, 4:30's high tea had long since become necessary and ancient-seeming as any memory of Africa. Castalia's busted Wedgwood gravy boat was well fitted with a new teapot lid bought at Lucas' (employees' discount). This mended piece has got further sealed with river mud. Under smeared brown, you could yet see the original sky-blue white gods gathered, partied, round its sides. Zelia supervised the sugar bowl—a chipped enamel cup. She used tongs fashioned from flat sticks joined by two lengths of leather shoelace Xerxes had brung home.

Lately, that boy didn't sleep here much. He spent most nights on the itchy cast-off customer bibs wadded underneath his shoeshine stall at Stark's. That offered a toastier nest than this. Paydays, Evidence Anne was sent to follow Xerxes everywhere till he shelled over his share of community food money. For fun, he sometimes flipped coins her way just like his clients rewarded him. White fellows had begun standing young Xerxes to drinks, asking him to "do" each of them: tones of voice, rollicking bowlegged walks. Odd, men felt both semi-ashamed and a good bit clearer thanks to the nervous boy's mummery. "So that's me, is it?"—a scratching of the scalp. "How long it take you to figure all that out, Slick? Been watching me right along, I bet. —Oh, *I* see you grinning, Xerxes buddy."

Even when the child slept here in the home crate, even when his friends from Lilacs days begged him for imitations, even if he felt untired enough to give free samples, it just won't the same. Xerxes' new subjects, the big-time somebodies of Falls, were mostly strangers to these women and children living cut off in a box by a mud river. You can't exactly ooh and aah at copies of folks you ain't ever seen. This first audience lately proved right dull for Xerxes.

Finally, one night, bored and eager for some usual appreciation, he agreed to do a last turn as Lady. "Beg me," said he. "Consider yourself begged," Cassie snapped back, proud but eager. The boy had traded in his homespuns for a fine mended once-store-bought cotton shirt. He now slipped out into the night. You could hear him somewhere in the black, clearing his throat, hopping all around getting limber. Others braced, like they were about to once more see the ghost of It. Seemed it was part of the last century, out of date as cornstarched wigs, as boating parties come to view nice bushes.

IN THE low entryway, you-know-who playing you-know-what appeared. He entered the box just like she would, pretending not to notice how low-ceilinged, sad, and smoky it was. "Why . . . you-all have done so much *with* it! Why, it just so quaint. It so . . . you!"

On he went. But tonight, his accuracy only scared the others. Made them imagine her out yonder, haunted, busy being her own guard, her own slave, her own ghost.

Some folks setting here smiled, uneasy. Didn't nobody laugh. Odd, during the months since Xerxes last tried doing Lady, he'd grown weirdly better at it. Being free of her made him more responsible to Lady More Marsden's *facts*. If you watched him close, you'd of noticed his own pleased surprise at the improvement. That was always part of Xerxes in action, the steady joy his talent gave him! Even later, as a pro, backstage, Lady stayed his yardstick, he ofttimes loosened up by lovingly redoing It of Her.

A Falls dweller, the child now understood just how the mistress was like and unlike other rich white women. He saw how her living so isolated on The Lilacs had made Lady behave all the more flibbertigibbety. But— fine as Xerxes did it tonight—the more of a mirror he became, the stiller did his audience grow. They seemed sunk so far into their mixed memories. Finally the big-eared actor flopped down, worn out, hollering, "What *good* are you? Give you the one thing you done ever seen, and you all freeze like you scared to let on really knowing It. —You ain't no *fun* no more, for me." Then he stuck his tongue out and swerved into the dark and back to town.

THIS AFTERNOON'S tea yet steeped as rain got worse. Company was present—a child from the residence next door (seven pickle barrels and one slab of rusted tin nailed overtop). When the brew was judged ready, Cassie poured, such slow hostessy care. Portions threaded into green keepsake demitasses. Thunder made rude claims and counterclaims, rattling—lawyerish—along the river Tar. Big trees lashed nearby littler trees—and vice versa (though the littlest felt it most).

Sipping, the group hushed. Folks felt soothed by this old liquid ritual, but somewhat saddened by it, too. That was part of the pleasure: one pot, the many cups—it linked you. Lightning palsied overhead, children scuttled nearer each other—but slow, not liking to appear afraid of nothing.

"How you reckon she getting on in this?" Z nodded towards puddles darkening a Baby Africa invented of paperboard and branches.

"Bout like us," Cassie answered. "Only worse. We got a future."

Evidence Anne (who would be grandmother to my beloved orderly Jerome, and who'd live long enough to work on the line in a Detroit Chevy plant), she shared her cup with the little next-door neighbor. That boy, son of field slaves from outside Tarboro, considered this ceremony—with its slow cup-filling, with the women's careful sipping—nearbout as strange as any religious rite. The child wouldn't of been surprised to find that yonder gravy boat held molten gold or blood or some sky-blue liquid.

Little Venus looked up at adults, "Do *this* be our at-home day?" Grown-ups laughed, less because they wanted to—more because they couldn't not, child. "Bout as good as any, I reckon," Miss Zelia coughed, shrugging. The worse it rained, the steadier and louder did folks' voices rise over this cloudburst.

They mentioned what might come next. How, onct it finally did happen, what they might get to wear, what they'd maybe finally know enough to finally feel. Each person here had already snagged a few first flirting wingbeats of it. For the visiting boy, it meant: this ritual. For Evidence Anne, the one yellow sour-ball candy bought from out of a great glass globe decaled with the world-map in Lucas' All-Round store. For Cas, it was the freedom of going anywhere you liked along Main, of talking back while wearing a new dress printed with one hundred redbirds. Z felt the rustle of it in sudden shoes that scooped you more toward citizenship—the first high-stepping parade before blisters laid a tax on what's too new. —You got one small thing first, then more, see, until these mosaic-like feathers overlapping, braiding, corn-rowing, rag-rugged into being a body's own personal wings. To let you finally fly free. Was that so much to ask? Did you want a Summit Avenue mansion, or the right to be a meadowlark and go anywheres, luggageless? Might a body request . . . both?

The Young Man Linking was yet semi-expected. Late, sure. But these things happen. Squatting under a tarp that kept filling with heavy rain—using a chopped broomstick to poke its belly-center and spill silver out the edges—their hands pressed cups' warm sides, folks endured the smoke. Even in a storm like this, people canted a bit forward, seeming to half listen. Primed to welcome the huge Giant Him, they would shoehorn Him into this home crate—finally offer Him some tea. Today even the children sat with their chins half lifted—appearing to wait for something good.

Rain flopped, a greater frying roar. The river, having onct turnt red to impress Pharaohs over wrongdoing, now ran black from hundreds of upriver plantation fires. Marsh mist rolled past reeds to shore then snuck into a cramped piano crate.

In her choice back corner, Old Miss Zelia got the croupy shakes again. Venus and Evidence—with the neighbor boy's help—just piled more drop cloths up around her. One night whilst taking a break on the funeral parlor's portico, while cleansing the pince-nez with her apron then looking hard at nowhere like she owned it, Z'd caught some kind of ague that would take her off come August.

Castalia sat coiled nearby wearing a turquoise scarf, a butterscotch-colored shawl, and the rare redbird dress. Cardinals, her favorite, the future state birds of both North Carolina and Virginia. Good choice. Cas kept hoisting its hems up onto her lap, trying and keep cloth clear of mud.

After the livery-stable fellow bilked her, she decided to change, try self-defense. "Something wrong with me. Seem like cheaters can see Castalia coming. I gots to leastway *look* stronger." So she found a pair of cast-off white man's trousers, these matched her farmer's brogans.

(Lady's all-white all-silk clothes had bored Cas very much.) First, she risked a scarf overtop her mannish outfit, then she added copper earbobs. Nice. Finally, she made a last payment on the African-bright getup of choice. Dress, hat, bag, shawl, scarf, pin, shoes. Cas wore it all one whole Saturday up and down Main Street. Her body wound in some bold national flag, she kept glaring at all shoppers she met, daring them not to admire her, and hard. When they did gape at the ten proud contradicting colors, she understood: they envied her, they wondered how she'd found all the nice tints first.

While dressed in mannish homespun slave clothes, Cas had heard Falls' male idlers praise her. Now, done up so, that trail of groans and checkmark whistles slacked. She figured she'd just got too sleek for them. She knew they felt it: she'd quit dressing for *here*. She was living Practice, becoming a Lady of New York City town. They smelled her unslave future. Weak men hated her for it.

(Two months from now, yet living in this crate—a spot by then improved with oiled-paper windows and little home-stitched curtains no bigger than Xerxes' ascots—Cassie, saving for her pricey Northbound fare, will feel right happy to accept temporary work as a full-time maid. She'd got offered work by three families. She was finally glad to be hired by a returned soldier name of Marsden. She hadn't really understood all that much about them other families. At least, she *knew* him.)

HIGH TEA in a piano crate can be a comfort. Folks didn't mention how they would soon head off to clean the homes of local whites—both quick and dead. Didn't seem a worthy topic for no in-town high-tea talk. They failed to chat about old Africa, half a dream now—rich as a dream but hard to translate into table talk. These people had come too far from Africa and way too long ago. They were yet too close to bondage here. So, naturally, they talked about the Future. What else is there, honey?

"You usually take one cube or two, child?" Z hollered to be heard over thunder, asked the silent boy from next door. Tongue-tied, he first shook his head No—then his hand did rise, despite hisself. A single finger lifted. Next, as him and others watched, a second finger—like some snail's dainty stubborn horn—grew beside the first. Others, finding this sign hopeful and familiar, chuckled. Lord but they knew a person's greediness for good things. It could be set alongside your seriously doubting your ever getting much. Before Cassie repoured, Zelia took the boy's Spode cup, she rolled in three rattly cubes like dice. "Child—don't you worry none. You our guest. Long as we gots sugar, you gone drink sugar."

Sipping, he settled back, eyes half closed, hardly believing this here luxury. Such fancy talking, such sharp red-winged patterns, the real peacock feathers Xed on one wall. What ladylike refinement: strong brown hands using tea things. Honey, to this boy, awed at being here, all this seemed too good, too fine to really happen in this our world of mud.

Folks sipped, waited, mapped it all out. They seemed to know the Future far better than anything they'd lived through so far.

Friends leaned back, staring noplace, hands curled half prayful around small English teacups held real close against their chests. They seemed so willing to wait it out, they'd chose to hang on just a few days longer.

He was coming. It was coming. Who was coming? What?

THEY CALLED it By-and-By, child, By-and-By.

IN ENDING

SO, to tidy up our paper's end—settle the freed folks near the river Tar at their piano crate's warmest end, please. Set the lady of the house, the ex-house, into puddled ruts of her freed slaves' garden. Place her son on his own two feet. He's a ex-soldier, it being late May of the year of Appomattox. Have him getting home from all that mess as best he can. Lilac bushes that outlived the fire show new green. Crusts of brown foam still hang ragtag here and there proving, yes, trees tried blooming earlier this year.

Now, do like you're a bird. You *can* here, darling. Go on up, it's a freebie. Paddle high, then hold—tipping—semi-quiet in pure county air. Look leisurely down upon the muddy crossroads, footpath shortcuts, farmers' cemeteries set within their choicest upland fields. From here, what stares back up at you is like some comfortable and tragic face you've always known. Its features are scars. A face plowed till it understands: Living means steadily learning to live on. The most you can hope for is a life sentence.

Nearer town, the settlement of black squatters shows. Six miles off, a figure plunked out in her garden gasps during rain. Along the river's twist, see great black bite marks where plantations stood. Then notice a getting-home soldier, seeking shelter from the rain, dodging under tobacco barns' tin roofs. Each force and person of the old days moves back toward each other, old strands, new knot. Everything seems so simple from up this high. In fact, it's so simple it's impossible to understand. So spoon on down, settle on a fence post, tilt your head, fake being just another watchful meadow-lark—draw nearer the last things we must see to end this right.

The King is in his countinghouse counting out his money.

The Queen is in the parlor eating bread and honey.

Lady's been gnawing final collards. Moving row to row, using her stick—everyplace she goes she pulls the heavy needleworked family crest behind. Does she consider this a pass card like the ones she signed so her slaves might ride for supplies in Falls, might slide past owners' patrols? Nights, she must abide the sounds of large-bodied animals scratching, trying and get at her in the quarter. Lady's been forever accustomed to third-floor safety. Now, one hour before sunset, she must begin to pull the logs and branches across her shelter's door. One hour past midnight, she'll hear the first arrive. Their snorts and snufflings sound as hungry as *she* feels. Lady, after trying a long time, finally finds her voice, screes straight up, something like "Who, who?" Some beasts scurry off. Others—hearing—only paw the harder to get at her. Mornings she finds fresh burrows dug half under her barricade. Are these dogs, raccoons or wolves or foxes, rabid Yankees? Is it the Bogey Ghost of the Swamp that young overseer Winch onct jokingly confessed inventing? Now she believes in it.

Most neighbors that've chanced onto The Lilacs' grounds consider Lady either dead or spirited off to Falls. Some owners out this way were killed—most by fires, a few as freed slaves' first act. From her hiding place in the woods, Lady hears one young woman call her name. Lady onct offered this girl a beauty tip about a person's always moving, white, amidst a guarding armada of oiled dark torsos. Lady bends still lower in the elderberry bush, stays out here till dark, long after her neighbor's given up and buggied off.

Sometimes just at dawn, once she's dug free of the quarter's barricade, the Widow Marsden goes on her cane, moving back and forth in the burned home's side yard. Her soles keep testing wet grass before her, toes scything through the green. Like a person who has dropped—into high weeds—her only house key and is now hunting the one item that might let her back, back in.

Not two months after the fire, her son enters Nash County. He moves along the highroad towards his home. He has passed the other showplaces, burned. Cool Spring and Ashland. Willie was once boated by slave oarsmen to fellow rich kids' birthday parties, to the docks of all these homes, with Uncle Primus posing, hand in shirt, at the Marsden rowboat's helm.

Now, passing burned familiar gatehouses, Will won't let hisself quit hiking—he just trudges on. He knows he will be finished once he stops. "Mustn't expect," the gawky ex-soldier tells hisself. "Mustn't even *mind* its being gone. Why should ours be different?" Almost home, he's scared that he'll be recognized. When he hears a wagon coming, Willie jumps off the road. Hides in a ditch. He spent last night at the edge of a lake, standing up—stunned after one half-glimpse of a certain spindly somebody reflected in the water. Oh, to be home. On land you own, who can really criticize you?

Before he turns a bend that gives all southbound travelers their full and sudden view of The Lilacs set uphill among its famous hedges, before he braces hisself for a vista that makes many first-time passersby pause here, Will Marsden says aloud, "I believe there's not one stone's left on another stone." And nods to prove he feels this, and deep.

He knows he won't be savoring the foreground's red Chinese half-moon bridge crossing double lily ponds that barbell out to either side. Bridge won't lead now to a winding white stone drive bordered by famous lilacs and—three hundred yards up on the slope—the drive will not now curl around the big white place fronted by four guarding marble pillars. No. Portico ain't likely to be there, shielded and half hid back of five humongous magnolias. Gone, the windowed dome—his mother's bedchamber conservatory—topping all. Nope. —And Will accepts this. He does. Having hoboed clear home from Virginia, ignorant of how he's grown eight inches taller in the last two months, with so many dusty miles to warn hisself from hoping, how easy he can picture all that's lost.

So the haggard boy says in advance, "Nothing, I expect. Less than that." Stronger for speaking this aloud, he takes a goodly breath, he turns the last bend, he stares. He falls down in the road.

THEN—so tired—Willie, on his back in wagon ruts, laughs onct.

Setting up, brushing at hisself—he uses a good stick he's found, gets to his feet. Struggling to appear almost jaunty (for whose sake?), Willie nears a red bridge. First he tests it, pressure from one home-rolled "shoe," a leather upper wound with strips of gunnysacking. The bridge holds, which is something anyways. Underneath it, cup-shaped white water lilies are ribbed with soot, spotted like decayed teeth.

Will calls his mother's name. "Expect nothing," he reminds hisself. But once he's nearer the mansion's smoldering foundation, he's already calling her so loud. Willie climbs up onto a flagstone veranda. (How high its steps look, leading, like they do, to nothing now.) Willie stares straight down. Only whilst bellowing her name does he hear how his own voice had deepened. First he shouts "Lady," then "Mother," finally "Momma." The boy trots everyplace, choppy little visits, dodging into here and out of there.

Moving fast as his raw feet allow, Private Marsden even stumbles through woods towards a little woodside cave. He's always considered it his secret. Nights at the front before a coming battle, Will would sometimes picture this here tunnel, its hidden drippings steady as a tent dweller's dream of mansion clocks. He ofttimes wished that, in 1861, he had just slipped inside this den. Will could have lasted out the war here, happy to be a coward, a deserter and wise man. Think of all he might have learnt if—for every minute that he'd felt fearful these long years—he'd been snug here reading, getting stuff straight, making up his mind. He could've maybe become a hardworking scholar like his late dad who ofttimes mentioned Aristotle's owning thirteen slaves, Plato fifteen.

Soon Will has checked most everyplace but the slave quarter. Will never once saw his mother out here—except during state visits, a few christenings. Stooping at its door—"Have I grown?"—he ducks into a single long low bunkhouse. Sixty-odd people slept here—so many died and born in this one chamber. Its walls, alive with handprints, seem smudged now from all these spirit entrances and exits. Will has never understood before—the place has no windows. Maybe planned that way so, come night, the single bolted doorway could be guarded by Winch's men.

The main dormitory, rows of corn-husk mattresses, looks to've been deserted in a hurry. Will remembers the little annex running alongside this hall. Was known as Dr. Marsden's "office." Willie now slips into that narrow chamber, finds it wholly draped with dingy sheets. He recognizes his mother's monogram, the two thorny M's making a pedestal, one looping L set—a curly boot shape—not unpleased to ride on top. This alcove's tenting makes it seem a pitiful slave copy of his mother's brocade tower music room. Or maybe somebody's memory of a household game: On rainy days, as a boy, Will—with his mother—played it hour after hour. Always with whatever slave children he chose.

This cell is so dark, he first mistakes the tall mirror yonder for a corner exit. Then Will sees glass give back a sliver of the open doorway where he stands. "You in here? Momma?" Mirror's mahogany frame has buckled from weather. The glass—though losing conviction in some spots—still works. He moves toward this brilliant oval. In his daze from hunger, with both feet bleeding—Willie has yet to understand that *he* might register.

The boy only hurries here because he knows it's hers.

When he has got six, now five feet from the glass: a standing giant in gray looks back at him. The beast is half again as tall as Child Willie should be. Like him, it turns aside, but way too slow. A uniformed shape is on its hind legs. Sad part: You can tell by the creature's vexed face—it wants something better. You can someway tell it plans to try and maybe school itself back towards being . . . what? . . . half human again. The creature's eagerness sickens Will the most. If only, like that great Bible King, this thing would simply go down onto all fours, would just eat grass, be done with trying. Willie Marsden presses the real beard of it. Yes, it's a boy's thin beard. Yellow furse shows three cockleburs tangled in. Will slides one hand clear through a great rip in the outgrown tunic. He touches something's left nipple—this mark seems some one-of-a-kind defect.

And people have noticed him like this! Throughout two ex-Reb states, during steady hiking—strangers have been viewing this for free. The shape is worse for being—these long weeks—such a secret to itself. "When miniés stopped flying, did I think I'd gone transparent? Coming through towns, everybody stared so. —Now you know why, Willie boyo." And he understands, this is exactly what his absent mother would reel from first. Having *others* see her at a loss, that always grieved Lady worse than any loss itself. If people gaped at her too long, and even in a manner too admiring, she'd inhale, "What?"—she'd touch herself as if some secret stain was giving her away.

During battles, for comfort, Willie Marsden decided war had one hidden advantage: Yeah, he'd almost lost a leg to the surgeon's overeager saw. True, his side's army—after giving up so much for victory—went and sacrificed the war itself. Fact, he'd lost his friend, his friends. But at least there was this: He'd found the terrible cure for Marsden family vanity. Might be war's single benefit.

Willie recalled his daddy's self-justifying scholarship—Dr. Marsden's pleasure with his own mildness (a person can be proud of anything). Will knew his momma's high-handedness about her music, her beauty—things she expected the world to daily help her improve upon. Walking home, the boy told hisself: At least *some*thing good has sprung from all this ruination. At least—along with everything else—he'd finally lost *his* share of the inherited vanity.

But now his mother's mirror tells Willie M.: His present case is maybe forty times worse than the one he marched away with.

Understanding he's gained nothing from these three years, what breaks across the side of his neck, against the brunt of Will's forehead, is so strong a shame he feels a moment's blindness. Needing steadying, he reaches for the quarter's wall.

IT'S THEN that he hears something shift.

Something else alive has claimed this room. It has made a burrow of sheets in the tabby hut's corner. Crimped breath can now be heard to rattle behind the mirror. Will's war reflexes come back so swift—knees dip, weight's center lowers, arms fling out, stick hoists off the floor—gone from cane to cudgel in one instant. The boy half stoops, primed for danger even before noticing the sound as sound. Will is about to leave the mirror (glad to), he's ready to sidestep his reflection and check behind the glass.

When three dark fingers curl around its frame.

The boy all but cries out.

By dodging behind glass, Will finds—huddled in deeper shadow here—a prickly swaddled shape. Its matted eyes reflect all the daylight streaming from behind him. This creature acts so frightened by the staff he holds, he throws it willingly down. But the noise of wood striking flagstone floor makes the victim draw in even tighter.

On a filthy cot, she smells the way we all would if we just quit on niceties, admitting being animal. A rank gamy lanolin sweetness—like original sin. And about as hard to shake, child. Shouldn't people at least get to naturally smell like . . . lilacs, minimum. That too much to ask? She clutches a picture frame against her chest, holds it like some shield or crucifix. The granny-woman tilts back, gasping. Her head looks sheared. The face shows black blisters, partly healed. Her body needs washing so bad—it's gone gray-brown as a fresh-dug potato's jacket. Knowing she's been uncovered, the crone makes even worse pleading sounds. Her tone itself plainly asks, "Don't hurt me more."

She has failed to know him.

And, child, he don't know her.

Stepping inches nearer, Willie first believes this squaw to be vague Old Zelia, finally unstrung like folks'd long predicted. Then Will takes this person for some mad black stranger, hiding out from damage suffered elsewhere. He leans over the hurt one. "It's all right," a baritone echoes in this stone vault, half surprising him. She curls deeper under one sheet, she pulls further into the corner, frowning from the hurtful white light framing him. Her face's whole left side is mashed flush to plaster, her one visible eye bugs out so, blinking. He can hear the wet eye snapping, snapping.

Will wants to help the creature. He's not certain how. She moves—one fist yet gripping the gold frame. Her other pulls the sheet aside. She's naked underneath—he hadn't planned to look at her, it. But the boy's too curious about a signal she keeps making.

She shows him small burned breasts, keeps pointing at her neck. She tips here, quaking. Something like a laugh keeps breaking through her, blurring features to a smile, baring her blacked gums. She signals and signals at one side of her throat. Will's own tired mind moves so slow today—but he begins to understand: this person is so beaten, so at the end of hiding— she is exposing her jugular to him. She presses against plaster, racked by small spasms like giggles, ones she fights in a manner almost genteel, grinning behind her hand in a way that sickens him for being someway familiar. Head tilted left, she's offering this shaggy upright beast the right to end her.

"No," he says. Meaning: I won't hurt you. But a marveling sound echoes in his own voice, gets his own attention. And it's only now that Willie sees— just where this person's shoulder meets her throat—how the crusted darkness gives way. In one protected seam, a paleness. First, it appears to be a scar. Then, slow, Will begins to understand that all the rest is—scar. That this poor raddled creature has been fully scalded down to this—rendered— down down the way fat's reduced to make candles, soap.

It's now: The locked muscles of a boy's knees give. Will seems to fall some inches while yet standing. He says just, "No. Not," and turns aside.

She stares up at him.

Then he speaks, but to the wall. "—Not *you?*"

She seems to understand. Slow, he risks facing her. She begins to nod. She soon offers big-eyed head-wagging child nods. One blacked finger then taps warped glass. She keeps pointing to a family motto in Latin. She gives off small asking sounds. It's soon plain she wants this read aloud to her. Will learned the legend by heart at age five. So, moving like somebody old, settling onto the stone floor beside her unclean cot, he quotes it and loud, and with some great simple patience seeming older than a boy's. "*Morus tarden moriens moru cito moritum*. 'The family members, like the leaves of the mulberry tree, shall perish, but the tree shall live forever.' "

Seeming strengthened, not onct touching him, she throws her feet over the cot's edge, takes up her own walking stick, motions he should follow. Willie has not even brushed against her—he feels afraid to, child. Seems one squeeze from him might crack her to a hundred ashy bits.

She now leads him on a tour of ruins. He keeps close behind her. Under the one bedsheet, she's quite naked. Scar tissue gleams across her back. Willie, staggering, numb now, hopes he will eventually forget to be shocked. Please. He tries so hard to forget the crippling family pride. (His only hope now is to lose that, quick.) He can plainly see how his mother moves.

Barefoot over gravel, she goes forward in a scurrying heedless way, so determined. Helpless against it, she's grown right rangy, taking no care over how she looks, not understanding that. Now that Lady has started living from the inside out, and not the outside in, she's become visible to him. She looks like a body turned inside out, flayed then tanned as saddle leather. But, odd, only with her broken like this, does the boy see how strong she has forever been. "My mother."

Her readiness to be so hurt while agreeing to stay on, alive—it seems to Will the strangest miracle of all. (A woman whose idea of luxury was forever resting, chattering, fanned by others, blindfolded with silk.) He almost feels sorriest for her first self.

And Willie, following, head down, aware mostly of his own breathing, now feels a prickling light his scalp. *Now* he feels the deepest pride set in. That's it—he feels so proud. Proud that—even rendered down to this—his mother's found no choice but to stay alive, to really really want that. Cooked stupid, she has noticed her life.

Trailing Lady, studying his own hurt feet, Will needs to know: How has she eaten? Who has tended her? Willie guesses she has made this tour daily for the many weeks since everything was leveled. From a barn's coals to the flattened summerhouse and back, she scuddles. She seems to feel that by watching each site hard, she can maybe bring each back to life—can maybe teach them by her own example. She says nothing, she leads her son past a browned lilac hedge three-quarters killed by fire.

At each blackened foundation, the woman props herself up on her stick. Like at the stations of a tour, she makes such pitying sounds. Finally, faltering onto the stone porch, she points, lets the stick's end drop, stirs ashes still smoking in some spots. Seems she hopes to offer each pile the will to rise. Lady keeps going, "Unnh. Unnh."

"Yes," he says like to a child. "All gone. —You do know me, don't you, Momma? —It's Willie. It's over. I didn't get killed. I'm home. I can see it's you."

They're both standing on the stone veranda of nothing. When he speaks this, the second he says it—she nods to show she's recognized him, to prove there's still a little memory left—which means a bit of hope.

And it's just now that both these people seem released—sprung like from some trance that's run years too long. It's now that Lady E. More Marsden finally shoves away a stick that's held her up and, spinning, drops toward flagstone. With what great glad energy, she falls. Will catches her, but must break her toppling by going down hisself. Even in collapsing, their hands are on each other. And only when all possible falling is done can they sob. They do and do. It might sound comical to you, child, if you yourself had never cried. You have.

To them, these noises are more satisfying for sounding like beasts'— just so many gulps, brays, yelps. Sounds are way below anything as dignified as language, far under the best hopes of a civilization refined as theirs was.

They keep pulling at each other, one trying to jolt the other like fighting to recollect some important errand they both at least recall forgetting. With un-words—her in peeps, him in strange broad trombonish blasts—how they comfort each other!

Sun begins to try and set. Barn swallows still spin around blacked chimneys. A May breeze rises. On the third-floor mantel among intact figurines, one French clock's pendulum is stirred by wind. Unexpected—the bedchamber's white onyx timepiece, all sooty now, gives three unasked-for gongs, then falls still. The two former owners below, they laugh at its happening. They chuckle and hoot, they cackle together. And scream together. And scream.

NEXT DAY, wearing a overcoat some neighbor has lent him, riding that neighbor's only mule, Will turns up at Falls' best boardinghouse—he carries a child-sized person wrapped in a borrowed quilt so that nobody might see her and laugh. After his bossly trip to the livery stable to announce he's back and has lived through it all and is taking over—he soon fills his mother's rooms with what furniture Castalia's managed to save, masterpieces she hoped to maybe sell for herself, or maybe peddle to her former owners, but certainly to save, which she has done. Was a warehouse's worth and though it yet smelled of the great fire, it all got packed with Chinese box-in-box skill into double rooms, chairs handstanded upside down on chairs, mirrors making much of far too much to start with, chandeliers like great marine catches hung up for dockside drippish weighing.

And, thirty years later, it's just me, a stubby pigtailed schoolgirl knocking on that door, three sharp pencils slippery in one hand, a list of hard-strict questions (don't push me) bunching in my other. I've come, ready to pull from the Mummy and others such rude facts as braid and latch and link semi-together till—it becomes this story I've just told.

BLACK, white, and lilac. Well, darling, I got me a Satisfaction Minus. Miss Beale never did give a Satisfaction Plus, not in her whole half century of teaching here. When Emily Saiterwaite (hooked on teacher praise) asked why not, Beale only replied, "Satisfaction Plus, in *this* godforsaken bush-league wilderland?"

I didn't even mind the Minus all that much. Poor grammar was ever the millstone/albatross strung around my neck.

"While Lucille would patently prefer unbridled narrative to the discipline of composing a history theme, one nonetheless senses she has posed many difficult questions to many willing persons from various walks of life and has made, from all she's gathered, this lurid showy pie. True, she fails to use the semicolons required but the pupil does attempt an organization involving a three-color scheme. She hopes, This Reader believes, to demonstrate how relative our moral standards truly are, how war can reverse forces even so seemingly immutable as the planet's very colors. Perhaps

Lucille collaborates with history too readily—as if its terrible pageant were being daily staged to simply amuse, horrify, and entertain our little friend. Even so, she has spared herself no end of legwork. Lucille has, I believe, when it comes to the spirit of events chronicled here, entered in. With Lucille's theme, as often occurs in both my own historical vision and in History itself, I am left wondering what worse could possibly happen next. Seemingly, something always does, does it not? —Lucille's acknowledgment of suffering as a constant, argues, I believe, the beginning of this child's compassion. Therefore—dear one—Satisfaction Minus."

(Bless you, Miss Witch, our silk purse stuffed with the big bills of History and Taste. You knew everything but how to save yourself from the folks you most hoped to save. Lord rest your martyred heart.)

THERE, pretty much done. Except for a final question. And I am asking it, darling, of me and you and of flint-hearted History itself.

What *is* black, white, and lilac?

If this here query had been put to me at age eleven, I would've bragged, "Why, that's the modern history theme I just wrote for Miss Witch Beale and that she liked right much. The one that Poppa helped me age the new brass hinges of."

At twenty, I'd have said, "A school paper done by a very innocent little girl very, very long ago. That, plus maybe some new multi-tone boudoir-decorating trend mentioned in a recent number of *McClure's*?" At fifty, "Three names of three popular shades and whatever on earth happens to be those particular tints. Period."

I think, at seventy, I had enough on my mind so I'd probably forgot ever doing the twenty-six pager I've tried breathing new life into here. Asked the question then, I might have said, "What is this? three colors? a joke? Maybe one about some nun hooked on red wine or something? Tell me it."

At age ninety, I ain't too sure if I'd have recalled Mr. Goethe's naming colors "the deeds and sufferings of light." I do now. At the end, so much comes back to you, and clear as day.

With me creeping nigh onto a hundred (imagine), I've grown more cautious about blabbing any off-the-top-of-my-head ragtag answer.

Look, by now, I know what I know.

By this time, honey, so do you.

Miss Beale, the best thing I found out: How much they'll tell you if you trust enough to ask. True, my paper don't exactly mount up to no national document. Still—ma'am? it's what I learnt.

Today, if some pushy eleven-year-old shoved to my bed's edge, if she offered me the old question, child, I believe I'd try a shorter truer comeback.

Q: What is black and white and lilac?
A: Depends.

BOOK THREE

Give Strength, Lord

Back
to War
Again

And though I bestow all my goods to feed the poor, and though I
give my body to be burned, and have not love, it profiteth me
nothing. Love suffereth long, and is kind, love envieth not, love
vaunteth not itself, is not puffed up. Doth not behave itself
unseemly, seeketh not her own, is not easily provoked, thinketh
no evil, rejoiceth not in iniquity, but rejoiceth in the truth.

—I CORINTHIANS 13:3–6

CAPTAIN wanted to name our oldest boy Ned. I didn't think it was too good of a idea, seeing what'd happened to Ned the First. More babies followed—knit one, purl one, turn around, you got a afghan—family spread across your knees and spilling down, warming the very ankles that're swollen so on their account.

Those days, it was either one end of your use or the other. Like being a broom that's strawed at both ends, north and south, you circle yourself to keep cleaning up after him, even after lamps go out. —Those days, I can't tell you, you that's always had the vote, that got to go to college and can smoke anywhere so easy it never even dawns on you to start, which is good. You, who can discourage babies in advance of seeing what they'll look like and then falling in love with their first smile instead of saving your own self! Well, comparing then to now, it's night and day. I'm ready to start over.

WE GOT us a Ford car, was the first in all of Falls. Model T, black of course. Oh, spluttering to church especially, we were mighty stuck-up for about four weeks. Till we got outshined by Doc Collier's Pierce-Arrow. Then near-strangers would say right to our faces, "Yours is just a Ford." Jealous. Still, it was good for me—overnight I'd grown snooty as Lady More Marsden in her prime. Went out and bought me the goggles, a driving hat and veil, gloves. Some days I wore them around the house, as a joke for the children. Cleaning in those. I was just a girl myself. Captain drove that thing as if he'd done it all his life. Children begged for the privilege of washing the Ford. I caught Louisa, a enterprising darling, charging neighbor kids admission to scrub our auto—big kids, too, boys! I felt proud of her. "How much you clear?" I called her aside. She acted ashamed, "Not enough for nursing school."

"That what you salting it aside for?"

Lou nods.

"We'll get you in, Miss P. T. Barnum." She held out a nickel, offering to rent my goggles, hat, and gear. I give them to her absolutely free.

One noon, Cap drove home with this look on his face, fingers kept carving maps all through his brown beard, he paced, counting platinum watch-chain links like the Pope doing beads for dear life. Kept talking about a pilgrimage. Revisiting the war. By then we had eight of the children. Yes, child, eight. Happened just that fast. Many of my wee ones were in their diaper years. Sure made traveling harder. Won't like now, where you just throw them paper things away. Oh my no—had to wash each one, had to keep the evidence on hand, you had to love your children then, just to stand it.

Auto was a hand-crank Model T. Not like these station wagons you see these days, ones with added playrooms for your babies to go be busy in. Children were either on the floorboard or in your lap, period. I'll skip the arguments I gave for not traveling. It come out, he'd bought the auto-car just so's he could go. Here was the twentieth century's big breakthrough and what'd he want to do with it? drive back to war in the nineteenth!

We set out one Thursday just at dawn. I had told him he should go alone. He said, "Lucy mine, fact is, I'm frightened to." That got me, naturally. I packed enough picnic stuff to feed a regiment. By then, we were one.

Leaving, our town looked sourish but pink with waking. My baby in my arms, I stared out at all the unfamous things I knew best: the school, the church, a tree where me and my best girlfriend'd built a tree house and practiced our first kissing on each other, the courthouse monument to Our Fallen. I sat worrying we were bound for something that we shouldn't see. "Say 'Bye,'" I told those children awake in back.

"Bye, everything," Lou said, waving at the Courthouse Square's highest-shooting water fountain, the green bench before Lucas'.

Took us nearbout three weeks all up into Virginia and Maryland to find his basic war spots. Cap had left two trusty black men in charge of the stockyard. By now, they mostly ran it anyways. They scolded the Captain, growing more frank the more work they did for him—at the selfsame pay. Fellows explained he was crazy to buy the first local autocar. Here they were, trying and sell Marsden horses, Marsden mules—and he went tooling around the counties in this show-off backfiring boat unhitched from any animal at all. He shrugged, he told them flat, "I wanted one." It's all the reason a boss ever needs.

We bumped into a few other vets, men nosing around old acreage, men fingering fence posts for bullets still wedged there, men pushing their wives' and children's fingers into brick walls and tree bark so's they'd feel the lead there. Treated kin like Doubting Thomases that didn't believe it'd all happened, that *wouldn't* believe till their hands got poked wrist-deep into the sticky maw of it.

I heard one wife say, "I am not jamming my finger into one more thing, Stan. *I* know it was rough." Us wives, sisters, mothers followed our men. Some vets were on crutches, some got lugged on stretchers by hired black men. But all vets were looking overly alive. Us wives give each other tired grins. We rolled our eyes, overeager for peace, quiet, and a good couch. Counter-pain. The children thought this open land was just a playground. But, for vets, it sure was not, and you had to keep your babies quiet and in rows. It was hard.

And you think the Captain would let me tend our brood in the autocar whilst he stepped off battle events, maps held nestled up near his brown beard? Not bloody likely, child. We had to follow every last stride. So the babies would remember, he said. Was like pacing off a hunt for buried treasure, only without the treasure. The second-saddest thing to fighting a war is remembering it inch by inch decades later. I told my husband that a child has got to be seven or a mighty smart six before such fine print stays recollected. Our babies couldn't recall their home address much less which Reb regiment under General Thus-and-so tried holding on to which Reb ditch.

Captain did name our oldest boy Ned. I let him, had to. "You pick the girls' names," he said. Well, Ned was old enough to notice the trip. He was bright, eight, all eyes under sweet humid blond ringlets. His curls would tighten up and ease, our own live-in barometer. "Come here," I'd call. "Let's see, oh yeah, says: Clearing by late afternoon. I thank you, messenger boy." "No trouble," said he, running off to organize those younger. His curls were noticeable, like ones in the picture of Ned number one I'd found during our honeymoon. No girl or woman could resist wrapping her pinkie finger inside a bouncy little ringlet and asking, "How does he *do* it?"—like he stayed awake nights. Lolly, my beautician, avoided Ned. Forced to see Ned's curls, she went glum. "I do excellent work—but sometimes I lose heart. God sure is the hair burner to beat!"

Such flattery never really spoiled our oldest boy but, too, his big eyes did register each compliment. Took after his poppa in that way—and, come to think of it, his momma, too. A great gatherer, our Ned. If there was more than two of something, loose, free of charge, and small enough to pocket, why he'd collect them. His corner of the boys' upstairs bedroom looked like a magpie's own ideal museum. And now, during Captain's pilgrimage, Ned had already snagged stones from each battleground, plus leaves and—whenever possible—bird feathers he found.

There was something about Ned. For one thing, he seemed as smart as I *remembered* being. Which was, truth be told, and allowing for mistakes of recollection, pretty crack-outfit bright. On balloon tires as we rattled through Virginia—me holding our newest baby—I sat recalling how one morning when Ned had been nearbout a year old, his eyes were just starting to like the middle distance. His eyes'd finally settled into their true color.

I was bending over his cradle. It'd been the Captain's. Castalia and other slaves had hid it with The Lilacs' choicer furniture when Sherman's torches swarmed through Falls. I was just tucking blankets around my baby's feet. I felt something strange, like a sudden lift in temperature or some dip in the wind outside. I, quick, looked up to his face. It was framed by the cradle's dark hood. Studying me, they were, the eyes. Eyes made up most of his face. Hair was all white-blond and eyes were shiny, bounded by pale lashes. Ned's eyes shone broad and gray, speckled as birds' eggs with these flecks of amber set way in, lids hardly blinked. For the first time, eyes really saw me as one person, whole, as me. They fixed right on my skin, bored in, moved from my ear down my neck to breast to breast and back again. A dog barked two blocks off. I felt I should be learning something from this. Ned's eyes seemed about to ask for help. Thinking he was hungry or that a diaper pin was sticking—I bent closer.

And I had pulled right down over his rosy face when I felt something catch in me, this kind of hiccup got me just under the rib cage. You see, I'd recognized the eyeballs. I pitched back, then drew nearer, saw how his eyes were less asking for my help than offering some of their own—giving off a kind of baby-animal curiosity, guessing, "And what do *you* need, sister?"

I had to lean against his cradle, counting on its rockers for support. Because see, darling, here they were. The same. The eyes—old and young all mixed in them, those eyes I'd first seen peeking (civilian) from the Captain's fort of a face. Now my boy batted his lashes, showing this 20/20 sweetness. He proved to me: My faith had been rewarded. I'd helped to free them. It was my small part in Emancipation. Just when I thought I would never reach the boy I'd first spied hid so deep in the smug reviewing-stand officer, just when my own tiredness made each dawn feel like a huge new horizontal subtraction mark, I looked down at my child's blue blankets, I saw he'd torn that whole set of eyesight free from trouble.

Saved! Here were eyes aloose again and full of peace, a fresh start in the open air. "It worked," I spoke to his cradle. I stood there, one exhausted girl, half laughing. He watched—a mild careful expression. His hands kept moving in round baby spasms like planning to someday somehow clap. Ned's eyes seemed smart enough, they *trusted* so. Our house was real quiet just then. Mantel clock ticking in the front room. Oh, I felt like everything was possible at last. I felt honored to be at home with a gaze this safe and sure. "I did it," I told his face in his father's cradle. "*I* did it." No shame, I wanted full credit. Ned couldn't talk yet but he could see. Me. Among others.

so, at age eight, here he fidgeted in the car's back, watching farmland sweep by, plenty old enough to love such a trip. Ned's rock/leaf/feather collection was under his father's front seat and it looked more and more like the nest of some scruffy mammal half beaver, half bird. (And I knew he'd catalogued each scrap of it.)

Riding along his dad's war path, little Ned stood, leaning on the back of Captain's driver's seat, arms crossed, head bobbing level with his seated daddy's, listening hard, Ned's yellow-brown curls bright against the first grayed touches in Captain's temple. Times, gazing forward, they looked like two heads of the same thing.

We would see a low stone wall, Cap would pull the motorcar over, would sit there parked, hands fisted on the steering wheel, motor still going, his forehead warping. In back, our other babies—all but Ned and Lou, our oldests—kept picking at each other, squabbling like all children on car trips will: "Did so, did not, did too, unh-uh, bet you anything I own, you don't own one dry bean, do too, do not."

Ned, tilted forward, hair full of predicted weather, waiting for whatever news his dad would choose to spill. Lou wet the tip of her pencil, ready to jot into the travel diary I'd bought her. Good calfskin—it locked. I made sure of that. Lou's broad hands held her precious book, she was a large-framed girl, built like her poppa (but with the fine skin of *his* momma, plus such a memory for figures).

Captain would start, "First Gunnery Sergeant John B. Morris, grit aplenty, broke his left leg right here, just there, a fall from a maverick mule." It didn't mean much to me, it meant nothing to our babies, meant everything to Cap. I'd nod, looking out, playing interested. So would Ned, then Lou. She'd write down this much, she'd wait for the rest. It rarely came. After twenty minutes' melancholy, you could all but hear a memory churning towards curd in the poor man. Then he'd open his door, ready to go hand-crank the engine starter again. Then I'd have to tell him he never cut the motor *off*. He'd go, "Oh . . . right, silly of me." Lou would be heard to lock her diary shut. Ned would stand straighter so our Ford's forward lurch wouldn't knock him back into the others' laps. Then we'd get two miles or three. Out the window would poke the left-hand-turn signal of memory, and over we'd pull again. —Oh, but it was a long haul, honey.

i hoped that seeing the lake where his childhood bud had got ambushed might help ease Captain past calling out the warnings in his dreams. He still did. I hoped a visit would get him over repeating the whole story aloud his usual every other week or so, to us and strangers. I expected that by facing up to it again, he could let the bugle practice slide.

He'd lately taken to dragging out into our toolshed around eight or nine at night. Just when I was upstairs getting all the children settled in and was listening to their prayers—right when they again asked God to let Poppa see his way clear to letting our family own just one cocker spaniel dog, please—"We will share it"—the durn horn would start out back. First time he did it was the anniversary of Ned's dying. If, as a boy, Cap had ever learned to do reveille right, he'd sure forgot it. —At the corner grocery next morning, neighbors give me certain looks and the clerk goes, "I didn't know our Captain was musical." "Nobody knows that," I said, and tried explaining that his music was, you might could say, a war-related wound. The clerk holds up his palms to show I don't need to apologize, he understands. Not a soul complained except through frowns and stares. One mother from two blocks off cornered me near the bread to ask, "And what time do you try and get *your* brood to sleep?" Finally I wished somebody would just yell at me—or, better, at *him*. There's a certain type of soggy understanding look that your Lucy here finds most galling of all. Between pitying glances and what his bugle did to dogs' ears—the din of hounds howling over half of Falls—I felt ready for a cure.

FIRST, I figured I'd been wrong to fear the trip. Bound to help. Between familiar battle zones, while pulling over more often than some from-around-here tractor on a state road—he stayed right patient with the children. They played their usual rumpus seat games: Mules and Graves, busy with questions both silly and sensible and both at once.

"Daddy," Louisa touched Poppa's nearest suspender—he'd taken his jacket off in the heat. "See those hogs penned over there?"

"I do," he said. "I ever tell you about the farmer whose shoats were so skinny he had . . ."

"Yes. The tails? You have." I laughed at Lou's honesty. Good girl.

"What *about* these hogs, Louisa? Those'd bring you three cents a pound in market. No more, wormy-looking beasts."

"Poppa, hogs aren't smart enough to know that they're alive, right? Does it mean they're *more* alive for that or less? Are we smarter because we know what 'alive' means or are we maybe less? Are we smart because we're alive or is smart something extra added on overtop?"

He whistled. "Excellent question, Louisa. You must take after my side of the family brains-wise. Little joke, Lucille." Cap drove on at the speed limit (in them days the upper limit was however fast Henry Ford's skills could push you forward).

"A hog is no less alive than us. Do you children, when you see a mother sow wade right into the mud and flop down, ever think, I certainly wish I could do that?" Back-seat opinion split between yes and no answers adding "yuck."

"Well, we *could* all wallow in the muck but know not to. Shoot a hog or shoot a man, they're just as dead. A man . . . simply wants more, wants to live. He wants his family and friends to. —I guess we're all about third cousins once removed from hogs, Lou."

One twin piped up, "Except Louisa. She's kissing kin to a Duroc." (Times, Lou could have weight problems.)

"For saying that," their father spoke, "you've just lowered yourself far into a sty. Do you hear me? You've set Louisa high above the angels, and she and the angels are looking down on you."

"Well then, I better take it back," the one twin goes.

"No. There's never taking anything back. Done is done. Try calling back a minié to its starting place. —Ned, you have any questions?"

Captain, praising Lou, often turned aside—unaware of creating contests—he asked young Ned to better his older sister.

"Ummm, no. I will, probably, but so far . . . no."

"Well, speak up when you do. Fine thing, questions. Did I answer your last to your satisfaction, Louisa?"

"Not yet but I'd rather think it out myself, thank you."

"Sounds like her mother," Cap says to nobody present.

"I thought one up," Ned's voice was vague as air but pressing. "If dogs hate cats and chase cats, do dogs eat cats when they catch cats? Everything has enemies—and everything's against rabbits. But who is *our* natural enemy?"

"We are," Louisa answered. Her father, driving, shaken, turned and looked at her. Ned still sat waiting.

"What she said." The Captain stared at the road. "Exactly as your sister put it, son."

2

ON WE RODE, me figuring we'd go right to that infected spot and, being there, move right *through* it, like lancing a boil. We'd dry out the badness for good. Our whole family would be in on the balm, too. "The Family That Heals Together . . . Can Deal Together" or "Mends Together . . . Can Fend Together" or something.

But, child, the nearer we drew to the hurtful place itself, the more I commenced to worrying I'd been wrong. For one thing, he started telling whole new facts about his friend. Here I thought I was already Ned's very encyclopedia. I mean, I knew exactly which foods Ned liked (he favored custards and creamed corn, if it matters one whit). I knew every song he had by heart. I still recall his favorite canary's name. He bypassed his momma's title of Von Himmel—instead giving his the moniker of Waverley because he'd read Sir Walter Scott and he figured a canary's song moves like that, kind of waverley-like. But Captain's memory was now marching double-time. His eyes stayed locked on the bumpy road, his mouth now telling children all this fresh stuff about their "Uncle" Ned, who'd never

turned fourteen. Cap tale-told to our youngsters and—along for the ride—
I got to eavesdrop. That's how it felt.

—How Ned, in a letter home two weeks before he hit the lake, wrote
Winona Smythe: "And, Momma, I want to ask you not to worry so much.
If I do get killed, I'll only be dead."

—How Ned, in battle for the first time, vowed to act manly and bold
as possible, a regular Ivanhoe. He smudged a little mud across his face to
make hisself look older and more blended with landscape. He crammed all
bugle-colored curls up into his cap. Marching orders were hollered. With
his bugle dangling, with his bayonet jabbed forward for show, Ned goes
walking alongside others, moving stiff-legged through a batch of scattered
Yankee casualties from the day before.

Ned soon passed a boy fourteen or so, boy lying down. This child was
redheaded and resting prone in a very tidy blue uniform, stretched out on
his back. He must have known that he was dying (though no mark showed
why). He'd crossed his arms over his chest the way his momma'd probably
taught him to. Some children in them days were trained to fall asleep that
way—"If I should die before I wake." None too cheering for a young mind
with insomnia tendencies. —This boy'd set his blue cap close beside him.
Squared away, perfectly dead, he was still pretty and rested on this mat of
dried oak leaves, not a foot away from two pink-blooming ladyslippers. Face
up, his eyes were open, each yet fresh with luster. You could not believe
that he won't just playing possum. He had been a corpse just under twenty
minutes, no more. Ned stopped. Ned noticed how some other Rebel soldier
(from his own division) had just robbed this body. Pockets had been slashed,
a thief hunting some coins, a watch. Instead what spilled out was homemade
sausages and ginger cakes, food probably sent by a Northern mother and
sisters. This meant some sacrifice for the women, mailing such treats to the
front. The dead Yank might of been saving home-cooked sweets for some
choice quiet moment.

Ned, wearing gray, set his own rifle alongside the body. A file of fellow
Southerners stalked on far ahead. Nobody had missed him yet. Not even
young Marsden. Ned plunked onto sod beside the Northerner. The whole
idea of manly conduct gave way so quick. I sometimes want to ask: Who
forced men to feel they *had* to strut like that? Other men? Men's idea of
women's idea of men?

Years later, I took my children to the moving pictures, to see this *Nanook
of the North* picture. All about how hard this one lonely Eskimo had it,
hunting blubber, pretty thankless work. My kids set there—big-eyed—all
during, not saying a word. While we wandered toward daylight, I asked how
they'd liked it. One, Baby, turned to me, her face curled with worry. "A good
one," she nodded. "But, Momma? who makes him live there?"

It's that question I want to ask of these here bullyboys. Bluster ain't
assigned. Takes nerve for one to finally holler, "I didn't pick this. This ain't
me."

In '62, Wee Willie Marsden circled back and found young Ned seated, his mouth full, studying the Northerner. Mouth stuffed, Ned tried explaining, "These'd be wasted, otherwise. I'd have fed him mine. I'd want Momma's stuff used while it was good."

Ned chewed, sat watching the dead soldier's eyes cloud over, waved off the gnats. Ned had just quit the hero stuff cold turkey. For the rest of his term of duty, he'd be sneaking off to pick raspberries for cheering others, he'd turned up baby rabbits carried in his hat with dry grass all around them—naming them Natchez and Nashville, he'd practice bugle and sing his nightly songs. He learned quick to avoid this Seeming Brave. He hid whenever possible. Nobody could make *him* live there. In my book, that made the pip a choicer type of hero. He stayed on the ground beside the dead boy, the sound of muskets cracking through the woods beyond, his face all crumbs, sucking fingertips, saying, "Somebody made these. They're still so fresh. Here, have one. A lady baked these, Willie."

WELL, Ned, *our* Ned, wanted to hear everything. His face aimed over his poppa's shoulder, nodding at this story, looking awful serious. He started asking better questions about the boy he'd been named for. He needed to know—it's only natural. I could hear Lou's pencil scratching now, jotting down all facts. Our Ford bounced along washed-out country roads. We rambled all over creation, hunting good scorched spots, finding one-night bivouacs Captain and his pal had shivered through like puppies in a box. And I kept quiet, Mrs. Perfect Listener, but getting more edgy every mile we chugged. I heard my husband tell so many other full new stories about his true love, ones with details all in place like the miracle of your baby's ten speck-sized fingernails. Fuller and richer fine-grained lore pulled out of him. I soon come to feel pure shocked by the number of untold tales. You could see why anybody'd be fond of the sweet dead boy—a sentimental nervy child, game for most anything but shooting people, simple as his momma was pushy, a lad tender as a tadpole nub. From the back seat, I heard Lou sigh. I understood why she admired the boy's small deeds. Still, he didn't sound quite real. First I wanted wartime Ned to be a good person and then—while he grew sweeter, story to story—I got grouchy about all that virtue packed into one green pip.

I asked myself how Ned the First would have turned out if he'd had to live. If only the good die young (what does that say about *my* present age, sugar?), maybe that's how come the young *stay* good? Would Ned be a governor or even President by now? Actor, preacher, probably anything but regular. It was left to us who'd survived—getting through having turned out only Ordinary.

Oh, but I wanted this autocar to head back home, and now. To move away from tracking that lake, from seeking the very tree where it all happened. Ned had got killed near the start of Captain's war but Cap held off visiting that death site till the very last of all.

· · ·

WE NOW circled, looking for it hard. The rest we'd mostly seen. My husband had even acted cordial to the Yankee vets swarming these same boneyards, their accents duck-harsh as the winning side's *would* be—wives just as bored, just as busy being neutral as myself.

By now, on the trail of it, Cap would stop and ask directions of farmers: a gristmill on a oblong body of water, please? We got a lot of head scratching. The pond didn't have a name my husband could recall. Even the most brittle memory, like his, gets groggy with the weight of forty-some years hammocked over it.

We'd been gone from home eighteen days, then nineteen. Nineteen days in a Model T with eight squirming children—four of them in diapers—is forever and beyond. Time seemed something we had given the slip—like we would always live like gypsies—me washing in ladies' rooms or doing diapers in none-too-glad-to-see-me little roadside streams. Children using our Ford's running board for their dining table. Kids invented games: the Seven Wonders of the World—but you could only use sights from home. Like me, they were missing known streets. The bench in front of Lucas' All-Round Store—painted a hundred times and rubbed in the fanny zone to show a candy counter's worth of color living underneath. The water fountain in the Courthouse Square. Our house. Our vacant lot. Castalia's many mink cages. Like scholars, they made lists. It soothed me listening. Worried me to notice: Captain by now heard not one syllable of what our young ones said in back. We bought food in grocery stores, not restaurants. Day twenty, Captain told our children bickering in back that, if they'd stop their spatting long enough, he'd tell them how Ned the First had actually sung songs for J. E. B. Stuart and General Lee.

Hearing this, my jawbone sagged. Like Castalia, copying Zelia, warding off the world's blows, I crossed arms over my chest. As many times as my old man'd been over all this territory in my company, alone and at banquets, through rain and dry till death do us in, imagine Captain Marsden leaving this part out. Even if he made it up, you know he might have made it up a little earlier, and for his lady-wife alone.

My mother once told me that, of all the electric feelings on life's totem pole of bargain-basement emotions, Jealousy and Self-Pity are the tackiest. Momma always felt more at ease lecturing about emotion than showing any. Still, this didn't make her wrong concerning personal hunches. I remember her changing subjects, claiming every local family had its own built-in gene-prone weaknesses. Ketchums stole. Cogdells stuttered. The Williamses always suffered kidney complaints and, after forty, their backs went. So I asked, "What's *ours*?" She blinked. I pressed her, being pushy me, "What's our own clan's biggest sicknesses?" Momma got a strange large look on her narrow face. She felt to check if her cameo was pinned on straight. She looked dead ahead as her voice wobbled some. "Jealousy and Self-Pity," she said.

Early on, I'd vowed to never feel any envy for the slippery child my husband missed. I told myself, "Lucy, in that direction, craziness waits." I swore I'd blow the whistle on self-pity every time it licked its way within a foot of me. But now, hearing what the Captain had been holding out on me, it smarted afresh. Saving back his most name-brand story (Stuart *and* Lee!), well, that flat hurt my feelings. No telling what else he'd filed deep in his ponder heart, hid there, refrigerated—forever sweet while I risked spoiling out here in hot open air.

Said (over babies' lowered voices, some still counting mules and tombstones) how one evening (Cap waited for the game to die—one backward glance from him soon killed it) the great men had been camped near his regiment, there came a lull in the fighting. Supplies were due any day. Was time for oiling your musket, time to jot brave cheerful letters home while, on another page, writing your will. The boys from Falls were just fixing to do their nightly skit. Word arrived that entertainment was being sought for the High Command. Generals need distracting, too.

Private Ned, as his division's all-time favorite, got handpicked for the tryout. Meanwhile, the big-toothed kid who did Ned's musical arm gestures, he won't even asked along. Nobody half thought of Will, though he stood around, chin up, chest out—right winningly ready. —See, everybody knew: Lee might be a genius at strategy and a saint at duty. (What other general *ever* stuck his beloved youngest son in a risky artillery unit as a buck private and made sure other boys got promoted quicker? Fact.) Lee's might be the candidate for the handsomest face in Christendom. (The argument always run: if good looks had been ammo, the South would've won the whole mess two weeks after Sumter.) Yeah, Lee maybe boasted the finest pedigree this side of Upperville thoroughbreds. But, child, levity was probably beyond Marse Robert. He was not what you'd call no laugh riot. Saints ain't often all that big on comedy. One of self-sacrifice's big loopholes, to my mind.

So for this reason, the singing team got split up. The pretty young talent part got escorted by the General's aide-de-camp, on towards Command Headquarters. The silent partner, freckled, thinking of cute hand signals to try, he followed at a distance.

Out by the horses, out near a tent that Lee's famous animal, Traveler, had all to hisself (huge horse for a big man—I seen him stuffed in Lexington, later of course), Fitzhugh Lee, one of Stuart's division commanders and kin to Marse Robert, held a kind of audition. Four tenors from four other outfits did their level best, one by one. A fifth fellow offered rope tricks. Good, but he ended with a trick using a noose made with one jerk and he added some patter about Lincoln's swinging in it. Would Lee go for *that*? No way. Then Ned sang. Everything went stiller, then still, including horses. Even night bugs took a brief intermission. Ned got picked. The others agreed. Some tenors come over to shake Ned's hand and ask his name. The rope one pouted off into the night.

First the child was fed extra-fine rations. He got groomed a bit. From one tiny black bottle, a drop of what smelled like expensive perfume was daubed behind Ned's either ear and on his wrists. Later, a strategy meeting broke up, leaders exiting Lee's tent. Imagine a little soldier's excitement. It'd be like a Bible believer catching sight of a Prophet Convention, Moses and Abraham talking shop, prophet shop.

The map boy came out carrying tubes and rulers and calipers. He sure flung our little singer one jealous look. Then Fitzhugh Lee ushered in young Ned Smythe, introduced him. Two generals were left seated on folding camp chairs. They'd just finished their meal. History books will claim that Lee prided hisself on using the same tin plates and cups your average foot soldier ate off of. But, according to Ned according to my husband, here rested a full-sized Dresden soup tureen, fine porcelain plates out here in the viny woods. In bowls, remains of a clear French soup. By the light of one lantern, two bearded gents turned to study this silvery newt of a boy.

Stuart was a knobby dandified wag, personal congratulations in his every fidget. Lee—the white beard, gray suit, brass buttons—looked, in lamp-light, metal! Ned swallowed hard. He didn't know quite what to do with his hands now that all of him showed. He clasped these before him just like a hometown choir director once made all the solo ladies do. Ned announced he would now try "The Last Rose of Summer." He chose to offer his best selection first. Oh, he had show-business instinct, that lad! He understood: Such faces didn't want no tinselly minstrel jokes. (It was a bad moment for the Southern fortunes. That sure showed in the generals' grave features. Victory at Bull Run was just a memory. What'd seemed destiny's first win was looking more like beginner's luck. The long unmanly wait for supplies had worn everybody out.)

Standing up—both men would've been over six feet tall. Even sitting, Ned saw that they were massy and real *there*. Both waited. So Ned, willing, sang it out. He faltered at first then judged that these figures expected but little from so young a recruit. Which freed Ned up considerable, relaxed him into usual sweetness. His tone lifted, pure as duty going on its rounds from verse to verse. The voice, unchanged as yet, hit even highest notes with simple and sensible spirit.

When the song was done, Stuart asked for it again, please. Then Lee, with typical kindness, wondered aloud if Ned felt strong enough. (A saint can understand most everything but ease, child.) Ned nodded he was fine. Scared as he felt, with his pressure points just pounding, the command tent now stank of the lilac-ish perfume he'd been touched with earlier. Ned re-scaled that sad song's every peak, did it even better. Still thirteen, he showed a face wide open as his open oval mouth. He looked and sounded like one thing: the winning side.

Them elder males sat soaking up his every note, basking in the scent his pulse was broadcasting. Lee—upright in his chair—looked like a chart for ideal posture. Stuart slumped more forward, studied his boots, fondly petting his beard's one side and then the other.

When singing stopped, Stuart rose up very straight, barked, "Our cause is just." Then he nodded respects to Ned, saluted a Lee as still and silver as any Lee on any coin might be—and, riled afresh, sporting a yellow sash around his waist, J. E. B. took his leave like some rash bighearted operetta prince. (In two years, he'd be a lot more famous but completely dead at thirty-one.)

Ned now faced the Supreme Commander of the Army of Northern Virginia. Moths kept pestering the lantern's chimney. You could hear laughing from the three hundred tents downhill. Lee sat, legs crossed, looking hard at the handsome child. He spoke, "Where's your mother, boy? Where do your people live?"

"Falls, North Carolina . . . sir."

The great man asked Ned's age. "Thirteen, sir." At this, Lee lowered his head, pinched the bridge of his nose.

"*Four*teen come May, sir," the child tried helping out. It was only August.

Next the General muttered what he was later quoted as saying elsewhere, what he finally admitted at Gettysburg when requesting a pitiful Reb company to resist impossible odds. Lee, seated in lamplight, bugs peppering the tabletop and getting in the soup, said, "Of course, it's my fault. All of it is my fault, son." (The man *had* read his New Testament.) Then Lee's eyes seemed to shut, fretting. Ned, still waiting to be dismissed, considered contradicting this, about the blame and all. But, polite, a private, he decided against. Then he noticed: the Supreme Commander was napping. Ned would wait till Lee woke. Beginning to be tired, Ned shifted from foot to foot. Maybe he should clear his throat, or else just leave? What would his stern mother scold him to do next?

Then Ned told hisself: Fool, here's your big chance to notice Marse Rob. Ned knew to study this hero that enlistees admired "with a love surpassing that of women." Finally Lee's sad eyes opened one at a time. He sat straighter, smiled a close responsible smile. He took something from his tunic's inner lining and waved the singer nearer.

The old man held a picture of a child. She'd posed, a dimpled ideal person—ten or twelve—one finger pressing her right cheek. Ned, nervous, nodded to show he approved and saw how pretty a girl this was. Lee sat looking at the tintype, moved it off at arm's length—squinted—a nearsighted man in his fifties—too vain or busy to use glasses. "My nickname for my baby girl here is 'Precious Life.' Is that a foolish name?"

"No, sir. Girls' nicknames always sound like . . . that."

"Like what, son?"

"You know . . . Puddin' or Kitten. Mushy such as that. Nice but mushy."

Lee actually laughed. It appeared to cost him a good deal but it was a sacrifice made nobly. Then he thanked the boy for singing. —Smiling, Lee reached up, almost touched the front of Ned's neck. (Lee would not have done so without express permission from this bugle boy private.) "You have a gift here. Guard it." The General looked back at his unlatched picture.

"My daughter here sings. Some evenings on special occasions, her nurse will let her wear a bit of cologne. Nobody would believe it but, times, young boys your age come in at night to sing for me—and I feel—I can smell it."

Lee directed Ned to step a bit closer. Ned did so—uneasy, his eyes watering, feeling guilty—he had *tricked* Lee, the single greatest American strategist. Ned saluted, needing something to do. The old man seemed to be dozing in his daughter's scent. His beard now rested on his chest. The General still clasped the portrait in one palm. Ned—for good measure— hummed final bars of "The Last Rose" again. "Sir?" He finally backed away. "Dismissed?" he whispered just in case. Then he saluted the sleeper once more. He said, "Sir. Sir? . . . We *like* you."

Ned slipped out.

He was sweating, fearful he'd made a mistake that might disgrace all Carolina regulars. Had he done enough for the great Lee, or maybe too much? The smell of girl still hung around Ned Smythe but by now it was mostly his own smell too. Confused, he found his buddy waiting by the horses. He told skinny Marsden everything, and fast. The perfume, the song twice, the old man's great silver weariness. Shy, Ned even offered his own pale neck for the other to sniff—even jerked his collar open. Even so near horses, Marsden went, "P.U.—nice. Precious Life!" and Will made comedy kissing sounds. Arm in arm, shoving each other, getting one then the other into headlocks for no good reason, boys walked to their part of camp.

All the fellows had waited up to hear. Salvador Smith, the sentimental corporal, was circulating pictures of *his* girls, he forced Ned to sing it three times through, just like for the big brass. "Boy," Sal asked, "what'd Lee say to *that* note? Just look what that did to me," and rolled back a gray sleeve to show goose bumps. Others did the same, it was a beautiful form of bragging. And Ned was about to tell his chums the rest—the aide's strange trick of dousing Lee's nightly visitors with a familiar scent, the old man's battle-weary catnaps. But Willie flashed him just the ghost of a frown (they knew each other like Siamese twins sharing one snack's candelabrum in-digestion). Ned thought better of it, hushed. Nice to spare the Supreme Commander a little pain. Instead, Private Ned Smythe hummed one final "Last Rose" refrain. A man studying his own goose bumps called, "Amen," and added in his own dusky voice, "Boy, when this is over . . . one spring, when this is over . . ."

Five days later, the inspirational boy soprano was floating dead in the water.

MORE DIRT roads, more dead ends. One farmwife rushed onto her porch lugging a shotgun as Cap did a real gingerly U-turn in her yard. Two more days we rambled, looking. Tires kept going flat. They soon appeared about as nicked and patched as I'd commenced to feel. I could see my husband sitting more forward. One-eighth of his beard kept shifting where his molars clamped and slid. Hunched nearer the windshield, he had a stranglehold on steering. In Cap's side glances, I noticed him decide what'd be around a curve—his head fixed square on that very feature when it appeared. By now, Cap had quit asking locals. He was homing in on the bad old place like moving toward a sound. "Lucy," said he, quiet. "We're near it." "I could tell," goes I.

Behind me I hear a strange sound: it is our children holding still.

FOUR A.M. in a tourist camp. A low-lying walnut grove, moon at three-quarters full, all my babies sound asleep. White shacks looking like a combination of necessary johnny houses and the ideal cottages songs talk of. I woke to find the Captain missing from our bed. Where to now? First I slipped next door, checking on our young ones. —This is not too dainty of a subject but it's a fact of life: My children had pinworms. I don't know if Yankee mothers put up with this. It was early fall and my kids played outdoors and sat right in the dirt. Worms were in the dirt and kids were, too. Meeting of the twain. Get the picture? What you going to do?

Doc Collier'd given me a medicine I spooned down all of them, this stuff turned worms a purple color. Made them easier to spot when, around midnight, worms came out onto their only porches—which also happened to be my babies' private rectums. So I got up, pulled the cardigan around my shoulder, grabbed my pen flashlight, and scuffed off to be nurse.

Heavy walnuts kept dropping from trees, loud slaps, thudding like practice ammo in the dark. My seven oldest children were all heaped onto one bed, leaving the other empty. My beautiful litter, busy being each other's covers, pillows. I smiled seeing so many arms and legs overlapped, blond cordwood. I turned each child over, untangling one from the others, yanking down undies, scouting—hankie at the ready for those minor worrying vermin. —How routine all this was for me. How odd to remember, with me this old, with them all now dead.

Worms!

Maybe Captain was off exploring on foot. Done, I finally wandered to our Ford, arms curled around myself, head down. I watched my moving shoes. I half admired my own plain shadow in the moonlight.

I knew my husband loved our children. Of course. Sometimes he lit up—watching them, he laughed his pleasure. Their back-talk sass pleased him more than it did me. "Shows their grit," he'd say. "They'll need it, Lucy—ease up on them." But every summer night, he felt me rise from off the bed, he heard me shuffle in to check their backsides. Did it ever come to him to say, "Get back under covers. I'll do that tonight"? No, child. Never.

I knew my husband loved his missing friend. But if that friend was alive, one cabin away and still a boy, could the Captain find love enough to get up, grab the flashlight, drag over, settle on the bed, tug those Confederate skivvies down, check? It give me the shakes—the picture of Marsden so big, bearded and grown, helping his pal in a way that personal. Did he love that boy enough? Oh dear, yeah. Seemed to me, he did. And I hated him for it. Ned, I mean. Right then I hated Ned the First.

Cap sat, sleeping hard at the wheel, like ready to roll again. I let my flashlight play over his thick sheeny beard. Platinum watch chain glinted white. Why had the man brought all of us with him? Alone, he could've traveled at his own quick pace, could have chewed the fat with anybody, he might have bypassed all them wayside bathrooms that eight little ones— and a pregnant wife—require. Did I mention being pregnant? Honey, by then it'd got to be a right steady state—eight little ones in something like eleven years. So, yeah, I was, again. Number nine, the last, I vowed.

Dozing, Captain looked handsome. Awake, his opened eyes ofttimes prevented me from noticing him proper—eyes threw this zone like a helmet and a dare before his face. —Now I could safely admire him. Aloud, I said, "You're a fine-looking man. What *good* does it do you?"

I switched off my light, settled on the running board, leaned against the rear door just in back of him. Our Ford's springs squeaked as I set both feet on the ground, my mended maroon sweater drawn closer around me. Across the road, beyond a field, over a woods, the moon gave every stem a fine and serious shadow. —Dignity. Is that too much for a person to ask?

I sat here marveling at the headlock History still had on my man. I wondered, chilled out here, what tales I had to match his own. Sometimes I worried I was jealous of his charm around our watchful children. Above me, in the car, Captain now muttered—something about the three missing tent staubs, where were they? "Not again," sighed I. Marshland behind the cabins sent a knee-high mist our way. Above walnut trees—black and lacy-looking—a yellow moon burned off to one side, cocked like a Saturday hat. Clouds kept interfering with moonlight so the brightness looked anemic, cramping, gaining confidence then losing face.

He claimed aloud he had to know who'd took that tent gear, and why. Child, I felt so bored of acting nice, of being Mrs. Nurse to every soul but me. Listening, I longed to give some marching orders. Then, not even expecting to, I yelled at Captain. Just said in a voice as strong and hard as your most superior superior officer's, "Marsden, listen up." Then I heard my husband—fast asleep—stiffen, his wide breath faltering, gone quiet as some bullied kid.

"Do this, Marsden. You run and get that Ned of yours, hear me? Go fetch your young friend right back to this spot. That there's a direct order, soldier. Got me?"

I waited.

Two touring cars rattled past, headlamps on. A mule-drawn hayrick creaked by, slow, black children headed out to harvest something for somebody, nestled half asleep amongst the straw. —I'd been in on the ground floor of my husband's nightmares all these years. Before, I had only told him to roll over, quit jabbering, calm down. Ofttimes that worked. But till this minute, I'd never thought to holler, try and bluff my way into a sleeping head, to go—a double agent, so to speak—down into that bitter dreamed old war of his.

And what if it worked? What if I really finally managed to set up a person-to-person talk with this famous Ned I'd never heard the voice of? What should I *say*? I figured, Lucy darling, you'll probably think of something. You usually do.

Biding my time till it seemed one boy *might* go bring another obedient boy, I waited. Cap kept rigid up front, I could practically hear his posture. I cleared my throat, swallowed. "Private Ned? I sent for you. You getting this? You present and accounted for?" I leaned shoulders back against the car doors, requiring support. I touched my throat, for company.

"Ned, son," I made my voice dip froggy/manly as I could, "you sure have been a big help to us, boy. I mean, you've stuck right with us all this time. No shaking you, ever. Job well done. But, look, you've stayed on long enough, hear? You just got permission, from the higher-ups, the top in fact, to clear out. Congratulations, son. You got the orders every warrior wants. It's over. Go pack. Singing voices count. Head home to your poor momma yet waiting with her birds. Go be civilian as possible, lad. Your days of service they just ended, honorable, too. So, bye-bye. You can leave us be now. Oh, and, son? That's a direct order, son."

I waited, braced for back talk, maybe a little whining. Oh but I longed to hear his voice squeak through that grownup snoozing at the wheel. Ned's voice that would never ever stop being thirteen. But no sound came. Finally I hollered Private Marsden's name. I had to know if his excellent dead friend was following commands. (Prayer: Dear Lord, in who I doubt, do let these discharge papers go through for my sake. Amen.)

"Is your buddy packed yet, Private Marsden? He fixing to clear out?"

A boy voice finally spoke. "Sir? in the woods yonder."

I asked—hard: And what was he doing over there, following orders?

"Sir?" my husband told me, "he's just crying and crying. And, sir? Sir?"

I give a snort. I sounded mean as a mean man can—which is mean.

"Sir?" The tone came out all pinched and reedy. "Sir? please don't make him. If he goes, I'll be in it all alone then, sir. Sir?"

A shout. I felt the chassis hop inches, Captain's great weight jerking to. His own holler woke him back into a peacetime adult. "Wha . . . ?"

"It's okay, honey. I'm here," speaks I. "The tourist camp, remember? Your babies are asleep. You were talking out loud again is all."

"Had this dream. Had another one, Lucy."

"What about?"

"It was then—only, I'd been . . . betrayed."

I sat looking out at the road. Moon made all Virginia look gunmetal gray. Deeper in the walnut grove, falling nuts gave sharp stupid thuds, both grim and funny.

I thought, If I ever smoked cigarettes, I'd surely stoke one up right now.

At last he crawled out, he bent over me, said, "Night, buttermilk," kissed my dry scalp, and then—rubbing his either eye—Cap dragged back towards our cabin. His bulwark back seemed wider than our rented hut. Either very early or very late in the day, Cap could act sweet as your secretly favorite child.

NOW, alone, I pulled either foot up onto running board, tugged skirt down over knees. I clasped myself around the ankles. If it won't for my age and experience, I could of been a girl. But I won't one. Never would be again. Maybe one reason my old man looked so young so long, he'd never quit being basically a boy. I didn't know if I'd been old since birth or if this present tiredness would finally roll back and leave me feeling a kid again.

Dawn was just trying to start, and I wondered what I'd of done if Ned hisself had answered up. I imagined the kid soldier, still off somewheres in the woods, leaning against a young tree, sobbing and sobbing. Poor thing. It won't enough that he'd been dead for a half a century, *I* had to come along and ride that child still more. I didn't hate him. He was—after all—like one of mine. Lost prior to my own turning up on earth, someway, he felt like my firstborn. But, oh, I wanted him planted finally, and stilled. Won't nothing personal in that. Was for me *and* him. Oh, for a stake through his heart to let him *sleep*.

I pictured my own kitchen, my house standing alone without me— clicking like a empty residence does thinkingly click. And, you know, I wished that *I* was missing somebody. I wanted somebody back there in Falls to be missing me in a active way this very second. A person would wake with this same dawn, to mumble, "Wonder where my Lucy is *now*?" and then they'd slide back to sleep imagining me. I wanted my absence noticed, just half strong as Captain missed his Ned. I wanted it so bad. Who—in all of Falls—did I long for even partway as much? And who . . . who liked me back?

I ruled out all the ladies at church. I passed over my own fussy mother, who didn't want to know the truth, which she called Morbid. And Poppa— who loved me because, half lazy, he almost had to. The older I got, the weaker he seemed—the sweeter, too, but helpless someway that made even three hours on the porch with him a torture. Almost by forfeit—I recalled Castalia. Cool, on fire, my first true enemy, a victim, another soul whose proportions seemed somewhat on the secret cathedral scale of mine. I pictured her in her orderly ruin of a house held up mostly by the mink cages around it. I remembered her pressing cold washrags to my forehead and how she always knew just when a scented compress had faded to plain room temperature. Her touch could feel almost rough but quit just at the edge of being careless. It felt all the truer for that. She had lately told me a few more stories about slave days—sometimes even funny tales from then. She talked about her plans for one huge mink farm—it always made me picture lettuces of minkskin, growing in a thousand plugs, rich brown and round as her. She described the coat that she was growing for circling her own great girth, cultivating it animal by animal. I heard her voice, ripe-sounding, rolling from her bolster couches of breasts. I recalled her barking orders at my older children while I heaved to bring forth the next little rude one. I'd be stooped over a basin, thinking this should get easier with practice though it won't. I pictured her hands—so gray-brown on their backsides—ivory in the underpalms. Work had burned palms with deep coppery pleats. Cassie looked out for her own six children, but had never bothered marrying any of their separate fathers. Seemed to me she'd squeezed the very best out of her men—good times, fine memories, their seducer's charm, distilling from each: a single snifterful of crucial seed—one souvenir child apiece. Her men had sense enough to clear out, sometimes even before true happiness stopped.

I sat here in Virginia's first light. I listened for my kids—none stirred yet. Castalia spoke of her former boyfriends so fond-like, if full of comic pity. Castalia could honestly praise each one's tricks, talents, looks, styles of lovey-doveyness. Plus, she got to keep the kids without having all them extra bosses right there on her case full-time. Once at our house, Cap caught me talking to her over coffee (Cassie and me were hooked on the stuff, could put away ten cups a day—needed it, two cups per child, minimum, our day's dark jazzy fuel). Maybe feeling jealous, Cap tried and make Castalia look bad in front of me. Undignified.

Our long cozy talks worried him. He didn't much like how our children played mingled all day long in the white neighborhood. Even after his own long complicated history with Castalia, Cap still kept a eye out for her shape, her skin like smoked round glass. "How come you never married any of them, Cassie? Six children and not one spouse in sight. A God-believing woman like you, it seems you'd feel ashamed."

She just laughed, a gilled edge ridged under each chuckle. "Ooh, I tell you—I done lived with all six of them men. All fine-looking, good with they hands, better steady company than *you* usually makes, sir. I tested them in this, checked them out at that, I give each one them pretty clowns a good fair tryout. But you know what, mister? Won't even one of them my *type*."

He laughed at this. Had to. He recognized some truth in what she'd said, he knew her answer was fairer than his hard question deserved. I remember we all sat in the kitchen, holding identical white coffee mugs. Each of us looked each other over (appraising, tender, realistic, sobered). We sat here laughing like the equals that we were. Some of our children trailed in to ask something and stood in the doorway, not daring interrupt for once—jealous of our union, stepping from one of us to the other, asking, "What? *What?*" Kids felt cut out of it and they were right. We didn't want no children in the room just then. They spoiled things. We were grown!

—I stood now, rubbed my lower back. Yeah, I'd feel the happiest to see Castalia. Did she half miss me? Was it her I loved? Was Captain just another of my children and Cassie some truer mother bulk, more my own and only equal? Was this a stupid crush like my children sometimes got on teachers and friends' older brothers? "Self-pity and jealousy," I warned myself—the family curse. Sunlight broke through pinewoods across a field—the center of it red as your own eyelid closed against noon. Light let me read a sign, "Heart O' Dixie Tourist Cabins." It'd been hid in the dark all night, not nine feet from our black Ford. (Child, the word "motel" had not even been invented yet—all of this went on that long ago.)

3

AND IT WAS this very morning, not three hours later—us underway again and me nodding off, he stopped the car. I woke fast, so did the one baby in my lap. I looked over. There Cap sat, swallowing hard. Grinning like some bridegroom trying to hide his nerves and second thoughts. The few children awake in back had been playing their first games of Mules and Graveyards, counting, sounding sleepy but half interested. No farm in sight, no lake visible, just weeds and way up ahead a rusted mailbox, like a case of lockjaw on a stick.

Now all our young ones piled out. To them it was just another stop. Older ones led the babies into tall weeds to do their duty. Lou and Ned took charge, giving me a break. Captain still sat at the wheel. It was a misty early morning but he was perspiring pretty bad. "So," he said, looking around. In the bushes, one of our twins still argued game rules, whether cemeteries canceled solid-*white* mules. True, I was yet holding the baby but I got out, I come around to Captain's side, opened the door for him like *he* was the wife. The big fellow thanked me, unfolded hisself, patted down his graying brown hair, a single stubborn cowlick left, he buffed shoe tops on the backs of trouser legs, shining shoes. Like keeping a appointment. Somehow pitiful to witness. We all followed him. We had to.

I was getting aware of breathing—mine and the baby's I held—my heart grew busy, expecting what? I glanced around, prepared for smoke, for rifle fire, a long scream, anything. I didn't see no water yet. I just wished I *looked* better. We heard late summer bug sounds, a tractor working uphill maybe two miles off—it was that still out there. Captain hopped a ditch, us trailing after. My children had hushed. Even groggy, they sensed some change. Cap had cleared a little rising when he spied a low woods up ahead. Soon as he smelled the water beyond it, I saw his whole chest swing aside, front muscles locking like a horse's shying from a high jump or from open flames.

"What?" I asked him, trying to be helpful, wondering if I could. I half heard the man. He kept whispering one foreign-sounding word, like trying to steel hisself and using it as a charm. "*What?*" I asked, feeling I had a right to know. Only weeks later would I figure what he'd sputtered again and again. "Gethsemane," he said.

Needing no guidebook now, he was like sleepwalking, arms lifting partway before him, half tripping over sticks and roots. Hurrying so. I lugged one baby on my hip, our youngest napped snug in the picnic hamper I toted. All our little ones pulled along after, ragtag, not wanting to get left. Soon as he saw water, Captain, stiff-backed, commenced to checking his Swiss pocket watch, like it might tell him how many holdout Yankee marksmen still hid waiting up them trees before us.

"Everything's taller," he said. Something in his voice caught my heart then, nearbout sideswiped it. I'd never heard him sound so plain unguarded. It reminded me again: he was a victim just like the rest of us. Different things get everybody: For him, war. For me, the setup, or what war'd done to him maybe. For my babies, what this mix—his battle past, and my stab at side-street peace—set off. Who knows? We all keep trying, darling.

I followed. You do that if you love somebody. Otherwise you leave.

My children huddled closer. Our group waded through a field of tall sedge. The back of the Captain's black suit was flecked with green triangle sticky seeds. They're called beggar's purses, a good name since they're worthless but'll grab whatever's unlucky enough to move past. My children's hair was already spotty with these. I figured it'd give kids busywork once we got back to the Ford (we will, we *will* get back, I promised my own self). It soothed me for a second, picturing small hands going over one another like young grooming monkeys do.

I'd made the Captain wear his civvies on this trip. Said I wouldn't be seen with no man sporting a feather in his uniform hat—especially when I didn't even own one hat with a sprig of plume to its name. Too, I hated how that sword was always knocking against our Ford's gearshift. One hint at how off-center war is: the awkwardness of living life with that size a weapon tripping you up. Whenever I called the Captain's uniform vain and dandyish, he cited peacocks: how the man ones have more colors than a Rit Dye sample board at Woolworth's, while the lady birds get born washed out, khaki being about their finest effort tint-wise. I'd scold him, "Don't talk peahens to me, mister. I'm white as you, and not no hen. Besides—what's the use of quoting Nature at a person if it only makes her feel worse. *That's* not what Nature's for!"

NOT a marker, not one path. The gristmill standing on the far east shore was in ruins now. Vines had made a trellis of its waterwheel. Not one other sightseer. No battle had happened here. Just one boy got killed and only Captain Marsden remembered who.

A big blue heron at the lake's far end flew off like a judgment on our nosiness, our family's size. Everything got way quieter. Us, too. Bug noises—interested in us—tamped back a notch.

The shore narrowed more. Trees on our right, stagnant water to the left. I shoved children all before me, hoping none would slip and fall into that filmy mess. I remember thinking, What are we looking for? What are we *do*ing here? He needed witnesses, I guess. You marry, it means you've signed on as a witness to that person's pain—meaning their history, entire. We trailed him—so he'd have somebody with him. Could've been anybody. But it was us. Required to, we all tripped along, fighting to keep up.

He stared to his right then. Saw one tree wedged among the many. They all appeared alike to me. Must of been the one. Because: Captain stepped left, Captain fell three and a half feet downhill, Captain sloshed away from us, Captain backed into the lake. He was getting the full view of it, looking up. He bogged knee-deep in bilgy mud among floating water hyacinths. He'd sunk to his thighs.

The pocket watch popped free of his vest pocket and—on its chain— swung back and forth above the shallows. Minnows, drawn to platinum, bunched there churning before him. Some fish broke water, leaping for the watch like they figured Time was edible, the fools. Cap's vest and lapels were speckled like a telegram with green seeds set in rows. He mashed one hand around his throat, up underneath his brown beard. For every breath, his voice gave one moan. Fish kept stitching water all in front of him. He pointed up at that tree yonder.

Our children held tight on to one another's sleeves and shoulders, they grabbed my skirt's whole hem. On all sides I was soon sectioned like a pie, my honor guard. Captain finally saw us, gaping from uphill—our faces so worried about his toppling right into water. Proud as ever, he must've hated what pity showed in our wide eyes and open mouths. Lake weeds clinging to black britches, dripping, he now climbed, hands and knees at first, onto our mossy bank. He moved through our group—which split—on towards the tree. It was a big old sycamore. It'd grown a lot since that August day in '62. But then, too, so had Captain.

Strange, this breeze came up, wide sycamore leaves turned to show their whitish backsides. I felt for a minute, against all my common sense, that the tree had someway recognized him. Then Cap, he shinnied right up into it. Muddy legs and shoes went last into the rustling green. He was now hid total from our view. This was early September. All at once, I felt the heat.

Ned, who'd heard about this tree his whole life long, whose very name was stuffed so full of this sad spot, kept bouncing all over, just dying to climb up after. But I clutched him by the wrist, no way would I let him budge. Our group stood looking up at one knotty sycamore, hearing nothing. Even the baby in her hamper was awake, her Marsden gray eyes open, fixed straight up. For a while it seemed my husband would never come down again. From behind broad leaves, no sound. For miles around us here, such stillness.

IT FELT like that wicked old war—after too long a wait—had got its way at last, had finally sucked him up. I stood here, every neck muscle tightening from gawking overhead too long. I wondered: Girl, what will you do if it has finally funneled him up into its very craw? "Live, I guess."

That was my best answer. And still is.

Then we heard the slightest cry. I figured he'd come upon a skeleton, something dangling up there still. I'm sorry, I just didn't want my children near this. Was I wrong? I wished that I could drive the motorcar. I'd leave, I would. Up high, he parted greenery. He was nearer the treetop than it seemed any fellow his size could find support. A full fifty-five to sixty feet in air over the lake and us. Green divided, he popped out before it, all in black. Cap said, "Look, love." He meant me. He never called me that at home. I felt like he'd just spoke to somebody else.

"Still here, it's here." His one arm crooked around a bough, his other held out what seemed part of a crisp old harness yet knotted there. Cap posed so high above the water. You knew that to just swing from such height into a lake so shallow would kill a diving boy for sure.

By kicking two limbs aside with a free leg, then pinning branches back, Cap could show us: One branch had someway swollen. He had a hold of something. Wood looked puffed, like bordering some tourniquet, the leather maybe wedged inside its deep grooved dent of bark. "I was right," his voice bounced out over the lake and back. "All of it's true." He sounded fearful he'd been making up each word for fifty years.

Which bothered me. At my arm's end, our child named Ned kept wriggling side to side, pleading to please go up, could he, could he please? (And I stood thinking just, Uh-oh. Was wondering, If Cap has talked about it so much when there was still some doubt, what now—which last few square inches of the man's attention must I try and fit into next?)

The man held out a leather cord. It was half white, looked salty with age. My husband stood far up as an angel in the lush folds of this tree. Our heads tipped back so as to see him. He leaned forward, moving to test the rein's strength. Our babies edged nearer me. Many short spines pressed against my legs. "Don't, Daddy," Lou whispered straight up. We expected he would now fall: break his neck. Canted forward, he was sure trying. I saw he'd half planned this. Maybe to drop, maybe to bust his skull in the same shallows where his friend'd died. I didn't understand. His logic was diseased but, for him, it was logic. And yet, the leather, it held—supported even a man grown to this serious size.

After slumping forward, his watch a pendulum above us, after he'd heaved out like begging that line to snap, Captain tipped back to safety. Then, behind the crook of one arm, he covered his face, started making the shrill sounds of a boy upset. Crickets hushed a hundred percent now.

Finally my husband called down to us and the lake, "What'd he do? What'd he *do*?" —Like we had killed that child.

On ground, our children gave off unplanned little groans. Not understanding anything, feeling everything. I almost sobbed, for reasons of my own. Part rivalry. I knew that nothing I could ever do or say would compare with my real enemy—a boy-corpse since '62. My crying jostled the hamper

I still held. Our baby girl started, loud, too. It got almost funny, all of us crying out here in the middle of nowheres, the noise.

Well, recovered some, Captain now wanted each of us—me and every last child—to come up in the high tree and be with him, to see the leather thong. Right now, he said, this instant. Fifty-five to sixty-five feet straight up. Well, honey, that's where I drew the line. A mother she has to. Eight youngsters from age nine years to eighteen months. Half accidental, I let Ned's hand aloose, he practically ran vertical, laughing as he commenced the scramble, hidden by full September leaves. He hadn't yet connected death with the famous story of this place, was just glad to climb, a child. Even scared of Captain, I someway allowed our eldest, Louisa, to go struggling up too. Maybe to guard Ned? She went carrying her diary stuffed into the back of her skirt's elastic. She'd said she was going to have a jump on her first school assignment, "What I did on my summer vacation." (Big-boned, watchful, up she slid behind leaves, lost to me.) "Call them back," I told myself. "No. They're half his. Not half, but some. A portion his."

Our youngests, hopping every which way, begged to go. They couldn't half walk yet, much less scurry ape-wise straight up into air. Baby, she sure whined. "No way," said I. "Baby *miss*," she yelled, meaning she always missed the good stuff, fun.

Well the Captain glared down on me and gave what he now called a direct order. His face—seen from underneath—was a pink udder full of blood. He didn't much like my staying on the ground, sparing my wee ones. Didn't like that a bit. Wanted each infant to see one piece of cracked horse harness choking some treetop. I watched him frown and mutter down at me. Next his tone changed, he went, "But please, Lucy, I've come all this *way*." And I felt for him then, I did. I knew that a softer decent-er woman would have passed her whole brood—whole life—into his hands. But, listen, staring up, I understood, I wasn't so much scared he'd mistakenly drop one of my wee ones. Fact is, I felt spooked he'd *throw* one. Into the lake. On purpose.

I could someway tell he wanted to. I heard my eldests move higher, nearing him. I saw branches quiver with their minor added weight, tree's tip nodding with a man's great size. That sycamore kept shivering. I knew the Captain had some strange plan. Maybe he wanted to chuck a live child into water for a offering, maybe he hoped the sacrifice would let his friend swim ashore, awake and new, speckled with greeny film.

Captain waited for Ned and Lou to hand-climb within reach, he looked so odd up yonder. In black, one leg holding tree limbs aside, he was scoffing down like a naysaying Jeremiah, one minute nagging me up to him, next promising things like some sly salesman, saying Lucy this and Lucy that but looking grim and black there on high, looking like something hungry.

Honey, I shook my head No so many time I nearbout lost balance, I almost fell back in the lake itself. "No way, mister. You cannot have these ones of mine!" I was quaking so bad I had to set the baby's hamper down before I dropped it. I screamed, "Ned! Lou! You come down from there/ this/second/and/no/questions/asked. It's me or him, you hear? Get your bodies down here if you plan to stay living!"

I heard them stop their long crawl up. Then, without one little gripe (God bless them), I felt both souls ease, branch by branch, back down to me, towards ground, and breathing a bit longer.

To this day, I don't know if he'd of hurt them. It was something I felt. And listen here, I knew him, didn't I? I knew and know that man.

When they dropped back into my sight, I expected they'd act peeved. They each bolted over and held on around my hips—like they'd been scared all during and were just waiting for some order stronger than the old man's.

Well, we all stood on firm ground, shaking as a group. Well, when he seen how they'd turned back, had tricked him and were safe on land with me, oh the things he said.

Older children hid their eyes, like that'd help shield them from what he bellowed at us from on high. He was rocking side to side, the whole tree rustling, creaking, pitching with a man's unnatural weight up top. He yelled I was a turncoat, a lady Yankee spy that'd helped them burn his family's place, a camp follower, worse. Then he let limbs go. One hiss covered him. Bits of bark came sifting down on us. No telling how long we waited. It was so hot. The end of a long humid summer. We stood. We sat. I saw Ned notice a whitish rock he wanted to collect but felt too polite or fretful to go after. "Grab it," I told him, and he smiled, dashing over.

Finally we heard Captain start his own glum climb downwards. Whole flakes scuffed off the sycamore's wallpapery trunk. Bark drifted down before our upturned faces like so many ashes or diplomas. Parchment all around us. First his black-buttoned shoes bobbled into view, then dark mud-crusted pant legs, striped jet-black silk socks, and then the rest of him. On the tree's far side, away from us—he fell, landing square and heavy, one wet thud.

When he rose up, the man looked over one shoulder, his back to all of us, him muttery, bent in. The face looked puffed, ruddy from being so angry, like some venom had worked loose in him. He hunched over something. He had cut a piece of the harness to carry home. Kept holding it close up to his chest and beard, like we planned to steal it. He moved twenty feet across a clearing, stood guarding the thing like a splinter from the Cross itself.

I figured he needed time alone. I told him, We'll be waiting in the Ford.

"Don't *leave* me," he spun our way, voice pained, pure child now.

"Won't," I promised—stepping nearer, playing totally unscared. "None of us can drive it, remember?"

We'd waited an hour and a half (Ned had gathered half the white rocks of Virginia). Cap finally turned up—breathing like he'd swum that lake. He smelled of bottom mud, his face looked neutral. He held the harness mashed between two hands like some small life he'd trapped.

4

THE WHOLE trip home, Cap said nothing. Didn't eat. The children tried to keep hushed but that lasted about ten miles and who can blame them? Usual noise gave me such comfort now. I listened to many wayward bits of their jabber. Baby was trying to make her baby talk understood. "Baby *miss*," she repeated a good bit. Not easy to make out, yet forever poised, that one. The others teased her. She seemed pretty able to take it and I soon quit fighting for her. Cap stopped at diners now, not groceries. Didn't seem to care about saving money anymore. Whilst we ate, staring (guilty) out the restaurant window, he'd stay right at the wheel, like being another part of the car. Underway, he went slower than before, a perfect driver, with that bit of leather clamped betwixt his wide red fist and the black steering wheel. After we'd finished our diner breakfast, Ned or Lou or me had to step before the Model T and crank the motor, get her going. Cap would not climb out. Them whole two days bound home, I never once saw him go to the bathroom.

We started seeing landmarks we knew. I hoped he'd turn, by degree, more into hisself again. The children commenced pointing at things. "I *knew* that was over there," Ned boasted as we rounded a curve. A fancy lattice gazebo on a farm lawn—six funny whirligigs spinning at its six corners, one little jigsawed farmer chopping wood, another cow-milking—all inspired by wind into a joy of blurred enameled moving parts. Then, one half-burned barn. A low creek without no name. These all felt famous. To me and us they did. I loved hearing the kids predict sights I thought that only I had noticed. I recalled my honeymoon return. I remembered my own husband's long walk from Virginia wearing hand-rolled tow-sacking shoes, fifteen, every step a decision. We passed four charred chimneys of the Marsdens' spoilt plantation home. Captain, our Captain—speeding us back into civilian life—man never even glanced The Lilacs' way.

Finally just outside Falls' Baby Africa, Castalia's place. Unmatched non-painted shanties seemed to have grown in a circle the way mushrooms'll spring up after May rain. Her house's wood had silvered to the color of a nickel. She'd made her outhouse from a Bull Durham backstop thrown out of the ballpark. Its sides showed a salad of red paint and chopped lettering. Gave you something to read whilst sitting in there.

Cassie had kept expanding the stilted mink cage herself. It grew by seasons like big wasp nests do. Thing now wrapped around her shanty—so she could hear whenever dogs stopped in to run the minks, make them lose weight and dull her future coat. Its single tube of screening looped round her lot like a long tossed fur stole, a boa maybe. Her four youngests were playing outdoors—towels tied around their necks as capes. Her baby—hearing our Ford come chugging—bolted from the outhouse trailing a towel cape, pulling up knickers with one hand, waving the other. "Look," Lou called. "It's Leander, Reba, Aubergine, and Antwan. Stop, Poppa. Look, they really want us to."

"Do. For the children." I reached out and touched Cap's arm—he flinched like my fingers were live coals. Ford coughed on, past running kids. I turned, glad at least Castalia hadn't seen.

As we pulled down Summit Avenue toward our place, children stayed quiet in back, we passed our town librarian supervising six high school kids. Their arms were stacked with towers of books. The librarian nodded Yes, grinning. Then we approached Winona Smythe's home. The house itself was present but her yard was now just flat lawn. A crew of neighbors worked with saws and they too smiled on seeing us. Without Winona's jungle, the whole street looked bald. "Gone!" they called when Cap slammed on brakes, jumped out.

"Where to?" I hollered.

"Thin air!"

We all patrolled a home now totally purged of its Winona-ness. Weird for 1910, its lack of weirdness. Ladies who'd said for years—"Ooh but I'd love to spend one day inside that health hazard," they sure had. The house reeked of ammonia, of everything but the ticklish history of dynasties of yellow birds.

Captain stood in the small second bedroom. He was leaning in its doorway.

"Near as we can tell," the Mayor's sister's husband explained to Marsden's back, "she just took clothes, her birdcages, and the bed out of here, her late son's, near as we can tell. All the doors were open. That got my wife's attention. No note, no nothing. We're not even sure who owns the place."

"I . . . do," said the Captain. Then I saw it come to him—there might be a note for him, one Winona'd mailed to our home. He got us home right quick. I said nothing. I knew not to. After his recently trying and lure my babies up the tree, after finding that his Thursday pal since '65 was fled— I kept real real still, child.

I worried how all this would change him. I recalled his saying the one word, "betrayed."

Soon as we pulled up before our own house, Cap stomped indoors. Cassie had seen that mail got stacked on the hall table. By the time I'd supervised our rumble seat's unpacking, and started making the first few forays indoors lugging stuff—I found envelopes thrown everyplace, him seeking the Widow Smythe's reasoning. I was unloading the boot of our Ford when my husband strides out right past me. "Nothing" is the only word he says. Headed downtown, the man was already wearing his full-dress uniform, feathered hat and all. He wore that getup for a week, ten days. Put it on for General Forrest's birthday, July the thirteenth. Come winter—when he got it out for Lincoln's (and not the day Abe got shot, but his borning date)—well, then I knew the Captain wanted to *live* in the thing. He pretty much did.

Mrs. Peahen quaked to think what plumage-saber rattling lay ahead.

Home again, our car covered with great sprays of red Virginia mud, I myself set to cleaning with a unhealthy vengeance. Ned's latest mineral trove stayed underfoot all up and down the back-porch steps. (I would not let him tuck rocks under his bed—the place where his poppa stowed guns.) Ned says, "But they'll get rained on." "Honey, where you think they been since God wore knee pants? They *love* rain. That's what chipped them off of mountains and made independent rocks of them. They lap rain up. Rain's their . . . travel agent."

"That true?" He squinted, moist gray eyes fixed on me. I touched his humidor curls. "Go think about it," I told him. "And if Momma's wrong, come tell her something truer." You got to keep them busy, honey. Was one thing I was good at.

ALMOST immediately on getting back, our Baby started talking plainer. She'd been goo-gooing whole sentences for weeks but now we sort of understood them. She made sense earlier than any child I've heard of. This, for her momma, proved both a novelty and a pain. Her *starting* words were: "Bay might *miss*." Meaning: Baby might miss something. You couldn't leave that one anyplace by herself. Try and you'd hear a tiny bubble voice say, "Bay *does* miss." I felt for her, I knew the feeling. Mostly we just left her cradle parked smack in the middle of our living room. Not nine months old, but you couldn't put a thing over on that one. Had to be the center of everything from Word One, honey. Pretty as the cover of a candy box. Everybody said so.

Returned, I got busier than need be. I do that. He stayed away more. I rarely knew if I'd see him at dinner or no. By day, you never witnessed such housecleaning as mine on returning. Now I understand that it was superstition. *His* voodoo meant driving north, cutting magic charms down from trees. Mine seemed to involve purging dust kittens from our upstairs halls. Maybe I'd been inspired by seeing Winona's yard timbered and purged of muskrat nests. Got so evening itself looked like a form of dinge trying and settle on all my just-cleaned home surfaces. "Oh no you don't, darkness!" I bleached the linens till some got tiny holes at their edges, shaming me. I believe I thought—don't laugh—that I could someway clean his sadness from his life and mine. I'd get our one white house just perfect.

Someway, everything felt changed.

Since the tree, our kids acted half afraid of him. I saw him notice. I regretted how that kept him from the house still more. He went to poker games and steeplechases. On the Outer Banks, in our lieutenant governor's company, he shot many a innocent duck.

Nights he did eat at home, our table talk grew sparser, his and mine. The children gabbled on—like trying and take up the slack. They stared at him a bit too much. Cap left off telling me his stockyard news. I risked making a joke about the sheep counter that divided by four. On the foot-treadle Singer, I made myself a new dress—a nice flashy gray worsted. I feebly hoped to get his attention. Not that I wanted it, but more to cure him. What am I saying, darling? Of *course*, I wanted it. I asked Cassie's advice. She said he was remourning his young Ned, and then to come home and find Ned's momma needed mourning too. Rough on anybody. I saw that. Still. . . . Our kids'd bravely ask him to pick them up and twirl them in his arms like usual. He looked down at them like they were Martians talking French. The man's moods turned more dark, they really lasted now. Earlier, his tempers were what you might could call Washable Blue—now they ran towards Permanent Royal Black. Too dark to ever wash out, too dark to look through, into or past.

At Lucas' I bought petunias—last of the season, marked down. I lined clay pots in our kitchen windowsill. Some smell, but did he notice? I volunteered to be the Room Mother for all six of my children in school. (That's a heap of cupcakes, honey.) I ordered new lino for our kitchen floor, paid for it from a fund I'd personally set up to get my Louisa into nursing or social work school. I begun to find my sadder husband better-looking. Strange, his straight-facedness had begun to working on me. He'd quit paying nightly social calls on my side of the bed. I thought, Now we are back from the Front—we're finally ready to learn to love each other right. But, you know me, I was always thinking that. My nature to. The sight of him dragging up the porch steps, slow, at six—it broke into a whole new zone of my heart (Sorry for Our Appearance—We Are Expanding for Your Shopping Convenience). It was my heart's fatty rind, a annex that I figured he'd done used up years earlier.

On the road I had feared him. Home, I mainly pitied the fellow. That made me need him more. I hoped, at the very least, for Cap to come home every night, to do what he said he would. Well, he didn't. Maybe he couldn't. But he sure did not.

One odd thing, after seeing the tree again, his hair went white. And real fast too. I thought he must be dyeing it—or else that he'd finally quit. Almost seemed like my own scrub-bleaching of the house was having some effect upon his temples. Ten weeks, four months—and by deepening wintertime, my man's mane and beard showed no color in it whatsoever. His momma's hair had done that, due to Sherman. Happens, I'm told. Doc Collier explained to Cap: A shock can do it. Our GP then asked the Captain what *his* shock had been. He said, "Nothing I didn't know already. Is this exam about over, sir?"

Downtown my man gathered crowds—him in that outfit, the gray wool, the white hair and beard now setting it off more. I remembered when he'd been *shy* about his war doings. It got kind of tacky, his dressing like that so much. I stayed home alone more. The house I'd hoped would lift his spirits after work each day failed to air out mine. Frost got the petunias. I kept busy, though. I had them IOU class-mother cupcakes—I decorated for Halloween, Christmas, and could it already be Easter? I tried to encourage Baby to do more with her first language than complain and brag. I visited my parents, who were running down like rusting clocks. I watched this with a cool sad eye that scared me some. I crocheted booties for my latest one, due any day. I'd already wove enough booties to stock many of the East Coast's looser unwed mothers. I could stitch booties while cooking and helping with math homework and talking to Castalia in code about which person on what street had done what smut now. Little pitchers have big ears. I made more booties still, it kept me moving, busy. Only when I stopped did I tend to collapse. Sitting quiet, I remembered the long trip north and my old man's strangeness up a tree and even back on flat land. Like Winona, he seemed disappeared.

And I missed him. Missed just having him in the house every evening at a certain hour. Missed how on good nights he'd tell the children stories, he'd let them take turns sitting on his knee—them sometimes using his Swiss pocket watch to time each tale. I missed how, after breakfast, he set that fine watch by my kitchen clock, how he got a stern regretful look before stalking out to earn another day and dollar, how he'd asked—sly—of my Seth Thomas, "Now you're *sure* this is right?" I'd nod, "Was right yesterday, won't it? What do I look like, anyway, Greenwich Mean Time?"

"Well, you look Mean," he'd smirk, he'd flirt. I would stick my tongue out—like clockwork, clockwork—and the kids would laugh. Those days him and me failed to do something like this, children's breakfast digestion got thrown all off. "You forgot to stick out your tongue at him, Momma. Poppa, watch her. —There."

"Baby *miss*!" was screamed from the cradle. Louisa held Baby up, then I did the tongue again. She got replaced. "Satisfied?" I called. "That child's going to lead the cotillion if she has to invent or hire one. Ain't nobody going to get *her* goat. And more power to her."

THEY LEAVE you alone, and no matter how much you've played like you wanted that, when it happens you miss them. You even miss wishing they *would* . . . leave you alone. Don't ask me to explain it. If it was logical, then you could go buy a algebra textbook, check the answers in the back. If love was something you could balance like a checkbook, we'd have CPAs, not Cupid. Cupid's arrows hurt. Arrows *do*.

Sickening, ain't it? that I loved him yet. I did, though. Odd, at first, it almost seemed half pleasant—I'd be sipping coffee near the pre-frost purple petunias that come sundown put off a mild bruised-smelling sweetness. (They gave up too easy—petunias' only drawback.) I'd have Baby propped up nearby, teething, in the high chair opposite me, her ringlets nearbout good as Ned's. Nothing calmed her down like a little hand mirror—she could study parts of her own face for hours. The others'd be out playing Indians in the vacant lot in this powdery perfect early evening. Supper all but ready and me not knowing where he was. With me alone at home, it was easier to love him.

He was out all hours visiting other aging soldiers, Monday-morning-quarterbacking Jeff Davis' several mistakes. I missed the regular bulk, fine appetite, coarse jokes he repeated as if I was once—for him—at least the equal of his colored stockyard workers. Even now, I miss being taken for granted. Even this old, I *still* hope he will change.

5

CAPTAIN hired a private detective from Raleigh to track down the absent Mrs. Smythe. She'd took along her pup tent with her thirty birds and her son's little blond-oak bed. How she slipped away lugging all that, how she got past the Mayor's nosy sister right next door—that'd keep the busybody neighbor wide awake for months, regretting. Captain brought more guns home. I knew that he was wagering our money, he was winning big. He bet on artillery now. I'd hoped that seeing the swimming hole might help—but it'd upped the terrible ante for us all.

Seems to be like that strict sage says in Corinthians: Love suffereth long, and is kind, love envieth not, love vaunteth not itself, it thinketh no evil. Compared to the Captain since our war outing, felt like I'd once had a semi-model husband. As they say, sug, it's all relative. Relatives especially. But even with the gift of prophecy, and if I understood all mysteries, and if I had all knowledge, if I didn't have love, I'd be nothing. Not nothing. Or so the Book says.

Of course, I was not alone—not with eight children, the ninth (a kicker and a turner) percolating past its due date. But still, too, alone. Stuffed with the company of babies but feeling real alone from the outside in—a losing combination. Castalia would stop over and pour java in her favorite white mug—the chipped one, that's how she knew it from the look-alikes. And this saucy wide woman would sit at my kitchen table and talk and talk. She'd tell me worries about her oldest boys still at home, or midwifing news from all over Nash County, scandals brewing at the bank. I pumped her for slave-days lore. I wanted to know the full scoop on what it meant: being in the boat from Africa, being a member of what her people called the Tribe That Answers. She let me have it a little at a time over ten thousand cups of coffee dark as her, addicting as she was. We had our spats but, times, it seemed that she was the one factor kept that your Lucy grounded, not half mad. I stayed moving. If I stopped onct, it was over. Water boiling all day long.

UH-OH. Where's your car parked? "Relatives and Visitors"? Well, that's good. Otherwise, they *will* tow you. It's one way our Home makes money to support the penniless ones in here, like me. Fact is, the director gets a commission from the tow-truck company. Don't tell.

We had a troop of Pixie Scouts in here last week . . . What? Well, Brownies then—what difference could that make? And they just swarmed from room to room singing camp songs whilst wearing green beanies. They read us only the cheerful Bible verses. One gal explained to me she got extra merit-badge points the older her old one was. Word leaked out. I was surely popular that day. —Anyhow, the girls' leader, she was full of smiles and wiggles, so sugar-sweet you longed to let your dentures drop into your lap, just to see what-all she'd do. She prayed in every room, loud. They's some that think a prayer is a Hallmark greeting card, only less expensive. The Pixies kept their eyes open all during, watching her be perky and overfamiliar with God. I could see they sure had *her* number. Some winked at me during Prayer, and I can't say but that I didn't do it back.

After going, "Amen," the leader lady chirps about me: "My, girls, but isn't this lady a colorful old one!" And me right here, still breathing halitosis and feeling full of potential. Acted like she'd brung her Pixie troop to the monkey house at the Asheboro Zoo. I told her straight, "Colorful? Lady, I'm white as you and a pile more honest. It's rude to talk about folks like they ain't even in the room. Especially when it's *their* room you been invited into." Pixies giggled over that. —Well, her car got towed. While she was visiting my cubicle, thinking she was the magic wand of youth twinkling from room to room, they dragged her station wagon off right quick. She found out when she was standing right over there and oh you could hear her clear down the hall just cussing a blue streak. Them Pixies learnt a word or two that day. I loved it. —But, yes, "Relatives and Visitors," that's a safety zone.

We got quite a antique-filled parking lot out there, don't we? Some days when Jerome slides me in my wheelchair, I'll just set at my window yonder, gazing out at all them cars. Makes me proud. So many of us residents brought along our old sedans. Try and sell them, you can't get half what they're worth. Anybody hates to part with something that's served them good through the years. We got many a fine touring car out there. We won't all always as poor as we are now. Strangers sometimes come to the Info desk in front, ready to pay a fifty-cent admission. They think we got a museum going here. We do, in a way. —Six black Packards in a row! I don't care what's come down the pike since, don't nothing touch the hem of a Packard.

I can't brag much on my old green Chevy out yonder. It's the '46. I made sure it got parked next to Mrs. Minnie Lytton's Cord-Airstream. My Chevy's somewhat akin to me—a low-priced one-owner vehicle, a hundred and ten thousand miles on it. Car may be too antique to risk on the interstate but it's just a bit too nice for use as scrap, thank you.

You let your automobile set around long enough, magic happens. Its fins and chrome will first get to looking somewhat lumpy, mumps-prone.

Till you hit around year fifteen or twenty. Then your model finally commences to growing on people. First—it only seems a "novelty item." But soon it begins to gain a dignity especially around its running boards and headlamps. Why, Dignity has even sneaked up and pounced on my trusty ugly Chevy. Our Mohawked candy-striper, Zondro (she's taking art classes and she's *good*), she told her boyfriend that my old buggy had upped and turned into "a classic." Child, I can't wait till that happens to plain me.

Listen, on your way out—you flip the canvas tarp back, get you a goodly look at Minnie Lytton's Cord-Airstream. She lets people. Her car is proof of how much we expected of this century. Sleek, child. That roadster looks like our Future ought to, like the Future used to!

A Hunger
to Be
Vertical

BACK FROM war zones, I Dutch-cleansered even harder—feeling half ashamed, like dirt was mostly my fault, my own fluffy leavings. My favorite maroon cardigan was getting thin around the elbows. I loved it too good to abandon now. My ninth was kickishly near due. Childbearing in them times, you didn't check into no hospital for a week to ten days. Didn't have these fancy breathing lessons, with your cooperating husband hovering right there to help. No, ma'am, I'd send word from my home bed over to Castalia's mink ranch. She'd swoop in modeling the coat she'd begun to making for herself.

It started as a collar piece of mink that grew into one of those trailing wraps where you can see the shape of minks as minks and where the eyes are glass and where they bite each other into staying round broad shoulders. Then those fused into a short cape that soon added on others at the bottom and was dropping more toward a stole. She wore it in most weathers. The pelts were good but I worried a wee bit about her skill at sewing them together. Still, mink is mink and her pride in it dared you (like her clothes' bold color combos) to do much past admire.

By then, Cassie was delivering most every new baby in town. Doc Collier didn't like this fad. She'd come running with her famous basin, she'd set her fur wrap on a far chair—out of harm's way. She'd make you climb out the bed, stoop over that tin bowl, squatting-like, efficient (but no way to have your picture took). With Cassie's good coaching, out'd eventually drop your latest, that was it. I begged her—when it happened this time—she should please gag me so my screams wouldn't upset the little ones. I feared I'd yell things about my husband. I could imagine Baby, hearing me shrieking like Mrs. Lon Chaney through our home's thin walls, and Baby going, "Baby *miss*." Lucky Baby.

If you didn't die in three days, they called you back to work. First they'd ask you how to do some one thing right. Family'd inquire if you could maybe get up out of bed, step over here, and show them how. "Now the *best* way to peel a potato," you'd lecture, knife in hand, and you'd turn around and there you were, alone in the kitchen again, so you knew you'd lived. If you didn't pass on by day three, they figured you'd probably be good for at least a year and a baby more. If you did die, well, you did. Many did.

And Captain would have remarried fast enough. He'd made that plain. There was always some other woman nearby (living with her younger brother's big brood), some unwed woman that didn't quite cut the mustard lookswise but won't the least bit scared of work. She'd earned her own unpretty way for all these years. She'd had to. Cap kept his eye on one each time I was laid up.

Some fine morning just before I got ready to spring my ninth, here he came to stand near our bed (I'm sure it was his backhand idea of encouraging me someway) and he told me which woman he had in mind this go-round to be my babies' future stepmomma. He asked did I approve. Imagine. Just said it to make me mad so I wouldn't fade off and perish on him. He knew I'd never leave my precious ones to some hatchet-faced workhorse that'd beat them for not being her blood own, that'd pinch them when Captain went off into the country buying more edible livestock to dress up Sunday platters countywide.

At fifteen, why I'd been able to do everything. But at twenty-six? No. Before, the world had been going at me only from the outside in. Now it was hardship from the insides out. And, child, that's way different. Calendarwise, I was young yet but my tiredness soon felt the age of Lucy now. No, older. Older than the Old Testament. Back pre-everything, lacking form and voice and the will to even be toilet-trained. It soon felt like such a gray and important tiredness. Was the gray of circles under all the eyes that ever longed to shut for good. The fatigue was so huge that no one night's sleep, no month of good nights' rest, could whittle one initial in it. It just sat there, on you.

Our trip back into his war had everything to do with this great dip in Lucy energy. Till that, the whole war was a paper-doll chain of stories, a litter of ditties and tragedies, mostly true, if stretched out lacy, newsprint. Now it was a actual location, and not that far away. Imagine you could drive over one state line—and visit Hell. Not "Fort" Hell. Hell itself. Like looking down into some tourist Grand Canyon. Only, you can witness tormented souls frying in their juices like a zillion rafts of bacon popping on the canyon floor. And along the crater's upper ridge, shutterbugs taking Kodaks of Purgatory. Postcard vistas for sale, the foldout kind, heavily colorfully retouched.

The war now seemed a place for me. I understood—it still daily licked its greasy chops, eager for some whole new cast of characters, recruits. I felt it had our names now, me and all my babies listed, even the unnamed one yet drubbing in me. —A weasel is so sly that it can suck a hen's egg through one hole in the egg's underside, your average weasel knows how to leave the thing looking perfect. Poor hen'll set on it forever, waiting.

Before our trip I'd stayed untired as possible in resistance to something. I'd been getting steady if quiet help from him. Now he was off God knows where. He was wagering with money from my own dowry—a good-sized lump, I later discovered. He was risking my children's futures to win yet more collector's-item guns. They stacked under our bed till some nights, shifting, I'd feel them, rigid and not-nice beneath the mattress. Our weight would rattle hammers, triggers, stocks. Gave me the willies, bad. Suddenly the enemy seemed so near, right well equipped.

War: a fiery lake squirming with people I was pretty powerless to save. I felt smaller.

Castalia then weighed just 230–260.

Captain, he weighed 198–210.

Lucy—even pregnant—just broke 109.

BEING this old makes me remember how it felt then. My tiredness now is right on schedule. I'm really doing pretty good for somebody that should've been dead long ago—if she had a shred of decency left. At this age a person thinks, *Of course* I'm fatigued, after all I'm nearbout as old as God. But when you ain't yet twenty-seven and get so low, it feels way worse. Out my home's front window, I'd spy—walking back and forth to town—the spinster Cap had picked to fill in for me at my death. She wore her clothes like a Pilgrim, toted a handbag big enough to carry a stolen orphan in. She cut her own hair, you could tell from sixty feet. Was I being crazy, or was she sizing up our home, our yard? "So," I said, rolling over, with something in me rolling over in me. I meant: "So be it." I was starting to get too tired to stay mad long. For me that means near death, child.

After Cap dragged us to war again, with me laid up and ripening towards Cassie's handy help, I started fading in a final way. Was feeling, child, like everybody's inconvenience and eyesore. I was the one stain rusting something otherwise white and good. I was extra. By degree, I'd sunk, I had become the fuzz under furniture, I was the brown that made new wallpaper go stale and used-looking. In such a state, sleep avoids you like the plague. Just to lift your arm, just to manage dozing off for twenty minutes, you deserve the Noble Prize. You'd risk anything to try and shake this deep of a exhaustion. Louisa herself had started packing her brothers' and sisters' school lunches while I supervised from a yard chaise lugged into one corner of the kitchen. I felt sorry for my daughter, up at six-thirty. I made her keep the water boiling on the stove. I wanted to explain how water helped me to stay interested. The explanation seemed it'd require a full day's energy. "Just do it," I said. Sounded like her poppa, whose main reason to child-questions stayed: "Because I said so. Because you're eating my food is why."

I hated who this tiredness and further pregnancy was turning Lucy into. That changed nothing, honey, nothing.

The kids were at school, Baby was bored and actively saying so in the other room, and I soon got feeling like I knew what-all I needed. I grew crazy hungry for some one thing. You're *sad* for it, like everything you lack is waiting in one food group. I asked Louisa to bring me a Monkey Ward catalogue, please. She did. Lou always did, poor thing. I flipped through it like through some menu of what-all I'd missed. "Let's try something *new*," my husband had sometimes said in bed. I spoke that to the pages now. I needed, what? A snack of window caulking? no. A saucerful of face powder? no. Or did I need, like Wise Winona, to run off, to disappear no place?

I'd never before got that famous dill-pickle-at-4 a.m. yen you hear of pregnant women having. But now, waiting on number nine, there seemed some one dish that might make everything up to me. Captain had once told us: Sows eat their young owing to a lack of niacin. Ain't nothing personal. Starving for some one thing, I understood my sister sows better.

I sampled flour from the sack. No, it won't that I craved. I chewed a quarter pound of cloves (which is a lot of cloves, honey). I moved on to baking soda. Not quite. I hollered would Lou please bring some Niagara starch to my bed. Starch was sold in blocks then. I hacked off a good-sized piece and settled into eyes-shut chewing. I did the cud till my whole mouth felt soapy in a blank and sudsy way. Close. I swallowed half the bar that afternoon. I'd heard how black women downhill ate this stuff like candy. I recalled Winona's bartered hardtack. I moved on to trying soil out of a flowerpot. To make it go down easier I used a tiny silver teaspoon as my genteel shovel. Felt I was on the brink of everything I needed. Soon the subtraction would reverse, I'd once more begin to get added on to. I needed . . . supplements, something. There won't enough of me to fill the space requiring my being on guard these twenty-four full hours a day. Just thinking "twenty-four hours a day" made me get real tired, honey. —You still awake? You know the feeling?

My children, out in the yard, had just been playing round my bed. I saw they'd left their crayons in a old fruitcake tin. I bent and scooped that up. Guilty, I commenced to nibbling crayons like bonbons, peeling off the wrappers first. Honey, I did have *some* pride left.

Dainty, my eyes closed, I sat sampling crayons. Sky Blue tasted chemical but vague, Sea Green had a tang in it, but the sweetest two were Berry Red and my all-time favorite, Flesh. I stuffed myself, poking through these waxy sticks to find one little extra nub of Flesh, then gobbling it. Four kids filed in to ask me something. I tried hiding crayon peelings littering my counterpane and sheets. Seemed I had been snacking at my little ones' expense, nibbling fingers, someway gnawing *them*. Flesh of my flesh. Well, being mine, they noticed. They backed some steps away from me. I longed to call, "Please understand. With crayons, it's my first time—honest."

"She *ate*," Baby, merciless from birth, pointed at me. Ned told younger ones, "Uh-oh, Momma's turned wax eater on us. And I think she *swallows*."

I fought to explain but felt my molars cushioned in a film of smoothness. Kids looked back at me, sniffling—now right horrified, small hands on their small faces. Then I stared ahead. In the oval mirror opposite the bed, I saw myself—a gray person. I made a face, smiling, drawing back my upper lip. The teeth were rotten with all tints. I cried out. I tossed the fruitcake tin onto the floor. Crayons fired to far corners of the room, chattered out into the hall. I rolled over. I was shaking, I was facing the wall and I was shaking so.

I heard my children crying in the yard.

I onct had a husband. What do men do all day? Where was my husband?

EVERY TIME Mother came calling, I perked up, played like all was well. Why couldn't I tell anybody what was wrong? Why didn't I know? There she stood in her tailored suit, white gloves, hat on, bringing me three more Lady's Lending Library books, always three, always with titles like *Her First Mistake* and *The Heart Is a Funny Thing, and Frail*, plus *Blood on the Delta*. Just what I needed. Literature's got to be a ticket *into* your own life, not out of it. For my momma, escape stayed the single luxury. I begun to imagine making Getaways literal . . . if I ever come back to being the full-moon phase, I'd let Lucy run away from home. Out of here, Eclipse.

Momma had purchased a gaudy perfect bunch of zinnias from the colored ladies that peddled such things near the post office. Some days Momma told me she had grown these herself, specially for me. Now why did she lie? She'd always feared bugs (after a near-fatal childhood mishap with those). The lady hated yardwork. Still, I appreciated the thought. But, as I jammed zinnias into a bedside jar, they looked to me just like crayons come alive on stems. I knew that after Momma left—I giggled once, which spooked her some—I *was* going to have to sample one teentsy zinnia—nibble, nibble, little mouse.

My mother's the most fearful person I think I've ever known.

Momma now offered news of far worse male and female troubles than my own. "*You* remember that cute Winnie Murchison, the one from the expensive scarf-dancing class I tried to interest you in but couldn't? She was, what? two grades under you at Lower Normal? Remember how she always looked up to you so? You *know* the little Murchison I mean? Well, at least *nod*, Lucille. Seems the maid came to work, saw little Winnie's shoes sticking out the pantry door. Well, Winnie was *in* them. Stroke. Never knew what hit her, doctor claims. One minute here . . . next minute? Dead at twenty-four. What can you say? *That* Winnie Murchison. And you recollect the oldest Thorp boy, the only really handsome one? Well, and remember the dangerous quarry swimming hole? Well, not a week ago, that warm Monday? . . ."

She did half cheer me, but (as usual with mothers) for all the wrong reasons. While the strict lady jabbered sloppy tragedies with great good cheer, I sat up straight in bed, pretending I deserved to be talked at and was as basically alive as your next adult. It was easy to feel more alive than the weekly obit list she offered. With her here, my children gathered in my room. I felt ashamed—seemed that only when company arrived did they feel sure I'd behave regular. Outsiders were chaperones against my acting weird for 1911.

Lou got my hairbrush from off the dresser and, listening to her grandma, my daughter groomed me. Then we traded off, me working on my eldest's thin hair. Louisa pretended like we did this all the time—not just once a week when my momma visited. Mother watched, she set over there with her posies and news of maimings, her books about good women cornered on stormy nights by bad if handsome men.

My children piled right into the bed with me. Grateful, I didn't bother them about taking their dirty shoes off. I saw my mother wondering at this but saying nothing. As my life pretended to be hale and regular, my mother's lipless doubting mouth grew tinier and tinier. Here she was: Mrs. Bianca McCloud Honicutt. How had rude me ever slicked out of a body that dry, that cripplingly polite? I pulled covers up over kids' legs and gathered them against me, lumped under my either arm. It was all a show for her—the clatch of us backed up by many pillows. My children liked it, so did I. It was all faked but—during—sure felt nice.

The minute Momma said, "Well . . . this *has* been . . . Lucille, you certainly *seem* . . . don't budge . . . no, no, I'll show myself out" (as if I *could*, budge), soon as Momma closed the front door, children dragged down from my bed, my grasp. They didn't blame me, see. Kids didn't even seem too sad but acted like this had just been part of their duty, pretending I was basically okay. They seemed to hope that if they played-like once a week—they might help stave off further crayon gorging—might keep me *with* them and not off the edge where I usually wavered. "Don't go away mad," I called at them.

" 'Just go away'?" Ned added, turning back, and shrugged. They didn't hold it against me, darling. That was what worried me the most.

HONEY, once my stiff well-meaning mother had cleared out, when the children had moped off to the side lot, I would lean back. I'd be remembering my own big bedroom upstairs in the homeplace. Frilled sunny room, it was. I'd once had no worries but homework, playing with my pal, Shirley, fretting over what to make Momma, Poppa, and the maiden aunts for Christmas.

Come morning, I told myself that being so romantical about the past won't good or healthy. I was the mother of eight, soon nine. I told myself: Lucy, try, girl. I would get the covers thrown back. Then I rested. I felt the ceiling was looking down with pity on the swollen legs I'd kept well hid from Momma. Ceiling looked down on my lower body pumped up like a balloon tire about to rupture with a cannon-firing sound. Then I pulled quilts back, decently covering myself again. No. Couldn't. Compared to moving out of bed, a hemorrhage seemed a holiday. Two days after crayon snacking, I cleaned my teeth on the sheets. Every color in the world rubbed off. I wasn't only ready for the worst, it seemed I *was* the worst, the trench that others' runoff ran in. (I'm enjoying telling this!)

A sparrow chirping in the hedge outside my bedroom window, got so I would weep over it. That little dun-colored bird sounded so feisty, a factory's worth of willpower. I admired every creature more than myself. The baby turning in me, getting ready for the world by practicing to flex and strain, it seemed the President of the U.S. and me the cut-rate hotel room he'd been forced to stay in overnight thanks to a unexpected storm. I was a service, a waiting room designed for others' comfort. I felt sorrier for the crayons I'd gobbled than I did for my own self.

And where was the man I married? Off making more money, I guess. Off winning bets, off doing what he said he had to.

HOW can you keep going? I'd be in the brass bred—bugle-colored—one Captain later made famous by lying in it till somebody thought up television and finally sent a camera to film him propped up there. My face was turned to the wallpaper. The upright bars at the bed's far end looked like St. Peter's gate and like a jail cell I'd hand-polished. Cassie was in the next room making a fuss over my latest (I've skipped that part, it wears on me to speak of it). Cassie was yelling orders through the window at my eldests in the swing out back. Castalia kept croaking snatches of a hymn, "Sweet Jesus, Don't Nobody Work Like Him." Captain was off God knows where making deals and mischief on some county farm. I was twenty-six. I was near a child's weight myself. Here I rested, nine deliverings into my own life, nine passengers frailer.

And was then, just past my bedroom window, outside on the vacant lot, I heard my third from oldest boy fall off the rope swing. (Hadn't I told them: No more than three on the swing at onct? Hadn't I *told* them?) From indoors, I knew the breath'd been knocked clean out of him—that terrible pause that can wake a mother from the dead.

When he cried finally, when I heard he *could* gasp—that helped. Another boy kept whining from crabby hunger, from being overlooked too long. Baby was crying, "Baby *miss*," scared the world was a party being held elsewhere. You know how your kids get frayed and wild and varmint-cranky without regular attention? The steadying word or touch to smooth them down some?

Two crying and a third now tuning up. I could always tell the Why of each one's sobs. For every child in turn, a whole new independent language. Maybe I only do speak English but I sure felt fluent—a college of college material—in my every baby's fresh tongue.

Lunch was late. Baby had sprained her wrist and was crazy to have its dingy bandage changed, hated dirt. Report cards wanted signing. All those lacks waited heaped out there: tree climbing, falling down weepy.

Honey, was my own children made me turn my head back into the room. First they got me to sigh, a beginning. Then they got me propped up onto my elbows. Which let Lucy finally fling covers back, swing one bare foot at a time onto cold floorboards and a few stray guilty crayon rinds (my eyes opened from the chill—which helped). The room a wreck, dust every-where like lintish buzzards gathered in far corners to watch me lose it all.

Before I knew why (much less *how*), by using the bedstead as a early form of walker, practicing at the Vertical, I'd waddled off to make my peace with ragged smaller lives outside. Here comes Lady Crayola, Mrs. Spit-Polish and Heal.

My arms sprung out, automatic balancing, I tried for my sea legs again, hoping to get back on gravity's good side. I made it to the hall (so far, so good), I depended on furniture and the wall to help me find the staircase and then get down it, inching, but proud of progress, fighting faintness like it was some bad smell you can just decide decide decide not to notice.

My loved ones pulled me back toward the fray. For a while more, I would be their chef and referee, their witness. Then I hoped to leave. I saw that now. Elsewhere looked real good.

Four to the swing, they spied a shape leaning in their kitchen's back screen door. Ned cried, "Momma's up!" And they hurled into air and tumbled this way, running at me, colliding till they all but knocked me over. Then half on purpose, I did fall. But they were back of me to break it. I was going down onto a waiting curl and surf of bodies I had someway borne. They were all around me on the floor. They knew not to settle on my lower body, tender, sore. Castalia laughed from off the edge of what I saw. Her laugh swerved dark and rich and striped as her mink coat lowering into her idea of elegance at last.

A convention—kids' faces gathered round this fast-aging body, their first home. They thought I'd come downstairs to encourage them. But— hands all over my face and shoulders, ears: they didn't none of them know that—for a while there, they were really all that kept me in the world, honey.

Every single time, my loved ones teased me back to standing. (A trick!) Castalia come up then, holding our latest. She stood over me, here on the lino with my eight now playing with my hair—me powerless as Gulliver, pinned. Cassie looked me over with a touch of admiration, a great remembering tiredness of her own. "Again," she smiled. "Here we goes again?"

"Something like that," said I, straight up. She stooped closer. Her strong hands put Archie, my weak newborn, on my breast and—Cas indulged herself—she leaned down, let her own big head rest for one second on my shoulder. "You," I said so glad. And tears slid back to fill my ears.

Here we go again. Before the kids run off—forgetting to remember me for another six weeks—we were for those few seconds a unit, like one centipede with many different shoe sizes on all sides, the tired willing legs of one long long long life.

LOVE endures all, like they tell you. All. You can't keep somebody truly stubborn down too long. But everything sure does try, right, child? And things most certainly do seem to get bunches better at it year by year. But look, I'm still sitting up here, right? Lucy ain't all the way down even yet. Love suffereth all and is kind—though it really should eventually know better.

Stubborn, love.

Maybe even stupid. But who cares?

AND WAS two days later, into the kitchen pushes my old man, home from nowhere after being there too long—he's wearing the full-dress uniform—he bears a cordwood stack of guns and rifles. I'd been setting with Cassie over coffee here at the kitchen table. She'd tucked a quilt around my slowly unswelling legs. Cap, he steps right by us, not one word, and him gone these four days without my knowing where.

"So where *you* aiming, Fort Alamo?" Castalia most hollered. He paused, right-faced, and then, with great care, set weapons between Castalia and me on my red-and-white-checked-oilclothed table.

"I didn't hear the motorcar," I said. He frowned to prove I had but little right to ask. Then Captain reached down, stroked stocks of guns between Cas and me. Such fondness in his touch. You could see they were old ones, you could see how some of their handles were hickory, others pinky-gold fruitwood. Brass hinges had greened a bit. Two musket butts looked notched, somebody's scorekeeping. Ducks? Colored boys? I didn't want to know.

"This," he touched one, "*is* the Revolution. And that exceptional specimen there saw duty in 18 and 12. Here's a fine weapon that thundered on our side during the Mexican Expeditionary. And this," he lifted what looked to be a squirrel gun, no better or worse, "belonged to the great Forrest himself."

"Let me axt you something, mister. You just give away your Ford car for these, right?" I felt glad that Cassie'd spared me saying it.

"I have a museum here. They make more autocars. As for masterpieces such as these, this are all she wrote." Then he started piling them again into his arm—weapons stacked clear to his beard.

I stared at him. "And where you plan to keep them things, sir? Oh, by the way, nice of you to ask, it was a boy."

"That a fact? Well, how about that. Cause for celebration. I'm putting them under the bed, where a person's guns belong. In handy reach. Too many children in this house for me to feel easy hanging firearms over the mantel."

"First sane thing you've said, husband."

"Besides, they're far too valuable."

"Thank you. As their mother, I thank you."

"The firearms, Lucille. These museum pieces. Aren't you pleased? Don't you understand what we now own?"

"It's just guns to me, darling. *One* is one too many by *my* lights. And now we have no better way of getting to church than the old Pat and Mike method. So I ain't exactly bouncing up and down, no. Been busy, got other things on my mind, I guess."

"It takes imagination to understand our nation's history, Lucille, and how these items gracing your own kitchen table figure in that struggle. —Requires imagination." Arms loaded, he left the room and us.

I set here looking at Castalia. She shook her head. Her mouth was all pursed with irony but her eyes burned full of redbird fury. I pretended not to notice. I had enough on me without further fearfulness. I dreaded knowing what was coming next. Even in advance, I half understood. Even now, even stuck safe here in a Home where serving ladies with hairnets make three meals a day for me, I pull back from saying that next part. Like, by polevaulting over what's ahead, I can maybe leave it wholesale right out of my life. Can you, darling listener, handle a few detours?

But, of course, our bargain: A person's got to tell. Tell it. Tell it all.

Just, please, not yet. —Okay?

Good
Help

A good name is better than precious ointment, and the day of death than the day of one's birth. —It is better to go to the house of mourning, than to go to the house of feasting: for that is the end of all men, and the living will lay it to his heart. Sorrow is better than laughter: for by the sadness of the countenance the heart is made better.

—ECCLESIASTES 7:1–3

*E*VEN WITH the nine, even mostly managing alone, I never wanted a servant to boss.

Momma grew up in a household staffed by twenty-four black helpers. Most tended the yard and horses. Her enjoyment of good service got stunted early on. The accident taught her. She passed such fear to me, her only daughter. Even at my present age, I try helping every waitress who tries serving me. "Here, honey, that looks *heavy*," I stand, sometimes jostling her tray, sometimes spilling stuff.

Momma'd just turned five when this here mishap grabbed her. It proved nearbout fatal. She ever after blamed a certain nurse, one Bible-believing older lady named Maimie L. Beech. This woman dozed off whilst minding the white baby. Accident. Child Bianca floated in a coma for three weeks. Neighbors brought casseroles enough to pave a modern-day patio.

Bianca's poppa—the "Indigo Baron" of Falls, North Carolina—had three smart older daughters. But he favored his unruly baby. With her now drifting beyond help and love, past the power of money, young Angus McCloud nearly lost his mind.

ONE poisoned baby girl, my future momma, had been considered the local hellion of all time. Darling, this is truly saying something in Falls: Brat Capital of the Tidewater. Wealthy Summit Avenue spoiled its kids because it really could.

Soon as Bianca learned to walk, other walking and crawling children hid from her. Some parents did, too. The town's fire chief all but ordered the McClouds to keep li'l Bianca "observed" after what'd happened in a flammable shed near the lumber mill. She was bad about matches. When Angus donated a fire wagon to Falls' Volunteers at a brass-band ceremony, his youngest was discouraged from attending. She was off kicking the Collier twins in all four of their shins. Hopping around, these decent older girls asked, "Precious, why *us*?" Bianca spat back, "Go check the mirror, bug-faces."

HELP! Maimie L. Beech got summoned, a last resort. Among certain rich folks who'd spoiled their children seemingly past help, Miss Beech was called the "secret weapon." Nobody knew this woman's method, nobody asked. She herself had been a orphaned slave girl doing laundry in a Pastor Beech's home. His six rowdy children started orbiting around Maimie like bees fretting one brown honey log. She did nothing to woo or humor them. Fact is, Maimie scoffed, pinched. Kids couldn't get enough of her brimstone disposition. Maimie was the single household slave that didn't fear these devils. They sensed this and admired her for it. Kids' wildness soon tamped down some. Preacher noticed. Word spread.

After Freedom made her a semi-free agent, young Maimie Beech found she had a skill that sure beat ironing all to pieces. Decades gone and monsters later, Maimie was much sought after. J. V. Vining, Sr., had nearly got J. V. Vining, Jr., age eight, thrown into military school or a state reformatory or some weighted sack suitable for river tossing. Maimie turned up, she stiffly tended the boy for two months, he showed first melting signs of being almost human. Now "Vining's Cotton Mill" bore a extra gilded plaque: "and Son." Maimie got part credit and a bonus big enough to help her buy the little riverside home.

Other McCloud servants were soon jealous of a new-here woman given nothing to do but mope around the energetic youngest. Castalia remembered seeing Maimie around town, a spindly steepled lady nearing seventy. Maimie admitted to some Tuscarora blood. This showed in her thick straight hair, the stalky high-boned face, something in her surefooted stride. Beech's upper lip wrinkled every quarter inch with a ruler's evenness. She wore a cross-shaped brass locket she touched right often. Her nurse's cap looked pinned to her—some unopened envelope. She was long-limbed and springy as the daily switches she forced some brats to go cut for their own whippings. Beech jumped at loud sounds. Everywhere, everywhere, she carried her dark Bible big as a child's tombstone.

First, Maimie served as Bianca's jailer. No stranger to shinnying down drainpipes, the child often slipped away. Baby Bianca collected neighbors' rotting jack-o'-lanterns (she'd slyly waited for a nice frostbite decay to set in). Then the scamp sneaked indoors, pulled over a chair, climbed up, mashed four spongy pumpkins apiece into metal workings of her sisters' three signed Steinway grands. The older McCloud girls cried but proved saints in not biffing little sis. Angus' eldest three, in dark high-buttoned clothes, were tidy yet unbeautiful as furled umbrellas. They enjoyed just the kind of impractical tastes that female children of self-made men were then supposed to have. The day of the pumpkin mash, my momma—a pointy quail-boned crinolined little thing—took a lawn mower to the neighbor's Persian cat. She did. The cat survived but its feelings never recovered. It developed facial tics and therefore whiskeral tics, too. Every few minutes, its whole fluffy head went off like a alarm clock. Something to see. Legal action was mentioned but Angus McCloud paid nextdoor cat owners fifty-five dollars—held to be a fortune in them days.

Doubts were soon expressed about Maimie's secret powers. Had she met her match? Nurse kept muttering from the Bible she carried room to room the way some women honor their purses. Miss Beech stuck right in there. To Bianca, the woman quoted scripture: How if you spare the rod you just *are* going to spoil your child. Nobody knew what private punishments went on. Momma later hinted about *somebody* making a certain child kneel in prayer position whilst bare-kneed on a purposefully sandy floor. The squatting Naughty was then made to pray while forced to hold a heavy flatiron level at each shoulder. (Was this Beech's Christian ritual? I wouldn't be the least surprised.) Honey—what's nowadays known as Child Abuse, folks once called Just Good Maintenance.

The McClouds soon noticed their Bianca did seem tired, then worn calmer by a notch. All around the mansion and back yard, Bianca listened to Beech's tales of wicked children and harsh angels. The child's face grew sullen—a bruised, building reverence for her jittery and Pilgrimish Miss Beech.

2

BEFORE his favorite's accident, Mr. McCloud, Glasgow-born, figured you got pretty much what you purchased. Till then, Angus made almost a religion of cash value. Hisself a foundling, he'd become a ship's cabin boy. In 1839, he sailed into the port of Wilmington, North Carolina. He liked its looks. It appeared familiar—the way unlikely Heaven seems familiar to so many. Unnoticed on deck, a little scrappy redhead spoke under his breath: "It's on these shorres that Angus herre'll found . . . whateverr Angus here can find to found." Thirty years later, he sure had. McCloud employed over three hundred souls, he owned five freighters for transporting his cotton bales and the patented secret-formula blue dye. This local legend believed in something called the Verrra Best. His brogue burred "Verrra" till it seemed to mean even more. —You did things right, because you did things once. Your every transaction and employee lasted you jolly well forever. A king couldn't beat the quality of McCloud's major household items. What ever outranks the verrra best? Made you a potentate on earth—and certainly in Falls. Your four daughters: princesses exempt from everything but Poppa's treats. Angus' favorite hymn: "Under His Wing, Everything Prospers." Of McCloud, locals said, "Whatever the rogue touches . . ."

Five years before my mother's mishap, Angus came inland from coastal indigo growing, home to hear his oldest girls play six-hand pieces in their teacher's parlor. The elder sisters McCloud were then real young but musically already mighty good. Angus felt it. Though he lacked formal education, Angus—with his pure pitch for quality—knew this in the very gristle of his kilt-worthy calves. Family talent called for "seed money." The man didn't even wait on recital applause to peter out, he bounded right toward the telegraph office. Angus, man of action—distant acquaintance of his idol, Mr. Carnegie—wired direct to Steinway and Sons in New York City, New York. By next train, causing great interest at Falls' little station, here came three matching ebony/ivory concert grands in crates of boat-sized and seaworthy-looking blond wood. A minor Steinway cousin actually rode along to "install" the things. Such are the benefits, child, of buying only the you-know-what. A party at the house was wrote up in the *Falls Herald Traveler*, photos inclusive. I've seen these yellowed newsprint pictures of my square-jaw grandpa and his plain musical girls. The Indigo Baron is shown being taught scales at three different concert grands by three thin gifted daughters. One giggler hides her face behind a raised hand. Another uses sheet music plainly marked "Humoresque," that camera-shy.

3

DETERMINED to succeed here, Famous Maimie Beech soon doled out unexpected treats for good behavior. She'd granted just such privileges at earlier homes, even to her little white boys. For some reason, they loved it, too: Beech let them plait her silver-black hair. In back-yard sun, Nurse unpinned her cap, set it atop her Bible. She pivoted Bianca on a high stool opposite and child fingers were soon maundering all over a dignified woman's nobbly head. Senior McClouds and three older girls smirked, worried, from their house of windows. Miss Maimie rested down there in daylight, patient, nodding forward like some African-and-Tuscarora elder saying Yes. She spoke lanyard hints as corn rows sprouted off of her. Beech's hairdo— under Bianca's loving if stubby touch—come out somewhere betwixt Medusa and a Maypole.

Nurse and girl soon set to work on one another. Seeing this felt wonderful if creepy. Maimie would brush Bianca's mud-rich curls around a long expert black finger. Maimie tallied curls aloud like treasure. Bianca would quote rhymes she loved to scramble: "King is in the countinghouse counting out his honey. Queen is in the parlor eating bread and mon-ey." The brat— tongue pressed between baby teeth—improved Maimie's hair into a mass of plaits each ending with its own rag bow. Miss Beech's scalp soon looked to be some dandelion seed puff sprouting kite tails.

You saw this talkative pair enjoying long strolls across the county (leathery-black six foot one/marshmallow-pale three foot two, hand-in-hand arms swinging). Maimie, nodding toward bees, mud, hogs, explained: "What'd I tell you? 'Earth is the Lord's and the fullness thereof.' It *planned*." After hiking through Meadows' Pasture and beside the bright river, Bianca rushed home with major news: Jesus could walk on any water He chose and whenever He liked, couldn't He, Maimie, hunh? Tell them . . . they don't know *any*thing. —Maimie, pure authority, nodded. Onct. Though the McClouds had surely heard about His Knack for the Buoyant—why did it seem like Maimie'd just made it up? And if she had, who here would contradict her?

When Bianca made a clover bracelet for Nanny, Beech wore the thing till you found its last brown twigs sprinkling the mansion's Oriental rugs. Nurse and child settled in back-yard clover, shooing away bugs, weaving jewelry for each other. The Indigo Baron wandered out, smiled down. "Ye take bees, for instance," he began. Beech, somber, nodded. Angus asked if his favorite ladies knew: Bees weren't even native to North America but, like him, came over on a boat. Like him, they soon slipped free, diversifying, which meant "branching out." Even by 1750, bees still hadn't buzzed beyond the river Susquehanna. But Indians soon called them "white man's flies." Indians learnt that such bugs moved a hundred miles in advance of the troublemaking westbound settlers. Fact.

Maimie sat here, appearing knowing, nodding but amazed. She took this bug news right downhill to friends. Bees? they asked—brung across the water in rope hives, captive as slaves? Whites had shipped in America's every bee and black and bird, too? Hogwash. Nobody believed Maimie. Which only made the Mansion McCloud mean more to her.

On Bianca's bad days, Beech hand-fed the girl. You'd walk in, you'd hear this seemingly joyless old woman stifle certain nasal buzzing sounds, a spoon had just been flying around one crimped pretty mouth. Maimie hushed saying, "Miss Flower? Open Up. It Me. Here Come You Main Admirer, Marse Bumber Bee . . ." Feeling your presence, child and nurse would practically leap. Bianca gulped down that spoonful so quick, she chewed hard, nervous as if caught at spy activity or kissing.

After three smoke-free weeks, Beech invented a extra treat for polite little girls: they got to go downtown with Maimie's five best women friends: Saturday lotion-and-notion shopping at the Woolworth's store, hooray! Maimie called her favorites the Sisters. They were Beech's age or younger but their shapes bosomed where hers slatted. These ladies were as hardworking, faintly medicinal, as fully respectable and semi-religious as their boned corsets. They moved in a talcumed pigeon-breasted rack, all talking at once side by side under similar wonderful hats. You saw their dark cluster window-shopping led by one bossy pointy white star of a child. Bianca, meeting whites she knew (most everybody), loved introducing all of Maimie's friends by name and very slow. Just more of her mischief. Castalia knew Beech and friends. Cas had no time for them: Freed from slaveness, they signed on for a white Jesus, gossiped about white bosses, lived for Christmas bonuses, married the men they lived with, named their daughters Letitia or Mary Grace. Cassie's own pals made everything up—from their home-rolled redbird religion to their children's names.

Bianca, well served, now got to hold Miss Beech's hand throughout dinner. Nurse supervised each spoonful, she napkined Baby's mouth clean. Even when the Governor came for Christmas, Maimie was allowed to sit right at table. Otherwise, my momma flat shrieked.

Elder McClouds did feel twinges of jealousy, they admitted these but only in jokes. You almost missed Bianca at her most overwound. Still, there were reassuring flare-ups. Especially if Cook, against strict Angus orders, left out tempting kitchen matches. But four months of Maimie: and Bianca started seeming like somebody nicer, if maybe somebody else, somebody *less*. Four months' Jesus tales offered like bribes of promised powers, four months' stern hypnotizing care and feeding ("Open up, it's me"). Sure looked like Nanny'd half tamed Summit Avenue's champion Rounder.

4

TO HIS paneled upstairs study, Angus summoned this miracle worker. He sat toying with a inkwell made from twelve deer hooves all on point. Behind his massive desk, in glassy golden frames, a fine collection of arrowheads—arranged on honey-colored velvet, by size, like money.

"Come in." He admired Beech's strange heron-long limbs, the silver hair kept seriously knotted behind her like some hostage that—if not watched—might try some funny business. Angus McCloud looked straight into her black Bible of a face.

He asked Beech to sit, please. She would not. She seemed to expect reprimand. Instead Angus smiled. The fellow dispensed charm like twenty percent interest accumulated daily. He handed Beech a blue business envelope. "Your bonus for managing . . . her. But tell me, miss. Off the record like, how do ye *do* it?" It was his favorite question. He put it to many men and a few women. Asking this, Angus always seemed to beg for some sexual-type favor, his eyes twinkled that much, you felt his palms were sweating and God knows what else. The world was a secret formula like his personally improved richly rewarding powder for home indigo dyeing. When it came to necessary celestial blue, he'd cornered the international market. —The man usually got a answer.

Maimie L. Beech met his gaze with a stare that was a dye: a stare too darkly like Angus' own to be transparent till it dried later. Looking into these jet eyes—Angus saw one word waiting in each slot: "Patent" "Pending." He nodded, touched the inkwell's doe cuticles, for luck. He felt the washing joy of it—Beech too was his, the verrra best.

This woman's lot in life might prove real dicey, but—given that—she knew her value absolutely. McCloud leaned forward, reviewing the amount he'd stuffed in her envelope—enough? *"How?"* He was still waiting.

She studied her dry hands. "You maybe after Maimie's secret, sir? —Don't half know it my own self. Maybe that the secret. Got something to do with remembering what worked last time. —Sir, could be it come from Maimie's having . . . you know—Talent?"

He laughed hard enough to slap his upper leg, causing the deer-hoof thingie to skitter over desktop, spilling not a drop of ink. This let Miss Beech risk one pleased snort, gnaw slightly on her lower lip.

"We'rre going to get along just fine here. Sense of self-warth. Nothing like it, Beech. Hold on to that, ye hear me?"

Came shouts from downstairs. Whilst Maimie let herself be buttered up with flattery and cash, Bianca'd requested the head gardener's six children to please strip naked. Her being the boss's kid, they did so. Bianca next locked them into a gazebo. She set it cautiously afire. Dragged up to Poppa's study, Bianca was soon being severely scolded by her folks, loud, "Why? Tell us *why*?"

Without knocking, Maimie rushed in. The blue envelope still plugged her uniform's breast pocket. She posed—arms outstretched—between the girl and parents. Everyone acted startled by her doing this—especially Beech herself. She answered the Indigo Baron's dangling question. *"Why*? Marse Satan. He *after* her. Times, my baby here just feel so left out, them three sisters all in a clump. Satan got *His* Eye on her. —And I tell you: she *shy*."

Hid behind a white uniform, the child grabbed its starchy hem. Tears came to her great eyes, she tried blotting these onto Maimie's crackling whites. The cloth was too stiff for absorbing much, teardrops rolled as if down plaster. —But, listening, Baby Bianca suddenly found she *was*. That. That Maimie'd said. —Only Maimie Beech truly knew her.

ONE of Angus' competitors tried luring Beech away, hoping she'd come "break" his own namesake scamp and son. He offered Maimie a goodly raise—she snitched to Angus. A lover of loyalty, McCloud gave her this exact amount right then and out of pocket. Bianca now semi-behaved. Maimie's love had done it. Miss "Secret Weapon" knew no name for her secret weapon. Talent? No, more Love.

Her brats shaped up because Beech got them totally used to her own terrible complete attention. When she arrived mornings, kids could spend thirty minutes telling Maimie what she'd missed since they spoke last night. She taught them to mistrust their little playmates and everybody but the Need itself. She then met the Need completely. Everything Beech knew and guessed, she told them. Her earnestness, they felt. Kids met it with their own. In these soft spoiling households uphill, she offered them a single certainty, one gauging straightedge. Maimie then scared her brats: They might lose their Maimie's love. How would they like *that*, hunh? Who would they have *then*? —Her love was strict as the Old Testament contract. God often told His chosen children, "I'll call you 'chosen' if you choose Me back . . ." And if not, His brood got extensive wilderness, boils, bears, bugs, the deaths of favorite children. Maimie's love, like His, kept a flashy mirrored sweetness spelled across its front. (This, the hiring parents saw.) But, behind, you found a hundred slapped-on crusted layers of black lead. And yet, this very blackness made the mirror mirror.

Maimie was a strict addiction for which there won't a known cure. None except her kids' outgrowing it, their being packed, weeping, off to school. Children soon found: Learning to read was not a fair exchange for having been so lovingly decoded under Beech's complete attention.

Thanks to my feisty mother's smoothing-off, Maimie's reputation now lifted past nanny, more towards governess almost.

5

LIKE MANY of us, this woman worked hardest to hide one precious secret— and it was the very secret everybody knew about her first. No fair.

Arriving at McCloud's hiring interview, Beech hand-delivered fourteen excellent references. But these were notes she couldn't read and, see, sugar, that's the secret. One letter claimed: "Beech is a genius with children. My little Sandra called *her* 'Mother' first and, though my blood just absolutely positively boiled, I saw how, in most ways which mattered, Maimie L. actually was, alas. So be it."

Maimie Beech's major vanity? Pretending she "had" reading. (Some letters she herself handed Angus lightly mentioned this.) He instructed others in the house never to tease poor Beech about it.

Like I already told you, she carried her Bible everywhere, often opening and closing it, glowering around, daring anybody's doubt. Beech used the Book as her moral guide but, too, her pedigree in these fine homes.

Prior to doing for one self-styled Baron of the store-bought color Blue, Beech had served born blue bloods. These aristocrats pinched pennies, tried saddling Beech with changing brats' diapers *and* washing them. "Plenty talented *launder*esses around here," she threatened quitting every time.

But not in Angus McCloud's openhanded home. Everything he touched . . . From Maimie's first day on the job, his forty-room house—with its stained glass, its mantels like altars—seemed almost a weekday white folks' church, some church you'd never have to leave. "McCloud's Mansion"—it sounded worthy of the 100 Psalms that Beech had memorized. Corridor walls were paved with thirty paintings of one castle. The place rang all day with three pianos, players good and getting better. Skylighted rooms sprouted potted palms even taller than Miss Maimie. Though Maimie knew that the word "Psalms" had more sighs in it than Palms did, she'd seen such plants in Sunday-school lithos. She let herself enjoy blending the Bible with this house. Before the accident, while chasing Bianca through downstairs chambers, Beech seemed to aim towards palms, smiling, eyes shut as stray fronds whisked her face. On the huge stairwell (a makeshift pulpit when won't nobody around), she mumbled the sweeter Psalms. She recollected her favorite book's incense, its cedar tabernacles and marble steps, its chimes, the pretty sounds of captive nations' native tongues offering praise to the Lord.

When Angus came inland from indigo growing, he entertained local mayors and some foreign guests. French was sometimes talked at dinner. Maimie listened at the cellos sawing underneath French's surface jabber. Working in five decades of rich folks' homes, Beech's manner had slowly changed. She now kept her long neck extended at a haughty angle. Her pleated face stayed wide open with a look of full entitlement. At table, she was spared having to speak the native tongue of strange nations herself. This way, she could just enjoy the sounds—follow them from mouth to mouth. (Letters printed in Maimie's Bible—the antlike dots and dragonfly squiggles—looked to her lots more like choir-book sheet music than signs for plain dull English. To Beech's ear, French sounded much more Bible-days Oriental.) She sat here, awestruck but contained, following its music back and forth. For Beech, French became the official Psalmish gong-and-tinkle she heard steadily belling in her head.

And little Bianca eating right here—one hand stowed safe in Beech's— this darling babe-and-suckling spoke the holy tongue.

6

TO FOLKS *most interested in rightful owners' control, parenthood can be the hardest job of all.*

Later, waiting to know if his high-tempered pet would live or be a vegetable or what, handsome Angus McCloud lunged around the overdec- orated home. He avoided a second floor where doctors buzzed near one baby swollen unrecognizable. Experts wore dark wasp-waisted coats. They'd buggied from far-off Richmond. Young local Dr. Collier had been bypassed, not good enough for this. Till now Angus had believed a person got what a person paid for. The oldest daughters hunted their addled poppa, floor to floor. Since the accident, girls wore black full-time. They'd sacrificed their major joy: they locked the lids of three massive pianos. Household mirrors were covered with jet crepe. Angus' wife and elder girls found him crouched alone in the attic. Poor man was slowly tapping his right temple against one wooden upright. Strapping McCloud then galloped downstairs, he yanked velvet drapes off windows in twenty-nine steep and perfect rooms. "Light," he called loud. "It's light she'll be needing more of." He didn't blame skinny zealous Maimie L. Beech for his daughter's accident, though the culprits had been black as Miss Beech. Nurse could be heard now weeping out in the garden house, tearing strips from her white uniform. ("I won't asleep, just resting my eyes after ex-cess Bible reading.") Angus' womenfolk followed him chamber to chamber as he ripped down curtains. Daylight showed rooms full of floating dust—gold, yes, but gnatlike—a terrible corruption working everybody's air. "Will ye look at it all," he studied motes. "Two dozen people cleaning a house and they canna keep out pieces *this* size? —No wonder."

Loved ones allowed this temporary madness, just the way they'd admired his earlier gift for managing.

"*Let* him"—for some ladies, it's a whole philosophy of life.

ANGUS respected America's Indians ("Ye have to hand it to them"). Angus praised Beech in front of company and mentioned her Tuscarora forebears: chieftains and lairds, no doubt. How could Maimie fall from being so wedged and high up, chapter and verse, in the House of Palms? Child, I'm getting to the accident and lapse.

Like lots of religious unschooled folks in those days—Maimie'd memorized well over a third of the Holy Scriptures. But when quoting from memory, she preferred to fake a somber reading of it. Didn't matter if her selection came from Genesis or Revelation—Maimie always opened the Book midway to Psalms. At impossible speed, her finger blurred over printed lines. She sometimes paused, rubbing her eyes the way she'd noticed other readers do. Maimie Beech seemed to feel that reading—with its joys and power—must be very thrilling but mighty wearing on you. Jealous McCloud servants said they'd often seen Beech check the gold cross engraved across her Bible's front. This was her guide in holding the book right side up. If the cross's T bar was near the top, she knew she was safe from being discovered. Then her deep voice spoke God's word with fresh, level authority.

Before the trouble, Maimie and her Bible arrived to work hours early. Long before Bianca woke around eleven, here came the black spinster armored in the crispest of white uniforms. She fondled the brass cross bobbing at her throat. She forever wore that perched unaddressed envelope of a nurse's cap. While tiptoers waited for the baby of the house to rise, Cook let Maimie go sit in a place of honor, on the low three-legged in the stove's corner of the kitchen. Maimie's outfit was so starched: the first time she sat each day, you heard her break like pasteboard egg cartons.

She could rest over there for the longest time, staring down into a Bible big as any cookbook. Other servants sniggered. The chief gardener sometimes asked, "What *you* studying on so hard today, Miss Famous Maimie Beech?" And—convicted—furious, without even lifting her head, the woman would suddenly spout four minutes' worth of Leviticus, citing chapter and verse, finger blurring at a angel's speed over one page of Psalms. She seemed to consider that a book was like a bucketful of water—pretty much the same contents floated on its top as on its bottom. Dip in anyplace, all water. The text she wanted would rise, up up through pages—drawn to the bait and lure of so hardworking a fingertip. Maimie got no credit for these feats of memory. She could sure concentrate. The selfsame focus she usually pinned on some scared flattered child, Beech now pegged square upon one page. The old woman paused only to massage strained eyes. She did it with such conviction, child, you found: your own had started burning.

IN ACCEPTING this job, she'd told Angus, "Can't stay here long. Maimie likes them young."

Miss M. L. Beech always gave notice the day her babies turned six. White folks believed Maimie just specialized in toddlers. But truth is, she couldn't bear it when the children found her out.

Till school spoiled things, Maimie might sit, with some beautiful picture book opened in her lap, a living baby tucked snug under either arm, and— free as air or water—spin out any tale she chose. It felt like swimming and walking at the selfsame time—a promenade along some river's glassy lid. Her lore was partly fairy tales like one about a poppa-king whose golden touch proved butterfingered. Her lore was partly Bible rehash, part neighborhood gossip from Baby Africa downhill, partly whatever stepping-stone footholds the pretty pictures gave. Her finger was careful to skim to and fro, fro and to—a dorsal fin keeping her afloat. Beech's tales ofttimes starred little dervishes she'd tended at other rich white homes in Falls. Her latest charges felt right honored to join a list of local children already so famous they'd been wrote up in national books.

Years back, a child Maimie'd shepherded through six years and thousands of changed diapers—betrayed her. This blond-ringleted boy, a Saiterwaite, was the first to do so: She never planned to live through that again. He sat listening—he watched her needling clockly finger move over the dark wasp shapes swarming in rows, shapes she'd patiently explained to him were Letters. He had only been a schoolboy for six weeks. He piped loud in front of adults, *"That's* not what this book says, Maimie. You just make it up. I think you made up every book you ever told me. Did you, Maimie, hunh?" She smiled at him, tears stood thick as lenses in her either pouchy eye. Come morning she politely resigned, moving next door to the neighbor's brand-new baby, a baby who'd admire and forgive Maimie Beech till school unlocked the mystery of a black-and-white page.

Maimie might have stayed the honored servant in one home forever. She might've lived on long after the household children grew up and moved out. But she felt determined: learning to read by *seem*ing to read. That and some restless curiosity kept her changing jobs every six years, minimum. Maimie'd considered asking one trusted employer to please help her learn her letters. Beech knew how avid, grand, and Old Testament her own mind was. She surely had the deepest *will* to know. But asking meant admitting, didn't it? Doesn't it always? Bosses would find: She'd been lying all along— they'd go and tell their children (hers). False-reading was Maimie L. Beech's only lie. As a serious Christian woman—she suffered for it daily.

7

A GIFT Beech bought my momma led to both their downfalls. I often wondered who Momma might've been without this—and who, in turn, child, I
might've managed becoming. Actress, scholar, teacher—anything! Beech
lost her place of honor in the mansion and at table. Her Main Street dignity
toppled, too. A child thrashed half dead upstairs. The mansion and its staff
stayed unmusical and overlit in penance. Everything was said in harsh un-
Psalmish English. Doctors refused to even let old Nurse go near the little
victim. They idly blamed Beech without quite saying so. Twice they'd found
her sleeping on the hall floor outside the sickroom—her head resting on the
huge black book.

Next dawn, Mr. and Mrs. McCloud heard Maimie arrive for work that
early. She had banished herself to the back yard. She'd asked to spend the
night in the gazebo. She was denied permission. What first sounded like a
mourning-dove reunion proved to be Miss Maimie's endless scripture-
quoting vigil. Angus rose, looked out. A fat Bible rested open across Beech's
long bone thighs. Her black finger speeded so, it tore one page's precious
tissue. She pressed it back, apologizing to the Book, mashing the tear like
it might heal. Beech, her prim hat knocked off-center, sat hunched on a
lawn bench whose cast iron made it look formed all of ferns—petrified ferns
wanting more than anything to serve one person as group-effort fern
furniture.

From the upstairs window, my grandpoppa, Angus, listened at chanted
Old Testament lamentations—ones so suitable for awful troubles and, therefore, child, too often far too suitable for you and me. (Might be one reason
the Book is the second best-seller of all time. Behind the Sears and Roebuck
catalogue. A fact. Look it up.)

McCloud came lordly down the stairs. Cook still slept. In his tasseled
robe, Angus personally made tea for Maimie. (A newly rich Jack-of-All-
Trades, he loved mornings best—each one seemed born with a message
printed on its lower left border: "Imagine your name in this space." Angus'
pride was worldwide shop talk plus knowing how to do most everybody's
chore just a bit better.) Of his efficient household staff's two dozen souls,
he'd only felt awe at Maimie's mischief-squashing talent. Now, she too had
proved mortal, disappointing. Why was Angus always surprised when another minor wizard slipped? It hurt him every time.

Wearing just his robe, he carried out a tea tray, one warmed scone.
Beech blurted what she'd had all night to prepare: That day it'd happened?
She'd only blinked after reading the Good News too long in a row. Her baby
slipped right off. "*Now* look what's gone and grabbed her. Lord bound to
punish Maimie. Unh-huh. 'Eye for eye.' Exodus 21:24, Leviticus 24:20, Deuteronomy 19:21, Matthew 5:38. 'Eye for eye.' You watch."

"We must never talk like that," Angus said. He explained he wanted Beech to eat and drink while he could see her. She'd lost weight she couldn't spare. His indigo-blue robe's hem was wet with dew. He pulled satin around his red-haired legs, settled beside Maimie. Both folks could hear the household waking. They could see three daughters' heads peek out. Servants soon studied this odd pair resting side by side in a green back yard as green as greenbacks.

Angus said he remembered how, like him, Maimie was a orphan. He said he understood how this made such family as a person finally found (and founded) mean all the more to that person, did it not? "That person . . ." she began but nodded instead, "person . . . so sorry." Her hands kept opening and closing her Bible, its cover flexed the way a perched butterfly will cure its wings in sunlight. Angus, watching, understood she hardly noticed. He reached over and—with a tender manly touch—stopped her. "Oh," Beech said, ashamed.

Angus shifted more her way. In full daylight, she looked refined and yet—blinking—seemed mystified at where her power'd gone. McCloud regretted that her secret weapon must stay a secret now—unpatented. He onct imagined having Maimie dictate a short book's worth of how-to's at one of his secretaries. Since the accident, Miss Beech looked so stranded—something with its wings clipped, a poor buzzard forced to hobble forever along the ground. McCloud asked that Beech please go home today, just rest. He swore he'd send word if their wee child's health changed, either way.

"Our wee child," his ripe baritone allowed itself the sloppy luxury of repeating. In him, words' sweetness released a wallop so dark and syrupy it became almost a poison. The big man let hisself again feel what losing poor Bianca'd mean. The last time Angus indulged this, he'd raged around the homeplace tearing down stifling drapes.

Now, not even planning to, he reached out, took up this old woman's black bone-rake of a hand. He squeezed it, saying, "*We* underrstood her." Maimie only nodded. Angus saw her face split, podlike. Weeping, her wrinkles softened from the deepest center creases outward. Each of Maimie's braids, tipped with rag, seemed worn to blot one tear.

These two people, holding hands, soon felt semi-embarrassed, child—but not enough to stop. Angus, consoled by Maimie's touch, saw fit to cry in a steadied determined way. Tears, leaving him, seemed Grief's most natural dividend. Beech sat still, swallowing hard, admiring his ease, fighting back her own strange need to scream, to fall against him, begging, blaming. Fifty-nine years of doing good. Now this. No credit. A person got no credit. Her account was all Checking. No Savings. Nothing saved.

Maimie waited to know what emotion—if any—would be possible here with everybody looking. Angus' solemn gulps sounded so much like his baby daughter's. Beech had comforted hundreds of crying white children but never a grown white boss, and surely not whilst holding that gent's pink cabbage rose of a hand.

She knew that under his slippery Bible-days robe, Angus must be naked as a boy child. This held no mystery or charm for her. Just made her feel the sadder for them both and for Bianca upstairs.

Needing to sob aloud, Beech tried not to (a knot of push and pull). The shoulders shook—her fingers moved in short accidental jerks—and Angus' hand, scaring her, returned the pressure—his usual "Let's do *this* now" authority.

Soon these two practically Indian-wrestled, strength matching strength, wrists locking. They almost hurt each other and respected doing this. They found it someway helped. Neighbors, servants, and children watched amazed from many windows.

Down there, Angus quaked, bucking, steadily moaning, "Oh Lard God." Unashamed, he coughed and shook so. Out sounds came. Stripes of salt water ran clean down his smooth ruddy face. He hadn't shaved yet but the pinkish stubble didn't check the tears. Soon his wet chest and belly shone. Healthy amounts of water cooling his butterscotch skin, Angus quieted some. "Well," he said, wiping cheekbones with the back of one free freckled hand. "Well well." Tears had darkened his indigo lapels to black.

Maimie's wrinkled brown face could've been a mosaic made of wild rice. She still dared not make a noise, she hardly let herself breathe now, elbows punishing ribs. If she blurted even one raw sound, it might explode, might prove more shaming than breaking wind beside the Governor during some long mixed-doubles seesaw Psalm of French. Don't.

Angus McCloud had profited from crying a pint. He sat here steaming, spent like some lover cleansed sleek. Maimie'd released two crooked thimblefuls of tears. But this wetness kept so busied, was so mazed inside her face's crevices and folds, the woman's starchy collar stayed bone-dry.

—Hands still gripped but less hard, each too polite to break the other's hold. Neither person dared look toward the sickroom, the only second-story window still bandaged behind velvet draperies.

From adjacent homes and many household windows, people in pajamas stared down. Sunlight found this fern bench, a man and woman seated here, facing dead ahead, stiff as any King and Queen park statue. It was already getting hot. All over town, rough-sounding local roosters crowed.

Straight up.

The earth is the Lord's and the fullness thereof. Roosters called direct toward sky. To Beech, their cries sounded like a homemade Psalm she'd chanted down down at fifty-nine years of fussy eaters:

"Be nice. Open up. It's me."

BUT I WANDER. What had to happen has to happen—even in the story of it later, child.

The accident itself. With personal money from her taming-Bianca bonus, Maimie L. Beech, sixty-eight, bought her dear child, newly five, a birthday gift: some grown-lady perfume. The price of the bottle has been lost to
us but we know it came from Woolworth's and was very, very sweet—even
for a humid magnoliaed back yard during three pianos' practice in green
Falls, mid-May. Too much sweetness can become dishonest and a poison.
Remember that. (And, child, I'm just guessing here, but do you figure too
much polluting poison might reverse itself? Couldn't *poison* come full cycle
and swing back to sweetness? For our clogged spoilt world, I dearly hope
so. We deserve it. We deserve better.)

It's the day after a party for fifty handpicked children, my momma's
brown cigar curls need yet another washing. Maimie carries one edgy child
into the back yard, she places Bianca on two dozen thirsty towels. The girl
feels tired from behaving right well during her party. A few lapses: she
pinned the donkey tail onto/into two bossy visiting mothers. Then she purposely broke her sisters' gift, a brown celluloid hatpin box. ("It's *ug*-ly, it's
too old for me, I hate it.")

In such pre-hair-blower times, damp-headed ladies enjoyed setting outdoors in direct sun. Just take along your brush, a novel, a talkative friend,
or all three. Nice ritual—one now lost to us, as is the wholesome scent of
clothes dried by a passerby spring breeze.

Bianca—deeply trusting somebody for the first time in her five jumping-
bean years—lets herself now be arranged face up, formal as the corpse of
some exceptional Egyptian princess. Glad to finally be recognized as shy,
she closes her blue eyes—eyes so richly lashed they're awninged. Maimie
counts the curls aloud—Bianca's hairdo averages between forty-nine and
fifty-one, depending on humidity and whim. Beech tugs out each curl so
it's at its fullest length sunning along terry cloth. I picture all of this (and
Momma) from above. Feels like I'm in air or else well hid up the loftiest of
McCloud pecan trees. From Bianca's head down there on white towels
overlapped in grass—damp curls spoke every which way—they shoot like
rays from off some spongy young sun in training.

Maimie occupies a ferny yard chair. The Bible rests against her like the
next infant she'll tend when reading spoils this present darling. Looking
over at Bianca, the old woman feels so gladdened. Many casework kids in
turn have seemed Maimie's favorites, but especially this one. It pleases
Beech, reviewing simple secret weapons: Never talk "down" to your baby.
Treat yours the way *you'd* expect to be treated—which means loving, hard.
Love is a secret weapon, a serious profession and not (like for these uphill
parents) some fond sideline hobby.

Bianca has steadily begged to attend Beech's Wednesday Night Prayer
Meeting. Earlier this week two wary parents finally agreed: "Only because
you've been verra good, only owing to our implicitly trusting your Beech
here so." Parents later worried that a child's getting this Good might mean
her getting a bad dose of that Old-Time Religion. Privately they said, "First

we'll get her civil. Then we'll discourage the rest." At Afro Gethsemane Baptist, Bianca arrived in state. She allowed Maimie's five favorite Sisters to come out of the choir and make much over a stiff white dress, white hat and shoes. On request, she said ten things in French ("Pass the butter, if you please, dear dear Maimie of mine"). She apologized for a accent that her big sisters swore was perfectly shameful. Bianca soon went forward and got saved. Just like that. Out loud the girl admitted how bad she'd acted, said she regretted putting poor Maimie back there on the sixth row through pretty much total hoops but promised she wouldn't ever be that again, bad— if possible. Then she looked around and begged to be dunked. "Not while you wearing that, you don't," Nurse called aloud whilst beaming. Everybody laughed. Bianca didn't feel taken real serious here.

She'd believed that Baptizing water would—under your feet—go thick, instantly lidded like chocolate pudding's leatherish cap. Water would support the walking weight of a saved little girl. Imagine hiking over any wet you liked, be it bathtub, be it flood. Your sisters would just hate you, they'd feel sorry as they sank and drowned like Pharaoh's troops. Bianca pleaded now for Baptism, swearing that *Her* Jesus would keep *Her* outfit dry, she knew He would. Bianca announced, "My Jesus will be Water Wings." She sounded sure as her poppa sounded at his surest, darling, which was sure. This deeply impressed the entire congregation. Amens sprouted row to row. Older ladies rolled eyes, shook heads, sighed, "Tell it." Friends had *heard* their Maimie Beech brag on this most recent child, and sure enough.

And: Here in present sunshine, Maimie, remembering all this, feels so pleased with a girl's Christian progress, feels so exceptionally appreciated at this address—she trots inside the mansion, fetches back the birthday perfume. Beech kneels on towels. (Maybe she should ask Mr. Angus hisself for reading lessons? "Go to a busy fellow when you want things done." —If Beech finally admits her lacks, can't she finally rest? rest here?)

Maimie douses her favorite's every fat sleepy curl. The dime store calls its best perfume Instant of Joy. Out flows all that amber liquor. "Noint/you/ sweet/head/Maimie oil/Cup/runneth/over . . . goodness/mercy/dwell/house/ Lord/ever/'men/."

Her baby will soon wake in a cloud of sweetness bought with Maimie money. It'll be a surprise—like your coming to in a tailor-made halo all yours. This smell—addressing the earth's mysteries, feeling on a first-name basis with earth's fullness—this smell will say, "Open up. It's me." Kneeling, Beech closes her own eyes. Scent lifts a choir of chemical amens.

SUNLIGHT only swells the scent. It grows close to a sound like Psalms' own trumpets. Scent competes with upstairs pianism of a right high order. —Sweetness sends Bianca pegs deeper into honeycomb sleep. A six-hand arrangement of one Schubert song reaches her. Maimie adjourns to a Bible waiting—warm as life—on sunning cast-iron ferns. She opens to Psalms, shuts her eyes tight, sniffs her own excellent-smelling fingertips, dozes.

—The good lunch was heavy, the good sun feels hot. Four black helpers are assigned to tend each white one in this hive of mansion. A McCloud future is based on the poppa's sought-after secret formula: the most convincing available Blue. Everything in sight seems certified: the verra best. Life comes with a warranty.

THE ACCIDENT is gathering, unnoticed.

MAIMIE, nodding, dreams dreams. Swans are on a bright river—upper bodies white and easy-seeming, hidden colored rubber feet are paddling hard to read the currents—and suddenly it's Jesus alive in person astride one row boat—His a Scotsman's pink-orange beard. He leaves the boat to walk, He's wearing a manly white bathrobe so starched it's caulked solid as a upright buoy, pretty as a good girl's crinoline. His pockets are leaking bits of gold. Coins fall straight down through deep water He's exempt from and just strolls.

I'm mostly guessing here.

Fact: My Baby Momma wakes. Where? Oh, out in sun, on shampoo day, must be the birthday perfume so strong everywhere like evaporating shellac or doctor's office—music, sisters . . . Oh, okay, home . . . But a new sound seems the one fact out of place. (A drone, snipping, clicks like from castanets being demonstrated downtown in the Courthouse Square six blocks off.) Any person peeking from a pecan tree overhead would notice one change: Bianca's pale brown hair should've dried a fairer color than when wet, but it's gone darker. See, two or three hundred black wasps have been drawn to this maybe overly literal Woolworth's perfume. Gathered bugs now fret and fidget, sucking at the sweetness sogged along each out-spread curl, roads all leading to one Rome, the soft white head of a child who don't even know yet. She's been behaving lately, so why *is* this?

Bianca's hair fans out around her. Her feet are bare, she's dressed only in clean batiste panties and a pretty little satin shift. Bianca sits forward, scared to look behind her. Something's about to happen just in back of her. She knows this. Bianca's head feels covered with a new weight, shawl or helmet. War bonnet. The sleepy child, curious, now touches the back of her own skull—mashes twenty jet-black stingers into pale scalp.

Here the scream should come. Here fur on the neighbor's cat should lift, all pianos hush, Maimie jump, and everyone like mad come running. But in Bianca's mouth's—complaint, warning, fury—can't, quite, move, through, teeth clamped this tight owing to a kind of pain she's never known before or even guessed at.—Till now, what's been amusing? the fires you set, seeing animals try and get away in time, grown people's ugly faces when they find out what you've done now. Those, plus Poppa always, and dear Maimie lately. —But how can anybody this spoiled and five be prepared for a first grief and so close in?

She's quiet, owing to a tongue that suddenly feels swollen to the size of a dead trout some days dead. Poison makes the backs of Bianca's blue eyes spot with blackness then go wider awake. Her mind shoots everywhere—a new emergency of chemicals and thoughts, smeared.

Bianca—dainty, gingerly—hops up. She scampers, barefoot, off the towels and onto grass. Silent, graceful, how she hurries. She wears pretty white underthings and the three glossy pounds of black. Bugs' humming means they're starting to be upset. The child runs in seven hushed and urgent circles all around around one chair. It contains Miss Maimie Beech snoozing, mouth open toward her Bible. The child runs so light, she could be flying, winged herself.

THE CHILD's logic is poisoned, plus it was a child's to start with.

Logic tells her: Get past Meadows' Pasture and down to the river Tar and drown them, baptize them into being nicer to you, you. —Logic tells her if she moves quick enough they'll blow off her like gnats do at a gallop. Meanwhile, rushing, she makes some other mistakes—one being: hitting herself many times across the head and temples, ears, the neck. A cloud of black is out ahead of her and right into that she runs.

Through a rear garden gate, down cinder alley, soft bare feet go. She sacrifices shade. She leaves the safety of her sisters' doing rounded guardian Schubert. Bianca, soundless, somehow gets six blocks, seven. Courthouse Square is baking, totally deserted at siesta hour. She runs around the whole downtown alone.

9

FAT Mrs. Luke Lucas of Lucas' All-Round Store sits eating cheese. It got marked down today but is not moving. Nothing doing here at 2 p.m.— except just now, fast as one of them squiggle shrimps of bloodshot ghosts that flit across your eyesight when you're looking from a shady place into a brilliant one, past the front door of this dim emporium—Mrs. Lucas spies a child dart by so quick, so white in sun it seems a spirit. The body part looks snowy, bare. The head smoked blind—busied with darkest thoughts seeping out into a cloud, a mask and hat.

This black/white ghost lasts just a fraction second. Mrs. Lucas' jaw hardly misses one chewing beat of cheese eating. And yet this good-sized woman, even whilst doubting her eyes, decides to act. Something decides *her*. (And God bless the lady for making my life possible by saving poor Momma's.) Mrs. Lucas, mouth plugged with discount cheese she is trying hard to swallow, the mother of eight herself, is now in air, is off her stool, goes up like the least likely rocket ever launched. She's been shot vertical by the sudden panting strength Disasters can bring out in certain people— especially usually fairly slow parents secretly packed with just such save- our-babies surplus. She is no longer a fat red woman bored betwixt customers. She is a blurry flour-white angel, she's Diana in fast motion. Whipping off her apron, she runs on tiptoe.

Barging out the door, she leaves a cash register and every all-round item totally unguarded. She is seeing she was right, it's real, it's spastic, roughly thirty feet beyond her. Mrs. L. is half past the store's sidewalk tool display marked: "It's May. Think of your Neighbors. Get Your Yard Right This Year." She grabs a pair of hedge clippers—not sure why till later.

What has changed this often lazy woman into such a jump-back Savior? Something called "You must." It can make heroes of us in one second. It can just as easy show how deeply cowardly we are, can leave us knowing that forever. Which hurts. But her? Hey—she's running—it's the longest such trek she's made in twenty-seven years since—during a church picnic— she ran unsuccessfully on purpose from the huge and horny Luke Lucas, then eighteen. She is now flapping her apron all around her like some bullfighter's cape, clippers are hid beneath. Mrs. L. chases a child she recognizes from behind as a definite McCloud, the wild youngest one that stole so bad till right here recent.

Nearing Courthouse Square, Mrs. Lucas (made a temporary genius by adrenaline that will, in a short time, fail her the way genius fails some people early—a woman blessed with sudden juice that'll leave both thighs chafed, her body taxed from two years' effort spent in six good goddess minutes), Mrs. Lucas draws alongside one fast little barefoot child. The child is galloping with eyes closed, hands wavering in front of her like a drowner's underwater hope to please grab hold now, please. Mrs. L. sees: The child's head is already twice a child's head size owing to what's released by shiny stingers stinging yet. And the woman throws her apron over this entire buzzing noggin. She uses her own running bulk to knock the youngster off her legs and onto grass beside our War Memorial. The girl goes into a cartwheel that looks almost planned. Mrs. Lucas is seriously falling, too, one prolonged respectful thud. A girl's worked-on head is now resting in a woman's lap.

The perfume that Mrs. Lucas suddenly inhales is so strong and unexpected, it almost makes that marked-down cheese come up. She shouts at the slit-eyed features because they seem so far away. She bellows past bugs curtaining a blue-white face. She does what you are always told in First-Aid Classes: "Remember to assure your victim aloud." It's something that, in being victimized by the *sight* of your victim, you can easily forget. A fine stout voice cries, "I'm here. It's Doris Lucas, honey. It's okay. I know just what to do."

Like all of us, this lady during lunch hour is really only inventing it as she goes, child. She's horrified all during. Sometimes you act because you're less scared of making a mistake than of *not* making one in time.

Quick here: *fake* it.

. . .

HER OWN palms are being bitten so, stingers pock each hand with little map lights. Mrs. L.—hedge clippers in one fist—chops off long curls, throws brittle clotted curls as far away as possible. She's staring down into the open mouth of the poor head she's pruning. She swats and crushes insects in the air but never on the flesh itself. And even as wasps bite Doris Lucas, she keeps yelling kind words down at what might be a corpse by now: "Almost over, nearly done now, hold on, sug. They're off you mostly. You're with *me*, it's Doris. Lucas. Doris's got you. Fine, we're going to be fine here. We're almost through. It's over with, I swear to you, we're done. Breathe, you, *breathe*. For Doris, do."

And she pounds a child's back, pounds, she pounds it.

AT HOME: Schubert continuous, Caucasian Jesus wades in dreams.

As for personal property during such valor—the Collier twins arrive at Lucas' to buy rickrack for edging a round felt tablecloth. Finding the All-Round Store empty of every last Lucas for the first time in human memory, these stalwart girls choose to stand guard and are actually sweeping up already. Tending the counter, they're acting like this is their usual shift— Doc Collier's twins, who'll never have to sweep their own place, are really loving playing store. They even sell a little marked-down cheese to a good-looking colored fellow in from Apex. They even offer to wrap it.

A shorn head is finally opening to sun, free of hair—a child mouth, breathing at last, allows a scream to fountain out of it. Scream cuts past and over the fat woman, whose own breath stops dead. Bianca is a siren that stills the action of eleven hundred souls—napping, lovemaking, piano playing, store minding. First: The scream brings Maimie L. Beech out of sleep and onto her shoes and into the act of running—Bible held against her chest like a shield for discouraging bullets. She is bound the six blocks toward the sound, she feels capable of going headfirst down into the troubled mouth of her beloved Bianca. All this before Maimie even understands why she's moving and toward what and who she is and how she is not Jesus on some pond promenade but one employee, mortal—before she knows what her beloved job is, was, and why she has just lost it.

TO MAKE a long story less gory and more short, the swelling finally commenced to shrink after three weeks of what sickroom lingo still calls "touch and go." Puffiness slacked, but not before it'd made a independent gargoyle-type beast out of just the head of one small girl. Bianca's face had widened to the width—gossips said with their genius for citing things' dread sizes— of a beehive—"face spread that broad till skin actually tore from the insides of either eye, or so one hears." Bianca's hands—from trying to save the head—were near as swollen as the head was.

Downstairs, well-wishers arrived each afternoon and evening. They spoke in low voices, many wore black. Mrs. Doris Lucas herself turned up, rouged, fists bandaged, saying, "Anybody would've. Lucky to've *been* there, really," a heroine. The cook had given word that no more donated casseroles would be allowed into *her* kitchen. "They think I don't know my job here?"

In the parlor, instead of lying, offering the usual story improvements granted Falls' sick and perishing—folks told true tales. About the languishing Bianca, they recalled her spunk. No angel, her. They skipped all recent advances Maimie'd brought about. They told of serious former naughtiness. Vandalism they called High Jinks. Arson they named Playing With Matches. They made up hymns to the Calamity Jane momma I might've got. Quiet elder sisters, longing for keyboards—secretly mourned their young Mozart and Schubert along with the family baby. Sisters now heard of fresh Bianca crimes. Confused, they risked minor-key smiles. News: Several occupied privies suddenly in flame—cats granted hairdos, dogs found tied in human clothes. The time Bianca sat on the brand-new maroon velvet church pew cushion and smiled a strange smile and said, "A test. P.U.," and you know she had peed on and deeply into it. Why? Shyness? You ever try removing pumpkin meat (and later its smell) from seven hundred piano wires? Well, don't if you can help it. —Folks today made her brattiness a litany. Their stories of her brilliant no-no's tried to pull Bianca back from dimness. Folks wished *they* had been way worse when young.

"Nice" seemed counties closer to Dead than "Bad" was.

WHEN BABY Bianca finally opened her blue eyes, everybody rejoiced. Maimie most especially. (If prayers were books, Maimie would've been through every library of the Western world since her child got stung.) Afro Gethsemane Baptist had steadily petitioned for the life of its recent fresh-mouthed visitor. True, that girl had lived, but she'd brought bad stuff out of her three-week nightmare in the dark. Maybe she confused the color of her coma or the darkness of wasps with skin tones of poor Maimie Beech. When that loving nurse finally got squired upstairs for a first viewing, when she stood in the open door, ashamed, hopeful, grinning, holding out a scentless bouquet bought with her own money, the child took one long look. The child swallowed hard then went straight up over the back of her carved bed, clawing wallpaper, trying to get away. The girl, covering her puff-pastry eyes with puff-pastry hands, screamed a scream that again cost people three heartbeats apiece for blocks around. Even birdsong lost its place. "Black!" is what Bianca shrieked. *"Black!"* was the first word of her scared new life. Black, child, is the presence of all colors. Colors are the deeds and sufferings of light.

Poor Maimie's one mistake had been dozing off whilst hired to guard. The white girl (white is naturally the lack of all color) blamed a black nurse for that—and through it, child, for all the pain on earth. No fair. But wee Bianca felt it was this simple and this fixed. Angus McCloud gave Maimie L. Beech a large chunk of severance pay. He handwrote five pages concerning her sterling character (a letter Maimie carried home stuck in her

Bible and later learned, with help, was maybe her all-time best). So then—nicely taken care of—she sat in her small clean house by the river and slowly understood she had been fired, if verra genteelly. Since her livelihood had forever been tending rich white troublesome children, since news traveled for as far as she could walk to work, her single nap had cost Maimie L. Beech a good deal. She could afford to retire but—without work—she had no baby of the moment. Without that, what use in wearing starched whites, in staying up to iron? Alone at home, there was no need to fake daily Bible reading—this made the Secret Weapon feel less worthy. *She* knew she couldn't read. God, all-knowing, all-sight-reading, surely knew. Still, Maimie missed going through the motions. —So much of the grandeur in our lives comes, strangely, from certain loving daily habits. "Here I am, doing *this* again. —Amen." Yeah, grandeur. In a second, I'll explain her chancy later life.

—I now want to mention how the L in Maimie L.'s name stood for Lucille. Odd, that young Bianca—not remembering just *where* she'd learned to love that name so much—later came to call me, her only child, after the sad nanny she'd got fired. Another story.

Little Bianca McCloud, now age five going on forty, no longer needed a zookeeper. Before the accident, fear meant nothing to her except a nice taste in her mouth. Like Poppa's secret blue, she manufactured it. Fear trailed her everywhere, a wake of knee-high calamity. Cats scattered. Neighbors shut the lids of their spinets and, for good measure, sat on the shut lids. Now it had *her*. Fear did.

People change. Even children do. Especially kids. Catch them young enough, you can twist a poor baby to most any bentwood shape you choose. To make a violin, you wet the wood and *hold* it there till dry. What did a five-year-old believe about her perfume accident? Maybe she thought it was a punishment for all her early mischief? Did she see it as the dark race's revenge on white folks' strutting—all blackly visited upon young doughy her? Considering this version (a child's, fairy-tale simple, fairy-tale wicked), I reckon it's no surprise: Bianca never again exactly cottoned to residents of Baby Africa. That'd be putting it mild, honey.

She'd no longer go downtown on Saturdays when the Courthouse Square was most swarmingly "mixed"—sixty-some percent colored. If a big black dog ran across the McCloud lawn, the little girl stiffened with something like shock. Her body temperature dropped and Angus had to rush her in the house, rubbing at her pink toes and fingers.

After the accident, whilst Bianca convalesced in bed, her sisters—working shifts—did just what the un-brat asked. They taught her to read. Her early favorites? How-to books on Manners. She soon demanded that her plain upstairs nursery be re-covered in the very best of polished chintz—but only patterned in flowers—no birds or butterflies and certainly not no bees. She said *she* wanted a Steinway concert grand, and sighed, and did they come in white? She was soon scolding her big sisters for their wallflower ways, pasty complexions, hours spent practicing in shaded rooms, their murksome dowdy clothes and social panic. Bianca had once speared her way through a neighbor's populated goldfish pond while farmers, in a wagon parked on Summit, watched. Now, head shaved wholly bald (that way it'd grow out even and not clumpy), she observed high tea at age five. For Bianca, everything had to be just so.

Before the perfume, her poppa'd secretly loved paying off the grumblers who brought in items she'd broke or accidentally set afire. For Angus—the former up-and-coming cabin boy from Glasgow, a man who had his tartan vests and kilts made only of "hunting" plaids, not "dress" ones—Baby Bianca's every shredded frock once seemed some flag of victory.

"Just like me," *a parent's fondest prayer, a parent's worst fear*.

Now he mourned his wild child's passing. (Secretly, he felt his son had died. He hadn't known he *had* one till that imp got stung out of this world, drowned in a blackness Angus felt to be as cold as the North Sea around 3 a.m. on some off-night, midwinter.) The Indigo Baron now noticed: His Bianca was just a girl, just like the others, was she not? He missed being the weest bit afraid of her, that was it. It's how the truly strong recognize each other. "Uh-oh" turns to "Ah." Fear can be the start of truest love.

10

HAVING CHANGED into a hedge that clips itself, Bianca McCloud later tried teaching her rude Baby Lucille such personal topiary. With me, darling, it didn't really take. Back of Momma's misshaped character stood what she considered one oversight made by one servant, black. And Momma never tired of blaming. A terrible destiny. To think: *Others did it to you*. To know the others' color, to live in a hamlet whose citizens are sixty-odd percent that shade.

Adult Mrs. Bianca ofttimes criticized our neighbors' gardeners and maids as "exceedingly insolent." She claimed that the verra rarest commodity on earth was something called: good help. Momma swore she wouldn't trust black servants far as she could throw them. And Castalia later told me: In Baby Africa, Bianca stayed the one white blacks loved to hate—turnabout being fair play.

Alone amongst the white ladies of Summit Avenue's better end, Momma did her own housework. Something of a union buster. It just embarrassed everybody. Me, too. Others' maids—bound for work—clucked, saddened to see so finely made a white woman out washing her own windows, hanging perilously off the side of our house, her head wound in a ugly-making indigo cotton rag and sweating like . . . a stuck pig, waving down to all and calling, "Hot day, nasty job. Must be *done*, though." And basically loving it, child.

She'd grown up in that showplace home based upon some idea of order in Edinburgh (Angus McCloud hisself hailed from less tony Glasgow, but stocked his place with huge oil paintings of Edinburgh Castle, aiming in everything he did to be Edinburgh fine-grained, Edinburgh worthwhile). Someway, knowing that Bianca McCloud Honicutt was *his* heiress made our neighbors find her willful clumsy housework all the sadder.

"Lucille, it's a race that does not *mean* to steal." (In 1900, this view made my momma a liberal by local standards.) "They simply take a shine to something and the next thing anybody knows (themselves included) a person's signed Paul Revere silver sugar bowl, my dear dead poppa owned one, is in their handbag, soon to be displayed on some pine mantelpiece downhill. One doesn't blame a magpie for hoarding certain bright items in its nest. So, we mustn't blame *them*, is how I see it."

The earth is the Lord's and the fullness thereof.

—Poor Momma.

AND, oh yeah, what of Maimie? What about my Bible-believing namesake who—in her day—had made so many white children "straighten up and fly right"? She could not get work. Not anywhere. In six months, nothing. Once she was put in charge of a promising new bed wetter but, second day she turned up, news had struck. Beech was asked to leave at onct, please. Nothing *per*sonal. People now claimed she was just bad luck. Sleeping on the job, they said. Luring harmful Nature to the one whose nature she'd been hired to iron out.

Finally a committee of five black ladies from her church took a train, then hired a wagon, arriving unannounced at the flagship indigo plantation of Angus McCloud. High walls surrounded his headquarters: Angus—with two chemistry majors' summer help—had concocted the secret formula for making semi-colorfast indigo dye. Others wanted it. The trip cost Sisters a two-day journey. Showed how much they meant it. Maimie's onetime employer recognized this, asked ladies to sit down, please.

"She ain't set foot in church since the day it happen," one woman started. "Which ain't *like* Maimie," one lady added. "We been worried sick," a third chimed. "Over her," the first put in. They talked like this, such tag-team sentences. Though not related by blood, at Afro Gethsemane they called each other Sister and were. They'd belonged to one choir since childhood and now seemed to think and move the way they'd sung forever four times weekly: one harmonized, quietly fiery unit.

The group let on as how Maimie sure pined to see her little girl. Angus said that just won't possible. Doctors' orders, another scare could set Bianca off. Unfortunate but true.

"Maimie ain't *just* sad."

"She running out."

"Of cash money."

These friends knew better. Maimie lived alone, she'd saved for life, she only spent on church tithing and treats for her former children. (Beech hand-delivered a gift on each's birthday. She carried presents in person, hoping to see how another year'd changed each lapsed child. This also spared Beech having to address the package, write a card. Maimie's first brats were nigh into their sixties now. "Well, look who's here," they'd say to shy smile. "Like the proverbial elephant, never forgets, does she?")

During the long trip to the coast, Sisters decided: If they couldn't get Maimie rehired, if they couldn't get her back on visiting terms at McCloud's Mansion, they'd at least try squeezing more retirement funds from Person County's third-richest man.

"Cash," that man now admitted, "might be forthcoming from me. Lord be praised. Especially considering my family's feelings for Maimie. Terribly devoot. Starling character. Ever sa prompt. A genius with children, Beech was, is." He took out a checkbook big as a Bible. The Sisters noticed: Twelve joined checks made up every page.

"Lord be praise," ladies answered, a solemn breasty sigh rolled forth. What'd made these women travel so far and act this bold? Maimie's absence from their midst. It felt killing. She used to move and breathe and speak with them like this. Downtown with her on Saturdays, Sisters grew flustered, pleased and troubled when fancy white folks, knowing Maimie from the McClouds' very dinner table, nodded, touched hat brims, said without a whit of question in their voices, "Beech." They said it like you'd factually say "Day" or "Night" in greeting. Maimie took this as her due. Made the Sisters feel a bit more visible and Maimie-famous. Beech's memory for scripture was much admired at church. Her absence from these oldest friends felt like a amputation.

She'd been the unit's single skinny one. Sisters loved carrying food to Beech's house, forcing her to eat it while they watched. She stayed their only unmarried member, the one un-mother. —First they'd tried matching her up with their Bible-believing brothers and flashy brother-in-laws, horse salesmen for Captain Marsden. But the men came back, sat down real hard, rubbing their tired eyes, whistling, "I already *finished* school. She only talk about some cute wicked rich white twins uphill. Do *I* care? She din't notice me not all night long." So be it, lady friends decided—Maimie'd stay more truly theirs. These five appreciated Beech's refined ideas—they loved her unlikely spying news from the great homes. Mail-order bees! Though two of these Sisters taught school, they felt like Maimie's years uphill made her almost their educated equals—whether she could technically read or not. Maimie had no family. These friends were her age or younger but forever treated her as something of pet, their secret child. Odd, Maimie let them. She knew just how to sulk and give way after years of white brats practicing on *her*. To Sisters it now seemed their oldest dearest child was fading quick. This made them fearless. They'd do anything to revive a woman who could be prissy and had real high standards but—if in the mood—might make low-down grumbly jokes with the best of them.

"Does this seem fair?" McCloud had written a check for eleven hundred dollars.

"Lord *be* praise."

He told ladies that their own food and carfare should come out of this. He stood and thanked them for their trouble, for being such good friends to Maimie L. Beech. Angus said he personally missed her verra much but that it couldn't be helped after what'd happened, which was nobody's fault, was it? Who's surprised that wasps are drawn to sweetness? So much awfulness in this world just cannot be blamed, can it? On hearing this, four women cleared their throats. One friend held the blue check, others grouped around. Soon one fingertip of each Sister touched a part of it. The unit didn't seem disposed to leave McCloud's office yet. A board meeting waited, mumbly, in the antechamber.

Angus leaned back against his desk. He didn't say, "Ladies, I am, I fear, quite a busy man, I fear . . ." Instead he grinned his ginger grin: "This *has* been a fine visit. I believe you've got everything?" They then looked at him, they did so very hard and very neutral. The center woman spoke alone, slowed by trying to become others' choir and quorum all her self. "This gone probably seem like a lot to Maimie. But she ain't herself no more."

"You feel my amount's insufficient?"

The speaker got nudged by four soft shoulders from behind. She shrugged then, but left her own blank check of a look aimed Angus' way. He thanked the women, hard. A gent fitted to do well in this world—Angus chanced adding, "Lorrd be prraised?"

"Lord be praise," the unit sighed. And left.

MAIMIE's friends were headed home, not unpleased, taking turns holding a blue chit. Their preacher was knocking at Miss Maimie's door. Smiling, the elderly gent explained: *He'd* found a way of easing Maimie's mind. God had whispered it to him after supper last night. Hat off, Rev. stepped in, uninvited. There were, he said, so many *black* children hereabouts who might could benefit from MLB's years of uphill practice. In Baby Africa, so many youngsters were flat starved for Maimie's one-at-a-time kid-glove-type care. Why didn't she cheer herself by tending *them*, us, ours? Beech's plaits had come unfastened and dangled like risky laces trailing a untied shoe. She'd lost weight you never knew she'd had. She looked more pure and vertical. Less a virgin, more a warrior.

"*God*," Beech said, "whispered you that? Free babysitting from *me*?"

She had not offered Preacher tea or even water. She stood, proving this'd be a short visit. On the table behind her, partly wrapped presents: fifteen leather pen wipes and twenty bath talcs. Hat bunched in hand, Pastor said: His job was delivering God's word. What folks *did* with it was their business.

"Well, sir." Maimie rubbed her eyes like a reader burned steadily by the world's finer print. "One thing is, I real used to being *paid* for it. Got pretty good money uphill, too. *You* should know—I been tithing right along, paying *you*." She explained she'd steadily worked for "quality." Maybe that'd ruined her, who knew? But these ragged weedy little young ones from down around here? Well, they just didn't rightly *mean* as much to Maimie, you know? Did that surprise him, had she gone and hurt his feelings? "Not to boast none," she went on wrapping gifts, "but I been called a genius at getting the Spoilt to do right. Could be, all my time *around* the Spoilt has done spoilt Maimie, too. But, way I see it, if *I* can't cure me of my being ruint by spoilage, then can't nobody else. As to my doing for these little black ones, free of charge? Noo, that don't really draw Maimie un*to* it all that much, sir, but thank you."

He turned to leave. "Sister," he tried a last time. "You know this, but . . . Charity begin at home."

"Fine," Beech snapped. "Go start at *your* place. In this house, my re-membered babies keep me steadily busy, sir. I believe they calling Maimie right now. Good day."

She saw him ease down her porch steps, the man looked caved in, that disappointed with his old favorite who knew the best 100 from the Book of Psalms' 150. She grabbed up her Bible (dust was on it—troubling, the strange deadly feel of grit there). She ran to her porch, didn't even bother opening the Book but mashed one hand across its cover. Then—like re-ceiving telegram knocks—she quoted aloud at his bent hurrying back: "Preacher? We all 'discipline problems.' You, too. Who is ever going to take us in hand? Psalm 14 it say, 'Lord looked down from heaven upon the children of men, to see if there were any that did understand and seek God. They *all* gone aside, they are all together become filthy: there is none that doeth good, no, not one.' —Everybody a brat underneath. Maimie ain't the only one spoilt rotten."

Three children (one of them Castalia's) were playing with a wagon wheel on the dusty street. They went still, watching. Miss Maimie'd once been this neighborhood's example. Some mothers told brats, "Get out that lazy bed and come to this window and notice our Sister Beech." There she strided, stern uphill in virgin white, Bible clutched against her, bound daily toward making children of the grand do godly. She now knew from street kids' faces—one-half year out of work and she'd become a witch. Beech touched her untended hair. This uniform seemed soiled. "You so ill-*bred* to stare," she shook her Book at them. "You bad." —She hurried indoors, leaned against the wall. It crackled with hundreds of children's yellowing drawings.

How could she ever tell her preacher and Sisters what it meant to eat alone, a meal without one living child nearby to stroke and cleanse and stuff? Food interested her none at all now—Maimie by herself hardly seemed worth cooking for. She was accustomed to dining at the Governor's fancy table or else lolling in a sunny nursery alongside her darling—or even sitting at the staff lunch, Bible opened before her so she wouldn't have to talk to simple under-gardeners and such. Sent to her home downhill, Beech first struggled to make one nice meal a day, she'd tried amusing herself. She uselessly ironed her uniform at night. All day, she wore the nurse's cap around her kitchen. She told herself kiddie stories—the one about a king that turned everything he touched into refined genteel gold—a king that couldn't keep his mitts off of his favorite little girl—that made her too be valuable, twenty-four carat and dead, dead.

Bored of food (a rich person's ailment caught uphill), Beech used tricks perfected on five decades of fussy eaters. This woman alone at a table in a house, lifted a spoonful of hominy grits. She held it before her own resisting mouth. The mouth called singsongy, "Knock knock? It me. Open *up*, Maimie's Sweet Flower. Cause here come big fat old Marse Bumber Bee."

Then she heard herself. The woman, alone at a table in a house, lightly set her spoon aside. She mashed both palms flat against wood. She stared ahead.

FIVE SISTERS, returned to Baby Africa, brought McCloud's blue check direct to Maimie's home. She didn't look so good. Her face was ashy as she thanked them. "I hopes," she said, her back turned toward these dearest friends, "you didn't beg him for it or nothing. I right fixed, money-wise. It ain't the money so much. I hopes Mr. McCloud give it free-will-like."

"He seem real glad to." "He tell all kinds nice things on you." "We figure he got off mighty cheap." Maimie thanked them but cried again. They all prayed together, holding hands, hoping to regain their nice old working unit. Traveling ladies then dragged on home, exhausted. Wilmington's "True Blue Unltd. Indigo Camps, Inc." was as far from Falls as many of them would ever go. Only on account of loving Maimie had these Sisters made the sacrifice of distance.

Towards their houses, women scattered to pray for Beech whilst bathing, steeping. (Water can be a form of prayer—a lightning-luring conductor even for the Spirit.) Tonight was Wednesday Night Prayer Meeting. Again Preacher would mention Maimie's health. For nearbout seven months, he'd kept her on the "Favored Shut-in's Church-Pillar Prayer List." Secretly, while praying under a flutter of Amens like pumping wingbeats, all of Afro Gethsemane sat, eyes closed, blaming blaming one white child.

Sisters back from duty found their home porches alive with husbands unworthy or overworthy. Their sinks were piled with days of dirty dishes. The back yards were littered and too loud with children less refined than their chosen mascot Maimie. But after *her* bare box of a house, a person did feel joy in greeting loved ones' noise, the pleasure of this much friction waiting to welcome a body room to room. Just another soul's saying (without even being real deeply interested), "So, how *was* it?" That helped. You compared your life to Maimie's choices—walls coated in baby scrawlings, total silence, one big calendar Xed grand with bigwigs' birth dates. Maimie—and her kindergarten of white ghosts—ghosts that hadn't even held the door or waited for her. Ghosts that'd betrayed her—not staying baby ones but growing up on her and coarsening, forgetting.

. . .

MAIMIE L. BEECH, alone now, paced. She appeared to seriously read one upside-down piece of blue paper—indigo blue for purposes of advertising and as a little joke. To her, the amount seemed huge. Embarrassment ran just that size. This, stashed with her own savings, meant she'd have enough to live comfortably forever. Why did that now seem a endless jail term? McCloud's gift felt rigged, each dollar had a stinger hid inside it. Money meant to slowly numb her, hush her, keep her calm downhill and minding rowdy children her own color. Once Maimie turned McCloud's blue paper into hard yellow gold, she would sign away her last true claim. She tried and calm herself with scripture, "Psalm go: 'If his children forsake my law, and walk not in my judgements, if they brook my statutes and keep not my commandments, then I will visit their transgressions with the rod and their iniquity with stripes.' " To the blue check, Beech explained, "I been famous. Fa-mous." She kept pacing.

The "secret weapon" they'd called her. This payoff meant goodbye to remembered French at table, so long the Book of Palms. Bye even to the scary half-fun of smelling smoke, dashing toward it, screaming, "Sugar, sug, what *now*?" Beech was being asked to cash in her Bianca like a stack of soap-smooth ivory chips.

"No way," said famous Maimie Beech. "No way in *this* world." She walked back and forth, the check pulling nearer her long face and weak eyes. She pictured what gold this paper'd draw her at the bank. She imagined it: a head-sized pile of rattly yellow light, coins that someway rhymed with all the thousand gold/brown/yellow ringlets sprouting off pink babies for all those uphill years. Around her finger, she'd created them from fluff, from nothing much—the definite and separate curls, proud years of them. Baby ringlets seemed a type of coinage, too, maybe this earth's tenderest denomination. Rich folks, out all day earning still more money, had onct felt proud to leave the costly Maimie Beech guarding their true treasures. Even as a slave girl decades back, Beech'd understood: The hellions, her chosen specialty, were oftentimes their parents' best-loved. Everybody considered that being bad—wild, willful—meant both a sadness and a luxury. There was heat in badness. Beech knew. The homes might change, the children might look different, but out of baby blues and baby browns one thing scoffed at her. It made house calls and so did Maimie Beech. "How you hanging, Marse Satan?" she said with a silent nod. And He snarled back, *"You* again?" They were old enemies. She was His Laundress. He was her filthy livelihood.

Beech had onct felt so in charge when big spenders called her in, tried bribing her to come and tame their lively worsts. She felt she'd pulled a fast one all these years—*loving* the brats had been her trick—it was that simple, that cheap. (McCloud believed a person got what a person paid for. Beech now saw—a person surely did. And she wanted it back, fifty-nine years of it. Might be a seller's market but she'd regather all of it she could afford.)

Everybody got issued a certain amount of love per household—even residents of Baby Africa found their rightful share. But hers? Oh, she'd been real clever, she'd rushed uphill and squandered it on sets of thankless twins, she'd spread it—gilding powder—over idle little clumps of strangers' babies. Her share went to end their fevers, to hush their stammers, it'd urged their first steps. She'd burned her share in reading kids the finest things a hired head could make up. Years of it—sunk into scoldings and Bible lessons, the changing of those million diapers, all the rubber sheets.

No gentleman caller ever returned to her home after visit number three—not even when local gossip hinted how much cash old Beech had squirreled away. To her, no gent ever buzzed, "Open up. It's me."

Pacing, Maimie wondered: Was she one bit better than the women who accepted white men into their houses for a fee? Name the difference between loving these men and loving these men's brats? At least the other act was over with lots quicker. Even if nobody quite meant it, that deed was at least *called* "love." Wouldn't it have been a faster, more honest livelihood than her years of patience—this gallery of scribbles, a few bronzed baby tokens, her tended calendar of honored births, and for what? Her birth date was now nine weeks gone. Who had honored her?

She'd been whites' "secret weapon." Love had seemed her secret weapon against them. Now she saw, love had been their secret weapon—against her.

Beech studied his blue check. It was, she understood, a polite white un-invitation. Marse McCloud was taking back that time he'd held her hand. A genius with children—kept far from children—why, she ain't no genius no more. Mostly she has sunk to being a bleachish watered ghost. The bank is broke.

Maimie shut her Bible on the check. She tucked both underneath a pile of white hand-me-down plates. But even from the far side of her room, a tongue of indigo showed. She dressed to go out, she chanted verses Bianca'd liked: "Enter into His gates with singing. King in his countinghouse counting out his honey. Know ye that the Lord He is God. Queen down in she parlor eating bread and money." Maimie pulled the check out, weighted it with the salt and pepper. These shakers: metal-plated baby booties—fitted with clear-glass inserts. Beech fetched her own unopened bottle of perfume—just like one she'd given to a birthday girl. Instant of Joy had been Maimie's mirror-image gift to herself. She slipped into her best white governess outfit, one kept back in case she ever got offered work again. She pinned on her crispest cap. Beech stowed the perfume in one pocket, clutched her Bible big as a Welcome mat—hiked off to Wednesday Night Prayer Meeting. She was greeted with screams like the dead returned to life.

I'VE ONLY heard this next part third-hand, fourth-hand. Still, especially if such events changed your coming life, especially if you're named for the person, you try and understand what went on in her head that evening. We know the service ended around eleven. Sisters walked Beech home. They all kissed her good night. They kissed each other. Friends felt they'd saved

Maimie's life. They were grateful she'd allowed them the excellent, justly famous sensation of doing right. (Wrong-doing is exceptional, too, and maybe has more variety, but right-doing's pleasure lasts longer. Or so somebody as old as me must tell herself, darling.)

Maimie waited till loved ones meandered home. She already missed them. They'd always admitted envying her uphill reputation, amazed at how whites kowtowed. Friends forever acted kind to her but, in the end, they always left to join their real families. Beech knew: If she got sick, they'd tend her. If she died, they'd carry on proper and noisy at her funeral. But— even after years of kindness—Maimie knew what her Sisters knew: For a whole lifetime, it just won't enough. The tally wouldn't do.

Maimie—richer now—figured maybe she should haul off, hire herself a nurse and stranger (maybe even a white one). This person would come and stay with Beech tonight. The lady professional would bring along her knitting or letter writing but she'd first tuck in Maimie's covers, she'd say, "I'll be right here if you need anything," she'd say, "There there," or whatever honey-tongued hired comfort said.

The nurse wouldn't have to mean it. Fact is, her words'd help Beech *more* for having nothing personal in them. For being bought at the going white rate, pricey.

FIRST BEECH embarrassed herself by hiking uphill to the McCloud home. She guessed this was a humongous social mistake in the making. She couldn't stop. Being "bad" was suddenly of major interest to her. "*You* again," she muttered, and knew she was greeting Satan, Satan stationed on-duty in herself. If Beech set her mind to being bad—considering the years of observing little wicked geniuses—who might be better at it?

A party was underway. Chinese lanterns lit the trees. Lanterns drooped from a harem of palms dragged onto the porch. Every pastel lantern glowed with one squiggled Chinese letter. Maimie had learned: No McCloud could translate these. Each character looked like Beech's vision of Oriental-Bible-English writing. Each looked written by some ink-dipped wing in flight.

Folks packed and jammered all over the McCloud lawn. You heard so many clinking glass ladles against glass punch bowls filling glass cups— sounded like the Caucasians were made, mouth and hands, of glass. Maimie mingled easy enough at first. Two young women asked her to please go get them some extra napkins. When she looked hard their way, one said, "Sorry. We thought . . ."

Three pianos sounded from indoors. The visiting Collier twins played flute. Music leaked through open windows with the candlelight. A gate-crasher moon looked on through tree limbs. The mansion's hundred points and edges showed black against a sunset. This sunset was the color of cut-rate foreign rubies or the best local berry jams.

All in white, the second gardener stood carving rare roast beef on a banquet table dragged outdoors. The smell of food made Beech feel giddy.

Seemed she hadn't eaten for the longest time. How many days made a week and what was her day off? The nearer she wandered to the churchlike home, the weaker did her legs feel. Finally—bumped and milling among glazed white strangers—Beech sat down on the lawn. She had to. She'd been staggering.

Waiting here in dewy grass, Beech held more tight to her Bible. (People would see the Book and know her.) She touched her scalp, was the hat on straight? Facing the three-story uphill home, its stained glass burning from inside like with a fever, Beech spoke as to some choosy eater . . ."Open up. It's me."

She only wanted rest. She felt like she deserved to rest right here. To someday be buried in this pretty grass—a gravestone white as a salt lick. Soon Bianca would know Beech was here, Bianca would dash out holding tailor-made clover anklets, a five-strand clover crown.

Guests—though busy admiring, addressing, and fondly criticizing each other—did slowly notice the curious sight: a black woman wearing a white uniform—sitting in grass as if stationed here for some useful chore, to read "fortunes" from her big black book, or to bodily plug the yard's worst geyser, or give guided tours of clover. Nested among the pretty open-toed shoes of white ladies, shiny summer shoes of gents, the seated woman was careful to keep her long neck stretched in a way half grand—her pleated face wide open with a look of full entitlement.

Out-of-towners' fancy shoes first edged away from her. Then one pair of white suede oxfords did come nosing nearer. "Might we be of service?" The shoes had a young white male voice helping them from high above. "You're feeling a tad woozy, I take it. Well, welcome to a fairly largish club. My friends were just asking what our Presbyterian Angus uses to spike this stuff. Certainly sneaks up on one. Not that you don't look perfectly at ease down there, but, listen, should you ever *care* to stand, I consider myself still steady enough—possible mistake of mine—to maybe assist a person. Say, are you a nurse? We were just wondering over there. Couldn't help notice your tidy little hat. Young lady in my group, see the one? she was admiring it. Look at her giggling. Definite drawback. Don't you hate it when they giggle?" "Tell Marse Angus my name. He know me. I used to help around this place. Set right at the table. Tell him Maimie L. Beech back on the job. See what he say do."

Beech understood: McCloud must now be sent for. Her order had been given. She was glad. Enter into his presence with singing. Sound the gongs, burn incense, waste precious precious ointments. When the gates swung open, when Beech was asked to enter again, she would know what to say or chant. She felt she did not need to plan it now. Her favorite hymn was "Something Always Sings." Just trust, she told herself—she gave herself some credit.

But Beech was down here shaking. Her dark legs—little wider than the bones in them—poked straight before her, ending in great blockish white shoes. She always wore flats to shorten the distance she had to bend toward her children. Now hugging the Book, she waited among other feet. Her face changed, mouth almost gloating, mumbling, ready to greet the man. She sat stubbornly grinning at nothing—plainly eager to become more naughty. Beech was laboring at it.

The young white shoes went off to others ("Seems to actually *know* Angus"), then both shoes moved to the house, climbed nine front steps, returned: a message.

Clumsily, one whole young man bent down into sight and breathed whiskey. Beech closed both eyes. She never expected to see a whole person lower towards her like a diver coming down to join her underwater. This was the first direct order Beech had ever sent McCloud: "Hear my petition. Come unto me." Where was the man?

"Angus insists you meet him on your back-yard bench, on you two's bench. You *do* know him, don't you? Boss told me to tell you, at all costs, 'Bleach must not be seen by the youngest,' that little one who always wears the hats, their baby one . . . named . . ."

Eyes shut, Maimie hoarsely announced with great tired feeling, "Bianca."

"Very one, yes. Boss said, under no circumstances should you be seen by her. I hinted as how—maybe you'll object—you'd perhaps imbibed a drop. Not that *I* haven't. (But then I have due cause. I still work for him.) And Boss goes, 'Bleach is not to be seen by Bianca. Bleach will know this herself, in whatever state.' He said you were devoot! But why 'Bleach'? Anyway, my advise'd be go and try him now in the back yard. You know, Clara's right. Especially up close, this is quite a cunning little hat you've got. Clara might even want it. I think I'm going to go *ask* Clara."

Maimie Beech nodded, careful to keep eyes mashed closed. She started to unpin her cap but the voice walked off. Beech let her hat stay while repeating in a dulled locked tone, " 'Cannot be seen here.' 'Cannot no longer be seen here.' He acting so rude. He *rude* to me."

She had asked for a moment's credit and right out front where folks could see a person get her due—prepare a table/presence mine enemies. He had not come out to her. "Open up," she'd asked. The household would not. Few saw the minor spectacle. Through groves of ankles, cuffs, pale shoes, paste buckles, one lean black woman in outsized whites, eyes mashed stubbornly shut, clutching her Bible, scrambled away on hands and knees. She slipped from the lantern-lit yard, was soon just white shoes scuddling out a hedge's hole, was lost to the safety of the darkness of the street.

At midnight Beech someway trekked into countryside, never more than six minutes from Falls' most urban center spot. At Meacham's farm and apiary, something happened. Versions of it change with whoever chooses to tell you. Some claim Beech tried drinking the perfume as poison. Most agree she drenched herself with scent. Next morning, footprints proved she'd walked back and forth before the hives, kicking a few. But bees, helpless day workers, stay home at night.

The broken perfume bottle was found under one of three rope beehives that Famous Maimie Beech overturned. Seems she smeared herself with honey. Morning showed a hillside clotted with wax comb and gritty syrup. Many trapped bees floated under amber, stuck in sweetness they'd spent lifetimes making.

Maimie Beech then marched herself through Meadows' Pasture to the river. Maybe bees were stinging her the way she wanted bees to. Maybe she was only sticky and perfumed, a mess, disappointed. The river seemed the one place a person could be safe. Maimie opened her Bible and placed it on a flat rock near the roadway, the rock where ladies fished. No name was written in the book, just one X traced over many times to make it clearer and more hers. But the volume was bigger than anybody else's hereabouts and would be recognized. Its center had been most worn away, leaving Psalms a frilly cavity betwixt the terrors visited on faithful Job and the bossy hope of Proverbs. I imagine Maimie smelling the river, sighing many Psalms aloud, practically chugging them. I see her noticing the moonlight wavering on water like some flaming path or giant tongue. I imagine her good shoes testing water's temperature. I hear Famous Maimie Beech saying to the river, to the night and world: "Open up. It's me."

She steps off a rock into our river Tar. Easy to picture her starched cap becoming a little folded-paper-looking sailboat, breezing away without her. Maybe she planned to briefly run over the water's moonlit top, maybe she settled for walking on the surface, only to discover that she couldn't stroll much of anywhere except along the mud bottom, a bottom that dips to thirty-five feet there by our town's namesake Falls.

THE BODY didn't turn up for the longest time. Later rumors swore that when four scared shad-seeking white boys fished her out near a factory up near Tarboro, she had traveled further from Falls proper than ever before during her lifetime. With sun's bleaching, with her soaking in the tannic acid from a shoe-polish plant outside Tarboro, the bloat of her had been someway bleached. It made identifying all the harder.

Tarboro authorities announced finding a "possible elderly Indian nurse." Falls had sent the official missing-person notice but if you're a town Tarboro's size you don't absorb the expense of having a body crated up and put on the Atlantic Coastline spur train till you know whose body it's been. The Tarboro sheriff looked for ways to learn this. Not by dental records, since this particular person's dental work had just meant taking out the hurtingest tooth one at a time. Nothing was ever put back in (which is all that really helps you to identify—the gold and silver additions. Those, people keep track of).

Sheriff Cooper (cousin to *Falls'* Sheriff Cooper) spied a cross-shaped brass locket round this neck so swollen that he had to break the chain to get it off. He opened the latch and pressed a pulp of wet paper inside, paper oozing water like a eye. Sheriff then set the locket near his office wood stove all day. He found he could finally make out what each dried thing had been. Using a knife, he peeled off one layer at a time. In order, here were modern type of photos moving back toward daguerreotypes, then tintypes: likenesses of thirty-nine white children. Some grinned. Many looked forced to do so. From a mischievous-looking curly girl at the front, Sheriff worked backward. Then, against the locket's very metal, he saw a red sticker and, finally, some writing that looked promising as ID.

"Okay, now," he took the locket to his cleanest office window. He held it up, squinted hard, then read aloud to sunlight:

A Woolworth's Special Value
29¢

SISTERS found the bank check on her table still un-Xed. Blue paper was weighted by bronze salt and pepper slippers. The loving choir members had already scanned every page of Maimie's sticky Bible, looking for some jotted clue. Friends plundered Maimie's house till they destroyed its true first order and couldn't get stuff back the way it'd been. Still, they kept seeking some explanation. Maimie had got the McCloud tribute money. She had returned to church. So why'd she go and do this godless thing?

Maimie Lucille Beech's best friends kept patiently ransacking her shelfs and counters, seeking a note. It would maybe accuse my granddad, Angus McCloud, it'd maybe say he'd done some deed beyond unfair hiring/firing. Maybe he had "touched" Maimie. What if something off-color had gone on? This seemed unlikely but the women wanted to see blame placed where it belonged. They felt ready to accept Maimie's word for who to accuse.

Sisters quit hunting long enough to sit around her kitchen table. They sat looking at the bronze booties, one filled with white salt, one black pepper. Who had these tiny shoes once fit? Some plump sixty-year-old grandpoppa uphill? It made them sick to wonder.

Sisters felt tired and cross—almost cross with Maimie. The harder they looked for her last message, the deeper they felt: She'd never exactly been *like* them. Maimie had believed. That'd forced her to do so foolish. She believed too much in Them uphill. She disappeared when Them uphill stopped seeing her. She considered their eyesight some Sun that can kill you by just looking away. And ladies decided, Maimie'd partly valued the Sisters because, like her, they'd been so shamelessly interested in the ones uphill, in Power of such bright white voltage that it sometimes passed for love.

Maimie had once seemed these women's aging child. That now made them group mothers of a suicide. (If the hardest thing on earth is losing your own child, how much rougher losing that child *to* that child? —Why?)

They rose again in grouchy unison. "Well," two said. Rubbing lower backs, they turned and hunted the note in places they'd already checked twice. (Sisters had their own reasons for sadness and the little daily rages. But their friend's reasons interested and puzzled them. They wanted to give Maimie Beech a last fair chance at listing hers.)

Finally one lady snapped strong fingers, "She *couldn't* . . ."

"Read nor write," somebody added.

"Which mean: no note," another explained. "No way she *could* tell us."

Then they all went home. They felt guilty but released into their safer crowded lives. Afterward, even as their needing one another grew keener, the surviving Sisters would never again be quite so much a unit. At church, even while singing, they would look at one another, hard. They'd always known everything that loving friends can do for each other. Really, so much! But now these women knew what they *couldn't* do for each other. It made them afraid. They resisted this but: it made them almost afraid of each other.

11

ONE excellent final question can often run you: *The money that set so much motion, where'd those big bucks come from?*

Well, like I said: Cotton and 1851–88, a small but profitable shipping line out of Wilmington. But mostly indigo—one cash crop that proved of short-lived value. The plant itself was suitable to marsh-growing conditions that rice favors. Indigo got named for first being used in India. Its dye made a violent if heavenly violet blue. One drawback: the tint tended to streak. It got replaced by quicker, easier chemical processes just after our story ends.

Since indigo's moneymaking days are gone forever (and even if they should come again), I want to now reveal my grandpoppa Angus McCloud's unwritten-down but passed-by-word-of-mouth secret recipe. If he knew I was telling this, the man would probably spin in his bronze casket. Angus who lived such a long full life and ran for governor twice and lost twice. Angus who gained enough gold so one day he turned around and saw it all behind and under him, who suddenly understood the value of his touch and soon got stiff and precious over it, and frozen. He panicked he would lose everything. He stopped finding ways of making, and turned to ways of keeping, and was lost. First he became a Republican and then moved beyond that till folks claimed he should've run for state office—not on the Republican ticket, but on the Royalist one. These things happen, even to the self-made, especially them. Child? Beware of using up your last forty years in being the curator of your first fifty. *That* ain't getting ahead!

The chemicals you need I've never really laid eyes on or touched. Still, their names I know. My poor old magpie mind just works this way. So here goes the family money's secret finally in black and white:

Take one part powdered indigo to two parts ferrous sulfate, combine and stir. Steep with three parts of slaked lime. Then, before allowing your brew to perk for the three needed days, add—finally—two hundred parts water.

AT MAIMIE'S funeral, most white McClouds and nineteen of their black staff arrived in a right stately queue. Angus and his silent diplomatic wife were accustomed to doing the right thing. Locally they'd grown famous for it. Servants hadn't planned attending, they'd disliked Maimie's privateness, her scholar's airs. But one direct order from Angus, and here they mostly were. A skeleton crew had been left to mind the Mansion McCloud. Of course, young Bianca McCloud won't present at this particular burial.

Her three big sisters had offered to play suitable six-hand funeral pieces. Their poppa even volunteered getting the three Steinway grands downhill from Summit to Gethsemane Garden True Gospel Afro-Baptist here near the river. Preacher felt certain whispered doubts about his old church floor's willingness to support that kind of show-off weight. And though he thanked the young ladies, Rev. did let hisself wonder aloud if *their* type of Europe music would be sufficiently homey or fitting for the end of a person as Christian, local, and unemployed as the late Miss Maimie Lucille Beech.

These quiet girls, denied permission after practicing two days straight, still felt determined to do something right for Beech. They hinted to Poppa: He might offer pallbearers use of the healthiest palm plants, might have greenery sent down to Garden True Gospel for the service. Maimie'd onct asked permission to come uphill and water all the palms one Palm Sunday (her day off, too). She seemed to like these plants for secret reasons all her own. Girls sometimes caught Beech standing under one's droopy overhang, green fronds throwing louvered shadows on her dried dark skin. Her eyes would be closed, loose braids poking like feathers through a leafy weave. Her thumb and finger might be joined to hold the tip end of one branch that she tugged slightly. Seemed its fibers sent her coded vibrations: news or poetry, the fullness thereof. So Angus said: Liked palms, did she? fine, sure. And after breakfast he called aside his third gardener, mentioned which wagon should be used. Angus said to deliver, say, the mansion's twelve top plants and get them into the church and set up well before the service began, and to retrieve them at a decent longish interval afterwards—so black folks would remember just their being beautifully *present*, and not get confused by seeing them fetched back home too overcarefully, and so forth. Understood?

Parents had left their little Bianca uphill today, unsupervised upstairs. She'd never let them hire a replacement nurse. Bianca's hair was now growing out, if somewhat darker. (Angus'd wanted to buy a wig for his invalid, one made of real human hair from Irish girls who arrive at the hair brokers every five years and let theirselves—whilst weeping, quiet, resigned—be practically scalped for the money. It pleased a Scot to purchase Irish hair for his American daughter. But Bianca's mother, in the one thing she will say within our story, rose up during dinner, slammed her fist on the table, shouted how: a wig of stranger's hair would only further lure death and tempt fate. "My child will wear a wig over my dead body." And sat again, having stated this strange picture.)

MR. AND MRS. McCloud felt like their Bianca had meant it: in asking to stay home and practice scales on her new piano. Starting so far behind her sisters, the girl was really struggling to catch up. You had to admire the hours she put in, even if she maybe lacked their natural gifts. Worried about leaving her, parents finally decided that, after all, the cook, groom, and head gardener would be just downstairs if Bianca needed anything and called out for a snack or help.

Angus McCloud now listened at the white-robed church choir clapping near Miss Maimie Beech's pine box. Its lid was mercifully shut. Borrowed palms swayed, semi-African, trembling with music and the choir's pooled breath. A blue envelope stuffed with bills crackled inside Angus' breast pocket. His check written to Maimie had never been returned for payment. He planned making a notable donation to her church today. But Angus slowly recalled: Collections aren't taken during funerals.

Which was pretty silly—especially with *him* present. Angus sat staring into one of his rosy hand's opening and closing. A fly kept buzzing on the windowsill nearby. Angus imagined profits that would've gathered by now to the importer of that first beehive from Holland in 1602. Imagine if the guy could've just kept bees under lock and key, then issued further hives to other immigrants—franchises. But of course, if your company bees are going to bring home decent honey, you *have* to let them fly off loose, free all day. They'll soon branch out on you. They leave. You cannot hold them.

Angus had liked Maimie. He tried imagining how any employer might've treated her more justly. Accidents will happen, what the boys in insurance call "acts of God." Head lowered, he half smiled: There'd been the first time Beech ever saw him come downstairs in full Scot regalia. She'd spied his kilt, she lost all usual dignified reserve. Beech clamped one hand over her mouth and giggled, pointing. Everybody laughed along with her. Angus—fists knuckled on his hips, feeling handsome and powerful and patient astride the third stair step—grinned, "So, what *is* this I'm a-presently wearing, Maimie Beech?" (One reason you keep servants—getting their news of you, how they "read" you.)

Beech answered, shy, pleased, "A diaper, a plaid diaper, and on a man!"

SUICIDE seemed so *unlike* her. "Self-warth," he'd felt it—a solid floor bid—living stubborn in and under his Miss Maimie. (Maybe she had caught a disease from the aristocrats who'd hired her prior to Angus: they believed a person either had standing or had nothing at all.)

McCloud now asked hisself why he should always feel surprised when others disappointed him. He steadily searched the world for people with the kind of grit and springiness he'd had when young. He longed to find just one member of the deserving poor who was presently as poor and deserving as he'd been there on deck—skin and bones and rickets, but already planning, planning.

A first business partner had told Angus he was a fine judge of others' characters—that he noticed everything but luck. Part of McCloud's own luck meant: barely admitting to luck's wild-child wild-card effect upon hisself, his fortunes. —That really *is* luck. Or is it?

But the well-made fellow straightened now, no percentages in sulking, why dwell long on sadness? Just vanity, this hating to be wrong about your staff. Your sadness only burdened those around you. So Angus slid one arm along the pew back, guarding the three homely gifted girls here on his right. Maybe they'd been unduly upset by the excess emotion pounding here-abouts: Girls were crying as they'd never done (disappointing Angus) when their own little sister got so maimed.

Hedged by weeping and the handclaps here, McCloud determined to feel cheered. Yes, you made your own luck. He imagined that first hive on open deck, bound for the new land. Bugs had been silent during the six-week crossing. Fed sugar water from a pan, they seemed groggy from the rocking and the salt air. But before even the keenest land-loving sailor sensed a continent waiting forty miles ahead in fog, bees knew. They smelled its fullness, the perfume. Nervous sailors gathered—smiling—around a hive suddenly humming, unsticking, groaning with a churning life—wholly charming, totally menacing. Kidnapped bugs sniffed it first: green profit dead ahead.

Angus could so easily picture his Bianca alone at home now. She'd be straight-backed before her new white Steinway. He had never offered her anything but the earth's fullest and finest, its choicest help.

And—for all the sadness of this Maimie business—my granddad supposed that here, too, if half on the slant, he had somehow managed. Again he'd come out in the black. Maimie'd at least given Angus what he *claimed* to want. Even from Beech, he'd got the verrra best of help.

So, sure: His youngest could be trusted alone at home for the hour and a half one funeral'd take.

She was, after all, such a good little girl.

Why
I Say
Ain't

God setteth the solitary in families . . .
—PSALM 68:6

S O ONCE, YEAH, happiness. Once fourteen prisms hang in another little girl's room, these prove that even whitest daylight lives packed with secretive wild colors. God assigned me to the household of a grown lady once also a wild child but stung so strict! Let's skip it, child. Let's commence with happiness, my own, and work our way down, okay?

I picture my gold-haired best friend, Shirley Williams. Nine birthdays into things, Shirl ofttimes slept over at our house. It had three stories, one corner of each: stained glass. Shirl was born poor. When stepping into our place, she forever whispered.

I'll start at Happiness. Okay—once—that.

Just tuck Shirl and me into separate high-backed rosewood beds carved with garlands. My room's bay window had prisms playing starring parts. Prisms decked my quilts and wallpaper with blobs of color like the very rainbow's droppings. One white enameled drawer-pull beat with changing tints, kind of gulped with light—like the gill on something living. Across Shirl's slip (strung neat as her across a chair back) six raw colors held a powwow. Down the street, from Winona Smythe's open porch, canaries sang, announcing daylight like they'd got the patent on it. Then I would start jumping up and down in bed, I chucked two pillows towards Shirley, I commenced hollering our favorite Mr. Robert Louis Stevenson poem, loud:

> A robin with a yellow bill
> Hopped upon the windowsill,
> Cocked his shiny eye and said,
> "Ain't you 'shamed, you sleepyhead?"

Though Shirl was dozing in the bed opposite, her yellow curls looked right awake. She always groomed herself alive. Now she slumped forward, fingers plumping each ringlet, laughing, puffy, "You old so-and-so. It's day again! What'll we do *first?*" She grinned, she stretched, maybe she looked too excellent to stay mine long.

We bounced on beds, chanting, "Ain't you 'shamed, oh ain't you 'shamed?" Lilacs sent excess stink to our second floor. You heard bacon frying downstairs. Momma—still fearful of hiring black help—argued aloud with bacon over how its ends kept curling up, not behaving like choice cuts she'd paid for. Honey—I didn't know that this was happiness, not then. Looking back, over a pile of guns alive as brown-and-silver snakes under your bed, you understand.

The one complicated sight that morning—blood on our sheets. See, the day before, my friend and me had cut our wrists. There's a story here. That much I know.

So, yeah, sacks of seasons before hitting my nineties' city-limits sign, back when men were men and women weren't so sure they liked it, in advance of being queen bee to my own busy hive, why, prior to even getting engaged, I was the mischief of a child I've skipped over total. Back, back, back, a bucket down a well. Let hemlines fall where they may.

My momma looked dignified as a dictionary (everything in it). Was straight-backed as our front hall's Shaker chair (where no soul ever sat— only company's hats). Her words seemed counted in advance, party favors, one per guest. She kept hands clasped before her. She kept her hair all baled behind her in one breast-shaped bun. Momma's long dresses glided like on wheels. By now, folks feared her. Folks were right to. A cultivated person in a hick town, Momma ofttimes praised Mr. Bizet's *Carmen*, claiming it'd done for the Latin temperament what Mr. Wagner'd failed to manage with the German one. Only her sisters knew what she meant by this but they disagreed. Besides, she hadn't spoke to them for years. —Some folks' tragedy, child, is not caring what anybody thinks of them. Others, like Momma, are forced to care too much. My own early roughness didn't just irk Momma—it scared her so.

And him? Red-haired and rawboned even in how he sounded. Poppa spun a chatter full of homemades: spur-of-the moment words like "scuzz-budgets" and "hoity-toilets." Momma traced my own foul grammar right back to him. I admit he wouldn't win no diction certificates. Poppa's agreement between his subjects and verbs was broke about as often as Indian treaties. But in the contest betwixt what's proper and what's fun—he come out as Champion every time.

The man would shuffle downtown (in no hurry, auburn everywheres, shirt misbuttoned—face as bristled, useful, centered as a Welcome mat). He'd soon tote home the bread she'd sent him for. But in the nine minutes he'd been gone, Poppa's broken English had stored Magellan's own amount of info—man had hints, gossips, lapses, he'd seen whose Episcopalian lap-dog was in heat and which twelve pagan yellow yard dogs knew it.

Momma punished me for any echo of the man. She said that Ain't was such a no-count mongrel, it had never even got into the social register of English. And, looking back, I see she had her reasons. It's too late to improve or reconsider now. At the time I figured she was just being extra snobby. Now I understand—Ain't changed my life. Ain't forced me to marry at fifteen. Ain't was the crowbar that shoehorned me into bed beneath a certain wide tough gentleman. Old Ain't. And Momma warned me.

ME AT NINE? That's easy. Hell on shoe leather. A porridge of freckles, two stiff auburn braids spouting off one stubborn streak. Like now, my front teeth were missing, but then I had a chance of new ones growing in. Through the gap, I'd spit and whistle. I stayed busy masterminding ropes and pulleys, tugging planks and found furniture to a tree house sixty feet up. Across my knees and elbows, I had so many knots and scabs and bug bites, these could've spelled a book of verse in Braille.

We were rich enough. We were rich. We lived along Falls' only crest. Hill towns are too easy to read. Rich folks stay up top where breezes make life possible. The single view for miles is like a club you join by paying dues.

Our Summit Avenue was a regular museum of gingerbread porches, competition yardwork. By the curb, horse's-head metal hitching posts were painted the rich mahogany of black people's skin. Some hitching posts were metal colored boys enameled into clothes the tints of carousel hobbyhorses. Our street said: A place for everybody, everybody in his place. Us especially. Others? Eat your heart out.

County hay wains and buckboards would tool in of a Sunday to check us out. Summit Avenue got paved before any road in eastern North Carolina. Farmers drove back and forth—mouths open, choosing which house, if one was offered free of charge, they'd pick. To my knowledge, no house ever was. —From our porch swing, I wanted to bellow, Go on home, you-all have whole fields, so what's a measly yard to you?

While they oohed at our front walk's cheese-even boxwoods, where was I? Off downhill visiting my favorite poor girl, Shirl. Or maybe indoors getting knuckles slapped for saying Ain't again. For this, I ofttimes got hurt, always by Momma. She believed in discipline, wanted me to act rich, hoped I'd protect myself. From what? I wondered. "From *them*," she answered, whispering in our servantless house.

Thanks to her money, we lived on this street I never felt entitled to. Poor kids stole home from school along Summit, big-eyed—even brothers and sisters tended to hold hands. They pretended to have dibs on some fine mansion. And Miss Entitled? I went slipping along side streets, I followed ditches clear downhill via Baby Africa. Except on wettest days, this stayed Lucy's long route home. I dodged in through our back door, the former servants' entrance. I appeared scuffed and ruddy as a farm child. Like Poppa, I was raw, carroty-colored. Momma, a true white woman, stayed more like cauliflower baked to that sad innocence past texture.

Girl snobs and mother snobs had already commenced to snubbing your little Lucy. Was thanks to my copycat Ain't, a tendency to pick my general nose area, a trend towards pushing small dull facts into taller more worthier tales, a knack for imitating others, a fondness for the noisy. The stable-keeper's daughter was fast becoming my one friend. Momma took me aside, let me know: *Noblesse oblige* had its limits. "Sally who?" I said. She explained: I could do better socially than this Shirley person. Momma warned: No self-respecting family would keep asking me into finer homes if my company and English didn't straighten up and fly right, "You hear me, Miss Poverty Lips?"

2

POOR as Shirley was, she spoke proper as a teacher. After she slept over, I'd find traces of her tucked back of couch cushions—homemade vocabulary flash cards: "Incorrigible." "Obsequious." Which broke my heart. When did daily talk ever ask "obsequious" of any living soul? Shirl seemed to think that onct she'd trained me right, the two of us might go—almost a couple—into the high-ceilinged parlors of Falls' tip-top society. Seated high in our secret tree house, Shirley asked with pity if I even knew what gerunds *were*. I scratched my head, copying a ropy Poppa, "Gerunds, gerunds. —Sounds like . . . sprouted wheat?" She didn't laugh. I never stopped trying to make Shirl laugh. I wondered if her lack of money subtracted that much humor from the world.

Other Summit Avenue girls had already titled me Miss Lucy Trench-mouth. It hurt to hear and, even now, it smarts a little to admit the grief I got—even from their mothers. Especially from them. "Lucille, Emily must go in and practice her *En*-glish lessons. I believe I hear your parents calling you."

"From six blocks off? You don't no such of a thing, lady. I can take me a hint. Bye, Em. Boy, that ain't too nice. And you all call *me* rude!"

At the time, I tried and play like I was half proud of being sniffed at on by my street. I hid in our cozy tree house. With Shirley as my choicest friend, I felt stronger than them Episcopalian fussbudgets. Like me, Shirl was totally Baptist. Full of dread, we had been dunked the same day. Shirl's mother stuffed her child's golden curls into a kind of rubber bathing cap. I went bareheaded. Sun had cooked my hempy braids bone-dry by 2 p.m.

We sat together in every service, as far from our stern parents as possible, we constantly passed notes. Our great trick was pretending we'd dozed off during the Reverend's dull whinings. Other preachers raged and hellfired. Ours just scolded. Many adults slept, too. Snoozing, snorting, Mr. Pember drooled onto his tie. We saw, it like to made us die giggling. Every time we looked, the stain got worse and wider. Some total stranger seated behind me, now bent forward, thumped me on the skull. Shirl straightened at onct. Then, improved, safe herself, using a little gold mechanical pencil she carried, Shirl wrote on our church bulletin: "Ain't you 'shamed, you sleepyhead?" This made me pretty much unravel. I got thumped again. Savagely. Hilarious! We stifled ourselfs by biting the backs of our hands. Afterwards, we compared, studying whose skin had turnt reddest, counting girlish teeth marks. Finally, service ended, Pember woke with a pig grunt and stared at his ruined tie and hid it under his coat, and we nearbout perished from the humor of it, tears all down our cheeks. "Did the spirit descend on you two?" Shirl's heavy mother touched our wet faces. Shirley, better at faking than me, nodded Yes. When adult eyes got right in front of mine, I shook my head No, admitting, "Mr. Pember drooled, during." "Well," Shirl's momma said, "the Lord sure moves in strange and mysterious ways," and laughed. Onct home, my mother burned my knuckles good, the ruler.

HAVE I mentioned Shirley's looks? Oh, Lord God, that Shirl was the very ore to make a princess of. Poppa bragged: My pal was so much prettier than any highborn Summit Avenue girl, it won't funny. When rich ladies put white frocks on their daughters, Pop claimed ladies just prayed (if Episcopalians *did*) that their lumpy girls'd turn out half so fine as our Shirley in simple school clothes.

Still, Shirl's dresses were never exactly plain. Her hefty mother nursed ambitions for the one child. The Mrs. forever added cheap trims, brass lockets, net panels onto poor Shirl's sleeves, hems, collars. Shirl was forced to wear straw hats in warm seasons, furry felt ones fall and winter. Her smocks stuttered with frills. Tired cloth roses drooped everywheres. Talk about colorful, her frocks tended towards your raw mint greens, overly pinks. Shirl had one outfit made of bitter yellow that could made a citrus grower pucker. Local folks pitied a child forced to walk around like some dime store's notions counter. Fingering the latest fringe, some asked, "Aren't you *hot*?" But Shirl, pure dignity, never onct complained. When Shirley Williams visited us, Momma often eased into my room's open doorway, mother's mouth set, hands clasped before her like some solo soprano waiting for her cue. She'd come to check on Shirl's latest getup. I knew and it burned me. Shirl smiled her two-and-a-half-dimple grin, "Your mother acts so nicely towards me. She really takes an interest."

"Right," said I.

Later, alone with me, Momma played piano whilst explaining just how sad Shirl and her mother really were. We'd earlier seen my friend downtown strolling arm in arm betwixt two huge adoring parents. "You know your Shirley's mother's idea of perfect beauty?" Momma asked. "Goldilocks is."

"That's mean!" I backed off, pointing.

Music ceased. Momma turned my way. "You're right, of course. And I repent, Lucille. It's just, I want so much for you. I get ill-tempered when things interfere."

I studied the freckled hand I'd pointed with. "Ain't Shirley's fault. You should be glad *some*body still comes around. Blame me. I look funny. I talk bass ackwards. It's me but, Momma? I try." I poked one ivory high low note, I felt soiled and weak. She leaned forwards, lifted my either wiry braid, wound them into overlapping circles on my scalp. I reached up to touch this topknot, grinning, "Feels like a beanie."

"Tiara," she corrected me. Momma bent off her ebony stool. I looked at its feet, claw-and-ball and brass. She kissed my coarse tight crown. Momma kissed and kissed it. "You'll do," she purred. I saw: Her eyes were closed.

A TRAIN wreck brought my folks together. Momma was twenty-two then, already a old maid by Falls' standards. She'd been pursued by several likely boys who'd scented the inheritance. Not one fellow interested *her*. "Clothes-store mannequins," she called them privately. Bored, she went on a trip with her older male cousin. This was a country outing into the godforsaken terrain near Bear Grass, North Carolina. Backwoods, all ponds there stagnant. The rich reckless older cousin owned a duck-hunting lodge out there.

To make the long story quick: Momma's fifty-year-old cousin, jilted by a young lady friend, got drunk and—with my terrified momma in his buggy—someway decided to race a northbound train toward the Bear Grass crossroads. He did not actually decide this till he *saw* the train. His horse, it never decided. The black train barely noticed. Momma did. Her screams were mistaken for the crossing whistle by passersby. The drunk cousin's timing proved terrible, fatal. His horse, forced to turn right at the crossroads, was struck at once, so was the dandy cousin. Momma got thrown free of tracks. She later said she recalled last thing, one thought: "So this is flight."

When she woke nine hours later, she saw a makeshift splint—lathing and newspapers—already improving her broken right arm. "Lucille, I found myself in a tiny filthy farm hut. I'd seen better-looking stables but the humble folk there did act so generous. I hardly understood their speech. First I thought I was in Heaven, and that Heaven was a kind of Peasant Europe. Everything the color of straw. There was a rough boy hovering over me, pressing cool cloths to my forehead. My first sentence, hours later, was to ask his name. 'Samuel,' he said, and he winked. I laughed and fainted. I woke knowing more. The boy understood nothing of who I was, what I stood to inherit. Finally he asked me whom to notify. First I couldn't remember, then pretended not to know. I pretended that for four sweet days. My poor parents suffered so during those days. But Samuel's wit, his . . . well, his personal heat—contrasted so with my stuffed-shirt suitors from Summit. Samuel told the most charming stories. I drew strength from them. Especially the ones about cunning woodland animals. Delicious. I rested in the sun, my eyes closed, listening. I felt like the child I'd been before a childhood accident I had. The older peasant couple gave me milk, still warm, directly from the cow that looked to be as much a hick as its owner, ribs all showing. Slowly, I grew stronger and finally felt quite certain. I never understood one word his parents said. Their kindness was replete but they were, well, *primitivo*, my dear Lucille. Your poor father seems to have been allotted the collected wit of the last four Bear Grass generations. One day he carried me, bodily, out into the tomato patch, direct sun. Tomato plants have an erotic odor. I asked him to please brush my hair. When he was behind me, doing so with a currying comb for horses, I believe (which I preferred to his mother's far-from-hygienic hairbrush), I joked about some-day finding the courage to ask a boy such as himself to marry a girl such as I. He did not say 'Yes,' he said, 'Try me.' It was the most precious thing I'd ever heard. I turned. He lowered the currying comb. He had tears in his eyes.

" 'I'm Bianca,' I said.

" 'Hot dog,' dear dear Samuel replied. That is how my happiness began. I refrained from informing him about my being a McCloud as well, as in the Angus McClouds. (He'd never heard of us, or Poppa's fortune in indigo. Which shows you how intensely rural Bear Grass then was.) My reckless bachelor cousin had sacrificed his disappointed life so I might find my own."

Four days, Momma'd been considered killed or lost. People searched the train tracks for three miles, seeking jet buttons from her dress, her satin reticule maybe tossed into a ditch. Nothing was found. The locomotive wheels were scoured by police told the color of her hair. Grim business. The strain shortened her loving parents' lives. Samuel Honicutt had dis-covered her groaning in a ditch. He'd seen the crowd around a derailed train nearby. He carried her home to his folks' cabin one mile off in piney woods.

Now, feeling stronger, she had herself buggied into Falls so's she could plan a wedding. Folks downtown at first considered Bianca McCloud a ghost. Her girlfriends thought she'd made up this romantic meeting as some by-product of concussion. Humoring her, they agreed to be bridesmaids. It pleased some girls how Bianca's wedding freed up her three serious suitors—plenty now for everybody. Local society soon heard about the noble rescuer, and they acted right excited to meet my poor poppa.

Now, darling, in most families there's this split. One bunch is rich and graceful and not a little proud—their genes a tea party of p's and q's. The other clan is, well, a hornet's nest of public teeth pickers, dud grammar, weak kidneys. But I got to say in all honesty, rarely was the split as wide as happened in our odd home.

Having chose a man from the suburbs of Bear Grass, Momma must've found his rough-cut history someway charming. At first she did. But the woman lacked the strength of character over time's long haul. Her people claimed one college vice president and many piano teachers. Is anybody more high-toned and refined-feeling than a small town's three very best piano teachers?

Whereas my poppa's great-granddad had been shot for being A.W.O.L. from the Revolutionary War. Family glory had been downhill from there. The Honicutts' role in our national life had been deserting it right regular. Pop swore the shot soldier was only home for a day, just to lay in firewood for his pregnant wife, their kids. Momma said nothing for or against. Pop's motleyest relation (low even for Bear Grass) perished of tapeworms. Fact. The wormy case got more interesting as the patient grew more peaked, and before the fellow knew it, his riders held the majority. Outvoted by his major stockholders, Pop's poor cousin was kicked downstairs.

When Pop, as was his habit, tried making light of his unpretty history, Momma ofttimes said, "You, we love. But as for those others, we remain unamused."

INDULGING reasons all his own, Pop's first service at All Saints Episcopal, he chose to make lower-body-gas noises (with his mouth) then flee the sanctuary.

After that, Pop was never exactly welcomed into Momma's former set. Time hung what you might call heavy on his hands. When my little girlfriends came near our house, he'd pepper them with well-meant but dumb pranks. He'd cook up instant nicknames for each. The man would lumber at them on his knees—child-high across our marble foyer—one raw hand foremost, him saying, "Shake, Wee Jake." Emily, she ran.

Nobody knew what to make of this grown fellow living in the porch swing all day, and working full-time at only being company for Momma. He begged my friends for tastes of their milk or cookie, he barged right into my door without so much as a knock. Odd that only Shirley, bashful as she was, knew how to talk right back to Pop. She called him "Mr. Card." Once— when he rushed her, his hand out, running on his knees—she shoved him so hard he fell sideways and laid there, laying, saying, "Again, again."

I stood apart, watching them together. Seemed I could be the mother or sister of them both. I crossed my arms. Felt like pleasure has swung open my whole chest, a mirrored medicine cabinet stuffed with patent cures.

If Shirl visited, Pop got all bossy, joshing. He loved to peeve Momma by misquoting scripture. In marrying him, she'd done her post-accident life's one wild unexpected thing. But with that in place, she become a slave to the letter of the law in all else. She longed to be invited to the homes of her old girlfriends, now married to her three ex-suitors. Yes, old pals spoke to her on the street and at neighborhood do's, but Poppa (home on the porch) stayed her social albatross. That I favored him seemed likely to drive my poor mother crazy. She never regretted choosing him, but his side effects sure made her sad around the house. All her ambitions turned on me now—

I would send the precious family genes diving back into the social swim. Good luck.

Pop was no churchgoer, claimed that his own funeral would be attendance enough. But he soon whipped out a pet Psalm for Shirley. He used it on her every night she slept in my room. "Why, look who we done trapped under our quilts," he'd come in, teasing. "Shirley Goodness and Mercy, will you follow me all the days of my life? Please?"

She pulled sheets overhead—a modest thing to do but (from in there) chuckling proved she considered herself Miss Surely Worth the Attention.

When Pop finally left us alone, we played our secret game called "I Am Chicken Little." For our own child reasons, with fingernails and hair pulling—with a wicked little hatpin I dearly dreaded—we'd hurt each other, sometimes a lot. Once when I caught a fever and Momma was undressing me, she reeled back from the sight of marks and nicks. "What *got* you, child?" Maybe Momma was recalling bugs. (Shirl always left worse marks on me than I seemed to manage. I felt sorry for her, stopping short. Shirl's mother kept Shirley's fingernails glazed in colorless lacquer, filed pointed, terrible.) Whoever gave in first had to squeal after long torture, "I *am* Chicken Little." I never knew why we did this to each other. We played it once every ten days or so, for years.

POPPA might've been cut dead by the fast crowd on Summit but he had another following. A certain kind of happy-go-lucky local bachelor and politico, pool sharps, black sheep from your best families—they stopped around each November, especially. Till this flush of company, Pop seemed pleased enough to sit alone on our porch swing, pretending not to know how unpopular he was.

But busy Novembers, people climbed onto our porch, come to ask Sam Honicutt's election views. Like me, the man was a magnet for others' gossip. The postmaster was a close buddy. Expecting company, Pop shaved for once, wore a boiled Sunday shirt. I helped him with his collar studs and cuff links. Even Captain Marsden stopped by, young then (for him), mid-forties. Rich and busy as Cap was, he arrived on our porch steps, hat in hand, nodding all around, a practiced quiet charm. I claimed the swing, bobbling, proud, silent for a change. Even the Captain (gloomy usually behind his warrior's face) gave Poppa's jokes wide grudging smiles.

Visitors asked for certain of his well-known stories. Especially the one where Jefferson Davis, hoping to avoid Yankee capture, dresses up in women's clothes. Soon enough somebody'd say, "Well, Sam? What news of the Republican candidates this go-round?"

Daddy, democratic, started. "Listen, I ain't hinting that their one up for mayor might dip his hand into our fair city's kitty, but you've seen the size of the man's wife, ain't you, boys?" Pop paused to scratch his scalp. It looked like he was choosing what-all he'd speak next but, weeks before the election,

I'd watched him pace our back yard, planning, lips going. "Yeah, that poor Republican's got to keep his wife in pastries someway—why, I ain't claiming that his wife is *fat*, but I hear tell . . ." Pop looked around, lowered his voice, milking his crowd of respect. "That she's so plump, she has to put a book-mark in her neck just to find her pearls at night. —Fact!"

Men yahooed. It was what they'd come for. They slapped porch uprights. "God's native truth," Pop kept straight-faced but barely. "Ask Lucy here. Ask my little Second Hand if it ain't Gospel." My job was to nod. I did so. So hard the porch swing squeaked its chains. But, just inside our screen door, I noted Momma's stiff shape, arms folded, one foot tapping. Momma was already planning my coming-out party. She didn't like to find her one child out here serving as a Little Xerxes minstrel-show straight man.

Only Momma counted Poppa's Aint's, and mine. When others swore that her Samuel could charm the birds out of the trees, couldn't he? she'd draw herself up and, defended, claim *she* would know—having neither feather nor leaf anywheres on her.

Still, I figured she'd picked him, hadn't she? With her indigo inheritance, with her good blank check of a face, Ma might've chose most any pretty rich boy in eastern North Carolina. Now, as then, there are thousands, God be praised. Instead, she'd proposed to a skinny county wag—one who'd saved her life, she claimed—a man Bianca McCloud Honicutt felt she could totally boss and totally enjoy.

IN OUR shady front room, along cool halls as wide as ones in good hotels, my folks and me kept busy living like we talked: Momma pretty much perfect if unnoticed, Poppa wrong but witty, me mostly plain mistakes. Momma worked at playing—bridge and semi-classical piano. Poppa played at work-ing. He whittled and was visited. He often sat picking at the calluses his farm boyhood had cobbled him with. His palms were ridged and horny as toenails, worn amber brown. Marriage had sprung him from manual labor but the man never tired of studying his paws—wide and naturally quilted as any catcher's mitt. Never dawned on him (or me) that *I* might someday have hands worn raw as his.

Sometimes Pop chewed his palms' tougher spots. Ofttimes, staring into hands the hue of beef jerky, he retold:

"No way you can imagine it, Lucy of the silver spoon. Before your momma landed at my feet, literal, like manna from the heavens, I was poorer than poor. Be out chopping firewood at four in the morning, blisters bulging off my blisters, hands'd get to dripping like tears were weeping out before the blood came. Four older brothers with no more curiosity than logs. Mornings, Momma'd ask them, 'How you boys sleep?' One'd say, 'Log.' Others'd nod. Logs, redheaded logs, forever beating on me. Nobody in the family knew a A from a Z. I'd sneak off into the woods with books hid down my britches. At least Honest Abe read by hearth light. I had to snitch matches, build campfires for to be my lantern. Oncet I burned up two acres of pinewoods by accident, for the light. Your momma makes fun of the troubles I went to, just to read my Westerns. But, Runt Funny, I'll tell you, compared to where I started, I'm already about up with Mr. Shakespeare. People in Falls wonder what I *do* all day on this here porch. Oh, I keep occupied, got plenty to think on. You know my trouble?—and don't laugh. But, see, I got me a Harvard College mind in this Burgaw County body— and the split between them is so blamed wide, all it'll let me do is set right here and mull about it."

The man wrote weekly letters home to his folks that couldn't read. Whenever we visited to the outskirts of Bear Grass (another story), my grandfolks had pinned up every envelope—unopened, neat on one log wall. Like Poppa, they loved to get mail and they displayed it for the beauty of the stamps' pastel colors. Still, Poppa admitted that even this busy with whittling sassafras (some smell!), even with porch swinging, cowboy novels, cheering his visitors, some days around 3 p.m. he did feel a tad bored.

His train-wreck angel had saved him from working. "But, Runt Funny, *should* she of?"

3

ONE IDLE morning, Pop decided to become local assistant postmaster. (He'd dreamed he *was* that.) Might get him off the porch a while, put him more on the cutting edge of local gossip. Hearing her husband speak his first ambition in eight years, Momma practically percolated. With only her mouth appearing overjoyed, she dressed quick in her finest black outfit and, looking feetless as a gyroscope, the lady glided chin-up to City Hall. Her former suitors were now mayor, alderman chairman, and city manager. She'd never asked them a favor. They sure owed her for her having married another.

Pop waited, swinging, soaking his rough hands in corn-husker's lotion. He waited at home for sixteen more months. He speculated on changes he'd make (extra daily mail deliveries to each home—postmen hired to read important mail to the unlettered). Pop praised the beauty of fine stamps. Why, he told me, there are stamps as pretty as . . . as Shirley, pretty as anything we've ever seen and from whole countries we've never even heard about. Momma had a uniform made for him, just in case, just to keep his spirits up. Poppa was helping Shirl and me engineer the addition to our tree house. He told me more low-down salesman jokes—warning me not to pass these on to Momma. He bathed too seldom for Momma's taste, he asked after Shirl's health like it was my wife he spoke of. He avoided church, waited for work, he was liked even by some of those folks that could never invite him socially into their homes, liked even by men who envied Samuel his wife's small fortune. —Finally the offer arrived. "Influence," Mother did a little dance, unlike herself.

Poppa was to report for duty the next day at 8 a.m. sharp, downtown P.O., bring own lunch. Momma threw a select party the night before. I invited Shirl. Place cards were shaped like parchment envelopes. On them I painted little stamps from nations as beautiful as possible, unknown to me until I made each up.

Pop left home early, waving back to us, uniformed—like a warrior finally headed, bold, towards enemy ammo. Momma cried, "What a perfect darling he is, a child really. I think the way we met is perhaps the most romantic thing I've ever even heard about."

Around 2 p.m. I noticed a fellow, dead ringer for Daddy, right back in our porch swing. He slumped, wolfing the show-off lunch Momma had packed for him. He sat shaking his head No, muttering. Seeing me, the man grinned but acted ashamed. He tossed his official cap my way. I wore it, bill backwards. Momma bustled out looking for some sheet music she'd been studying, she spied him, froze, patted towards a wicker chaise.

"Samuel?" She settled, elevating her feet. "Does this mean the end of your postal career?"

Pop explained with so sweet a shrug. Said he felt more disappointed than her, really. Claimed he had hoped the P.O. would prove local gossip's very temple. Not so. Can you believe the present postmaster, decent fellow but ignorant, didn't even understand how Rev. Vickers' daughter *hadn't* spent six months visiting some aunt in Newport News but not yet fifteen was in the family way and put there by the church janitor! "How does a man who can't count to nine on his fingers hope to call hisself official? How? Besides," Poppa said each word slow: "I hate alphabetical order."

Only Momma, his best audience and single sponsor, would utter what she now said: "Why?"

"I told them and I'll tell you, pearl of my life. Ain't no way M should come before N. N is like a practice for M. Only after one good try does N get to skin the cat and loop the loop and double itself into good old M. I mentioned this down there, M before N?—something's wrong. And you know, not one soul in the sorting room had even *thought* about it? I ain't saying they lack real vision, but those boys looked at me like I was foaming at the mouth. You can see it was on principle I quit. Had to. Point of honor. Talk about pigeonholes—that's all they *do* down there all day. Who needs it?"

Upon the wicker chaise clicking like a cricket tally of her troubles, Momma kept both eyes closed, lids sealed. I settled beside Poppa, cocked his cap over my right eye, checking to see did he approve. He pulled me against him, lifted my braid's brush end, spoke into it. "Does my Minute Waltz mind having her old Pop underfoot some more?" I hugged my answer. (His pet names for me: Pocket Watch, the Second Hand, Runt Funny.)

Momma's eyes stayed closed as traffic clattered along Summit. Canaries at the Widow Smythe's hopped from nervous perch to perch. It was Thursday and dashing Captain Marsden was at Winona's, indoors, visiting. Upset with Pop's unemployment, no inch of my Mother moved.

"What's wrong?" Pop sounded mad. "Don't forget, Queen England, was you married me."

"That much is clear," and when her right eye opened, Pop fell off our swing, left me bobbing alone. He knee-walked to her fainting chaise, he offered (up nastily close) his best horrible face—two fingertips yanking down eyeskin, two others mashing the nose tip up so you saw not nostrils but mossy caves.

She touched his face the way a blind woman would, "My excellent successful fool. But, Samuel, my darling, you need a career. Men do."

He mumbled to her neck, explained he would be playing more post office at home now. "Besides, you're my career, Peachness. You two are my daily duties. You ladies are all I'm really good at. But with you two I feel— don't laugh—like I'm . . . a Harvard professional!"

Stooping there, he hugged Momma's girdled center, grazed at her lace jabot, his rude witty tongue lifted her gold brooch. "You," she sniffed. April sun kept fighting to come out. Along Summit, a wagon knobby with seed sacks, slowed. Faces gaped up our lawn, thinking that bigwigs must live here. Ha!

Pop whispered to her waistline, "Special Delivery, upstairs." For once, Momma was enjoying being floppy. He helped her to stand, he told me, "This is how I found her in the weeds thrown twenty-some feet from train tracks, her bodice tore open, her hair come undone and tumbling all around her. A angel fallen from God's sky, my COD gift from Heaven's Postmaster General." He led her to my swing. I whipped off the hat. I took the fingers of the milk-white hand she offered me. I kissed my mother's spongy knuckles. Then kissed his: toffee-colored leather. "You'll go far," Pop told me. "A retired postman says so."

He tried lugging Momma over the threshold like when they were lovebirds home from the honeymoon. But Momma'd since gained some dividends. Pop was years from strengthening farm work. He dropped her leg half. Out of character, she cackled. Laughing seemed to hurt her like some deep cough would. But, too, you heard some air funnel deep into her corset. Momma kissed the man's stiff auburn crest, said, " 'What mortals these fools be.' "

"Yeah?" He winked my way. "Well, it's a job."

I heard them rush upstairs. I knew they'd nap for a hour and a half. Afterwards, they'd act extra kind to one another. Each would corner me to say what a dear, despite everything, the other was way underneath. Left alone together, they were among the happiest couples alive, child. Strange marriage but a good one. Fated, they both swore.

Sun arrived, canaries sang news of it. When I turned and looked, birds'd all pressed to their cage's brightest sides. They appeared nearly yellow as the sun itself, like downy bits of it fallen and trapped here but whistling straight back up, "Remember me? Remember me?"

The buckboard had stopped before our showboat home. I waved but farmers acted scared. One skinny boy in back looked around for something to show. From behind stacked bags of meal, he lifted a strand of pond fids— too small to keep. He pointed at his chest proving who'd hooked them. Wet fish glistened. I gave the boy a Postal salute but the buggy lurched forward, tossing him against burlap.

I heaved our swing side to side, feeling lucky. Birds sang. Sun shone. We had plenty to eat. I was the only child of two good foolish people. Poppa would return to our porch where he belonged. I had Shirley for my friend. Now, for Pop, I quoted his favorite from Mr. Stevenson's *Child's Garden of Verses*. (Poppa's judgment was: "I like my poesies like I take my bourbon, short, neat, no funny business.")

> *A Happy Thought*
> The world is so full of a number of things.
> I'm sure we should all be as happy as kings.

Shirley was due over at four. I owned a new hat. Our elms were alive with bug music, elms would keep on pushing up and up forever. School, that prison term, was ended and sweet summer only just about to start. What, during my whole lifetime, could ever really go wrong? What?

—Whatever could.

4

THAT YEAR, a dead man was found in the livery stable. He'd sneaked in for a nap, he climbed to the hayloft without being seen. A old hobo. First clue: Horses tossed and bucked conniptions. Then men followed their noses to the unhappy sight. The fellow had forty cents on him. A folded Wanted poster showed this same face, only younger. A scandal attached itself to the livery establishment then. Shirl, in our tree house, told me in her quiet way: *Her* poppa couldn't help who slid into his place of business to doze then die. Trying and cheer my friend, I asked if the fellow who'd tried rousing the corpse had hollered, "Ain't you 'shamed, you sleepyhead?"

Shirl turnt sullen. She used a pet phrase learned from my momma. Ma had read how the reigning Queen of England spoke it about most everything from storms to headaches to Indian rebellions—"We are not amused." I now told Shirl what Pop unleashed on Momma if she stayed unamused too long. "Yeah?" He smiled. "And who's this 'we'? You and your tapeworm?"

Shirl slapped me. Then she climbed from our tree house but her exit was slowed by crying so. I pressed one palm over pink stripes stinging my cheek. Up this high, my head swam, ears popped, I swallowed. Through leaves I watched her mope around our mascot elm.

I saw Shirl pick at bark. She leaned there muttering. Then all those gilded curls (one arbor's worth) commenced bobbling as she sobbed apologies to herself and me. She lisped into a knothole sixty feet below. I knew exactly what she'd said.

THE TEACHER forced me to stay in and chalk up three hundred "I must never again dishonor my parents and community by saying Ain't again" 's. I saw *her* out there on the schoolyard swing set, knees pressed together, breath fogging, waiting. Winter, she stored fists inside a false-fur muff. Blue clouds left her pink face, the vapor scallop-edged as much else Shirley dressed in.

Loyal, my sidekick. Since the hobo died at the Williams stable, other girls acted extra mean to Shirl. "Shirley's way too curly," they chanted after us as we walked home hand in hand. "And Lucy's sure a goosey." I didn't know what this meant. At that age, it don't have to mean much—it's the spirit that counts. I did notice—out under winter trees—our girl enemies, two different preachers' fancy daughters, loitering about, studying my friend.

I scribbled faster, keeping a eye on them. High-flown girls tarried in the cold long after the playground was deserted. I saw them admiring Shirley, eyeing her like folks at some auction drifting around before bidding starts, singling out their pick. They knew Shirl was waiting on me. Seeing them appreciate my pal, I understood afresh: My poor Shirley had just two strikes against her. One—being a horse renter's child. The other—having, for her only friend, a rough-acting tree-climbing rule breaker like yours truly, daughter of a mixed marriage, socially. I knew: If ever one of these drawbacks got hauled away, the most la-de-da crowd in all of Falls would snap my Shirl right up. But, too, I figured neither fact'd ever change. Not if I could help it (and I could).

I broke chalk into dice-sized bits, shook them in one fist like some gambler practicing.

I was keeping her back. She didn't know. Knocking on window glass, I waved. She wagged her muff overhead then settled again, the patience of a sheep's wife. Behind Shirl—unknown to her—the stuck-up ones, spying me, huffed away in their own steel-colored clouds. Who could blame me for wanting to keep Miss Shirley Beautiful to my own self? There was— besides my folks and maiden aunts—nobody else. Even my teachers, knowing that our money sprung from Momma's dowry, not no backbreaking work of Pop's—treated me a bit harsh. Momma spoke to teachers like they were our very hirelings, which didn't help their moods. Ma's having the fortune made it mean less. Till I got a teacher called Beale, the Genius of Falls Lower Normal, I noticed: Ladies showed a right limited respect for other ladies' clout. During class, teachers'd call the boys "little future gov-

ernors or better." Me, they kept indoors writing a different "I must not
. . ." every week. I hurried now to finish. In each sentence, a single word
was missing. At the very last, I got to scrawl three hundred Ain'ts—and big.
Kind of defeated the whole purpose. Ha.

I rushed downstairs to winter sun, ran up behind my quiet friend, who
sat humming "Frozen Charlotte." I surprised Shirl with a good swing-shove
clear off the ground. She grabbed chains, flapped out ahead of me, squealing,
"You!"

Ruffles took wing.

I NEVER slept at her little house. I dearly wanted to. My mother seemed to
fear that some strain of my poppa's genes would grow vexed and stronger
via Shirley's downhill company. Momma seemed to fear that Falls' poor
section, the stink of its peanut mill, would abduct me. Shirl loved the story
of how my folks'd met. When she and Pop and me were alone together,
she'd say, "Mr. Card, tell how you saved the lady." If Momma was around,
Shirl clammed up. She never seemed to connect the broken bodice in the
story with a handsome practical woman who, brandishing Falls' fastest
flyswatter, patrolled our high cool corridors.

Shirley's big-boned folks explained to me I couldn't stay the night—I'd
feel too cramped sharing my friend's single bed.

"Our house," Shirl's momma said, "is planned to be more—what you'd
call—compact than yourn." She pronounced compact "compack." I didn't
correct her. I marveled that my own pop had picked up manners and a
certain sleekness of manner compared to my friend's folks. I managed to
eat Saturday lunches in their unpainted bungalow—just a stone's throw
from Baby Africa itself.

The minute I got home, Momma always pumped me for lowlife details.
"I suppose," she said, straightening the front hall's art folios—fanned ar-
tistically on a marble-topped table, "I suppose that you expect me to believe
their luncheon china matches. It would surprise me if they even *have* a
dining room, not—of course—to pry." She never asked a thing point-blank,
just gave me openings the size of a canyon. And I wanted to tell her the
whole strange truth. But I saw it'd please her too much. If she married a
man from a log cabin, why this glee over my friend's lesser hardships? So
instead of telling my momma all, I'd go, "Oh, they're pretty much like us. I
reckon folks is folks."

"Folks *are* folks."

"Why, that's just the way *I* feel," I put in to get her goat.

When my staid momma made that Republican purse mouth (too greedy
for news of poor folks' sad tackiness), I shushed up. Momma figured being
rich was her biology, not her luck.

Fact is: Right on Shirley's lunch table, there were kittens, moiling, mewing, doing worse. They were free to lap out of any of our dishes they could
reach. Shirley liked kittens, but not cats. She would only have the little ones

around. I never questioned where they went onct grown. I suspected that Shirl's obliging ham-fisted poppa made a trip to the river Tar with a weighted sack every few months. The house smelled of talcum, frying, kittens. Shirl's folks ate grits on everything, three meals a day. The mother slopped them over cutlets and turnip greens. I hate grits. The daddy soaked his corn bread in a red side dish of vinegar. He burped into a napkin without one "Excuse me," just said, "Ooh, that was a bad 'un." He shook so much pepper across his soup, it looked like a inch of ants swimming. Mouth full, he talked horseflesh and feed prices, he wiped his lips with the back of one hairy hand, and, at meal's end, I spotted food samples (the menu) smudged across black bristles. Like the kittens squiggling everywhere, the sight made me feel ill and excited, both.

My momma later said, "They treat you like royalty, I suppose, the two Bear Grass bears and Goldilocks?" Fact was, Shirley's folks made so much over Shirl, I only got leftover attentions. Them two'd be running to fetch her a pillow off a bed to make Shirl's kitchen chair set easier. The daddy, when he looked Shirl's way, would sometimes give a hoarse sigh. You'd think he only just this minute noticed her—born perfect and grown—like Venus nudely enshelled inside our myth book at the Normal School.

During lunch, in the middle of saying something, the momma would jump up, whip a comb and brush set from her apron pockets. She used a sawed-off broomstick as a guide to forming cigar curls. Spiraling yellow hair around the thing, she set to work remaking a even better Shirley, curl by curl. The hairdo was so complicated that—when it was done—you felt you'd watched somebody build a chest of drawers from scratch.

At her own place, Shirl changed, she made sure we talked about what *she* wanted. In my house, she tiptoed and followed everybody's leads. Now, with her mother's hands still scooping at the finished hairstyle, Shirl asked me across the table, "What do you *really* think of Emily Saiterwaite?" I worried, looking at Shirl's parents in the room. Shirl said, "It's all right, they keep up."

"Emily's a total snit," I admitted. She was the Episcopal preacher's daughter I'd seen scouting Shirley.

"And what," Shirley's mother started, shy, "do you reckon young Emily thinks of . . . well, our Shirley here?"

"She thinks she's pretty," I admitted, though it was against my own interest.

"She never tells *me* these things," Shirley told her momma, about me.

Her mother asked if it was true that Pastor Saiterwaite of All Saints Episcopal had once proposed to my own momma, as had both the handsome Streeter twins, including the one presently our mayor. I shrugged, "So Momma claims . . ." Shirley's mother said it was kind of Momma, marrying the farm boy that'd saved her. Mrs. Williams claimed she'd heard that certain boys in Bear Grass now hung around the train tracks, wandering weeds, seeking *their* heiress. I didn't know if this was meant as a joke or not. Again,

I shrugged, but smiled. I hated hearing other grownups describe the curiosity of my folks' uneven marriage.

But Shirl's parents did love me. Of all Summit Ave's rich brats, only I paid court on their prize. The family cottage had low ceilings (unlike our rooms' eighteen-foot lids where shadows and thick plaster moldings made their peace with the spiderwebs my scared momma called "Yankee lace"). Shirl's tight house kept the smells so strong, made two red hefty adults seem way larger as they fidgeted around her beauty. —My own folks were both right good-looking—even Poppa had a fine straight nose and high cheekbones. And yet I'd only turned out a little less than regular. But here sat Shirley, a masterpiece sprung from nowheres. Seemed like her rawboned folks, without even needing bodies, had *believed* her into the narrow front bedroom, they'd dreamed their child alive.

My job, her parents made clear, was to help others notice, spread the word from mansion to mansion along Summit—big news: a thing had happened over by the peanut mill, this here ample pearl and miracle delivered by accident.

Still, I won't allowed to sleep at Shirley's itchy kitten-smelling beauty-parlor dollhouse. I begged to. Nobody'd let me.

ODD, if folks on Summit weren't ready to admit her total beauty, the children of Baby Africa considered her just this side of a fluffy tinted goddess. Sometimes—on the way uphill to my house—Shirl would make a side trip to this vacant lot adjoining the colored section. A house had onct stood here. Now just a few sample bricks hid among the weeds—just a stone staircase with a landing at the top and steps leading noplace. Shirl—in full crinoline glory, hair just done perfect by her momma's farmwife hands—would come and stand here like onstage. I waited on the lowest step, fatigued if respectful, looking up. She faced the poor black section and soon children would be glumly stealing out across the rubble. They whispered at the sight of her there, patient, stiff. Sometimes she held out the hems of her stiff yellow dress, mostly she just stood—appearing a bit bored—but like it was her duty, letting them inspect her, offering them inspiration and incentive. Kids would approach in little groups—dressed worst than the poorest whites in town, wearing castoffs we sometimes recognized as having once clothed our classmates. In bands, a step at a time, they drew near Shirley's level. She waited, stiff as some celluloid Kewpie doll on a stick sold at the fair. Black girls, hair in ropy plaits tied with rag bows, would finger the hems of her stiff clothes, they dared touching one yellow curl while Shirl waited. Bold as any flag and just about as passive—she let them admire. Once a very little boy grabbed Shirl's hand and held it to his mouth, but she jerked it back, not mean, just stern. "No kissing," she said. So—if Shirl won't yet admired uphill—down below, she had been practicing ways to accept certain tributes, practicing a lot.

5

MOMMA overheard two preachers' wives make wisecracks concerning a certain young somebody's contrary Bear Grass grammar. When I explained I probably couldn't change, Momma stopped speaking to me. For three weeks. Shirl and Poppa shuttled room to room as go-betweens.

During this long hush, I found myself watching Momma more. I wondered why somebody as smart as her would be so fearful of others. Any biddy on our block could spoil the woman's week with just the hint of a snub. When Momma finally spoke my way, she took another tactic. The woman set me down and started reading me a long English novel, four whole chapters at a time.

I hated the scenery parts most. In a story, a little dew goes a long way. But, bored as I was, my sense of justice made me start to notice something. All the servant characters talked funny. Being poor (cooks, gardeners, fish sellers) tripped these people into speaking real unschooled, dropping off *h*'s. It made them offer a chuckle for any reader rich enough to buy this book. I hated that. Momma, slit-eyed, seemed pleased to note me fidget whenever some low-class person had to talk, and she really got to be a actress—making every maid as broad as Pop's jokes about Republicans. Poppa sat, surrounded by shavings from his sassafras whittling, snoring nearby. Finally, I crossed my arms, announced, "Ain't fair." Momma closed the book, shut her eyes a second, asked, "What 'Ain't'?" (She could sure handle that word with tongs, I tell you.) When I spelled out my gripe, she looked so overjoyed I saw I'd been set up. She explained I was right, of course. Said she didn't want any child of *hers* getting stuck into no minor funny character part. "You'll become a lead when you sound like a lead. These 'Ain'ts' are pure mannerism, Lucille. I agree with the Englishman as how 'naturalness is the most galling pose of all.' My child, whenever you get tired, when you lose the will and forget to concentrate on this fixed idea, why you become as grammatical as anybody. —So, which will it be, scullery help or leading lady? Choose. Now. Which?"

I caught her drift. But, feeling mad about this old unfairness—the gyp to my dad's hick parents, to Shirl and them ones downhill—it made me stick still closer with old Ain't. Seemed a point of honor. *Somebody* had to.

Times, I did try otherwise. At school and especially around Shirley's folks, I struggled to sound legal. (If I talked like a lowlife near them, they'd think me unfit to be their daughter's helpmeet.) But I figured *rich* folks shouldn't like a person only because she spoke fancy. Good grammar is a type of conspiracy showing others you know code words, proving you belong by birth and bank account. I got so I enjoyed being grouped with Shirl and other rougher downhill children. Struggle as I might, I never changed enough. Whenever I grew happy or excited (happened right much in them days), I fell back. Poppa's salt canceled Momma's sugar. And, out my mouth, that shameless old toad Ain't leapt forth, warts galore, scaring everybody but me. Me, and Pop. And Shirley, who forgave. Plus, my unwed aunts.

MOMMA hadn't spoken to her three older sisters for nearly sixteen years. They lived not two blocks from us. In a town the size of Falls, you *know* when somebody's cutting you dead. The sisters occupied their birthplace, the inherited McCloud homeplace, one twice the size of our excess house. This one had gables atop gables, a garden house big as Shirley's whole home, and it all needed paint. The only garden was whatever perennials sliced through ivy and high weeds.

My aunts—like lots of folks who live together from birth till old age—had divided up who to be. They were each good at different-type emotions—they respected one another's territory. You couldn't quite think of them as separate, more like three plants sprung from one pot—root-bound, leaf-entwined hybrid ivies maybe.

The three girls had loved one boy. He'd gone off to college up North, he'd come back sick, he'd published one poem in *The Atlantic Monthly* while studying at Cambridge. The poem, my mother said, a little high-handed, was about spring—how everything looked bleak and bare till your buds came and your birds got back from Florida—not all that original.

The poet signed his work with his middle name only, Randall. He had ghost-colored skin, he drooped across furniture, looking boneless. The sisters played piano for him constantly. My stern Scottish grandpoppa didn't like artistes. Grampa Angus McCloud had turned into a gruff old self-made stiff. His opinions were writ large as the handlebar mustache he oiled and nursed. He was one of those men of the day who bragged on his four girls' purity, men who ofttimes managed to keep the virgin bevy a few rooms away throughout men's long old age. If it hadn't been for Momma's train wreck, Angus McCloud might've had a perfect track record. Ten years before my pop turned up, Granddad worked to discourage Randall, beloved by the oldest three girls. Randall—when finally pressed about which adoring sister he would marry—got tactful: his color improved and then, roses in his cheeks, the poor boy died of consumption at age twenty-three. Randall had no aptitude for marriage.

My Granddad figured his grieving girls would finally, as he said, "brrranch out." But the three sisters formed a kind of permanent memorial fan club. They copied all the poet's work in fancy script, they made the first letter of each page sprout birds and flowers and gold-leafed tree limbs. Their music room was soon plastered with Randall's ditties, framed. Grandpoppa kept bringing young men home. He imported Scotsmen to manage his indigo works outside Wilmington. Such boys got invited to dinner. The sisters quoted Randall to all comers. Girls offered to play guests a piano setting of Randall's famous *Atlantic* poem, "O, Awakening Bud—A Young

Man's April Reverie" by "Randall." Grandpoppa couldn't forgive his oldest girls their taste in gents, dead ones. He came to favor his youngest child, Baby Bianca. She'd been eleven when Randall—after tinting hankies red for two months—perished. To Bianca, he won't no dashing poet, just the One That Coughs. Her older sisters thrived on their shared moods, hunches, poetry, piano music, "issues of the day," which they debated with a skill that impressed then scared young Glasgow boys from the indigo works.

Bianca's second accident involved the train. Then she'd had enough bad luck and good. She retired to her porch with her new husband. And though Poppa McCloud disapproved of Bianca's crude new spouse, the old man preferred a living gent to that cult the other three had built around one sissy ghost. So when old Angus died, he left my momma everything except the homeplace. Locals cried unfair. Everybody seemed outraged except my momma and the three sisters theirselves.

After Momma accepted every last family cent, she ceased speaking to her unwed sisters, not the other way around. Ever after, the sisters earned their meager keep by teaching piano to all girls from your Summit Avenue families. —My own poppa would slip the sisters envelopes stuffed with cash at Christmas, Easter, and on the anniversary of the Poet's death (the Ides of March, as it happened, a coincidence the classics-minded ladies found fitting).

Like me, Poppa visited them often but always by the servants' entrance at the back of the mansion. It wouldn't do for Momma to find out. It'd only hurt her feelings for no reason. The generous sisters considered Poppa "droll" and "original." They taught him things. When he confessed to having a Harvard intelligence in a Burgaw County body, aunts nodded total straight-faced sympathy. Poppa said Harvard might've happened to him if he'd been born in Falls, not on the outskirts of Bear Grass. "I'm sure you'd have done superbly at our Randall's college," the oldest sister said. Poppa got still with the pleasure and his eyes narrowed as he picked at his once callused palm. "Thank you. You can't imagine . . . how I . . . thank you for that."

THOUGH the three well-bred McCloud sisters looked alike and spoke only kindly of each other, their piano-teaching techniques varied a good bit. Their many students never knew from lesson to weekly lesson which sister would sit waiting at which Steinway. The three's idea of top-notch poetry seemed right unanimous (Randall's was). But the ladies' notion of what they called the *ex*-quisite in music, why that rambled all over, child. Their differences made for troubles in a pupil's learning. The differences caused fear. One week, the youngest of the three McClouds would tell you to play more dreamy-like: "Think of moonlight on a lake and let your fingers find that glimmering just under the ivory, dear." Next week, you arrived with your practice piece all moon-sopped. But the dreamy sister was on the wane upstairs with one of her sick stomachaches and in her place you'd find the next-oldest, who just loved pedal work. She wore felt slippers (a Indian chief on each—though nobody liked to say they'd seen eighty more like these at the Woolworth's). She would scold you for ignoring the drama of foot dynamics. The thrill of swells and mutes, surges and hushes—"Think North Atlantic, child. Wake up and live. Become *la Mer, toujours la Mer!'* Your playing feels so . . . inland. A farm pond. Flow, child, crash, exult."

And, of course, darling, the next week, a pupil would turn up with a seasick foot-stomp version only to find the eldest, grimmest, and most technical sister bone-cracking on the bench. She ignored all comparisons with water. She hated the new murky French music that her younger frailer sister swooned to. When folks asked her opinion of Mr. Debussy, she'd slowly say, "Algae." She admitted she "worshipped at the altar of the Germans." As a child, when my momma called Mr. Bizet superior to Wagner, this sister laughed, took up the little soapy white busts of Handel and Gounod off her Steinway grand and primly threw them Momma's way.

Pupils found her waiting, a varnished ruler in hand. When a student knuckle wandered to a wrong note, that knuckle soon knew it. Her pet line was: "Imprecision *is* Immorality." These three ladies charged competitive rates, held recitals twice a year. My aunts were said to be the very peak of a local musical education.

Townsfolk called them Lake, Sea, and Ruler—behind their backs. And though generations of children had dreaded walking up the weedy garden path, through huge boxwoods (smelling of cat box), and on to the front room to find (Lady or Tiger like) one of the three, nobody *knew* better. Piano technique was considered another needed part of a young girl's hygiene.

Lake, Sea, and Ruler acted very sweet to me, their only niece. In fact, this is how decent they were: They never forced one lesson my way. The colder my momma treated them, the more they offered me raw benefit of the doubt. I always felt welcome in their place. I was hardly the perfect little lady (not at all like the Emily Saiterwaites you always saw traipsing, blanched, into their parlor weekday afternoons). But the sisters kindly compared me with the adored poet. Like him, they claimed, I was, yes, a wee bit red in tooth and claw, but underneath serene, accomplished secretly. I accepted this. I felt glad to have one house where nobody didn't correct my talk or manners. I brought friends to meet them, Shirley inclusive.

Aunts listened to my tales of climbing through two miles of underground ditch pipe. Or scrambling to the tops of dangerous swaying elm trees during lightning storms. How a person can bring salamanders, unknown to her mother, in a bucket to live under a person's bed. They stared and nodded with open admiration. "So like . . . Randall," one would finally say. They seemed to think their poet had passed, gene-free, into me. Only *they* had seen his outdoorsy ruffian side. They remembered how, after "nature walks," quests for "material," the author of "O, Awakening Bud" collapsed in their reception parlor. Sticky mud and burred seeds would be glommed to Randall's tweedy legs—like the world was something that a poet had to roll around in, personally becoming a sort of breaded veal cutlet of the spirit.

I begged Ma to forgive her sisters. I asked what their big crime had ever been. "Pretension, complete silliness, and the scent of martyrdom they trail everywhere. As children, they were a club, baby nuns, I was never invited to join. They seemed to always pity me whenever I made any small fingering mistake. They whispered. When *I* practiced piano, they all sat in the next room, with their eyes closed and the draperies drawn, sighing—audibly. They once admitted, listening to me decided them on all becoming teachers. No, you cannot imagine being baby sister to that. Them learning German hours on end and giggling over some irregular verb form. Lucille? You're so lucky to be an only child."

But Momma herself had helped to turn Lake, Sea, and Ruler into local saints. Finally I understood that the crime, if there was one, rested mostly with Ma. She might, at the reading of the will, have handed a fair share of the booty to the mild older girls. Instead, Momma honored her poppa's wishes, and had taken all. Now, nearly sixteen years later, she could not forgive how, without one whimper, the threesome had sat right there and let her rob them of their birthright. So she ceased speaking to or seeing them. At church or on the street, Momma would do a U-turn to avoid the ladies in matching paisley shawls all calling after her (Lake, Sea, and Ruler's tone—two parts liquid, one part solid), "Lovely day, sister. You look so *well*, sister."

Their separate voices could be sharp. But when the three spoke together, their pooled sound—to nobody's surprise—was not just musical, but music.

6

BY NOW Shirley, our audience and favorite, slept over twice a week. Poppa really tried to keep his calluses to hisself but it was never easy. If he admired Shirl's naturally yellow hair by touching it, if he invited my pal to just come settle on his lap a second, Momma would dart into the parlor, clear her throat. "Samuel, I believe young Shirley here feels properly welcomed without these extras. Don't you, Shirley?"

Shirl sighed, nodded, hopped clear of Pop's grasp. Fiddling with her hem, she stood there, a girl ringed with lace the way a tree-trunk wears its years.

Pop still eyed her, winking a comic tic. "Old Shirley Goodness and Mercy is okay in my book. Ain't like certain other hoity-toilets little girls I could name on this street. Noses held so danged high they'd get drowned in a April shower. Shirl hain't no snob."

Momma straightened inside a legislature of whalebone.

Even her voice sounded corseted: "Samuel, any person who'd come this frequently to the home of a person so ignorant of our mother language must be, by nature, a forgiving Christian girl. At least young Shirley here speaks properly. —I hope some of it wears off on you over there, Miss Lucille Slang."

I made a grumpy face, then laughed.

SOME WARM nights during lightning storms, I heard my folks pacing the hallway carpet outside my room. I felt honored. I believed they guarded me from lightning. I pictured a blazing stick figure—white-hot zigzags, light for its blood—come to fry or kidnap me. I imagined them fighting him off using the brass umbrella stand or a huge pink wedding-present vase kept out there. But, listening, I found: Momma was secretly petrified of electric storms. Sure, she joked about it, acted real ashamed, but (at first flash) she always hurried to my hall, the only one without a window. Pop rose with her, in his nightshirt, never sounding cross. They had their good talks then. I could see the candle come and go under my door's seam. I used to feel spooked of big gales till I found that Momma feared them. Then it seemed she was being scared for the both of us. Through my keyhole, I had seen my folks holding hands while pacing. To keep Mom's mind off death by fireballs, Poppa teased and imitated townsfolk. She would sometimes sit in a side chair and coach him. "More wrists," she'd say. They squabbled like brother and sister, I decided, but being a only child, I could just guess.

Some windy nights I let their voices stay a murmur that lulled me off towards sleepyland. But whenever Shirl got mentioned, I sat up big-eyed. Blue light crackled everywhere, it showed me my staying-over friend curled just one bed away.

Momma, agitated by thunder, pitched into my pal again, Momma said she'd send Shirl packing if it wouldn't make me think of her all the more. "Lucille will get over this craze. Those two are seeing entirely too much of each other. Our baby has yet to notice how her Shirley cuts the other poor children point-blank dead. Oh, Shirley's gotten quite grand since she's been coming here learning her forks. You'd think we had adopted her."

Then I couldn't hear: they'd got to the hall's furtherest end. On turning back, Pop pointed out how a fellow had to own the horse before he can rent it—he claimed a stablekeeper makes a decent living. Pop again called Shirl good company for me, like a sister. "This Shirley," Momma started bold—then lowered her tone (first sign she knew my friend slept one thin door away), "Miss Shirley . . . will forever act nicest to the richest person presently acting nice to Shirley. You forget *my* childhood, Samuel. Two upstairs play parlors stocked with beautiful wax dolls. Any girl for a hundred miles would've risked positive hellfire to get her hands on those. They were cold as dead babies, those wax things. I so loathed them. They all looked swollen. How often some little visiting pest would say hello to sisters and me downstairs then bolt to our four furnished dollhouses. Oh, I know whereof I speak. We shall simply give Lucille's pet enough rope, enough leash. She'll do the rest. Outright banishment would be a tactical faux pas. Even I see that."

Pop claimed she was wrong about Shirl, adding, "I know. I got eyes."

"That, dearest, is your problem. Remember: 'For sweetest things turn sourest by their deeds; / Lilies that fester smell far worse than weeds.' Do you recall that, Samuel?"

His voice went deadpan. "What, have I been talking in my sleep again?"

They tussled. I saw candlelight flicker as she laughed her strained locked laugh. The storm was grumbling itself still. Back to bed they gossiped, happy. My door's sash went yellow to pinkish to brown to black again.

"Shirl?" I asked, praying she'd slept through Momma's insults. I heard only easy breathing. When my friend shifted under sheets, this new wave reached me: a milky smell she had about her. To me it seemed the scent of health itself.

POPPA'S parents were like I am *now*: too old to care, too mean to quit. They still lived in boggy suburban Bear Grass. They hoarded his letters but never sent him mail—owing to their not being able to sign nothing but X's. They each had a different *style* of X: their signature. Pop felt he had to visit them every few years minimum. Mother's more refined parents had died. "They would," Daddy said. "Never really liked it here anyways. Hated me on sight. They were grateful for what I'd done, rescuing their beauty and all. They knew she'd twisted my arm into marrying her. Before meeting the McClouds, I went out, bought a new suit of clothes, everything. Combed my hair, the works. I walk in and—setting in these big wing chairs—they both take one look at me and they just groan. Literal. I call old Daddy Angus aside, I tell him I don't like it one little bit, him grunting at first sight of me. He liked me for talking back at him, nobody usually did. —Yeah, Lucy mine, for your momma's folks, the population of this world was way too huge, too unselect-like. Now, if the earth had maybe only about thirty-five people on it, why her folks would've liked it here. That'd mean they were chosen-like. McClouds! But rabbits and gnats got to live here, too. If bugs got breath, what good was it? *They'd* be ex-clusive. They checked out."

If Poppa liked making jokes about his perished in-laws (whose cash he lived on), he said little about his own folks. He hated how they'd whipped him when he was little. Still, the man was so embarrassed, he couldn't admit it. We packed a huge picnic lunch. Bidding my bye-byes to Shirley, I cried and so did she. Momma, bored with such extremes, said, "Honestly," for miles. Poppa made us come, Momma and me. Going home for visits, Poppa said, it's something nobody should have to do alone.

Momma had taught me how to read. She loved to hear my voice sound everything out. In our buggy, I worked through a novel she'd brought, one of her English ones (governess comeuppance), one written by a Mrs. Something. I squinted with the dust. It took four days to find a damp bulrushy county where Pop was onct born. Red-winged blackbirds rode dried reeds, singing their fair knifing little songs. The swampier that land got, the nearer we drew, Pop grew quieter (for him), then silent as anybody.

As we pulled over the county line, countryside seemed to go stiller and the roads got worse. Up ahead you'd see a little crossroads store, and after so many weedy miles you looked forward to the sight of two faces and some tin signs advertising poultices, cigarettes. The store was boarded shut and you felt sadder for counting on it. Soon we passed ramshackle farm huts and—having heard our buggy—people waited by the roadside for us.

Nodding, they seemed to recognize Poppa though he'd been gone fifteen years. Folks went running back into the hut with news. We heard a woman shout mush-mouthed to somebody inside, "Momma, come quick. It's that durn Sammy Honicutt and His Rich Lady." My mother sat, horrified, eyes straight ahead. But Mother never blamed Poppa for putting her through this. Between my folks on the cushioned buckboard's seat, I tried and imagine how we looked. I saw Momma in her tailored gray suit, her cameo that she left me later, her hair swept back, the solid evidence of a foundation garment keeping her solid and true, wasp-waisted. How beautiful she was! I compared her with the seed-sack dresses at the roadside, the sallow faces and rude open mouths that followed us along our trip. I slid closer to her. I tried reading more of the book where the downstairs maid at a great English house falls "rather hopelessly" in love with the lord's second son. A long kind lecture from the village preacher sets her aright and she signs on to be a missionary and is rather honorably killed by brown folks in India. Out this far in rural Burgaw County, even reading aloud seemed a form of showing off. I pictured Shirley's city beauty. This far into the country, they would worship her, my saint of the crinoline.

Pop's people lived in a cabin made of real but flaking logs. Three pigs roamed free and looked too thin to ever butcher. Poppa had explained: Smart hogs out this way under-ate as self-defense. From the door, two old people came forward, walking just alike, side by side. They looked varnished brown. They appeared roasted, like they were past ever dying—like everything moist in them had been baked, like what stayed on would last. Their faces: little fist-sized hams. What English they spoke took getting used to. They left off any word they could.

On tiptoe near our buggy, they kissed me and asked, "Hong?" Right in front of them, Pop said, "Sugar, they mean, 'Are you hungry?' "

"Tell them No," I whispered, then—troubled—turning to my own grandfolks, I shook my head sideways hard, said, loud, "NO!" Momma huffed, "Honestly." The old ones laughed.

"Doll mesh," the yam-colored woman said. She looked like the old man (only with some extra hair, her pant legs joined to be a skirt). "She said, 'Darling mess,' " Poppa sounded tired already. "That's considered nice," he explained. "Say 'Thank you.' " I thanked him but he then pointed off the wagon at two tiny farmers. "Oh, thank *you*," I said. They wheezed. It was their way of laughing.

POPPA had written ahead that we were coming. They couldn't read. We always came ahead anyway. They would definitely be home. Momma refused to sleep in the cabin. She claimed to be allergic to insects and straw but everybody knew what she really meant. Poppa drove her to the county's only boardinghouse six miles away. My folks always stopped near a rail-road crossing not far off—the spot where a lady, thrown twenty-odd feet by a locomotive's striking a wagon, dropped directly in his path. I was left alone with the little varnish people, brown as beetles. My poppa seemed to be taking hours getting back. I grinned harder at the country folks. The inside of their cabin was just backs of the logs on front, wood cured with years of greasy cook smoke. Holes had been plugged by some of the hundreds of Poppa's unopened envelopes pinned up on most inside walls, brown now, too. I smiled more. They sat in chairs facing mine, they stared. They could. It was their house. I was new here. Once the old woman hobbled over and felt of my braid, nodded, said, "Liquor popper," sat again.

A half hour later, "Like her poppa's" done occurred to me.

When my loved one finally got back, oh I hugged him so. Night really settled. Such night, too, a pitchy dark that our bright glittery downtown Falls kept at bay. Dogs could be heard howling in a ditch nearby. Bug noises sounded like a coded insect plan to take over the world. Let them, I thought. Our only light came from a lantern burning oil as brown as the old people. Ridge-backed bugs chimed its smudgy flue. For twenty minutes, more, not one soul said a thing. I gulped a lot. "Sure is quiet," I offered. They all looked at me—nobody'd noticed.

"Lucy here can read." Poppa sounded both proud and mad.

"Naw," both old ones said. I looked young for my age. Poppa promised I actually could, whole rows of words, pages even. The old woman scurried to her cabinet, brought me a Bible fat as a couch cushion. On my lap, she opened it, pointed to one verse. (Since I knew that neither of these folks could read and that they'd punished Pop for doing it in the house—I felt ashamed and irritated, weak now.) Their open Bible smelled like a open grave.

Poppa stood behind me, jittery. He slid the lantern nearer my side of the table. One bug hit my neck. It felt so big. Dogs kept barking. I looked down into the Bible. I feared that the brown people would punish me. I pictured Momma alone in a room, explaining to boardinghouse wallpaper how honestly hideous that very paper was. (Poppa had onct burned a whole woods to cinders just to try seeing the black and white of a cowpoke Western story he needed to finish.)

I looked up at him.

"Do," he said, sharpish and vain-sounding as Momma at her worst. He touched my shoulder. "Show them," he said. "This here's important to me. I'm with you. *Now*." His worn hand weighed on me, a comfort.

Gulping, I went slow, not wanting to seem bratty or too good.

"Chap-ter Thirty-two. Give ear ye heav-ens, and I will speak, and hear, O earth, the words of my mouth. Verse Two. My doctrine shall drop as the rain, my speech shall distill as the dew, as the small rain upon the tender herbs, and as the showers upon the grass. Verse Three . . ."

I peeked up. Water lit the dried face crinkles of the old ones watching me. The little man one jumped up and ran to a cupboard, seeking some prize to offer. Every shelf slowed him, he found less and less. Finally he brought me a sugar bowl, one rusty spoon stuck in it. "Eat some," Poppa spoke, hoarse behind me. I looked up. Pop's face was fisted. "I'm so proud of you," he stroked one pigtail, then turned toward the log wall spotted with his life of letters. He said to that wall, "Eat some sugar, sugar. They believe it's a treat." So I took me a spoonful. I felt it melting at the edges. My mouth full, I tried grinning. Their Bible, heavy in my lap, put either leg to sleep. The book smelled black. It stunk of olden times, bitter as tar. In the Bible, the earth opened and swallowed children for bad things their folks'd done. I could smell that. Mouth full of sugar grit, I smiled. Howling dogs got closer. They sounded not so mean, just hungry. My tongue burned with sugar. I couldn't hardly swallow. Three country people now chuckled, shook their heads amazed at me, they sniffled some. My momma was allergic to all bugs and straw. Sitting here, the days of buggy riding caught up with me, plus the hardship of sitting here on my own with the old ones. I thought of Shirl, home alone and missing me. I nodded off.

I soon felt Poppa lift me, tote me to the attic loft. A mattress, stuffed with corn husks, whispered, guessing my weight. I felt three hicks undressing me. I heard three rubes talking that strange unborn English. Now he talked like them. With me too tired to help and guard him, the poor man had lost hisself it seemed. He had become them now he thought I slept. The old woman placed her lamp near my feet. I could feel all three of them studying my pale city limbs. They jawed and grunted in their strange farm language. They studied every part of me. They turned me over. They looked between my legs. I laid there. I let them. I had to.

Years after, whenever I heard somebody say, "She speaks a foreign language," I heard "farm." A farm language.

HOME, this invitation waited, my full name in roly-poly cursive. Our mayor would throw the year's most important party for Summit girls. Being poor, being connected to a stable, having hayseed genes, Shirl won't invited.

Before the shindig, in our tree house, she cried a little, begged me to remember everything and tell her it afterwards. I said Okay, I said we should now practice our first aid. A class at church concentrated on helping fainters. Those years, many more women fainted—they did so thanks to corsets, too tight shoes, and, yeah, the *fad* for fainting. Honey, never underrate the power of fashion. Step One: Loosen all constricting clothing. Shirl always played the swoon victim. Her pink cheeks still shined from crying. I set to work unfastening twenty-some buttons hiding white collarbones from air. I'd got good at this. Her clothes had more buttons than a concertina's tail end. When I'd unlatched a fair number, I chanted down into her open dress our favorite ditty. Ended: "Cocked his shiny eye and said, 'Ain't you 'shamed, you sleepyhead?' " On " 'shamed," she showed signs of becoming un-faint. I pressed one ear to her chest. Since the country visit, she looked more soft and fair and perfect. I listened to the humid center of her, a middle spot where old Eve got built around Adam's spare funny bone—a knot of garden yet in there. Oh, to get at it. Squatting on our platform in the privacy of leaves, I watched my Shirley giggle alive. Laughing, I stared along the whole girl—prettier, longer, simpler, lots more kind than me. I could not believe the Mayor'd forgot to ask my Shirl—and here I had grandfolks that looked like salt and pepper shakers made of tanned raccoon hide. No fair. Something had to happen. I longed to *do* something for her.

I GOT let indoors with Momma, me decked out in a itchy crinoline—it felt like wearing a place mat. Momma'd paid a clever black lady to sew this outfit, special. (The seamstress was in such demand, Momma'd already made a down payment on my debutante's gown, some years in advance. When I poohpoohed this, Momma said, "We have simply avoided the rush. You'll thank me later.") Our country trip had soured me on all this fancy society junk. It'd further glazed my poor mother's eyes with party ambition for me. From visit to Bear Grass visit, she forgot how bad Poppa's people really looked. She had turned them into hearty hunting country-squire types. But then there they stood and she bitterly knew. She feared for me, my future—even for such genes that were presently aloose in my own wiry unfine body. Oh, but Momma hoped I would prove she'd not made a terrible mistake by marrying the one she did. I see that now.

At the time I sat around the party, got dozy, and then, half thinking about Shirley, half remembering rough country manners, did something. Idle, but meaning it, I reached up under my dress and scratched a certain something, yanking at panties. Mothers around the grand room (my own included) experienced facial paralysis—their shoulders fell, then all their backs locked. Such dredging—far from ladylike—had got me a certain amount of attention. I did feel a little bad when the Mayor's wife looked from me to my dignified mother, then turned aside. A bit later, when other frilly little things lined up to pin the donkey tail, all obeying orders (just three feet tall but acting high and mighty as their mommas), Mrs. Saiterwaite tried pinching me into place. What got into me? What made me bellow at the center pole of Summit society, "Keep your claws to yourself, nightmare face. I ain't *yours*."

That pretty much did it.

I found poor Momma on the front porch, her cheeks so full of color, she looked half changed. She sat fanning her forehead and neck, hissing, "The shame, Lucille. The shame." I told her: I didn't know just what made me do it. Underneath I was basically nice, but felt like we were wrong to try and lord it over everybody not invited. I'd looked around the huge room and all I seen was: who won't here.

Like Daddy, maybe I was too much of a democrat—not even Republican enough to save myself.

I patted Momma's linen skirt, counted her long fingers, played like I was the nicer sister of that wicked snit that'd talked so countrified and loud in there, that'd sounded like a reform-school boy paroled into a lettuce of a dress, that'd then excavated in the pantaloon territory.

"Socially," she spoke like in a trance—not even mad no more—which upset me. "What you did just now in there was suicide, Lucille. You know the term 'suicide'?"

"Like . . . ?" and I dragged one fingertip across my throat, made a raspy sound.

She nodded. "That," she said, and held my hand—tender, almost re-laxed-acting—all the way home. "Change your clothes," she said at our front door. "May as well make yourself comfortable. I know you might not recall this moment when you're grown. But you should understand what you've done, my poor baby. It's over. All my plans and hopes are ended here. This means that our family will never regain the place we lost when I married my darling Samuel. We had a chance. You could not or would not help me in the only thing I've ever wanted. Go on, change. Put on rags. From now on, nobody will care."

IN STREET clothes, carrying a book and a butcher knife in a sack, I shinnied down one drainpipe.

Up our tree, Shirl sat waiting, long-suffering and calm as any spouse. Eager to hear about my social triumph, she hollered hostess questions down through elm leaves. I climbed towards a sweet voice pleading: Had they served mints both pink *and* green? Types of floral centerpieces, please? I moaned. Around her, a full skirt was spread. She'd worn, for me, what she would of worn to the party if they'd asked her. Perfect, she'd tied bows of crepe paper to our household twigs. It broke my heart.

In one of Poppa's Fenimore Coopers, I'd read where this friendly Indian and white man cut open their veins to become blood brothers forever. I wanted my heart now circulating some droplet souvenir of Shirl for good. I understood—after digging at my privates publicly, after snarling at a holy Saiterwaite—high society was now but a thing of the past. I was ready for the next part: Shirley. For her, I'd given all of it up, I'd half killed poor Momma. Odd—I only believed in Momma's pain onct it'd finally happened. Her strange calm had made me think of her when young, when hurt so.

But poor Shirl sat pumping for the Mayor's punch recipe. I was not often stingy with details (as you yourself should know by now!), but I just shrugged off Shirl's every question. Seeing I was in a darker mood, Shirl said she'd settle for a last teensy fact: How did the inside of our mayor's finest mansion parlor really look?

My answer: "Big."

Shirl smoothed her skirt (a painful green) over knees, she made her either dimple show, she tossed the curls and spoke to our tin tea set arranged just so before her. "But *how* big, Luce?"

Behind me, I undid the sack, pulled out the book, leaving the knife for later. I read the Mohican rite where your blending of veins happens. "Sounds mighty good, don't it?" She half nodded, still eager for news of a party I only wanted to forever forget. "Sounds mighty good, okay," I answered my own self. "Let's us do it. Only, we'll be blood *sisters*."

"But how?" When I whipped out Momma's best butcher knife, Shirley slapped a palm to either cheek, gave this squeal I thought was absolutely precious. My hip bones went pure sponge. Below our elm, on sidewalk, the postman spun in circles, looking for a crime. Then I did one hour of fast-talk convincing, told Shirl how this swap would make us stronger, we'd each catch half as many colds.

Finally I offered to go first—just a light scratch, see? You could only feel amazed at all the color waiting inside a skinny white girl. It filled my hand, red coated each finger in its bright new separate glove. Then I cut Shirl as—eyes closed, frowning—her free hand pinched her nose. We made the magical mingling (I'd agreed to be the Indian, leaving her the choicer white role). Our wrists nuzzled wetness to mother wetness. We invented vows, shivered, spoke Red Indian place names aloud.

"There," I said when all felt done. Shirl even kissed a red pinkie fingertip, pressed it to my forehead, left pink streaked there. But onct our blood was swapped sufficient, drainage didn't quit. It longed to be transfusion. We used old curtains as bandages, we ripped down crepe paper but party favors proved flimsy tourniquets. First we snickered, seeing our losses flung on leaves, boards. Then we went, "Uh-oh." What had started as a poem was ending as emergency. (Like life, child!)

One-armed, we gimped down, and—even with her leaking pints and ruining good clothes—Shirl called back, "Crust on the finger sandwiches? Cut to triangles? Watercress and what?"

We later found that each of us, when mothers asked how it'd happened, said, "From picking blackberries. A thorn."

NOBODY spoke to me after the party where I dug into, up, and beneath my underpants. Girls that'd been present turned away. Girls that wished they'd been there really gave me the works, peeved that homely me had been so careless with my good luck. Come school on Monday, I was shamed like some brat who—in a land of famine—throws away a banquet of leftovers and has not shared. On my way home from class, some unseen person chugged a heavy green walnut at me, over a fence. Luckily, I ducked. I couldn't exactly complain to Momma, could I? All invitations quit. That, she noticed. Three meals a day, she kept her diluted half-cheerful air and sometimes smiled my way. She said, "Hello, suicide." Poppa asked her to please ease up. "Samuel, have you written your sophisticated parents a thank-you note? No? Why, they'll be mortified," she then apologized to him, scared of herself.

If I told some colorful story at table, she'd rush me for the letter of the law, "How *big* a pumpkin?" Pop said it just showed I was having my way with the world, peeling a bit off, adding a inch on. "An inch? Hold up your hands, young lady, show how large. I'll go get my tape measure and to-morrow we'll just march downtown and we will simply check. I cannot abide liars."

She swept off to her needlework room. I sat picking at my bandaged wrist. Pop gave me his crooked grin. "My wife," he shrugged, nodding her way.

"Our wife," I said without thinking. He laughed agreement.

I THEN decided what I'd known: Coming out would always be beyond me. After my party setback, after being fortified by my chosen sister's blood, I could now act more myself. Momma would never shoehorn *me* into no ball gown at seventeen. I'd give it to the poor or shred it into silky kite tails.

I had always tended more towards Poppa. Now I got up from my place at table and I announced, "I'm climbing into your lap." He pushed back his chair, made room for me, I held on to him like a monkey. "You'll see," he said, like trying and soothe me with a promise, but he never said what I'd see.

Soon I plainly copied his bowlegged walk—Momma feared I'd caught the rickets. I chewed on grass's white stem ends, read dime-novel Westerns, made water willy-nilly under shrubs. I memorized Pop's funnier lines and sprung them on poor Shirl. Something got lost when I scratched my head and used his shambling swamp-boy manner. —Momma meantime played piano, paced, sulked, dragged me to church more. She made me give her a penny every time I imitated somebody or stretched the truth or said old Ain't.

The night I turned twelve, I already owed her a hundred and thirty dollars plus change.

CAME a visiting evangelist, a real pulpit pounder, young, all shoulders, full of examples, using a voice with more ups and downs than any foot-treadle Singer. He wore too much oil on his hair so he could flop it side to side and make a point. Other Baptist girls and women praised him. Shirl and me decided they were hypocrites. Instead of saying, "I dearly love the way that boy looks. He's sure got one Mount Zion of a chin on him, don't he?"— they'd go, "The Lord has certainly given our visiting pastor a pleasant ap-pearance, to the greater glory of God." "Full of the spirit of the blood of the lamb" can mean "Cute."

This bold boy devoted six Monday nights to Genesis. Church was jammed, women mostly. When the preacher took off his black coat and slowly rolled up his shirt sleeves—admiring his pale arms' own beauty—it seemed our communion for the night would be his white-bread biceps, honey—probably a taste treat, too. He was full of lingo and brackets, that one. He told us, right off, how out of all the churches he had faced, he'd never seen such good-looking Christians under one consecrated roof. Folks lowered their eyes, grinning a little. Then he added that *he* knew the extra temptations of the flesh thrown into the paths of those cursed with beauty—*he* could read minds just by looking pew to pew. Faces sobered, eyes aimed at knees, at handsome knees. Soon the boy's voice rushed at you broad and deep as you heard the Mississippi was—not like our usual preacher's frozen ditch of sound.

"Yes." The boy wonder unbuttoned his collar and the shirt by accident fell open on a chest surprisingly hairy for a person his age. "Yes, as your youth nowadays might put it, those two gardeners 'had it knocked,' were 'made for each other,' went 'hand in glove' with the green world. They walked around unclothed. Why dress if you never set foot out of your own green-house? Their one job? Enjoy the grounds and animals and love each other round the clock."

Of course—he explained, a regular scholar—there won't no clocks yet. Clocks came with clothes. Clothes were clocks. What need of a clock if you're never going to die? Who'd bother setting a alarm clock if there won't no Death to put the "dead" in "deadline"?

Shirl and me sat holding hands, studying each other's cuticle condition.

Since I got permanently cut out of the Summit crowd, we'd had some hard times but finally—when she seen that I was It for her—we drew closer. First Shirl complained that Emily Saiterwaite'd blamed *her* for how I'd misbehaved. I urged Shirley to spend more time in our tree house, where we both forgot the ranking and squabbles below. The catchy preacher was giving hell to Adam and Eve for messing up a good thing. "They didn't know when they were well-off, did they, brothers and sisters? This pair got offered the deal of a lifetime but could they coast on it? Well, could they?" Everybody grew still, like fearing they'd be called on, blamed. Why did church always point the finger our way? Preacher after preacher told Lucy she was a Sinner. A tad of mischief was all I'd admit to. Maybe I *wanted* to do wrong but I'd never really got the chance.

Instead, I sat in church planning what I'd bring on our next elm-tree picnic. "My friends—my pretty-is-as-pretty-does loved ones—back then the whole world was a combination resort and greenhouse. The only two people alive were the perfect couple—most likely to succeed. They got free food. Everything grew on trees then. No rents, no taxes, no maintenance, carefree as monkeys. Every day in Eden was another brand of Sunday. It never even rained in that garden. Genesis tells us how a nightly dew refreshed things on a frequent basis. No umbrellas, no nothing. These caretakers did not

even have to (I'll use a farming term in this fine farming community of
yours), have to 'weed.' There weren't any. And what'd they do with this
bounty? What?"

I sat holding Shirl's perfect hand, I sat remembering her first visit to
the tree house. I'd built the place with Pop's help, hoping I could one day
know one friend good enough to let her in the club. If you put a floor inside
a elm tree's bell shape—you've made you a perfect dome-topped room. For
wallpaper? Why, yellow and green leaves, moving. You can peek down
without others seeing up and in. A tree house is the most private public
place in the world.

That first time up, I'd climbed ahead of Shirl. I stared back, warning
her which handholds were rickety, which sure—I couldn't have her fall on
her first visit. I sat back on my haunches and waited. I had heard how babies
arrive in the world headfirst. Shirl's forehead slid into sight. Blue eyes
seemed about three-fourths of her whole noggin. She'd never been up so
high in her life. Seeing how cozy I'd made it shocked her into saying, "Ahh."
To have her in this leaf room—was like being both in a church and on some
private dirigible kite. With street sounds squawking far below you, you felt
a sweetness akin to best lonely moments of clear thinking in the privy.

"This," Shirl announced, "is our *real* home." She commenced tying this
limb to that one, swagging green aside like drapes. How safe I felt when
she spoke, "Home."

Next visit, Shirley brought two cloth-covered hangers. Warm days, we'd
shuck our dresses. We'd play Mom and Poppa while wearing just chemises.
She hooked our clothes over some handy limb. Dresses turning in the breeze
looked like bright flags flying. A whole nation we'd discovered and founded.
We were its two co-presidents, its favorite actresses. And nobody knew.

Even on street level, we lived out our own treasure map. Other folks
saw Falls—but the true one was ours. We hid flowers for each other inside
empty lampposts, in a statue's hand that unscrewed off the war statue downtown. Nobody knew. We adopted one step of the courthouse to be our
message board. On my way to school from the highroad on the hill's crest,
I'd lay out two magnolia leaves under a blue rock alongside a store-bought
seashell. Hurrying home, I'd find—on our holy spot—my things vanished
and her substitutes: a rhinestone button missing a few back molars, plus a
nasty green comb she'd found somewhere. I sat down beside this news from
her. I laughed. Adults stepped past me. Nobody noticed my chuckling or
cared. Such tidbits were our code and meant something definite. They
meant: Us. They said: We live in this town, too. We count in general because
we matter to each other. Us, separately, we ain't one whit more interesting
than we find each other to be. Which is pretty interesting. Every grownup
on Falls' sidewalks knows our names, our folks. Nobody really knows us.
We like it this way. We go to school—we don't care about school. We sleep
in grownups' houses. Those ain't our true home. Us two lived *disguised* as
little girls. We only put up with it because it frees us for one another, we

can hold hands right in church while being hollered at, we can sleep so near each other. We carry a garden in our looks at one another, a secret garden—the best kind.

Now the boy preacher was heading down the final stretch and—no surprise—here come Jesus. Nailed to the tree for our sins. The tree of the knowledge of good and evil, run through with pikes and set upright with perfect naked innocence, pinned to it. Shirl and I knew, you could do more things with a tree than just get tacked there. I kept my fist around the knuckles of a pink fine live girl.

"Blood of the Lamb" didn't hold a patch to the cut-wrist sisterhood betwixt Shirl and me. So, in the nobbed and worked-up church we sat trying to look like all the other wicked ones. Only, we won't wicked! During the last hymn that ran for forty verse, one called "Just As I Am, Without a Prayer," the boy ordered Sinners to come up front now, admit to having fallen off and dropped and lost it. Get right with God. You'll feel better. Tell every soul present how you're stained and soiled within. How you've lost hope of all garden possibilities but how you want back in. Others shoved past us—coarse bear-sized adults, faces bunchy with regrets—dragging forward right in front of everybody, scared as hell of hell, fearful of their weedy crimes. Meantime, we just settled lower in our pew, shoulder to shoulder, hand in hand, alone together in peace. If you *are* the secret garden, how can you be turned out of it?

7

CAME the year of drunkenness by accident. Shirl played Virgin Mary in our church Christmas Spectacle. Folks still mention the day: many a teetotaling and Bible-pounding Baptist got knee-walking drunk through no wish of their own.

Since Luke Lucas was Deacon, he donated forty-some gallons of cider, long in storage. For a man so known as tightfisted, this kindness seemed a switch. Fact is, the cider'd been in storage for right long. Lucas must've had his doubts about how hard the stuff was. His worried wife, plump Doris, loaded this heated brew with cloves, nutmeg, sliced preserved pears. That only made the children line up for *their* share. Everybody stood around waiting for the pageant to begin. It was late starting every year.

While folks milled about till the Mitchell twins quit tussling long enough to have their angel wings belted on correct, men/women/children kept bellying up to trestle tables for another ladleful of tasty mulled cider. The weather was warm that year. First sign: six people, outdoors, saying in a chorus, "Is it hot out here or is it just me?"

We're now talking about Christians that hadn't let one drop of devil water ever cross their God-fearing lips. To find yourself four sheets to the wind for the first time and on Christmas, that felt new.

Our churchyard was soon strewn with folks seated right slam in the bushes. They kept swallowing cup after cup—still sending staggering children for refills while they kept puzzling about what'd happened to them. Everybody felt overwhelmed with holiday warmth. There'd been such a line around the cider, I hadn't got myself one drop. Pitifully clearheaded, I wandered from bunch to bunch. A straight-A student from my Normal School class, oldest son in a family of nine, reeled up to me and slurred, "What's Thursday's geography homework?" then angled off, muttering about responsibilities. One set of ladies, overcome, decided to hold a Bible lesson (in self-defense), but somebody was reading the part where Easter happens.

The ancient bachelor choir director, known for his tenor voice so high it stepped on certain sopranos' toes, known for his begonias, known for once going North to the Juilliard School, where he had a quick but total breakdown, then come straight home, a fellow famous for the long patience he showed his own foul-tempered mother—the very choir director who'd been so taken with Ned the First and who wore a black armband long after the killing and who once admitted considering hisself Ned's secret widow—*he* seemed changed today. I found him standing between the boxwoods and our church—he was beating fists against the church's boards, and hard, loud, punching whilst muttering many bad words I'd never heard yet but someway knew were totally illegal here. His knuckles really bled. "Look," he smiled, showing me raw fingers' backs, the matching red marks printed on our white church. "Look, Lucy, you didn't think I had it in me, did you?" and—glad-acting—went back to pounding.

I hurried to my own folks. Momma, plunked on cold dirt, was all but spread-eagle, had her skirt well up past ankles, not minding who saw. She kept touching Poppa's cowlicks, saying that she wanted herself a farm. She adored turkeys, Irish wolfhounds, peacocks to drape every bush. She just loved Christmas and she dearly loved a snowy farm at Christmas. "Just think, Prince Consort, on our property you could go out and cut any Christmas tree you liked."

"Hate farms," he grinned, then went serious, holding up one finger: " 'The sweetest wings tour sourest by their needs; / Wilies that lily fester worse'n . . . deeds.' "

"Close," Momma said and—in front of everybody—pulled his head her way, kissed him wet and full on (in) the mouth. Then they struggled to their feet and hurried home, willing to miss Shirley as the Virgin Mary. A mistake.

In the cemetery nearby, I couldn't but notice Mr. Kingston chasing Mrs. Buxton, plump and the mother of seven. She quaked and danced and finally fell back onto a new grave. He said, "I've had my eye on you since we was eight, gal," and they thrashed about. Well, such changes upset a child plenty, honey. Nobody hates surprises like dogs and children do.

I ran near tombstones, looking for my aunts. I passed a huge lady and her short mild husband. She was complaining, "DeWitt, for the past fifteen minutes, I've felt distinctly sick." He told her, "Ruth, for the last forty-eight years I've felt sick. For the last fifteen minutes, I've felt wonderful."

In the midst of this hurly-burly, two well-known local dogs (both yellow), having followed their owners to church, now stood very still. Posed side by side, hounds only let their eyes move, catching a crazy behavior pattern never before glimpsed hereabouts, especially on the church grounds. Mutts seemed scared of how—if primed proper—even your strictest local Baptists could act more decidedly doglike than most casual dogs. —Worrisome.

I cut past our hefty bank president, cornered by four sketchy little boys, their hands out. Kids were just drunk enough to finally come up and ask the great man for a quarter (apiece, please) and—today only—he was stoned sufficient so he reached into pin-striped trousers and fished out a dollar gold piece for each big-eyed boy. "Gol-ly," one said. That, sugar pie, is how long ago this happened. People still said Golly. Still meant it. Then, believing that the banker might change his mind, one kid yelled, "Scatter." They all did.

Seeking everyday decency, I found my maiden aunts. Dressed alike in black, they perched at graveyard's edge, one per headstone. They rested not twenty feet from where one fellow and another man's upended wife still grappled, petticoats a type of salad that they swam in. Aunts—backs to graves—hadn't noticed. Instead they were talking shop: piano. These three ladies were cruelly overeducated for a town this size. A wind blew and they all held on to their dark hats but otherwise seemed fine.

They addressed a pupil and, though the aunts looked okay from a distance, as I drew nearer I saw they were maybe making a mistake. Standing before them, Mary Eliza Woolrich, supposedly their best student this year.

Ruler, the oldest sister, said, "You call yourself talented?"

(Now, honey, everybody knows that a small-town piano teacher cannot afford to tell her students the whole truth about their long-range career goals.)

"Well," argued the Lake, youngest of my aunts, "at least Mary Eliza here *works*. Imagination might not be her middle name. But our only gifted one in the last nine years could think of nothing but M E N. Myself I'd rather have a plodder like her here than some genius who quits. No—it's a lie what I just said. I'm not myself today. Genius is always worth it. —Now run along, Mary Eliza, you've leached enough free coaching out of us for one day."

I watched the girl weave away. I felt glad to notice: She was far too looped to understand what-all'd just happened.

Ruler pitched into a favorite topic. I understood that she was three full octaves drunker than her sisters. "I am often asked about Maestro Liszzzt's nationality. By birth, he is Hungarian admintentlyly, admittided—I admit. And in Liszt's social faddishness, in his easy morals, *un soupçon français* perhaps. His sense of design is, I'd be the first to add, not *un*-Italian. But, as a moral force, in sheer uplift, Liszt the idealizer—can only be called German, High Churman. His sweep, his . . ."

Her cowed younger sisters usually sat still during this but today they all spoke at onct. Lake said, "Oh, pack it in."

Sea went, "You're *al*ways talking Liszt."

And I watched the two youngests skip away, stand to one side smiling, then start playing patty-cake. "Aren't we something, Lucy?" Lake asked grim little me. "Why, I haven't had this much fun since Andrew Johnson died."

I swung around our church's rear, needing peace, some pouting room. Shirley's hefty mom sat slumped on back-porch steps, swilling her cup's dregs, sucking cloves. Around her free finger, she now twirled Shirley's silver halo. The Mrs. saw me, waved me nearer. "Feeling funny, Lucy. Maybe stage fright for our pet. Was up all night putting last touches on her costume— powder blue and white. I hate how the veil is going to cover up our darling's curls—but you cannot have a bareheaded Virgin Mary. Everybody knows how Mary looks and *I* ain't going to break no new fashion ground. —Here, take a load off your dogs. Been meaning to talk with you. Woman to woman like. Lucy, child, I see you sometimes a-studying me, squinting when I get out my brush set and go to freshen up Shirley's curls again. Don't judge me too harsh. For one thing, I'm a fool for holidays. Especially ones where she gets the lead."

First off, the Mrs. claimed she wanted to make something clear: She didn't blame me for how Summit Avenue was called Summit owing to its being the highest point for five counties. It won't *my* fault that the blue-blooded folks who'd settled this town had picked the choicest view and coolest area for their own. Only natural. The valley was close, yes, and the peanut mill that made so much cash for those atop the heap did throw a heavy smell over certain houses at the big hill's bottom, but, she wanted me to know, I was a child and innocent. "Thank you," I said, unsure. She accepted.

"I like my darling having friends good as you. Let's not hide our light under a bushel. Now, concerning our favorite topic, yours and mine, about how she came to be. I hail from way out in the country, swampland. You want a clove to suck? No? Mine is your own pappy's home ground. You probably think your daddy's folks are dirt poor. I knew the boy by sight, but not to speak. See, out Bear Grass way, Lucy, why *his* people are the rich ones—like your momma's here in Falls. Give you some idea. The Honicutts owned a fine cabin, five whole acres.

"Us? We hardly had a full roof. Why, when it rained, only rained a bit less indoors than out. Young ones on a damp straw pallet—brothers and sisters of a age where they can't help but to notice one another, nights. Daddy cut his foot, died of his jaw locking. Momma, on her own, had no more idea of how to farm than some city child would. The one pretty thing in that tatty hut: oiled paper for window glass. (Can't afford glass, you rub cooking grease on a paper sheet, light gets through, some of the rain'll bead up on it.) Pages got cut out of this *Godey's Lady's Book* my brother found by the roadside. One page—glued in the window near our sleeping spot—

it showed two beauties, Lucy. They were all rigged and stirruped in this lace and finery. Every time the sun came up, it showed me them. One was walking a squinchy little dog no bigger than a dinner roll. Both strolling in a park as pressed and like cut on the bias, as the ladies' frocks. —Darling, that picture kept me going. Won't much, Lucy, but it proved plenty for a thinking girl like me. It give me this notion, see. Oh, even then I knew how *I* looked. Maybe we didn't own no looking glass but the ponds'll show you enough. I saw I was too big-boned to ever wear them bows and sashes and suchlikes. But every time I studied the ladies from *Godey's*, yellow as they'd turned and out of date as the styles already were, I felt I ought to be *around* a person that could get spiffed up that good. I'd then wade out in the swamps, I'd tie a pink ribbon round some cypress tree's trunk. I'd slide the sash low, then tiptoe off and turn back, saying, 'Middy style.' I'd cosset the ribbon higher, then I'd check back, smiling, 'Empire style.' I longed—don't think it silly, child—to just help dress somebody up each day.

"Thinking on this got me through, got me out that shack before my big brothers laid a unclean hand on me, it pulled me to this here fine hill-top city. When I hitched up with my Silas and we had us a girl—it was only when the nigger midwife, all compliments, handed me this child in a blue blanket, when the baby looked right at me and I noticed how her eyes matched that very blue—was then I seen that oh, the Lord God of Hosts, Stitcher and Finisher of Our Faith, why He'd give me exactly what I'd asked for. All them nights of wishing on the stars that you could see, due to a lack of roof (nice when it didn't rain), all them dawns that held up two example ladies in a far-off park—I'd been rewarded.

"So you got to understand how I'm feeling today, nearbout drunk on it. My girl: Virgin Mary herself, pick of the litter. Our Shirley, she's the answer to a simple woman's prayer. Shirley is my Amen, with a dust ruffle around it. So you mustn't think me too set on this one joy I been given. I knew what I wanted and it came true, came true out of my own big body here. —Darling? I'm probably the happiest woman alive."

A FEW minutes later, the preacher (knowing how crocked his sheep were but not willing to fess up to this and make them all feel guilty), he called us in to see the Holy Play. A few things did go wrong: The star lit up too soon and Bobo Kingston's shepherd bathrobe fell open, him jaybird naked under it and too drunk to shut the thing by hand. Others, on the front row, helped. Then we found that our Virgin had gulped her own fair share of cider. Fact is, her mom had fetched extras for Shirl. That year the pageant used a real live baby (a little Buxton whose momma had been seen rolling amongst graves earlier). Halfway through the play, came time for Shirley's speech. A long quiet fell. Even the nodders-off (it *was* hot in here) woke up for this part.

Shirl's cheeks burned pink under her white tablecloth veil—she looked more perfect than the plaster manger scenes at Woolworth's. But soon as

she tried talking, she appeared way too looped to recollect a speech memorized with my help and her momma's. So instead, seated up there in straw
as fresh and yellow as her hair, she was—I could tell—going to just make
stuff up. "Don't, stay still," I longed to holler whilst I chewed my knuckle.
Poppa had said we might help Shirl move up in life. I feared that my adopted
friend might spoil her reputation forever. I knew something about that.

She spoke finally—sweet if a wee bit fuddled-sounding—she faced her
sentimental audience, whilst the little Buxton pretty much behaved hisself
in her arms. Went:

"This my own baby boy. He's new. Nobody'd even let me inside a house
to have him. Why, I tore up my own good coat to wrap this poor naked
thing in. I had him out here in the straw like a yard dog would. The stable
was all I could think of, wasn't it, Joseph? I said, 'Well, let's try the stable,'
and so here we are. Ooh, someday folks will look back and say, Boy, was
that ever tacky, not letting *them* in! Why, we should've been 'obsequious.'
Did we ever slip up! But for now, nobody knows us. One thing, at least the
animals have acted real nice and seem interested and peaceful about our
being out here. They certainly have warmed things up, too. You need that
with a baby this young. It's cozy enough for now. I want more for this child,
though. We're trying as best we can for our new boy. This," she held up the
living child as he tugged one golden curl from under Mary's veil for all to
see, "this baby here," Shirl looked out at her audience (her momma, standing
near the back door, holding a hairbrush in one hand, weeping, the other
hand covering her mouth), "he feels just like my very *own* little baby. He
does. True, we may be mighty poor. And college for him is out of the
question. But, you know, I'd just die for this baby. We just love our pretty
pink little Christ child almost to death." Then, overcome, she really hugged
him. Our Virgin Mary sat right there and cried and cried. Couldn't nothing
stop her.

The organist came in with a quick low carol to save the day. It almost
seemed planned. Shirl's talk had sounded lots more natural than the stiff
words she'd forgot. It reminded you that the gal she played would've been
this innocent, just a few years older and nearbout as upset. Well, everybody—pew to pew—felt so stirred. Even the twin angels (regular hellions)
quit fidgeting with coat-hanger halos, stared out at their mother and daddy—
holding hands on the front row. Every person present, drunk as skunks,
swore this had been the church's best play ever.

Yes, it'd embarrassed us when several Lutherans and Episcopalians
stopped by earlier, buggies halted in the road before the church, and—for
half a hour—watched our accidental shenanigans. They'd trotted off and
blabbed it to the entire Christian world, seemed like. Next Sunday, our old
choir director led the anthem with both his hands bandaged like a boxer's
and he acted forceful and showed off some, seemed pleased. Then our
preacher got up and said it'd been inspirational how—with help from Christ-

mas—everybody'd contrived to use their blighted accidental drunkenness to help them feel as deeply religious as possible.

And ever after, this year became well known. Being small-town people, we did a lot of labeling. This year of Shirl's perfect local stardom went between the Time When the Tar River Almost Flooded and The Year the War Monument Fell Over One Night for No Good Reason. It was on the list with how Mrs. Tom Yount had a baby, got up and walked around four days, fell over, and—nobody was more surprised than Mrs. Tom Yount herself—had two more. Count them. Shirley's was the year of the really good show. The year when the tiredest if nicest pageant of the church calendar broke through to something colorful and fresh for onct. I've told about the year we cried in church and really meant it. World without end, Amen.

FROM THAT Christmas to April, Shirley practically lived with us. Much as Momma railed against my friend in private, she always treated Shirl polite face to face. (That, if anything, made ladylikeness seem like something I might someday look into.) As spring rolled in, Ma put a silver bud vase on Shirl's bedside table, kept it pretty with whatever bloomed around our yard. By this time, not one soul spoke to me at school excepting teachers who got paid to. Some mornings, just at dawn when light is glazed the colors of candy, I'd wake, roll over, look at a straight-backed chair—Shirl's shift hung on the slatted back—sunlight getting through, making a spectacle and hobby of her underthings. I knew someday I would be old then dead and so would Shirley. If she went blind first, I could *do* more for her. I got tears in my eyes without knowing why.

Things changed when Momma enrolled me and Shirl (I wouldn't go otherwise) in a Saturday china-painting class. We played hooky from daubing nasturtiums onto finger bowls. Instead, we frolicked in the hayloft of Shirl's daddy's livery establishment downtown. He kept white hens underfoot. Hens ate what oats horses spilled. Using eggs he found in straw, her poppa had earlier made us little omelettes (grits ones) on his office wood stove. Off we run, annoying chickens, tussling. We rolled everywheres, stuffing hay down each other's socks, giggling so hard we got wheezy from fun. I'd been warned everywhichaway about going near horses. Poppa hated farm animals because they lived on farms. Momma called such beasts dangerous and seemed to feel that every horse was male. Whenever we passed one with its manhood lowered into resting position, she'd point out clouds, weather vanes. Rough-housing at the stable, Shirl and me were new to the age of twelve, that giddy minute before your grimmer changes set in with a vengeance. You play then with a rangy energy that lets you guess what waits for you ahead. We kept daring each other to roll across the very spot where the drifter's corpse got found. We pretended we could smell a human body. Other than our own.

I overturned a bale of straw, we noticed—hunched in a dark corner—one small furred creature. It arched itself, then backed, sissing, against barn wall. It'd been feasting on a stray hen's egg. White shell was gummed across a snout as black as patent leather. Now its nose gleamed glossy yellow with yolk. "Here, kitty." Shirl knee-walked closer. Out she reached when the critter spun around. White stripe bristled into view. Up lashed this splendid tail. The thing went off like some alarm clock. We fell blinded into straw. We'd been coated in a stench so strong it ended breath and eyesight for some seconds.

Shirl's dad heard our screams. He rattled up the ladder quick. He got his nose to our level then clattered halfway back down, "Ooo—eee!" We rolled around, hands mashing eyes, we gagged, flapped skirts, fanned our stinging features. "I've *told* you girls about teasing skunks," he shouted. Honey, the man had never onct mentioned it.

Mr. Williams eased us (one under each arm) from the loft, lugged us into a dark tack room. He backed off, swearing through a hairy omelette-smudged hand. The door slammed on us. We stood near one old bathtub sometimes used as a watering trough, not hooked to pipes. Dark mildewed oats were heaped at one end. Along the far wall, harnesses and the wicked metal bits that hurt all horses into learning right from left.

Her daddy hollered we should clean out that tub, quit our blubbering. Off he cursed towards Lucas' All-Round Store to seek a cure. He swore what a botherance girls are—like that skunk wouldn't have squirted boys!

All over the stable, horses whinnied, kicking stalls, rankled by such a stink. Hens set up a coffee-klatch racket just outside the door. Shirl and me stood gasping, arms held out from sticky sides. We studied each other, we sniggered once, then really sobbed. "I look *aw*ful," she cried, laughing while holding out one long curl's stinky end. "Poor Momma!"

After a knock, her pop asked if we were decent. We didn't know what he meant and never even answered. Through the cracked door, he handed us, a few cans at a time, one whole crate of tomato juice. Then in came his pocketknife, its opener yanked forth. "Empty every last tin into that tub, shuck off them nasty clothes, kick them out to me for burning. Then you climb in and scrub each other good. Soak till you're nearbout shriveled from the acid in it. This here's the onliest way you'll ever get that evil stink off of you—hear me, rascals?"

First we thought he was joking, a tomato-juice bath? But when he stalked off, muttering, we finally started opening the two dozen cans. We weren't too good at it. Knowing we had to climb into the grimy tub, we really set to cleaning it. We unfastened our Saturday wash dresses, we used those to scrub stained sides. Shirl sniffed, "It looked just like a kitten, Lucy. And I dearly love kittens and every single one so far has liked me back—till this. No fair."

"Fair don't average into it," said I, smarter than I knew.

After half filling the tub with cold red juice, we kicked free of bloomers and—modest, every finger a fig leaf too narrow—wriggled in, complaining. Upstairs at my house, we undressed for bed without much thought. Today, in this musty dark storeroom, it felt different, we looked barer.

On a nearby saddle pommel, we found one ragged sponge. Full of jokes, we started scrubbing. Shirl claimed that nobody around town would even be*lieve* this. We picked which momma and teacher we'd tell first. We guessed what each person would say. Purse-mouth, Shirl imitated the haughty cool Episcopalian Emily Saiterwaite. This scrape with a wild animal would've killed her. But us? We'd lived. Baptists are just tougher.

Our only light got filtered through the transom's dusty glass. Shirley's dad had stationed a young groom outside to guard us. (Later, when I thought he might have peeked, I nearly perished of the shame.) Shirl settled with her back to me. She scooped every yellow curl atop her head, nodding forward whilst I scrubbed her tapered neck. I told her she should really wear her hair up like this full-time. I hinted she ought to, for a change, buy a plain white dress, not her usual strongish pastels.

"But Momma wouldn't *let* me," she said, simple. And I felt ashamed. Here we were, buck naked, and I was jabbering clothes advice, just like my own society-minded mother would. How strange it felt to be stripped, mid-day, downtown. Warming, the red juice started smelling summery, it welcomed us like we were our own lunch.

From Main Street close by, you could hear horse traffic clopping. Men talked Commerce and Women. Women talked Bargains, Children, and Disease. We overheard everybody. They could sniff skunk (some remarked on it) but they couldn't spy two girls sloshing jaybird naked in this strange wet. Even seated, even from the rear, Shirl looked taller than me.

Happy, we grew stiller. Tomatoes' acid seemed to peel the stink from us and cure a dome of air above our tub. Other smells came forward, shy. You got the nice fustiness of leather harnesses, salty saddles. From two dozen horses, a rankness, half between sharp urine and the sweetness of new straw. I thought I could smell Shirl, too: milk, sachet, melba toast, one housebound kitten too many. Horses still sneezed but were calming some. Even hens forgot to sound hysterical. And skunks *eat* chickens.

I washed her. I leaned forward. I whispered to her shoulders, "We're having us a adventure." I saw her head nod, "An adventure," Shirl's low voice added, "like we're in our tree house. Only, instead of being windy and green, this is more . . . red and wet."

"Yeah," I said, idle. "Wet and red." I kept thinking I'd forgot something, there was something I was supposed to *do* now. It concerned Shirl. Of that much, I felt sure. We sat, already sisters *in* the veins, coated now with outside red. From the waist up, from the back, Shirl still looked mostly angel white, gold, pink, sweet and blank as cake. But from the navel down—liquid could've hid most anything, fish scales, a sateen porky tail, raw mystery. Slow, so she wouldn't spill any bath juice or scare me, Shirl sloshed around, faced my way. She looked determined now, taking up our nappy sponge, commencing to clean my front. She did it pretty hard, no nonsense. Every swipe tried proving this was just required—not much fun—only something that a poppa'd forced on us. But . . .

My chest knew better. Her long hands got to going over collarbones then scooted down along my many ribs. Shirl dragged coarse sponge across two tender points my front was just coming alive with. They perked: small lights, birthday candles. Shirl didn't understand how these were definitely noticing, were getting used to their Aunt Shirley's funny heavy touch. I closed my eyes. I leaned one to nine inches nearer. "You old stinker," she said, mashing soggy sponge against my ear. Warm juice rushed, skittish, down my neck and front. "Someday," she said. "The two of us will be sitting on the veranda looking out on a whole yardful of babies, Luce. I imagine our children will be 'incorrigible' darlings, and will have names like poetry and will be best friends."

I smiled, shaky. "Where," I couldn't help but asking, "did the husbands get to?"

"The what? Oh, they've died by then. Maybe the next war got them. Wars are rough on husbands and ours were nice while they lasted. Now it's just us. We got willed every cent. All I know is, it's just us up on a fine porch, plus our yardful of babies. And, Luce? the babies get along."

"Well, that's good."

Then her voice took on some growl. Said I knew, didn't I, that we'd have to clean each other *right*, right? I understood, didn't I?

Then like dreaming in broken English, a farm language, I stammered, "How clean does he wanted us?"

"Well, my momma always says, 'There's clean and clean.' And I believe I am going to want you *clean*, girl." I caught the sharp meaning-it tone Shirl used when she was about to win big at "I Am Chicken Little."

Then she really went to work on me. When I opened either eye, Shirl had moved closer. She'd become Flo Nightingale set loose, after ten cups of coffee, on the whole filthy Crimean War. The war was losing. I heard a sound . . . it was me, not talking, not breathing—but somewheres on loan in between. I tried speaking but my tone shook. You couldn't help but to notice (I, I couldn't) how Shirl's breasts (where else could you, a short person tubbed with her and facing the front parts, look?), though about as recent as my own, had seen fit to pout a little farther into air—more interested, less stay-at-home. Hers appeared achy—nipples pink as anything, the size of quarters—sad, but extra ladylike. Prim as cameos yet matter-of-fact as drawer-pulls.

Main Street still sounded money-mad, overtrafficked. Shirl's knees were up so we could both fit in here, so were mine, my knees up, too. We were real close. Just a courtesy, I scrubbed. I got excellent at it. Lucas' store's cash register pinged its toylike give-and-take. I loved our town so. Scrub scrub.

Happiness flustered me some. I dropped our sponge. Under the dark juice it sank. Then I had to pat around down there, hunting, fishing. Blind luck, I groped.

By accident, my best friend's right thigh got touched. By this. By my hand. She didn't flinch. I did. I pulled back, but Shirl, sleepy-looking, reached under the rich liquid we sat basted in. She lifted my hand, wet with red, Shirl kissed my palm, hoisted the sponge herself. I couldn't help but notice how her rosy nipples had now closed past nickel size, got down beyond pennies and on towards tightening to perfect dimes. Sponge: four pounds of dripping black wet.

"Here," her voice, a grown boy's, "I'm going . . . to clean . . . *you*." And when she whipped it forward, mumbling, "You're so nice, Luce. I think about you all the time, you're just the best, best friend," when, without no warning, she clutched that rough old naughty thing and touched it hard to me, Shirl Shirl Shirl sure triggered a secret that, till now, had stayed mostly secret to that secret's keeper. Whoa. When the scratchy old sponge hit, first try, fresh down up beneath me, Lord—but I rocked back with what-all news she'd let loose . . . "Best friend a girl ever . . . had . . . whole world wide, wide world, Luce."

"Whoa," I tried saying, but what slid out instead was "Ahh-mm, err . . ." I pitched forward, took hold of Shirl's either slick shoulder, me—moving to some state of both jump-up and collapse. I was a real bad spastic, I was a excellent firecracker, I felt crippled but the sturdiest person on earth. I deserved, I deserved.

All below my waist went part sneeze—like just before you do, sneeze, when you know you can't help it, not for a zillion dollars, not to save your entire nation, family, and South, you cannot . . . quit . . . now. (Strange when one timid unnoticed portion of you all of a sudden starts having its own dreams, dreams important and colorful as ones your nighttime head burns with.)

I couldn't stand it. I reached down, snagged Shirl's squirmish wrist hard, stopped her, yelled, "Don't, please. I'm nearbout clean, Shirley. I'm really nearbout all spanky whistle clean down there now, promise."

Then this: She cursed the vilest string of things I'd ever heard out of a man, woman, or toad, she stuffed that sloppy sponge into my hand, mashed my fingers overtop it so rough, three knuckles popped. She got hold of both my braids, she yanked my small face up in front of hers—big, pink, with straw jamming angles through her curls—and, really hurting me, Shirl said her English wrong for the first time, ever—hissing wet across my eyes, says she, "Well, listen up, Lucy fuss-priss. There's two of us in here. And I ain't clean yet, selfish. I sure as hell am far from clean just yet . . . So," Shirl rerouted my whole handful of sponge, straddling it, and next—into my mouth, her entire mouth arrived. It someway fit. A exchange student. I felt the long serious visit start. Hands across the water: only, tongues. When Shirl relaxed some pressure on my braids—when my eyes got unsquinted sufficient to blink again—I commenced to catch the drift of this.

I had heard how pregnant women ate for two, but seemed like Shirl and me now breathed for one, one big one. Her hand, friendly again, gave mine a hint of how to scrub just far enough up, then turn back with serious purpose, redoing the whole round-robin swoop. Her face, so close to mine, looked as pained as pleasure gets. Next, quick, up out of liquid like a rainbow trout rising at right angle—Shirl leapt inches. And, Lord, child, I was just getting the hang of this, just getting actually pretty good at it, when a whip handle hit our door.

Her dad yelps, "My two petunias sweet-smelling yet?" Well, we jumped three feet to the tub's either ends. Mid-spin, we turned, faces hid from one another. One full red gallon sloshed the wall and harnesses, dropped a gory fringe. Through the open transom, her poppa tossed fresh clothes. He'd gone and fetched my finest Sunday frock from Momma's very hands. (Momma!)

Shaming to see my good blue dress belly-flop onto straw, one sleeve sickled over empty cans. Gaping across my red-splashed shoulder, I managed to give Shirl one sick whippet of a smile. Big-eyed, we both stared— each wondering which child was guiltiest—and guiltiest of *what*?

Her poppa chucked in towels and two clean horse blankets, then left, hollering, "Take your time, cherry tomatoes." Slow and rickety, we hunched clear of tub, we dared not view a single inch of one another, red or white. Bashful inside blanket tents, we dried, said nothing. Air in here got to feeling tense and awful. A horse nearby made water (lots of water slapped dirt comically loud). We quit breathing till this rushing stopped. I felt chilled, my teeth chittered.

I saw how the bath's acid had shriveled my legs and hips—I appeared wizened as pouch leather, crimped as somebody old, old old. At last, in tones most quavery, I went, "Some morning, huh? First a blamed skunk. Then to be sheep-dipped in doggone tomato juice!"

That eased things. It let us laugh a bit. We giggled, pained-sounding. Soon we overdid. Dressed, we jabbered, readying our stories for others— we left in the skunk and cold juice—we skipped the mystery: what made us do all that just now? Do what?

Our pitch of cackling grew shrill, even for us. Shirl's pop opened the door, clamped hands over his ears, "Pipe down." A terrible fact: The first horse was being led into our room to drink juice from our tub. When I asked why, her dad shrugged. "Be healthy for them. You think I'd waste all that? Cost me good money, gal."

"But," Shirl's eyes lowered, "we *sat* in it."

The boy groom who'd guarded us made his eyebrows go. "Be all the tastier. Heck, we might could bottle it." He winked our way. Shirl's dad give the boy a sharp look then laughed anyhow.

Shirl and me pretended we'd not heard this. We parted, claiming we just dearly hated to. I did not set eyes on her for three whole days. Then four.

· · ·

ONLY AT night, my second one at home, could I let myself remember.
Something strange and huge had happened. I felt we now knew more than
any other folks—grown or not—in all of Nash County. I believed we had
someway invented it—it that'd happened. I still knew no name for it. Just
had Shirley's name. Shirley Goodness and Mercy. Before I fell to sleep, as
a reminder of it all, I did sometimes allow myself to reach under quilts.
Yeah. I found it all still there. Complete and perfect as a hidden garden.
Even alone, I could recollect a lot. I only did this to recall Shirl sitting
there—pale as wedding cake from her waist up, the rest coated in nice
slippery red-wet. Only with my eyes squeezed tight did certain pictures come
over me, but random:

I pictured Shirl wiggling free of the perfect wedding dress. In my head
she moved to a jump-rope song we liked: You marry in brown, you'll live
with a frown / Marry in gray, you'll go far away / Marry in yellow, you're
'shamed of your fellow / Marry in green, you're 'shamed to be seen / If you
marry in blue, you'll always be true. —But I figured, Shirl, she'd marry in
gold and pink—her hair, her skin. What'd *that* mean?

I pictured how, summers up the tree house, we just wore our slips. The
family tree we called ours, we talked of it as "she"—our nurse, pet guard
and dinosaur. The elm didn't exactly love having us and our boards up in
her but, like some girl forced to wear teeth braces for a season or two, she
got accustomed. She even forgave me the ten-penny spikes I'd drove so deep
into her. I apologized at every hammer blow. Next day, I found sap, cut-
glass doorknobs, coating each spike head. Touching these clear amber
knots—suffering and jewelry mixed—I worried like for some human I had
hurt. Surrounded by these gems, Shirl and me sat happily bare, packed by
leaves on every side—greenery, our excelsior, us feeling like two pale valuable vases in shipment on the high seas.

I now only touched myself as a shortcut to imagining my friend just
one bed away. Tonight, the bud vase stood empty. She should stay here
every single night from now on. We could spend winters here and summers
up our tree house. Seemed like Shirl and me just belonged together. How
strange: that we were, through some mistake, locked into different houses
blocks apart, one mansion too big and one cheesebox too small, prisoners
of that peculiar luck-of-the-draw adults called family. Odd that, though we
liked each other so, Shirl and me hadn't talked in four full days. What had
happened? And yet, even confused, even apart, I could yet communicate
with my friend. There rested, under quilts, this beginner's key—tiny yet
powerful as one at the Telegraph Office downtown—even in bed, far from
one another, we could send and receive our dots-and-dashes heartfelt messages, at night, in code, by hand.

TWO DAYS later, Poppa (seeing me look so grave) offered me my birthday
present early: forty feet of good hemp rope, it'd be our tree house's new

entry ladder. "Yellow as a certain person's hair," he smirked his widest. I nodded, grateful for permission. I lugged new line, looped over one shoulder, to that certain person's side-street house downhill. Near the peanut mill, air smelled about to fry. Seemed you could gain weight just through your nose.

I knocked on the unvarnished door. Then I stood straight, posing holding our new rope to show. Shirl's mom appeared, that wide kind lady red-cheeked from excess cooking. She lumbered onto porch, closed the door quick, smiled, wrestled off her apron, settled on a splintery bench, then eased me down beside her. She held my hand, hard, whilst explaining. Sad to say, Shirley's language had gone to Hades in a hand basket lately. Barnyard language. Bad talk was like a fever, the Mrs. said—was catching, won't it? Four days ago, Shirley'd come down with a right bad case.

"I know my own English it's not up to much, but we want only the best for Shirley. I know you do, too, Lucy. Our Shirley's pretty and plenty sweet enough so's she can go most anywheres, be most anybody's friend. After the skunk, I'll tell you straight, we got extra worried, girl. Shirley acted feverish, even crazy, kept to her bed, talked out of her skull, couldn't say nothing but Ain't. I pointed to the window, did she want more air? 'Ain't, ain't.' Shouldn't we get her downstairs to the privy? 'Ain't, got to ain't.' She missed choir practice, she threw up, calling, 'Must've been something I ain't.' She had her a kind of fit. Don't tell. I know you won't snitch. I always know who sees our Shirley's best parts. Me, I've always trusted you, Lucy."

Mrs. Williams stared forward, held my hand tighter. I heard fifteen, twenty kittens mewing in the house. I commenced to feeling sick. She spoke of Shirley like a dead girl, one who'd left us. She explained that Shirley's state had got way worse. Doc Collier came. Her health only made a turn for the better when our First Baptist preacher's wife and proper young daughter paid a sick call. They asked the ailing Shirley: Would it cheer her to attend this here private-type party? They even let Shirl borrow a nice white dress that'd look decent for so formal a birthday tea.

"And our girl, why she's over on Summit right this minute. At little Emily Saiterwaite's. I'm surprised *you* ain't there, Lucy." Shirl's momma gazed off nowhere special. Her grin looked deformed it lasted so long. "You ought to have seen our girl leave here. That frock was something to respect. Way too plain for my eye but of a high quality anyhow. Didn't weigh not one ounce. You could've ate it like cake frosting, pulled it through my wedding ring. Too, we plaited her hair in this tight circle on top. A crown, like. Was preacher's idea. Here all along, everybody in town has been thinking up how to dress my child, hoping and fix her up even better than I could. It flat touched my heart to see them others working on her half the morning. Like decorating the Maypole. And I don't need to tell you, Lucy, she didn't mind one little bit. When she danced into our kitchen all done up like that, why her daddy took one look, put his head down on the table, and Silas cried like a baby. I'm still shook from it. When she left here, child, she looked . . . well . . . to pass her on the street, you wouldn't even know her, Lucy."

"No, ma'am," I said, trying and sound a sport.

So, Shirl's momma finished with me. No hard feelings. There'd probably have to be new friends now, ones with finer mouths and smoother manners, a notch up. There'd be other dresses maybe even fancier than the one today— important dances—we'd both be finding our very own Shirl listed in the *Herald Traveler's* "Society Comings and Goings" section, understood? Less tree climbing. No telling where Shirley might end up society-wise. Did I see? I nodded, said I did. The Mrs. claimed there won't nothing personal in all this. She patted my hand, she even kissed one grubby palm. She thanked me for having had Shirley as a friend. I thanked her for having had Shirley at all. Then I knew to stand, I knew to hitch up my yellow rope, I knew to leave.

SLOWED, I passed our tree house. I needed to get off ground. The earth was my only problem. Gravity had a grudge against me. Once up, I made my rope circle be our table—inside that I placed our tin tea set. I tried arranging everything just so, like she'd forever laid out stuff for me. I had been spoilt: me, Poppa just home from work, grousing up into the family tree, extra bossy from the world's street-level chores. She (Momma) always seemed pleased to spy her breadwinner climb up.

Breadwinner: And how are the wee ones, wife?

Wife: Half dead from mumps again, they are, I fear, high-strung peevish little things. All twelve have sties all over them and won't quit squabbling— same as always. And how was the Governor's office, sir?

Breadwinner: Today we mopped up, we are set for life, my pretty one. What's for supper?

Wife: Any dessert you want that I can make, sir.

And on and on. How stupid it now sounded! Like kids, just playing! Had this poppa been bullying this momma—or the mom this pop?

Shirl blamed Ain't for everything. But what we'd done in secret (like a man and wife must), *that* had forced her through the spasm of bad grammar. Now she'd come out on the other side, cleaned up word-perfect. I climbed higher, scaring off two nesting jays. Good riddance, I didn't want another thing on earth, especially a living couple, to have a home again, especially in this tree.

Around me broken stools and chipped trivets toted up here from Shirl's folks' place and mine. On blond boards below, rusty stains left by our ceremony: blood, that old sorority. I'd told my handpicked sister that my red would double up her strength. But it seemed that, by mistake, she'd got the toughness. I had took on all my friend's diseases, plus my own. She was yet working—a terrible white sugar—in my veins.

Across right wrists, the pink lightning-shaped slash mark still puckered like a zipper. With jays swooping at me, I commenced to slam that arm's

veiny part against rough bark. Then, when it hurt sufficient, I figured this
was mighty silly. Everything unasked for had already punished me enough.
I didn't need to add on pain. So I climbed down, rope around my shoulder,
wondering who would help me. Help me do what? First I took a long mopey
tour of Baby Africa. I knew nobody there. If Momma hired a maid, I'd visit
that beloved maid's house. My rope got a few uneasy looks. This all happened
just four years after the Raferty lynching. Soon I shambled towards my
aunts', hemp dragging.

Lake and Sea sat on a shady side porch, eyes closed. Through a open
window, Ruler played some anthem with real power. Favorite pupils were
scattered here and there on hassocks and old wicker. Children's eyes were
clamped shut too—girls wore white dresses so starched that, if you put a
stamp in the upper right of their bib waists, they'd be honored by the
postman, they'd go places. Each child seemed half blind under a steep paper
cap showing one composer's features copied from some somber old engraving. "My *Personal* Composer" was written overtop in letters arching like
those on a gravestone. Under stiff foreign black-and-white genius helmets,
rosy local faces blinked.

Seeing my aunts, all busy, I felt sadder still. I started crying. Each eye
opened. Ladies rushed me to the farther side porch. Music stopped. Ruler
appeared, squatted before me. Other young people (she barked Kaiser-like)
should remain seated, with eyes closed, should allow the music to resonate
continuously within, beginning *now*. Aunts—having lost their own loved
one—seemed to know right off what'd happened. They huddled nearer me.

"Now," Ruler began. "Lucy dear, whom? Whom have you lost. It's your
little Shirley, is it not? Why is it always the *one* that goes? We'd let Falls
tiptoe off to its deserved doom if only it would leave us just our *one* to love."

The three sisters had been giving my friend free lessons. I'd brought
Shirl to call, aunts figured her folks had but little money, they saw how
Shirl stood (none too subtle) plunking dreamy at one Steinway's keyboard.
Aunts kept their donation a secret. All as a favor to me. At Shirl's name, I
blubbered, feeling so ashamed to spoil their concert. I wanted to move right
in with these exceptional women, ones unlucky enough to've been cheated
at love early, but smart enough to have never given up on it.

"What precisely did young Shirley *do* to you?" I shook my head no, eyes
streaming like broken blisters. I tried to keep things hushed so's other children wouldn't hear and gossip at school come Monday.

"Well," Ruler sounded logical, "what did you do to *her*?" Again I couldn't
tell. The love subject, a difficult farm language that I could not speak.

Ruler, full of pity, straightened now. She laid one hand across my scalp,
she took a stance. On me, she used a line she'd once paid me twenty-five
cents to memorize by phonics (I still have it by heart). Ruler ofttimes quoted
it about Maestro Wagner, at whose altar she admitted worshipping right
regular. " '*Er wurde entweder verfolget oder angebetet—zwischen diesen zwei
Extremem pendelte sin Leben.*' "

And again the Sea, who hated Ruler's overuse of distant tongue on native soil, chimed in: " 'He was either persecuted or adored. Between those two extremes his life dangled to and fro.' "

"The women of this family!" Lake added, placid, cheated. "The destinies of the women of this family."

I'd never heard Tragedy expanded to apply to sixty-eight pounds of me. This omen spooked me some. So I kissed my good aunts' hands. I dragged my rope down off their cultured porch.

They later told me that—in my mood—it was the rope that worried them the most.

8

YESTERDAY we sat in the lounge watching *My Children, Right or Wrong*. It comes on at one and is the show I've mentioned where everybody's good-looking but it don't ever seem to help them a bit. Honey, whatever can go wrong in their lives, does—but every single day. Tiring.

I keep up with it but not like some of them in here. I do have other subjects. I hate being what you call dependent on anything. Good as I love to eat—if I could, I'd quit food for three days at a stretch just prove it ain't *that* big a deal. —Maybe my not wanting to lean on anything come partly from finding that everything I onct tilted towards is missing now. *My Children*—child, some days just the name of the show sets my four teeth on edge. I out-aged all of mine. But I told you that. You have kids partly so they'll be company for when you're as brown-green with time as I've got now. They're supposed to keep a eye on you, put banisters on your back porch to prevent the Broken Hip. They're to bring over pear preserves and your straight-A grandkids, right? They're to keep you out of a State Charity Home like this.

Anyhow, yesterday we sat watching our program and, all of a sudden, there's this haze over the set like the angel hair we used to trail across our mantelpiece at Christmas. The set blows up. Then comes the vilest wire stink you ever did smell. One old lady—*real* old—she cried, thinking that the entire group of all them children had burned up. Some folks get more superstitious as they age. Woman had once been a schoolteacher, and now she was back to thinking that actors were tiny and lived, blow-dried and wife-swapping, in that box year round. Today, riding her chair, same lady wheeled in here holding a tin can in her lap. She'd come collecting to have the set fixed. The Home just shelled out forty dollars for repairs. Our director said we'd have to go without for a while. But the frail teacher collecting dimes, she is just dying to know about two divorces, one murder, and who Debby's daddy really is. I told her I didn't have not a cent to chip in, though my heart was in the right place. She looked mighty let down. So I reached into my bedside table, wrote on a scrap of paper: "I, Lucy Marsden, offer

my total support to this here effort at repair." I slipped that in her tin can.
Well, it cheered her right up. She saw herself to be Miss Joan of Arc out
gathering ransom for them pretty young folks locked in, waiting to see
daylight and troubles again.

That's one thing about getting on up in years. The Lord giveth and
sometimes the Lord, in taking *you* away, He handeth back a bit. One woman
down the hall died last week, nothing new. Room Twenty-six. But, just
before, I rolled in to set with her. She was like me—the last survivor of a
long line but ended up alone as if she'd been the one and only all along. I
double-parked beside her bed, got hold of her nearest hand. Our nursing
staff is real overworked and Jerome was probably off doing some set-and-
dry-and-dye job down the hall.

Those of us still clear-thinking (more or less—I have my *days*), we
sometimes try and help out where we might. Keeps you from getting stir-
crazy and thinking that the daytime shows are the onliest things left spinning
in the world beyond our parking lot. Well, my patient started talking out
of her head somewhat, talking about planting a three-row bed of zinnias.
But when I woke from a little unplanned catnap, she was laying there looking
right square at me, concerned, like she was *my* nurse. Handsome woman,
always very particular in her clothes, didn't look a day over seventy-five and
she was, like me, gnawing towards her first century's end.

"You know, Lucille," she recognized me and everything. Sounded just
as reasonable as Woodrow Wilson in his steel-rimmed prime, says, "I
thought it'd *hurt*. I mean, yes, certainly it's quite a shock to the system,
ending—but there's not the kind of pain I'd been dreading since around,
say, sixty-eight. It eases you as it slides out from under the person, like a
favor your body pays you at the end. I worked as a waitress at the Virginia
Beach one summer as a girl. They'd leave your tip under their plate when
the meal was done. You'd think: Here's just another stranger's dirty dish—
no reward for all my smiling help—but sometimes something *was* hid under
there for you. The suspense was seeing how much you'd got."

"Well, that's good," I said, clutching her old paw in mine. "It's some
mercy, anyways."

But then she was right slam back to being six, bullying me (like I was
her long-suffering black mammy) to go fetch that child's red watering can
from off the window ledge. Plain, she saw it there. I made to roll over for
it, humoring her. Well, she pulled on my armrest. "Now wasn't that foolish
of me?" she laughed, but, too, it was the slow heaving's starting up. You
learn to know the sound of it. I soon had to go call Jerome and our head
nurse.

Still, I figure the more exits a body is in on, the clearer you see: You
do have some control over how you slide out. People manage it in their own
peculiar style, you know? Me, I used to think it was some dark chute you
fell down. You'd be standing in line to buy some cheese, Death dropped

over you, conked you blind. Into that you'd slide: blackness and a jaw as big as the state capitol.

Now I see—it's *in* you all along. It ain't no net that falls from up on high. It's there—like a gift for music, this appetite long hid, waiting. (It just happens to be your final knack, is all, and it's one talent that—right dem- ocratic—don't nobody escape.) Comforting to see how it's tucked inside our marrow from babyhood forwards. No way can you stop its happening. Thing is, it's still personal. So when old Death rears up—you can control and shape it some, it being *you*.

To Lucy here, that feels a blessing. See, I'm learning: Cradle to crypt, we get to stay who we are.

Only fair, really . . . we die in character.

9

MOMMA, seeing me mope upstairs, called, "Well, who stabbed you?" I made sure the bathroom door was locked, I struggled free of clothes, slid into hot hot water. Before Shirley, I never sat in a tub with anybody else. But now, whenever I climbed in alone, this much porcelain looked huge as a tooth- colored mausoleum. Plus, clear water (unlike juice) made a magnifying lens the size of a oval tabletop. I hated how much of you you saw aquariumed under there—still you, but now all sprigged and changing, swollen some. I propped the bath brush at my tub's far end. I pretended that the brush was human. "Hi," I said.

"Sister?" Momma stood calling from the hall, jiggling the lock. "Are you crying? or sniffling with a cold? You're crying." I refused to tell what was wrong. She hurried downstairs, made a quick social call downhill, dashed back here. She'd never before visited Shirl's cottage. I imagined her queenly taps (three only) at the planked door. I felt ashamed of Mom, of us. We'd been rich in all the wrong ways. I had forever played poor, and Shirl, ashamed of being poor, acted semi-wealthy. We had never been straight with each other. Maybe we should've *both* played Poppa or both Momma or switched more regular?

My full-time momma kept retesting the doorknob. She knew something but wanted to hear my own reason for crying. I finally hollered, "I ain't crying!" Well, then she really roared like I'd never heard a person do. I slid underwater for cover. She kept hurling one shoulder against door. Screamed I was a wicked wicked child to go on using that dreadful word—and after Ain't had just cost me my one and only friend on earth.

"How, can, you, still, say, it, child, how?" She struck my door hard, risked ruining her pianist's hands. She staggered to a hall table, grappled with something and chucked it (the huge pink vase she'd never cared for) down our stairwell. The sound—across marble foyer—scattered purest terror. In water, I lay whimpering as Momma cried: "*Ain't* is the dagger you have driven through your mother's heart. In our town, as of right now, you are truly dead, child. Even the horse renter's daughter has dropped you cold. You have nobody now. Satisfied? You are not yet thirteen. A corpse cannot make her debut. Socially, Lucille, you're a little . . . blue little dead girl. —My life is over."

I was in water, shaking. Water was so cool now. "Monster," she was kicking busted crockery off the stairs. Doc Collier was called. He stuffed her with many a pill, ordered her to lay flat prone in a dark room till strength came back. I worried she might use returned strength to throttle me. Poppa, sullen-acting now, hid me from her all Saturday and Sunday. He acted hurt, treated me like I'd purposely left Shirl, not vice-a-versa. Saturday night, I looked out my bedroom window, saw more things dropping, heard breakage chime our brick walk. From upstairs, Momma was throwing forth all bed-clothes. She'd tossed two mantel pug dogs. In smithereens: matching Strat-fordshire cockatoos she'd owned since she was six. I laid under covers listening: Pop tried talking loud but nice, then loud, then slapped her. Next a stillness dropped with only me awake right in the middle of it, me the cause of everything. I felt like a tooth so rotten it prays to be yanked clear of where it hatched and stayed and spoiled, a thing so brown and bad it longs to be thrown away forever. On the city dump. Maybe, for good meas-ure, burned. Yeah. Burned, too. (I want to be cremated. Pretty soon too, child. I probably said that.)

Sunday on the porch—with her tucked in bed upstairs—he acted like his lady wife was dead, like Momma was a form of Shirley—too perfect and so, lost to us. "I told you about my greatest day of all? In Bear Grass, was walking to shoot pool, carrying a cue I'd whittled from aged hickory. I'd sewed a little broadcloth sack, riveted on a suitcase handle to give it the official look. Hiking along train tracks, thinking nothing. The 2:04 that never stops in Bear Grass seemed to slow down on my left.

"Its blamed whistle was sure blasting when I hear a splinter and a sound like forty gallons of water, a huge balloon breaking over the cowcatcher. That was the horse, hit. Woods stood off to my right and I catch a rustling amongst the highest limbs, Runt Funny. Then I seen a thin trailing cloth fall into sedge grass. We'd had rain the night before and so our ground was soft, a mercy. I took the falling thing for maybe some eagle swooping off its tree-limb perch. I go over. It's a very pretty young lady face-up, eyes closed, her wearing a cape. Cape was lined with white silk, it rested open all beneath her like wings fanning out. Her bodice had been tore but not so much as to look cheap. A little blood was on her but that was scattered too—artistic-like. Up ahead, the locomotive grinds still, great scuttling and sudden shouts. I didn't rightly connect all that to what I'd found here. Not right then. I dropped my pool cue, I fell onto my knees beside it. (I didn't yet consider it a human but some bird or angel fallen from on high.) I mashed my ear to her/its chest, a beating, good. 'Sammy, you appear to be in such luck, boy,' I told myself while pulling her cape as a kind of sled into deeper woods. Then—after dabbing at her face with spring water—I toted her on home, she weighed next to nothing in those days, child. I hid my pool cue to go back for.

"Them at the train, picking up the pieces of her cousin, noted how half the horse was on one side of the track, half on the other. They believed that she must be scattered, too, a mushy goner. People who'd watched the foolish buggy chase from the train's smoking car, they told our sheriff, 'A girl was with the unlucky gent, handsome girl—pity, really.' We had her three days all to ourselves before she come to. Ma and Pa acted impressed I'd found her. I was always lucky about finding things, but never a whole girl! I used to set near her pallet, watch her sleep. One day she opened her eyes. Someway I knew she'd know me if ever she woke. She seemed to, too. She looked around like thinking that our plain cabin was some stage set or a joke. 'Am I alive? This is Heaven, is it not?'

"I nodded to my angel from the treetops or the sky. 'Heaven. Yes'm. Whatever.'

"Finally I went to town and told the sheriff, 'Look, I found somebody.' Her rich folks had offered a reward. I didn't know. I didn't know who-all they were, though her silk-lined cape proved something. Soon as I confessed to the sheriff, I regretted it, child. When he asked me for her hair color and all, I shook my head No, not yet. Couldn't surrender that, not yet. I would only repeat what I'd said to him so far, 'I found somebody. I found me somebody.' "

Poppa now reached over, touched my shoulder. "After all that poor Bianca's lived through—that accident when she was a wee girl, plus the train mess—this latest thing is small potatoes, Runt Funny. She'll do fine. High-strung is all."

"Yes, sir," said I, and held on to his hand.

10

THEN for me it was Monday (oh, how I dreaded school). I saw *her*. Waiting for the bell, already huddled with that fancy bunch, she wore white. The Baptist preacher's girl stood near Emily Saiterwaite, the Episcopal one's. They'd decided to share her. Both were touching the back of Shirl's new hairdo. They gossiped with each other, not her. How could my Shirley let them poke at her like that? Hair all ringed and crimped on top made Shirl (alive under this pie and crown) look older. It showed off her fine stem neck—she already appeared way richer, better, nearbout up to princess, but cooled off, too. They'd plucked all drab cloth flowers from her, they'd pared her of lackluster lace. I missed the pretty junk. You won't be surprised to know: Tackiness has always interested me. I'd forgot that Shirl was so much taller than me. A person *had* to look up to her.

When I shuffled past their group, the Mayor's daughter laughed, "Shh. Here comes you know what." Hurrying, I let myself give Shirl a look. It won't a mean look nor was there a mess of forgiveness in it, just a look. I knew she wouldn't tell a soul what-all had really happened. We couldn't tell, no words of ours (town talk or farm language) covered that.

I made my walk seem cocksure and boyish as I could. I crooked thumbs under my skirt's waistband, jammed my chin out. Shirl gave back half of one ill nod—her mouth, the basis of a smile that never formed. She looked like their prisoner but, I saw, she'd picked her jail. —She'd always been a bit too easy to boss. In the privacy of our tree, she forever agreed to play Wife, a role (like Indian for massacring) nobody chooses first but somebody's got to undertake. Maybe it served me right, losing my friend to others' orders? But oh how fast those scuzzball hoity-toilets had got their claws into my pale blood sister!

They all now turned from me. Two caught Shirl's white puff sleeves. Snorting, they spun her clear of my smarting face. Shirl's lifted hair showed off, at her neck's nap, two shy silvery fluffs—not long enough to reach up, join the plaiting. Out these wavered, looking so sad and sweet there, surprised by daylight after years spent under curls' humid awning.

Even from the back I still admired her.

POPPA sulked all over the house. He stood thirty minutes in our dark pantry. He helped Momma to her piano, where she sat playing back issues of Prelude of the Month—her music precise then forgetful. Pop looked off the porch and out at envying farmers, envying them. Felt like our place had been quarantined because of me and my foul mouth. Pop blamed hisself, his swampy history. He missed Shirl's coming over, grinning at Mr. Card's stupidest stunts. When he called her "Shirley Goodness and Mercy, follow me all the days of my life," I knew that he half meant the invitation. Whenever Shirl told me she flat liked the way my daddy *looked*, I'd report right back to him. He beamed, "Surely not. Shirley said that about this gooneybird face?" and he'd rush upstairs, shave, come down in plaid suspenders, yanking on them, walking bowlegged, asking, "How'm I doing?"

Now he fell into the porch swing, not even moving. I wanted to tell him not to fault old Ain't. Maybe he should blame a skunk, a handy sponge, a weird itch. Blame how two girls got squirted by a unexpected animal. Blame how, though vegetable juice was strong enough to squelch the stink, it couldn't stop girls' noticing each other, couldn't stop their feeling so warm towards one another—from clinging like the honest little animals that they were. Blame how vegetable cannot cancel animal. Only Animal can cancel Animal.

All language starts as Farm Language.

I tried lightening things by telling jokes. "Thanks kindly," he says after a set of my level bests. "But, Runt Funny, I've heard those ones." Of a sudden,

I understood: All my jokes were his. I'd never considered it before. But he'd never squashed me before by pointing this out. It was, I saw, adulthood setting in.

AROUND then, he started squinting at me, he'd take a pinch of my calico dress between two fingers, testing it: "Your momma can do better'n *this*." Poppa would hoist my braids and—like Momma—pull them to a lump atop my head. He grinned disappointment, shook his head sideways, dabbed my nose with my pigtails like repainting me. "Poor weegie, you got more freckles than your speckledy old man."

Poppa'd never complained about my non-prettiness before. He always said my being the perfect Runt Funny was what kept me snug on the porch with him. I thought (because of this) my face was someway lucky. But now I caught him studying my ankles, my hands—Pop's eyes (nobody's fools) working like the appraiser folks hire to come in, tag the furniture of somebody that's died.

Poppa commenced wearing nicer clothes on weekdays. Something about this weighed on me, like he was trying to look nice so *I* wouldn't be bothered. He showed a sudden interest in our yard, strolling out there in a white shirt to clip the box hedge, smiling half-toadying to all nice folks that passed on foot. Farmers he still cut dead.

Poppa had always kept close track of the social scene that never let him in it. That season there was a full-tilt scandal: The plumpish daughter of the peanut-mill owner got engaged to a strapping Italian scissor-sharpening drifter who'd been working around her poppa's house. The fellow was handsome but (word had it) couldn't read a lick. Folks let out as how, when the bride-to-be's heartsick mother asked the dark boy for *his* wedding invitation list, he coughed up two names: a circus barker from Providence and his own parole officer out of Newport News. Poppa said he was shocked, flat *shocked* that such a family had fallen to such bad luck. Pop claimed the boy should be horsewhipped and the girl must either get sent to Europe on a slow boat (to get over the romance) or else have her trust fund punished. Momma and me sat still during Pop's high-falutin speeches. We didn't mention how these selfsame charges had been aimed at Momma's own marriage choice. "And if *you*," he turned to me one day, "ever did that to *this* household, if you put a boll-weevil blotch on *our* fine name . . ." "What?" I asked, not caring. "You'd do *what* to me, you redheaded hicky clodkicker?"

I saw his face fold in on itself—double—like hands clapping—then smartly release. He turned aside. "That does it," he whispered. "Boy, Runt Funny, that really does it for now. Cut me down, why don't you?"

Hand over my mouth, I rushed indoors and upstairs. All kids live in secret fear that there's one thing they mustn't do or say. Once they've blurted that, love and home will never take them in again.

· · ·

MOMMA, after six sad weeks of this, mellowed into Mrs. Peacemaker. She tried to make me feel I won't too underfoot. I knew otherwise but where else was I welcome?

One Sunday Poppa sat heavy in our porch swing, and for the first time in ages, I crawled up onto his lap. His arm made a easy automatic bundle of me. His face, the color of a flowerpot, grew gold and silver nibs. Along his jaw, I did Itsy-Bitsy Spider.

"You're a royal mess okay," he said, and wrapped me closer to his bony front. "Look, just because your old pap lives in the doghouse full-time, that don't mean *you* got to. If you're smart—and you are, seeing as how you take after your momma's side and your aunts—you can choose anything, Minute Waltz. 'Anything' covers a peck of ground. If you've got all that, why in this world try and act like me? Heck, I wouldn't if *I* could help it. I got assigned it. —Tell Poppa why."

He waited. I clamped on, spooked he'd set me down, shove me away like Shirley had, like Momma did.

I held for dear life on to his shirt, like I was some baby monkey, petrified of heights but treed for good.

He pushed on, "Because you know what your old daddy thinks *you're* getting ready for?" My cheek pressed Poppa's breastbone. I made a questioning sound—balled and locked against him, either eye gone huge. I was about to hear everybody's unspoken plan for me. Church bells rang. Mrs. Smythe's canaries made their feathers sputter.

"Why, choosing the perfect fellow, silly britches." I held on so. "Look, after all, you'll soon be going on fifteen, right? A long engagement. How does that grab you, My Second Hand? Let's face facts, pip, you ain't ever been what you'd call a good student, not like Shirley and them others. Which ain't to say you're not smart, understand. But what your momma calls 'higher learning' don't seem real likely for you, right? And you'd go pure stir-crazy sitting forever on this porch with the likes of me and her. So, what's left a girl? What? I'm asking you. In your own words."

I felt thick-mouthed, slow. I leaned harder against him. People seeing me from the street wouldn't think it a bit strange that a child my age could sit in her poppa's lap, and yet what was this poppa hinting? He caught my upper arm, just a wee bit rough, proving he was asking me for real here.

I mashed closer, wanting to be either safe or noplace at all.

"Tell Poppa. What'd be good for you, gal? What comes next? What? I'm asking here."

I swallowed and tried it, "Perfeck fell . . ."

He nodded, "Perfect fellow. Glad . . . Glad that dawned on you, too," he wagged his head Yes. Only then did our swing move.

I was just coming up to fourteen. "And don't you worry," he squeezed me in a nicer way. "When it happens, Runt Funny, and once you've moved, you won't be able to even keep me out of your house. Why, your momma

and me we'll come visit most every Sunday you want us to. You see if we
don't, why wild horses . . ." I held this man. Had to. Who else?

I felt too bushed or dulled to cry. "Runt? You in there?" he tried and
tickle me alive. He made his best worst face. His hairy nostrils looked like
burrows where shy animals live. It scared me suddenly, a whole grown man
this close.

"I'VE STOPPED blaming you," Momma told me at dinner. "I think of it as
'we' now. You worked to capacity—some genes have held you back, is all.
We are poison. Even when certain persons try speaking to me downtown,
it feels a good deal forced. Invitation-wise, this household is a ghost ship,
The Flying Dutchman, return to sender. —Lucille, no cotillion would touch
us, not for a sizable bribe. Believe me, I have made certain overtures. And
even if we *should* turn up on a list now, *I* couldn't go through with it. I
mean . . . it'd be like traveling all the way to the New York Dog Show and
expecting a blue ribbon for . . ."

"Enough," Poppa yelled, struck the table.

"For some three-legged animal. Some three-legged dog!"

She wobbled from the table, coughing up the stairs. Two of us were
left.

Since she'd dashed off like a child, that made us left here, a couple. He
said, "Pass the butter beans." I did. I knew, if we were the couple, our
marriage was a bad one. I missed her being here. I knew she tried. I forgave
Momma's not yet feeling ready to forgive me. Years I'd seen the woman
playact at being hurt over little snubs. Now that she really felt it, deep, her
pain scared and stirred me. She wore the same dress all one day and clear
into the next. She bumped into the furniture like some old-timer losing
eyesight.

Before the skunk, she daily planned my debut guest list. Worried which
florist to use. Now when Poppa recalled the down payment on my gown,
when he asked if we could get us a refund—Momma give him her most
unamused look to date. I was her one child and her schemes for me had
always felt a mite ruthless. If only I'd been born as simple as Shirley, that
willing to take orders, born as pretty as my onetime friend—store dummy
for others to dress up and sell things off of. Not even *I* thought my face was
such a bargain—I tried not to blame Momma for agreeing.

She played piano more. Stayed home all afternoon, the house dark. She
left windows open even on cold days so Summit passersby would at least
hear how she was the sister of fine piano coaches. She sat rigid: her very
upright spine, three octaves of ivory. She concertized, as she called it: This
was the large daily favor she doled out to a wormy undeserving world.
During her open-windowed afternoons, Momma only risked pieces she knew
perfect and by heart. This meant repeating the same five numbers, always
in the selfsame order. She never made a single mistake. But Momma had
no confidence in one new piece she'd learned for twenty years.

Came the Tuesday afternoon I sat bathing, thinking about nothing—grateful for that. One floor below, in our dim front parlor, Momma stayed after her music, reliable as wallpaper, the same, the same, the same. Then I looked down and saw, between my legs, this long red stripe, a kind of cylinder in water, pushing out past knees. The thing went frayed and feathery at its far end. When, fading pink, it reached my ankles, I stopped smiling. For a second, crazy as poor Shirley with her fit of Ain'ts, I thought that tomatoes' color had been saved in, then sent out—some stranger knickers-level form of weeping or remembering. But by scooping up bath water near my face—by touching myself—I found: This was no juice but my own. All the red in white me, leaking out.

Slow, moving like somebody real ancient, I crawled free of the tub. I kept eyes aimed forward. I tied on my baggy robe. I went barefoot down carpeted stairs to Momma's music. There she sat doing her reliable cross-hand runs with no more ado or mystery than a person making toast.

I stood by her black Chickering grand. She wore a Sunday dress on weekdays now, trying to fluff up the self-esteem I'd helped flatten. I waited till she finished her fifth and final concert piece. Done, she turned to me with no expression whatever. I said, "Look, there ain't no reason I should be bleeding from between my legs, is there?"

Sitting, she drew herself up, fingertips touched her beautiful cameo. "No," she said. "No fair reason in this world." Then her features broadened from the inside out. "Yes," and she fell—face in one arm's crook—onto keyboard with this slash of spine-crack sound. She laid there weeping, her back bucking like a child's. I stroked Momma's neck, the fine and upswept hair. "It's nothing." I left out Ain't this time for her sake. "It's nothing. I just asked."

NIGHTS, I heard my people strolling the hallway, no lightning to scare them awake. Discussing the future: mine. Two weeks after bleeding in the bath, I took first serious notice of a big ex-soldier. He'd been keeping eyes on me. (Otherwise how would I have seen so much of his eyes in his eyes?) The uniform, jaw, body all seemed made of solid shoulder, one upright wall—painted mostly gray. For years I thought "soldier" and "shoulder" came from one word. Poppa's friend looked back with a readiness unknown since Shirl. Alone as much as I was, I had too much time to think about his gazing at me so. Captain seemed to offer what a best friend my own age was supposed to. —He claimed I brought out the boy in him.

He lingered around the house some evenings, sat beside me in the old porch swing. Poppa joked, flattering the man. Pop kept giving me slow grins and cagey winks I fought not to see. I figured Momma would make quite the fuss over my first caller, and such a wealthy one. I expected her to flirt, to overdress. Instead she acted like Distance come indoors. All day Poppa mentioned how Captain was nice-looking, had a good share of fame here-about, the big house on Summit long paid for, rental properties aplenty.

How onct when General Forrest, old by then, came through here by train, the General waited at the station, asked some black child to run fetch the Captain. From the waiting room's far side, a crowd watched these two catch up on old times until the 5:42 whipped a grizzled hero off again. Pop pressed his case: "Who else you waiting for, woman, the Lord Jesus? He's a confirmed bachelor, wouldn't know what to *do*. He'd probably throw rocks at it. You expecting Jesus Harvard Vanderbilt Astor or what?"

Polite as Momma acted toward the Captain, she could make her handshake leave a blue icicle bracelet dangling on any person. Pop scolded her afterwards, said that, around Captain, she carried on like Queen Victoria unamused mid-migraine.

Now every night, my folks paced, talking in low solemn tones about whose house I'd be living in for life. Nobody asked me. Momma admitted she was the one who might seem to favor such "an alliance." True, other local mothers had perked up, even Mrs. Saiterwaite, on hearing talk of Captain's interest in unlikely me. I was up to seventy-some pounds. Momma knew this could put us back on the social map. She might just use my debut invitation list for the wedding roll call. Without a coming-out, my value marriage-wise had been cut way back. All this she knew. "But," she said. "For one thing, the age difference."

"Happens all the time," Pop announced. "Juliet won't but fourteen."

"Juliet who?"

Silent, Poppa was enjoying the moment, "Mrs. Juliet Romeo, ever heard of her?"

"But, dearest, her young man was that age as well." Momma always considered Literature the biggest name a person can drop. I sat up in the dark bedroom, listening. But not even Shakespeare had swayed my mother.

"I see Captain's hand with those yellow nails, huge. They look like a war veteran's hands would. God knows where they've *been*. And I study our child sitting there, knowing not a thing, Samuel. I'm sorry but it makes me the slightest bit nauseous. It just does. I cannot picture any of it together in the same frame. —You think marriage is easy for a woman, just because ours has been so fortunate. But, dear one, marriage has . . . more excruciating high F's than the Queen of the Night's second aria. Everybody cannot *do* it. She's so young, she's not even seen Europe yet, or for that matter Washington, D.C. I want Lucille spared, is all. I promise you, I'd rather have her remain unmarried like my stick-in-the-mud sisters. I would. You mustn't rush me on this. She's our only one—she's been my hope all these years. Of course I've known she lacks finish, but still . . . ."

When Pop started in about Captain's war record again, Momma—pacing—got louder, claimed she didn't care if he'd won the thing single-handed. It didn't matter if he owned controlling interest in the world. "Samuel, he's older than *we* are."

"Look, woman, he *wants* her. I mean, not to be overblunt, but have you got yourself a good long gander at our sweet Runt Funny lately?"

"Do not call my baby that. You know I loathe your doglike nicknames for her."

"But have you? I mean really *looked*?"

She rushed him. I heard her, he'd be holding Momma's wrists to stop her pounding his shoulders. In bed, I leaned back, hands laced behind my head. She started crying in a low, lost, sour way.

In dark, I grimaced, smiled, I panted out of fear. For years, I'd heard the woman define who-all I might, by accident, turn into: a scholar, society butterfly, overnight beauty? But now—in her tone, the ugly gasps out there— I felt her really fighting suddenly for me myself. Me, plain—like I was and had been all along. But, odd, instead of feeling honored, I turned mean. I did. Just kept hardening my heart to the woman who might've saved me. After all, I wondered, where had Mrs. Queen of Night been when I needed her? She'd forever hinted I should keep a eye out for some male person, one holding property and a known name. She had criticized my old girlfriend till I dreaded bringing Shirl downstairs into Momma's royal presence. And now, for once, I decided I wanted to do exactly what Momma'd told me to, back then. Seemed my best way of repaying the woman for all them daily stings, the sighs, small freezing glances doled my way. —Honey, I believed that, by wedding the Captain, I'd be spiting *her*.

THAT's how young I was. I couldn't know that Pop—a dirt farmer who'd married money hisself—would want the same for his child. (He forgot we now had some dollars of our own.) He'd been so pleased with his own odd step-up, he couldn't imagine anything finer for his girl. Too, I hadn't taken this into account: Poppa was a man and so was this admired fellow he planned handing me to. That, you find out later, counts. My being Pop's blood-own single child, Momma's being his life and chow line forever— these were listed in one column. In the other rode Captain's being he-horse male. It won. No amount of years in the porch swing with us females had thrown the ledger balance our own way.

Looking back, I pieced all this together. As Mrs. Married, I'd have lots of household hours to mull on how it'd happened. But at the time, it was me alone in the dark. Me, minus a best friend to test things out on. Me, at fourteen, with a gland where a brain should be, one headful of revenge, no notion where babies even come from—me, stretched out there in that fine garlanded bed, hands behind my skull, feeling in pretty complete control for once. Ha! I could weep, remembering. —I want to break into my own story, child. I'd scream, "Fire!" I'd rush my own skinny self free of that big white house, get me out in time. Of course, you can't ever save yourself in time, can you? That's one thing *about* time—it's like the spring water that has to sit a while before it comes quite clear enough to drink, and by then it's too room-temperature to quench your thirst.

• • •

POPPA would not take Momma's No answer. He grew sly (I saw how many lessons he'd picked up from her all along—or her/him?—by now it was hard to chicken/egg them). Not since he got excited about the P.O. job was Pop missing off the porch for two days running: He'd bought a box of sticky caramels after finding out these were a certain seamstress's favorite. He visited the black lady who still held layaway cash on my deb gown. Sweet-talking, passing around candy to all her children and her whole Baby Africa block, Pop egged her into carrying deb-dress money over towards the wedding one. He whipped out a wad of bills, then went to her best bolted silks and flipped through, picking a perfect royal blue for Momma's gown. Brides-maids? There would be none—we wanted it to be simple but elegant, don't you know. Besides, I had no girlfriends. He knew the Captain had a right to wear his uniform to church. Poppa, born too late to fight, he envied that. So my daddy paid for a tuxedo to be built on him, from scratch. (Honey, the man was serious.)

Inviting the seamstress to our house for a unannounced measuring session, Poppa laid in some champagne. He settled beside Momma, showed her a invitation he'd scribbled out in smudgy pencil. "Wrong, wrong," she had to laugh. "This is on a level with the things young Shirley used to copy, scraps I'd find under bolsters: 'The Maharajah of Raleigh and Mrs. Incorrigible Maharajah-ette request your presence at a Fountain Gala.' Pathetic. The only thing you got correct is our names' spelling. Otherwise, darling, I'm afraid this is so far off it's nearly 'original.'" And when she took the pencil he held there at the ready, Pop gave me this chastened little wink. I got—at that very second—my first strange uh-oh kind of roaring in my ears.

Then I knew I was about to make a major step. Pop, playing dumb, had drawn Momma into so many fidgety details. She had just said Yes without half noticing. Which meant, darling, that *I* had just said Yeah.

As for my would-be bridegroom, I felt he knew me pretty good. At fourteen, who-all was there to know yet? He offered me my due, right square in either eye. Since Shirl ditched me, nobody'd really met my head-on stare. Captain did.

One night, walking with him, I chose to point out my (our) old tree house. He said he loved trees, certain trees where important things had happened, they could be like friends, could they not? He gave me a rose geranium for my bedroom's bay window, showed me how to break the leaf and let out scent like a rose's. Only thing troubled me: To catch you a whiff, you had to go and ruin a whole leaf. He asked did I like pets. Wanted to know my favorite color. Wondered did I love marching-band music as much as he did. I went, "Probably." Answering as best I could, while seen walking around town with him, I felt right interesting, almost adult. The snooty Saiterwaite girls, out under a new fad for parasols, spotted the two of us, arm in arm. I felt them covet me the Captain. Maybe I was wrong.

Pop, less than three months later, off the books, really set up the engagement. Honey, what'd I know? I believed wedlock's strongest half was the "wed" and not the "lock." I thought it would feel like being in a nice clean tub (owing to modesty—one filled maybe chest-deep this time with suds and this go-round in the company of a sweet hard-scrubbing boy my age). I wanted to try everything. Besides, as Poppa pointed out, before Captain came along and proposed, nobody had ever asked me.

The ring itself—offered that autumn, by moonlight in the back-yard garden—was one and a half full carats, it had belonged to the addled Mrs. Marsden, who'd saved it from Sherman's fires. A beauty, pear-shaped, just alive with lights. For a gal my age, this helped. Alone with it, I talked to my new rock. "Cocked his shiny eye and said, 'Ain't you 'shamed, you sleepy-head?' " I spoke to it the way other girls of my years were yet chatting up each other or their dolls.

11

SHIRLEY was, our local paper claimed, the recent and unmistakable central belle at a tony Hunt Club Ball in faraway Raleigh. Me, married off, in a house alone a lot, minus the fired Castalia, pregnant with my first (it happened about this quick, too, child), I had long afternoons to think back on my long spell with Miss Shirley Popular. I heard, through local tongue-waggers, how the girls what'd taken up our stablekeeper's daughter sure did rue the day. Quick study, that quiet Shirl. Why, just after she quit me cold turkey, Shirl switched to the Episcopal Church, leaving me and her own folks stranded as abandoned Baptists. She'd taken to wearing white and left all us cheap earnest pastels behind. The Baptist preacher's wife and daughter, ladies who'd first "discovered" Shirley, let it be known around town that they felt, yeah, right . . . well, *used*. They'd been Miss Shirley's total-emersion stepping-stones towards high-society sprinklers. Episcopalians thought that liquor was just a digestive aid. They thought good genes were the equal of good works. They thought the Godhead had stationery with a list of charter members engraved on it. They believed God was a club. Shirley, she agreed. Shirl joined.

Soon she was attracting—at musicales and charity benefits (first in Falls then on up to Rocky Mount then Durham and finally to Raleigh itself)—attentions of the very boys her fancy early friends expected to interest. Emily Saiterwaite was, you heard, just livid over it. Ha ha ha.

Shirl still remembered how to keep her mouth shut: a asset. The Summit gang had fixed Shirl up a mite too good. They'd even hinted early on as how she should use her middle name—the neutral Ann—to help offset a certain low-class brassy aftertaste that Shirley left in folks' mouths.

I sat breast-feeding my Louisa—eager eater, that one. I had Shirl's picture (in the daily paper) propped on my right knee. I realized afterwhile that my knee was rocking, like you'd keep a colicky baby amused. It was just a picture. The leg jiggled it happy anyways. I sat remembering a certain clean dairy smell she carried with her. I did wonder. Maybe if I hadn't said old Ain't so much? Maybe if she'd stayed plain Shirl and my good friend, maybe then I wouldn't have married quite so young? Maybe. Of course I knew better. Still, it pleased me to think that a finer-quality speech might've let me rise. (I'd still be fifteen but someway unpregnant, a non-mother—not that I regretted my dear hungry baby Lou here.) I would rise then, to a safer lighter life. Who knew? Maybe because I spoke rude Ain't so much, I had to say "I do" so early.

ONLY Animal cancels Animal.

MY FOLKS regretted losing me. They hadn't known what a round-the-house spark plug Lucy was till they'd done shipped her off. The first time they visited me in my husband's big underfurnished house (two pieces of bachelor furniture in the middle of each huge room) the two had to go home early, holding on to each other, their faces fists. I played like I didn't understand exactly what—in the sight of me, dressed up and trying—had saddened them so much. But soon as they were off our land, I run upstairs and sobbed, too proud to follow them, follow them home.

Maybe my parents then decided that without me around they each needed projects. Who knows? But things changed for them not three months after my June wedding. Momma was sitting on the porch watching a squad of hired black yardmen rake first September leaves up and down Summit. The men all knew each other and often stopped to jaw, leaning against the cast-iron lacy fences, leaning on their rakes and brooms. "Look at them," she said, never too patient with black servants' slack. "They don't know *how* to work." And while Poppa sat blinking, she dodged into the house, put on old white gloves, grabbed a broom, and set to work on our own yard—one that Poppa had fitfully took swipes at or hired boys to clean. It was low maintenance till that day. From then on, she started a contest with hired gardeners along the street. By spring, she was wearing Poppa's oldest clothes and chose to work in garden gloves but liked to show you that her palms were still starting to get brown and tough as pecan husks. She did fear bugs and once had to be sedated after finding three mantises riding her hat. But people—seeing her out there, scraping—spoke to her more often and seemed to feel less scared of her haughty tongue. They liked her sudden mannish getups. "Bianca seems almost 'human,' " they said. Only Poppa, stranded on the porch, appeared doubly lonely.

But even that changed when the postmaster—still on speaking terms—brought over a newspaper article about a new grownup night-type class being offered by a certain Harvard College. Harvard gave official certificates and everything, so Poppa wrote away for their list. To make a six-week story quick, him and Momma soon boarded a train, took many suitcases, found nice rooms up in Cambridge, Massachusetts. On his happy return, my three aunts threw Poppa a party. One beautifully hand-lettered banner read: "Welcome to Our Sam, Returned in Triumph, Gentleman and Scholar." In six weeks, proudened toward a kind of quietness that pleased me, my own poppa come back with his certificate of graduation framed.

"To Whom It May Concern, This Asserts that one *Samuel Honicutt* has completed to the satisfaction of the Harvard College Extension Night Annex course work for *Introductory Carpentry*. Be Informed He Is Entitled to ALL THE RIGHTS AND PRIVILEGES Thereof." This he hung right in the homeplace foyer, he showed it to a trail of visitors. Poppa stood beside it, scratching his head and admitting, "Things moved faster up there than here in Falls, folks talk about a mile a minute, and there was times I literally doubted I could keep up. But my darling Bianca believed in me throughout. Many's the day I'd come home with my britches covered in Harvard sawdust, hands covered with Harvard nicks and Ivy scratches—but she had only tea and kind words. Said she, 'You're Harvard College material and all the more perfectly preserved by that rough-hewn manly Burgaw County exterior.' So Bianca said, and well, turns out . . . must of done *some*thing right—says here 'to the satisfaction of' that school in Cambridge." He was now so much in awe of his own Alma Mater that he sometimes—religious-like—didn't want to say its name direct but used the town instead. "During my time . . . in Cambridge," began many of his sentences. He wrote news of his certificate to his folks outside Bear Grass. And there was a happy ending, at least for the school in Cambridge. Happy for them considering how much of my mother's money the graduate-husband wound up willing to his favorite college and not to the settled married daughter down the block.

As for Shirley Goodness and Mercy: I told myself—a sad public nod is all I'd ever get from her now. But, reading papers, keeping up, I felt proud of her and happy for Shirl's folks. She did take them along to this big "do" at the Governor's Mansion, coaching both in advance (according to rumors) to talk only when spoke to direct and then to see if they couldn't weasel out of answering by using a nod or shrug. But, still, she took them with her. I knew it must have meant her mom's idea of Heaven come to Earth. Seemed like, as I whipped through each day's "Society Comings and Goings," ready for my friend's advances, Shirl was my own daughter, not a girl my age. I felt right old already. Maybe I looked it. I spoke right to her picture sometimes, talked so loud that my baby daughter looked up from a teat now vexed by uses, I half hollered to the paper, "You show them, child."

Was three full years later, I spoke to Shirl. In person. Just the onct. The shortest conversation on record. Whilst shopping downtown with Lou new to walking, with Ned in my arms, it happened. Lou had just turned three, acting headstrong from her birthday forward, like she'd read the warning Baby Books. Ned talked early and explained he wanted a second piece of horehound candy at Lucas' All-Round Store. Then Lou chimed in. I'd tugged her out onto wooden sidewalk, her squalling that she was *so* planning to have that extra piece. The boy in my arms said, "Am too." "You ain't." "Am."

"Ain't." "Am so." "Ain't, pip, I'm here to tell you, you just ain't, ain't, ain't."
I stomped sidewalk.

Was just that second, I moved to let a lady pass. She wore this cream-
colored silk dress, a hat, a veil. All her motions, even from a distance,
whispered news of mighty finery. She was just sweeping past when, slowing,
this lady stopped, looked down at me. She'd kept on growing. I'd stayed
nearbout child-sized, still had to stare up at her. Mrs. Wren remeets Miss
Still-a-Swan. She smiled through the star-shaped speckles that netting cast
over her features. We stayed locked like this a minute, her toting two packages and a hat box. She didn't let her eyes stray down over my tired wash
dress, my favorite stretched-out cardigan. It was my appreciating face that
Shirl's face still held, considering. We said nothing, but our eyes lived again
through everything good.

She shifted her parcels to one arm, reached for pearl buttons on her
left glove. Maybe moving to show me a new bracelet or watch. All during,
her features stayed aimed right flush with mine. But then, fickle like she'd
always been, the lady made a face, changed her mind, grew brisk again,
rearranged her shopping, she appeared about to leave.

And that very second, Shirley, maybe noting my allegiance to old Ain't—
my four-letter word—she spoke. In a new voice, through the netting, a
pressed and beautiful mouth said, "Incorrigible." Sounded like she approved.

I smiled back, not knowing what else to do. Finally, with a nod all curt
yet dreamy, the lady gathers up her hem, sweeps past me and my hushed
scruffy brood. Louisa stared after, she'd been put on best behavior. Kept
peeking over one shoulder in the lady's direction, then back at me like asking
who that was, like she could no way connect the two of us. And in my arms,
Ned turned to Little Lord Fauntleroy, behaving all the way home, improved
by just the sight of Shirl. That sight had perked and stunned me, too. I
strolled, openmouthed, moony, going over what'd happened. I'd said, "Ain't,"
right? And she'd said, "Incorrigible," which meant—I reminded myself (not
quite recalling how I knew)—a toughness akin to stubborn, unbeatable.

Well, I figured I could settle for that. Was something anyways. And,
honey? I held on to it.

I WAS expecting my third when I read that Shirley (her Ann had sprouted
a *e* by now, spelling's pinky finger up) was to marry. Her choice was the
tall son of the second-richest lawyer in Raleigh/Durham. (The very richest
only had daughters.) She'd made the finest match locally available, both
society- and money-wise. Her young man's granddad had been governor
and there was, the paper said, "every reason to expect the new generation's
prospects are similarly august." I'd seen her choice just onct, buying gardenias from a black lady downtown. His face was smoothed and upright as
the celluloid collar that held it—like a vase—from underneath. Of course,
I didn't get no invitation. Didn't expect one—though, of course, you hope.

My poppa was bitterly let down, not to be asked. Now that he'd been to . . . Cambridge, he expected his prospects to improve. "You reckon she's even *heard*?" he asked me of Shirley and his college standing. Momma only nodded at our being overlooked, both confirmed and pleased to be off *that* list.

But I sure studied every last word written about the event. Two full pages got devoted to it in the *Herald Traveler* with, thank heavens, plenty of pictures. I hung around the florist charged with decorating the Hunt Club for the local reception. (It was the same florist shop Momma had picked to prettify my unhatched coming-out party.) I learned that white garlands of gardenias would be swagged everywhere, floor to ceiling, and to heck with the expense. Ballroom all done in white, like her dress, the only pink there would be the bride's now famous complexion. Rumor hinted that the in-laws, while right taken with young Shirley Anne's natural looks and manners, were somewhat worried by her strawy history.

A year later this changed when her first child was born a boy. He was the only male grandchild on either side, he got dubbed something Hamilton the Fourth. Then Shirley (Ann or Anne or nothing extra), why she'd arrived. She was Mrs. White Lady born to bear Blue Bloods. It was plain she'd outgrown Falls and everybody in it. To save face, all ambitious local folks claimed her now as "our" lovely Shirley Anne. Emily Saiterwaite got Shirl to turn up at one of Em's Books and Issues club meetings and you'd of thought that Victoria herself popped in for a quick tea break. Summit Avenue mothers now held up Shirl as Mrs. Example to their own cakewalking piano-tinkling girls.

When Shirl left me at age twelve, she quit speaking to my folks, my aunts. Seemed to feel a wee bit ashamed for taking all them years of hospitality and free lessons, giving nothing back. Since Momma had long since ceased even nodding at Shirl, Momma took this silence to be her own idea. But Poppa, hurt and interested, stayed posted on every tidbit about his old Shirley Goodness and Mercy. Momma called this pathetic, but Pop kept me abreast of every detail about Shirl's second pregnancy. It'd commenced, rumor had it, whilst the young folks, away on Cook's Tour, were visiting Venice, Italy. "Probably at night in one of them long ski-nosed canoes," Pop guessed, still a regular romantic about our old yellowhead. He seemed— through solid postal gossip sources—to know of Shirl's every morning sickness by that selfsame afternoon.

ONE EVENING I wheeled my babies to their grandfolks' place two blocks away. "Care to know something new about your old buddy-ro?" Pop waved me out onto the porch. Momma, in her gardening getup, sat playing piano (same five preludes) for my three wee ones. Can you feature childish me with that many of my own? that many a two o'clock feeding? I couldn't either, sugar.

Pop settled on the weathered swing. Since he "graduated," he seemed both happier and sadder. Was like—having got most everything he wanted— he could think of nothing else to wish for. Both his folks had died within three days of each here recently. He spoke about them now with great new tenderness. He forgot how they had whipped him just for wasting time, reading. Now he sat here checking his hands like some fine farm map might yet be stamped across them. In fading daylight, I saw how much he'd aged, the stripes of gray now added value to his spiny orange hairs.

He smiled but a tired sickly smile. "I been remembering: Was one summer evening when your Shirl slept over here. I did something. I don't know what got into me, Runt Funny. I found a little candle. (It'd been your birthday, a long loud dinner. The three of us had such a lively time, your mother'd left the room with a headache, remember? No?) Anyhow. I lit the candle, I walked up into your room. I told myself it was to see if you-all were safe. But, my Second Hand, I knew better. I lifted up the sheets . . . off of Shirl, I mean. I studied our Miss Shirley Goodness and Mercy . . ."

Waiting for the rest, I nodded. But he just shrugged, like there won't no more, he squinted at his palms, his dwindling calluses. I commenced to fill in what he meant. He must of done something like: hitch up covers off the girl child's muslin nightie, then hiked *it* up. Then considered all the candle showed under the sheets, sheets I knew would be filled with a fond milky smell she trailed like a cure. After, eyes full, he maybe resettled linen, kissed both our foreheads, tiptoed out. I was just guessing, of course.

My older wiser Poppa sat watching me—he nodded, like he saw I'd got it. "Me," he pointed at his chest. "*I* did that."

He confessed all this to a grown woman, nineteen.

"Next morning Mr. Card here woke up," his voice grew raspy. "Heard you children a-bouncing on them beds, chanting, 'Ain't you 'shamed, you sleepyhead?' Well, that flat spoke to me, gal. Couldn't hardly believe that a fellow such as myself would *do* a thing so low. And all these years I've just played like I didn't—but, my old Minute Waltz? Did. I did. I only just wanted to see. Even then I felt like she might up and quit us cold. Before she got the chance, I hoped to check for one second only, just to study all of it, what I'd never get to be . . . near my own self. Wicked, wicked—go on, say it. I knew better, I know better. Now I have my diploma, I own most everything I want. But that's been on me all these years—how I let everybody down." He sat beside me, hands open on either knee, eyes lowered, braced like for a verdict.

Indoors, Momma played two full selections whilst I twisted my fine wedding ring in circles. I finally tried explaining. "Poppa—it's just . . . we both loved her so much. Was only natural, probably. We hoped to save her, to make stuff easier for her, cause it'd been so hard for us. You loved her. So you peeked. And, listen here, Pop, in my own way, me, I looked, too."

Then I saw he sat ripping at the coin-sized bunions that wouldn't never go away, I saw he was near crying. "Shouldn't ought to have, is all. That, I know. But I appreciate your hearing me out. Had to tell. I thank you, my Lucy Luck."

I slid nearer, he put his big head on my shoulder. Brushing my cheekbone, one of his cowlicks, cactus-stiff as ever. My husband was off in Dare County, buying/selling. My mother and children were one room away.

"Why did you leave here?" he asked me. "If I'd of known what I was trading to a stranger and right off my own porch, why I'd of shot any man looked at you. It ain't ever been the same, gal. *I* ain't. My own blind Cambridge-type ambition, it seems to undo me every time. —Us climbers suffer."

MIDWAY through Shirley's second pregnancy, two specialists got hired. I grilled Castalia, my favorite midwife, for news. Of course, richest families used white doctors and not her. Still, Cassie stayed privy to news of carryings for sixty miles around. She told me, "They done sent telegrams to doctors from away far off. And that baby ain't been but five months in the oven."

I fixed a ring of homemade aspic. Poppa buggied me to their fine home out of town, set up on its own green hill. We rode fast so my present wouldn't melt. On their polished veranda, a live pinky-white cockatoo in a frilly cage give me this look like "What do *you* want, white trash?" Pop, waiting—shy— out by the horses, signaled I should go ahead and knock. I handed my present to a brown maid. All in black and white, uniform and cap, she looked stern, starchy, printed-like as the Queen of Hearts.

"Just tell them to keep the plate." I backed off, then added, "But, how about her health, Mrs. Shirley Anne's?"

"Miss Lady," the maid stepped towards me, pulling the teakwood front door closed behind her. "They's a doctor up them stairs from Washington. And I mean Washington *State*."

I asked, could I leave a little note? She fetched me two engraved cards: "Mr. and Mrs. Cheatham Hamilton III, Hilltop Farm." It took me a while, bearing down on a porch banister, biting my tongue, writing careful: "Shirl, Now 'ain't you 'shamed, you sleepyhead?' Rise and shine, girl. A friend still. Luce."

Jotting, it came to me—our poem was probably Mr. Stevenson's only one with Ain't rearing up anywheres in it. No wonder I'd picked it. Then, uneasy at this huge home with its view of miles of view, the foyer's marble statue (a boy getting a splinter from his foot) and the stained-glass cool as ice cube in the hall yonder, I printed the other card. "Do get well soon. Sincerely, Mrs. Lucille Marsden." I handed the maid this last one. She'd watched me write out both. She sighed, like disappointed with me, said, "My man used to work at her poppa's, shoveling out them stalls. Me and her goes way. Now, don't you be standing on no ceremony, not with her like *this*. You give me both them." I did. I thanked her. —People are always surprising you.

Halfway back to town, Pop decided *he* wanted to go indoors, visit Shirley. But soon as he turned our cart around, he lost his nerve. Once home, he got as drunk as I'd ever seen him. Captain was back by then and Poppa came over to our house, nearbout woke the children. Mr. Marsden, disgusted, sent Poppa reeling back to his own end of Summit. (All along, Poppa, he did drink some. Did I say that?)

TO BUY the flowers I wanted, I used half a week of food money. I would just serve more rice next week. I didn't care. I ordered a spray of white gardenias (Greek-vase-shaped) with two rosebuds tucked deep into it. Nobody but me would understand what it meant: two red children playing in a white tub.

Momma babysat my three. Poppa walked me to the funeral. From other liverymen, Shirl's dad had borrowed six matched white horses to pull the black-plumed carriage waiting out front. The crowd was talkative and huge. The Governor hisself was present. His police escort smoked out front. Daddy and me'd just slipped in when ushers shut the doors for lack of room.

Among the dark clothes, I noted three real wide black hats, veils thick as mosquito netting. Headgear was so dark, the owners had to pull layers aside before I recognized my aunts. They looked relieved that Pop and me had wedged in before the doors shut. Their stark faces welcomed me like to some club. They looked odd, clothes too tight, long out of date. Slow, I understood: They'd wore their outgrown widow's weeds from the day, ages back, when they buried their un-husband/poet.

They hadn't loved (or even much liked) my Shirley. But they offered me a nod and, onct they saw us settle, lowered their veils, turned to face the front, moving like one unit all rehearsed. (By now they knew what I might expect of married life. Maybe that'd helped them decide that Shirl, from earlier, had been among my life's true loves. I believed them. As always, I felt honored to be loved by these worthy women.)

Shirley's mother could not be present. She just won't able to believe it all. Poor woman had been taken for some rest at a hospital out past Durham, a place the Baptist preacher got her into, still pulling strings for the lady. (I figured she had enjoyed nineteen years of daily happiness. It was, I told myself, more than most folks ever get.)

Though Shirl and me had barely nodded in seven years, sitting here I felt as close to her as ever, closer. Only feelings for my own children could compare. I saw the two of us riding in a bath the very color our own histories would be. I saw us up a tree—veins opened as a sign of sweetest feelings, not spigoting off when the ritual quit. We won't ever able to stanch whatall we'd unlatched in each other. Going our separate ways had been the only answer.

I stood in line with strangers. Curiosity seekers, some of them, come to see a woman said to be this beautiful, known to be this rich, now as dead as anybody gets. Shirl's dad waited on the front row, his face swollen something awful. He saw me—reached out one flat hairy hand my way, I broke line, gave his fist and shoulder a good squeeze, kissed his forehead. "Lucy," he said. "Somebody got our girl. They's been a mistake."

One row behind him, the Summit crowd who'd offered Shirl her first step up, who'd acted so mean about her later successes. Now here they sat clumped around Emily Saiterwaite, all in deepest mourning. I knew that, forever after, they'd speak of their dear dear departed friend. They watched me with Shirl's poppa. Two of them—cautious—nodded. My mother's daughter, after all, I looked right through them, cut them purblind dead. And it felt excellent.

I WANTED to walk past her open coffin. That way you know it's true. Her infant daughter's small casket was shut, Shirley's not. Seemed important to see my old friend stretched out in white silk, wearing many more yards of it than had ever been needed in real life. White, always her best shade—laid safe between tufted margins of it—here she was, perfect finally.

People were dropping roses, violet bouquets across her lap. Shirl's face showed this sheen like porcelain or the wax-smelling tuberoses banked around her box. Some grim priss at Black's Home of the Funerary Arts (the best) had seen fit to link Shirley's hands in prayer and place them on her chest. Honey, it looked tacky. Shirl would've just hated that. Lilies of the valley had been stuffed between her palms and, under joined fingers, at the edge of her silk sleeve on the left, I saw it, plain.

Not as bad a scar as mine, not near so raw-looking—but a puffy pinkish Z shape. What she'd almost showed me when she moved to take her glove off that last day we met. Nobody knew I won't just tossing in a nosegay like the others. I bent, touched the spot. It was, no surprise, right cool—somewhere between feeling of marble, chill beef fat, tomato aspic, and somebody alive. When I shuffled back to my place beside Poppa, when I slumped down, it seemed like I'd just run about twelve miles.

"A ideal wife and mother," the preacher was saying. A Baptist and a Episcopal one (their bishop, no less) shared the pulpit. Four times they mentioned the Governor's being here. The young husband sat, neutral in his starched collar on the front row. He held their baby boy all dressed in a black velvet suit and matching beret, some of Shirley's gifts to him from Europe.

Listening, I tipped against Poppa (he had refused to walk up, look at her). He bent forward clutching the tasseled vellum program that Shirl's husband had got printed fast and special. It was quality, like the keepsake leaflets passed out at graduations.

Pop kept studying the Order of Worship. Then he groaned loud enough for others to hear. Did it so noisy that three folks (fancy friends of the husband's family) half turned, strict. I didn't know what'd hit him. He rocked now, frowning, shaking his ragged head side to side. He reached out and caught my hand—its palm now worn nearbout as leathery as his. Holding on, he was hurting my knuckles. I saw how, across his fist's back, among the pretty pinkish freckles, new brown age spots had creeped, lording it over boyhood speckles. Finally he let aloose but only to mash two big mitts over his either ear. Then I knew. Then I heard four-hundred-odd voices, every throat but our two go: "Surely goodness and mercy will follow me all the days of my life, and I shall dwell in the House of the Lord forever."

AT TIMES, I still wonder why I picked to speak like this and not the way Momma wanted, full of quotes, rich with a tense for each tense occasion. My husband's grammar was a good bit better than my own and he never let me forget it, neither. Got where my children (their grandma's pets) ofttimes scolded me for talking like some hick. My oldests griped they felt ashamed to bring home fancier friends from school. Especially little pals from Summit Avenue's best end. —I think of poor Momma—dead so long now. But every time I commit Ain't again, I feel her spinning like a wood lathe in her crypt. And, times, I do feel bashful about certain slips. I know I ain't even consistent in my being wrong. But, Lord knows, it's too late for me to try and get it letter-perfect now. Crude as I may sometimes sound to others—*I* understand what I mean. And I always did know this much, darling:

GRAMMAR's just a way of talking about something else.

WHEN LOU, my own girl, got up around nine, a serious reader, she found this grownup book where some young fellow, desperate and broke, jumps off a high bridge over frozen river. The book said, "Then Gerald took his own life." Well, Lou admired that phrase, new to her. She repeated it out loud three times. I was settled beside her on *our* porch swing (I'd got the model just like my late poppa's). I sat shelling butter beans. It was raining out and all my children had been forced to play on the porch. Lou—a patient, sometimes gloomy child, full of methods—she reached into my colander loaded with green, lifted my pink right hand, turned it over. Lou placed her own gnawed fingernail along a zigzag still printed in my wrist.

Tracing it, she asked, "Did you, Momma? One time, did you try and . . . 'take your own life'?"

"No, ma'am," I said right off. "Tried to double it."

"What happened?"

"*This* did. Because, see, once . . ." But I'm holding the wrist out and away, turning it side to side, tilting my head, squinting like Momma always did to make me go blurrier and maybe be pretty finally. I sat recalling everything at onct, a crunch and stew of pictures: Two little girls in a bath the color their own histories'd be. And especially the nails I'd drove so deep into our favorite female elm, how amber had coated each spike's head overnight, lumps smooth and sizable as a big man's pendulum parts, but clear as jewels, nuggets such as only pain can hatch. I sat modeling my scar like some fine lady's choicest heirloom bangle. "Because, see, once . . . upon a time . . . way back, like the Grimm Brothers say, when wishing still helped, there lived . . ."

My other children set down their toys and spoons and pebbles quick. Got off floorboards and scurried towards me. What was nice: They won't doing this to please me. They'd come for selfish reasons. Made me feel good, thinking I had something to tell, after all. My English may be ugly as a mud fence but I know what a story is.

Anything I picked to parade aloud after "Once," anything true, why my brood would gobble it. Louisa, being sensitive, knew to shut her book. Both my hands kept snapping the beans I'd serve kids later. A fine rain spray blew off our gutters. The street was a fat gray river and our walkway a silver brook. I wanted to offer children my entire messy tale. But I knew: Maybe you can tell kids about grownups' carryings-on . . . but never the whole truth about the full range of what other children feel and do. Scares kids too much.

So I winged it. "Once . . . back when money yet amounted to a hill of beans, when every water fountain in the world still overshot its own drain bowl by a yard at least, when your grandma's grand piano got tuned twice a year by a blind fellow on contract to buggy clear out from Raleigh, it or no, there lived what might—to anybody not from around here—seem the dullest thing going: two little girls, best friends, in a town where nothing ever happened."

"That's *here*," one twin pointed through porch flooring. "Here," our other twin puts in. "Well," says I, "it is and, too, it ain't." Then I really got rolling.

Rain kept at it, the day stayed blue and—like this one has—my story drew up to where I might could close it. I felt my audience's attention span droop a bit but as I sneaked up on the famous words "The End," it come to me—it might not. Ever end.

My young ones would get some size and years and seasoning on them and—if I told it right—they might repeat this selfsame tale (plus all their own yarns). Then other kin would tell yet other babies on other porches in far countries and states and maybe even galaxies. Who knew? Woman down the hall says the weather's so strange now owing to those astronauts blowing up that time. Cameras were on their poor relatives, staring overhead. But I fancied blond children living long enough to rattle this to *their* big-eared little pitchers—on and on, a ocean of waves each cresting Once, Once, Once . . .

"Once, in the earth days, in a tale my great-great-grandma weaned others on, there lived two little girls, innocent as anybody gets to be, bored as possible, liking each other too much to stay legal in a town where nothing ever happened but what you got to go on in your own head and heart and, sure, your knickers. —So, one fine morning, these children, wrists bleeding on the sheets, commenced chanting a pet rhyme and bounding on their beds. Once, two . . ."

And on, so much to tell before "The End."

The end, no fair how soon its cowcatcher strikes us all. Shirley went at nineteen when I was nineteen. Momma was fifty-two when her turn came: I'd just turned thirty-two. Poppa stopped at fifty-eight, and me, I was thirty-six. My husband lived till ninety-two, me then fifty-some. And, oh yes, don't let me leave out my aunts, please, darling. I was in my middle forties when they drifted off—in a group, like always. They were old after all. You expect people to die. You should, I reckon. It's supposed to be natural and all and you're considered wise to say that you accept dying. Fact. But, honey, lots of ways, it still seems right weird to me. Not to mention: Unfair.

Now all my assistants in the telling, my little witnesses, they're flat gone. Not you, though. Many thanks. And me? Well—all my friends are new friends. I've got to start the whole thing over every time any story wants saying out. They still do. Yet twitching a mite. As for the telling, darling, I reckon *somebody's* got to.

So, see? child, it ain't over yet. Nope.

Ain't, ain't, ain't, and amen.

A Little
Self-
Pity

*Folly is set in great dignity, and the rich sit in a low place. I have seen
servants upon horses, and princes walking as servants upon the earth.
He that diggeth a pit shall fall into it . . .*

—ECCLESIASTES 10:6–8

*B*EWARE of feeling sorry for yourself. It's mighty tempting.
Private Marsden, still a kid, sat slumped—filthy—by a ditch
near Appomattox. He held a jar. He was trapping bees in it. One musket
rested across his lap. It'd killed three people (with his help). The boy kept
crying but no longer noticed doing so. Four thousand other ragged fellows
rested here in open countryside. All were Southern, most seemed stunned
by being called "non-victors" after so much work. They now waited to see
Lee. Lee and his horse would soon trot by here. Rumor claimed he would
sign away Reb soldiers' rights today. Boil a whole document down to one
word: "Uncle."

Some vets stood balanced betwixt homemade crutches, forked saplings.
The seriously wounded laid on pallets. They asked friends: If and when the
godlike Lee passed, could their pallets' head ends be propped up so they
might see, please?

The best talker in each platoon kept slinking off to one side, preparing
a speech meant to buck up friends and the humbled Lee. Our mighty hath
sure fallen. "SOUTH LOSES IT." How would all these fellows get home,
child? Nobody knew how to behave.

Where *is* a soldier when his war gets yanked out from under him? Not
yet a ripe civilian but not quite military, either. He is some type of Milque-
toast or pirate caught betwixt. Unscrubbed Rebels played cards, dawdled,
built fires just for the comfort of doing that. Most sat still, looking at each
other or nowhere. Poker run quieter than usual. Willie set his bees aside
and, unnoticed by others, placed his empty musket in a roadside ditch.

Solemn, he scooped loose clay over it. He cried like he was burying some dear old household pet. He would rather let his out-of-ammo weapon rest in peace than have it claimed by Northern hands and shown up yonder as "captured armament." Once he'd sprinkled dried grasses overtop, Will turned back to busywork, bee gathering. He was fifteen. There'd been this empty mustard jar by the roadside, there'd been all these clover-loving bees, wasps, yellowjackets.

Sal Smith and other cardplayers today acted edgy. They were like some sawmill crew the morning their foreman is sick: Workers arrive to find the whole plant locked. Everybody mopes around outside its gate. Should they run off or stay put, getting credit for the hours they've already waited? Men find, by noon, they're really missing their loud splintery jobs. They love their work, cut off from it. Even war, people really get used to.

Wee Willie Marsden had fought on the losing side. Darling? it sure showed. His knee had healed, leaving only a livid purple scar. By now, his boots and the mud inside his boots all felt like boots to him. His pal's footgear still dangled from his belt but the soles were missing. Over one shoulder a bugle rode its red cord, mud-crusted. He wore a man-sized sword around his waist. Gray britches were gummed across with sticky seeds, cockleburs, and mildew from his lying in a ditch these months—face-down—eyes trailed along the sight of a musket, empty since February. His striped shirt was a civilian one. This old lady in Roanoke had pitied the boy his sleeveless tunic. Seeing him march by, she snatched this off her clothesline, passed it to him over her back fence. He seemed confused. "For you, the youngest one," she said as other men around him laughed. Will had doubted her goodwill. His being picked surprised him. He'd felt invisible and old. His musket had been useful lately either as a cane or just as something he'd got used to holding. Where *was* that thing?—he couldn't quite decide—oh, yeah, he'd buried it just now. Yeah. It, at least, was safe.

Sal Smith had somehow lived through everything. The longer Salvador Magellan lasted, the deeper blue were circles under trusting eyes, the redder and more oakum-stiff did his hair look. Now him and others loitered near this road, bent toward cards, admitting they worried about starting over as farmers, as clerks. Off in New Bern, Sal's twin boys were commencing to talk. He'd never seen them. The absconding Chinese tailor and that flashy local matron had, so far, failed to send along a Florida address.

Will listened to others wonder how it'd be—returning to their civvy jobs. Curled off to one side, Will felt: He hadn't really *been* anything before finding himself a soldier. Nothing but a child. And he sure couldn't go back to being that.

The fellow whose farmhouse had been picked as the location for today's signing, he'd surely fallen afoul of luck. Rumor had it, his *first* farm got caught ambushed by First Bull Run up near Washington. So he'd upped and sold his bullet-riddled barns, moved deep into the sleepiest available Virginia. To Appomattox.

Willie studied captured bees. He'd stayed at least this much a kid. Numb, he held the clear jar up against sky, he played like these bugs had chose to stay (renters) in this particular plug of blue. How they battered, trying to work free. Nearby, another Reb sat whittling one little spread-eagled woman from a forked branch. She was mostly open white thighs. "Bessie," the man held up his masterpiece. "Bessie, spread 'em, pride of my pride, because here Poppa comes." Others laughed but sounded a tad spiritless. This runt had been carving open homecoming thighs since two weeks after Sumter.

The platoon's orator stood off behind some pokeberry shrubs, talking to hisself and trying hand gestures. "Sir? Saint and Genius, our sacrificial . . . something . . . genius." His words drifted as he checked over his shoulder, guilty. The speaker hoped to stir both Lee and these beloved hungry comrades, the kids and louts he'd fought beside these many years. Almost forever, it seemed. That was the weird part. These fellows might've been sired in these ranks, birthed in foxholes—literally sons of guns.

Fires won't needed in April but many burned along this road. Fires and horses, *they*, at least, would never have to know we lost.

"Where *is* he?" Sal stood, craned over the heads of thousands milling near the road that led to one farm outside Appomattox Court House. In the distance, one trace of dust lifted. Nearer, a few pallets' ends were being hoisted onto ditchside stones. "You know he's punctual as any man on earth. If anything, he'll get there earlier'n Grant, you watch." Sal, cooling his face with a fan of playing cards, resettled and said, "Oh, fighting dirty? Well, I'll see you and raise you, you sly dog." Poker won't being played for money now. None around. Unshaved recruits used fistfuls of promissory pay chits. Each slip said this'd definitely be made good by our Confederate Treasury. There won't one, but men used chits anyhow. Made your poker seem to matter more. All a game anyway—the whole four years' worth, somebody had to win, somebody had to . . . the other.

Sal kept checking on little Marsden, slouchy upon the crest of the low hill. Marsden sat cross-legged. In one hand, a jar of bugs, in the other a fine gold pocket watch he kept opening to hear chime. Boy's eyes were closed as he cupped the metal timepiece to his left ear, as he pressed mason jar to his right. Will looked browned or grayed, no longer plump and shrimp-tender but—from living in the open—parchmenty like some old-timer. Quietly, the boy was crying in a hapless kind of way. It bothered those gents that noticed. Cardplayers sometimes checked in Will's direction. Some glances seemed to say, "Grow the hell up." Others, like Sal's, hinted, "Me, too, mostly."

Will kept naming bees, kept losing track of which he'd named so far. Before burying his musket, he had used its detached bayonet to jab nice air holes in a jar's tin lid. Careful, he now undid the thing, he slipped in clover for bees' comfort, their civilian furniture.

"Something's coming," one sergeant called.

Others yet half listened for the old sounds: cannon rumble, thunder man-made. Instead, birds kept singing from the thicket close by. Where had loud birds *been* these last four years? Hiding in vacation trees of border states? Now they sure let rip, songs sent straight up—almost taunting, like they approved the Bluebelly Sapsuckers carrying off top prize. Cardinals, mockingbirds, turncoats.

"Somebody pretty big-brass bound our way from the look of what the crowd's doing."

Fellows stood and stretched, like waking. The whittler had just peeled dark-bark knickers off yet another innocent forked branch. "Sister to Bessie—she'll wrap them pudding thighs around you, squeeze you half to death, and you'll feel Sherman's fire but where you'll love it, hotshots. Melt your miniés! Look at the size of the thighs on *this* 'un." Nobody looked. Somebody said, "Grow up, loser." It was noon. You felt sick from hunger, numbness, and the dullness of these mortal un-winners you had fought alongside too long. How perfect daylight looked. Paint. Nothing else bad could ever happen again to the person, could it? A fellow just wanted to go hide inside a smooth wallpapered room and then look out some clean window when he woke. First a man might sleep one solid year, then the smell of homemade flapjacks floating in pooled clover honey, that'd wake him, plus the sound of some live tolerable not-half-bad-looking woman humming a hymn or ditty down the hall, the smell of maintained linen—the lady's personally, and this bed's—that'd cocoon you in hard-earned middle-class delights. Surely that won't much to ask, plus some bacon cooking maybe? Could the losing side expect so much? Would the losers' women cut them off lovewise for losing it so bad? *Would* home let you back in?

Sal, dealing a last hand, watched Will not even know that Will was crying. Will probably considered it just Confederate *thinking*.

Some wag climbed (and ruined) a young maple as he hollered, "Dust getting nearer, might be Lee. Best get ready, just in case. Wouldn't want to get caught playing cards and miss this, would you?" The whole poker match rose then, stepped closer to the place, claimed certain choicer spots. You saw how others from other platoons were also lining up with a certain fuss. Men on crutches now crossed the road, but in that shy quick way people jaywalk between floats in a parade.

Those on pallets complained about the many legs now blocking their view. The wood carver set the twin thighs upon a mat of leaves like some kid putting dolls to bed, "Don't go noplace now. I thigh for you." Nobody laughed. They'd heard it. They'd heard everything before. In the grove, clearing his throat, the orator went, "On behalf of myself and others, sir, perhaps a few remarks are in order, sir, considering the momentous . . ."

Willie turned his back on such commotion. It was him here and the clover and the bee wings fraying their rare film against the glass. Plus a ticking from one excellent German watch. Boy closed his eyes. He'd pretty much had it. The jar's cool side he rolled against his forehead, he forgot to wipe his streaming eyes and nose. Too tired to feel ashamed, he sat face-up toward a peaceable sun. *We lost it. I cannot be seen. I will have to live hid the rest of my whole life and I'm not all that old yet, numbers-wise.*

On the road below, Southern voices churred like bees' wings eager to get loose, to go hive on home. Will should want that, too. Shouldn't he be missing something? Somebody, maybe? Squeeze that trigger like it's everything you love. You do—as a gentleman—love something, right? Food. Food maybe? With food's help, he'd aim due south, he'd ask directions on the way. He knew who probably waited—the widowed Momma, that ninety-pound overload of silk and charm. Maybe with Castalia taking care of Momma yet. He knew who did not wait—most of Momma's sixty-one slaves, including all their babies.

"Will? Come here, saved a excellent spot for you. Lee, boy, Lee coming."

Will sure had slept on the ground of many states lately. Some days it rained all day but that changed nothing. You still fought. They still came at you. His voice had lately dropped in fits and peeps while, underneath gray worsted, other unasked-for changes started threatening. To kill a person (several) before you've even got a sprig of pubic hair, and to be praised to Heaven for doing that! Yikes.

"Will? *Is* Lee, I'm told. Best get your young butt in motion and on down here. He's no more'n a eighth of a mile off, look alive. —Will? 'Why does the ocean stay so mad?' Little joke, boy, why?"

Now, listening to his bees like for smart gypsy advice, holding the cool watch closer like some pet, Will heard hoofbeats gathering and couldn't for the life of him remember the answer to Sal's corny riddle, or just *why* he'd gone and shot three whole other fellows. The "how" part stayed way too clear, every inch and droplet of it did. But the "why," way less.

Maybe Lee could tell him. As if Lee had a human moment for any soldier shy of colonel!

Sal was sounding seriously miffed. "I got to come up there and drag you down here and lose *both* our spots? Or what? It's important, it's our commander. All over but the shouting, so come shout some. One last Rebel yell while we're still *called* Rebs."

Will would have no part of Lee. Lee seemed too fine to ever feel such sloppy stuff as now rocked his enlisted losers. Lee had always been too handsome to live, Lee too noble to ever need a real bath or to long for a snack or to break wind, even whilst imperially alone.

Little Marsden—secret-like—had come to flat out hate this Christian gent and others' slavish praise of him. The hungrier Wee Willie felt, the more he longed to call Marse Rob aside and ask, "Look, where's a certain fellow's dinner, fellow soldier, hunh? Not to whine, mind you . . . even so . . . no shoes, this wet out here, to lack all miniés for my musket, and then starve on top of that. There are, sir, limits, sir. You invite people into your war, there's a Southern hospitality thing you should remember."

But Lee was made of platinum, not blood like us. Lee must eat communion wafers for breakfast and sleep with crowns of thorns under his pillow. Lee could've led the side that would win today. Yanks invited him to. But, no, Lee rode over the Potomac's bridge. From Move #1, a genius at martyrdom. Will had just one question for Lee: When can I leave here and leave you, sir? Lee = Leave.

Marsden opened eyes again, saw soldiers drawing to attention. Some slapped dust from uniforms or whipped hats cleaner against uplifted knees. The orator waited, front and center, hands clasped before him, about to pounce into his solo moment. Hoofbeats. Some fellows tilted forward, a few stooping lower to spare others their big heads.

Will had never told any soul his irreverent views of Lee, not even Sal still beckoning the lad downhill. Sal called: "Last chance . . . saw Traveler's ears just now. Miss this, and your momma'll wear your rump out with a switch and she'd be right to too, Willie mine. Come on. It's history, son. If I hated officers less, I'd give you a direct order, Will," and Smith smiled uphill, offering his snaggled loveless lovely smile. Finally he asked others to save two places and Sal ran uphill graceful as some makeshift goat. "You even *in* there, Will? People are so goddam disappointing. What is eating you?"

Marsden then whispered up at the friend who'd saved his leg that would sure make the long walk home much easier. "*Can* we yet, Sal?"

"Can we what, son?"

"Leave."

"Leave . . . what?"

"Leave here. Leave it."

"Leave me, us?"

"Leave. Because, see, Sal, we lost it. You lose, they make you leave, right?"

"First, you come and watch this—I'm not ordering, I'm begging." His Adam's apple bobbed from nerves as he kept checking over one shoulder. Sal explained: Willie's army had been outspent, outnumbered, but never outclassed. And all thanks to one dude forty feet away. Sal gave Will the sternest, most fatherly of looks. Then he bolted, calling, "Suit yourself, ingrate."

Because Marsden set up on the clovered culvert, because he twisted his head about three inches to the right, he could see it—right through the clear glass jar he held—defense. He could see it better than most soldiers by the road. The Boss was already upon them. Men along either ditch bank made the straightest two lines possible while men were quite this tired. Some even left viewing gaps for the wounded on the ground. Will saw hurt ones—pathetic in full sun—salute straight up at sky and for the longest time before Lee even got to them.

Downhill, the raggedest-looking bunch since children walked their crusade to the Holy Land. Men held each other up. The wood carver tossed a blanket over sweet-tempered letter-writing Lieutenant Hester, shot last night and already putting off a stifling sweetish smell beyond the ditch. Soldiers didn't want Lee to note one extra bad thing. God knows, he'd seen enough. They all had. Every platoon's Cicero stood, face full of his planned long speech, but even from up here, Will could see: Nothing ceremonial was going as planned. Of the worst-hurt side, all too typical.

Here came Lee all right. No bodyguard. A squad of mounted officers followed one quarter mile behind. Will used his jar to keep from witnessing this straight. But, through glass, he knew Lee—even with distortions—you knew Lee from engravings, and from that one time with Ned. But now Will had a reason for studying Marse Rob. Hadn't this man once sniffed a Ned Smythe doused with girl's perfume? Hadn't Lee heard one of Ned's last "Last Rose of Summer"s? Lee'd become of interest and Will watched, lens of bees lowering.

Sal saw Willie notice now and stand. Sal clapped once and turned with relish toward the great man. Now *Sal* could watch.

Slow and stately, hushed, here Lee came. He first seemed calm in the confusion that his calm set off. No speechmaker could say word-one of the planned talks. The woodcarver held up Bessie's thighs over assembled heads. Lee, high on horseback, moved along his muddied troops, a sweep of whisper spread before him. When fellows saw him setting straight on Traveler, the pearl-gray horse near famous as Lee, men's plans changed. Not one person hip-hooorayed. No arm waved. You instead heard low and manly moans—hundreds of questioning groans told you—the Chief was here with us. Seeing him, that made you know we'd lost.

Even his proud horse advanced with a gait gloomy and half-broken. Maybe our horses *did* know. Seemed Traveler understood on behalf of all pack mules, Rebel Arab chargers, and enlisted quarter horses. He too was bound now to surrender, like *their* representative, and Traveler sure hated doing so.

Everybody'd taken off their hats. Down came gents' broad-brimmed planter's ones—if stained, off with rake's dusty caps. Hats got mashed to chest, the way you do for a passing lady or some stranger's funeral. Someway you knew Lee's face better than your own after these years away from household mirrors. Lee's uniform looked brand-new. It'd been sewn special for a Victory ceremony—kept back for that.

Men expected to be noisy, expected to toss hats aloft like the graduates at West Point, where Lee'd been second in his class and then the school's head honcho before Sumter. But Will heard only stilted greetings spoken up to Lee, little grunts, questions, some male kind of keening. As the General drew nearer—fellows went stoop-shouldered, losing ramrod posture that'd cost them a good deal. They acted ashamed—like, by losing, they'd let their Lee down. And, to judge from studying him, proud as ever but stunned-seeming in raw sunshine—you saw Lee felt responsible. He seemed to bodily apologize toward men staring up, memorizing his every silver inch.

Then Will understood that something had gone really wrong, with Lee.

"No," Will heard the voice of Salvador Cortez Drake Magellan Smith, a bleat: "You know not, no." First it disappointed Willie: seeing emotion leak out of this general amongst generals—right unseemly. Lee was a man over six feet tall. Here even in the saddle that showed. Plus, his horse was huge. Lee's chest didn't buck a bit. His chin was raised in a way that might appear vain in a gent ten years younger or one whit less religious. First Will noticed how some hurt soldier, in trying to touch the General, had left a whole red handprint on the horse's shank. Then, slow, Will understood why everybody'd flinched. Imagine the headline: "Lee Weeps Here." Unbelievable, *him* doing it. Water moved—orderly stripes—from either eye into the beard. Only later would Private Marsden figure: The General never undertook anything by accident. A gentleman is never unintentionally rude. Lee had chose to let hisself. It showed such manly strength. Was probably the kindest gift the Great One could still offer his men. Don't you see? —His crying let *them*.

Standing troops now dragged nearer, stood facing one another, men flattened hats tighter over hearts. The closest fellows did what those miles earlier had done. Happened like they'd practiced this for years. Soldiers lifted tattered hats, soldiers held these at arm's length. And through this double line of outheld floppy caps and hats, Traveler moved.

When the horse breasted parallel with your spot, you made darn sure your own hat's soft brim reached, eased first along the creature's potent foremost withers, then slid back across a crying person's stirruped legs and over the shiny boots of Marse Rob hisself. Next your hat whisked against the animal's smooth flanks again toward its silver tail—until your hat and hand moved once again into free civilian air—so lonely! Till finally your headgear dropped forward and touched the hat and hand of that enlisted man just opposite you.

Warriors all did this so gentle, the great horse never onct spooked. Lee'd passed. His stiff back, you saw now. Men in the roadway twisted sharply right face. They stood, not feature to feature now, but shoulder pressing another's shoulder. They shifted two by two. Lee moved off from them for good to sign the cause away. Had to. Fact.

Bye, Lee. We have, sir, attempted honoring you. We sure tried. Pleasure to work for you.

Marsden noticed Volunteers already turning aside, fondling their old hats' crowns. Surely men would show these stained felt scraps to waiting families. Everybody would try stroking a sweat-marked brim containing traces of the famous general and his almost just as famous horse. Who says magic don't exist, child? History can make any greasy hat go heirloom.

The crowd commenced to settling, now melancholy as you'd imagine.

Marsden walked downhill, and not unjaunty. He felt ready. It showed. Will tucked the treasured pocket watch into its case. Boy lowered his jar— its ticklish bugs striking and restriking curved glass. He tied a rope around the jar's notched lid, bound rope around his waist, where glass sometimes clanked against the butt of his sword's handle.

Sal, still looking after Lee's dust, turned toward Willie, face haunted.

"Did you see, boy? If Christ had got to live to be fifty-some, I bet you any amount of Northern cash Christ'd look just like that, nearbout that good. My girls are going to want to hear this part over and over, plus my twin boys—I still sometime forget my boys. You *see* him?"

The private nodded, shy, straightening the bugle's red cord straight around his neck. "Yeah." Then Willie added as how the General *had* looked right handsome, yeah, and it was good that it'd got beside Lee to where Lee was really crying. "But, Sal? after what-all we been through, Lee just—maybe it's just me, but for me, he just didn't look quite good enough, you know?"

Others, hearing, stared at Will, then snorted, remembering his tender age. He appeared real worked up over something.

"Sal, I believe I'll be heading home now. Can we, do you think?"

Sal looked around, checking for Lieutenant Hester, noticed him there under a blanket where two sea-green dragonflies had landed, flexing wings. "Nobody around to ask."

"That means we *can*," Will said. And his adulthood started.

Then Smith held out one big freckled hand. He didn't believe that Wee Willie (wiping messy eyes and a worse nose onto his sleeve) *would* shake. But how spiritedly Willie did. "I'll say it to the rest, first," Willie said. The lad then wandered, hurrying some, from man to man. He hugged a few, he threw fake punches at others, said, "Bye. See you. Bye now. 'S been real." And Marsden said every person's name aloud like reciting this list of names broke a last fine chain that kept him tethered here.

"Bye, boy," they grinned back, awkward. They needed time to make up speeches. The orator had just stormed into the grove, pacing, sick at having missed his chance with Lee.

Here were men who'd survived. The twenty left from a ninety-five-fellow unit starting three years earlier. Here stood some of the very ones that'd been swimming on Ned's death day. These same fellows had buried that boy in a secret place near the millpond, they'd tied up Wee Willie to save him from going out too much at night when he felt wildest with some fool kid's notion of revenge. Now the wood carver handed Will the last slick pair of thighs. "Take Bessie's sister, for good luck. Free. No? Well, whatever. Soon you'll start shaving, son. You'll find out. Bye. It's been a regular education, ain't it?"

Some ex-soldiers asked if Marsden didn't want to stay till other soldiers begun taking off. Wouldn't he like to have company when he heard how it all turned out? Others planned remaining till they learned the exact conditions of surrender. (Later, when they heard the word "unconditional," they would cuss a blue streak. Some even railed against their semi-holy Lee and even his departed momma.)

Marsden just said, "No. Now'd be better." At fifteen he as yet stood about five foot five. In hugging pals, he'd grab whatever part of taller ones he could reach easiest: belt-buckled waists, a knee, unwieldy holsters.

Marsden noticed his best-loved red-haired corporal moping hangdog near a dying fire, lips going, face crumpled. Will stepped up beside, tugging at one sleeve to get Sal's proper attention. "Never thought we'd get to say goodbye like civilians and just walk off from one another, did you? For a while there, didn't seem I'd have most of what I needed *to* walk on!"

Sal wouldn't turn Willie's way, Sal just wagged his big head no.

Corporal Smith finally said to his feet. "You just leaving for Falls, just like that? How you plan to get there, Will?"

The child lifted either boot for demonstrating. "Same way I've stumped all over Virginia and Maryland these years. How'd you think? We lost it, Sal. I mean, wake up. You been dying to go see your folks, the twins. Now you can set off for New Bern. Come *with* me?"

"Naw, got to see how it turns out. I don't much like your hauling off like this. You got to see a thing *through*, son. —Besides, I got stuff to tell you before you walk off—only thing is, I can't think of one pointer I meant to say."

Then the Corporal shifted his back on the kid who stood here. The hum of bees was coming off him like a body sound, forlorn. "Say," Will touched Sal's back. "Why *does* the ocean stay so cross?"

Sal smiled but begrudging, "Not 'cross.' You can't say 'crossed' in the lead-off. That's the whole joke and you'll spoil the answer part. Boy, you couldn't tell a joke to save your momma's life, could you?"

But Sal saw the former private's half-smile, he understood Will had messed it up a-purpose. "Scallywag, you *must* be feeling better," and he ruffled Marsden's plentiful cowlicks.

"I am, better. It's over. Well . . ."

"The worst thing is—Willie, I'll never know how you look, grown. It kills old Sal to think that he might someday pass you on a street and not even know. You'll stop me, right? To be strangers on a street after everything we hiked through together—that's a pisser, ain't it?"

"I'll know you," Will said. "*You're* not going to get a bit better-looking," and he punched Sal hard. They hugged each other—determined not to cry now they'd seen Lee do it—to protect Lee, by not.

"Sal, I hate asking: but which way's due south?"

Smith pointed, "That's it. You ain't due much else."

Then Marsden backed away. You can't believe you get to walk off from those many others. Free. But Will straightened all the gear strapped to him, evening its weight. He cut through stranger soldiers on the road's far side, he stepped into the sedge grass of the field there. "Don't go away mad," the wood carver hollered, dancing two wooden female lower bodies. Will saw that Sal—in what looked from the back like a lover's fit of pique—had stomped off into the pokeberry bushes, hiding from the sight.

Then Will just walked.

Others watched his progress. It was steady. You could see he'd planned this for a while. They had offered the lad usual parting words. They knew him as arm gestures backing up a perfect singing voice, they knew him as the poorest bugler on either side of the War of Northern Aggression, then they knew him a groom and then a marksman who'd scored a fair amount of hits and who'd chose, they decided, to loot at least one little victim. They knew his family's name, one of the twenty flashiest in North Carolina, easy. Now—idle—they watched him stroll off, determined, bound Home.

To him they'd said nothing better than "Never do nothing I wouldn't if I got the chance." "Have yourself the fine long life you've earned, son." "Don't take any wooden Confederate nickels or, for that matter, Reb metal ones." "Listen here, pup, my advice'd be: try and keep it in your pants, hear?"

Goodbyes are never excellent enough.

WILL started out on foot. So simple his stumbling forward, a determined trot that saddened men to see. They knew he'd known as little food as they had lately. They knew his being fifteen helped him find this sudden needed spunk—must be coming out of sinew, a backlog used to get the heck out of here. How young he still looked—from behind at least—and after all of this! Men saw him try and keep his every step aimed south as possible. He had his buddy's boots yet dangling around his waist, one outsized sword and scabbard, his pal's brass horn on its grimy tasseled cord. He had, at his waist, a jar of bees that nobody'd mentioned or asked about. Superstition maybe, or childhood? Early on, he'd collected and abandoned many museum-worthy rock crystals in three years. But these had been left buried careful among various ditches.

Ten minutes later the kid chose to turn back, planning to wave gloriously at friends. But when he turned, Will found he could hardly see the ridge road now. Vets were just a thin line. Men he'd known were only part of a grainy stripe, now as gray as their uniforms and not the rosy tint of the faces in it. At the front of this line, Will saw a hand-sized bit of dust lifting. Must be Lee, slowed by all them tribute hats, Lee headed where he must.

And so the child soldier waved anyhow, even knowing he could not be seen. "Bye, mess." He turned and walked some more, walked hard as he could go. He ran some, clanking with gear and glass. The field was deep in gummy mud. You had to lift each boot quite high to make a decent step. Every step became its own decision.

TO HEAR him tell it later (and you have to trust the person by then)—while he tramped south, not rightly knowing much about southeast or southwest, just using for his guide the sides of trees opposite their mossy flanks, while he took it a day at a time, begging and stopping for handouts at ladies' back porches, his body started changing on him. Female voices were even more beautiful than he'd recalled. Did they help him change? These ladies asked if he'd known their soldier sons or sons-in-law or brothers, husbands. He met many women who spilled long breathless lists of names, names he sometimes *did* know and sometimes knew were dead and gone or bad hurt, but he never admitted that. Let others bear such awful news. He had plenty of his own and planned to keep it to hisself.

Instead Will ate what he was offered, stayed still, trusted word to follow. Willie—being among the first returning soldiers to walk past farms and through small towns—got a bit more pie and attention than would the next ninety thousand.

He grew more superstitious. Bees in the jar kept dying and he felt he had to stop at some clover and catch more. He told hisself that if the bees kept living in the jar, he'd get home—they hummed and helped, a supplement heart. And he was collecting bees when he heard a train whistle and here came a southbound freight moving slower than a walking man because the thing was covered with vets. Even the locomotive was piled with homebound Johnny Rebs, wearing bandannas to make breathing easier in the blowing soot. Every inch of roof, vestibules, and couplings seemed mosaicked with limbs and hats and gray cloth. Grant—at Lee's urging—made transport on any train free to any now unsalaried Southern soldier. Several vets were urinating off the caboose roof, their wetness struck near a ditch bank where a boy, acting ashamed of doing so, sat trapping bees. Men looked at Will, he stared at them. Nobody recognized him. He seemed to fear them, as if everybody grownup on earth was a Yankee. The hunger put a fuzz on some things, hurt you with the bald brightness of others. There was a scent, too. Call it puberty. Say he had been on the road less than three weeks, he had been sleeping in haystacks and farm-gear shanties when this started happening to our Willie M.: the lad commenced to truly sideshow *growing*!

One sign was, to be blunt, his gentleman's bauble stayed perpetual on guard—which might (what with his outgrown trousers) explain why passersby avoided him. Seemed his body'd waited for a truce. You don't want to bother expanding till you know the feeble organism gets to really live through present jeopardy—just good business practice, really. Now it decided to enlarge.

He was walking in the post road's dust when he slowed, seeing how his own pant cuffs seemed to be splitting from the bottoms up. Pant tubes seized now at his own widening gristled calves. Will noticed how tanned ankles showed a whole inch and a half of skin—burned raw by everyday sun.

Slow, he understood he had grown that much, this fast. It scared him— weeks back, Sal had said, you'll change and I won't know you. Willie hadn't quite believed this. Now he understood. He had no mirrors handy to gauge if his face was lengthening like his wrists and shanks were. He got even more superstitious than during the Great Struggle. Example being, he felt sure, child, that if he walked back north—he would shrink into the little boy he'd been, mile by centimeter smaller, smoother, less a bristled goat and more the sleek young fawn he'd been.

It happens to some boys all in one early summer. They'll get the majority of their adult inches, they'll go weedy-rangy and then dense, all in one most haywire mighty upshot. These boys sometimes feel right dizzy during this. Their joints ache from expanding like a pregnant woman's pelvis bones will, such radical unlatching, but with boys it's all over. Boys then sure do fall down a lot. They will trip over the smallest root, over nothing. They've got to nap often and they have to eat about enough for four, minimum.

Considering the increased appetite, growth's timing sure was hard on Willie Marsden headed home. It being late April, blackberries won't yet ripely black or even very red. Poor child ate the greenies. If it won't marked Poisonous, he *would* put it in his mouth and try and chewing. Dandelion leaves sure get old fast. When Willie drew near settlements, he was interested in two things: newspapers—full of details (Grant had let the Rebs take their own horses and mules home)—and food. Every town smelled of frying, baked goods. Your nose and your spit glands were, Will found, first cousins. Downtown, noticeable to strangers as his scent seemed, the kid's stomach also groused and yodeled. A whole zoo lives, secret, in your lower body, waiting to go ape-noisy if deprived. Will held one palm to his tummy and another over his mouth when people passed. Spittle sprung out near a bakery. Uh-oh.

He knew something was really wrong when—unable not to—he stole three cooling hunks of shortbread off the windowsill of one Virginia matron. Will had been about to knock and ask for free food when he saw these buttery things. He knew that, at best, he would only get a smidgen and just of one. That would not do. He grabbed the three and ran and jumped behind a large blooming hydrangea bush and sat there, wolfing, trying to keep his loud groans quiet as he could. Every time he ate, he felt faint from how much blood his new erection hogged. His brain had competition now, below.

"Gypsies!" he finally heard a lady's shriek. "Or else Yankees or else gypsy Yankees. What could be lower? Here we lose our war plus my first peacetime all-butter shortbread to such vermin. Hattie, run call the sheriff!"

He bolted for the woods and then stood there, confused, laughing. Years later, he forced his wife, who I am, to try and work out a recipe for Scottish shortbread that'd equal the taste of that snitched stuff, pure gold. He claimed nothing that'd ever gone into his mouth since came near it—except he said, lovely lovey-dovey, except maybe portions of honeymoon me. The rogue and liar. I worked and worked but—though my own homespun recipe won the state-fair blue ribbon seven years running, count them—for him, it won't the same. I finally told my big old quilted bellied man, grown, overgrown, "You'll never find the jolt shortbread gave you because you'd have to steal it, and get a war to be the meal's first course. And you'll never again be that hungry, sir."

"God willing," he laughed. "I ate bark off trees. Ate clay from clay banks like our black folks do. Saw a dog being fed one night, coon dog. I threw rocks into the shrubs beyond the dog and when he ran in there, barking, I got right down to his dish. It was leftover stew gone just a little gamy.

Mighty fine. Boy, was he ever mad. Nice thing was, he could never *explain* to his owners, beyond barking, naturally."

When my Willie departed Appomattox roadside, he had stood five five/ six, in there. Captain swore to me later how—by the time he finally planted his bleeding feet onto the turf of the Lilacs seven weeks later (I hope I ain't blowing the story's suspense, child, but in order to marry me thirty some years later, he had to at least get back home)—the young civilian stood six feet one and every long bone in him was throbbing—not knowing what'd stretched it so. So much quick growing made him pant.

Springing up that quick is way better if, say, you're a rich boy working at the country club as a lifeguard, say, during the summer your inches come upon you like a angel visit and a seizure both. That way, you can drink gallons of milk and sit in sun and be admired and sleepy, bronzing in plain view, tripling like somebody's good stock.

But try walking through two states—not wanting to hock your buddy's bugle or your victim's pocket watch or your own sword with the real gold hilt.

Will Marsden, bound most duly south, found a splendid walking stick, five foot high and twisted with hardship and authority. He used it like Moses used his—minus the ability to turn it into snakes. Folks seeing him in his dingy state, growing shaggier each day and with his clothes less likely to cover the increasing amount of him, folks moved to the road's far side. His uniform (what was left of it) drew a nod from them at first—but when the hordes from Appomattox and elsewhere overtook him in their getting home, folks looked right through him. They had woes and troubles of their own. They could catch a whiff of their own losing side—plus the scent of a young man who'd grown considerable since last bathing. They moved away from Willie, who was grinning, hoping to be liked.

Sometimes the pilgrim would make half a day's progress and find he had got turned around, was headed north. Then he'd run hard south a ways like north was a magnet that a fellow had to most boldly fight. Years later, looking back he'd see that, hatless, it'd been sunstroke that'd helped to make him addled by day and sick come night. Night shakes—hidden behind others' sheds—vaguely recalling the scripture where the wandering son plans going home to Daddy and saying that even your servants live better than I have here lately, take me back. But *had* his father's servants?

Confusing at midday to walk into strange crowded little towns. People stared at first and then—when all towns teemed with ex-Rebs taking breaks in their journeys—nobody noticed. Once Will passed a cotton mill on fire. He had been walking since dawn and it was eighty-five degrees at 6 a.m. Now—a volunteer bucket brigade and the sight of a building burning in this kind of heat made a healthy person feel real thirsty, pretty ill. Somebody yelled that he should set his stick down and he should get in line, help. Marsden did both, he felt glad to be included in a group again. Suddenly living alone like this had been a kind of torture. He understood how much it helped, whining *to* somebody. Now, stunned, when folks passed a first tin pail his way, Will smiled to those in each direction, thanked everybody, lifted the thing, and drank down a good part of the water in it. Citizens were swearing at him then, they pointed to the city's southmost limit. "Get, madman." He took up his staff then and, clinking like a traveling hawker, jar against sword against boots against jangling watch chain, walked where they had shown him to—the burning building crackling at his back.

Odder stuff went on: Two hummingbirds decided to measure him. He said one minute he was standing in the road looking back at a town marked by its great bookmark of black cloud, the next two ruby-throated things appeared before his face—aloft without even trying. Their beaks were pointed sharp as awls, their wings moving so fast wings made five o'clock shadows on the shimmering noon air, such glinting bodies seemed the work of jewelers and made them seem the two most perfect cuff links ever made. Will swore they then zoomed up to the crown of his head—a sort of bird's "Who goes there?"—and each begun measuring him, buzzing down one inch at a time, one bird to the left, one right—seemed like they were working for some cunning native coffin maker that'd set out two hawkers working on commission. Then birds veered off at right angles into cool blue woods beyond. I don't usually bust in and say I doubt that something happened. Stranger things've happened and why would Captain bother making all this up?

The next afternoon, he heard a mule approaching and he moved out of its way. But on the creature's swayback proved another Johnny Reb, real old. He gestured Willie up onto the thing. Men didn't speak any more than their tired mule did. The three seemed one thing, reunited. The owner of the mule was yellow from the jaundice, the whites of his eyes the color of late forsythias still blooming all along this pretty Maytime road. The mule was all but white with dust. To Will this seemed in keeping with a world where ruby-throated emerald-blue-green birds come out of woods to sum up your inches, only natural: silently offered a ride on a white mule by a yellow fellow. At a crossroad some four quiet miles later, the mule distinctly coughed. When you are on said mule, its cough means more to you and you feel that cough's high-up hitching seriousness. This, Will knew at once, had been a last cough. He knew because his crotch was in the saddle of the rattle and his sensitive crotch had been rubbing against the back (couldn't help it) of one old yellow man. The zone between Will's legs was becoming a area of increasing and fairly shameless sensitivity (as I would much later discover). The mule spun left then two-stepped right and staggered like some melodrama's drunkard. A single back leg buckled, the other copied it, just as folks say a camel kneels to let passengers off easy, the mule's right front leg caved in and only when the riders had dismounted did the creature let the left front one totally go. And when it hit the road that polite beast was dead. Dust lifted off of it like some flour soul was rising.

The owner muttered something like a prayer, patted the poor thing's mangy pelt, and sneezed. Rising, staggering some hisself, staring waves of hate back here at heavy Willie—he left hinting how Willie's growing weight had killed the creature, which it maybe had.

SOUTHBOUND Marsden, back on foot, would pass northbound blacks. Sometimes they spied him from a good ways off—his soiled gray uniform trousers. Ex-slaves, though free, took nothing for granted where ex-Rebs were concerned, they sometimes hid in woods while the gangly boy dragged past, depending on his staff, laden with clatterish glass and metal extras. Will, polite, half guilty feeling, played like he hadn't noticed them—also polite, half guilty, lurking off in yonder alder bushes.

For a while, Will felt he was the very first Reb walking home, but as he got nearer the Carolina line, he found that others had beat him. Some hadn't been lucky. Maybe they had tried too hard. Propped against one county mailbox post, a fellow wearing a Carolina insignia. The man had got to the hallowed border itself but perished from out-of-state wounds. He'd chose this public spot to die. Hoping to do all he could to make sure his corpse'd be honored—he had, poor thing, shoved up the mailbox's red metal flag. And he'd rolled his right sleeve back to draw attention to a hand that held a envelope, his people's address inked there plain. "Let them know. See they fetch me home please." The body sat there, dignified, undead-looking. A cat sat beside it. Two little girls stood staring at it. One, pointing to the corpse, said, "Look, mister."

Willie nodded. "Go home. Go tell your momma to come help." His own deep voice scared him. Will's presence scared the girls more than a dead man had. Girls ran. The cat did not.

NIGHTS, Wee Willie tried sleeping in strangers' barns—but any sound could wake him—he'd come to, he'd already be standing, his arms flung out and whirling a protected zone around his upper body, so automatic this desire to guard your head, your eyes. (Seemed he'd spent half the war: with arms wound around his skull like some schoolboy warding off one single threatened blow.) He again woke standing in a barn in blackness in the middle of strangers' property outside Crewe, Virginia—woke because somebody very male and bass-voiced had hollered, "No, you don't!"—woke boxing toward what turned out to be one snaggly-sounding insomniac hog, and the man that yelled at him was him, him warning him away.

A NORTH Carolinian can tell when passing over the Virginia line into green home safety. Let it be night or noon. Let the blindfold be satin, let it be burlap, just keep them North State nostrils open-eyed! Almost at once, things smell different. Don't believe Virginians. They'll say their soil smells historical. They'll say Carolina smells of dirt farms—not soil, child, *dirt*.

For us, for him, the air at once refines some. It smells not of wayside but the houses beyond. Scent tells you there are not just weeds but plants set in window boxes all along this road—petunias grown from seed each year, from seeds saved back from our last try at home pride. These might be hidden beyond shrubs and hedges but your nose opens. Takes scent in as clue and ticket, lets scent out as sigh.

On a clovery bank, Will stopped to replace yesterday's bees. If he ever let the whole bunch of them perish, he knew he was done for and lost. The man later told me how, shortly after he left his pals (maybe owing to the constant motion of growth whilst walking?), his male member stiffened out, permanent, it seemed. What he had instead of a compass: his jar of bees and his trouserful of blood. It all but led him home, a dowsing rod. Was it the idea of Home that so excited a boy or was it his picturing Momma or Castalia or the soft red mud along the river Tar? His certainty stayed most solid and almost visibly growing during his seven weeks of southbound march. Times, he told me shy—and don't say I'm keeping nothing back from you, darling—he had a hard time making water, was like trying to get a upturned drainpipe to aim a thread of water downward please. In town, he shifted the heft of his sword, the load of bee life, the dangling bugle over the unsightly lump, his infant part turned infantry armament. (Infantry is named, as you might could know, for those infant young ones who went out to fight in a early crusade.)

Meanwhile he walked. Mornings, calves and blisters hurt you. He'd long since been barefoot as any Indian holy man wandering the world with a begging bowl. But by noon he got limbered, your leg moves for no better reason than that, a second back, the other leg done so. There's a kind of momentum that momentum gives momentum. On. I'm almost done and there.

At a general store near Sharpsburg, N.C., Will finally met a notions salesman, who said, "We know some *Carolina* Marsdens." "Same," the boy could hardly speak for grinning. He stood scratching head lice that'd bloomed in every crook of him just after he crossed into his home state (lice eggs seemed waiting for a decent setting to hatch in). The salesman asked where Will was bound. The man said he had been there, along the river road to Falls, not three days earlier.

"Is The Lilacs standing?" Will managed to ask. He and the well-dressed gent were now sitting on crates outside a store. "Don't know the names of all those farms, sir, but most were burned. Prepare yourself. I hate to tell this to a young man who looks as . . . much a veteran, sir, as do you. But while you were away up there, Sherman pretty much had his way with us. Diddled, we've been. And savagely. Everything fine got leveled. Everybody low is trying to rise up and rush in. You never saw anything so grand as the black folks walking up and down the streets of Falls in their mistress's old clothes. I hear tell that some Yankee whites have put up a nigger to be mayor of your town. He can't read English but can spout some Latin. You figure it . . . I don't want to get you upset in advance. Could be you-all's place was spared. Hope so. But son? don't count on that is all I'm saying.

You think the *war* was a shock. Sherman made a point of wiping out all monuments of ours worth remembering. In the 1812 one, the English burned the White House up in Washington. This go-round the pagans from Washington have come to us and burned every fine white house on every river in our Holy Land. Sherman took the best. He should have left the very tip-top ones. Only civilized to. What will we show your grandchildren, boy? They'll think we made the whole thing up, about how good it was, how grand. We'll never find the money or the will to build such ones again. Each mansion might've one day become a museum. Each already was. The jackals . . . is their sleep troubled? I dearly count on that. As a salesman I had the honor to be admitted to many such homes in a three days' buggy ride. I tell you, young man, Solomon in all his glory . . . ashes now."

And the two just sat side by side—the salesman appeared not to mind Willie's scent. The two looked out onto the noontime main street of Sharpsburg. They stared at six square feet of bleak and glittery dust.

Finally the salesman apologized, learning that the boy was one of those Marsdens, those proud people with the very beautiful lady in the house, the lady people only saw at her own parties, ones that persons such as sale staffs never got to go to. "I apologize if I offend, but might I offer money, such money as I have on me?"

Will noted that several silver coins were being held before him. Mostly they looked very clean to him. He took them, careful not to hurry, glad to speak his thanks. He started to offer repayment, soon as he was settled at The Lilacs. Then—for many reasons, polite and practical—did not. Accepted. He'd learned to take what others gave.

"That'll do for food, sir," the man went on. "But might you need cash for a room?"

"A what?" Marsden looked over—he'd slept outdoors or in tents for two and a half years. The idea of a House!

And finally, this commercial gent volunteered his buggy. He would drive Will the last six miles toward whatever was left of a fine home.

"No," Willie said very loud. "It's just I want to tell my wife and children—when I get some, if I do, sir—that I walked down clear from Appomattox."

"Say no more," the other held his hands up.

Will explained he knew he should take these coins into this store here and buy food. "Cheese'd be mighty good. I thank you for the money. And then I should set off while there's six hours' light left. I could make it by this evening, I bet, with the cheese in me but . . ."

The piece-goods dealer asked, "What, son?"

"I'm scared."

The other fellow told him, "Under the circumstances, son, that is very wise." The salesman asked leave for a last question: Why bees in a jar?

"For direction. And company. It's been pets."

Then Will stood and turned so fast toward the salesman that the man tipped back. "You know what I'm most scared of? The very most of all? The thing you got to watch or it'll kill you quickest? You know what that is, sir?"

The other shook his head No.

"My feeling sorry for myself." Willie said it staring straight ahead. Then without goodbyes he stepped indoors and bought some cheese they wrapped real nice for him. The salesman watched him walk away, jangling, steady, half out of his mind.

You already know, child, what he found at home.

Bunting,
Wrinkleproof

When I kept silence, my bones waxed old
through my roaring all the day long.

—PSALM 32:3

CAPTAIN HATED being ceremonial out of town. Older not-from-Falls vets recalled he hadn't been a officer, just one walking-home boy who'd overdone. Now he was in his sixties and these men made certain remarks. Mr. Marsden's hide couldn't stop such insults. Back he'd come to me with a headache, sensitive as some nun-loving girl mocked at school by Antichrists. In Falls proper, he lived safe from such questions. His looks, his vesty sureness, the family name—all these gave Cap a goodly credit line.

One day after our ninth was born, he took the spur train to Tarboro on hog business, sat reading another moving memoir about Stonewall. The colored porter, recognizing Cap on sight, sneaks up, says low, "Er, excuse me, Captain. We couldn't help but to notice, me and the boys yonder, that you fly is right fully unbuttoned, sir, thought you'd want to know."

"Yes," my husband tells the book, not raising his eyes. "I wear it this way sometimes."

When Falls' Daughters of the Confederacy asked would he please go lead their big yearly parade in Raleigh, Cap hemmed and hawed. They said *Liberty* magazine would be there, the photogravure. Finally ladies flattered him, "Simply your manly duty to." Them's fighting words. Ladies iced a cake like the Confederate flag. Nothing meant what it *had* meant. Gals used marbled batter, red and white. They hoped it'd appear patriotic. Myself, I couldn't eat a bite. To me—looked like the locomotive wreck that'd tossed my momma into my poppa's life.

Ladies planned squiring my man to Raleigh on a chartered train, all picnic hampers, cloche hats, bunting. Day before, they gathered in our back yard to primp him. They'd decided that such white hair and beard needed more of a blue-gray cast to it. Six slim younger D of C's stood out back wearing pastel smocks. They sopped a crimping rinse (donated by Lolly's Palais de Beauté Féminine de Falls) throughout my only husband's beard.

Gals now had his white mane up in pin curls. If he didn't look silly! But you think *he* knew it?

Focusing on certain narrow Junior League waists, Cap sat grinning like some hog admitted to a heaven all mocha mud. At my kitchen window, I mumbled toward chipped dishes I rewashed. Captain held still like posing for some City Hall portrait. It was just a hairdo!

One girl on a low stool filed away at his big hand, a manicure. Maybe showing respect for Cap's death-dealing trigger finger? I refused to join in, wouldn't leave my kitchen. Nobody out there missed me or exactly begged. Three of my children were playing on nearby lino, face-down near my ankles, coloring. Our Seth Thomas—clicking reliable on the wall behind me—sounded to be on *my* side. "I know, I know," I heard Time say.

Then Cap (who'd earlier done some swilling from his sterling flask), he asked his young Society manicurist, blond, did she care to see his authentic one-of-a-kind minié scar? Since most of these well-off girls were residents of historical homes, the one said, "That'd be *int*eresting, probably. A person has to care about history, self-defense, especially around here!"

Covered in his barber's bib, marcel lotion dripping white minié-sized beads off his spit-curled beard—my husband—in plain view of me and neighbors and the D of C's—leads this flighty matron into our toolshed-garage. Before he closes the door, man winks back out at nervous others. Worried, they laugh. (I felt most ashamed of having anybody see our garage's insides: his mess of duck decoys, last year's rotted lawn furniture. I'd *told* him to clean that place.)

Well, the gal soon dodged forth, looking flustered, one palm pressing her cheek. "Why, you naughty old trooper," she rolled her eyes. "He didn't tell me *where* that particular scar was." Others shrieked, basically pleased. Maybe they thought Captain was one of them codgers too old to do more than pinch, one with all his starch long since shot? Child, I knew better. He moped out then, looking shy but pleased with hisself—bobby pins biting his chin, ears bulking out stiff in sun—reminding me of his Lady mother's ears after Sherm burned the perm clear off her, poor thing.

He stands there, playing with his fingertips like Ollie Hardy. The manicurist goes, "It's all right. You're probably keeping in practice for hand-to-hand combat." A group giggle. I seen fit to clear my throat then. This'd gone about far enough. A few heads turned my way.

I ventured—loud—a ditty Momma'd taught me, "Fools' names and fools' faces always appear in public places."

Captain blinked, he calls, "Oh, let me have a little *fun*, you stick!" And then he bellows this—which changes things—"*You* know I love you."

Said it right in front of everybody. Almost made me drop a gravy boat. One thing about Captain Marsden—just about the time you'd give up on him, he'd sense it and he'd reel you in three inches closer, keep you dragging in his wake. He was a killer, that one. I hated how he knew I loved him. He used it.

One gloating old man resettled in his white bib. Here at my sink, wet fists on hips, I tried and gauge my feelings. I ofttimes do, sug. What *else* have I got? To be honest: The strange part was a steady kind of pride. All these foolish younger women drawn to my old vinegar puss like bees unto a honeypot. Why? His history? His charm? Some virile pull they felt under his joshing? They made a pretty picture, pastels clashing yonder in the sun. He croaked some choruses of "A Old Reb" and, around me, on the floor my youngsters took it up while coloring, hardly noticing that they sang.

Ned rested by my feet on a spot already worn bald on lino tile, then worn into the lino scrap put over *that*. (A kind of clock, the damage use leaves.) Ned was supervising our rude twins. I'd bought kids a big coloring book at the Woolworth's, told them they could each do just one page per day. That way I found they took more care. "Momma? Are all skies blue? Aren't some black? Night ones are."

"Skies are every color that there is. What tones are certain sunset ones? Each child name three, please." And as I hear a list of tints, I tell myself: If that young woman takes a certain man's shoes off and starts filing them hoary toenails, I am *out* the front door, gone. Then I feel Ned's finger moving up my ankles, swollen from bearing this many in quick order. His fingertips make clarinet stops along my shin. I peek down at Ned's eyes, staring up, gray eyes—part spaniel's, half angel's. Maybe too local to be perfect, but almost as fine that anybody's eyes *can* be in a town of just eleven hundred mortal souls.

Now Ned tells twins, his crayon tracing jagged blue marks across my leg, "Look ya'll, poor Momma's got very-close veins." I laugh. What else can you do?

I soon listen to a singer out yonder yowling in his bib, doing another verse of "A Old Rebel" by Mr. Innes Randolph. Was Cap's favorite song along with "Who's Sorry Now?" later. He is musically joined by children coloring around my flawed legs.

Kids sing like it's some antique hymn. They hardly notice words learned before words meant a thing. A man and his babies croon:

> Oh, I'm a good old rebel, now that's just what I am.
> For this "fair land of Freedom," I do not care a damn.
> I'm glad I fit against it, I only wish we'd won.
> And I don't ask no pardon for anything I done.

I was standing at my sink then, suddenly shaky. Ladies discipled around Cap, laughed at bitter-funny words, ignoring the harsh voice of my "lip singer." I suddenly heard how deep he'd already sent his song into our children, down down their very gullets to a fishhook's depth.

"Too late," I thought. "Will it ever end?" Can a body ever counter-pain it drowsy, then Appomattox it forever asleep? He'd walked the whole way home from war. When oh when would he finally get here?

2

BORN pretty rich, a only child, how come I'm in this ward for the openly broke? Well, start with the dowry. Twenty years after I married, I was flipping through my husband's boyhood war letters, needing again to feel for him *then* so I could stomach him *now*. Out falls a note in my poppa's crabbed script, it stated the amount: fifteen thousand dollars. First I set there feeling wonderful, finding I'd been considered that worthwhile. Then, slower, cheated. For one thing, I never *knew* a cent had changed hands . . . over me, over my head, like. I asked my darling Professor Taw how much fifteen grand in 1900 would amount to now. He judged: a quarter to a half a million. Imagine it. Me?

When Poppa died and his will was read and Momma had been dead four years already, Pop's Alma Mater got the bulk of everything, including proceeds from the house's sale. Twenty-odd years later, my girl Louisa, scientifically minded, she visited Harvard to see the lab Poppa donated and named for his own kin. Lou told me that, by then, the school had changed a lot, but she finally discovered one bronze plaque near a door in the building where they store glass flowers. The marker read: "Given to celebrate the memory of Pearlie Gupton Honicutt and R. R. 'Rusty' Honicutt." His farm-language parents. Louisa found a janitor, who opened the locked door. The room had once been full of Bunsen burners and student curiosity. Now it was a real large and, she said, real nice storage closet. So much for my fortune, child.

I spent my life taking care of folks. Somebody had to, and I learned a lot. Now, of course, I wonder what else *I* could've done, without the others, solvent and alone. College material myself, secretly. Oh well. Lee's favorite word was "Duty."

The odd part stays: happiness. How stubborn it is, whatever bracket you land in. When I think over the list of my losses and time's take-backs, the household accidents, small everyday betrayals, the way your genius kids turn out to be just regular, if nice. Times, happiness surprises me. It keeps you as its hobby, Lord be praised. For some of us lucky ones, child, happiness stays our daily habit like any other. Happiness: that beautiful duty.

TOWNSFOLK had long since titled him "a character." Seems like characters can get away with lots, including murder. I was not held to be no official character myself, just the wife of one. Which don't quite count. Nobody marveled anymore at my young age compared to his. Nine children later, the old man, he'd kept very still, looks-wise. And why shouldn't he? *His* part in our babies' arrival took just a few forward-bobbing seconds, a rocking chair with Johnny-jump-up heaves, one hiccup, muskets away, the itch soon gone.

But, for me, each child meant spending nine months growing stationary as Mrs. Couch. Cap's face was making only local stops. Honey, mine was the downhill Express, mine was the Speed Queen.

We had fun, though. I ain't saying that. One night when he was off seeing Sal Smith's twin sons—both fathers now (Sal had died at age eighty-one, rich)—I went upstairs to check on my own sleeping kids. They all jumped out from nowhere, like to scared me witless. In comes Baby with a day-old cake from Harbison's bakery (that Castalia patronizes so). Candles on it, my birthday. They'd all made hats. And no hat was a soldier hat, which pleased me. I sat at the end of Louisa's bed—I accepted the usual hairnets. (I never ever wore one but my children ignored this since these were the cheapest thing at Woolworth's in the zone marked LADIES. When I sold the house, I found one whole kitchen drawer was most full of them still in their packs. That was the worst thing that whole day. No, the worst was: The painters for the purchasers, a nice young couple working from the radio station, the painters painted over my children's growth chart under where the old Seth Thomas hung. Our "ups," Baby called that. "Mark my up," she'd say.)

But to get a cake I didn't bake, store-bought *new* candles, all one color, not just gathered from the pantry piecemeal! I loved kids for remembering when I had clean forgot. I wondered why my husband stayed away from me so much. Was I harsh? Go on, tell me.

CAP had been investing money, his and mine (the secret dowry, I mean). He'd picked a company that did long-shot oil-field schemes in the Louisiana bayou country. "How's that sound?" he asked me onct. "Fishy," says I.

I kept wishing a gypsy fortune-teller would come to town. I kept hoping I'd finally get invited to do something responsible and smart-requiring, like teach Sunday school. I *wanted* to. People like me never got asked. Maybe others thought I was too busy with all my kids? Apart from Castalia, I had no real women friends to talk with. Her being black made her seem a *shadow* friend in others' eyes. Made her mean more to me, considered off on the side but really ever in the foreground. With her, I didn't need to apologize for nothing I did—or, worse, that *he* did. Hadn't she known my old man inside out forever? She was old as him if way younger-looking. By now, what might still surprise Castalia, African princess come down in life? We still had our arguments. She was still a very touchy person, easily insulted.

Pride maybe kept me away from neighborhood white ladies. Pride's always there to take its cut right off the top of everything. It's been my failing till right here recent. No, still is. Pridefulness can keep a person sort of alone—though I ofttimes have a crowd here near my bed. I see to that and am proud of it.

Understand me: I'm sneaking up on the subject, a topic not unlike, well, wife beating. Now, here at Lanes' End, we sometimes watch a TV talk show and they have the beaten woman sitting in shadows saying stuff like "He only hits me when he's drunk. He's bad for me but I love him. What can I *do*?" Burns you up. *You* want to shake her and say, "Leave, fool." But me, I said those selfsame unproud things. Pride made me tell them to myself alone, and to Castalia, who knew anyway.

He only struck me on a few weekends, only when tanked up for some big anniversary. Not ours, of course, but war ones. Might could be the day that Prothero got killed by cannon fire, or the day Cap plugged the young watch donor from up Massachusetts way. I'd be sitting there, darning the twins' socks. He'd veer in smelling of Irish cheer but looking like Potato Famine. I'd announce that he'd forgot to sign the kids' report cards—on the kitchen table for him—and that I needed school milk money by Monday, and I just sat nattering my usual blah-blah lists and lore, not a witty am- bassador's party quips, but important to the principals *involved*, you'd think. He'd pass my couch and something snagged me side the head, and there was, with us in the room, a sound. It was hand bone meeting cheekbone. It hung there. It seemed exactly the size of a piece of toast.

Then regret struck *him* and he'd be rushing for ice, saying, "It's not bad. Here," and me feeling scareder of his help than usual hindrance. "Today's our anniversary, his and mine, it's Simon's dying date, Lucille. That's why." I told him, every day meant another grisly holiday to him, another excuse for doing further dirt. Appomattox, Indian name, had occurred fifty-odd years back. He'd *been* there, remember? I wanted to be treaty right. It hap- pened just twelve times, sixteen, tops. For a real short while. Otherwise I would of been out of there. Look, ain't I just told you? I got my pride.

It happened seventy-something years ago.

Even to tell you it now, I'm so ashamed, honey.

CAS huffed up our porch steps and, seeing my lip, touched it without cer- emony, lifted a corner of my mouth. "Cut the lip against you front teeth, look like," she stated. Mouth swollen, I said, "Tut ze wip ginst fwunt teef." We laughed. The laugh you'd only share with a veteran loved one, another veteran of the veteran. What *hadn't* happened to us both already? Her clear from Africa and me starting more local.

She settled for coffee, she pointed out: Only since Winona Smythe left town had Cap got so heavy-handed. Since he owned Winona's house, still had the key, the man yet spent Thursday afternoons there in the empty place. Winona's boy and now her: Seemed most of Cap's more important pals were the Missing in Action. Times, it seemed he planned making one of me. Cap let Winona's yard run back to weeds then shrubs, jungle regained its foothold, some twisted tribute to the absent Widow Smythe's weird ways.

Cassie, yet winded from climbing front stairs, promised she had some decent gossip for me. Then sat there gasping. I told her (ice on my lip): If you die before you spill them beans, I'll never speak to you again.

Word was that our own Mrs. Winona Smythe had run off with a Italian

man—all round arms, sharp sideburns—some fellow sent here to re-tip the
War Dead monument blown over in a storm. Rumors swore he'd taken the
hefty woman and her every canary bird to the Pettibone Academy pour les
Arts Equestriennes. Cas claimed that Mrs. Smythe had slowly rose up
through its management ranks, from being bookkeeper to reigning full
Madam. Winona'd put her missing years to good use.

All this would've been common knowledge if the Riding School, two
miles east of Rocky Mount, had been even slightly on the level. It won't.
Child, it was a house of ill fame. Imported fallen Yankee girls played like
students. I sat openmouthed (which hurt the lip) as Cas explained how
certain local bankers and bigwigs faked being interested members of the
school's board. And why? So men could pay frequent quality-control visits
to check up on a certain new girl's riding progress, her posting. They soon
took little Agatha's five-gaited saddle education in hand. All I knew about
the school was: A lady from our church whose daughter really *did* ride,
horses, she went out there to check on tuition, they told it was ten thousand
dollars a year for "townies." No local gent guessed as how some women in
Falls—black ones especially—knew exactly what went on out there. Castalia,
who knew everything about everything, mapped out the full setup for me.
Named names. (She knew everything about everything except how to save
herself—our usual blind spot.)

But Winona, living there? The Widow Smythe who couldn't even stomach the hypocrisies of First Baptist Church, who'd reclaimed her Tiffany
glass off its altar? Winona who brooked no disagreement and who called
sympathetic casserole bringers "leeches and their young," Winona who'd
onct told Cap she felt qualified to be a real ambassador someplace? Her at
a whorehouse? Won't that beneath a person's dignity? Seemed unlikely to
go from a homebody to a house mother. And yet, the more I thought about
it (now eating my ice compress), the surer I felt: Nobody could've invented
this. There are facts like that—standouts, ones so far into the next world
you understand they got to be extremely genuine and local. "You didn't
make this up?" I asked Castalia, who, rightly, glared and pretended to try
and stand, leave here.

"Sorry. I know better. I just say that because *Momma* would. Nobody's
perfect," and smiled, which hurt.

I tucked info about Weird Winona to the back of my head. I refused to
mention it to Captain. He *must* know. There was a lot we didn't tell each
other now. Unlike me, he seemed to have a bit more to withhold than which
child got bad comportment marks at school. I felt glad for Winona, out
there busying being the Head of Something—even if just of that.

MY own momma, hearing man-handling rumors maybe, invited me to tea
and, though the lip was yet puffy, I accepted. She stood in the foyer, said,
"Ran into a door again, did we? How *are* the children? I hear that our

Louisa's papier-mâché volcano was the absolute pinnacle of the Science Fair." And Momma dared me to tell all concerning my marked face. Her eyes, a sufferer's, warned: If you can't say something nice . . .

So I said very little. I predicted Lou would be the next Madame Curie—only, Lou'd know to wear gloves whilst handling *her* radium. We'd had this talk before. I deeply wanted to drop the Winona whorehouse gossip on Momma but it was too good to share with somebody who couldn't even look her own puffy daughter in the face.

When I left, she slipped me a five-dollar bill (like a fifty now). "*Do* something with your . . . hair, or whatever. Broaden your vistas, Lucille."

"Yes, *ma'am*," I said real sarcastic, and regretted it at onct. She meant: I hope the lip's unswollen soon. Why can't people *say* stuff? I chose to take some cash to "Lolly's Palais de Beauté Féminine de Falls (avec manicurist on duty Vendredi and Lundi)." I went the whole hog, announced to Loll I'd want me both a wash and rinse. I did this twice a year, need it or no. My visits to the Palais dearly counted.

I first put on my white pearl-button gloves. I used them only for weddings, funerals, and Lolly's. Castalia gathered in my preschool brood at her place and let them slip Pet Condensed Milk to her latest baby minks. "Pet for pets!" Baby lisped, and Cas and me looked at each other. "She act like a certain Lady I done worked for." "I'm afraid so," said I.

I was alone today—with nothing hanging on to me at either side. Felt like I might float away into the elm trees that'd grown so much since my girlhood. Even back then they'd seemed high enough a place, safe from groundlings and the trouble we then summed up in one word: BOYS!

Lolly always squeezed in a spare appointment for me and did a real nice job. Loll give me more attention than any non-regular deserved. She'd been ahead of me in school (she was older, but held back—though she was really quick as she could be). I'd acted nice to her back then. She had a memory, Lolly did. I come in smiling. She always made a fuss. You can know that somebody's trying hard to cheer you and you can *still* be cheered, if you are smart. Permanents were new then. I couldn't really afford one, which is just as well since Modern Science has since proved they absolutely fry the person. A rinse'd do.

Only one building in all of white-owned Falls was stucco painted a let-her-rip wedding-cake pink. "Palais avec manicurist," the sign said. Momma made great fun of it, but I maintain, Is Lolly's work professional or not? That's what matters. Classiness—blue-chip classiness—is something I been turning my back on since age four.

The Palais, entire, was only about sixteen square foot, but oh, honey, so much can happen in so tiny a place. Felt like your getting in a sloshy lifeboat with six to nine other women and when you again set your foot on dry land you were stronger for the ride, real ready to stride home, but sensing you had really *been* somewhere.

Lolly was her own best walking ad. She had a long horsy face, but that never discouraged her copying any hairdo seen anyplace in any magazine, on any human movie screen. If, later, Ginger Rogers in Wednesday night's picture show at the Cameo wore her gold hair swept in one frothy teapot storm all to one side, count on finding a long-faced Lolly grocery-shopping in that very "do" tomorrow. If you called attention to it, Loll forever acted like she didn't have the foggiest idea what you meant. "Oh, this? Just a stab at it. Ginger's's more extreme but she's got the features to go *with*, me . . . well . . . I saw this photo taken of her talking at a garden party, talking with . . . David. I *like* Ginger, but she's not up to the Prince of Wales. For all her moxie, it's something a little coarse about our Ginger."

Seeing the "do" on Lolly, any local lady could then decide whether it might someway suit *her*. You heard women say, "You *know* if it turned out even so-so on Lolly, 's going to be fabulous on you. I believe she even guesses that. If only she had a man . . . I mean she has *men*, plenty, from what she says, but Loll needs one good *steady*. Who deserves it more?" Lolly agreed, and said so often. Thing about Lollie (she spelled it either "y" or "ie," depending on her mood and last night's movie), her love life had been what you'd call checkered, plus her oft-described digestion was a mess. She was Falls' one white double-divorcée. Lolly's only son, a juvenile offender, had been in every federal prison on the map, but through each tribulation, her hair and nails remained a perfect wonder of the world. It almost seemed enough.

She settled me at the sink for a hot wash. I dreaded her noticing my almost-down-to-normal lip, her feeling the two goose eggs on my scalp.

My child Baby thought the sun rose and set in Lolly's hair. Never the same twice, always a different shade of brown. Loll was savage in condemning peroxide and those who used it on anything but blisters. "I don't *dye* people," she said, proud. "Lolly transforms, Lolly improves, but this is not just some some crude henna hut. At Le Palais, I want to bring out the real woman underneath, not lay on a paint job that hides Inner Glow. Real beauty comes from Inner Glow, not bottles. All my customers have that certain something, Inner Glow. See anybody here that doesn't?" We looked around at each other—all deformed in pin curls, slopped with lotions, egg whites tightening pouchy eyes—we figured we were all in the extreme outer progress headed smack *toward* Inner Glow. We gave each other the benefit of the doubt. Benefit of the doubt: darling, that's what small town beauty parlors are there for.

During the shampoo part, while she hummed her favorite tune, I leaned my head into her specially notched sink. Loll stood over me, wetting the scalp. I loved being here because I forgot everything. The kids were in good hands. I could've been anybody. Her pet song was "I Danced With A Man Who Danced With A Girl Who Danced With The Prince of Wales." (And Lolly had, with two such gents, though she wasn't mentioning no names.) Her first love was Edward but when he got kinged, she fixed on his nephew. Her shop walls were soon lined with professionally framed photos of her

David—him wearing pure-white polo togs but never really playing. "Too refined to need to even *try*, at least publicly," Lolly said. "His chin, I'm the first to admit, is a touch weak. But me, it works on me. It proves his Inner Glow even more. The boy's nation feels his IG. I mean, don't you want to just take him home with you late some Saturday night, and tuck him under a blue blanket and just *see*?"

Down the pike, David—as history tells us—gave up his kingdom for the woman he loved, though God knows why he picked that one. I believe: she *made* him. Lolly somewhat resembled Mrs. Simpson—knobby, long-nosed, doubly-divorced-looking. Loll was not to be consoled over David's poor choice. On the couple's wedding date, Loll took down every picture of either Prince of Wales, carried them to the courtyard behind her Palais. Squirting them with some lethal hair product, Loll threw a match, watched glass pop, watched David's greyhound beauty curl and brown.

"A entire country's Inner Glow is . . . doused, and for what? some tramp golddigger with a butt like a boy's," said Lolly. We'd never connected the name Palais with Loll's interest in her Crown Prince. But not a week later she had the sign changed. Reduced to just "Falls' Beauty and Inner Glow Headquarters." You could tell some dream had died.

So on my visit that day, before England changed hands, when Le Palais still had its name, Loll was humming the Princely song, squinting in her Lucky's back-smoke, and passing along less international trashy news. Was then that strong fingers touched my scalp's worst knot and I, though I'd vowed not to, flinched. Couldn't help it. This came during the brief brief period when Cap was playing out his Hit Parade of Battles on my youngish noggin. Loll's smart fingers with their red talons right off found the biggest bump. Fingers skirted it like magic, not missing a beat in her tale of misplaced North Carolina highway funds and a certain lieutenant governor's love-nest casino in the nearby countryside.

There might have been ten other women in the sixteen square feet of the Palais, tucked under industrial-size blowers and soaking in some necessary cream or shellac dedicated to the torturing to the surface of Inner Glow. Some such glow rested stubbornly farther *in* than others, and I placed mine among the deep-seated problem glows. But even with this high-octane gossip, and even considering close quarters, not one soul ever knew that Loll was working around a Asia Minor relief map conked on my head. Fingertips treated my each welt like secret royalty.

Chattering, she quick gets me in pin curls to hide the goose eggs. Before she whips my bib off I feel Loll do some serious backcombing of my thinning hair. And all the while, she's scurrying from other head to other head. Wouldn't hire no assistant. One queen per Palais, but a cross one: "Estelle, I swear to God, look at you. Your moisturizer has clogged, now didn't I tell you to call me when it clabbered up on you, honey? Well, does that look clogged or clogged? Now wake up and put down that back issue of *Liberty*. Your glow'll just *stay* inner without some cooperation here. *I* want you attractive at the Daughters of the Confederacy Antebellum Belle Bash, but do *you*, Estelle? All right then!"

And those many years, Lolly told nobody. She never blamed me for the welts and bruises. (Blamed *him*, I mean, blamed him.)

3

TIMES, while ironing, I'd find myself haunted. The people I stood recalling weren't any souls I'd ever seen alive. I only knew them through a grown civic leader who'd been a soldier, aged thirteen, and *he* only knew these three from having killed them.

I stood dousing a terry-cloth middy belonging to Louisa and I was picturing a man shot while smoking a pipe. (I had no other info on him!) Trying to imagine his features, I'd be hoping to apologize. Sometimes my husband's curtness hurt locals' feelings, and I would then go over at a gathering and pay folks a little extra attention. I would be making up for what he'd done, a little social slight he had but half intended, child. And, like that, while ironing or shopping—these three victims would sweep into my head, good shirts hanging drying on one line. I soon wondered who they *were* to me, and how sick I was to feel accountable, say, to the Yankee boy who trusted a Reb with his heirloom watch? I told myself that if *I* ever had to kill somebody, well, I wouldn't, couldn't. I'd die first. And even if I did— how would I then walk around eating snacks and taking catnaps? Life would not allow a moral murderer her everyday joys and pleasures. The ghost of who you plugged would be there like state and federal sales tax on niceties great and minor. And so I paid secret tariffs—forty-odd years' worth—to the puzzled spirits of three strangers my boy-hubby'd slaughtered. It seemed a duty—as I ironed—but, too, I got half used to their being there, like the sound of water boiling just across my kitchen. I became their protector, their volunteer Madonna on a real real smalltime level. This might sound odd, child, but, over the years, so upset was I by the idea of murder, of his doing them in (even if he *had* to), I signed on as their loyal representative. They swarmed in—faint as steam but at least that real. They each became my silent partner, okay company.

I slowly knew: I had willingly become the mother of the men my husband killed.

4

WELL, at Raleigh, Cap found he could now act ceremonial and bossy as possible, he would finally get away with it forever. See, by this time, many soldiers who'd once doubted his war record, they had aged past life's more lucid parts. Half had one mental foot already in the vegetable patch. Their tempers improved.

They'd been full grown during our terrible Rebellion. Him? he was just a shaky sliver of a child. But none of them elders now recalled Cap's tender age back then. At the last reunion six years back, doubters had made comments. Now men believed Cap looked so strong because of what a rough, exceptional soldier he'd once made. Older fellows still recalled the Marsden family name, still considered Captain's mother the Tidewater's ongoing finest-looking woman. They forgot how she'd got burned, and how—after years of living under veils and clutching teacups through flamish nightmares, after living back of drapes to hide scars—the poor thing died, Spode in hand, her last words, whispered toward what she imagined were still more gentlemen callers, "Tell . . . them . . . I'm . . . out."

But there in Raleigh, milling around, waiting for Fort Bragg's spiffy marching band to arrive by bus, Cap got grilled by his momma's last living senile admirers. "She's doing exceptionally well, considering," Marsden valiantly lied to the valiant boys in moth-eaten gray. Cap didn't want to spoil their final parade.

"High-flung as ever, I guess? A handful, our Lady is, but Lord such skin."

"I'm sure, if she were present, my mother'd ask to be remembered to you."

"Well, well. Same back. Recalls me, does she? Oh, I'm no fool, I know I was but one of many. Not like our 'Lady' is . . . one of a kind. Now *she* can flat-out flirt." They sighed in their wheelchairs. Behind them, talking at each other about more recent topics, were young black men hired to push these geezers along festooned Hillsborough Street (the black helpers discussed not no mealy has-been war, but Last Night).

The veterans wheeled with Confed flags as lap robes, they had perfect memories for every little thing but what'd happened these last fifty crowding years.

(Dear God, never let me lose my marbles—all I've got—but I ain't complaining.)

Captain Wm. More Marsden let hisself be liberally photographed and admired before the parade moved. His crew of D o Cs still worked on him like he was a whole Rose Bowl float, them his keyed-up florists. I understand some eyeliner was used, but I didn't like to say nothing too critical at the time. —A photographer from *Liberty* come up and snapped him. There he stood, one fist delved into the tunic of a uniform that had about as much to do with his skinny wartime self as Hollywood California did The Holy Lands. My man posed, with wheelchairs being background to prove *he* won't yet in one.

Pearl-gray outfit, feathered hat, white gloves I'd scrubbed myself by wearing each one while I bleached and scoured the thing on my own burned hand, cock-spur cut still stingsome. The man answered only direct questions *Liberty* asked but otherwise never opened his mouth. Soon, everybody present accepted as how Marsden had once god-Blessed the great Lee's every sneeze.

Our dashing lieutenant governor was photographed smiling, slapping Captain on the back, inviting him to a floating poker game, after. Our *Herald Traveler* did a full page of Parade Pix. The local chapter of D of Cs made sure. I studied the fleet of wicker wheelchairs, old-timers waving out at the crowd, what vets still had use of their arms. Time had paralyzed several, and yet their *eyes* still could chop side to side, self-styled 20/20 salutes, poor things. But my man was the only one that later got showed in *Liberty*, worldwide.

REMEMBER "Red," our Tailor of Genius? He was fifty-some when, around this time, Wong Chow died downtown at his solitary Singer. Must've happened sudden, he stitched a seam across two fingers, joining them to the oldest Lucas girl's white satin wedding dress. Huge funeral "Riceyman" had. Preacher praised him, "Knew what a day's work meant." Under the shop's floorboard, eight thousand hard-earned dollars was found squirreled. Ignoring foreign addresses among his things, our Town Council voted: the money should go to keep our public library open longer hours on the weekends forever.

MYSELF, I was home in Falls with the kids, four head colds and the twins had fallen from the side-yard swing trying to get a neighbor's collie up onto it. I *told* them not to. Then our first household case of measles. Me up and down them stairs—not yet old but feeling I deserved a flag and lap robe myself, and a wheelchair (which I now rate, you notice). A two-story house with that many children, I deserved a elevator chair on wheels with wings. But also, after the Raleigh vets' march, I felt proud of him, and that's a fact. In downtown stores, people kept coming up to me.

One month after the parade, there he was in *Liberty*, on newsstands worldwide, plus the one at Lucas' All-Round—Captain hogging a whole page and looking fierce and fatal and content as God hisself on wartime R and R.

When that issue come out, our house was all loud joy. We received two casseroles, and without even a death or injury to any of us personally! Baby, who proved nimble early with our mother tongue, noticed the occasions when such dishes usually turned up. She dubbed such donated casseroles "Disasteroles." We all sat stunned at supper, Cap too, amazed how apt it was—how bright she'd have to keep on being all her life to stay abreast of her own starter wit! She pretty much did, too.

The magazine got so many letters, they wrote us saying it'd be nice to do a feature article "on what we hear is your surprisingly large and surprisingly youthful family, sir."

Cap set a date and, two weeks later, two days before *Liberty*'s cameras arrived to check up on my housekeeping for all of planet Earth to see, my hubby thought to tell me. Can you imagine? Is that even fair?

Food
and
Rifles

*B*OYS LOVE GUNS. Dads, being both ex-boys and members of the NRA, encourage this. Me, I watch from outside and wring my hands and hope it's all a phase every man on earth'll outgrow in time to save theirselves and us. I mean the rest of us at our sinks and calendars and chores—us, trying not to listen for the crack of weapons from nearby woods, trying not to expect open season and the sky on fire.

Meaning: Back then, my oldest son, Ned, was about to turn twelve. This meant his poppa planned to take him hunting soon. A rite—blood rite. Ned's older sister I cornered for a warning talk concerning womanhood, her own. I wouldn't be a coward like my mother had. At table alone with me, Lou idly touched veins on the back of my hand, Lou whispered, "But, Momma? how will I know when it happens, the woman . . . hood?"

"Blood . . . will . . . tell . . . us . . . that. Nature marks the occasion, see? Ain't that something? They think of everything." I felt sick, like I'd foisted the whole darn setup on her.

I thought how my hubby would someday have the fun of taking Ned down to Duck, North Carolina, to shoot mallard blood from out of a whole migrating skyful. Heaps more glamorous than living like Louisa, scanning the comings and goings of her own plump stay-at-home body. But then, darling, like I said: the mystery with us and fairness stays: how we ever came to so steadily expect it. Maybe we're all banished, at birth, from some dim land of perfect decency, maybe our hopes for it are just homesickness for that first remembered justice?

"I will not permit your taking our Ned to no Outer Banks in the company of professional bourbon drinkers whose main joy is not shaving for three days straight. Most come home looking worse than what they bagged. Ned's a bit nervous, and the sounds of guns won't help. You want meat? I'll go buy some from Luke Lucas'. These ducks you bring back have so much shot in them, it's like eating fricasseed tooth fillings. Leave Ned be, Cap. Leave me one. You get your way so often, sir. Do me this one favor, please."

Ned hated hearing me call him "nervous," a mistake. This was during another lovely evening meal—peace, communion, and good digestion. Ned claimed *he* got to choose what he liked doing: he'd soon go twelve. Captain said our lieutenant governor would be among the hunters. "Imagine a lad firing his first shot in the presence of the North State's second-in-command. Might almost constitute a civics lesson."

"Don't push this," I said, just as the twins raised their hands to contribute. I welcomed a change. "Yes, petnesses, what's on *your* mind?"

"Baby just called us a wiener-head."

"I did not, called you 'Hot-Dog Breath' but not 'Wiener-Head,' because that'd be . . . *crude.*"

"When can I, Poppa, 'fire my first shot,' hunh?"

"In time," Cap answered, eyeing me. "More corn, Lucille? Ned, we will bring her around. I plan to personally prove what an education this outing's going to be. Ducks, natural history, elected official, a motorcade with State Police to lead it."

Says I, "Waste of taxpayers' money, ask me. Anyhow, it's final. He goes over my dead body."

"So, is *that* the way you want it? —Just joking. *You* can joke constantly, can't I? Relax, voice of doom. Further corn anybody? Your mother's done a fine job here on this corn."

"Please pass the Wiener-Heads."

"*Enough,*" my fingers snap. "Besides, he's young for his age."

Ned threw the saltcellar my way. I couldn't blame him basically. Nobody likes being discussed like they're missing.

"Twelve's not young," my husband said. "You know where I was at twelve?"

"No, remind me." I stooped to irony.

"It's high time Ned learned a few things. Time the lad got . . ."

" 'Broke in'? Kind of 'broke in'? Where have I heard that before?"

Captain excused hisself to go back downtown to work at 6 p.m.

"You hate fun," Ned sputtered at me. "You want to keep me safe in some house all day with *girls.*"

Louisa lowered her eyes and Ned told her he was sorry but *she* knew what he meant. "Men have the fun. I can't be safe forever, Momma. I'm twelllve."

I looked at him—how reasonable and sharp he sounded. How clear and fair a face. What a shrew I was, driving my old man from this house at night.

"I'm trying to save you, son. Don't hate me for *that*, please."

Ned sat there behind those long lashes that looked stowed nightly in tailor-built humidors. For Ned, eyes won't just something to look out of—they made surfaces to rest behind. We stared at each other and he said, "Be excused?" rising, tossing down his napkin. "Wiener breath," one twin remarked. "Breath wiener," come the other's reply. Nobody laughed.

"CASTALIA time!" I hollered minutes later for a change of pace. Some kids cheered. We would head downhill to re-view Cassie's mink ranch and neighborhood rec center. Ned said he'd stay home with *Water Fowl of Our North America*. Said they showed you birds flying in black outline so you'd know which to aim for.

I started to joke aloud: Maybe baby ducks had library albums showing boys like him, only pictured from on high—so ducks'd know to flap away quick? But I let it rest. My will to have the sharp last word—my desire to ofttimes be proved right—it made me harder to be near, both as mother and wife. Everything that now makes me a sometimes-okay talker with strangers, that could turn me to ground glass around the house. And, look here, it's a weakness I've admitted, right? Okay, then.

Though the temperature stayed near seventy, Cassie barrels out to greet us ridged inside her ripe brown mink. The coat now struck Castalia mid-thigh, new pelts added along the bottom one at a time, like some Sunday-school perfect-attendance pin accumulating your prestige and longevity at once. The collar arched high as Elizabeth I's, framing Cassie's noble neck, backing her up.

Her hair tonight was all braided corn rows—glistening with pricey pomade. Like us, she had no phone—so all my visits (trailing my kids and their stray pals) were unannounced and more a pleasure for that. Castalia was, like me, a stay-at-home. Our usual problem was the swallowing of pride it took to walk ten long blocks to one another's house.

She showed us how pit bulls had been disrupting her minks' needed beauty sleep. She pointed near front porch steps where she kept her sledge-hammers. Cas explained how satisfying it'd felt last night when this particular hammerhead met bulldog teeth trying and pry through the mesh of her chicken wire. Minks, saved, hissed in cedar breeding boxes. The bulldog had staggered home, head dented but barely fazed. "You gots to hand it to them," Cas respected any enemy's true merit—even when a sledgehammer was needed to fully investigate it.

Black friends visiting her, they shyly took off at the sight of white us, me of course protesting. Cassie poured iced tea, using mason jars for glasses. My kids had tried this at home but uphill it looked silly, here it seemed a fine idea. Once we settled in a bright red kitchen that made up most of Cassie's home, Baby stepped toward the great fur wrap our hostess wore. "Can I, Cas?" Baby would then point to a pelt. Castalia, seated, eyes closed—feeling Baby's finger prod—announced the name of each pelt's contributor. "Dixie. Dixie Too, that's Dixie daughter. Chenille. Flyboy. Compote. Max. Foxy. Tater. Toothy. Back to Chenille again—you a sly one, ain't you, Baby?"

The game soon bored kids. Who could prove Castalia wrong? She sat inside the sheeny pelts fed table scraps donated by my family and many others. No game is fun long if just one person's cornered all right answers (I'd tried telling Captain that for years).

So our kids scattered after Cas warned, "Feed them by dropping just one peel at a time—you, don't you lost that finger, got me?" Off mine dashed with Cassie's youngests and the neighbor children. Minks are like professional beauties of the human type: staying pretty seems to use up most of their dispositions—not much kindness left. They wear their limited love right on their backs. Then people skin them for that love. I once asked Cassie if she minded wringing necks of all these beasts she'd raised. "Never met a mink I liked much—except to stroke 'em—which you can't do till they done checked out. They ain't pets, they beautiful excuses. —Talking furs, you ought to of seen Lady's. Kept hers all in one cedar closet, used to have us bring up ice from out the icehouse in hottest August and only when the room got cold unto meat lockers would she try on one fur at a time. Let *us* do it, too. You learn to get accustomed. August, and your breath blowing white and you in snowman chinchilla, silver fox. One way of softening the world some."

I confessed worrying: Captain's toting Ned to some seaside duck blind for a overly male weekend. Cas disappointed me, saying the more I fought it, the more fun it'd seem to boys who will be . . . "Can *I* touch your coat?" I asked.

Out come a whole ringtail sleeve of her—stuffed full of flesh as dark as mink but smoother, harder. Seemed mink might make some fuzzy truce between Castalia's cast-iron silhouette and the light air all round her. Up close, I again saw the coat's sad imperfections. Twice in ten years she'd shifted its fastening frogs outward as her girth grew. Each expansion made a mark that caused her garment to look walleyed or scored with udders in twin rows. The skins grew lusher as the coat eased toward the floor—Cassie'd started throwing slaughterhouse fat to her more recent stock. Minks were out there making squealing rustles as our kids pelted them with leftovers. The beasts could strip a cow skull so clean so quick, you might practically sell the bone to some nice science class. "So pretty," I touched fur, she nodded.

Her neckpiece in the 1880s had become a glass-eyed boa by the nineties, then a "chubby" by century's arrival, falling to a wrap, a stole, then drooping towards the fabled glory of "full-length mink." Though you saw how pelts were joined with fishing-line stitches peeping through, the coat still seemed Luxury itself. A log cabin of earned fluff, it covered her huffing all over town and in most weathers. Castalia didn't trust the world enough to leave her coat alone at home, no, not even in August.

2

MY KIDS hated visiting Momma—she made them play board games, she set them in groupings here and there. They always claimed to have lots of homework waiting back home. So today we passed her place on tiptoe practically, me guilty: a only child trailing all these grandkid dividends. She sometimes acted jealous over the hours I spent at Castalia's place. She once said, "What *can* you see in that obese bulldog wrapped with rats?" (I didn't speak to her for six whole days.) But here *comes* my mother, and carrying a armful of hydrangea blooms, too blue to seem earth-grown. The more acid the dirt, the deeper your blue. Dressed in black, she had dark bags under her eyes (first sign of her undetected liver cancer), she was wearing a hint of cologne (unlike her), and she'd rushed right past both me and ours. Ignoring me, she interested me suddenly. She wore a crepe armband. I spoke into her homegrown flowers, "Who died?"

"Nobody that recent," the bouquet shifted, I saw Momma's softened face. My own mother looked different. People change. I believe this, even now.

"She would be a hundred and five today." I figured Momma meant her own bland mother, Mrs. Angus McCloud, a woman everybody seems to've loved but nobody could ever make *real* to me in stories, the author of a shortbread recipe I've got to give you, a lady who had no motive or gumption past wishing for her family's well-being, not enough. Not enough to make it into History.

"You never knew her, Lucille. I've lately come to see things a bit more clearly. It was most unfair—no doubt of that, quite dreadfully unjust. But blaming!—we all blame. Ugly in the extreme. Why *is* that, Lucille? We want a reason, I suppose, or—better—some culprit. But so little of value can actually be traced that way. I regret her losses. Along with Poppa's love, it was she who got me through much early difficulty. And yet—sad, only on her hundred and fifth birthday do I get around to taking certain . . . tokens."

Along with flowers, Momma held a little gift-boxed bottle of cologne. That's what I'd smelled. Momma never wore scent, said it only courted harm.

"I dreamed of her. And in my dream it was her birthday. I had your father go check her stone and sure enough, today's her hundred and fifth. My nurse loved me but couldn't spare me any pain of note. We cannot save each other, Lucille. In regards to a certain man in your own life, dear, do remember that. We must let each other go down independently and that's maybe why we come to detest each other so. We hate how much the others' pain reminds us of our failing them, our likely going down as well. —'Basta.' Probably sounds silly. I am off. She was ever the fool for birthdays."

I turned and watched her rush, the notorious Bianca McCloud, acknowledged monster among all the virtuoso brats of Falls. How had time and tricks turned such a rogue into this skinny society lady veering past me, hiding behind flowers and trailing a flag of good cologne? Change, always so mysterious in people. I guess we should be grateful it can happen to most any of us anytime. Can't it? Can't it? Live and hope.

CAP was growing broader through his back. Though he'd been fifty when we married, the fellow was in right good shape—a little cello notch at the center where those first saddlebags of stored plumpness settle in the midst of mid-aged gents. But now his trunk thickened. If his chins'd doubled, trebled, the white-silver beard spared anybody's seeing that. Only when he slipped into his nightshirt did I—the one on earth allowed to—notice how plump he'd grown from the extra water whiskey held. His cheeks got rosier. He was now looking—all the whole year round—like some vice-riddled Santa, drawing unemployment clear up till late fall, hard on the elves in the off-season. Darl, ain't nobody more depressed than Santa between shifts. And yet, remembering, it was a good time, too—one of the last we had. When he was "up," he kept slipping me fistfuls of twenties to buy groceries— back when a twenty seemed Gibraltar. He was rich as he would ever get. He only hit me once or twice for six whole months there. He quacked his mallard mating whistle around the house. That year and the next we had a genius mockingbird nesting in our black walnut where the kids' swing hung. This creature could copy the duck call. Only the male mockingbirds sing, and they can "do" up to seventy-five songs but (like with all of us, darling) a few repeats. I soon heard this bird do a cat in heat, a window fan, and the first half-bar of what I swear was Rudy Vallee's latest, "I'm Just a Vagabond Lover." Bird also did other birds. They'd answer, thinking he was one of them. Cas sat with me in the back yard one August evening, shucking corn. Our kids were gathered—her youngests and all mine. The genius bird was tearing through every local color. Cas heard Captain's decoy mallard-call decoyed. She coughed one of her un-laughs, said, "Who *can't* that Xerxes do to pieces?"

" 'Who *can't* that Xerxes do to pieces?' " I gave right back.

"That ain't *me* Luce done done," Cas defended herself.

"Is, too," her own daughter nodded. "Just like."

Louisa confessed then, "Momma, while doing dishes especially, she *practices* you, Cassie."

I faced my victim and inspiration. "Someday I want to tell The Tribe That Answers just like you do."

She give me this look I cannot describe. "Best do it right then, or not a bit."

I only nodded. We turned back to detasseling corn. We listened. Evening fell on one bird doing everybody's music.

3

RUTH, a abandoned wife, twenty-nine years old, lived right next door. The mockingbird did *her* Rudy Vallee record. Ruth's husband had gone alone by train (on his railroad worker's discount) to Washington, D.C., to see the April cherry blossoms. Turned out, Willard liked them cherry blossoms so much he wrote Ruth: He felt a yen to stay right on till their *next* pink go-round. "You don't mind, I know," his postal card said. Poor Ruth brought the thing over, showed me it while smiling out her worry. "It's a *pretty* card," she said, like its attractiveness mattered. "That darn Willard. Some dreamer," she said twice, then left. I sent over some of my famous Scottish shortbread in time for poor Ruth's dinner. Have I given you the recipe for that? I have to give you that before we're done, remind me.

Willard never mentioned how Ruth might get along till spring next arrived in D.C. Lucky for her, she had a little money of her own. Her mother's people had been Pomeroys, though it didn't show. She stayed put and smoked and, from her quiet porch, watched me gather all of the Captain's growing mail, invitations to "appear." She seemed to think her strapping Willard wrote *us*, not her. Ruth daily waited for the postman or Spring, whichever got here first. She waved over at me, poor thing, she called, "Guess who's having a very juicy lamb chop for dinner?"

"You?" I tried being polite but she broke my heart, Ruth. Ordered stuff by mail order, just to give her something extra to look out for, postally speaking. Like my poppa, poor Ruth was addicted to the mail. Like Pop, she got little. Still, it's one of Falls' joys that makes us like most other spots. True, our local bedsheets always needed changing, and so did the program at our moving pictures. True, this year's fashion was last year's, let out an inch with one tired flounce more—but Falls at least got recognized by the U.S. Postal Service, receiving some six days per week. Made you feel more *here*.

A radio turned to *Mary Worth*. A Victrola rigged with tangos, a carton of Luckies with three clean ashtrays: Ruth set up shop on her front porch near the mail basket. She got out there around 9 a.m. sharp though our delivery won't till one-thirty to two. Willpower might bring her strapping Willard home. "Poor Ruth," even our kids called her that.

Every time she drifted past one of our town's three competitive hair-cooking establishments, beauticians rushed to their windows, stared out at her, longing. Lolly couldn't pin a curl for minutes after.

"I'd pay *her*, Lucy. Love a challenge. I hate to say it about another woman in my hometown, and I remember that her Willard was nice across the shoulders but otherwise no great shakes, but no wonder he left. I can see Poor Ruth's split ends from fifteen feet—they're 'tridents.' 'Tridents' is trade talk, Lucy, it means you got one hair in a three-way tie of splitting. I have dreams and in my dreams, they've turned to three-headed snakes and are underfoot everywhere in Falls. I kill them with a pitchfork that's my favorite silver styling brush, only huge and barbed like frog gigs are. Send Poor Ruth to Lolly for help, free. On Le Palais. My civic duty to a town this size. Her and her hair are everywhere."

Waiting for Willard, Ruth installed our block's number one telephone. Maybe she hoped he'd call. She got her own name listed every possible way—maiden name, initials. Helped flesh out Falls' early phone directory, Ruth's moniker tridenting too. Poor thing tattled on my own children over our shared fence. I'd go out with yet another eighty pounds of wet clothes and Ruth'd say, "I worry about the twins going down that drainage ditch again. Maybe it's just me."

"It is," I said under my breath. I knew I was supposed to rush around like a chicken. I was supposed to beg to be led to the drainage sump hole where my matched set was gasping, maybe stuck. But I had explored that same death trap as a Runt Funny child. "They usually come home," I said. Then felt I'd hurt Ruth's feelings.

Willard had worked for the Atlantic Coastline Railroad like half the folks in Falls. His job was he signaled train-to-train, first with kerosene lanterns, then—as modern times hit—with twelve-battery flashlights.

One night, my Baby admitted she had lost her new Junior Princess wristwatch I had paid much more than I should've at Woolworth's for her birthday. Missing it, she was crushed, I saw that, Baby doing her Katharine Cornell dramatics about how she'd never sleep till it was found. She lisped, tragic, "Baby's best ac-cethory, ever." She'd been near our swing out back. So I grabbed the kitchen flashlight. I kept the Eveready in the (hairnet) drawer nearest our back door.

So I'm out there by the fence on my hands and knees. Baby's been forced to wait at the back screen door, where she's just whimpering for it, and I'm aiming my flash at the scuffed spots that hold puddles under our swing set, when I hear a whisper.

"Willard? lover? that you?"

I felt bad telling Poor Ruth, no, just Lucy seeking Baby's Junior Princess Accessory watch.

"Oh," she said. It was the sound of a soul going down a long sliding board towards nothing. "Oh," she tried brightening. "Thought it could be. That Willard, he does dearly love a flashlight." And she drooped toward her big empty house.

"Night . . ." I called, and watched her go. I heard her Victrola crank up loud to help her through the evening. I thought: At least I ain't alone. Times I long to be, but having Poor Ruth right here, it proved to me—this life would have to get worse before I'd really leave. —I'd *thought* of leaving. Did I say that?

From next door, Ruth watched me flip through a stack of mail for Cap, post-Raleigh speaking offers so fancy they called the fees "honorariums," like he was some Roman emperor. From half of Dixie, they poured in. Was it jealousy I felt?

The Elks, the Lions, the United Mooses. Cap was now welcome by every form of club wildlife. I thought it fitting that these men chose to be known as types of missing animals. Imagine naming yourself for exactly what you've gone and shot the last of. Falls even had a club called the Lodge of Redmen.

Momma claimed our family failing was: jealousy and self-pity. I *have* been known to cave in to self-pity. Nobody's perfect, all right? But maybe this I was feeling, with two pounds of male mail in my hand, was that other: Old Jealousy.

And—a hard thing to admit: The more of a celebrity he started being to the world, the more motorcars we got with state flags on their running boards, the more motorcycled State Police turned up before dawn to escort hunting expeditions clear down to the beach—sirens making everything including ambulances pull over—the more of a moving-picture star he expected even *us* to feel he was, the more some part of me believed he was becoming, well, cheesy. Tacky, he'd started turning. Here he was lending money to wealthy poker pals. Imagine, *me* falling for *this* fellow. But, hateful as it is to say, I did, I had.

Once, I went to lift his civvy vest off a chair back around then, I jabbed myself on something sharp. Really sliced my palm. From one pocket, I pull forth this little curved metal barb. Was a lethal-looking doohickey, thorn-shaped, three and a half inches long, bright silver as some dental pick. Two leather thongs tied onto it, like laces of something you might wear. Seemed a cross between hypodermic needle and the nastiest brass knuckle ever.

Having scratched my palm, I stood staring at my open hand, like some fortune-teller finally measuring her own artery Life line. Red beads, a new seam. Alone in our quiet bedroom, I said, "Lucy, I see rubies in your future."

His shirts lately required extra bleaching, speckled with small rusty flecks. He stepped up behind me now, unexpected, silent, home for lunch. When he touched my back, I jumped like somebody shot. He saw what I held. He grabbed the thing, tucked it behind him. He stood here, a foot taller than myself, giving me this guilty pluckish smile, straight down. Whiskers, still tinted parade blue, widened like some tomcat's.

"What cut me?" I asked. Typical, my curiosity coming on account of bodily damage, *my* body, and afterward.

"Equipage from a recent sideline, Lucille—game fowls. You see, this gets strapped onto a fighting cock's legs. Allows the victor to achieve his end more decisively."

Downstairs, I heard Ned and Louisa start bickering over a nickel. She was money-mad and always saving.

"Sir, you mean that makes this one chicken quicker to slice off the poor loser's head?"

"Something along those lines, my dove. You do have a way with words,

don't you, Lucy?" and he laughed like a boy caught shoplifting, a boy whose
daddy owns the store. "Do wrap something around that hand, I worry about
you. And next time be more careful in sneaking through my pockets? No
telling what might turn up."

"I'll ignore that. And them dark specks on your white shirts? Just dried
rooster blood, hunh? They fling it off in such amounts, do they? and you're
right there up front with a fistful of bills, egging them on, I bet. You enjoy
that, sir?"

"Everything sounds rough when flattened that way, Lucille. Everything
does. The sexual act, bravery, everything can be reduced as you've just done.
And you have a gift for doing that, I fear. It's your fable-making. Ironing
out certain distinctions. There's so much I'd like to explain to you, really.
But so little I actually *can*, you know? Lately you resist the best parts of
me. Maybe the age difference. I don't know. But fun is one thing you never
seem to *get*. Two different languages seemingly. And what I keep trying to
make clear, it's probably nobody's fault. I mean that. Here, come here . . ."

He motioned toward the bed. I heard the nickel fight approach getting
physical. I'd need to go downstairs and referee. "Come, please." He beckoned
and was smiling and I saw that it'd only take three minutes, tops. He just
sat there, seeming so sure, so ready, and looking at me with this appetite I
knew had love in it. For me. I felt a kind of weakening under my apron and
at the knees' very hinges. He was so much bigger than yours truly. I'd best
keep my wits about me just to survive here. "Fun," he smiled, "ever heard
of it, Lucille?"

Then I figured: What the heck? You know me. I can resist anything but
a dare. "Why not," I flirted, "for 'a mature man,' you ain't totally un-cute."
I hate myself. He reared back on our shared bed. I heard his boot strike the
muzzle of a rifle under there, he kicked it gingerly aside. He eyed me like
a hypnotist and, slow, commenced unfastening his pants. I told myself I'd
have to go through with this now. Somewhere, in so much of it, things often
shifted toward a somber ugly feel, brown, some service I provided. Me
wondering where *I* came in, though he sometimes acted so sweet and patient, dwelling on every sigh I made and coaxing forth more.

"Hel-lo," he said, mouth gone grave in its white pretty beard. I stood
between the legs of him sitting here. We kissed. He'd learned how from
Castalia and he was real good at it and that in itself made married life some
better. I touched his white shirt and his hands were all up suddenly under
me and welcoming theirselves to what was always mine and sometimes his.

I pressed his shoulders, then remembered and jerked back, I saw I'd
bled onto his shirt. "Oh, look," I said.

He sleep-talked, "Whaa . . ."

"I've gone and spotted your shirt. If it ain't the roosters' blood, it's mine
because of them. I'll never get this clean."

He pinched me then—not mean but, being betwixt a person's legs, surely attention-getting. He craned up to be level with my face—which he nearly was, even sitting. His bass voice whispered, "Who gives a flying fuck about one white cotton shirt?"

I leaned back into his goodly grip and looked at him. I wanted to say, "*I* do. Since it's what you put me in charge of. I don't love doing it but since I do, I want to do it okay, okay? So, yeah, I care about the shirt." But he was right. *He* could afford another shirt. Why'd I bother even bleaching them? But how might I admit all this, honey? Then I'd seem *really* powerless. Instead, I chanced sounding wifey and conventional and chill. I hated how few choices I had. "I'd best go soak it in cold water. Blood *takes* that. I'll . . ."

"You haven't answered me, about the importance of one shirt," he said. "For years you haven't answered me. Someday I'll get your attention to the point where you'll answer."

"That a threat?" I asked, and his hands at onct abandoned my lower parts and I wanted to mourn their leaving me, yeah "mourn." Right then, for reasons of my own (a puzzlement so often) I really wanted him so much. Wanted somebody.

"Ned owes me thirty-five cents and now . . ." Louisa was right here beside the bed before she noticed what was what.

"It's okay," I said.

"Yes, fine," her pop got very still. But he spoke under his breath to me, "You people," he said it with tears in one of his gray eyes only. "Nickels and shirts and shirts and nickels. And you wonder why I'd rather sit around anyplace else remembering *real* things."

I didn't answer him. I caught his drift. I should not have abandoned him there on our bed. I think now: A better person than myself would've touched his beard or hair, touched anything but the traces of red on his second-nicest business shirt. Instead, I put my arm around Louisa, who was upset at interrupting what she didn't understand but surely felt. "Now what's all this about your famous bank account?"

And he was left there on the bed. Alone. He had his side to everything. I see that.

And later that afternoon, when he'd locomotived back to work, I came in looking for my scissors and found a handkerchief on my pillow, a hankie closed around a gram of his own ivory seed. He'd left that for me, a love song, a ransom letter, a poison-pen love note shot right my way. I decided not to wash then bleach that hankie. I just tossed it out. But it'd been a perfectly good Irish linen handkerchief and, in tossing it—why?—I felt a little guilty. A waste. I sometimes think I felt more guilt and love toward the laundry than I did some days for him.

It's a thing I live with, sugar, year in, year out forever. I blame pride.

But then, that in itself is cowardly, that in itself is pride.

A
Minstrel Show
for God

Vanity of vanities, saith the preacher, all is vanity.
—ECCLESIASTES 12:8

JUST WHEN I'd chose which cardigan to consider packing (my worn maroon but with the deepest pockets, naturally), something nice happened. I'd hoped for a gypsy or a job. Wouldn't you just know, right when woe is getting your life organized in straight deep ruts, you get a canal slashed right through your jungly Panama and, zip, you can now look from sea to shiny sea.

A Baptist committee came to call with exceptionally fine news. Seems this lady at church had got cancer (that won't the news) but she'd had to quit teaching Sunday school after thirty-one years and I was being asked to take over her class. Would I, please? —Imagine . . . teach!

The committee said it'd been a oversight, my not being pressed earlier. One deacon went, "We figure: You want something done superbly, Lucille, ask a busy person." Flattery. I've stayed a sucker for it. My failing.

As the world goes, such a job might sound right minor to a person with some choices, like you. But living like I had, being who I was, I took it serious. It was what they were giving away that year . . . I wanted some.

My brightness'd mostly been used in learning how you cut eleven pieces from one pie, in telling kids how many colors our single sky gets to be. My husband was somebody long since "discovered" by a vet-respecting world. What did I usually receive for trying hard? A chance to go unnoticed yet another week. So Sunday-school teaching made me stand up straight. "Here goes. I'll sure give it a whirl, with God's help." I added that aloud to cheer my visitors concerning my credentials. I meant it.

No sooner had the committee in dark clothes set down my best teacups and cleared out, I rushed to look up next Sunday's lesson. I fetched the massy marbleized volume inherited from my grandad Angus McCloud, and still pressed full of four-leaf clovers that him and his youngest daughter had collected amongst backyard bees in happier days. It was a Scottish edition, "The Testaments Old and New in King James' Peerless Translation, With The Apocrypha in an Annotated Version Intended For All The Daily, Scholarly and Devotional Uses of The Modern Family." Well, child, today that seemed exactly me and us! Lou'd been hanging around the kitchen, waiting for the crowd to leave. "Who died?" She drifted into my sewing room, where I now sat, scholarly and devoted, reading the pre-assigned text. I told her of my honor, asked would she please keep the wee ones quiet for a while. Lou did, of course, after closing my door quietly behind. Lou most always did what we asked her to. That was *her* tragedy.

Next week's text was where: Judith cuts off the head of her people's worst warrior-enemy, a man she might've come to love. That, plus her getting him drunk and cutting his block off, was *their* tragedy. Okay, good—something juicy to start with. A story with stuff really happening in it, my favorite type. I'd practically memorized the scripture when I hear a scratchy sound— was Ruth, my sad neighbor, not the Bible character. Ruth, having seen the group in black leave, is now tapping at her window screen and, mouth moving, sounding out, "Hi. Who's died?" I waved her away with a smile, pulled all shades on that side of our house.

Holding the Good Book, I paced my narrow mending room, door locked. The children lived on tiptoe suddenly, the hush enforced by our long-suffering Louisa. In print, Judith's story was so lively and severe—full of gore and a love life, the heroine with ideal looks and patriotic reasons. I soon thought of her as "Judy" almost. But I well knew how in Sunday school it'd come out dull as Thursday's leftover rutabaga. I was stalking back and forth with growing stage fright. I asked myself: What is ever more boring than a boring church-school lesson? I had to find some way to make this *mine*, a Lucy-type lesson, something real as life, something New. A *story*! I'd suffered through so many Sundays.

Shirl and me had sat in First Baptist's big back room, it was sectioned off by curtains on wired rings indicating your age group. You could hear the class you'd soon grow into, droning on, just as uninviting, behind a cotton drape. Our teacher's voice was so nasal it twanged like a Jew's harp, sounded like her nickel-plated spectacles spoke each slow word. "This here is just so deep," she always said, lifting the book within inches of her eyes. "A uneducated woman's got no right to even touch the hem of this in here. Still, somebody's got to, so we'll try, but, boys and girls, I'm not up to it, it's just so *deep* . . . It's the *Bib*le." "No lie," says I under my breath, drawing snickers from Shirl and others. Our only joy was counting Mrs. Snipes's pet word on our fingers: "deep." We compared after class. Her one-day record was thirty-one. Fact. I hated Sunday school. And now, my first time in the spotlight, I risked turning into just such a spiritual dud. I told myself I'd never apologize for lack of education. Artists never apologize. "Consider the lilies of the field, they neither sow nor reap nor have a fancy B.A. degree but which of them won't knock your eyes out with beauty?"

The one chair in here rested before my foot-treadle Singer. I settled, book in hand. I'd just finished making a bottle-green jumper for Lou's first tea party (at the very mayor's house where I'd disgraced myself only seventeen years before, dredging in my knickers). I'd just been tearing up one of the Captain's rooster-bloodied shirts for rags—it was stained so serious, made Forty Mule Team Borax cringe. (I had *not* given up on purging bloodstains, a matter of pride really.) Sitting here, I drummed fingers on the tabletop, started fooling with leftover scraps from Lou's frock, then with Cap's ruined shirt. My class would be the nine- to eleven-year-olds, plenty old enough to notice. Lou and Ned would both be my own pupils. I didn't want to embarrass them.

Picturing Judith, I held up one scrap of dark green velveteen. I saw my Judy as a redhead, though carrottops were probably right rare in Bible days. Who cares? I imagined her a patriotic child, half Irish. Ain't sure why. The green maybe.

Next, I bunched a sleeping tyrant from a swatch of onct-white Egypt cotton. This I placed on a horizontal bias to become the fighter, snoozing at night. Then it seemed only natural to let the green hop right onto this speckled white, a battle pitched. Him Punch, Her Judy. I sat (glad to be hid from nosy neighbor and questioning kids), my worn hands pushing remnants here and there, making them stand, then lying each down.

I'd been telling my brood, about their Halloween costumes, you can't get any fancier than what you have on hand. So I now surveyed my sewing table. You got your hatpins, thimbles, a pincushion shaped like a tomato with a pet of a red pepper leashed to it (for needles). During a camping trip with his pal Billy, Ned had gathered me some hickory nuts, now resting in a little yellow bowl here. To make decent Pirate of Penzance mustaches for my trick-or-treat girls, I'd bought a pack of pipe cleaners and held these over my stove to get each good and black. Had half the box left here.

This is how Sunday-school history was made: I reached for a hickory nut and, using my biggest darning needle, bored a goodly hole into one end. I wedged a pipe cleaner's wire into this hollow. Then, for feet, I found two silver thimbles, I hooked a V-bent pipe cleaner to each. Then I Xed arms over the neck stem, keeping the nut up. You getting this? Before me stood a simple little human shape, six inches high and recognizable as just one of us.

From the same supplies, I made a Man one. I shoved him beside my first. I'd chose to think that the Lady was my first and that he come after. I'd made Man from her ribbing starter culture. I could. I could do anything I liked. I was the boss in here today, the shades drawn, door locked. I soon felt powerful as Eden's single landlord and subcontractor. Like Adam, I got to name stuff, a caretaker's tender joy.

Outside in the hall leading to our kitchen, I heard Lou shaming quiet the nose-picking and sometimes lackluster twins, I heard Baby telegraphic in her tap shoes on a rug today to hush them, plus Ned and Billy suddenly whispering pig Latin. I loved my kids for sparing me part of a half hour. Sometimes twenty minutes clear of your own kids' eyes can save your life.

I'd soon made more decisions in a shorter time span than had maybe ever happened previous, child. For me, I mean. I ain't making claims that I turnt up a cure for cancer, mind you. But it was honest fun—which is something anyways. I hadn't hurt anybody.

Half tranced, I turned to my trusty Singer and, feet at pump, started dressing my new doll thingums. A few simple tubes—wide one for Judy's skirt, two skinnies for sleeves. (Put gold rickrack to edge all and to provide a certain Bible-day Oriental gypsified dash.) In a minute I ran up Holofernes' nightshirt—white cotton flecked with blood which played right into our story's hands. I worked in a blur, like I'd redreamed all this for years, like it had taught me how to play each angle. I recalled being a kid, inventing in a tree house. How if you made one thing be so, others followed. I felt— how to say this?—a dampening in my hurry—a quickening lower-body thrill.

It was a smear of time those minutes I come up with Puppetry Gospel. Like Ned sliding towards home plate during side-yard baseball—I felt myself flopping towards some goal my body knew better than my poor young hickory-nut head did. *I felt certain.* That's it. Part of me understood how my husband's inborn certainty had long been one of his big continuing advantages over me. How, if you seem certain, you are. And if you don't, people sniff it and that is that, for good.

But the person could change things, couldn't she? Yeah, she could. Certainly. Even Ruth sensed something with her X-ray eyes through my lined drapes. Poor Ruth knew I was on to something good, so she cranked up a tacky tango, loud. Nothing bothered me.

I jammed a darning-needle sword in Judy's right hand. And there she stood over her sleeper. I'd emptied one of Cap's cigar boxes of scissors and such, I covered it with red tinfoil off a handy pot of immortal if uninspired Christmas poinsettias in the windowsill. With the stage all set, I reread the tale three times, then moved my dolls, puppets, whatever, through sensible paces. They soon did like folks *would* do.

The second they each had yarn hair, my cast became real to me. Their logic easy to figure as anybody local's—even with Ruth blasting a dance that'd be shaming in your nicer Argentine circles, Holofernes was a older man who snored nights, a meat eater and sound sleeper after a day of war's bloodshed then red beef. Judy sprung to her dark work.

ONLY THEN did I bellow children in, "It's show time, li'l Chrustians!" Which froze them on tiptoe. My tone must've spooked them, they were so unused to me excited about anything except both twins getting gashed on the same grape-soda bottle. *Certainty* they heard. Kids packed my sewing-room door, faces braced to find me jerking in some fit. I apologized for how selfish I'd been, hiding in here for twenty-five full minutes. Couldn't get the tone right yet, the tone of feeling "artistic," "entitled"—the deep pleasure all this'd given me already. Sinful—fun for me felt sinful then. (Lately fun is holy.)

My kids' playmates hung back but I called them into the dark workroom. More the merrier, I needed honest child reactions. They grouped on the floor before my worktable as I slid behind, standing there. I flicked on my gooseneck lamp, aimed it at a glittery cigar-box stage like some real theater. I then quoted the whole story straight through.

"Now," said I, so stirred I felt ashamed, "let's see how all that might could *look*, shall we?"

I was winging it, child.

But you can't let them know that, see? Children, dusty from our vacant lot, tipped nearer our one light source. In light, my hands coached strange new little figures through a drama that was, it seemed, way bigger than them, bigger than us. I had this vision as I told and showed, both. It sounds cheap but it happened: felt I was being puppeted by something with me in its hands and these figures in mine—something lowered into me. I thought of these shapes not as dolls but figments. Like in "figments of your imagination."

Finally I'd moved my couple to their outcome. I followed word for word—like some slow chef working through a cookbook. At last, when my lady figment—with a goodly sweep of her silver needle-sword—slashes the sleeping tyrant's neck, and when—with a playful yank—I accidentally on purpose jerked that old soldier's head right off (felt *good*!), all the children made one swallowed gasp. The hickory head of Holofernes rolled across the floor under my Singer and four kids scrambled for it, checking its neck end, seeking bloody traces. Give me goose bumps, their belief. *I* believed.

Then they just clapped like crazy and Ruth's record stopped, the entire trumpet of her Victrola seemed trying and listen, too.

I made the figments both take bows. Even our headless wonder hopped up (bald of brains), receiving credit. When babies kept whistling and stomping, asking for the whole thing once again, well—like they say, I believe, in the Moving Picture Industry—I knew I had me a hit on my hands.

In my hands. What more can I tell you? Fame spreads. A good thing, in a town this size, is soon unbusheled into broad daylight and I had requests to "freelance," you might could call it, at other Sunday schools. Everybody invited me but my friends the Jews, who still met in their secret rose-covered gazebo. I think they only held back out of shyness. I would've done them a freebie just to see inside. Nothing to offend, either: Most of the good stories are *Old* Testament. —Of *course* I'd like the Old Testament best, darling, look who I married.

After that second time through my premiere, after reattaching the head just so Judy could have her way again (you won't be surprised to learn it's harder to hook a head back on than to just yank it off), I asked kids for tough criticisms. "I can take it, believe me. Don't treat me like anybody's momma. Treat me like a . . . equal. I need to get this right by eleven on Sunday for church school or I stand to look real foolish. Mess like this, it either works or it's pure pitiful, you know?"

They nodded. They knew. I felt that.

WELL, them kids were right on the money. Said I needed a better stage, more lights than the one, and a bulb that wouldn't hurt the audience's eyes, please. I hadn't *known*. Maybe some tiny furniture, props. "And phonograph music? Something with bugles?" Ned—those eyes on me—asked in his usual absentminded way. Said he would go borrow Ruth's Victrola, and what records? "Maybe something more towards *Aida*?" says I, already sounding like D. W. Griffith on the set. "No, don't ask Ruth. She'll be over here in a jiff anyway. I know her, she'll soon be giving all my trade secrets to the Methodists. Those Methodists got to copy churches above or below them, not one idea among them, Methodists."

Power had gone right to my head, child.

Kids' good help surprised and pleased me. The right question is all you ever need to discover this again. Kids speak in questions so often because they love to be asked, only too few grownups *do*. I had. And today I benefited. Ned and Billy adjourned to build me a stage with a proscenium so it'd hide my rooster-spur-scratched hands, or the wrists at least. My girls had good ideas. I thought: You, Lucy, of all people, should steadily recall how smart kids are. Yours especially. You've hardly said three sentences to anybody else but them, Cassie, and him for ten breeding years. —But, too, the more children you *have*, the harder you got to work just keeping them stocked with basics, the less time you're free to notice sideline bonuses, to notice the only reasons anybody'd ever bother.

It stirred me, their smartness—and those quiet twenty-five minutes before. I didn't care if kids much noticed my trying and keep the house clean, or how I left their macaroni and cheese in the oven extra long to brown on top the way they liked. But their loving my figments mattered to me, child. As they filed out, talking amongst theirselves, like folks leaving some *real* performance, I stood behind my worktable feeling nervous. "Thank you," I called after them, and one child visitor, that lovely Billy Preston, called back, "Thank *you*, Mrs. Marsden. Didn't even *expect* this today."

"Nor me, Billy." I was now gathering up scraps and spools tossed everywhere while throwing my idea together. Usually you'd find me tidier than this, but for onct I had let loose. I spied my Louisa lingering in the doorway, half in the hall. Toying with her braid, she looked back in, said nothing, didn't smile. Just nodded onct, her eyes on mine, then Lou left behind two words, "Was good."

I stood here at my worktable where I usually made and mended their school clothes. But today I was backstage, full weight resting on my arms, head forward. "Was good," the girl had said. I felt grateful—grateful as a child praised honestly by other kids.

And it was later that evening, after dinner and when little friends had all dragged home, our house got strange and quiet. Captain was in the country for a week, buying has-been racehorses at auction. Just us here, us chickens, but the place was strangely still. I went looking for the trouble. Soon as such a hush sets in, watch out. They were in our front room doing homework, face-down on couches, grinding through geography, arithmetic, asking each other answers, shushing each other. Always surprised me how they could concentrate with all them *others* antsy in one room. Only later did I—a only child—understand. Of course, being there were nine of them, they pretty much *had* to.

I found they'd quieted because Louisa—it won't like her, really—had slipped out and changed into the new green velveteen jumper. She just waltzed around among lined paper and notebooks. She glided among brothers and sisters who—hunched over their work—looked up a while, made Lou a short-lived one-girl fashion show. She was a hefty child and stayed a large-boned woman. Her braided hair was too thin, but she moved so nice, already a presence. Tonight, Louisa stepped with this stiff grace, she held one braid up in the air, a fine silly fanciness that rivaled Baby's. I tarried in the hall's safe dark, not wanting to spoil her moment. Others—faces neutral but not disrespectful—stopped long enough to at least admire her. Then quick—not trusting the moment—Lou swept from the room. Imagine, she'd put that dress on because, earlier today, my pipe-cleaner Judith had wore that selfsame color. For a minute and a half, Lou felt famous.

I hadn't got a compliment like that since 18 and 96.

2

THE MONDAY after my first figment play was such a smash at the Baptist Fellowship Hall—then known as just Annex—my husband lost his shirt. Ours. He had, along with half the gaming gents on Summit Avenue, sent our money to this broker up in New York, who sunk funds into Louisiana oil. Men did it on the advice of our lieutenant governor, later indicted. It only happened to the best known of Falls' several good old boys. It was a rehearsal for '29, when the rest got hit. It was our Crash and struck us local but real hard.

I first knew something was amok when I saw the bank president—a portly man who'd given away coins at the Christmas play, this gent as dignified as a beautiful tufted club chair—he's running down Summit Avenue, pocket watch bouncing its links in the air before his belly like some escaping convict's ball and chain. Then around the corner came forty citizens waving papers and bankbooks, fists. I sat on my front-porch rail, touched my forehead, thinking that in my desire to put on good shows at church I'd flapped over into fantasy land. Our banker had used official money for personal gain, and had lost the gamble. Same second I heard a shot from the Wilgus home, two doors past Ruth's. (These are the folks that, from behind curtains, watched Cassie deliver twins in that wagon.) I now noticed Mrs. Wilgus, fifth-richest lady in town and a invalid since the eighties, come sprinting out of her house like Bill Tilden playing the net (and eyeing the ball boys). Her white hair hung down, her face was wild, she ran to me, the one person not chasing a bank president, and cried from our sidewalk, grinning in her nightgown, barefooted as the day she was born, "Unless I'm very much mistaken, my husband just put a shotgun in his mouth and pulled the trigger. It seems to've ruined, though maybe I'm wrong, the embroidered Spanish shawl covering our Baldwin. Unless I'm very much mistaken . . . I've not the faintest notion why Robert *did* that . . ." and then she gracefully drifted around the corner of Summit and Sycamore, a ghost.

Next Sunday's text, Paul's letter to the Corinthians, proved harder to act out than Judy's revenge on her lover-enemy. But even choirs of angels— live and in person—wouldn't of been noticed by children who'd just seen two men jump off the roof of the bank, our one Falls building tall enough to do the broker-jumper major damage. It did. One fall each did it.

I'd made my hickory-nut Paul sit at stage left writing the letter and then a larger group of believers opened his little letter while I recited it. Dull, I'll admit. But who noticed? That day collection plates were not passed at First Bible-believing Baptist. Was the single time in our history that us big-time losers weren't asked to give a dime. I almost blamed my so-so figment performance. Broke, we deeply appreciated our preacher's tact.

THOUGH Captain confessed we'd lost a good deal, his gun collection grew. I now see he was doing a pawnshop's business with weapons he'd admired for sixteen counties. Wives of the weapon collectors were all too happy to get these out of the house, considering the local rate of self-done death lately. Some pistols had been gifts. Cap claimed one was ruined by the brass plaque our trophy shop had screwed into its cherry-wood handle: "The Elks (BPOE) in fond appreciation of Capt. Marsden's patriotic Confederatism, selfless service to others," etc. The plaque eclipsed half a curving stock. "Imagine putting a brass name tag on the face of the Mona Lisa, Lucille, and you have some idea of the desecration." People were jumping off roofs and he was raking in the dueling pistols of the dead, and with no worse sign of strain than bags under his eyes.

When he bought the very gun that Mr. Wilgus used to spoil a valuable shawl, I knew we'd best watch out. Sunday morning—just as I was loading up my cast of helpers to carry stage and lighting and Ruth's on-loan phonograph to church—in Cap roars back from some county overnighter, in he bounds, arms stacked with further muskets, two pirate-looking pistols tucked under his belt. "We should've had *those* for Halloween," said Baby in a baby talk I'll spare you (she'd just tricked or treated as a tapdancing Miss Annie Oakley).

"Over my dead body," goes I, rushing back to my workroom for David's harp made entirely of paper clips and rubber bands.

We stood waiting for Cap to stow the new ones under our bed. By now he came home with a few items weekly, sometimes dumping prizes on the table like he hoped I'd plop them, calibered carrots, into some family stew. By now, beneath our fourposter, he had a elephant gun, cute ivory derringers about the size of dice cozy in their own velvet caskets. I thought of the Alamo's own arsenal under our mattress at night, there on the dark floor— daring any dust to accumulate around them. Guns soon felt somewhere between being our roommates and a snake farm, one that might snag a woman's ankle when, at 3 a.m., she trotted off to get three wakers water.

THERE's good news and bad news: The good is that soon our Sunday-school Annex's curtains, still screening your present age group from your past and future, soon fell open like a Jericho of shower curtains. And all to see my "show." I tried avoiding the word "show," which, for Baptists, has a low tinselly tone. "Show" hints at loose women and high admission prices, sin sin sin. If the wickedness us Baptists Imagined was half the fun of wickedness only Lived, we'd have reason to go somewhere and be real bad. I called mine "presentations" or "visual aids," but "show" made kids happier and they wouldn't quit calling mine that. Let them say Show.

If youngsters soon hung around our house, pointing at the shut door of my sewing room and listening, whispering to Lou (who, I believe, charged admission)—kids whispering, "Is she in there, doing it for Sunday?"—if kids loved the undullness of my visual aids, other long-suffering church teachers, long starved for a novel way to teach the Bible, struggling many years for some new tack to take, decided one by one that this won't it. Mine won't. Someway I knew this when I seen them lined against the back wall's bulletins and fruit-tinted lithos of Our Lord. Arms all crossed, each was dressed in mourning dark. I soon saw them as a set of black castles, eager limits towering over the low foreground of curly golden laughing children's heads. The more noise kids made when Saul threw his spear at the harp-playing David and so forth, the quieter my grown fellow-teachers got. Joyless, no lips, the lot of them. Just made me gush and imagine all the more. I dared them to fire the best darn Visual Effect by a Supporting Baptist. Let them try. My young audience would have their old dry lipless heads on a platter! See, I'd turned Gloria Swanson overnight! Vanity about vanities.

Soon, other religions were after me like ducks on a June bug. I even got a feeler from the twenty catacombed Catholics over in Rocky Mount, but I wrote a note that said I only did short-range travel with my sho . . . visual aids. At Lucas', I ran into my old Sunday-school teacher whose voice was like the sound her nickel-rimmed spectacles might make. She was still at it, one lowered cotton drape from mine, still complaining. "Well, well," said she. "Aren't *you* the clever one, it's our Lucille. Everybody's talking about your little Old Testament flea circus or whatever it is, and though it charms the children to the point that when I pull my curtain afterwards and try to discuss the holy mysteries, pupils're keyed up to talk only about the color of the *wigs* on this week's nuts, and though I think you're smarter than I ever thought you were when you and the late Shirley gossiped through your years under me, I must say that, bright and 'modern' as it all is, one thing I feel sure your lessons aren't, my child, is DEEP. Good day." I was left feeling stunned and shallow in the extreme, darling. Cheap.

The playboy lieutenant governor still hunted ducks and took along a certain white-haired vet storyteller. The state spent gas money and probably bullet money, too, for a motorcade clear down to Duck, North Carolina (the name given to a town by wishful thinkers—a form of decoy). Limos zipped past shanties of those who should be fed by the state funds. Captain spent all his charm with the big boys of our state. News of our small-time Gloomy Monday finally seemed to reach him. Not even new guns could cheer him up around the house. While I was enjoying newfound fame among the youthful Baptists of the Greater Falls area—and here's the earlier-mentioned *bad* news (how should I put it gentle?)—he hit me a few more times. Two. Maybe three.

Here I was, bound onstage weekly before the entire Sunday school, and suddenly I was sending Louisa to the dime store for foundation makeup to disguise a blacked eye. The first. Ruth, next door, noticed one day while I was out hanging up the clothes. She had the face of a secret drinker (though—to be fair—we never caught her). Poor Ruth bent over our fence, spied a lump above my eye, and said, just so I could hear, "There's worse things than a husband who loves but leaves. Some of us'd rather be proud and alone, Lucille. Is what *I* think," then drifted inside, limp as her wash dress. I pitied her. And mostly agreed. But I now knew to hide my war wounds better.

My husband still muttered in his sleep, shouts of artillery danger, naming childhood friends but mixed with recent daytime news. A whole night's worth might run: "Nine dollars a head and not a nickel over . . . said I shouldn't . . . vines'll just *grow* faster . . . got face cards every time, Ned. Ned? Duck, duck!" I'd lay awake listening, still trying to feel like feeling sorry for him. Not so sure, a ice pack on one eye.

I will say: This was the last of that part. Seemed connected to my puppet reputation at First Baptist. The more times folks came up and complimented him, the less he went to church.

Onct when he was being sweet, I asked him what him and the Lieutenant Governor and other poker guys discussed at Duck, in blinds at dawn. We were alone in bed and my husband turned to me without a pause, "Pussy."

"Oh."

"Pussy 'n' money, money 'n' pussy. The order varies."

"Don't mind my saying so, sir, but it sounds kind of strange to go all that way to the coast just to grab-ass each other, you know? To me, anyways."

"We *know* it's dumb, Lucille. That's what you women never seem to recognize. We *like* that. We find it a relief from all these duties that you and these children are always weighing us down with. Do you know how much is *eaten* in this house? It's fun to act like boys again when we get to, and you know what, Lucille? We *get* to. But enough small talk, there's a topic I've felt a certain burning urgency to discuss with you and you alone. Only you can help me with it."

I felt wary but, too, half drawn. "So what's that? Shoot."

"Poos-say. As my black brothers pronounce it. Pussy, Lucy. Specifically, your own."

This is sick. It was us, though, and I'm telling. I put up with it. Probably I was asking for trouble. And you might think me twisted, child, but someways, most parts that mattered, I liked it. When he breathed his own sad smut my way, I stayed for it, didn't I? You either stay or leave. For now, till what-all happened next, I stuck right there and took what he dished out. —And I blame myself for everything that followed, child. Really, I should be in jail now.

HE WAS not a happy drunk. Losing the money set him back. Drink made him talk war. "Sorry," he'd say after biffing me, and sit on our horsehair couch with his face in his hand. He knew it was rolling out of him, him muttering figures, how eleven states left the Union, twenty-three stayed, twenty-four counting West Virginia, rough odds at best and no wonder the two hundred and thirty thousand fellow Rebs had been so wounded, two hundred thousand of his Southern brothers killed outright, and on and on he kept the score. He seemed to want (some Fridays especially) to hit me. I saw that look, I handed him a pillow, "Duck feathers are in there, hero, go to it." Fridays were bad. I'd rather it happened on Monday—Friday meant a shiner really bloomed in time for my precious Sunday-morning hour onstage.

The last shiner, I gave him notice. He'd just hollered, "That's for Wilson's Creek." A war skirmish's name, I guessed.

"For *what*?" I screamed and ran his way across the room and pulverized his shoulders. "I plan to get out of here if you lay a hand on me ever again, ever! Give me it back, now. I want back everything you've ever took from me, which means most everything."

From behind two huge hands covering his face, he said, "Where would you go? You having gentleman callers?" I saw he was smiling, so certain.

"Very funny man," I said, not sure.

Then we'd make up. You figure it out.

· · ·

NOWDAYS folks get divorced if the other person looks puffy at breakfast or has what these TV ads call "morning breath." Meaning halitosis. Typical, such ads change two of the most beautiful words in English, "morning" and "breath," into the title of a stink curable with one product only. Back then you contracted till death do you part or till your husband's body parted from its spirit, whichever came first. I rode it out, God knows.

Ruth's Willard used to knock her cockeyed twice a week and she'd come over with a beefsteak mashed to one eyeball, a beefsteak that I, being on a stricter budget, would've loved to swipe—even with Ruth eyelashes on it—for a nice little lunch. And now here she was giving me lectures on the joys of being alone and uninjured.

Some tacky tango cranked up, and we could see Ruth through the window, cross-stepping in the middle of the floor of one huge unfamilied room. "Poo Wooth," Baby sighed, watching. Once more I scolded my prettiest girl for lisping so. Ned was, I reckon, finer-featured than our Baby. She had a kind of ready surface peachiness, she flared it at all comers, working on them curls and nails, mad for matching accessories, at age eight. Ned, quiet, favored some statue from Greece, a perfect if eyeless boy whose features seemed more natural that far into the past. His face was almost too refined to bear a world as spiky and overtinted as this recent one is. Neddie was one of them kids where: if we were out and he ate candy and his hands got sticky, he stared at them, whimpering, half crazy from the goo till you *had* to find a sink for him so he could see the world again. He moved dreamy. When I attended to some back-then version of a PTA open house, his this year's teacher, always a lady, would call me aside and say, "What *is* it about our Ned?" They were not complaining, they were showing me they'd caught the dreamy quality in those eyes that rarely seemed to blink, that steadily stayed a good gray percentage of his face. It was a privilege to be around that kind of beauty and made your waiting on the others almost easier, him silent at their middle, watching your very-close veins very close. I kept learning from his patient eyes. —Oh, what do people *do* that don't have children, child?

NOT ONCT did Captain mention how folks had praised my shows. Not onct did he ask me what I was fixing to stage come Sunday. Never did he tell me that the time I spent in yonder was a nuisance, or that I had his full permission. He withheld it all, and me? Darling, four wild horses and boiling hot oil and all the vexations visited on the saints couldn't have made me ask his opinion of myself in this. Over my dead body. I figured that if they put up signboards downtown praising me as some new local attraction mentioned by the Chamber of Commerce "Register of Sights: Curiosities of Interest in the Gateway to the Threshold of the Peanut Capital of Eastern North Carolina," if my shows were on every lip, it'd be good in how it showed up his stinginess, begrudging me my one new pleasure. I wanted him to be ashamed of being ashamed of me.

Then he arrived at one of my shows. Adults had started slipping into the back of the Annex. They'd arrive for church a bit early or their own Sunday-school classes would break up. "Young Adults" especially never lasted long. I was there, being helped by my own kids—envy of all—while Ned worked the Victrola that Ruth donated after seeing a certain episode based on the Book of Ruth—which she took grandly to be about husbandless her. Cap arrived during the escape from Egypt of a sizable number of hickory-nut players, pursued in chariots of Blue Tip Match boxes on wheels from certain busted toys of Ned (some he busted just so's we'd have a suitable Pharaoh fleet, greater love hath no boy). I seen a familiar black suit and white beard. A easterly span of platinum watch chain over vest, all a sideline blur in black. He watched the show. He stayed for the applause. He left and never mentioned it to me or the stagehands, his own flesh and blood.

I could've throttled him.

3

NEXT SUNDAY, churchbound, our babies were lined two by two behind us when, on sidewalk up ahead, I seen a short dark girl handing out pink leaflets. She won't colored or Cherokee—but a foreign-looking ragamuffin with tangled black hair that just cried out for some mother's comb. She was barefoot, on Sunday! Cap swept past her. I wanted to grab a flyer but thought better of it. So when, regretting, I looked back, when I saw that six of my nine now walked whilst reading one flyer apiece, I felt relieved and blessed.

Only after service, at home, whilst hanging up their Sunday bests, did I pilfer a few pockets. I found one such notice that Ned—during church— had folded into a paper football, one that him and the twins thumped back and forth over a hymnal. I stood by a window in our boys' dormitory and opened the pink page:

DESTINIES TOLD, cheap.
Have Love Left You? Is the Best of Everything Forget Your Present Whereabouts? Do Dark Forces Try and Keep Your Potentailities Hid Away from YOU? Where *is* The Getting Place? Mrs. Williams know. Her Advice concern Love, Fates, the Money, all Human Knowleg. Where you do Belong? Not Here? OK. Mrs. Williams Knew this. Mrs. Williams Understand where You might finally Fit In. Trust Mrs. Williams. Who *else* can you? —Price of first Reading?—the best 50¢ You ever to let Go of. Come on! What's waiting? Your True Future is all!

Well, well, well. It listed a chancy side street down by the peanut mill near where my Shirley onetime lived. In my hand, pink paper felt cheap, it'd bled rouge onto skin healing from a rooster spur's scratch. The notice's

printing looked done on some press the size of a toaster. Ink plugged all
o's and a's. But for some reason, this and the intuition spelling made the
Mrs.' promises seem truer and more dear to me. Plus, behind the flyer's
address, somebody'd handwritten: "Walk Up one Flight." Which made me
think of a whole new promised level waiting, angels one floor and a cut
above.

I reread the thing, liking how Mrs. Williams went just by the Mrs.,
keeping her mystery gypsy first name to herself. She sure knew her local
market.

SO MONDAY, during school hours, I left my lap and crib babies with Castalia. Then it was me in my good hat and shoes, with a dollar's change and
my excellent rings stashed in my bag. One bell was marked just "Mrs. Williams, Specialty: Futur."

Here in Falls you can't throw a rock without hitting some Williams or
other (Shirl was one). When the uncombed brown-eyed child—still barefoot—peeked downstairs, I asked to see her mother. "Her seester!" cried a
woman's husky voice from inside.

The second-story apartment door swung open on a wide sour soothsayer
breast-feeding the most beautiful child. Room's wallpaper showed every
early layer like a cut tree shows all its hidden holy rings at once. This room
had four cots, a spindly card table, one radiator, and, atop it, a clicking tin
pie pan full of water. On one low ledge, a hot plate glowed. Its pot sent off
spicy steam that smelled of curry, paprika, something. The girl went back
to cooking, she unscrewed the lid from a medicine jar, dumped orange
pellets into some mess of foreign stew.

"Howdy," I told the grumpy older woman. I'd hid my wedding and
engagement rings—not wanting to sway her or give a free ride. Of course,
certain rusty grooves showed on finger number three. Mrs. Williams said
she already knew what I wanted, but why didn't I ask anyhow? Her accent
was a puzzle. I *think* that's what she said. "Okeydokey," I explained a bit
more than I'd planned to (like usual!). Said as how when the Opera Company
of Raleigh did their show here last May? there'd been this fortune-teller in
it with some elixir of love and that'd given me the idea of getting mine told
someday. "My, you know, future, destiny, what have you?"

"Unh," goes she, nodding a lot. "Chess I subspeck."

Then she motions I must sit in the chair at her card table. Tabletop's
loaded with her children's blocks. The baby is smacking to beat all. Since
I'd got Cassie to babysit, I must say I felt someway disappointed at finding
kids packed in here. *That* destiny, I knew.

About sixty alphabet blocks were stacked between the soothsayer and
yours truly. Hoping and be helpful, I commenced to clear them while she
fished out her cards, tea leaves, crystal ball. Well, you know, that woman
slapped my hand! I quit tidying. (If I'm left in a bus station long enough,
I'll try and clean it up. Just nerves, I think.)

Setting opposite me, she said nothing. Her ears'd onct been pierced but the only decoration left them was two long holes. These seemed to show that Mrs. W. had used, not gems, but bricks. She flared a testing look my way. I quit gaping at her lobes. I knew to ease two quarters from my black change purse. I laid coins on the table. (Glimpsing rings in the bag gave me comfort—my secret life!)

Uneven towers of red wood bricks were heaped between me and the huge sullen woman. I couldn't quit studying her suckling child, someway envying his pleasure. Dark lashes rustled with the joy of feeding. One reason I knew his sex, he was buck naked, a stranger to the hygiene of circumcision. Mrs. W.'s nipple, wider than the boy's mouth, was exactly as black as it was red.

She peeked over the small city of blocks, spied my coins, then lifted one wrist of her feeding baby. She waved his slack hand, swatted it toward blocks' three steepest points. Some clattered off the table. Most stayed. Then Mrs. Williams placed her son's arm back on his chest and bent across him, studying my fallen letters. Half her child was eclipsed under the free-swinging breast. Hid, he whined. I tried studying my blocks, my seeming destiny. Red letters were carved on two sides. Silhouettes of familiar animals decorated the others.

She pointed to one marked P. (I'd got me a porcupine—good sign?) Mrs. W. stared me dead in the eyes. Her pupils were too black to read.

"You," she said, "know Pain."

"So far so good." Then I half covered my mouth—hadn't planned to give that much away. I wanted Mrs. to guess who I'd been so far. I hoped she might predict what and who I'd get to be next. I figured, for the fifty cents, it'd be a buy. Errands I understood. Fate, not.

Her fingernail scratched a U block next.

"I see," Mrs. Williams said, "local travel."

"*Local?*" This miffed me. My husband had once told me that the word "gyp" is based on "gypsy." "I got me a question, Mrs. Williams, ma'am. —Can I *call* you Mrs. Williams? Little joke there. But how can it be 'local' *and* 'travel'?"

Preparing a answer, she cleared her throat. Her son (or brother) sucked on.

I heard the barefoot girl, interested, face our way, tapping one bare sole on dingy linoleum. (It'd needed straight bleach and ammonia by now.) I heard the child licking steady as a cat along the wooden spoon. And when I next looked across my alphabet of fate at Mrs. Williams, I found that all of her appeared suddenly blue—like hid behind some midair shower curtain. I figured the spirit world had already spread cataracts across my sight. Jumpy, I leaned forward when I saw the Mrs.' nostrils flex, I noticed her son retching like resisting milk's bitter new taste, I heard the woman tell me, "A far-off child . . . in dip dip trouble," she screamed this as she spun toward the hot plate, crying, "Sees," "Cease," or "Sis." The pan and wallpaper were all on fire. Flames showed blue and orange, smoke filmed my view still more. The girl turned her face toward the wall and just stood gazing like at some spectacle she'd paid to watch. Mrs. Williams grabbed a apron off a chair and—lugging her baby—rushed beating at the flames. I swept past her, snatched a hot pie pan off the radiator, and pitched water on the hot plate. It shorted out at onct, with a sinusy snarl. Then one nasty chemical stink sure rose. Wallpaper, stained dark, smoldered now.

"A far-off child in dip trouble?" Maybe she'd got her wires crossed, picking up her own bad news instead. I slipped back to my place, took up my purse, kept stalling, not sure what was polite. I did feel entitled to getting my money back. Local travel and a distant kid in trouble? Come on. I needed these coins for Louisa's college fund. Mrs. seemed mad I'd spoiled her hot plate. She stomped nearer, bent over colored blocks, pushed the fifty cents my way. I picked up one quarter only, left the other. Then I set the first one down again, superstitious. I backed, half smiling, into the hallway. A black janitor, busy sniffing, bolted past me, hollering at her, "Fire *again!*"

I got down that flight quick.

Once home, I wondered if I'd been seen down near the peanut mill and if so why did I mind. I sat, rings still hid, in my good clothes at my own solid kitchen table. What had she predicted? After ten minutes, I recalled my babies waiting at Cassie's and walked down there, but very slow. "Pain." "Local travel." "Child in trouble." Whatever happened to tall dark handsome strangers? I deserved a refund.

And yet, that morning helped me decide: I would make sure my kids had decent winter clothes. I'd ask Castalia if she'd come and housesit till the Cap hired somebody permanent or remarried, whichever came first. It would not be actually abandoning my babies. More like saving some of my own self. For them. For later.

These decisions shocked me and yet didn't. Was it him I was escaping or them or Falls or his diehard war or all of it? How long had I known I'd have to someday clear out?

Seemed I had to hurry.

I was like a bar of gift-shop soap. What of me would be left, after everyone was done with me? Their best compliment? It's all gone!

Local pain would now travel far. I'd leave before a child got into trouble.

Mrs. Williams became a bargain. She let Lucy see, destiny was cinched, fate was elsewhere.

4

IF YOU cannot trust the trusties, watch out. It was 19 and 10, a pretty good year, and the local donuts (Castalia's staple) were ideal, thanks to Gurney Harbison, unlucky sod. His ill luck told me, "Pack, quick." Now, looking back, I see, was Gurney caught it first, all of this.

He'd been a member of the town council that commissioned the Gateway To The Peanut Basket arch, Gurn also served as superintendent of Sunday School at First Baptist, plus he was a fanatic about his yard. Nice quiet redheaded modest fellow till things changed and sudden. Harbison had been regular and sentimental as we *were* then: a sucker for kittens, too openhanded with his six sons. To the Lutheran Orphanage, he donated much-craved week-old jelly donuts (their filling beloved for being so cherry-red ruby-red). Foundlings remembered Gurney in hundreds of nightly prayers, powdered sugar dainty upon moving baby lips. Gurney Harbison turned fifty. Some blamed that. Others guessed his slaving over deep-fat-frying all those years had battered Gurney's gray matter. For whatever reason: He woke one Monday feeling he must have three bake shops in three *other* towns. He'd been a local grinnish sort of guy, ready with a joke, lazy with news. Now he bought a fast horse and in all three distant bergs hired rough overseers to push Harbison's addicting jelly donuts. Every fry-shop worked, and soon Harbison had scads more money but piles more woes. He resigned his council seat and—after he missed Sunday School four times running— was asked to let others take over. He cussed the Preacher who'd remarked how careworn and gray our once-pleasant Gurney looked. Dark countable rings were gathering like franchises under either mother-office eye. School plays featuring young Harbison boys as pilgrims, bunnies, and The Green Leafy Vegetable Food Group were now attended only by the Mrs. (One son, starved for male attention, wandered into the scary anvil clutches of Bertram, the genius smithie, slow to rouse but soon breathing crackles and sparks like his bellows.) Gurney, altered, soon took flowers to Lolly, asked the still-around-here favorite to be his mistress. Loll both refused and announced she planned telling pretty much everybody, which she sure did.

Our beloved baker soon jumped at loud noises. I saw him check his pocketwatch a lot. Donut donations to orphanages stopped. Sugar-deprived orphans now prayed for Gurney's doom. He accused lifelong menfriends of being jealous over his new bracket, said their small-change problems didn't interest him now. All we could find to say of his sudden hurryings, his polluted moods: "Maybe Gurney had a real bad temper all along?" "Gurney'll be his old self in no time, watch." "Gurney needs more love, but Gurney *had* so much, he gave it up." The more he succeeded in sating the discriminating tastebuds of three counties, the less he enjoyed our free and easy present. He never hung around the Courthouse Square with pals, sunning, watching hicks make much of the water bubbler. He quit listening. No fun lately, The Jelly Donut King.

Then, a final strangeness as, one October afternoon, sipping milk to coat his successfully expanding chain of peptic ulcers, Mr. Gurney Harbison patrolled the curb before his home. Wearing baker's whites, he pressed a pale shoe against walnuts scattered on Harbison-owned sidewalk. For years the neighbor's tree had dropped such nuts across Gurney's curbing. If you've ever cracked black walnuts, child, you know they leave permanent tobacco-colored stains. Gurney'd never mentioned just how much such splotches bothered him. The plump neighbor stood yonder raking his lawn. Gurney called the fellow closer, pointed to the pavement's yellowing, whispered, hoarse, "Fifteen years of filth from you. I know your plan, and there are limits. You people keep fouling everything I own. This is where your kind gets off and my kind takes charge, you fucking pig." How mad *was* Gurney? From under his starched whites, he whipped forth a brand-new forty-five, the price sticker still gummed, pink, onto its muzzle. He instructed his neighbor to clean up these nut stains, and he meant *now*.

"What *with*, Gurn?" the gent sensibly asked, smiling, hoping this was April First but knowing this was Autumn. Seeing the business-end of a pistol's solemn snout (has there ever been a *witty* gun?), the neighbor chose to fall upon his knees and—with the pistol still watching very close—decided to prove additional good faith by clawing at nuts' markings using his very fingernails.

"Lick it up." Gurney's voice was now cut off from everything but the voice itself, his sadness had even lost the community feel of others' sadnesses bordering his. "Said to *lick* your mess up, dog, lap it, you."

The neighbor bent, either weeping or chuckling, he pressed his tongue right onto gritty pavement and—for his trouble—caught a slug just at the base of his skull. He then stained the offending stains with his own mortal losings as Gurney walked directly to the bank, withdrew a lifetime's savings and, grabbing two sweetrolls from his downtown shop (raisin I am told), jumped his fast horse and rode out the east end of town while, at the west, a crowd gathered near one neighbor, dead of what? Killed for what good reason? And nobody understood. 19 and 10.

This, see, was new.

GURNEY HARBISON never got recaptured. I think our law enforcers were afraid to. They could determine no motive and that scared them most. The dead man had not owed Gurney one plug nickel, the gent had never touched Mrs. Harbison or even the prettiest son. What if Gurney had killed the guy only for a sidewalk's stains? We remembered how our baker had overnight grown somber and ambitious, how lovelessness had claimed him like of some unknown virus or ague. How listening stopped. Our Falls *Herald Traveler* wrote weeks of editorials guessing what could've gone wrong. Often mentioned: Mr. Stevenson's popular *Dr. Jekyll and Mr. Hyde*, news since it appeared in 18 and 86. Only now do I understand: that book is about a man caught between the old age and the new, a gent turned brutish by times way worse than him.

Now, of course, daily newspapers are full of such killings. People walk into grammar schools and shoot kids they've never even seen before: because last week's paper described somebody walking into another school and shooting other unknown kids and because something in that appealed to them. Gurney's change of heart, child, has become a way of life. That mammoth rage at little things, it's old-hat standard equipment now. Even those of us who *say* we do not understand it understand it a little.

So, from this bed parked at the creaky end of the century, I see now: Gurney Harbison, the discriminating tastebud, he was just our first one locally to come down with it.

Nice family man, Bible believer, excellent baker, he, among us, caught the Twentieth Century first.

5

BUT STILL mostly all innocent of that: the Fad of the Sleepover struck sudden, struck giddy. All Falls children felt this epidemic need to wake elsewhere. (I knew the feeling.) Kids were test-driving far-flung wallpapers, trying other mommas' breakfasting techniques. Girls Lou's age longed to be harassed by girlfriends' older brothers, boys named Lex and Ray, boys whose rooms stunk of used sock, hair oil, and secret sun-colored stains stiffening the mattress. Ned bragged that him and his pal Billy Preston had Peeping Tommed a third pal's older sister who owned a vanity dresser with a heart-shaped mirror and its own lace dress full-length as Cassie's crispy mink and that the sister talked to her mirror while pressing her own eyelashes with what looked like some ice tongs for the human eye.

Got so I never knew whose children would traipse downstairs come morning, or where my missing were. On the wall under my kitchen Seth Thomas, I seriously tended the growth chart of our kids' shooting-up. The Sleepover Fad confused such stats—stray initials entered, meaningless heights. Everybody's got to get into the act. Finally our superintendent of schools sent notes home: "Parents: Re: The Rash of recent Pajama Parties. Please restrict to weekends since school-day sleeplessness results. Books claim that children like routine and so does local higher education. Bands of children tend to sneak out bedroom windows and meet up with other bands. The Methodist church was just found occupied by ten sleepers (several straight-A ones, in fact) at ten on a school day and there is no telling what happened right there in God's House. Parents are to use discretion and for once, please, a little common sense."

I well remembered fibbing to my own folks and I knew when my own brood did me: "Her mother says it's okay with *her* if it's okay with *you*, oh please, Momma?" We had Ned's Billy with us the night Captain set to work making Duck Lore seem deeply educational for one and all. Billy acted impressed. "Fine boy, that young Preston," Captain said—he always sounded like some army recruiter, judging twelve-year-olds.

At dinner, Cap asked would Ned please run fetch a duck decoy from the garage. The man had been pure charm the whole night and I knew something was in store. He could work it like a faucet. Once Ned got back, all eyes, Captain held a wooden drake, quacked it along over interested head. He said, "I admit, this does look reasonably fake. But . . ." He turned the thing so we now stared straight down onto its back and upper head. "Say you're eighty feet up, and this has all *your* colors on it, and you're fatigued, you're looking for your own to rest with, well, who does this appear to be? Why, the very image of your favorite first cousin, perhaps the love of your life."

Our children smiled, glancing at one another, both cautious and amazed that their father was acting his old best self again. He said he'd show us where each sort of decoy should go so each breed feels easiest on a given inlet.

The vinegar cruet became Canada geese, who always land close to shore. Our pepper shaker proved how pintails settle farther at the pond's quiet end and forever in pairs. "Pintails and geese mate for life," Cap gave me a smirk I didn't understand. "You children might think animals are too crude to find the love of their lives and stick right with her, would you not? You'd consider that only higher forms such as your lovely mother there and myself would have undertaken that. But Nature is a wonderland of virtues." I stymied a groan.

"Ducks are smart and pigs are smart but pigs can't fly," Baby intervened.

"Correct," goes Poppa, not impressed. He shifted dessert plates, proving that certain ducks always face into wind, so your decoys must do that, or else live ones'll think, "Fake," they'll fly right on. Teals and widgeons and black ducks tend to keep to theirselves—you can't mingle wooden those with others.

"But here's what we call the pièce de résistance."

"Tabasco?" Ned asked.

"This is not Tabasco, son. Get your eyes checked. This is our life-sized painted-plaster great blue heron. My friend the Lieutenant Governor keeps one in the trunk of his car full-time. You know how nervous herons are? Ducks know so too. And this becomes our very trump card, fellow hunters. Ducks in the air spy a jittery heron down here, acting calm. It acts upon them like the all-clear bugle. The false heron stands a yard tall and is placed off to one side all by itself, this is what we call a confidence decoy. —Can you say that?"

They did. They went for it. It scared me. My own brood. They sat gaping where I did—at the smooth oval of table space he'd cleared so we might imagine landing, imagine trusting it after a long night on the wing. Our eyes did now. Land. You saw how attractive it'd seem if you hadn't eaten since the Chesapeake Bay or earlier. Sad, that your need for food, shut-eye, and friendly company was what'd get you hurt.

Ain't it always the way?

"Nothing to it," their poppa showed us his palms. "Just total and complete expertise, years of patience and simple know-how. —So when you see Daddy here come home with a carful of birds, next time you'll better understand what skill is exercised in bagging them." My husband leaned back, pleased, thumbs in his vest pockets.

"Can I say something now, Poppa?"

"Proceed, child. Might we venture at its having to do with ducks' intelligence?"

The twin nodded, disappointed. "It was just that 'ducks *are* smart.' "

"True enough. Not as smart as you or me, but to give you an example: Even after you *shoot* the duck, there's no written guarantee you'll get it home." Cap claimed that, if a duck is winged but not yet mortally, the dazed creature will do anything to keep from being taken. Anything. That's one reason a truckload of dogs must follow your limousines to Duck (N.C.). You better hop into your boat quick, get out to the downed bird. Even then, if it sees you coming, a duck that's hurt but far from killed—it will plunge underwater, see? It'll clamp its bill to any stick or reed and will hold on down there with all its might.

"Till it dies, Poppa? They drown . . . by choice?" Lou asked. "Taking their own lives?"

Sad-acting, respectful of the breed, Captain nodded. "It's quite something, isn't it? But a fact of nature. You have to hand it to them. Marriage and suicide. Both they understand. Both they practice. Ducks have will-power. That's why hunting them constitutes such fine sport."

"It wouldn't be fun if ducks just *let* you?" Lou asked.

"No, that would not, my girl, be sport, it'd be . . ."

"Murder," I entered the conversation.

"Yes, perhaps, as your mother puts it with her typical succinctness. 'Murder' . . . no fun. You need a competitive intelligence to make it fun. Look at everything we've done here just to draw them down to us in the first place," and he gestured around at our table rearranged. My bread pudding in its pretty yellow bowl was cold as death.

Cap went on talking—a great talent at it, center of any party he chose to adopt—a great confidence giver, often set off at the edge at first. Our babies and their guests sat asking smart questions. I cleared away dessert, uneaten. When did the kids last forget to jump on my handmade sweets? I moved around the edge of our crowd at the lighted table. I seen Ned, quiet, smiling, feeling honored, soaking up this lore of how to trick beasts we only respect because: they're smart enough so we can try to gyp, to lure on down, to blast them.

I stopped at my sink, I shifted pudding from one bowl to another the same size—absentminded. See, I was picturing, with my own children's low murmur and comic quacks behind me, I was seeing the whole thing but from the duck's viewpoint. For her to spy the perfect marshy spot, to oar the air on down toward it, a spot turned rosy by dawn which means, light itself a confidence decoy: "Here, finally."

You're scanning all the signs and are, say, nine feet from the water when a outcropping of weeds pops up the shapes of spindle sticks that empty fire and smoke and cold, you're on your back, feet up in freezing water, your left wing shuddering. You flip around as best you can and see a boat, occupied, splash towards you, a dog, huge figures seeking you here in the wet, and now, by choice, by will, just as all that nears you—local travel, down you go with such determination. It takes each scrap of your last strength to plunge as fast as you can from giveaway light. You wriggle straight down till your beak hits a bent stem, furry with silt, and as you bite on it very very hard, your air all leaving you in bubbles sent toward the dark of a boat passing right above. And you, clamped here, eyes on bottom mud, now drown, but do so dignified, because you're still your own. Because you chose this. I leaned against the cold metal sink and looked at my own outline in the night-blacked window before me.

"Hey, where'd that fine dessert fly off to?" my husband calls in four more minutes.

"I threw it out, I think."

"But isn't that it there, just in a new container? You're getting dottier, old girl. Louisa, go fetch us our dessert. Might be a little cool by now, but your mother's bread pudding's worth eating at any temperature, am I right?"

Later, clearing the dessert bowls, I saw how kids had someway respected the table's free space. They left every eating utensil in its position as a confidence decoy. They were afraid to touch these changed things, things they handled every day. I went to put things back right. *I* was briefly spooked to touch my own trusty salt and pepper shakers.

But I did.

MY WEEKLY show still gave me a booster shot I craved. To get letters on church stationery from as far off as Wilson with my name spelled right and *typed*. Well . . . all this finally helped me leave but—by then—it was too late.

I was setting up the Sunday puppet stage on Saturday, readying my run-through for my Daniel in the Lions' Den—a instant classic, I felt it in my bones. In comes our thin-lipped preacher. Baby was working with me, offering vocal tips. Preacher leads in the same committee that'd begged me to come be useful to Our Lord. Preacher had a funeral air. He told me my puppet lessons had been appreciated but, unfortunately, were *"too* good." Baby come up and stood beside me. It was her first unpleasant experience with Theatrical Management but, thanks to her later well-known stage career, I am glad to say it was not her last.

I told Preacher I couldn't think of a crime I would prefer to that of making the Book too vivid for young thirsty Baptist minds. I said that my swan-song sho . . . visual aid might well change his opinion. "That seems unlikely," he said, looking at my tinsel stage and all them little rope-maned lions I'd worked on till 3 a.m. "There won't be 'a show' tomorrow."

Baby wedged between me and the preacher. Looked like she was screening me from him. The child gave him a martyred Lil Gish eye-roll that could make Saint Paul like girls, that could melt a ceiling fan and, holding onto my legs, Baby bleated, "She . . . Teaches . . . Us . . . God."

I saw even the preacher bend a second. He recovered, smiled as much as a person minus lips *can*. "You're young," he said.

"And you . . ." Baby pointed at each face in turn and spat out with a mad vamp's power, "jealous. Jealous. Jeal-ous!"

"Come, dear," goes I, grand as Sarah Heartburn. "Pastor, Have your people bring my supplies to my headquarters, please? You'll find the street address written on the Figments' Dressing Room Door. Oh, and this is my last day ever in *your* so-called House of God, *Wel*don." (His name was "Weldon" Otis. And I'll risk saying: I hope he's frying in Hell this very second. I just do.)

My child and me left there in perfect step and with our noses held up. We were plainly Bianca McCloud's adoring female kin and—in Baby's case— also that star, Lady More Marsden. Only when we were well off consecrated ground (so called) and far from those crows in black did I turn to Baby. I said, "Times, I've wondered about your character, child, which can—we both know—be right self-interested. But you must understand you got just unbelievable acting talent. It was good, what you did. Made me feel wonderful and I do thank you for that."

But this close to her face, usually so controlled, I saw I had completely misread her. She stood here crying, not caring how she looked. She was stunned at them turning me out, furious over it. A child, she hadn't seen it coming like I had with that first round of wonderful un-Baptist applause. She hugged me there and said, "Momma? I will miss you."

I knew she meant Me, the puppeteer celebrity. But, too, I heard her mean more. I heard her life beyond me starting. I heard her guess my restlessness. I heard her own. We were sure related.

But, see, what I'd got out of the puppet thing was: Ned's being so good about building the stage and choosing me that perfect music every week (a early form of disc jockey, now I think of it). I'd got Lou's "Was good." And now this strange tribute (and great performance) from Baby.

I'd had my golden public moment but, like always, I gauged it most by how my loved ones saw me there, where I was happiest, making things up around the house.

I LEFT six weeks later to the day. But by then, see, it was already too late.

6

I DATE the changes from our Ned's twelfth birthday and that magazine article. A year after Cap's picture appeared there, here come *Liberty* into our lives, switching everything. They wanted the vet's formal picture, in uniform of course. Our nine kids should line up like a army in our back yard. Each child ("Over my dead body") should shoulder-arms one rare gun from Poppa's collection. (I'd spent all afternoon wrestling my brood into Sunday clothes, then this magazine man says he wants them in "play togs," he said—a bachelor for sure. Later, I saw that the Yankee he *wanted* them to look like hicks. The worst was: They *did*, looked just like the dolts the fellow'd hoped for. *We* did. No fair.)

When time came to do that mug shot, I bolted. I won't sure what got into me, I just felt the camera would turn into a cannon. I run into the house and the prissy photographer was asking Cap to *force* me to come back. "Fat chance," Cap said. I waited at the back screen door, yelling—temperamental around company—"No way. *I* know how I look."

Cap was too joyful then to mind much. He'd got our babies out there, had nine souls with him, what was one less? I watched through my kitchen window. The cameraman told my brood to look stern, like folks had in old-timey duty portraits. It scared me, seeing my wee ones there in the sun, fine eyes all sunk in shadows: he *planned* that. Ruth had got on the phone and—through no merit of her personality or hairdo—drew a crowd to her porch. There they were, watching the big time descend on side-street us. Lolly—with a new "do" for the occasion and in a smart polka-dot number she rarely wore—her eyeing Ruth's straw. There stood Luke Lucas in his apron, and all our neighbors. But what bothered me most was, on the back row, going up on the tiptoes of gold dance slippers, Castalia. She was welcome here any hour of the day or night. But it's being National Attention must've drove her to the sidelines, shy of us. She'd dressed. Under her fur coat, clothes this colorful made a crowd in theirselves. The glitter of cut-glass doorknob earrings I hadn't seen since my being lugged across the threshold of this very house, me a lightweight bride. She now looked heavier and therefore sadder, Cassie did. She ate starch for snacks. Maybe she'd dressed in hopes of being asked into our picture. Maybe she should take my *own* shy place? God knows Castalia Marsden belonged in any Marsden photo, but she stood off aside on the gallery of Ruth's instead. I was out of *Liberty* and so was Cas.

My own darlings, shouldering weapons, set their faces like Captain's. Most kids were holding muskets taller than they were. Louisa gripped both a flintlock and our youngest, Archie, six months, and him grinning to beat all—baring his gums in a way that always cracked up both drunks and matrons. The photographer kept saying, "This is a definite wrap. That baby redhead just won't quit. Does he ever stop smiling?"

Baby, eager to be "discovered," said, "Archie even smiles at the sun."

"Archie? An infant Archie? My dear, we're onto something here." My husband, keeping kids cheered during slow exposures, eager to entertain Ruth's porch crowd and the Press, asked kids to sing every word of "A Old Rebel." (I'd forever crammed them with Mr. Stevenson's *Child's Garden of Verses* whilst Captain force-fed this 1868 ballad, favored in every roadhouse of the sore-loser South.) Beneath the picture, the magazine later printed all the words. Most Yankees had never even heard the secret cankerous thing, Yanks seemed to find it right cute. They didn't know enough to understand what fear they should've felt. At my sink, I burned with shame whilst Captain, using the butt end of a dueling pistol for the conductor's stick, led my sweet-toned innocents in verses I still know all too clear.

Oh, I'm a good old rebel, now that's just what I am.
For this "fair land of Freedom," I do not care a damn.
I'm glad I fit against it, I only wish we'd won.
And I don't ask no pardon for anything I done.

I hates the Constitution, this Great Republic, too.
I hates the Freedman's Buro, in uniforms of blue.
I hates that nasty eagle, with all his brags and fuss.
The lyin', thievin' Yankees, I hates 'em wuss and wuss.

I hates the Yankee nation and everything they do.
I hates the Declaration of Independence, too. [It does go on, don't it, honey?]
I hates the glorious Union—'tis dripping with our blood—
I hates their stripéd banner, I fit it all I could.

I followed old mas' Robert for four years, nearabout.
Got wounded in three places and starved at Pint Lookout.
I cotch the roomatism a-campin in the snow.
But I killed a heap o' Yankees and I'd like to kill some mo'.

Three hundred thousand Yankees is stiff in Southern dust.
We GOT three hundred thousand before they conquered us.
They died of Southern fever and Southern steel and shot.
I wish they was three million instead of what we got.

I can't take up my musket and fight 'em now no more,
But I ain't a-going to love 'em, now that is sartin sure.
And I don't want no pardon for what I was and am.
I won't be reconstructed and I don't care a damn.

And there in my back yard, all cables from cameras, light boosters shaped like silver umbrellas reminding me of my dead mother-in-law under black-held parasols, a show we made. Like good planning, just the sec my crowd stopped singing their cute horror, I heard the Falls High Marching Band come pounding down our street. "Oh no." I hit my kitchen sink.

After the band drifted off and Cassie hurt my feelings going home without onct speaking to me, I ventured forth. Cap never looked happier. He pointed to the guns just held by children, rifles now tilted in a kind of tepee Ned was making. "This," Cap said, signaling at them weapons, "is history."

I lifted Baby Archie from Louisa's arms. "Sir," says I. "Sir? This is."

BOOK FOUR

These Things Happen

Archie's
First
Appearance

Thou art my hiding place, thou shalt preserve me from trouble . . .
—PSALM 32:7

T HE CHILD born after our return from war, the one who'd ridden me during that scene at the sycamore, he got named Archie. Cap picked it. Told me I could name our future girls, him all males. Each boy was dubbed for a buddy of Cap, some gents alive, some Missing in Action.

Can anybody six months old be said to have a sense of humor? Yeah, I know from Archie. Even his name was ridiculous and he seemed to half guess this. "Archie," a good joke. He arrived redheaded like some firecracker party favor, something built to break you up on sight. Louisa, spying the fire-engine hair, blamed my gobbling crayons during Arch's brewing. "He will probably never be beautiful, will he, Momma?" "No," I answered, holding him up, "but look here," and—glad to be in air—he bared them gums and grinned till his eyes hid in folds. We laughed: he knew he'd made us laugh, then joined. Character, it starts so early.

From his wicker carriage parked on our Courthouse Square, Archie would beam at anything. Sun, dust motes, street sounds—all these made his fists roll like some baby fighter who planned to *grin* the opposition to death. People that'd never been good with kids revised their opinion upwards. Archie's pleasure had just warmed them from under a much-used carriage's cowl. His eyes were sea green like that wild man Samuel Honicutt's, my jollifying poppa. I managed to make Archie's middle name Samuel and Daddy took a extra shine to the baby who looked weirdly like him. Poppa set up a bank account marked "Archie's Harvard College Fund." He claimed the pip, even prior to teeth, appeared college material. After Captain's Money Crash, seemed my kids would need such schooling help.

When I nursed our Arch, he'd play tricks. He'd leave off suckling me. I'd look down and find his face aimed square at mine. He had only quit to get my attention. His eyes mirrored a mischief I'd long recognized as Lucy's own. It almost tired me, seeing such energy re-arrive this fresh, so ready to try again. Next time he stopped nursing just to get noticed, I told him I had eight *other* kids and—not mean but definite—I set Archie on the floor. He didn't cry, he seemed to understand this had some rough justice. Later, when my carrottop's mouth quit pulling on my Shredded Wheat of a championship dug, I found his eyes fixed on me. But right then, he latched quick back on to Momma's taste treat. A game! His eyes danced—he'd got both my notice and my thin blue-white milk. Something in the timing of this showed a flair. I can't explain it. Strange that wit can come forward a goodly distance before talking does. Seeing my boy's pranks at my own bosom, I laughed once in our quiet house—Seth Thomas chopping up eternity into a temporary salad. I laughed so hard it pulled my nipple free. Arch just kept staring where it'd been, grinning at my breast. Biting air, a joke. I could feel his weight twitch then with hiccup giggles.

Must've been October when things shifted, October because we were again arranging who'd be a bum this Halloween (burnt cork for beard smudge), who'd go as ghosts (my ruined sheets worsened with eyeholes), who'd be something original ("Go and make it your*self*, child. Branch out"). Baby was eager to try a angel again, which meant my making wings. I'd *told* her to save last year's. I remember I was pinning buckram feathers to a coat-hanger shoulder rack—the kids were glad to be home from school because there'd been three cases of scarlet fever out in the county. Was a hot fall afternoon, wide open, one pumpkin per house.

I break from wing creating and, straight pins lined in my mouth, reach towards Archie's bassinet for to test his diapers. Child seems asleep when I lift him, arms loose-jointed all akimbo. Then I touch his forehead and the child's so hot I yank my hand away and suck the fingers. Next I'm yelling at Louisa, pulling a pink cotton blanket over my naked child—blaming myself for not touching him onct since putting him down to nap two hours back—"Mind the others. I'm at Doc Collier's. Get word to your daddy if you can. Our Archie's fair burning up."

Baby stood at the oval pier glass (one inherited from her vainest granny, Lady More Marsden). She tugged at her own left wing and said in baby talk, "Arch have burn up." It stopped my heart, something in her idly mouthing that.

I was at Collier's—a six-minute walk—in under two minutes, without no memory of locomotion beyond speed's whistling over earholes.

Three people set in the murksome waiting room reading the only two *National Geographic*s that'd ever been there. All local mothers of three or more had memorized each issue. One such person belonged to the church committee that'd recently sacked me. Plus, Emily Saiterwaite was there looking peaked. It won't like me to cut in line out of order. But these three knew me and I held up Archie, me smiling like a idiot, "Seems . . . serious, excuse me, not that you all ain't . . . serious."

Nurse Milgrom—old as God and a heap more efficient—half stood from behind her desk. She touched Archie then jumped like I'd done. "Ice, we'll be needing ice, come right this way," and led. Her voice sounded low like Castalia's, a grateful kind of baritone that made its every swerve matter. Fast, Miss Milgrom was down that lino corridor, her uniform rustling ahead of me like white wings or wonderful stationery. Things will work out, the rustling told me. I studied the child here in my arms. All I could think was selfish thoughts:

How I'd had him in me while waiting under the Virginia sycamore— how the sadness I lived through whilst carrying the funny gum-baring child had nearly killed me during my gray and longest tiredness—but what pleasure his silly rust-red presence soon offered. I told myself, lips moving: "If You take this child, Lord, I'll never . . ." But I knew that all I had on my side were small-time actorish threats against a God who owns the theater and writes all plays. I knew I didn't even directly believe in Him but, look, I *would*, to save this child.

"Ice." When it was ready, Nurse took my red sleepy baby. From me. Lowered him into a porcelain vat of water so cold it seemed blue. Archie's green eyes bulged so open then. He looked up at me and knew me, and his silent question run: Must This Happen?

He seemed soothed by my being here. Slow, most sunk in ice, he bared his gums—from pain but like a practice, too. It was what'd have to pass for now for smiling. I moved my hand to touch him, but was scared to feel his face. It would be very hot or very cold and which was worse? Collier stood behind me. Archie had gone redder than any of my children ever sunburned at their worst. Overhead a ceiling fan chewed nothing. I heard people mumbling in the waiting room. Concerned, they sounded. Doc and Nurse Milgrom made this whirl of white around a whiter basin: one pink-orange-purplish shape was in it—but the head was out of water, gasping like some witty little put-upon starfish. And Archie knew me. That's what really gave me hope, see?

"I'm right here," I said up closer. They lifted him from wet and bound him in a towel and I heard his teeth chattering, though Archie had no teeth.

Doc walked me out. I said, "He knows me, you saw." "Good thing, fine sign, but this might just be scarlet fever, Lucille. It's around. Keep close, we'll maybe have to quarantine your others, I'll send word they must stay at home. You wait on our porch. Captain been sent for? Good. Look . . ." He pointed at my ankle. It was bleeding some. Taking shortcuts across strangers' lawn, I'd snagged a croquet wicket and the corner of one low fence.

" 'S nothing. Tend *him*," I pinched Doc's sleeve. He nodded behind smudged spectacles and left me.

The three patients got grave, seeing me, eyes on my ankle. "Sorry to bust in and all," I shrugged and flashed my gums, a good sport. "It's just . . . it's just my boy, he . . . and they . . ."

I hated that somebody from First Baptist saw me here like this. She'd later say it was all God's Punishment. That's the way those people's minds work.

The street was not busy enough. I paid attention to six potted plants along the porch rail. Several needed water, a spiny mother-in-law's tongue plant, huge it was. Two young dogs nosed each other's opposite end. A group of boys saw one mount the other, boys tried to break it up. "Let them," I cried from Doc's porch. Beside myself, I was, without quite knowing. "Let 'em." I then added, "Sorry," but boys cackled, "Yeah, Roy, *let* them fuck. You heard the old lady." I sat in the single rocker—eager to run home and calm my others but scared about leaving here. If the Health Department came up and quarantined them with me gone, it'd shake them something awful. They'd instantly believe the worst of Archie and I could not have that.

He had recognized me. Yeah, I told myself, nodding, rocking. Excellent sign, Doc said so, yeah. Forty minutes I was out there on hold. Everybody knows how elastic time is. Those forty minutes, as a example for you, if they'd been shifted into land, not time—would've meant most of Antarctica explored on a person's hands and knees. I was out there feeling very cold. I did not look at my own hurt place. The *new* bargain was—if I lost the whole foot then Archie could live. I pictured my husband, a child, his leg spared thanks to pistols held by a good friend. How might you thank the person for that? What could I offer, who could I rob to save that funny yam in yonder?

He knew me and had grinned his puckish simple grin. Fine indicator. Doc even said so. We'll see.

Walking fast, Captain arrived. "It's not scarlet fever," he said first thing, like giving me direct orders. I nodded, willing to obey in this at least. He said, "Lou mentioned his having a fearsome temperature. But it's not scarlet fever Archie has, I know not. It's in the county, everybody says so. What, are you walking around with a bloody ankle?"

I reached over and took his hand. I made a mouth. "Sorry," my man said and sat beside me. "Sorry. You know how one gets. —He's our card, Archie. Something to look forward to with him. Sorry," my husband said.

I felt grateful I had not yet been forced to contribute nothing aloud.

We just sat there. It was nice. He was in the un-rocking chair beside mine. To feel another person's big mitt close over all five of your own fingers—I cannot tell you how calming this was just then, how precious. He had been my partner in getting myself with Archie and now he'd interrupted work and everything to see us through this. That too was a very excellent sign about our smart boy's future, yes. That pulled me back partway from the South Pole. We had our differences, the Cap and me, but in emergencies . . . He said, "How'd you do it?" I knew he meant my ankle but only for . . . conversation purposes. "Just getting over here quick enough." Then he said, "We've been very very lucky with ours, Lucille. Measles, nothing more. Great good fortune, God help it to continue."

"Yeah," I said. "Yes." But I felt he was talking too much. Bad luck.

Two of the three patients left and I could tell that they had not seen Doc yet, that they were not pleased but couldn't gripe aloud. They gave us the respectful head bobs that dramatic bad luck gets.

Collier spoke behind me. I turned to see him drenched, ice water, his own sweat, eyeglasses about to slide clear off the tip of his long nose.

"May I?" I stood, held up my finger, showing I planned to push them on.

"Please, many thanks." Doc nodded at Captain. "As you were," Doc said, hinting we both should sit again, a military order. I hate military orders, not too good of a luck at a time like this.

Doc had the kindest voice, just like his nurse did. Collier's twin daughters, the flute geniuses, had run off with a paper boy one third their age and, since that, folks said Doc'd grown vague-headed and that he overprescribed. They said he had got Old Lady Helms hooked to drugs but, me, I trusted him. I was thinking how it helps when your family practitioner and his old nurse both have such beautiful kind talking voices. "Lucille," the total voice now said. "Lucille, child, it's not good. He's gone into fits. It's the fever. He's resting. The crisis is occurring just now. It happens this fast sometimes. Have you taken him downtown? He's so young and it's just profoundly contagious."

"It's not scarlet fever," Captain told our doctor. "Because that's out in the county."

"Doc, I did take him to Lucas' with me in his buggy. I mean, I had to buy *food*, where could I leave him? You got to live."

"It's fine, you two just sit right here. News could be okay. Look," he went back for a second, then carried out the tray, "I brought you both a nice Cocola, on a tray."

I pointed to chilly sweating glasses. "Ice," I said. "You got enough back there? You don't need this? And your plants want watering. He knew me, didn't he, Doc? Tell Cap. Good sign, Doc said."

Then Nurse Milgrom come out, wiping her hands on a towel. "George? best go in." I'd never heard her nor anybody else call Doc Collier by his first name. Then Nurse said, "I think it . . . went against us." Doc moved quick but he was back out here so fast. Had he even checked, really checked good in so little a time? I mean, you want to be sure.

They had this look. A look about them, standing there, white uniforms shoulder to white shoulder. I cannot tell you. (I knew—like on the side— that they had been lovers for forty years. "George," she'd said. Death made them forget to hide it for oh maybe twenty seconds. Staring at It, that scared, they drew nearer for a flash, then distance remembered itself. I saw this out the corner of my eye-like. It made me sad for them, their secret, even their happiness, it made me sad.)

Doc touched the sleeve of Captain's black coat, said he was just as sorry as a person could ever be. "These things happen," his choir voice said.

"It don't seem possible," I sounded bouncy, wrong. "Boy, not three hours ago, he was all appetite and making faces, you know our Archie . . ."

"I'll bring you out a nice Cocola on a tray," Nurse Milgrom said.

"I did, I did that," Doc pointed.

I said loud, too loud, "What do I need with it being On A Tray? That's supposed to help us now and be fancy, a drink On A Tray?" My husband reached for me. I shook him off, I turned my back on everybody. "It's just it takes so long for them to finally get born, and then it's over with so quick. —Ain't it? It's just so quick . . ."

Captain reached for me, nervous I was being foolish and I knew he was right, I really *was* this time. Because I seen them dogs come back and start rutting. "Look," I signaled, "look, two dogs are fucking and the baby's dead. They get to fuck. And nobody even knows yet. Who'll miss him?"

Oh, darling, forgive me this dropping all this on you like this.

It's just that if you can tell your own son is going to be funny—and how he might offer that fine a level of company—you get ready to enjoy some *ben*efits from Archie along up ahead. He came into a person's body and out of a person's life—quick as some hat trick, gone. He is recalled today only as a nineteen-dollar marble block saying:

Archibald Samuel Marsden
infant son, six months
"Called Home. Saved from the Damage to Come."

Oh, dear. I swear I'll never mention him again.

The Tribe
That Answers

Look not upon me, because I am black, because the sun hath looked upon me: my mother's children were angry with me, they made me the keeper of the vineyards, but mine own vineyard have I not kept.

—SONG OF SOLOMON 1:6

WHITE FOLKS' Bible say, "In my Father's house is many mansions." But, Mrs. Lady? down here, for now, this the only one *you* got. House about to burn, ma'am. Is.

You still wants your girl to tell-tale Africa aloud?

Castalia's been being you slave for most her fifteen years, entire. I forever listened at tales of your great coming-out ball in Charleston. You always say that's partway like my coming out . . . of Africa. —Well, Lady, today and today only, since you wiggling there on the piano stool, since we slamming fast towards this bad deal's end, I believe I *is* going to tell you . . . all of it, for onct.

Just to prove what a fine mood this slave's in, you stay at you keyboard, keep on tinkling out that icy tune. (Do it make you feel better? Good. Cause from now on, Mrs. Music, you gone need all the comfort you can get.)

Soon as them Yankee horses snorts up to this Big House, soon as Northren torches find us, I can shuck my apron, do one serious jig on it. Here at the end, I can *afford* to talk of my folks' coming out into evil. But, Fancy Nancy, you best listen good. This my last run-through, ever. You perch right there, fretting if you pretty enough to get captured. Spread that fine white satin all round you big old feets (oh, Castalia knows how huge). Your Castalia's gone paint Africa, gone try. Be my final gift to you.

PICTURE it. I seems to recollect a certain perfect root-bound jungle. Picture it like through smoked eyeglasses, lenses cured green, mustardy and gray. Castalia were most definite a princess over there. Oh yeah. Everybody what floated from our village to work for you here, they says so too.

Now, *in* this particular Africa, Mrs. Picky Eater, we had us more trees than you could shake somebody else's stick at. You think this plantation's two thousant acres of woods be wooded? Ha. Africa feel ways more thicker/ older than here. Our trees? why every one wore forty good-sized coconuts up top. Vines hanging every which a ways, drooping so you didn't know if roots was fastened in the sky or steaming up off jungle floor. Now, *on* them vines, growing free of charge, bunches of the flowers you folks calls "orchids." For us, they bout like weeds. In Africa, luxury's second nature.

So, while I dust you English figurines, while I dabs lemon and linseed on this mahogany, try and notice me a bit better than usual (meaning: start to). You forever says what's "bad form," "good form." Castalia's kidnap might help you get, good form, through yours. Yours gone happen in thirty-seven minutes. Watch.

Our coming out—it hinge on one old lady, King's great-aunt, my great-great-one. We talking the meanest thing this side of a open grave, a doubled-up antique croaker, name of Reba. Reba would disappear for weeks, she live off by herself. Right when you first notice Aunt's been gone so long, right when you figure she done finally died from snakebite (Auntie's body shown a scoreboard of fang marks), just when you believe she been claimed by quicksand, here come the scratch of her knob-topped stick. Here into sight do Reba hunch, scolding you for some tiny silly thing you done—a slip-up you figured hadn't one soul but yours noticed. Reba been so weaned on Legend, she nearbout creaked with all that she done tried and ceremonied over and then spit out as "wrong."

You think *my* disposition's nasty when I get into my door-slamming fits? Should of seen Miss Reba's dark-day moods. Throwed stuff, and not just around, I talking *at* folks! Chucked rocks towards teasing children. Good aim, too. When you spied Auntie in her gloomy figuring state, you'd best run.

NOW, Miss Sick Headaches, in our time, we all done seen some messed-up fish-faced folks stumping round. But this Reba were so ugly it almost got honorary. Been clubbed around the head and shoulders with the Ugly Stick so many times, Stick broke, splintered. Some people they so bad-shaped and crookedy, it almost starts to come up on the slippery side of beauty all over again. You seen it?

You know them things you call crow's-feets? ones you been fighting with every import balm-salve known to God? Well, Reba's each wrinkle ended in a three-way tie to start another set, and on and on till she look to be a regular schoolhouse for creasing deep. (Not like you, that wants your face to be a stopped clock. Which ain't natural.) Lack of teeth meant Reba Woman's nose most chafed against her chin. Poor thing had nostrils so wide open, they about like spare eye sockets waiting for eyeballs to roll down in there on vacation. Un-hunh. Her little eyes be twin flint judgments cushioned into sacks of feathery folds, all earned. Every soul what'd knowed her in her life's first half, they long since gone total dust. She alone. She living in that Old past pretty old. It the spot where the worst done long back happened. Time's just keeping you around—a chained pet—feeding you table scraps (the odd half-days). Our tribe claimed Auntie acted so cross cause she way too smart. Hurts, that high-up of a mind.

Everybody considered that she fed mostly off the meats of these huge snakes she kilt. Wherever Reba padded barefoot, guided by her walking pole, you'd hear the jungle shudder, frying with snakes sneaking off, grumpy over kin snakes lately stomped into being Reba snake steaks. Folks went to Auntie for advice.

She too lizard-quick not to mostly know, too cruel to ever lie. Sometimes, during a fine late-night dance, you'd look up from shaking you new parrot-feather anklets, and you'd spot her, most hid by leaves, squinting right at you, little pointy eyes ever smirking in a way that seem halfway admiring you, half finding you flat pitiful. Miss Reba eyeballed warnings at the world. Come time, Aunt looked right into the face of that great judging thing what grabbed and changed us all for good. Was Reba led us over here.

BEFORE getting stole, we didn't understand what Sin meant. No missionaries yet been kind enough to paddle upriver, point out what-all we doing wrong. Plus, nobody'd ever laid eyes on any Wedgwood china needing careful scouring after dinner. (Remember how you had me whipped, Madam Sassy, for busting that gravy boat by accident, ten lashes cross my back in front of all the others? You don't recall? I can take my blouse off, smack you memory a bit. You already forgot how my mother lived here at The Lilacs with me? She blonged to you, along with me. By the time I got ready to axt Queen Mother my full history, she gone. Momma left me alone here, to make up a truth, homemade as me. So true it'd seem like what she might could have told. This that truth. Recollect what you had done to her? Castalia remember. A good servant, I gone carry that around *for* you.)

But, back over there, come dawn for miles of jungle, won't one Wedgwood salt dish to wash, no boll weevil needed pulling off a local boll. And, Missy, just to show you how backwards we done truly been, we didn't miss either Bible wickedness or hard labor. Not yet invented: Sin or Work. Now, won't we simple!

SEEM like I were quite a princess over yonder. I said that, but it *do* bear a certain mount of repeating. Each morning here at The Lilacs when I goes to empty you nasty chamber pot, I chants to myself, "Were one, were one." It help. Even here, I gots to keep some them old slave folk (my cousins) from bowing down to me. Bad form. Say we out working the collard patch. I'll hear a muttering in some language I don't half know no more. I look over, there they is, kneeling mong the ruts of a field, just bending low and calling me the newer queen of our old-timey misused tribe of Reba the Wiser. Well, I just won't *have* folks rolling round under my feet. (Unlike *some* people.)

Strange as it might sound to you, Lady Chilliness, onct I been brung
over and was working like something store-bought, I didn't feel the leastway
surprised to recollect my royal blood. I could *feel* the kingly squish in my
arms, a joyful extra doodad pounding in my throat. Even while you sits
over there hitting patchwork chords (I glad I made a dent in that Stephen
Foster tune, your usual weed and orchid), even while I stands dusting things
not rightfully mine, why I is yet a princess. Maybe you can't see it. But no
weak Blue eye can see Brown blue blood true.

Today, with Yanks bout to bust me out of housework's jail, I done quit
being overmodest. It tiring.

If folks stays as far off and alone as our tribe done, you ain't got
no earthly picture of how outsiders might could view you. For them, is
you gods? is you all Reba catfish faces? what? The only tribes living
roundabout us (ones sharing this holy river that brung us water, fish,
and the steady trickling we figure was the sound of everyplace on earth),
they our enemies. Sometimes us wandered far to the edge of home territory, us find strange fiber ribbons and crossed bones tied to home-owned
trees.

Some nights, we heard the hated strangers' drums get rolling. Bad tribes
be signaling among theyselves. Bout us! One hot evening when this far-off
pounding rode the trough of river, Miss Reba decided us should talk right
back. Playing hippo ham bones. Using our own genius drums. Slapping
forty holy rhythm instruments, we begun right brilliant pounding, sure. Our
steady pulse just seek to say, "Look out, we here." Thing is, once you starts
competing, you can't quit till *others* does. All night, enemy shake and knocks
keep cutting through miles of vine and bog, kept lulling mosquitoes big as
you fist. Two days later, quiet settled. Nobody could say which tribe had
left off message making first. Afterwards, evertime we heard war thumping
from whatever direction, we challenged it with smart noises of our own.
We got excellent at it. We meant such pounding to stand for long-distance
warfare, only safer. But what happened: What start out as war turned into
everyplace music. Answer, answer back. Sound good. We ain't full enemies.
We more a duet.

Us soon captured one skinny foreign-tribe girl, copper-colored, trapped
while gathering fruit on our land. We felt shocked that so stranger a young
lady spoke a language most like ours.

The King axted her many hard questions. She a mess of shaking, begging. Finally old Reba poke up from nowhere, "What does your folks *call*
us?"

All us listeners look hard at one another, puzzled. Took a leap of mind
to know that—past ourselfs—we might, by others, be *named* something.

Girl, she heavesome quivering, "You ones is called . . . 'The Tribe That
Answers.' "

Reba cough with joy, then done a satisfied jig. "And, child, what the
name of you *own* folks?"

But now this girl look mighty troubled, staring round. "My tribe? . . . be onliest . . . *my* tribe. It . . . just . . . us."

"Same here," nods our quick-to-answer Auntie, hobbling off humming.

OUR ROYAL work been mostly leisure. We took pride in getting good at it. That's how come they caught us off our guard that day it happen. Of course, I personally were just a baby. Age three but still at suck. Now, *some* black folks out in you quarter, they'll try and tell you (if they dared talk to you at all) that I been far too young for remembering all I swears I can. Some claims I won't even born till we wobbled off that ship at Charleston's pretty harbor. But, part my memory (some of everybody's) is what I overheard. I always been one nosesome little child. (Who else round here done listened to your "Debut" lies and braggings umpteen million times?) You know them jigsaw puzzles—views of Europe—you forever lingered over out on the veranda? Well, it's the same with my patching Mother Africa together. Find outside corners mashed to be a frame—two parts sky, two lowers land— then the rest just fall so neat in place. And every last trace of the whole picture I gone puzzle forth in high and fiery colors, it true. Trust me here. I'd stake my own six hundred dollars life on it. Castalia's bout worth that now, ain't she? You better listen hard—because, in thirty-two minutes, Owner Mine, I gone to be flat worthless. Once them Yankees hit here—on the open market—I ain't going to bring one penny more than *you* would.

2

COME the night before they grabbed us. Big dance, a few privileged elders (all uncles mine) wore outfits what tried looking like our holy local bird. Uncles' getups never come no closer to the bird's perfect color than say grape purple. But, for then, for that late on a humid jungle night, it'd pass for red, it'd do.

The Festival of Our Rare Red Bird, we talking. Round home parts, this one flying creature ranked as the most beautiful and hardly-seen. The only bird couldn't nobody shoot no legal arrow at. That was owing to this sparrow-sized thing's feather shade, a color we didn't have one berry, no tint of clay nor any ground-up mussel shell to help make. I speaking Red here, Lady. Picture it.

Now for you, pale as mail-order powder, ghosting round this white room, wearing that blank satin wrapper and playing them mostly white keys (with a few black ones sneaked in on the back row to do the dirty work), Red must sound a wee bit raw. It were! So full of heat and hoping, about as cheap as life. That bird stayed so all-out for us, owing to how pretty Red look flying alive in a world made from a trillion greens. Seem like every tribe along our river had one color held to be most holiest. It been the tint most hard to make. Times, some local child'd find a dead one of our precious birds, it feets up, eyes missing life's smart shine. Child'd stay famous for a day or two, folks axting her where she turned it up, how come she checked *that* spot.

Only Reba, oldest person on record ever, only she got to save up bodies of every red bird what'd yet been found. In her way-off hut, she stowed some birds been dead fully thirty spans her own musty age—all handed down. By now, just greasy fluffs we taking Time's word for.

Till the earth turned tables on us, was only three ways we could look on the holy red we craved so bad: When neighbor tribes made night raids and cut or kilt our own, or better, when us hurt them. (Though no blood looks redder than you own—expecially when it flow cause you done dropped a gravy boat!) Another was the red seen in once-a-month personal lady blood. But our favorite unslashed uncramping way stayed how these flamish droplets of birdlife sputtered past on high, making us fall onto our knees, heads tossed back, gaping.

Well, seem like the Bad Ones learnt about our tribe's longing for redness. Soon as others figured how one hot color were such a craze with us, why we won't safe no more. (Be careful bout letting anybody know what you loves most, Lady Ownership-⁹⁄₁₀-the-Law. Whatever's sweetest to you gone get turned to perfect bait.)

Happen the morning after our Dance of the Rare Red Bird, second-biggest "do" of our jungle social year. We been mostly dozing under different palm trees or deep inside cool palm-wood huts. Of a sudden, all dogs every-where start barking louder than us ever heared and in a different whinnying pitch. Every child out making mud pies start quailing like the world's done ended and this shrill sound be one last echo rolling back from then. Sleepers wakes, even some what's been missing deep down with the sleeping sickness for long weeks now. We come to—expecting all our enemy tribes is raiding us at once with perfect timing, right when we the most hung over from our fine palm wine.

In your dark hut, you can't help but notice, by ear, past dogs' stunned yappings, our whole jungle—upriver and down—have grown still as death is dead. Cat's got the tongue of every monkey, screechy bird, and wild boar, too. Scared air feel about to bubble like on boil. Finally, out our huts us run, we stops, then seen it. Most folks dives right back in. Once hid, our breaths just heaving, we looks to one another, not considering it possible that all this might be happening at bald-headed and everybody's noon. No.

Because,

Along our brown slow river in plain sight during the bare-assed brassiest of broadest day, here rides one dugout canoe built bigger than our village's whole straw council hall. Not a soul aboard it, here drifts a island-sized pontoon/tree house/temple thing rigged with rails and windows, with great palm-high poles spouting out the lid of it, these hung with broad stained sheets, each one blowing the floating place nearer nearer us and to our one home.

Till this, all we knowed bout floating was—things we made by scooping innards from logs, leaving such side bark as might keep water out and let us sit safe in. So a boat this big, unpaddled, was big news. But, oh, White Lady Mine, what make this thing the most outstanding and terriblest and way most beautiful of all, be its *color*. Because this huge slatted thing, bowed like a drum, point-ended as any anteater, it done been painted. And you know what shade? Good guess (you getting quicker with Man-cipation rolling in!). Why, yes, it bout as red as red can be.

Imagine you only seen maybe one gold coin in you whole life and then, up our local river Tar out there, glides the entire gleaming Confederate Mint (if they *got* one). A choir of cash registers clinking towards you, pay-drawers full of glitter yellow. Hurt you eyeballs. And oh, to feel Red coming, without a single sound (not one oar slapping).

Somebody'd guessed how good we dearly loved even one rouge cake's own amount of what you white folks calls crimson. Made the village stomach turn with a most pleasuring fear, most fearful pleasure.

LADY, I talking redder than the shiniest line of fresh blood moving down the driest blackest dusty leg in Africa.

CAN TOTAL stillness get even stiller? Cause, it did. Even old Reba—what lived in her own snake-skinned shanty set way far off from us—even Reba got tuggled downhill towards this quiet. She finally stick/drag into a village what seem empty of all life, including dogs'. Hounds done barked first, then—following examples—jumped *behind* us. Now, in huts, dogs just eye-watered. Dogs smart sometimes. Not in the whole jungle were a single birdsong squirting. Expecially still, the simple-tuned red birds, stunned to know that, in the world of rainbow, they won't near so rare as our jungle'd figured. Nothing but river gossip miles upstream.

Using her knobbly-topped walking stick, old body bare as anything, here come our pinched nerve of a blue-black Reba, late. Never married, never wanted, she look to be a sweet potato left some ages out in hurting jungle sun. We studying one what's got three teeth left, but is still vain enough to brag bout them date pits. Her black legs so skinny they like snakes what's swallowed rocks. From behind canoe-sized leaves, we all watch our tribe's one unwed and most grouchy woman. She usually a-scared of nothing but how stupid others act.

Someway we hoping that, this once, Aunt gone scream and double over like we done done. Maybe Reba ain't so brave, just nosy. We bet when Miss Reba sees that redness yonder, her stringy heart won't hold. She now mumbling bout something, one stiff seed necklace chattering round her falling-off neck. We keep gripping heads and shoulders of the loved ones we hid with, we holding on to dogs, letting the smarter of scared dogs hold on to *us*.

First, her usual crotchet frisky, then she slown a bit—then crank, to, full, stopping. Her hollow gummy mouth glump open, her old body grown dead stiff. But seem her crooked walk staff's just way too interested for letting Reba stop. Stick itself, a good one she found when she was six then waited to grow into, it now drag Auntie nearer water where the Red Visitation wait.

Usually Reba only enjoy others' accidents or fits. Now, in plain view, our Miss Mind Over Matter start materially jumping up and down, necklace made of common garden seeds just chippening every way it can. Cept for river whisper, these dried pods pepper forth the only sound for miles. Reba carrying on like a bad baby—meaning, yes, ma'am, she wet her own self, then start striking her very Reba mud puddle with that stick's knob end. Arms doing wing flaps, she shout, "I dreamed all this. And, friends, it now *so*. Come out and see what Reba done thunk up." Just *like* her, claiming. But the strangest part was hearing Reba call us "friends." In two seconds, Queen Eater of Serious Snakes done got out "friends" and smiled. Strange. Her face wedge open like with its own first blinky look-see at the world.

(This sudden boat from noplace felt to us like one big typical dream, on a scale with such dreams as folks only dreams in Africa. I ain't talking the weedy paltry chicken-scratch hot flashes what pass for a dream in *this* land. No, ma'am, I speaking big-scale—the kind us Africans only seemed to have while still in Africa. Dreams of living wrapped in perfect pelts. Dreams so rich and huge was just one the things we lost on our long trip over. Back home, in our greener country, a dream it slaved hard to out*do* the jungle's lushness. Some dreams could run you so river-deep, could twist your mind so many viny ways at once, you'd lose you footing, you'd drowned and tangle, both. Come morning, family'd find only a ashy one-eighth of you left in you straw hammock. The white milky self-part of who you truly been—like the sweetness you hears locked slopping round inside a coconut—why, that choice part stayed sealed in a dream too good to let anybody leave it alive. American dreams, compared to my home/monkey/orchid/jungle trances? why they just little windbreak stands of poplars. American dreams, they bout money. African ones—majority of nights won't only bout magic, they *was* the rawbone magic its own slippery fish-snake self.) Right then, with Reba cackling out there, grinning welcome—the boat stirred. From one slot underneath—some force slid a walkway towards us. Seeing this, folks that'd stole inches free of hiding was right far back in. Reba mashed one eye shut, waited. Down boards did plunk on shore, planks tinted a red as harsh and fancy as the pretty rest.

Seeing how Aunt could pose within touching distance of such rougeness and still live, some our bolder royal children sneaked out, run right up onboard. King's kids is brats, Mrs.! No news. Then dogs commenced usual bothersome barking. Next, mommas could scream for children to come back here this instant. Was then that all our banked-up jungle sounds— bird and monkey ones, the barely-there hum of The Sound You Could Never Name—all it start to life again but richer with a miflion thousand fears built up inside ten minutes' silence. With noise helping make us all feel someway safer and more us, we come inching into full safe sun. Talk about pretty, ooh that boat! If the thing itself look good, river reflections flat outdid it.

Red coat each rope. Even the sails had got pure-soaked in your most beautiful of bloody dyes. Still, it took our King and the rest of he court (cautious because they Kings, Kings because they cautious) round three hours to find gumption sufficient for drawing right up near it. Aunt Reba, though about as you-can't-hurt-me as any of them snakes she'd skinned— Aunt didn't plan to risk no royal life—expecially Miss Reba's own.

She stub up to King, showing no particular respect, she huff something towards tall Poppa's ear. Nodding, he quick orders six guards, Go force some common fellow to sidle over, touch that ship's probably poison side— a test. Guards had to jab umpteen-ten spears against the spine of one poor handpicked commoner. Royal Guards push him towards that gangplank where, to stay alive, the fellow *would* have to feel of red. Not expecting to be around real long, he call Goodbye at his kinfolks and, shaking, whimpered so. But once he close eyes and do it and find he yet alive, man laugh so hard, he got to slapping bright boards, showing off. When we seen how that nobody-special done managed to keep living, our royal crew of a sudden felt right brave. Full of leadership, don't you know.

Soon three giggling baby semi-princes scampered all the way to the ship's far side, proud of being so wild, so first. Scolding mommas run to fetch them, and once these court ladies was up there *on* it, they stand blinking, shocked as how they breathing yet. Myself, I were then carried up the gangplank by the Queen, my mother—at the breast of which I done happen to be a-suckling at the time.

Reba scurvle on board fast as her tall walking staff could rudder her. She muttering bitter, like mad she didn't rush on earliest. Ship's shiny paint yet be so sticky-new, it gum off onto court folks' feet. Pushy younger princes hoist they soles, shown their big royal feets to eager folks on shore. Ooh, but them others was flat dying to climb up where us high-ranking ones now sure primped and strutted.

We a-crawl all over it, nodding greetings at lower-downs on land. Not acting too nice, now I thinks back on it. Say fifty-one the King's toppest-ranking peoples all stands clumped on high, milling round like at one of *you* fine Lilacs boating parties back before war ended such silliness. We chuckling, touching sides of stuff, teasing, double-daring one another, leaning over the rail and taunting, but all in a right royal way, of course. We busy describing what do it feel like; being stationed here in ruby shiny glory. Ship start moving. Walkway draws right up. People on the shore, they screams. People on the ship, they screams way worse. People on the bank runs same way ship be headed. People on the deck trots back to where they left the land and wants to be. Screamers off the bank wades fast towards a boat all moving. Screamers throw they spears.

My second-oldest uncle dive off, splash, try and swim to where it safe and dry. A great sound make us all to yell, to flinch, to cover up our mouths then ears. Smoke hang in the middle air, my old dark uncle gone so still, be just a face-down arms-out spot in brown river. Next we seeing how that rare color done commenced to leaving him. Red, like this, us didn't want. One tribe elder holler, "We on a Blood Canoe, sure. We being took someplace to die. Oh, tell me it a dream. Please somebody tell me I be dreaming!"

Reba hunched most scythe-shaped over railing, she just squint at eye-level coconuts, vines, weed orchids whipping by so quick. She say, mostly at sheself, like half admiring whatever just snagged us way too easy, "Ain't no dream. Be bout the truest thing what's gone on round here in *my* time." And Reba just rest there—acting proud like she on some ride she paid to take. Us trots away from Auntie's talking crazy. "Witch," folks spits. We be dashing, wildness, all round that open deck. She watching, cool, right disgusted. "You can't run but so far. Keep still and see what-all do Red got in mind for us. One achy knee tell Reba, this mess ain't what it seem."

Right then, loud, from underneath, all that boat's doors, ports, plugs of floor wood slam wide open. Next, slithering into plain daylight—like they deserves the holy healing of our African sun—paste creatures lunge. Paste! Such shrieking you never heared. Even Reba cough, "Yikk," she join us in quivering at the boat's back end. She didn't run, just walked—but with that stick rowing her mighty quick out the way them see-through monsters.

(You like how Castalia's dusting here? Oh, I done had so many years' practice. Notice how Cassie's fluffing ostrich feathers round this shepherd-lady figurine with six plaid bows on her crook. A working gal! Watch how I cleans the marble mantel with soap and lemon oil to make it shine good, like *so*. Remember this. You gone have lots of time for practice.)

All them holes and trapdoors unhitch quick and—pushing up into plain day, alive on this runaway canoe—more monsters unhatch. This boat they termite egg nest. Men-shaped but huger, they got too little color in them anywheres. Whole faces be stitched up only out of lacks. Instead of hair, they have grasses, straight blades, sprigging forks off seamed scalps. Some faces let brown moss cling everywhere but eyes. Some noses have silver metal water bugs of wire settled cross them, knots of clear dead river armoring each eye. Twelve my old kinfolks—seeing these creatures pale as yanked-up plant root—vomits on the deck, down into our river. I toss my arms round Momma's neck, I tries and crawl clear past her shoulders. The whole court sprints lickedy-split to the dugout's back and waits here, panting, hand in hand, faces hid.

These ones wear cloth tied in tubes over arms and legs and chests—like hiding even worse sights. They stalks all round and, no-nonsense, just sails they ship. One he wearing a log for a leg! They got no nostrils you can see, just sneaking slits hid underneath long birdish bills. Faces butter yellow or milk white—pored like sponge or sleek as suet. And they eyes!—the worst yet—eyes burn about the blue of sky but feel like you looking clear through eyeholes, far in as the brain and—since they don't seems to *have* one—right out past it. Us would sure have a mess of trouble fighting these trickers—they appears to be mist ghosts. If you drawed near one and went to hit it, your hand'd freeze right into him. Whitenesses seem carved only from columns of river mist, a core plug of cold wind. Ain't nothing *to* these monsters. That make them seem more monsters yet.

All my family gasping theyselves hoarse. Everbody cept Reba. First she cowering at the boat's hindside with the rest of us mashed in one clump: darksome gooseflesh, quiverish parrot-feather anklets, faces so scared, lips drawed back. But then Reba just step out of us. She soon hobbling free in the open. Air on all sides, she alone. Aunt following two wiry Bleaches. We calls at her. King done give a direct order in he lionest King bass voice. Reba busy acting deaf, trying and stare into such faces as got the rest of us so spooked. Them ones stands so much taller than her (she short for *us* and on them be no more than thigh-high), she nearbout tries climbing her walking stick to get a better view. Reba so bent up with age, so turned in on sheself, she look like a fishhooking black question mark—one using the stick, strong exclamation point, to keep Miss Question propped up, axting. (Oh, the truth be out. Yeah, I done studied some reading, ma'am, illegal though it be. Listen, you know how all these years you kept sending me with letters and love notes to other plantations, how you'd hand any private thing to me, sure you was safe as with somebody blind? Well, truth's had its coming-out at last—Castalia's read every word, or, leastways, most! — Yeah, I figures that: naming/spelling/owning can comes to the same thing. I—C-a-s-t-a-l-i-a.)

Two my old kinfolks was already dead on boat floorboards. First sight of blade-faces done kilt cousins that quick. Two pink monsters—busy ignoring Miss Reba's trailing them—bent down and listened at my kins' chests. Then whitenesses just chucked our old ones over ship's rail, three swings, gone. We run to the red boat's back. Man cousin and lady cousin float on off. Out past them, we can yet spy a wide dark spot of river where our hurt uncle he still bobs.

Past him, the village—already looking like something sharpened and shrunk down by distance into being just a learning toy of its own self. You feels you know, of a sudden, how to go back *right*. You thinks extra clear, "So *that* where I been being all my life."

We can see each known dog running circles cross the mud, barking, going crazy over losing our King scent. We sees our subjects crying, some stands with arms vined round they loved ones. Some waving hard at us, other old-timers holding on to they heads. Folks keeps crying out our names, not knowing who gone order them to do what tomorrow. Half our people has waded nipple-deep into the bright river. Some still throwing spears at where this boat just been. Others now pulling big leaves off shore. They rip a hole into greeneries' middle and—heads poked out—stand wearing these like shawls over they shoulders. Were our funeral custom. You wear the leaf till use and rot lets it drop off, natural. That mean you rightful time of mourning done started ending. And—us? Us waves back, trying one last time to look in some part royal.

Then, with dead kin drifting further and farther behind (our lady relative washing face-up, the men turned face-in), were right then that this big boat just ease round one bend, ma'am. How simple. How quiet do it happen. River curves the once. Green ease out from water's right side. Green now hides you from everything you ever knowed. All you thought was so, all that made you be the lifelong king/queen of something fine, why every bit of that can't see you no more. The home what held you up as so high placed/ big shot, that home just ain't there. You? You, now only this—you head/ you hands/you feet. Now you are however strong and useful such a head/ hands/feets might be to others.

Oh, fine Lady what bought me for next to nothing, how lonely a body did feel then in her total bones. I held on to Momma. We'd already got all the red we ever wanted. You just standing there high in the breeze, wind go by—whistling you earholes—moving faster than you can credit. Feel like flying with red cloud sails for wings but pulling you the opposite of where you longs to be. You can still hear—riding out cross river the way sounds carry—our whole home village wailing, shouting, wailing our full names, like we was already dead.

And, Lady Migraines/Musicales? most ways, we was, we was.

3

IF WE standing on some rope that air ghosts needs, they just pulls it out from under us but didn't hurt us, no, not yet. One young wide-walking bleachness act real nice towards us children but we feeling way too scared for opening eyes. He squat near us. From out a flap in cloth over hips, he pulls a yellow metal heart, it ticking like magic at the end one yellow chain. Its front were filmed across like fish eye. He snap the lid open, a frog mouth upglomping—out juts music sounds so sweet so sharp, they cuts into you tear holes/nostril linings, like do wickedest eel gills. When us childrens, hearing, hides our faces, this smooth bleachness give out hacking sounds, a copied type of human laugh.

Bleach sailors got this boat well along our river. They look out for the sandbars/shallows. Seemed they done managed this before. Us stands and shakes while studying the shore uncurling, be so much *of* it. Finally, the haze of first panic starts letting in small things round our edges: we notice a pet monkey. Pale-heads keep it chained to one big pole that carry the most sail. This olive-greenish monkey have on a little blue tunic, yellow cloth tubes trap he legs (a hole to let the tail wave loose). Gloomy under a mud-pie cap, the ape sits a-picking at heself, staring down on us. Looks right pitiful, like he don't *wants* to be a monkey—not even no monkey what's free to live up trees, but specially not no creature forced to wear all this hot mess, to set around in chains and pass for some Bleach boss's idea of funny.

That monkey give us a look like advice. Advice run: "Go drowned youself. End it while they ain't yet got no leash winched round you neck." Monkey's chittery sounds—sad though they be—give us the only comfort we could come by. Us called him "our" monkey. He were the single thing on this giants' dugout that we knew one fact about. From now on, Mrs. Keeper of the Keys, we would reconize Nature this way:

Be whatever had the chains around it.

STRANGE THING: how soon strangeness left off feeling full out strange for us, the Kingly children. You spend forty minutes beating fists gainst the wood of this canoe, you soon hollered youself most sick. Children got flat bored of being scared. A young one can't concentrate too long, even on something like fearing getting kilt! Soon, little ones commenced finding seed husks and banana peels near our monkey's perch. Us kids scurried over and watched such bits fritter-spin to water twenty feet below. Elders watch youngsters being frisky, acting usual. Elders grown the most scared yet, all glazed/quiet. Some snatched sons and daughters, shook them good, nodded toward the boat's sick ghosts. Tribe olders point, "Look what's happening here. And you off fooling all round. What do you all *see* when you gazes on such devils as has grabbed us here, *what*?"

And us childrens? pinched by ears? we answered, "Don't know. But them poor things sure is some kind of ugly!" Then, too pleased by the ride for staying scolded long, we skipt off. Regular mischief let us fool with ropes, turn knobs, try all kinds new gear. This busyness left grown folks puzzling in a knot. What seem to scare them most? —How fast us all gets used to, gets used most anything, Missy.

Is it fair that a orchid can't live if you move it four feet from where it been used to growing—but us humans? We can be tricked and captured and dragged halfway round the muddy stacked-deck world.

You gone learn youself. Red fire's coming here.

"In my Father's house be many matches." Right now you believe you can't live through losing these twenty-foot ceilings, Queen Anne furniture, them chinchillas, Frenchy gowns, maybe even you one son.

But, Lady, I believes you gone surprise yourself. You about to live, and live, and live. Through any/every/thing. You don't know yet but: You a bunch like me. Secret sister, I warning you: You can hold on. However hurt or poor you get, you gone pull through. And can you even guess, Silly Butterfly, the very saddest part? You gone feel so glad you *did*—live. *That's* your punishment. Yeah, my pretty tired old gal, you own true Coming-Out it just about to bust you free. But where'd I leave us? Crouching on the open deck? Had no more plans nor weapons than might a herd of snared gazelles. Felt dizzy from moving so fast so long. —If you ain't ever skimmed no quicker than you can paddle with you own strong arms, to now be twenty-some feet over river water, up along the middle of the thinning trees, to be moving where we used to only see the red birds fly, it nearbout make you ill, how nice it feel while zipping past all good help. Usual mud and river stink be gone. Up this tall?—we catches smells of flowers, ones growing big as you white lace-edged parasol but set there blooming, ten thousand high and vain in treetops.

We floats right by the village of our most enemy tribe. They been killing us forever. And us *has* been know to stab them back. This the outfit what named us "The Tribe That Answers." Today, here we is—getting rustled off nobody knows where. Our hated ones come right down to the water's edge. Seeing these fearful flesh eaters, we naturally runs to the boat's safe side. Us hides behind such little huts and boxes as been built onto this dugout's lid. You expect warriors on shore to point/laugh/dance at seeing the Kingly cream of they river's smartest tribe get grabbed. But then, well hid, we notice how they stand so stark-faced, watching.

Finally when no arrow didn't fly, when no war drum didn't sound, us checked on busy Bleaches' whereabouts. We inched nearer our black enemy's side. Surprise, they mourning.

Suddenly we feeling different bout the longtime slaughterers of us. Suddenly they our favorite all-time killers of us, ever. Our enemies wait quiet near the water. Arms hanging heavy by they sides. Maybe they done lost some of they *own* tribe like this, loved ones disappeared by other such big boats. Our hated ones starts putting on funeral leaves. They acting much like us! Too much. Be easier to hear them laughing of our bad bad luck.

From our high spot we stare across they heads to huts, to village poles yet stacked with dozens of the skulls of our own kin. We know these white bone helmet-heads of our very grandfolks, great-great-great, our dead going farther back into the dark than even Reba's vine-tight memory stretch. Our King, then all us, slow commences waving—signaling down at the bones of our lost ones. Bye, bones of the early us. We ain't been waving at our enemies but they wave back, so we do. So long, familiar beloved enemy—beloved because familiar. Bye.

4

UNANSWERED drums spike our way down a river longer than we ever even dreamed. Some dye bled off the boat's back, staining milky-brown water a nasty pink. Three arrows stung the mast—shot by tribes we didn't know was there. Bleach-heads only hunkered low till we done turnt another twist. Now my kinfolk just standing in the open air, weeping, tired of weeping, partway weeping bout that. We feels homesick for all our old troubles. We even miss the sight of our dead kinfolk drifting back there in the wet. Compared to here, that all seem perfect home.

Four days' river uncoiling, trees started having spaces in amongst them. We been used to miles of jungle growing with a thickness that not one of us has ever found strength to wander to the back of. The Sound You Couldn't Name thin out considerable. Next, sky come falling clear to shore, dipping betwixt scraggle trees. Green soon getting sparse as Reba's teeths. My people grieved to see the heavens let so near to earth. Feared a bad explosion or a lightning fire, some sky bruise. We'd forever thought that jungle was the world.

Well, everybody just stand clutching each other. All but the children, off making up new games and even partway commencing to flirt with bleach-nesses-in-charge. Reba, tired of getting shoved aside by the two yellowheads she been dogging, now sets festering to one side, hunched there holding on to the stick, making mutters, counting something on time-yellowed finger-tips, touching hurt spots on her wrists and knees. Me, I sure did sleep a lot. A mercy, that. Plus, I was busy just being a baby princess (a fat one to start out with). I felt happy in the arms of my momma and Queen. She cried so much, her bitter feelings got spelt out to me in milk. Flint. It soon taste like flint and ash. But I sucked anyways, playing like I loved the taste. That forever been my nature. Trouble all they is to eat? Just make a pretend dinner party out of it. You know me, and ain't you lucky?

The river broadened, going foamier, lighter. Cascades happen, rapids crackling so, churning theyselves white. In one bare tree ahead, we seen waiting—a whole flock of the holy red birds, more than ever lived in our village for the dark fan-spread of time. Thousands, they nearbout coats the slick old limbs, they each sit facing our passing ship like taking lessons in what final crimson might could mean. The King go, "These red birds are all our dead ancestors, ever, more birds than there is drops of water in the river, and all come out to see us go." Others stare at Reba, checking and see do the King be right. Aunt just shrug, "Possible, but . . ." Look like Reba plotting some grand escape. We lets her.

Nights seem safer. We slept on deck, scared to wake and find what world change would hurt us next.

TWO months before this terrible debut sneaked in and grabbed us, Reba had done fell to a terrible tribe unfavor. Aunt always stayed alone, but she kept out of sight weeks extra. During this dry time, ugly Auntie cricketed into Village, she cried loud that a flood was coming. Everybody best take all they mats and pots to higher ground. She say this right during drought, land all cracked, a river hardly there.

Reba Woman, after speaking it the onct, just slunk back into green. Folks laugh over Auntie—foretelling flood in parch days! Three nights later us slogged, dripping, most drownded, onto safe high ground. That morning, waters had swept off all holy shields, two babies, and many a complaining dog. We lost most cooking pots and our fleet of dugouts. Now we seen: curlt on our highest viewing rock, Reba sleeping, surrounded by her ninety twelve-foot snakeskins, all her jars and pods, the saved bodies of four hundred dead red birds plus them sticks she kept because they shapes seemed funny only to our Auntie. With one rude big foot, King woke her. Hey! Loud, he axted why come Aunt didn't work harder at *making* us believe a flood would steal and kill so much?

"I say it onct. You heard it onct. Enough. Ain't fair to blame somebody my old for being too right." Then she turn, stretch back out, already safe asleep, her bumpy helmet of silver hair still flirting with the moonlight. Then everybody yet drenched, stand round her snoring. Folks decide Aunt were a witch, sure, and have no heart. She a eyesore irritation. Folks got to hollering names at her. Loud, they told again how one time when Reba been young—way back in the early days when our river were yet a trial stream, back when all the warring tribes still been one big family (ours), when birds could dive and live underwater for twenty minutes—her folks, the old King and Queen, tried marrying Reba off. To a blind boy. Though Reba's blood be of royalest stock, wouldn't nobody else come near her. (Were always the *mother's* family that our kings done hailed from. Now, Lady, I don't know bout you but I calls that *civilized!*) Court folk led this blank-eyed boy to Reba. Folks mash he fingers up cross she face. No sooner did he touch them bunched-up features than his hands jerked back, and no sooner did the fingertips leave her omelette nose than Auntie's teeth (Reba had a full bucked set then) chomped that blind boy in the left wrist, hard. Boy run off screaming murder, sucking the bit spot like a snake done nipt him. The whole tribe watched, cackling. Reba laugh too—but just so nobody could later say she *didn't*. Reba even force a joke, "They can't keep they hands *off* me. I loses more husbands that way." Then proud, shamed, she turned and nimbled off, shaky, to live alone for six more jungle weeks all by her lonesome. Far from mockers (talking smart to herself only), Reba stayed the homely secret mascot to our rubiest birds.

Now, on the red ship, nobody asked for Auntie's vision. She the one that eased us onto this.

Fifth day on Redness, we woke right before first light. The Sound You Couldn't Name you couldn't hear no more. First sun told us trees'd give out total and complete. Land itself done also quit on us. Ship just slid around a misty curve like any other, be nothing left of the earth on earth. Even tribe children—seeing—rolled around, holding one another, screaming. You eardrums popped, you braced for falling off the edge of everything. Was then we seen it, we be *on* it already—more pale gray-green water than could ever hope to fit on one world. If the sky was turned to water, this might be that water sky's huge hammock hiding place. A new country, only made of drops for dirt clods, fishes for it rocks. Wetness kept buckling up, trying and play like hills. At the water nation's edge, these false hills give way, ridges collapsing outwardsly, axting land's forgiveness, tired of faking being dirt. "I'm not, I'm not," each breaking water hill admit to the earth it copied. And earth shown the same patience with each mistake that break/lap/break onto she breasty self, "Hush now, hush." "I'm not." "Hush." "I'm not." "Hush."

We looked frontways to the far side of wet. We hopes and see a little scrap of waiting jungle. That could mean this just the widest river ever. But nothing green were there to hold on to or hope for.

A spray blown up and my poppa got a taste of salt and he call, "Tears. I names this 'A Country Made of Something Even Bigger's Tears.'" None of us had ever heard of water what's born salted. Even Reba, set off to sheself deciding stuff, she cried, tasting it, rubbing some into her terrible-wrinkledy face like for to heal or numb it, like she trying and turn either young or dead, one. "Exceeding strange. Sure do make any person to wonder, it not?" and Reba sat uh-ohing, sat shaking she head No.

Waterland laid sticky varnish on us. Being fresh-water-loving river folks—we won't used to it. Someway, it made us feel more naked-like. That, and watching the cloth tubes on the unpersons, guessing how they looked without.

Free to roam on deck, we still kept near each other. Reba trailed the two youngest lard-backs. They didn't pay her no mind. One—the yellow-hair with his chained heart what sings shivery like fish scales overlapping—he step to the rail, pull something out the front slit of his cloth leg tubes. Reba be right there. Sailor arch water frontwards then down into passing current. Reba lean forwards, checks, barks back at us, "Ooh, it he thang. Nasty. Pinky white as the rest of him!" Three ladies was sick all over the deck.

Then, bold, Aunt, breathing deep, stuppering nearer, tried to up and talk at this same Bleach-face what'd acted kindest to us children. Auntie been biding her time, picking the choicer of young foamy ghosts. He the yellowhead with smoothingest pink face. He got a ivory-looking chest drawn tight as a answering drum. It inlaid with strange dark ironwood pellet nipples. Reba sheself now sinuate close up to him. He done stuffed he thang back in cloth leg tubes.

Aunt weans off she hex part, crank on the charm, try putting this one at he ease. Tilting on the stick, Reba a-chattering far up. She axting (slow, out of kindness) bout bleachness's idea of a good time. She admit wondering: Is white ones born from womens or—as seem more likely—break like turtles out big sponge eggs? He wink down at Reba just gumming away in a language he won't smart nor lucky enough to know yet. He grinning, his white fangs just spangle in the day. You seen that—though all paste ones is ugly— some be less bad off than others. First this Bleach pats Reba's scalp. Tribe folks we ouching—to see a white one touch a one of us—not thinking Reba gone pull through. But she just smirks this way, winks at us, like saying, "See? I done made a pet of it." Then he called at buddy monsters, he points from my wise gabbling great-aunt over towards the monkey. The huge Bleach with outshoot sun ray for hair, he now signal from a chained ape to Reba. Blanks, seeing this, laugh, one slap he knee. Reba hush down then. Pride always been her failing. Nobody figured she could live through this much insult. Well, Aunt just gather herself up and, with the stick for only company, scump off away from laughing. She alone. We watch Reba resting to one side, hands knotted round she staff, her back bent, old woman staring for a long while out cross the Tears of Something Even Bigger. What she deciding? Might she use her walking staff for cudgel weapon on the one what hurt her royal feelings so?

A jealous niece—long scared of going face to face with Reba—now holler at Aunt's back, "Was you that coachened us onto this blood boat. Know something? Aunt Unmarried/Unmagic? I glad you ain't ever gone be listened to again."

Now, madam, in holy Africa, us had another longtime custom. Reba now performed it on the niece. Without bothering looking behind, Aunt just hoist her veinish blue-nailed snake-gnawed right hand. Then oh so slow, its middle finger lift straight up. Boing! Back home, this act been called "shooting a troublemaker 'the bird.' "

You can use it on them Yankees in twenty minutes. —Here, look, I gone show you how it's done.

BELOW

THEN whitenesses hurlt open twin doors built flush with deck. Bleaches led us into a great ribbed hollow where they'd hid earlier. Going down, suet-faces didn't shove us much. Politeness made us think some treat be waiting. Whatever'd got hauled down here before had left dark smearings. We seen a single handprint (human) mashed onto one beam, like a message for us. Off to the end, on cleaner wood, tracings by childrens—butterflies and such—smudged there with what? Only then did chains come out. Hundreds pounds of blue-black links. Up these got ritually lifted from out great boxes.

All our royal cousins, uncles, aunts, cranky Reba, start getting bolted to floorboards in the dark bottom of a high red boat. Didn't nobody fight harder than Auntie, slugging. You never heard such cat shrieks, never seen a blur like her knobbed stick swung sideways wild. Aunt's skull top come to about manliness level on a few sailors. Her stick sent them howling, doubled, back upstairs. We admired how Reba carried on. But, after, it come to my relations—not only did Aunt not like getting chained . . . she didn't want to be chained onto *us*. This old one was so used to going off alone. Now being hooked, permanent, by hands/feets/round the neck, clampt like everybody else *to* everybody else, it must mean a extra little death for her.

Bleachnesses found that babies couldn't be shackled right. Metal arm and leg manacles clamped too wide for trapping babies proper. So we got to crawl round free among the chained big ones, we was passed continual from hand to hand. Us youngests felt right free till trapdoors flap-flap shut. Then we all known we been locked down here with one plug of African night—another royal captive. They taking our homeland's Lateness cross Tears, too. It almost give comfort to be hid down here so *in* it, spared studying them spear-nose hair-bellies, kept from seeing the strangeness of a world all teary mist, the oddness of no vine, no tree. In first dark, Reba's chains got to jingling, tests of how far each bond would let out. She starts throat-making red-bird sounds. Folks linked closest to Aunt was getting tugged here/there by her tries at usual freedom. Jerked sideways, they flat *told* her bout it.

Home rumors once said Reba—when she disappeared from out our sight (she mostly lived that way)—disappeared from out the jungle, too. Gone, except for a spirit marker left to help her find her place and come back solid when the crinched body needed seeing. Reba—not caring for the kind of smooching middle-village friction-care us others had to have—lived some freer, hidden. Now, we would see how far she got and did she vaporate.

Is Freedom not needing too much? Or maybe always having more than you can use? Tell me, Lady. I myself ain't yet made its acquaintance, though this French goddess clock I'm dusting tells me my appointment with it's close at hand.

Storm heave up our sixth day out, seventh maybe. Such sickness you never heared nor smelt. We didn't rightly know what, besides the rocking, kept making us so ill. By then, won't nothing in you *to* throw up. Still, you did and did and did till you spitting out bile itself. Seem bile be the very last of brown-black Africa wearing off. Leaning forward, spent, you did and did heave, feeling emptied of all home dyes. In shadow, the King (hoping to get our minds off sickness) now try explaining *why* the boat ones looks so awful. He claim that they been staring at the sky so long (up where nobody can't go). Cold sky done hooked deep into these animals' up-aimed eyeholes. But us? see, we been gazing down at our own brown river and home earth for so many years, we been adopted by both. As a type of honor, each one's turned us—eyes and all—towards they own personal family shade.

Folks commenced to blaming Reba even louder when a bigger rain blown and bob and slap us round all day. Storm's sounds! Thunder un-hitching right overhead, every plank in this here tub trying and decide whether to stay hooked to the others for one more roll, or float off and take its chances alone. The ropes was all whining-biting with the strain, white voices screaming orders at each other or the wind. And every bit that red dye done scrubbed off, Lady Listener What's Forgot to Play Piano. (I takes that as a token of respeck, being the princess I am.) Dye done dripped all salty in on us, down through curved boards and straight. Blood-red wet be drumming over me, sucking Momma's bosoms. Her breasts'd started drying up from not getting enough drink nor food. Our Queen so thirsty, she now gulping all the red paint droplets what fall in reach. Hands out, her mouth be stretch wide open in the dark, eyes mashed so tight-shut. My Queen don't care do this downpour red be poison or no. (Maybe hoping it *were*.) She lift her face to where she think that, back in our country, over the jungle of clear streams, long vines, and loose monkeys, a rightful sky'd yet be.

Me, I kept curled, dreaming bout the milk wall-safed in sweet free village coconuts. Bleaches fed us something like what we calls oatmeal nowdays. It got served in one long wood trough, one slid by ropes down our narrow footwalk. I say "served" . . . a word I learnt from you. Some joke, speaking "served" bout a trough pulled over chains that bound every adult ankle. Our court folk had to bend forward cross they own legs' bolts, then each'd drink it, head in, sadsacks sucking up a soup what sounded made out of the kidnapped African dark itself. Bad form. Picture it.

A week into chains, some hungry kinsman call, "Oh, Auntie, down there on the end? Kindly pass us that seed choker from round you baggy neck. We gone soak them pods in tears. Seeds gone swole all up, be right good to nibble. They's leastways solid. —I plans to share. Give over, everybody's favorite."

"Come kill me for it, you. I done had a sign. Reba here, she saving this back."

"Why for? We hongry, witch breath. What matter's more than food?"

"Plenty. These seeds be messengers. They wearing *me*."

He yell, "Listen, how that bitch be acting ever crazier than to home. She the mud-face what teased us onto this."

Right after our daily feedings, kin commenced they loudest rattling of chains. See, broth just didn't fill you. Were mostly water. Every day us waited for this mash to make things better. Every day after it failed to half help, us roared, tried breaking bonds.

Reba, she say nothing. Our tribe magic seem all spent. But, soon enough, things changed, luck it shift. Our old pride, it soon down-deepened.

Aunt Reba made it happen.

2

MASHED in irons (minds free-wandering, everything else right much the opposite), us'd hear Bleach-faces singing they tribe songs. A strange hooted heron language. They played one reedy whistle, plunkt something rigged with strings. Didn't even use no drums! They sure needed schooling. White song sounded thin as the gruel whites slopped our way.

Two older Blank ones come down, stare around and pointed, unlocked three our young womens. Took the girls with early breasts poking out at sassy angles couldn't nobody living in this down-pull earth keep high-riding for long. Bleachnesses didn't even choose the royal sisters us considered our most beautiful. (No-colors have they own odd unperfect idea of what bout us look good.) Off went handpicked girls, each just shrieking for our King to save them, please. He done nothing. Him said not one word as they got pulled, fighting kicking, towards day. Both doors slammed shut. Sunk down here in home night, we had to set, eyes open in the dark, and listen at our three maidens screaming so. One sailor had a wood post to support he un-leg. We heared him thump around, chasing. We heared other white-bodies laugh. We heared that tree leg strike and knock, tackling and holding down one princess onto deck. His wood foot beating, beating as she screech so bad. Sound like he drubbing her to gruel.

Two days later, when Bleach chanting start again, we got quiet in our chains, guessing that by now our three tribe girls be floating dozens of blue-green miles underneath the Tears of Something Even Bigger. Then we heard own maidens giggling, our home girls trying and hum along with the putty-faces what wanted nothing but to harm us all.

King announce in his boominest boss bass, "Ladies only doing that to throw them water-bodies off guard, soon girls gone slip down here and save us." Reba—chained at the very end, keeping even more to one side, slouched in on herself, chains tensed up off her neighbors, still holding that stick upright in stale air like she bout to go land strolling—she just cackle at the King's explaining. "Reba say, first: Let them save theyselves." Others (mostly ladies) moan, agreeing.

Then we keened for our lost maids-in-waiting to the Queen. Us call they full names upwards, encouraging. Our three missing was probably being touched by the white blotter hands of twenty-some bleachnesses, our dark girls might be losing color now—one handprint, one wet mouth bite at a time—our girls maybe having they very lives leach/sapped by all that white male bleach spread, spilled, shot, and burning on the deck.

WHEN we still lived aloose, each time Reba turn up in our village, all peeve, snub, and mumble, folks *would* gather at they own risk. They drawn close, but only in groupish knots to see Aunt's truest skill. After being axted a question, Reba'd reach down and blind-touch some feeble part of her tough hide. The snakebites' shiny scars lumped in either palm, a long spear wound in she side that someway, pure miracle, healed over after enemies raided when Reba won't but nine years old—back when the world itself were all unmemorized names, fresh paint. Aged to slowness now, face both open and decided, she'd prod her own flesh wounds. Then—eyes closed—our spinster would tell-tale her old hurts' freshest answers. Like the star charts you keep forever reading out you Fashion Quartlies, ma'am—no wound ever says the same fact two days running. And, look here, Missy, folks generally *believe* whatever Auntie tell them do. Be it for their stomach dropsy, a bad son, or a hut what's smoke hole ain't been drawing right on windy days. — She alone. She know. She, alone, know.

—So, yeah, Miss Reba had what everbody *claim* they want. But—still nodding from her pointy answer—folks might then study this old walking-away toadstool, all folded in and cranky, folks see her over-with breasts that'd never invited one drop of milk into theyselves for giving on to others. And, spying this never-kissed stump—three-toothed—living freedom out, you sure had to wonder, Mistress Mine, What's the point of being free if you gots to go off and do it all *alone*?

SAY WHAT? But I don't *wants* to quit my dusting. You done owned me seventeen years and you never thought to tell Cassie "quit" before! Only with Yanks headed here to spring me, only now does you grow milk-of-human-kindness mushy. This shade of white is new to me. Listen, if you think Castalia's going to slack off for her last someteen minutes of your ownership, you out you silly gourd.

Oh, I know you ain't *all* bad. (When the chips is down, all the wicked say that.) I *know* you been giving me the party dresses you gets tired of but, answer me this, where is I going to *wear* them? Green watermarked silk with lace side panels—should I slip it on for a corn husking? Bad form. I done caught that disease from you: Knowing what's "put on," "climbish" and "too free and easy." But except "climbish," except heartsick for "free-ish," Lady, you ain't left me much to be.

OUR KING, using he deep rich voice, flexing chained arms overhead, he say he'd about *had* it. He finally shout, It time for our own best warrior guards to spring out of hiding, get they tailbones down here fast, set us free, "Now!" Everybody rustled to bossy regal life again—loving hearing our most royalest person roar so.

"Free us!" King bellowed good, and others start to chanting it, us children too. "Free!" sound so fine, no matter that the bleachnesses didn't know our word for it. King act like a king what always gets his way (though we knowed he chained as tight as us). We tilts forwards, each eye open in this rocking, whining stink-dark. All waiting for our guards' brave shouts, for a scuffling as they kilt off unkind Bleaches. Came no sound. Except. The slapping. Of more water hills. Then more. —Our guards sure is staying quiet though us give them time aplenty. Finally you hears the King fall back against his metal links, a great ramshackle crashing like his proud feelings been powerful hurt by such rudeness from tribe serving folks. (See, ma'am, good help's always been real hard to find!) And—Lady Whalebone Stays, was right then that all our tribe's rich magic seemed clean over. Our saving ceremonies had gone silent as The Sound You Couldn't Name. Our Our-selfness felt spent the way sweet water, dropped into the salted stuff, be right off ruint.

To fill the time, my Daddy King, he axted us to describe our missing village, act like some lost-and-found. King figured if—even in this wet dark—we spoke our local truth true enough, maybe it might save us. Each elder soon added on a fact till it seem you really *could* be walking back to the safe-beaten center of our home. Somebody would recollect how one crazy yellow dog always slept in this certain doorway and how, after a week's snooze, when the cur finally built up decent spunk, he'd stand and chase hisself in total circles. Always. Some boy say, "That dog ain't *ever* been right in the head." Then—out of this being-lugged-away scrap of African shade—tame mild laughs rose up from loved ones. Folks talked in order of their chaining. Odd, but I recalls that order of folks' answering. The one real thing had shrunk down to my kin's voices, laughs. Voices stayed our shields and totems—we was chained but *they* won't. Even now when I thinks back to the home time before Red bamboozled us, I someway recollects our group along the same two rows where we sat chained. Soon every child add on one knee-high fact about our missing village—everybody say a picture. Our tale-told darkness, it were full of pain but full of Equalness.

All us spoke but Reba. She just snort like belittling this whole boat and us ones too.

Mrs. Got to Have She Marmalade from England, they can do a lot of badness to you. They can hurt you and hide you and cart you off from where you always knowed the rules, but maybe the worst deed be how easy they can switch you inside out—I mean: set you gainst youself, gainst each other. Happen on day ten/twelve. Packed in this foul spot, one lonely husband, chained to the row just opposite his wife's and missing her terrible, call out that all he want to do is touch her breast, just one she breast be plenty. Bolted in this bunch, he feel so alone. Breast'd help. Shy, she whisper then—with him so far off—call louder—yeah, she wouldn't mind. Soon others try and get at others for to feel and rut. Chains clanking. Childrens soon shrieking. Soon folks do like animals—try anything for comfort.

I were still three years old, stationed at my Queenly mother's perfect breast. Of a sudden, I won't too alone there in my worship. From out the dark's every which a way, I/her/it was being stroked/milked/squeezed by the hands of whose?

Now, Lady Place Cards, you get you forty-some folks carrying on like this, it bad. Our home tribe's religion didn't credit no Hell. We just expect one hammock limbo, plus a long long waiting list. But now we learning bout the Blanks' idea of Hell. Because they made one. Put us in it.

Some my kin crying bout having been fumbled with. Others crying bout *not*. But worse sounds were the childrens'. Don't know what happening here, they squeaking to their lovey-dovey parents for advice, parents' hands on anybody round them, including children of other parents. None too pretty, for a royal group.

"No more!" King shout. "They gone *hear* us, gone think we copying they savage ways." Then our regal clan sniffed a new smell, half old, part new, total scary. Were the scent of people worked up love-wise (forgive my French, Miss Prissy—but if you lived out in you own quarter with all that matrimony in one room, you'd of smelled it, too). But this time, honeymoon perfume took on a tangy edge. The more us smelled of us, the more we caught uprising whiffs off the heated metal binding us. Just now, the tribe's wild flurry of feeling free caused a new mix: our scent and our bonds'. After just twelve days in chains, us reconized the iron smell nearbout like we knowed our own. Us tried and name this deep stink of unfree. Something'd edged into every head with steel bent round the neck of that head.

A shaming quiet snared us in our chains. What if we someway deserved this? What if being royal caused us to be punished? Our language didn't even hold no word for Sin. Closest one—maybe: "Fun" or "Necessary Hurt" or even "Too Much of a Good Thing." But *Sin*? And yet, this sin idea? already it be working in us like undertow. A contagion so soon picked up off the bleachnesses above.

And where Reba been during such sad mess? She still embunched off yonder, wrapped in chains that she keep shifting over shoulders like some shawl that she done knit. Folks, slow, turn more Auntie's way. We done tried all else already.

Ship's upper deck had a few chink holes knockt betwixt planks. Sometimes one stray arrow of yellow day would fall and settle on our rocking under here. Sun—bobbed side to side by waterland's false hills—Sun would find a brown hand flexing in its blue-iron hoop. Light might pick out a child's cheek pressed gainst one dry breast and—for dear life—sucking Nothing. Just now the beam settled across one of Reba's filmy eyes—brown/green/gray/amber/black—her pupil un-laxed wide, staring straight ahead like looking *at* something.

We can nearbout hear her map-plotting something. Such purr won't like Reba's usual jagged cut-yourself disposition. Back home, she been so quick to accuse you . . . and for next to nothing. Now, she keep so still, seem peaceful as somebody beautiful and kind stuck down on the far end. But how? How, *here*?

Finally a sassy princess speak. Girl's sharp clear voice coaxened Auntie, Why *didn't* she care for our Put Home Together game? Reba finally grumble, We all been taking it from the wrong side, should be figuring where-all we headed, not feeling of each other, not trying to remember what we knowed already. Waste of time—recollecting a place probably not one of us would ever going to see no more. Hearing this, two girls commenced whimpering.

"Shut up," Reba tells them but not not-kind. You could hear Aunt using all her spirit to mull on something way far off. Aunt'd already got past the appetite for petty messes that kept her so stirred up/mad back home.

"Us needs to recollect the *new* place. Us needs to remember the future. —That what a true King'd keep you busy with."

The King heself, in a voice used to being listened at, axted right loud, How *does* you call back a spot you ain't never seen once, hunh?

Reba giggle-coughed over this silliness, then give a marshy answering sigh, "Look, sir, we'd best get ready."

Our tribe had right good drummers/storytellers, had even better drum and story *hearers*. So we noticed at this very second how Reba's corner share of darkness now seem singed with something strange for Aunt back home, but truly odd for anybody clonked down here.

Happiness!

That right unusual since we talking a rake-bottom boat what stunk so bad of you not having no jungle to go use (a different willing spot each day) for personal toilet needs, we talking hands and feets and necks past feeling anything—irons what fit you like your total-turned tourniquets. We talking a slow leak someplace what let in salt water, not enough to sink the boat but plenty to wash over you, to baste you in leavings, to trick under them irons and sting you hurts way worse. We talking a place where roach bugs lived, bugs that our three semi-princess forced to race down the center plank. Bugs growed so big they sounded, when stomped on by a chained foot, like a walnut busting. We talking the fear of being in another storm and only hearing *sounds* of the storm.

"Know what done happen to us, folks?" Reba volunteer now. "Guess. Go on." Ain't like her, bothering to even axt what *you* thinks, but now? She say we got time. "Got nothing but," Aunt say.

Her quextion make a target over chained heads. It hung up there in dark like a memory of moon. Drifting at Reba out of the pitch, ragtag answers come. "Our lives ain't ours no more? Bleach-brains someway stole our souls?" Another party venture, "We all having one big dream, see? it from something bad we et. We bout to wake up, dog-sick but happy in home hammocks, right? Right."

"Wrong. —*We been picked*."

Reba's voice grind extra deep, layered. Her voice made all our warriors and ladies chained down here—ones that'd felt of one another earlier—tip closer, now hearing what they'd sought love-wise. Reba's smoothened young-ened voice now offered sufficient room so it'd hammock all desire. Nothing'd be too wild or strange for resting in there. *What* she'd got so ready for us, we couldn't know. It hum. It drawed us.

Our language didn't even have no word for "future." Closest we got fell somewheres twixt "more of the same" or "Heaven Early" plus that handy jungle standby, "Too Much of a Good Thing."

"They a pattern here. —You figure it by accident them sad beasts got windblown so far up river, up *our* river? Do it be a mistake that only just the King's kinfolks be stuffed down here on this great tipping shell? Well, Reba, after considering a good bit, after trying and overlook you-all's silly gabbling, Reba believe, No. Ain't a bit of this by chance. Childrens, it have all been planned. I bout to tell you what gone happen next."

US WAS listening in metal, hearing big frisky fishes slam against the boards bowed under us, like fish saying, "We free, you ain't." We was floating in our own messes (nobody can tell you how *much* mess you makes per day till you gets forced to stay right with and in it, Lady Fair!). We won't ready to *accept* nothing yet, but we felt willing—like always—to let Reba do first backbreaking thinking for us.

"All my life," voice roll forth with right much energy, "my pet pleasure (nigh onto my *only* one) been scheming and figuring the Hows and Whys of world mess. Your Reba's fought to stay not nobody's wife, nobody's momma. That way she ain't got to be running back home to check bout what's true, what ain't. The more heads you got adding onto this and hacking off of that, the less *so* a thing be. I kept myself aside and apart (and maybe even a wee bit above) the rest you folks. Still, I ain't saying it done been without a cost.

"Not that I now looking no extra pity or nothing—because, mostly, it were worth it and a pleasure. But expecially on rainy bad nights with me hid off so far from out the village in my hut, me hating the damp like I do, well . . . let's say it ain't all been *pure* gift. I earnt what little seeing I done managed on my own. I got by on a few Whats at a time. That made me nearbout happy enough. Not quite (who ever is?), but close. Then the big Why done slipped up on me, done toted me off—raw reward—me, laughing all the way. Reba ain't *never* had no fun that touches what she's knowed since they done trapped us. This the ride home I been waiting for."

Well, that drawed some right loud groans/grouching, you can bet.

"This time," rolls the King, "you gone too far, dog-woman. If this be your idea of a fine time, you ain't no fit blood of mine. And listen up, Miss Old, if you so smart, then why come you tied down here among the bugs with the rest of us, hunh?"

Reba just give a snort. Us heard her cross them bony scarred old arms (chains following). Aunt lets out a long huff that back cuts towards coughing. (It the damp.) First we figured she about to go off and hide inside sheself to tend the meaning of it there. Sassy princess (Reba's favorite niece) begs, regretting a un-answer when we most needs telling. But soon Auntie's chains start clinking. One by one, wound by wound, she begins testing her own signs. You hear her shifting. Medical fingers soon be finding every place she ever got scalded, bit, or stabbed. Long years *will* leave a history of marks on a person living wide open to this world of bruise. Soon we hear Auntie turning scars to she advantage, ouches pressed to being telling mouths.

"I believes Bleaches been sent to fetch back home a royal family whole. You all seen how pitiful them pale ones is. Why, they bodies missing so much. True, they do got a few dark spots on the shoulders, cross they spiky noses. But I calls that beginner's luck. One them young ones have great egg-size blisters rising on he back and just from living in plain view of our holy sun. Don't you reckon it bound to hurt? Why, just looking out through pinchy blue eyes must make the whole world throb like a palm-wine hangover. Fancy having a medcine tint locked in you eyeballs full-time, like stale water sealed rattling/crazy-making in you ear! Ain't natural. But listen, ignorant though they is, they did have sense aplenty to come collect all *us*. Right? Wants us to go cross, be they guides, they medicine peoples, examples. To help teach them and other bleach-bodies how to do and be.

"Bleaches *gots* to hide us down under here. And why? My busted hip say (a ache-glinch drumming out the pulse) it to keep other white ones from spying such prizes as been stole from out our land's downriver. There'd be wars if other jealous Bleaches was to learn about us here.

"Someday, my snakebit left palm say by tingling like some third eye trying and rise up like a boil and look right out my bony wrist, this boat going to cease it wicked rocking. True. We gone quit smelling how they onetime hauled fish down in here. Finally our noses'll tell us Land Again! Bleaches will toss open both them wide doors, gone sclump down, all sorry-acting. Yeah. I figures that, waiting on us up there—our honor guard and help—we gone find the selfsame holy sun. We the only ones knows how to use the sun proper. These un-colors, why them it mostly hurts. They dead to know why our women be so beautiful, our men so strong, how come our children act so smart and bold? They flat palpitating to understand. Poor things, gone needs a pile of help. I don't likes to say they slow but I reckon that poor monkey up yonder would be better at sailing this thing. Sad part, how hard they try and look in charge. You notice? that's what they seems to care about the most! Poor creatures so confused. That where us comes in. We gots to let them finally see the folly of this owning/grabbing mess. They figures that anything or anybody they likes (and has a boat big enough to tote away) be theirs."

We all set here listening, Lady. We hear Miss Aunt's chains clinking, ironbound hands prodding some ouch plowed deep into her left side: "My scar, bunchy far in, twining with a nerve wit all it own, say: Once us on they shores, we gone see other whitenesses bow down and smile. This proves they know what-all luck they had in finding us wizard ones come clear cross Tears to teach them right. Bleachnesses is bringing us to finish off they own missing gredients. They got a big tribe—be like a pot full of village food—I talking: mealy, pinky, blank. *They* knows it ain't too tasty. They done zigzagged everywhere seeking spices/flavoring/hot stuff what'll put some lively bite into they paste. We the dark and quickening herbals they sought. —Right now, blood kin, these chains do hurt, unh-uhnh, they smarts for old me, too, but the ones sailing up in daylight, they keeps dancing and singing cause they know how good they done by finding us. Oh, yes, they gone be rewarded mighty rich for turning *us* ones up. I mean, don't we be famous? After all, childrens mine, ain't we 'The Tribe That Answers'?"

Everybody got pent all up so still. One person commenced crying in a ordered kind of gulp. Somebody that glad to finally know the reason for this pain we going through. A few bold aunts start axting Reba more, to clear things up. But right off we mostly blieved what Aunt just say. It help us to. Blieve.

Patient as anything, old Reba croak-spill answers. She never have acted more willing to prove she our blood own. Reba touch another tender under-rib spot, "Say here, one reason them bird-beaks behave so lazy bout hurting us: so much hurts *them*. They figures the world's *gots* to feel that bad. Won't trust what fails to pain/bind/cut them some. Maybe they ashamed all the time, be why they hide theyselves in leg and arm hammocks? Might be part of they religion, staying dammed all up with fears. Us got our healthy river gods, bird and fish and mud gods. (Like your King say, they probably just has sky ones.) They very eyes show it. Sky gods? Can't nobody fly up to no sky. Be nothing to touch. No wonder they looks so miserable! Still, that why they sought us Answerers out, to show them how. They after some holy help."

Somebody axted bout the food part. If us *was* such a find, why don't they feed us proper? She say, "Bleaches soon gone prepare a long feast. They bout to let us up into the sun, they gone give us more real eatings than our whole hungry home tribe could down. I see this picture, starting like a spiderweb pult out my thumb joint and leading to the base part of my skull. We soon be sitting on thrones in a huge room. We all feel proud-ened on a high stage. I sees many Blanks come to study what it mean to be a person that ain't ashame of knowing all bout color and the sun, facts of they own body. Spirit don't dwell up in no cold sky but right much nearer, it right here bodily beating plain as the million drums them poor Blanks ain't yet discovered. —We going to answer mist men with all us knows that's solid, color. Just be our leading family duty to. They the un-world, the not-yets, pitiful spongy like shelled pink crayfish. Our best luck gone come this way: teaching through example. Secret is—they needs us and they leastways smart enough to know it."

Then Reba rock rearwards among chains, feebled by the long tell, her voice, dry as years, ashed back to a old woman's. "You been listening?"

Us answer in no words, just low, meant sounds.

"You blieve Reba's hurts been spout/fountaining what's least partway true?"

Again our answering grunts make a group Yessing.

Were then, from her quiet place, Reba give low "huck, huckle" sounds. First us think she got some food caught in she throat—but ain't no food down here. Then we know, pleased, she'd started laughing. Reba just laugh and ackle. Seem like she got tickled, couldn't hold nothing back. Health and un-health rubbed and kindled in her, side by side, on right good rattling terms.

"Ain't it something?" she axted, not axting. "Ain't that great white shore-line going to be a sight? No wonder our river enemies weept and carried on so bad. They wisht it was them. We been let to come here apurpose. And ain't we going to do the un-ones up top a world of good? Putting tints onto great waiting blanknesses. You each go in on you best self, you choose one color and one law to tell out first. Get both ready. And, listen, you'd best to keep it simple. —Prepare you answers, Answerers."

(If we hailed from a land where one leaf could grow wide as your front double doors, just think how huge/to/beautiful our transplant answers might could bloom!)

And so, yet in the limits of chains, we pick which color—of all the pretty tones on earth (beautiful and homey)—we plans and slap up earliest. What in our way of looking at the earth, should each/us speak the first? Some folks nested here in links wonder if—once we *does* teach blanknesses, once them starts to knowing rules, once us makes them become more human and upright animals—*then* can us head back where we come from? Reba say out, "No. That part over, friends. We this now."

"Oh," the sassy princess answer for all.

My kinfolks stays locked down here in dark, and yet we each sat deciding how to rule the very rightest. What would you first tell?

Though many arms sure smart and though our legs is cut right deep and though we a-laying in floating personal messes—all my kin yet starts picking what deeds want speaking first, then second (second's right important, too). How do you coach chain lovers in proper ways to rule, to carve they art and live a life where shame and sin and joyless work ain't yet got barb hooks into every single soul?

You could hear folks' chains being somewhat neatened now. Like for inspection. Like we soon gone be led up onto deck to view the anything-possible white village Reba promised. We best start practicing for how to act. Down here, we got to show no pain, we best give lessons to the very dark, these chains, and each other. Mostly each other. For this great task, we gone need our all-tribe strength.

Reba'd helped us understand how water-faces be so ignorant. And we commencing to change our feelings towards them. Not to loving them, no, but at least offering the pity you shows animals, even animals what'll turn on you, ma'am, the flesh-eating kind. We *is* the King's family, after all. Patience with risky fools stays part of being at the center of a setup. "We will do right." In the dark, our heads rise, like Reba say. In the dim gut of a boat, we knows that—though rude whitenesses got it all wrong—this trip is yet a clumsy try at invitation. So, now us royals has got a new un-leisure job. May be our hardest yet. But, yeah, we will teach. We gone try and start a colony of courtesy, of answering river calm.

Were weeks of days then a new half-week gone (try like you will, you flat lose count). Us yet waits, hoping only to live long enough to go on expecting deliverance. Folks wants a chance to say first speeches in the big promised tooth-white court. Eight my kinfolks died. Of fear, hunger, from age, of this water prison's excess strangeness. Fifty-one had started. Take away the one uncle louded to death within sight of home, plus two cousins what perished from first scare of monster seeing. We down to forty-eight and now subtrack these other eight new dead, make forty. Should we count the three maids took up on deck for purposes of purposes—girls not heard scampering for days? Three more equals thirty-seven but, no, let's say the three maids yet lives. So we just down to forty. Eight bodies got toted out, us yelling they names, announcing who they be to The Country Made of the Tears of Something Even Bigger. Us hears kin splash.

The Tears be where all rivers go to die. And maybe all us, too. Rivers headed to form *this*, just like we is washing to our next level and test—this training-up-right of a animal race toward kinder natural thinking.

"But," the sassy princess call, not honoring Auntie's tiredness for a single second's pausement, "how come one river's sweet water, when it meet another's bound-to-heaven drinking water, go so salt, turn straight to tears? Why, hunh? Guesswork long been my secret hobby. —So how come, Auntie?"

"That part," Reba go, laughing till a slow geyser of cough done hook-leap all up out she, scarring air. "That part," Reba scrap for breath (chains clashing while she feel her boils, cuts, bunions), "I ain't been lucky enough to've got hurt in the right place so's I'd know. Yet. But, sassy, I checking. I can't keeps my hands *off* me."

Folks chuckle at a newfound modesty what'd overtook our old-time crab woman. Odd, sometimes seem like all Reba's skills if ladled into a married-man warrior would've made him King of Kings for sure, and since the age of twelve. But them same gifts, sewed up in a wither-spinster and un-wife, mean she been, for life, called Witch.

Later, when more strength seep back, folks put harder questions to the sadder parts of Aunt's nicked body. We hear irons' slow shift. For us, Reba woman stir up all them embers hid under her ashy scars. You wakes a pain to axt a one-word question, you can't just hammock-rock it back to sleep for another twelve years' snooze. Fearless for us, Reba. Auntie now admit she ain't *ever* had a better bunch of painting-pains to read, never. Finally out his corner, the King speaks one home word to put her back in place . . . our word for "Too Much of a Good Thing."

A man, he feeling scared of all the tribe notice freed toward Reba, scared she'd took over most complete. King go, "Seem like the best sign would be: You didn't have not one single ache *to* read, Respected Aunt."

Reba never even bother answering. Our tribe elders, in chains, done noticed the King's selfish tone. They heared him trying and keep Reba's full truth from us, and only out of personal vanity. Then Daddy King heself, ashamed, listening at how he sound, knowing he bout to be scolded by the council/elders—say, "I sorry." Be the first time we done ever heared He Majesty admit that. And—to give you some idea how Reba'd took over: Didn't nobody marvel for more than a second on hearing He High-Up pologize like any hangdog mortal. Her spell were already that fixed upon us, Mistress mine. All evening, she stay hush till her giggle led down to the up-pull of one deep cough. In the slow-coming stillness afterwards, Reba found enough oddment air to sigh over at us: "Oh, soon, soon."

MOST others they now trying and sleep. Wee bit later, sassy princess call, shy then not so shy, "Uh-oh, I just heared what I thought was gone for good. Know how we been blieving that The Noise You Couldn't Name come out the center of our jungle? riding from some hollow tree or whistling cave what led down to the Nother World? Well, now, I figure, couldn't be, cause . . . uh-oh, right here, me, I just heared it." She grown uneasy, acting not much like her sassy self.

Reba, bent into a black crescent resting on one side, Reba go, "Tell."

"When we been scared," the girl admit, "it grown real still, the sound. It gone and hid. Now us is calmer cause of Auntie and . . . listen. Friends. It back. Eavesdrop on youselves. Each one what's still awake, you try. Might could be, I out my mind. —You tell me. I gone believe you."

A smoothening happen, listeners concentrating so.

"Well? *Does* you? Hear?"

The Sound Us Couldn't Name. Now we down here in dark—unorchided, unsunned—folks found, plain, that all along it ain't been coming from the jungle, it mostly been us breathing. It the ear blood living in you hearing, and when no listening work be required, just playing house, and having servant fun and trying not to break nothing.

We once figured such sound rolled to us from miles out of our land. But all the while it just been sawing/hushed inside our throats, our lungs, and home-owned mouths. It our own bodies' river-drums answering others', staying brave.

Down here, you felt now others listening so hard. That added another purring noisement.

"All *I* hears," goes one cousin, "be Uncle Thus-and-So's hoggish snoring!"

But slow, come nodding, general muttering. "The Sound You Couldn't Name?" princess axted. "Well, look, *I* can. Name. It just us. We ain't so lost as us done felt. We brung it. They's more us here than we done guessed or knowed. We now our own main home. Us, bodily."

LADY, might I bust in here and speak right frank? You *better* nod Yes.

All these years you figured you the lucky one. But, Mrs. L. E. Marsden, Jr., but that ain't the full way true. You hear those scraping sounds cross you marble foyer downstairs? Them's the left-here slaves saving all you fine picture portraits and settees from out the seven parlors. Well, don't get *too* misty-eyed bout it, Lady Ladyfinger. Slaves ain't saving them for *you*.

You know something? After all us clears out (us what didn't have no choice but to act loyal these long years), when us stops cooking, and sets down the long mending, quits that hardest chore—listening at you chatter-birding all day (the Sound Couldn't Nobody Miss)—why then, Lady mine, you gone crave us lots more than we does you. They's some sweet revenge in knowing that. Don't set there shaking you semi-pretty head No. It flat True.

All these years, once the long day finally over, we could all go stretch out in the crowded quarter. We done had each other for complaining to. But you? You couldn't complain bout slaves except *to* slaves. You poor pale thing weighing not much more than a skinned rabbit, you been left upstairs, blinking in the dark of three floors pretty as a funeral home. You been the only live thing left here nights. Hiding in yonder ivory four-poster tall as a ship what needs a gangplank to help you crawl to sleep. You done dwelt alone since you got widowed, then young Master Willie left you here by heading off to war. He march north to keep me down here at The Lilacs doing windows. They a hundred and seventeen windows in this barn and, by now, Castalia, she know every one by heart.

Facts be coming down on your fair head, don't they, Beauty Nap? Is *too*. You got ten, eleven minutes, most. Castalia would feel sorry for you if Castalia could. Castalia might be sadder now if you'd let *her* feel a wee bit sadder for you—day by day—all along. Secret is, You only had to axted! I were right here, won't I?

Oh, I plans to go on storying while hand-and-knees polishing the rest this bedroom's flooring. And you, stay cross-wristing it up and down you white piano there. (I never did understand why come you painted that fine ebony thing flat white to match this bedroom's color. White ain't even a color, Mrs. Decorator, or ain't you heard? Black be the gathering of all tribes of every color in the world. White the lack of even one! Black be total Tribal. White: alone off by itself. So when Castalia say she's colored, she means all-colored with every color, all!) Play on. Keep them boneless-looking fingers working good. You soon gone need them for something other than ebony/ivory stole out of Africa. Like what? Like for maybe hoeing round you own okra and field peas. In minutes flat, you gone look up, you gone really finally need Castalia. She be *gone*.

ABOVE

BUT, till then. That same night us heared shouts, another boat seem to draw alongside. First we figured it was the pirate Bleaches that'd learnt bout us—valuable cargo—come for to kidnap us off kidnappers.

Next morning, hatches done flop open nearbout blinding us with a full dose of regular day. That's what punishment can do—turn what you wants most into something that'll hurt you when first you gets it. Then your jailer can say, "See, you didn't really want that. Look at you, all fally down. I knows best." Darkness, chains, un-food, un-drink, un-dignity of bobbling in you bits and juices, it had turnt us weak and sun-spooked as them pale things what done did it. We finally sees, through shielding fingers, plain up in air (the sky!), sees framed by ship's salt timbers white birds, too bright to watch for long. Picture them. They keeps circling high up yonder, letting out twisty cries like the souls of lost children. They sobbing, "Go back. Not now. Head off. Hey off, hey off." Birds keep swinging over, trying to peek down in on us—the dark guests needed by a spirit-starved land.

Sailors pulled us up, our legs too out/practice for working good. It hurt you feelings, being so floppy and for all to see. Still, remembering Reba's words, our necks done managed to pitch upright. Maybe our knees *won't* ready to lock in place, but jaws lifted, tribe eyes did fight to stay proud-open.

Reba got lugged up last, too worn down for taking a single step, maybe too pleased. They left her famous walking stick below, the exclamation gone and just one old rubber question mark now glomped on deck. Crouping, Aunt keep checking all round, eyes full of water from hacking so. But even while coughing, Reba signs towards salt water. And what do us see down there? Riding them Tears, green leaves bobbing big as life, chips of barky tree limbs go drifty past. Then her find sufficient air to boss us, "Somebody young, look to all sides, does you spot it? Anybody spy a white village? Is they land?" Our second-from-youngest semi-prince soon jump up and down, he pointing, "*There*, what Auntie say, it lined up over there." Reba, level with the deck, only nods the once, grinning her crixcrossed squint, "Which way?" Her eyesight been so good till now. Sad to know it leaving her, us look at each other. Then we just aim her shrunk body in the right direction for enjoying the clay-and-greenery smell at least.

Our skin—from weeks' steady soaking in stray salt water—looked time-withered. In full light, we was wizened to a tribe of Baby Rebas. Bleaches now shines browner than when us seen them last. (Already Auntie's magic cure be working!) Sky-eyes just laughs to see us carry on—so glad bout viewing they own shoreline. They think us don't know better. They ain't yet offern Reba no credit. Time's coming.

Our monkey still skittering, scratching, tugging the little collar out away from he neck what's worn right raw. Nobody sees the three prettyish princesses what got dragged up here. No trace of our high-breasted sisters what tried to do pleasing things, tried so hard to stay alive they probably didn't have no pride left to stay alive *with*. Not a sign, and us not daring mention it among ourself. We studying all round for them, not wanting anybody else from home to see us scouting. Odd, to feel ashamed, like this sin were someway ours.

One smooth new Bleach-head must of slunk aboard last night. He young but wearing this old-seeming long black robe. It fall over he feet, trips him sometimes. Have on a high stiff collar so full of white paste, seems it cinching off the blood to he long blinky face. He got sky eyes so sky they purple. Soon as we been dragged hissing into sun, hands shelling eyes, this fellow in black start milling round among The Tribe That Answers.

He soon moved everywhere with two long sticks tied crossways, a staff like Reba's missing walking pole. He wore other little sticks crossed on a belt, trapped to a leashing chain of beads. He keep smiling/signing in this tender careful way. He the first one seem to know he dealing with the royal sixteenth of a good tribe. Eyes closed, he somewhat talking to heself. Keep stooping before each one us thirsty folks. This boat mighty low on sweet water. We ain't had no drop to drink for three days. You know how long three days can run without one drop of wet floating anywheres in it? Fancy you own thirstiness while hearing the splash of all them Tears you sailing through. Our lips feel made of salt. This black-dress drags among us. He child-looking, hid in such long robes.

Then he whips out a little silver bowl, pours water in it. Well, when us spied that cold-looking drink, we took proper measure of this sad-face, sure. We now seen how the crossed sticks have one tiny clay man nailed to them. Being earth color, this toy person look somewhat less Bleach than our sailors. Clay man been caved in, skin-and-bones as us after long weeks' floating noplace and eating just oatmeal. Seem a good omen, earthware man arms out on the stick, even with him *tacked* there. Plus, oh listen at that black-dress's cool blue water sloshing in he silver bowl. He pulls each us off aside. Reba among the first he notice. Her lung-unravel cough seem to draw him, like he gots to work fast. He dip three fingers into wet. Reba point at Reba mouth hole, proving where that water oughts to go. Black-dress bend right over her but his fingertips, dainty-like, press just a few sample drops on top her nappy gray hair. Quick, Reba wags her head, pokes out a extra-long brown clever tongue and, sly, catches wet flung off her shooken scalp. Others oohed, admiring. Reba holler over at us, "Sweet water, sure. Get ready." My practical old Auntie pats stray beads off she pate, then quick scoops damp to her few-toothed mouth. Seeing this, the Bleach boy slap Auntie a good one down side her head. Hollow-gourd thwak. He then seem to feel half bad, instead he stroke her old noggin. But when the next thirsty person tried Reba's stunt, why that one got cuffed way harder. That cousin's nose done bled from it, Mrs. Pisscopalian.

All during, Reba told us, "My baby snakebite on the ankle, the one I got when both me *and* the snake was babies, say Bleaches is a superstitious race. Believes in spirits, all like that. But, listen, they religion just going to make them riper for finally obeying our will and lessons. They ain't yet got no codes, no true rules. We they living help. That one sprinkling us, with black tent trying and stretch long enough to hides he *feets*!, he remind Reba of how back home, we sometimes got that hunger what'd drive us to rush downriver and eat a good piece of soft clay. Remember? That like what's forced these palenesses clear cross Tears to us. We bout to fill that deep white maw what's felt real empty way too long. You think it a accident how that spirit-minded Bleach boy be wearing black? It the hue of mysteries. We the very nourishment-answering earth they lack so bad. They ready. Kinfolks? Listen up. Prepare your color, prime you starting talks. —We on a mission to civilize."

2

NEXT DAWN, with us stretched across the deck, scent of it woke us long before the sun done let us peek. Dirt, a campfire, the sweet smell of one mild flowering hedge blown this far out into the night's last scrap. Your head be turned in the exact right direction—your eyes both knows right where to wait so—working—you could help hatch land out of wishing and into plain holy sight. Even us little ones perked like old animals at the smell of remembered earth, our new home.

We runs to the rails, least so far that way as chains'd let us. There! Where sky and water meet—a gray line soon say, "I here all right. You ain't making me up." It start so blue, next dip more grayish till final daylight sharpens land to being bitter parrot green. The King (what's acted so sulky-quiet for some days) finally speak up in he finest purple-black grapey voice. He claim Reba been wrong all along. "Where the white village she kept telling us gone be here?" King swear that this boat just turned around, this be our home again. "Full circle," he go, trying and sound wise. Soon, Poppa promise that our own fierce warriors gone paddle dugouts into view. Old Reba don't even speak, just rest on she back, flat as her crook neck gone let her lie. Aunt's front side spread open to the sun, her breaths frizzing/crackling in her (the damp, weeks of it, so little food/drink, why it hadn't agreed with the old lady). Reba shake her head No, onct. Us look at her, at King, and then to bleachnesses—their boat's red sails rain-washed cream pale as them.

They guides this thing direct towards one new speck cut from the strung-along green. A little rain come up, cooling us, making our irons wear better but stinging cuts hid festering underneath. Now, in light, some our folks tried peeking under metal to see how bad them hurt spots be. Reba, sensing this, screams mean as ever, "Keep *every* eye on shore, don't *pif*fle with you nearby no-count woes. Do what Auntie say do, you."

Folks did.

Sailors grown busier after spying a far-off fleck the same no-color as them. White birds give louder hoots, wing-spinning, like glad we here.

Bleachnesses start washing us in sweet water, they heaves buckets of it our way, laughing to see how good us like it. Ain't we river people! (Why is sailors wasting good water for *this* after keeping us so thirsty for so long?) Once our bathing's done, suet-faces pass us coconut butter (the home smell!). They shown us how to rub it on our bare legs and arms and chests, all into scalps. It lets us look somewhat like the healthy gleaming crown-heads we once been a goodly while ago.

Our sailors then make another of Reba's promises come true. Out pulled bananas in huge bunches (baby-sized to rotten ones, all tribal in a single shape). Came halfs of coconut, fruit, cooked meat what must've slipped on board last night when that young mumbler-in-black did. First, gobbling, our throats closed up. Strange to find, it takes practice even to learn eating anew. Then we got a few morsels down but spit them up. Food seem scared of being sent down to dark belowdecks but got sent anyhow and learnt to stay. Flat on she back, Reba—like the rest of us—just stuffing it in, laughing, she crackling bad.

Whitenesses start jattering, excited, pushing each other, pointing. One young one seem near crying, clutching a small picture. Some us peeked—

it looked to be a female Bleach. (Hair piled up, face even more lizard-belly white than him. Make us sick!)

Boat soon drift close enough so us seen a settlement sharper. Glide near, glide nearer. Be truly something. White houses and white temples maybe built to honor made-up sad white sky gods. Seem like Reba done announced it right. We been brought here as a bridge between all-color in our world (home/mud/orchid/mud/jungle/free food) and this blank polished port, this lack of anything but pure space waiting to be filled/drummed/scribbled right. We feeling proudened, ready. Every texture what's been missing, it done finally turned up. It have arrived at last—it here, in us.

Steep village sent more white boxes creeping onto hills piled round the harbor. You eyes just smarted from how much white aches here. Great cubes, columns, blocks, all painted bright, rising high and sure off ground, not once falling. No end to how these waterside huts could add up and up and link in rows. Like chains. This much seem clear—bleachnesses' favorite shape is—chains.

Kinfolks lift Reba so she can see more good. Heaven's village appear to be missing everything cozy (no straw, no color, no mud, no dogs) but it still must mean home to sailors. Too weak on deck, Aunt been peeking out twixt slatted rails. Now Reba (in air) spreads wide her wobbly arms to greet the holy city.

Reba's either hand ease open, snakebites' knots shown pearlish double fang marks yet sunk into each palm. Legs and arms be all uncrossed in open sun, but each still dangling chains what hooks her firm to us.

She hoist she head, she greeting imagined on-land whitenesses. With all her strength, Reba now grinning a grin ain't none of us ever seen out her before. Be a smile that almost scared us. Her face alone won't grinning—the whole head, whole top half of she crinched body beaming. If anybody'd ever doubt Reba's plans for us, the truth of all she prophesighed—doubts ended with a face this lit.

Our wide-backed King heself be among gents not hoisting, holding her. With both hands braced under Aunt's sharp shoulder blades, maybe King were spooked to feel this brittle witch, most blinded but squinting so at shore. (Who among us last *touched* Reba?) Did it scare Poppa King to know that Aunt, for all her power, only weighed bout as much as a good-sized jungle mantis? Now he craning hard to see her strange smiling face hooked to a twiggish spine he helping to uphold. While pale birds circle and air-oar, King announce in a voice not like his usual bass boss, "From now on, I just another kinfolk of this woman. Reba stay righter longer than I ever hope to. I only proud to be so full she blood. What her say do, we do. Or *I* do . . . cause I no longer gots the right to boss no soul but mine alone, if that."

Reba, not seeming to notice, stare off towards the waiting white village, she now hoarsely speaking to it. "We here. Not to worry no more. We done gots to you in time, you lucky. And after us have taught you, you ain't never gone look so cold nor strange nor dead again. You watch."

The monkey, swallowing same foods as us, still keeps chittering a coded monkey warning at us all. Reba cough/say, "First they done bathed us, they then anointed us with coconut oil. Nextly we been fed a feast prepared by our own enemies. Soon they gone lead us off of waterland and onto shore and towards our rightful thrones. So carry on like who you be by birth."

Our folks now treating Auntie roundbout like a river goddess. All Auntie done said, its every particle keep coming true. The sassy princess look right bothered in her face, maybe dreaming she might one day turn out a third as smart as this woman what foretells worlds. Once the old one is lowered onto deck, the princess squats at Reba's left hand. Be three princes per Auntie foot. Our boat drift near to boats way bigger. They all rope-chained onto land. At harbor's edge, a thousand white faces start slow-turning our way.

"Prepare," breathing hard, our old one ratchets, "your subjects waits you. Be ready . . . to answer, but . . . do it slow. They gone need time to learn . . . what a real language sound like. You bout ripe for you shackles to be shed? . . . Our time's at hand, my blood kin. We here. We done got Heaven early, but we been let to stay alive to *notice* it."

OUR SHIP got drawed in by ropes, then was boa-ed around with chains even thicker than our own. Past the docks, we seen strange animals—brown-black as us—but long-nosed beasts pulling carts they strapped to, eyes eclipsed by shells, and some was being whipped to make them move. At the gangplank's end, we got greeted by twenty mens in white hats, white tunics, holding whiter papers. They stand looking honored to come out and welcome us proper. We all yet linked—ankle, wrist, and neck—one group.

Our sailor Bleaches led us—naked, shining, our metal knocking out a kind of music down the plank wood. Long the shore, great crowds of idlers turn. "Hold up them heads. Look to it. I done *tolt* you," Reba screeing shrill at us. She fighting for air but smiling down on dockside Blanks. She nodding while bossing us out one side her mouth. "Don't stare *back* at them, fools. Square them shoulders, stick out you bellies. Act proud as you feels, Regal Teachers of the Law. —We done brung them answers cause it us they axted."

Quiet onshore water-bodies studied us all over (which won't too hard). Two sailors lug Reba on a stretcher. She too frail for walking. Weeks in wetness sure have made a dent in such wiry health as our oldest started with. Not caring, she yet grinning in her wild-eyed way. Three brown teeths shown, proud. She just laying back on that stretcher, hands behind she head like some great dying queen—long expected. Auntie wave, cackling down, nodding Yes to this brute's face and that's. Reba signal greeting at ten little boy Bleaches now trotting beside her stretcher and hollering up salty-sounding words. (Auntie just love them for knowing who she is.) The plain sight of her royal extra-ugly self seem to fill Blanks with such pleasure, made some nearbout hoot with joy. Some pointed, grinning, laughing at our Reba. Already, bleachness heathens learning joy!

Then, like Aunt vowed, us got led into a little toolshed and, magic, off them chains did fall. Ooh, the sound of so much weight dropping! Once unlocked, instead of running off apart, everybody clumple gainst each other. Grinning so, eyes wet, you gasping at this feel of semi-free. Arms and legs seem so light, you was like a pile of feathers what might blow clear home cross all them miles of Tears. We keep rubbing wrists and ankles and expecially round our blistered necks. Did I say, Lady Fair? how all the grown folks had steel hoops clamped round they necks. Should of. Did. (Boss, you see how strange the sun looks through third-story windows? Fires. You gone soon be running out you mansion in the next six, eight minutes. Trust me in this.) Feeling free air move once more gainst all parts, we got readier to forgive Bleachnesses, forgive them just for *un*doing some the pain they'd put to us.

Sky-eyes eased out vats of black tarry paint. Brushed this mess at chain sores on our wrists, ankles, necks, at fever blisters on you lip. Paint hid the damage but it sure did hurt way worse to have you open cuts so smothered. "Medcine," Reba speak from her pallet on the floor. "Damn crude, but medcine."

A heavyset Bleach what'd greeted us now counted heads. Made sure he didn't get tricked out of even one rich-blooded royal. He helped squire us into the palm-high teeth-white room. Hall be so huge you didn't know how it could hold itself up. Us—all fed, looking sleeked with coconut grease, our hurts sealed under paint too dark to match us but still covering wounds— we now got nudged up onto a platform. (Only somebody strong as Reba could keep from calling out, after foresaying so much, "I done *told* you so!") The stage it sunk inside a pit, seats curled inside a fancy funnel boring down on us. All high up around, many empty chairs was lined—some paradise council hall.

We known now, sure. We here to offer solid teachings to these watered ones.

Each of us got busy—unchained, finally fed—memory-mapping our first real talk. Reba'd warned, be patient how we starts off telling. Take it slow. They dim.

Whitenesses what'd sailed with us now got paid many yellow tear-shaped bits of metal. They rush off, doing jigs. The tree-legged one was leading our chained monkey, he done a joyful spin on he wood foot. Ape's leash wound partway round it, little creature shrieking. Off went our tall yellowhead with the chained spare heart. We watch sailors march away from us, arms ropey round each other. Our sailors didn't even look back to thank us proper or say bye. Odd, but we already almost missed them. See, Lady, we had knowed them ones the longest. We all loves what we knows because we knows it.

Greeters start to opening our mouths, fingertipping all round. We turn towards where Reba lay smiling yet, shaking her grizzledy head Yes, yes. We seen how Aunt's black skin had growed right ashy, bad sign in somebody she old. Though it hot as anything here, Aunt'd pulled the stretcher's sour blankets all up round her, shaking bad. We heard how much it cost her, trying and explain, "They studying how teeths should be. Maybe . . . gone copy ours for ones on they idols. They a bit too eager in learning. Try and act patient with them, friends." After hearing Reba's news of what this mean, why even the King open he mouth full wide, acting proud to show off royal molars to these glum-faced fuzz-cheeked grubs. The plump-set boss one kept tracing down messages bout us in long snaking lines.

I clung on to my mother—watching everything. One un-dark, he eased my beautiful Queen and me, plus four my younger aunts, into a side room. He pull a curtain behind us. Six young bleachnesses stand waiting there, grinning, they white hats tilted fancy to one side. They have on fine pale suits what make their faces glow a riper pink. One these Bleach bucks just rubbing hands together, that pleased to finally spy he race's new Queen. Next, us got led to the mens, mens begins touching our sassy princess all over she. Her go stiff as dead, unsassy, lost to who she been. Mens even starts handling my mother's breasts. Milk got on the fingers of one bleachness. He joke and shown this milk to others, seem to dare he friends to lick it off. Momma, a-scared, call through the curtain loud at Reba. Tell Auntie that, uh-oh, the young whitish ones seem to be prodding, uh-oh, sad to say, opening the Queen's nearest and most, uh-oh, herself-type body places. One the Queen's new pupils now be down on he knees and peeking up and under, oh such cold-fingered studying. It hurt the person.

"They just trying and learn what real womens should be. Behaves strong, beautiful child, forgives a bit more. I know it hard, but remember—being so famous a beauty do have its duties to it. You the first queen them un-souls done ever met. You a model, royal one, so be it, full." Then Momma just suck in air, brace both legs. But all while chewing she lower lip, fighting not to cry out none. I felt her straining to act worthy of all tributes what these many chilly hands keep paying her and paying her.

When we got finished being felt of, us were led back out to stand again together, which been nicer. Then we seen a mess of other black people lockstep in at the great room's back. New tribe yet chained. They ain't been lucky enough to have a vision-filled Auntie knowing how to read she aches and make—of old days' hurts—a new world be. These folks never was told *why* they got brought unto this teaching temple. Oh, the wails they making, a sound to wash you eyes with tears you ain't expected. Poor things was being sick and some kept tearing at they faces with fingernails and two boy bleachnesses with terrible whips was keeping them in strict strict line.

Reba now stare hard towards them, eyes narrowing. She shade she face with one hand, trying and make out the shapes of poor folks shivering back there. The pawed-over sassy young princess (yet looking struck half dead) bend down, whisper bout what going on. Weak as Auntie'd got, you felt her mind flat buzzing to fit *this* part in. Right off, Reba tell us, "That tribe, I believes, be our court substitutes. I afraid that they somewhat inferior to us, manners-wise. Wouldn't nobody consider *them* a royal clan, now would they? Such screeching. Ain't seemly. —But the Land of White Unfilledness done brought these ones over, courteous-like, so, on days when *us* be feeling somewhat tired, these ones'll go on out. They gone meet the weak-minded pale questioners *for* us. Is probly who these ones be."

Our substitutes, seeing us, growed quietened. And right off. Them stared so. Our heads lifted, we kept lined up here, sleek and willing—we already seem this pale, chain-loving Lost Tribe's very favorites. We models. And just the sight of our true royalty worked on black others quick as any lixir. Our substitutes stood straighter and more calm. They now known that *everybody* on the shore of this dry unjungled Nother-world won't a body-shamed blankness. Soon as they got soothed by seeing us, we felt again—our tribe's potent answering magic be steadily at work. No stopping its ruddering strength on all what meets it.

Then a loud loud bell chimed. And into this huge room stacked high round a stage where we waits, hundreds of whitenesses swarms, jawing mong theyselves. It such humid weather, and each was dressed in pale cloth sacking bandaged round he arms and legs and chests. Each had one fine-colored cloth piece knot—gathered at he throat. Another white bit flop and billow out a patch stitched to he tunic's left-side front. Equipment, but—what for?

Entering our court, Blanks took off they hats, a superstition we appreciated, pure respect. Following them, scampering black children dressed in cloth as white as any whitenesses'. Some these young ones was wearing turbans, single earbobs, such fine trappings. They each carrying a big peacock-feather fan for keeping flies and heat from ever settling onto our subject bleachnesses running towards seats, that eager to hear first lessons bout living a more natural human life.

(In so short a time, our own tribe had already learnt to look right into the faces of these white ghost totems and not to throw up. Now here sat two hundred or more of them and nobody mong my relatives got sick even onct. Hard to believe what-all a royal group *can* complish when it put its mind to something, ain't it, though, Mrs. Mine Own Owner?)

Stout deep-voiced Bleach man stroll up behind a box. He hold papers covered with snake lines bout who-all royalty we be. He hit the box's top with a fancy wood hammer. Everybody hush down. Then, one at a time, us got pulled forward. Headman hold up he fingers, him lift our strong arms, him point to a good face or to one particular fat high-riding breast, its nipple wide across yet prim as any of you teacups.

"Childrens, the worship have begun," Reba grinning so from under blankets, face hid down underneath, mouse gray while nodding only Yes. Water-bodies soon admire all handsome folks in our Kingly group. Blanks out on benches, real young to real old, be every one a male. They would start to maybe pull on one ear or lift a eyebrow. (Almost like they was admiring us but shamed to let they *brothers* know.) When the hammer man seen some such sly high sign (he looking round right hard), him call out one word loud, make a quacky happy rattle song, strike one serious blow to wood.

Course, us stare towards Reba, needing help. Two more young princesses have stoop down to hold Miss Auntie's hands and help her know things Reba eyes can't find. She quits coughing long enough to try and give a mild grin. "I believes they making up a name for every last one of us. Yeah. Bleach trying and guess . . . our true titles, home ranks, and what-all we each gone teach the best. Maybe you men gone talk bout fishing traps and . . . like that. This stubby one keep helping them . . . decide . . . which name suit us best, see? True respeck, first questions, Children of the Blood Royal, just about to start. Prepare you basic lessons. But Reba gone be straight with you, from the look of this here group, you'd best keep first talks full . . . of examples. I talking *simple*." Then her lapsen, worn, back into the waiting hands of worried princesses.

Hammer rapper chant a loud notched row of names. He yodeling so. It the best Bleach music us done heard, full of passion bout something. It excites all what's listening. First hint: maybe they *is* a winion of Drum locked in these mealy selfs somewhere. Hammer man holds a hand over the head of my relatives, one by one by one. He singing bout them. Praise.

Blanks lead forward my shy momma the Queen, me hanging on to her for dear life, me, three, small for my age. I taking everything in, scared so bad. Out among the seats high above us, broad rocking peacock fans looked to me most like our home palms, waving bowing. I stare round for anything what's like I knowed before. Plump head fellow, making a big face towards he crowd, smiles approving noises bout my momma's looks and station. Next, the man took slow hold of her left breast. He cause a drop to pearl out its end, then—squeezing hard—he shoot one thread of holy royal lady milk angling down towards the school's front row. Bleachnesses sure did move they shoes out the way right quick. Laughing, all them pink sponge faces split wide open. Out roll hard hard sound. "Hard, hard, hard," they say. Many fought to guess my momma's name.

Then we was being prodded off in smallish side groups. Whatever pale one chose our names the best, seem like he got to take us off with him. Whichever name got sing-sayed last and loudest and three times—that become our winning title. (Just by the repeated sound of it, so scared that everything done stuck, I remembered my momma the Queen's new one. Only later did white language make a shelf for me to put that name up on. Our Most Royal River Village Queen's new bleachland title be: "Four Hundred.")

The Blank what'd thought this up, what'd rubbed both hands together so, he seemed right frisky bout naming Momma, me, and three my kin. (He titled one the semi-princes, plus our two older cousins.) This gent I describing be nobody but you own late scholar-bossman-husband, Mistress. Does you reconize the hand-rubbing, or was that saved only for he special "nap" chamber out yonder in the quarter? All right, *do* keep quiet, then. I gone live.

One fan-carrying black child under a glittery turban hurry over, smiling clucking at us. He could talk the Bleaches' own bird language, be just chattering away in it, giggling, shaking his head bout us. Acted like we hopeless ugly things and not the royal family long waited for, sought after halfway round this mud-wad earth. Some my older kinfolk yet stand out front— bare to all them pinch-blue eyes—still being named. Maybe to honor our old ones, the head bleachness had saved them back for last.

Momma and me was already being hurried off by that young yellowhead what'd felt hardest of her behind the curtain. We turn back and tries studying what gone happen to the last of us.

We seed the hammer man posing over Reba now. He set he shoe tip gainst her ribs to prove Reba should stand and let the namers look her over good. Then the chief Blank changed, nudged her somewhat easier (easy as any shoe toe *can* nudge one old naked lady's onstage ribs), seem like of a sudden he recollected being the son of some old Bleach-bag root-pale mother somewheres. Reba just shrug, proving she feel too poorly for moving very far.

Auntie rested there, panting under blankets, but grinning round at every subject in this huge white room. With her body shaking so, Aunt's teeth would've been chattering if all three hadn't of been lowers. The most Reba could do was ease onto elbows and blink out at all them pale admirers with so much yet to learn. Not seeing too good, she still seemed right interested in the *feel* of being surrounded with this much blankness. Didn't scare Miss Aunt—how much space so much white makes. All here for her filling, for our filling up. Reba woman yet believed, ma'am, that Ignorance were just the lack of smarts. 'Tain't so. Us soon found out. Ignorance be a whole force unto itself. Trust you Castalia in this.

Reba grin out them mist men's way, her narrow slotted face opened to its widest beaming.

"I plans and go slow at first," her cried, crackly yet loud as she could. "Starting off, might seem real hard. But then, one day, just like things done dawned on Reba here, you gone see what-all we come to teach . . . Tribe's lessons bout to break over you heads like so many rare red birds' eggs full of light. You going to say, 'So, it *that!*' Then you sure will laugh. Even took your old Reba here a day or six to see *you* reasons for toting us on over here. Did. Oh, I slow sometimes. I winded just now . . . It hard but, boys? it possible. And, listen, even fore I gets rolling on your first lesson, I wants to let you know (here, has to catch my breath a second) yeah . . . let you know: where I been? Yeah, you was right. You already took the first sure step towards a wiseness sufficient—saying what you *needs* to understand.

Now . . ." Round in here, somebody starts to clapping, grumblish. Aunt took this as encouragement. Naming went right on, plump man going bout he chores, axting Blanks to title others. He keep casting side looks at the old one, yet unnamed, jammering away her loudest. "Maybe you Blank boys been wondering why you all been axted here. Well, that cause you Reba wants to tell: We feels for you. Pities you. And you sure is lucky. Why? Cause, well, don't like to brag none, but you done found The Tribe What Answers.

"For my starting lesson, I gone speak" (hollering got worse) "bout the need for Tribal Kindness. I put it frank . . . Don't test us too much, please, not at first. We still partway homesick. Remember, Blanks, under . . . everything runs this need to treat each other right, to try and . . ."

Most bleachnesses now slapping hands together, like they knowed Auntie were trying and make a speech, like they found that right comical at first but only for round about one minute.

Water-bodies clangored to finish naming. But Reba, bad eyes working this room, she act most sated. She yet took clapping to show how some of these heathens had already understood, and first thing! She just lay there, peeking round (bashful but pleased like some old sunning turtle), grinning so's her three brown tooths' nub ends showed. Well, her students just loved that, sure. Oh, you never did hear such hooting, whistling, kicking on seats. Paste-faces in back, grinning, talking mong theyselves, stood for a better view of her down there on the floor.

Chief singer man come closer, held his hammer down onto addled head of our good King's greater great-aunt. Reba shuddering, eyes unblinking mong blankets' stains, been waiting to hear what-all they gone title her, smiling with a edge of fun, vain to the end. Reba use the hammerhead to scratch some stray itch on her scalp. Water-bodies laughs. Man cup one free palm behind he ear. Hammer man lean clear across Reba and nearer to her hundreds pupils. Didn't one crag-face try naming her. Probably not one soul in the big white room felt worthy of guessing Aunt Reba's full title nor her rank. So the headman snort out a name of he own for our most holiest of all. This, too, me and my cousins would remember later just by how it sound. Seemed that important. Head whiteness named my answering aunt "No Takers."

Man just pull a face, roll his eyes, pass on to our next-oldest person— a body young enough to yet be standing, waiting, looking not at hammer man but, like all us kin been doing, down at her, down at Auntie in last trouble.

Reba yet wear that spiny necklace made out pods. Acting confused, staring all bout, Auntie yank it off. Only then did us notice how her whole head, all along, been mostly a skull with six tanned crisscross strips of hide and one million earned old crinkles covering it, cooperating in hiding bone. Someway, that necklace—forever tied in place below—always made your eyes go there to it instead. Now you seen only the answering skull bulking there a eighth-inch beneath. You seen how Reba's eyes was testing in they sockets, pulling deeper, going back to where and home to what?

First Auntie, fuddled, reach down, start a spastic feeling of her shiny scars, grabbing one old handful of snakebit thigh skin, prying, twisting it for news bout what-all this mean, fighting to understand she own new name. By now, Auntie'd lost even her deepest wounds' true voices. Still, even so confused, Reba considered her hurt spots the only things worth trusting.

(Lady About to Maybe Meet Her First Slap, much as anything on earth, your scars is *yours*.)

Auntie dangled the seed choker for Momma to come fetch. Guards finally let our Queen stoop and take it, me going down with her. Queen then press necklace to she mouth, kissing it good while looking right at Reba. Flat on the floor of our first great stage, Aunt, addlepated, were yet grinning out at multitudes what lacked skin tint and any kindly mind for others. But, while nodding towards them, Reba still joked quiet up at my mother, "Us flat got us a *task* all right. What Festival Dance Day do . . . this be? Seem like I were trying and remember something."

(Necklace's seeds would be the start of you plantation's only okra, plus the first peanut plants in this whole northeast end of Carolina . . . foods you-all never would of tasted or knowed about without they being saved from holy Africa in this Tear-crossing witch jewelry.)

Our King heself were getting pushed off by some dough-head what'd named him best. Momma—watching—start shaking the worst yet, got shuddering nigh as bad as Auntie. Reba turn our way. Not seeing nothing clear, but feeling all what's going on in her every crook and bone, her final strength cried to us (bove the loudness of our lasts being named), "We soon gone meet in the Court of Our New Whitenesses. We just . . . being led off to go get dressed up fine, to sleep some. Oh, a nap! Where my good stick? Had that thing a long while. Hard to find the perfeck one. Good sticks don't grow on trees, well . . . yeah, but . . . I trying saying we is soon to . . . Meet . . . glory . . . in a room what makes this one look like my little shack . . . back home . . . built to hold our dead red birds. Remember, young ones? So, go on off with them. Trust." She coughed bad. "Do. Us'll see each other directly. Remember: act kinder than them does. That our best lesson. They always gone be . . . watching. In a land so bleach, black skin bound to show up plain. The un-ones knows you started off as kings—gone expect you to be forever better at everything than them—and just to break even. Anybody seed a fine stick staff? Round here someplace. Can't go far without. —Look, royalty, try."

Two young straw-hairs lift Reba's pallet, starts toting her wherever they takes the extra ones. Where do bleachnesses store they leftovers? They had to lug our Reba by the unchained group of us. When her stretcher drawed close near, Auntie been set high onto sky-eyes' shoulders, us couldn't see up that far, we only spied one edge her blanket, one dry Reba wrist dangling down. The other hand still tested her mute hurts. Then us all broken line.

We tried and touch her while us could. Great-aunt Reba goes bouncing past on a bed of sticks, two long, two short crossed at either end. Us press forward to feel one hand's rough knuckles. Our fingertips quick traced Reba's broken blue nails, quick felt a snakebit knot set—one great bulb jewel—in the middle of her ivory palm, us reach to squeeze them stiff old horny fingers what'd finished off so many snakes, what forever pointed out things to us, what pointed so at *us*, accusing, schooling, teasing. Then two boy Bleaches and one old shrunk unmarried woman—they was quick gone round one corner. Gone.

Black child in the shiny turban set aside he fan. Acting bored official, he yanked cloth tubes out a sack. Then he shown us how to pull these over heads, round our limbs. Our coverings looked like the namers' own, just darker in color, coarser in weave. You felt smothered cross you shoulders, tugged at under arms, expecially clamped twixt legs. Clothes be a softer kind of shackle. Black tar meant to hide our hurts—like how you'd wax away a scratch on furniture—it rubbed off, spoiling cloth. Was then—from far at the end of one long hall—us heared something, a sound, the caved-in leaf-mold voice.

Us perkened so, staring at each other, not rightly knowing one the other—such a goodly percentage of familiar skin now been quenched back of hiding cloth. Her cough reached us as a warning and a promise. Then something else done rivered up underneath it, calmed us so. Be her snaggle laugh. Us stood, mouths open, eyes salt, listening harder than us ever had. By now Auntie's laugh and cough done braided into being one turn-taking sound. We love to hear it working in her still.

Out from under such rasping—she trying/saying something. But couldn't none of us understand. We look to each other, worried what-all we missing. Something good, we bet, something to remember. King draw hisself up to he full tall, lift he chin, go, "I believe Reba probly mean, 'Closest things I gots to childrens, go on out. They can't hurt us now. We kings. Go make the world over. But, this time, get it right. Show them how. We royalty. We *they* royalty. Why we answer? Cause they axted.' "

But a long stillness stretch clear from down them arched brick halls. On the floor, back yonder, under blankets, in the Chamber of the Leftover, "No Takers" hush herself.

Blinking, sun's favorites, we now squinting on a street. Port town's market day swelled so, buy and peddle. Like a storm on Tears, such haggling and push, hurrying bout, outdoing one the other. Close by the slammed back door of our strange temple house, three open wagons.

Chain-hitched to them was roomy black-brown creatures bent low under the biggest whips we done seen. After us got pushed up into carts, we noticed how—in a fancier leather wagon at the very back—our first female-type whiteness be setting, quiet and nervous as a bird. Seem like, if you bothered her, she could sputter straight up into the air, all wings and spur, sliced wind. For now, she perched there, not so sure, not so *not* sure, spar-

row-sized but face set in a high-strung manner big as bossy life. (Like the
Bleach men, she steadily pretending to be human!) Bout her neck, and left
wrist, in finest gold, dainty as possible, two narrow chains showned—ornament for proving who be boss.

She rest, surrounded by many packets of store-bought shiny things,
round boxes and paper wrappings piled. Seem her couldn't stay propt upright wivout store stuff's help. From under one these bumbles, two white
dogs popped, yibbing-barking seeing us. White fluff piles not no bigger than
a coconut apiece, they faces act stuck-up, even while they teeth stay bared.
She try hushing dogs while holding a new hat. It so fine she afraid to crush
it in some shipping box. That hat proving the day's breeze, twelve egrets'
worth of whitest feathers, shifting. Spying us, her of a sudden gone still.
She mighty white. Scared, she let feathers hide her face's bottom part but
them blue eyes of yours just stared so hard and cold, two metal linchpins
fixed right at us.

That day, the sash round you white dress's middle were blood red, the
color what'd got us into this.

Our King, on another wagon, clatter right by us then. His hands looked
clamped again. And King been stuck into the ugliest checkedy shirt I ever
seed since. Liver-colored, yellow, red, and green—shirt seem nearbout
harder-going on he dignity than them chains did. King appeared headed in
a whole direction other from us ones'. Me, my Queen Momma, one semi-
prince, and two old cousins hunkered here—we was all fussed at by that
clean child turbaned up. Someway, trusting Reba yet, we figured the King
and us all bound on one tour. Maybe we going by different paths but bound
a selfsame place, the spot where they'd have Reba lifted high, all brown/
black/blue/gray/silver, and at they very center, axting useful answers out of
her.

You know, Mistress mine, even while seeing each other being droven
off in all forked scattering directions, even when King's wagon round a turn,
even losing sight of one the other's face for permanent-ever, us didn't even
know enough to think hard, "Notice. Notice this."

MRS., I still scrubbing. Happy? See how I clumped them silly little gilded
chairs all in one corner. Moved them easy as you shifted us from Africa to
Charleston, then upriver to here. Simple as you pushing us into the kitchen,
out to fieldwork, back again. You the person stuck my Momma Queen in
this Big-House scullery, scrubbing pots. Her one revenge been never learning
English right. They'd bring her great stacks dishes dirty from you sit-down
dinner parties for fifty. Momma known only to point, she say, "I these? I
these?" The Queen! Do you wonder that she tried and steal away?

You forever let your overseer, Marse Winch, take care "discipline." A
certain lady one time say, "I'll trust you to do whatever's necessary for
maintaining 'slave morale,' my dear Winch. I offer you complete authority
on one condition: that you never trouble *me* with the details." You recollect

saying that, woman? I heared you. It cost me Momma. The redheaded sweet-faced Winch, a good and faithful servant like Castalia, he never onct troubled you over how he troubled us. Oh, he really do his job.

Lady? You got so much to answer for.

One day, eleven years into our being owned, my momma got sent to kitchen garden for picking supper okra. Sun was setting. Momma took the colander nearer sun. Sun looked ripe, promising and ready. Like for to pick. She walk to the garden, in the garden. Sun there. Through the garden. Sun yet there. Go to the Marsden property line. Closer sun. Next thing, she been you personal property but off you personal property. Without no excuse nor wrote-down pass. Uh-oh. She come to herself in a woods six miles from here. Momma decided in African, "My my. I late. Supper bout over. No okra. They out hunting me, sure. I lost. But, no, I now gone do *this* instead of dishes." She look around, breathing like when you seriously know you breathing. "I *this*," Momma say. "Now, I Queenly free."

She were bout thirty-five years old. Didn't look one bit like the beauty what been brought over young. Her shape missed Africa so much, it'd swoled, changed, dropped on her. Which left the Queen being somebody else, somebody heavy but less. Sent out to fetch okra, sent barefoot, she had no smart plan for leaving. (Other runaways been known to first steal atlas maps from out the Master's study room.) This woman just walk when walking feel right. This woman only understood you two thousand acres. How *could* she plan ahead when the one thing she known best was what she most hoped to forget?

Momma yet carried the big house's best colander. It were blue and white made to look like marble. Later, when they caught her, she still had holt that thing. Momma felt the Law might go easier on her if—while trying and free herself—she didn't lose nothing rightfully blonging to you. She slept in ditches, up trees, hid nights in haylofts on bandoned farms. Even with no food, she got clear cross Nash County, then on to Edgecombe.

A lady over in Tarboro put a fresh-baked cherry pie on her kitchen sill for cooling. If Momma had took the pie *and* its pan, she could of got away free, sure. Instead she stood out there in plain view, shaking from she hunger and the jitters. Queen tried and dump hot crust and scalding cherries into her borrowed colander. See, Momma wanted not to steal nothing *but* her freedom plus the food she needed. Queen's mistake been trying and stay out of worse trouble than she been in already. Her mistake was trying and stay out of worse trouble than Freedom its own self is.

They brung her back in ropes. The colander rested pretty on the wagon seat beside her. Colander looked boastful like it'd turned her in. Seeing us lined beside the farm road, Queen smiled but shy. Maybe she was troubled over how she'd failed at getting free. Maybe how—leaving—she hadn't said bye to any one of us. Not even wiry Princess Me.

Without no food past blackberries, acorns, and the smell of white folks' cooking—she'd still walked eighty mile in three days. Good form. Hearing, we all felt proud. Didn't own no compass. Turned out, all along, Momma been headed south, not north. Winch nounced this at the lashing.

"And where did our wandering minstrel here *go* when she slipped free as the balmy breeze? Towards Georgia. Hopped out of the frying pan and into the fire, she did." Then Marse Winch, just a boy hisself, personally peelt off Momma's clothes. I don't likes to trouble you with the details, ma'am. I know how delicate you system is. Winch, he made example of Momma. Made red hash out she back. He offern Momma a stripe for every mile she'd got nearer free. Standing, watching but not watching, hearing while listening only at the blood in my own ears, I wondered: Was Momma trying to keep sane during punishment by picturing every one them sweet-snitched miles? Ma'am, do eighty sound like a small number to you?

My Momma Queen got tossed into the root cellar. Is a favorite slave prison here, or did you know? Yeah, it far enough off from this room of yours. Screams get lost halfway up you perfeck three-acre lawn. Momma had no skin left for to be she back. Had just a front she got to hold up, like a dress all dangling unfastened behind. Headmen chain-bolted the cellar's storm doors shut. Men left her (three weeks, no food, no drink). Cellar means a dark hole twenty feet long, six deep, meant to hold potatoes only. First, bosses had us take out every nourishing one.

Winch hired a white boy from Falls. Boy come out to live in a tent pitched right beside the padlocked cellar doors. Boy been there to keep us slaves from slipping Momma any food, any word of kindness.

Down in dark, woman must of stayn on her stomach. Did that to spare dirt's working into a back cut so wide open. She crawl/dragged round a trench of busted crockery thrown there to help to drain things right. Momma found, buried mong old bricks, a busted Wedgwood teacup. With it, the Queen commenced her tunnel north. This time she figured the right way out. Nobody come down to check on her for ten days, twelve. Rest of us aboveground, we made the Queen our own example. For us, she been the one that nearbout got away, good form even in the wrong direction. That don't matter—it the trying counts.

On ground level, every night in the quarter, we stood round her corn-husk mattress, we turned down her flour-sacking coverlet. We saved her place by talking to a bed like the Queen were yet in it. Us'd tell her a day's worth of work news, gossip, anything the least bit funny. Silly hurtful bossy little things you done that day, you.

Underground, by touch, she found your cellar's dampest corner, she pressed Wedgwood down there long enough for scooping up mud droplets to drink. Enough. Gouging with the cup, Momma come upon a few dried potatoes—seasons old—locked brown and blind in dirt as her.

She kept a strength sufficient for getting that tunnel five foot long. Then eight. Eight and a half. White guard boy, he lounged up top reading penny dreadfuls, carving branches, catching up on naps, whistling. He was a boy innocent of everything but what he'd been axted to do. They a lot of boys like that. I chanced bribing him with a fine stole pudding. But Winch kept that child fed too good to care for seconds. Still, little fellow didn't turn me in for hoping and get stuff down to her. "She my mother," I say. "Bet you'd do the same for yourn."

"I would, but mine's not down there. Lucky." Then he go, "Sorry. I've been paid. She's alive, all right. Some days I hear her, some days I get so bored out here, I talk mostly in *her* direction." Leaving, I screamed from forty feet, "Momma! It Cassie. We up here, Queen, we ready for you!" Boy chased me off a short ways. Never planned to catch me. He just had to do like that. I couldn't blame him. We all slaves to something.

Quiet in she un-light, Momma cut away. Steady—she prove herself to be Reba-tough, be proud as my own missing poppa. Down she went, deep enough so's nobody'd hear her chipping at red clay. She work clean under the farm's main road. Her thin cup got used with oh such care. She hack through tree roots a few fibers at a time, frayed herself toward free. (Be like you said, ma'am, that Wedgwood's right good stuff. It wedge the wood!) Momma swervt round rocks too big for one raw shoulder's budging. September rains come on. Her digging got easier/spongy. The boy guard hid in his tent: practiced fancying his whistling, practiced his cussing.

A hayrick heavy with harvested pumpkins, with slave children fooling round, getting a free ride, pushing at each other, having fun (me and my weight too), it wobbled along the road. Not knowing, hay wain crosst her secret under-tunnel.

Four days later, Queen's example time finally been done. Men unbolted double doors. They found her gone. Winch blieved she had excaped thanks to African magic. First he grabbed the guard boy by the front he shirt. Then somebody noticed a tiny northbound hole. With potato roots, she'd mostly closed it up behind her, modest-like. Didn't seem big enough for no full human person to fit into. Aboveground, seeking the buckle and turn of it, men followed on foot.

They couldn't figure where it finally push up into daylight. Fellows went back in the cellar. Their shovels trailed one teacup's forward progress north. They bugled open that burrow-tube. Took one morning and three men to try and trace the cave. Bosses hoped to find Momma still hacking at the front and freest end. Tunnel wound twenty-seven feet. It curve then straightened, bent then evened out, you seen it learning its way north. The longer white ones dug, the quieter they grown. Respect or interest, dread, they superstitiousness? What? Us slaves been hiding in the woods—we watching, we seasick from hoping's up and downs. Tunnel headed right towards the Reba-seeded peanut field. Tunnel started to go shallower. Tunnel been coming up for plain good gulping air. Men done dug a full canal across the farm road. There they hit a spot where the great wagon had passed. Been like a huge shoe sole stomped hard on one mole's dug path. A bit nearer free they found her. From above, shovels let light in on somebody face-down. Queen's grimy back was yet unhealed. Queen's arms been drawn up close to make sheself a smaller fit, not axting much, even of space in the world.

Momma wore dried potatoes on they vines, a braided necklace so she wouldn't ever have to come back for more Marsden food. Held before her one brown-smudged Wedgwood cup. Was a sky-colored thing. Had white gods porcelained into it—talking lords, they ladies park-benched playing lyres under heaven's own willows. Chalk royals been standing blank all round the blue, too little to do at some paradise party.

Winch, he ordered Momma buried the usual four feet deep in the slaves' boneyard. It out near your livestock pens. You ever gone there for a senti-mental visit? I ain't ever seen you. That night, all us ones stole forth. We scared, but yeah we dug her up. And then us laid her back so Momma's head be turned due north. Us pressed that busted Wedgwood teacup back into she hands. Us give Momma a decent chance at getting out right next time. Come Judgment Day, she wouldn't rise looking skywards (what help do sky gods be?). Our Queen were now aimed north, she cocked and ready.

I believes Judgment Day gone be your fancy Coming-Out at last. *Every-body* bound to be there, the living and the dead, the owned and free, all watching you. —See me clean the crystal on this fine French clock? Ooh, its big hand do be headed north most quick. Yankee hoofbeat clicking closer wiv each tock.

Madam? Madam, get you answers ready.

3

I NEVER could learn the story of what happen to my Daddy King nor any other blood kin. None except the ones you bought to work here at The Lilacs. And *they* story, being mostly mine, I knows too good. —If only I done leastway heared bout my poppa's life, the tale of where they sent him, how he getting on, do he be dead, did they make him to sire another family, do anybody at the new home know bout he famous highborn history on a river?

Might sound strange to you, you what's traced the legend bloodlines of everybody on you either side since England backwards—but, Lady mine, if I knowed even *two* such lately facts bout my King now, I wouldn't mind so much not seeing him again. Cheated out of my own poppa, it strange, but I'd of settled for the history of a poppa, any history but specially he story.

Remember when I begged you to please look up the record of my King's sale? You said you would, you said you would, ma'am.

You know what might be you worst deed yet? Ain't the gravy boat you lashed me for. Ain't even what you-all done done to Momma. Maybe you biggest crime is: how you took me out the story of myself! You stole Castalia's true life-tale. You left her here to find the puzzle pieces' odds and ends, to make up all this stuff as best Cas might and then to feel she should apologize for just in*vent*ing a history, for not getting a good one assigned to her, like you.

So, every new slave what got shipped in here, I'd quiz them steady bout where they been before, I done described a king and missing court. "Won't no king anyplace *I* been," them said. "Leastways, not a black one."

But the person I forever fretted bout and axted after the most be a old catfish-face woman what trained us up with such fine hopes. She taught us to try taming the mist men and ice ladies what brung us over here to help and thaw and heal them (whether or no they seen our true purpose at the time).

But, to end up, to mop round the back of my housecleaning life: See? Whites—using Red for bait—done tricked us Blacks on board. They coaxened us out the Green and Brown with Red. That one slip-up in colors be why come I standing here, already up to fifteen Carolina years but still carrying a headful (like milk heared slopping safe in home coconuts) of missing Mamma Africa.

—And now, to make a body truly water-sick on colors—Blue be fighting Gray for young Black me. Red brung Black over here, now Blue's about to spring Black up to the White Riveredge City I been ready for so long. Ripe so long, Castalia nearbout rotten. The Blues is just one farm away, less. (I reckon I bout scared of them as you. Seem like I keeps *on* getting kidnapped. I just hope this go-round it be by the forces of right.)

Yeah, Woman What's Named "Lady," I fell from a right high station in life. Done dropped clear down to this cooking/dusting, this being-barter stuff. Odd, if my people hadn't been the King and Queen type family, why I'd yet live over yonder. I know I'd be fifteen there, too. Only, it'd mean something different. My name wouldn't be Castalia. And I would not be wearing no more than a body needs in a riverland where it stay so hot so much—wearing nothing much past a good disposition, new parrot-feather anklets, and one orchid/weed pinned behind a ear (for luck). I'd yet eat for free and anytime I likes. Dressing up for the dances, then getting over the afterwards palm-wine headaches—that'd be Castalia's major princess pastime. Oh, I'd probly be silly as you! But I ain't, I ain't there, so that ain't me. I right here and still be yours under the law, ma'am. But, with all due respeck, not for long, Mrs. Test the Tops of Furniture with Her Villain Little White Glove.

Any second now (where *is* they when you needs them?) the Blues gone clomp over the highroad's red Chinese bridge. Then I can finally end up starting my own true journey. I bout to hike off on a trip that Reba seen so long ago in visions milked from scars. I finally heading towards the Great White City Great-aunt expected just a few tribulations too soon. It *there* that my people gone finally get treated right. That tribe is the true nest where Justice live, where every house turn out to be something between a school, a all-night dance, a Kingly court.

The North, I talking. My linking Canaan is shining there, map-upwards of this South, cross the River of Jordan and the Mason of Dixon. For freedom, I bout overdue. New York City, the new place Reba seen dancing—pure and perfeck welcome—in she ugly head. I hear it's got rivers on all sides, bound to make my river kin feel most welcomed in. City's streets (some passing runaways done tolt me) is just strewed with beaten gold, roads running full of coconut milk, guttered with free honey. Lady? In my Auntie's house be many mansions.

And you youself? Please brace for a fall. You bout to learn the pain of being the cleverest person alive in a language don't one soul speak. You gone see that nobody much cares *what* you been princess of if that place ain't around no more.

Odd, how all these years you's called me Castalia. Yet I couldn't call you nothing but ma'am or Lady. That changing. All along I been knowing the secret middle name you hates so bad, Enid, Enid, *E*-nid! —Names count.

Someday—when Marse Sherman's cure-house smoke finally clears—you gone to recollect a certain flown-away Castalia spending her last unfree minutes telling you the story of her coming-out, her people's debut to the world of sinful work. I done gifted you with the whole thing one last time. Right now, the Favorite Owner I Ever Had (besides my own self, of course), my story's all I gots to offer. But, from out these Reba-wizened hands, it yours. For free. Up North, I gone again be a type of princess. But this time, my title will just run "Miss." One "Miss" all mine. I tired of sharing. I plenty Reba-vain to take "Miss" for my birthright.

What I hopes: On a fresh-painted Northern trolley car (maybe red), some fellow (a gent) will see me come on board by streetcar's foot-ladder gangplank, my young arms just heap full of hatboxes, nice fur coat, store packages, all new stuff (not *nothing* secondhand), and he gone rise, gone touch the front he hat, gone say deep and nice and civil, "Might could I offer you my seat, Miss?" —Miss! Music!

YEAH.

I has earnt a mite of glory, Lady. And you—how bout *you*? Uh-oh, them's the hoofbeats. Finally. Let's get you down them rosewood stairs, get little old you hid safe for watching Blues make this Bleach house go red then black. Quick, down these spiral stairs, gal, let's us scramble our young asses off.

I ain't helping you out of no tribal kindness. Enid, I *won't* be thanked. That just real bad form. I only being selfish. You got to stay alive long enough to finally start. Know what? You just being born. That why it hurt so bad. You done hit you own true coming-out at last.

It commencing glorious. New York City of Heaven, here I comes. Our mansion's whole first floor gone soon be lit so spiffy. Pretty house make pretty fire. Here go.

Auntie? I running. Auntie? I think I free. Us answerers been answered, Reba. —Free!

In Which
Our Heroine
Pretty Much Catches
the Works

Unto the woman he said, I will greatly multiply thy sorrow
and thy conception. In sorrow thou shalt bring forth children,
and thy desire shall be to thy husband, and he shall rule over thee.
—GENESIS 3:16

D arling? We all got to represent each other, try.
Jerome danced in here yesterday wearing a blue ribbon behind either ear. Won them at the State Fair for his quilts and boy was he
ever proud! Hand-stitches every one. His designs outdo most of them prim-
mer granny ones.

I told him, said, "I don't know what deserve more high-type praise,
Jerome, your workmanship or your flash, probably your flash." He accepted
that with a bow. He's done one quilt to mark the twentieth anniversary of
these girl singers, the Superbs, or Supremes, and it was silver and all three
of them were holding mikes and then the mikes' cords formed a kind of
lasso spelling out the group dates and their names, then each singer had a
trademark wildflower over her head like a halo. No surprise *that* won, hunh?
Creative, Jerome.

He's offered to do a quilt for Professor Taw's bleak old room. It'll feature
Taw's Theory of Combustion spelled out in fine cloths many ways. Jerome
has done commissions for some Lanes' Enders (they pay dear, I'm told).
They offer him favorite clothes from their most choice old outfits, baby
blankets, you name it. Fabrics then get mashed to a original design. Yesterday he told me all those've just been practice. For the one he's planning
making your old Lucy here. For free. The price is right!

He said he'd stop back by in six weeks' time. I should set aside my favorite all-time garments, silks, whatever. (This shamed me, since they only brought four dresses in here with me when I got committed. They said the rest needed dry cleaning, just left them in five closets.) Jerome announced that all his quilts tell stories. "This one shall reflect your . . . Lifestyle, Lucy."

"Okay," says I, a fool for tributes. "Glad to know I've *got* one. I'll file through my stowed heirlooms, choose the colors for my famous counter-pane." He discoed over here, he hugged me. I thanked Jerome via a hard grip. When he left my cubicle, I beamed for whole minutes. I feel lucky. Why are folks so good to me?

You know, honey, nothing in the world beats a hundred percent cotton. And you can quote me on that.

2

BY NOW my husband was the Old South's Uncle Sam. Newspaper reporters tried and monopolize Captain's office hours. He welcomed one and all. Cap was good copy with a face like that, a mouth so apt to wave the flag then send forth "The Man Who Loved His Wife Too Good." "If the Shoe Fits." All over the New Dixie, you could read versions of his old holy tales on Sunday feature pages.

Invitations soon clogged our porch's wicker mail basket. Most for him— "and family" some kindly added. To be blunt, I felt semi-envious recently fired by Christ's own church myself. Soon I was down at Lucas', child, I was pricing luggage. I wanted to clear out before worse happened. I could feel something coming, even then I could. Some nights it'd wake me from the soundest sleep. A noise right in the room with me, a shout, like a boy soldier's cry from right beside our bed.

I'd sit there, one hand pressing my sternum, the other patting over to feel his great sleeping bulk. "Imagining things," I scolded myself. I'd lay back down, then throw aside the quilt and go to check on all our kids. The sound of that much breathing made a palm-frond thatching over me, soothing and half-tropical it seemed. I pictured the palm trees haremed on a side porch of McCloud's Mansion in its indigo Steinway heyday. I imagined baby Castalia climbing Africa palm trees loaded with lettucy orchids. I touched child counter-pains and blankets. Then, calmed, returned to a bed straddling guns.

(In my day, husbands worked at stores and offices. Us wives minded the houses. Now wives get to work in stores and offices *and* mind the house. Progress, who's she? "Lib" for women? You know what that still mainly is, sug? "Lib" is just another nickname for Elizabeth.)

SINCE Billy Preston slept at our place last Saturday, Ned asked permission to stay with Billy the Friday following. I said then what the world has so often told me, "We'll see." Captain said, "Of course"—which is what he's heard most from the bank and others.

Ned packed a clean shirt and rolled two pairs of socks. He took a little windbreaker and, seeming overpleased, said bye to me. He stood around the kitchen then, like wanting something else. "Need a dime, sug? Tide you over?" But he shook his head, looked at me with those eyes, took off.

My kids usually dragged home from sleepovers by one the next p.m., acting all bushed and sore, grumbling they'd never do *that* again. Then our kids'd sleep ten straight hours and wake recalling the best time ever humanly had. Captain was to be off hunting on the coast that weekend and I planned taking my whole brood to see a new (to us) picture at the Cameo. When Ned won't home by four on Saturday, I asked would Louisa take a note to Billy's momma. Mrs. Preston had a phone—but we didn't. Cap hated the idea and I won't none too keen. I could've stepped next door and borrowed Ruth's but hated being beholden for small stuff.

Lou was pleased to go talk with Billy's mom. The lady published cute verses in our paper under the name Neva. Her poems were meant to draw a nod of recognition on subjects like how kids always slam the screen door. Well, I wanted to say, *some* children slam *some* doors. Most of Neva's ditties involved a child's galoshes and his messy room. I felt for Billy, her one kid. Maybe this give him his sense of outraged justice that led him to the federal bench later? Anyhow, Lou got back right quick with pretty blue notepaper, sealed. "She is so intelligent, Momma. It's fun speaking to a real . . . writer. I keep a diary and all but I'm no *real* writer." I grumbled something. I never much liked hearing my kids praise other minds in ways they've failed to mention my own. I'm sorry but I'm like that. Besides, being terminated by First Baptist, I felt touchy right then, a fallen star.

Dear Lucille Marsden,

We thought you understood. He said he had your blessing in taking Ned away to the seaside. They left last evening at six. Your husband kindly offered my Billy the chance to join their hunting party. Billy and myself were somewhat in awe of the motorcycle police and state vehicles. I think Billy would have considered going had he not chanced past a truck full of bird dogs. They scared Billy and myself and perhaps Ned too, though he seemed to know to hide it.

Captain M. kindly introduced me to our young Lt. Governor (fine-looking and no doubt about that). Unless I'm very much mistaken, the Lt. Gov. had been celebrating something since he'd left the state capitol four hours previous. This was, I admit, a factor in my keeping Billy back from them. Captain introduced me to the Lt. Gov. as a "poetess," not knowing I avoid the term. I feel it is, by nature, a lesser and therefore dismissive sub-category. I know he meant well. I hope I did right in allowing young Ned to leave here without your express permission but as the Captain is Ned's father that seemed reason enough to pass the child on to him, or so ran my thoughts at the time. Your note, delivered by your most charming and respectful daughter (I've given her a few of my modest latest quatrains by way of thanks), disturbed me and I trust I've not made a mistake. I know how careful we both are about our sons.

"Neva"
Ann Preston

We did go to that movie. Was a silent about this fraternity boys' prank and one boy gets tied to the wrong train track and he loses the leg. They show it when his mother first spies him hobbling up her porch steps using a cane—you see her trying to be brave and not let him catch her crying. I got mighty upset. I embarrassed my children with a few stray sounds I made. To me, such noises seemed in keeping, but afterward, near-strangers came up and told me it'd got them *too*. I felt foolish then. I hate that: Everybody *says* they cry in movies but when you do, they blame you. Something about living with the scar on Captain's leg for all these years—a nasty scar. Surgeons never thought a man's leg'd be out of pants (long before Bermuda shorts) and so who cared about suturing's crude looks? Too, it was something about my Ned loose with unshaved poker players down at Duck.

I made the other kids stop by and see my lonely parents on our way home from the pictures. As a bribe, we first patronized the new soda fountain in Lucas' and kids got ice cream. Lou always ordered vanilla and became furious in defending her doing so. Baby tried pistachio, this week's novelty, and vowed she'd be faithful to it for life and was. My folks now asked after Ned's whereabouts and Lou said, "Sleeping over another night at Billy Preston's," and I looked at her and felt grateful that Neva had not told and worried Louisa too. It relieved me, thinking only *I* understood Ned's absence. That gave me more control over my own organized wishing. I would do a lot of that tonight.

I grew lively then with jokes beyond my rude usual. Bargaining with the fates: If you laugh enough, bad things skulk away from you. I pretended I could play Momma's grand piano—kept faking arty entrances like some grand concert artist and then really messing up. Poppa, of course, had to try it too, right after. But I agitated my own children to where the laughing twins knocked over a bamboo end table and chipped the inherited deer-hoof inkwell Momma'd always loved. She was good about the accident, at least better than expected. But I got my crowd out of there—worried that my own emotions were out of whack. Here I was pulling sideshow pranks in my folks' dry parlor, plus turning our Cameo Theater into the Wailing Wall.

Once I got my brood abed, avoiding looking at Ned's tucked-in bunk (made with care when he knew where he was bound, the brat), I wondered would I sleep. I heard out the kids' singsong prayers—pointless chants and yet, tonight, less so. "Add Ned," I asked. They said he was just at Billy's but, used to the whims I ofttimes forced on the poor things, kids stuck in "And bless Ned if he needs it. Amen." That was that.

I felt better. With people like me, it don't take much.

Downstairs, looking out my kitchen window in the dark, I seen the glow of poor Ruth's latest Lucky. She'd been on her side porch listening to me wedge seven kids between the sheets. I got a crawly feeling that she knew how Cap had tricked Ned out of town and clear of me. Seeing her over there waiting for her Willard to finally wise up and phone home, I turned out all the lights and went to bed, recalling Momma's lecture on everybody's awful need to blame. I dozed off quick, trying to ignore the Fort Knox of weaponry stowed in glass-fronted cases just downstairs. (Did I tell you he had taken over my sewing and puppet room, put up a museum to the gun? He waited, polite, till after I got sacked from church.) "I blame no one. Because nothing's happening," so said I. Sleep saved me.

We can be saved.

Sleep will, if nothing else does, save us, honey. Death will come and fetch us all to peace at last. I ain't afraid of that. Times, this long life seems the insomnia that's keeping me from what I most dearly deserve.

3

NOW it all lines up in memory—how, deciding to keep busy that next morning, a Sunday, I chose to make potato salad in volume. I figured I'd give portions to everybody, Cassie, my folks, poor Ruth, everybody. More superstition. Act nice enough to others, maybe the dark stuff'll avoid you, it'll think you gave at the office and will go next door for dues. Though this was October, a heat wave held on—flies yet everywhere. In Lucas' yesterday I'd heard a lady remark, "I think the flies are *worse* this year." She waited for credit like she'd discovered a new moon slung near Jupiter. Sometimes, even for small-town dwellers, small towns sure seem small. The idea of escape got funneled into my famous potato salad. Very local travel. (My secret? Lots of celery seed and fresh-ground pepper, don't spare the dried mustard.)

I boiled every spud in the house, had two pots gurgling that lovely sound of water changing, resentful if resigned, into dense air. I stood chopping onions with a knife too big. One bluebottle fly (they *were* worse) lighted on diced pickles and—moving to snatch it—I someway crossed the waiting knife, and really cut myself. I studied the sliced thumb, knowing it'd have to bleed a lot before stopping, one of those.

I judged: If I was a single woman living alone or even a Neva, I'd be rushing to Doc Collier's for five stitches. But being here and me, I just wrapped the whole left hand in a old white apron soon bloodied, went right ahead with fixing. I wanted to look generous and productive and in charge— mostly out of self-defense. My kids were loud swinging on the vacant lot. Church bells started their competition clanging earlier described. I'd told kids they need not go to church today, since the Baptists' follow-up letter had informed me my hickory-nut figments were "graven images" to boot! Can you imagine? I heard Lou pushed by the complaining twins, Lou calling one verse on each shove,

> "How do I love to go up in a swing,
> Up in the sky so blue?
> Oh, I do think it's the pleasantest thing
> Ever a child (higher, you dummies) can do."

Ruth's phone rang. I hate it when the person telling a story breaks in too often, like wanting credit for inventing the whole idea of all stories and not just this one she's guiding her hearer through. But when I say from this semi-toothed mouth, "Ruth's phone rang," I get such a push of kind sad rage, I want to bust in. I long to edit life and hack this out. "Which part was *your* favorite part of the trip, Momma?" my kids'd ask me after even a visit to Castalia's. "This part" I would skip in any ideal world but this world sure ain't that. So, it's in to stay. Come ahead. We have to.

Ruth's phone rang. At the sound, the Wilguses' simpleminded collie, Gladys, barked to hear herself. Loss of blood from my sliced thumb made me feel chilly suddenly and—both hands covered with egg yolks, celery seed, standing before a counter of peeled cooling potatoes—I'd just pulled on my bagged-out maroon cardigan when I see poor Ruth posed at our screen door, sniffling.

"It's for you, Lucille. I better tell you, something has gone wrong."

"What else is new?" I spoke this all surly and flip, trying and make it not be so. "They say what? I'm busy here, Ruth. You want some potato salad later? 'Cause I'm making plenty."

"Lucy, you have to come to my telephone. They won't tell me all of it, they need you." She was weeping out there.

I cannot explain to you, darling, how much I hated Ruth then. She had to own a modern telephone that siphoned others' bad news to them faster.

"Step in, Ruth honey." I wiped hands on my apron. "Sorry—coming."

Poor Ruth slipped into my kitchen like wishing she was air-colored, less trouble. A cigarette dangled from her mouth and it looked like her cause for crying. Ruth's small eyes were wet, the weed burned very dry. That seemed to matter.

I peeled the apron from my cut, egg yolk all powdery across my red thumb. I followed Ruth's gaze and understood I'd also bled onto my gingham wash dress and over a few of the white potatoes gleaming on the counter. My eyes still streamed from inhaling onions.

"Cut myself," I apologized. "It's not bad. Where they phoning from?" and I reached gently back, I held on to my counter.

"Out past Duck. It's some stranger. There was . . . hurt. Somebody's apparently been hurt apparently, Lucille."

I said, "Oh. —Ruth, I ain't had a cigarette since I was ten. Give me some breaths off yours? Steadying, are they?"

She stepped nearer, unnailing the thing from her lip while both eyes played over me. Then I viewed myself like she must. The bun had come undone behind, a pouchy sweater, the bloody palm and apron, onion eyes, egg crumbled on everything. I got a tea towel, I bound up my left hand like a boxer's. I inhaled onct.

Then Ruth backed off, Ruth sobbed, she said, "You poor old thing."

I was twenty-nine. She was thirty-one.

I GOT led out my own door, down the steps, and through a latching gate that joined our back yards. Louisa made the twins quit swinging her the second she saw me. She always seemed to know, right at the instant, but maybe I misremember, needing another noticer to have lived in my own house.

At Ruth's wall-mounted oak phone with its ear cup, I went onto tiptoe. Five foot one, it's never enough. She settled at her nearby table and made a show of lighting two cigarettes, of getting her clean ashtrays ready, like having busy hands would prevent her overhearing. Of course, it was her house, her phone. I wanted to ask Ruth to call Louisa in. But that didn't seem quite fair to Lou, almost thirteen. It's just I wanted family here for this.

"I'm Lucille Marsden, who'm I talking with? Who got hurt? *Did* somebody?"

At that, there come a long crackling. All I needed was to get cut off! A man's voice finally said to somebody, "Go tell June they fetched the Marsden lady. Here, June. June, good, you talk. Woman should." I heard a scuffling as folks changed places.

I leaned, my eyes closed, tipped against the white enameled wall. My chin I pressed toward my chest and I was bowed here like preparing for a blow across the back and shoulders. I swore to at least conduct myself right. Lately, so much had made me act so crazy. Bad things won't personal. Stuff happens. Worse things've happened to better folks than me, I told myself.

But, honey, I knew what I was wishing. And it scared me to admit but I did admit it. One of my two hunting relations had likely been killed or damaged, right? If it had to be one? . . . dear God, no contest who I'd pick. After Cap done made this end run around me, snaking our boy out of town for gun play? No contest. I did not regret it either. I was learning not to be so guilty. It takes you a long time to learn that part.

"Yes," the lady said. "*Is* she, Jim? —Yes, are you there?" I answered I was. She said good and then she asked would Jim bring over her coffee, please. Said, "Yes, they put me on to tell you. I live right beside our general store here down in Duck? I'm June? And look, they asked me to. —Look, is this the mother?"

THEN I waved around for Ruth to slip a chair beneath me and she scooped it perfect and I settled with perfect dignity, I did.

"Dearie?" the woman said. "They told me I should. You his momma?"

"Probably," I said. "How bad? *Please* just tell me it quick, ma'am."

"He's alive, it's okay. It's just . . . it's been a accident. They took him to the hospital near Wilmington. I hear it's real nice. The one whose gun went off it was the one with the white beard—they say his safety won't on good— he was holding bob wire open for the boy? the shotgun went off, honey, in the direction of the boy. He'll likely pull through. So it's not that, honey, no. He caught the burns more than the shot really, which is good. But, see, he caught it more in, well . . . look is somebody there with you? Are you near your home?"

"Yes, a neighbor. I'm next to home. My kids are outside, my other children, tell me please and don't stop."

"See, sugar, it's the eyes. It's more in the child's . . . the eyes is what."

"They're burned? You've got to, Mrs.? Miss? you've got to be real specific here with me here. To hold back is not fair on me now that I know this much, honey. Please."

"Okay. It was hard to tell what was wrong when they had him in here— you know how it gets, I mean there's blood in any accident, but my guess is that, I'll level with you, that the eye-type damage is 'extensive' . . . my guess is they're really hurt to the point of being . . . To say it straight, well, they're more or less, the eyes, sugar, the eye *parts* are pretty much scorched, gone, sugar. But *he's* fine. Such a little soldier right through it too. All us near the store, we still cannot get over him. He was comforting the beard one—his granddad? Now *he's* the wreck because he knows he did it to him. He said call. The State Police took off with sirens going. Here, I got a number at the hospital."

"June? I'm going to put somebody else on now, June, to copy that? but look, June, I want to thank you for doing this part. I can fancy what it's like to tell even a stranger, and please leave your address 'cause I want to write you when I get a minute or send you little something, June. June? my name is Lucy. I thank you."

" 'S nothing, dear. You'd of done it for my boy. Of course, I got all daughters, which I'm glad of."

"Yeah, do be. Here's somebody who'll copy."

Ruth was right there with a pad and pencil. I thanked her. While I'd talked to June from Duck, I noticed a *Stage and Musical Personalities* magazine folded under on the low table nearby. Its mailing label had Baby Marsden's name on it but Ruth's address and I knew Poor Ruth subscribed to things for all my kids to draw them over here. I rethanked Ruth, backing out. I was just thanking everybody.

LOUISA stood at Ruth's screen door, nose grated there, one hand visoring her eyes so she could see in.

I needed to get by. "Here we go," I said so she'd back up.

Sunlight struck me and I sneezed. "It's your brother," I said. "Poppa took Ned hunting."

"With Billy Preston?"

"No, Billy's momma had the sense to keep hers home. I *thought* I had the sense. I've had no sense, Lou."

"What happened, something happened," she told me, taking one hand. By then we were in our own yard. We stood beside the clothesline, where wet sheets hung though it was Sunday and most neighbors felt it dead wrong to do laundry on the Lord's day. We stood near enough damp white sheets so when a breeze come up, one cloth pressed against us like a cooling compress. I took hold of Louisa, she was almost thirteen but nearbout taller than her mother here. I whispered to her. The sheet was lightly lashing us, all chill, and it felt wonderful. I needed to tell her what'd happened. I couldn't say it at regular volume, knowing as how—more than news of her own monthlies coming—this'd change her, probably. I hated to change them.

"Ned's alive," I whispered. I said, "There'd been a shooting accident and the gun went off, nobody's fault, but there's some certain burning and it could be near . . . his eyes. Burned Ned's eyes. But we can hope. We'll do things till we hear more. Ruth's calling the hospital." I said how she's been good in this and I was ashamed of how I'd carried on about her. "And the woman from down there told me and was just unbelievably nice. It must be hard, to tell."

Louisa looked unchanged except I watched all color leave her lower lip. "Ned's eyes. Not *Poppa's* gun?"

"Something like that, honey. But, look, we need to stay moving here. I believe I know what needs doing. We got us a project till we learn more. Come help Momma. Because—this is ending. I am ending all of this. I don't want it in my house ever again. Such a fool I was. Who did I think I was living with?"

4

HONEY, at that moment I become this force of nature. I headed to get the guns, and it was like going to drive the wasps out of a hive, every last poison one. I turned into a sleek goddess from the Greeks and Lou beside me, my sister in efficiency. It soon felt like flying, light and vengeance mixed—that whitest spot where sunlight splits to rainbow that can set a world afire like paper. Past my other kids beneath the huge black-walnut tree and its black swing-tire hanging like an udder. They all turned my way—and seemed to know, sharing a sound too fine and hurtful to be heard by normal un-Marsden hearing. "Ned!" They knew, and I felt that understanding enter their bodies, and as much as I hated their father for doing what he'd done to our boy down there, bloody on the coast in some bad store, I hated their father almost more for forcing all Ned's sisters and brothers here to *know* the nature of a world where crimes spread and cannot be contained and a second's carelessness can change stuff in far lives forever. I think what we were hearing was the cry that second of a child *not*-screaming on the floor of a sawdust general store, a boy trying and spare his poppa's feelings, a boy who'd refused to let his mouth grieve for absent eyes above the mouth. Our silent heads picked up a noise Ned had denied hisself, and we took his scream and we nursed it, and oh we valued it. But we appeared silent. All my children's eyes were huge, knowing then. But folks filed past for church, ladies' matching purses, the pastels. Nobody knew. Nobody knew yet.

"OKAY, get organized," I told myself. I heard a rattle that each breath made, caving into me and pushing out with waste air, keeping me alertly me, a angel of revenge and purpose.

Passing through my kitchen's coolness, I grabbed a new blue-handled broom. Striding to the arsenal, I saw a oval label on the broom, the label said: "Blind-made quality. Thank you for continued patronage of we, the deserving unsighted." I'd never noticed that before.

I wrapped my uncut hand in rags, the bloody fist still in its bloody apron so's I wouldn't mess up anything else. Then I stepped into his trophy-room, scene of my former private life.

I ordered Lou to close the door and keep every living soul out until I finished, no matter what the noise. "Yes, ma'am." But I decided to first run fetch a pair of high rubber boots from among old decoys and, with these on, shut myself away in the onetime sewing room now housing one hundred and ten instruments for flying pellets ready to cause damage to anything anywhere. I tugged at three of the twelve brass padlocks—he had the keys on his person. He had everything along with him. I noticed which cases showed empty slots. I tried imagining what the gun'd looked like that'd done that to my boy, but canceled such-like thinking. I used the broom's stick end to bust out twelve huge sheets of otherwise good plate glass. I danced clear of many icy zigzags falling, ambitious to be harmful, aiming towards me. No way. The sound brought people running from three blocks off. I knew it would. Half of First Methodist milled outside the hallway door. In my house already. Leeches. (I didn't hear quite right for two full days after, such was the noise, and I kind of liked that—sealed me off from some of what followed.)

I knew June had paid me the favor of not holding out false hopes. She'd paid me that favor, woman to woman, not lying a bit or being sicky-sweet.

I knew the worst already. *Had* known during last night's moving picture (was it only last night?). I had known when the sound of one boy's scream woke me Thursday when I scurried off to do a mother's body count upstairs. Maybe I'd known during my honeymoon or earlier.

When all panes were ruined good, I used the stick to knock loose jagged pieces from wood framing. Then I could reach in, begin to gather weapons, picking up pawpaws, picking up poison. Out you all go. When I opened the door onto the hall (having a time of it since blue-green glass stood inches deep), when I stood here with my first armload of rifles and told Lou to take these direct to our side yard—I saw concerned adults, shirts and ties and ladies in white gloves. In my home uninvited. I considered hollering like wild Winona. Faces told me they all knew already. They wanted to help but, as usual, didn't understand how. They also longed to keep well clear of me. I must've looked a sight, and it'd only started.

I sent Sunday-school adults into our yard, each toting guns worth thousands. They agreed to, but like humoring me. They didn't know where to grip each one—like I'd passed them severed human limbs. Pistols, muskets, all the lethal things soon started moving outdoors in piles, and nobody quite understanding what I planned. Me not knowing either till I told Lou, "Child, build a fire. Let's us make a big fire and have done with it." "Yes, ma'am." Ruth stood in the middle of a group, her telling them it again and crying. I asked for more news—she yelled: They won't at the hospital yet but were expected, the Lieutenant Governor had two doctors from Chapel Hill headed to the coast by another siren motorcade and Cap's message was, he promised everything that could be done would be done, Lucy.

I said, *"That's* for sure."

Lou soon had kindling glowing and a wad of *Herald Traveler*s joining in and all my other kids held a log apiece and stood there crying waiting to be useful. I took them off to one side. We'd never been a family for hugging constantly and kissy-kissy and like that. They dropped their fuel and clung to me. In trying and purge the house I had forgot them. I felt bad as they hung on to me. I told them nobody was to blame. I lied to them because they had to hear that at their age. For six minutes, we were fused there, turned aside from gathered watchers.

Since the day Cap's guns got shown in *Liberty*, new men had been filing in, reverent, to view them. These same fellows now stared envy at these museum pieces nude here in sunlight, lit by nearby flames. I made many dashing trips. Out came ivory derringers that slipped into my apron pockets, cherry-wood dueling pistols with cursive curlicue ivory garlands inlaid, two German revolvers black as oil and snub-nosed like terrible lizards and so cold to the touch. I lifted my apron's outmost ends and lugged still more, knowing that my bare thighs probably showed, not caring who saw. These legs'd stopped interesting anybody long long ago. Me especially.

The children tried being useful and so were picking up what rifles I dropped. I told the grownups worried all around, "See they hold those by the handles, not their tips, whatever. Baby, not by the tip." To show you how stunned my kids were, Baby—our dramatic one—had said not a word, had shed no tear but ran everywhere helping, dead white.

I got a shovel and begun digging a hole. Then—disorganized—I laid first rifles into the decent little fire Lou'd made. One sinewy black teenager, eyeing dueling pistols, he lunged over, said, "They loaded, any of them? Don't be sticking guns in no fire, all these folks around, they go off, *then* where you be?"

I thanked him, mortified right proper. I ordered all the things unloaded. I was taking charge, but of what? Where was any help for me? The bullet check let men do what they'd longed for, pick up each gun, crack open the works, look down its sight. Unloaded ones among flames won't burning too good. I saw now, even charred, the things would still have worked, metal latchings stay intact even on a charcoaled stock.

So I hollered, "Take them off from here. Get them far from this house and my children. Go to the river with them, melt them down, I don't care. Just let it all be over please. Hide them."

The colored teenager grabbed them cherry dueling pistols right out of the fire. They burned him till he jammed them under his belt like a pirate. Boy wagged his hurt hands but was smiling at his luck. I knew those guns had garland inlay on them and might be called works of art, but any artwork on a weapon had misunderstood something basic and, for me, won't.

Boy ran off fast and two white men after him, keeping track for Cap. I saw that. Other fellows lugging cordwood armfuls now went zipping off in all directions whilst eyeing who'd got what. Once men stepped off our land, I seen them halt, admiring their own loot. Some were standing there across Summit's sidewalk, wearing Sunday suits, a Bible tucked under one arm and aiming their ill-gotten guns up elm treetops. The wives beside them looked back over here at me, very very tired. I saw what a mistake I'd made. Once you got the weapons, what do you *do* with them?

I sat right beside the fire still burning peaceful. Nearby was one old pillow slip the kids'd stuffed with sand and pine straw to be home base. I crawled over to it, hunkered here, seeking safety. My children come and bunched around me, in a circle, like being my guards until my mind would clear. Resting under the swing made me think of Mr. Stevenson's poems someway. I said one, numb, trying to calm my kids:

> "When I am grown to man's estate
> I shall be very proud and great.
> And tell the other girls and boys
> Not to meddle with my toys."

This crowd of spectators watched us from the sidewalk. I heard Ruth's phone keep ringing. More news I could not bear.

Lou stood beside me and her knees were there. I put my arms around the backs of both her knees and hugged her to me, one ear tipped against her stomach as she stroked my hair. She said, "Let's us go in the house. They're looking, Momma. This is bad. We're outdoors."

"Yes, ma'am," I said, and tried standing. I saw the crowd, everybody afraid of me, my bloody hand worse now, stains all over.

Louisa helped me up. I bumped into the rope swing's tire. It now seemed some dark lynching victim. I filed indoors with my kids. We moved like people ashamed of ourselves. We were ashamed. We had let this happen. We could not clean up after ourselfs.

CASTALIA, ripe in mink, winded from her trudge uphill, both hands still coated with flour from baking, right massively appeared, put Louisa in charge of other kids, sent strangers from my kitchen, guided me to the front parlor. I always kept it covered with cloths to spare my best furniture till fancy enough company eventually came. They never did.

Castalia heaved down onto the davenport, sighing relief. Coat still fastened, she patted her wonderful and ample upper thighs. I did as told, I settled in the vast deep lap of all of her. No mink on earth could've given a person more pleasure then, more comfort. Her arms, enminked, closed round me, her hands' skin felt so cool and smooth. The pressure from a human squeeze released me so, I felt pooled, grown right smack into the front of her.

She smelled of dough. And not just because of interrupted baking. There'd always been this yeasty and producing kind of scent around her. Marigolds, dust, basil. I patted her minks like living pets she'd brung to cheer me. I looked into her eyes' yellowed whites, the black black centers that'd never let daylight make them less than solid jet. She seemed, if possible, larger than before. Could she be gaining at her age? Castalia had been named, like many Marsden slaves, for a local city. Maybe this added to her sense of scale, child, made her seem both a person and locale, a principality, almost.

"Look at you," she said. "No wonder they all running from you. Look like *you* the war one, blood all over place. How you cut that hand, on them racks you busted?"

"You know what my husband is begging for, don't you? *Our* husband. He wants us to kill him, Cassie. He's like some foaming-at-the-mouth dog that is basically just dying for release. He needs the help that'd only come from being dead."

She clucked as how Cap had not much more control in this than I did. I should go wash my face and calm some, go take my other children off into one room and tell them what this was about, because some of them— to judge from their faces—didn't really know and I was scaring them myself. She knew I didn't mean to, but I was. These strangers milling around Marsden property, it won't fitting.

I was inches from her jack-o'-lantern face, more of a mask it seemed as she aged. It grew extra chins in valance rings like her mink accumulated. I felt her list of instructions calm me, narcotic nearbout, it give me simple things to do. We all need, at such ransacking moments, such a person to step in and be specific and to help. What endless aid this woman had been giving me for life. How could I repay it? I think I wanted so much to be with Ned right then, I turned all that banked kindness on the person who'd been truest to me longest.

I heard Louisa playing hostess and I knew it must be aging her. She hated outsiders, shyer even than I was. Nothing was coming at me right just now. I had maverick thoughts like how smells travel in my house—how while cooking cabbage for supper, the kitchen stays surprisingly unstinky but my linen closet, two rooms and a hallway off, seems to suck all odor to itself—household currents I could never figure. Now, my respect for this free slave, my pity for a missing son, my rage against the husband, it all registered as a desire so sudden it hit me in the lower spine, the wallop made my lower carcass dampen instantly the way tears can literally leap out of your eyes at certain news. Leap. I was here in her lap already. Was easy. I kissed her then and saw her eyes accept this as one type of kiss when it started, then eyes widen as the kiss opened to being another sort. Castalia kissed me back, but out of pity? I hoped not. I won't ever know, I reckon.

A collaboration, okay, but this became such a kiss that it grew like some thought we shared. All I knew was the great massive chifforobe fact of her below—and her mouth's wit. I wanted to escape into her head forever. At the edges of us two, wrapped in her beautiful if someway tacky mink, I felt a crackling like some circus's electric air. I heard people standing gabbing on sidewalk clear around our big old house. Thousands of dollars of free merchandise had just been given away by a seemingly crazy woman and maybe other prizes would pour forth and people waited on that.

Again I heard Louisa opening our front door, Lou saying the word "thank" and the word "casserole," already those were rolling in. How could women *bake* them so fast? Or did ladies keep some constantly on hand for any possible maimings of local kids, specifically Captain Marsden's? I hated the feel of disorder in my home, I despised the notion of strange adults' hands calming my twins, or Baby, touching Lou's thin braids. —Cas now told me it won't just me, she said as how the Marsdens had done killed Castalia's mother, suffocated underground, they'd sold her poppa like potatoes. They'd *let* the overseer and his men touch the slave girls, babies practically. "You bend over in a field out there, you skirt ride up? men they come and have they hands on all you, couldn't do much about it. So this just part of that, seem like. Just the latest. It's something wrong with how it's set up, seem like."

I nodded. I saw that. But, myself, I had other things to do, I was someway unbuttoning Castalia Marsden's blouse. It was like the peeling of a planet. She must now weigh near three hundred and some, who knew? She looked down at buttons released, surprised, not shocked. "What? What you after, girl? Ain't exactly no milk in there at my age." "The sight," I said. "The sight. Am I acting like a madwoman here? Because you can tell me."

She shrugged. "It'll pass. You just getting used to the idea of him hurt. You gone get by, I reckon. We do. Got to, seem like."

THEN I grew real White on her, middle-class, regretful, I commenced to fasten her back up. I heard Louisa rise to the occasion of her brother's blinding, saying to more food, "For *us*?" Castalia's hand slapped my hands, their nervous buttoning back. "You think it'd help? 'Cause this's the one request for anybody's looking at 'em I've had all week . . ."

I watched mighty hands undo thin cotton. I watched the dark flesh be a V and then a U and then be everything, dark as the mink framing all. I watched hands dip into the strained D cup of a overwashed bra, bleached to being furry nearbout. I watched both hands offer my own eyes these breasts. "So," I said, not knowing what that meant. "Okay," I said, and did feel better, seeing her, seeing somebody else. I wanted to hold Ned, or be a child myself. I don't know what I was doing. Her nipples were salmon color inlaid in this ripe brown field. Her palms held breasts like scooping up great drinks of spring water. Her breasts right here, all used and perfect, badges, burdens, you name it, hers—they were Castalia's. That was why I'd wanted them.

"Thank you," said I. "Can't explain. But it helps considerable."

"Give us a last kiss and go about you business. Because getting these things back in'll take a sight longer than whipping 'em out usually does. At my age, seem like everything's a job."

We kind of laughed. I kissed her near the mouth but she said, "Give us one real kiss. Nobody been kissing you enough, that's part the problem," and we kissed. It held me against somebody living.

ONE SKINNY white woman stood up from that couch, disgusted with her bloodied wash dress, straightening her apron and feeling a little single pistol was left careless in one pocket there. Miss Priss pinned her hair in place. It was me again, and back.

"Go on out to them, go greet." Cassie pulled fur over her bosom, modest suddenly and dearer for that. I saw it'd cost her, opening to me. Everything I asked of anybody costs so much. "I will," I smiled. "I'm fine. I plan to kill him the first chance I get, and now I'm fine."

5

WHEN I looked better I felt better (but that's the middle class). A washed face, nice bandage on the hand, hair brushed, clean Sunday dress, new apron (with my one remaining pistol transferred from the pocket of that smudged first one). I circulated, shaking hands, meeting eyes. People seemed relieved. I saw they'd heard things about my being wild earlier. They hugged me like I'd been on a long trip but'd got back home. I told Lou she was off duty. I thanked her. I heard men talking out front and later realized our front porch had become a kind of company store, see, guns they were coming back. Men'd heard Captain was returning, and his buddies, they'd retrieved almost all the weaponry. Thank God I didn't know this at the time—otherwise, I'd be in jail or the nuthouse now for sure.

I excused myself, held another powwow with my kids in the girls' dorm. I repeated the phrase "nobody's fault." Of course, they'd seen me try and burn his guns, but even so. You had to say "nobody's fault" to kids this age. I recalled my Archie's look at me, the un-smile, his accepting question, "Must This Happen?" I tried recalling other things. Nice stuff mostly.

NEWS had reached us: Cap would be bound home late tonight, come to fetch me. I couldn't believe he'd leave Ned alone on the child's first night of blindness. But after everything else, why should *this* small lapse surprise? I wondered, are all men like this or was it just the luck of the draw? I pictured my son with his head bandaged, massive as a small world globe (the neater the bandage, the sadder the picture).

Were there other children in Ned's ward? Were the mothers there? I hoped. I hoped the nurses were not male ones.

I entered our second-best parlor and talk hushed: one man ended a joke. The other conversation had been about Braille and some outfit in Lumberton that trained good Seeing-Eye dogs. I asked that the name be wrote down and given to Ruth or Lou, please.

I excused myself and stepped in to try and sweep up glass in his ruint trophy room. It always soothed me, cleaning at times like this. Typical, my trying to go undo my nervy earlier damage. Here I'd just been staring at Castalia's breasts, and now I was off trying and impress the world with my housework skills! I bent to scoop a pound of slivers, felt something sway in my apron pocket. "Oh," I said, "this little thing." I studied the last weapon left in the house besides my Sabatier butcher knives. Then, cheerful-like, I set to work, opening all drawers under his show racks. Three were rattly full of bullets—boxes colorful and pretty like they held good stationery or even candy. I squatted, pilfering ammo cartons, doing so with a great yawning patience, almost good humor—seeking the perfect tear-shaped bullets for this silver pistol, pearl-handled. It seemed plain for one of Captain's fancy guns. I wondered if it might really work. Round and blunt, pointed/ sharp, I tried many types till four fit snug in "the chamber." I think it's called chamber. Then I snapped shut and repocketed the thing, I glided off to be the kind of perfect hostess my momma, Bianca, always hoped for.

Momma was there by then. Somebody'd gone for her. Somebody handed me a empty casserole dish with this note taped in the bottom: "Good for one rinse and set whenever you're ready. Lolly. Your Inner Glow will get you through this mess, you see if it doesn't."

. . .

TWO A.M. and twelve casseroles (six topped with potato-chip crusts) later, we hear sirens enter Falls. The Lieutenant Governor's motorcade roars up before our home, waking kids all over town, especially our own that I'd tried singing and lulling off to sleep. Children had prayed. This time Ned got mentioned first. Cassie's in the kitchen in her mink, writing down which dish goes back to which house, tasting a corner of each casserole and the two unexceptional peach cobblers. Mother circulates, chin up, in dark blue. My poppa murmurs on the porch. Ruth drifts into groups, says things like "Can you even be*lieve* this, the poor things?" I go wait in the center of our foyer. One hand slips into my apron pocket.—Now, child, I see I was completely in another world. But who could point this out and stop me? I myself could not.

The children are all out of bed, footed pj's dangling through the banisters above and behind me, kids also facing the front door. Men gathered on the porch to smoke now greet somebody. I hear them offer the person condolences. Some neighbor says plain, "Here . . . these yours, I believe." Then I understand my husband's buddies, the Elks and Moose and Redmen, they've collected Captain's scattered valuables. Men are handing back his precious guns, doing so before he even steps in here and sees us, sees me—before he explains. "A smart young nigger got your Aaron Burr dueling ones, boy ran fast but not quite fast enough, hunh, Charlie? There *they* are."

Front door flies open. Every soul in this house jumps. Behind me I feel children draw against each other, like bracing. Even Castalia behind me and watching from the kitchen, even Castalia flinches. Takes some doing. *That* scares me, her cringe.

I'm feeling glad I just took the bandage off my paw. He's always telling me I'm accident prone. Me! I look right good, I straighten my shoulders, and in he comes. For onct, I'm ready. I live here.

What a tall and handsome heavy, heavy handsome tall man now barges in like owning the place, mammoth in his khaki, plaids, and brown. He's wearing rubber waders, hip-high, frog-green. He seems broken-winded like he's run a ways. I see he has been drinking. Who can blame him? I must, as ever, look up to him and something in his eyes turns me ways I've not planned going, honey. He is weeping, in public, tears move direct into his white beard. "Lucy," he says. "Forgive me." And so much that's gone between us all these years is like some web gauzed from my sternum to his, my skull's front side lacing to his own. I feel I'm sinking. Can I forgive myself forgiveness one more time, with all these people watching?

Then, he sets something down, it's a sack, he settles it beside the door a burlap tow sack stuffed with returned guns. Points and muzzles jab out. He has a white beard and his sack it's stuffed, some Santa's satchel, but corrupted—infection slung indoors for Christmas. I picture my Archie's pink gums bared, Must This Happen?

Above the white beard, one grown man's face has aged five years. I see that and I feel for it and him. I do. His eyes look wild with a grief older than our hurt son. This haywire aspect touches me. It is mine. Nobody understands us, two sadsacks in love despite it all. I cannot help taking a step toward him. It would be right to hug him now, to know he's helpless in all this as *I* feel standing here with a mob watching. I do that. I think it might feel fake but it's sure worth trying. I want to be generous, or at least *considered* generous. Two steps nearer, I see he's holding something behind him, could be flowers, for me. One second, I think he's got a little child back there, alive or dead? I've started towards him. I'll step on, I have to.

My head comes chest-high on him, nipple-high. Men have nipples, too. In my apron, I release the little gun, hand-warm. Then he reaches behind him and right up in my face he jerks these shapes, dangle dangle.

First I cannot see nothing but fluff. He seems to feel this is some justifying tribute, a apology. Man shoves six dead canvasback ducks toward my confused face. Neck-broke floppy, some still trail sad skummy reeds, and when I see one's this-side eye and its gummy glazed hole, I am gone then.

"Tact," I say. "You're all tact, sir. *Now* I remember who you are."

Nearby folks have gasped at what he's done. We stand here with these strangers peering from four doorways opening on this hall. He has not hugged me. Our kids in the gallery behind and around me are waiting. My hand again finds metal. My hand is glad the metal's still hand-warm, hello.

"Lucy," the vet says, hiding ducks he sees I haven't liked. "It's nobody fault, Lucy. The safety came off."

I'm thinking of our children all behind me. I want them to remember me as being a good person at this moment. I want to do right here and act openhanded as Castalia, not like him, scorekeeping. But I see that ducks are dripping on our pale hall floor, pink droplets coming down.

"Your idea of a present? Dead things I should clean till they're of use?"

"The safety came off," he says. "Could've happened to anyone. Ned's really okay, considering."

"Don't you even speak his name to me."

I pull it into light then. I point a weapon at him, cool, I feel so clear it scares me. I know exactly how this veteran will look, on falling backward.

I hear my children rustle up behind me, a menace of whispering lifts from all rooms. Just that second comes a tap on the door and some old bachelor from down the street, in his bathrobe, holding three rifles, plainly scared of Captain for a long time and eager to endear hisself, sees fit to barge in smiling long enough to say, "I believe you'll be wanting these," sees my gun aimed right his way, grins, " '*Scuse* me, folks," closes the door. Men! a club, a army.

My wrist goes out at purest right angle. I mostly focus on the area between his eyes. My hand is shaking none at all. This nearbout worries me. "Children?" I say back of me. "Go to bed. *Now*." They do not. I feel I've got to say, to him, "This is a real pistol and I loaded it."

"Seems highly possible," his voice comes deep and rich and capable. "You've had any number of weapons in circulation all day long, it appears. Lucy, give me that. I cannot believe you're doing this to yourself in front of everybody. —Forgive her, she has no idea . . . she's grieving . . . she has not a clue what this means, doing such a thing in front of people. Lucille . . . look at you."

"How could you leave him alone? He's never been *away* from home one night except at Billy Preston's."

"Oh, he's in good hands, the nurses were making much over him. I wanted to come fetch *you* back there, is all. Seems more your line."

"Taking care of them is more my line? Cleaning up after you, plucking your dead things?"

"There are flash burns but *one* might well be saved. —You think I haven't suffered over this, Lucille?"

Castalia stands beside me. She has her hand out, palm up. The palm is copperish yet ivory and quite beautiful.

"Sir, if you'd really suffered," I ignore her, "you wouldn't keep doling it out. The 'safety' came off the minute you were born. You stole my boy off from here and me. You're misery, you know that? You're misery and need ending for your sake and all us others. You should thank me for letting you rest finally. Here's Appomattox at last."

The gun shoves forwards. Castalia gets between him and me, there's a great deal of her between him and me. "Better ways," she's saying sad to me. "Folks here. Children watching. Come on, girl. I ain't got you this far to see you do this mess."

Hearing my kids mentioned, feeling very glad to look away from the somehow-father of them, I turn to see pajamas' legs and feet, pink, blue, yellow, little white scuff-pad soles—very still now locked betwixt white railings. They could be on some Christmas card. I smile, even wave, I count them. But I find Ned is missing. Must still be at Billy's. Then I remember. Then it seems I am the duck diving down to bite on something far beneath dim water, a bird who's chose to spare herself through drowning. I am ending, having black and oily earmuffs put on, things like blinders grab my temples then claim my eyes so cold on either side. Cold on either side. I am falling backwards backwards into dark.

6

HONEY, here's my famous grandfolks McCloud Scottish shortbread recipe I been promising, the one that snagged me so many State Fair blue ribbons:

Take 2½ cups sifted flour, ¼ teaspoon salt, ½ cup confectioner's sugar, one cup butter, some blanched almonds, candied cherries, or angelica or citron for on top and decorating as you like. Be "creative."

Sift dry ingredients into a bowl. Child, you'll want to work it with your

two hands till the mixture's right smooth and then feels blended. My visit
to the hospital I am avoiding telling. You halve your dough then roll each
half into four, a unit, say, six inches round and maybe half a inch thick. I
know I didn't ride with Captain, I must've had somebody's car follow him,
and me along with them. To see your son the only child in a bed up there
on the Men's Ward. To see him bandaged but perking to the sound of your
familiar footsteps on the tile. His neck drawn up long and pert and delicate,
head twisting your direction, a wad of orderly gauze big like some baby
bird's goggle eyes not open yet. Aiming almost your way, both his arms are
pumping up and down, held out to where he thinks you will soon stand.
With tines of a fork, outline six wedges into each round pie shape made.
Place on buttered cookie tin. I'd brought him a note written by his brothers
and sisters, all of them got to say four lines apiece and I read these to him,
but in their voices. Tried. Managed Louisa's, then I Little Xerxesed our
twins taking turns alternating lines—and our youngests, and finally lispish
Baby, easiest of all to do. I am right good at this type thing when I put my
mind to it, and—for him that day—I was inspired. I almost wanted to do
Ned for Ned. Encouraging maybe. Reminding. He laughed, like I knew he
would, wanting to prove to me he was the same as before, though he wasn't
and would not be, never. His father waited in the archway at a distance,
watching, keeping aside, feeling he should, the man all politeness now. I'd
brung our boy some shortbread still warm in its toweling and he was nibbling that (no appetite, I saw) and Ned was smiling and nodding his head
like eager to prove that he was brave and all, trying to laugh while eating
and for my sake. I had pushed too hard with comedy at first. You know
me, child. I fall back on that, a habit really. You're terrified underneath. It
was the best I could do at the start of my first sight of damage done to him.
Preheat oven at, say, 275 degrees. He was in the ward and concerned men
around all watching. The mascot, they had made him. Through no fault of
his own. Men saying nothing, sitting there with their own woes and bandages
and fevers, but listening to the mother of their new human interest. No
privacy but you couldn't blame *them* for that. Anyway, when had I ever
known privacy? I thought of Ned, the First Ned, pet to a whole division and
dead so long. I sat on the bed of this hurt boy, wishing I'd not let his poppa
name him for a child killed at this same age. It was a mistake, names are
contagious, I knew that now.

   Ned, my Ned, leaned back in his starched pillows and took the shortbread from his mouth and put it on the bedside table after feeling for the
table's edge, and said the bread was so good he would save it. He said I did
the voices right. "Do the twins. You get the difference. That's what's good,
you get the difference between them." Put cookie tin in oven. Maybe I said
that. Preheat. So I *did* the twins, but not as good as earlier. I can't repeat
on request, which means I ain't a true performer. He smiled though, behind
the huge head bandage (so white) and leaned back grinning, shaking his
head sideways, pleased in a man-sized bed. He kept shaking his head side

to side too hard maybe. And I felt pleased—I'd cheered him with my baking and my silly stunts. Okay. It'd be fine soon. It was a good sign, basically, underneath all of it. Cassie had lost all her folks and only *this* had grabbed me. We were lucky. One infant and one accident. Many had it worse. We'd get by. Then I saw this mark on his neck, and when I drew near it, I understood, child, it was moving, it was dark, his laughing had sent forth this exploring into daylight out from under gauze. One small red line had spilled under bandage and was now easing out from where the eyes has been. After removing from slow oven, shift to wire rack, allow to cool at room temperature. Decorate tops with almonds, bits of cherry, or angelica or citron as desired. Be "creative," let yourself go.

Then break apart. You will not be dissatisfied.

I NOW planned running away. Get out. Had to. Of course I first took Ned to "see" these schools in a car with a hired driver . . . who helped to teach me driving as we went. A handy skill. I didn't want Captain Marsden along, glad-handing headmasters, throwing his name and war record around to open doors for our son. Captain was now living at the New Ricks Hotel near the depot. I asked him not to show his face for a while and no hard feelings. I said I needed time off. He was nice about it. I mean *really* nice.

That was what perpetually confused you.

I drove Ned to a training camp near Lumberton where we got assigned Moxie, a yellow Labrador. Ned's brothers and sisters grumbled that they had always wanted a cocker spaniel, not a Lab, but now here Ned got a big gold Lab and trained, a *whole* one to hisself.

Family! Darling, what're you going to do? *You can't live with them, and you can't get born without them.*

I'd had the ruined arsenal turned into Ned's bedroom since the stair steps became a problem. But he asked to go back up with the others anyway. I understood that and said sure. When he moved out, I got my Singer right in again. It stayed till Sheriff Cooper evicted me from the old house some decades later.

Throughout this whole mess, my children had been unbelievable. Bricks. Not just Ned, the others. They could handle most any occasion, seemed like. They were good at anything but boredom. I took all eight out to restaurants, the two in town. My daddy had started giving me some money at this time. Captain was having trouble covering his counties-wide poker IOUs and I felt sad for him, I did. You know? I missed him being in the house. Can you *stand* it? Am I sounding like the battered gals you see in shadows on the Magnavox out there in Multi-Purpose?

Even so. I could see our children missed him, too, especially at dinnertime and breakfast. The thing I can't seem to find is a way to say how potent his attention was when he was "up" and with you, really there. He had the deepest, finest, most beautiful speaking voice. The only actor's like it was young James Mason. He's dead, too, they all are. But like Mason's,

Captain's had this kind of light in it. He'd just comment on the weather—
and it would seem to *mean* something.

Here lately Cap was becoming kind of a town embarrassment. People
knew what he'd done. Low on funds, too. He was beginning to forget things.
Yeah, and the house seemed huge without him—and me wiping fingerprints
off new spots low on the walls and wondering, Why there? Till I remembered
Ned's condition.

Good as my other kids acted, they would talk about our hurt one like
he won't in the room. "What kind do you think Ned wants?" Baby asked
about a choice of dessert. "He's sitting right *here*, honey. Ask him. It ain't
nothing changed about him." But her face told me that there *was* too. And
that I had embarrassed her. "Chocolate or vanilla, sugar?" I asked him, my
hands plumping his sideburn curls that the smoked glasses always flattened.

I got the best possible harness for Moxie. There was a store of Blind
Supplies in Raleigh, a whole display of short short canes, red-and-white,
the sight of which—a rack of twelve models for your well-equipped blind
child—I cannot tell you. "*You* choose," I said, and sat here like some mother
in a shoe store where, instead of walking on carpet, your kid he tap-taps
into everything. They'd set up a little obstacle course of boxes and stuff. "I
think," the nice salesman said, "he's tending toward our lighter-weight
models. The modified bamboo has been a big favorite this season." "Good.
Whatever." And all during, I am sitting here considering—with a inward
sound like some giant amount of wind lashing over a cave's fixed open
mouth—escape. My own. Just mine. Maybe someplace with palms like ones
in Cassie's home village, like ones Maimie Lucille Beech so loved? I'd *had*
it with this taking care of others. Seemed like I had tried this—staying in
place and being kind and making school lunches—and had failed. I'd been
put in charge of shirts and nickels and children. One child was dead, another
blinded. I really should let others, better qualified by nature, try and get it
right now.

"Let's see. Is this cash or a check? How will you be paying, ma'am?"

Out of my bone marrow, I almost said. But didn't. You don't. I was
done with acting crazy. That just gave them too much satisfaction, their
seeing that they'd got to you, their hurting you that much. But I stood, I
walked to Ned, smiling, him knocking into walls, using his cane like a fencing
sword and grinning under dark glasses. I stood beside the register, my wallet
out, and I noticed that the register had Braille on all its keys. I looked at
the salesman who'd seemed so at ease. He was young and smiling at the
sound of Ned's cane whooshing through air. "It's a good weight," the man
said three inches too far left of me. "He'll do well with that." My problems
seemed so silly compared to others', but to me how huge and gray and lardy-
real they felt.

Revelations says, "And he that overcometh, and keepeth my works unto
the end, to him will I give power over the nations . . . and I will give him
the morning star." I changed the "him" to "her," of course, and waited.

Forget nations. I'd settle for some favor as small as breakfast in bed some-place foreign yet sunny. I'd grown so primed for a reward: two weeks' rest would do nicely, thank you.

I walked all over Falls with Ned, making sure Moxie did right by my son at street crossings. People give us unasked-for respect, closed-mouth smiles, eyes that turned down at their outer corners. I felt almost glad Ned couldn't see—pride had been his sin, too. These grins seemed embarrassed at knowing the whole history of our loss and my collaborator's part in it.

ONE DAY a little Pomeranian bitch in heat turned Moxie's head and I was there to catch that fool dog after his quarter-block run, him yanking along my Ned, who—when I got to him—was laughing. "He sure *liked* something," Ned told me. The child still wore bandages, but only over the sockets now. He put smoked glasses over them to make gauzed dents look less scary and a tad more human. From Ruth's I telephoned Lumberton, concerned about Moxie's roving eye, and they said it was time to have him altered, his being altered would help him keep on giving Ned good help.

"Altered?" I asked—it sounded like having his dog-collar style updated.

"You know . . . de-maled," the gent said after a tactful pause.

I laughed, "So *that's* the way to get good use out of male ones! Why didn't I think of that be*fore*?" I chortled like a lunatic longing for escape. Silence from the head Seeing Eye man.

Captain kept his own hours now. He sold Lady More Marsden's final farm. He asked me for formal dinner invitations. He was sleeping in the back of his livery stable, a little room with two cots, his former poker headquarters. He turned on the charm while at home and I appreciated the effort, I did. He made things easier. He brought over gifts I knew he couldn't no longer easily afford. He mail-ordered a rocking horse for Ned—covered in real pony fur and with glass amber eyes that spooked me. Ned, just gone twelve, and way too old for hobbyhorses now. I see how much it bothered Cap, coming in like some uncle, not their father. But none of it made me want to stay. I was right far gone. I tend to get righteous, it's a failing. But the sight of Ned caning around the house, and being such a good sport, oh Lord. I worked hard to stay wide open to our other children. I took each, alone, on separate outings downtown. They might sulk about Ned's getting Moxie, but they basically pulled through with many kindnesses. My children already seemed like solid moral little people.

That made my leaving them seem easier.

NED dearly loved to sit whole minutes touching Cassie's homegrown coat. He made up his own names for each animal donor. Captain, a model of kindness there for a while, told me *I* should take a day off, he'd mind the kids. I worried about having Ned alone with him again, unchaperoned, but then I figured, sounding bitterer than I thought I'd ever sink: What else can the man *do* to him? I got granted a day all to myself, my gang comedy off seeing a farm where gamecocks were bred. But I spoiled time off with pacing, laundry, and regrets, with plans to run away. I picked the date. I again explained to myself why I would have to leave alone. I was cleaning up the house and in every room there seemed a spare red-and-white cane tilting up against some wall. You know how some absentminded folks leave a pair of bifocals on every table in the house so they'll never be without? When would I get used to it? I literally feared for my own mind. Sounds simple, put like this. But if you ever been through it, child, you know the jeopardy each minute brings. One more tiny thing might set you off over some border that turns into a armed frontier. You will never see your house again. Cap put in extra hours with our blind son. What these divorced husbands today call "quality time" spent with bartered kids on weekends. Men call it "quality" to make eight hours a week feel more important in their busy lives. Fine that Cap was driving our boy around in a borrowed car. But was I too harsh in feeling it was too little and too late?

I saw our other kids slowly come to trust Poppa again. Even Louisa. First an honored guest, then asking permission for an overnighter, and then, someway, back in here. Playing like he was a human one of us again. And oh he was, I guess. I didn't trust my judgments anymore. I avoided Castalia. Couldn't say why. Her strength begun to irk me. Who wanted to be brave and beaten down? I wanted to have things fun, wanted to feel free.

There were nice events that happened in this period, I'm sure, but I forget them now. To wake up in your bed beside your returned husband and the father of your brood and to hear that noise first thing, a light child-scaled tap-tap along the hall toward the bathroom at 3 a.m.—because he has to go and can't see when dawn comes so he might wait and not wake others. It can strike a person many ways. To me, it said one word, "Leave." I wanted to save them or else take them all far far from harm. I could not, so I would spare myself for now, for them, for later. Or so my logic run.

Sometimes I'd find Ned in the pantry (crying in the darkness for our sakes, plainly, and not his). I knew he wept: because his shoulders bucked. I knew that way and not through tears. The Chapel Hill doctors told me that the tear ducts had been cauterized, were gone. Mostly Ned tried acting cheery. The nicer he behaved about the whole mess and the better he moved around the place and the harder he worked at his Braille, the readier I felt to pack by the fourteenth, D day. The closer I felt to reconsider murdering Ned's father. Seemed *some*body had to. My boy never asked for special favors. He took to Braille right off and said it was a little bit like rock collecting, recognizing dots by touch and groups of words waiting there in the far dark, spelunking. Some stormy midnights, I'd find him abed in the boys' dormitory, fingers reading under the covers, mouth sounding out the harder words whilst staring straight ahead.

Cap was asked to do more parades all over Dixie and he'd go off with his extra uniform in a dry-cleaning bag. He had a livestock convention coming up in Richmond on the fourteenth, the day I'd head elsewhere. All travel starts local. I felt almost serene about the leaving.

We'd reserved a place next term at the best blind school in either Carolina. Therefore I could go now. I planned to first buy him lots of beautiful little new cashmere sweaters at Ekstein's. I figured anything that'd be nice to feel of, Ned should have with him always, no matter the cost. I got out the trusty honeymoon carpetbag. Sent Cas a note and, despite avoiding her of late, asked would she come and sleep here the night of the fourteenth. She turned up to say she would.

"Where you headed?" She held the page I'd sent, folded it with care, pocketed it—evidence she'd keep back from Him. No trace. Disappeared without a trace. Castalia handed me a jar of her famous watermelon-rind pickles.

"Where?" I shrugged. "Someplace they don't know me. Someplace *else* they don't know me."

I frowned at her like blaming her. She'd seen me, a bride fifteen, she'd known this was in store for me but what had she done to stop it or spare me? "We'll see," I said, to take it back a bit.

Lately, every sentence I spoke or heard had "see" or "eyes" in it. All my life people answered my requests that way, "We'll see."

THE DAY before leaving, came time to take all Ned's bandages off. Us two would usually go off to a far corner of the house to change his dressings. I didn't want the other children to yet be bothered by the sight I'd learned to look right at. Somebody must. I was his mother, I loved him.

The twins were enduring matched-set bad dreams right along in here. I was up and down all night those first six weeks after the shooting. Ned slept better than his brothers and sisters. He seemed determined to be easygoing, I tried telling him he didn't have to. Then I worried I was spreading my own darknesses to a boy already wound in dark enough. He told me he saw more than blackness. The blind see slow colors, spots, the deeds and hidden sufferings of light. His rich curls—without living eyes to be beneath them—appeared suddenly heavier, some wig, like Harpo's.

Once the dressings come off for good, once he'd gone downtown a few times with Lou's help and that of drowsy (altered) Moxie, Ned called me aside. "How do they look?" he asked me. "Because I must have scars that show over the glasses, Momma. Because, see, when I walk into Lucas'? everything stops for a second then they all get real loud and come over like everything's okay. Something must show, Momma. Lou won't tell me. When I ask, Lou gets mad."

"There is a little scarring here and here," I touched Ned's forehead, which didn't flinch, glad to be touched, eager to know all. "Doc said these ones will fade. Otherwise you'd never know with your glasses on. Son? the eyes are like mostly blank, son. Everybody's got whites around their eyes, yours just have more now. That's what people see."

"So not that bad-looking or anything, hunh? 'Cause, I need to know."

"Folk're just getting used to you with a cane, is all. Plus Moxie. That Moxie loves you to pieces but is lazy at times. Smart, though, our Moxie."

"Okay then." He was finished with the topic forever and I watched his narrow back bound off outdoors, to play tap-tap-tapping, trusting the world.

Doing breakfast dishes I remembered Mr. Stevenson's poem "Travel," starts:

> I should like to rise and go
> Where the golden apples grow—
> Where below another sky
> Parrot islands anchored lie.
> And, watched by cockatoos and goats,
> Lonely Crusoes building boats.

Another sky. Sounded good. I felt ready as I'd ever be.

BOOK FIVE

A

Treaty

with the

World

How
to
Leave

For all our days are passed away in thy wrath:
we spend our years as a tale that is told.

—PSALM 90:9

THIS IS how God explained it was my time to run away: Ned's bandages were all off and he felt he looked okay, Lou had finally won her local Spelling Bee, and though she'd just lost the state part (giving the world "plebeian" one more "b" than it deserved), she still got the tri-county trophy and shined it twice a week till the brass rubbed off. Twins' croup was breaking up. My potato salad cut healed to a mere scar. And, at long last, the leak over my kitchen ceiling had been patched—by me—with a bucket of tar and a fistful of brick dust from our vacant lot. It seemed a right good stopping point between disasters. I figured: Lucy, better clear out now before the next batch starts. The thing about setbacks: In a family with eight living children—there are more coming.

At my kitchen table, after midnight, I drank a cup of tea, decided to make sure the young ones had decent winter clothes. Castalia would housesit till my husband decided who'd mind our brood or which orphanage to use, whichever happened first. I knew it was time. —Sure, I'd considered taking my babies along. But, honey, running away with eight children, that ain't running away—it's moving.

I'd started to feeling like a waning moon that might never come back full.

THE DAY I packed, I saw a newspaper at Lucas': how a woman in Ohio had killed six. She took a hatchet to her husband and five children while they slept. Police asked her why. Woman said, calm as you please, "Because things were too hard for them alone. And *I* couldn't find a way to help."

The *Herald Traveler* showed her picture. You know? she looked nice.

Had on a pretty suit. When I read all this, when it made perfect sense to me, I knew that—as a decent wife and mother—was time to go.

I sized up the honeymoon carpetbag, its tapestry showed roses. It was already long out of style. How fast things had moved. Everything but me. I made no plans beyond the need to clear out quick. The kids were tucked in. I'd given them hot milk so they'd sleep through my goodbyes. I'd made Cassie take money to come tend them till Captain got back from the hog growers' convention up in Norfolk. I'd read the leaflet they sent. The meeting was called "Recent Advances in Technical Butchery." I just laughed. He give me his worried guilty look. I kept thinking about the Ohio lady who'd killed her own brood. She'd done it because she couldn't spare them, couldn't save them from the world's messy future waiting, a set trap, for each. —Packing my best things, I felt excited and rotten.

I tiptoed around and kissed my children as they slept, first the girls' long row of beds and then my boys'. I righted the cane that'd tipped to the floor beside Ned's bed. I said the full name of each child aloud, and though I am not now nor never will be a Catholic, I made the sign of the cross in the air above their blankets. Humid milky smells lifted from the covers, reminding me of Shirley. But I felt less emotions than I'd hoped. Soon as you plan your feelings in advance, child, they'll go substandard on you. Different, anyhow. —At least I hadn't hurt them or killed them. Unlike certain others. That was something, anyhow.

Was a cool clear night. I had most of a moon to guide me. Falls, North Carolina, at 2:49 a.m. looked new, more like I'd pictured Europe. I headed to the station on foot. Felt scared that cabdrivers (the town had two) might recognize me and get nosy. I swung my carpet sack at arm's end, like a child toting her book bag away from school, not towards it. Before, when I'd imagined my big getaway, it meant foreign adventures. Funny, kind new friends were eating in restaurants with me and laughing. But the nearer escape got, the quieter my picture of it grew. By now I just saw a rented efficiency I'd have somewheres. A single bed, one chair and table, a bureau with a oval mirror to back it up, some one window looking out on anything green, just a place for a afternoon nap with no interruptions. One longish nap alone. I didn't want much, I told myself. *Was* that much?

I wore my black straw hat, my finest gray suit. I wondered how long I'd last without seeing the children. (I tried not to think how they would feel waking to find Castalia scrambling their eggs.) I imagined my babies to be some kind of vitamins, a necessary food I'd shrivel without.

Still, maybe a diet wouldn't kill me. If I stayed, I'd hurt him or me, or maybe even them. I felt sure of some rash act, though I knew that toting a hatchet bed to bed would always be beyond me. Your Lucy walked.

Took the long back way to the depot. I'd saved one hundred and five dollars even. Seemed like a lot to me then, maybe because of Cap's recent losses, maybe because of the six years it'd taken to stash that amount without feeling I'd cheated the children out of extras. Before leaving I'd showed

Cassie the coffee can in the pantry marked "For Lou, my oldest daughter's education." In there, two hundred and forty-two dollars and some cents. Head to toe, my girl, a spelling champ, was college material. Twelve or twenty cents at a time, I'd squirreled aside her tuition and my getaway money. I figured Ned, even considering the accident, given his brightness and beauty, would win a scholarship someplace. Lou, maybe not. I knew her father couldn't pay.

Dogs barked at hearing my good shoes squeak. I come on a tree house in the elm where Shirl and me had built one years back. Up there, near the road, two boys sat smoking. One heard me, and he struck a match to question who I was. I stood looking up. I don't know what made me tell them. "I'm running away from home," I said. "Good," one called right down. I didn't recognize them. They were about Ned's age. Eleven is the perfect age for a boy. "Where to?" the other asked. I swung my satchel back and forth. I felt very free and nervy. Imagine, out at 3 a.m. talking to people I didn't even know by name. I hollered, "Where sounds good to you?"

"Florida," they both said nearbout in unison. They must have been talking about it right when I stopped, about where *they'd* go, given the ticket. Everybody has some escape route they would pick, their alternative to the humdrum terror of right here.

It made me feel better, how I'd told my plan, how I'd asked their advice. Almost made me feel I could head back home now. Even getting this far was somewhat satisfying. But I reminded myself: Troubles are troubles and plans are plans. I forced myself to hike toward the station. One boy hollered, "Good luck, but hey, supplies, come back." They dropped a cigarette for me. I thanked them, tucked it in my bag.

I hadn't set foot into a train depot since the honeymoon trip fourteen years before. Our Falls station, clean and white and gingerbready, always looked beautiful from outside. Inside needed painting. The waiting-room ceiling was steep. Big fedora-brim flakes of enamel had popped loose, like trying their own getaway.

Only seven people sat inside, not counting the one caged with the tickets. I'd expected a minor Ellis Island crowd, a little bustle, your finer clothes, steamer trunks marked with foreign stickers. Something.

Instead, two old men I knew from around town stretched out on benches. Their possessions rested bunched in sacks and shoe boxes nearby them. I'd gone to school with the daughter of the one snoring. I felt ashamed for her and him and for our city. Since so few local people traveled, ever— few would know that this fellow, so polite downtown, always giving chewing gum to my children, was really somebody homeless.

I eased away from the man I knew and who knew me. I settled near a dark woman in a loud tatty shawl. She had two children and, while she slept, sat breast-feeding another. A suitcase rested beside her and a hot plate in the box it'd come in. Mrs. Williams. Something about how greedy her smacking child sounded, how his mother's eyes pressed shut, mouth slung open like amazed to again be in transit. Her pretty oldest girl kept kicking a cigar butt back and forth. The child seemed to recognize me, winked.

I rushed over and read every place the Orange Blossom Special stopped. Eeny, meeny, miney, mo. I liked the train's name. I had carried a orange blossom bouquet in my wedding. Remembering the smell still pleased me, despite everything. I chose St. Petersburg because I'd once heard Poppa say, "St. Pete." Going to see St. Pete made me think of heavenly reward. I'd picked my next hometown with no real reason, the way Cap sometimes bet on horses for their catchy names alone. Now that I knew my destiny and destination, I wanted mainly to talk.

The train would leave in an hour and a half. I saw a few stray men and boys trail into the station's men's room and linger there a while. I saw a handsome woman in her fifties. She wore all shades of off-white, was busy repacking her one suitcase. A undignified task—your personal things spread out along a bench for all to see. But she conducted herself with a style downright royal. Between trains, taking her own time, she was a tall edgy white woman, tidying up. Her shoulders and fine neck she held all as one unit. Even in her mumbly state, she *presented* herself like somebody entitled to high society but on the lam from it. She wore all her jewelry at onct. It won't safe-deposit-box fine—it won't bad either. Way better than anything I owned except my carated engagement diamond. She had on pale fingerless gloves nobody'd worn since the Jackson administration. "Morning," I said. "And where are *you* going?" I didn't know how travelers acted. She took no notice. I'd been willing to wing it, though I saw I'd failed. I stood here, both hands clutching my satchel bunched before me. I just smiled. She gave me a look weary and familiar (like I'm a type of train rider she knows coming and going). Then she bent back to reorganizing white clothes. I saw they were finely made but could sure use several serious washings. Maybe they were too far gone already. Close as I stood, I couldn't help but see that— pinned to every piece—a bit of scrap paper described it: "White blse w. Belgn lace cffs cllr." Odd, since one glance'd tell you that.

"Sorry," I said (about speaking), and turned aside towards other benches, when—low, so nobody else could hear—she goes, "You're running away."

I swiveled back, waited, a little scared, my chin lifted.

She counted on her fingers. "Too many children. A husband who's ceased knowing you. No strength. Everything's sad, routine."

I nodded. "You're a wizard," I said.

"Just a woman with a memory, child. Take my advice." Her voice sounded ripe and powerful.

"Yes, ma'am?"

"Don't."

I asked why not. She settled beside her open suitcase. She patted the worn oak seat, showing where I should sit. I did. She looked around like afraid of being overheard or busted in on. Our shoulders lightly touched, I trusted her. Still refolding her fine dingy satin things, she give me the hem of a slip. I held it whilst she pressed the upper half to mine. We worked through her clothes, refolding as she spoke. It was a wonderful chore to do with a stranger, who is not one afterwards. She said, the way lots of older people will when they commence their telling, how she'd once been good-looking or better (you never heard *me* say that, did you, darling?). She claimed that three or four folks with extra-good eyes had called her full out beautiful in her prime. I told her it still showed, but she gave me a slighting wave of one glove.

"I only mention it since it matters in *my* story of leaving, and what went wrong."

Her voice was so refined. Her nails looked grimy as a miner's. I felt ashamed to notice.

Well, the lady said as how she married, moved to Baltimore, had three fine children, soon felt trapped, lost, and wasted. And tempted. To try anything. Anything but what she had day in, day out. One Saturday morning at a street fair, waiting for her young ones to get off the carousel, bored with waving at them *every* time around, she was approached by a gentleman and dandy, a man of commerce. He acted so nice. She saw him three times in secret, finally went to his rented rooms once. She bought the best stationery Baltimore had to offer, wadded up twelve sheets before she got the note right. While her children were at school, husband on the job, she left the note. It said, "I simply must." She took the express to Niagara Falls with her notions salesman. He was ten years younger than herself. He loved her, seemed to really see her as she was, a person full of promise, depth, and sense. Without even being asked, he ofttimes did pocket magic tricks, tipped his hat to strangers, was everybody's idea of a man's choice companion and any woman's darling. He wore a jade monkey on his watch chain. Said he'd got it, not at a pawnshop, but in Singapore proper. He planned to take his new love to the Orient come spring. He promised this, he showed receipts for down payments with a steamship company out of Seattle. She felt rewarded and somehow famous. She slept late. He bought her fine white brocades, lacy blouses, and a little jar of face paint which she'd never worn before. She turned heads. She gave her old ginghams and bright-sprigged calicoes to the poor. He worked days. He found a job up there in Canada hawking industrial laundry products and restaurant supplies.

One summer evening, rocking on each other, fastened perfect, she heard him cry out his pleasure, extra loud, too. Then she overheard herself join in even noisier till they both sobbed and gasped for all the boardinghouse to hear. Not caring, even proud. Next morning while dressing for work, her young man found a neighbor's note shoved under their door. It said, "You two lovebirds sounded like cats. Cats. Some restraint, please. This is Canada." He handed the paper to her, still in bed. She cried, shamed, till she heard his low laugh. He'd put on her best hat and paced in a braggart clowning way. He made her laugh. But, later, seen alone on the stairs by other shy tenants, greeted by the wizened old Indian janitor, who smiled, she felt right notorious, right unworthy.

She took a trolley to the Falls theirselves. She'd seen them many times but never tired of their force. She claimed you could hear their roar a mile off, easy—said you could see their white steam rolling to a mountain's height, steam as alive with rainbows as a greenhouse full of plants. At a overlook cave, she read this tourist plaque that told how a young girl onct slipped off this very observation deck, how her older brother jumped in and pulled her back to safety not twenty feet from the brink. Other sightseers formed a human chain and tugged the children safe ashore. Standing, reading this, shielded from spray by a new white parasol, she felt she had experienced a sign. She missed her children with a wallop long postponed. The Falls' roar seemed an abscess hollow, groaning to be filled. Her children's favorite phrases, their flukes of coloring, the very way each slept at night, curled in, sprawled out—came to her in a great and dizzying rush. She closed her parasol and used it as a prop to keep her standing. The white dress was soon covered with fine haze. Mist weighed her mutton sleeves and chilled her neck. The heroism of leaving wore off all at once—like, she explained, a prescription you cannot refill. And when she passed an arcade mirror, she saw how her face's rouge had beaded in this haze, was bleeding—dainty— down her jaw. She left a note (on fine paper) for her young man. It said she still loved him. It swore she'd be back by return train. Her letter ended: "I forgot something."

She took a express to Baltimore, caught her a taxi to the old address. The landlady wouldn't open the door. Neighbors came out, saw her in the hallway, and—clucking—hid from her. Everybody felt she was worse than a murderer to leave her children and a good man. Her family had moved. They'd left no forwarding address. She traveled by a local train to her husband's parents, their farm in far-off Indiana. It took three days. The in-laws wouldn't come out onto their porch to even see her. They hollered through their mail slot—not even *they* knew where their son and grandchildren had got off to. They also waited to receive the new address. They blamed her, and said so with a frankness she admired more than herself. Through the brass slot, three small framed photos of her face and shoulders dropped. Glass became blue powder at her feet.

She caught the fastest rail connections back to Canada. She'd promised to be home by return train. She vowed she would treat her salesman now as brother, child, and lover, he would be her family. The key to their room had been changed. A girl on crutches and a heavy man answered. On her former dressing table, she saw a parrot cage. She found that her young salesman had quit his job, cleared out. He'd stored her bags with the janitor. This man, a East Indian with a bad limp, led her to the basement. When he saw how sad she looked, he admitted that her friend had given him a two-dollar tip. Now, studying her face, the old man offered to give back half.

She thanked him but refused the money, said how very kind he was. Then, in the dark storeroom, he told her he had heard her through the walls—enjoying a certain thing. He tried to touch her neck, her bodice. She screamed at him. Nobody understood. She'd been pawed and underestimated all her life. The salesman had left no word, though she suspected the Far East. With her luggage, she revisited the Falls, deciding to either find some decent plan or jump. —"And so, my dear, when you ask me where I'm going, you see I can't say—and not from being rude, more from not actually knowing quite where the next hint might come from. I wait for leads, the news of everybody's whereabouts. Oh, they're out there, I know. I first hired a Canadian detective, then a man from Baltimore. But I ran out of money before either turned up anything. I accept jobs—I was a governess once. I've been a paid lady's companion. I get clues from time to time. A girl named what I named my girl graduated from Bryn Mawr two Junes back. My salesman turned up on the payroll of a lumber firm in Eugene, Oregon. I took the train there. But nobody would talk. You can lose your place, you know. It seems there's one groove mapped out for each of us. I slipped free of mine. I made one wrong connection. I cannot find the right track now. I can't find it."

Then she described her husband and young children in surprising and complete detail. Next she told me each tic, joke, and plaid-suit color of her missing salesman. But I felt sure her descriptions were thirty-some years past due. She said that if I saw them, any of them, or even possible look-alikes, I ought to contact her at once. She said she would jot down her address for me. The lady found a scrap of envelope in a depot ashtray. Tongue pressed between teeth, she did a very careful scrawl. The dark child shuffled past in slippers, still dreamy, still kicking around that vile black cigar butt. Her mother kept nodding so far forward, baby still sucking her, I feared she'd lean across and smother it. Local boys in nice clothes and in shabby ones kept piling into the men's room looking glazed and guilty, coming back out in pairs. Must have been fifteen in there by now, doing what? I saw our superintendent of schools, who wrote the Sleepover bulletin, father of four, slip in, glancing left and right to see if he'd been spotted, and at 4 a.m. What loneliness drove people to do this, and right in my own Falls, who'd have guessed? Everyone but me seemed homeless. She handed me the paper, she acted pleased to have yet another person on the lookout for her absent ones. The scrap said: "Contact Mrs. Carlotta Webb, care of the Atlantic Coastline Railroad (will be in club cars mostly)."

I looked at her, thanked her. I creased it, said that if I did . . . see her folks, I'd surely be in touch. I said I was grateful for the advice of her story. She smiled, seemed tired again, went back to organizing her one battered case. She noticed my concerned look at her grayed clothes. "I *am* a tidy person." She touched the folded things. "It's just . . . I wash these out with the soap in railway lavatories. Their soap's harsh to start with, then they dilute it. I have found a clever way of hanging things up to dry on a moving train—but then, you see, you risk the soot. I've finally faced it: You can't keep clean. You can't keep clean in transit."

Then she smiled, then shrugged. I walked out.

I eased on home, my neck feeling stiff, like from a long trip. I took off my good shoes, went barefoot. Sidewalks felt dewy, road's tar felt smooth as suede. Dawn was just happening by accident again. Why does dawn always look like a secret, some shock, sort of a accomplishment? Every sunrise is walled off by the dark, from like company. Maybe each believes it is the very first. Our town looked like a rosy tour of itself, news again.

I passed that elm and, in the breeze, saw a blue blanket moving, drooping off the tree-house platform. I listened hard and thought I could hear the two boys breathing. Asleep as only eleven-year-olds (outdoors with a friend on a weekend night) can sleep. It pleased me. I imagined their shouting down, "How *was* Florida?" I invented answers. I considered smoking my cigarette but needed a light. I've never bought any kind of matches but the kitchen ones.

I let myself in and found Castalia dozing at the table, one of Baby's moving-picture magazines open before her. She looked handsome spread there, her precious coat almost alive as company on the chair opposite, her twin. I felt grateful how earlier, when I'd told her what I planned, she hadn't tried to talk me out of it, just sighed, nodded the onct. Now I touched her shoulder, she looked up surprised, then she grabbed and kissed my palm, said just, "*Knew* it." Without a word, I give Cassie twenty dollars of my trainfare (maybe partly as a bribe to keep quiet, not that she wouldn't). She shoved it back, I poked it in the deep pocket of her mink, then I sent her on home to *her* children.

I started making cinnamon toast for eight. I knew the smell would lure them downstairs early. Because of the sugar, plus the value I placed on their first teeth, I'd usually only do cinnamon toast twice a year. "How'd you sleep?" I asked my first ones to trail in towards the spice-and-butter smell. Kids arrived in groups or singly, rubbing their eyes, smelling of a bitter metal smell, footed pajamas scuffing. Sleep for them is taxing, they do it so hard. I heard Ned's cane on the stairs and tip-tapping along the hall baseboard and the sound made me feel as wonderful as I'd felt terrible before. At least it was still *him*, you know? Alive and mine. Seated at table, all the children appeared fresh to me, like I'd been away a long long time. I felt myself regain—in one long greedy look—everything I'd sacrificed by leaving them. "Like logs," come their standard reply.

"How'd *you* sleep, Momma?" Lou asked, taking rag rollers from Baby's hair.

"Like there was no tomorrow," says I. She nodded but asked if it was cold in here to me. "Not specially," I told her when she looked me over. See, I was still in my good suit, even had the hat on. Near the stove, my tight shoes rested. The honeymoon satchel looked full and floppy, collapsed.

I unpinned my hat, touched the back of my hair. Nobody would ever know. In this at least, I was spared feeling ashamed. I studied them eating—each did it in a peculiar way. Baby nibbled cinnamon toast from the soft best inside out. Others came from all four corners inwards. Ned holding his with both hands now, did circles left to right. The twins chomped every which a ways. Lou, helping others, let her own get cool, then bit in perfect side-by-side squares like a mother's spelling champ *would* eat.

And standing, barefoot, my arms crossed, overdressed for here—I saw that your Lucy here, why she didn't want to murder nobody anymore. Not even him. For six or eight weeks, I felt better. Not exactly great, mind you, but better. My own true geographic self again.

Was in the ninth week, I found that—finally—I could.

This I've told you is how I got ready to run away from home. My first try had been good practice. *Then* I was ready to leave.

2

BUT with them. All eight. You didn't think I'd abandon a blind child and them darling cranky others, did you? The person, she might consider it, but when it comes to the very departure minute, she saw she couldn't. Cap, back from the good-time Norfolk hog fest, was now off to one in Richmond. Good timing. The kids were excited. I'd sent notes to school, our excuse? "A outing." True, I wanted to save myself. A person does. But that self had grown so root-bound tangled with these babies, semi-babies, plus my weedy half-growns. How could I live, separate?

They were either at school or in the yard and I was up in the dorms sorting their going-away things into piles. I'd told them: One summer and one fall outfit apiece, one toy, plus a hairbrush per three. Tidy. Baby'd asked if we'd stay overnight in a "vine-colored cottage." I'd said, "How many times I got to tell you: 'vine-*covered* cottage.'" Come a knocking now at our front door, scared me good. In Falls nobody knocks. If they know you good enough to visit at all, they come on in, and if they're nervous about walking into your rooms, they yell "Woooo?" for politeness. Captain's timing, as usual, proved awful.

A telegram: "Possible stroke of yr. Husbd. Hospitalized Richmond Livestock Convention. Not that oriented." I tipped the boy a dime and then a quarter. I stood here, one of the twins' corduroy rompers in my hand. I wondered where I'd planned going. To Winona's vine-colored Riding Academy maybe? Would she take in me and mine—as her cleaners, yard help? Local travel. Real local.

I hired a high school girl to move in with my brood whilst I took a train north to see how bad it was. My husband hadn't known me by telephone. Cassie acted insulted at my choosing this girl, not imposing on *her*. But I saw that as a tribute to my friendship with Miss Cassie Marsden. I was done with assuming stuff. You can't just assume where a friend's help's concerned.

When Ned got hurt, I learned driving. Now Cap was stricken and I hopped a train like some professional gal in the movies. Tough, but kind underneath. Riding north, I felt mixed, so mixed I got lulled neutral. I arrived there weirdly relaxed and determined. I took a taxi, glad for my recent visit to Lolly's. It all reminded me of that rough trip to see my son in the Wilmington Hospital. Only this was easier. My old man looked rested and I felt I looked good, too. But Captain couldn't notice that in me. I took his hand. "They hurt my mother," he said, almost cheerful, information. "Yes, they did."

I was glad he recalled that much. "Know who I am, sugar?"

He took a while to focus on the question and then me. He nodded, smiling behind this sudden catlike spread of whiskers.

"Who am I?" I pressed, thinking he'd give me some advice, like Mrs. Williams'. I had his mammoth hand and squeezed it. Other robed men scuffed around the ward, watching, jaded. "Who?" I bent near the father of my children. "Who *am* I then?"

He tilted back into the pillow and closed his white lashes and said very tired but very grand, "You're a little girl. You're a little girl I'm responsible for but, the curious part is, I can't remember your name."

I stood here, considering weeping, mixed, mixed up. Then something in the ward's decor—framed infantry coat of arms, crossed rifles—made me coach him. "Tell me about Simon's pocket watch. Private Simon P. Utt."

First I thought he would be sick. He leaned forward and, like some epileptic released into the joy and necessity of a perfect lavish fit, half yelled, drawing the attendant black man, "They'd get too close. You'd tell them to stay back. They wouldn't. You saw they had their muskets ready. Officers forced you to or maybe knowing all your friends were watching. Maybe just the scariness of another body rushing over the hill at you. You could see their faces . . ."

The attendant, who reminded me of Jerome—now I think on it—he come up and touched my shoulder. We both stood watching this man with the white beard nearbout hollering a story no soul here knew quite how to take. Sounded memorized. Sounded acted.

I turned to this young man in starched whites. "I think I'm going to want to see his doctors."

"You the daughter?"

"No." I shook my head. "But he's a old man I'm responsible for."

Then it was nine children and not eight. And you know? it was better.

Poppa had been fronting me some cash to keep eight kids and one old bedridden gent in shoes and sandwiches. I had a brainstorm one morning, straightening Cap's bedside tabletop. I took his pound of keys to the home of a black man who'd long worked at the livery stable. "And what's this to?" I found myself asking. And was being told that Captain still paid rent on his dead mother's boardinghouse rooms. No wonder we were broke. He'd paid for Cassie's home. He owned Winona's abandoned digs and here he'd kept Lady More Marsden's rooms for sentiment's sake. For what possible reason? " 'Cause all she things still in there," my husband's ex-employee told me. I explained that this man would receive a commission on a maybe-profitable forthcoming sale and that I was good for it. I walked right to the boardinghouse, then, at the last minute, lost my nerve. The kids were just arriving home from Lower Normal. I explained our expedition. I told how a little girl had once gone to those grand rooms so many years ago to write a school report that got a Satisfaction Minus. Ned said that was not so good. I told him it was the most that anyone could hope for. The key fit and my children picked up on my jitters. They begged permission to wait in the two filthy rockers left on the porch. I would not take no for a answer and opened the door onto the smell of smoke. First it seemed so urgent and so fresh, I wondered if we'd arrived in time to douse a fire. And then I knew the stuffy closed-up rooms had held the smell of Sherman's torches fifty years. Louisa bravely went over and jerked back velvet drapes and then we seen the armoires full of spiderweb chandeliers. There were punchbowls of Venice glass shaped big as real swans. I spied a set of the plain white Spode like the cup Lady'd clutched for her last addled years. I thought of her poor son in bed three blocks away—a family cursed. The kids felt nervous and got grimy quick. I did, too. I locked it up and found the name of the finest prissiest bachelor antique appraiser in all eastern North Carolina. I let him in and he acted stiff with me at first, but soon reserve give way and I could hear him knee-deep in some Biedermeier desk just whistling.

"Will you look at this," he asked hisself, not asking, thrilled. On the sales money, we lived. I held back no furniture, no plantation memento.

I kept nothing.

A Body
Tends
to Shine

*It is the glory of God to conceal a thing: but
the honor of kings is to search out a matter.
Take away the dross from the silver, and
there shall come forth a vessel . . .*

—PROVERBS 25:2,4

ON DAIRY CREAM nowadays, they write: "Best if used before . . ." Well, faithful visitor, my last safe-fresh year was, oh,
around 19 and 51. But here I am—subject to blackouts now and again, eyes
most gone, but still cross and talking. Old filbert face. Jerome hates it when
I run myself down. He scolds me like sticking up for a child what can't
protect itself. I just laugh.

I'd like to end with happiness. Memory stacks the deck that way, thank
God. I'm lately recalling a summer before Cap's stroke took the civilian
porch off his memory's total war museum. Before Cap blinded Ned. Some
days here in bed, I'm grinning about the good stuff. Fronts of my eyes
might've whited over like a Frigidaire's double doors—but what's locked
behind stays crisp and cool, child. And till the end, I'll fight to keep it safe,
preserved. He was often out of town. So my final blue-plate leftover special
is the perfect troubled summer of 1910.

My children would gobble any bright thing. Whatever shined, our babies
ate it. They took light to be a type of snack. I warned them, "All that glitters
is not food." But gulp, then here they'd come running to me, crying. One
June day in nineteen-aught-ten here's Lou, holding the hand of our then
third-to-youngest. "Tell her," Louisa orders baby sister. "Tell Momma what
you ate now, pig breath."

I bow from the waist, I quiz Baby: *Has* she swallowed something? (A
nod.) Please describe the missing item.

"It . . . siney," Baby explains. "Siney" was her favorite word that summer.

Lou, bored, bossy by nature, rolls her eyes. "We *think* it means 'shiny.' "

I give Louisa the glare. "Listen, you, we're lucky our Baby here can talk. Just pipe down, Miss Mouth."

"Darling?" now I'm on my knees before Baby. "Look at me. Look at Momma. Lead Momma to where Baby found whatever Baby put down Baby's throat."

Then it happens: my child, my five-year-old, our all-time prettiest girl, points to my third finger, to a callus, the brown married-life groove that shows what's missing. I glance at the drainboard where I left it.

"You ate Momma's diamond ring."

Baby nods a whole lot, ninety fat curls jostle. She gets real big-eyed, she gulps as a test then points to one side of a neck banded with chubby folds. Next the fingertip slides lower, lower, clear down to her breastbone's top. "It . . . tickle . . . Baby." Hoarse, she keeps us posted.

"Does it hurt you, pumpkin?" I shake her by the shoulders. "Tell Momma how it feels, *tell* me."

Baby smacks her lips, tasting. Baby looks off to one side, concentrating. Finally Baby reports, "It feel . . . siney."

Seems like Baby swallowed my finger and the finger is crooking itself inside her, signaling, hoping to be noticed and called back. Finally, Baby sobs. I'd been expecting that. Her yellow curls, her jumper with its animal-cracker smocking, her pearly nose, the pinkness otherwise—poor beautiful Baby.

"Are you still *married*?" Louisa, ten then, is tugging at my apron. Lou can drive you absolutely crazy. Now she bolts off, a hefty interested child, to tell brothers and sisters: Baby has swallowed their parents' being married. I half believe her. I'm that tired. I feel illegal and alone. Captain's off traveling with his business. Like lots of young mothers left at home with kids—I speak to my children like they're the grownups. I talk to adults like they're my kids. —Too, I'm swallowing mouthfuls of iron pills for anemia. Eight children, no outside help.

Luckily, my particular eight interest me. Few dull moments hereabouts. I now promise my weepy one that everything'll be fine. She'll see. "Whatever goes in has got to come out. Understand, Baby?" The poor child pries open her mouth, stuffs many dimpled fingers down her throat. Quick, I stop her. "No, the other end, darling. We'll wait. It takes a while. Let's play like Baby is a river and, say, we dropped something into one part, then we can fish it out when it floats upstream (or is it downstream?)—anyhow, you see?— not to worry. We'll check on everything you . . . on all your little . . . you can use a whole separate potty and you'll bring it to Momma every time, okay? Now, ain't this going to be fun? The pot will be your own special one, and nobody else can have the use of it. You catching the drift here, peachness?"

"Yeth," says Baby in baby talk. "I a river."

"Correct." Still on my knees, I waddle toward the cabinets underneath our kitchen sink. My burnt and bent pans always end up here last thing before they hit the garbage. Here's a old white enamel saucepan, red-rimmed, chipped with deep black flecks like worrisome moles. It was amongst my wedding gifts, some centuries before. Used to be my favorite all-time pan, especially for boiling my morning water in. I know I'm sacrificing it forever.

I hope to get Baby excited about this, like a project, see? When she acts calmer, studying her own personal pot, wearing it as a hat, trying to squint into its hollow handle, I question her. In my lightest not-to-worry voice, "Tell Momma why you swallowed Momma's engagement ring, honey dimple. What . . . ?" (I almost say "attracted you to it," but that sounds pretty dumb, so I wait.) "Just . . . why?" I grin. She must not feel judged.

Baby acts like some famous opera singer answering reporters on the deck of a ocean liner. " 'Cause . . . it . . . siney."

"Siney, yes," I say. "Shiny."

Outside, my older children sing how Baby's done gulped the bride and groom, how this couple's kids will all stay orphans till the bridal team squirms free again. Then certain brats chant:

> We know where *they'll* come out.
> We know where *they'll* come out.

I yowl for kids to shush this very instant. Cherishing her new toy, holding it by the red handle before her face like a personal hand mirror, Baby hears their teasing. She dreads the neighbors' knowing. Baby stands here dripping tears. Her face, heart-shaped, curdles.

"Say 'shiny,' " I coo to get her mind off what lays ahead. "Say it."

"Shiny," she tries. "That mean 'siney.' "

"Yeah," I smile at her. "Go sit on the pot."

SHE DID. The poor thing couldn't budge from it, for guilt feelings. I asked a favor of idle Ruth next door: Please run to Kress's. I wanted to ease Baby's mind. I ordered myself a ten-cent ring with a clear glass rock about as big as an acorn. Rhinestones are tacky, yeah—but the sunshine they trap inside theirselves ain't no different than a diamond's daylight.

For Baby, I modeled the flashy thing. Poor child already wore a pressed-looking face, like she was straining while just walking around. "See?" I acted Lady Bright. "No hurry. Momma has got lots of rings, Tulip. You only ate one. Things take care of theirselves. Just be natural and live like usual. It'll happen."

This Kress's ring was way too small. It cut right bad. I wore it full-time anyhow. Maybe it'd help my Baby to relax. I showed it off, smiling.

"That's not your *real* ring." Louisa can be right whiny when she puts her mind to it. "You're nobody's wife now," Lou points at me, using her left braid's tip. "Or maybe you're just the wife of Baby's stomach. I bet it's fake. Yeah, that's probably just a one-cent *toy* ring."

"Will . . . You . . . Shut . . . Up?" I mouth across the kitchen, but our darling, hurt, dashes screeching down the hall. Then, timid, Baby scuffs back, grabs up Pottie. (She's made a pet of it. In her loneliness, she's named it Mr. Pottie.) Baby pouts off, shy and wronged. She turns back and, full of self-pity, a family disease, full of it even for *her*—she puffs, hugging the saucepan even nearer, "Baby's onwy fwend."

It about breaks my heart. It does.

SHE SWALLOWED my ring at a bad time—but then it's always a bad time, you know? Still, I was bushed just then. Cap stayed gone weeks at a sweep then, selling and buying livestock. Kept gallivanting off, jawing with other vets about the happy bloody olden times. I felt every inch the vet of the vet. He left me high and dry in the gory present. Doc Collier had explained: Since Archie's birth, my body lacked so much iron, I could eat our entire eight-burner Wedgwood cookstove and still not break even.

Was one of them moments: I'd finally get the children all pajamaed, watered, tucked in, and storied out. Coming down the stairs at last, I'd settle on our landing's window seat just for a second so's I could rub my lower back, just so I could look out on a sidewalk clogged with family trikes, bikes, scooters.

In them years, at such a time of night, you never heard one sound you couldn't name. The Wilguses' collie and the Thorps' corgi-mix stirred each other up, barking over nothing. The Orange Blossom Special, two minutes fast, outraced its whistle. (That's how long ago this happened: some trains ran early!) Doc Collier's buggy creaked on home: he'd visited a tenant farmer's wife weeks overdue. Wind in the trees—you knew whose elms and which direction the breeze came from and what it meant for tomorrow's weather. A nod later, still slumped in the window seat, I reopen eyeballs: on morning and, already, my children nearbout late for school. What kind of mother is that? Eight hours' sleep was just a blink in the bucket of my swarming backlog. So—this here ring thing seemed the straw that broke the spine, meaning my own.

But—as will happen—Lord be praised—disasters can often interest you the most. They make you feel like a Sherlock, hired to solve your own sad case. They perk a person up and prove that World Drama is basically a homebody.

Tell me: How do you usually get your valuable rings out of *your* Baby's sweet gullet?

I don't plan to make you ill with the crudest details of my ring search. Let's just say: Motherhood! Let's say I borrowed many old newspapers from the neighbors. These unmarried people hoarded paper for just such family emergencies. But, not having no families, they lent their bounty to us instead. Seemed our house stirred up troubles enough to keep a radio soap show in daily episodes forever. Times, it felt like I had more problems than Dick Tracy. I asked poor Ruth and other neighbors to please not tell the ring news to our well-meaning pharmacist, deal-maker, and jack-of-all-trades, Luke Lucas. Folks agreed but grilled me.

Why'd she swallowed *that*? They had every right to ask and, of course, each did. "Because," I admitted, "it was siney . . . shiny. That's all Baby'll say. I just slipped it off whilst washing dishes. Always do, scared I might otherwise lose it down the drain."

"It surely seems that's precisely what's occurred here," one old bachelor smiled. (These non-parents can really Monday-morning-quarterback your life for you!)

"Yeah." I fought sounding surly. "Yeah, sir, it's a drain, okay. But the human body is the one drain that gives back. You wait. Just watch." Then I remembered to thank him for his extra *Herald Travelers*.

"See you in the funny papers," he hollered after it. It was something people said then but, that day, I took it personal.

I FED my lover of shininess prunes. Many stewed prunes. I whispered it'd be Baby's secret food. She asked me to eat some, too. "Baby feel so . . . only," she confessed. (She meant "lonely.") Baby acted scared these prunes was poison. So I gobbled the same number, matched her prune for prune—and paid for it afterwards. Seemed the least I could do.

I begged our other children not to tease her. And they tried. Kids fought not to giggle but it struck them as funny. Ofttimes, it did me, too. But I could not let on. —I worried I'd mess Baby up. I pictured Baby—years later—in the office of some counselor or social worker, certificates paving his walls, and Baby's mouth near his face, telling him the many mistakes I'd made. I imagined him going, loud, "She did *what*?"

No, I wanted to behave right. I mostly do. Odd, nobody much speaks of how hard we all try and be clever at not hurting others. That's so much of every day in the world. And yet, it's only the wars and muggers that get wrote up. How do you figure it? Stories of real-life kindness stay left out every time. (This one's bound to be lost. I mean, how minor can you get, darling? One ring, a woman running a side-street house in a town whose Main Street won't within a hundred miles of the beaten track.) Meaning: I thank you for listening so far and hope you'll stay and see how it all turns out. You keep coming back, God love you. Soon, another meal. They'll be wheeling in the chair that fetches me to Wednesday's chicken à la king, never my favorite.

Meanwhile, Baby dragged to her room, whimpering. I listened from the hall, not wanting to seem pushy. Mostly I felt glad my stone was pear-shaped and not one of them spiky claw-and-ball ones you see. I told you the gem had been my husband's own rich momma's. White gold, her initials and some Latin engraved inside of it. I pictured the grand old lady hearing of her jewel's damp whereabouts. I saw Lady More Marsden, gorgeous, spinning—like a wood lathe—in her grave.

What'd helped to smooth my ring? What'd made it a safer passenger through Baby? The wear and tear of years of household days. Why, just my taking it off every night to do our dishes, just my popping it back on, finger soapy afterwards—that'd whittled extra harm and angles off of it, that'd sent it—without a hitch—on a tour of tender vitals. There's some justice: Effort is streamlining!

Late evenings, with the wee ones finally in bed, my man counties away, me alone downstairs and pretending to read (just to prove I'd had a chance), I started thinking of my absentee diamond. My thumb and little finger kept reaching for their pet and sidekick. In stores, I'd commenced studying other ladies' rocks. None came near comparing to the shine of what I'd lost.

My ring—a minus—made me recollect my own small circle of history: me, a fourteen-year-old kid being offered that fine gem whilst seated in my momma's garden one autumn night. The moon was a witness as blue and white as the ring which moonlight lit. My breath came and went with his— one mixed huff and curl. The moon proposed. The face-up diamond blinked, "I do." Or how, left alone in my husband's big house before our first baby dropped into view, I would wander the place, bored silly, a child myself, that ring held up before one open eye. Hoping Cassie wouldn't catch me at it, I'd be bumping into walls, seeing corridors and furniture through my good-sized rock, squinting at twelve versions of every andiron and fern. It was like, needing company, I made my husband's house flash into nervous copies of itself—my practice family. How, though they shaved me every which a way for my ninth childbirthing, nobody thought to take the ring off me. And during the worst of bossy Castalia's "Push, push," my stone someway got turned around and trapped inside my red fist, got mashed so hard into the center of my palm that, afterwards, it looked to be one nail hole bruised there.

I now sat downstairs, alone, a novel open in my lap. (I'd been faking reading this same book for a year and a half.) I sat—my right hand's thumb and index finger busy being the left one's departed ring. It got so I missed that diamond, like on the very worst days—you feel you've someway missed out on your whole life.

SEEING how low she'd sunk, I started calling Baby "Momma's favorite safe-deposit vault." I told her to look on the bright side: If a robber jumped us, he'd never find the most valuable thing that Momma owned. Baby barely smiled—she was usually a genius at pleasing—too much of one. (She'd been caught curtsying to mules downtown.) She half grinned, but later I found her eating whole handfuls of salt, trying to make herself sick and lose it. I carried her around the house then, rocking the poor thing, saying, "Trust time, sugar beet. Time will bring us what we want. You wait and see."

Did I mention it was 19 and 10? Honey, that was one of our last safe years, ever. This mousetrap of a century waited up ahead of us—a whole miniature golf course of pits, traps, rapids, mines. "Trust it," I told my third-to-youngest. "Time is—like everybody says—a big nice river, sort of. And we can all float."

"But, Momma," she frowned in my arms. "You told Baby *Baby* was a river." (She was like what they claimed of Teddy Roosevelt: "He wanted to be the bride at every wedding and the corpse at every funeral.")

"Okay, fine. Go ahead and be one. I reckon there's always room for another decent river." That calmed her. I told Baby to trust time. So she did, poor thing. She would become an actress, she would begin succeeding when she died at thirty-one. They called her Baby to the end. "Trust time," I kept telling her. What choice do we have?

Then I gave her a lid for the saucepan. Nothing had happened. I wanted to nudge her memory. "It's named Mr. Pottie," Baby reminded me. "And his lid's name will be . . . Miss Lydia."

"Fine," I smiled, and hoped. Soon Baby brought me Miss Lydia tight in her place on top. Grinning, Baby looked worn but proud. "Thank you, sweet pea. Momma's pleased." I grabbed my second-best yardstick, snatched up many a newspaper. Lugging pot and Lydia, I bolted our bathroom door and spread the business section in the tub. It was all I could think of. I'll spare you the rank facts of my long long search.

To think back, seems like it took weeks, whole Sunday *Herald Traveler*s. My one wish ("Seek and ye shall find") used up all the want ads. I didn't usually have time to read a daily paper, not even a Sunday one. But now I let myself get hooked on little human-interest items off along the edge. Hadn't seen a funny paper for years. I now spared the funnies—kept them back for myself. I was usually so busy trying to save everything and everybody else—just to squirrel aside Mutt and Jeff for a midnight read seemed sinful. Which shows you, child, how far off course things'd drifted. Only now, with me nigh onto a hundred, with me alert in my last leisure, with my whole family missing—only here recent do I have hours on end for telling tales to cornered strangers and to loved ones like you. I can nap when I please. I got no chores left. Except to concentrate on staying alive another day. The *Herald Traveler* promises to send a photographer over if I hang on till my hundredth. That keeps me interested. I ain't been in the paper since a flattering wedding picture taken in nineteen aught aught. (The veil was down.) My nurses pull for me. One pretty one is pregnant and I want to stick around and see if it's a boy or girl. Zondro's now off at art school in Philadelphia. I miss her. She felt so sad about the six other freshmen girls with Mohawks, she shaved hers. She has a beau and brung him to meet me, she's answering to "Sandra" now and wearing *a dress*!

These days people let me be. It's nice but I miss work. I have substitute children. You, for one. I still can't believe my own youngsters are gone. Every one, and of what? Natural causes, mostly. Even Louisa, the practical nurse, she went like the rest—her medical knowledge no help. Times, I pretend *they're* the missing diamonds trapped for a short while in something's dark intestine. They're all lined up, ready for a comeback in the light. Their characters yet seem so stubborn, real, and hard-cut to me. Permanent. Makes me think of these ads you hear: "Diamonds Are Forever." What if my brood is still hid, safe in some spot that's body temperature exactly? Of course, I know better. Still, you hope.

Anyhoo—my older children took to camping outside that bathroom window, listening, laughing when they heard me start to rustle newspapers. Lou, standing on a apple crate like some carny barker, hung out there lording it over neighbor kids. A rounder, that child. But I could tell: Her gloomy imagination, like my own, had been kind of snagged by the human-interest angle of Baby's stem-to-stern ring toss. Louisa (named for the author of *Little Women*. I said that.) usually behaved herself. She would help me around the house—but the child always grew rangy during disturbances. Now she stood outdoors, eavesdropping on our brick home, tucked behind bushes, telling others, "I bet Momma finds a real pearl, too—one worth . . . about six thousand and something dollars. Nobody's missed it yet but it's in there okay. And I bet Momma finds the good red cat-eye shooter marble I lost when I was about Baby's age, way long ago. I bet . . ."

Ned said, dreamy as ever, "She will find . . . a whole cocker spaniel puppy in it, alive."

Then Lou asked little visitors what *they* hoped for.

I hollered till I felt dizzy. "Go away. Life is hard enough." Besides, I suspect that Miss Louisa had been charging neighbor kids admission, two pennies apiece for standing out there, listening, picturing, wishing.

Growing famous, poor Baby kept to her bedroom, burrowed under blankets, the shades drawn, ashamed like a little plague victim. She would rest, face-up, thick lashes mashed tight, one hand rubbing her tummy, another testing her forehead. Mr. Pottie and Miss Lydia sat on a chair a piece nearby. They waited like two interested cats. To her own lower body, my poor blond child kept muttering, "Hurry, oh hurry."

Three meals a day, we all waited, trying not to seem to wait. We watched her chew. Unwed neighbors, the non-parents who'd loaned us *Herald Travelers*, strolled over and, half smirking, asked, "How'd it come out?" " 'Tain't funny." I'd squint. That old bachelor sure burned me up, going, "So, is our silk purse free of the sow's ear yet?" Fists locked on hips, I snapped, "I sure see why *you* never married. You know nothing of a lady's finer points. For your information, sir, it's *all* silk purse."

Most of Falls, aisle to aisle at Lucas' All-Round, pumped me for nastier details of my ring hunt. I crossed my arms. No way would I betray my darling. As I looked and looked for the family jewel, my search's background—the daily paper—seemed to bulge with one word. "Ring." (There must be a name for that—how, once you find some fact or notice a phrase—the earth just rushes forward to show you how often it's been right there

under your nose.) "Ringleader Confesses." "The Raleigh Opera Society hopes
to do—one work at a time—the entire *Ring* in the next six years." "Prosti-
tution Ring Exposed." "Ringling Brothers and Barnum & Bailey's four-ring
extravaganza opens." —I commenced believing: *Soon, everything I'd ever
missed would be returned to me. With interest.*

NIGHTS, I started picturing it in there.

Just as I dozed off, I'd be drifting in that half-life state that's often smarter
than my daylight best. Then the jewel came clear to me as in some X ray.
I knew exactly where, inside of Baby, my solitaire had rested for the night.
In darkness the exact size of my child, it winked. Sometimes, when I'm
upset, I'll twist the ring around and round, hardly thinking. It now seemed
to do that on its own—lonely inside Baby, "only" inside Baby. I'd snooze
and make up crazy thoughts (or, no, they'd made me up):

How, say, the ring's clear stone is really a eye, see? Faceted for storing
every sight. Each facet is like another angle in its high IQ. The gold band
behind this eye is the circling skull that holds the eyeball steady, that saves
up memories of things it sees. Then I let myself imagine what-all it was
getting to view, for free, right now, as Baby breathed just across the room
(I'd moved into the girls' dorm, she was scared of sleeping alone with It in
her). Easy to picture the ring's total voyage. A Cook's tour, it tours where
this cook's own home cooking tours, breakfast to dinner. I see my prettiest
girl's interior views. Here's a canoe's rocking route: It passes through great
pink caves, blue arenas, slick and necessary tunnels of love, sluice gates,
sewers of museum beauty. On a floating pleasure cruise, the diamond swims,
inching through a whole coiled map of rivers. It swims so slow because it
really likes it in here. A year-round 98.6 degrees—the Florida of my infant's
health. —But, wait, what if it snagged somewheres inside of Baby, what if
it chose a spot, settled down, started gaining carats month by month? My
own five-year-old will carry it full-term. Newspaper reporters wait near
Baby's favorite swing set, hoping for interviews. Finally, I've told her what
to expect. I hold her hand, I go, "Push, Baby." Out slides a gem big as a
goodly coal chunk—hot ice shoots into the rubber hands of waiting Swiss
doctors. Over their surgery masks, they wear dark glasses so's they can bear
to look onto such brightness. "Never in all our years," they say. Headlines
in the *Herald Traveler* and other world papers:

SUDDENLY FAMOUS TOT BRINGS FORTH HOPE DIAMOND, ONLY QUADRUPLED
Authorities Mystified

These were my odd selfish thoughts whilst half asleep. Maybe I was
going partway crazy. My child's medical glamour was running away with
me. But, honey, even wide awake, this much I understood: No painted
picture, no treaty, nobody's genius can compare with the wonders one ring

might be privileged to glimpse on its ride through a regular baby's ordinary digestion.

You know, right often the body is the best thing we've got going for us. A body itself is a shiny object. Something!

"LET'S MAKE this accident a mite more educational," I told myself and then the kids, my usual conversation's echo. I bossed Lou and Ned into looking under D in their school encyclopedias. "I want A-plus oral reports," says I. Even neighbor kids gathered. For all I knew, Lou charged them for the honor. Archie grinned in his high chair. Lou cleared her throat, announcing the *Britannica* claimed: It takes your sifting six tons of ore to find one pound of jewels. "Like life!" goes I. "Imagine." And they all did, I could feel them—the echo again. Then Ned quoted *World Book*: How famous diamond cutters, at day's end, will gather their floor sweepings and burn these to make sure no stray carat gets chucked out with the daily dust. "Fancy that," I shake my head. "Fire means nothing to them. They eat it for breakfast. —But wait, where's Baby herself? *She* should be here."

Only then did we notice: Nobody's heard the usual pacing, not a sniffle since her breakfast of hot prune juice and bran. We found the door locked. I sent Lou around to shinny up the drainpipe. Lou came across a plug of Baby's best crinoline, ripped and flying from our gutter's metal cross brace. Onct inside, we saw she'd taken Mr. Pottie and Miss Lydia. One of the twins mumbled, "Uh-oh, the dish run away with the spoon." Baby'd hit the road.

Louisa knew where we all filed our secrets. She rushed right to her sister's sock drawer and announced that the savings passbook was missing. (My husband had started all our children with five-dollar accounts. Most soon whittled deep into their capital, owing to excess candy purchases.) Not Baby! She deposited a few coins each week. We never knew how she earned a cent. Whenever Baby turned up at the bank with her white calfskin handbag clutched before her, the head teller, a maiden lady, made much over our thrifty dumpling.

Now our diamond reading group rushed downtown to People's and Farmers' National Bank. Miss Pritchard, the head teller, smiled her best savings-account grin. (She had no checking anywheres in here—a young woman already far too willing to start being old.)

"Well, well. We understood your third-youngest is heading for Hollywood, California, to be a moving-picture star. She even had her cooking gear along."

"Of course," I tried to sound in charge for once (though my honor guard of kids gave me judging looks). "And when did our famous one take off for points west? Look, Miss Pritchard, tell me how much my child had stashed with you-all. What might Baby's nest egg now total, please?"

"That," Miss Pritchard, bun in a snood, eyeglasses on a black cord, pencil held by a silver chain, brass sweater guard preventing any wind or vandal from getting her black cardigan even two inches out of place, "is confidential. Bank policy, alas."

I turned to leave—ain't no arguing with such rule-book souls. (Not five years later, she'd be stretched out here on the marble floor of People's and Farmers' after trying to stop a holdup, after body-blocking some drunk man who'd grabbed sixty-one dollars, a drunk that our duty-proud unfairly unloved Miss Pritchard *forced forced forced* to shoot her.) But today she stopped me, one touch on my shoulder. She whispered she'd lift a certain number of fingers. I'd draw my own conclusions about what she was signaling, okay? That way, see, she wouldn't compromise a soul. Soon as she broke a rule for me, I liked her very much. The more you love the law, the more you love the ones that break it right. We all cried at her funeral.

By the time Miss Pritchard, using both her ringless hands, poked up fingers totaling thirty-two, I felt ready to call in the State Police. I pictured my poor Baby, footloose, full of jewel, headed west toward stardom. How does a unemployed five-year-old earn that kind of money? Beside me, holding my right fist, squeezing it so the dime-store ring hurt me even more, freckled Louisa, a bit jealous but real worried, gaped my way, eyes large, and admitted: Each Saturday, Baby'd been bustling downtown—all starched and rosy. Then, on the sidewalk before Robinson's Billiards (rough trade at its most lubricated), our Baby danced. For money.

"*Now* you tell me," I scold our eldest. "Eating diamonds, plus panhandling nickels off of sentimental drunks? That child's got a future if we can catch her in time."

We rush past Lucas', where Luke hisself hollers, "A certain hurrying young person purchased a lifetime's supply of breath mints here not thirty minutes back, is all I'll say." So we check two country roads bound west. Find nothing. Then we scout the train depot, looking under each booth of the ladies' room, making enemies. Luckily, it being but 19 and 10, there won't no aeroport yet, which saved us a trip.

Well, I had to go back home, had to settle at my own kitchen table before choosing what step to take next. By now, child, you know me: one of those people that's no good whatever at deciding important things on the street amongst total strangers. My house was always like bifocals that jerk world-blur to something sharp and clean. (This Home I'm in, it ain't home. No wonder I can't see good.)

I'd settled at my kitchen table, sighing, debating between sending telegrams or screaming, when I notice this tiny gift-wrapped bundle near my right hand. I take the thing up, rip it open. I half believe Baby herself might leap out of this four-inch casket. Here, slotted in its rich brown velvet case, I discover a ring—not my own, but a real gem—I'm not sure what type of stone it was—purplish, full of light, bound by a simple yellow-gold setting. At the bottom of the box, I find a price sticker (from Cuthrell's Jewelers of Distinction—locally our best). "Thirty-four dollars," I make a little cry and sprint upstairs. I find her doubled over in bed, sobbing.

"Your life savings," I shout. I test her for fever. "Your short life's total savings. No fair."

I explain, though the ring's beautiful—amazingly tasteful for a five-year-old to pick—we'll have to take it back. "And you're never to go spend any such amount on your mother ever again, you understand me?"

Baby confessed to her pillow, "It not nice as your one, Momma. I show the man the one I want. I put my finger on their big glass box. Baby point and point. But he look at all Baby's money, he say Baby can only have *that* one. Yours is better but . . . Baby ate. I point and point, Momma. They won't give me it. Baby feel so . . . only. All Baby's money not enough money, Momma."

"Don't," I say. We hold on to each other, blubbering while my family (and strangers' children) mill around watching us from the hall. Their eyes go narrow, their arms folded. Louisa circulates among them, collecting a few more pennies. For kids, this day has turned out even better than expected. Meaning: worse.

SOON. It had to happen *soon*. I couldn't go on like this. When I seen just how low Baby's morale had slipped, I invented a trip for her, not to Hollywood, but at least around town. We'd sock her money back into People's and Farmers'. We would do chores, just me and her, nobody else. The others begged to come. I let my child wear all four Sunday petticoats plus a little white-sprigged hat from last Easter. Baby did love that hat. (Some five-year-olds are already as vain as any grownup ever gets. It's funny to see.)

Making a fuss over the poor child, I was halfway down our front walk, was holding Baby's spongy little hand, when Louisa yells, running out the house. She's carrying Mr. Pottie and Miss Lydia. "You forgot you-all fishing net." She jiggled these by the handle, like popping popcorn—clowning. But I saw that Louisa, left in charge here, was dead right. Away from home, it might happen anywhere, our golden moment.

In the prescription wing of Lucas' All-Round Store, Luke, who'd taken a night-school course in pharmacy, nodded toward my child. He studied her—all gussied up and puff-sleeved. Baby held her pot and lid in that proud quiet way she has, had. "So, ladies," said now-white-haired Luke. "Covered-dish supper at the church tonight?" That man had to know everything.

"No, sir." I saw my child flinch, scared I'd squeal on her. "Nope, let's say we're carrying around a family recipe." I winked at Baby, full of shine and secrets. She liked that. Luke was forever running "How Many Jelly Beans in This Jar?" contests. He was a demon with his mortar and pestle.

"So," he looked up. "A dish made with some secret family ingredient, is it?"

"Yeah," I admitted. "Luke, this pot's kept aside, special-like, for . . . the secret ingredient all to itself. And you know what's odd? This particular ingredient's found in every American home. But nobody ever stops to consider it. The stuff is the opposite of attention-getting. Oh, yeah, it's been in our family for years. Whole generations. Goes way back."

"Secret, hunh? Ingredient, is it?" We'd got Luke interested. Baby and me pivoted to leave. "Wait. I bet it's . . . baking soda," Mr. Lucas hollered. I squinched up my nose: meaning a No answer. "Okay," he leaned over a display card of toenail clippers. "I'll go with . . . bay leaves!"

"Is he even warm, Baby? Tell our favorite storeman that much. No more." I hunkered down beside my darling and jewel.

Luke bribed her with some butterscotch candy. Just one hint? Was the secret ingredient liquid or solid? Bigger than a bread box? What color? Shrugging, the child acted bored but willing. "Baby gives him one teentsy hint—it siney!" I saw she hadn't understood. Just as well.

We dragged past the baseball park, bound home. It'd sure been a long long day and I felt this in that achy clock: my lower back. I was ready to admit—I'd lost the ring. I felt justified in acting extra bitter for a week. What *good* is the world? That same second Baby starts the dancing. "Oh Lord." We just made it to a grim ladies' room behind the dugout. It was all gray cement, green mold, and lipstick on the mirrors. In my panic, I slipped Miss Lydia under Baby, then quick replaced it with Mr. Pottie proper. Both Baby and me heard something, metal, loud, go clank. Sounded like some shrapnel from her poppa's stories, like it weighed eight pounds easy. A red-faced Baby grinned. A red-faced Baby laughed, then, pale-faced, cried and cried. I clamped Miss Lydia on, real tight. Finally semi-happy—with results warm before us at my wrist's far end—the child and me marched home, hand in hand, arms swinging.

The human body *is* the only drain that gives back all it's given . . . more!

2

WE DECIDED to make a party out of our regaining everything. I offered Baby a lot of the credit (trying to build her up, don't you see. It's what we called "just good psychology"). Soon as we hit the kitchen, I soaked that ring for four straight hours in a brew of ⅓ straight ammonia-bleach, ⅓ Oxydol soap (which could blister rowboat paint), plus *scalding scalding scalding* water.

Pottie and Lydia got drowned in the same solution till their last red enamel flaked off. Baby was allowed to keep these utensils. By now they meant something to her. She took the clean Mr. Pottie outdoors and planted zinnias and one Easter lily bulb in him. Settled on our back porch, she taped her pot with a sign she'd dictated to me: "Here It's Baby's Secret Garden. Keep Out or Pay." Miss Lydia waited alongside. Baby'd nested betwixt them and—when I looked out my window over the sink—I saw her, arms Xed across her chest, face set, muttering—guarding friendly items like she'd heard Austro-Hungarian spies were out to kidnap them. My third-youngest stayed there—relieved, jumpy, proud—explaining things to herself till dinner.

Come mealtime, the twins waltz in with construction-paper place cards shaped like big rings, tinfoil being the diamonds. "Such clever children. Whose *are* you!" I touch their heads. With my grizzled husband away, I put out six Kress's candles—meaning: a special event. We will now celebrate the stone's homecoming.

My children all line up to study the now-famous ring. (Famous to us, at least.) "No pushing," says I. "There's plenty for everybody."

"Show Archie, Momma," Baby says. "Look, dat so coot. Archie wants to see." I peel off my apron and settle. Ned pulls out the chair for me. News of my jewel's comeback should be in the *Herald Traveler* but, of course, it won't get mentioned noplace.

Soon as we've started on the corned beef and cabbage, Lou announces I can consider myself married again. I take off the rock then slip it back on. The twins hum "Here Comes the Bride." Looking around the candlelit table, it seems—for one second—like I had these children without any man's help. All solitary mothers must get these flashes. A willful woman's stubborn self-seeding—just another inside job and daily chore. Of course, my wee ones look so much like him. I can never believe very long in my being a self-starter.

Lou, especially, setting here beside me, shows her pop's sober open mood of a face. Observing it all, believing but little. Tonight, she droops, real sad. Slow, I understand that, in trying to keep my high-strung Baby calm during this upset, I've ignored my brightest if maybe plainest-looking child. Lou (an entire planet on tap betwixt her braids) usually behaves right well. Till she feels left out. Then, honey, you better hire somebody to watch her.

With my free hand, I find hers under our tablecloth. Lou's grip bites into my Kress's ring. I now slip that jewelry off, awarding it to her hand, in secret. (Oh, but kids respect secrets—everybody's trust fund.) The rhine-stone ring, too small for me, wobbles on Lou's knuckle. I bent its soft metal hoops to fit.

Now I show off my real diamond, one Zelia couldn't work off Lady's scarred finger, one lost to me then boomeranged on back. "It ain't ever looked better," I say. "Will you all just study the fire in it? Like it's happy to be back. My ring means more to me than ever. Why, I'd quit noticing it. Now I'll never take it for granted again. Thank you, Baby. Really." Smiling, shy, Baby nods, accepts. (Odd, I only said that to make her feel better. But, in the way you do, of a sudden, I found I meant it.)

How lucky I am to have pretty smart and really healthy children, plus jewelry that comes back when nature, daylight, greed, and gravity all call.

Lou now stands, formal. Others have been nudging her, whispering.

"Okay," she sounds so serious it scares me. Under the cloth, she lets my hand fall free. I miss her heat. "Okay, I made up a poem that some people on our street have already memorized. *They* want me to say it"—grinning, she points at brothers and sisters, who cheer. Baby goes extra still.

Myself, I do not particularly care to risk hearing Louisa's poesy. But— no matter what the topic of it—you cannot squelch a poem from your own child. Especially with candlelight at dinner and your husband out of town. So I say, "I'm sure yours is a very good one." We all wait. I tense some. I notice Baby fidgeting like hiccups looking for a home. Then Louisa clears her throat.

"Okay . . . No, not yet . . . Yeah, okay . . . Now."

POEM
Baby at the sink, saw something "siney."
Baby ate it up, came out her heinie.
The End

Three laughing children fall off chairs. Two chime their water glasses. I turn quick to Baby. There's one second when, batting wet blue eyes, she's about to go screeching down our hall. Then, slow (it's hard for her and that makes me feel real proud), she shrugs. She makes a "who cares?" mouth. Baby's already grown older! It's like she's admitting: Louisa's poem is true. Which, though blunt, I reckon it mostly is. We all study Baby. Others crawl back up onto furniture. They quiet some—waiting for a usual Baby con- niption fit. But, knowing what we all expect, the child acts right dignified.

"So what!" says she. "Baby didn't know, and Baby not ashame. Look here," she points to my fine gem, unharmed by her body's best tries at making food of it.

To cover up my kids' earlier picking at each other (I just hate it when they do like that), I stand to clear their plates. Ned is asking, "What's for dessert?"

"Tonight, I've got you all a light dessert," I say. I shove my expensive worldly-wise diamond down toward Kress's candle flames. Gem light flings itself all over our dining room. My inherited ring makes coleslaw of the rainbow. I aim my stone side to side like some smart salesgirl, demonstrat- ing. Pear shape throws mild specks, bright watercolor dots, stripes, X's, a short-lived chandelier across walls, over my children's living faces, onto window glass with night pressed black behind it.

Louisa, still standing, seems quieted by the show. She blinks then steps around my chair to Baby's. She tugs off the dime-store ring, grabs her sister's left hand, and—moving bold as a groom that means it—shoves the jewel hard onto Baby's pudgy finger. Then Lou bends, tightening soft metal yet another notch.

"But . . ." Baby lifts her right shoulder, tips her right cheek to it, dimples deepening. "But . . . why . . . me, Weeza?" (Some folks' whole life is a fishing trip for compliments.)

"Because I'm oldest is why." Lou, square-built, truth-telling, straightens.

" 'Cause they expect me to and because you're such a . . . total . . . baby. Because you're our baby, Baby. You're all our Baby."

"Sanks," comes the answer. Our eldest sits. I resettle myself and find Lou's hand. I keep my ring held still on tabletop, hostess to light.

Other children have hopped up (no "May I be excused?" tonight). They run now, really chasing colors that keep beating with my pulse. Wallpaper takes on light as a project, meal, and spangle. Kids fling up their arms as eyes go animal wild. Twins jump to reach the really good spots burning above the sideboard. Ned drags over a chair so he can climb up quick and touch a circle. His head pokes into spotlight as he pretends to eat all brightness before it dies. The deeds and sufferings of light. Such noise in here. We're all laughing some. Kids trot around and round the table. Only Louisa, Baby, and yours truly are still seated, watching. (I know: All that glitters is not gold. True, too: All that glitters is not food. But, honey, all that glitters glitters. That is fact—like your body is a fact.)

Lou's grip tightens. My mouth swims to her nearest ear. "You been so good during this long wait, child. With Poppa gone so much lately, I depend on you. I overdo. And I know what being considered a strong person can cost a girl—you're so fine, Louisa."

"Not really," says she. "Thank you."

"What?" Baby slaps tabletop. "You all talk about Baby and talk about Baby. *Tell.*"

I can only offer her my elbow to hold—I've got to keep this ring hand in the middle. I aim my light just so and our dining room is a stained-glass window, chicken-poxed with happy tints. Such a noisy excellent madhouse we've got going here.

That yellow near one wall sconce, it's the exact farewell yellow of a healing bruise. And on the tinfoil of a place-card gem, coppery light flips itself to crib-quilt pink then turncoats to the greenery of seaweed, gills. Oh, sixty shades of blue. And, as I watch, my children—skipping through these broken plates of churchy light—change, bit by inch, into the silly saints. One diamond lays a million checkmarks on us all.

NOW THAT's over except the recollecting. Time has come and turned me this hickory-nut brown. Not that I was ever no front-page beauty—my face was Section C at best. Time's made a oversight in leaving me propped up here but, oh, it'll be back. Maybe a person is "best if used before . . ." but I'm still enjoying full sunlight and your softer foods.

Even so, some nights in this place, sleep gets real hard. The world's grown noisier—these roars and booms and sirens you can't trace or figure. (Not like Falls then, when every slammed door was on a first-name basis with you.) Nowadays you hear our new aeroport, and you were never ever on a plane. You lay in a bed that, within two days of your dying, will be another person's bed. You hear the world's static a-hissing and spitting right outside your window. You don't even need a wireless set to pick it up. Wired, you *are* one! —A person rests less and less at my age. It's one gentle way they get you ready. Finally you've grown so homesick for quiet and a good night's sleep—you'll throw yourself at Eternity just to enjoy them first eight restful hours of it.

Sometimes, trying to doze, that ring story will come back on me, like a rich food. Some nights, half asleep, I feel I've done become the thing. I tell myself: It's always been like that for me, lost and found. "We'll see." Maybe I'm a permanent stone washing through some darkness? But, to me, the blackness itself seems familiar, kind of personal—like it's the shadow zipped inside one of my babies. Seems like I helped to start the darkness where I'll end. I'm *one* of its mothers, anyhow. —Other nights, *I* get to be a baby. But some item that's supposed to be real valuable (the world) has turned into a fishhook, has snagged—caught and killing—somewhere deep in me.

Now I have time for thinking up such silliness. Which is good.

NOT TWO days ago, I was laying here at 10 a.m. full of French toast, recalling what the *World Book* said way back when: about the diamond-cutting district in Amsterdam, which is Holland. Come shop's closing time, the boss is naturally scared he'll throw out some lost chip of preciousness. So he makes the evening cleaning ladies do this: They dump all their sweepings into a open metal pot. They set such gunk afire. Flames take care of paper scraps, burn the usual lint, scorch what threads and nameless crud will sift into corners of any busy place by workday's end. Then, all the cleaning lady does, see, she pokes through them ashes. And sometimes—sure enough— there, still safe among black crackling soot, she'll find a few beautiful lost stones—blue-white brilliants—too pure to let fire bother them, gems stronger than the earth's best damage.

Honey, I think: My life has been like this—the frying off of extras. And whatever is left, whatever still shines in the hand—why, that's what I call Mine, darling. Them's the keepers.

I LOVED my children. My children are all gone.
I loved my ring. Here . . . look . . . I still have it.

Music Changes
During
War

Sing unto him a new song. Play skilfully with a loud noise.
—PSALM 33:3

Here's the last of his better tales:
Once, in a time of smoky war on a cliff with the clearest of Virginia river views, there lived a peaceable young rich girl—musical and plain.

Virgin-ia. The commonwealth was named for Elizabeth I, the Virgin Queen.

Given the personal talent and hygiene of our last tale's heroine—young Miss Randolph sure deserved to be her poppa's dream of a youngest child. Three roustabout blond older brothers gently teased baby sis, their worthy favorite. Unison Randolph turned fifteen the day her father and brothers rode from the plantation house to war. Unison and her mother stood on the portico waving lace as big as flags.

In Virginia at this time, child, lace sort of was . . . a flag, to save.

Men left girl and mother to tend the place and mind the family name. Off gents trotted toward General Lee's Army of Northern Virginia. Unison was not fifteen long when word arrived: She now had but one relative left living, Momma. These things happened—especially in Virginia '61–'65. Unison's poppa had been killed outright by a cannon volley that'd also claimed his beloved Arabian horse. Her eldest brother, a strong swimmer, drowned under strange conditions during a river crossing. The other two were shot within three days of each other while foraging in different parts of North Carolina's Piedmont.

Six months later, a division of Southerners chose to encamp around her big house and across family acreage. Till now, the ladies Randolph had turned their grief toward good works amongst local sharecroppers and the few blacks who'd not run off. Unison endured on the comforts of her expert keyboard playing, she lived with her mother's quiet patriotic woes. Most every night, skinny Unison took to her huge four-poster, where—under quilts, so as not to bother Momma—the child cried, saying names of her three older brothers over and over again, "Edmund, Billy, Keane, Edmund, Billy, Keane." Maybe this might keep her favorite boys real? Maybe this would restore them, blond and fresh-mouthed, to the world? Brothers had all been flirts and hell-raisers, brilliant horsemen and big spenders. How she missed their constant pointless noise.

With a division of fellow Rebs bivouacked near the mansion, two grieving ladies had sudden company, assured work. Oh, to be needed again. The yard and acreage sounded and smelled once more of men. Young Unison could stand on the veranda and stare at a zone dusty from ridden beasts, prickly with tent tops. She could hear a gritty raucous clanking she connected with hardware and with the weapon-prone male of the species. A graceless sound, brutal, smacking more of physics, less of niceties—but even to Unison's trained musician's ear, it had a order, child. She noted each passing gray uniform's rips and missing brass buttons. Unison so longed to act kindly towards every Rebel present, even the enlisted ones. She succeeded—faithful listener, as we soon will see—little Unison Randolph oh she succeeded all too well.

My husband was a groom then. Thirteen years of age, he'd been demoted from bugle boy. Being seriously tone-deaf proved something of a drawback. Your waking at five-thirty under a dew-sogged tarp is never easy . . . but when what's waked you is flat then sharp every morning—it'll wear on you, child.

But, by now, you, a veteran of the veteran's veteran, *know* all this.

So . . . another billet was offered young Marsden. He got sent to help tend horses. What harm could he do there?

Will now lived stuck off with beasts at woods' edge. Birds gathered to be near the oats. Willie liked that part. He liked birds. He was good at keeping horses well watered and nicely groomed, not that anybody noticed. Nights, he got to talking to his charges—he explained how his own people's home stood near a river much like the Randolphs' grand pile yonder. He described his favorite home spots for finding muskrats' burrows. Will told horses about a nifty little home-woods cave that dripped steady as a mansion's clocks'll click. Horses absorbed his voice's sound waves natural as couches will indoors—but remembered little, understanding little, being horses.

Will and others admired Unison Randolph, her kindnesses around camp. Sometimes she made cookies and distributed them by hand till she ran out. Some fellows saved the cookies, good luck, in their pockets.

A new lieutenant arrived in camp, his magnificent bay wobbled under gear enough to equip a minor traveling circus. Lieutenant Prothero owned a three-paneled mirror—how it glinted during his gallant approach! It almost seemed that mirror was a kind of cannon: sunlight dragged to earth for purposes of warfare.

Lieutenant Prothero was handsome in a plump obvious way. You almost resented noticing that so fast, and of course, the splendid whiskers. He brought folding camp furniture made of ebony and sterling. Plus he traveled with his own portable potty seat to spare his visiting the common latrines. All these extras had arrived strapped onto the Lieutenant's thoroughbred. The Morgan walker seemed to hate that. Who wouldn't? The beast snorted as asthma sufferers'll snort. This gelding boasted its own after-hours outfit— a tailor-made blanket stitched from the Fraser clan's hunting plaid.

Prothero's first night, he set up his looking glass. He got out two monogrammed solid-silver hairbrushes. The young Lieutenant kept four kinds of French perfume in squirt bottles for spraying during tense times onto warrior pressure points. Not even Miss Unison Randolph owned so many Europe scents.

Boy he rigged his three-part mirror with candles. This got others' attention. His mirror, like music stands of the day, featured slots for tapers around its frame. Evening fell. The Lieutenant arranged his ebony camp chair, clamped on his pince-nez, set to combing his silver-blond whiskers, trimming sideburns. He did this in plain view of everybody. From a distant veranda, Unison Randolph and her sickly mother sat in rockers behind hand fans that fluttered just beneath uplifted chins. The fans slowed, ladies watched a man groom the way some touring actor in a sideshow might. What did it mean really?

A poker game in progress, other men gathered just opposite, near the campfire. They turned to study young Prothero, new here, exceedingly new here. He lounged at his makeshift table (the mounted platform of a rolling cannon). He was staring into hinged silver. Many times apiece, he combed his either platinum eyebrow.

It hurt your feelings, watching. You felt like an intruder, but shouldn't *he* feel odd? When rowdy enlistees hollered certain wisecracks, the young officer absentmindedly waved them off. Salvador Magellan Smith, homely as ever, finally hollered, "See something you like, sir?"

Prothero called back, "I see three times more of it than anybody in this wilderland has any right to, thank you, soldier." Then he made a show of jutting out his excellent profile and he groaned with seeming pleasure.

Well, men laughed. They more or less had to. When people joke about their little failings, they dare you to dislike these. Sal shook his homely head. "Boy's handsome. But ain't nobody *that* handsome."

Who would complain about mirror gazing by a young man so seemingly lonely at the front? Who, except other lonely men here? Who but the surviving mother and sister of three boys and one older man, gents once maybe even better-looking than this dandy?

Prothero's careful treatment of hisself seemed less sissified way out here.

The care was so direct and simple. His perfumes, more a superstition than a comfort. Grooming came to seem a joyless maintenance on some large investment.

Passing Prothero's mirrors, other fellows avoided viewing theirselves. If you've been living in open fields for two years straight—it's better not to see the damage up close, all at once, and from three cruel sides, magnified.

THE YOUNG Charlestonian introduced hisself to everybody, twice. He asked for names and hometowns and you saw him memorizing these. Even Willie Marsden, Prothero's assigned groom, seemed worth the Lieutenant's notice. Prothero's voice was smokesome, rich—sleek black like caviar. The new man walked in a rolling particular stride. He used a pince-nez fastened to his vest's lowest button, held by a two-foot-long grosgrain cord. Prothero circulated behind solid handshakes, acting like some candidate overripe for office. He took time to ask his thin groom about the boy's hometown and folks. When the Lieutenant found he knew a Charleston cousin of young Private Marsden, he showed the pip a new respect. Prothero remembered all that Willie told him. The Lieutenant loved hearing about Will's tantrum-prone talcum-white mother. Prothero would wander from his mirrors out where horses were tied. While Willie curried the officer's Morgan named Target, the Charlestonian asked to hear a certain tale again, again.

Young Willie enjoyed grooming Target—a creature russet, high-strung, and overpretty as Prothero hisself.

Unlike Yankees, who were issued their mounts, Confederate soldiers brought their own animals to war. Plugs, Arabians, swaybacks, mules—you can imagine: any Animal Army gets all kinds, too. I maybe said that.

My late husband considered Prothero's steed to be the Thomas Jefferson of quadrupeds. Other beasts looked at Target as if into some candlelit mirror that showed them their own raw spots, swaybacks, flyspecks. They bit Target. The officer's blooded Morgan was out of Upperville's top-drawer stud-book. Target had been overbred for peacetime. During war, what with so much noise and shouting and all, Willie claimed the creature seemed a pinched nerve, five-gaited. Sounds of shelling so scared the beast, it often shook. Instead of whinnying, Will heard the poor thing give off a kind of low humanish cough, "Ah-her, Ah-*her*." Tied amongst grouchy quarter horses and stinky pack mules, Target seemed some visiting celebrity in its satin-lined plaid. Only when young Will commenced to brush and talk to the poor beast did its trembling ease some. For a few minutes at a stretch, it half forgot the war. But—like with soldiers—never for long, child.

Prothero had inherited a silver sword from his great-granddad. It'd been awarded for bravery by the great Washington hisself. It said so right on its scabbarb and Lieutenant Prothero, if asked, would show you. Others said that, out here, the Society boy's oily cordial habits sure seemed wasted, kind of sad. "Way I figure," one private remarked. "He can't *help* it."

Nobody liked him.

. . .

EVEN SO, the Chaplain felt sure Prothero would become a favorite of the division's present hostesses. Reverend set about arranging a fittingly formal first meeting with the Widow Randolph and her refined daughter. The Chaplain had retired from teaching classics at Chapel Hill. He was a walking bloodline studbook for the entire South—he had personally met the Lieutenant's father when Prothero, Sr., was governor of South Carolina.

Unison Randolph and her mother issued officers a invitation to tea on Thursday. Told of this, Prothero smiled and spent extra time at his mirrors. For all his courtesy, something felt unfastened and wide open just under his grins and compliments and bows. Something comical in his confidence charmed you. To muddy soldiers, he identified nearby trees by their full Latin names. When one corporal said, "So what?" the Lieutenant grinned and shrugged. Prothero's certainty seemed to take its own silliness into consideration and to feel even better for that. His nightly vigils at the looking glass told one and all, "I know that I risk *seeming* ridiculous." It someway made him less so.

Two days before tea in the ladies Randolph's west parlor, gossip followed: The Lieutenant had deeply miffed superior officers at his last post. Rumor didn't yet say how. "Cowardice" seemed likely.

Unison Randolph was not glimpsed the full forty-eight hours before the officers' tea. Maybe she was being mysterious for the Lieutenant of the mirrors. Maybe she was sewing herself a new black dress. Troops missed her.

Prothero had already heard much about the young heiress. How she reminded every single soldier of some one cherished person left at home. How eager she was to make all the fellows stationed here feel natural. Unison (it was a family name) showed officers no favoritism but circulated among enlisted men, asking after their well-being, remembering the names of their children, their hometowns. She wrote letters for the illiterate (there were many) and the wounded (there were many). She had a talent for cutting silhouettes from black paper. She did "sittings" of men who waited in line for hours, who then mailed likenesses home. Outlines were merciful in how they eliminated splotches, three-day beards, and the crow's-feet even boys developed from living out of doors for years now. Strange to see a hardened old soldier walking around with a weightless him-shaped piece of paper curling in one hardened hand. "Look, buddies—me, only little!" What gentleness we show our own images! Unison explained to some subjects: The very word "silhouette" had a curious history. It was the name of a stingy French Minister of Finance—a man so tightfisted that newspapers of the day showed him only in black Punch-and-Judy outline. His name became the name of this itself. Monsieur Silhouette. Unison smiled, her scissors creating a nose.

"You don't say," soldiers said. "Live and learn," they said.

She was not beautiful. Her face was too oval and her hair—pulled back— could make the earnest head seem almost egglike outdoors at noon. Her hands might be beautiful but she was not. Unison Peyton Randolph carried herself with a quality of patriotic mourning that men found moving and familiar. Suffering, which breaks down some people's bearing, makes others' even grander, prouder. This is hard to explain, but the dignity of her public-spirited pain made the division see Miss Unison as more a man—less girlish. Made her more womanly—her good sense, the readiness to help, to chance being awkward in the service of a fine idea. —She inspired many sighs.

Unison sat inside the tent containing boys most newly dead. There she sketched portraits of the corpses stretched on cots. Other men looked in. They considered that this made a beautiful and strange picture. They considered Unison one brave girl. They knew that her three older brothers and her father had been killed within one week of Manassas. Had that made a child who looked so frail grow so darn fine and stubborn?—What stirred men more than just the sight of their dead friends? Seeing dead pals solemnly sketched by "a Southern maiden of surpassing sensibility." That's how they talked back then, child. Unison mailed many such sad noble drawings to families of the deceased. She sent letters telling of last days, final words. And every man who camped here felt she had special feelings for him alone. When troops arrived, that had been her secret vow and plan. She had succeeded.

Every afternoon, men camped on the lawn and barnyard of this mansion heard Miss Unison practice at a keyboard instrument. Chaplain—who'd led the Seminary Glee Club at university—explained the thing's distinction. Their hostesses owned one of the three finest harpsichords presently at large in the commonwealth. Dutch-made in the 1600s, it had been barged up the river James to this plantation's dock.

UNISON's fate is of interest. Warriors *expect* to die—or should. Those who survive them learn to live around the hollow that their absence daily makes. But just the way you hear how kids—playing near a brook two dozen years after a war—find this nice metal ball and beat it with a rock to see what-all's inside and set off an explosion that costs kids hands and eyes—just that way, the punishment of survivors, child—it's what really interests me the most.

That's what grabbed me, and boy, I hate it. Even at my age, I still expect a little fairness! That's the meanest trick of all. How do they keep *do*ing that to us, darling?

Who can teach me to quit expecting?

AS FOR Prothero in battle, nobody hoped for much. Watching him preen, others guessed that under siege the Charleston heir would prove both bossy and gun-shy—a losing comb. A skirmish happened the one morning before his first meeting the ladies. Northern scouting parties had been spotted down the river James. Prothero and three young officers plus a ragtag crowd of thirty volunteers rode out from the Randolph farm.

Others predicted Prothero would falter or bolt. But on overtaking the enemy along the riverbank, the Lieutenant was seen to jump out front right quick. Pince-nez in place, he led a charge that caught the Blues unawares and sent Vermonters scurrying like allergic girls.

Under fire, the highborn Prothero seemed to grow both chestier and taller. Beckoning and scolding, running, swearing, pointing—the youth appeared fearless—he was exposed during the heaviest of firing. His blue eyes would widen, blond whiskers stiffening like some riled lynx's. He waved his silver sword around like he was some French warrior posing for a picture. Prothero's Rebel yell—especially coming from so genteel a officer—terrified even his own men. When the Lieutenant gave off this hellion's screech, veins big as garden hoses forked across his temples. At the sound you could hear enemy fire cease for about three seconds, like taking a break to swallow onct, hard, then blast again extra loud. In battle, on foot or astride his asthmatic animal going "Ah her," this smiling Charlestonian seemed to swell toward the perfect target and then press beyond that into some screaming scarecrow puppet exempt from harm.

Well, even the lad's worst critics had to concede Prothero's unexpected mettle. The night after battle, he seemed changed. He plainly did not sleep, he did not plan to sleep.

Prothero stayed near his lit mirror. Nobody blamed him now. The evening of his first great showy battle, men watched the nightly ritual with a warier respect. What was Prothero primping *for*? The memory of some sweetheart? The idea of young Miss Randolph in her cliff-top mansion pouring tea tomorrow evening? Civilian life awaiting him in smooth clubby Charleston? Or did he groom for tomorrow's slaughter of the enemy?

That same night while young Willie cared for and whispered to Prothero's horse, older men started wandering out towards the animal. They acted eager to pat the officer's beautiful jumpy Morgan. Will felt proud of the attention Target got. He took part credit. Admiring hands all over the gelding made it really go, "Ah her, Ah *her*."

(Later, the braver Prothero acted on a given day, the more nightly comforting Target got from shy enlisted men.) Still, everybody agreed: Target was a poor name to give your own war-horse.

2

NOW FOR a tea party in the Randolphs' beautiful west parlor! Just four-thirty and the March sun had a strawish pink tone. Head-on light made this mammoth farmhouse seem a palace. The whole hilltop home sat circled by porches like hoopskirts. Porches offered quite some view of the James River's most dramatic (and strategic) bend.

Men found the mansion's mirrors yet hung with black crepe. Both hostesses wore dark clothes and four armbands apiece. The parlor's walls were nearbout paved with family oil portraits of now-deceased men. The sons had been painted as young boys. They were shown gripping the reins of favorite ponies. In the background—one mild-looking black manservant held his cap and watched riders (the same man from picture to picture, hair going whiter), approving, grinning.

The Chaplain smiled at Prothero. "And may I, sir, present our division's chiefest ornament, Miss Unison Randolph?"

Prothero noted the girl's lowered modest eyes. He took the hand she offered, shy, he bowed and kissed it. Other officers smirked, rolling their eyes. But, undiscouraged, Prothero studied only Unison. Her face was a fine and simple oval—maybe too much of one. Her hands, he saw up close, were very good. Black clothes set off her stark half-transparent complexion.

Prothero, stirred by Unison's severe Virginia charm, soon filled the west parlor with his own perfume. It was a wonderful scent, not manly exactly— but not silly. There was simply way too much of it. He told a story of a riding accident he'd had before the war. He made it funny—he made the faults all his own faults. He made the ladies like him. He praised their home, its view. He talked in a way he never talked to other men, even ones he seemed to like. The aged Chaplain stood smiling in the corner. He gloried in this olden style of conversation—confiding, gentle, light—the type of talk the war had sunk for good. Chaplain sometimes said how this wasn't the *least* of war's crimes. War hogs conversation, kills it.

Prothero soon offered Unison Randolph the very highest praise. He jokingly claimed she was almost worthy of Charleston. He grilled both Randolphs, trying to turn up some well-placed South Carolina relation of theirs. Prothero joked that he was sure such fine ladies could not be mere Virginians.

The mistress of the house excused herself at onct. She held a lace hankie to her face. The young daughter smiled at the Lieutenant but her face looked tense, "You mustn't mind Momma, sir. You meant it civilly, I know, but— in the first place—you do bear a strong resemblance to my eldest brother, Edmund, in the picture there. Secondly, Mother feels that Poppa and my brothers died less for our Confederacy, more for Virginia itself. So, you see, it's hard on her just now, sir."

And Unison smiled. Prothero apologized, he bowed. Like the other gents present, he'd found her speech most pretty and most kind.

Unison treated all soldiers the same. That way they all could love her equally—and purely. Around the girl now, Prothero acted agitated and charming but glazed. He had told both the Chaplain and his groom: Back home, he depended so much on the company of women. Unison was the first refined young lady he had addressed for months. Ladies of his circle had always checked and improved his moral progress in the world. By teasing and scolding, they kept him well in line. He seemed to need that, he admitted. To meet another such young woman—after so long—it half alarmed him, he admitted, smiling, stroking his platinum mutton chops.

He was scared that, while learning certain other, ungenteel skills in battle, he'd lost his oldest, surest knack—his luck with ladies. Prothero now explained how he regretted causing Mrs. Randolph grief on his first meeting. Young Unison accepted this and said she must go attend her parent, if you gentlemen will excuse me. The party broke up.

Prothero wandered to the latticed garden house with its view of a far cliff now shadowed purple. Armaments could be heard to echo up the river. Other officers watched Prothero mulling there, his Revolutionary scabbard glinting in last light. It seemed right romantic to them. He had gone off to pine for the young lady. Okay. Fine. He was hardly alone in adoring Miss Unison. But, seeing that the dandy could be moved, men liked him more. Tried to.

3

THREE youngish officers had regularly led the charges before Prothero arrived. But, understanding how freely this new man lunged into the open, hearing the donkey-devil sounds pump from that boy's bow-mouth, older leaders soon begun holding back. Seemed they could now afford to act a wee bit less courageous. And—once Prothero rallied for a second then a fifth attack—these men started to feel a stupefying type of relief, child.

By that I mean—when recalling their own earlier exploits they grew amazed, dizzy, even almost ashamed of their onetime swagger. Nights especially, as they watched him prepare for battle (or for maybe meeting Miss Randolph over tea), gents wondered: Had *their* reasons for bravery been any better than jolly self-satisfied young Prothero's? Was he being brave because his great-granddad had done so whilst fighting Cornwallis? Had the lad noticed or chose this? In some way, he didn't seem to know he was at war. In other ways, he seemed born to be cavalry. —Both.

You studied him there at his nightly mirror. Fog would roll uphill off the river James and one hundred yards from the central campfire, you'd spy him there near his four candles repeating theirselves glass to glass, a glimmer set off in the blue haze.

Unharmed on the evening of a battle day when others had fallen all around him, the young man's candlelit grooming came to seem a strange new putting on of armor. His power appeared to spring from those three mirrors or the scent he wore into the field—some kind of magic. Will Marsden noticed that other older men now started borrowing one of the division's communal combs. When combat seemed surefire, when you heard the clatter bounding through the woods this way, big-eyed troops—using fingers and shared combs—commenced a new and frantic primping. It was pitiful. It distracted some. They got hurt.

. . .

AMONG his own enlisted men, the Lieutenant inspired a gloomy boldness. But at night or during the long days between fighting, nobody much spoke to him unless he addressed them direct. Around this society boy returning from the woods and his private potty chair, even the cordial First Lt. Hester grew stiff, formal. When Prothero strolled among his troops, some men wearing arm slings or on crutches would hold their noses, pretended to gag in his sweet trailing scent.

But nobody made such jests to his face. Though nobody quite said so, men understood—he was really needed here. But this very respect meant: People were a bit afraid of him. He'd have been the last to guess their fear. This spooked them even more.

NOBODY could figure why his last division had transferred such a overwilling soldier against his will. Even so, little Willie Marsden and the others watched him hard.

An expeditionary party rode out from headquarters at the Randolphs' river home. It was after Prothero's fifth successful charge. Two Southern privates noticed him circulating among the fallen enemy. A sorghum field lay strewn with groaning Northern survivors. Men too wounded to march away as prisoners of war waited till battle lines shifted, till their own medics could scurry out and attend them. Prothero was seen to walk from Yank to Yank. He carried a ladle and a oak water bucket. Reared an Anglican, he was so High Church, he crossed himself and often. He did that now, drifting among the wounded, speaking to them. But the privates, admiring this aristocrat's kindness, later reported: The Lieutenant would first speak to those Northerners who begged loudest for water. He would stoop, lift a man's head onto his knee, use the dipper with great care, finally lowering the fellow to the ground. Then, making sure the soldier was conscious, Prothero stood back up and—onto the person he'd just treated so carefully— he would slop more unexpected wet. He sometimes emptied the whole bucket over a wounded man's head. Then speaking to this fellow gasping in the dust-gone-mud, Prothero would ask, "Thirsty? Still thirsty?" He crossed hisself, refilled the bucket, moved on to help a next victim crying aloud for water. While the privates watched, he left a dozen wounded men gasping toward the sun, half drowned.

News of this little incident spread fast among enlisted men and, slower, worked its way up to other officers. The white-haired Chaplain defended Prothero against such tales. Chaplain claimed the lad's family on both sides were deeply civic-minded, great patriots and patrons. Chaplain recalled Prothero's governor father—a man, the Reverend said, of exceptional grace, talent, piety. "I care very little for this mumbling against him." Chaplain acted hurt.

AS PROTHERO seemed to get on better and better with Miss Unison, he grew haughtier and tighter. He freely told now about his father's two terms as governor, how his granddad—Washington's buddy—served in the U.S. Senate's earliest days. If he'd had a nip to drink, he fell to a kind of ruthless Charleston name-dropping that—considering this present city of tents, given the deep Virginia mud and this probably losing cause—impressed nobody and would've angered a few if they hadn't considered Prothero, with his fuss and toiletries, frivolous to start with, frivolous if lucky.

One night after a downriver skirmish with the enemy, the much-talked-of gent abandoned his mirror. He wandered over, settled near the others' fire and card game. He must've had a drink or two: Prothero grew quickly sentimental. His was a dry splendid accent, the voice ran deep, full of surprising wayside compassions. Touching his pale whiskers, still holding one heavy silver hairbrush, he sat praising his mother's musicianship, he described his family's homeplace. (Off in the distance, Prothero's three-panel mirror reflected its lit candles.) He loved to quote pet sayings learned from some wise old slave woman who'd helped rear him. His favorite: "The soul of another is a dark forest." Tipsy, the lad would speak this line at the end of his own tales and others'. To the Lieutenant, it seemed the moral of every story. Men, watching him with unsure feelings, would sometimes nod at the seeming truth of this, but all whilst giving each other certain serious side looks.

Courteous and drunk, Prothero crossed his arms, pulled both knees together, stared into flames, and bored everybody by recalling finer social seasons in the great city of his birth. The poker games roared on around him. Only a few men even pretended to listen. If Prothero seemed huge in battle, how wizened and kidlike he looked talking here. He described which chandeliers in which hometown ballroom he counted among his town's five most beautiful, how each distributed the brilliance of hundreds of candles. (When he started in on Charleston street addresses and the merits of their crystal lighting fixtures, men began filing away from the campfire, taking cards with them.) The Lieutenant mentioned certain accomplished young women who'd once considered him a wit, a notable skeet shooter, excellent churchman, fine practitioner of the waltz. (More fellows cleared out quiet.)

When Prothero spoke, you *could* imagine his civilian charms. You wondered why they so failed to translate into this other, harder time. The Chaplain sat nearby. Maybe he'd grown worried by reports about the lad. Now he smiled at a new, more human side to Prothero—but even the Chaplain was surprised by the Lieutenant's going on like this for fifty minutes straight. His pince-nez, dangling, turning on the end of its cord, would catch campfire glow. Lenses seemed to burn with independent and unhappy sights. The few men left here watched the Lieutenant with some concern.

Next morning, Will found that Target had been badly whipped—great welts were opened along the gelding's back. Prothero's enlisted men begun remarking his strange shifts in mood. One day he praised these fellows as the bravest in the war. Next morning, before assembled troops, he called the well-liked Corporal Sal Smith "exceedingly ill-bred." When first complaints were made, the Lieutenant's family ties, his strange and handsome certainty, all helped protect him. Prothero had never onct been wounded— not a scratch on him, he wore more decorations than did most seasoned majors. He seemed shielded both from usual damage and regular regret.

4

PROTHERO admitted to Willie: He saw Miss Unison as a test of his own flair with womankind. He felt determined, he said, to "annex" her.

Downriver action took the Lieutenant away on a ten-day scouting mission. Others could now talk of nothing but his genius, his recklessness in the fight. But the boy himself seemed to have no memory beyond his having upset, that first day, his distinguished elder hostess.

The Randolphs sent a graceful note welcoming returned officers. A little celebration would be held next evening in their best parlor. That day at three, Prothero went on a foraging detail with nine men. They came upon a group of stray Northerners bathing downriver. Prothero placed his troops in brush at twelve-foot intervals along the bank. He himself forded the river upstream on Target. He fired from the eastern shore, his men from the west. Ten Northerners, confused and caught in cross fire, were killed. All Prothero's men handily survived. The Lieutenant returned to camp acting winded and exaggerated. He handed Target's reins to Will while talking far too loud. He hurried to his mirror, preparing for the party. He'd made sure to get back with time to spare. Ten men dead—now tea.

Prothero civilized his uniform with French perfume. For those who'd heard his scary Rebel yell today downriver, this proved comforting—his grooming, hard. It hinted that the young officer got gussied up for others, not just himself, not just as a battle ritual.

Greeting the ladies, he gestured and purred. You could see that Mrs. Randolph looked on Prothero with strange feelings. Maybe it grieved her to see a face so like her late son's. Could be she was straining to forget his earlier remark about Virginia. But both ladies seemed right well disposed to him. He quoted: "The soul of another is a dark forest." In such a time and at such a party, nobody argued. Prothero's charm—lost on his enlisted men, his horse—now seemed placed where it belonged. He told three stories in a row that were funny, clever, kind. Other officers who'd felt muddy and graceless in this brocaded room were grateful to the dandy. He kept cleaning his pince-nez while staring at Unison. Prothero drank more mulled wine. Then he did something that startled everybody, especially hisself. You could see he never planned to nor expected it. You could see he only wanted to be liked. Standing near Unison, within easy hearing distance of her mother, Prothero made a joke about girls' loving duty toward soldiers who're about to lose their lives. He said it was a patriotic duty: There should be no female

Confederate virgins above the age of thirteen. Prothero drew alongside Unison, he stared directly past her armbands at her bodice.

Silence fell and then a real loud attempt at talking. The Chaplain asked could he please speak to young Prothero out of doors, at once, please? The Chaplain was a dignified-looking man, a gaunt gentleman of exalted standards. He'd been entertained in the best homes of the Southern nation and he said so often. He smiled a lot and was held to have a good heart but his interest in the Confederate Army seemed a snob's. Loss of life among the leading families' sons made him speak of tragedy. Deaths among the sons of grocers seemed to him inevitable, if sad. The Chaplain's features appeared to have benefited from sixty years of German music and the most serious available reading. As a preacher, he was cursed—or so his untutored men felt—by a fondness for musical terms. "God," he would say, "has transposed our parts down a minor third and *still* our voices crack." On the veranda, he now grabbed Prothero's arm, almost twisting it. "I resist saying so . . . but you've just acted nearly unchivalrous as our barbaric enemies. Why are we *fighting* them if you choose to adopt their very debased style? In a boy of your connections this resounds with especial discord, sir."

Prothero strolled off to one side, cleaned his spectacles, he was smirking, shaken. He put glasses on and, absentmindedly, crossed himself. When he returned to the party (probably a mistake) old Mrs. Randolph cut Prothero directly, then rushed upstairs. The pale daughter seemed nervous to be near him now. He twice tried to joke with the girl. She twice drew other gents into the conversation. The Lieutenant, acting hurt, stepped away from her and stood, silent, in one dark corner. For the rest of the party he looked only at her. Prothero's respect for the girl appeared to slowly turn into a jolly kind of hatred.

Next afternoon, he was seated alone in the Randolphs' garden house. Unison had been out gathering the season's first grape hyacinths and an armful of forsythia. Seeing him here, she braced herself. First she headed the other way but then duty or resolve or interest changed her route. "April!" she said to him. It was a general comment and intended to be harmless.

He jumped to his feet, fumbling to set his pince-nez in place. "My sentiments exactly. Forgive me . . . Spring forgives everything and you must, too. The strain works on my mind in ways I fear I cannot quite predict, Miss."

They talked then. Alone with her, he relaxed. She settled as far from him as the small round gazebo would permit. He spoke about his entertaining married sisters. He frankly said how lonely a warrior's life was. He said he'd heard her practice, he sensed she was a brilliant musician, he longed to hear Unison play something difficult straight through. He stared at her. Dark mourning clothes handsomely contrasted with the spring bouquet. She held flowers with the same brisk care Unison brought to everything she did. He said, "I so wish I could lay my head upon your lap. If that sounds scandalous, it shouldn't . . . in these times." He said how propriety must alter along with the great historical events.

She told him that she feared for his reason. She sensed how he had behaved before the war—she felt like war had made him rash and wild, quite bitterly unhappy. She advised the young man to make adjustments as he could. She said she pitied him.

Her own honesty surprised and moved her. Her honesty surprised and moved him. He admitted to terrible confusions. He told her he had killed up to nineteen Northerners already. "Nineteen," he said. "And I have not one wound to show for it." Boy sounded regretful.

He smiled at her and Unison felt astonished: Orderly fat silver tears rolled down his either cheek from under the pince-nez. Eyeglasses held bright accurate copies of the river past the gazebo, the river behind her. Tears came down his cheeks on alternate sides—the way, from a distance, she'd seen him brush his hair with two silver brushes. One-two, one-two.

He spoke loud, "Think of your brothers on the night before their deaths." Her face she hid behind beautiful lifted hands. Prothero kept right on. "Imagine if some young lady of breeding had been kind to them that final evening. Can you not find it in your heart to help me here? It's so little that I ask. One simply wants to rest one's head on your lap, among the flowers of your lap. One's head will be more on flowers than on lap. —My sanity, dear Unison, depends upon it."

Somehow, while she yet screened her features, he dodged over, silent. He stretched out along the gazebo bench. Her hands parted and a whiskered tear-streaked face was already riding her upper thighs—looking direct at Unison, seeming her own disturbed reflection.

"Why? Why are you *like* this, sir?" Exactly at that moment Willie Marsden and two young pals who'd been bathing in the river strode back towards camp. They passed the gazebo, noticed this spectacle, saw young Unison's face contort. Discovered! Boys stopped dead, then hurried off, trying to keep their expressions neutral. Word soon spread: Either the pair was engaged to be married or else Unison had seriously compromised herself. A whole division felt jealous, they blamed not the society wag with his scents and whiskers—they blamed a very foolish and surprisingly unstable girl who had succumbed, who'd been successfully tricked, who'd lost her virtue and her precious standing in their hearts. He might be odd. But her? She seemingly was loose, far worse.

Next day she appeared with a tray of cookies hot from the stove. The first three men she offered treats refused them. Others accepted but their faces stayed narrowed, grudging. They seemed to be doing her a favor by quickly gobbling warm sugar cookies stamped with a cutter, heart-shaped.

After this she refused to see Prothero on the grounds or in the mansion. Old Mrs. Randolph felt a change. Unison had told her nothing, not wanting to trouble the widow. Prothero began stealing into the big house uninvited. Unison was at her harpsichord. The Lieutenant asked why she had, like so many others, turned against him. She told him she was his truest friend but that his being so unpredictable made him hard to be near, impossible to help.

The young man offered light jokes about her makeshift wartime wardrobe—the three black dresses. He held his pince-nez in air between her face and his. He predicted that, with the slaves run off and her being mostly orphaned, lacking a dowry as she did now, she would quite possibly never marry. Yes, he added, he could picture her—maybe working as a nanny to brats of the newly rich. He claimed he knew just how a lady like herself would look, dry at fifty.

She had been trying to practice. She stared at him. "Your voice sounds so much like my brother Edmund's. It's a kind voice underneath. I can only think that the war has done all this and other things to you, sir. I wonder, would I prefer our Edmund to have died when he did or to have been subjected to such changes as you have endured. I must tell you, sir, that your being treated cruelly gives you no right to treat me so. I wish you nothing but good. The first time you walked into our hallway, I felt quite giddy. It was the pleasure of how you looked and how you pulled your scabbard aside so you could bow as deeply as you did from the waist, sir. The hand-kissing, however, struck us all as affected, I fear. I always speak plainly. Some of us have no choice. A blessing, finally.

"The war will end and you will return to yourself. You are not essentially *like* this, and I feel that. Even so, my mother, who knows little of what's happened, will never let me come near you again. The Chaplain fears rumors are in circulation concerning untoward events in our garden house. I feel innocent of wrongdoing. I only hoped to save you but I fear it is beyond my powers. That is all I have to tell you, sir. Good day, Lieutenant."

She ignored him after this, she tried. Mrs. Randolph begged other officers never to leave the girl alone with the odd, pretty officer. But when the widow asked this favor, gents stiffened as if with some secret. Unison's coolness only drove Prothero to mutter further insults. He treated the girl as if he was her loving taunting elder brother. His pranks ran darker and darker. He found her working in her cutting garden. He stood upon a clump of irises. Silently, Unison drifted upstairs to practice her recorder. He took to patrolling the home without permission. In its basement, he found remains of a fine liquor cellar and many kegs of maple syrup brought South before the war. He ordered the company cook to annex these. "Flapjacks for everybody. And on our charming hostesses," he said. Mother and daughter kept silent. They watched him drink their dead kin's last brandy. Noticing their faces, the Chaplain later apologized.

On the evening of a hard day's fight two miles southeast, women found young Prothero inside their home and now upstairs. He was sitting, eyes wide open, in a gilt Venetian chair along one dark corridor. "Yankees are abroad. Therefore I am guarding you," he smiled. "You would not believe what some of these dogs will do to ladies, no matter their age or basic attractiveness. To Northerners this matters but little," and then he crossed himself and smiled. "Savages," he said.

Prothero soon joined poker games near the nightly fire. He often won. His daily face was hard enough to read. At cards, this became an advantage. His betting was unpredictable, full of bluffs. No one could find the pattern. They envied his success with women. They hated his success at cards. They finally blamed him for compromising Unison.

Fewer and fewer men would sit near Prothero in the Officers' Mess. Just his mentioning Charleston brought groans. Card games were soon organized in secret. One evening Prothero stepped away from his mirrors to go fetch a cup of water for personal hygiene. A Yankee sniper opened fire. Candles and mirrors were blasted like a shooting gallery—nothing left but silver bits, the splintered walnut frame.

"That was a gift, you!" Prothero ran—exposed to harm—shouting toward black woods. Others, well hidden, watched him grab a sword and pistol from his tent. Target still suffered from a last beating. Prothero jumped onto the animal unsaddled, wearing its plaid blanket. At high speed, lacking orders to do so, the young man galloped off alone into the dark.

Will and others waited, very still. The ladies Randolph waited in the safety of their marble foyer. Fifty minutes later, everybody heard a single shot. Everybody looked at each other. Shortly afterwards, Prothero came trotting back into camp. He jumped off Target, passed reins to Will. The Lieutenant hurried to a wagon's flatbed where the broken mirror was. He gathered the shards with great care, setting these inside his tent. Prothero then returned to the same spot and—on wagon's slats, overtop glittering blue glass—he mashed down one small item. The youth then went off mumbling to his tent. Will and others gathered. Here among mirror bits was the tip of something fleshy—maybe cut from a Yankee person's earlobe, maybe from a person's nose.

No more sniping happened for some days.

5

IT LATER came out how, drunk one evening on borrowed brandy, the Lieutenant had pushed into Unison Randolph's very sleeping chamber. Her fourposter was a hundred years old and required a stepladdered gangplank for entry. She woke to find a blond young man sitting, grinning—boots off, cross-legged at her bed's end. "Edmund!" she cried, and reached forward. Then, seeing who it was, Unison jerked back, one hand covering her mouth.

As a joke, Prothero had unbuttoned his fly. Through it, he had poked her blond recorder. "Hello. Can you see how lonely I am."

The young lady's brown hair trailed down her shoulders. She tossed it behind her and pulled covers high around her neck. She asked the Lieutenant to please leave, now. Prothero explained he only wanted to talk to a woman, alone. "This," he pulled out the recorder, "was just a joke. Not a terribly good one, I fear."

He said that a lack of contact with women had, he felt, confused him about certain rights and wrongs. "Please, I'm not the kind of person I must presently appear. You can help me. You know the story of the toad who was a prince. You can send me back."

She agreed to have a conversation but only if he'd please go sit in a chair across the room please. Instead he rose onto all fours and, pince-nez dangling off its ribbon, stuffing the recorder in his mouth like a beak, scurried nearer, hopping.

Only then did Unison Randolph reach under her pillow. Her father, last thing before riding away, had presented her this little pearl-handled revolver. Using both hands, holding it at arm's length before her, the young lady aimed directly between the gentleman's eyes. She held the pistol very steady. "Manners," the young lady said.

He sobered then, climbed off the bed, smiled, took her instrument from his mouth and set it on a bureau, collected his boots. "Goodbye, you," he waved from the doorway, his tone gone grave. "You see, I now feel even lonelier. I expected better from you. I shall not forget this unkindness. Women should go to war, too. Just for living in tents, so we might come and talk to them after battle or before. Especially after—no, especially *before*. I'm held to be talented at fighting. It's only willpower. I haven't the gift. Some of us need women's company. It would be a service. 'The soul of another is a dark forest.' There'd be less war if women were nearer to it. You had a chance to help a fellow know his rights from wrongs. You failed him fairly badly. There will be consequences, I fear."

She considered telling the Chaplain. Finally Unison knew she'd speak to no one of the visit. She felt she was protecting the Lieutenant. She sat here in her bed, listening hard till dawn—listening to what? for what?

Something in his wildness she recognized. Something in his high blond craziness she felt to be the joined ghosts of her missing brothers. Edmund, Keane, and Billy's love was communicating in some code she might eventually break—the way you can break algebra or musical notation.

BY DAWN, she regretted sending him away.

6

THE CHAPLAIN kept mercilessly working music terms into his riverbank sermons. He soon lectured enlisted men about the actual harpsichord they heard played daily. (He mentioned how one side of her instrument's inlay showed a shepherd on a hill, lutes and horns and ribbons crossed its other.) He asked young Unison to give a concert for the division. The Chaplain knew how she had fallen in the group's esteem. He felt this might help.

Always willing to do her duty, Unison said she worried that her instrument was in too poor repair. She blamed the river James's humidity. She said she'd learned to tune the thing herself but that new strings, much needed, were impossible to find now (plus, such a use of metal would be downright unpatriotic). The Chaplain insisted. He asked leave for his enlisted men to gather on the Randolphs' portico. The boys, he assured her, needed uplifting. Certain unworthy behavior was emerging in the lower ranks and—he added, watching her face—among junior officers.

Unison looked back at him. "If it will help . . . that. And generally, sir."

River's acoustics always bring sounds from great distances. Men heard rumblings from Northern artillery far downstream. But all that afternoon soldiers concentrated instead on a young woman's serious tuning and retuning for tonight's event. Will noticed that even Target kept all hooves on the ground, calmed by steady testing notes. While men cleaned their muskets, as they marched their ragged formations back and forth in the paddock—how fine the sound of one delicate instrument trying to get better, finding then losing and refinding its own thin voice. Cannons' downriver roars sounded like something huge was being steadily blasted and chipped away. But bright metal notes from the house seemed to try and lightly pin that back in place.

SUNSET, and the company assembled. All the bivouac's lanterns had been set into the upstairs windows, placed around the portico's broad columns.

Clumsily and as if by accident, it seemed to be spring. Tonight a body noticed. (Spring is the earth forgiving itself.) In spite of war, between tents, a plantation's quinces and dogwoods and jonquils bloomed with great sad almost-stupid lushness. The more flowers opened, the more mail boys sent home. The lovelier the grounds, the sadder a soldier could feel—evenings especially.

Forty muskets were stacked on the veranda, there if something went wrong. Windows and French doors stood wide open to enlarge one instrument's faint sounds. A chandelier in the music room had been lit with one hundred candles for the first time since Manassas—a spendthrift move. Coarse yellow army-issue candles were jammed among satiny tapers placed there before the war.

Women and children invited from nearby plantations began arriving. Mrs. Randolph—in mourning black but of a richer fabric than usual—glided out front to greet guests. The old woman seemed so animated she looked silly to the soldiers who'd known her only six weeks as a solemn staid old thing. Her pale daughter waited on the porch. Dismounting from makeshift mule carts, deprived of servants, of their husbands, fathers, sons, these women—old friends—embraced. The children seemed startled at finding three hundred soldiers in cleanest uniforms. Women had worn their best remaining gowns. Binding long white gloves and fair satin sleeves, dozens of black armbands. On one old woman's right arm, soldiers saw a tourniquet of six. Some ladies wept at finding the great house lit and wide open again. "Before," they smiled. They meant: Tonight the place looked like it had for some spring ball held prior to Sumter.

Enlisted men were forced to sit outside far from the ladies. They'd scrubbed hard anyway. In sunset light, boys' washed faces now showed pink, freckled, baked. Supplies were long-awaited—new boots especially scarce. Barefoot fellows borrowed at least one boot. Along the big-house steps, they set in ways to hide single naked feet. Boys meant to reassure the patriotic ladies.

Chaplain convened things, sparing folks his usual long-windedness. He just stood and quoted: *"Musick is an insearchable and excellent Art, which rejoiceth the Spirit and unloadeth Grief from the heart, and consisteth in time and number.* To our intense good fortune, Miss Unison Randolph shall now demonstrate."

At her instrument's first tart note, everybody breathed a single "Ahhh," then, looking around, laughed at their own simple delight. Though the harpsichord did at times sound somewhat sharp, after all this recent hardship you felt so pleased to sit, newly bathed, out in the air of a warm May evening without one duty beyond listening. Given such weather, considering the talent of the girl inside, given that group "Ahh" just now and the smell of narcissuses blooming near the porch, how could a war last even ten days longer?

Folks sat through two rollicking if prickly Italian pieces. Then the ranking major asked after some Stephen Foster. "For my men," he smiled, nodding toward the nearest open French door where eager boys in gray sat clumped. Chaplain was about to protest this too rapid descent into the merely Popular when there come such a crashing from the cellar. The young lady quickly pitched into her sprightliest of French jigs.

At the parlor's arched door, Lieutenant Prothero soon leaned, grinning. He wore his hat. On one shoulder, he carried a wooden cask just lugged upstairs. His uniform trailed cobwebs. You could see he was drunk. Young mothers in the room tugged youngest children closer. First it seemed like Prothero had fetched up a libation for others. But chalked on the barrel's side you could read "Maple S." and a date. The Lieutenant hoisted this here container. As the crowd watched—as the young lady continued to splash safely behind a thousand skillful notes—he stepped towards her, smirking. Prothero seemed fixed only on Miss Unison, hardly noticing dozens of strangers crowding each downstairs room.

The Chaplain rose. But the keyboard player, glancing his way, hinted that, no, she could most probably manage whatever the young man planned.

Prothero moved towards her, passing many officers and guests. He stopped directly before the player, his back blocking others' view of her. Music came forth with greater and greater nervous spirit. Swells of it rose. Over the ivory and ash-wood keys, Unison's fingers made two blurs like wings. For one second, it seemed a contest was shaping up betwixt the power of music and whatever mischief this war hero planned. Will, the groom—seated at an open window—tipped further into the chamber. He saw only how the posture of those indoors had suddenly improved in a way most locked and deadening. He leaned further: Prothero, oh. Now Willie understood.

Without ceremony or explanation—smiling, bitter—the Charlestonian opened a harpsichord's lidlike soundboard to its fullest. Then, as if cracking a huge egg, he busted the barrel, staves splintering. Into the young lady's instrument, across its fine workings, he dumped a gallon and a half of dark thick syrup.

Listeners inhaled one sucking hiss—the exact opposite of "Ahhh." The Lieutenant threw cask's slats and metal cinchings into the harpsichord's casing. Some syrup had smeared onto his hand. This, he wiped onto decorative inlay. The surprise was: just how long music lasted. Child? The surprise always is!

Though the young lady kept on, her face had already blanked itself. You saw skin go older all at onct, her color draining noplace. Unison Randolph, age fifteen, leaned nearer and nearer the small keyboard. Her oval face was inches over ten palsied fingers yet working so. Her elbows lifted at determined awkward angles, but as you listened, syrup found and coated every wire and bolt and pick of it. Men/women/children—every person in this and other rooms slowly tipped towards the dying instrument: because they listened harder and because they seemed to think that this'd someway help it. The player—shuddering, head fighting to stay upright—resisted a minor spasm. But Unison stayed gray-faced at her post. Music lost some clarity, all edge, it soon glued over. Then just many finicky damp slappings, sticky separations.

The rooms now grew so still. For a second you could hear the river James sloshing at the bottom of the lawn, currents pushing and searching along the cliff below.

The girl pulled her fingers off the keys all at onct. Otherwise it seemed she might never find the strength to separate herself from this instrument where she'd sat daily since age nine.

Unison kept still for a second. Then she stared—not at the culprit. He had swollen to his fullest heroic size as if he'd just performed some right witty parlor prank. Instead Miss Randolph looked to other officers. And they'd just turned toward each other, trying to decide what to do next—when the Chaplain heaved forward. He lurched direct for Prothero's throat. Others grabbed the old man, held him back. One little girl, snickering, not understanding, dodged behind a love seat, peeked above its edge.

Chaplain had prayed over hundreds of deaths, he'd witnessed the torture of many more amputees. He had seen the finest young men of his region maimed, burned, and dismembered. But through all these horrors his features showed little real outwards emotion beyond his thin lips moving in the act of rational prayer. Now two burly colonels could hardly hold him back. Enraged by the dying of this harpsichord, pointing to it, thrashing side to side, the Chaplain screamed, "Monster! Why, mon-ster? *Why?*"

Some children—feeling the strangeness, missing the music, bothered at being so near all these men after seeing so few lately—sniffled, then cried. It was only at this sound, only on hearing ladies' rustling dresses that the governor's son seemed to notice. He turned, looked, understood who'd sat watching him.

In other rooms, guests stood, craning around doorjambs to see why music had stopped. Prothero lifted his pince-nez, studied the assembled women. He seemed to find them suitable, even agreeable. And with an almost comic pleasure, the Lieutenant moved his scabbard aside, did a profound full bow their way. He clumsily removed his hat.

Meantime the ladies glanced elsewhere, everywhere, anyplace but him. Children wouldn't meet the young man's stare. Some hid eyes behind their mothers' skirts. Other youngsters held their hands before their faces, screening him from view, dreading him without quite understanding.

But then, who here understood?

Children's hiding from him seemed to stun this handsome boy. You saw something register. Standing at the center of a parlor alive with candlelight, banked with cut spring flowers, paved with pictures of privileged little boys and their ponies, the young officer broke into a strange fetching grin. It was not his recent leer. It seemed that something opened in his face. He panted. He'd suddenly noticed a chandelier ablaze directly overhead with pendant lead crystals, silent pink/gold light wavering on the features all about him. He smoothed back his blond hair. He gave off one closed giggle. He'd not seen so many dressed-up women and children in months, even years. He studied each woman with a shy respect, hands now laced together over his belt buckle, as if called upon to make a speech. As if he could think of nothing, but expected everyone would wait.

A one-shoed enlisted man—puzzled by the hush—flapped through a French door, squinted into this cramped parlor. There at the center stood Prothero. Two officers still held back the Chaplain. The player stayed at her instrument. Not one soul spoke. All at onct you smelled a rush of the perfume escaping from some person, like a body gas. Suddenly, great veins swelled at Prothero's temples. He actually staggered, and, as others watched, he leaned for support against the harpsichord. Soon as his palm touched it, the young woman screeched, "His *hand*." She leapt to hide herself behind a group of officers who'd gathered at her back. These men now advanced. Flattered, they drew nearer to the culprit.

Everybody watched this young lieutenant with a sort of medical interest, almost a horror. He seemed on the brink of some seizure that you couldn't bear to witness, child, but dared not look away from. Everybody stared so. He knew this. It made things worse. His shoulders lowered, knees now met each other as if for the first time. He seemed to lose whole years and inches. It was like watching a real real good umbrella slowly shut.

His voice sounded higher than usual. "I see, of course," he cleared his throat. "Only some vandal would do this. It must prove, what? How thought-less one has become? Everybody cried the day I left Charleston. True tears. Even Uncle's slaves, and a good deal more than they had to. My sister fainted. I was the one everybody loved. Ask them. My own mother's greatest joy is her piano. —Miss," he turned but saw only the girl's dark eyes half hid between tall officers. "I can't say why anyone, myself especially, would choose to do such a thing. I will—pay, of course. It's that . . . 'The soul . . . is a dark forest.' By degrees it must come upon one. I know what it means to be loved by people. And to offer that back. It's by degrees this other happens . . . Do please excuse me, all of you. —Also, I want it known, I've never touched that girl there hiding from me, though oftentimes I've wanted to. Her, I do not blame."

Then he started for the door but slowed, looked overhead, then whipped his silver sword from its scabbard. Several ladies jumped back whining against the wall. Prothero just used his saber's point to touch the light overhead. "This is actually not a bad chandelier." Even his barely tapping it caused the thing to sway so—the whole room rocked with swinging shad-ows. And, rushing, mumbling to hisself, Prothero tripped past rigid officers, past the openmouthed Chaplain, down marble steps mobbed with young Will and dozens of others. The Lieutenant left a room's seasick faces going from shadow to not, shadow to not.

Prothero stayed away for two full days. Willie fed his blooded horse. He felt ashamed of all assigned duties that now connected him to the in-famous gent from Charleston. Some claimed the man must be a Northern spy. Only this could explain his incivilities to women, such affronts to the joys of Southern standards.

When the Lieutenant did turn up, his uniform looked torn like he'd been wandering through swamps as punishment. Prothero appeared milder now. You could see his face more clear—it lacked earlier bloat and pride. He looked thinner. He acted so ashamed of himself you felt sorry for him despite everything he'd done. He avoided meals in the big house, kept clear of its owners. He ate alone in his tent. During the next day's drill, he over-praised his men, which just upset them. Someplace he'd found extra oats and, by hand, fed these to his badly treated gelding.

The division received orders. It marched away from the fine house, the grounds in bloom. Two kind Randolph ladies waved further lace from their veranda. Many soldiers looked back. Three days later, when a flurry of fighting commenced, when it came clear that there must be a running charge across this contested field, others crouched low. They were waiting, waiting for Prothero's famous forward lurch. Those officers who'd slacked their own charges when Prothero arrived now checked over their shoulders. Stooped, muskets at the ready, men braced to hear the terrible yell. But, silent, the Lieutenant held back. First Prothero looked around. Seemed that he, too, was waiting for some leader's sound. Then—starting to understand what was needed, slowly finding others' eyes all on him—the blond boy straightened his shoulders and, inhaling with greater and greater gasps, visibly steeled himself. Setting glasses on his nose, making the sign of the cross in air before him, he quietly said to those nearest, "Would now be good?"

The Rebel yell he gave that day sounded strangled by embarrassment at its own rooster crudeness. And when, on foot, he struggled up across breastwork and out into the sunny open spaces, Prothero's gait seemed weighted. His slowness endangered others and—rushing by—they knocked the boy aside. Prothero's face was set behind a terrible grin, apology. He was just struggling to catch up, was just calling others' names, when a cannon volley struck him full across his chest and spun him clear back twenty feet into the woods.

7

THE CHAPLAIN, despite Christian principles and his breadth of learning, looked broken now. Despite a strong partiality to founding families, despite having onetime sipped bourbon with the boy's important father, Reverend stayed unforgiving about that harpsichord's ruination. "Why?" he kept asking—speaking of the instrument's ending, not a certain young man's.

Past the division's new encampment, just beyond horses tied in rows, a former cotton field was presently sunk deep with mud. Here fellows were to bury Alfred Huger Fraser Prothero III.

They learned his full name off his papers.

Though the division had moved miles inland from the river James, the harpsichord's owner someway learned about this death. She buggied six miles through a war zone and at real danger to herself. Miss Unison Randolph arrived just after the burial service commenced. From their field with a new hole in it, men watched her carriage advance. Men turned to see her high-stepping this way across the bog. She half smiled at her trouble in unsticking each foot from mud like gumbo. Her pursed mouth showed disgust at sloppy sounds each small boot made sucking loose. Clutching her handbag, she kept skirts' hem wound against her shins. You saw she'd worn her best calfskin boots, ones far too good. Four black armbands had become five. The men here respected her long trip and the trouble she'd taken. But they remembered how she'd compromised herself with the dead man. They felt sure: If *they*'d got killed, she would not be present. Even so, Will and others nodded as this girl, sixteen now, took her place amongst them near the open grave.

"We all must fight," the Chaplain had been saying, and he took up there again after a somber bow. "But, I fear, this young man *enjoyed* said activity too much. I believe, as he promised, he had been quite the decent boy before war changed him. Diatonic gone cacophonous. And I consider that he understood what dreadful things he'd done of late—especially toward objects

worthy of veneration. Difficult it is to understand such wickedness. To ap-
proach the one beautiful thing: to end the one beautiful thing. I must tell
you," he smiled at the newly arrived young lady, "how every season in my
Glee Club, one boy walks in who is plainly gifted with the most perfect ear.
He is elected what we call 'pitch pipe.' Others—less skilled—place their
voices near to his as possible. This makes them all more nearly correct. Our
Saviour remains that for each of us. He is the variable bassoon that we—
His orchestra—must tune to, if you will. No one is so unmusical that he
cannot hear the perfect guiding Tone and—through it—find his own true
voice. Though I do admit—this particular youth here proved as nearly pitch-
deaf as any I've encountered." Others stared into the open grave or at the
tips of Unison's spoilt boots. The Chaplain looked only at the sky. He could
not bring himself to speak of Prothero's finer traits. Instead, the sermon
turned one boy's killing into the topic of tone-deafness.

It was then, like acting out of mercy for the Chaplain's stilted speech
and lack of love, like she now meant to offer true music and not just its
shop talk, one young lady opened her black reticule. She pulled forth a small
blond recorder. How simply she began the Doxology. Unison's face looked
so white in the late-day sun. Her egg-blunt features' main beauty: their
discipline.

The field was mud eighteen inches deep, seven open acres of it. The
western sky was piled with battle-gray clouds. Nearby horses chewed hay,
they stupidly noisily relieved themselves. One mildly said, "Ah-*her*." On this
brown bog—trees at its edges splintered by yesterday's shelling—the pull of
a girl's piping came at you so pure. It started by sounding clean then grew,
while daylight faded, patient, nearbout unearthly.

She performed two hymns. Her elbows poked way out, the upper body
slid subtly side to side tipping with the melody, her eyes were lowered as
notes she piped fell into the open grave. "Jesu, Joy of Man's Desiring." "Sheep
May Safely Graze." "He was Despis-ed." Loose ends of five black armbands
shifted in the breeze. Men and boys felt embarrassed, they were so stirred
by these direct songs. They felt ashamed of earlier dark thoughts about this
strict young virgin. She had cut their silhouettes, she had written their
letters, she had sketched their fallen comrades.

Here in tents, Will and others lived glumly alongside each other—always
checking fore and aft—sure only of likely damage. To each other, they acted
numb if semi-courteous. But every good personal feeling seemed lost way
in the past or hidden far far up ahead. Even now beyond pinewoods, heavy
shelling could be heard. Then came the random tenor snap of closer musket
fire. But steadily threading above all this, much nearer—her reedy tone: "A
Mighty Fortress Is Our God." Notes came out unornamented, simple as the
breath they rode.

Something in her traveling this far, honoring the man who'd stolen her
best music and last civilian pleasure—it upset and surprised the forty men

gathered here clutching hats in hands. She reminded the division of almost too much. Maybe they worried at how like Prothero they'd each and all become. One fellow now trudged toward the woods—one acre of mud away. He just left—something in her tune upset him. Unison Randolph had been playing six full minutes.

Chaplain now turned and watched the young lady. He listened hard, some new amazement complicating his face.

Her piping worked on all the men and boys. They soon felt moved that *any* fellow should be dead, especially a gilded boy like Prothero at twenty-two. Soldiers naturally thought of theirselves, of their own ends. But what seemed even worse than war's claiming a person was: its making you a brute before it got to do you in. Music—starting as a simple statement of the young lady's faith—had twisted, had become a question. The more it shaped that question, the more men shifted weight from foot to foot. Some turned partly aside from its odd growing force. A wind came out of the east. The horses, soothed before, now tossed and snorted.

When the Chaplain spoke again, his lofty unyielding tone had deepened. He now stood looking not towards sky but down at the winding shroud. How small young Prothero appeared there in his personal hole! Somehow, the pince-nez had resisted wrapping and its black ribbon looped out between two twists of cloth, lenses catching round bright bits of sky.

"Lord, we never noticed," the Chaplain began afresh. "That he was quite mad. He was, though. 'By degrees,' he told us. And here I have been holding him to blame. I've been asking 'Why?' as if this boy invented our circumstances and didn't simply fall prey to them.

"Father? such is the nature of our times. Derangement passes, Lord, for what? for valor, Lord. We profess to admire those among us who fight best and kill fastest. We condemn the rest as weak. This boy walked among us, and we recognized him not. I'd met his father, charming man. That changed nothing for me. We might have stopped our Prothero here. I don't quite know how. In such moments as ours, Holy Father, it is not simply hard to become good, Lord. It is so hard—O Father—to *remain* good. Let those parts of us that still are, stay. 'A dark forest'—Lord, as are Thy ways. *Keep* us suffering for our misdeeds. Let our virtues stand separate from our madness, Father. Let us know which part is which." The Chaplain ended: "Do not necessarily give us all *per*fect pitch, Lord. Only give us pitch. Some. A little pitch, Lord."

IT WAS the funeral of a man nobody much liked. And yet some stranger passing on the road—seeing all these downcast eyes, men holding caps against their ribs, the one girl (his sweetheart?) with her instrument—might have taken this for the burial of a great favorite. It became, for many present (for Will, the groom), the single most upsetting funeral in a long war of those. Because of music? Because of a woman's saving presence? Because

Prothero had finally grown still and let people forgive him? Nobody quite understood the power of his ending—no more than they'd figured out his bright odd swerving presence.

Then men started filling in the grave. Bending closer, you still smelled his stubborn perfume rising. Will shoveled dirt, aware of Target over there wearing a Fraser's plaid blanket, tied among mules, eating oats, not knowing—of course—what'd happened. (Soon many others would ride Target in turn and badly till he dropped.) Six shovels were used. Everybody helped but Unison. The boy's grave had seeped half full of boggy tea-colored water. The young lady went on playing a German instrument. You saw fingers shifting on their pear-wood stops. Her face wet, upper body moving—sinuous and natural, comfortable rocking side to side. Whatever she wept for now (her brothers and father? a lost love?), how perfectly she piped hymn after hymn. Now she did a little country dance air, whatever came to mind, continuous. Her eyes weren't lowered now. They bore into other mourners, hard requests. She'd found a strange fearless stance—ruined boots planted farther apart. Men looked away from her. Soldiers stared at their feet.

Done, men filed away to camp. They moved in small clumps. Will and the Chaplain waited last, they left the grave together hinting how Unison Randolph should follow. But the young lady stayed out there a while—her trim silhouette made the only vertical for acres. Her back was towards them. Her purse was yet strung over one arm, she kept playing in the middle of noplace, playing to the newly heaped mud. Wind toyed with her armbands: From camp, others watched her braided bun. They listened. Had to.

If this was not true story, it might perfectly well end right here, child. There would be decisions made, sweet resolve on all sides: to act better, to really learn from this.

But fact is, it's a war and it's not over and it's always harder than you think. She'd soon kept at it for nearabout a hour. That's a right long time as the day is ending and you want to get on with things and eat your dinner. The man who'd walked off to the woods came hiking back. But when he got some nine hundred yards from her, the others saw him pause, hear, then turn and stalk right back toward trees. Above those pines, the sun had lowered, gone a somber red.

The ranking major now left his tent, he settled in a canvas chair. He studied the young lady, listened to the start of her second straight hour's music. Men slouched against cannon's wheels and in wagons' flatbeds. Men watched her. Miss Unison's dress was black, the field brown, the late-day sky a rosy saturated gray. It made a right sad picture. Some soldiers started fidgeting, wishing she'd stop. Ten or twelve, though right eager for chow, retired to their tents. It wore on them, her style of music—the pure simple quality, tireless. Some serious brilliance ran straight through her ditties, now came hymns, now jigs. It was so *true*. Truth always leaves a pleasure asking questions.

First men told theirselves they worried for her health, her being too long out there in a marshy field behind enemy lines. Then guys had to admit they'd had enough, thank you. Her music changed from being a pleasing statement of one girl's homey faith, it went moving on through asking and more towards a challenge. Now its perfect lightness weighed on them. Miss Unison's music seemed a lesson: *"Why have we lost these people? Who is making us do this?"*

Finally, the Chaplain sent Will out with a cup of hot coffee. The blue willow mug sat steaming where the boy put it beside her feet. Will looked up, ventured a dim smile. Her face was swollen, wet. She saw him, nodded curt, but Miss Randolph never missed a note.

Now the sun had nearly set. She kept playing. The company doctor, known as See and Saw, went next. He stood where she could plainly view him. He bent closer, said, "It's time. Thank you. Your own strength to think about. My advice . . ."

But with a shrill note she turned away from him. Seemed rude. Doc came back shaking his head, miffed, hating to look powerless before other men.

One corporal eager to *do* something, wanting to give her a sign, reached into his vest, pulled out a good-luck brass piece shaped like a horseshoe. Bashful, he straggled out, held it near her face—made the highborn lady know he gave this as a loan and not a gift and mostly as a bribe to shush her. He placed it near her small caked boots, he walked back, looking smug. But it didn't work. Two others dragged out separately, put down a ring, a keepsake handkerchief.

They were hungry. What did this woman *want*?

She never stopped. She seemed to be mourning *them* while blaming them. Her tone grew wilder if more sweet. Two full hours into it—some listeners felt accused. Felt sick. Imagine this girl's mother pacing their veranda, worried. Under Unison's boots, in final light, the Lieutenant's grave rose just a little higher than its field.

How could she go on? What would stop her? If a battle came out of the trees yonder, that'd pretty much shut her up, wouldn't it? If she got hurt, she'd need them then—that'd quiet her! Soldiers felt they couldn't go about their business. Music had them like a trance, a taunt. She was nagging them, that was it. The cook made no move to start the fire for supper. Darkness settling. You could barely see her—and then you only heard her out there. Nothing of the war could continue with her out here right in it. She'd probably *planned* this!

When the division had been camped on Randolph property, men had found Miss Unison a touching mascot, even her sadness: a inspiration. Here, out here, no. Men wanted to get on with things. They were hungry. Night had fallen and Prothero was buried. What next? Let's get it the hell over with.

More fellows withdrew into tents, but the canvas proved porous. Her sharp music still reached them. One boy said just, "No." Some men started

cupping hands over their ears. She played anything that came to her. Southern fifes and bugles only dared "Yankee Doodle Dandy" during the firing-
squad execution of traitors. Unison now chanced choruses of that alternated
with holy "Dixie," weird. Was like listening, privileged, to the sound of
another person's ransacking inside thoughts. Nursery jingles, little love
songs, scales, anthems, everything. She seemed to play about promises. The
pipe sang about something her listeners had all lost but could still perfectly
remember. Her music would sometimes smear a bit, maybe from tiredness,
but melody pushed on into another hour—even more urgent. It ran shriller.
In the distance, munitions' rumbling sounded worse with the sun gone.

"Unison?" The Chaplain called in his grand voice. "Thank you, Unison?
You've done more than your part, that is enough. I ask you on behalf of
your father and brothers . . . Unison."

She didn't stop. Now, only fifteen fellows waited in the open, all others
were on cots in tents, staring noplace. Finally, one man (nobody but hisself
later knew who) slipped around behind the others still turned towards her,
seeming held here. Unnoticed in the blackness, this fellow lifted a single
dirt clod. In Unison's direction, he threw the thing. He stood near the road
out by her buggy. He tossed his pellet over the heads of other infantrymen
yet facing her field. The Chaplain and the Major, sitting forward, pretended
not to notice. In darkness, that was easy. A second and third toss. You could
hear the man give a little grunt as he hurlt one after another, using all his
strength.

Nobody stopped him.

Finally, one struck her back. You heard her pipe give off a extra squeal.
Though the melody ran on—determined—a second pebble hit her, harder
yet. Music held its own. Someone joined the stone tosser on the road, then
a third did. Soon over the piping, a snapping sound out there like some
hailstorm centered on one grave. Finally, her tune did falter, stop. You heard
a whimper follow her each breath. Rock throwing ceased.

All the men wandered out of their tents, so glad for silence. There was
a moment when anything might've happened. Some stone thrower could've
run toward her—might've pushed her down on the mud of Prothero's new
grave, could've yanked her skirts up, pressed one hand over her mouth, and
done whatever. Whatever, repeatedly. Men might have found a large rock
and beat her head to paste. This didn't happen. Instead, silence seemed
Unison's new kind of accusing. Felt almost worse than music that'd bravely
kept this massive stillness back.

You heard bug noises, frogs croaking. Nothing else. In camp no lantern
had been lit. Only now did soldiers hear the girl's feet squishing mud, moving
in rushes and halts, as she headed fearful back this way. They heard Miss
Randolph walk right through their ranks. Somebody saw her holding one
side of her head. Soldiers eased aside to let her pass. Once in her buggy,
she clucked, "Effie? Good Effie," probably to the horse. Unison turned her
cart around in three bad tries, then trotted off—bound back, unescorted,

those six miles to a fine riverside house that Sherman's troops would burn in '65.

Men stayed right where they had been. And for some minutes. They waited till something happened next. More music? enemy fire that'd give them a excuse to move? Then there came another dragging step from out there in the black black field. Two men ran for firearms. But, oh, it was just that fellow who'd trudged off to hide in the woods. Only when he returned did Cook stand, yawn loud, say, "So. We got us any willing fire builders?" He struck a match to his oil lamp. Tonight ten noisy volunteers came forward. Others stretched, feeling meaner maybe—but easier. Just them here, just men/boys/males, honor among thieves, all do-gooder outsiders gone.

Among the troops, nobody ever spoke of what'd happened way out here. They never mentioned Unison again. She'd lost their respect. She was dead to them.

This I've told is just a little incident of war.

It won't show up in any of your more official histories, child.

I heard it from W. More Marsden, Falls, North Carolina, born in 18 and 49—my late husband—Will, the groom for Target, the horse of young Lieutenant Prothero from Charleston.

This happened March through May of 1863.

Poor men, poor boys. Understand, two more whole years of it were waiting for them up ahead.

RECORDS show us: Unison never married. Until 19 and 41, she was teaching piano to the children of the prominent in Richmond (Virginia).

8

—YESTERDAY, on a home outing, Taw and me rode the blue Chevy bus. Among others we sat, not hand in hand but at least pressed wheel-to-wheel-chair. Bus stopped alongside a shiny hearse. In back, one tapered mahogany box. Taw looked down at it. He snorted for all to hear, "That's what *I* need. A nice, dry, lined coffin." Many laughed. At our age, the laugh of recognizing. We'd all thought that.

Still, it got me down a bit. I went back to quilt planning. It's comforting, nights specially. I know what fabrics I would choose but guess Jerome can't find them. Still, just telling makes them so.

Requested cloths so far?: a nosegay of dotted Swiss from Shirley's pinafore so yellow it'd cause a citrus-grower to pucker. One pair of long johns, cashmere—red/white/blue, knitted by a mother for her iceberg-bound soldier boy. A white snippet from Lady More Marsden's stay-at-home silk wrapper charred the faintest ivory. Maybe one of Little Xerxes' tuxedo tails—white satin fine as Lady's silk or better, and as a tribute to her. Baby's plaid organdy hairbow. The piping off one aunt-stitched honeymoon travel-outfit, seriously stained. One pink cotton blanket I wrapped naked Archie in and ran for help. A stiff plug from Maimie Beech's starched uniform that broke like cardboard when she sat first time each day. Poppa's blue serge postal outfit, worn but rarely. My granddad Angus McCloud's hunting-plaid kilt. My own momma's narrow batiste slip, hacked by garden shears whilst chopping off curls and wasps. One small square of gauze from my Ned's eyes that day on the Men's Ward. A swatch dyed with Momma's people get-rich indigo. Maybe dingy lovely Belgian lace from a sad lady in transit on club cars. Gray worsted off the tunic of a child soldier that so unhappily outgrew it. Jerome's best gold-lamé disco "top." And surely samples from a home-bred, home-fed, home-killed, hand-tanned real mink coat. Plus green velveteen off a costume shared by Bible Judith and my regretted Louisa. And stuff it with the down from Reba's holy red birds.—That'll do for *one* side, child.

What a counterpain to sleep under or die in. We all got to represent each other. Every color is a deed and suffering, a prize. Our quilt'll be, oh, quite the winding cloth and glad rag.

—Pull it over me!

Enough

By night on my bed I sought him whom my
soul loveth: I sought him, but I found him not.
I will rise now, and go about the city in the
streets, and in the broad ways I will seek him
whom my soul loveth: I sought him, but I
found him not.

—SONG OF SOLOMON 3:1–2

I'D ALWAYS been married to a old man but now I was onto oldening
up myself. If I'd started aging, he seemed ancient as some minor
pyramid and about that easy to pocket. For years now, he'd been mild, lost,
furious, lost. He spent most days in one of his nightshirts. Slave-made things,
they'd outlasted slavery and most that sewed them. Beautiful with monograms—frayed at cuffs and collar but irreplaceable, being 100 percent mortal
cotton. You can't beat the stuff.

His presence in the back bedroom became a demand every minute. I
counted my distance from the brass bed (even whilst out shopping at Lucas'
Superette—big-time, Luke'd got). Cap kept usual relics hanging on our bedstead—the bugle, its blood-red cord faded all but purple now, the twig off
a sycamore where something bad happened, the handsome heavy scabbard.
If my man stayed quiet too long down that first-floor hall, I worried. Like
with my children—ours—only silence meant you needed to go check, and
quick.

Castalia helped. Over she'd come, bottom-heavier and slower-moving,
with a countable number of silver hairs like watch mainsprings curling at
each temple. In all seasons, she honored the homegrown masterpiece of
mink, long about ankle length it struck her by now. Seemed more a cren-
ellated fort she peeked over the top of. Only up close did you see how many
tiny pelts had gone to make it, poor conscripts signed into some glue of a
army.

She spoke less but, when she did, talked more about Back Then. You
heard her make things up about a Africa now sprung almost wholly from
her head. People I knew she'd known in Falls would turn up in some tale
of long-lost tribal uncles. Did I stop her? You kidding? *Me*, child? I poured

more coffee the color of her coat and her. I tried not to listen for my massy male baby down yonder hall, a genius at interrupting good parts.

Cas's skin had lately lost some of its sheen. One of our pet beauty aids was olive oil and—while she talked—we'd rub some steady into our chapped knees and elbows. Though it helped considerable, it left us smelling like two portions of one salad.

At corners of Castalia's generous mouth—the starter culture that'd taught my husband to kiss, and his daddy, and had even kissed my mother-in-law and had, I well remembered, seriously kissed me—excavations showed new sinkholes of wrinkles. Under eyes, new folds were working crisscross, tic-tac-toe-ing. Ashamed, I thought of a elephant's skin seen onct at the county fair. Her clothes tamed down to browner, golder tones—the hot pinks and yellows lost or given up. She was quieter around town and people got even more scared of her. Merchants now gave her merchandise at cost, and called it tithing. She'd sometimes laugh and you could still see maybe half a inch of the first beauty near her eyes, but here, too: a puzzle of boxy lines made the slightest mirth feel a little bitter. Even when she looked at me, I felt some edge—like "Is this shrimp all I can find to call best friend?" If I *was* that. Sure wouldn't have minded hearing Cassie call me it. Never really did.

Her weight grew, the arms rarely lifted from her sides. Couldn't, probably. She acted nicer to fewer and fewer loved ones (the list had never been long) but she behaved more neutral to old enemies.

Sometimes she'd shed her coat in our house (a honor), she'd kick her shoes off and pad down the hall and bellow at our patient, "Look, what ails you, High and Mighty? The fight gone out you carcass finally, you menace to womankind. Know who I am? Well say it then."

I waited, clearing the table. She shrieked, "Luce? He say 'Cassius' . . . I believe he *do* know."

Like me, she wanted him to *be* here. All here. We would rather take our chances with his wild side. We liked that better than this other drool and fade. That seemed a judgment on us both. Her and me won't ready. Men lapse faster. We get some catch-up ball at the end—a little justice.

OF COURSE, I still knew folks around town. The checkout girls at Safeway sometimes called me by name. I didn't have no idea who they were till they asked how one of my far-flung kids was doing. Louisa now headed her whole hospital's nursing schedule assignments up in Newport News. She wrote regrets that her skills won't more help to me here with her cranky pop. Ned taught boys at the Travis Methodist Home for the Blind, Plymouth, N.C. Only saw him on holidays. He'd come home by train, him with his cane and one leather satchel, the dark glasses, and a head balding early—under his mad-professor hair I'd see that perfect smile, the same. He was often the last off, helped by conductors who treated him like more a guest of honor than he ever made of hisself. Ned might bring home his latest prize pupil, some boy who'd lost his sight and his folks in one car wreck—and who was glad to be someplace real for Christmas. I always felt glad and nervous, having Ned home. Like he was a celebrity. We got many letters about how good he taught, how selfless and all. I would sit at my kitchen table (same one, naturally—"if it could talk") and just read praise of him and feel so proud and yet I'd wonder what he might've done . . . Well, but, the truth is—this sounds bad, I'm sure—but times, thinking back, I can't rightly remember him unblind. That's how long it's been. That's how good he took to it. Times, I recalled how he once used his eyes as cover while he thought back in there mulling somewheres—eyesight a wall to hide in the shadow of. Here lately, too, the two names Ned have merged till it almost seems that our blind beautiful Ned's father was not Captain but the first Ned, who'd someway managed to have a son *through* Marsden, so we got one Smythe instead. Let that pass. Confusions. You'll hear more of them from me in time, I fear. Others here forget what hour our dinner's served. My failure I'll call overremembering. It gets a jumble sale and crazy quilt of this beside that, identical, but eighty years apart and never met. As I listened to our blind son chatter bright over some new listening machine at school, one bought with money he helped butter up the local rich to win—I found I was forgiving Captain Marsden more and more. For that, at least for that part. Seems we each have got some set shape to our lives. You can change degrees in that bend, but you never get to challenge the whole basic shape beneath it. Other times, the opposite seems true, so let that pass. What do *I* know?

Our twins were business partners of the rarest kind—them what trust each other through and through. They'd *married* twins (and the wedding was a little rich in symmetry and gingham darlingness for my blood, but I didn't say nothing critical at the time). They were together in the real estate game, as they call it, pistols them two. Coming up, they'd never been my whiz kids but now riches were raining down on them like another part of the plan. Didn't matter they'd been held back a grade. They had money, were my only children not in nursing or teaching or some service to others. Except Baby, of course. But I reckon acting is a service. She had a walk-on part as a French maid in *Her Second Marriage* and walked off with the reviews. She sent us copies by the fastest possible mail. One said: "How many things can be done with an ostrich-feather duster? Consult 'Baby' Marsden, currently seen as Fifi, the scene stealer in our latest parlor drama at the Roxy. Other cast members must loathe 'Baby' precisely as much as last night's audience was thoroughly hers." In the margin, Baby'd put a exclamation point beside a question mark. Wanting Mamma's approval, not sure the review was rave enough?

Things moved and changed and I knew I'd been through most of what'd have to happen next. Experience has a way of working for me in threes. It now seemed more than two-thirds shot.

One day at the Superette, I spied this September sale on new school notebooks, a bright stack, and though my children were off being grown or beyond, I bought just one. Red. I opened it at my kitchen table. I planned to get something down at last. I've forever loved a fresh chance. My kids had told me a couple times I should write down what'd happened in my elastic lifetime bandaging century to century, a tree graft. "Nobody'd believe it," Louisa smiled. I wished she'd lose some of that weight, she still had such a pretty face. —Well, I drank three extra cups of my vice, coffee (nobody's perfect) and wrote: "In the town of Falls (N.C.) a plain little girl was born . . ." I crossed that out. Awful, bland as anybody. So then I jotted: "Me, I started out young . . ." Too sassy by half. I wadded up the page. There seemed too much to tell while I was setting here alone. I needed a crowd, or one questioner's "Yes?" Needed to *talk* it out. My single major knack. And so I took the almost virgin notebook to my husband's room (I'd just got it "broke in" good). He looked at me, suspicious, pleased. I put a pencil into one big tawny fist of him, the book I opened in his other. "Get busy, Mr. Man. Write your memoirs. You've loved all them other war ones. Mark Twain wrote Grant's and they made a fortune, pulled them both from debt. So, start. Get us out of hock."

He tilted his head my way, more the way puppies do or parrots in movies. Trying to understand, cute but by accident.

"Memoirs means memories, nothing fancier. Write your memories in here. List them. I'll be back at four and I want to find a goodly start, boy, hear me?"

When I stepped in later, he was sloppily asleep. But I saw marks on page one, and oh, my heart did a little skedaddle snare-drum roll. Odd, after all this time to grow excited at the thought of your old man's life being wrote up (or down). His years might finally achieve a start, and mid, and end. That'd help it *mean* something to both him and me. He had made a drawing looked like this:

I stood in the late-day side room (you'll be relieved to hear we didn't share a bed no more). I studied this sketching of his major war loss. Marsden's memory was in there yet, in some Miami of the nervous system, fled as far south as The Confederate Scared can get. I looked over at the moony-bearded face, one now watching me. Eyes suddenly open—still that gray and wildly young-looking.

"Take me," he said, plain if croakish. First, alarmed, I thought he was being lovey-dovey again. (When I bathed him, he still revved up right manly but he'd mercifully forgot what-all to do with it.)

"To . . . where, sug?"

"Back . . . to tree, war, Ned's tree where . . . back, please, Buttermilk."

The nickname got me. "Really want to see all that mess again, sug? Think it'd help you rest more easy? That it?"

He held his massy finger up before his face. "One," a sleepy voice said. "Once . . . more. Poor Ned. Lucy? they shot Ned."

"I know. Was a loss to all of us. Yes, they did shoot him."

SO WE went.

I'd become a good driver while taking Ned to schools, learned from Cassie's third-oldest son, handsome gray-eyed Antwan. I stopped by a Lucas-Hedgepath service station—another business owned by our great merchants' families' enterprising inbred children. (Tied to Falls by inherited property, they stayed put, unlike my scattered tribe.)

"You think you're up to this?" the fellow at the pump asked, a second cousin of Ruth, our old neighbor. (She'd killed herself at thirty-nine when Willard finally broke his cherry-blossom silence to petition for a legal divorce after all that time. He couldn't just stay merrily gone, could he?) "Sure," says I. "Been before."

Cap was in the car beside me. The filling-station man give us every map of either Carolina and Virginia. I was determined to do this last thing right for my Captain. Figured this would put me well ahead on what little of the tally sheet he might still remember.

Castalia helped me strap him in with rope. Man couldn't sit up, chin'd be on the dashboard otherwise. This was, I believe, the world's first seat belt but did I get one nod of credit for inventing it? Not a penny.

The joy of knowing how to drive—having a purse temporarily stuffed full of green, a brisk October day, the chance of maybe later doing a surprise side trip and seeing our daughter, the top nurse. The sky that day glowed the color of a dare.

"You know where we're getting ready to go, sir?"

"Get," he repeated. "Get . . . even?"

"Darl, we'll get to Virginia and maybe we'll get you some nice car-trip memories. But 'even' is one thing nobody ever gets. Not even you."

He seemed cheerful, hearing our destination. The few neighbors that knew our mission come down to the fronts of their yards and waved. Cap saluted for the first time in six months. I said, "You do know, don't you?"

So, back to war yet again. Would it never end? We passed the Mall, flattening a spot where the beauty of The Lilacs mansion once literally stopped traffic on land and water. Where the Big House stood, a Toys "R" Us! We're the gods' playthings okay, darling. Toys "R" Us!

Then all up into Virginia did the happy couple tool. Me helping him with the ropes and then his zipper. This was in the roadside weeds. We never stopped at rest rooms because I could hardly squire the Cap into the Men's side. The Ladies would've squealed seeing shoes that huge in the next booth.

Took me two days and at least one fleabag motel I checked us out of fast on account of pre-used sheets, imagine. On up to Gaines' Mill. Onct in the town proper, I aimed forth from there, fanning in all directions, asking farmers of both races at the few farmlike stores left. Mostly there were basket shops and cute antique places that would, you knew, charge you a fortune for something they probably "aged" in their garage last weekend.

Two men told me that such a lake was long since landfill, ancient history. "Who you got there in your Chevy, ma'am?" "A old man what fought at that lake. He's needing to see the spot again." "Well, I declare. Not the Civil War, you know not. He must've been a baby in it, how many are left? I do declare."

I hate being interesting to strangers. Now, honey, don't sulk. I wouldn't count *you*—you? a stranger? After all *we* been through together? Why you've kept on coming back remains a central mystery that warms my heart.

Him and me wasted two more days searching, Captain wearing diapers I'd made from some old dormitory sheets. You have to really love the other person, since this was previous to the Adult Pampers that are very bread-and-butter necessity at Lanes' End Rest here. I invented seat belts *and* Adult Pampers. Meantime, *People* runs dumb articles on Dog Groomers to the Soap Stars! I ask you.

Another day and him all-a-fidget like some child.

I got testy, hearing his ropes creak. "You still even *in*terested?"

It was a mean thing to say.

"They shot Ned," he told me. Then he repeated the same thing for forty minutes, put the emphasis on a different of the three words each time. "Didn't they?" he ended.

I agreed. "I sure wish they hadn't of. Why, if Ned Smythe and his wife and their kids had become our kids' friends, wouldn't that've been ideal-like? if your Ned had come home and hitched up with somebody I considered worthy company, some woman, well, like . . . Castalia," and I laughed. He did, too. I almost had a wreck, seeing—or thinking—he'd maybe understood.

Finally his "They shot Ned" made me stop to ask again concerning bodies of water hereabouts.

It was another pottery place, a big stone barn, and inside I found a shaggy boy throwing this slick vase at his kick wheel. He sat there shell-backed and when I spoke over his classical music, he jerked but threw hands far *from* the pot and, thank God, didn't spoil it. Even in surprise, he was graceful. I described the MIA pond. I told more of the story than I usually let out. Music played and a aged finch hopped to and fro in a pretty wicker old-time cage like one of Winona's.

The potter cleaned his hands on a filthy apron he wore, so crusted it seemed a starter garden with armholes. He asked, "This pond wouldn't have had a mill on it, a gristmill?" "Sure did." Thought I'd said so, getting addled, hate that. Happens a lot lately. I fell last week. I don't want to talk about it.

He walked to the back of his studio and opened the wide doors and led me out onto a kind of stone ramp beside a suburban pond.

He told me how his girlfriend's mother had inherited this bankrupt gristmill. At the pond's far end, cedar-shingled homes clumped, all alike.

And yet, just short of a motorboat dock, some older trees had been saved back. I pointed across water, "I think that's where it happened."

Potter said, "And the participant is actually in your car out front?"

"The one that lived is."

So this boy hurried out there with me, checked, said, "Wow. Some patriarch. Looks positively Mosaic."

"He's way older than me, always was."

"I saw that at once, of course."

"You'll go far, son," and I climbed into the car, thanking him. Imagine driving right up to the right gristmill. He told me I couldn't pull close to the water on that far bank, said he'd follow in his jeep and he'd help. The potter turned over a sign on his studio door, it read: "Closed Creatively." No comment. He locked up like he was going to Paris, France. (The modern world! the trusties are the last ones to be foolish enough to trust others.)

Our old Chevy followed his jeep, mud-flecked as the potter hisself. I think his name was Wade or something. Wayne. Call him Wade, I could find out if I really had to know.

He finally pulls down a dirt road I never would of found. "We're here, I think," I told the Captain. And from nodding in sleep, he went to being so fully awake. He had come alive so quick that it seemed to me (for a instant anyhow) his whole senility had been faked. As a personal convenience. As a decoy, waiting out death. I left him in our car while me and the boy with clay in his longish hair patrolled the shoreline. We passed deep ruts and I asked him about them—Wade said it was from the motorbikes young kids ride all back in here. I pictured those tires passing over the unmarked grave of young Ned Smythe, Confederate, and thought he'd like that, twelve, thirteen hisself. "Bike noises travel across that lake like you cannot believe, drive us up the wall. We thought we'd found the end of nowhere after Manhattan. You never have, I guess."

"No," said I.

He took my arm, polite boy if filthy. We had to gallop down a real steep bank. I think his name was Wade. Waylon. No, *was* Wade, definite. I walked, wondering would I know the sycamore if it jumped me. Did it even matter if I found the exact one? But yeah, it always matters. Has to. I'd come this far and, if only for myself, I wanted to do this right. Wearing my nice little linen dress with the light jacket and a new leather belt, flats but good ones. As Captain lost interest, I'd took to seeing Lolly monthly and buying clothes a bit. Along lake's edge, Wade and me stepped over milk cartons and used French letters. There was clots of junk mail in bright IOU colors. The mess made me sad.

"It's awful, I know," the potter apologized.

"*You* didn't do it, you want it *nice*. Don't blame yourself for what you didn't do, Wade, Dwayne, no, Wayne." Or whatever. Definitely Wade. (Memory is a muscle—one that needs constant flexing. Lose it or use it.)

• • •

I KNEW which sycamore. It told me. Fact. A wind come up and leaves turned sides and it was the granddaddy of them all. It stood on the little hill but most of its land had been lost now to the lake and all these roots showed like them twists on the surface of some great brain. But the whole tree was yet alive, I saw that.

"And somebody was killed here? Skirmish?"

"Snipers," I said, and looked quick across the water, just checking.

"Imagine. And he knew them?"

"Loved him. He was here when it happened. Kids, both of them. Left home holding hands the way girls that age would."

We trudged back to fetch my Captain. He'd someway untied hisself and got his uniform tunic from out the honeymoon satchel where he seen me store it. He'd tore a hole in the old rose-patterned valise instead of using its clasps, but there he stood, ready. As we drew nearer, Wade said, "Your husband looks like God in Michelangelo's 'Creation of Adam.' What a noble head."

I said, yeah, well, Noble is as noble does. I asked if that was like *Michael-angelo* and he said, "Actually Mick, I'm told, is correct. Mick-alangelo."

"You don't say. Live and learn." I thought of Momma's *An American Child's Sistine* folio I won't allowed to touch with my grimy mitts and blood-sister bandage. Odd how jumbled every moment is.

Down to water we got Cap, him trying to stand at attention while we tried and keep him easing along pitched red clay banks. "He knows," the potter told me quiet over Cap's shoulder.

"He knows," Captain agreed, embarrassing Wade. Wade didn't understand Cap was referring to Ned. Cap meant: knows we're here, Ned does.

We led the old soldier to the shade under that largest sycamore. I saw how its huge shadow had stunted lesser trees struggling near but under it. Captain stared up into the thing. "Right," he said, and gave me a look of the old wild intelligence, and even a little sexual something underneath. I loved him then!

"You're most welcome. We got fewer kids along this time, don't we, honey?"

He beckoned me to stoop down where he rested in the weeds. Wade turned away from what he expected to be some tearful tender scene maybe.

Cap pointed up its trunk. "There's more," he said, and rubbed fingers together. I knew then he meant the harness, maybe a grain of it still up there.

I WANTED to put all this behind us. The chances of discovering any findable horse tether this many years after, it seemed impossible, but you are either *in* on something or you're not. I stepped out of my flats and leaned against the sycamore trunk to pick off a few corn plasters that might get in my way and—considering the strapping helpful Wade blinking yonder—might be also unsightly.

"He expects you to . . ." Wade pointed at its top, ninety feet above.

"Yeah, oh he *expects* . . . he's still good at that."

"To *climb?*"

"You got it, honey. And I still can, I bet. Was onct a pro. Someways I never have felt more relaxed than in a tree house me and a good girlfriend built. —Whether I'll find what my husband's hoping, that's another matter. But I didn't drive all this way not to least *try*. Here goes nothing."

"Wait," I told the Cap, like he had a choice. I bent and he caught my hand, he kissed my knuckles. I said, "Don't expect. It's later than you think, century-wise."

His face was spread rosy with widening memory, the old light, the old poison maybe raring up on him but seeming sweetened some. All I need, thought I, is his dying on me *here*. And yet, as I set my handbag in a prominent spot, that really didn't seem so bad, Cap's exiting here. I might borrow a shovel from Wade. I'd dig a slow but good-sized hole, just past complicating tree roots. I'd buy a nice jug from that boy and set it at the head of Cap's grave, a purchase to thank Wade—Dwayne? no, Wade—for helping. Sweet boy.

He now offered to give me the first hoist up. He laced his fingers and knelt, stiff arms V-ed before me. Touching his shoulders, I stepped up. His powerful palms joined, toughened, under my sole. And just the feel of my weight swung in young Wade's fine hands, it gave me a sudden twinge. "Oooh," I said, old enough to act right trashy for a change. "Oh, honey, but all them sinews feels *so* good." He laughed, breath on my leg. "Two, three . . ." And then I was up. Heavenly breeze.

Hadn't been inside of a tree for years, tens of years. Leaves of years and time. Felt like being let in some temple/home. To arrive high and invisible in the safe hollow of it. Talk of a Child's Garden of Verses. Here was what a person had, just shy of the flight I'd always longed for. I went on up, slow, but limb for limb, I did him proud. Did me proud. Did Shirley, Cassie, Reba, Maimie Beech, and fearful Momma proud. I really scouted for some cinched spot, traces. It mostly was a smooth-barked good-climbing tree. You didn't burn your hands too bad.

"Call me," Wade hollered due sky, "if there's a problem or . . ."

"Thanks, but I like it. I can see your mill. You're lucky to have a whole stone mill and all. Must stay cool right along. Your wife pot too?"

I didn't listen to his answer. Round flaky logs were underfoot. It being October the big yellow leaves scraped against each other everywhere, looked the size of certificates, like I'd climbed into a courthouseful—the family tree. I thought of hollow African logs, ship's masts. The potter was trying to chat up my senile husband. Wade asked Cap about his Captain's uniform. No answer past a belch Caruso could've envied. Woodwind.

Wade had offered to climb *for* me. I said it was my duty to. I wanted to manage this while I still could. Cap won't talking. So Wade stole off into the woods a ways to pee—not daring to go far from Cap but worried that

I'd see. Young Wade kept checking modestly over his shoulder. From my spot, I could plainly look right down onto it, his pinkish decent standard deal from direct overhead. You know me: I considered whistling a catcall but didn't. From this high, that stream from Wade looked silver.

I'd at least drove to this spot. For all the grief the old coot down there had given me, along with good laughs sometimes and the bonus of our own particular godsend kids—this seemed my last offering to him.

I found one set of branches where the flesh of wood seemed double-scarred. But if this was where one poor bugle boy tied a mule harness for a goodly swing toward clean pond water, I would never know. I touched the spot for luck anyhow. Soon I'd been in that tree forty minutes. To tell you honest, I was still somewhat of a monkey but not a young monkey.

Then I did what I been doing throughout this whole told record, child. I took the best facts available and tried making them connect and last and maybe stretch some. I imagined *with* facts, around them. I did history the favor of believing it literal, meaning I invented some of it! I unbuckled my natural-toned leather belt (ten good dollars last month at a Ekstein's Finer Women's Fall Apparel sale). I rubbed it hard against a broad boll. I worked thin leather against coarse wood till heated rawhide frayed then snapped. And now I had a thong stretching fourteen inches. I scraped both sides till it did look old—older than me, if maybe not so old as the vet down there, patient, eager, jaundiced on his back. Odd, the going down was harder and way scarier than my getting up. Ain't it ever the way? coming down in this life. Was I really up that high and must I now fall?

The potter jumped when my feet poked free of green.

Captain had slid off asleep while I ranged up yonder knocking on heaven's very gate for him. Which pleased then peeved me and I suddenly thought, staring at his peaceful lowered white lashes: He's dead and gone! Why, oh why should my life have been *this* one, with *this* one?

But warrior's peepers opened on that same gray I'd fallen for (and into) in 1899 when he flared them off a reviewing stand where the doomed McKinley spoke. How huge these eyes looked under me, like they were the pond that a shot person, seeing he was shot and knowing he was falling into water, would choose to free-fall into. I thought for one second of the canceled color in the blank eyes of our son. "Find?" Cap swallowed hard.

"Sir? We *are* in luck!" and I squatted, dangled the thing before him like some prize snake just discovered. Near me, Wade's sandals took one surprised step back till he saw it had to be my belt.

I held the thing in air over Captain's face. He smiled so, the gums long receded but teeth almost eerie in how white and perfect they yet were. He grinned, and it was like Cassie's dwindling inch of beauty near the eyes, all his charm and sweetness, the full child seemed greenhoused in that rare grin widening beneath me. I admitted, "You're a darling, in a way." He didn't hear me. He held the precious thong between his hands and snapped it. "Good, still good," he said. I was grinning, stupid, down at his delight. As usual, half ashamed of my rich pleasure. Wade's dusty feet were good feet waiting like Mick-alangelo statue-feet nearby.

"*They* killed Ned," and Cap pointed back past me, and up. I glanced there and when I turned again, he again yelled "They" at my face but like "They" was my *name*, honey. He next gently pulled me near his mouth framed in its white mustache and the mouth said, simply, and with force, but only for my ears and lucid as anything, "You never have been enough, but . . . thank you." Tears sprung in my eyes, furious. But he seemed to pull me down for one quick kiss, him making up like always, and I was just compiling a long list of wounded comebacks when I saw these pieces of fabric floating between his face and mine. Then I felt a sort of brace around my collarbone and only slow did I understand how cleverly he'd got the thong behind my neck and then up under it. I understood how powerful his hands still were in cutting off the wind. My wind. First you feel embarrassment at Wade's seeing and then you think I better stop this anyhow and then you hear a hiss like prolonged jingle bells, which is blood ringing early warning in your either ear. Next you feel the gristle in your neck creak like a tested door lock before the full word "strangled" hits. "Closed Creatively." Thumbs pressing so and from directly underneath. "They!" he called like warning others off from me. "THEY!"

When I sensed the world was turning yellow and now gone spotted with red enameled daubed *over* that yellow—when I found that I did miss having my air in personal savings where I could control it, my legs shot straight out, and I tried beating him. I give it everything I owned. Child, all's fair in love and war and I had him on both counts. But a life of strength seemed saved in him. He was Savings and had been, I was Checking and too I was checking out. You are face to face, eyes working good enough to see the huge gray eyes below you—merry—noticing your tone declining into Northern blue, and it is Satan's own shit-eating grin. Excuse my language.

"Mrs. . . . is this a . . . family? . . . I mean should I maybe?" And I give a sound like a rabbit run over by a Model T and the potter was stooping on and around and over us, was working to dislodge my recent belt and maybe please pry Captain's mitts from off my general neck area please. I finally rolled free and gasped, so glad, both hands massaging my bashed windpipe. I tossed my own head back hard onto rocky soil to try and knock some wind deep into me. I heard Cap then get young Wade by the throat. And I was looking at the sycamore above me. A struggle nearby. How beautiful its yellow leaves. Just as I heard "They're *loose*!", out I passed.

I woke in the jeep. Cap slumped over in our car. How still everything was, just one mockingbird's song, highway noise far off. The potter who'd saved my life, he'd been busy tying up my husband—hog-tying him this go-round to our front seat. The boy, neck ruddied, stood pouring Cocola into a pretty handmade mug, goldfish brushed in glazes on its sides. I admired the fish a while before he saw I was awake.

"I knew you were okay. I checked your 'vital signs,' as they say do. I considered the hospital. I secured him. Unbelievable. Your neck is cut in back, you feel that? Never saw such strength, what possessed him? Did he know what he was doing to you?"

"When?" I asked.

2

I DROVE home quick. I didn't stop at the roadside weeds for his bathroom requirements. I knew that onct I untied the man, he'd maybe dive at me again. Instead I let him soil hisself. I'd just open the window. I'd pretty much had it by now. I trust you won't think me hard-hearted Hannah, but I'd hoped to wheel past Louisa's garden apartment on the drive home. I hated his spoiling that: "Guess where *we* been?", I'd wanted to phone Lou. Driving, I considered her and her life in Newport News. I had always enjoyed imagining what a perfect mother our Louisa would make (way more natural at it than I'd ever been with all my edginess, my pointless extra, slowing thoughts). Now Lou lived alone—kept her place's white area rugs perfect, was devoted to three girlfriends, two always trying and lose weight and one forever trying to gain, and, in my opinion, they talked about it too much, weight. Their big thrill was getting dressed to the gills and going out to Friday night restaurants. Flirting with waiters, making a four-way pact to sigh at him a lot but finally to always go home as a group. If Lou had been in love with one of these other lady un-beauties—respected wonderful people like her—I would have been real pleased, I swear I would. Instead she had a dog named Moxie in honor of Ned's first and she talked about the dog mostly and her work. I had hoped for another Madame Curie. Heck, I'd have settled for Miss Greer Garson *as* Madame Curie. To my mind, honey, I do not believe that being a virgin at sixty argues a wasted life—no. But here was our Louisa, who, like Winona, could've done any job on earth— ambassador, you name it. Me too, I would add my modest self to this list. Lou's life seemed a trifle hollow to me—just not enough *to* it for a person as sturdy and worthy as my adored and secret favorite. I wanted everything for her. I felt like I'd been planning that. I felt I *could*.

I had lots of time to think during that trip home. I couldn't bear to focus on the ex–hog dealer hog-tied to the Chevy's seat beside me. I took my choicest energies to thoughts of my children, ours.

Onct home, I need not tell you he required considerable restraining at first. The new doctor in town put Cap on tranquilizers, then he just swabbed my cut neck with rubbing alcohol and docked us forty-two bucks. No comment.

I missed Doc Collier with the lovely speaking voice, though I wondered if his being, like we found out later, a addict had hurt his treatment of my child I'd brung Doc at such a gallop. Who knows? Back home, I would stride in and look at the bearded one tied to the bed, the four-poster where everything had started and would probably end. He was irritating as a bad child, huge in adult power, irksome to consider as this wife's only likely future. (I made a mental note: Send Wade a Xmas card.)

Castalia's presence seemed to calm him. But as always, I kept wondering: What was in it for *her*? Otherwise he brayed sometimes and when I stepped in to check he'd get pop-eyed, yelling, "Sal, Ned, duck—it's them, Them!" Hurt a person's feelings at times.

"For God's sake, I was born a hundred and ten feet from here and *south* of this spot, so just pipe down, you old fool, Lucy ain't turnt Yankee yet." Then I'd come over and comb his beard, which soothed him but not as much as Cassie's being in the house. Others stayed away. Word was out— the young doctor gossiped, I was sure of it—unlike dear hooked Collier and his dear hooked nurse. Folks knew my man had nearbout succeeded in choking me and so the high school journalism students soon shied away. A warrior of antique fame was one thing, a wife strangler another. For me such differences had long since blurred, child. (I got to say this, in case you're wondering or have wondered: There were only two divorced women in Falls then, one was Lolly and the other a very loose waitress. Won't done then, and I obviously was not the leaving type. Obviously.)

Castalia came with leftovers, feeding these to us and not her minks. "Folks say he try and kill you. Someway I wishing hadn't nobody heard. I don't want our news all up and down these streets." Her saying "our" pleased me so.

But I told her what was worse, way harder than these marks around my neck. I said how before he tried to do me in, he'd said . . . said . . .

She stood, took her coat off, laying it careful over the living-room couch. "What he say you that so bad?" She settled beside me.

Though alone with her, though he was silent down the hall (untied by Cassie in honor of her visit, since only she was big and strong enough to "handle" him), I *still* whispered, "He said, 'You were never enough, but thank you.' "

"Whoo," she gave a barricaded smile. "They can *do* it, can't they? But, Lucy honey, we gots to consider the source. Look around you at these men. Ain't never had to axe theyselfs one real question. They start out, they a little boy baby with a congratulations in they didies. They don't got to wonder much (like us). They start out like being a state-ment. They never gots to question nothing. Gliding, like. They born—they name's already signed down at the bottom of the deed. But, Lucy? They the real losers. Those of us as had to start everything for ourselfs, as has woke up every day with questions right in the bed with us—'how to get through it,' 'why to get through it'—we done turned ourselves flat *into* somebody. We our own best answers, we a tribe of answers—we self-made."

"But it's so tir-ing, honey, always reinventing the wheel, at the bottom of every blooming hill!"

She laughed, "That do point that out. But they tells me: we gone inherit

Mother Earth, us meek. Well, semi-meek. Men like yours, like ours in yonder, why they ain't punished *for* they sins to others—they punished *by* they sins. Some justice in this world! He usually stay tied up, he done lost his mind, and us? why, we free. I free, you free, he all troubled in the spirits."

"Yeah. Free. Free to go shell the butter beans for supper."

"Or *not* to, far that go."

I went off then to check on him. I left her going through today's *Herald Traveler* (just a weekly now, no "Society Comings and Goings," mostly news-service stories, mall ads, a few Boy Scout advances, the crowning of the new Miss Falls, which always sounded to me like "misfire"). Cassie rested there, at home in our house, humming nothing, humming hymns and hits and a sweet smudge of hit hymns.

He seemed calm, chewing on something. "What've you got in your mouth, spit it out." It was a nightshirt button, it'd *been* a nightshirt button, nearly mawled to powder now. I wiped his tongue with the bedspread. "You be a good boy, hear?" I looked back, sun gleaming on his fine brass scabbard and giving one patch of wallpaper sudden value.

Everything suddenly felt fine. Cas and me adjourned to the kitchen and *did* shell the beans. Canned ones tastes like tin.

While we ate beans and fatback and collards, and cholesterol be damned, I started worrying. Got a crawling on the neck. I set some aside to feed him when she left. "Too quiet, don't like it, best go check on our favorite. Be right back." I left her to eat the rest.

I'll never outlive that walk down our hall, the hall I've strode ten million times, I bet. Sunlight was all but faded. Some children were setting off firecrackers on our vacant lot. I reached for his room's light switch, I heard a grunt, a heaving swing.

The light bulb seemed brighter than ever before. The room smelled of human filth. I saw he'd pulled the bedpan up onto the bed and that he'd smeared mess all over a rug there. But as I stepped nearer, as he kind of smiled at me like some boy child pleased in being caught at manly mischief, I saw what he had done.

Child? He'd got her coat. He'd smeared each inch of it with his own yellow stool. Her coat covered our bed—the bed where we'd conceived our children, the bed that'd sheltered his stored guns—a bed hung yet with his war gear.

"Willie," I said. "What have you gone and done to us, son? *Explain*."

He crouched over the thing, grinning, some double-daring bulldog in a manger. Seemed if *he* couldn't have this, her best, our best, everybody's, then nobody could. He squatted heavy on it, kneeling. His nightshirt was hiked up around his fine-skinned white white hips, and as I moved nearer, my arms out far beside me for needed balance like I was walking some wire above Niagara, I saw that he had got his old male self in hand, he'd got it up and functioning (old habits *do* die hard). And—on his knees in our bed—he'd just shot a lightning bolt of pearly seed across Castalia's prized, named minks.

The coat was matted, ruined *permanent*. He'd made sure. Even at quarter-speed, he had enough destruction left in him to be real thorough.

He eased back onto haunches. The grin was what just killed me. My first thoughts were of her, how to hide it from her, where I might could find some genius dry cleaners in Raleigh, experts. I would use up all his final money to make this right for Cas. But it was past help, her coat and history. I cannot describe what he had done to it, all over, sug, all over.

I felt adrenaline bloom inside me like a roaring sudden drug. I felt almost elated in some weird way—strong about how he'd so surprised me. He *continually* surprised me just when I thought my outrage was all peaked and spent. Now here he'd come up with another crime to add across our son's eyes, to pile over my own peeled loving life.

"So," I said. "You been planning this? or'd it just sneak up on you? —*No*," I said then. "You've gotten everything but this she grew from scratch for her own self. And this, you see, we needed, Willie. You can't have this."

He smiled like some man at a party who's just said the tip-toppest wisecrack and is unbeatable and clever and knows it all. Nothing of my own was left worth vandalizing, but hers?

"It's useless now," I said, praying she'd keep eating. "It's useless to anybody now but, on principle, I think I'll be wanting that back. Give me it."

I touched one corner. He pulled the thing away like believing this was just a game. I tugged and saw that he meant business. And I knew *I* did. He leaned against our headboard, breathing, mighty against the decoration of Ned's bugle and the twig and his own scabbard.

The room stunk of him. Or maybe us. Our years all come to this. Seemed like when I'd left my kitchen just now I had been a girl and here, seeing this, I was fifty-five going on ten thousand. Old as vintage dust, older. Old as colors.

"There are limits and you're way over now. *No*." I grappled for the hem. On knees, he lifted a sleeve of it to dangle, like some bullfighter, luring. I caught the hem of her mink. Just seeing his huge corded hands there galled me—sacrilege. We were waling each other within ten seconds. I was half on the bed, trying to yank the fouled rug out from under him, and I was managing, despite his greater weight. He saw I was winning so he got me by the voice box again. I lost all air, all, honey. This time he meant it. His hands, around my throat, felt ceramic.

Soon onct more: them little stamp-sized silky fabric swatches, just floating betwixt my face and his eyes wiry with bloodshot. I wanted to scream for help but dreaded Cassie's coming, seeing her masterpiece, then I tried screaming anyhow. He choked me whilst muttering, "They killed . . . *They* . . ." I flailed around, my arms extended to their furtherest. Hand open, I touched the cool brass upright of our bedstead, knocked aside the twig, and found a cool cool scabbard. My air seemed a thing of the past but I had enough sensation left so I still felt how cold the metal was. I welcomed that.

The rest is history—which means: You would've done it, too.

I worked the scabbard off our headboard. I was down to final oxygen. Likeways, I was under him. I let that whole arm straighten free of him bent over me . . . out to its full length, my own arm came back sideways at him and with last energy—with all my life really really meaning it, with purest glee and rank conviction and a joy just shy of, oh, exceptional sex—honey, I'm bringing that scabbard's heavy handgrip up hard hard against the ribs and then toward collarbone and finally up against the head of *it*. Of him. Trying and send him back to It where It belongs.

I kept chopping, blind I was, a steady chipping sound. And yellow was the only sight I saw. I heard a noise out in the hall and tried shouting to her, "No! Don't look," but he still had such a vise around my vocal cords, child. I heard just metal meeting bone, nice sound. I did that more, a kind of spasm dance betwixt us, hooking us like in the old days, but for different final reasons. "His temple," go for his temple, and in adrenaline's wild cascading calm (always my friend, Adren, and a pal ofttimes called upon) I had time to realize that Temple was a church and holy place, plus the pivot trigger of a brittle head. Here's the church and here's the steeple, open the door and free all the people.

There came two noises, one a long shriek from behind me that I knew was not from the sight of me being strangled—not from the sight of me bludgeoning the man back, a sight by now grown almost humdrum—no, it was her, understanding that her coat was dead. The sound rolled endless as some great tire screeching flat, as a great ship's sinking.

For the coat's sake, I kept at it. I got a pinch of air, and finally after one serious break and splinter, wind rushed into me with such a sissing welcome sound, like, gasp, my flying up, inhale, to freedom finally.

"I'll live."

A skull is a fairly tough old egg but can be broken.

He was bowing across a fur coat smeared in liquids yellow and white and now smudged with added red. Half his face and head were black-red, messy. I regretted that. But I was busier screening her coat from her, me crying, "Don't look at what we've done to it. Go out, go wait. I'll fix it." The blood *I'd* helped to add. I wadded fur behind me, I pressed it there, hiding it, and blubbering.

"Embarrassed"—I literally felt that, shielding her garment as I squatted over Captain Marsden's sideways carcass.

Cassie stood there in the doorway, hands joined, fingers laced before her, wagging the head side to side and looking completely and totally detached from me and from him under me.

She said two words, very quiet. She said, "White people."

I REMEMBER it was Election Day. I'd volunteered as a poll watcher and was due in two hours' time and felt guilty about missing that. Cas and me stayed like this the longest time. The unfailing Seth Thomas chimed in my clean kitchen and I longed to be there with it, out of this, all this. How had this occurred like this? Ugly.

She stood in the door looking at my husband and myself and doing nothing. Nothing left to do.

She said, "Wants it all, they take nearbout everything good, these god-dam whites."

I clamped hands over my ears. I'd rather look at him than hear this out of *her*. Despite the mangling of the head's one side, there was just a bit of pink across his white beard—not bad, like damage you spit out when you've brushed your teeth too hard. He appeared, child, unbelievably relieved. Cataracts filmy. Calm for the first time in decades, or maybe ever, maybe since that day he left our beloved town holding hands with his buddy like girlfriends that age might.

Finally I said something pitiful and male and *really* white: said I'd spe-cial-order a sable for her, would she like a sable? After I'd tried that crude type of bribery, she come over and dully helped me get down off the bed. "Well . . ." she said, resigned, exhausted. "Well, so it like this, is it?" and she looked him over. She spoke. "Oh, Willie Willie Willie, look at you."

She lifted the chenille spread and I feared she'd toss it over him before I was even sure of his state, though I basically was sure already. Instead, Cas eased the cloth over her coat. She yanked mink free of his weight via many unsentimental shoves. She carried her mink like a burn victim, child, to one corner closet and in there, bending to the floor, Cas hid the thing.

Next she dragged back over and pressed one ear to his chest. "He gone," she said. "*You* ain't got nothing to worry bout," she said, like *she* sure had. "Be self-defense."

"Self what?"

I'D SAID I would relieve Lolly at the firehouse polls by six and I got there just in time. Naturally I cleaned myself up first. Cassie wouldn't talk to me. I sent her home in a cab. Silent. No winter coat of mine would fit her. The sheriff and the undertaker had finally left. I'd phoned them all, cool as anything, and told each what'd happened. My tone of voice was samish, boring—I just laid out how I'd killed my own spouse, around three-ten, in there.

At the cinder-block firehouse, wearing a scarf and a clean jersey dress and after bathing my late husband's shit and cum off me, I settled there greeting people, smiling some, Lucy Regular. Nobody really knew yet and I was enjoying this part because I understood it couldn't last. Had to end. I got there around six and had thirty-five minutes' grace before one of the Lucas children came in and gaped at me—not able to hide her shock—and said, "Lucy? Should you *be* here like this, after . . . this afternoon? Are you all right?" I said nothing. Other ladies at the table cut their eyes my way. Lolly did, she'd stayed to chat. The Lucas girl, Jean, sweet person, Jean, she says, "May I? I know this is chancy, but may I?" I shrugged. She pulled my nice silk neck scarf aside. The others gasped at the four-inch blood blister, clear around. I hadn't let myself even look at it in a mirror. At my age, you can bathe and brush your hair away from mirrors. Maintenance.

"I am going to ask to walk you home, Lucy, may I? I think we should, really, or stop by the new doctor's on the way. May I do that, please? Let me walk you over to Summit, sweetie, now."

"I don't want to be there in that house tonight, Jean. The polls don't close till nine. I believe I'll work straight through if that's okay."

SHERIFF told me there would be an inquest.

I told him in glum flat detail how I had beat my husband's head in with his sword holder and how I was really ready to take my medicine. I'd known Sheriff Cooper since childhood. His granddad and dad were both Sheriff Coopers before him. He pointed to my neck and *he* pulled my collar open (Jean had snitched!) and Sheriff said, "Looks like you've already taken some your medicine. No, ma'am—Mr. Marsden's death will likely be reported as on account of 'a fall at home.' If I have anything to do with it, and as elected county sheriff, I do, ma'am."

"Maybe a *serious* fall at home," I said.

"Okay then, serious. He did have what doctors call a violent streak. Them that lives by the sword . . . Ma'am, I'm out of line here but some of us never got over the thing with the gun and Ned. Ned was my age at Lower Normal, my class. —In all my years of police work, I've never come near to throwing up until today. The sight of it sickened me."

"I know." I looked down at my own hands that'd done it. "I'm so ashamed. I used his scabbard on him. I told you, Mr. Cooper. I don't know if I *had* to hit him that number of times to slow him down."

"No, not him. That, I seen before. Not him, the coat, ma'am—what he did to her coat she grew. She's been wearing that since I was knee-high to nothing. That was the worst. Excuse my professional opinion at this time of mourning and all, Mrs. Lucy, but? Ma'am? he was one sick motherfucker."

"Was he? I guess so, sir, but . . . you know. Right along, he was also sort of . . . you know. It's day to day, ain't it? You just take it day to day."

DIED on me finally.
  I had to.

3

I DIDN'T clean his room up, couldn't face it yet. Felt surprised when the undertaker cleared out Captain on a khaki stretcher but not it, not her coat. It was still in our closet there under chenille, like personally ashamed.

Sleep, I didn't expect. But I slid right down into the famous rabbit hole.

Major final thought: I'd get a new one for her, genuine sable. I would phone Mr. Ekstein—use my first and only in-jail phone call, if it came to that. I'd order sable floor-length. His store's motto: "If you don't know furs, know your furrier." True, Cas wouldn't have no access to the names and dispositions of each li'l beast in it. But I did at least have sense enough not to go and buy her a new *mink* one.

Next day downtown, Ekstein said he could, for a price, get the sable here by Friday and the funeral. It'd come clear from Raleigh in a truck with just that in it. I ordered it against the Captain's life insurance and savings, and though it cost a pretty penny, I loved news of its expense. It *had* to cost a lot to even start to mean something. It could never mean enough.

I hand-delivered it, but all I'll say is, I knew it was a pale imitation of the real ruined one. (I'd taken the original to the back door of Ekstein's in a big shopping bag and, with him stone-faced at the smell, showed it to him, asked, "Is there a chance of . . . cleaning it up?" He finally held his nose and shook his head and said that this coat had cost him more fur business in Falls for more years than I could even imagine. A homemade fur coat scared people off from getting a real one.)

All I'll say is that she acted mighty mighty cold to me. Cas was eating block starch when I arrived and she barely stopped that long enough to take the sable out the box and try it on. The new coat looked, to my mind, just excellent on her—a perfect fit, which made it cost more, getting pelts aplenty to cover her with some to spare. "You done tried," she said, but withdrawn-like. Then she took it off and tossed it on a chair. I'm talking "tossed." You know how she gets.

It hurt me, though I saw what had been took away from her, and I sure wanted to understand. I'd hoped she'd see, child, it won't *me* that did it— but too maybe it was, partway. That's what kills you.

She come to the service but wearing no coat. And in November. I'd wanted the new one *on* her. I longed to hear others praise it. But she'd know that every compliment for *this* one meant it looked piles better than her last, her first, her real one.

THE BURIAL was quiet for somebody so famous. Embarrassment maybe. "Died of a serious fall at home," the Falls paper said. Most all my living kids turned up in black clothes, only Ned's red-and-white cane adding color to our row. There were flowers from the Meltons' barbecue place and civic clubs, and Lucas-Hedgepath Enterprises someway sent a huge batch of glads with a note: "An ever-faithful customer is gone and regretted." The local chapter of the National Rifle Association sent a football-mum bouquet, the only one I refused to have at graveside. Tacky of them, if you ask me.

Castalia refused to take the first-row seat we saved her though Lou went over and asked Cas to join us, asked in a way few humans could refuse. Cas stood back there, her arms crossed, glaring at everybody. I had imagined sitting in the crook of her great arm, and that arm suddenly all sabled.

Nothing turns out quite like you expect, does it, sug? Fact is, for all my loving the woman, I've never really known her all that good.

NOT ONE tear was shed at the grave, and though I couldn't manage myself, I do wish *some*body had. —It's slavery, being middle class!

I never did get locked up for doing it. There was a type of hearing—so called—but nobody there truly heard me. You'd think I was having fantasies while I sat telling all, telling and retelling the stubborn truth. "Fine, fine," said Billy Preston, handsome in black robes, "accidental death. Would you like some water, Mizz Lucy?"

I considered running a confession in the *Herald Traveler*. I got as far as calling their new young Yankee editor. He said, Was this another of these sick Southern jokes and who *was* this, and hung up on me. That did it. I tried relaxing. You've heard of the perfect crime? Usually takes months of preparation, honey. I had onto fifty years to get it right.

WE GOT thirty-nine casseroles before, after, and during the funeral. A household record. We also got the modern kind, called quiche—the first I'd seen. History! Ned and Lou and the twins were perfect and Baby got home after the funeral but in the company of the best-looking young man anybody'd ever seen. She had more luggage than Barnum, but *good* luggage. And she was dressed like Jackie Kennedy did later. A picture.

Then everybody cleared out and it was me alone in the humongous house. I had bad dreams at first and slept on the living-room couch, nearer the door. But slowly it got to be tolerable and finally a silent joy. Some of the old folks in here talk like a side-street house, with just *you* in it, is a curse of Satan. I got to like it. I asked Castalia over for meals. She refused three weeks straight, then finally managed the porch steps. She'd gained still more weight and, next time we had supper, I had to go call on her. I did not feel all that welcome. For one thing, she'd pulled down all her front yard's mink cages and those beasts left alive were living right in her home with her. Running free! Sanitary it was not—but I didn't like to say nothing. The hem of her new sable coat had fallen half on the floor and one lucky mink was hiding back of it. I bit my lip, said nothing. The coat was *hers*. I tried eating the chicken and dumplings she'd made but you could see mink droppings along the wall's edges. Minks scurried along the sides of Cassie's rooms. I went to fetch something for her and them little things in one cardboard box just snarled at me. Mostly she sat here eating and—in the next three months—her body spread and it was ugly to see now. Seemed the more there was of Castalia Marsden, the less there was of her. Bits of food and stuff, I noted, silent, had dropped right on the sable near her table. Her face was graying up on her, started being sunken. The last of her beauty was lost to view, but one day I snapped my fingers. I stared at this shrinking wizened head of hers set atop the body, mammoth. "You're looking like

your Auntie Reba. I never seen her in person but from what you've said
. . . you are a dead ringer."

"That a fact? Well, I can't see it but could do worse, seem like."

Then I got the inspiration. Her old coat was still in our garage uphill.
I didn't care to have it in our house but couldn't throw it out. I had asked
did she want it, or want it burned, or what? She wouldn't react none. Now
I said how we should bury it, proper, in the family plot—not next to Captain
surely, but there under the old magnolias where Lady More Marsden rests
along with famous others. "We'll buy it the best child's casket and put it in
there proper with some balms and some sachets and we'll say stuff over it
and I'll hire real gravediggers to lay it down there decent."

She looked at me. She quoted me at me and it was the first sign of real
life from her for many weeks. "Shows you you thinking, Lucy. Right good
sign." Then Castalia nodded. "That's fitting. I accept."

At *that* funeral, we wept.

Gravediggers didn't know what was in the bronze baby casket and
maybe wondered why no preacher man was present. The fellows lit cigarettes off to one side till Cassie hollered, "No smoking, clowns. We got a
funeral going on over here, ever hear of one?" They stomped them Ches-
terfields but quick.

We held on to each other. Just us chickens. I looked around at granite
markers. Already I knew most names on most stones. "So," I thought, "Falls."

November, Cas and me both shivering some. Oh but here I wished she'd
worn her new fur coat today. It was back yonder on a kitchen chair catching
crumbs and ferret breath. It's tacky to talk prices but I'd asked for the best
from Mr. Ekstein and I'd paid fifteen thousand dollars for it. Plus state sales
tax. I will say that I could not exactly afford it, looking back. I don't know
if I blame myself or Ekstein but I wrote one check for it and the check went
through and most of the ragtag inherited money I had on earth went with
it. And so, it was vain of me, I know—but I wanted it *worn* this day at least,
you know, at the other one's funeral? Though I see this is my limit. I had
learnt my limits, darling, and I am learning still.

Anyway, we were mourning the real coat and beside me this mammoth
woman (I had to drive right up to the hole cut in sod and to then put out
her folding chair), Cassie cried, "My babies. I never met one mink I liked."
And I heard this fond admiring in her tone. How strange, I decided, that
this most basically likable person I'd ever met should put a premium on
that, on keeping folks off, preventing anybody's nearness and pleasure in
her—but then I understood that this made sense for her, for Miss Castalia
Marsden, what with history and all.

THE DUMB SOLDIER
by Robert Louis Stevenson

When the grass was closely mown,
Walking on the lawn alone,
In the turf a hole I found
And hid a soldier underground.

Spring and daisies came apace.
Grasses hid my hiding place.
Grasses run like a green sea
O'er the lawn up to my knee.

Under grass alone he lies,
Looking up with leaden eyes,
Scarlet coat and pointed gun,
To the stars and to the sun.

When the grass is ripe like grain,
When the scythe is stoned again,
When the lawn is shaven clear,
Then my hole shall reappear.

I shall find him, never fear.
I shall find my grenadier.
But for all that's gone and come,
I shall find my soldier dumb.

He has lived, a little thing,
In the grassy woods of spring,
Done, if he could tell me true,
Just as I should like to do.

He has seen the starry hours
And the springing of the flowers
And the fairy things that pass
In the forests of the grass.

In the silence he has heard
Talking bee and ladybird,
And the butterfly has flown
O'er him as he lay alone.

Not a word will he disclose,
Not a word of all he knows.
I must lay him on the shelf,
And make up the tale myself.

It Ends
in the
Air

*. . . We, according to his promise, look for new heavens
and a new earth, wherein dwelleth righteousness.*
—II PETER 3:13

HERE WE GO. Up. You feel it in your breastbone and your wrists.
It's my first time on a aeroplane ever and me this scared and
you here with me. I bet you been before. I thought so, these days. Of course
I've *seen* them before, planes. Were you watching when that astronaut
teacher blew up in that rocket? Her relations were right there watching
from the ground. Don't think about it. Since Jerome's off in England with
his friend seeing theater shows finally, I figured I'd have to do this by my
lonesome. You're the only one I phoned when good news came and here
you are, big as life. Here *we* are, in the air where we've both always belonged.

How many times have I already showed you the letter? See, Agnes Scott
Nursing School in Atlanta, it's honoring "distinguished graduates living or
dead." And our Lou won one. You reckon her prize will be a plaque or a
cup? Friends at Lanes' End laid odds I'd wind up in Miami Beach, hijacked.
Think there's a chance?

Your taking time off and helping wheel my chair on here and your liking
my impulse-bought jersey suit and your settling right beside me, it's appreciated. Oh, here comes that stewardess again. Bet you she hennas. They
do stand straight. How can they tolerate those heels all day? —Why yes,
miss, I believe I *would* accept a compliment martini, I thank you kindly.
(What's in one, sug? You want it? It's free.)

You reckon the awards banquet will expect me to make a speech? Sure
hope not. I can't put two words together, I mean not in public for strangers.
Not chummy like us two together, hunh? Some joy it's been for me. Way
back, you just said, "yes?" The rest is history. Tell you what: On land, we've

sorted through *my* mess. Now we're up here in the air, it's your turn. Don't get shy on me. All I got is time.

Mustn't look now but the one on your left is smiling at you. He is so. I saw it. Businessman. Somewhat bald in front but kindly, cute. I *like* his looks. Decent Billy Preston kind of Southern boy, God love them. Oh, here's our new friend with my first martini. So, so this is gin, hunh? Bet it's silent but deadly. We're vibrating some, that normal? I did see my mended rose-pattern valise come up the conveyor belt. At least my speech notes are aboard. I did prepare a little something. Taw helped. Look at those cars, the color of Easter eggs from this height, live and learn. You know? flying already feels natural. So much does when its time finally comes. I count on that.

Bet I already told you my one about The Man Who Loved His Wife Too Good. Uh-oh, did? Fine. Well, there's still When the Shoe Fits. —That too?

Then it's Lucy's turn for pumping *you*. But first, scrunch over here close to my shotgun window seat, tell me what *that* is, darling. See yon two-toned stripe written all through the woods, how trees in one line only are a different color? You figure maybe acid rain did that? These Republicans look the other way while industry just poisons us. Or maybe a deep vein of potash or something. I wouldn't mind napping now, but first I got to find out what that is. You know me. This gin ain't half bad. Don't let me embarrass myself, beyond the usual. You're kind to let me hold your hand and all. You been so doggone loyal, coming back and back, I do love the idea of Loyal.

Look, Bill's already dozing over his personal copy of *Business* (I *told* you he was a businessman). Appears to be married. We'll ask him about that strange color brightening land down there. He's from Georgia and should know.

See? It's plainer again, like one lightning zigzag but with trees inside it of a changed color. Seems to go miles across in some spots, narrows at others. The mark keeps pushing southward under our plane's crossed-shaped shadow yonder. *Is* that us? Thought so. Green inside the stain looks newer than what flanks it. And all this feels familiar, like I knew about it onct. Let's wake young Bill. Don't be chicken, just nudge him with your knee, he won't mind, I know. The Bills of this world are wonderful. He just *drank* his too fast. If he wakes up mad, I'll take full blame. Promise.

TO ALREADY be pointing down there, eager to ask, when Bill goes, "See the stripe?" it freezes me, his guessing. I feel upset for no real reason I can name.

"Know what that is, Mrs.? They claim it'll fade on us in a few years."

I venture, maybe some mineral deposit livening the color of that land? But Bill tilts across you, apologizing, his nice face rests direct beside mine and I'm comforted by feeling heat drift from him. I like knowing I'm in air, plus semi-tipsy and about to learn something else new.

"Sherman's path," Bill says. "Still shows from way up here, imagine.

Ma'am, see how it changes at that river crossing? Going in at one spot, then wading out with the horses and torches downstream, there? Stretches clear to Atlanta, which he burned, you'll remember. From your history books, I mean." Bill thinks he's made a joke about my advanced age, child. But I'm in no pranking mood, knowing how that Struggle still shows—to God's eyeview and birds'.

I mash my forehead on the chilly plastic porthole here (half fretting for whoever'll have to clean this grease spot later).

"Yes, ma'am, the whole burned part grew back greener." Bill is ordering another round for us, a gent. "Maybe charcoal helps trees come up stronger? I've got a brother-in-law in wood technology at Georgia Tech, should ask him. But, yeah, that's what you found, ma'am. And on your first time up."

He retrieves his *Business*. Grateful for this hand you let me squeeze unmercifully just now, I am—like always—glad to know. But spooked some. Maybe it's the free drink or could be the danger of getting this high up and playing like I'm owed this, which I'm not. A while back, we felt how this plane worked to leave the dirt—this plane *prefers* the ground, makes sense. I don't know what I'm feeling here but maybe it's just: thrilled. Going to fetch a plaque for Louisa, or maybe even a silver loving cup, which would be more useful probably. And then *you* coming along, and my getting treated like Somebody by strangers and then to look down on this wonder of Nature over combat. Will I embarrass you? my forehead pressed here to cold plastic?

Fresh green is teaching me something. This burn rambles clear from Virginia past our hometown to Atlanta. What a beautiful map of a scar! Educational—a bitter, optimistic green. I recognize it. Up under my ribs, a sweet unlatching starts, a tallying. I stare down at that tint changed by hurt. Recovery has upgraded everything that blossomed after. I know scorched-earth policy. And I know about continuing, child. But I never knew that keeping on could, from this high, just *look* so pretty.

Colors *are* the deeds and sufferings of light. Fact. The fact is fair. People recover. Ain't it something, what folks can spring back from?

Today I feel right wonderful myself. I'm thinking fond thoughts of my husband and my children, child. To be riding our Southern sky, with me strapped up here in a seat belt I secretly invented, to be getting gently half plastered on a second free drink supplied me by a friendly moral man, to be going to harvest prizes my kids earned—oh, it's a day. And that a young friend such as you would take off work, and use vacation time just to shove my wheelchair on and off this silver rocket, well, it's more than anybody should expect, ever.

You'd think that all along I really *had* been college material! You'd think I was Mrs. Gotrocks, somebody you'd ask for more than street directions or her shortbread recipe.

I see that path down there, refined. Again I feel this wild ambition stoke up in me. I *want* to. What? Anything, darling. Everything. I have seen so

much and have someway been left alive to tell. I ain't told all, but most—
well, *some*. Now I need to hear *your* all. Start from birth and go till now.
First though, let my eyes stray back to that color yonder, as self-made as
me. I *am* listening. I know how. Before I shush, one last thing needs saying.
I want to speak a fact that Green just taught me. I've long waited to know
this. I got to say it now out loud to make it so. I'm mighty mighty glad to
have you helping, listening. It's just this.

    Nobody could stop me.

    Several tried.

    I am still here.

    At last, I get to say down towards our world, "The war is over."

A Note About the Author

*Allan Gurganus was born in Rocky Mount, North Carolina. His short fiction
has appeared in* The Atlantic, Harper's, The Paris Review, *and* The New
Yorker. *His prizes include two grants from The National Endowment for the
Arts, an Ingram Merrill Grant, a Danforth Scholarship, and Stanford University's Wallace Stegner Fellowship. Mr. Gurganus has taught at Duke, Stanford,
the Iowa Writers' Workshop, and Sarah Lawrence College.*

A Note on the Type

*The text of this book was set in a digitized version of Aster, a type face designed
by Francesco Simoncini (born in 1912 in Bologna, Italy) for Ludwig and
Mayer, the German type foundry. Starting out with the basic old-face letter
forms that can be traced back to Francesco Griffo in 1495, Simoncini empha-
sized the diagonal stress by the simple device of extending diagonals to the full
height of the letter forms and squaring off. By modifying the weights of the individual letters to combat this stress, he has produced a type of rare balance and
vigor. Introduced in 1958, Aster has steadily grown in popularity. Composed by
PennSet, Inc., Bloomsburg, Pa. Printed and bound by R. R. Donnelley & Sons,
Harrisonburg, Virginia. Designed by Iris Weinstein.*